Operation Lucifer

The Chase, Capture and Trial
of Adolf Hitler

To Linda —
In friendship!
from Will R
&

By

David B. Charnay

Squire General, Ltd.
23679 Calabasas Road, #515
Calabasas, CA 91302

ISBN 0-9675135-0-2

1 2 3 4 5 6 7 8 9 10

Library of Congress Catalog Number 99-96823

Contents

Book One
The Chase & Capture

Book Two
The Trial of Adolf Hitler

Of all the bigotries that ravage the human temper there is none so stupid as the anti-Semitic. It has no basis in reason, it is not rooted in faith, it aspires to no ideal.

> Lloyd George, Prime Minister of Great Britain
> 1916-1922

The Holocaust is a central event in many people's lives, but it has also become a metaphor for our century. There cannot be an end to speaking and writing about it.

> Aharon Appelfeld
> New York Times
> November 15, 1986

The people have some champion whom they set over them and nurse into greatness...this and no other is the root from which a tyrant springs.

> Plato
> The Republic Book VIII 565C
> 347 B.C.

The last year of the 20th century has burned with racial and ethnic hatred across America. Synagogues have been torched. Blacks, gays, Asians, and Jews have been murdered. Like acid eating through human flesh, hatred has sizzled through layers of indifference to the core of who and what we are. White supremacist Web sites have flourished...their target: children.

> Al Martinez
> Los Angeles Times
> Sunday, July 25, 1999

ACKNOWLEDGMENTS

With profound gratitude to these dear, wonderful people who believed in the premise of this book and gave unstinting help and support to my efforts.

My plaudits to the historians listed in the bibliography at the end of this book.

My special thanks to the Department of Defense at the Pentagon for connecting me with Kathleen Canham Ross, chief of the U.S. Army Office of Public Affairs in Los Angeles. This lady most professionally asked me how she could help. I explained my project. Within an hour she had a Sergeant Field call me and advise that a Defense Department Judge would call me. The next morning, Judge Wilford H. Ross, Administrative Judge of the Defense office of Hearings and Appeals, phoned me. His approach was professional as he patiently questioned me about my book. Coincidentally, he held court in the Woodland Hills section of Los Angeles. He agreed to meet for lunch. Over the years, we became close friends. He is an intellectually honest, most knowledgeable and amiable person who had served in the U.S. Army in Germany. His help has been invaluable.

My gratitude to friend James McEachin, actor and author of three successful novels, for his encouragement, support and efforts to have this book published.

Many thanks to Amelia Demnitzer Levin, former librarian at the Simon Wiesenthal Center, and Adaire Klein, director of the current library staff, for helping my research.

With great respect, admiration and appreciation to Professor Klaus P. Fischer, who received his Ph.D. in Cultural and Intellectual History from the University of California, Santa Barbara. He authored the acclaimed books *Nazi Germany - A New History* and his brilliant new book *The History of Obsession: Judeophobia and the Holocaust*. He most generously read my script, made corrections and wrote the Foreword for this book. His other writings are listed there. During my research of over fifty tomes on Hitler and the Nazis, I concluded that Professor Fischer is a giant among his peers. When Judge Wilford Ross and I met him for lunch in Santa Barbara, we were most impressed with his knowledge and charisma. He teaches at Allan Hancock College in Santa Maria, California.

With thanks to Christinna Chauncey, a budding actress and screenwriter, who served as special assistant to this author and transcribed my handwritten script.

My most sincere wish is that all Americans and our friends the world over born in the last half of this violent 20th century will read, learn and remember "The Nazi Holocaust." Racism and hatred are alive and well as we enter the new millennium, the 21st century. Complacency and apathy were the precursors of this most horrible carnage in the history of man. Can it happen again? To whom? Peace is priceless.

A special note of appreciation and love to my wife, Martha, who patiently tended to my creature comforts during three years of research and writing in long hand in the silent hours past midnight to dawn.

Kudos to her sister, Esta Arnold, for her encouragement after reading occasional pages.

Always in memory of the most intellectually honest people I've ever known, my parents.

David B. Charnay

This book is dedicated to the victims of the Holocaust, the millions of all faiths who were killed by the Nazis.

To the survivors of the carnage by Adolf Hitler and his Nazi minions, before and during World War II.

To the brave armed forces of America, Great Britain, France, Poland, Belgium, the Netherlands, Italy, Yugoslavia, Czechoslovakia, Greece, Denmark, Norway and Russia, and partisans throughout Europe who were killed or wounded, and those who survived this Armageddon.

FOREWORD

Countless efforts have been made to capture the quintessential nature of evil embodied in Adolf Hitler's Third Reich. These have covered such diverse fields of study as history, sociology, psychology, criminology, literature, psychiatry, medicine, theology, and philosophy. Over 100 biographies and 10 times as many specialized studies have been devoted to Adolf Hitler in the last 65 years, which vastly exceeds what has been written about the major world leaders of the 20th century combined. Robert Harris, author of *Selling Hitler*, has written not long ago that only Jesus Christ has had more words devoted to him than Adolf Hitler, a fact that attests to our fascination with evil as well as our inability to understand it.

There has also been a rapidly growing industry to recreate the horrors of Nazi crimes through imaginative literature, a subject treated at length in Alvin Rosenberg's book *Imagining Hitler*. This is an important genre because it can serve as another roadmap to a reality that is not fully accessible to the analytical understanding, quite apart from stimulating interest in historical events that fact-conscious historians are often unable to attain. As Rosenberg points out, it is only when the fact dies that the fiction has a chance to be born, and I would add that for many young Americans the facts about World War II and Nazi Germany have not only died but have never been born. This is not the place to bemoan the lamentable state of our historical knowledge in today's world, especially as it concerns young Americans, but to point out that there is a pressing need to remember the horrors of the Third Reich, either in scholarly or literary form.

This is why David B. Charnay's immensely stimulating and disturbing novel *Operation Lucifer: The Chase, Capture and Trial of Adolf Hitler* is going to serve a very important purpose, for what we have here is not only a painstakingly accurate depiction of what Hitler and his thugs were up to during World War II, but also a richly drawn literary scenario as to what might have or should have happened had Hitler survived the war. The book skillfully combines suspense and real history in a way that few other works on this subject have been able to achieve. It is a sweeping panorama of the post-World War II era with a cast of hundreds of characters, ranging from Hitler and his henchmen to Truman, Eisenhower, Churchill, J. Edgar Hoover, the Dulles brothers, Stalin, Eva Peron, Fulgencio Batista, Castro, the Mafia, the Kennedys, and so on. Although the action shifts back and forth between different locations such as Hamburg, Munich, Malmo, Washington, New York, Havana, Rome, Barcelona, Paris, and Buenos Aires, we never lose the thread of the narrative, as the hero, Barton Q. Milburn, relentlessly hunts down his quarry. Particularly gripping are those sections of the novel in which Holocaust survivors testify about their ordeals and the unspeakable atrocities they witnessed. Readers will be lifted into the charnel house of Adolf Hitler and the Germans who supported his mad dream of racial cleansing - a dream, as Mr. Charnay points out at the end of the novel, that is still alive in some demented minds today.

Operation Lucifer is not just another spy novel but a serious effort to retell an important and familiar story, while at the same time lifting it into a fictional dimension in order to stir our moral sensibilities and remind us that it cannot be allowed to happen again.

-Klaus P. Fischer

Klaus P. Fischer is the author of History of an Obsession, Prophecy: Oswald Spengler and "The Decline of the West" *and* Nazi Germany - A New History. *He was born in Munich, Germany, in 1942, and obtained his Ph.D. in Cultural and Intellectual History from the University of California, Santa Barbara. Professor Fischer teaches at Allan Hancock College in Santa Maria, California.*

PREFACE

This novel is predicated on the postulate of "What if?" The subject is the assumption that many historians and students have conjectured-"What if Hitler had escaped?"

Was it really Hitler's body in the Viking funeral pyre discovered by the Russians? Where is the top layer of Nazis who participated in the mass murders of millions of innocents? Where is all the money stolen by the Nazis? Do we blame one man or a half-dozen dissolute, power-crazed Nazis for the greatest mind boggling carnage in the history of mankind? Is it conceivable that just a small cadre of megalomaniacs could have organized the wanton and methodical annihilation of six million Jews, millions of Christians and created the havoc of that apocalypse from 1933 to 1945? Did all of Germany participate in this bloodbath called the Holocaust? Where was the Christian world during this macabre series of atrocities? Where were the other civilized nations during that period, while today, paradoxically, we are so concerned about civil rights and ethnic cleansing?

As this century embarks on a new millennium with our advanced technology of television, computers and web sites on the internet, we have a media devoting airtime and print space to excesses on celebrity scandals and political sleaze.

In the ebbing tide of time for the most violent century in the history of mankind, the world has gorged itself on the peccadilloes of a beleagured president in an onslaught of sleaze, 79 days of bombing by NATO in Yugoslavia and a first lady seeking a Senate seat in New York. Yet violence has not abated. The last years of the 20th Century brought us prosperity, a sudden political awakening to the existence of poverty, drive by shootings, the anti-semitic arson burning of three synagogues in Sacramento, the capitol of California, school children being slaughtered by fellow students in Littleton, Colorado and a hate killing spree by white supremacists in Illinois, where they killed a black man, wounded a Korean and six Orthodox Jews. Question - Where was the outrage? Complacency and apathy are alive and well in the media and our body politic. Will the "me" psyche of our populace spill over to the new millenium? Has the time come for a re-examination of our priorities? More than five decades have flitted by and students, parents, educators and the media still know little of the nazi carnage during 1933-1945.

In shocking contrast, the media's coverage of the Nuremberg trials was only a slight beat in cadence ahead of the world's complacency during the Nazi aberrations from 1933 to the war's end in 1945.

With apologies to the judiciary and our constitution, this novel is an attempt to visualize a hypothetical exercise of justice. This is a behind the scenes exploration of the "What if?" hypothesis which has been envisioned by millions.

Our research of powerful treatises by brilliant historians, the judiciary and academia has been most helpful in the exposure of the actual atrocities committed by the Third Reich of Germany. The unwarranted plunder of Europe resulted in the decimation of cities, towns and villages. Deaths add up to astronomical figures. The carnage was initiated by megalomaniac Adolf Hitler...the pied piper of death.

Military Casualties:

The US	300,000	dead	700,000	wounded
Germany	3,250,000	dead	7,250,000	wounded
USSR	6,200,000	dead	14,000,000	wounded
England	357,000	dead	6,369,000	wounded

Civilian Casualties*   50,000,000 dead and /or wounded

*Includes Stalin's Soviet genocidal excesses

The media coverage of the Nuremberg trials deserves a critique by experts. No attempt is contained in this novel.

This novel begins with the period seven years after the unconditional surrender of Nazi Germany.

We focus on the Nazis and bring its conclusion to New Year's Day, 2001.

For the anachronisms, the apocrypha, the abuses of due process and the tactics of our heroes, my apologies. This is poetic license to highlight a nightmare in the history of the 20th Century and a look back at our errors of omission and commission. Will a continuum of mea culpas absolve those of us whose complacency and apathy resulted in the subconscious three monkeys syndrome of hearing, seeing or speaking no evil?

At least, Dear God, let the <u>world remember</u>...for <u>what is past is prologue</u>. This is my epiphany.

David B. Charnay

𝔅ook 𝔒ne

The Chase & Capture

In Loving Memory of George Spota.

PROLOGUE

Tuesday, February 12, 1952 - 10:12 a.m., CIA headquarters, Langley, Virginia
General Walter Bedell Smith, director of the Central Intelligence Agency, was in his office studying a highly classified document. The subject matter dealt with two cargo ships being tracked by an American submarine off the coast of Chongjin, North Korea.

☆ ☆ ☆ ☆

Wednesday, February 13, 1952 - 3:12 a.m. - Wonsan, South Korea
A squadron of United States Airforce fighter planes took off from an air base 10 miles south of Wonsan. The six F-86 Sabre jets headed north over the Sea of Japan. At that moment, 30 miles off the coast of North Korea, the USS Tiger Shark, a Nautilus class submarine, was stalking the Eagle Prince and the Lone Eagle, loaded with tanks, artillery and assorted firearms. The fighter planes rendezvoused 1500 feet over the submarine, flying cover. The sub emitted an infrared blinker acknowledging their presence.

Ensign Paul Matthews was in telegraphic contact with Admiral C. Turner Joy at a secret naval headquarters contiguous to Kungnung, South Korea, awaiting orders.

☆ ☆ ☆ ☆

Tuesday, February 12, 1952 - 10:35 a.m. - CIA Headquarters, Langley, Virginia
General Smith pressed his intercom. Allen Dulles answered. "Join me, Allen,"

he requested.

"Be right in."

Smith dialed a direct line to Secretary of Defense Robert Lovett. "Yes?" Lovett responded.

"Bob, Smith here. What is the decision on those two ships heading for Pyongyang?"

"I'm to check with General Bradley in the next ten minutes, Beedle."

"Mind if I put my oar in?"

"Go ahead."

"Sink the bastards and get out fast," Smith advised. "No press announcements. Those ships are owned by an alleged high Nazi official who escaped our net."

"You're talking about Nordheim. Well, this is a delicate time. We're trying to arrange a cease-fire and are talking with the Chinese. However, I'm inclined to sink the bastards. We've been tracking those vessels ever since they left Vladivostok. They're loaded with tanks and other armament."

"Are you going to clear it with the President?" General Smith asked.

"Indeed, unless Bradley has already."

"Bob, if this action is done quickly without any fanfare, we can deny any knowledge of the action. If we stall, they'll pull into port and unload before we can discuss it. I urge immediate action."

"Yes, I agree with your scenario, with one note of caution. That sub has to dive fast and head for safe waters. They'll need air cover," Lovett observed.

"How about a diversionary bombing of Chongjin? Time is of the essence."

"Despite the gumshoe business you're in, General, you're still a gung-ho soldier. That plan is among our options. Stand by and I'll get back to you soon."

Allen Dulles, Smith's number one man at the CIA, puffed on his ever-present pipe, leaned back in a leather lounge chair and nodded his head. Smith looked at him as he hung up the phone. "Any comments?" he asked.

"Right on, Beedle. The Chinese are playing us like a yo-yo. What's Lovett's attitude?"

"He's going to try to convince Truman to go for it. He'll be calling back after he briefs him."

The direct line on Smith's desk interrupted the conversation. "Yes?"

"Beedle, the show is on. Truman approved. Bradley ordered the Air Force into action over Chongjin and the Navy sub attack on the ships immediately," Lovett added.

"Good deal, Bob."

"We should be getting some intelligence in about an hour or so. I'll stand by for a final report. I'll be in the situation room to follow the action."

"Allen Dulles and I will stay right here, awaiting your update."

"Fine."

Smith put the phone down, rose from his chair and paced the room, clapping his hands. "The show is on."

"How soon will we know?" Dulles asked.

"Within an hour or two, I would guess. Lovett's going to the situation room to monitor the air raid and the activity at sea. Damned if I wouldn't love to be there with him."

☆ ☆ ☆ ☆

Chunchon, South Korea - 10:30 a.m.

Ten B-29s, loaded with bombs, left the air base and climbed to 5,000, feet headed for Chongjin, North Korea.

At that moment in the Sea of Japan, twenty miles off the Coast of North Korea, the USS Tiger, a nautilus class submarine, was stalking the Eagle Prince and the Lone Eagle. Captain Clayton Lawrence was at the periscope. Alongside him stood Lieutenant Malcolm Thomas charting speed in the choppy waters. Heavy cloud cover and patches of fog caused the sub to move closer to the ships, which were in tandem a nautical mile apart. The crew stood ready at their battle stations. The tension peaked.

A message from the radio room was handed to Thomas. "Captain, orders are to go when our bombers start pounding Chungjin. We make quick hits and head home pronto. An Air Force squadron will fly over us for protection."

Lawrence, a veteran of the war in the Pacific, snapped, "When the hell will the bombing begin? We don't have a helluva lot of time before they pull into port."

"This cloud cover may delay the air attack."

The captain blurted, "That's it!" and invited the lieutenant to take a look through the periscope, which was scanning the coast. "See this?" he asked. "A beautiful fireworks show! Let's go hit em."

"Look at that lovely red sky," Thomas agreed as he turned the scope back to Lawrence.

The Air Force pounded the city and port of Chungjin. The captain gave the order. Tubes one and two fired the deadly torpedoes with direct hits on the Eagle Prince. "Full speed, ahead!" he exclaimed.

The stricken ship exploded, lighting up the sky. The Lone Eagle, pacing behind the blazing, sinking wreck, turned north, zigzagging in an attempt to evade the oncoming sub.

Tubes three and four shot their deadly missiles amidship and the Lone Eagle exploded. "Dive! Dive!" the captain yelled.

The flight commander radioed, "Good show. Bon voyage."

Back in Smith's office, the general placed the Nordheim file in front of him. "This is the damnedest enigma," he muttered softly to himself.

"Talking to yourself, Beedle?" Dulles remarked.

"You're damn well right. This Nordheim affair is getting under my skin. The identity of this mysterious bastard escapes me. I've drawn a diagram here with possible candidates to fit this alleged high Nazi and am coming up with a plethora of zeroes."

"Beedle, whoever that son of a bitch is, there is enough on his plate to warrant a thorough checkout. His activities in Argentina, his ships to Korea, his attempt to pose as a Jew, the reports from Israel's Mossad, his enormous wealth after VE Day requires our full and immediate attention."

"Agreed."

The intercom curtly announced, "Secretary Lovett on one."

Smith picked up line one. "Yes, Bob?"

"Two down and Chungjin afire," Lovett crisply reported.

"How did the air raid go? Any bombers hit?"

"No, our boys are clean and heading back to base. Total surprise to the commies. The sub submerged immediately. They are getting air cover until safe," Lovett continued. "The event is top secret."

"Good show, Bob. Congratulations," Smith said.

"Not so fast with the plaudits, Beedle. Depends on reactions from the Chinese, Eagle Shipping or the media."

"So be it. We've put a clamp on the entire operation. The three monkeys ride again. Have a nice evening."

"You too, Bob."

Smith turned to Dulles, "Allen, my boy, we hit the bull's eye. Two eagles down and Chungjin's burning. The president has been fully briefed.

CHAPTER ONE

February 13, 1952 - Washington, D.C.

A vicious winter storm attacked the nation's capital, sending gusts of icy wind and blanketing Pennsylvania Avenue with needles of arctic snow. Nature had capriciously emptied this corridor of power, its populace of wheeler-dealers, influence peddlers, functionaries and bureaucrats. The streets were barren except for the occasional bus and a taxicab attempting to daunt the ire of the angry elements.

Dusk brought an eerie silence to the city as the snow became sleet and continued its whirling-dervish dance to the doorsteps of the White House. The West Wing was a beacon of light that miserable evening. In his office, Dr. John Steelman, special assistant to President Harry Truman, was busy on the phone totally oblivious to the banshee wailing of the storm. He was Truman's confidential aide and chief factotum. Steelman's office was contiguous to the Oval Office where its occupant, Harry Truman, was deeply immersed in forty pages of highly classified FBI and CIA files dealing with the activities of one Frederick Nordheim, a recluse believed to be the richest man in the world.

The recipient of this dinner hour call was Barton Quentin Milburn, comfortably ensconced in his Rock Creek Park home den. Before a roaring fireplace he was balancing his five-year-old son, Michael, on one foot and his four-year-old daughter, Jenny, on the other while cradling the telephone receiver between his shoulder and left ear. His beautiful 27-year-old wife, Elizabeth, entered the den to announce that the cook was ready to put dinner on the dining room table.

"John, is this one of your tired jokes?" Milburn bellowed into the phone. "Have you looked out of your window?" He smiled and winked at his wife.

Steelman's rejoinder was a riposte, swift and to the point: "The President wants you in his office at 10 a.m. tomorrow. That's it. West Gate, as usual."

"Bad news from Korea?" Barton queried.

"No more telephone talk," Steelman snapped. "You didn't question Eisenhower or Patton when you bounced around Europe with them, did you? Be here. Happy Valentine's Day to you and your charming wife."

Steelman gently put the phone back in its cradle, then got up and stomped into the Oval Office. "He'll be here, Mr. President," he announced as Truman removed his glasses and looked up at his assistant.

"John, I hated doing this to Milburn, but we need to get him involved in this Nordheim situation."

In Rock Creek, Bart looked at his telephone receiver, which had suddenly ended his conversation with the President's aide. Smiling at his wife, he gently lowered his children to the richly carpeted floor and raised his 6'3" athletic body out of the leather chair, lifting both children on each arm. He leaned over to his wife, kissed her forehead and tried to wipe the frown off her classic features. "Something's bothering them at the White House," he said as he handed the children over to Mrs. Bishop, the 60-year-old English nanny who had been Elizabeth Lipton's childhood governess in London.

☆ ☆ ☆ ☆

June 10, 1940, Rome, Italy

On that fateful day, Sir Alfred Lipton was stationed in Rome as British ambassador to Italy. His wife, Dorothy, and 15-year-old daughter, Elizabeth, were preparing to leave Rome on June 8. That morning, Dorothy Lipton was stricken by a cerebral hemorrhage. She was rushed to the Ospedale de Santo Spirito where she succumbed two days later on June 10, 1940, the same day Mussolini declared war on Great Britain and France.

As the Carabinieri were rounding up the British and the French diplomats for deportation, two Gestapo agents accompanied the Italian police into the British Embassy. Ambassador Lipton was a secular Jew, or rather a monotheist, as was the family. He was less than gently asked to accompany six Carabinieri and the two Gestapo agents to the Italian foreign office. Despite Lipton's vociferous protestations, claiming diplomatic immunity under the Geneva Convention rules, they snatched the telephone from his hands and shouted, "*Juden* have no immunity!"

Lipton pleaded with the Italian police, who stood by mute, not understanding a word in the heated dichotomy that ensued. "Listen, you bastards, I am the British ambassador to Italy. What right do you have to detain me? My wife died this morning and I have to go to the hospital to claim her body for burial!" shouted Lipton.

"*Gut, schweinhund*, one less Jew to deal with," replied the taller of the

Gestapo agents as he struck the ambassador across the mouth with the back of his hand. Blood gushed from Lipton's lips as he leaped forward and threw a right hook at his attacker, decking him. The Italian posse stood by open-mouthed as they watched the tableau of Nazi tactics.

With that, the other Gestapo agent lifted his dazed partner, Hans, from the floor and then zapped Lipton with a blackjack. Lipton sank to his knees. By this time the rest of the British staff had rushed into the ambassador's office, horrified at the scene confronting them.

The leader of the Carabinieri awakened from his stupor, pulled a piece of paper from his back pocket and shouted, "*Arresto!*", then in broken English read: "A state of war now exists between Britain and Italy and all British diplomats and staff are to be deported under the rules of the Geneva Convention! *Capish?*"

The Italian police hustled the 14 men and women and two U.S. Marines out of the room. Their leader, a police captain, then turned to the Gestapo agents and in Italian cautioned them to cut the violence.

Hans, the one with a broken nose, held a bloody handkerchief to his face, attempting to stanch the flow of crimson spurting from his nostrils.

The chaos subsided and the staff was ushered from the blood-splattered chamber. Lipton, still groggy and bleeding from a head wound, pressed a button on his intercom and hoarsely whispered, "Mrs. Bishop, pick up Elizabeth at the hospital and take her to Archbishop Broderick at the Vatican. He'll know what to do. Hurry."

"Yes sir," replied Nora Bishop.

Hans reached over the desk, grabbed the intercom box and smashed it to the floor, stomped it to pieces, then tore the connection from the wall.

Mrs. Bishop, a very astute English woman, fully aware of the events taking place at that moment, picked up a private phone line and called the hospital. She managed to reach Sister Rosemary, who had tended the dying Mrs. Lipton. "Sister," Mrs. Bishop implored, "Please take Elizabeth immediately to Bishop Broderick at the Vatican and tell him that Ambassador Lipton has been beaten and is being detained by the German Gestapo and the Italian police."

"Oh, my dear Lord, how can they do that? This poor child is so distraught!"

"Sister, please hurry right this minute; Elizabeth is in grave danger. The bishop is a close friend of Ambassador Lipton. He'll protect her. Ask him to arrange to claim Mrs. Lipton's body for shipment to London and to call the Swedish ambassador to obtain Mr. Lipton's release. Hurry now. I'll try to meet Elizabeth at the bishop's office. Hurry right this second."

"Mrs. Bishop, I'm on my way; don't worry," the sister replied.

At that moment, Bruno, the other Gestapo agent, opened the door to Mrs. Bishop's office and in sign language imperiously beckoned her to join him. He pointed at her with his forefinger and wiggled his thumb as though he was triggering a gun. Then in guttural English he asked her, "*Vat* is *dein* position here?"

"I handle the food and supplies here," she adroitly answered.

"That's fine, *fräulein*, now you'll be back in England with the rest of these peoples waiting for Adolf Hitler to take over your country."

"Dream on, you fool," she muttered to herself, realizing she was trapped.

☆ ☆ ☆ ☆

February 14, 1952 - Washington, D.C.

The storm had abated during a fitful night for the Milburns. Bart and Elizabeth joined Mrs. Bishop in the breakfast room as Michael and Jenny greeted their parents with a lot of "Daddys" and "Mommys" and other love gibberish.

"Happy Valentine's Day, children," Elizabeth chirped, hugging both of them. "Daddy has a surprise for you."

They immediately jumped into Bart's lap. "What is it, Daddy?" Michael asked.

Bart reached behind himself and produced two wrapped packages. The children grabbed the gifts and plopped on the floor to struggle with the wrappings.

"Mrs. Bishop, please take the children into the playroom," Elizabeth requested.

"Very well," the nanny replied as she scooped up Michael and Jenny, entreating Elizabeth to eat her omelet *fines herbes* while it was hot. "You didn't eat much dinner last night, and Jacques was very upset because he prepared it specially for you," she said, referring to Bart's adopted brother, loyal friend and head of the Nazi Desk at the Central Intelligence Agency.

"Very well, Mommy dear," Elizabeth replied affectionately in her clipped British accent.

Bart finished his orange juice, reached into his jacket pocket and pulled out a small gift package. He placed it before his young wife. "Liz, Happy Valentine's Day to my favorite girl and best friend," he said with a sunny smile, in contrast to the dreary day evident from a large picture window facing a winter-shorn garden and covered pool.

"Tit for tat, my love," she responded as she opened her purse and placed a small package in front of Bart. "Let's finish breakfast and open our gifts."

As they consumed the morning repast, Bart looked at his wristwatch, then gazed into her sparkling hazel eyes. "Honey, I don't have much time to get to the White House. I don't like leaving you this morning; I know I promised to spend the day with you and the rascals, but one doesn't say no to the Prez."

"I understand. But try to hurry back, and don't stop at your office before returning."

"Okay, I'll try. Now, open your package."

Each in short order removed the wrappings. Hers was a black velvet case with a Tiffany imprimatur. His had a Dunhill label on a small blue box.

"Bart, you're a doll," she giggled as she held up a gold bracelet studded with assorted gems.

cigarette lighter with the initials 'BQM' on its top. "For one who has been picking on me to stop smoking, this is an oxymoron and I love it. Thank you."

"Well, if you must smoke, do it with elan."

He stood up and lifted her svelte 5'6" body, his normally steely blue eyes sparkling sunshine, stared at her for a split second, then planted a loving kiss on her receptive mouth. It was a very long kiss.

"Keep that up and I won't let you leave for the White House," she said as he gently placed her down.

"To be continued," he winked wickedly.

"Scoot, and drive carefully." She followed him to their garage and handed him his well-worn trench coat. It was 9:35a.m.

A benign drizzle greeted Bart in his Cadillac convertible as he tooled his way down Connecticut Avenue. The rain was melting the snow and splattered slush over the slow morning traffic. At 9:57a.m., he pulled up to the West Gate of the White House, lowered his window and flashed his security clearance ID to the guard. "Morning, Charlie," Bart greeted the rotund keeper at the gate.

"Morning, Mr. Milburn. You're cleared for 10a.m. Good to see you. That storm yesterday was a bitch."

"That it was, old buddy."

He parked and ran to the West Gate door. John Steelman, tall and scholarly, looked at his watch, adjusted his spectacles and, professor-like, intoned, "I'll say this for you, Bart, as a reluctant visitor, you are prompt. It is exactly 10 a.m. That's probably one of the reasons you became one of the youngest colonels in the Army."

"Flattery will get you everywhere, John," he countered.

"Come on, he knows you're here," Steelman said, leading Bart into the Oval Office.

President Truman was behind his desk. He rose and greeted his visitor. "Colonel, we pushed some buttons and cleared the storm out of town for you," he joked, pointing to a chair.

"Thank you, Mr. President, for that. However, I am a civilian now working in the trenches of our legal system."

Steelman chuckled as the President addressed Milburn.

"Quite rewarding work and hardly in the trenches, young man. Let me see now, for a 33-year-old-or should I say young man-you graduated at age 21, fifth in your class at West Point," the President continued as he waved a dossier at Bart. "You studied languages and became quite fluent in German, Russian, Spanish and French. A multi-linguist. Hmm..."

Bart's steely eyes focused on the President as the litany of his life was being recited. Steelman kept polishing his glasses, glancing intermittently at the discomfiture of Milburn, who indeed appeared much more mature than his years would indicate.

The President droned on: "You went from the Academy at the end of 1940, and from there Lieutenant Barton Quentin Milburn was assigned to Army Intelligence for a period of six months at the Pentagon. General Marshall thought very highly of you and recommended you as military attaché to the American Embassy in London, primarily to observe and coordinate with British Intelligence. That was in May of 1941 and you were only 22 years of age."

Bart squirmed in his chair, obviously anxious to determine why this exercise was ongoing. He looked at Steelman for help. None was forthcoming.

The dossier was still open and the President was not about to desist. Milburn tensed as he realized something heavy was about to come down. He mused with apprehension that he was about to be pressed into service. *Korea? Or what?* He was still in the Reserve. *Am I going to be called back into service?*

"So, there you were in London in the midst of the Battle of Britain when on June 22, 1941, Germany and her satellite nations invaded Russia. During the moment of a very brief euphoria, British Intelligence became highly interested in your knowledge of German and Russian. Churchill asked President Roosevelt to help them with the Russian Embassy in further contacts with the Russian emissaries to London. You became quite popular with the Brits. You met the Prime Minister frequently. Heady stuff for a 22-year-old, eh?"

Bart interrupted. "Mr. President, why are we…"

The President cut him off. "Let me finish and we'll get down to business," he frowned at Bart over the rims of his glasses, then continued: "By May 12, at the age of 23, you were leading an interrogation team, many of whom were senior to you. Your reports to Eisenhower were very helpful. He personally handed you a pair of Silver Oak Leaves, making you a lieutenant colonel. Not long after that you were assigned to the 7th Army headed by Major General George Patton. You soon became a favorite of his. In a way, you two were made for each other. The 7th Army landed on Sicily on May 10, 1943. What I never understood was that you were an intelligence officer and yet you were riding in those tanks through every battle all the way to Palermo with old 'Blood and Guts' himself. Patton loved the glory."

"Mr. President, despite his bad press and theatrics, he was the best fighting general we had. He got the job done," interjected Bart.

Don't let Eisenhower hear that," Truman laughed.

"I'm not demeaning Ike's abilities, but we all know he wasn't a fighting general. He was a tactician slightly junior to General Marshall, who was a planner," Bart countered.

"Right. Now I know why you went to law school at Georgetown and passed the bar, Counselor," Truman said. "Very analytical. Anyway, when Patton was relieved of his command of the 7th Army and replaced by General Bradley, you were back with the Eisenhower staff working Intelligence. Preparation for D-Day was ongoing. You finally made some bomber runs over Germany. You got hit with some flak and got yourself shuttled to a Sussex hospital. Some pain in the butt and a bruise to your dignity. After three weeks of hospitalization you were given a Purple Heart and a Bronze Star. Shortly after you returned to active duty, Ike made you a full colonel. Then came D-Day on June 6, 1944, and you were flying back and forth over Normandy making progress reports along with dozens of other intelligence observers.

"You were there for all of it. Patton got command of the 3rd Army and requested you. Eisenhower obliged. You were with Patton all the way interrogating prisoners.

"Then came the Ardennes Bulge with a savage attack by Field Marshal von Rundstedt on December 15, 1944, four days before your 25th birthday," the president went on.

As the President continued reading passages in the dossier, Bart was taken back to the day after Christmas, 1944.

It was a bitterly cold day. The snow was frozen solid and large patches of ice covered the landscape. Bart was looking over the hordes of German prisoners trampling through the snow. He spotted four German privates who piqued his interest. Speaking perfect German, he ordered them out of the line and brought them to a little hut just outside Malmedy. He assigned an American sergeant and eight soldiers to stand guard over the four. Three of them were very young in comparison to the fourth, who was much older and seemed more polished than the others. Bart tried to break them down. All claimed to say, *"Ich bin ein Soldat* - no Nazi, *Mein Herr."* Bart turned to Sergeant George Hillman, a Jewish lad, ordering him to take them out to the back of the hut and "shoot them one at a time," however, Bart handed his slip of paper to the sergeant, which stated, "Don't shoot anyone. Just fire one shot in the air." And as he handed over the paper, he stated loudly, "Here are your written orders for the execution." Hillman and his men, at gunpoint, shoved the three German soldiers out into the cold. Bart stared at the older man, detecting a sign of recognition of his understanding of the English language.

A shot was heard shortly thereafter, and the older man addressed Bart in perfect English. One of Bart's corporals tensed and pointed his gun at the prisoner in front of Bart. "You're about the coldest American I've ever encountered. Stop that killing out there now," he said imperiously.

Bart shouted, "Hillman, stop everything and come back here alone!" The door opened. The sergeant wanted to say something to Bart. He tried to whisper something in his ear. Bart told him "Shut up!"

"What do you want to tell me?" Bart said to his lone prisoner.

The older man stood up and the sergeant and the corporal alongside him pointed their guns at the standing figure.

Bart shouted, "Sit down now, whoever the hell you are! You're certainly not a sergeant in that noncom uniform you're wearing."

"I am Major General Eric von Heiser of the staff of Field Marshal von Rundstedt and I demand the respect of my adversaries," he pronounced as he stood saluting Bart.

Bart returned his salute and in gentler terms told him to be seated. "General, you tried to hide your identity by wearing a sergeant's uniform and as such you were accorded the treatment that all POWs receive from the Americans."

"Yes, but you killed one of my men back there."

Sergeant Hillman broke in to say, "Colonel, that's what I was trying to tell you. Those three kids back there were pleading for their lives and told us this guy was a high officer. They didn't say who. We couldn't understand German."

"That's okay, Sarge. Nobody's been killed either. That right, Sarge?"

"Yes, sir. They're okay, but scared as hell. None of them claim to be a Nazi. They kept saying, '*Nein* no Nazi.' "

"And neither am I!" roared von Heiser. He slowly sat down and asked Bart for a cigarette, which he obliged him and lighted. "Colonel, I would like to speak with you alone," he requested.

Bart dismissed the sergeant and the corporal, despite their protestations. Before the two left the room, von Heiser said, "Maybe you're not the coldest American I've ever met, but the sharpest. You tricked me and those poor boys out back. Can you get them some food? We haven't eaten in the last two days."

Bart ordered, "Segregate them from the rest of the prisoners and rustle up some chow. This is high- level stuff and I don't want you or your men talking about what took place. Write up a report, mark it confidential and hand it to Colonel George Spota to hold for me. Got it?"

"Yes sir, will do." Sergeant Klinger saluted as Bart unsnapped his holster and placed his Colt .45 on the table in front of him with the safety catch on. Bart remembered Klinger putting this incident in his report, which Truman read through, as Bart pondered the past.

"Colonel, I demand to surrender to General Patton personally."

Bart said, "I don't think that Patton has time to see you. He's chewing the ass off your whole effing Nazi army right back to your rotten evil murdering son-of-a-bitch, Adolf Schickelgruber, in Berlin, or wherever he is hiding."

"Colonel, I want to make it clear that there have been bad feelings about Hitler in the high command of the German army for some time."

Bart snapped, "Bad feelings or not, do you realize what you sons-of-bitches have done to humanity? Hitler, with his cadre of slime, has turned the allegedly intelligent country of Germany into a cauldron of evil. How do your people stand still for this?"

"Colonel, this career army officer disapproves of what Hitler, Himmler, Goebbels and Goering have done to Germany. I was disenchanted with the Nazi movement from the beginning and particularly with that maniac Hitler, who has taken over the command of the German armed forces. There is a spell of fear all over Germany, as well as the high command. Several attempts have been made to kill that bastard, but they've all failed. I am not going to make excuses to fall on deaf ears."

Bart said, "Herr General, no one is capable of apologizing or excusing the execution of our American prisoners of war just a few days ago, not far from here."

"I swear, Colonel, that I know nothing about it. But if it's true, I would be happy to personally execute the perpetrators of that crime. I don't want to go back to Germany until Hitler is removed from power. I will be glad to cooperate with the Americans if it would be kept secret because I fear for my wife and three children, two boys ages 13 and 14, and one girl, age 9. They live in Munich. Hitler would order them killed if he thought I was talking to the

Americans. I'm asking you to see that the three young soldiers be treated well and held somewhere away from the other German prisoners of war."

"By the way, General, what did you do with your uniform?"

"I ripped it to shreds and took the uniform of one of my dead soldiers."

"All right, General, come with me. We'll put you in a room in a nearby house here. I'm assigning ten men to guard you, to feed you, to treat you with respect and to ask no questions."

At that point, Truman captured Milburn's attention away from the pictures being framed in his mind. "You had a hot number on your hands. It took you two days to reach Patton, who told you he had no time. And the record shows that the Bulge wasn't cleaned up until January 31, 1945, although the Nazi drive was halted by December 25. So, Patton ordered you to get word to Eisenhower, who sent a plane to pick you up and bring von Heiser to London. This German general proved to be a font of information. You became Ike's fair-haired boy and got another medal for your efforts. Silver!

"You stayed in London at Allied headquarters making a few European field inspections with Eisenhower and his staff. Churchill had you over to 10 Downing Street to recount the von Heiser capture. He sent a letter of commendation to Roosevelt for you. Churchill was very impressed with you and presented you with another piece of military candy, a British medal for something or the other. Not bad for a 25-year-old American colonel. Well, we're coming to the end of this saga of one Barton Quentin Milburn...am I boring you, my friend, or am I setting you up for something else? The answer is both. I can see it on your taciturn face. Roosevelt died on April 12, 1945, and I took this office, which I never expected to occupy. The war ended on May 7 at 2:45am, French time, in our Rheims Headquarters, but was celebrated here on May 8th. You were there with Eisenhower and the Allied hierarchy. What a career for a youngster your age. You matured very quickly, especially when you accompanied Eisenhower, Bradley and Patton to the first concentration camp freed by the allies. I have a picture here of the three generals, with you right behind them, inspecting the devil's handiwork at Ohrdruf. None of the Generals and staff members could have envisioned the horrors of hell they observed. Your own account makes me shiver now in recollecting the carnage committed there. Piles of bodies, cremation ovens, gallows, and the emaciated walking and crawling almost-dead victims of Hitler's and Himmler's unimaginable maniacal inhumanity."

"Mr. President, after the Allied troops took the town of Gotha, the generals decided to inspect Ohrdruf. The press was there, and Eisenhower's orders were to let the world know what the Nazis were really like. No one could possibly dissect the horror on a person-to-person basis of what was done to the victims of what has come to be known as the Holocaust. Dante's Inferno was a walk in the park compared to those sons of bitches who tore apart every moral code in existence. This was the premeditated murder and torture of not only Jews, but Christians, Gypsies and citizens of every country in Europe."

"I've thought of that many times, Bart, but I can't for the life of me understand why any decent German with a Christian background would stand for the horrors that took place. However, I realize, on analysis, that this was a country living in fear of its next-door neighbors and even members of its own family. All you had to say was 'To hell with Hitler' instead of 'Heil Hitler' and you would be shipped off to a death camp. But, let's go back to Ohrdruf. There you found a young English girl about 15 years of age, emaciated and being beaten by a Nazi captain of the guards. While the media were photographing and interviewing some of the survivors, you decided to walk over to the camp commandant's office. You heard the girl screaming and the Nazi Captain Hugo Schultz swearing at her in German."

The picture was back in Bart's mind again as the President continued to relate the incident at Ohrdruf.

As Bart walked up to the door, he heard a Nazi voice saying, "I have orders direct from ReichsFührer Himmler to move you out of here before the Americans arrive, and if you continue to resist me I will have to drug you. Now behave yourself, you little bitch! I will kill you before I let you talk to the Americans. Be good and Herr Himmler might exchange you for one of our people being held by the Americans." At that moment Bart kicked in the door, with a couple of GIs behind him, and with his Colt .45 he shot Schultz in the groin. He fell to the floor screaming German obscenities at Bart, who merely replied, "Go for your gun, you Nazi piece of dung! Shut up or I'll put another bullet between your eyes." One of the GIs patted down the prostrate Nazi and removed his Luger.

Although emaciated and weak, blood streaming from her mouth and nose, the girl ran to Bart and hugged his knees. She had a Star of David sewn to her prison garb, and in a clipped British accent sobbed, "He was going to rape and kill me!" It turned out that she was Elizabeth, the daughter of Alfred Lipton, who was the ambassador to Italy and had been taken into custody by the Gestapo the day Italy declared war on England and France. She had been shuttled from camp to camp as a pawn to be exchanged for a high Nazi prisoner of the Allies, possibly Rudolf Hess.

Bart looked at the sheet on Hugo Schultz' desk, found the extension number for the front gate and dialed number 12.

A voice answered, "Captain Mark Hower, U.S. Army, here."

"Mark, this is Colonel Milburn. This is very important. If there are any reporters around, you just answer my questions with a yes or no, got it?"

"Yes, sir."

"Is Ike still there?"

"Yes."

"Talking to reporters?"

"Yes."

"Are there any medics around?"

"Yes."

"Many?"

"Yes."

"I hope this line is clear."

"May I say something else, sir?"

"Short and sweet now."

"I think all the krauts have been rounded up."

"Get someone to relieve you at the gate and get a couple of medics to come quickly and directly to the main office here where I am. And tell them not to run but hurry over and bring their kits with them. After that, nice and slowly salute Ike and tell him there is an important call for him on extension 2 and he can use the phone you're on now. Don't hang up, just get to it. Medics first, and then Ike."

Within minutes two medics knocked on the door. "I'm Captain Frank Winslow, sir."

"All right, I just shot this miserable fucking Nazi scum. He's the commandant of this cesspool. If you can save him for a hangman's noose, fine. And if not, so be it. Go to work and keep your mouth shut about this and now, what's your name?"

"Lieutenant Charles Kivovitz, sir."

"Treat this girl very gently. She is a very important lady and one of your landsmann."

"Yes, sir," he replied, opening his medic's bag.

Elizabeth, still in semi-shock and bloodied, stared at Bart as though he was Sir Galahad.

He remembered being called that later.

The phone rang and Bart picked up. "Colonel Milburn here."

The caller was Dwight D. Eisenhower, who said, "Bart, what the hell is this about an important phone call?"

"Sir, I had to use that ruse to keep it privy from the press. Two things, sir...that girl you were asking about, well, she's here identifying herself as the daughter of Sir Alfred Lipton."

"That's wonderful. How is she?"

"A little worse for wear and badly beaten by the camp commandant, a Nazi colonel, Hugo Schultz. I shot him as he was about to assault her to keep her from talking to the Americans."

"Where are you now, Colonel?"

"I'm in the last building, eyes front, straight back, with that big Nazi flag on top."

"Where's Commandant Schultz right now?"

"He's on the floor here, with a medic trying to save him. The girl is being tended by another of our medics."

"All right, if her injuries can withstand it, bring her up front here. This will make a hell of a story; that is, the discovery of the ambassador's daughter. Churchill has been bugging me about her. Let's keep the Schultz shooting quiet. I'll send an ambulance over if he's still alive and can be saved for hanging after a fair hearing."

Bart asked the bloodied little lady, "General Eisenhower asked if you could face the press for a short time."

"I'll try my best," she sobbed, holding his hand tightly.

A sergeant pushed the wheelchair toward the gathering of generals and media. The photographers rapidly clicked away. General Eisenhower leaned over and kissed her forehead and whispered, "You'll be with your father soon."

"Thank you, General. I'll do the best I can," she haltingly replied.

A medic wiped blood off her bruised face. A reporter shouted, "Can you tell us what you can about this camp?"

"Sir, I have just been extracted from the horrors of hell by this office," she replied in her clipped English accent, pointing at Milburn.

"What was that, Ike?"

There was a long pause. Not a sound was heard. Elizabeth slumped in her mobile chair.

"I suggest all of you go back there, talk to survivors and look at the cadavers."

Elizabeth fainted and Bart embraced her. Eisenhower eyed Milburn, indicating the ambulance. Bart carried her to the Army medics. BBC reporters described the scene. Margaret Bourke-White then photographed the horrors of the camp and Life magazine devoted twenty pages to it.

Bart's journey into the past was interrupted as John Steelman came back into the Oval Office, announcing that two men were there and waiting.

"All right, Bart, now to the nitty-gritty...have you ever heard of a man named Frederick Nordheim?" Truman inquired.

Bart answered, "Yes, he's reported to be the richest man in the world, controlling a financial empire called Winston General Associates, Ltd."

The President intervened. "The total issue of stock in that company is 100 shares, all owned by Nordheim. He holds no executive position in any portion of that company. The officers of that company and its subsidiaries are all personal nominees of his. And that's going to be the subject of our luncheon with these two men from the CIA who will brief us on what could be a very disturbing pain in the American psyche. You've got top clearance, as do all the others. Come on, Bart, let's have lunch, and when you hear it all I want your reaction."

"Mr. President, am I here as an observer or participant?"

"Both," snapped Truman.

"What has this to do with my dossier? Am I involved somehow?"

"Not with Nordheim, but you're surely involved with me."

Steelman patted Bart on the back and said, "Relax, you might enjoy this session."

"Like a mustard plaster," Bart whispered. "I have to call home and tell my wife I'll be delayed."

"Use my office, and join us in the dining room straight down the hall."

☆ ☆ ☆ ☆

Elizabeth responded to Bart's call with "Don't tell me...you'll be delayed. I expected it."

"Honey, the President wants me to stay for lunch. I can't refuse, can I?"

"Bart, darling, don't fret. I understand. I've been invited to have lunch with Hazel Norris, Grace Davis and Beatrice Cardley at the Carlton Hotel. You remember them? They are with the BBC. And afterward I intend to do a little shopping at Garfinckel's. Mrs. Bishop will keep the children occupied. The sun's shining through now. See you at home later for dinner. Take your time. I love you," she gushed.

"Love you too, my doll. See you later. And thanks for being so under-standing. Please don't mention my visit to the White House to your lady friends."

"Of course not," she bye-byed.

Bart made his way to the President's private dining room. where Truman was just greeting the two men he had mentioned. They were Lloyd Sedgwick and Richard Maybrook, both assistant directors at the Central Intelligence Agency, the successor to the old Office of Strategic Services during World War II.

Steelman said, "I believe you men know Bart Milburn."

"Indeed we do," Sedgwick replied.

"Rick Maybrook and Sedge worked with me doing a little hedge-hopping, checking out those brutal concentration camps," Bart acknowledged. "Let's see, yes, it was the spring of 1945 at the war's end. That was Ike's assignment to me. Good to see you men." Hawkins, the butler and all-around man for the President, put a bourbon and branch water before Truman at the head of the table. A scotch and soda for Steelman, a glass of sherry for Maybrook, a vodka martini for Bart and a glass of Riesling wine for Sedgwick. The libations contrasted the diversity of the five men.

All opted for a Caesar salad, Southern fried chicken, french fried potatoes and a potpourri of mixed vegetables.

"Dig in, gentlemen," Truman urged, "and don't hesitate to eat the best Southern fried chicken east of the Mississippi with your hands. We're all ex-Army folk here."

Over steaming hot coffee and apple pie a la mode, Truman turned to Maybrook and invited him to do a quick rundown on the subject of Frederick Nordheim.

Maybrook began, "The gentleman we're discussing has a most interesting ca-reer, though very much under-publicized. He shuns publicity. He is socially very much a recluse, yet he has had contacts with the royalty of the world and kings of the underworld. Met with Lucky Luciano in Cuba, January 5 of this year."

Truman, Steelman and Bart looked up at each other after that disclosure.

Sedgewick transferred the passport copy around the table, first to the President and then around the table to the others. It showed a round-faced, double-chinned, gray-haired man with matching brush cut, wide mustache and a Van Dyke beard. He seemed rather distinguished, although his brown eyes were squinting, possibly due to the flash of the camera.

Steelman commented, "He looks more like a professor than a tycoon."

"What a tycoon," Maybrook added. "He's reported to be worth over forty billion dollars with a big B, we have learned. But that's ahead of Mr. Sedgwick's report."

Sedgwick, a little annoyed at the interruption, continued his report. "His full name on the passport, as you can clearly see on this enlarged photo, is Frederick Avram Nordheim, born February 16, 1890, which would make him 62 years of age two days from today. His birthplace is listed as Stockholm, Sweden, but he is now a naturalized citizen of Liechtenstein and listed as an ambassador without portfolio, representing the principality in the world of commerce and trade. The total population of this tiny state is 23,000. It is a monarchy. The country is Catholic and its language is German. Rick, pick it up from here," Sedgwick said, turning to his counterpart.

"Mr. President, if I may, I'd like to thumbnail it from here and then present you with four copies of our joint report."

The President nodded assent.

Maybrook continued, "He's had visits to the rulers of Saudi Arabia, attended the crowning of King Idris I on December 24, 1951, and met three times with the Duke of Windsor, the governor general of the Bahamas. He met the former Prince of Wales, who later became King Edward VIII and abdicated his throne December 11, 1936, to marry an American divorcee named Wallis Warfield Simpson. Now, here's a very strange set of coincidences. On September 21, 1949, the People's Republic of China was announced as a national entity in Peking by the People's Political Consultative Conference under the leadership of Mao Tse-tung. Chou En-lai became premier and foreign minister on October 1, 1949. Shortly thereafter our Soviet friends, true to their colors, signed a thirty-year treaty of Friendship, Alliance and Mutual Assistance with this newly born republic."

"Come on, Mr. Maybrook, that's all distasteful history to us; let's move on."

"But, Mr. President, to quote Lewis Carroll, it gets *curiouser and curiouser.* A former FBI agent, Darren Mayfield, fluent in Chinese and having watched the Chinese underworld while working for the Justice Department, quits his job at the FBI in May 1945 and is next heard of visiting Peking on February 20, 1950. Next we know, he's with Nordheim on his 175-foot yacht in Monaco. We have photos of Mayfield and Nordheim on the rear deck of the yacht, appropriately named The Flying Eagle. Here are the pictures. The guy in profile with the Van Dyke beard is Nordheim, and he's in animated discussion with a full-faced Darren Mayfield. There are several snaps here.

"Five days prior to that visit of Mayfield's to Peking, the USSR, on February 15, 1950, repudiated the Yalta Agreement. Later, in 1950, Great Britain recognized the People's Republic of China.

"Nordheim and Mayfield fly to Peking," Maybrook continued. "They meet with Chou En-lai and sign a multi-billion-dollar deal to furnish China with arms of every nature. The plane leaves there and flies straight to Moscow. As you well

"Nordheim has a team of reps all over the world map. All of various nationalities. We are not certain yet whether his activities are political or financial. We don't know where his money came from originally. Our contacts with Israeli intelligence at the Mossad have brought us a mixed bag of answers. According to them, Nordheim claims to be Jewish, but they haven't been able to validate the accuracy of this detail. He has provided Israel with arms and money in their battle with the Arab countries. But they believe he has fed Egypt, Jordan, Syria, Lebanon and Iraq with equal or more materiel. They have no solid confirmation of this except that they have captured Soviet arms and tanks. The Mossad believes that the arms had been sold to the Arabs and Israelis by Winston General Ltd.

"They are fully aware of Nordheim's peregrinations and they are trying to sort it out," Maybrook went on. "They've recruited some Irish, French and Swedish agents to check on him. We understand that our State Department is attempting to ameliorate past differences between the UK and Israel. A Sir Alfred Lipton, of Jewish faith and a member of Parliament, has been having private talks with Israel, the U.S. State Department and the British Foreign Office. The Mossad reports some progress is being made."

Bart cut in. "The gentleman you mentioned, Sir Alfred Lipton, happens to be my father-in-law. I had no idea he was involved in this activity. He's a secular Jew and more of a monotheist, if that means anything in this equation."

"Well, maybe you'd also like to know," said Sedgwick very quietly, "he has British Intelligence working hand in glove with us on Nordheim."

"My wife and I had him here with us this last Christmas, but he never said a word about his activities."

"We know that," Sedgwick and Maybrook chorused.

"We had a visit with him the day before he returned to England, Sedgewook added. "We asked him to let the President talk to you first."

Nonplussed, Bart's response was simply, "I'll be damned."

"That's the way it goes in this gumshoe business, Bart," Maybrook observed.

"Well, what else do we know about Mr. Nordheim?" the President queried.

"In a capsule, Mr. President, he is, without a doubt, one of the richest men in the world," Sedgwick continued. "He has a mansion in Buenos Aires, a hundred-acre farm in La Plata, completely fenced and gated. He has a large spread in Vancouver, Canada, and another 175-foot yacht moored there. He maintains a large twelve-room apartment in Paris in a new building next to the Hotel Plaza Athenee. He has bank accounts at the Banque Lorraine in Geneva and at the Bank Royale in Zurich. He has accounts and friends in the National Pacific Bank in Vancouver, Canada. He also has friends and stocks in two Wall Street brokerage houses, Thornton & Wiley and Fenwick Brothers. All of the foregoing property, bank, stocks and yachts are in the name of Eagle General Associates, a subsidiary of Winston General Ltd., headquartered in Vaduz, the capital of Liechtenstein. They own another subsidiary, Eagle Shipping Ltd., with a fleet of twenty-five — ten freighters and fifteen oil tankers. They have interests in West German oil refineries and steel manu-

oil tankers. They have interests in West German oil refineries and steel manufacturing, Bordeaux wine, French food producers, and Sicilian cattle and sheep farms. They maintain an office in Caracas, Venezuela, mostly to monitor its shipping contractors for Eagle freighters carrying coffee and textiles. We have reason to believe connections exist between the drug cartels and Eagle. One of the most powerful drug lords, Pablo Cortez, has been seen entering the Eagle Shipping Ltd. offices. The FBI and the American Customs Service have been checking their ships at American ports and have found nothing so far. If the Eagle has contraband, they must have transferred it to other carriers outside the twelve-mile limit. Our Coast Guard has been alerted," Sedgwick concluded.

"All in all, Mr. President," Maybrook remarked, "we are concentrating on the shipment of arms to North Korea and China. As per your instructions to the Secretary of Defense, the Navy has been stalking all ships headed that way and, in particular, the Eagle fleet. Two of their ships were deep-sixed a few days ago."

"Okay," said Truman, "this mystery man must be fully investigated. Who is he? What is he? And what's his game besides money? He smells bad to me. Thank you, gentlemen. Keep me advised. Good afternoon. Bart, come back to my office," he ordered, shaking hands with the two departing guests.

In the Oval Office, Truman's secretary waved a handful of message slips at the President.

"Bart, give me fifteen minutes and I'll take care of these. You probably have some calls of your own to make. Steelman will stay with me while I appease a few senators. You can use Steelman's desk. I'll be with you shortly," Truman gestured with a wave of dismissal.

Bart lifted the phone to the White House operators. "Yes, Dr. Steelman?" one of them responded.

"No, this is Barton Milburn. I'm trying to reach my office. The number is…"
She cut him off, "I have it."

A voice responded, "Graybeal, Arnold & Milburn."

"Sheila, this is Mr. Milburn. Put me through to Nancy."

"Yes, sir, your secretary is in the library. I'll have her in a moment."

In seconds, a very efficient 48-year-old woman who had been acting as Bart's right and left hand came on with "Mr. Milburn, I've been trying to track you all over town. Your wife wasn't much help. She didn't know where I could reach you. Where are you?"

"Sorry about that, Nancy, I can't tell you now. You'll probably learn all about it when I see you. No more questions, please."

"Very well," she snapped. "Sy Fisher of the American Trucking Association has called here five times. He's at the Mayflower. There is a meeting there at 5p.m.regarding the Pennsylvania Trucking Association's lawsuit against the railroads."

"Nancy, cool him down and tell him that I'll be there with some information that should please them all," he soothed her. "And you know what it is, but say nothing more."

"Oh, yes, you mean the meeting you arranged with Walter Tuohy, president of the Chesapeake & Ohio, and Jim Syms of the Pennsylvania Railroad."

"Right on, Nancy, this weekend at the Greenbrier. Oh, I forgot to mention it to Elizabeth. She's going with me, but doesn't know it yet. I hope to come by the office before too long. Anything else?"

"Just that Mr. Graybeal wanted you to know that he filed a writ of certiorari with the Supreme Court on the Brewer's Board of Trade matter. Other than that, everything can wait. Oh, the Cafritz Building management gave the okay for us to take over the fourth floor as of April 1."

"Good, see you soon," Bart replied.

Steelman opened the door and beckoned Bart into the Oval Office. Truman pointed to the chair behind his desk. "Sit there for a minute or two, Bart, and try to imagine some of my problems."

Bart and the President were head to head, *one on one*, as Bart put it later.

"I went through this exercise with you, Bart, for more than one reason. You've got a good legal mind, from all I hear. Your record in intelligence matters is excellent. But I'm fully aware of your antipathy to the Nazi scum who are scattered all over the world. We only nailed a small cadre of the higher-ups in that miserable *gang of world's worst thugs in the history of man* at Nuremberg. I am going to tell you something that is not in any of those reports we heard today."

Bart's interest was captured, so he leaned forward and said, "You have my full attention, sir."

"Colonel, what I'm going to reveal to you dies in this room for the present. Israel's prime minister, David Ben-Gurion, reached me last week. His boys at the Mossad, their CIA, have handed him a super-confidential *for your eyes only* memo. But he decided to share this with me after pondering it for several days. He remembered that I ordered recognition of Israel shortly after their declaration of a new state on May 14, 1948, so he is grateful for our support. The Israelis believe Nordheim is <u>not</u> a Jew. The Mossad is of the opinion that he is a high-placed Nazi whose death has never been verified."

Bart's interest was more than piqued. The wheels were turning in his mind. His memories of the death camps were vivid, and his nostrils flared like a toro entering the bullfight ring.

"Don't tell me they believe he's Martin Bormann, Heinrich Himmler, Joseph Goebbels, or the man himself? They shoveled billions into Swiss accounts knowing the end was in sight!" Bart exclaimed.

"Hold on a minute, counselor," Truman cautioned, holding up his hand as a stop sign. "There is not a scintilla of evidence in anyone's hand to support that theory, nor does Ben-Gurion vouch for its authenticity. But that very suspicion by the Mossad calls for a red light to start blinking in this office. Apart from all that, we learned that he was delivering arms to North Korea, and that's why we sank his two ships."

"Well, why are you sharing this with me? I can't blame the Israelis for being paranoid on that subject. But with nothing more than a firm belief without a substantive iota of evidence, it means very little," Bart observed. "However, his Korean activity is another matter."

"Look, Bart, I didn't ask you over here for a walk in the park. I haven't discussed this with our White House counsel, Clark Clifford, or Don Dawson. Only one person besides you knows of that call from Ben-Gurion, and that's John Steelman. No one at the CIA, FBI, or anyone on the White House staff knows it. I just don't want rumors being leaked to the media. Besides, Clark Clifford has enough to do here."

"Okay, why me?" Bart asked.

"Because I want you to track down this Nordheim character on a very confidential basis. I know you have a very lucrative law practice, and I don't want to put a dent in that. But I'm asking you to accept an ambassador's role as a roving trade representative so that you'll have diplomatic status. Do some traveling in an effort to unravel the mystery of Frederick Avram Nordheim. Avram. That's a Hebrew name, isn't it?"

"Mr. President, *why me?*"

"Because you're the best outside man I can think of. You'll have a large enough budget to put all of our facilities at your disposal. I'll set up an office for you at Commerce, which will be a no man's land for anyone except you and a handpicked staff. You can look into your law practice quietly at your leisure. Think about it over the weekend. Talk to your partners and your wife without revealing the true purpose of your assignment."

"How do you expect *me* to be confirmed for the job of ambassador - not that I'm thinking of accepting your offer?"

"You've got two buddies in the Senate who'll push it through pronto for you, Senator Earle Clements, the Democratic Whip, and Senator Styles Bridges, the Republican powerhouse."

"Mr. President, please let me ponder this until next Tuesday. I've got a few chores to attend to and a lot of thinking about your offer. I am not one bit honored by your proposal."

A tight-lipped Truman stared into Milburn's eyes and with a grim smile said, "The word *proposal* - is that what a lawyer uses when trying to mediate a client's settlement controversy? Get back to me Tuesday. Regards to your pretty little wife. She's a stunner. Both Bess and Margaret like her very much."

They shook hands, then Bart went by Steelman's office and waved goodbye to him.

CHAPTER TWO

February 14, 1952, 2:30 p.m. -Washington, DC

Bart Milburn's mind was spinning as he drove to the Cafritz Building. Tires screeched as he drove up the ramp to the fifth floor, which comprised the offices of Graybeal, Arnold & Milburn, housing twenty-five lawyers, six paralegals and two dozen secretaries.

Nancy Telford, slightly plump, well dressed in a beige jacket, skirt and light blue ruffled blouse, greeted Bart with "At last, we can get a few things done. Please sign these checks and that stack of letters you dictated two days ago."

Bart feverishly scrawled his name to the checks and seven letters to clients.

Nancy swept up the checks and letters, then "harrumphed" out the door.

"No note for my records?" she called to him as he went out the door to talk with his partner, Martha Arnold, and filled her in on his upcoming meeting with the American Trucking Association at 5pm and the trip of peace between the railroads and the truckers.

A beautiful 38-year-old woman originally from Knoxville, Tennessee, Martha Arnold had wavy, shoulder length, red hair and was well dressed in a pink blouse and navy skirt, her eyeglasses lodged on her forehead. "How did you pull that off, Bart?" she inquired.

"You know I have weekly lunches with John L. Lewis at that back table he's occupied for years at the Carlton. Well, we were doing our usual chitchatting about this and that and I happened to mention our lawsuit on behalf of the Pennsylvania Truckers Association. He got interested and pressed me for details. I pointed out the railroad's control of the legislature in Harrisburg. They forced the trucks passing through the state to unload part of their cargo because of the 45,000-pound weight limitations on their state highways. The PMTA was seeking a 60,000-pound allowance. The railroad stopped them in every session of the legislature. I finally hit the railroads with a lawsuit with which you are familiar. Anyway, Lewis arranged a meeting with his longtime friend, Cyrus Eaton. After meeting with him, I got calls from Walter Tuohy of the Chesapeake & Ohio Railroad and Jim Syms, president of the Pennsylvania Railroad. The Chesapeake & Ohio owns the Greenbrier Hotel in White Sulphur Springs, West Virginia. They invited me and the key truckers and their wives to join them at Penn Station in New York on Friday night, where several private cars would await us to carry all to Greenbrier for a weekend of golf and socializing and a short meeting to settle the impasse. Just the luck of the draw in my friendship with John L. I owe him one, or maybe more than one. He's a very self-educated man. Knows all of Shakespeare and the Bible and quotes them frequently. Well, Martha, we may have a winner here without depositions and court wrangling."

"Good work, Bart, and good luck. Now, I've got to finish this settlement agreement between Mack Truck and Ward La France. See you."

☆ ☆ ☆ ☆

February 14, 1952, Same day - 5 p.m. - Washington, D.C.
The trio awaiting him greeted Bart as he entered their suite at the Mayflower. Simon Fisher, Harry Gorman and Louis Schramm, CEOs of three of the largest trucking firms in the country. Sy Fisher, the smallest of the three, appeared more like a college dean, in contrast to public opinion of what had been considered to be a rough-and-tumble business. He headed a fleet of 200 semi-trailers operating out of Chicago and serving the 48 states. He was a former attorney, erudite and articulate. He was chairman of the committee representing the industry in its battle with the railroads.

Louis Schramm, head of Allied Van Lines, and Harry Gorman of Gorman Transport, tall and executive in their mien, were the other two of this special committee of the Common Carriers Conference, a unit of the American Trucking Association, headquartered in Washington.

"Have a drink and tell us the good news," Fisher said, pointing to the bar in the large suite.

"No drink for me, men, thank you, and I'll come right to the point," Bart replied. Then he filled them in on the upcoming weekend at the Greenbrier. "We can wrap up the PMTA lawsuit and get our 60,000-pound law through the legislature in Harrisburg with their acquiescence. The case will be on hold till that becomes fact. This get-together is to build a rapport between you men and the railroad tycoons. Even Alfred Perlman, president of the New York Central, is on board and will be at the Greenbrier for this peace-pipe-smoking affair."

"How did you pull this off, Bart?" Schramm asked.

"This isn't a trap or a ploy of some kind, is it?" Gorman questioned.

"Come on, Harry, I didn't fall off a turnip truck. We're dealing with very honorable men under auspices I'd rather not delineate at this time. Besides, they can't afford the risk of a far-flung series of depositions. Bring your wives and expect to be treated with kid gloves. Now, I have to go with one plea. I expect you all to be charming and on your best behavior. I firmly believe we've got a winner here. I've got to go now."

After the routine back-slapping and hand-shaking, Bart was gone.

Dusk was rapidly enveloping the city, and Bart, hardly aware of the homebound traffic, had blocked out all but his meeting with Truman and the mystery figure of Nordheim. His personal and professional life was caught up in a quagmire of red and green lights. As he maneuvered his convertible along the road skirting West Potomac Park, he slowed down, stared at the Lincoln Memorial, looked at good old Abe and unconsciously shrugged his shoulders. A couple of honking horns behind him automatically caused him to resume his speed on the way to his Rock Creek Park home.

Elizabeth, Michael, and Jenny, and Squire, their Dalmatian pup, with Mrs. Bishop standing behind them, greeted him. He kissed Elizabeth, lifted both children in one swoop and hugged them, put them down, patted the tail-wagging Squire and acknowledged Mrs. Bishop. The warmth of this welcome cleared his mind.

"All right, children, let Daddy change his clothes. It's time for your dinner. Go with Mrs. Bishop. You'll see Daddy later," Elizabeth directed.

Things at the house went back to a normal routine. The kids were fed. Half an hour with Bart and off to a bath and bed for the little ones. Elizabeth and Bart were in his den sipping martinis. Bart suggested they have dinner served in that room.

Bart briefed her on the Greenbrier weekend and stopped there. Liz, knowing her man, bided her time before satiating her curiosity about the White House visit.

"How was your day?" Bart broke the silence.

"Dinner is ready," Mrs. Bishop announced, tapping the den door gently. "Jacques called and left word he would be working late this evening and to eat without him."

"Thank you, dear," Elizabeth replied.

Bart held his wife tightly and kissed her forehead. They sat down at a mahogany table with two leaves lifted for such intimate occasions.

"My day was fine. Lunch with the girls and a little shopping. That's it, and besides, that question is a non sequitur in light of *your* day. So?" Liz responded with that all-too-wise smile, a cover for her piercing glance at Bart.

"Honey, it was a tortuous morning with the President, who read me my dossier down to the last period. Then lunch with Steelman and two other guys, followed by a one-on-one private meeting with Truman. The import of it all is top secret, and the bottom line is…" He stopped.

She waited apprehensively. A pregnant pause ensued. Dinner was getting cold on the table, so he rose and locked the door of the den.

He held her hand and looked straight into her anxious eyes. "Truman wants to appoint me ambassador at large as a roving trade representative. He was very adamant that I accept it. Remember, I am an Army reserve officer, and if I try to wiggle out of this, he more than hinted that I could be called up for duty in Korea."

Liz broke in: "He won't do that, since you have been handing him all that intelligence material that those Chiang Kai-shek's generals who were here last month gave you for delivery to the White House."

"That's speculation, Liz, my love. Truman's got a stiff spine and the instincts of a bantam rooster."

"Bart, there's a lot more to this than you're telling me. This has as much to do with trade as our garbage collector does."

"True. Let's compromise for the moment, and I'm swearing you to silence on this much. It's a cover for an intelligence gathering operation. And are you ready for this? Your father, who spent the holidays with us, never mentioned the subject matter, although he had knowledge of the Truman problem and left town without a word to us."

Elizabeth's mouth was open, but nothing was forthcoming. She stared at the window, which picture-framed the garden and park grounds beyond.

"Where's Jacques? Is he upstairs?"

"No, he called saying he's working late and will have dinner at the office."

"I can understand that. He will be involved in this matter."

"Mmm, I won't probe."

"Liz, believe me, it's heavy-duty stuff involving the CIA, British Intelligence and more."

"Bart, darling, I never probed you or Jacques on delicate matters, and I have no intention of doing that now. This is a decision you'll have to make on your own. And I know, in due time, sweetheart, as always, you'll tell me all that you think I should know. We've been through a lot together. I'll back you, no matter what you decide."

☆ ☆ ☆ ☆

Sunday, February 17, 1952 - White Sulphur Springs, West Virginia

The trip to Greenbrier proved to be a welcome respite for Liz and Bart. Mother Nature cooperated, with sunshine, blue skies and an unusually warm winter weekend. Temperatures ranged in the middle to high sixties.

The business conference between the truckers and the railroad execs lasted 75 minutes and proved to be a total success for the warring parties, as well as a great victory for Bart and satisfaction for all concerned.

The host, Walter Tuohy, pulled out all the stops. Champagne, caviar, Beef Wellington and a variety of goodies at each meal.

Despite the question mark that hung over the Milburns regarding Truman's demand for an answer by Tuesday, Bart and Elizabeth managed to enjoy their sojourn as a honeymoon holiday.

☆ ☆ ☆ ☆

Tuesday, February 19, 1952 - Washington, D.C.

Bart and Elizabeth spent their breakfast hour at home with Michael and Jenny. Mrs. Bishop ushered the children out of the breakfast room. Liz and Bart silently sipped their coffee, each waiting on the other to get to the subject they had been pondering after their holiday at Greenbrier.

Bart less than gently put his coffee mug on the table, rattling the other dishes and silverware. Liz, startled for a moment, looked up and blurted, "What was that for?"

"I've made up my mind," he replied. "I'm not going to be stampeded into a rash decision. I'm not interested or cut out for an ambassadorship. There are other ways I can accommodate our President without going through this charade."

"Hear, hear!" Liz applauded approvingly, emulating her father in the British Parliament.

"And that's that," Bart acknowledged her plaudits. He rose, bent down, kissed her on the lips and waved goodbye.

"Good luck," she whispered as he left the room on his way to the office.

Bart had completed most of his backlog of client problems on Monday when Nancy Telford brought him his dictation of the previous day. He read them through and nodded approval to Nancy, who smiled her satisfaction. They had brought everything pending up to date, and she was pleased, but waited for some explanation of his whereabouts on the 14th of February.

"Nancy, please get John Steelman on the phone for me and, yes, that's where I was last week."

She turned to go and, as she exited, looked back at him, then shook her head from side to side.

"He's on," she intercommed.

"John, as ordered, I'm reporting in, but I've got to have a little time with the President."

"Problems, Bart?" Steelman asked.

"Not really; it's just a matter of tactics that I would like to lay before him."

"Okay, Bart, let me see what his time is like and I'll get back to you at your office."

Fifteen minutes later Steelman called back. "The President will see you at 4:30 this afternoon. He filled me in on your private chat with him. He wants me to sit in on the meeting with you. See you then," he clicked off.

☆ ☆ ☆ ☆

Tuesday, February 19, 1952, Same day - 4:30 p.m. - White House

Bart, prompt as always, was ushered into the Oval Office by Steelman.

"Well, my young friend, have you reached a decision on my proposal?" Truman asked, leaning back in his chair.

"Mr. President, I've done a lot of thinking about this Nordheim problem and, quite respectfully, I do not believe that we can penetrate the shadow for substance by cloaking me in diplomatic garb. There are several imponderables that have to be evaluated, sir."

"Bart, you're not in court right now. Let's have some plain talk. What are you getting at?" Truman snapped.

"Okay, sir. Most respectfully, as an ambassador I would be subject sooner or later to some media attention. Secondly, if I were to undertake this investigation of Nordheim, I'd prefer to do it in the guise of a civilian entrepreneur and attorney, possibly with CIA cover and assistance. Also, there's the problem of how long this job will take." Bart paused for a couple of seconds.

"Go on, counselor. You obviously have a few other things on your mind. Let's have it."

"Very well, sir. You have made it clear to a few insiders that you're not going to seek another term. And should Eisenhower, who has already announced his campaign, or someone else fill this office, the Nordheim chase could end abruptly. And some newshound, congressman or senator could start asking questions about 'what have we accomplished' in the way of trade and commerce."

"A point well taken," Truman acknowledged.

Steelman nodded assent and stared quizzically at Bart.

In a much more conciliatory tone and with an air of relaxation, Truman leaned back in his chair and waved both hands receptively while smiling at the unfeigned young man. "Let's hear it. What exactly do you propose?" Steelman interposed, "Bart, relax, we're all on the same team. Let your hair down and get it all out."

"Okay, Mr. President, bear with me as I go through a little reprise of our last meeting."

Truman glanced at his desk clock and noted, "We've got until six or 1800 as you military men put it. However, Bess and Margaret expect me to entertain some friends from Kansas City upstairs. So, shoot."

"When you went through the litany of my career in the dossier, I had pictorial visions of events I lived through during my service. Each event is deeply engraved in my mind. I freely admit to a deep and abiding hatred for the Nazis and most of the Germans who professed ignorance of the atrocities that took place for the 12 years of Hitler's regime. I cannot erase this bias, predicated on what I encountered and observed throughout the war. Not only that, sir, our American hands were not too clean prior to the war."

"What do you mean by that, Bart?" Truman queried.

"Mr. President," Bart said, raising his voice, "need I mention that we turned away over one thousand German Jewish refugees aboard the German liner SS St. Louis. Then there was the infamous refugee conference in 1938 at Evian-les-Bains on Lake Geneva in France, where the Nazis were willing to release or sell Jews for $250 apiece, and thirty-two nations, including ourselves, refused the offer."

"True, true!" the President exclaimed. There were some bitter fights about that in FDR's cabinet meetings, as I later learned. If you recall, I was in the Senate then, and a first-termer at that. But, Bart, I *was* aware of the Jewish problem in Germany."

Bart interjected, "Mr. President, I did not mean to imply that you were in a position to open our doors to these beleaguered, hapless Jews. Those Nazi bastards, a German government run by a bunch of hoodlums, the scum of the earth, were slaughtering Jews and Christians by the millions, and America and the world stood still. This century will go down in history as the worst in civilization. I saw it with my own eyes; the carnage defies every tenet of morality. 'The extirpation of a whole people.' "

"Hold on, Bart," the President entreated. "I share your anguish. Let me remind you that my best friend and former business partner is a Jew. I heard his cries of pain over the atrocities in Europe. There was little I could do. But I assure you that, in retrospect, I am ashamed of our immigration policies during those days. That's why, despite much opposition in my own cabinet and in the Congress by members of both parties, I moved quickly to recognize the state of Israel. Your passionate hatred for these Nazi bastards is understandable and is shared by me. I know they are still scattered around the world. I would like to round up every one of these lice and, like Judge Roy Bean, give them a fair trial, then hang them en masse, if possible. If Nordheim is one of them, we've got to get him."

"Okay, Mr. President, let me present a scenario. Whether Ike or a Democrat succeeds you, we need a bridge to them to continue the search for our suspect."

"Bart, I promise to fill in Eisenhower and his opponent with my urgent recommendation that the investigation not be thwarted, but backed to the fullest. First, let me hear your plan."

"Very well, sir," Bart replied. "As you probably are aware, the director of the CIA, General Walter Bedell Smith, and I are very well acquainted. We worked closely together under Eisenhower during the war. I propose that I be permitted to work out a cover plan for our Operation Lucifer with General Smith. I do not mean to be presumptuous, but I assume that if you approve my suggestion you would first discuss it with him."

A long, pregnant pause ensued. Truman templed his hands, tapping the fingers against the others. Steelman stood up and reached for the electric coffee percolator, waving it at both men. They assented, and cups of hot coffee were placed in front of them, then one for himself. After a few sips, Truman looked at Steelman, who nodded his head. He glanced back at Bart. "I like it, Colonel, but I won't approve it at this moment until I chat with the 'Beetle'. Operation Lucifer? That's good. You'll hear from me. Regards at home."

The meeting was over, and after Milburn left the White House, Steelman called General Smith at CIA headquarters at Langley, Virginia. "General," Steelman said, "the President would like you to join him for breakfast here at the White House tomorrow at 8:30 a.m. if that's convenient."

"Look forward to it, John," he replied.

"One more thing, General. Is this phone clear?"

"Hang up, John, and I'll call you on your private line."

Steelman reached into the bottom drawer of his desk and picked up the receiver of his direct line. "Okay, General, pick up the Nordheim file from Maybrook, Sedgwick, or Jacques Laurent and read it tonight."

"Gotcha," he replied, and clicked off.

The following morning this tall, impressive man of military bearing met with Truman. He had served his stint as ambassador to Moscow and had retired from military service with no political bent except to serve his country quietly.

The breakfast meeting came right to the point. The President first tested the waters by asking General Smith for his opinion of Bart Milburn.

"Mr. President, it is rare in a lifetime where you have exposure to a young man who is knowledgeable beyond his years, trustworthy and as likable as young Milburn. If he stayed in the Army as a career, he would undoubtedly become a general, and probably Chief of Staff. In short, we worked together and I found him to be an excellent intelligence officer and a fine human being."

"Quite a laudatory appraisal."

"Deserved."

"Well then, General, I want him to head up a team to track down this Nordheim character. I even offered him a roving ambassadorship, with trade and commerce as a cover. He turned it down, saying he would much prefer to work out a cover plan with you. He said he worked with you during the war and felt that you and your agency would be able to work out a cover and a staff to go with it. If you approve, I'll arrange all the necessary additional funds for Operation Lucifer, as he called it."

A laugh followed. "Mr. President, is there something more to this than what appears in our files?"

"Yes, Walter, and here it is. Prime Minister Ben-Gurion called a few days ago. He had a *For your eyes only* memo from Mossad. He thought about it for several days and finally decided to share it with me. Now, without a specific piece of evidence they could put their hands on, they have every reason to believe that Frederick Nordheim is not a Jew, but is masquerading as one. They believe that Nordheim is one of the top Nazis who escaped and is now one of the richest men in the world, if not the richest."

General Smith's handsome face hardened into a sinister look, his jaw jutting forward. "Mr. President, I've seen some of the pictures of Nordheim in our file, yet I can't place the profile or the girth of the man to match any of the five heavyweights of the scum of the Nazi leaders. Yet, it's seven years since the war ended, and a lot can be done to alter or disguise one's image. But it is the *who* that bothers me. We have more than one reason to investigate this man: his Peron connection, his Chinese connection, his arms connection with the North Koreans, the drug connection, his Mafia connection, and now this possible Nazi connection. What a plateful."

"For sure, Walter. But there is one caveat: I don't want this Nazi allegation spread through your agency, for fear of a leak. Trust only those you are certain you can trust. How do you feel about Milburn spearheading this investigation undercover?"

"I think he's perfect. I wish I had him full time. He's a sharp lawyer, has a great mind for detail and doesn't jump to conclusions until he has all the evidence to back it up. He proved that during the war. For security reasons, I would rather not meet with him at Langley. Also, I believe it would be wise to include Allen Dulles, my number two man, who, if Ike is elected, will probably replace me. Forgive that reference to Ike, sir."

"Not at all, Walter. I admire Ike, but I'm sorry to see him get caught up in a political maelstrom. This is a dirty business. But I want to be kept up to date during my tenure here."

"Of course, Mr. President."

"The safest place for a meeting would be this building on Sunday. I'll make the Cabinet Room available for you. Bring Dulles, Laurent, Maybrook, Sedgwick, and a handpicked team. I'll have Milburn here. Say, 8 o'clock breakfast served there, and none of our people will be around to bother you except my kitchen staff. How does that strike you, General?"

"Sounds fine."

"I'll meet with Milburn privately before Sunday. Dr. Steelman will get you all cleared and settled, then you will be on your own."

"Yes, good idea for you and Milburn to meet first. Thank you, Mr. President," Smith said in parting. "I'll keep you advised, sir."

"Good luck."

☆ ☆ ☆ ☆

Sunday, March 2, 1952 - 7:30 a.m.

A mini-bus with six men and two women aboard left the Langley headquarters of the CIA bound for the White House. The man driving the minibus was Richard Maybrook, assistant director of the CIA.

At the West Gate, he flashed his credentials and the other seven held theirs up for inspection. They were quickly waved on through. Right behind the shuttle bus, a blue Cadillac convertible pulled up to the security guard. Bart Milburn reached for his ID, and the guard waved him through with a "Good morning, Mr. Milburn."

"Same to you, Frank," Bart replied, waiving.

John Steelman greeted the retinue and guided them directly into the Cabinet Room.

The table was laden with a variety of breakfast foods: pitchers of freshly squeezed orange juice, a variety of dry cereal boxes, milk, half-and-half cream, strawberries, bananas and assorted fruits, croissants, bagels, cream cheese, smoked salmon and thermo-lined pitchers of hot coffee. If eggs were required, Nelson, a pleasant, elderly white-haired butler, was in attendance to oblige.

At the center of the table was General Walter Bedell Smith. Alongside him on his right sat Allen Dulles; on his left was Richard Maybrook, next to him was Barton Milburn, and opposite Dulles was Lloyd Sedgwick. The two women faced each other: Katherine Wharton, in charge of classified files, and Margaret Wilson, internal comptroller. At the end of the group and across from each other were Phillip Berger, chief of covert operations; Anthony Fuentes, heading the South American desk, and Jacques Laurent, chief of the Nazi desk.

During the next half hour, small talk took place while the food was being served and consumed. Nelson cleared the table and left a large electric coffee percolator on a buffet table behind the seat occupied by the general. He excused himself, saying, "Just press this button behind you, next to the coffee, if you need anything more. All doors will be closed and you will not be disturbed."

The meeting got under way with Smith introducing each individual and his or her ken of expertise or responsibility. He said, "While all of you from Langley know each other, some of you know Colonel Barton Milburn. He's a reserve officer and now a practicing attorney. He served with Eisenhower and me throughout the war. He's a very experienced intelligence officer. Mrs. Wharton will pass around a short file on Mr. Milburn's background and experience."

Maybrook and Sedgwick waved their hands in confirmation of Bart's credentials.

Fuentes spoke up. "I was a captain who worked intelligence in Italy with Colonel Milburn. He's good to have on our team."

Berger chipped in, "I know all about Colonel Milburn and his tour of the concentration camps. Great piece of work, Colonel."

"Thank you," Bart acknowledged the plaudits.

Dulles said, "Colonel, glad to have you aboard. Now, let's get down to business. First of all, Colonel Milburn has the highest security clearance, as does everyone in this room. All of us are fully up to date on Frederick Avram Nordheim, the target of this exercise appropriately named, Operation Lucifer by Colonel Milburn. General Smith will delineate three specific reasons for our interest in this man and its importance. Jacques Laurent has a detailed file on Nordheim and his associates."

The director of the CIA came right to the crux of the matter. "All of you have the file on Nordheim. Let me spell out three items. One, his company, Winston General Associates Ltd., and its subsidiaries, specifically Eagle Shipping, are delivering arms to China and North Korea. Two, it is believed that his ships are plying the waters between South America, particularly from Argentina and Colombia, to our shores, carrying contraband, arms and illegal drugs. Our Coast Guard searched their ships at sea and found nothing. It is believed they disgorge the illegal stuff to other carriers outside our twelve-mile limit. We have followed some of his fleet by air en route to China and within North Korean waters. In fact, we sank two of his ships headed to North Korea loaded with arms. Three, Nordheim is not an officer of any of his companies, yet he owns 100 percent of the stock in these entities. He is believed to be the richest man in the world. He professes to be a Jew. Israel disputes this, and their Mossad suspects he is a high-ranking Nazi who escaped the Allied net at the end of the war. He is a recluse. We have some photos of him - a passport picture and a side view of him aboard his yacht in Monte Carlo. Neither his face nor his physique equates with any major Nazi fiends. I've matched his profile with every one of those miserable bastards. Hitler, allegedly dead. Himmler, allegedly dead. Goebbels, definitely dead. Goering, definitely dead. Martin Bormann, whereabouts unknown, but sighted once in Argentina. However, he is too short to match with the pictures of Nordheim. Could it be the man himself, Hitler? I doubt it, but the KGB will not cooperate. They found the funeral pyre of Hitler's alleged remains. One of their generals? I doubt it. A conundrum? Yes. Enough here for us to go all-out to solve this puzzle."

Dulles took over. "This man is quite a formidable adversary. He has interests the world over. We have to chip away at his empire covertly. No leaks of any kind will be tolerated. No overt action which would alert him or his people. Colonel Milburn, what say you?"

Bart replied, "It is my opinion that Nordheim has completely changed his appearance. First of all, that photo on the yacht shows him to be as tall as Darren Mayfield, the former FBI agent who acts as his spokesman and contact man. Mayfield, according to your files obtained from the FBI, is six feet tall, and Nordheim standing alongside him seems to be the same height. Now, look at your photocopy and examine it carefully. Nordheim is wearing Western garb, a cowboy Stetson, and his boots-look at them carefully and tell me if that isn't one of those specially designed boots with one-inch uplift inside the boot and two-inch heels. That would make him three inches shorter than Darren Mayfield: 5 feet 9 inches tall. Now, look at his passport photo - a sweeping mustache and a Van Dyke beard. I would venture a guess that this man had an expert job of plastic surgery. Surmise? Yes, but worth consideration."

Silence enveloped the room. Eight pairs of eyes gazed at Milburn. There was an air of respect for their new colleague.

Dulles turned to Bart and said, "Well done, Colonel. We need to super-enlarge the photos we have and examine them closely. In addition to that, we need some more pictures of this man. We have to track him down and, if necessary, get some aerial shots of him. We should put a tail on Darren Mayfield. Have Customs here put a marker out for him, if and when he comes back to our shores."

Katherine Wharton spoke up: "Our file on Mayfield indicates he has a brother, Paul Mayfield, living in New York. The brother has a sordid past."

Jacques warned, "Be careful how we approach them. A little surveillance first. No contact until approved here."

Smith asked Dulles, "What about Stellar Security Services, better known as Triple Security?"

"Oh, yes," Dulles answered. "They have state-of-the-art equipment, plus a few gimmicks beyond the best in the field. Heading it is Michael Paterno. They have a building of their own on 12th Street."

Bart cut in, "Not Magic Mike, the guy that tapped Mussolini's lines?'"

"The very same. Do you know him?"

"I sure do. He was a captain assigned to our intelligence group when we went into Sicily. He's an effing electronic genius. Excuse me, ladies," Bart apologized.

"Oh, we've heard it all, Colonel Milburn," Katherine Wharton said, smiling.

Smith interjected, "A final plan of operation will be worked out by you people over the next few days. Work closely with Colonel Milburn. This is to be a team effort, with Milburn in charge, subject to reporting to the President and then to Dulles and me. Margaret Wilson will meet with you, Bart, to go over financing, cash withdrawals, passports, billing your fees and other such matters."

"A delicate question, sir, for all concerned." Bart said.

"What would that be?" Smith asked.

"As is well known to all, I am a partner in the law firm of Graybeal, Arnold & Milburn. I will not be sharing any of our activities with my associates. However, we have a client that can be of great assistance to us. I am referring to the state of Israel. If this is a roadblock to my association with the CIA, I would like comment on it now."

A momentary silence ensued as heads turned to one another. Smith and Dulles whispered to each other. The rest remained mute. Bart's steely eyes focused for a few seconds on each face in the room, coming to rest intently on the conferring general and his deputy. The silence was deafening in the two minutes of the hush.

Dulles, who polled the room, vented the secrecy of the confidential colloquy: "Does anyone here visualize a problem with Bart's very proper question?"

Maybrook raised his hand for recognition.

"Problem, Mr. Maybrook?" Dulles asked.

"On the contrary, sir. Considering Prime Minister Ben-Gurion's report to President Truman regarding Nordheim, and the Mossad's revelation to the prime minister, it would hold that the Mossad would cooperate with us more openly."

A chorus of "ayes" followed.

Smith affirmed the reaction to the question. "Mr. Dulles and I concur. In fact, if Mr. Milburn's current schedule permits, we would advise the colonel to make an expeditious trip to Tel Aviv."

Bart smiled. "I can clear my decks for all of next week. I have a short court appearance on the calendar for the week following. If I am detained in Israel for more than a week, my partners can opt for a continuance or proceed in my place. I'd appreciate an early answer on the timing of this trip."

"I'll speak with the President the first thing in the a.m.," Smith replied.

"Bart, who do you want on your team?" Dulles asked.

"My choice would be Maybrook, for his familiarity with the Nordheim file, and Phillip Berger, for two reasons, one being his fluency with the Hebrew and German languages and secondly for his experience in covert activity," Bart specified. "Plus, Jacques Laurent, who heads your Nazi desk. I want him as my deputy."

"A good choice," Dulles declared. "I recruited Captain Laurent. He's sharp, dedicated and multi-lingual. Now, I would suggest that Maybrook, Laurent, Berger and Milburn have a coffee klatch here to discuss their agenda. This meeting is adjourned," Smith uttered as he slapped the Cabinet table.

After the group's goodbyes, the four filled their coffee cups and sat down at the end of the massive mahogany table.

Berger, 5 feet 10 inches in height, nondescript, but neatly dressed in a blue blazer, white shirt and knitted black tie, was known for his ability to adapt himself to many disguises. He had been known to dress as a cab driver, longshoreman, scholar, rabbi or priest, or college professor. His record in covert actions had received approbation from his supervisors in the OSS and the nascent CIA.

He looked at Milburn over his cup and spoke gently: "I want to thank you for asking me to join your team."

Maybrook also expressed his thanks and added, "Bart, including Berger was a very wise choice. I've worked with Phil on a number of projects, and there is no one I have more confidence in than this Lon Chaney character. He is indeed a man of a thousand disguises, and fun to work with."

Berger cut in, "The accolades are appreciated, but before we go any further patting each other's backs, suffice it to say that both you men have more than distinguished yourselves in the service of this country, so let's get on with the job ahead."

"Should the President succeed in getting Ben-Gurion's approval of our visit, it would be wise for the three of us to familiarize ourselves with Israel's history, placing emphasis on the period just prior to their existence as a sovereign state and its travail over the past four years," Bart cautioned. "Laurent needs no briefing. He's an expert. Check with him."

"I believe Phil and I have had full plates dealing with trouble spots around the world," Maybrook responded. "We are quite familiar with Israel's problems, but a refresher course would be helpful."

Berger asserted, "The Israeli problems have always been of profound interest to me. But I agree, Bart, that an update is advisable. Would you care to emphasize some items?"

"Allow me to make some personal comments about the leadership, particularly, and the general population as well. We must understand the psyche of the people. By and large, they have what I would term a healthy paranoid attitude toward strangers. Many of the citizens of that new country are survivors of the Nazi death camps. They are a melange of inhabitants from all over Europe - Russians, Germans, French, Hungarians, Romanians, Hollanders, Belgians, Germans, Italians, Ethiopians and others who managed to escape the bondage of those evil fucking slimeballs, Hitler, Himmler, Goering and Goebbels," Bart said.

Berger and Maybrook looked up in shock at Bart's emotional outburst and the use of street vernacular. Not that any of those words weren't commonly used, on occasion, in military circles or by either of the two men. It was the intensity of his delivery.

"Bart, I take it you don't like Nazis," Rick responded facetiously.

Bart's eyes cut a look at Maybrook. "It is very difficult for me to wipe the pictures from my mind of our tour of those concentration camps. I wrote a report, which has been classified, and I must admit that I am highly suspicious as to why it hasn't been released, at least to our Congress. There is still a lot of anti-Semitism in this country and throughout the world. And the Israelis know it. They are a tough bunch over there. Just let me go on a bit more. On May 14, 1948, when Israel declared itself an independent state, within hours the armies of Jordan, Syria, Lebanon, Egypt, Iraq, and Saudi Arabia attacked. But they were soundly defeated and driven out. Israel is surrounded by hostile neighbors. The mutual hatred goes back thousands of years. My bottom line is to know as much as we can about them so that they recognize not only our feelings toward them, but also our sincere empathy. We need to have the confidence of the Mossad."

"Bart, you have made yourself manifestly clear," Maybrook declared.

Berger spoke up, "Bart, I commend you for your little diatribe about the Nazi bastards. I just want to remind you of my heritage. I lost relatives in the Holocaust. I have strong feelings for the Israelis, and I am more than anxious to participate in Operation Lucifer. Laurent lost his wife and children to the Nazis. We both have a stake in this operation. Thanks for the opportunity."

"One last thing. If Nordheim was a highly placed Nazi, we've got to nail him and his cohorts alive. Then we will milk every drop of information out of them," Bart concluded.

Laurent maintained his taciturn comportment. The men admired and respected the knowledgable warrior.

☆ ☆ ☆ ☆

Monday, March 3, 1952

The conference room adjoining Austin Graybeal's office was sealed by a *Do Not Disturb* sign hanging on the knob of its entry door, indicating that something important and confidential was in progress in its confines. Orders had been conveyed to the switchboard to hold all calls.

Graybeal pounded the table, raised his voice several decibels above his normally soft-spoken demeanor and railed at Bart, "I will not tolerate any talk about leaves of absence or resigning from this firm! Hold fast, my friend, we're here to discuss and solve a dilemma. Nothing more and nothing less. I wish to make that manifestly clear. I'm certain Martha agrees."

"Of course I do," Martha responded. "Bart, we understand the problem. It's a question of how do we handle it."

"I'm sorry if I offended either of you, but I felt obligated to present alternatives to my partners. Let me lay it out in forthright terms. We will be representing the U.S. Government without binding the hands of this firm to represent any of our present or future clients in matters opposing the government in any of its agencies, even the CIA itself," Bart said.

"Explain that, Bart," Graybeal calmly requested.

"Simple. This is a highly vital matter involving a clear and present danger to this country. I cannot, at this juncture, reveal the objective other than to advise both of you that it is a highly classified matter, which I will handle on a security basis and reluctantly be unable to share with you. At some point in time I will seek permission to brief both of you. We will be billing several corporate entities. I will oversee the financial aspect of this task and share the information with you without violating the classified nature of my activities. I assure you that I will not neglect any of our clients, but I will need a little leeway and your cooperation. One more vital note to this discourse. At its terminus, if successful, you'll be proud to have been connected with this venture."

"My dear young associate, rest assured of our confidence in you. Accept my blessing and support in this cloak-and-dagger operation, which I have surmised it is," Graybeal asserted.

"Well, I'll let a little cat out of the bag," Bart stated, smiling. "We will be serving one of our clients in a very important way."

"How's that and who's that?" Martha asked.

"Firstly, the client is the state of Israel, and secondly, this is something that Prime Minister Ben-Gurion has shared only with President Truman," Bart revealed.

"Why didn't you tell us that at the outset?" Graybeal inquired.

"I guess I was saving that for the punchline," Bart replied. "Actually, it was incumbent upon me to obtain your joint acquiescence to my suggested m.o. for our new clients. I also need your assurance of secrecy *vis-à-vis* this situation."

"Bart, you know better than that. Nothing will leave this room," Martha chided.

Graybeal said, "Godspeed, my friend."

Martha shook her head, and in disengaging herself, said, "I've a few chores that need attention. Good luck, Barton."

Graybeal patted Bart on the back as he left the room.

Milburn entered his office, abstractedly juggling the reaction of his partners, the portent of his engrossment in a covert intelligence operation and the placid productive life of two weeks prior to his entanglement in the Nordheim affair, or, as he titled it, Operation Lucifer.

He was subconsciously ambivalent, his martial instincts, polished by five years of frontline experience chasing and evaluating Nazis, stimulated his vital instincts. He was jarred out of his tangled abstractions by Nancy Telford's exasperated outburst: "Was your conference so important that you couldn't be interrupted for a call from the President of the United States? Our switchboard said *No calls*. I told a fib to the White House operator."

"Calm down, Nancy."

"Well, I don't like lying."

"How long ago was the call, and what exactly did you tell the operator?"

"It was 9:45, and I said you were at a conference, not *in* conference, implying that you were not here."

"Oh, come now, Nancy, you didn't lie in the full sense of the word. I *was* at a conference. The operator didn't ask where, did she?"

Nancy, somewhat mollified and blushing, quietly said, "There you go with your lawyer's analysis, making me feel like a witness who has just been corrected on the stand."

"What was the message?"

"Oh, shoot, Mr. Milburn, all she said was to have you call the President when you have a chance."

"There you go, Nancy. You didn't really fib, did you? I appreciate your concern for me. You're a dear friend. Now, will you please get John Steelman on the phone at the White House?"

Bart was shuffling some papers on his desk when she announced, "Steelman's on."

"John, I understand the Prez called," Bart began.

"That was me. He wants to see you at 3:30 this afternoon for a short visit."

"Can do. See you then," was the reply.

Milburn cleared the White House gate at 3:25 p.m., and Steelman met him at the west entrance, then steered him to his office.

"The President is tied up for the moment, so how about a cup of coffee?"

"Fine."

As they sipped the hot coffee, Steelman whispered, "A Democratic congressional group is in there trying to get him to run again."

"Will he consider it?"

"I doubt it. He hasn't gone on the record either way. The end of this month he'll announce his decision."

They heard the meeting breaking up. Voices in the outer hall chorused, "Thank you, Mr. President."

"We're up next," Steelman declared.

They placed their half-empty coffee cups on his desk.

At that moment, Truman opened the door to the Oval Office and said, "Come in, gentlemen."

They walked in and seated themselves facing the President, who remained standing.

"Barton, this will be a short meeting. I wanted to update you personally because of the sensitivity of our Israeli friends. Prime Minister Ben-Gurion and I had a very frank and pleasant talk. They are tracking Nazis all over the world with limited resources. They welcome our help, but, they don't want us to become a runaway horse in any of our joint efforts, or for us to interfere in their ongoing, highly secret trackdowns of Nazis other than 'Nordheim, alleged Nazi,' is the way he put it."

Milburn began to fidget in anticipation of the bottom line. He reached into his pocket for a pack of cigarettes and held it up for Truman's approval. The President assented, and continued as Bart lit one with his new Dunhill lighter.

"Ben-Gurion agreed to receive your visit in two weeks. He has his intelligence people preparing for an in-depth meeting with your team."

As Bart blew spirals of smoke toward the ceiling, the President, in a *non sequitur*, remarked, "Those coffin nails will certainly shorten your life, my friend."

Smiling, Bart extinguished the cigarette in the ashtray before him.

Truman continued, "The next few weeks of updated intelligence could be rewarding. Argentina, we know, is a Nazi haven. We need more information about Nordheim's relationship with Peron."

"I agree, Mr. President. This hiatus period is a godsend. Anthony Fuentes, head of the South American desk, is the perfect man to send to Buenos Aires."

"Fine. Don't pour the details on me, Colonel. All I want is the results," Truman retorted.

"Sorry, sir, I didn't mean to interrupt," Bart said blandly.

"All right, let's get on with it. I've other business to attend to," Truman said. Obviously, the President's mood was dour. It also indicated his preoccupation with other matters. Bart surmised that the preceding meeting with the Democratic congressional group had soured the President. "Now, it is clear that there is and has been tensions between our British cousins and the Israelis. There are remnants of the Cliveden Set, the pro-Nazis, still in high places in England. Churchill is very much on the side of the Israelis, but he has opposition from the royal family and the House of Lords on down. Sir Alfred Lipton is close to Churchill and has been working with us to enlist British Intelligence, their MI6, to cooperate with the CIA."

"Sir Alfred is my father-in-law," Bart interjected.

"I know, I know," Truman said. "That's why I've mentioned it."

"Sorry, sir," Bart apologized.

"Bart, I don't mean to snap at you, but I need to finish this meeting and get on to some other problems. Finally, the last item, Mossad believes Nordheim has purchased a new 210-foot yacht. It is expected to be delivered to Monte Carlo on March 22. They learned this from the dock master at the marina. He may be there to check it out. Dr. Steelman will pass a copy of this memo on to General Smith within the hour. That's it. Make your own plans with Smith and Dulles."

"Thank you, Mr. President," Bart said as he rose to leave.

"Okay, Bart, keep Steelman advised if anything definitive is unearthed. Good luck."

The peremptory dismissal was unlike the usual demeanor of Truman.

Steelman and Milburn exited into the adjoining office. Both men were silent, and Bart's discomfiture was apparent. John waved a bottle of scotch at his guest. Bart nodded acceptance, and no sooner was it poured than he picked up the shot glass and swallowed its contents.

"Got to you?" Steelman ventured.

"What the hell is biting him?"

"Nothing personal to you, Bart; he's pissed off at that crowd from the Hill. They were obviously pressuring him to make up his mind. In other words, they were telling him to shit or get off the pot. They want to pick a candidate if he decides not to run for another term."

"Everyone is entitled to a bad day," Bart said in parting.

Once in his car, He drove directly to his office. Miss Telford handed him three messages, one from his wife, one from Maybrook and one from Margaret Wilson.

He called home first.

Elizabeth answered.

"How's my sweetheart?" he asked.

"Which one?" she giggled.

"Oh, that big fat lady I married."

"Ouch, that's what I get for teasing you."

"What's up, honey?"

"Dad called. He wants you to call him this evening at home on his private line."

"Let me do that now and I'll call you back."

"Love you."

"Right back at you, schweetheart," he said, mimicking Humphrey Bogart. "Miss Telford," he called on his intercom.

She entered.

"Please call Maybrook and Miss Wilson and ask them to stand by. I'll call them shortly. I need to place a call first to London on my private line."

"Will do," she replied.

A cultured British voice responded, "Lipton residence."

"Jennings, this is Barton Milburn. Is Sir Alfred there?"

"Yes, sir. How are you, sir? How are Miss Elizabeth and Michael and Jenny?"

"They're all fine and send you their best. By the way, Miss Elizabeth is now Mrs. Milburn."

"Oh, I know. It's a habit, sir. Here is Sir Alfred, sir."

"Bart, thanks for calling so promptly. All's well, I trust."

"Yes indeed. What's up?"

"I understand you are preparing for a visit to Israel."

"Yes, but not for several weeks, based on a meeting I had today with the head man."

"That's the reason for my call to you. I think it would be a rather large plus to your mission if you were to come to London first."

"Sir, if you believe in ESP, extrasensory perception, that thought has been running through my mind. For two reasons. One, I know that Elizabeth and the children would love to spend some time with you, if you would approve. Two, I need to talk with you about our agenda."

"Bart, I would be delighted to have a family reunion. As to your agenda, there are some experts here who would be willing to share their expertise."

"That settles it," Bart replied. "I haven't mentioned this to Elizabeth," he added, "but I'll surprise her shortly. We can be there within a week or so. Rather than fly over, I would like to spend some time with them crossing the Atlantic on the Queen Mary. I believe the ship sails this coming Friday."

"An excellent plan, Barton. We have plenty of room to accommodate a small army in this rambling house. I assume Mrs. Bishop will be with you."

"Yes, indeed."

"I'll be at the Southampton pier."

"No, no, we'll take the train to London."

"Very well. See you at the station. Love to all."

Using his private line, Milburn then dialed Maybrook. "Rick, sorry to delay my call back to you. What's up?"

"Need to talk."

"My office, Cafritz Building, at 10 tomorrow morning. Drive up the ramp and park on the fifth floor."

"I know the building. See you then."

Milburn dialed another call.

A voice answered, "Yes?"

"Mr. Fuentes, please."

"Speaking."

"Bart Milburn here, Tony."

"Yes?"

"Can you be at my office at ten tomorrow morning? Maybrook will be here."

"I'll be there."

"Check with Maybrook and you may be able to ride over together. I'll have Laurent here."

"I'll do that."

"Thank you."

He dialed home, and a child's voice piped, "Hello, this is Michael."

"This is Daddy."

"Come home, Daddy. I miss you."

"Very soon, my son. Let me talk to Mommy."

Elizabeth got on the line as Michael's voice in the background was heard to say, "I wanna talk some more!"

"Later, darling. I must talk to Daddy now."

Mrs. Bishop's voice was heard placating the youngster, enticing him with a toy.

"He raced for the phone before I could pick it up," Elizabeth breathlessly explained. "When you're not here, he's the master of the house."

"You know, that's the male instinct."

"We'll see about that," Elizabeth retorted.

"Honey, I spoke to your father. Have you any special plans for the next few weeks?"

"Barton Quentin Milburn, what are you up to now?"

"If you are going to be nice to me, I'll reward you with a big surprise. Are you ready?"

"Please, I promise. Don't tantalize. Let's have it."

"Elizabeth, my love, could you stand five uninterrupted days of my company?"

"It will be difficult, but I'll try, Sir Galahad. How, when and why? Don't toy with me. You know I would love it."

"Fine. We're leaving on the Queen Mary for London next Friday. The whole gang- Michael, Jenny and Mrs. Bishop. Your father is delighted."

"Barton, I'm overjoyed, and I'm not going to ask any more questions. I have to start packing," she giggled.

"Love you…see you soon." Bart laughingly smacked a kiss over the phone.

CHAPTER THREE

Monday, March 3, 1952, Rock Creek Park

Bart's arrival at home resulted in a tumultuous greeting. Michael and Jenny came marching to the entry door attired as a miniature fife and drum corps. He was beating his drum furiously while she was feebly blowing discordant notes on her flute. Squire, their Dalmatian, followed behind, barking loudly. Elizabeth and Mrs. Bishop were bringing up the rear, laughing at the Yankee Doodlers. The children kept up their impromptu parade, marching in circles.

Mrs. Bishop apparently couldn't resist joining the pageant, and quipped, "Yes, and the British are coming," as she put her arm around Elizabeth's shoulder.

Bart hilariously embraced the two ladies as the children kept up their strident concert.

"Where in the world did they get those fife-and-drum corps outfits?" he guffawed.

"That's what you bought them last Fourth of July, you ninny," Elizabeth chortled.

"Why now?"

"That's the way they wanted to let the British know that the Americans are coming. I told them that we're sailing to England for a visit with their grandfather," Elizabeth explained.

"Mr. Milburn, I haven't been able to contain them since they learned the wonderful news," Mrs. Bishop joyfully announced.

"Mrs. Bishop, how many times have I told you to call me Bart? We're family, you know."

"I've tried, but just can't. How about Colonel? Will that appease you? It's just my English upbringing," she conceded.

"That's fine."

"Well, Colonel, I can't tell you how happy I am about our trip. I'll be able to see my sister and brother. Thank you so much."

Bart bent over, pulled Mrs. Bishop close to him and planted a huge kiss on her blushing cheek.

Teary-eyed, Mrs. Bishop turned and called to the marching fife-and-drum corps, "Come, children, it's bath time."

Squire wagged his tail and followed.

Elizabeth pulled Bart into the living room, puckered her lips and invited him to lean over and join her in a lingering kiss.

"Your surprise has made us all so happy. I will get to see my aunts, uncles, cousins and, of course, my wonderful father," she declared.

"All right, my love, we'll have five wonderful days on our trip. Now, let me change my clothes and I'll join you for a martini in the den."

Later, the children, much calmer after their bath, joined their parents in the den. They climbed up on their father as he gave them a seesaw ride with one on each of his long legs. They asked questions about the ship, the Atlantic Ocean, England and Grandpa. Elizabeth and Bart answered them until the youngsters became sleepy, then Mrs. Bishop took them to bed.

Bart sipped his second martini, lit a cigarette and advised Elizabeth of his trip to Israel after his stay in London. He told her that expedited passports for all were being arranged.

"We should close up the house while we're away," he suggested.

"What about Jacques?" she inquired.

"I have plans for him, which I'll discuss with Jacques after dinner."

As usual, Elizabeth dropped the subject. She knew instinctively that Bart had an assignment for him.

After a pleasant dinner, Bart excused himself for a short meeting with Jacques Laurent, stepbrother and friend.

The broad-shouldered, husky, 6'2" man entered the door.

"Sit down, Jacques. How about a little brandy?"

"That would be most welcome," he replied in a clipped English accent.

"Cigar or cigarette?" Bart inquired as he pushed the humidor containing the Havana specials and a smaller box of cigarettes toward him on the mahogany coffee table.

Jacques, sensing that something important was about to be unfolded, reached for the cigar and the brandy snifter in one dexterous motion. He picked up the large table lighter and lit up the Havana special.

Bart opted for a cigarette. He lifted his brandy snifter in a toast, "To old times and better new ones, *mon ami.*"

"Colonel, *c'est si bon,* as Edith Piaf would sing. Merci, to you, my benefactor, and the Milburn family, which also is mine."

"Jacques, I love you as a brother. We've been through a lot together, haven't we?"

"This is true. You have made me an American citizen and given me a home here. I am very grateful. I have a family in you, Madame Elizabeth,

Michael, Jenny, and Mrs. Bishop. I am a very lucky man."

"Jacques, indeed we are your family. On this Nordheim matter, I want you to take a trip."

"I am your deputy," he declared.

"First of all, I am going to ask you to undertake a mission, something like the old days."

"Chasing Nordheim?"

"Right on." Bart poured a little more brandy into both snifters.
Jacques pensively puffed on his cigar and emitted spirals toward the ceiling.
Colonel, lay it out."

"Okay. I want to send you to Monte Carlo to observe and study a yacht that is being delivered on March 22. It is 210 feet long and will carry a helicopter on its rear deck."

"That is all?" Jacques questioned.

Bart smiled, "*Mon frere,* let me be very frank with you. I trust you the most."

"Colonel, I understand. Who, or what, are we after?"

"Before I go into that, I want to ask you a question."

"Okay."

"Are some of your fellow partisans still around? Would they be willing to help you in a good cause? Are any of them located near Monte Carlo? Are some of them connected politically or with the Sûreté?"

"Yes to all of those questions, but it would depend on the cause."

"That makes sense. All right, but you must be careful with what I'm going to tell you. Assume that Frederick Nordheim *is*, or rather *was*, a very important Nazi."

Jacques' nostrils flared, his back straightened and he leaned forward, staring intently at Milburn. He was ready for the spoor. "Who could he be?" rasped Jacques.

"We don't know. That's the main reason why I am asking you to go to Monte Carlo."

"You don't have to ask me to go. I beg you to let me go. After what those vultures did to my parents, my wife and children, I would give my life to kill those rats."

"Now listen to me, Jacques. I trust you implicitly, and I don't want anyone killed. If this guy is really a high-up Nazi, we want him alive so that we can capture as many as possible of the Nazis who escaped to Argentina, all through South America, Canada, and here in America. Do you understand me?"

"I am a good soldier, Barton; I will do exactly what you want," Jacques warranted.

"Well, you prepared the Nordheim file. The yacht being delivered on the 22nd is his. If you can get aboard that yacht on some pretense and plant some bugs, listening devices, in some of the key cabins, the dining area and wherever people would gather, that would be a real success. But, in heaven's name, don't board that yacht illegally. I don't want you to get caught because that would ruin our whole investigation. Understand?"

"Yes. He claims to be a Jew?"

"That's what he is trying to do. He wants everyone to believe he's a Jew. The Israelis say no. We will equip you with a small special camera to photograph the yacht inside and out. You will also be given the most up-to-date bugs, listening devices that will be directed to antennas at a suite in the Hotel de Paris. Follow me so far?"

"Yes, yes, but who will be receiving it?"

"Your fellow agents, Phillip Berger or Mike Paterno, who will register at the hotel under phony names. They act as multi-millionaires. You are not to see each other or talk to each other. They will have all the equipment to record anything said on that boat if you are lucky enough to get those bugs placed. Then, Jacques, you will meet with them before you leave for Nice, which is about nine miles east of Monte Carlo."

Jacques laughed. "Are you telling me about my homeland? I've been there many times. I have friends who live in Nice. I have old buddies who are in the Sureté. The partisans keep close contact with each other. I write to them and they write to me. We were very close, as you say - *knit together,* during the war."

"Well, don't let them run with the ball. One of them might want to kill Nordheim or blow up his yacht."

"No, no, they will follow my instructions. Colonel, you know how I operated during the D-Day invasion. Have confidence in me."

"Of course, brother. By the way, Jacques, we're closing the house next Friday. Giving our cook, Chloe, a paid vacation. The family is going with me on the Queen Mary to London. You'll be on your way to Nice and Monte Carlo."

"Same business, Colonel?"

"Yes, and tomorrow afternoon I'll have you meet with Berger and Magic Mike."

"Oh, yes, Mike bugged Mussolini's lines," Jacques recalled. "I worked with him in Paris after the American army chased the Nazis out."

"He will brief you on the equipment you will be using to bug the boat. All of that stuff will be sent over there through our embassy in Paris and will be delivered to you once you are settled in a hotel. You will have a contact man in Monaco or Nice. I don't know yet who it will be. Remember, you're in charge of this operation."

"Colonel, I feel like I'm back to the good, or bad, old days. I feel like an old warhorse. I'm really excited, and maybe I can find out what happened to my sister Joyce while I'm there."

"Good, I hope you find her alive."

"I pray for that."

"One last thing, Jacques. You are going to be well paid for your services."

"No, no, the CIA pays me well."

"Jacques, this extra money will come from the U.S. government. Also, the government is providing all your expenses. They are paying everyone involved. So, do as I say and be a good soldier and accept the bonus."

"As you order, Colonel," Jacques mocked, curling a smile.

"I'll see you at my office at 3 p.m."

☆ ☆ ☆ ☆

Tuesday, March 4, 1952 - 9 a.m.

Anthony Fuentes and Richard Maybrook left CIA headquarters at Langley, Virginia, at 9 a.m. en route to their meeting with Barton Milburn. The turnpike traffic was bumper to bumper as they approached the 14th Street bridge.

Maybrook was driving and cursing the tieup, so he turned on the radio for a traffic report. The cause of the jam was an overturned truck that was spilling oranges all over the highway leading onto the bridge.

"Of all the frigging days for a juice party," Fuentes quipped.

"We'll have to lay back and enjoy it," Rick commented.

"What do you think Milburn wants to meet with us for?" Fuentes asked.

"I have no idea, except he's probably got some plan in mind that he wants to discuss with us," Maybrook speculated.

"You've known him a long time, Rick, haven't you?"

"Yes, and he's quite a guy. Got the balls of a giant and a brain to match. Woe unto anyone who crosses him. A verbal executioner. On the other hand, if you're his friend, his loyalty is unbounded. He'll go to any length for his intimates, as he did for his men in the war," Maybrook declared.

"One has to feel comfortable working with a guy like that," Fuentes acknowledged.

The traffic started to move. Up ahead, Virginia state troopers were directing traffic into a single lane.

As they neared the bridge, Fuentes pointed ahead. "Look at all that Vitamin C going to waste."

The road was strewn with squashed oranges, and the highway's asphalt had taken on a yellowish hue. The Ford they were in participated in the juice-squeezing rampage as they finally picked up speed crossing over the Potomac River into Washington.

They reached the Cafritz Building at 9:55 and raced up the ramp to the fifth floor in time for their 10 o'clock appointment.

Miss Telford led them into the dining room, where Luigi had croissants, whipped butter and percolating coffee on the table. Bart joined them with a warm "Good morning, gentlemen. Welcome to our humble quarters."

Luigi began pouring freshly squeezed orange juice into the glasses before the three of them.

Maybrook and Fuentes waved at Bart and broke into uproarious laughter. Bart and Luigi looked at each other, nonplussed by the reaction to the orange juice.

Maybrook outlined their experience on the highway, causing Bart to vouchsafe that the juice had just been delivered from the scene of the overturned truck.

Luigi nodded his head and retired to his kitchen.

After that high note of hilarity, they got down to the business at hand and Bart filled them in on his assignment of Jacques to Monte Carlo.

"How capable is this Frenchman?" Fuentes asked. "I see him at the Nazi desk, but he's a loner and doesn't fraternize."

Maybrook stepped in. "Tony, believe me, he's the best. His work behind the lines on D-Day was spectacular. After Dunkirk, he and his partisan comrades were right in the center of the Nazi defenders. They were holed up in a broken-down barn, dot-and-dashing Ike's headquarters with positive positions of Nazi artillery. Our planes pounded away at these resistance centers and saved thousands of lives. He's a brainy and gutsy French Jew who's now an American citizen."

"Wow," said Fuentes. "Hey, I'm convinced."

Bart beamed at Maybrook's description of Jacques, then added, "If there's a hand-to-hand brawl, I'd rather have him at my side than anyone I know. He was a captain in the French army training troops in martial arts. He's a whiz. A giant of a Nazi came at him with a bayonet, and in the wink of an eye he kicked the bayoneted rifle out of his hands and landed his foot on the kraut's jaw, knocking him cold. The Nazi was coming at me."

"Wow, he saved your life, Bart!" Tony exclaimed in admiration.

"That he did, and he's been my brother ever since."

"What's up for me, Bart?" Tony asked.

"Tony, I would like you to go to Buenos Aires. You know the outline of Peron's visit with Nordheim. There are allegedly ninety thousand escaped Nazis in Argentina. Maybe you can hit some pay dirt there."

"I wouldn't mind that assignment at all."

"Go there high style in business or as a tourist. Use whatever front you want, and arrange a contact man down there who is on the CIA payroll."

"That suits me fine. Should I have a wife or go solo?"

"Is there a female agent who speaks the language the way you do and has the talent to nose around?"

"How about Sophia Carrera?" Maybrook asked.

"Yes, she's beautiful, she's tough and...no hanky-panky," Fuentes groaned. "She's a class act. Like myself, she speaks impeccable Castilian Spanish. She is reputed to be distantly related to King Alfonso XIII, who was dethroned in 1931. She was educated in England, which explains her English accent."

"Enough said," Bart declared. "Tony, contact Sophia, or better still, I'll call Allen Dulles and try to persuade him to talk with her about acting as your wife on the trip to Buenos Aires."

"Good idea," Tony said. "As a matter of fact, I wouldn't mind her being my real wife."

"Save it for when the work is done," Milburn cautioned.

"Just voicing a latent thought, Bart. I realize the seriousness of the venture. Rest assured, it will be strictly business all the way."

"Tony, besides plowing the field for information about Nordheim's relationship with Peron, if possible, without being too obvious about it, try to get socially acquainted with Eva. She is alleged to have been a spy for the Nazis. Among Argentina's elite, they whisper about her as having been a failed actress with a shady past."

"Where did you learn that?" Maybrook broke in.

"I admit that information is strictly rumor. Ask Allen Dulles to brief you. I'm sure he's heard lots about her," Bart declared.

Maybrook chimed, "I've heard a few whispers about her. For one, she was the bastard child of a peon. Two, she failed as an actress. Three, she was and still is a social climber. Four, somehow she contrived to get Peron to marry her and allegedly has him wrapped around her little finger. She's a power down there."

"Sophia and I will have to figure a modus operandi on how to get to her," Tony suggested.

"One cotton-pickin' minute," Bart said. "A thought just struck me. Sophia has some roots to King Alfonso XIII of Spain. Could she possibly have some royal blood? A countess or a duchess, perhaps? Check it out with her. If so, we could plant a story in one of our papers that *American banker Mr. Anthony Fuentes and his wife, Sophia, the former Duchess or Countess of Whatever, are planning a vacation in Argentina and a possible tour of South America.* Then, we get Reuters to wire a story to the Buenos Aires papers."

"Bart, that's brilliant," Tony commended as he clapped hands.

"Hold it, Tony," Bart interjected. "There are a few *ifs* in this scenario.

There has to be a shred of legitimacy to her royal background. Also, we have to establish your bona fides as a banker."

Tony heaved a sigh of disappointment. "For a minute, I thought we had it."

"One second, men" Maybrook intervened. The hypothesis, as suggested by Bart, becomes ephemeral if Sophia can't establish the royal link. However, the second part, *vis-à-vis* our proposed banker here, can be brought to life with the approval of General Smith or Allen Dulles. We have a financial front on Wall Street, the American International Finance Corporation. If the royal part jells, the banker will be activated, pending hierarchy approval."

"What else do we have to cover?" Tony asked.

"Richard, we need passports for Jacques, Tony here, his new wife, Social Security IDs and whatever is required for our upcoming activities. As to money, talk with Miss Wilson. Jacques is to be put on the payroll, one thousand a day starting next Friday and two thousand a day when he is at the danger scene in Monte Carlo and wherever it takes him."

"I'll take care of it, Bart. Is that above his CIA salary?"

"Yes, and one more item regarding Mike Paterno," Milburn continued, holding up his hand as a stop sign. He reached into the bottom drawer of his desk and pulled out a red telephone. He looked at a pocket- sized address book, then dialed. "Mr. Paterno, please?" he said into the phone. "Colonel Milburn calling..." He held for a few seconds, then said, "How's Magic Mike doing these days?"

The loud voice on the other end could be heard by all in the room. "Colonel Milburn, I've been waiting for this call."

"Sorry for the short notice. Can you join me here at my office about 3 o'clock this afternoon?"

"No problem. I know your building very well."

"Up the ramp to the fifth floor."

"See you then."

Waving the phone at his associates, Bart said, "Mike will equip Jacques for his snooping detail. Stuff to be shipped by large diplomatic pouch or trunk." He dialed the phone again, waited, then said, "Allen, Bart Milburn here."

"Yes, Colonel, what's up?"

"Would you or General Smith have a little time today to take a meeting with Tony Fuentes and Sophia Carrera?"

"Subject matter?"

"Argentina."

"I'm clear after 2 o'clock."

"Sir, might I impose upon you to have your secretary ask Miss Carrera to stand by? She doesn't know the subject, but Fuentes will lay out a plan for your approval."

"No problem, bye."

Bart looked at Tony. "Dulles will see you at 3 p.m.. He'll have Sophia stand by. It's up to you to present the plan as succinctly as possible. Tell him I suggested it, so that if he turns it down, I'll be holding the sticky wicket."

"I'm glad it's *your* plan. I don't want Miss Carrera to think *I* concocted this idea. She knows I have eyes for her. We're friendly enough, but I've never made a pass at her."

"Like I said, save it for later," Bart advised.

The meeting was adjourned.

At 3 p.m., Nancy led Jacques Laurent into Milburn's office.

"*Merci, Mademoiselle* Telford. *Vous êtes très jolie*," Jacques said, bowing.

Blushing, she retorted, "You say that to all the girls."

"Only to you and Madame Elizabeth," Jacques demurred.

"Nancy, he speaks the truth. You are a very pretty lady," Bart added.

"Oh, shush to both of you," she chided, then exited, closing the door behind her.

"You charmer, you. Would you like a cup of coffee?"

"No, Colonel, I just had lunch."

"Okay, here's the plan. Make some notes."

Jacques took the proffered pad and pen. "I'm ready."

"You'll have two sets of identification - your regular passport and other ID. We will furnish you with a set of fictitious papers and a passport to be used as a cover, in case you get in trouble. In Nice, check into the Westminster Concorde Hotel, 27 Promenade des Anglais. Do you know it?"

"Very well. It's on the beach promenade, and some of their bedrooms face the Mediterranean."

"Exactly. You must have one of those that face the sea. You will have high-powered binoculars to keep track of incoming yachts."

"Good."

"You will use your legitimate passport at the Westminster. Keep that room all the time you're over there. Leave one of your bags in the room at all times, hang up extra clothes in the closet, and keep some items in the drawer. Leave some money and valuables in a safety vault at the hotel. Also, leave all legitimate ID material in the safety box. Understood?"

"Will do."

"Now, what is your *nom de guerre*?"

He came right back at him, "I am François Joffre, like the famous general from World War I."

Bart smiled, "Very impressive. You will have a passport and other ID in that name. In Monte Carlo, you will register at the Balmoral Hotel, 12 Avenue de la Costa. Do you know it?"

"It is against the cliff in the middle between the Casino and the Royal Palace. They have rooms that face the yacht harbor."

"Exactly. You will have a perfect view of the yachts coming in, going out, and those docked there."

The intercom broke in with Nancy announcing, "Mr. Paterno is here."

"Send him in, please."

Paterno, handsome and slightly overweight for his 5' 10" stature, entered the room. His brown eyes sparkled, matching an infectious smile.

"A welcome reunion, Colonel," he whistled softly. "And here is Captain Jacques, my Paris buddy."

"You two know each other?" Bart asked.

"Right after the war, this guy showed me a side of Paris that tourists never see. We bar-hopped all over the city and got into all sorts of trouble."

Jacques' usually serious demeanor gave way to a loud laugh.

"You'll have to fill me in on the mischief over a glass of bourbon. But for now, let's get on with the order of the day."

Bart outlined the plan for Jacques to scout the Nordheim yacht and to possibly get aboard and bug it.

"Not bad, not bad," Mike approved. "They usually also have a hookup to telephone lines available when docked."

"If you're not under special assignment now, how will a little journey to Monte Carlo appeal to you?"

"Are you kidding, Colonel? When do I leave?"

"Not so fast, Mr. Magic. First, I need to clear you with General Smith or Allen Dulles. Secondly, you and Jacques cannot be seen together in public. Any meetings would have to be clandestine."

"I understand that. I believe I can tap into Nordheim's lines. I can receive and record their conversations. I can also put a bug under the hood of a car and point the vehicle to a location on the street 100 yards away and record any normal conversation. Whispers are difficult, but we can treat a tape and raise the decibel count. This is something new."

"Amazing. All right, Jacques will be in Monte Carlo under the name of François Joffre. He will also have a pad in Nice, nine miles away. That one will be registered in his name. If you have to confer, it will be there in Nice. Now, I have to clear you at Langley. Hold on." Bart reached for his red phone and dialed. After a few seconds, he said, "Allen, I want to clear something with you. Do you have a minute?"

"Shoot," was the response.

"I would like to press-gang Magic Mike into the service of Operation Lucifer. I could use him in the Monte Carlo operation with Phil Berger."

"If he's not on special assignment, you've got him."

"Great. One more small item. The name of this operation from here on in should be called *Lucy*."

Dulles chuckled, "Colonel Barton Quentin Milburn, you're in the wrong business. You should be over here with us. You've got a knack for this gumshoe profession. Lucy, *Lucy* - I love it. I'll memo our agents to apply that moniker to our target."

"That's it, sir."

"One minute, Bart. I thought you'd like to know - Sophia Carrera is now Mrs. Anthony Fuentes until further notice."

"I appreciate that."

"There's more. She admits that she is a niece of Alfonso XIII and her Royal connection entitles her to be called Countess. Her father, Felipe, had a hand in pushing Peron into the war."

"That plan was a shot in the dark. Never thought we would hit paydirt."

"Further to all that, Colonel Milburn, Mr. Anthony Fuentes, the multimillionaire husband of the countess is now the chairman of the board of the American International Finance Corporation. There was a meeting of the board of directors half an hour ago electing him to that august post. A press release will be sent to the business wire services shortly."

Bart guffawed, "How the world does turn."

"Not bad for a day's work," Dulles commented. "Good work. Bye."

Turning to Michael Paterno, Bart advised, "You've been cleared by Dulles. So, for the next few days, get your ducks in a row. You'll be traveling with your own passport. Remember that Jacques, my deputy, is in charge."

"Colonel, it'll be my pleasure to serve you and Jacques."

"Gentlemen, you heard me tell Dulles...never refer to our subject by any other name than Lucy, short for Lucifer. If you see Mr. N, report that *Lucy has been sighted*."

Both men nodded their heads in concurrence.

"Jacques' buddies from the partisans are all over France in well placed positions, anywhere from the waterfront up the ladder. Some are in the Surete. Remember we're chasing an alleged Nazi official of the Third Reich. Hatred runs deep in France, as well as other parts of the world. Do not discuss or even allude to this venture. You may inadvertently tip our mitt to one of Lucy's paid informers. Caution is the watchword."

Jacques kept writing notes on his pad.

"Okay, boss," Mike said with a grin. "I'm ready."

"Instructions, Mike. Make note of what I tell you now."

He produced a pen and a notebook. "Shoot."

"You are to reserve a suite at the Hotel de Paris. It overlooks the harbor. You should have high-powered binoculars and a long-range camera. Keep shooting pictures of the yacht as it approaches the dock on March 22nd. I'm fairly certain we'll have some aerial reconnaissance while it's at sea en route to the Monaco harbor."

"How do we communicate with you?" Mike asked.

"The point of contact is the team of Lloyd Sedgwick and Katherine Wharton. Reach either one. If Sedge goes into the field, Wharton will act as the conduit. If either of you need immediate help, let them know. You've got all the confidential numbers. Draw money from your usual sources. I'll have Margaret Wilson supply funds for Jacques. Take plenty of cash and travelers' checks, and make all travel arrangements through Gilbert Travel. That goes for both of you. Case the casino, but don't go overboard. Look for anyone connected with the yacht. One more important caveat: if it becomes necessary to contact each other, be discreet, work out a system of codes."

Mike looked at Jacques. Both nodded yes.

At that moment, Nancy announced the arrival of Phillip Berger. Mike and Jacques looked up in surprise as the chief of covert operations entered the room, immaculately dressed in a blue blazer, taupe trousers, cordovan shoes, white shirt and navy-blue tie. He removed his tinted gold-framed glasses from his scholarly face and bestowed a broad smile on the gathering.

"Sorry I was delayed," Berger apologized. "Had to set up some background for my trip to Monte Carlo."

Mike looked at Jacques, who maintained an apathetic countenance in contrast to Mike's bewildered facial expression.

"No problem, Phil. You know these men?" Bart said.

"I've never met this gentleman," he replied, pointing at Mike Paterno. "But I know his face and I'm familiar with his exploits. Of course I've seen Jacques Laurent at Langley," he explained as he stood up and embraced Jacques. He turned and shook hands with Paterno.

"All right, your timely arrival is fortuitous. I haven't mentioned your stopover in Monaco because I wasn't sure if your cover has been worked out. If not, we were going to forego your presence there."

"Am I to assume that these two gentlemen are going to sojourn in this idyllic resort?" Berger surmised.

"Your crystal ball is accurate, as usual," Bart jested. "Magic Mike here is our latest addition to the Monte Carlo team. He will handle all the electronic surveillance. Jacques will attempt to plant bugs aboard Lucy's yacht, and..."

Phil cut him off. "Lucy's yacht?"

Bart laughed, "Yes, from now on our target, Mr. N, is to be referred to as *Lucy*, as in *Lucifer*."

"Neat," Phil approved.

"To continue, Mike will have a suite at the Hotel de Paris and will be the receiving end of the bugs, and will also try to tap into the telephone hookup to the yacht supplied by the marina facilities."

"Hold it, Bart," Phil interjected. "I have a suite reserved at the Hotel de Paris facing the yacht harbor under the name of Philipe Bergere, with a passport to match."

"That's fine. Mike will try to get a suite also facing the marina. You, Mike and Jacques are to be strangers at all times while there, except in case of an emergency requiring contact. Jacques and Mike will fill you in as soon as we finish here. You can use our conference room to work out details."

"That's fine," Phil said.

"Now, tell us your cover story and we'll wrap it up here," Bart declared.

"I am now chairman of the board of Oceania Shipping, courtesy of our board of directors, Dulles et al., and the acquiescence of Timothy Fitzgerald, president of the company." He handed an impressive raised-print calling card to Bart in affirmation of his new occupation.

"We're *impressed*," Bart exclaimed, as he held up the card for Mike and Jacques to observe.

They nodded an admiring approval.

"Now, what's the caper?"

"As is universally known, Aristotle Onassis and his brother own and operate the largest fleet of cargo ships in the world. They are headquartered in Monte Carlo, with offices facing the harbor. Aristotle has the largest yacht, with a helicopter on the aft deck tied up there at the marina, and with a direct view to his boat from his office. He entertains on board frequently. Also, dines there almost daily," Berger added.

"Very convenient," Bart observed.

"Here's the plan. Fitzgerald knows Onassis, so he is going to set an appointment for me with Onassis and his brother, or brother-in-law, I'm not sure of the relationship. My initial mission, as chairman of Oceania, is to talk about a joint venture with him to try out a couple of ships, one of theirs and one of ours, in a trial conversion to containers. I will then have the opportunity of probing Eagle Shipping and its parent company Winston, its ownership, and, lo and behold, that new yacht in the harbor."

"Phillip, that's ingenious. As usual, your planning is excellent. That should squeeze some oil out of a dry hole."

"Thanks for the approval. I might be able to get Onassis to ask for a neighborly tour of the new yacht. Just a shot in the dark, and we might get lucky."

"By the way, Phil, if that should occur and you should see Jacques on board or near the yacht, just ignore him. I don't know what he has up his sleeve in his attempt to get on board."

Jacques smiled grimly. "I don't know yet either until I make some contacts over there."

"I know that," Bart acknowledged. "Now, gentlemen, this meeting is adjourned. Please retire to our conference room and exchange plans and codes for emergency contact if necessary."

They shook hands all around as Bart asked Miss Telford to lead the trio to the meeting room.

"Thanks, Bart, for including me in the hunt," Mike said, shaking hands with both men.

"This meeting is over, and I'll see you at the house, Jacques."

CHAPTER FOUR

Friday, March 14, 1952 - the same day -Washington, D.C.

Plans were being made for a reception in honor of the recently married Countess de Cordoba. The meeting was under way in the catering department of the Mayflower Hotel. Present for the arrangements were Frances Horton, director of catering; State Department assistant protocol officer Janis Fulton, and Countess Sophia Carrera.

Mrs. Horton inquired for details as she filled in an order form, "When and how is this to be held?

"On Saturday evening, March 22nd at 7 p.m.," Miss Carrera stated.

"For how many guests?"

"Sixty-five, no more than seventy-five," Janis Fulton replied.

"Buffet serving?"

"No, seated, with about ten tables. We can confirm that number in a few days based on the RSVPs," Miss Fulton guessed.

"Champagne cocktails and canapés?"

"Yes, top-drawer please," Miss Carrera suggested.

"Music and dancing?"

"Yes, indeed," Miss Fulton replied. "Ten- or twelve-piece orchestra. Soft music, some violins, oldies and goodies, you know...low-key, please."

"Menu?"

"What would you suggest?" Janis Fulton asked.

"Appetizer caviar, vichyssoise or lobster bisque as a soup choice, small dinner salad; chicken Paella or bouillabaisse or rack of lamb as entrée choices. For dessert, cherries jubilee, spumoni or sherbet. Coffee, tea, cappuccino or *café latte*."

Miss Fulton turned to Sophia. "How does that sound?"

"Fine to me."

"If there are any changes, I'm certain we can accommodate the countess," the director of catering said as she handed over the list.

Sophia opened her purse and withdrew an envelope. "Here is a check for five thousand dollars. Will that suffice?"

"Oh, certainly," Mrs. Horton agreed. "Would you folks like to see the Grand Ballroom, which I think, if condensed to half-size, will be perfect for an event like this? Fortunately, the room is available that night."

"Not necessary," Sophia declared. "We've been there on other occasions."

On the way out, the protocol officer invited Sophia to join her in the coffee shop just off the lobby.

When the ladies were comfortably seated in a booth, each ordered coffee, croissants and fruit preserves.

"I love their freshly made croissants," Miss Fulton observed.

"I do, too."

"Well, that went well. I will prepare the invitations for gilt-edged engraved cards. I'll send it over to Dupont Printers for rush order delivery to Mr. Anthony Fuentes at the Shoreham Hotel...is that correct?"

"Yes, and have Dupont bill him there."

"No problem. Your people, I assume, are preparing a guest list?"

"Correct."

"It's been nice meeting you, Sophia, and good luck with the soiree," she gibed.

Both smiled.

☆ ☆ ☆ ☆

CIA headquarters, Langley, Virginia

Across the bridge in Langley, Allen Dulles made some discreet calls to Capitol Hill urging a few senators to make contacts with the doyennes, social arbiters, grande dames, ambassadors and the high and mighty to be sure to respond affirmatively to the RSVPs they were about to receive. He made a special call to the amiable Alben Barkley, the septuagenarian Vice-President of the United States.

"Now, what legerdemain are you up to, Allen?" the veep said.

"Indeed, Alben, you're clairvoyant."

"Okay, my friend, how can I help you?"

"Quite simple. I would be very beholden to you, sir, if you would accept an invitation to a dinner on Saturday evening, March 22nd, in honor of the Countess de Cordoba."

"Is this a gag?"

"No, sir, I am quite serious. We're also trying to get some of the elite envoys, especially Argentina's ambassador, to attend."

"This some kind of scam, Allen?"

"You don't want an answer to that. Check with your President. This is rather important. Your presence there will be the imprimatur of the lady's authenticity.

This is in our national interest, Alben. Besides, you'll have an enjoyable evening and a great dinner. Let me have Dr. Steelman or the President call you."

"Do that, you scoundrel."

Dulles dialed the White House. "Allen Dulles for John Steelman, please."

"Hey, Cloak and Dagger, to what do I attribute this honor?" Steelman jested.

"John, your friend and the President's choice for Operation Lucifer, Colonel Milburn, has a special dinner going on March 22nd honoring a Countess de Cordoba. We need you to clear an okay from the Prez for Alben to attend that affair."

"Have you spoken to Alben?"

"Yes, and he will go if Truman approves."

"Say no more. I'll attend to it forthwith."

Fifteen minutes later, Alben Barkley was on the phone with Dulles. "All right, you rascal, I'll attend with my lady. Where and when?"

"You'll receive an invitation. Please answer the RSVP. It's at the Mayflower, 7 p.m., in the Grand Ballroom."

"Glad to help, Allen."

"One more thing, Alben. Do you know the ambassador from Argentina?"

"Yeah, I've played poker with him and a couple of guys on the Hill. I think he cheats at cards."

"Are you sure?"

"No, but he always wins."

"Who are the guys on the Hill?"

"Senators Magnuson and Fulbright."

"Fulbright on the Foreign Relations Committee, haw haw."

"What's the 'haw haw' for?"

"Naturally, Argentina is trying to make time with us. Do the senators win at poker?"

"Now that you mention it, yes. Fulbright most of the time...mmm...mmm."

"Thanks, Mr. Vice President, I am going to twist some arms now. I want those guys at this dinner with the Argentine ambassador, bye."

Dialing feverishly, Dulles reached each senator and explained his mission only insofar as the dinner was concerned. He impressed them with the confidential nature of his request. They agreed to attend, and Senator Warren Magnuson took on the chore of urging the envoy to join them at the reception, with a little poker game to follow.

A list of the invitees was placed on Dulles' desk that afternoon. By 5 p.m. the invitations were motorcycled to the Shoreham Hotel. Tony Fuentes personally approved them and rushed them back to Langley. A calligrapher was standing by to elegantly address the gilt-edged invitations. Seventy-five invitations were delivered to a Washington post office that evening, March 14.

☆ ☆ ☆ ☆

Barcelona, Spain

That night, a 210-foot yacht quietly left its moorings in Barcelona and floated silently to sea at a speed of less than five knots. It was cloudy and fog bound until the magnificent vessel reached a point ten nautical miles away from the Spanish coastline. The wind abated as the boat sailed into the Mediterranean Sea en route to Ajaccio, Corsica, 115 miles east-southeast of Nice. It flew the Liberian flag.

☆ ☆ ☆ ☆

Saturday, March 15, 1952 - Washington, D.C.

The Langley operator phoned Allen Dulles at his Georgetown home as he was planting rose seeds in his mini-garden. His butler handed the phone to him, then he stepped into his glass-enclosed solarium.

The operator advised him that Senator Magnuson was on the line.

"Patch him through," Dulles ordered.

"Allen, I spoke to the Argentine ambassador, Diego Sanchez. He was delighted for the invitation."

"Good work, Warren."

"He gave me a little gossip while we chatted. He's not certain, but there is a rumor that Eva Peron is being treated for cancer."

"Oh, shoot," Dulles scoffed. "Is she bedridden, hospitalized or what?"

"It's just a rumor. She gets around and is still making speeches."

"I hope she holds up for a while."

"I didn't realize she was one of your favorites, Allen."

"Oh, yes, as much as a 100-to-1 shot in the Kentucky Derby."

"Gotcha. It may be her opposition floating that story. Whatever your interest is in the lady, I know better not to pursue it."

"Routine, just routine, Warren. Thanks."

As Dulles mulled over the import of Eva Peron's health, he walked into his cozy den and plopped himself into a comfortable swivel chair behind his desk. He tapped his fingers on the world globe on the stand beside him. He spun it several times until it came to rest with his left forefinger on Buenos Aires, which is contiguous to the southwestern corner of Uruguay on the Rio de la Plata leading into the Atlantic Ocean.

He put his elbow on his desk and leaned forward, resting his chin on his right fist in a fair simulation of Rodin's sculpture of "The Thinker." He pondered the effect of Eva Peron's ostensible illness on the planned visit of "pseudo Countess de Cordoba" and "husband" Anthony Fuentes to Argentina. Was the planned reception an exercise in futility? Should he scrap the expensive charade? As these thoughts flitted through his mind, he reached for his very private line and dialed CIA Director Walter Bedell Smith at his home.

"Yes," was the greeting.

"Beedle, Allen Dulles here."

"What's happened now?"

"A possible dilemma."

"What is it?"

"Just got word of a rumor to the effect that Eva Peron is being treated for cancer."

"How reliable is the source?"

"Senator Magnuson, from Argentine Ambassador Sanchez, his poker buddy."

"We'll check it with our man on the scene."

"Better than that, I thought you might call Dean Acheson to get some intelligence from our ambassador in Buenos Aires."

"I'd rather put that on hold. Dean's such a fussbudget. He would be full of questions, and at this point in time it's not in our interest to furnish details. It was ticklish enough to borrow that protocol lady from State."

"You're right. I'll handle it with our man Ernesto Nogales. I'll code a message to him."

"Let me know if he verifies the report, or what the lady's doing these days."

"Will do. Sorry to bother you, Beedle."

"No problem, Allen, bye."

At the South American desk, Octavio Flores was struggling with a cross-word puzzle in the Washington Post. His prosaic endeavors ceased instantly with the call from Allen Dulles.

"Sir, yes, sir, Mr. Dulles, this is Octavio Flores."

"I know that, Octy. Listen carefully. Get our cryptographers to phrase this message for you and send it posthaste to Ernesto Nogales: *What is health of Eva? Is she active? Send details pronto. Love, Papa.* Got it?"

"Yes, sir. Right away."

"Octy, don't leave for the day until we get a reply," Dulles instructed. "Call me at my usual number. It's on your emergency sheet. I'll be here."

"Yes, sir." Flores then told his secretary, "Hold the fort, I'll be right back."

He ran down the hall to the back stairway and descended to the floor below. Half a dozen men were pounding at technology's latest version of a typewriter.

Gregory Watkins, chief cryptographer, was at his desk in a glass-walled office protected from the clatter of the machines.

Octavio knocked on the door. Gregory waved him in. Watkins, in a short-sleeved polo shirt, white slacks, white socks and sneakers, his feet on his desk, and green eyeshades over his steel-rimmed glasses, greeted his nervous, ro-tund visitor. "What brings you here, Octavio?"

"Mr. Dulles wants this message coded and sent immediately to our man in Buenos Aires."

The calm, laid-back cryptographer stood up suddenly. "Wait here. I'll have it for you in a couple of minutes."

He walked over to the man at the first machine as Octavio watched through the thick sound-proofed glass. The action resembled a silent movie. Watkins' lips moved as the man at the machine took the sheet of paper, pounded on the machine, and handed the original sheet and a second one to his boss.

Watkins came back into his office and handed the coded message to Octavio. He glanced at it and ran back to his office, where he handed the coded mes-sage to his gum-chewing secretary for typing. "Attention Ernesto Nogales, attorney at law, care of the American Embassy in Buenos Aires. Rush."

She handed the freshly typed copy to Octavio, and he raced to the wire room demanding immediate transmission.

Tom Hayes, communication chief, took the copy to an operator. "Stop everything," he ordered. "Send this now."

"Thanks a lot, Tom," Octavio said gratefully, adding, "Let me know immediately as soon as a response is received. Decoded, of course."

"High-priority item?" Hayes questioned.

"Dulles," Octavio said.

Hayes whistled and nodded acknowledgment. Flores went to his desk and studied his copy of the encrypted message. He tried to compare it with Dulles' original.

My wife and I separated. Every detail of settlement verified. Waiting for her to confirm alimony payments. Claims to be ill with flu. Think she's stalling. Advise when she is up and around. Call her attorney. Regards, Adam.

Octavio scratched his head and went back to his crossword puzzle.

Two hours later, Tom Hayes sent a decoded answer to Octavio. It read, *Lady still active. Rumors of illness denied by spokesman. Nogales.*

He called Dulles and read him the deciphered reply.

"Thank you, Flores," the deputy director replied, and hung up. He then called Tony Fuentes at the Shoreham, first asking, "Is the countess with you?"

"Not at the moment, sir. She's out shopping for her reception and the trip."

"We've been checking a rumor that the lady down south has cancer. Our informant just confirmed that there are rumors to that effect. But she is still active. Urgent you leave on Sunday, March 23rd, or Monday the 24th."

"Yes, sir, will do."

"Call Gilbert Travel now. Best hotel, best suite. Travel first class. I will notify our ambassador to arrange motorcycle motorcade police escort, ecetera, and to meet you at the airport. A little fanfare is in order."

"The countess and I are very grateful for your efforts, sir," Fuente joked.

"Don't let it go to your head, now that you're a big financier. Incidentally, let me or my secretary have dates, times, flight numbers and hotel accommodations promptly. Press releases on your appointment as chairman and on the reception have been sent. A further press release will be wired regarding your trip. Get to it."

"Thanks again," Fuentes replied.

Friday, March 14, 1952, 3 p.m. -New York City

The Milburn entourage boarded the Queen Mary at Pier 9 where she was docked in the Hudson River.

Bart presented his tickets to the purser's assistant, who was checking names and directing cabin stewards to lead the boarding passengers to their staterooms. Upon his being identified, the purser stepped forward, took his tickets and baggage stubs, then led the Milburn party to the side of the entry so as to let other passengers proceed.

"Sir, there is a gentleman here who has identified himself as your brother-in-law. He told me that you have left one of your bags in Washington. He maintains that he would prefer to hand it to you personally."

Very coolly, Bart queried, "Did he give you his name?"

"Oh, forgive me, sir. It's Richard Maybrook."

"Well, of course. Where is he?"

"In the lounge, sir. I offered to put the bag in your suite, but he declined."

"Could you get us settled, please, and have someone bring him along?"

"Certainly, Mr. Milburn. Just being careful, you know."

The family stood by during the colloquy with the purser.

The purser snapped his fingers and ordered a steward to lead the Milburns to their two adjoining suites on the M deck, above the promenade.

Elizabeth took charge as Bart instructed the cabin steward, who was awaiting them, to see if he could locate their twenty pieces of luggage.

"Some of it is here, sir, and the rest is on its way, sir. My name is Evans, sir, and I'll be serving your family, with the assistance of Alice."

At that moment, a pretty young English woman appeared.

"I'll be going next door to help Mrs. Milburn and the children, sir," she said as she curtsied her way through the connecting door.

In the adjoining suite, bags were arriving as Mrs. Bishop was entertaining Michael and Jenny with a jigsaw puzzle of Mickey and Minnie Mouse.

Elizabeth helped sort the luggage and directed Alice as to where each piece was to be placed in either suite.

There were bars in both suites. The one occupied by Mrs. Bishop and the children was amply stocked with soft drinks, milk, and bottled water.

Elizabeth handed each child a bottle of cherry soda and stuck straws into them. Jenny and Michael took the proffered drinks without looking up. They were concentrating on the Disney puzzle, and automatically began sipping their drinks.

"I'll stay here," Elizabeth announced. "I think Daddy will be busy for a while." Her instincts always blended with situations such as the unexpected visit of Richard Maybrook. She knew it was important and that Bart needed his privacy.

As some of the luggage was routed to Bart's suite, a smiling, handsome man stood outside the open door of the living room.

"Room service, sir. Did you ring?"

"Yes, I did, Mr. Maybrook. Won't you come in?"

As he entered, he placed an expensive leather flexible case at Bart's feet.

"You left town and forgot your briefcase. I thought I would bring it to you and see you off at the same time."

"That was very thoughtful, Rick. How about a drink?"

"Why not?"

"What will it be, gentlemen?" Evans asked.

"Scotch on the rocks," Maybrook opted.

"Same here," Bart seconded.

After the drinks were served, Bart addressed Evans: "Will you see how they are doing in the other suite? We'd like a little privacy now."

"Thank you, sir. If you need anything, just ring. We sail at 5 p.m., sir." He closed the door.

"What's with the briefcase? It's a large one, I'd say, and heavy," Bart observed as he lifted it.

"First, let me show you how to open it. A combination lock. Like a safe. See these three sets of rollers with numerals on each? Well, line up these three numbers, 3-1-7," Rick whispered.

Bart spun the rollers to 3-1-7, pulled the safety catch, and the case opened. Before he looked inside the expanded bag, he looked at Rick, "Why did you set it at those numbers?"

"I didn't want you to forget a certain birthday."

"You sly devil, that's Liz's birthday, March 17th, St. Patrick's Day."

Maybrook reached into his pocket and handed a neatly gift-wrapped box to Bart, "For Liz's birthday, my friend."

"Very much appreciated, but why don't you hand it to her?"

"No, save it for Monday when you celebrate."

"All right, what's all this stuff?" Bart asked, pointing to the briefcase's contents.

"Allen Dulles has gathered up some material pertinent as to who is still alive to fit into the role of Lucy, and I don't mean Lucille Ball," he laughed. "I couldn't resist that bad joke."

"Why send you to New York for this? You're a pretty high-priced messenger."

"There are some top-secret files in that case, as well as some books on the Nuremberg trials. Besides, he didn't order me to bring this to you; I volunteered."

"Why?"

"To be quite frank, when it came up I stepped to the plate because my family lives in Westport, Connecticut, so I thought I'd spend the weekend with them."

"Ah, that sounds more like it."

"Okay, now, Bart, Dulles wants you to go through all this stuff before any meetings in London with MI6 or whomever."

Chimes resonated throughout the giant liner, followed by an announcement through loudspeakers notifying visitors to leave the ship.

"Time for me to go," Maybrook said, shaking Bart's hand. "I'll say my farewell to Elizabeth. Have a nice trip."

"Here, come with me," he suggested, ushering Rick through the connecting door to the other suite.

"Elizabeth, I want to wish you a very pleasant journey."

"Oh, thank you, Richard. You know Mrs. Bishop?"

"Yes, indeed. Nice to see you again for so brief a period. May you have a very pleasant trip. I'm certain you're anxious to visit your home town."

"Very much so, Mr. Maybrook, and thank you. Michael and Jenny, say hello to our visitor," Elizabeth said to the children, who were still engrossed in their puzzle.

"Hello, sir," Michael said, then stood up and shook Maybrook's hand.

Jenny, still on her knees holding pieces of Mickey Mouse, waved at Rick.

"Nice trip, children," Maybrook said with a smile.

"You too," they responded, still absorbed in their endeavors.

"'Bye, you-all," Rick said, then Bart escorted him to the hallway exit.

All the luggage had arrived. Alice and Evans appeared with extra towels and buckets of ice for both suites.

"We'll be leaving the dock in about ten minutes," Evans announced. "May I suggest that you and the children might enjoy watching our departure. Here is a box of paper streamers and confetti. It's a most pleasant sight."

"We'll be back to help you unpack," Alice asserted.

"Thank you. Come on, children, Mrs. Bishop, and you too, Bart," Elizabeth beckoned as she handed the box of streamers to him.

Evans escorted the group to the portside deck, then placed two chairs at the rail for the children to stand on. Bart held onto Michael and Elizabeth, while Mrs. Bishop had a firm grip on Jenny.

The ship's horn bellowed loudly as she eased out of her berth. Hundreds of people on the pier below waved as streamers and confetti rained down on them.

Jenny and Michael giggled as they intently unfurled the streamers with the help of the Milburns and Mrs. Bishop. Huge tugboats were guiding the giant ship in a southerly direction into New York Harbor past Battery Park at the tip of Manhattan, leading to the open Atlantic Ocean.

The Milburns had a very restful and enjoyable family communion on their trip across the Atlantic. The seas were unusually calm. The children, Michael and Jenny, had the run of the ship, with either Mrs. Bishop, Elizabeth or Bart chasing after them. The Queen Mary's crew enjoyed the little ones, helping to spell the huffing and puffing Mrs. Bishop and the Milburns in their daily chase.

On St. Patrick's Day, March 17th, a birthday party surprised Elizabeth. A pile of gifts was delivered to the Milburns' table with a huge birthday cake. Maybrook's gift was a gold chain bearing gold four-leaf clovers.

Bart and Elizabeth had lots of time to themselves, so they took advantage of every free moment. They were two lovers on a honeymoon. During rest hours, Bart read the material Dulles had sent.

☆ ☆ ☆ ☆

Wednesday, March 19, 1952

They arrived at Southampton and, after customs and immigration clearance, boarded the train for London. At Victoria Station, Sir Alfred Lipton and his retainer, Jennings, greeted the Milburns effusively. As Lipton hugged and kissed his daughter, Elizabeth, the children pulled at his coat. "Grandpa, we're here!" they squealed. The distinguished, youthful-looking patriarch bent over and hugged them.

Bart shook his hand and hugged him. Sir Alfred hugged in return.

Two cars awaited them, a Land Rover and a brand new Rolls Royce sedan. Jennings and the gardener, Tri, an East Indian man, collected the luggage and placed the bags in the Rover parked in front of the station. A uniformed butler was standing guard. He saluted Sir Alfred. "Nice to see your family, sir."

"It certainly is," he replied.

Tri pulled away with the Rover. Jennings drove the Rolls up to where the family was standing.

"Mrs. Bishop, would you care to sit up front with me?" Jennings said.

"Me, too!" Michael exclaimed.

"No, no, you'll sit here with us. You, Michael, on Daddy's lap, and Jenny on Grandpa's lap," Elizabeth ordered.

As Jennings drove the Rolls Royce into the left lane of traffic, Michael blurted, "We are on the wrong side, Daddy."

"The adults laughed as Bart explained, "All cars drive on the left side here in England, Michael."

"Why, Daddy?"

Bart, momentarily stuck for an answer, was rescued by Sir Alfred. "Michael, it's always been the custom here."

Elizabeth diverted the children's attention to the sights of the London landscape.

"Look, there is Buckingham Palace, where the Queen lives," she said, pointing. "And there is Hyde Park."

The car was entering Belgravia, the most fashionable and exclusive quarter of London. Jennings slowed down and wheeled the Rolls into the driveway of an English Tudor home situated behind a well manicured lawn and neatly trimmed bushes. The door was open. A stout gray-haired lady and red-haired, freckled young woman, both wearing starched white aprons, greeted the arrivals.

Sir Alfred introduced them to the family. "This is Maggie, our excellent cook." The older lady nodded. "This is Bridey, who is an assistant to Jennings." The Irish lass curtsied. He then presented Bart, Elizabeth, Mrs. Bishop, Michael and Jenny. Jennings and Tri were taking the last pieces of luggage to the respective rooms allocated for the family.

☆ ☆ ☆ ☆

Wednesday, March 19, 1952, the same day - 9:22 a.m. - Paris

Jacques Laurent had arrived in Paris on Monday morning, the 17th, aboard a TWA flight from New York landing at Orly Airport. He rented a Renault at the Hertz desk and drove to the George Cinq Hotel on Avenue George V. Gilbert Travel had reserved his room, so he checked in under his own name.

After a quick shower and shave, he drove the Renault to the vicinity of Paris police headquarters. Circling the building, he spotted a bistro that had outdoor tables with a view of the Sureté's front entrance at Ouzi Des Orfevres. He found a choice table at the sidewalk café and ordered a bottle of Bordeaux wine and a salad Niçoise. He opened the newspaper Le Monde and placed a pack of Gaulois cigarettes on the table, then lit one. He looked and acted like a native.

After two hours of observing the traffic of uniformed and civilian men and women in and out of the main headquarters of the Paris police, he focused on a heavy-set man in civilian attire. The object of his attention was crossing the Quai d'Orsay. Jacques tossed a handful of francs on the table, scooped up his pack of cigarettes and ran toward the man. He put two fingers into his mouth and let forth three shrill whistle blasts. The husky man turned and looked directly at Jacques, who waved at him.

As they approached each other on the sidewalk closer to the bistro, a look of recognition flashed on the face of the stocky man as he ran forward, smiling. "Jacques Laurent?"

"*Oui*. Felix Gaumont!"

They embraced with heavy backslaps and rocking each other in deep emotional friendship, all the while rattling at each other in French colloquialisms.

"*Mon ami*, you have time for a drink with me?" Jacques invited.

"All the time in the world, *mon frere*."

They retook the table previously occupied by Jacques during his surveillance of the Sureté headquarters, then consumed half a bottle of Pernod as they reminisced about their days in the French army and later as partisans.

"When you whistled our old signal, I knew it had to be one of my comrades from the past!" Felix slapped the table, rattling the bottle and glasses. "*Monsieur*, you are talking with Captain of Detectives Felix Gaumont."

"I am very impressed, *mon Capitaine*."

"And you?"

"I am an American citizen living in Washington and working with Colonel Barton Milburn and the U.S. Government."

"What brings you here, *mon ami*?"

"Felix, how would you like to have an early dinner with me at the George Cinq and I will tell you a very interesting story of my mission here. Strictly confidential."

"*Oui*. Let me stop by my home to see my wife and three children, then I will join you at, say, 6:30. How is that, my dear friend?"

"*C'est si bon*," Jacques replied with a big smile.

More francs on the table, and they left.

Jacques tipped the maitre d' handsomely at the George Cinq and reserved a table against the back wall of the posh dining room. He waited for Felix at the front door. When he arrived, he escorted him to their quiet rendezvous.

Two bottles of Beaujolais and lamb with crayfish in a tarragon cream sauce, followed by a chocolate soufflé and espresso, sufficed for the two comrades. Later, over two Napoleon brandies and puffing Havana cigars, they reached the moment of truth.

"Felix, my dear friend, what I am going to tell you cannot be shared with your superiors or anyone else. Do I have your word on that?"

"It depends, Jacques, on whether it is legal or not."

"Well, let me put it this way...if I am tracking down an alleged escaped Nazi, would that be illegal?"

"My partisan comrade, you have my word on secrecy. How can I help you? Who is he?"

Jacques filled him in on the hunt for Nordheim. He explained his mission to get aboard the yacht to plant the electronic bugs.

"You have a photograph of this man?"

"Yes, here is a copy of his passport picture."

"Mm, it's hard to place that face. Maybe a little plastic surgery?"

"Could be."

"When are you going to Monaco?" Felix asked.

"First, I am going to Nice. I'm planning to leave in the morning."

"Can you delay it until later in the day? I want to do some checking. I have to make some phone calls. We have some of our comrades in Nice and Monaco."

"Sure, I can do that. I can spend that time in trying to trace my sister Joyce. I know she was alive when the Russians liberated Auschwitz."

"My God, Jacques, you mean to say that you haven't seen or heard from her since the end of the war?"

"No. I contacted all the refugee committees, and the French-Jewish committees tracked her to East Germany, but those Communist bastards in East Germany and Moscow refused to help. In fact, the Russians wouldn't release their own Jews who wanted to emigrate to Israel."

"That Stalin bastard is just as bad as Hitler was," Gaumont said, shaking his fist. "If I can help in any way, just say the word."

"You're a very good friend, Felix. We were always close, weren't we?" Jacques reminisced, his eyes becoming misty.

"I haven't forgotten, Jacques, that you saved my life when we were behind the German lines, about a month after D-Day. That Nazi was coming after me when his gun jammed. You kicked that rifle right out of his hands, shot him between the eyes and killed those two other Nazi bastards. I'll never forget that moment."

"Oh no, we protected each other. Our partisans were very close. You did your share. Everyone fought to the end. There were one hundred in our group, and seventy-five of us survived."

"Yes, yes, we lost some very good men. I keep in close touch with our survivors," Felix said.

"That's wonderful. I'd love to see some of them before I return to America."

Felix smiled. "You might be with some of the brothers sooner than you think."

Jacques looked at him incredulously. "Why are you smiling?"

"That's why I want you to wait until tomorrow. I may get you some help in Monte Carlo. Don't press me. Let me see what I can do."

"All right. If I am out when you call, leave a message."

"Here's my card, Jacques. It has my direct phone number, and I'm going to write my home number on the back."

"In the morning I'm going to the French Refugee Committee."

"Good luck there. Her name is Joyce I remember."

"Don't let me hold you any longer, Felix."

One more thing. When is Nordheim's yacht expected?"

"Sometime on Saturday, March 22nd."

"Okay, we have a few things to do. Thanks for a wonderful dinner and reunion."

"Mon plaisir, Monsieur."

Same day, Wednesday, March 19, 1952 - 5 p.m. - CIA headquarters, Langley, Virginia

The intercom buzzed, and General Smith's secretary announced, "Ambassador Stuart Bingham calling from Madrid."

"Yes, Stuart, how are you?"

"Fine, General. That yacht left Barcelona an hour ago. Our commercial attaché, Arthur Ryan, is here with me. He'll summarize."

"General, Ryan here. The yacht took on provisions early today. It's a magnificent piece of work, 210 feet long. Seagoing. Only the crew on board. Flying the Liberian flag. Named The Flying Eagle with a picture of an eagle in flight painted on the hull. Maybe they're heading for Genoa. Not certain. Could be a phony report."

"Thanks, Arthur. Put the ambassador back on the phone."

"That's it, General," Bingham said.

"Much obliged, Stuart. We'll pick up the trail from here."

Allen Dulles waited for Smith to fill him in on the short conversation.

"Nordheim's 210-foot toy pulled out of Barcelona about an hour ago heading for Genoa," the general advised.

"Why Genoa?"

"Your guess is as good as mine. To pick up Nordheim or to get some more goodies on board, or people, or who the hell knows," Smith reported, exasperated.

Dulles studiously filled his pipe and puffed smoke to the ceiling. Then the intercom announced, "Arthur Ryan on the line, sir."

"Put him through," Smith ordered. "Yes, Arthur, what is it?"

"My contact at dockside just called me. He says the Genoa destination is a smokescreen or, as he described it, *mierda del toro*, or in English, *bullshit*."

Smith laughed. "What's his reading on it?"

"Says he learned second hand that the captain, one Leif Sandstrom, Swedish passport, made a phone call to Ajaccio, Corsica, from the dockmaster's office. He made another call to Porticcio, a suburb of Ajaccio. My contact is friendly with the dockmaster, who eavesdropped on the calls. He said Sandstrom spoke in English. He heard him say they would reach port on the night of Thursday the 20th. On the second call, he asked for Mr. Nordheim. He then broke into German, saying *Herr Nordheim*. He couldn't understand the rest."

Smith motioned to Dulles to get on the connecting phone. "I've got Allen

Dulles on this line with me," the general said.

"Hi, Arthur, something brewing?"

"I think so," Ryan replied.

"How do you know it was Ajaccio and Porticcio?" the General queried.

"I laid a fifty on him to check the operator for charges and the phone numbers called. In a split second, he rattled away in Spanish and obtained the information. I've got the two numbers."

"Shoot, let's have them," Smith demanded.

"The first call to Ajaccio, the number is 52-09-33. The second one, to Porticcio, is 25-05-55. Do you want me to check them out?"

"No, no, Arthur, you've done a great job. I'm glad we placed you there. Do you want us to bring you home?"

"General, I *love* this assignment."

"I thought so. We'll take it from here."

"Arthur, take care," Dulles said, and signed off.

"Good day's work, Arthur," Smith praised in parting.

Smith and Dulles grinned like a pair of Cheshire cats.

"So, Mr. Nordheim is going to visit Napoleon's birthplace," the general mused softly. *"Très intéressant."*

"Have you been there, General?"

"Indeed I have. I flew in there, September of 1943, when we were mopping up after our invasion."

"Why of all places would the yacht be heading to Corsica?" Dulles wondered.

"That same thought is rambling through my mind."

Dulles picked the extension phone and said, "Connect me with Sedgwick."

"Yes, sir, Mr. Dulles."

"Lloyd, check out these two numbers in Ajaccio and Porticcio, Corsica. Tourist-type check, understand? Call me back in the general's office."

"Yes, sir."

After a brief moment, the phone rang. Dulles picked it up. "Sedge?"
"Sir, the Ajaccio number is the harbor master. The Porticcio number is Le Marquis, a brand-new hotel."

"Thanks, Lloyd."

Smith and Dulles silently contemplated the import of this latest intelligence.

Drumming the desk with his fingers, Smith said, "I'm weighing the idea of sending a man into Ajaccio. On the other hand, is Nordheim going to board the yacht for its trip to Monte Carlo, if it actually is going there?"

Dulles took several deep puffs on his pipe, then laid it down noisily on the coffee table. "Beedle, sending a man in there could be a bad gamble. Nordheim must have eyes and ears all over the place. Spotting a stranger in town could alert him that he's being surveilled. That might cause him to change his present plans. I doubt that he will be aboard that yacht when it docks in Monaco."

"I'm aware of all that," Smith countered. "Bart Milburn has a team waiting for the Flying Eagle to dock at Monte Carlo. What if the vessel doesn't go there?"

"Let's try this scenario. From Ajaccio to Monte Carlo is half a day's run.

Nordheim wants to see his new toy before it's delivered there. My guess is he won't spend time aboard as it travels to its destination. He'll probably fly there and take possession after Monaco's customs clears the boat."

"That's a fair analysis. But what is the reason for the layover in Corsica?"

"That baffles me too, Beedle. However, in my opinion, let's play the cards the way they were originally dealt. We can track the craft by air, should it seek a port other than Monte Carlo."

"I'm inclined to go along with that, Allen. Check the Navy to see if they have any ships close by, and the Air Force for a discreet surveillance flight over the vessel. Allen, nothing overt in either case."

"I'll go back to my office to set it up. Be back shortly."

"By the way, Allen, when you return we'll update Bart Milburn. He must be in London by now."

"Good idea, General."

Smith sat back in his chair, contemplating Nordheim's true identity. He mused to himself, *It can't possibly be Hitler or Himmler, or can it? It could be Bormann, but he was too short to fit the photograph of Nordheim. Are we chasing a myth?* "What a riddle," he muttered softly to himself.

A short while later Dulles returned, and Smith dialed Bart's number at the Lipton home.

It was close to 1 a.m. in London when Jennings answered, "The Lipton residence."

"Please tell Mr. Milburn that the beetle is calling."

"He might be asleep at this hour, sir."

"That doesn't matter," Smith snapped.

"Yes, sir. One moment, sir."

In less than a minute, Bart Milburn was on the line, "Are you in your office, Beedle?"

"Yes."

"Hang up. I'll call you on the red line."

"Fine."

Shortly, the secure phone rang in General Smith's office. "Sorry to wake you up," he apologized.

"I wasn't asleep. What's up?" Bart asked.

"Just wanted to update you. Allen is here with me. I'll put you on the speaker phone and you can talk with both of us and vice versa."

"Okay, shoot."

Dulles filled him in on the planned reception for the Countess de Cordoba and her newly acquired husband, Anthony Fuentes, the Wall Street bank executive, also their planned trip to Buenos Aires.

The general detailed the embarkation of the Flying Eagle from Barcelona to Ajaccio.

Bart, in turn, advised the two men of Jacques, Berger and Magic Mike's mission in Monte Carlo and his prospective meeting with Churchill and MI6 in London.

"Well, we're acting on three fronts, Tony and Sophia *vis-à-vis* the Perons, Jacques *et al* in Monte Carlo, and you there in London. Not bad for starters," Dulles summed up.

"Keep us advised on your meeting over there, Colonel," Smith said, then signed off.

CHAPTER FIVE

Thursday, March 20, 1952 - Paris

Jacques Laurent entered the French refugee office, and a pleasant, middle-aged woman came out of her office after the receptionist announced his name.

"Monsieur Laurent, I am Blanche Lefcourt, we've spoken on the phone before. Please come to my office."

"Merci, Mademoiselle Lefcourt."

"Oh, no, it is Madame," she smiled.

"Ah, oui."

As she returned to her desk, she pulled a file with the legend plainly printed on its cover, Joyce Laurent.

"We have traced the name of Laurent to Leipzig, East Germany. But we haven't been able to determine who is the person with that name. You know, we have to be very cautious in locating people in this Communist country," Madame Lefcourt reported.

"The name of Laurent would be very unusual in East Germany, is that not so?" Jacques leaned forward, trying to control the emotional surge he was experiencing.

"Most unusual," she concurred.

"How did you learn that someone with that name is in Leipzig?"

"When we were debriefing a young man who escaped from there, he told us that there is someone named Laurent teaching French at the University of Leipzig. He didn't know whether it was a man or a woman."

"Where is this young man?" Jacques asked.

"He is in Israel now. You see, he is Russian, with relatives here in Paris.

He made his way here to obtain funds and papers to help him get to Tel Aviv. He has family there. He left here three weeks ago."

"What's his name, please?"

"Dimitri Kosov, twenty-three years old, speaks a little English, no French."

"How did he learn of the name of Laurent?"

"He was thinking of taking a course in French at the university. Then he was invited to join two other young men for their escape. A very daring one indeed. All he knew was that a Professor Laurent was teaching French there. He didn't have a first name or whether it was a male or female," she explained.

"Do you have an address for his relatives here in Paris?"

"Unfortunately, they all left for Tel Aviv."

"Well, I thank you very much," Jacques stated.

"Monsieur Laurent, do not be discouraged. This is a very warm lead, and we'll keep after it. Keep in touch with us. Is your address in Washington the same?"

"Yes, please. I'll be here in France for a few days, and I'll call you before I leave." Jacques felt a warm glow of hope. Most certainly, his sister was capable of teaching French, he assured himself. In the taxi on the way back to the George Cinq Hotel, he was anxious to pass this information on to Bart Milburn, whose connections in high places could bear fruit, he mused.

There was a bounce in his step when Jacques inquired for his messages at the hotel desk.

"Ah, yes, here is one for you, Monsieur Laurent," the clerk said, handing him the slip.

It stated, 'Please call Felix,' so he placed the call from a public phone in the lobby.

"Captain Gaumont here," was the response.

"Felix, it is me, Jacques."

"Meet me at Chez Paul in one hour."

"Oui, I'll be there."

Laurent stopped at the concierge's desk and checked out flight information for Nice, both day and night flights. He took the slip on which the concierge had written the schedule of Air France.

The weather in Paris was unusually warm, so Jacques strolled several blocks on the Champs Elysées before hailing a taxi.

At Chez Paul, he seated himself at a table where he could face the sun. He ordered a bottle of Pernod and two glasses, threw his head back, closed his eyes and felt the warmth of the rays, his mind dwelling on the fate of his sister.

The waiter noisily placed the bottle and glasses on the table.

"Merci, garçon," Jacques snapped, angry at the rude interruption of his reverie. Then he poured a drink and sipped it slowly.

"Jacques, how are you?" Felix Gaumont said heartily, slapping him on the shoulder.

He stood up and greeted his former army-cum-partisan comrade warmly.

"A little Pernod, Felix, or something else?"

"This is fine. Just like the old days."

They raised their glasses and clinked them together.

"To friendship," Jacques toasted.

"Oui," the captain said as they both gulped down the sweet French liqueur.

Jacques offered a cigarette to Gaumont, who waved it off. In turn, he took two cigars from a silver case, proffering one to Jacques, who accepted, smiling. Each man pulled out his old army lighter, and they puffed heavily as the smoke drifted skyward.

"Sit back, Jacques, I have some news for you. Do you remember Claude Colbert?"

"Of course...he was a good soldier and a great marksman. Also, very charming with the ladies. But more than that, he was with us to the very end."

"Yes, and he remembers you with great affection."

"What is he doing now?"

"Claude is with the Sûreté, stationed in Nice. He is the French liaison officer assigned to Monaco."

"*Mon Dieu*, fantastic, what a coincidence. Will he help me?"

"Without question. I pledged him to secrecy. When I told him of your mission, he said to tell Jacques we're with him all the way."

"What does he mean by *we*?"

"There is another name you might recognize. Remember Pierre Dernier?"

"Ah, *oui*, we called him *the surgeon*. He would sneak up on a Nazi and in seconds he would slit two or three throats before the rest of the patrol knew what happened. I was with him on a couple of those sorties."

"Well, how is this for your luck, Jacques? You know that Prince Rainier stood up to deGaulle and refused to stop providing a tax shelter for French businessmen in Monaco. So the general retaliated with a customs tax. Pierre is France's customs officer in charge. He, too, will help. And he sends his best to you."

"Felix, I am overwhelmed. This is all too good to be true."

"But it is, just like that, *mon ami*. You will find out anyway. So I will tell you. Claude and Pierre got their jobs, on my recommendation, not long after the war ended."

"How do I contact them?"

"Both of them live in Nice. They also share a pied-à-terre in Monte Carlo for nights they work late. Here is Claude's home number. He expects your call tonight. When are you going?"

"There is a flight at 5 p.m."

"All right, where are you staying?"

"In Nice at the Westminster Concorde under my own name, and in Monte Carlo at the Balmoral as François Joffre."

"Two passports, *mon ami*?"

"*Oui*."

"I don't want to know that," Gaumont laughed. "By the way, I may fly over to observe this activity."

"Leave a message at the Westminster Concorde and I'll call you back. Just say Uncle Paul called."

"Real spy stuff, eh?"

"*C'est la guerre.*"

"You had better leave now if you want to make the 5 o'clock flight."

"Felix, I am indebted…"

"Go, go."

Jacques tossed a handful of francs on the table and hastened to seek a taxi. He checked out of the George Cinq and was on board the Air France flight to Nice at 4:55 p.m.

☆ ☆ ☆ ☆

Thursday, March 20, 1952 - The same day, Monte Carlo

Earlier that day, a well-dressed man had arrived at the Nice airport, and after clearing customs he entered a taxi to take him to the Hotel de Paris in Monte Carlo. During the nine-mile ride, he viewed the splendor of the beautiful stretch of beach and the shimmering waters of the Mediterranean.

A bellman greeted him when the cab door opened. "Welcome to Monte Carlo, sir."

"Thank you. My name is Philippe Bergere. Please bring my bags in, and please be careful with the golf clubs."

The baroque façade with its marble and nude mermaids extending from above the entrance captured Phillip Berger's attention for several minutes.

The luxury hotel was indeed everything he had read about in Frommer's Guide to France. The travel book had described the Hotel de Paris as a *Rolls Royce and caviar experience.*

When he presented his passport at the reception desk, the manager, a robust, white-haired man, greeted Phillip effusively. "I am Laurence Montaigne. It is my personal pleasure to meet you, Monsie*ur* Bergere. I will show you to your suite, which faces the sea, as you requested. Just sign the registration card."

The manager clapped his hands and ordered the bellman to bring the luggage.

When they reached the elegant quarters, a maid was there drawing the curtains and opening the windows. The large living room and an ample-sized bedroom were luxuriously furnished and immaculate in every aspect.

"I trust you will be happy and comfortable here. If there is anything special we can do for you, just call the concierge, Paul. I too am at your service, Monsieur Bergere." The manager bowed and took his leave.

Phillip tipped the bellman and shut the door behind him. Then he strolled to the open windows and raptly stared at the yacht basin, which was a panoply of assorted boats, from small sails to oversized motorized yachts. A knock on the door pulled Phillip away from his momentary trance.

A bellman entered with a basket of fruit, crackers, and assorted cheeses, plus a bottle of Dom Perignon champagne, compliments of the manager. After tipping the bellman, he loosened his tie, spun the bottle in the ice bucket and audibly said to himself, *Why not?*

Phillip opened the bottle and poured the champagne into the tall flute wineglass. As he sipped the bubbling drink, his thoughts returned to the object of his mission. He opened his briefcase and pulled the material that Dulles had handed him before his departure from Langley. Sales brochures of cargo containers and a history of Malcolm McLean's Sea Land's revolutionary breakthrough with the conversion of his recently acquired Waterman steamship fleet into container ships were spread on the table.

Phillip had studied all the materials several times in preparation for a meeting with Onassis, which was arranged by the U.S. Commerce Department at the behest of General Smith.

Berger reached for the phone and called Onassis' office, a short distance from the hotel, facing the yacht harbor.

A pleasant female English accent greeted the caller: "Onassis Shipping."

"This is Philippe Bergere. Mr. Onassis is expecting my call."

"One moment, sir."

A male voice in a slight Greek accent announced, "This is Alexis, Mr. Onassis' assistant, Mr. Bergere."

"Alexis, I would like to confirm a time for my meeting with Mr. Onassis," Phillip said.

"Mr. Bergere, we have you booked for 2:30 p.m. Saturday, March 22nd. Is that convenient?"

"That's fine."

"If there is any change, we can reach you at the De Paris. Is that correct?"

"Indeed." Phillip signed off, then changed into white ducks, white shoes, a blue blazer and a white open-collared shirt, and strolled along the marina docks.

At that time, Michael Paterno registered at the reception desk of the Hotel de Paris. Manager Montaigne accorded him the same effusive greeting he had extended to Phillip.

"Monsieur Paterno, we have placed your trunk in the suite. It was delivered here this morning."

The routine and the words were the same as he escorted Magic Mike to his room facing the yacht basin.

After the manager departed, Mike went into the bedroom and examined the trunk. It was locked securely. He took a key from his pants pocket and opened both locks.

The large steamer trunk was in a standing position. He gently parted it and viewed an assortment of electronic devices, telescopic glasses, tools and wires in the six drawers, three on each side.

A knock on the door and the bellman entered with the standard basket of fruit and the bottle of Dom Perignon.

Mike tipped him and went back to the bedroom to examine and sort out the materials for Jacques' use. He took the long-range binoculars, adjusted the focus and scanned the yacht basin and the docking area.

Nodding and smiling, he spotted Phillip sauntering along the marina.

The sun was setting when Jacques checked into the Westminster Concorde Hotel in Nice. His room faced the Mediterranean, and he stared at the spring sun dipping on the horizon.

Jacques went to the lobby and found a public telephone booth, then dialed the Hotel de Paris and asked for Monsieur Paterno.

Mike answered, "Yes?"

"Your Aunt Lucy is in Nice," Jacques announced.

"Tell her to wait, and I'll see her in an hour."

"Yes, sir."

Laurent dialed another number.

"Allo?"

"Claude, this is Jacques."

"Mon ami, where are you?"

"I'm at the Westminster Concorde."

"I can meet you there at ten this evening. I'll bring Pierre, is that okay?"

"Fine." He rang off, then dialed the Balmoral, advising them of his late arrival. He also ordered a car rental from the concierge.

An hour later, Mike Paterno arrived, carrying a heavy suitcase. Jacques met him at the entrance and led him to his room.

The next hour was spent in an indoctrination course by Mike on the proper use of the bugging devices. After a few run-throughs, Mike complimented Jacques. "By Jove, I believe you've got it," he mimicked in a pseudo-English accent. "Test this bug at 8 a.m. tomorrow. Set it to my room."

"*Merci beaucoup, Monsieur*," Jacques quipped.

"What's your schedule?" Mike inquired.

"Two war comrades, a French police liaison officer and French customs officer will meet me here at 10 o'clock."

"Fabulous contacts. Are they going to help?"

"All the way, I've been told by my dear friend, the captain of detectives at Paris headquarters."

"Marvelous. You're really well connected."

"The three of us were part of a partisan group after France surrendered. We were in the French army and went underground after Dunkirk."

"I better leave before they arrive."

"You're welcome to stay, Mike."

"No, no, they'll be more comfortable without a stranger here, Jacques. I can meet them some other time."

"You're right, Mike."

"When are you checking out of the Balmoral?"

"I've phoned to advise them of my late arrival tonight, so I'll drive up there around midnight."

"Good luck to all of us, Jacques, and goodnight."

Jacques unpacked one suitcase and hung a couple of suits in the bedroom closet. He laid two pairs of shoes below them and placed underwear and shirts in the dresser. He carried a garment bag on his left arm and lifted a suitcase with his right hand. He entered the elevator and alighted in the lobby. He beckoned a bellman and handed the baggage to him. The concierge presented him with the car rental papers. He filled them out and took the proffered keys. A Renault sedan was at the front door. The bellman placed the bags in the trunk. Jacques handed some francs to the bellman and the doorman. "Could you keep the car here for a short while?" he asked the doorman.

"No problem, Monsieur. Leave the keys with me. Are you checking out?"

"Just overnight to visit my sister."

Ten minutes later, a Mercedes Benz pulled into the driveway.

Jacques bounded down the steps and greeted the arrivals, "Claude, Pierre, I will follow you to any place where we can talk."

"*Bon*," Claude approved.

Jacques retrieved the keys for the Renault, then trailed the Mercedes along the Promenade des Anglais for a mile and a half. The cars turned into a darkened side street and stopped at a blinking neon sign flashing *Le Bistro Marcel*. The trio paused and, in turn, Jacques hugged Claude and Pierre.

The two comrades, tall and trim, expressed their delight joyfully in the reunion with backslaps and hugs, then the trio entered the dimly lit and tastefully decorated brasserie.

Claude and Pierre waved at the bartender.

"Is that back room occupied?" Pierre asked.

"Go right back."

As they passed the sparsely occupied leather booths, they were greeted by the proprietor.

"*Allo*, Marcel, this is our friend, Jacques, our captain in the war."

"*Enchanté, Monsieur*. Welcome to our humble chateau," the heavy-set owner said, bowing in jest. "You must be careful with the company you keep," he added, pointing at the two officers.

"We're here to close you up, you rascal."

"With friends like these two, who needs enemies?" Marcel retorted.

The group entered a cozy room with heavy leather chairs placed around a thick oak table. The walls displayed Impressionist paintings of fair quality.

"What will it be, gentlemen?"

"How about some wine?" Jacques asked his comrades

"I have some very fine Pouilly Fuissé, Chateau Lafitte Rothschild 1938."

All three nodded in assent.

Marcel quickly returned, placed three glasses on the table, opened the bottle and poured the choice wine.

As they toasted each other, Marcel announced, "We have a very special bouillabaisse this evening."

Once again, nods of approval.

As they drank and ate with gusto and high spirits, Jacques outlined the spoor for Nordheim, the alleged Nazi. Pierre and Claude asked Jacques for details. He pledged them to total secrecy, pointing out the intricacies of the operation. "I beg you both not to reveal anything about this operation or the name of Nordheim to the authorities here. The American officials will be contacting the French government in due course. Any premature leak could destroy a delicate mechanism that has been launched," Jacques implored.

"But, Jacques, we have a loyalty to France," Claude rejoined.

"How do we justify our silence?" Pierre added.

"Look, my friends, there are a number of Vichy French in government here. All it would take is only one such Nazi sympathizer to upset the apple cart, and Nordheim, who is believed to be a high-up Nazi, would go underground," Jacques heatedly reasoned.

"You have made a good point. However, there will be a point in time, say, when your people are ready to zero in on this supposed Nazi, that France has to be included," Claude said.

"I'm sure that the Americans will ask France to join them in this venture, but not at this moment. Getting Nordheim isn't the total objective. It is the beginning of a roundup of all those rotten bastards who escaped from the Allies. So, you see, it's bigger than one man," Jacques passionately explained.

"Okay, Jacques, we'll play," Claude agreed.

"*Oui*," Pierre echoed.

"All right, can you get me aboard that yacht?" Jacques said.

"Pierre and I have already worked that out."

"How?"

"Tell him, Pierre."

"You will come on board the yacht with me. I am the French customs officer. And you, Monsieur Joffre, will be my supervisor, who has come to see this beautiful new boat, because you are an aficionado of world class yachts. The dockmaster, Guy Bernarde, is my friend."

"Suppose Nordheim is there and wants to question me about other boats in his class?" Jacques said.

"You will have a book on famous yachts delivered to you in the morning at the Balmoral. Read it, and in half an hour you'll be an expert," Pierre gleefully declared.

"How about credentials?" Jacques asked.

"I will present them to you personally in Monte Carlo, Monsieur Francois Joffre," Pierre laughed.

"We have a *pied-à-terre* on the Boulevard des Moulins. Here is the address and telephone number," Claude said, handing him his card with the information written on the back of it. "We can meet there when necessary."

"By the way, walk along the marina dock tomorrow, and you will see a variety of very expensive vessels. There is one docked there with a helicopter on the aft deck. It belongs to Aristotle Onassis, the world-renowned shipping magnate," Pierre advised.

"Friends, I am very grateful for your cooperation. Felix said he might come to see us in action."

"Yes, he mentioned that," Claude said.

"I must be on my way to the Balmoral," Jacques declared.

The trio rose and entered the bar, where Jacques beckoned Marcel. "L'addition, Monsieur Marcel, s'il vous plaît," he requested.

Jacques pulled out a large handful of francs, which included a handsome gratuity for Marcel.

The Bistro owner dropped his flip manner and in extremely polite tones thanked Jacques. "You are most generous, Monsieur. Please come again."

"See, Marcel, we bring a little class to your humble chateau," Claude scoffed.

They shook hands all around and departed.

Jacques waved and headed the Renault for the drive along the Corniche to Monte Carlo.

Twenty minutes later he checked into the Balmoral on the Avenue de la Costa. The venerable hotel had been built in 1898 and was beautifully maintained. It had a homelike ambiance, and while being constantly refurbished it still maintained some of the elegance of its early years. The building was lodged on the side of a cliff halfway between the casino and the Royal Palace, directly overlooking the yacht harbor.

The suite pleased Jacques. The furnishings were immaculate and low-key. The views from both rooms were spectacular, encompassing the array of yachts and the sea beyond.

Jacques opened his double-locked suitcase and removed shirts, underwear and socks. He lifted an expandable briefcase, which contained the bugging equipment. He replaced it and locked the suitcase, which he slid under his bed. He called the night concierge and ordered a wakeup call at 7 a.m. and a continental breakfast for 7:30.

☆ ☆ ☆ ☆

Friday, March 21, 1952 - 8:30 a.m., Monte Carlo

After a quick shower, shave, and a breakfast of orange juice, croissants, strawberry preserves and hot coffee, Jacques Laurent was ready for his microphone test.

He turned on the radio and selected a music station. Edith Piaf was singing "La Vie en Rose." He placed the bug ten feet away from the electronic device, then adjusted the bug as instructed. He was hoping that he was zeroed into Paterno's room at the Hotel de Paris.

Speaking softly over Piaf's melodic rendition, he announced in French, "We are pleased to bring you a medley of Edith Piaf's hit songs. Hope you enjoy this presentation."

Five minutes later, the phone rang. "*Allo,*" Jacques answered.

"Monsieur Joffre, your Aunt Lucy received your message. She is fine and sends you her love. She enjoyed the concert."

Jacques smiled and replaced the bug in the briefcase. He dressed in casual clothes, carried the briefcase with him and set out for an inspection stroll along the marina docks. The strap around his neck holding a camera marked him as a tourist.

The sun bathed the tranquil waters. The blue sky was flecked with small puffs of white clouds.

Jacques studied the montage of dissimilar boats plying the waters and the luxurious vessels tied up at the dock. He paused in front of Aristotle Onassis' 200-foot yacht. Conscious of rubbernecking tourists, he focused his Nikon speed camera and clicked off several shots of the impressive boat with a helicopter on its aft deck.

A deckhand waved at Jacques, who acknowledged his approval of the vessel by waving back with his forefinger and thumb of his right hand joined in an "okay."

He returned to his hotel, checked for messages and was presented with a gift-wrapped package. Back in his rooms, he tore open the wrappings and found a book titled "World Class Yachts." He spent an hour poring through the book, where a wealth of information, plus photographs of royal and affluent owners and their luxury craft, were contained in the compendium.

Jacques picked up his high-powered binoculars, went to the windows and surveyed the harbor and the Mediterranean to its horizon. The phone rang. "*Allo*."

"Dinner at seven o'clock at the De La Roya, 21 Rue de la Turbie. Back room. Can you make it?"

"*Oui*," Jacques said, then exited his room.

Upon leaving the hotel, Jacques paused in the hotel lobby to purchase a newspaper. A bellhop was paging "Monsieur Joffre."

Laurent waved at him, "Young man, that's me."

"This way, sir. In that booth, a long-distance call."

Jacques pressed a couple of francs into the pager's hand, then picked up the phone.

"*Allo*."

"Monsieur Joffre?"

"Oui."

"This is long distance. I have a person to person call for you from Paris."

"Put them on, please."

"Joffre?"

"Oui."

"Your Aunt Lucy should arrive about 2 p.m. tomorrow," an impressive American male voice recited.

"Thank you," Jacques replied. *Must be the American Embassy*, he mused, as he hung up.

Then he sauntered leisurely to the Avenue Albert, entered the portside Quick Silver restaurant and requested a table in the sidewalk café. He ordered a bottle of Heineken beer and a seafood salad. Lighting a cigarette, he exhaled, and noticed Mike Paterno seated four tables away to his left. Quickly he unfolded his newspaper and seemed absorbed in its contents. Mike spotted him and turned his attention to a pretty cocktail waitress, striking up a conversation with her.

The proximity of Paterno's presence vexed Jacques, yet he found it fortuitous. He finished his repast quickly and wrote something on a small piece of paper, which he crumpled in his left hand. As he departed, he tripped into Mike's chair, dropping the small ball of paper in Paterno's lap. "Pardon me, Monsieur," Jacques excused himself, and quickly exited.

Mike adroitly retrieved the ball of paper and put it under his napkin. He casually scanned the area to ascertain whether anyone had observed the split-second encounter with Jacques. Satisfied that none of the diners or waiters were interested in him, he smoothly reached into his jacket pocket for a pack of cigarettes, depositing the crumpled paper there. He lit a cigarette, waved at a waiter and asked for the check, then walked briskly to the Hotel de Paris. In his suite, Mike unfolded the crushed note, on which was clearly printed *Lucy due tomorrow about 2 p.m.* He tore the paper into shreds and flushed it down the commode.

Jacques returned to the Balmoral and sprawled himself on the king-sized bed, staring at the open window. Thoughts of his sister Joyce flashed through his mind. He wrestled with his desire to contact Barton Milburn for help in tracking down the identity of the Laurent professor at the University of Leipzig. *Better to wait until the mission here in Monte Carlo was completed,* he counseled himself. Soon he was in a deep sleep. A faint knock on the door eventually jolted him to his feet. "Who is there?" he demanded harshly.

"Maid service, monsieur," was the reply.

"No, not now," he snapped.

"*Pardonnez moi,*" she whispered.

Jacques looked at his wristwatch. It was 6:15 p.m. He took a quick shower, donned a Brooks Brothers light blue cotton, buttoned-down-collar shirt, a gift of the Milburns; a taupe-colored pair of slacks, a blue blazer and cordovan shoes. He applied a Windsor knot to a dark red tie. He hurriedly left the suite, encountering a plump middle-aged night maid in the hall. He handed her a few francs and apologized for his gruffness. She smiled. He smiled back and raced to the elevator.

The doorman sent for Jacques' rented Renault. He tipped the doorman and the valet driver who opened the door of the sedan. Jacques took off for the De La Roya on the Rue de la Turbie. Promptly at 7:00pm, he entered the plain, clean and unpretentious bistro. He asked for the back room and was ushered there by a pretty young lady.

On entering the room, Felix Gaumont greeted him. "Come, Jacques, sit here next to me. Claude and Pierre should be here any minute."

"Felix, I am so glad you could come."

The room was pleasantly furnished with an oval table and six armchairs around it. The walls were covered with prints of English foxhound-hunting scenes. Rose-colored lamps muted the lighting.

"The boys have you well prepared for tomorrow's sortie," Felix commented.

"Felix, my dear friend, what you have accomplished is far beyond my wildest expectations. I shall be eternally grateful to you."

"The cause is good and I am as anxious as you, Captain Jacques, to root out any of the Nazi scum that escaped the net."

"Especially if Nordheim turns out to be one of the big ones in the hierarchy," Laurent added.

Pierre Dernier and Claude Colbert entered the back room. Accompanying the two was a tall, muscular man wearing a pea jacket and a naval officer's hat tilted back on his head in a jaunty manner, which matched his demeanor.

Jacques' discomfiture was palpable. He slapped the table in disapproval and stood up angrily.

The stranger took off his hat, threw it on the table and laughed, "I see that my presence here disturbs you."

"Jacques, relax," Claude said. "This gentleman is a friend and is here to help us."

Gaumont put his arm around Jacques' shoulder, then stuck his hand out to the jovial visitor.

"Good to see you again, Captain," he addressed the stranger. "Jacques, I know you are surprised. Come, shake hands with Guy Bernarde, the dockmaster of the yacht basin."

Bernarde, smiling, reached out and shook hands with Laurent, whose dismay quickly turned into embarrassed charm.

"Captain, forgive my rudeness," Jacques apologized as he continued pumping the big man's oversized hand. "I am paranoid in matters like this."

"No problem, my friend," Bernarde graciously acknowledged.

"Let us sit down," Gaumont indicated, pointing to the chairs as he pressed a button on the wall for service.

An aproned waiter, with flowing mustache, appeared with five menus, which he placed in a stack on the table.

"Aperitifs?" he asked.

"Two bottles of Beaujolais," Jacques ordered. "Anything else, fellows?"

A chorus of okays ensued.

"Jacques, let me explain. Guy here is an old and dear friend. He was captain of a destroyer in the French navy during the war. When Vichy France was under the domination of the Nazis, he defied orders from Marshal Petain and with the concurrence of his crew, headed for England. He operated with the British navy and scored quite a few hits on German submarines. He was decorated by the British and the Americans, as well as General de Gaulle."

"I am impressed," Jacques said loudly in a salute to their new conspirator.

"Monsieur Laurent, I have been fully briefed on your mission here. I, too, have an abiding hatred of Nazis and racists of all stripes. I have sent my fair share of them to their perdition. So, rest assured, I am here to help you. In fact, I am honored to be part of this venture," Bernarde said. "I know of your role as a captain in the French army and later with the partisans, and I, too, am impressed."

War stories became the order of the evening. With much to share in memories of the previous decade, the five men drank, smoked and participated in an anecdotal soiree. They laughed, joked, and reminisced about their experiences in the great war. There were moments of tears for their departed comrades.

During dinner, the five consumed the food with gusto. The rapport among them was manifest.

Gaumont pressed the button on the wall. Paul and a busboy cleared the dishes. Jacques ordered coffee, a bottle of cognac and cigars.

After the coffee was served and the cognac bottle opened, Jacques addressed the waiter. "Now, Paul, please make sure we are not disturbed."

"Absolutely, monsieur."

The cognac was poured. The cigars were ignited, and a ceiling fan scattered the smoke.

Jacques stood up and raised his glass, "To success. *Vive la France, Vive l'Amérique*," he toasted. The other four joined in.

Then the captain spoke. "Messieurs, here is the plan. When the yacht arrives, I will supervise the docking procedure. As soon as the boat is secured, I will escort you, Jacques, Claude and Pierre to board her. The captain of the yacht should be there to meet us. I will explain that you gentlemen will make a routine inspection and determine the tax to be assessed. I will ask for an advance payment for docking fees. All of this should be very casual and in order," Bernarde said.

"I will check passports," Claude added.

"The yacht is on its way now," Jacques said. "It is due at approximately two o'clock tomorrow afternoon. The name on the boat is the Flying Eagle."

"How do you know that, Jacques?" Gaumont queried.

"I received a call a few hours ago with that information," he replied.

"That's good news," Claude interjected.

"The dock space was reserved over a week ago in the name of Eagle Shipping, from their Liechtenstein office," the dockmaster said.

"Felix, can I ask a favor of you?" Jacques asked.

"Of course, my friend."

"Where will you be when she docks?"

"Wherever you want me to be."

"I would like to have pictures of the yacht and any of the faces that show themselves on board, or boarding the vessel. I will give you a speed camera, fully loaded."

"I will be the perfect tourist and shoot as many pictures as necessary."

"Gentlemen, let us gather at my office on the dock at 1 p.m.," Bernarde suggested.

Jacques buzzed for the check, then gave Paul a fistful of francs, which included a generous tip.

The five exited, shook hands all around and departed.

☆ ☆ ☆ ☆

Saturday, March 22, 1952 - 9 a.m. - London
Elizabeth Milburn, Michael, Jenny and Mrs. Bishop climbed into the Land

Rover, with Tri at the wheel. Bart Milburn and Sir Alfred Lipton were seeing the happy group off to a tour of London. The sky was overcast and a slight mist covered the vehicle with driblets of water.

"We're meeting Aunt Rebecca at the Dorchester for lunch after the changing of the guard at Buckingham Palace," Elizabeth enthusiastically reminded the children.

"Yes, yes," Michael blurted, "and we're going to see the soldiers."

"I want to see my Aunt Becky," Jenny chimed in.

"Tell my sister that we are expecting her, Uncle Daniel and the children for brunch tomorrow," Sir Alfred said.

"She knows that, Daddy, but I'll remind her," Elizabeth said, smiling. "Let's go, Tri."

Bart and Sir Alfred waved goodbye as the Rover pulled out of the driveway.

The two men returned to the house and settled in the oak-paneled den. Jennings placed a tray of silver service containing coffee, cream and sugar on the Honduran mahogany coffee table, then stoked burning logs in the stone fireplace.

"Jennings, we'll be leaving at eleven o'clock for Downing Street."

"Yes sir, I'll be ready," Jennings responded as he gently closed the big oak door behind him.

Bart and Sir Alfred sipped their coffee, both meditating on their upcoming meeting with Prime Minister Winston Churchill at 10 Downing Street.

Lipton finally broke the silence. "Bart, as I told you last night, Churchill is extremely interested in this Nordheim affair. His curiosity is at feverish pitch. He has been hounding the lads at MI6 for reports daily. Being the old warhorse he is, he won't let up until this enigma is unraveled. His abiding hatred of Nazis has never abated. For that matter, neither has mine."

"Amen," Bart said.

"If Nordheim is not what the Israelis allege, then his delivering arms to North Korea by itself is enough to warrant extreme action."

"What does Churchill or MI6 know so far?"

"Well, they have come up with quite a few things beyond what you have told me. When I told Winston about your mission, he suggested you come here before you visit Ben-Gurion in Tel Aviv. He wants to meld your information with the MI6 reports. As you know, he is a self-confessed Zionist, going back to the time of the Balfour declaration for a state of Israel."

"What are some of these *things*, as you put it?"

"Just a few items, Bart, such as Egypt being equipped with armaments by Nordheim. King Farouk's reign is tenuous. Winston General is backing their strongman, General Mohammed Naguib, who controls the army. Attacks on British troops reached a climax in the Suez Canal zone in January of this year, just three months after Egypt abrogated their 1936 treaty with Britain and the 1899 Anglo-Egyptian condominium of the Sudan."

"I guess that is a large enough burr under the Prime Minister's saddle," Bart ventured.

"More on that, MI6 will spell it out. Nordheim is a duplicitous bastard. He is playing both ends against the middle, to coin a phrase. This is an evil man. He is grooming an Egyptian army officer, one General Abdel Nasser, to help General Naguib get rid of their grossly fat libertine King Farouk and to eventually dump Naguib. Nordheim has been pouring vast sums of money into Nasser's coffers. Just between us, Bart, we have some men well placed in the Egyptian army and the upper echelons of the Egyptian government."

Bart emitted a soft whistle. "Alfred, this is very heavy stuff. Nordheim is undoubtedly a very dangerous man. Let's cut to the quick for a moment. I have been diagramming the Third Reich's hierarchy from Hitler, Goebbels, Goering, Himmler and Bormann on down. For example, Hitler, according to all accounts, committed suicide and was given a Norseman's funeral. The Soviets have never matched the dental records of the remains. There is no empirical proof that it was Hitler. Yet it is widely accepted that he is dead."

"Do you really doubt that it was Hitler in that pyre?" Lipton challenged.

"Just begging the question. The Allies had no hand in the verification process. The Commies, for some unexplained reason, held their cards close to their chests and closed the book on Hitler. What would your answer be in a court of law, Alfred, to this question: Is Herr Hitler dead?"

"I believe he is dead," Lipton replied.

"Are you certain?"

"I can only base my answer on news reports."

"Not on empirical knowledge, based on factual information or observation, sir?" Bart parried.

"My dear Barton, that's the barrister in you. And quite good, I might say," Sir Alfred said.

"Going down the scale, we know that Goebbels committed suicide and Goering did the same. Himmler is not a positive, and Martin Bormann is believed to have been sighted in Argentina. So have Adolf Eichmann and Josef Mengele. Thousands of other Nazis are nestled in Argentina and throughout South America, Canada and the United States."

"The field is broadening, I would say."

"Alfred, the possibilities are extant. Just let me tick off a few names: Rudolf Hess, in Spandau Prison, but is it the real Hess? Joachim von Ribbentrop, Wilhelm Keitel, Ernst Kaltenbrunner, Alfred Rosenberg, Hans Frank, Wilhelm Frick, Julius Streicher, Fritz Sauckel, Alfred Jodl and Arthur Seyss-Inquart, all hanged at Nuremberg. Still alive are Walther Funk and Erich Raeder, both sentenced to life imprisonment. Baldur von Schirach and Albert Speer sentenced to twenty years. Konstantin von Neurath, fifteen years. Now the acquittals" Hjalmar Schacht, Franz von Papen and Hans Fritzsche, Nazis nevertheless. Those sentenced to long terms have to be checked to be certain they are still incarcerated. Those acquitted have to be tracked down."

"Apparently you've been doing a good deal of research on the Nazis," Sir Alfred observed.

"Yes, plus materials that were furnished to me by our intelligence people."

"Your euphemism for intelligence people, simply put, is the CIA, is it not?"
Bart laughed. "I guess it's habit not to be too precise unless pressed."
Lipton looked at his watch. "It's time for us to go."

Both men donned their coats and exited the house to face a brisk 38-degree temperature and a fine misty drizzle. Jennings, attired in his livery uniform, awaited with an open umbrella hovering over them as he held the open door of the Rolls Royce.

"Sir, I heard the early weather report on the BBC. They predicted a possibility of snow later today due to a northerly gale in the North Sea, which will cause a drop in our temperature to below freezing. However, they pointed out that the gale will not strike London."

"That's a relief," Sir Alfred sighed.

London's traffic was in its rainy-day crawl mode, so Jennings, impatiently struggling with the recalcitrant traffic flow, finally said, "Sir, if I may, I can avoid the mainstream a few streets ahead."

"Please do," Lipton fretted. "We can't afford to be late."

"I may have to break a few rules, sir, but, with your permission, we can make it."

"By all means."

Jennings wheeled the vehicle into a sharp right turn, cutting off an oncoming Bentley, whizzing through stop signs and splattering puddles of rain on pedestrians.

"Jennings could hold his own against our New York cabbies," Bart complimented.

"Indeed," Sir Alfred agreed.

They pulled into Downing Street at 11:28 a.m. A security officer greeted Lipton as he stepped out of the car.

"Sir Alfred, nice to see you, sir."

"How are you, George?"

"Fine, sir, fine. I presume this is Mr. Milburn."

"Yes. Bart, say hello to Captain George Dempsey."

"My pleasure, Captain."

"Mine too, sir. You gentlemen are expected at eleven-thirty and you are right on the button."

A liveried butler opened the door, took their coats and pointed to an aide standing in the hallway.

Jack Colville, personal aide to the Prime Minister, addressed Lipton. "Beastly out there, Sir Alfred?"

"Just the traffic, Jack. This is Colonel Barton Milburn."

"Welcome, sir. Please come with me."

They were escorted into the inner sanctum of one of the world's most powerful men. The room was adorned with many mementoes of England's history. Leather chairs, a large desk, a roaring fireplace and an air of informality contributed to the ambiance of Prime Minister Churchill's lair. "Sir Alfred and Colonel Milburn, welcome to my humble quarters," the 78-year-old

Churchill bellowed, pointing to two large leather chairs.

"Thank you, Winston. We barely made it on time," Lipton replied.

"Colonel, you look quite well since I saw you last."

"Thank you, sir. You seem to thrive on the affairs of state," Bart returned the compliment.

Churchill leaned back in his Victorian-era leather chair, adjusted his sweater and laughed loudly. "Alfred, your son-in-law may be a successful barrister in the colonies, but he sounds more like a diplomat."

"I'd venture to say the two professions are kin."

"Well stated, Alfred."

"Mr. Prime Minister, I am at your disposal in either capacity," Bart proffered.

"You've come a long way since the war, Barton. How is that charming wife of yours?"

"Quite well, sir. She is here with our two little ones."

"Yours is quite a story. I've told my spouse, Clementine, of Elizabeth's ordeal in those death camps, your rescue of her and the romance that ensued, which led to your ultimate marriage. Truth is stranger than fiction. She was enthralled and would like you to join us for tea one of these days. You, too, Sir Alfred."

"We would be delighted and honored, sir."

"Fine, now let's get down to business. President Truman called me last night, about 10 p.m.-that would be 4 p.m. Washington time-and he cryptically advised me that Russian Ambassador Gromyko has met with your Secretary of State Dean Acheson to register a protest about the alleged sinking of two cargo ships in the Sea of Japan off the coast of North Korea. You wouldn't know anything about that, would you, Colonel?"

"Is that a rhetorical question, sir?" Bart parried with a straight face.

Churchill snickered, glanced over his glasses at Bart and continued. "Acheson denied knowledge of the action and promised to make some inquiries. However, it seems those ships belonged to Eagle Shipping, a subsidiary of Winston General, Mr. Nordheim's conglomerate. If Nordheim is truly one of the high Nazi officials, it occurred to me that he is taunting me by using the name of Winston for his holdings."

"Strange you should mention that, sir. The conjecture crossed my mind, too," Bart said.

"President Truman asked me to have MI6 assist you in your mission to unveil Nordheim's true identity, but not to interfere with your plans. I assured Harry that we will let you run with the ball, as you Americans are wont to say, but we will continue our intelligence operations as usual. We will share any pertinent information with you and will not undertake any overt action without full consultation with you. That satisfied him, and I think it would you, Colonel."

"Quite, sir."

"Very well. I have arranged a meeting for you and Sir Alfred at MI6 with General Lloyd Forsythe and staff at 3 p.m. today. Now, give me a brief summary of your operation so far."

Bart outlined Operation Lucifer, starting with the visit of the Countess de Cordoba and her husband, Anthony Fuentes, to Argentina. He spelled out the plans of Jacques Laurent, Phillip Berger and Michael Paterno to check out Nordheim's new yacht docking this day in Monte Carlo. He capped the briefing by outlining his planned visit with Prime Minister David Ben-Gurion and the Mossad in Tel Aviv on the 29th of March.

"That would be on Saturday, one week from today, and you do know that is their Sabbath, Barton," the Prime Minister cautioned.

"Oh yes, we'll be arriving there on Saturday and I assume they will see us on Sunday or Monday. We will confirm a date early next week," Bart explained.

Churchill chuckled, turned to Sir Alfred and pointed at Bart, saying, "That son-in-law of yours has a penchant for undercover intelligence activity. Jolly clever trying to penetrate the inner circle of the Perons and bugging Nordheim's yacht. Code word *Lucy*, by Jove, sounds like a B movie."

Sir Alfred laughed. "Stranger things have occurred during the war, Winston."

"Right you are," Churchill agreed.

"Here, sir, are two photographs of Nordheim, one from his passport and the other taken of him on his other yacht talking to one Darren Mayfield, a former FBI agent who operates as his point man," Bart said.

"Have you checked out Mayfield?"

"Yes, sir, I have a sheet here, which you may keep. I learned that he left the agency rather suddenly. The Jewish Anti-Defamation League charged him as an active anti-Semite with connections to some hate groups in Skokie, Illinois. J. Edgar Hoover never followed through. The CIA is still digging and surveilling his relatives."

"Let's talk a little about Herr Nordheim," the Prime Minister suggested. "You must be aware by now that we have a deep interest in his activities, apart from his possible Nazi past. Sir Alfred briefed you on his machinations in Egypt's body politic, did he not?"

"Yes, sir."

"As you can plainly see, Barton, there is a tinder box there which is a threat to us and the state of Israel."

"No doubt."

The Prime Minister rose, straightened his Shetland wool cardigan sweater, then walked over to a picture window and silently stared at the spattering rain.

A pregnant silence ensued. It was obvious to Bart and Sir Alfred that this giant statesman was in deep reflection. After a span of several minutes, Churchill, still facing the slashing downpour, soliloquized in a somewhat Shakespearean manner, "Who is this mystery man? Where and how did this Nordheim acquire such wealth? Forty billion dollars? How can this be? With a treasury of that size, he could buy off all the despots of the world and mold an amalgam of evil capable of launching another Armageddon. China, the Soviet Union, the Arab nations, Argentina, Spain, Egypt and North Korea combined...What a scenario for destruction in this atomic age. Could any single man orchestrate such a cataclysm?"

The peroration ended, Churchill returned to his chair. Bart and Sir Alfred were entranced. "Let me look at this photograph again," Churchill snapped. "Colonel, come over here. I have this magnifying glass. Who does this bastard resemble, if anyone?"

"Let me point this out, sir. The man on the deck facing Mayfield is wearing Western boots. The heels are two inches high, and another inch inside the boot would elevate the man's height to at least three inches above his normal stature. Now, the Van Dyke beard and full mustache covers half the visage. We have to assume, following the hypothesis, that he is one of the Nazi hierarchy and that some expert plastic surgery has been applied."

"From what we see here, does the body sync with Hitler, Himmler, Bormann or anyone on your list?"

"Bormann is too short and stocky. Himmler is short and slight. He was stoop-shouldered and doesn't match the physical profile. Hitler would fit the comparison in stature. The passport photo of Nordheim shows a thin nose, whereas Hitler's nostrils were broad; however, surgery could account for the change."

"This is a bad dream," Churchill barked. "In reality it could be mankind's worst nightmare. Almost fifty million poor souls were deprived of life due to the machinations of Hitler and Stalin. Hitler, Himmler, Goebbels and Goering were indeed the Four Horsemen of the Apocalypse. The carnage they wreaked on this world from 1933 to 1945 is the nadir in the history of civilization. Only God saved this world from subjugation by this evil cabal. Yet our world leaders were stupidly complacent in a depression-mired economy while this band of guttersnipes robbed, plundered and mercilessly slaughtered millions of hapless, innocent Jews. We closed our eyes and ears to this orgy of crime. Like all bullies, Hitler smelled the fear emanating from the pores of the European Community leaders and bluffed his way into the bloodless occupation of the Sudetenland, Czechoslovakia, Danzig and Austria. Daladier, of France, and Chamberlain, of England, quivered as this devil incarnate hectored them into unchallenged submission. We cannot allow this malevolent phoenix to rise from his misbegotten ashes. He was as cunning as a sewer rat." Churchill poured himself a shot of brandy and downed it in one gulp, then he lit his ever-present cigar and puffed huge clouds of smoke skyward.

Sir Alfred and Bart were momentarily mesmerized by the Prime Minister's diatribe, then Bart broke the silence. "Sir, if I may, there are a few more items for your attention."

"Yes, yes, let's get on with it," the irascible statesman snapped.

"The wealth of Nordheim is undoubtedly the proceeds of ill-gotten gains from the estates of slaughtered Jews, art, gold fillings torn from the mouths of cadavers, and laundered money in Swiss bank accounts," Bart said.

"Indeed, that is the venality of the Swiss bankers who run that pseudo-pristine country. They were and still are pro-Nazi. Their spurious secret banking laws have made it virtually impossible to penetrate their machinations. They were the best non-combatant allies of the Third Reich. They have myriad accounts for the thousands of Nazi functionaries abiding in South America,

Canada, the United States, Germany, France, and right here in jolly old England. Six million Jews were robbed and slaughtered, as were millions of non-Jews. This was crime at a scale never before perpetrated by man," Churchill declared vehemently, slapping his desktop.

"On that note, sir, here is a sheet of the key officers of Winston General Ltd. The president of the holding company is ex-Swiss banker Gunther Froelich, former ambassador to England. The executive vice president is Sir Clive Fenwick, former British Ambassador to Germany prior to 1938. He became a key adviser to Neville Chamberlain. The treasurer of the company is Konrad Fliegel, Swiss citizen. He claims to be Jewish, entered Switzerland in a deal conjured by that American pro-Nazi, anti-Semite Joseph 'the bootlegger' Kennedy. He was employed as an accountant for the Banque Lorraine in Geneva. Nordheim has an account there. Fliegel was a key funnel for billions of pounds pouring into Swiss banks."

Churchill interrupted Bart's recitation. "Clive Fenwick? When did that rascal join Nordheim?" he queried.

"About six months ago, sir, according to the materials furnished to me by the CIA."

Churchill adjusted his glasses to the tip of his nose, leaned over his desk and scribbled some notations on a pad. He peered over his tilted spectacles and addressed Bart. "This Fenwick blackguard was believed to be a member of the Cliveden set, Nazi sympathizers. Cliveden was the home of Lord and Lady Nancy Astor, who along with the Duke and Duchess of Windsor and other Hitlerian sycophants steered Chamberlain into the abyss of appeasement. I will call General Forsythe to see if he has any knowledge of Fenwick's activities prior to his alliance with Nordheim. Talk to him about that, Colonel."

"I certainly will."

There was a momentary silence, then Churchill slowly sat down in his chair and pointed at Milburn. "You visited those death camps and wrote a definitive report, at the request of Eisenhower, which is now classified material in the archives of the Pentagon; this is so, is it not?"

"That's true, sir, and for reasons I cannot explain it has been stamped top secret," Bart wearily replied.

"Was it too graphic?" Churchill asked.

"No more so than the newsreels depicted."

"We must never let future generations be denied the truth of that inferno. Yet the horrors of the Hitlerian era seem to be fading from the consciousness of the world."

"Mr. Prime Minister, I couldn't agree with you more," Bart responded.

The door opened and Jack Colville entered. "Excuse me, sir, but lunch is ready, and I wish to remind you that the Chancellor of the Exchequer is due at 2:15."

"Very well, so let's have a go at it, gentlemen," Churchill declared, and the meeting was over.

CHAPTER SIX

Saturday, March 22, 1952 - 12:30 p.m. - Monte Carlo

The French Riviera was bathed in sunshine on that second day of spring. The Mediterranean was placid, transmitting sparkling, diamond-like reflections.

Yachts of all sizes were heading toward the open sea. Two sightseeing helicopters were approaching a landing pad in Monte Carlo. Tourists were awaiting the rotor bladed aircraft for the next tour of the Riviera. Among the waiting rubbernecks was Captain Felix Gaumont, attired in vacationer's garb, a light blue polo shirt, white Bermuda shorts, long blue stockings, white sport shoes, and a strap around his neck holding a long lens camera. When the first helicopter set down, two passengers alighted. The manager of the helipad waved Gaumont onto the copter amid the demurring sounds of the impatient queues muted by the feathered rotors.

The attendant manager soothed the agitated line, explaining, "This man is going up to test the propellers. It's for your safety. This is routine."

The aircraft lifted off and headed to the open sea. At the edge of the horizon, the pilot turned the craft east for ten nautical miles and circled back west. Fifteen miles off the coast of Monaco, Gaumont adjusted his binoculars and zeroed in on a sleek royal blue yacht approximately 200-plus feet in length, cutting neatly through the peaceful waters, leaving a wide wake in its path.

"Circle back and get closer," Gaumont ordered the pilot as he focused his camera on the yacht and clicked rapidly at the Flying Eagle.

As the copter dipped in the direction of the boat, Gaumont captured a series of shots of four people sipping drinks on the elongated deck. Two scantily clad, voluptuous young women, two older men and the boat's captain waved at the tourist copter. Gaumont and the pilot returned the favor and headed back to the Monte Carlo helipad.

Exiting the craft, Felix loudly addressed the waiting manager and, in earshot of the queued tourists, pronounced, "The rotors are in perfect order."

A murmur of satisfaction emanated from the tourist line.

Gaumont then headed for the harbormaster's office. Awaiting him were Jacques Laurent, Claude Colbert, French liaison officer to the principality of Monaco; Pierre Dernier, French customs officer, and Guy Bernarde, the harbor and dockmaster.

"The Flying Eagle is heading this way. She should be arriving within the hour. I believe I shot maybe twenty-five to thirty-five photos of the yacht, the captain on the top deck and four people on the huge aft deck. Two sensual young ladies in bikinis, I think, and two older men in bathing trunks," said.

"Marvelous," Jacques declared. Felix, will you be at the dock when the boat is tied up to take pictures of everyone going on or off?"

"Oh, yes, as you can see, I am the perfect tourist. I dressed for the occasion."

The men laughed.

"You've got beautiful knees," Claude chuckled.

"Better than yours," Felix bantered.

The other men were attired for the caper, as well. Claude wore his French police lieutenant's uniform, Dernier had donned his custom officer's uniform, Jacques was attired in a navy blue serge suit, light blue shirt and dark red tie, and Bernarde sported a blue short-sleeved shirt and white pants. Each man had a plastic identification badge pinned to his jacket, and Bernarde's to his shirt pocket.

"Now, let's go through the procedure," Claude asserted. A French health-department doctor will join us at the gangplank. He doesn't know what we are up to. He is there to make certain that no infectious diseases are being brought into Monaco or France."

"Won't he be in the way?" Jacques queried.

"No, on the contrary, he will ask all of the crew and passengers to meet with him in the ship's lounge. Thus he will hold them captive, while he has them filling out forms and taking an examination. That way, Jacques, you will be free to roam the vessel as you wish."

"Very good," Jacques exclaimed.

"Further to that, Pierre will have them fill out customs declarations. He intends to levy a heavy tax on the boat itself, and this will cause a serious argument. They will maintain that the boat is not being delivered here, but is just visiting. We'll keep the argument going as long as we can," Claude said.

"I will have them sign a docking agreement and waivers of any responsibility for damage to their boat. I will also discuss fees and rules of our La Condamine," Guy announced.

"All in all, the partisans will ride again," Jacques declared enthusiastically, somewhat overwhelmed by his good fortune in having his wartime compatriots participating in Operation Lucifer."

"I hope that the mystery Nazi shows up," Felix added.

Jacques went outside and scanned the immediate scene, looking for any suspicious characters or possible Nordheim employees. Satisfied that the area had the normal type of tourists, he turned his attention to the sea, focusing his binoculars to the horizon and panning the view for the approach of the Flying Eagle.

"There she is," he whispered to himself and rushed back to the dockmaster's office.

"Messieurs, I believe I saw the yacht," Jacques uttered excitedly.

"Lend me your glasses," Claude demanded and went to the window facing the sea.

"Wait," Guy said. "Here is my telescope; let me adjust it and I'll give it to you, Claude."

The harbormaster settled the tripod on the top shelf of his bookcase, pointed the scope seaward, adjusted the lens and exclaimed, "*Voilà*, there is our baby, coming home right on time."

Claude, Pierre, Felix and Jacques took turns viewing the oncoming yacht.

"Let's not go out there as a welcoming committee. We should make our approach when my two dockhands start to tie her up," Bernarde suggested. "Captain Gaumont, you should be out there, shooting your pictures as she enters the harbor."

"When do you estimate that will be?" Felix asked.

"Let me take a look," Guy said, focusing the telescopic sight. "Mmm, mmm," the dock master hummed thoughtfully. "Within the next ten minutes, at the speed she's going."

The office, while not small, was hardly big enough for the five men to start pacing. Cigarettes and cigars filled the room with a cloud of smoke. The minutes ticked away sluggishly as the four men stared at their wristwatches in prebattle stances.

Guy Bernarde looked out his window and announced, "She is easing her way to the dock, and my men are out there directing her. A few more minutes and we can stroll over there."

The men clustered at the window, observing the sleek world-class yacht as it maneuvered into the allotted dock space. The dockhands had the ropes and were tugging the vessel into position.

"All right, men, let's take a walk," Bernarde said.

Jacques grabbed his bag, and then the men exited. En route, they were joined by Dr. Marcel Levien. The gangplank was being lowered when the five men arrived. A tall man in a white uniform was starting down the boarding platform as the group was ascending.

"Hold it, sir," Claude authoritatively commanded. "I am Lieutenant Claude Colbert, the French liaison officer to Monaco. This is Pierre Dernier of customs, this gentleman is François Joffre, customs supervisor, and this is Dr. Marcel Levien, with the health department, and this is Guy Bernarde, the dockmaster."

"That's fine. I'm Captain Leif Sandstrom. I've got to check the lines to see if everything is properly fastened," the captain said in a Swedish accent.

"All right," Claude said, "but come right back up. No one is allowed to leave this boat until we complete our inspection and paper work. Monsieur Bernarde, please accompany the captain."

After the examination of the moorings, the captain and the harbormaster joined the team in the entry to the ship's main salon. The group proceeded to the capacious lounge.

"Captain Sandstrom, please have all passengers and crew join us here with their passports," Claude requested.

Sandstrom placed his captain's hat on a cabinet revealing a full head of tousled blond hair, then whistled, and a brawny member of the crew appeared. He rattled off a command in German.

"How many in the crew and how many passengers are aboard?" Claude asked.

"Seven crew, besides me, and four passengers."

"How long do you plan to stay?"

"I don't know at this time."

"Why don't you know?"

"Because I haven't been told," the captain rasped irritably.

"Are you expecting any more passengers?"

The captain didn't answer. He merely shrugged his shoulders defiantly.

The crew began to gather in the luxuriously decorated salon. The captain snapped his fingers and gestured the crew to the back of the room. Two men, one about sixty, the other his senior by ten or fifteen years, arrived. The older man, military in posture, white-haired, wearing white slacks, an open-collared pink shirt and a yachting jacket, entered officiously and in a Germanic accent demanded, "What is the meaning of this? Why are you here?"

The other gentleman, dark-haired and similarly dressed except for a silk foulard tie on a white shirt, spoke up with an upper-class English accent: "Gunther, I believe these gentlemen are doing their duty. We must cooperate," he purred placatingly. "Is that not so, gentlemen?"

"Yes, sir," Claude replied. "The sooner we complete our work here, the sooner we'll be gone."

"Very well, let us sit down and finish this now," Gunther said wearily.

"First, we want to know if everyone is here. I count seven in crew, and the captain, plus you two. Where are the others?"

"They are two ladies and they will be here shortly," the Englishman said.

"May I have all the passports here on this table?" Claude asked.

Two sun-tanned, blonde young ladies arrived. Both wore shift dresses and were in their late twenties. Each carried a passport.

Pierre reached them, took their passports and motioned them to a couch. He then passed in front of the standing crew and accepted their passports. He placed them on the table in front of Claude.

"Gentlemen, your passports, please," Claude requested.

"Is this necessary?" Gunther peevishly demanded.

"Absolutely," Claude snapped in anger.

"Come now, Gunther, let them have it," the other man cajoled as he handed his passport to Claude.

Gunther threw his passport onto the table.

"Is there anyone else aboard this boat?" Claude demanded.

"I'll check it out," Jacques declared.

"Thank you, sir," Claude added.

Pierre and Guy stationed themselves at opposite ends of the lounge, casually guarding the exit doors.

Jacques quietly picked up his bag containing the electronic devices and made his way to explore the cabins.

"Sir, I would like to know the name of the owners of the Flying Eagle. I would also like to see the documents of authentication," Pierre boomed across the room.

Sandstrom placed a leather-bound folder in front of Claude.

"Let me see now, this vessel is owned by Winston General, Ltd., of Vaduz, Liechtenstein," Claude read loudly. "Now we have here Gunther Froelich, a citizen of Liechtenstein, place of birth Stuttgart, Germany, November, 1885. Next is Clive Fenwick, British citizen, place of birth Sussex County, England, August 15, 1895. Then we have Captain Leif Sandstrom, Swedish citizen, place of birth Malmo, Sweden, March 9, 1901. What is the relationship of you two men to Winston General?" Claude inquired.

Froelich rose haughtily, and in guttural English intoned, "I am the president of Winston General, and Sir Clive Fenwick here is the executive vice president, not that it is any of your business."

Claude stood nose to nose with Froelich and roared, "Sit down and don't tell me my business! This yacht is being delivered here and it's my duty to gather all pertinent information about its owners and the contents of this boat. Officer Dernier will have to assess a customs tax on the boat and its contents. Do you understand that, *Mein Herr* Froelich?"

"Lieutenant Colbert, there is no need for acrimony. I am sure that Mr. Froelich is merely stating our position," Sir Clive stated softly in an effort to pacify Claude. "However, if you disagree, we will abide by your desires"

"*Wunderbar! Wunderbar*, Clive, always the diplomat," Froelich sarcastically noted.

"*Gemütlichkeit, Gemütlichkeit*, Gunther. They are only doing their duty," Fenwick implored.

The bickering between Claude and Froelich continued, getting louder as it progressed. Sir Clive intervened. "Lieutenant, may I have a moment of privacy with my associate?"

"Please do, but make it short, as we haven't got all day to sort this out. Dammit, sir, this should be routine. Why the recalcitrance to answer some standard questions? Do you people have something to hide?"

"Not at all, not at all, Lieutenant."

Froelich and Fenwick walked to the entryway. A uniformed French gendarme appeared, pushing the two back into the spacious room. Flustered, Gunther exploded, "What is the meaning of this?"

Ignoring the outburst, the policeman smartly saluted the lieutenant. Claude returned the salute and snapped in French, "Henri, you are late. Where are the others?"

"Stationed at the foot of the gangplank. Sorry, we were delayed in traffic."

"Very well. How many men?"

"Two, sir."

"Tell them no one is to leave this vessel without my approval. You will stand guard on the deck at the head of the gangplank."

"Yes, sir, Lieutenant." He saluted sharply and brushed past Froelich and Sir Clive.

"All right, gentlemen, confer quickly," Claude barked curtly.

Jacques was moving stealthily along the corridor leading to the lavishly accoutered cabins.

☆ ☆ ☆ ☆

Across from La Condamine, as the port of Monaco is named, were the offices of shipping tycoon Aristotle Onassis. On a second floor balcony overlooking the harbor, Phillip Berger and Onassis were occupied with their binoculars, focused on the Flying Eagle.

The building, separated from the harbor by Avenue Albert, had a clear view of the yacht basin.

"There seems to be some unusual police activity over there," Onassis commented.

"Could that be the customs people?" Berger speculated.

"Possibly, but why the gendarmes at the bottom of the gangplank?"

"Strange."

"Mr. Bergere, let us talk about these Sealand container ships that Malcolm McLean is gambling with."

"Mr. Onassis, he is not gambling. The railroads, the trucking industry and practically all the major industries have applauded the concept. Here, look at these photographs, which speak for themselves." Bergere handed a neatly prepared album to the shipping magnate.

Onassis studied the pictures of the ships: the cargo containers on the flatbed truck trailers, the monstrous machinery lifting the containers off the semi-trailers onto the ships, then off the ships back onto the ships, then off the ships back onto the flatbeds. They were driven to railyards and loaded on flatbed freight cars, which hauled the cargo containers across country and finally unloaded them onto flatbed semis for door-to-door delivery. "This is very impressive. What do you want with me?" Onassis asked.

"Very simple. These container ships will revolutionize the transportation industry. My company, Oceania Shipping, would like a joint venture with your company in a pilot study to convert one of your ships and one of ours into container ships, or just one ship if you so desire, either yours or ours. We'll try it out in the industry."

"Why do I need your company?" Onassis queried.

"Because we have the American connections with the industry and the trucking companies. If we don't do it, McLean will have a monopoly. I firmly believe that there is plenty of business for all of us."

"Leave these pictures with me overnight. I want to discuss it with my people."

"Fine, sir. By the way, I would love to see the interior of that yacht."

"So would I. Join me for lunch on my boat at one o'clock tomorrow. Do you see it there with the helicopter on the back?"

"I'd be delighted, Mr. Onassis."

"Good. Maybe I can get the harbormaster to arrange a tour. See you tomorrow, Philippe...and call me Ari."

☆ ☆ ☆ ☆

Phillip walked across Avenue Albert and past the Flying Eagle. Two gendarmes were leaning against the gangplank. No one aboard the ship was in sight.

Jacques had planted bugs in seven of the staterooms and was in the master suite. The king-sized bed was solidly fastened to the floor. There was no leeway underneath the bed. The teakwood finish extended straight down to the floor on all sides. There was no room for a bug. However, as Jacques explored the area he noticed heavy blue and white designer drapes behind the bed, matching the bedspreads. He placed his hand through the side of the overhanging drapes and found a small opening. He carefully placed a bug on the right side of the wall behind the headboard of the bed. He quickly went to the left side, found a similar opening there, and carefully implanted another of the electronic devices. He opened the drawers of the dresser and discovered a photograph of a beautiful young woman in an ornate silver frame, inscribed, *With love to my dear uncle - Geli.*

He set the framed picture on the dresser, drew the curtains and photographed the lady, his flashes lighting the room. He quickly opened the curtains, placed the framed picture back in the drawer and left the room. He went into the large dining room and placed bugs under a huge mahogany table behind the service buffet.

In the salon, Claude was busily writing on a legal-sized pad.

Pierre was interrogating the two young women, whom he took to the front of the room away from their male companions. "You are both from Malmo, Sweden. What is your relationship to these gentlemen? You first, Ingrid Leifer."

"We were invited by Captain Sandstrom," the lady replied.

"And you, Berthe Swensen?"

"Ingrid tells the truth," Berthe whispered cautiously.

"Have you known these two men a long time?"

"No, we first met them in Corsica."

"How did you get to Corsica?"

"We left Malmo on a private plane for Barcelona. We know Leif a long time. This new boat was built in Sweden and Leif was the captain, and he took it to Barcelona for electrical fittings first and then to Ajaccio, Corsica, to pick up Herr Gunther and Sir Clive. Then the boat was being delivered to meet Mr. Nordheim," Ingrid explained.

Pierre didn't miss a beat with that exchange. "What do you ladies do in Malmo?"

"Why do you ask all these questions? We are respectable persons. Why are you doing this?" Berthe petulantly demanded.

"Just routine, so that we are able to assess the truth about this boat," Pierre said.

"If you must know, we are nurses at Malmo General Hospital. Very good nurses. Respectable nurses, you see," Berthe declared in a tone of righteous indignation.

"I'm sure you are, ladies. Please try to understand I'm trying to do my job, just like you do at the hospital. Do you understand?"

"Yes, I think I do," Ingrid said with resignation.

Pierre scribbled some notes, then looked at the two young women, whose resistance had faded, so he pressed on. "Ladies, did you meet Mr. Nordheim?"

"Yes, why do you ask?"

"Quite simple. The man who owns this magnificent vessel is Mr. Nordheim."

"I am not surprised," Berthe declared. "I could tell by the way Gunther and Clive behaved with him."

"How did they act toward him?"

"They were very respectful and they were bowing to him all the time. Well, like he was the boss. It was *Herr* Nordheim this, *Herr* Nordheim that. Oh, it was like some people say, excuse me, like kissing his ass, like they were afraid of him," Berthe nervously asserted.

"How did Nordheim treat you?"

"He was very kind and polite."

"Did you spend much time with him?"

"No, not more than an hour in the dining room on this boat. We had a little lunch, and Herr Nordheim excused himself and invited Gunther and Clive to join him in the salon. He looked at us and said, '*Auf wiedersehen,*' and we didn't see him any more," Berthe added.

"I would strongly advise you ladies not to discuss our conversation regarding Mr. Nordheim with Herr Froelich and Mr. Fenwick. If you see fit to ignore my advice, you may find yourselves involved in a serious legal matter. Understand?"

"We do not wish to be involved in any police matters," Ingrid replied. "We will do as you say."

"All right, to your seats."

Pierre sidled up to Claude and whispered in his ear. Claude nodded. "Froelich, customs officer Dernier has a few questions," he declared.

"Very well, let us finish this business soon, because we have other things to do."

"How much did this boat cost?"

"I don't know, and if I did I wouldn't tell you, because it's none of your business."

"Herr Froelich, it is my business to assess a customs tax."

"This is a tax-free principality, and the Monegasques do not pay taxes."

"Yes, that is true, with the exception of customs taxes."

Froelich flushed and angrily turned to Fenwick. "Clive, this cannot be."

"Monsieur Dernier, we must consult a barrister. Can we defer this matter until tomorrow afternoon?" Sir Clive asked.

Pierre and Claude huddled, then Jacques appeared. He joined the conferring pair. He calmly tapped the shoulders of Claude and Pierre, gesturing them to the corner of the spacious salon.

"I was just about to leave the master suite when I noticed a small lump in the carpet near the bathroom. I got on my knees and ran my hand over it. There was a square cut out, barely visible to the naked eye. I lifted it and saw that the lump was one of those indented latches which, when raised, helps lift a lid. Underneath was a hole below containing bars of gold. I couldn't tell how far the pile extends," Jacques hoarsely whispered.

"Did you put the carpet back the way it was?" Pierre queried.

"Yes, yes, you would never know I touched it. However, I did take a picture of the gold and the carpet area. I also took a picture of a lady in a silver frame."

"We should keep a twenty-four-hour surveillance on the boat to see if any attempt is made to remove the gold, and also to watch for Mr. Nordheim's possible arrival," Claude interposed. "I will order the necessary men to maintain a round-the-clock observation of this boat. Also, I will alert our coast guard to stop this vessel from any quick departure."

Gendarme Henri knocked on the door, and Claude snapped, "What is it?"

"There is a man here to hook up the telephone, sir."

Froelich jumped up. "Let him in, Lieutenant. We need to call our lawyer and other people."

"Very well, send him in."

Mike Paterno entered, carrying a large bag. He casually surveyed the room, chewing an unlit cigar, and flippantly observed, "Nice of all of you to greet me this way. Where are the phones?"

"I will show you," Froelich volunteered.

"No, you will stay put, sir. Monsieur Joffre, may I impose upon you to show this man to the telephones?" Claude said.

"No problem, Lieutenant. Please finish up here. We have other jobs to do," Jacques declared.

Nodding his head to Mike, he led him toward the stern.

In the master suite, Mike whispered, "I had to see you. We need someone to monitor the tap on these phones. Is there room in the harbormaster's building to set up my recording machines? If my reception is not good at the hotel, the tape recorders will be a good backstop."

"All right, go to work on the phones, there are bugs in every room. I'll go back to check with the harbormaster." Jacques returned to the salon.

"The man is working on the phones," he announced.

"*Wunderbar*," Froelich said.

"I'll be out on the deck if you need me, gentlemen," Jacques announced. "Monsieur Bernarde, would you care to join me?"

Bernarde followed Jacques to the aft deck, where Jacques explained Paterno's problem.

"We have a small room, with a desk and telephone next to my office. It has an entrance from the outside. That way it will not interfere with our daily routine. You are welcome to use it."

"Fine. Now I need Claude to assign someone to monitor the wiretap recording."

"Stay here and I'll get him to join you."

"Good. I'll tell you later about the gold bars hidden under the floor of the master bedroom."

"Gold?"

"Yes, yes, later."

Jacques lit a cigar and observed a helicopter flying toward the Monte Carlo harbor. Claude Colbert joined him.

"I see our favorite tourist is taking our picture," Claude joked, smiling and pointing to Captain Gaumont at the dock.

The helicopter seemed to be heading for the Flying Eagle. Then a head poked out of the rotor-driven craft, waving them off the deck. The gestures frantically backhanded them away from the huge deck.

"I think that son of a bitch wants to put that thing down on this deck," Bernarde shouted, to be heard over the panting motor and the whirring blades.

"Yes, there is mooring equipment at the other end of this deck," Jacques said, pointing.

The Bell helicopter looked brand new; it bore the Flying Eagle logo.

Jacques and Guy retreated to the portside deck, watching the craft settle on the far side of the aft deck. It touched down with a resounding thud, rocking the sleek vessel and causing sizable waves.

Claude, Pierre and some crew members came running out of the port entry door.

"*Mon Dieu*, what the hell is going on?" Claude roared.

"We were expecting that helicopter to be delivered today," Fenwick explained.

A crowd had gathered. Gaumont and other tourists were snapping pictures.

The pilot and co-pilot busily secured the craft and made their way along the portside deck.

"Is one of you men Mr. Froelich?" the pilot shouted.

"That is me," Gunther answered.

"Please sign this receipt for acceptance of this aircraft."

Gunther scribbled his name on the paper.

"How do we get a taxi here?" the pilot asked.

"Just walk over to the Hotel de Paris," Claude answered. "That officer will direct you."

Henri was standing at the base of the gangplank. Claude waved at him and gestured as the pilot was led to the boarding platform.

Jacques had returned to the salon and was busily photographing the twelve passports.

All returned to the large room.

"Is there anything you people have to declare before our final inspection today?" Pierre questioned the gathering.

A murmur of denial echoed in response.

"Very well, we will now check out all of the cabins, the dining room and kitchen, and the hold."

"Just one minute. Aren't you exceeding your authority?" Gunther asked vehemently.

"Sit down, Herr Froelich. Don't dictate to me what my authority is," Pierre angrily replied.

"Listen carefully, young man. Do you realize to whom you are talking? We have important connections and will not be bullied by little bureaucrats," Gunther said gutturally.

"I don't give a damn about your connections, you Nazi *chiant*," Pierre exploded.

"How dare you call me a Nazi? Your foul language will be reported to your superiors."

"Please, Gunther, do not exacerbate this situation," Fenwick appealed.

"There you go, Clive, in your typical British manner, appeasing these *pfennig* bureaucrats."

"Please, Gunther..."

Gunther cut him off. "I will talk to your superior, *Herr* customs officer!" he shouted.

"Well, he's right here," Pierre yelled back, pointing at Jacques. "*He* is my supervisor."

Jacques imperiously addressed the agitated German. "What is it you wish to say?"

"You heard your man call me a Nazi and use foul language to me. I wish to file a complaint against this gutter servant."

"Your complaint is filed. Now behave yourself, or we shall be forced to take you into custody for obstructing our officers in the performance of their duties. That is a very serious offense."

"This is getting out of hand, Gunther," Clive pleaded. "We have nothing to hide. Let them get on with it."

"*Schweinhund*," Gunther murmured. "Go, go, get it over with."

The heated exchange subsided. Claude and Paul began their inspection tour of the boat.

Mike Paterno returned to the salon. "Your telephones will be activated in about ten minutes, gentlemen," he advised.

"Thank you, sir," Clive said.

"Who is the man in charge of the docks?" Mike inquired.

"That's me, sir. I am the harbormaster and dockmaster. What do you need?" Bernarde asked.

"The main line to connect these phones is down at your office. Is someone there now?"

"Come with me," Guy said.

Captain Sandstrom, who had remained silent during the confrontation between the two forces, sat down next to Jacques. "I do not understand this whole situation, sir. I assure you that my crew and I have nothing to hide. We are merely employees," he said.

"You have nothing to fear, Captain, if you have declared everything," Jacques replied.

Claude and Pierre returned. "We are finished here for the present, so let's go," Claude said.

They exited, somewhat casually, as they scanned about, then convened at the harbormaster's office, where Gaumont joined them.

☆ ☆ ☆ ☆

Same day, March 22, 1952 - 2:45 p.m. - London

A wall-to-wall carpet of snow covered the street as Bart and Sir Alfred emerged from 10 Downing. Jennings opened the door of the Rolls Royce, and Captain Dempsey held an oversized umbrella over the two as they entered the sedan.

Traffic was snarled. The snowfall was steady. Lipton directed Jennings to MI6 headquarters. "By the way, have you had lunch?" Lipton asked Jennings.

"Oh, yes sir. Mrs. MacDougal invited me into the kitchen after Captain Dempsey called me to join him," Jennings replied, referring to Winston Churchill's devoted cook.

"Is her name Frances?"

"Yes, and a fine lady she is."

"How did you like the casserole?"

"It was excellent, sir. Frances was fussing because, as she said, *His highness doesn't eat enough vegetables.*"

Both men chuckled.

"He ate them today," Bart remarked.

Traffic thinned out a bit, so Jennings maneuvered out of a maze of stalled vehicles and began an accelerated approach to Great Britain's counterpart to the CIA, the MI6 intelligence headquarters.

Alighting from the car, Sir Alfred said to Jennings, "We'll be at least an hour, maybe more. Find a tea shop and stay warm."

"Thank you, sir."

A security officer holding an umbrella approached the two men. "I was going to say good day, gentlemen, but it's not really," he said smiling.

Sir Alfred produced his Parliament credentials and said, "General Forsythe is expecting us."

"Right through those two doors, gentlemen."

A burly man at the reception desk stood up and greeted them. "Sir Alfred Lipton and Colonel Barton Milburn, welcome, and follow me."

He led them down a long corridor and pointed at a private elevator.

"Just press button number three, sir, and when you exit you will be facing the door to the general's office. Go right in."

A pert, neatly dressed young woman with a stylish coiffure rose from the reception desk and greeted the visitors. "May I take your coats?" she said. "Follow me to the conference room, please, gentlemen."

General Lloyd Forsythe, six feet tall, with a neatly trimmed brush mustache, impeccably dressed in Savile Row's best, and soldierly in his stance, met the two men and in congenial tones said, "Gentlemen, welcome. We are looking forward to this meeting."

Four other impressive men were standing around a conference table.

"Sir Alfred Lipton and Colonel Barton Milburn, may I introduce my associates. This is Deputy Director Courtney Wallace, Harold Bancroft of European Affairs, Federico Lopez with South American Affairs, and Charles Moore, a specialist in tracking Nazi war criminals."

There was handshaking all around, then Bart and Sir Alfred were seated on either side of Forsythe, pads and pens in front of them.

"Before we start, Colonel Milburn, do you recall our meeting during the war?"

"Yes, of course. It was at Eisenhower's headquarters, the night before D-Day. At that time, as I recall, you were Colonel Forsythe, then assigned to the RAF's role in the invasion."

"Good show. Excellent memory, Colonel. And, of course, Sir Alfred and I go back a long time. I was in Rome when he was Ambassador to Italy. I was stationed there before Mussolini declared war against the Allies. I managed to get out the night before. Sir Alfred was not so lucky, but was eventually released through the intervention of the Swedes."

"Those were treacherous days, General," Lipton added.

"Indeed, they were. Before we start...coffee, tea, or something stronger?" Forsythe offered.

Bart and Sir Alfred opted for coffee. Charles Moore did the honors. The others helped themselves.

"Colonel, would you care to brief us first on this Nordheim fellow, and we'll follow?" the general asked.

Bart opened his black leather briefcase and withdrew stapled copies of the papers and two photographs he had presented to Churchill. "These pages are self-explanatory," he said, handing the sheets to the general.

"I'll have copies made for you gentlemen," Forsythe said as he pressed a button.

A young man appeared. "Sir?"

"Four copies quickly, of the papers and photos, Thomas."

"Right away, sir."

Bart outlined the upcoming Buenos Aires tour, the Monte Carlo yacht caper, and his projected meetings with Israeli Prime Minister Ben-Gurion and the Mossad in Tel Aviv.

Copies of Bart's papers were distributed to the four MI6 officers.

After a short question-and-answer period, General Forsythe commented, "At the Mossad, I assume you will be meeting with director Ariel Rubin, a very knowledgeable and professional man. We have a very high regard for him. He is not only an intellect, but sharp as a barber's razor and easy to work with if you don't try to con him. He has a healthy paranoia and is a stickler for the unvarnished truth. Don't let his easy manner deceive you."

"Glad to have that profile," Bart noted.

"Now, we'll kick off with you, Charles," Forsythe stated.

"Herr Nordheim fancies himself as a very wily fellow," Moore said. "For example, the Liechtenstein passport of Frederick Avram Nordheim is just one of two or more. There is a second passport issued by the Swiss in the name of Yeshua Immanuel Nordheim. And he..."

"The bloody cheek of that blighter," Sir Alfred angrily interrupted, "How dare he! That stupid clod is twitting the religious world."

"How so?" General Forsythe queried.

"Yeshua is the Hebrew name for Joshua, which the Greeks Hellenized into Jesus. Immanuel means *With us is God*. Why in the name of common sense would he do that?" Lipton said angrily.

"I would agree, sir, that his choice of names is scandalous," Moore observed.

"Sorry for interrupting," Lipton apologized.

"That passport surfaced in Vancouver, Canada, a year ago. It was issued on April 20, 1951, in Geneva."

"The gall of that bastard," Bart cut in. "April 20th was Hitler's birthday. Nordheim is cat-and-mousing us."

"Please continue, Charles," Forsythe ordered.

"There are neo-Nazi groups scattered around the world. Our immediate interest in their activities is mainly those groups operating in the United Kingdom. Based on a recent incident in Liverpool, we have ample reason to believe that Winston General has been financing some of these groups. A bunch of these yobbos, under the title of the Aryan Swords, held a parade on Church Street, which is in Liverpool's commercial area. They carried banners bearing the swastika with four swords pointing at each open space of the symbol. The Liverpudlians attacked these white supremacists and a riot ensued. Thirty neo-Nazis were arrested. Scotland Yard's special branch sent a team there after being notified that two of the prisoners had cracked and were ready to talk. The bottom line is this: They were being financed by a Zurich bank. Scotland Yard briefed the general, and I was dispatched to Liverpool. I questioned the two prisoners. Based on their statements, a search warrant was obtained and the headquarters of the Aryan Swords was raided a month ago. We found pictures of Hitler, Himmler, Goering and Goebbels, as well as the usual hate literature. Most interesting was the name of a Zurich bank, which is on the list supplied by Colonel Milburn. It is the Bank Royale in Zurich. This is the very same one in which Winston General has an account, as reported by Colonel Milburn."

General Forsythe held up his hand and said, "I have a list of names found in their safe. One of them that appeared frequently in their files provides the tie that binds. Thanks to you, Colonel, your list of officers at WG shows one Konrad Fliegel as treasurer. We were under the impression that Herr Fliegel was an officer of the Bank Royale. The copies of the correspondence seized were addressed to him, care of the bank. Very interesting. Is that right, Mr. Moore?"

"Quite so, sir," Charles replied softly, apparently discomfited by the general's disclosure.

"Let's get on with it, Charles," Forsythe said.

"With regard to your action in Buenos Aires, we have reports in our files going back to the early Forties and up to the present on the financial activities of German industrialists and Nazi leaders." Moore said. "They transferred substantial assets to Argentine banks as well as Switzerland. Goebbels, von Ribbentrop and quite a few high Nazis deposited funds in Banco Aleman Transatlantico, Banco Germanico, Banco Strupp and Banco Tornquist."

"What about Martin Bormann, Charles?" Forsythe demanded.

"Well, I was coming to that, sir."

"Very well, get on with it."

"Martin Bormann was sighted in Buenos Aires on 5 December 1944. Our agents in Argentina tracked him to the German Transatlantic Bank of Buenos Aires. He was followed from there to a mansion in Mar del Plata. That was the home of Ricardo von Leute, who later became president of the Geneva Bank. On that morning in December 1944, he was followed discreetly to Avenida de Mayo and the Casa Rosado, government house. He was chauffeured there in von Leute's Daimler. We do not know whom he visited there. He left the building an hour and a half later and was driven to the airport. The Daimler drove onto the runway alongside a four-engine Lockheed Constellation. The plane's engines were idling. There were no markings on the plane. He boarded the plane, which revved up immediately and took off. Our man tried to check its destination. The tower there had no record of such a plane. Word was sent to RAF Headquarters here in London to be on the alert for the constellation, apparently on its way to Europe. The RAF did not spot the plane, but our man in Lisbon reported its landing at the airport on 10 December. Bormann debarked there and was met by two big men in civilian clothes, who escorted him to a Mercedes limousine. The plane took off. Bormann and escorts drove to Estoril, a resort catering to spies, diplomats and military men of diverse loyalties. Bormann stayed at the home of one Lord Caldwell, a member of the Cliveden Set, a close friend of Lady Astor. They were ardent Nazi supporters. Our people in Portugal maintained constant surveillance of Bormann over a two-day period. A stream of visitors called upon him during that stay."

At that point, Moore halted his recital and asked to excuse himself in order to retrieve an additional file in his office.

"This is a good time for a recess, men. The loo is to the right of the door, Sir Alfred and Colonel."

When Bart returned from the men's lavatory he approached the General at the wet bar.

"How about a bit of sherry?" the General said.

Sir Alfred joined them in partaking of the drink.

"This Bormann fellow was - or is, as the case may be - very close to Hitler," Bart surmised.

"Oh, yes, he served as an aide, confidant and a buffer for Der Führer," General Forsythe replied. "He incurred the jealousy of the likes of Himmler and Goering and most of the upper echelons of the military. Bormann actually replaced Hess as number two man. He was power-hungry, and chipped away at Himmler and Goering while eschewing the limelight. He was, or is, to Hitler what a *consiglieri* is to a Mafia boss. Shortly after Hess's hapless flight to Scotland, he replaced Rudy as head of the party chancery. Goering was Bormann's number one enemy. Bormann eventually became indispensable to Adolf," the general added.

Moore returned with the new file, so they all returned to their seats and the briefings continued.

"Go ahead, Charles," the general prompted.

"This is most interesting. In late July of 1945, two German submarines plied their way toward the coast of Mar del Plata, a posh beach town south of Buenos Aires. The war ended on 8 May and almost three months later the two subs surrendered to the friendly Argentines. Bormann was there, as was one Rudolph Freude, the top Nazi agent in Buenos Aires. Bormann and Freude supervised the unloading of a large amount of ill-gotten loot consisting of art, jewelry, gold bullion, diamonds and other precious gems, plus millions of marks, dollars, pounds, Swiss francs, Dutch florins and French francs. The total value was estimated to be over 100 million pounds. All of it was transported in lorries to the Aleman Transatlantico, Germanico, Tornquist and Strupp banks.

"Over a period of two years, Bormann made six visits to Buenos Aires." Moore continued. "In early 1947 he stayed at a mansion on a 100-acre ranch in La Plata, where he entertained Eva and Juan Domingo Peron, who was president of Argentina at that time. We also learned that Bormann was accompanied by Wilhelm Zauder, his personal assistant, who was with him in Hitler's bunker on the night of 29 April, 1945. That was the night of the alleged suicide of Eva Braun and the Führer. Also at the La Plata ranch was his secretary, Fräulein Else Krueger, who left the bunker, underneath the Chancellery, with Bormann, Zander and others on 1 May."

"Just one question at this point, Mr. Moore," Milburn said.

"What is it, Colonel?" Charles said.

"Have you determined the ownership of the ranch in La Plata?"

"No, not as yet. We've been given the runaround as we tried to check the property tax records through an attorney we use in Buenos Aires."

"Look at the third page of that report I gave you. It shows Winston General as the owner of a 100-acre ranch in La Plata."

"Quite so, quite so," Moore noted as he shuffled Bart's papers. "Very well, I'll continue. Later, after Bormann left Argentina, one of our agents located a husband-and-wife team that acted as butler and cook at the ranch. A handsome gratuity to the couple and they became quite loquacious. There was a heated argument between the Perons and Herr Bormann. He yelled at Juan and Eva and overturned a coffee table, disgorging dishes and a coffee pot, staining a beige carpet. They spoke mostly in English, the butler said. He gleaned, bit by bit they were bickering about money. He heard the word 'millions.' The Perons seemed to be trying to pacify Bormann. Eva was heard to say that it would be taken care of. She mentioned a meeting in Monte Carlo."

"Fascinating," Sir Alfred exclaimed.

"It gets curiouser and curiouser," Forsythe interjected. "Mr. Bancroft, will you take it from here?"

"Indeed. There was a meeting at the Hotel de Paris, in Monte Carlo. Eva Peron arrived in August of 1947 and registered at the Monte Carlo Beach Hotel. She was there to receive a gold medal from the principality of Monaco. After the ceremony at the Palace, she joined Martin Bormann and Konrad Fliegel, treasurer of the Bank Royale, at the Hotel de Paris. Eva, escorted by a handsome Argentine colonel in full white uniform, joined Bormann and Fliegel in the Grill Room atop the Hotel de Paris. After one drink, Eva dismissed the young officer. Eva and the two men apparently had a very cordial dinner and seemed to have resolved any purported differences with Bormann. Fliegel obviously was acting in the role of mediator, according to our observer. Eva, Bormann and Fliegel went to Bormann's suite on the third floor. They were there for twenty minutes. Fliegel escorted her to the lobby, where the uniformed colonel was waiting. Fliegel handed her a large manila envelope as she stepped into her chauffeured limousine. Our agent surmised that some papers were signed in Bormann's suite and were contained in the envelope Fliegel gave to her. She took a train to Zurich.

"Our man in Zurich observed Eva's arrival," Bancroft went on. "She was met by Sir Clive Fenwick and Konrad Fliegel. We identified Fenwick from photographs sent by our agent. Up to now we hadn't been able to determine his role. They proceeded to the Bank Royale. Now, based on your report, Colonel, the shoe fits nicely. Sir Clive, our pre-war ambassador to Germany, was a known Nazi sympathizer. Your report places him in the orbit of Winston General, Exec VP. The hundred million, unloaded in Argentina, and undoubtedly the subject of the Peron-Bormann controversy, I assume, was being resolved at the bank. That's it for me, General."

"Thank you, Mr. Bancroft. Deputy Wallace, it's your turn."

"In trying to put a definitive label on Herr Nordheim, there are those of us who believe that Nordheim is just a front for Bormann. Now, that's a hypothesis, which is purely conjectural. To carry that theory further, we have empirical proof of his existence, whereas Nordheim is a mystery man. Based on the Bormann profile, we conclude that he is a devious man who sought power in a cloak of obscurity while traducing the reputations of Himmler, Goering and others that were threats to his position next to Hitler. Further to this posit, if Hitler is indeed demised, what better way to inherit the plunderage and continue the fight for a Fourth Reich by putting up a straw man? That is one side of the dichotomy here. The other side of the contrasting opinions is more simplistic. Hitler, or any one of a number of high Nazis at large, could be lodged in the persona of Herr Nordheim. Yet, if it is not a plasticized Hitler, but say a von Papen, Schacht, or Fritzsche or anyone else, Bormann could be the key man. If in time we are jointly able to unmask Nordheim and he is truly the phoenix Führer, we must capture this... this devil. A loose Hitler is a danger to the world," Wallace concluded.

General Forsythe thanked his staff and asked, "Colonel, any comments?"

"The reports and analysis here have covered the subject very well to date. Our joint efforts, including the Israelis, should be intensified. With the resources in the hands of Nordheim and Bormann, the task confronting us is formidable. I am indeed grateful for your unstinting cooperation."

"Colonel, accept our gratitude as well. We must press forward."

"Lloyd, this was a very fine show of cooperation," Sir Alfred said. "I believe that pressure will be brought against the Swiss banks from our government. I will bring the question up at our next session of Parliament."

"Excellent, Sir Alfred. I have no doubt that the Prime Minister will hammer it through the wicket. Our boys here will be digging for anything that will expose those banks thriving on the ill-gotten gains from the millions robbed and slaughtered by those amoral Nazi bastards."

"General, here is a list of numbers at which I can be reached," Bart said, handing him an index card.

"You have my number here," General Forsythe responded. "Courtney Wallace or Miss Grace Ardmore, whom you met coming in, will track me down at all times. I'd love to hear from you after your visit to Israel."

"Will do," Bart said in parting.

The street lamps winked at the steady current of snowflakes. The wintry scene added luster to the well-lighted streets of London in the twilight hour. The Rolls Royce traveled slowly over the cushioned road. Sir Alfred and Bart sat back in contemplation as Jennings maneuvered through the snow, homeward bound.

CHAPTER SEVEN

Saturday, March 22, 1952 - 6:50 p.m. - Washington, D.C.

Connecticut Avenue Northwest was split into two lanes by Capitol police directing unusually heavy traffic. Four officers had placed wooden barriers separating the outside lane from the one closest to the Mayflower Hotel. A gentle wind flapped the pre-Franco monarchical flag of Spain over the façade of the famous hostelry.

The powerful, the rich and famous were alighting on a thick red carpet. Men in their tuxedos and their ladies in beautiful new gowns, bejeweled and smartly coiffured, paused long enough for the flashing cameras of the press.

White-gloved attendants directed the arriving guests to the Grand Ballroom. Janis Fulton, the State Department protocol officer, and a male assistant examined the gilt-edged invitations. They directed the invitees to the receiving line. Countess de Cordoba, a strikingly beautiful woman, gowned in a Maison Jeannette creation - long black tight-fitting silk gown, pearl necklace and diamond tiara - greeted the guests with a cultured English accent. The Spanish-speaking envoys welcomed in Castilian Spanish. Her husband, Anthony Fuentes, tall and handsome in his tuxedo, acknowledged the guests in a measured American accent and spoke to the South Americans in Castilian Spanish.

Argentine Ambassador Sanchez held up the line conversing with the countess. He was exceedingly charming and obsequious to the lady. He kissed her hand and suggested they chat later. He would like to point out places of interest in Buenos Aires and ventured a suggestion that she meet the Perons while there.

She rewarded him with a flirtatious smile. He moved on and commented to Tony, "Your wife is a very beautiful woman. You are a lucky man."

"Thank you, Mr. Ambassador," Tony admitted. "I believe you will be seated at our table."

"I am honored," the envoy gushed, then bowed.

The orchestra softly played "Lady of Spain" as the guests were led to their respective tables. Nine round tables were placed in a semicircle, with the hosts' table in the center.

Three society reporters were allowed to sneak in. A table was provided for them in back of the bifurcated Grand Ballroom, which had been made more intimate by heavy velvet draperies drawn across the large room. A small dance floor was established behind the semicircle of tables. The waiters and busboys were attired in old English service garb - silk stockings, knee pants, buckled shoes, white wigs and white gloves. Under the ceiling, bunting in the colors of monarchical Spain encircled the room. Each of the tables accommodated eight people for the seventy-two guests and the hosts.

Seated at the Countess' table were Vice President Alben Barkley and his wife, Ambassador Diego Sanchez and a Señorita Anita Vasquez, along with Senator William Fulbright and his wife. Sanchez sat at the right of Sophia Carrera. Barkley sat on her left. Tony sat between Anita Vasquez and Mrs. Barkley.

The room was bathed in a soft glow reflecting off the burgundy-colored tablecloths. The orchestra played George Gershwin, Irving Berlin, Cole Porter, and Hoagy Carmichael tunes and assorted waltzes. A buzz of conversation underscored the music.

The guests stared intermittently at the Countess. Words of praise for her beauty were exchanged. Questions were whispered. *Why haven't we heard about her before?* A few planted answers by Senator Warren Magnuson explained that she had spent the post-war years in Europe doing charity work, sans the use of her title.

Ambassador Sanchez appealed to the countess for the first dance. She smiled, rose and placed her hand, bearing a diamond-crowned ring, on his arm as he led her to the dance floor. A scattering of applause accompanied the Strauss waltz. The couple were accomplished dancers. The applause reached a crescendo as the ambassador whirled the countess around the floor. A few flashbulbs blinked in the dimly lighted room.

Sanchez whispered in her ear, "We must see each other again soon."

"Are you flirting with me, my dear Diego?"

"*Si, si.*"

"You're a naughty boy. I'm sure we'll be seeing you when we return from South America."

"I will call President Peron to make your visit a pleasant one."

"That will be very exciting, Diego. I would like to meet Eva Peron."

"That will be arranged, my dear countess."

The orchestra stopped playing, taking a break. A couple of guitarists replaced them with variations of flamenco music. When the orchestra returned, Sanchez tapped his glass with his spoon.

He stood up, raised his wine-filled glass and in a semi-shout declared, "May I propose a toast to our beautiful, charming hostess, the Countess de Cordoba, and her husband, Mr. Anthony Fuentes."

The guests rose, raised their glasses and cheered. The orchestra played "Lady of Spain" and segued into "For He's a Jolly Good Fellow."

The countess arose, raised both hands for silence, and in a polished English accent addressed her guests. "Please accept our deepest appreciation for your attendance here tonight. I am a very private person. I have led a quiet life. This is my first public appearance. I am grateful for your courtesies."

An enthusiastic round of applause followed. The orchestra, on Tony's signal, played "Good Night Ladies," and phase one of the Argentine caper ended.

☆ ☆ ☆ ☆

March 22, 1952 - 9:30 p.m. - Monte Carlo

A Lockheed Constellation set down at the Nice Airport at 9:30 p.m., then a Daimler limousine drove onto the tarmac. Frederick Nordheim and his point man, Darren Mayfield, debarked the plane and entered the limo.

"To La Condamine in Monte Carlo," Mayfield directed the chauffeur.

Twenty minutes later they pulled up to the brightly lit Flying Eagle. Sandstrom, dressed in his white captain's uniform, and Froelich and Fenwick, wearing tuxedos, greeted the arrivals at the foot of the gangplank. Two crew members in sailor's uniforms removed baggage from the Daimler.

Two gendarmes, twenty feet away, watched the greeting party. They couldn't agree later on whether Froelich had raised his hand in a Nazi salute.

Observing the activity were three pairs of binoculars focused on the yacht.

Jacques stared at Nordheim from his room at the Balmoral Hotel. Phillip and Mike were doing the same from their respective rooms at the Hotel de Paris. They saw Nordheim in his taupe-colored slacks, Western-heeled boots and Stetson hat shaking hands with Gunther, Clive and Captain Sandstrom. The boat's outside lights were dimmed.

Jacques attempted long-shot photos of the scene. He then raced to the elevators and out the front door to the area of the Flying Eagle.

The two crew members each carried two large leather bags up the gangplank. Nordheim led the entourage on a dockside inspection of the luxurious yacht. They paused at the aft side of the boat. Nordheim was gesturing to the helicopter. He clapped his hands, stamped his foot and applauded in apparent appreciation of his latest toy.

Jacques arrived at the gathering in time to view the inspection tour. He deliberately focused his camera with built-in flash equipment and clicked off half-a-dozen shots before Nordheim turned in his direction.

"*Nein, nein*, pictures, no, no," Nordheim bellowed, pushing Mayfield toward the flashing camera.

"Hey, you with the camera, stop that! You can't take pictures here," the ex-FBI agent shouted as he rushed toward the flashes.

Jacques stood his ground, shooting pictures of Nordheim and the oncoming Mayfield.

"Give me that fucking camera!" Mayfield roared, lunging to dislodge the instrument out of Jacques' hands. Laurent sidestepped and clicked off a shot of Mayfield tripping to the ground.

"You mother-fucking son of a bitch, I'll kill you for that!" Mayfield growled as he pointed a Smith & Wesson .38 at Jacques.

In a split-second maneuver, Jacques whirled and kicked the gun out of the assailant's hand. He dived for the gun, retrieved it and pointed it at Mayfield's nose.

"Listen, I'll pay you five thousand francs for your camera and the film. Let's forget our little misunderstanding," the thoroughly discomfited former FBI agent pleaded.

"What is so important about my pictures?" Jacques demanded, assuming a deepened French accent.

"We are married men here on a holiday and we don't want pictures of us in the newspapers for our wives to see," he lamely lied. "How about it? You're a man of the world. You newspaper people should understand our predicament."

Jacques shifted gears and decided to play along with the charade.

"Monsieur, first of all, you should never draw a gun on a journalist. If you are prepared to protect the sanctity of your marriage for five thousand francs, then it must be worth much more."

Mayfield chuckled, "Stop pointing that gun. So, it's a matter of price? Okay, my frog friend, how much will it take?"

"Frog? Do all Americans call Frenchman frogs? A Yankee trader like you should have better manners than that. If you want to bargain, first you don't draw a gun. Then, when you are at a disadvantage, don't call me a frog."

"I'm sorry about that. I'm a little upset. I apologize. Now, how much?"

Jacques lowered the gun to his side and simulated deep thought, scratching his head with the gun barrel.

After a short pause, Jacques waved the gun at Mayfield, saying, "I will not turn in my pictures to my editor right away. Let me think about a price overnight and I will meet you at the Monte Carlo Beach Hotel on Roquebrune Cap Martin at, say, 11 o'clock, Monsieur."

"Why, you extortionist son of a bitch!" Mayfield roared, charging at Jacques in an attempt to wrest the weapon from him.

Jacques pulled his right arm back and feinted with his left, evading the attack. Mayfield threw a punch, grazing Jacques' chin. Reacting, Jacques slammed the pistol across Mayfield's jaw, inflicting a deep gash along the right side of his face from the ear lobe to his chin, decking him. He was semiconscious and bleeding profusely.

Nordheim's voice shattered the stillness of the night. "Shtop that man!"

Jacques pocketed the revolver, departed the scene expeditiously, running toward a darkened area, and disappeared from sight.

Captain Sandstrom, two crew members and a gendarme ran to the prone man. The young policeman pointed a flashlight at the stricken figure. Sandstrom applied a handkerchief to Mayfield's cheek in an effort to stanch the flow of blood.

"We must get this man to a hospital," Sandstrom declared.

"I will summon an ambulance on my car radio," the gendarme offered.

"No, no," Mayfield uttered weakly.

"That is a nasty cut, Mr. Mayfield. It will require stitches," the captain said.

"Take me to the boat and find a doctor to sew me up," Mayfield implored.

As they slowly made their way back to the yacht, Mayfield held the handkerchief to his cheek and inquired, "Who was that hoodlum? Did you see him?"

Two members of the crew, along with Sandstrom and the policeman, agreed it had been too dark. All they could see was the outline of the two men and the short struggle that took place.

Jacques ran along Boulevard Albert to Rue Grimaldi and back on Avenue du Port to Quai Antoine to the rear of the harbormaster's building. There were lights in the office of Guy Bernarde.

A gentle knock on the door brought a sharp reply from the harbormaster, "Who the hell is that?"

"It is me, Jacques."

The bolt lock rasped loudly and a key followed. "Come in, Jacques. Why are you panting like that?"

"I've been running, and as soon as I catch my breath I'll explain."

"Come to the back where our captain of detectives is listening in to the Flying Eagle."

"Oh, good, I am glad he is here. I have to talk with him."

They entered the room behind Bernarde's office. The window shade was down, blocking out the street. A pair of earphones, supported by a wire brace on his head, was clamped to Felix Gaumont's ears. He waved to Jacques, holding his hand up for silence as he listened intently. Jacques plopped into an armchair alongside Felix, and his heavy breathing was beginning to abate.

Apparently Gaumont was nodding in tempo with the sounds he was hearing. He pursed his lips in satisfaction.

Bernarde and Jacques stared at him quizzically. The phone in Bernarde's office rang loudly. Gaumont nodded knowingly.

Guy answered the telephone. "Allo."

"This is Captain Sandstrom. We need a doctor right away."

"Somebody sick?"

"No, one of our guests has a bad cut on his face. He requires stitching."

"What is your number there?" Bernarde asked, already aware of the number. "53-12-25."

"I'll call you back as soon as I locate a doctor."

Bernarde called Marcel Levien at his pied-à-terre. "Doctor, a man on board the Flying Eagle has a bad cut on his cheek and requires stitching. Can you handle it?"

"Guy, I don't know if it would be proper for me to do it. Try the house doctor, Alexis Montaigne, at the Hotel de Paris. If he can't come, I'll do it."

"Good idea. I'll call you back either way." He dialed the hotel and was connected to Dr. Montaigne. Bernarde explained, and the doctor agreed to handle the case. Guy called Dr. Levien, who was relieved.

Bernarde then dialed the yacht and advised Leif Sandstrom that a Dr. Montaigne was on his way. He rejoined Gaumont and Laurent in the eavesdropping room.

Felix dropped the earphones to a hanging position around his neck.

"I've picked up the voices of Nordheim, Froelich and Fenwick, apparently in his suite. Some of it is in English and some in German. They were talking about a fellow named Mayfield who was cut up in a fight with a ruffian. The captain of the boat was tending to him and is sending for a doctor to sew him up. I recognized the German of Froelich and the English accent of Fenwick."

"I just got the call for a doctor from Sandstrom and arranged for Dr. Montaigne to go there," Bernarde confirmed.

"The ruffian they referred to is me," Jacques blurted.

A look of amazement was obvious in the expressions of the two men.

"What happened?" Gaumont questioned.

Jacques explained, handing the gun to Felix.

"Did anyone recognize you?" Bernarde queried.

"I don't know."

"They didn't," Gaumont asserted. "Their conversation indicates that no one was able to see the man in the dark."

"Well, I got myself in a bind," Jacques sighed. "I can't let Mayfield see me now. I'll have to stay out of sight until they leave. I just couldn't avoid this. That son of a bitch attacked me. Damn it."

"Easy, Jacques. You did what you had to do," Gaumont declared. "And by the way, you may not have to hide for long. Nordheim was talking about moving the yacht north to Menton."

"Why Menton?" Jacques snapped. "There is nothing there. It's on the border of Italy."

"You're right," Gaumont said, pounding the table and rattling the recording equipment.

"I'll bet you that insidious bastard is shooting for San Remo, which is just a few miles from here. Now he wants to get away from us. After he was briefed on our actions today, he wants to get out of French jurisdiction. They are going to Italy," Jacques heatedly postulated.

"Especially with all those gold bars, he wants to get as far away from us as he can," Gaumont agreed. "Let me listen some more."

An hour later, Gaumont asked Jacques to relieve him and passed the earphones.

Jacques began a running commentary. "They are in the dining room. Mayfield says he's okay. The doctor gave him a tetanus shot and a pill to ease the trauma. The wound required twenty stitches. Nordheim wants to know if the newspaperman will print the pictures. Mayfield doesn't think so, because, he says, the man doesn't want to be identified, for fear of arrest. That is good, Nordheim says. Nordheim now is telling the captain to go to bed. I can tell that they are eating. I can hear the plates and the knives and forks."

"You would be good on the radio, Jacques," Gaumont exclaimed.

Jacques shook his head and continued his report. "Nordheim is pounding the table and yelling, '*Dummkopf*, Gunther, how many times must I tell you not to lose your head. You have made enemies of the customs people and the French liaison police. Clive is right. Pay the two marks and avoid controversy. Did I say that right, Clive?' "

"Yes, sir."

"My English is improving, not so?"

"Very good, sir."

"I was only trying to protect our interests," Froelich whined.

"I know, but, how do you say, Sir Clive, be cold, ah."

"Cool, sir, be cool."

"*Ach*, that's what I said."

"I was concerned about Bormann's gold," Froelich said.

Nordheim shouted, "Whose gold? It's my gold. Mine, mine, du idiot!"

Jacques handed the earphones to Gaumont. "Listen, he's talking about *Bormann's* gold. He yelled so loud, he almost blasted me deaf."

Felix listened intently and began reciting. "Nordheim said he was going to unload the gold here, where it is tax-free, for safekeeping at a Monte Carlo bank for sale to the Bank Royale. That's why the boat went to Barcelona, to pick up the gold...He just told Darren to get some sleep. Clive and Gunther too. He's having those two young ladies sent to his room."

Gaumont lowered the earphones around his neck."I wonder if that Nazi skunk is getting horny," he conjectured.

"Nothing would surprise me," Jacques commented. "I need to make a call to London."

"Go right ahead," Bernarde said.

"No, not from here. I need a public phone booth. Is there one near here, or do I have to drive to Nice?"

"If you want a safe phone, go to the casino."

"Good idea. I'll be back soon to relieve you."

"Take your time. Guy will help me. This is tedious work."

Jacques hurried to the world-famous casino. Tourists and the rich and famous were absorbed in games of chance. He entered a phone booth and placed a call to Barton Milburn.

"Lipton residence," Jennings answered.

"Barton Milburn, please, Lucy calling."

"One moment, sir."

"Yes?"

"Jacques."

"What's your number?"

"52-49-49."

"Is that a phone booth?"

"Yes."

"Hang up."

One minute later the phone rang. "Allo."

"What's up, Jacques?"

Jacques reeled off a full report on his activities since arriving in France. He detailed his alliance in Paris with Captain of Detectives Felix Gaumont and the link-up with his wartime compatriots, Lieutenant Claude Colbert and customs inspector Pierre Dernier. He recapped the events on board the yacht, the altercation with Mayfield, the wiretap conversations and the discovery of the gold bars. He capped the summary with the silver-framed photos of the beautiful woman inscribed with love to her uncle and signed *Geli.*

"Colonel, I am sorry I fouled up my mission by getting into a fight with that FBI bum Mayfield, so what do you want me to do?"

"Jacques, you did a marvelous job. The encounter is best described as *C'est la guerre.*"

"*Oui, oui,* it could not be helped."

"Now listen to me, brother. First, that yacht must be boarded on its way up the coast before it gets into Italian waters. It is much too late to bring Italy into this affair. If the yacht starts to move, see what your buddies can do with the French authorities. I will call our people in Washington to try to get French cooperation."

"Do we have enough time?"

"It's midnight, London time. That would make it 6 p.m. in Washington. I'll call there when we finish talking. Jacques, we must get that gold before they sell it to the Swiss. Call me back from another phone in half an hour."

Jacques hastened back to the harbormaster's office.

Gaumont was listening to the wiretapped phones on the Flying Eagle. Guy Bernarde was scribbling notes of the conversations relayed by Felix.

"Hold it one minute," an excited Gaumont cautioned Jacques. "Something weird is going on in Nordheim's cabin. The girls are screaming. I hear sounds like a whip striking flesh."

Bernarde and Laurent were spellbound by the revelation.

"One girl called him an animal. *Mon Dieu,* he is beating her. The other girl is screaming, *You are going to kill her! Stop it!* Nordheim is *yelling, Harlots, get out, get out!*" Gaumont reported, sitting back in his chair.

"Nordheim must be a sadistic bastard," Bernarde swore, spitting in a wastebasket. "That Nazi prick should be shot."

Gaumont adjusted the earphones. "There is a lot of talking. It is Froelich and the captain. They are asking Nordheim what happened. The captain is very agitated and is demanding an explanation in English. Froelich and Nordheim are jabbering away in German. The captain is yelling, *Why did you whip those girls? One of them is badly injured!* Nordheim is yelling, *Get out of here, Captain, and mind your own business! Go to sleep!* Clive is in there now. Nordheim is telling him, *Clive, go see the girls. Give them a lot of money and tell them it was a misunderstanding. Captain, get out, out, that's an or-der!* Nordheim shouts. Clive says, *Captain, come with me."*

"Let me have the earphones, Felix," Bergere asked.

Gaumont passed the unit, sighing, "I don't believe what I heard. That Nordheim is one mad dog. I'd like to strangle the son of a bitch."

Guy held up his hand for attention. "Mayfield is in the room. Nordheim is talking to him in English. *Darren, see that Clive takes care of those whores. Calm them down. Then tell the captain to relax, give him a good amount of money. Also, call Nice to send the car here. We will drive to San Remo, Italy, at dawn. It's a short ride on the Corniche. Tell the captain to take the yacht to San Remo. You, Froelich, Fenwick and I will meet him there."*

"I'll be back in a little while," Jacques blurted as he rushed for the door.

He raced over Boulevard Albert to Avenue d'Ostende to the Place du Casino and opted this time for the Hotel de Paris. He casually entered the lobby and headed for the phone booths, where he called Barton Milburn.

"Give me your number and hang up," Bart answered. "I'll call you right back."

One minute later the phone rang.

"Colonel, the yacht is leaving for San Remo, Italy, in five hours, according to Nordheim's instructions to Mayfield on the wiretap. He and Froelich, Fenwick and Mayfield are going there by car to meet the boat."

"Jacques, I spoke to the brass in Washington. They are going to try to arrange with Interpol and the French authorities to seize the yacht. To make the seizure legal, they may have to plant some illegal drugs aboard the boat. I have to make a quick call back to D.C. with the information you just gave me. Is there another phone booth where you are?"

"Yes."

"All right, give me the number in that booth and stand by. I'll call back."

"Hold on."

"Hurry."

"The number is 50-39-87." Jacques lit a cigarette and waited. He scanned the lobby watching the bejeweled ladies and their escorts coming and going.

The phone rang. *"Allo."*

"Jacques, the French and Interpol will try to intercept the boat."

"Good."

"Call me later."

Bernarde was reciting the events and dialogue on the wiretaps, while Gaumont continued making notes. Jacques eased his way in, closing the unlocked door and fastening the bolt behind him.

"Berthe is the girl that was badly beaten," Bernarde related. "Ingrid tells her she will be all right. Berthe cries that the peroxide burns. *All right*, says Ingrid, *I'll put these wet clothes on you for a little while and then I'll put Vaseline over your back and it will soothe you. Don't cry.* Berthe asks, *Where is my clothing?* Ingrid tells her that her clothes are in Nordheim's room. She says, *My dress is in there, too. He tore your dress off and mine, too. I can't believe what that animal wanted us to do to him."*

"That rotten son of a bitch," Jacques snarled angrily.

Bernarde passed the earphones to Gaumont. He offered a cigar to Jacques, who chose a cigarette.

Gaumont began his recital. "The captain and Sir Clive were in the room. Fenwick asked, *How are you, Berthe? Not good,* she said. *And you, Ingrid?* Sandstrom asked. Ingrid remained silent. Fenwick said, *Whatever happened in there was due to his drinking in combination with medicine he is taking for his heart. He is very sorry and wants me to give each of you five thousand francs.* Ingrid broke her silence and screamed, *Do you think we are prostitutes? That degenerate madman called us whores!*"

"Good for her," Bernarde exclaimed, interrupting Gaumont's recital.

Gaumont held his hand up for silence and continued. "Ingrid is yelling, *He wanted us to do bad things. He is a sick son of a bitch!*" Fenwick is saying, *Calm down, please. The money is for your injuries. Please don't carry this out of proportion, for your own sake.*"

"That's a threat," Jacques interjected.

Felix continued his report. "Sandstrom raised his voice and angrily demanded, *What does that mean, Sir Clive? You people will not harm these ladies!*"

"*Of course not, Captain.*"

"*Then why do you say to the 'for your sake?'*

Just a figure of speech. He is a powerful man. I don't for a minute believe he will do them any physical harm. But if these girls intend to report this unfortunate affair, he could make trouble for them in Malmo. And Captain Sandstrom, that advice goes for you too. Come with me for a moment. Let's go into the next cabin. I have something to say to you privately."

Gaumont paused and handed the listening device to Jacques, who picked up the recital. A door closed and Clive whispered, "*Captain, you have a very well-paid job on this yacht. I am going to give you 25,000 francs to forget this affair. We are going to San Remo at dawn. When we arrive there, the girls are to leave the boat and fly home.*"

"*You are bribing me.*"

"*No, no, just asking you to be practical. Nordheim knows you a long time since his days in Malmo, isn't that so?*"

"*Yes.*" Sandstrom replied.

"*Well, you realize how powerful he is. I don't want him to destroy you. So keep your mouth shut. Get rid of the girls and keep your well-paid job. Understand?*"

"What a slimy bunch," Gaumont snapped. "I could strangle all of them."

Jacques reported, "The captain says he will do his best. He says the girls should be given 50,000 francs each and he would be satisfied with 100,000 francs. Sir Clive says, *Well, maybe you are right. It's only pennies to Nordheim. Okay, Captain, be prepared to leave here at dawn. Mr. Nordheim, Froelich and I will be driving to San Remo.* The captain says, *I have a suggestion. Don't send the ladies home until they have recovered. They would have to explain their bruises in Malmo. Let them stay at a hotel for a week or two.* Sir Clive tells him, *That is sensible. There is a fine old hotel there. It is the Royal Hotel*

San Remo. Have them take a suite and we will pay all expenses."

"That Englishman is very smooth. A real slimy diplomat," Gaumont said.

Bernarde took the hearing piece from Jacques, then recounted, "Sir Clive says, *I'll be right back, Captain. Talk with the girls and try to settle this matter quietly.* The captain says he'll try. Now he is in Nordheim's room. He is explaining his arrangement with Sandstrom and his proposal to the girls. Froelich is yelling at Clive, *That's too much money! That's extortion. You're stupid, Clive, to enter into a deal like that.* Nordheim yells at Gunther, *Schweig, this is better. This proves they are whores and we know we can buy Sandstrom. Good deal, Clive. Gunther, you are a hothead. Go tell them that I approve. Take their dresses with you over there on the couch. Oh, Clive, come here. Better to send the girls now by taxi to San Remo. It is only twenty-five miles from here. Don't look at me like that. Do it. And pay them now. And pay Sandstrom. Bring me that black attaché case. Here, take out 225,000 francs. One hundred for the captain, fifty for each whore and twenty-five more for their hotel expenses. Now, schnell, get rid of them!*"

"Guy, have you got your passport with you?" Jacques suddenly inquired.

"Yes, but why?"

"How would you like to join me in a trip to San Remo?"

"Again, why?"

"How would you like to take a statement from Berthe and Ingrid?"

"Marvelous idea. We need a tape recorder."

"I have an idea. I'm going to break a rule. What is the number at the Hotel de Paris?"

"I'll get it for you," Guy dialed and handed the phone to Jacques.

"Monsieur Paterno," he requested.

"Hello."

"Sir, your Aunt Lucy here."

"Yes."

"How is your concert coming in?" Jacques asked.

"Spotty."

"Well, your Aunt Lucy has a clear copy."

"Great."

"Do you have a pocket tape recorder?"

"Yes."

"Can you spare it?"

"Yes," Paterno answered.

"Bring it right away to the dockmaster's office on Boulevard Albert near the corner of Quai Antoine. I will brief you."

"Okay, see you soon."

Gaumont and Bernarde stared at Jacques questioningly.

"My friends, Mike Paterno is the man who set up this phone tap. He is a trusted associate. Why are you looking at me like that?"

"Jacques, it's just my amazement at how well you are set up here," Felix replied.

"Now, Guy, if you need someone to help you on these phones, Mike can stay with you while Felix and I are in San Remo."

"Won't be necessary, because once the yacht takes off, the phone lines will be cut off," Guy said. "I can always get Claude and Pierre to join me."

Fifteen minutes later, Mike Paterno knocked on the harbormaster's door. Jacques asked, "Who is it?"

"Mike."

He opened the door and walked outside, taking Paterno by the arm to the back of the building in the darkened area.

"Have you heard everything that was said on the boat?" Jacques asked.

"The transmission was full of static. I only picked up bits and pieces."

Jacques gave him a concise rundown, plus his altercation with Mayfield.

"Quite an evening. In fact, quite a day. Now what?"

"That is why I asked you to bring the tape recorder over here. I wanted to fill you in; otherwise, I would have come to you to pick it up. Our plans will change accordingly."

"What do you suggest?"

"You and Phillip, as a result of this turn of events, are finished here. Captain Gaumont and I are going to San Remo as soon as those girls leave to go there. We'll follow their taxi. You will have to get instructions from Colonel Milburn."

"How do we reach him now?" Paterno asked.

"Here's his number in London. When the butler answers, just say, *Lucy is calling*. Have Phillip join you at the public phones in your lobby. Tell the colonel I am going to San Remo to get a taped statement from the girls."

Mike handed the recorder to Jacques and raced back to the hotel.

Bernarde was reciting when Jacques came in. "The girls have accepted the money. They called for a taxi, which will pick them up in an hour. The captain is telling Fenwick that the girls will cooperate. *How about you, Captain?* Fenwick asks. *Tell Herr Nordheim the matter is settled satisfactory. That's smart, Sandstrom.*"

"I'm going to check out of the Balmoral," Jacques declared. "Felix, keep an eye on the boat while I'm gone. I'll come right back with my car."

"Okay," Gaumont replied.

At the Hotel de Paris, Phillip joined Mike at the phone booths.

"The Lipton residence," Jennings intoned.

"Colonel Milburn...Lucy here."

"He might be sleeping."

"Urgent."

"Very well, one moment."

"Jacques?" Bart asked.

"No, Mike. I've got Phillip Berger with me."

"What's the number in the next booth?" Milburn requested.

A short pause, and the number was supplied.

"Hang up."

The next booth's phone rang. "Mike here."

"What's up?"

Mike relayed the scenario described by Jacques. "Obviously our work here is finished, so what are your instructions?"

"Let me talk to Phillip."

"Yes, Bart?"

"I want you and Mike to observe the yacht as it goes north to San Remo. It's only twnety-five land miles from Monte Carlo to San Remo. I don't believe you can charter that tourist helicopter at this hour. You've got binoculars. Do you have a car?"

"No, dammit, we both came by cab."

"Never mind, hire a taxi and drive along the Corniche. You'll have a view of the sea. If they ply their way up north close to the coast, you should be able to spot them. I expect a team from Interpol or the French Surété or the French coast guard to board and seize the yacht. It's a long shot that you will observe the action. That is, if it is successfully captured. Report back to me in the late morning."

"Will do."

"Good night," Bart said, and hung up, hoping it would be a good night.

.

CHAPTER EIGHT

Sunday, March 23, 1952 - 3 a.m. - Monte Carlo

A taxi drove up to the gangplank of the Flying Eagle, and Ingrid and Berthe were escorted to the cab. Sandstrom and a crew member carried the ladies' luggage, which they placed in the trunk of the vehicle. The captain kissed each of the women on the cheek and waved them off.

Jacques and Felix were in a taxi between the Avenue du Port and the Quai Antoine. The headlights were dimmed. At a discreet distance, they followed the ladies' cab as it pulled away from the yacht heading for the Boulevard du Larvotto, connecting with the Corniche to San Remo. Traffic was light.

Forty minutes later, the first cab halted at the Italian border. A customs officer sleepily approached the taxi carrying Ingrid and Berthe. "Tourists?" he asked.

"Yes," Ingrid replied, waving her passport.

The officer ignored the passport and pointed to the foreign-money-exchange booth, then waved them on. Minutes later, Gaumont and Laurent went through the same cursory examination.

The first cab drove on the Corso Imperatrice 80, five hundred meters past the railroad station to the Royal Hotel San Remo. The ladies were greeted by the night doorman, then a bellman took their bags to the reception desk.

The second taxi pulled in right behind them, and Jacques stepped out of the taxi while Gaumont was paying the driver.

Hastening into the empty lobby, Jacques was recognized by Ingrid, and she looked frightened. He held two fingers to his lips as he approached her.

"Do not be alarmed. We are here to help you and protect you," he cautioned. Gaumont joined them.

"Help and protect us from what?" Ingrid demanded.

"From Nordheim."

She stiffened in fright. Berthe was looking on and holding a handkerchief over her bruised lips.

A receptionist approached the four of them. "Is there a problem?" he asked in Italian, French and again in English.

Gaumont took charge. "We are here as security for these two very important ladies." He flashed his captain of detectives credentials.

"Oh, yes, Captain. Would the ladies care to register?"

"Come, Ingrid, you *do* want a suite," Felix interjected, then smiled as he took her arm and gently steered her to the reception desk.

She produced two passports and placed them on the desk, then displayed a sickly smile to Gaumont and Laurent. Berthe signed her name with a trembling hand.

"We have a lovely suite facing the beach. How long do you expect to stay?"

"Maybe two weeks," Ingrid replied.

The desk clerk noticed the bruises on Berthe's face and commented, "Madame, may I send for some medical assistance?"

"She has been in an auto accident. She just needs some rest," Gaumont declared.

"*Si, Signore*, this way please," he directed, pointing to the elevator. He snapped his fingers at the bellman standing by the ladies' luggage.

Jacques and Felix each guided the ladies to their luxury suite.

Ingrid handed some lire to the bellman, asking, "Is that enough?" The facial expression indicated it was lacking, so she took a bunch of lire and stuffed it into his hands. He smiled and departed.

Berthe wearily retired to the couch. Ingrid stood in front of Jacques and Felix, then, with her hands on her hips, she irritably asked, "Why have you followed us here?"

"Please, sit down and we will explain," Jacques suggested in a soothing tone.

"We're very tired. If Nordheim sent you, tell him that we'll not file a complaint against him."

"You do not understand," Gaumont softly replied. "We know what that evil son of a bitch did to you girls. We also know he paid you and Captain Sandstrom to keep the incident quiet."

"How do you know that?" Ingrid angrily demanded.

"Please be calm. I am a captain of detectives in France. We have ways of learning things. We are not here to embarrass you. We are on your side. We will protect you if Nordheim or his people try to hurt you. If you do not want to talk tonight, fine; get some sleep and we can talk later in the morning."

"Come here at twelve noon. For now, please go. This has been a bad night."

Felix and Jacques left the distressed ladies and checked into a room.

☆ ☆ ☆ ☆

Monte Carlo - 6 a.m.

The Daimler was at the dock, alongside the Flying Eagle. Nordheim, Mayfield, Froelich and Fenwick entered the limousine. Their bags were deposited in the trunk by two crew members.

Phillip and Mike were in a taxi parked at the harbormaster's building.

A motorcycle ruptured the pre-dawn stillness, roaring its way down the Avenue du Port to the Quai Antoine and onto the dock of the La Condamine. It came to a screeching halt alongside the Daimler.

The helmeted rider dismounted and raced around the limo, then tapped on the closed window as it was pulling away. The car stopped abruptly.

The cyclist gestured to Nordheim, who stepped out of the car and engaged the cyclist in a whispered conversation. Suddenly, he beckoned Captain Sandstrom to come down the gangplank. He tapped the shoulder of the motorcyclist in a praising manner. Nordheim led Sandstrom a short distance away from the car and spoke to him confidentially, gesticulating for emphasis. Sandstrom nodded in understanding and returned to the yacht. Nordheim poked his head into the limo. He turned away from the car, then handed something to the cyclist and waved him off. He re-entered the car. The motorcycle revved noisily and raced onto Boulevard Albert.

"Who the hell was that?" Mike queried.

"Looks like a messenger," Phillip noted. "You know, that motorcycle is very much like the one the French police use."

Phillip and Mike saw the Nordheim party in the Daimler turn south on Boulevard Charles III in the direction of Nice.

"Damn, he's not going to San Remo," Phillip declared. "What do we do?"

"We follow the boat, as ordered," Mike asserted. "That wily bastard is up to something. Bernarde is sleeping in his office. I'll ask him to reach Claude and Pierre. Keep your eye on the boat. Honk if it moves."

Mike went quickly to the harbormaster's office and banged on the door loudly. "Bernarde, it's Mike Paterno!"

The bolt rasped and the key was turned. "What is it?" Guy Bernarde grouched.

"Nordheim and his group are heading toward Nice. Can you reach Claude and Pierre to help check if they are going to fly out of Nice. We are going to see if the yacht sails up the coast to San Remo."

"Come in. I'll call Claude now."

Bernarde dialed the pied-à-terre.

"Allo."

"Claude, this is Guy. Wake up."

"I'm up. What is it?"

"Nordheim and gang are driving to Nice, according to Paterno. He thinks they are going to the airport. Can you reach someone to check it out?"

"When did they leave?"

"Five minutes ago."

"I'll get on it right away."

Guy turned to Mike. "It's being handled. How are you going to follow the yacht?"

"By taxi along the Corniche. We have binoculars."

"That is fine, if he follows the coastline. Good luck."

Mike rejoined Phillip. "They are getting ready to take off," Phillip announced. It is now 6:30 a.m."

Both focused their binoculars on the activity at the yacht. The anchor was being lifted and the mooring lines were being hauled in. The Flying Eagle slowly headed out of La Condamine, leaving the Port of Monaco into the Mediterranean, but, instead of heading north along the coast, the yacht pointed straight out to sea, gathering speed by the minute. The taxi moved to higher ground. Both men got out of the cab and held the optics on the yacht and its wake. No other vessels were sailing the waters near them.

"No use getting on the Corniche if that boat is going straight out to sea," Phillip said.

The Daimler limousine arrived at the Nice airport and drove to a hangar at the far end of the field. After the Lockheed constellation's four engines were feathered, Nordheim and the other three boarded the plane. As he taxied the aircraft out to runway two, the pilot spoke to the tower and asked for clearance. Standing alongside the air traffic controller was Sergeant Marcel Tellier of the Nice police. The air traffic controller requested route and destination.

"North, northwest, destination Genoa," the pilot replied.

"Cleared, north at 10,000 feet," the controller directed.

The plane revved its four engines, taxied to the end of runway two, turned around and roared its way to a smooth takeoff, then climbed into the dawn over the Mediterranean.

Sergeant Tellier requested the use of a telephone. The air-traffic controller pointed to a phone behind him.

Tellier dialed Claude Colbert in Monte Carlo.

"Allo."

"Lieutenant, Sergeant Tellier here."

"Yes, Marcel, what is the news?"

"You guessed right, that party of four boarded a four-engine plane. They just took off and gave their destination as Genoa."

"Oh, that tricky fox. Thank you, Marcel, good work. Sorry to get you out of bed."

"*Mon plaisir*, Lieutenant."

Claude placed a call to the Nice police headquarters.

"What is happening?" Pierre asked, rubbing his eyes.

Holding his hand over the phone's mouthpiece, he whispered, "Nordheim, en route to Genoa."

A voice on the other end responded, "Nice detective bureau."

"This is Lieutenant Claude Colbert. Can you hook me up to Captain Letelier?"

"Lieutenant, he is home and it's a little early to call him."

"Who is this?"

"This is Sergeant Pelange, sir."

"Ring him and I'll take full responsibility."

"Very well, sir." He rang the home phone, then patched the call.

"Captain Letelier here," came a crisp reply.

"Lieutenant Colbert, sir. Sorry to bother you at this hour."

"No problem, Claude, I was just leaving for the office. What is it?"

"That yacht I told you about last night took off a little while ago. I have reason to believe now that it is going directly to Genoa."

"Claude, I was told that the French coast guard, in cooperation with Interpol, was going to board the ship before it reaches Italian waters."

"Captain, could you check with your contact at the coast guard to find out if they have spotted the yacht?"

"I'll place a call now. What's your number?"

Claude supplied it.

Captain Sandstrom stood at the wheel of the yacht, guiding her over the placid Mediterranean at full speed. Within an hour he was out to sea, twenty-two miles west of Monte Carlo. Then he turned the vessel into the Ligurian Sea and headed north toward the Gulf of Genoa. Racing toward him at full speed was the French frigate Lafayette. The vessel was four nautical miles behind the Flying Eagle. A single-engine police plane passed over the yacht.

The pilot of the plane, in radio contact with the frigate, advised the captain that the yacht was moving into Italian coastal waters.

A team of six Interpol officers was prepared to board the ship.

"Gentlemen, I am afraid we have missed the boat," the captain wryly declared. "That rascal has outperformed us. He is now in Italian waters. We cannot touch him. Either we had bad information or they changed plans at the last minute."

The Lafayette made a one hundred and eighty-degree turn and set out for the Port of Nice. He advised the police plane to do likewise.

Captain Letelier had just reached his office when the aborted plan to board the yacht was relayed to him.

He called Claude in Monte Carlo. "Claude, they outfoxed us. The Flying Eagle is heading into the Gulf of Genoa. The operation has been canceled."

"*C'est la vie, c'est la guerre, c'est merde,*" Claude swore.

"Everyone tried, Claude. You'll have to fill me in one of these days. This must have been a very important exercise."

"You had better believe it. Gaston, we'll have a drink soon and I'll tell you a very interesting story, in confidence, of course."

"*Bon jour.*"

The Flying Eagle plied its way toward the Port of Genoa, which was crowded with the springtime arrival of yachts and commercial vessels. Captain Sandstrom radioed the harbormaster, who suggested that the yacht go to the Portofino harbor just a short distance from Genoa. The choice of Portofino pleased the captain, inasmuch as Nordheim had advised him at the last moment, when debarking in Monte Carlo, that the four men would be checking into the Hotel Splendido on Salita Baratta 13, Portofino, east of Genoa.

The Flying Eagle then anchored in the Portofino harbor, and Sandstrom made his way to shore in a twenty-five-foot motorboat, which had been lowered from the yacht. He called Nordheim at the hotel and notified him of his presence.

☆ ☆ ☆ ☆

Sunday, March 23, 1952, the same day - 11:30 a.m. - San Remo, Italy

Felix called the gift shop at the Royal Hotel San Remo. It carried most of the sundries for travelers. He ordered shaving materials, toothbrushes and toothpaste. The men took turns at their morning ablutions.

Jacques phoned Claude. No answer, so he tried Bernarde.

"*Allo.*"

"Guy, this is Jacques. Where is Claude?"

"He and Pierre left here a couple of hours ago. The operation to board the yacht failed. Call him at Nice headquarters. Where are you?"

"The Royal Hotel San Remo. We are going to interview the ladies at noon. Thanks."

He called Nice and was connected with Claude.

"What happened?"

"Jacques, that son of a bitch Nordheim outsmarted us. When he was on the dock ready to get into his limo, he must have instructed Captain Sandstrom to head for Genoa. That's why the wiretap didn't reveal his final plans."

"Where do you think they are?"

"We tracked him. The yacht is in the Portofino harbor. Nordheim is at the Hotel Splendido there."

"I can't go there under the circumstances. But I'll call my chief and see what he wants to do about it. That gold will be unloaded there. Talk to you later, Claude."

Jacques rushed down to the lobby and used one of their public phones. He reached Milburn, who called him back on the safe phone.

"What's it doing, Jacques?"

"The yacht is in Portofino harbor and Nordheim, Froelich, Fenwick and Mayfield are at the Hotel Splendido there."

"Where are you?"

"I'm in San Remo with Captain Gaumont. We're going to tape the two ladies in about fifteen minutes. I can't go to Genoa because Mayfield will spot me. Do you want someone to survey that Nazi bastard and watch for the gold transfer?"

"Jacques, finish what you have to do. I may want you to meet me in Paris. I want you to develop your pictures. I'll call Washington and see if we have a man in Genoa. Call me when you get to Nice."

Jacques returned to his room, then he and Gaumont proceeded to the ladies' suite.

Ingrid opened the door. She was dressed in a light blue shift, a string of pearls around her neck, and white pumps. Berthe wore a white terrycloth bathrobe with the insignia Royal Hotel San Remo. Neither of them wore any cosmetics. They were pretty, despite Berthe's bruised lip.

Coffee, brioches and fruit preserves were on a table in the center of the living room.

"Thank you, ladies, for your hospitality," Jacques cheerfully declared.

The atmosphere was less tense than the confrontation in the early hours of the morning, so they partook of the brioches and coffee.

Captain Gaumont attempted to allay the fears of Ingrid and Berthe. "I hope you ladies feel a little better now that you've had some sleep. May I put this recorder on the table?"

Ingrid nodded in acquiescence, then said, "Captain, I want you to know who we are. Berthe and I come from fine families. My father is a respected surgeon in Malmo. Berthe's father is a member of Parliament. My mother is with the Swedish Red Cross. I have two brothers who are lawyers and two sisters, one in college in Stockholm and one married to a prosecutor in Malmo. I am an aunt to six children."

"Ingrid, I realize you ladies are of good, respectable stock."

Berthe spoke up. "I would like you to know that my brother is the young-est man in the city council. My older sister is married to a colonel in the Swedish army. My younger sister is engaged to marry the executive vice president of an automobile company. So, you see, we are not tramps."

"Please, ladies, if we thought less of you, we wouldn't be here. Herr Nordheim is the richest man in the world and a very evil person."

Jacques looked at Ingrid and Berthe, then began: "Ladies, I will speak to you in confidence. We have reason to believe that his name is not Nordheim. He is a dangerous man. We ask your cooperation in being open and frank with us. We have no desire to go public with what you tell us. We are more interested in exposing him than subjecting you to an official inquiry."

"Gentlemen, please understand, the last twelve or fourteen hours have been a nightmare. We have never been in a situation like this. We cannot have our names smeared by filing a complaint, if that's what you want. Maybe you should turn off that machine," Ingrid vehemently asserted.

"Before I turn it off, let me convince you that all that is said here will be confidential. When we are through talking, if you are not satisfied with our intent, I will turn the tape over to you at your request," Gaumont assured them.

"Very well, I'll accept you at your word. Is that all right with you, Berthe?"

"Yes, let us finish. I'm tired and need some rest," she agreed.

"Thank you. Now I will ask some questions in a more formal way, and please answer fully."

Gaumont leaned forward and spoke directly into the recorder. "The date is March 23rd, 12:25 p.m. My name is Felix Gaumont, captain of detectives of the French police. With me is Captain Jacques Laurent of the United States Intelligence. We are here in the Royal Hotel San Remo in suite number 412.

We are interrogating two ladies, Miss Ingrid Leifer and Miss Berthe Swensen, Swedish citizens from Malmo, Sweden. These fine ladies are nurses at the Malmo General Hospital. The subject matter is one Frederick Avram Nordheim."

"I thought your name was Joffre," Ingrid interposed. "You were the customs supervisor. What is going on here?"

"Mademoiselle, that was, as we say in French, a *nom de guerre*, a war name, which I used in investigations," Jacques explained.

"Why are you investigating Nordheim?"

"We believe he is a very bad criminal."

"Miss Leifer, when did you first meet Herr Nordheim?" Gaumont queried.

"In Ajaccio, Corsica, when he came on board the yacht."

"How was he introduced to you?"

"As an employer of Captain Sandstrom."

"Just tell us, in your own way, what you know of him. I will not interrupt."

"Leif Sandstrom told us he was a very rich man. That he owned one of the largest yachts in the world. Leif had worked for him for six years, since 1946. He worked on another one of his yachts. Nordheim was a mystery to him, but he paid him very well. In early 1946, Nordheim had been recovering from surgery after a serious auto accident. He lived in a huge mansion with lots of servants and doctors, mostly German."

"What kind of surgery?" Gaumont asked.

"I don't know, except his face was fractured in many places, according to Leif."

"Was his body injured in the accident?"

"I guess so, but I don't really know."

"What is your relationship to Captain Sandstrom?"

"Just a friend. He and my brother were schoolmates. He was like a big brother to Berthe and me. We didn't date with him."

"What else can you tell us about Nordheim?" Captain Gaumont asked.

"He is a low, filthy animal."

"Did you think that when you first met him?"

"Oh, no, he was very charming in Ajaccio, that snake."

"You knew he was a German when you first met him?"

"He told me he was a Swedish citizen from Malmo. Of course, he is of German ancestry. We have quite a few Germans who became Swedish citizens."

"Are they all Nazis?"

"What are you saying?"

"Just a comment. Nazis have fled the Allied armies and are hiding in countries all over the world. Isn't it possible that some Germans in Sweden might be escaped Nazis?" The captain observed.

"Is Nordheim one of them?"

"Ingrid, we don't know at this point. That's why we want your cooperation. Can you tell us anything that would help us determine his true identity?"

Berthe, who had seemed indifferent to the questioning, spoke up: "Ingrid, tell him about the American doctor."

"I am not too sure about him. I only know what Leif Sandstrom told me."

"Please, let me hear it. What did Leif tell you about the doctor?" Gaumont gently urged.

"Leif's information is only second-hand. He used to date a nurse. She had been attending Nordheim after his surgery. She told Leif that a close associate of Nordheim had a big argument with this doctor up in the mansion where the surgery took place. I don't think this is important. No more, please." Ingrid stopped suddenly.

Jacques handed her a glass of water. She drained it. An uncomfortable silence ensued.

"What is wrong, Ingrid?" Berthe asked, leaving the couch and putting her arm around her shoulder.

"I don't want to get Leif involved in this investigation. If this gets back to Nordheim, he'll lose his job and maybe have a lot of trouble."

"Ingrid, I assure you that none of what you tell us will get out," Gamont again promised. "Leif will be protected. Please tell us everything. You will be doing the world a big favor if this man turns out to be an escaped Nazi."

Ingrid and Berthe were startled by Gaumont's statement. Their shock and surprise were palpable.

"That's it, isn't it? You are hiding something. You are afraid of this animal that whipped you and treated you with contempt. Just like a Nazi. Why are you protecting him?" Gaumont pressed.

Ingrid rose from her chair and angrily began pacing the room. "Very well, I won't protect this animal. I just want to protect Leif Sandstrom, who is a good man. Don't harm him," she demanded.

"He will not be harmed by us. Please continue," Gaumont urged.

"All right, this nurse told Leif that the doctor wanted to leave Malmo and told this associate of Nordheim that he felt like a prisoner in that house. The nurse was in the next room, Leif said, and she heard them shouting. The man told the doctor that if he attempted to leave he would kill him. The doctor called him a Nazi bastard. The man struck the doctor. The sound of the punch was very loud. She then heard a sound of the man falling. The man shouted for a servant called Hans. The nurse left the room she was in and hid in the pantry."

"What happened after that?" Gaumont pursued intently.

"She told Leif she peeked out of the kitchen door. Hans, a very big fellow, and the man were carrying the unconscious doctor up the stairs."

"Did the nurse ever mention the name of this man?"

"Oh, yes, yes. I remember now...it was Martin. She said that Nordheim called him Martin. She described Martin as short and stocky."

"Where is this nurse now?" Jacques asked.

"See, that's just it. She disappeared from Malmo about one week after that incident. She told Leif what had happened when they got together that night."

"Does she have family in Malmo?"

"She has a mother, Emily Bauman. She is a sick woman. Joan was her only child. Her husband died five years ago. Leif helps her financially. The father reported Joan's disappearance to the police. They found nothing. Leif was in love with Joan. He still is. He talks about her all the time. They were going to be married."

"When did this all take place?" Jacques asked.

"It was either September or October in 1945," Berthe whispered.

"Did you know Joan?" Jacques pressed.

"No, we were finishing our nurses training in Stockholm at that time," Ingrid declared. "Berthe and I were nineteen years old. We are just two months apart."

"When was the last time Sandstrom saw her before she disappeared?" Jacques asked.

"He had dinner with her the night before. They had a date for the next evening. He went to her house to pick her up at 7 o'clock. He and her parents became concerned at 10 o'clock. Joan's mother called the Nordheim mansion and was told that she had left at half past six. At midnight they called the Malmo police to report her missing."

"What did the police do about it?" Gaumont inquired.

"They sent two men to the Nordheim house. That man, Hans, told them she got in her car and drove away after six," Ingrid replied.

"They never found the car?" Jacques asked.

"No, no car, no Joan. No witnesses, nothing," Ingrid decried.

"Leif went to the house and spoke to the servants. They all told the same story," Berthe chimed in.

"There is something that bothers me about Sandstrom's attitude in this affair," Gaumont asserted.

"What do you mean? What is wrong about his attitude?" Ingrid defensively queried.

"Just put two and two together, ladies...Leif loved this lady. They were going to marry, you say. Wasn't he suspicious of Nordheim and this Martin fellow? Did the fight with the doctor have something to do with her disappearance? Why is Leif so anxious to keep his job with Nordheim? Why is..."

Ingrid exploded, "Like all policemen, you are suspicious of *everybody*. Well, if you're so smart, what do you make of this? Nordheim paid for a private detective agency to trace the girl. Leif worked with the investigators for over a year."

"What did they find out?" Gaumont asked.

"I don't want to talk about it anymore," Ingrid snapped.

"And why not?" Gaumont said.

"Oh, tell him. He'll find out sooner or later," Berthe coaxed.

"Damn you, Captain, I have said more than I should. Leif has been hurt enough. The private detectives and Hans said that Joan ran off with a German banker, named Klaus Heineman, who had been a guest at Nordheim's mansion. They left in her car and were last seen at the Stockholm airport. They never found the car. They said they flew to Zurich. Nordheim said he represented the Bank Alpine. The bank said he was an impostor. Nordheim acted shocked when he heard that, Leif said."

"You don't believe that fairytale, do you?"

"Of course not. Neither does Leif. He has been hanging on to his job with Nordheim, hoping to learn the truth. He doesn't trust that German pig any more than we do. That is the reason he invited us on this trip, hoping we could learn something about Joan's disappearance."

"Isn't that a bit naïve?"

"That's what you think. Well, how about this? We talked with Froelich on the trip from Ajaccio to Monte Carlo. He let it slip that Klaus Heineman works for Nordheim. That garbage of the Bank Alpine is very revealing. Nordheim pretends he's shocked to learn that Klaus is an impostor."

"Did you tell that to Sandstrom?"

"Yes, we did. And that's why he took the bribe money and told us to take it. He wants to stay with Nordheim to find out more. Now, Mr. Detective, I'll tell you one more thing. When we went to Herr Nordheim's cabin, he was quite charming. There was caviar and champagne there for us..." She paused and stared at Gaumont and Jacques, then rose and paced the room.

"Come now, why the suspense? What happened?" Felix barked.

"I foolishly lifted a glass of champagne and toasted the dear, departed Joan Bauman. He went berserk. He ripped my dress right off me. When Berthe pushed him away, he beat her with his whip and tore her dress off, too. He yelled at us in German. Dirty words, I guess."

"Then what?" Felix demanded.

"That beast called us whores and demanded we take off our undergarments. He said, *I do not believe in sexual intercourse, it breeds disease. But I'll teach you sex like whores should learn.* When we refused to undress, he started to whip Berthe. I tried to stop him. Berthe kept screaming and then Leif and the others broke into the room. That's it. No more to tell."

"Thank you, ladies. Enjoy your stay here and don't talk to strange men," Gaumont advised. He motioned to Jacques and they left, staying silent during most of the trip from San Remo to Monte Carlo.

"I'll take the recorder and have the tapes transcribed, then send you a copy," Jacques commented.

"Yes, I don't want to have it done in my office," Felix said. "Jacques, this is very heavy stuff. My mind is spinning. Could he be who I think he is?"

"I've thought that right along. And now with the name of Martin, this staggers the imagination. I've got to reach Milburn. Let's stop and see Guy before we go to Nice."

They drove into La Condamine and parked at the harbor master's building, where Guy Bernarde was at his desk.

"Felix, Jacques, I am so glad to see you. Sit, I have much to tell you."

He recounted the events of the pre-dawn hours. The last word was that Nordheim had flown to Genoa. He speculated that the motorcycle looked like police issue.

"Is it possible that Nordheim had a connection inside the Nice police department?" Jacques hissed.

Gaumont slapped the desk with his ham-sized fist. "We'll soon find out," he snarled. "Come, Jacques, let's go to Nice. Do you want to pick up your bag?"

"Not necessary; Claude took it with him."

☆ ☆ ☆ ☆

Sunday, March 23, 1952 - 8 a.m. - Genoa, Italy

Nordheim, Fenwick and Mayfield were seated at the breakfast table in their suite at the Splendido Hotel. Froelich was standing, phone in hand.

At the other end of the phone in his home in Geneva, Konrad Fliegel, treasurer of Winston General, Ltd., had just been awakened. "Yes, Gunther, I am awake."

"Listen carefully," he said in German, "Call Peter Weber at the Bank Royal in Zurich. We want him to buy a shipment of gold bars for American dollars delivered here in Genoa."

"How much is it?"

"One hundred twelve million."

"I don't know if Peter will do that."

"Konrad, you know better than that. Either he does that or we remove a billion from our accounts at his bank. *Schnell*. Call me back at the Splendido Hotel. It must be completed today."

"*Jawohl*."

A nervous Konrad Fliegel spent 25 minutes arguing with Peter Weber, president of the Bank Royale, who was reached at his home.

"I am leaving for the bank now, Konrad. I will call you as soon as I have completed the arrangements."

Fliegel then was back on the phone with Froelich. "You know it's Sunday. Weber is on his way to his office to make the necessary methods of transfer for tomorrow. He also has to open the bank."

"Tell him to call me directly here when he has it worked out."

"*Jawohl*."

One hour later, Weber unctuously advised Froelich that he would be happy to accommodate Herr Nordheim. "Gunther, it is always a pleasure to do business with Winston General and all your people."

"How will this be handled? Despite the fact this is a Sunday."

"We have arranged with our associates at the Genoa Banco Internationale to accept the gold for us. Do you want the money to be deposited to the Winston account here?" Weber asked.

"No, no, make a wire transfer to the Winston General account at Thornton, Wiley & Farrell at their Wall Street office."

"Very well, as soon as the gold is delivered and counted."

"Have the Genoa bank send an armored truck to the Portofino marina. The Flying Eagle yacht will be tied up there. Have the bank arrange for a few

Italian police to escort the truck to their bank."

"Thank you, Konrad. It will be handled."

At 10 a.m., Leif Sandstrom knocked at the door of Nordheim's suite.

"Come in, Captain," Nordheim greeted him. "Would you like some coffee?"

"No, thank you, sir. I want to get back to the yacht. It's quite crowded out there and I am anchored away from the dock."

Mayfield spoke up. "Captain, it is urgent that the boat be moored to the dock. I'll go with you and see what can be done with the dockmaster."

"Good idea, Darren," Nordheim agreed.

At the dock, Mayfield took the dockmaster, Tony Spinelli, for a walk away from the dock. He held a fistful of American dollars in his hand. Spinelli stared at the money. "How can I assist you, Signor?" he addressed Mayfield in English. "We like to help you Americans."

"Good. How about five hundred American dollars if you can find space for that yacht out there?" he pointed at the Flying Eagle.

"Tell your captain to dock at the far end in one hour," he declared, snatching the bills from Mayfield's outstretched hand. The transaction completed, Mayfield joined Leif, advised him and departed for the hotel.

Nordheim, Froelich and Fenwick were in a deep discussion on the subject of allocating funds around the world. When Mayfield entered the suite, Nordheim asked if the boat would be at dockside for the pickup of the gold cache from the yacht.

"It will be moored in the next hour."

"Call Andrew Thornton at his home and tell him that Sir Clive Fenwick, executive vice president of Winston, will instruct him on the investment of the one hundred twelve million."

A person-to-person call to Thornton took ten minutes.

"Yes, Mr. Mayfield, how are you, sir? Nice to hear your voice," a booming voice greeted the caller. "How can I be of service?"

"Sir Clive Fenwick, our executive vice president, will explain." He handed the phone to Fenwick.

"Andrew, how are you?"

"Fine, Sir Clive. Nice to hear your voice."

"Andrew, one hundred and twelve million dollars is being wired to you in the morning. It is 11:30 a.m. here. What time do you have there?"

"It is 6:30 a.m. here."

"That's what I thought. Sorry to wake you up."

"No problem, sir."

"All right, the first thing in the morning, we want you to invest the $112 million in U.S. long-term Treasury bonds."

"All of it?"

"Yes, all. Any problem?"

"Well, that could cause a run-up in the price and affect the yield."

"We're not concerned about that, just do it."

"If you say so, sir."

"According to our records, Andrew, our Eagle subsidiaries portfolio with your firm shows our assets of stocks, bonds and mutual funds to be 6 billion 463 million dollars. Add the 112 million to that and give me an accurate total in the morning after your purchase of the treasuries."

"Yes, sir. I'll call you as soon as the Federal Reserve auction is completed, Sir Clive."

"Fine," Fenwick finished, and he hung up.

"Darren, do you have a home number for that law firm in London who handles our investments?" Nordheim asked.

"You mean Carstairs, Higgins, Schiffer & Stone. Paul Carstairs is the senior partner. I have his number."

"Well, call him and Sir Clive will talk with him, now."

Mayfield placed the call.

"Carstairs residence."

"I have a person-to-person call for Mr. Paul Carstairs from Portofino, Italy."

"Who is calling, please?"

'Sir Clive Fenwick."

"One moment, please."

"Sir Clive, old boy…"

"This is Darren Mayfield, Paul, Sir Clive is right here. Paul, sorry to bother you on a Sunday."

"No bother. How can I help you, old boy?"

"The Eagle Shipping portfolio, which your firm manages for us, shows a net value of 3 billion, 441 million pounds. Our board has voted to liquidate those holdings into cash."

"All at once, Sir Clive? My lord, that could jolt the market."

"In an orderly manner, Paul. We want you to buy U.S. Treasuries with the proceeds."

"Orderly manner would take several days."

"Hold the phone for a moment, Paul." He turned to Nordheim. "Two days, three days or more, sir?"

Nordheim looked at Froelich. Gunther raised one finger.

"Ja, one day," Nordheim nodded.

"Paul, I'm afraid it's one day, tomorrow, and that's it."

"I implore you, Sir Clive, make it two days at least. You do not want a market crash, do you?"

"Hold on."

"Herr Nordheim, discretion is advisable here. We might be hurting ourselves if we dump everything in one day."

"All right, Clive. Two days."

"Paul, two days is the best I can do."

"Very well, we'll do the best we can."

"Buy the U.S. Treasuries first thing in the morning, as well, at the prevailing price. You have four days to settle. Is that right?"

"I'll have a little leeway to cover the purchase of the bonds, in case the market slides as we sell."

"Act accordingly, Paul."

"Where can I reach you?"

"Here at the Hotel Splendido in Portofino, Italy."

"Fine. I'll call our brokers at Lightfoot & Warwick now to prepare them for an arduous day tomorrow."

"Do that, and good luck."`

"Next call is to Fontaine Frères in Paris. You have number, Darren?" Nordheim asked.

"Charles Fontaine lives outside Paris. Let me see, here it is. Seine-et-Marne, about thirty miles, between Fontainebleau and Vincennes."- "Yes, yes, I know where it is. Place the call," Nordheim snapped irritably.

The person-to-person call was completed. "Monsieur Fontaine? Darren Mayfield here."

"Ah, Darren, you are well?"

"Yes, sir, and I have Sir Clive Fenwick here, who wishes to talk with you." He handed the phone to Fenwick.

"Charles, how are you?"

"Fine, Clive, how may I serve you?"

"We have 3 billion, 212 million American dollars value in Eagle Shipping's portfolio with you. Is that correct?"

"If you say so, sir."

"Our board of directors has voted to liquidate everything into cash. We want you to purchase U.S. long-term Treasury bonds at the prevailing market price."

"Over how long a period?"

"You have two days to sell everything. We want you to buy the Treasuries first thing in the morning. What time does the Paris Bourse open?"

"At 7 a.m., but this will have a heavy impact on the market."

"Do the best you can."

"We may take a huge loss."

"Charles, you're an old buccaneer, you'll try not to lose too much. I rely on you."

"*Monsieur*, I'll go to work right now. Maybe I can sell some in Japan and other Asian markets. You've spoiled my Sunday." They rang off, and Froelich asked, "Herr Nordheim, we have been so busy going through the portfolio accounts, I haven't asked you why we are liquidating our stock holdings."

"Gunther, you are smart in many ways. But, when it comes to the science of war or intrigue, you are a *dummkopf*. Mayfield, explain it to him."

"The activities of the French police and customs in Monte Carlo were obviously a blundering farce. I don't believe they were regular members of the Sûreté. I believe this was the work of French Intelligence or Interpol. They were after Herr Nordheim and Winston General. Also, that fellow taking pictures, who attacked me, is a professional intelligence agent. Then, as we were leaving for the airport, that man on the motorcycle tipped us off that the French and Interpol were going to board the yacht. They were going to plant cocaine on board as an excuse to seize the Flying Eagle. We were lucky."

"What has all that to do with dumping our portfolios?"

"What, what, what, Gunther! Isn't it obvious that the French and British at least are mounting a campaign to bring me down?" Nordheim rasped.

"So?"

"*Ach*, Gunther! We must curtail our activities and channel our holdings into safe havens!" Nordheim shouted in German.

"All right, I can see the French in all this, but where do the British fit?" Gunther persisted.

"Because after the war ended, the British and French worked together with the American CIA and the Interpol. While I do not yet smell the dirty hands of the Americans in this activity, it is better to be cautious," Nordheim replied.

"Then why buy American bonds?"

"Simple, Gunther. America is the strongest economy in the world and the bonds are backed by the government. That makes the bonds the safest investment in the world. We will in the next few days move all our cash and bonds out of America, France and England into the Banque Lorraine in Geneva and the Banque Royale in Zurich. We'll keep an adequate amount of funds in the Pacific National Bank in Vancouver, Canada, and the Strupp Bank in Buenos Aires."

"Herr Nordheim, while I follow what you are saying in German, I would appreciate if you would speak English," Mayfield requested.

"*Ja*, Darren. My English is better than your German. Is not so?"

"Yes, sir. What we should also point out to Herr Froelich is what the MI6 has done in Liverpool with their raid on the Aryan Swords. They have two members singing their heads off. They might have picked up some correspondence from that group in Skokie, Illinois. They might try to link us with those groups. The American FBI, through my old boss, J. Edgar Hoover, is not cooperating with them. But the CIA might be," Mayfield cautioned.

"Darren, we must never show our hands in helping certain groups. We were very sloppy in sending funds to them," Sir Clive interjected.

"How you say, that's all chicken *scheisse*," Nordheim asserted. "More important now. We must curtail all of our activities. I have sent for Martin to join me in Havana. Sir Clive will go back to his desk in Vaduz. Froelich, you will go to Geneva and Zurich to check our accounts at Banque Lorraine and Banque Royale. When finished in Switzerland, Gunther, you will go back to your desk in Vaduz. I will be going to Havana for a vacation. From there, Martin and I will go to Buenos Aires. We will all be very quiet until January. I will decide our future plans early next year. Mayfield will be with me. The yacht should leave here after she unloads the gold. Darren, you should supervise the transfer of gold. Send Captain Sandstrom here before they unload. It's not his business to know about this. Send the crew for a tour of Genoa. Go now."

Mayfield asked the concierge for a shuttle bus. It was quickly provided by the hotel, using one of its courtesy buses.

At the dock, Mayfield dispatched Sandstrom to the Hotel, then called the crew of seven together and invited them to tour Genoa. He handed the first mate a fistful of money and gave one hundred dollars to the driver. He told him to take a long tour of the city and to finish with a meal at one of the better restaurants. He ordered him not to bring the crew back to the dock for at least four hours. He called the suite and told Sir Clive to detain Sandstrom for at least four hours.

Fifteen minutes after the crew left, an armored truck, escorted by four *carabiniere* on motorcycles, backed up to the gang plank of the Flying Eagle.

The driver of the truck and two bank guards, fully armed, approached Mayfield. The *carabiniere* stationed themselves around the truck, guns drawn.

"Anyone speak English?" Darren shouted.

"*Signor*, I speak it," the driver acknowledged.

"Come with me. I will show you where the gold is."

"*Si, Signor.*"

In the master suite, Mayfield lifted the carpet, pulled the indented latch and showed the cache of gold bars to the driver. He enlisted the aid of the two guards and began the arduous task of lifting the loot out of the hidden hold for transfer to the truck.

The *carabiniere* impassively watched the 112 million-dollar fortune being loaded into the armored van.

Mayfield handed each of the Italian police a hundred-dollar bill. He made several trips from the suite to the truck. One of the guards had to lower himself into the hold and hand the gold bar by bar to the other guard standing in the suite. The transfer was completed in three and a half hours. Mayfield closed the door to the hold and smoothed the carpet back in place.

He accepted a receipt for the gold cargo from the driver and spread five hundred dollars apiece among the driver and the two guards. Sirens rent the tranquil Sunday atmosphere as the motorcycles escorted the precious cargo to the Genoa Banco Internationale.

Shortly thereafter, the grateful crew returned. They thanked Mayfield profusely. He handed another five hundred dollars to each of them.

Mayfield quietly entered the suite. Nordheim and Sandstrom were intently staring at maps spread out over a coffee table.

"Here, you will sail south to Palermo, Sicily," Nordheim said. "Dock at the marina there. It is a big port. We will be at the Grand Hotel Villa Igiea in the Acquasanta District. Stock up on provisions and fuel. Leave here as soon as you are ready. I will have the hotel cater a lunch on board the yacht when I get there in two to three days."

"That's fine, sir. Is that all?"

"Yes, Darren. Give the captain whatever funds he requires."

"How much do you need, Captain?" Mayfield inquired.

"I have about three thousand American dollars on board. Another ten thousand will be sufficient."

Mayfield opened a briefcase and took two packets of five thousand each and handed the money to Sandstrom, who then departed.

"I take it, sir, that you spoke to Lucky Luciano?" Mayfield asked.

"He will join us on board the yacht for lunch in Palermo."

"Did you tell him what you have in mind?"

"No, but he must realize that we want to invest in the hotels in Havana, for the gambling, and also in Las Vegas. We had spoken about it the last time I saw him. How did the gold transfer go?"

"Perfectly."

CHAPTER NINE

Monday, March 24, 1952 - Buenos Aires, Argentina

The Countess de Carrera and her husband, Anthony Fuentes, arrived in Buenos Aires after an arduous flight, and the Pan American plane was met by an official welcoming committee. Sophia and Tony were the first to descend the steps of the mobile staircase to the tarmac where they were greeted by Alejandro Mendoza, secretary of tourism; Colonel Arturo Garcia, security chief; Maria Ortiz, foreign minister; Janis Fulton, protocol secretary; and Roberto Lopez, aide to President Peron.

Mendoza presented the countess with a bouquet of roses.

"Welcome to Argentina, Countess and Señor Fuentes. We hope to make your stay here most pleasant. Allow me to introduce our welcoming committee," he declared, pointing to the trio behind him.

Sophia flashed a sparkling smile at the group. Tony shook hands all around.

"We are overwhelmed by your greeting," she declared in perfect Castilian Spanish.

Colonel Garcia, in an impressive uniform, escorted the couple. They were whisked through immigration, where their passports were quickly stamped.

"Let me have your baggage claim checks. There is no need to go through customs," he said curtly, and snapped his fingers. Two uniformed sergeants appeared and saluted. The colonel handed them the claim checks and ordered, "Pronto!", pointing to the limousine. More salutes. The colonel waved at the customs officers.

Señora Ortiz chatted with the countess about their trip and the weather, and asked, "Are there any special plans for this evening?"

"No, no, my dear, this has been a very tiring flight, so we must rest to overcome this long trip," Sophia coolly responded, looking at Tony, who nodded.

"You have reserved the Royal Suite at the Hotel Phoenix. May I ask who recommended it?"

Not missing a beat, Sophia replied, "Last year in Paris I was invited to have tea with the Duke of Windsor and his wife, Wallis. During our discussion, he mentioned his stay at the Phoenix and spoke highly of the ambience and service. I remembered. Is there another choice we should have made?"

"Oh, not at all. It was curiosity on my part. You see, it's a charming place with only sixty rooms."

"That's precisely why it was arranged for us."

"I think you'll be very pleased," the young protocol officer concurred.

At that point, Colonel Garcia announced that all the bags were in a station wagon to be driven by one of the sergeants.

The Fuenteses were escorted to a waiting limousine, where six police officers astride their motorcycles comprised the security force.

The greeting party joined the countess and her husband in the limo. The motorcycles revved their engines, blaring a cacophony of sound, accompanied by a penetrating wail of sirens. Phase two of the CIA charade was about to begin.

The caravan, on a signal from the colonel, began its siren-wailing journey, then crowds began to gather along the route as Sophia and Tony waved at the gapers, who had no idea who they were.

As they arrived at the hotel, about fifty onlookers crowded the driveway to the hotel. Above the entrance, the monarch flag of Alfonso XIII's Spain was fluttering in a gentle breeze. Beneath the flag stood U.S. Ambassador Franklin Withers, flanked by two U.S. Marines. With them was Esther Carney, social secretary and protocol officer of the American Embassy. She carried a large bouquet of flowers, wrapped in red, white and blue bunting. Beside her was attorney Ernesto Nogales.

As the countess and her husband alighted, Ambassador Withers put his hand forward to assist Sophia. He was a tall, dignified man, gray-haired, with a youthful suntanned face.

"Delighted to see you again, dear Countess," he said.

"Thank you, dear Ambassador, for meeting us here," she replied.

He reached over and shook Fuentes' hand and, for all to hear, said, "Tony, good to see you. I hear you've been elected chairman of the board of American International Finance Corporation. Congratulations."

"Thank you, sir. It's good to see you again."

Esther Carney, a petite young woman with blonde hair and blue eyes that sparkled with a knowing look, smiled at Sophia, saying, "I'm at your service during your stay. I'll leave my card with Mr. Fuentes."

"Thank you, dear, dear girl," Sophia replied, joining in the act.

"We have prepared refreshments," Secretary of Tourism Mendoza announced. "We would be honored if we could toast you and your husband before you retire."

"Delighted," Tony chimed in. "That's a wonderful idea."

The crowd outside applauded as the colonel coached the gathering with hand-clapping gestures. Countess de Cordoba threw kisses to the onlookers and entered the lobby.

The hotel manager, Juan Porteros, bowed, and with a sweep of his arm invited the distinguished group to follow him to a tastefully furnished lounge. Porteros sidled up to the countess and Tony, saying, "Welcome to our hotel. We are honored. I will bring the registration card to your room. We will do everything possible to make your stay comfortable and pleasant."

A maitre d', dressed as a *vaquero,* escorted them to a settee. The rest of the party were seated at small tables with elegant heavy wooded armchairs covered with crimson damask.

A cadre of waiters, attired in Argentinian gaucho outfits similar to the maitre d's, circulated quickly, serving assorted canapés, large platters of caviar, toast points, hard-boiled egg yolks, egg whites and onions finely chopped for the gourmet palate. Bottles of Dom Perignon champagne were popping open in cadence with a four-piece orchestra playing Ravel's *Bolero.*

Alejandro Mendoza rose, champagne glass in hand, and intoned, "Join me in welcoming the beautiful Countess de Cordoba and her charming husband to our country."

All in attendance rose and clinked glasses.

Tony stood, held up his glass and in measured Castilian Spanish declared, "With gratitude in behalf of my wife and myself, I present this salute to you and all of the people of your wonderful country. Our wishes are for your good health, happiness and prosperity."

Glasses clinked in acknowledgment. Murmurs of appreciation were audible.

"I would like to say that I am an American with Latin roots. I welcome the friendship of Argentina to America and vice versa. I also toast my good friend, America's ambassador to your country, His Excellency Franklin Withers."

Applause, and more glasses clinking.

Holding up his hand for silence, Tony asked, "Will you please rise?"

He clasped the countess's arm, and they both raised their glasses. "I wish to convey our greetings and best wishes to your very distinguished President Juan Peron and his charming wife and first lady of your land, Señora Eva Peron."

Loud expressions of *Ole!* and *Bravo!* ensued.

Franklin Withers stood and signaled for attention. In diplomatic parlance, he delivered his toast. "In consonance with the sentiment expressed by Mr. Fuentes, I would join with all here in wishing for a strong alliance between the United States of America and the great country of Argentina."

More *Oles* and *Bravos* rent the room.

The Ambassador smiled and raised his hand for silence, then continued, "May I wish the Countess de Cordoba and Mr. Anthony Fuentes an enjoyable visit in your country."

The countess rose. Regally surveying the room, she stood at attention, pointedly seeking out each pair of eyes in a deliberate gesture of recognition and gratitude. "Please accept our deepest appreciation for your most cordial reception of my husband and me. I thank each and every one here and the entire government of Argentina. We also thank Ambassador Withers for his kind remarks. I wish you all a pleasant evening."

Flashbulbs lit up the room as the news cameras clicked.

After much applause and many handshakes, the couple were led by hotel manager Poteras to their spacious, elegantly furnished quarters.

"Should you need anything, we are here to serve you," he said, then bowed and closed the door behind him.

Tony stood in front of Sophia and held two fingers of his left hand to his lips, then waved his right hand, sweeping the room. Sophia quickly acknowledged the cautionary gestures.

"The Argentinian people are so warm and gracious, Anthony," she declared.

"They most certainly are," Tony dittoed as he began examining the lamps, walls, furniture, bedposts and all possible areas where microphones or other electronic bugs could have been planted.

Sophia assisted in the search and suggested, "Let's go out on the balcony, Anthony, it looks beautiful out there."

He opened the double doors and they both stepped out onto the spacious balcony overlooking Avenida San Martin.

She suddenly pulled Tony to her, gave him a hug, and assertively whispered in his ear, "Don't get any silly ideas. We've gone as far as we're going to with this husband-and-wife pretense."

"What does that mean?" Tony questioned as he started to push her away from their embrace.

She didn't disengage and answered, "We're not both sleeping in that king-sized bed."

Agitatedly, Tony snapped, "Is that what's bothering you? Relax. I'll sleep on the couch."

She released him and rewarded him with a warm smile. "I just wanted to clarify our respective roles, personal and business."

"Sophia, you know how I feel about you. When this is over, I might want to talk about it. But, for now, let's get down to business."

Sophia took a long and appraising look at her pseudo-husband, then smiled at him and said, "In that case, you can sleep in the bed, but just stay on your side."

"It'll be difficult, but I'll try," he smirked.

☆ ☆ ☆ ☆

Tuesday, March 25, 1952 - 8:15 a.m.

Room service delivered breakfast to the Regal Suite, and two newspapers were handed to Tony. He handed one to Sophia.

"Well, they've put our pictures and story on page one," Sophia gasped.

"Yes, this paper did the same," Tony declared as he kept reading the account of their reception.

The phone rang. Tony answered, "Yes?"

"This is Ernesto Nogales. Ambassador Withers would like you and the countess to join him at the American Embassy at 10 a.m., if that is convenient."

"Just one moment, sir, I'll check with the countess."

"Who is that?" she whispered.

"Nogales. Ambassador Withers at the Embassy. Ten o'clock?"

She acquiesced, nodding her head.

"That's fine, Señor Nogales," Tony affirmed.

"It will be my privilege to drive you there. I'll ring you from the lobby at 9:45, if that would suit you."

"That's fine, Señor Nogales."

"Tony, I'm going to change my dress for a more formal suit," Sophia advised.

Tony poured a third cup of coffee for himself, lit a cigarette and absorbed the detailed accounts of the arrival and reception for *the Beautiful Countess de Cordoba and Her Handsome Husband, Señor Anthony Fuentes.* Of great interest were the quotes of the countess and Tony regarding President Peron and his wife, Eva.

When Sophia appeared, she was a striking figure in a blue jacket, pleated beige skirt and light pink ruffled blouse. A thick gold chain with a cameo of a coat of arms dangled over her chest.

"I'd say you stepped right off the cover of Vogue."

"Tony, you're sweet."

"I'm glad you noticed."

The phone jangled. Tony answered, then said, "We'll be right down." He looked at Sophia, "Darling, the car's ready."

In the lobby an affable, heavy-set, bald, well-dressed man in his late fifties greeted them.

"This is very kind of you, Señor Nogales," Sophia addressed him, shaking his hand. "We didn't have a chance to chat yesterday."

"Well, we were overwhelmed by the reception," Tony asserted.

"My pleasure, dear people. We will make time to chat today, I am sure," Nogales said.

He led them to a chauffeured Cadillac limousine. The doorman had the car door opened. "Good morning, Countess and Señor Fuentes," he greeted them.

The limousine arrived at the Embassy promptly at 10 a.m. A U.S. Marine escorted the three of them to the office of Ambassador Withers.

A middle-aged woman with gray hair, a round face, dimpled chin and ruddy complexion met them at the door. She removed her black-rimmed glasses and flashed a warm welcoming smile at the countess, Fuentes and Nogales.

"Come right in, folks," she said in a broad southern English accent.

The ambassador rose from behind his desk. "Happy to see you all on American turf," he chuckled. "Miss Carling, hold all my calls, except from Washington. I do not wish to be disturbed."

"Yes, sir. I'll be at my desk if you need anything."

"Oh yes, would you folks like some iced tea or a soft drink?"

They demurred.

"Thank you, Enid," he said.

The door closed.

The countess and Tony sat in the two chairs facing the envoy.

Ernesto Nogales sat in a chair to the right of the desk, facing Tony and Sophia.

"Mr. Ambassador, I want to thank you for your cooperation," Sophia opened the conversation.

Franklin Withers leaned back in his chair, stared at Sophia and Tony, then laughed loudly, saying, "You two are devilishly good. Are you sure you're not thespians?"

Tony leaned forward, looking Withers straight in the eye. "I assume that's a compliment, sir."

"Indeed it is. That was as smooth a performance yesterday as I've ever seen, off or on stage. My compliments to both of you."

"Thank you," Sophia replied.

"General Smith - Beedle, as we used to call him when I served with him in the war, clued me on your mission here. So, I played my part."

"Our compliments to you, sir. You handled it with aplomb," Tony said.

"Well, it's necessary in my current profession. Let's get down to business. Ernesto here is a good friend. He's been very helpful to me."

"Thanks, Jonathan. I'll start by giving you the latest on Eva Peron. She had an operation six weeks ago. It was a hysterectomy. That's when the cancer rumors began. The Perons have denied the cancer, and Eva has been making some public appearances lately."

Withers said, "We may as well confer here on a first name basis, Tony and Sophia. Call me Franklin. Now, the object is to get you two acquainted with the Perons."

"Do you have any suggestions, Franklin?" Sophia inquired.

"Yes, I have a plan, but first I suggest we wait a couple of days to see whether the bait you threw at them in your remarks yesterday, which are widely quoted in the newspapers, radio and television today, will get a reaction from them. The lure is there, to complete the fishing analogy."

"She has expressed an affinity for the poor. Are there any special charities she favors?" Sophia asked.

"There is a student housing project right here in Buenos Aires, which occupies five or six blocks, and The Children's City. Those two are her favorites. She founded them. A visit to either of them, with a little press attention, might be in order."

"That sounds fine," Tony agreed.

"Well, simple enough," Ernesto chimed in. "Let's call Mendoza at Tourism. He should lead the visit and bask in the press limelight."

"Good idea, Ernesto. Use that phone over in the corner and see if he can arrange a tour for this afternoon. Try to get it on the evening news."

While the call was being made, Tony brought up the name of Nordheim.

"I've never seen him, but he was here all right. Very chummy with Peron. Promised to build some manufacturing plants in Argentina," Withers said.

"Have you been briefed on this alleged Nazi?" Sophia asked.

"Only to the extent that he is believed to have been a very important member of the Third Reich hierarchy. I have been advised that he is shipping armaments to North Korea and Arab countries antithetical to Israel."

"Our intelligence service is anxious to determine his true relationship to the Perons," Tony said.

"Have you any suggestions to add impetus to our efforts in arranging a tete-à-tete with the Perons?" Withers posed.

"As a matter of fact, I would like it if the word could be conveyed to the right person, sort of a conduit to President Peron telling him that my father, former Ambassador Felipe Carrera, advised him to enter the war against Nazi Germany," Sophia declared.

"My, my, that is really important information. I didn't know that," Withers exclaimed. "Roberto Lopez is the perfect man to receive that advice. Your father, of course, sends his warmest personal regards to the Perons, isn't that so?"

"Yes, indeed."

"Say no more. That will be handled right this minute." He pressed the intercom button.

"Yes sir?"

"Enid, get Bob Lopez, please."

"Ambassador Withers, it is so nice to hear from you," Lopez said.

"Bob, how are you?"

"Just fine, sir. How may I serve you?"

"This is not diplomatic business. For that, I would call your foreign minister. This is in the way of a personal message to President Peron and the first lady Eva. The Countess de Cordoba is the daughter of Ambassador Felipe Carrera. She brings a message of best wishes, good health and dear friendship from him to the Perons and the people of Argentina."

"That is wonderful. I will convey that message to the President and the first lady promptly. I am so glad you called me."

"We must have a drink at the club."

"I'll look forward to that, Franklin."

Withers hung up, turned to Sophia and Tony and rubbed his hands together, exuding satisfaction. "He swallowed the bait. I bet there will be a message at your hotel in the next hour."

"So soon?" Sophia said.

"Yes, I know these people. Have faith."

"What if Peron doesn't bite?" Tony queried.

"I will then have a reception for you and invite them. They will not insult me by failing to accept."

"Get on your way, kiddies. Go visit her charities. We'll soon know how this plays out."

"You have a 3 p.m. at the student housing project and a 4:30 p.m. at Children's City," Nogales announced.

They drove back to the hotel, and Tony invited Ernesto to join them for lunch. "Escort the Countess to the dining room and I'll check the desk for messages."

A few minutes later, Tony joined Sophia and Ernesto and, with a big grin on his face, smugly placed a message slip on the table.

She lifted the paper and without looking at the message, blurted, "Bingo!" Eyes closed, she pushed the message slip to Nogales. "*To Countess de Carrera and Señor Anthony Fuentes. Please call Señor Roberto Lopez, special aide to President Peron,*" Ernesto jubilantly read aloud.

They ordered drinks and toasted each other in triumph. After a pleasant leisurely lunch, they adjourned to the suite. Sophia retired to check her makeup, while Tony placed a call to the Presidential Palace.

"Señor Lopez, I am returning your call to the countess and me."

"Thank you, sir. I have the honor, on behalf of President Peron and Eva Peron, to invite you for cocktails at 5 p.m. tomorrow at the palace. I trust your schedule will permit."

"Indeed, it will. Convey our best wishes to His Excellency and his charming wife. My best to you, sir."

Tony then called Ambassador Withers. "Franklin, I am glad I didn't bet you."

The ambassador guffawed, "It's nice to be right. I've been studying people most of my life. I know, I've been invited to join you there. I'll pick you up at 4:30. See you then."

Nogales drove the couple to their tour of the student housing project and the Children's City. The media were on hand for both visits, and the TV and still cameras gave the events ample coverage. The countess addressed the microphones and graciously complimented Eva Peron for her charitable endeavors.

On the way back to the hotel, Sophia asked Tony to rent a convertible for the next day. "Tony, darling, let's drive to the Mar del Plata. We'll put the top down, get some sun, have lunch at the beach and maybe a swim."

"Great idea. Ernesto, do you think we can get a convertible?"

"No problem, just ask the concierge when we get to the hotel."

The next morning, they left the hotel at 9 a.m., and a brand-new Mercedes Benz convertible awaited them.

It was a glorious day of sunshine, blue skies and a light breeze. There was a hint of romance in the car as Tony steered south. Sophia's hair was caressed by the wind, as was Tony's. "This is fabulous," he declared, squeezing her left hand on the seat between them. She returned the gesture.

The handsome couple might well have been on their honeymoon, romping on the broad beach, taunting the waves and chortling like teenagers. Sophia was tumbled by a wave into Tony's arms, so she looked at him, laughed and suddenly pressed her lips on his in a lingering sustained kiss. Later, not a word was spoken as they walked up the beach. He wrapped a towel around her shoulders. She squeezed his hand. Both sat back and stared at the sparkling Atlantic Ocean.

"Tony, I..."

"Sophia," he interrupted her, "I understand. We're on a mission. But, you should know that I will want to talk about what's happening between us when we return to the States."

"Yes sir, Mr. Fuentes," she mimicked, then smiled, her beautiful eyes sparkling in the sun.

Shortly, they headed back to the hotel to prepare for their rendezvous with the Perons, and at 4:20 p.m. they were at the hotel's entrance. They were a striking couple. Both had acquired a glow bestowed by a beneficent sun. Sophia wore a black silk dress, a custom creation, simple and understated, with a pearl necklace. Tony was dressed in a navy blue serge suit and a crimson tie, with a pocket handkerchief to match.

At 4:30, a chauffeured Cadillac limousine, displaying American flags on the fenders, arrived. Franklin Withers and his wife were in the back seat. The ambassador stepped out of the car and helped Sophia to sit next to his wife, whom he introduced. Tony sat on the jump seat. Withers joined the chauffeur in the front.

The chitchat was mundane and discreet. Obviously the chauffeur was an Argentine. They discussed the weather, the beach and the beauty of the Argentine landscape.

At the palace, a resplendently uniformed soldier opened the door of the limousine, and an officer stiffly saluted the arrivals. He then ushered the four into the palace and showed them into the striking quarters of the President and his wife.

Peron, in a white uniform, ribbon slanted across his chest, bowed and effusively greeted the party. Eva, in a light blue dress, jeweled necklace and a large red rose pinned to her dress, shook Tony's hand while Peron held Sophia's hand.

Caviar canapés and champagne were served by two liveried butlers.

"How is your wonderful father, Countess?" Peron unctuously inquired.

"Quite well, Your Excellency. He asked me to convey his most sincere best wishes and compliments to you and your charming first lady."

"How very nice. You must return our high regard for him and our deep appreciation for his counsel and advice in parlous times."

"Thank you, sir. He will appreciate your kind words."

"Countess, what brings you to our country?" Eva Peron pointedly asked.

"My father has spoken very highly of your country. He admires you and your husband for your efforts on behalf of the poor and the working class, Madame Presidente. It was at my father's behest that we planned this visit." She looked straight into the eyes of the first lady, taking note of the dullness of her eyes. And behind the apparent heavy application of rouge, she observed a sallowness of her skin.

"Why do you call me Madame Presidente?" Eva queried with a smile and a momentary sparkle in her eyes.

"No offense, Your Excellency, I meant that as a compliment. I visited your Children's City and the Student Housing site, where the people sing your praises, and I was very impressed with your accomplishments. I wish to commend you."

"Dear, dear Countess, I appreciate your comments. I can see that we could become very good friends. I would very much like to have you join me for lunch tomorrow for some women's talk," Eva pleasantly suggested.

"I would be delighted," Sophia responded.

"Anthony, you see how it is. We men are women's possessions," the President sighed.

Tony laughed, with the President and the ambassador joining in the hilarity.

"I would warrant Your Excellency's statement has a great deal of merit," the ambassador agreed.

"Pooh-pooh, Franklin," Eva countered. "There are times when the reverse of that is true. In truth, each of us possesses the other. The greatness of a man in large part depends on the woman behind him, and in turn the woman reaches her pinnacle due to the man supporting her," Eva stated.

"Hear, hear," Tony said. "Señora Peron, that is an excellent analysis."

"Indeed, that's perfect," Withers said.

"That is my Eva," Peron proudly remarked.

The foundation had been laid, and Eva's demeanor was buoyant. Her eyes were brighter. She beckoned the countess to join her on the couch. The champagne flowed.

"Countess, you know we have a large city called Cordoba. Is it possible that it was named for one of your ancestors?" Peron asked.

"I've wondered about that. We have a Cordoba in Spain, too, so I would like to believe that."

"If we say it is so, it will be so," Eva giddily declared, raising her glass in a toast. She laughed. The others joined in.

"By the way, Your Excellency, we read in the Washington Post that the richest man in the world, Frederick Nordheim, is going to build some manufacturing plants here. How is that working out?"

"Yes, that is so. We are primarily a farming and cattle-raising country, but he believes we can industrialize our nation and help expand our economy. He is talking about investing billions here. We could manufacture autos, computers, radios, television sets, trucks, tanks, household appliances and all sorts of consumer goods," Peron proudly asserted.

"He sounds like a visionary," Sophia said.

"He is a very unusual man," Eva declared. "He could bring a lot of employment to our people. I believe he will follow through. He bought a ranch in Mar del Plata. He will raise cattle, as well. A team of engineers have been hired by him to explore sites for the plants."

Tony and Sophia glanced at each other, and in a moment of extra-sensory perception, decided to drop the subject. Sophia would follow through with Eva at lunch the next day.

They raised their glasses in a parting toast, and Eva walked to the door with Sophia. "That is a beautiful gown, Countess. Where did you get it?"

"This is an original from Maison Jeannette in New York City. It was designed by Madame Jeannette herself," Sophia said.

"Yes, they have quite a reputation," Eva said. "I look forward to our lunch at one o'clock, Sophia."

"As I do, Eva."

At the door, Eva Peron whispered to the countess, "Come to my house on Calle Teodora Garcia. I'll have my chauffeur pick you up at 12:45."

✩ ✩ ✩ ✩

Tuesday, March 25, 1952 - 9 a.m. - Paris

Barton Milburn and Jacques Laurent met at the Plaza Athenee Hotel.

"Are you sure, Jacques, that Nordheim had mentioned the name of Martin?"

"I have the taped conversations here in my bag. You can hear it for yourself, Colonel."

"My God, is it possible that Martin is Martin Bormann?"

The question was rhetorical and required no answer. Both men remained silent, pondering the enigma.

"Come, Jacques, a meeting with the American ambassador has been arranged by General Smith. Bring the wiretap tapes and the film you shot in Monte Carlo. We'll have it developed at the Embassy," Milburn indicated. "And you are coming with me to Tel Aviv."

"Thank you, Colonel. May I bring up something personal?"

"Of course, anything."

"I checked with the French refugee office when I first came to Paris, and they say there is a Professor Laurent teaching French at the University of Leipzig in East Germany. They don't know if it is a male or female, but it could be my sister Joyce. Could you help me, or maybe the Israelis might?"

"Jacques, we will do everything possible. Let's hope it is your sister. If it is, our work begins to get her out."

"Colonel, I pray it is she."

"Amen."

The colonel and Jacques were about to leave when the strident ringing of the telephones halted their exit.

Milburn picked up and answered, "Yes?"

"Colonel, this is Felix Gaumont. Is Jacques with you?"

"Oh, yes, Captain. And I will take this opportunity to thank you for your very productive cooperation. Jacques sings your praises."

"*Mon plaisir*, Colonel. The cause is worthy."

"Here's Jacques."

"Felix, are you here in Paris?"

In French, he said, "Yes. I have some news about the motorcyclist. They traced the motorcycle to a Sergeant Gaston Morizet of the Nice traffic control."

"*Mon Dieu*, don't tell me he is on Nordheim's payroll."

Bart Milburn, who had been staring out of the window at the traffic on the Avenue Montaigne, oblivious to French conversation, turned and stood over Jacques.

"No, no, Jacques, the sergeant was ordered to carry the message to Nordheim at the Flying Eagle," Gaumont replied.

"Who gave the order, and what was the message?"

"Well, they grilled the sergeant all night. He's clean. Says he was carrying out orders. The chief of detectives in Nice, Rene Poulier, gave the order to tell Nordheim that Interpol and the French coast guard were going to seize the yacht. The matter is being turned over to the Department of Justice."

"Hold on for a minute, Felix, I want to tell the colonel what you have told me."

Jacques relayed the development to Bart Milburn.

"Damn it, this is a complicating factor. France is in the act. Damn, damn, damn!" Bart exploded. "Let me talk to Gaumont." He took the phone and asked, "Captain, has this matter been referred to the Department of Justice?"

"As we speak, Colonel. They transferred Poulier to my office in Paris this morning. Colonel Paul Marchaud and Major Maurice Duval are handling the investigation. I may be questioned about my role in the Nordheim affair. Captain Letellier, who wrote the report, is my friend. He called me, and that is why I have called Jacques to alert you."

"Who else is there?"

"Letellier. He spoke with Maurice Duval and briefed him on your investigation of Nordheim. The DGSE are expecting your visit here."

"Excellent. Sit tight for a couple of hours. Jacques and I have one stop to make and then we'll meet you. Felix, thank you for calling this development to our attention. The American government will have to brief your government on this matter. Rest assured that we will express our gratitude to your government for your assistance and that of Claude Colbert, Pierre Dernier and Guy Bernarde."

"*Merci, mon Colonel.*"

Jacques took the phone. "I hope I have not complicated your life, Felix."

"Not to worry, Jacques. I am proud to have participated. If we nail this Nazi bastard, that will be my reward. *Bon jour.*"

Bart and Jacques hastened to the American Embassy, where a uniformed, beribboned Marine smartly ushered them into the office of Ambassador Clark Courtney.

The stately, white-haired envoy greeted them warmly. "Colonel Milburn and Mr. Laurent, how may I help you? I received a call from General Walter Smith of the CIA, an old and dear friend, asking me to extend every courtesy to you. I can do naught for the Beedle than comply."

"Our mission is highly confidential."

"I won't pry."

"Mr. Ambassador, we have been recruited to do a certain top-secret investigation. Now, based on a report I just received, I'll have to talk with the White House for permission to brief you."

"Why would that be necessary?"

"The French government will be involving itself inadvertently in our mission. Sorry to be so cryptic at this point."

"How can I help you, Colonel?"

"A few things, sir. If you can spare an office with a safe phone, that would help. We also need to develop some critical photos. And further to that, is there a machine here on which I can play some wire tapped tapes?"

None of the items mentioned by Milburn brought a reaction from the diplomat, who simply pressed a button and said, "Tom, come in, please."

A young aide, tall and neatly dressed in a Savile Row pin-striped blue suit, entered.

"Tom, this is Colonel Milburn and Mr. Laurent. Take them to Conference Room 2. They are to have full and undisturbed use of those quarters. Take Mr. Laurent to the film lab and tell Isaiah to develop some pictures for him. Further, have a tape machine placed on the conference table there."

"Your courtesy is deeply appreciated, sir," Bart said.

On the way out, Bart instructed Jacques to stay with the developing of the films and to join him in the conference room when completed.

The White House operator put Milburn right through to John Steelman. "Morning, Bart. What's up?"

"The proverbial is about to hit the fan, John."

"How so?"

He related the development in Monte Carlo and Nice, then threw the bombshell at Steelman. "There is every indication that Nordheim might be the beast of Berchtesgaden. The facts are not empirical, but the wiretaps indicate him talking about Martin, which leads me to Bormann."

"Martin Bormann? That defies all intelligence to date," Steelman said. "Have you talked with Smith or Dulles?"

"Hell no, I'm working for the President."

"Well, in that case, my feisty friend, you had better talk with him. Hold on..."

"Colonel, what havoc have you wrought?" President Truman bantered.

"Sorry, sir, but to coin a word, I'm not in the *wroughting* business," Bart testily riposted.

"Touchy, touchy. All right, Barton, let's have it."

"I apologize, sir, but we're sitting on a powder keg, and my nerves are slightly raw."

"Explain."

Bart, in a ten-minute narration, compendiously outlined the Monte Carlo, San Remo and Nice developments.

Truman ordered Steelman to pick up an extension phone.

"John, are you fully briefed on the colonel's report?"

"In short strokes, sir."

"Let's not jump to conclusions, gentlemen, before we have all the facts. Of immediate concern is the French development. I want Acheson, General Smith and Dulles here within the hour. If I have to deal with that egotistical sourpuss, de Gaulle, I want to be fully prepared. John, get on it now."

"Yes, sir."

"Colonel, anything you want to add?"

"Mr. President, I appreciate your quick action. There is another fact that requires attention."

"What's that?"

"A leak to the French press of their Department of Justice inquiry into Nordheim's connection with the Nice chief of detectives would put the whole Operation Lucifer in jeopardy."

"Dammit, you're right, Colonel. I'll put in a call to Churchill and we'll deal with DeGaulle."

"One more item, Mr. President. Jacques and I are heading over to the Sûreté, where they're investigating the Poulier affair. Sir, we must protect Captain Gaumont, Lieutenant Colbert and Customs Officer Pierre Dernier with the French authorities. They were invaluable."

"Noted. We'll be back to you, Colonel," Truman vowed, then hung up.

☆ ☆ ☆ ☆

Sûreté Headquarters, Paris

In the lobby of the Sûreté, Felix Gaumont greeted Bart and Jacques. They entered the elevator and pushed the fourth-floor button. As the elevator door opened, Maurice Duval was waiting for the trio. "Monsieur Gaumont, so nice of you to bring friends," he jested. "Colonel Milburn, Mr. Laurent, my pleasure to meet you," he said, shaking both hands.

"The pleasure is ours," Bart said, returning the gesture. Jacques nodded his head.

"Right this way," Duval directed, and led off down the hallway to an interrogation room. Approaching them in the hall was a tall man, military in stature. His collar was open, his tie askew, and he was mopping his brow. Major Duval addressed him. "Colonel Paul Marchaud, this is Colonel Barton Milburn. You know Captain Gaumont, and this is Jacques Laurent of the CIA. Colonel Milburn is in charge of the American investigation. By the way, we're meeting here rather than the Direction Generale Services L'Exterieur building because this is a police matter and we want to contain it."

"Welcome to the party, gentlemen," Marchaud graciously greeted them. "He's tough and denies everything. Two of my best men are in there with Chief Poulier. Come in and try your hand."

Seated in the center of a long oak table, Chief Rene Poulier looked at the new players in the game as they entered the room. He was stocky, 5 feet 10 inches in height, broad-shouldered and arrogant in demeanor. He rattled off in French, "What is going on here, Colonel? Who are these men?"

Marchaud introduced Colonel Milburn and Jack Laurent. Captain Letellier and Captain Gaumont avowed previous acquaintanceship with Chief Poulier.

Darkness cast an eerie ambiance over the room. Gooseneck lamps at the center of the table produced the only light. Drawn shades blocked out the daylight.

Jacques stood menacingly over the seated suspect. He stared piercingly at Poulier. The others in the room were silent, entranced with the ominous stance assumed by Jacques.

The chief squirmed nervously in his chair. He reached for a cigarette, his hand trembling as he placed a Gaulois between his dry lips. Jacques quickly brought his old army lighter to the dangling cigarette and struck the flint, lighting up Poulier's pale face as a spectral visage.

Bart approached Jacques and asked, "What is it?"

"Put the lights on," Jacques demanded.

Major Duval flicked the incandescent overhead lights on, bathing the room in a luminous glow.

"Stand up, you scumbag! How did this army deserter get to be chief of detectives? His name is not Poulier. He is Henri Steiner, a former sergeant in the French army. When General de Gaulle and the American Army freed Paris, this bum was a lieutenant in the Vichy police attached to Marshal Petain's office. I was there that day in August 1944. We were going to arrest him when he disappeared with the rest of the Nazi bastards who fled!" Jacques shouted, ending his *dénouement* with a forceful slap across Poulier's left cheek.

The dramatic denunciation of the chief startled the gathering; the room was frozen in silence.

The suspect buried his face in his arms resting on the table.

Bart, Duval and Marchaud huddled in deep whispered conversation. Letellier and Gaumont joined Laurent in a conference.

"This rotten rat fled the French army at Dunkirk and hooked up with the Nazis not too far away!" Gaumont shouted. "I tracked him, that dirty dog."

☆ ☆ ☆ ☆

The same day - 12:45 p.m. - Buenos Aires

A uniformed colonel was driving a black Mercedes Benz limousine. Countess de Cordoba, dressed in a brass-buttoned, double-breasted blue jacket, white silk blouse and white shoes, entered through the door of the car, held by the saluting army officer.

En route to Eva Peron's house on Calle Teodora Garcia, she chatted in Spanish with the colonel. She stressed the beauty of Argentina and praised Eva and President Peron. He responded with great enthusiasm.

They turned into the driveway of a ranch-style house with gates at both ends. Trimmed bushes surrounded a dazzling garden display of flowers. Evita was at the front door. She wore a light blue suit, a pink blouse and high-shined black patent-leather pumps.

"Welcome, Countess. *Mi casa, su casa.* You look charming. You are indeed a very beautiful woman."

"Dear Evita, I must return the compliment. You are *outstanding*."

Evita led her to the living room, which was, by contrast, more tastefully decorated and furnished than the quarters at the palace.

"Champagne, martini, wine, scotch or whatever, Sophia?"

"What's your preference, Eva?"

"How about a nice cold dry vodka martini?"

"That suits me fine."

A liveried butler prepared the drinks, then the ladies toasted each other. Sophia sipped hers cautiously. Eva gulped down her first one, and was on her third while Sophia nursed her first.

A bottle of Argentine wine was opened and poured generously.

A repast of *paté de foie gras* with toast points, cold cucumber soup, and green salad, followed by a charcoal-broiled pepper steak, was served. Eva consumed copious amounts of wine as Sophia gently sipped hers. Their conversation ranged from clothes to the cinema to politics. By now Eva was in her cups, and she became maudlin and teary-eyed. "You are so young and beautiful. You have a big life ahead of you. My life is almost over."

"Why do you say that? You, too, are very beautiful, and you're also very young."

"I don't think God has planned a long life for me. Yet there is much I want to do for our poor people. I was once poor, and I know what my people need. But, besides money, I need time to help the humble."

"What's wrong, dear Eva?"

"Two things. I am a sick woman, and I don't have the time to get the money that Nazi bastard stole from me."

Eva sipped an *espresso* and alternated with sips of Napoleon brandy. At this point in time she was feeling no pain, and became quite voluble and confidential. "There was over one hundred and twenty million dollars, of which I was to get half for my foundation. It was right here in Buenos Aires. That money was taken out of here against my will. They sneaked it out. It was gold, gold, gold, and that rotten bastard shipped it to Barcelona, Spain. Oh, I could kill him!"

Eva wept convulsively. Sophia rose from her chair and put her arms around her.

"Come, sit on the couch here with me. Bring your brandy with you."

Eva compliantly followed her to the couch and fell into Sophia's arms, sobbing loudly. The butler appeared, and Sophia waved him away.

"Who is this beast that cheated you?" Sophia gently asked.

"He is a rotten bastard. A second-hand *caudillo*."

"Who is he? Maybe I can help you?"

"Can you? Please help me. My husband doesn't want to upset those Nazi bastards. And I was good to them when they needed me, but now they've double-crossed me."

She filled her glass with brandy and feverishly downed it. "Sophia, you are the first person I have talked to about this problem. My husband, *El Presidente*, is too cautious. He doesn't want to shake up the Nazis. There are a lot of them in this country..." She stopped, blew her nose loudly and sobbed.

Sophia poured another jigger of brandy and handed it to her. The countess lit a cigarette and waited. Eva reached over, took the cigarette from the

Countess and drew long puffs. Waving the cigarette clasped between two fingers, she continued her diatribe. "We never bothered the Jews in this country, but Juan Domingo Peron let ninety thousand Nazis escape into Argentina. I was nice to them. Now this German pig has double-crossed me. How do you say, he bit the hand that feeds him. *My* hand. Oh, God, why am I being punished?"

Sophia hung on every word. With great restraint she gently prodded Eva to continue. "Eva, obviously this man has done you a great injustice. Where is he now?"

"He is here in Mar del Plata."

"Why don't you have him arrested?"

"I am ashamed to tell you, my husband is afraid of those Nazi bastards. He is also afraid to let the world know that we have given them haven here."

"Tell me, how did this one hundred twenty million in gold come here?"

Eva got to her feet, then fell back on the couch. "I trust you, Countess, so I'll tell you a very interesting story. Two months after the war ended in 1945, two Nazi submarines came to the coast off Mar del Plata and surrendered to the Argentinian government."

The butler appeared with a pot of hot coffee. He poured the steaming coffee and placed the cup before Eva. Sophia nodded approval, urging Eva to partake. "You think I am drunk, Sophia? Well, I am not," she declared as she sipped the hot brew.

"No, but the coffee is good for you, Eva."

"I will prove to you that the liquor doesn't affect me. I even remember the name of the captain of the first submarine. He was Lieutenant Commander Otto Vermouth. Our people gave him a nickname, Captain Vermouth Cinzano. They came on July 10, 1945. Other subs came eight days later. Martin Bormann appeared from nowhere to supervise the unloading on the beach of San Clemente del Tuyer near Mar del Plata. You see, my memory is pretty good."

"It certainly is," Sophia agreed coolly, although her heart was pounding at the startling disclosure. "What came off the boats?"

"I know exactly, because the gold, the currency and jewels were deposited in our names, Juan Peron and Eva Duarte. It was handled by Ludwig Freude, a Nazi undercover agent right here in Buenos Aires. He deposited almost 200 million marks, about 20 million U.S. dollars, 10 million Dutch florins, 25 million Swiss francs, 5 million British pounds, 55 million French francs and 100 million dollars in gold bars, diamonds and other jewelry. All of it was deposited in three banks: Strupp, Tornquist, and Aleman Transatlantico."

The revelation had a staggering effect on Sophia, who battled with her emotions to remain calm. She was trying to remember the names and the arithmetical substance of the loot. She wanted to go to the guest bathroom to write a list of the disclosures. She opted to stay, for fear of breaking the spell.

"When did you learn that the deposits were gone?"

"Two weeks ago. I checked the safety deposit boxes at the banks. They were empty. I had met with Bormann in Monte Carlo. We agreed there that half the money would go to my charities, the other half would go to Herr

Nordheim. I asked why. He told me it was none of my business. I just learned this morning that all the gold was put on Nordheim's new yacht in Barcelona. That's why I am so agitated today because the gold was unloaded in Genoa."

"Who is this Nordheim?"

"I don't know. He says he is a Jew, born in Sweden. He showed us tattoo numbers on his arm from a concentration camp. I have asked myself and my husband, how did a death-camp Jew get to be the richest man in the world? I am suspicious, because I received no sensible answers."

"Eva, is it possible that this man could be Adolf Hitler?"

Eva stared at Sophia. She no longer seemed to be inebriated. In fact, she suddenly became alert and startled by the question. "Nordheim has a hundred men at his ranch. Why, I don't know. Maybe ex-Nazis. That's all I know. If you think that the drinks made me ramble like this, you're mistaken. I have revealed all this to you, Sophia, for a reason. First, you must promise that I didn't tell you what I did. Then, I want to stop these bastards. You have high connections in the U.S. Make them go after these Nazi vermin. I do not have long to live. I have cancer of the uterus. I want that money for my *descamisados*, the humble shirtless ones. If I can't have that money, then I don't want them to have it. They and the Swiss stole it from those six million Jews they murdered."

"I will help you. Let me write down the facts."

"Emilio, bring us a pad and a pen," Eva shouted.

The butler appeared.

"Why are you standing there? Where is the pad and pen?" she angrily snapped.

"Señora, maybe you should retire. You had much too much to drink," Emilio said softly.

"How dare you. Do what I told you to do or get out!"

"*Si, si.*"

He returned with the pad and pen, shaking his head at Sophia.

The countess quickly scribbled what she remembered. She asked Eva to repeat the names of the banks and the persons she had mentioned. She added the name of Ernst Kaltenbrunner, the Third Reich's chief of the secret police, who had given instructions to the truck driver and the strange men unloading the large trunks. The words on the trunk, she added, were *Geheime Reichssache* (State Secret).

Sophia tore two pages of notes off the pad. Deliberately folding the sheets, she stuffed them into her ample purse.

Eva stood up and faced Sophia.

"Don't embarrass me or my husband. You must reach someone high up in America. We will not see each other again. You and your husband must take the first flight out tonight or in the early morning. You are no longer safe here," she emphatically declared. She pointed in the direction of the butler and held her fingers to her lips.

A strong hug for Sophia, and Eva pushed her to the door. The limousine was there.

At the hotel, Sophia checked with the concierge. A Pan American flight to Caracas, Venezuela, was scheduled to depart at 6 p.m., with a connecting flight to Miami. She ordered two first-class seats. Tony was in the suite. She took him to the outside balcony and quickly detailed the unexpected jackpot of disclosures and the warning to leave immediately. She began packing. Tony called Ambassador Courtney.

"Sir, we would like to come by for an urgent meeting with you."

"Come ahead."

"We'll be there in twenty minutes."

At the American Embassy, Sophia sketched her incredible luncheon with Eva Peron.

"I must reach Colonel Milburn on a safe telephone."

"I can't vouch for the safety on our phones," Courtney replied. "You would do better on a public phone."

"May I start the trace from here?"

"By all means. Use this phone."

She reached Lloyd Sedgwick at CIA headquarters in Langley, Virginia. Speaking in telegraphic terms, she declared, "Lloyd, leaving for airport now. Need Bart, re: Lucy. Urgent. Will call public booth."

"Will trace."

"I will see you off at the airport," the ambassador announced. He ordered two Marines to come along with their sidearms.

"Let me have your passports," Courtney requested.

Tony handed the two passports to the Ambassador, seated behind his desk. He called for Tom, his aide.

"Tom, take these two diplomatic jackets and seal them over each of these passports. I will affix them with our seal."

"Yes, sir." He was back in a minute.

Satisfied, Courtney rose and forcefully declared, "There will be no hanky-panky at the airport. If Eva's butler has alerted some bad boys, we'll be ready for them. Come along now."

He handed the official passports to Tony.

The ambassador, Tony and Sophia were flanked by the two U.S. Marines. Two formidable men in civilian clothes followed the party to the Pan American check-in counter.

"We will have to search your baggage," one of the men stated in guttural English.

"On what grounds?" the ambassador demanded.

"We have reason to believe that there are illegal drugs in those bags," the second man barked.

"Who are you people?" Courtney snapped.

"We are with the Interpol Drug Enforcement."

"Let me see your credentials."

"Who are you?"

"I am the American ambassador to Argentina. Now, who the hell are you?"

A line was backing up behind Tony and Sophia.

"You people will have to get out of line," the ticket agent at the check-in counter shouted.

"No, they will not," Courtney yelled back. "Get your airport police here right away."

The two Marines, hands on their holsters, stood guard alongside the ambassador.

A crowd gathered around the line of passengers attempting to check in for the flight to Caracas. Two other civilians joined the first two men and they too declared themselves to be drug agents with Interpol. Their guttural German accents were unmistakable, whereas the other two were Latins.

"*Que pasa?*" one asked.

"Speak English; I am the American Ambassador," Courtney declared, flashing his I.D. "Are you with the Argentine police? If so, let me see your credentials."

Both displayed their badges and identity cards with photos. They were Lieutenant Jorge Diaz and Sergeant Antonio Ramos of the Airport Police.

"Who are these two clowns who are harassing us? These people are travelling with diplomatic passports," Courtney declared in perfect Spanish.

"Let us see their credentials," Sophia intervened in her Castilian accent. "I am the Countess de Cordoba and I demand to know what is the purpose of this obviously contrived annoyance."

The two alleged Interpol agents started to back away from the line. The Marines, at a nod from Courtney, stopped them. They patted the two men down and removed two German Lugers.

"Arrest these men," Courtney demanded. "Tony, check in. Countess, you should make your call now."

The Luger pistols were handed to Lieutenant Diaz. He displayed his handgun and ordered the two men handcuffed.

In a public booth, Sophia reached Lloyd Sedgwick.

"Sophia, we'll put you through to the French Embassy on a scrambler. Hold on."

"Colonel, it's jackpot time. Take notes."

"Let's have it."

She detailed the bizarre tableau at Eva Peron's house and the scene at the airport.

"That certainly is an excellent piece of work, Sophia. Get on that plane now. I will call 1600 with a short outline of your report. I'll arrange to have security for you and Tony when you arrive in Miami. Ask Ambassador Courtney to call our Embassy in Caracas to arrange police protection when you change planes there. Report to General Smith as soon as you reach Washington. Good luck," Bart said.

The countess and Tony Fuentes were escorted by the two Marines to the Pan Am plane on the tarmac. Two uniformed police, assigned by Lieutenant Diaz, joined them. The Marines and police stayed until the plane taxied for takeoff, then watched as Pan Am Flight 100 became airborne.

CHAPTER TEN

Wednesday, March 26, 1952 - 4 a.m. - Paris

Fog shrouded the offices of the Sûreté. The government buildings on the Quai d'Orsay were dark, with the exception of the fourth-floor lights.

An occasional mournful foghorn wailed from ships and barges plying their way on the Seine, just behind the official structure. Seven weary men were seated around the oak conference table, partaking of food in an assortment of cardboard containers. A lone forlorn figure sat in a darkened corner of an adjoining room, guarded by two uniformed and armed gendarmes. The chief of Nice detectives, Rene Poulier, a.k.a. Henri Steiner, was a broken, exhausted man. He had rendered a complete confession of his duplicitous role as a respected police officer and a paid subservience to the iniquitous Frederick Avram Nordheim. Colonel Milburn, Colonel Marchaud, Major Duval and Captain Gaumont formed a battering ram of interrogators. They took turns in loosening the tongue of the alleged traitor.

Minute by minute, hour by hour, the questions flew in the face of a recalcitrant corrupted police officer. The second team, Captain Letellier and Jacques Laurent, used less finesse and more muscle in eliciting information from the equivocal chief of detectives. Jacques asked Letellier to leave him alone with the former Henri Steiner for ten minutes. Shortly after midnight, Jacques stood over the crestfallen but stubborn chief. "Steiner, you haven't got a chance. If you open up, they will make a deal with you. Don't be a *schmuck*, take my advice."

"Take the advice of a Jew bastard like you?"

Jacques pulled the husky, broad-shouldered man out of his chair and delivered a violent blow to the pit of his stomach. Punch after punch pummeled both sides of the stricken chief, who sank to his knees gasping for air.

Laurent avoided his face and finally kneed him in the chest, toppling him to his back, supine and in a state of semi-consciousness. Jacques poured a glass of water over the sallow face of the beaten man.

"Get up, swine! Get up or I'll kick the hell out of you. So, you are nothing more than an anti-Semitic Nazi piece of shit? Either you talk or I'll cripple you for life!" Jacques vehemently rasped.

Captain Letellier entered the room. "So, Chief, are you still denying the Nordheim connection?" he asked.

"Get this animal away from me. He has been using me as a punching bag. I think he broke my ribs."

"Captain, you don't think I would hurt a nice traitor like Henri Schteiner," Jacques added, with a Germanic lilt to the captain's true name.

"I don't believe you, Chief."

"Let me throw him out the window into the Seine."

"Keep him away from me," the chief begged.

"Talk, you bum, or else we'll both work you over some more," Letellier shouted.

"I'll talk to the American colonel, not you two."

Jacques walked into the adjoining room, and said, "Colonel Milburn, I think the dish in there is ready to be served."

Marchaud, Duval and Gaumont followed Bart. Letellier exited, saying, "He's all yours."

The beleaguered chief bellowed, "That Jew broke my ribs."

"I doubt that," Bart roared back.

"Are you ready to tell us the truth?" Colonel Marchaud demanded.

"If I cooperate, what will you do for me? I want to go to America or Argentina with my family."

"This arrogant asshole wants a deal," Bart said. "What has he to offer?"

"Plenty," the cornered miscreant cried out.

"Let's see what you tell us," Bart said. "It's up to Colonel Marchaud to make deals."

The next four hours brought forth a torrent of charges involving members of the National Assembly and other police officials in Paris, Marseilles and Nice. A few minutes before 4 a.m. the interrogation halted, and two police officers were assigned to guard the exhausted detainee.

The probers adjourned for nourishment, which was obtained by a policeman from a fast-food diner. They also offered some edibles to the defrocked chief of detectives. He declined.

Marchaud asked Bart and Jacques to meet with him at the Boulevard Mortier headquarters of the Direction Generale Services L'Exterieur - the French counterpart to the American CIA - to coordinate their final reports of what had developed that night. Each agreed to seal their reports.

☆ ☆ ☆ ☆

Wednesday, March 26, 1952, the same day - 11 a.m. - The White House
Assembled in the huge Cabinet room were Secretary of State Dean Acheson, Attorney General James McGranery, CIA Director General Walter Smith, John Steelman, and Secretary of Defense Robert Lovett.

Smith delivered a detailed briefing of Countess de Cordoba's dramatic luncheon with Eva Peron.

"We knew about the German subs surrendering to Argentina in July of 1945. Sorry, we did not know of money and other loot being discharged in Buenos Aires. However, Eva Peron's reference to the gold being delivered to Nordheim's yacht in Barcelona has been validated, and the gold was unloaded in Genoa this past Monday, March 24th," Smith concluded.

"Now, there are a few more tidbits," Truman said. "Mr. Dulles, please tell us about the wiretaps on the yacht in Monte Carlo, the depositions of those two Swedish ladies, the photograph of Hitler's niece, etc."

Dulles summarized all the activities and highlighted the most critical areas of Colonel Milburn's projected penetration of Nordheim's identity and operations.

"Some very strange moves by Nordheim are planned. We had an agent of ours observe the unloading of the gold from the Flying Eagle in Portofino to the Genoa Banco Internationale. Winston General and its subsidiary, Eagle Shipping, caused the stock markets in the U.S., London and Paris to plummet on Monday and Tuesday. They bought billions in long-term U.S. Treasury bonds, causing the price to go up and the yield to decline."

"Why do you think he did that?" Truman queried.

"As a guess, Mr. President, we think Herr Nordheim figures he is being scrutinized. We shook him up, and he intends a period of hibernation," Smith ventured.

"Mr. President, with regard to the photograph of Hitler's niece, Prime Minister Churchill at his meeting yesterday with General de Gaulle identified the lady as having had a two-year incestuous affair with Adolf," Dulles observed. "Our files also carried that piece of intelligence. That picture was found in Nordheim's drawer in his suite aboard the Flying Eagle. Jacques Laurent, head of our Nazi desk, is one of our best agents. He photographed the picture in a silver frame, as well as the entire yacht. He also bugged the entire boat."

"Why in the world would Frederick Nordheim have a framed picture of Adolf Hitler's niece?" Secretary Lovett posed the rhetorical question.

A momentary silence ensued. The men exchanged looks.

"Dear God. The possibility staggers all comprehension. If he is who I'm thinking he is, how the hell has he eluded detection over the last seven years?" Secretary of State Acheson wondered.

"More to the point, where did his vast wealth of forty billion dollars come from?" Truman said. "Joe Stalin will be chewing his cud if we capture this bastard."

"Now, here is a spicy nugget," General Smith said. "Colonel Milburn advised us that they broke the Nice captain of detectives. He spilled his guts and named members of the National Assembly, government officials and other French police as being on Eagle Shipping payrolls. Their contact was Darren Mayfield, an ex-FBI agent and Nordheim's point man, close to Mafia's Charlie 'Lucky' Luciano. Thanks to you, Mr. President, and Prime Minister Churchill, General de Gaulle has consented to treat this as an intelligence matter and will keep it out of their Department of Justice's hands until we agree."

"Where do we go from here?" said Lovett. "Despite that cautious protest from the Soviets about two Eagle ships allegedly sinking off the coast of North Korea, Nordheim's people have been silent. But that had to shake Nordheim up. Maybe that is another factor causing him to pull in his horns."

"At this point, gentlemen, the time has come for intensified action in what has been euphemistically termed Operation Lucifer," Truman asserted. "Not only do I want Mr. Nordheim captured, but I want to freeze his funds here. I will urge our English and French partners to do likewise. Further, we must investigate the Swiss banks. They have harbored all the loot that the Nazis stole from the six million slaughtered Jews. The Swiss banks' slimy cooperation with the Nazis is scandalous. They control the Swiss government, which has been a secret ally of Hitler's. This is where you come in, Mr. Lovett,"

"Why me, sir?"

"I cannot, at this stage of the game, go to Congress for the funds. So, it holds that your Department of Defense will bear the burden for what could be the greatest manhunt in history."

"Sir, Defense is on a tight budget now. The Korean War is draining us."

"Bob, you'll find a way."

"Under what powers will you conduct this manhunt?" Acheson asked.

"We haven't yet signed our peace contract with West Germany," said Truman. "That is scheduled for May 26 this year. As commander in chief, it is my duty to continue, under the Act of War, the pursuit of the enemy. If we do not succeed by that time, I'll sign an executive order."

"I guess you do have the powers to do that," Acheson conceded.

"This hunt is to be an all-out effort. If Nordheim is who we suspect him to be, then I want this most evil person in the history of the civilized world to be brought to justice. I don't want that other degenerate tyrant, Joe Stalin, to get his hands on this slimeball."

He continued, "General Smith, I am asking the CIA to draw up a plan to be submitted to the Cabinet next Wednesday. Colonel Milburn should have completed his meetings with Prime Minister Ben-Gurion and the Mossad by that time. I want him to brief you and then to participate in your planning session. I want the full participation of the Pentagon and every other agency of government. Now, as to the State Department, I want every ambassador we have the world over to keep their eyes open discreetly for a visit by Nordheim and his minions. No leaks."

"How about the UN in this matter?" Acheson inquired.

"Hell no!" Truman snapped.

"Mr. President, while the full-court press is on for Nordheim, shouldn't we pursue Martin Bormann?" Dulles asked.

"Absolutely. I want every verminous Nazi we can lay our hands on."

"What about lifting him out of Argentina?"

"If you can find him, grab him."

"What about Peron? He might raise hell?"

"To hell with Peron. We can make life tough for him. I'll brook no interference from that petty Nazi-loving dictator."

"Even war?" Acheson queried.

"He'd be crazy to even think about it. They have about 90,000 Nazis there. War would be a great way to capture all of them. Don't tempt me, Dean. I haven't lost my marbles yet."

"Mr. President, would you mind a suggestion?" Lovett asked.

"That's what you're here for."

"A meeting might be in order between Central Intelligence and our intelligence units in the Army, Navy and Air Force in an effort to coordinate our activities."

"Excellent. Arrange that with General Smith and include Colonel Milburn, who is heading up Operation Lucifer."

☆ ☆ ☆ ☆

Thursday, March 27, 1952 - 3 p.m. - U.S. Embassy, Paris

Colonel Milburn and Jacques Laurent were in conference with U.S. Ambassador Clark Courtney, as Bart summarized the unmasking of Chief of Detectives Rene Poulier, a.k.a. Henri Steiner.

"Quite a kettle of polluted fish we have here," Courtney observed. "What in the world of common sense will de Gaulle do with this scandal?"

"Sir, at the behest of President Truman and Prime Minister Churchill, the general has agreed to keep it out of the hands of their Department of Justice. The DSGE will now join the CIA and MI6 in maintaining it as a top security matter. Colonel Paul Marchaud of French Intelligence and Captain of Detectives Felix Gaumont will be in charge of the domestic side of this conundrum. They will bond with us on the Nordheim issue. Poulier, or rather, Steiner, has been put on ice in a safe house on the left bank, just outside of Montmartre."

"Colonel, I appreciate your detailed report. I assure you that it will be held in the strictest of confidence."

"I have a request, sir."

"Shoot."

"I wish to borrow your number two conference room again. Also, we need several copies of the photos developed here the other day."

"Granted. I'll have Tom take them back to Isaiah."

"I need three sets, which I'll mark, one set to the President and one to General Smith at the CIA. Would you please pouch them to the White House and Langley?" Bart requested.

"I'll have my secretary address stickers for the large envelopes. If you wish to enclose notes for each envelope, come back here. I'll insert them and dispatch them promptly."

"Much obliged, sir."

"I'm the one that's obliged, Colonel Milburn. My pulse has been accelerated by your account of this intrigue. I haven't felt this way since the war."

Bart and Jacques adjourned to the mini-conference room, where Bart placed a call to Langley and spoke to General Smith and Allen Dulles on their speakerphone. Once again, he outlined the proceedings of the past two days.

"Colonel Milburn, your plans are proving to be quite fruitful. The contessa hit the jackpot in Argentina. Your visit with Churchill, MI6, and later with de Gaulle has been a bonanza. Jacques Laurent, are you there?" Smith queried.

"I'll put him on the speaker."

"Jacques, I wish to congratulate you on your most successful efforts in Monte Carlo, San Remo and in Paris. The President is most pleased, Bart, with you and Jacques."

"Thank you, sir," Jacques gratefully replied.

"By the way, Jacques, I hope you get another shot at Mayfield."

"I would like the opportunity, sirs."

"Bart, what's your next move?" Dulles asked.

"Jacques and I are leaving Paris late tonight for Tel Aviv. Please advise Prime Minister Ben-Gurion that we will arrive in Tel Aviv on Air France Flight 200 Friday at 0900. Also, please have Lloyd Sedgwick join Phillip Berger to meet me at the Dan Hotel on Ha-Yarkon Street. I'll reserve rooms for them for a Saturday arrival."

"Where is Berger?" Dulles questioned.

"He should be standing by in Monte Carlo. If he moved, Sedgwick would know."

"Okay, Bart, we'll handle it. Now, the President has called a Cabinet meeting for Wednesday, April 2nd, and he wants us and you at the White House that day."

"That being the case, I'll call Steelman to advise Ben-Gurion of my arrival. I hope I can finish up with Ben-Gurion and the Mossad in time for my departure from Tel Aviv on Tuesday, the 1st. Yes, April Fool's day."

"I don't see the significance of that, Bart," Smith said.

"Oh, just smirking at myself. I've wondered how I got myself involved in this enigma."

"Obviously, the President thought you were the best man for the job. As a matter of fact, Colonel Milburn, you should be with this agency full time," Smith declared.

"Gumshoe work doesn't pay that well. I'm doing this on a *pro bono publico* basis."

"Yes, for poor old Uncle Sam," Dulles jeered.

"In truth, gentlemen, I can't think of a better chore than to bring this rotten despot to justice."

"Amen," Smith sighed. "Good luck in Israel, Bart," Smith signed off.

A call to the White House, and Milburn was quickly connected to John Steelman. "What's up, Colonel?"

"I am leaving Paris late tonight with Jacques Laurent for Tel Aviv. Would you or the Prez notify Ben-Gurion of my arrival Friday at 0900, Flight 200 on TWA?"

"We'll take care of that. You know, Friday sundown is the beginning of the Jewish Sabbath. Saturday is their Sabbath until sundown. Looks like your meeting with the Prime Minister will be on Sunday. Do you think you'll be finished there in time to be here on Wednesday, April 2nd, for a standby at the White House? There is a full Cabinet meeting scheduled to deal with Herr Nordheim."

"So the boys at Langley have advised. I believe I have Sunday, Monday and part of Tuesday. I will be there unless Ben-Gurion insists I stay."

"Hold it a minute, Bart. I want to check with the boss."

Two minutes later Steelman was back on the line. "The President wants you here for that Cabinet meeting. He wants a first-hand report by you to be delivered at that meeting. If Ben-Gurion needs you for further meetings, you'll have to fly back. Explain that to the Prime Minister, and I'm sure he'll accelerate your session with the Mossad."

"Dear John, flying me back and forth some six thousand miles each way sounds like fun."

"Jangled nerves, Colonel?"

"Not really, just stating the facts, ma'am."

"Hey, the President is real pleased with your efforts. You've done a helluva job, my young friend," Steelman said. "Have a good trip."

☆ ☆ ☆ ☆

Friday, March 28, 1952

TWA Flight 200 touched down on the tarmac of Lod International Airport, a forty-five-minute drive to Tel Aviv. A slightly rotund, bespectacled, scholarly gentlemen, accompanied by a young uniformed Israeli colonel, stood at attention at the base of the mobile staircase.

As Bart and Jacques alighted, the colonel stepped forward.

"Colonel Milburn and Mr. Laurent, welcome to Israel. I am Colonel Yitzhak Rabin. This is Abba Eban, our foreign minister."

"*Shalom*, dear Colonel and Mr. Laurent. I bid you welcome to the state of Israel. We are honored by your presence," Eban jovially greeted them in a clipped British accent.

"My pleasure, gentlemen. This is indeed a very pleasant surprise."

"*Mon plaisir*," Jacques echoed.

"The rest of our team will be arriving tomorrow," Bart advised, referring to Berger and Sedgwick.

"Very good. Follow us, gentlemen. We'll get you cleared with customs and immigration," Rabin suggested.

A Cadillac limousine sporting an Israeli flag on its left fender and an American flag on the right awaited them at the airport curb. The sergeant tooled through heavy traffic to the Dan Tel Aviv Hotel on Ha-Yarkon Street. The centrally located hotel on Gordon Beach, facing the Mediterranean, boasted the ambiance of a resort.

The group entered the Bedouin-style lounge. Bart handed his passport to Jacques, who checked them into a two-bedroom suite facing the sea. The group was partaking of freshly baked croissants and coffee when Jacques returned.

"Prime Minister Ben-Gurion expects you at his office Sunday at ten o'clock. That should allow all of today and tomorrow to rest and enjoy our beach."

"We look forward to that," Bart said.

That night Bart was in bed listening to Sinatra at his best when an announcer broke in with a bulletin. "President Truman, at a Jefferson-Jackson Day fund-raiser, a $100-a-plate dinner in Washington, announced that he would not be a candidate for re-election."

"Hmmm...that's that," Bart mused.

☆ ☆ ☆ ☆

Sunday, March 30, 1952 - office of Prime Minister Ben-Gurion, Tel Aviv, Israel
The short, white-haired man greeted the entourage in the reception room of his office, saying, "*Shalom*, gentlemen, and thank you for coming."

"Mr. Prime Minister," Bart said, "May I present my associates, Jacques Laurent, a *landsman* of yours; Phillip Berger, another *landsman*, and Lloyd Sedgwick."

"Delighted to meet you all. Colonel, President Truman sings your praises."

"Thank you, sir. Mr. Prime Minister, I will brief you alone, if you prefer."

"No, all of you come in."

The casual, open-collared executive beckoned the four men to his office overlooking the sea. They sat at a conference table. Bottles of seltzer water, glasses, and bowls of Israeli fruit adorned the conference table.

Ben-Gurion said, "We are aware of Bormann being sighted in Argentina. We know that Adolf Eichmann is there, as is Josef Mengele. Bring me up to date on all you've gathered with your Operation Lucifer. An apt name, I might add."

Bart launched into a concisely pertinent report of the intelligence gleaned in Monte Carlo, San Remo, Genoa and Buenos Aires. Jacques rounded out his efforts. Berger gave his viewpoint, and Sedgwick capped it with an overall picture of the CIA files on Nordheim.

"The Nazi desk, headed by Jacques Laurent, has been tracking Nazis the world over," he concluded.

"I understand that President Truman has called for a cabinet meeting on Tuesday, April 2nd, to deal with an all-out drive to capture this despicable creature. However, I am saddened by Truman's announcement yesterday. Thank God Churchill is back as Prime Minister of Great Britain. So be it."

"I am sure, sir, that our next President will be a friend of Israel."

"However, Colonel, we are a threatened nation. Our enemies surround us and pledge to drive us into the sea. We are no longer the lemmings of World War II. But I vow that if anyone is to go into the sea, it will be our assailants."

"Is there anything further, sir?"

"No, thank you, gentlemen. I congratulate you for your noble efforts. Go directly to the Mossad offices. Ariel Rubin and Sean Briscoe await you."

"Sean? That sounds Irish, sir."

"Indeed, he is an Irish Jew, a nephew of the first Jewish Lord Mayor of Dublin. Briscoe is a very valuable member of the Mossad. By the way, you might ask him about the Dulles brothers. *Shalom.*" He waved a startled Bart out the door.

At the Mossad headquarters, the group was warmly greeted by two tall, suntanned men, military in bearing: Ariel Rubin, blond hair, hazel eyes, rippling muscles in his short-sleeved, open-collar blue shirt, and Sean Briscoe, with red hair, freckle-faced, sparkling blue eyes and a broad smile, wearing a long-sleeved military tan shirt and black knit tie.

"*Shalom*, gentlemen, welcome to our humble quarters. I am Ariel Rubin and this is Sean Briscoe, my associate and deputy director."

"*Shalom*, Ariel and Sean," Bart said, and he introduced Laurent, Berger and Sedgwick.

Rubin got directly to the point. "Colonel Milburn, two of our people, who have been on undercover missions in Argentina, Uruguay, Paraguay, Colombia and West Germany, were invited to a gaucho barbecue in Mar del Plata, a resort town. It was hilarious in all aspects, but we played it straight. There were twelve couples there, some with their German wives and others with their Argentine ladies. It was all Nazi middle class, plus the Latino amours. They were dressed as pampas cowboys. Nordheim's name was mentioned a few times. They talked about his commitment to Peron to build several factories. In pejorative terms, I questioned why a Jew such as Nordheim would want to help Peron. They assured me that Nordheim was not a Jew. It was only a front. He was really one of them. I gave them a little 'Heil Hitler' and they quietly responded. Bunch of *schmucks*. Two of them whispered to me that they had served in the Gestapo. I asked them if they were getting interest on their money in Swiss banks. The answer was '*No, but it's safe there.*' A few of them wanted to know if we could help get them into the U.S. and become U.S. citizens. I told them it was easy if they paid $25,000 per person. The word went through the gathering faster than the fat drippings in the barbecue. I got a list of names and addresses, with more to come in a Washington post-office box. Our people in D.C. forwarded the names here. We know all about sting operations. So, if you want to sucker them onto American shores for easy apprehension, be our guest. I told them they don't pay anything until we get them settled in the U.S."

Bart took the list, observing, "This is a very tempting package. I'll pass it along to our Justice Department and the immigration people."

"Colonel, I am going to open up with you on a delicate piece of intelligence," Rubin said earnestly.

"Shoot."

"The Dulles brothers are of great concern to us."

"How so?"

"John Foster Dulles had connections in financial circles linking Nazi Germany with American banks. Allen Dulles was a former director of the German Schroeder Bank, headed by Baron von Schroeder. British intelligence should open up with you. Going back to 1930, the Dulles brothers represented German money. John Foster Dulles was the lawyer for the German industrial giant I.G. Farben, the backbone of arms supplies to the Wehrmacht and Zyklon B for the Holocaust. Farben held the patent for the poison gas at Auschwitz. Allen Dulles joined the prestigious law firm of Sullivan & Cromwell. They represented German interests. There is much, much more of the Dulles connections to the Nazis. Maybe their associations with these vermin may not be ideological, but they most certainly are financial. Whichever is the link and motivation, it is deeply disturbing," Rubin said. "Don't forget that Allen Dulles was the OSS's man in Switzerland."

Milburn's dismay was palpable. He sat back, stunned by the revelation. "I can hardly fathom the import of your allegations about the Dulles brothers. Allen has cooperated with me in every aspect on the Nordheim investigation. I am shocked. I have no reason to challenge the accuracy of your statements, but are you certain of your sources?"

"Colonel, check with MI6, although we believe they may want to cover up the Dulles-Nazi connection on a *quid pro quo* basis to force America to keep quiet about the royal family's alliance with Hitler just prior to the outbreak of war."

"My idealistic friend," Briscoe said, "let me play a scenario for you. Truman doesn't run for another term. That is now fact. Eisenhower declares himself a candidate. That is now a fact. Ike is elected, remains to be decided. John Foster Dulles is named Secretary of State. Allen Dulles heads up the CIA. Israel is hung out to dry. Your Operation Lucifer is down the drain. A bleak forecast, sir," he said with a sigh of resignation.

"I am sorry to learn all this, but I'll not be deterred," Bart said.

"Colonel Milburn, I admire you and your associates here. I see the dismay and discouragement on all of your faces. Do not be disheartened, just be forewarned. Plow ahead and we will cooperate directly with you," Rubin said.

"Ariel, may I inject a personal note here, aside from the Nordheim matter?"

"Yes, of course. Feel free."

"Jacques has a sister who had disappeared during the war. Last week in Paris, he learned at the French Refugee Committee that there was a Professor Laurent teaching French at the University of Leipzig in East Germany. They didn't know if the professor was male or female. I know that your people are active all over the world in helping Jews to repatriate, or to find haven here in Israel. Can you help determine who this Laurent might be in Leipzig?"

"What is your sister's name, Jacques?" Rubin graciously asked.

"Her name is Joyce. I would be deeply indebted for your help."

"We'll keep you advised if we have any success. At least we will try to determine if the professor is indeed a woman and, hopefully, your sister. As long as she is alive, there's hope."

"Thank you very much, Ariel," Bart whispered.

"Back to business, we found out this morning that Nordheim is on his way to Palermo, Sicily, for a meeting with that Mafia boss, Lucky Luciano," Briscoe declared. "For what reason, we don't know. The yacht is on the way there now. Nordheim will fly there. He also is going to meet Bormann in Havana, Cuba, after that. With regard to Luciano, he was helpful to the Allies in their invasion of Sicily and all of Italy. What would that misbegotten son of a bitch Bormann want with the Mafia? Our speculation that he wants to buy a hit on someone."

Bart whistled softly. His thought processes absorbed him. A pregnant silence pervaded the room. *Was this a case of on-upmanship or a token of trust?* he wondered.

"We will hold nothing back from you, Colonel. Just remember that it was Prime Minister Ben-Gurion's advisory to President Truman that got you involved in the Nordheim hunt. We were tracking that maggot for some time."

Bart relaxed, realizing the efficiency of the Mossad. "We must keep each other advised from this point in time," he observed. "This has been a fruitful session. I will probe the Dulles question. Thank you, once again, for your candor and forthright delineation of the facts."

"This was a fine meeting," Rubin said.

"If you care to see our profiles of these Nazis, we'll be happy to share them with you," Briscoe said.

"That would be very valuable. I will ask Sedgwick to stay over to meet with you for that purpose. He will file your info with the Nazi Desk at the CIA. Jacques and I will leave in the morning for London," Bart averred.

An alliance had been formed. The Americans and Israelis warmly shook hands. *Shaloms* were exchanged.

Back at the hotel, Bart assigned Phillip Berger to Palermo, Sicily. "You know your way around Sicily, so try to get a flight out today to Naples or Rome. There are shuttles to Palermo from either city. Check into the Grand Hotel Villa Iglea on Via Belmonte 43. It faces the Tyrrhenian Sea and the port where the Flying Eagle will tie up. I am sure the marina can be observed from the hotel. It is possible that Luciano will have rooms there. Be careful, and try to get some pictures of the odd couple."

"I know the place, Bart. It will be the war revisited for me."

"Here are two cameras fully loaded, one for long-range shots," Jacques said, handing them to Phillip. "Here is a box of film, enough for a couple hundred shots."

Bart called his wife in London, saying, "Elizabeth, my love, Jacques and I will arrive there about 7:05 tomorrow morning. We're taking a red-eye flight tonight. Start packing. We will be leaving London tomorrow evening.

With the time difference of five hours, we should be in Washington before midnight."

"Okay, scalawag. Thanks for the short notice. I love you in spite of that."

"I love you too."

☆ ☆ ☆ ☆

Tuesday, April 1, 1952 - 7:30 p.m. - Washington

Harry Truman greeted Milburn with an unusual display of warmth, as did General Smith. "Welcome back, Barton. Your mission in the Nordheim investigation has exceeded my expectations. Congratulations."

"Thank you, Mr. President. However, our work has just begun. We've got to chain this animal before we can gloat."

"Right on target, young man. Let me have your perspective on the overall situation, Colonel."

Bart reprised his report. "There is a possibility, sir, that Nordheim will be going underground for awhile, so finding him immediately may be difficult unless we make a precipitate strike on both him and Bormann. We should try to net the pair together."

"What's your proposal?"

"We have a report that Nordheim plans to meet Bormann in Havana after his meeting with Luciano in Palermo. Would you authorize a strike in Cuba? We'd have to send in a sizable team."

"That Army sergeant Fulgencio Batista, who just seized power in Cuba, is owned by the Mafia. That explains Luciano, Costello, Meyer Lansky, et al. Luciano was helpful in our invasion of Sicily, so I don't understand his relationship to Nordheim. If we can get him or his partner Frank Costello to grease the skids in Cuba for us, we might be able to make a clandestine arrest. An overt capture might result in some fireworks. What do you think, General?"

"Sir, your postulate has merit, but, we can't solicit Mafia help on an official basis," Smith answered.

"Heavens, no."

"Mr. President, if you will give me your official sanction, I believe I can be of some help with the Mafia," Bart said.

"And how would you go about that, son?"

"My brother, Douglas, writes for the New York Daily News. He knows Costello and writes objective stories about him. Douglas has been described in Time magazine as a unique reporter who walks and talks with kings of the world and kings of the underworld and shares the confidence of both. I believe he will be willing to introduce me to Costello, who is Luciano's closest associate. I think they control all the gambling in Cuba, as well as Las Vegas."

"Colonel, I can't and won't approve any solicitation of help from the Mafia. However, I'll close my eyes to any moves you make in that direction. Should there be a leak or any linkage to this office or official Washington, it will promptly be disavowed. Consequently, you would be hung out to dry. Do we understand each other?"

"You don't give me much choice, sir."

"Mr. President, I don't think this matter need be discussed in this office. At this point this is a CIA problem. Colonel Milburn and I will sort this out privately," General Smith said.

"Mr. President, if I may, I would strongly recommend that the Cabinet be instructed that the Nordheim matter be treated as top secret. No leaks of any kind will be tolerated. Forgive my presumptuous advice, sir," Bart implored.

"Well taken, Colonel," Truman replied and the meeting was over. That evening, the Milburn family, including Jacques and Mrs. Bishop, gathered for dinner at the Shoreham Hotel.

They retired early for a much-needed night's sleep after their arduous journey from London.

CHAPTER ELEVEN

Wednesday, April 2, 1952 - noon - Palermo, Sicily

The Flying Eagle sped over the tranquil waters of the Tyrrhenian Sea and entered the port of Palermo. Captain Sandstrom docked the boat in the marina, then tipped the dockmaster and received immediate service. A phone hookup was quickly arranged. He called the Grand Hotel Villa Iglea and was connected to the Royal Suite, occupied by Frederick Avram Nordheim. "Sir, the yacht is docked in the marina, and I can see your hotel from here."

"Captain, I am arranging with the hotel to cater lunch on board. I want you and the crew to be in full dress uniforms. I want everything spic and span."

"Yes, sir."

Phillip Berger watched the yacht maneuver into the marina. He shot a few pictures and walked back to the hotel. He sat in the lobby perusing the Herald Tribune European edition.

At noon, Lucky Luciano, attired in a tan gabardine suit and black fedora, entered the lobby. He went to a house phone. After a very brief conversation, he paced the lobby. Within minutes, Nordheim joined him.

Berger exited the hotel. He crossed Via Belmonte, adjusted his long-range camera and clicked off several frontal shots of Luciano and Nordheim en route to the Flying Eagle. He followed the two and took more pictures as they walked up the gangplank. They emerged from the entry onto the aft deck, where the lunch meeting was to take place. The crew wore white ducks and naval garb. Three hotel waiters were pouring champagne into chilled flute glasses.

Luciano removed his jacket and joined Nordheim at the linen-covered table. A sumptuous repast was being served. Berger raced to the secluded hotel on the hillside for a better view of the aft deck of the yacht. He focused his long-range high-powered automatic camera for close shots of the unlikely duo. He clicked off a myriad of shots from several angles. The crew and waiters were dismissed.

The two men seemed to be in a heated discussion. Nordheim was gesticulating animatedly, shaking his head as he spoke. Luciano sat back quietly.

"I will pay you one hundred million American dollars in cash if you are successful. That is one hundred million for each man," Nordheim heatedly rasped.

"Who are you really, Nordheim?" Luciano asked.

"What kind of question is that?"

"Either you're crazy or you're some Nazi who wants to create a lot of chaos."

"How could you call me a Nazi? I am a Jew. Look at these tattoo numbers on my arm!" he exploded, baring the digits.

"Nordheim, do you realize that killing Churchill and de Gaulle will trigger the biggest manhunt in history?"

"One hundred million for each one. How about *two hundred million a piece*? Cash in American currency."

"You must want them real bad."

"I'll give you twenty-five million as good-faith money."

"Let me talk to my associates. We may not want to participate. But I may find some *meshugah* jerk to do this for you."

"If you arrange this, we'll fly to Havana together."

Luciano entered his chauffeured Rolls Royce sedan. Berger photographed his departure. Thirty minutes later, Nordheim strolled to the Grand Villa Hotel. Phillip took up his post in the lobby, ensconced in a large leather lounge for a two-hour vigil. Darren Mayfield and two tall, muscular men, military in bearing, checked out of the hotel.

They entered a waiting limousine. Berger raced to the taxi line, entered a cab and directed the driver to carefully follow Nordheim.

After a while the cab driver said, "Airport, they go."

"Stay with them."

The limo drove straight onto the tarmac. Berger ran through the airport and found access to the field. Nordheim's escorts boarded a four-engine Lockheed Constellation. Phillip photographed the takeoff. Nordheim entered his limo and returned to his yacht.

☆ ☆ ☆ ☆

Thursday, April 3, 1952 - 11:30 a.m. - Waldorf Astoria Hotel, New York City

Frank Costello, gambling king, had just completed his daily ritual of a shave, facial massage and manicure in the barber shop at the posh hotel. The fastidious, expensively clothed judgemaker, spread his usual largesse in a flurry of green bills among his attendants, then took up his daily stand on the mezzanine reception area opposite the barber shop. Costello held court. The man who controlled Tammany Hall, known as the Prime Minister of the Underworld, talked with a Wall Street lawyer, next with a high-ranking police officer in civilian clothes, and finished with a banker. An elderly lady sidled up to him. After a few words he placed two hundred-dollar bills in her open hand. She thanked him profusely as he made his way to the elevators. He pressed the Up button. On the twelfth floor, he made his way to suite 1204 and knocked.

Douglas Milburn opened the door and ushered him in.

"Thanks for coming, Frank. Meet my brother, Barton."

"Mr. Costello, I deeply appreciate your presence here. We took this suite for privacy."

"Your brother, Doug, impressed me with the importance of your request for this meeting."

"I'll try to make that clear for you."

"Frank, I ordered a Cobb salad for you. Is that okay?" Doug asked.

"Just fine."

A knock at the door and two waiters rolled a table into the center of the posh room. They quickly served the food and departed.

"I trust, Mr. Costello, that whatever is discussed here will be held in the strictest of confidence. We are dealing with national security," Bart said.

"You have my attention. Call me Frank, please."

"I asked Doug to arrange this session with you, as I know you are friends."

"Friends only on the days he doesn't slam me in his newspaper."

The three laughed.

"How can I help you, Bart?"

"Frank, have you heard of a Frederick Avram Nordheim?"

Costello blanched, and reached into his pocket for a silver cigarette case, then deliberately flashed a gold Dunhill lighter, holding the flame to a long Sherman cigarette.

"Why do you ask?"

"We have every reason to believe that he is a very dangerous escaped Nazi criminal."

"What is your role in this matter?"

"I am in charge of a government investigation in tracking him down."

"This man is alleged to be the richest man in the world, isn't that so?"

"That's the current intelligence."

"What do you want from me, Barton?"

"I would appreciate your cooperation. Nordheim had a meeting in Palermo with your associate Lucky Luciano."

"How do you know that?"

"We had him under surveillance, and photographed Lucky dining with Nordheim on the aft deck of his yacht, the Flying Eagle."

"You people are pretty good. I'm impressed."

"In a way, I'm doing you and your associate a favor. Neither of you should have any dealings with this slimeball. I know how you helped the Israelis. I'm sure that your other associate, Meyer Lansky, would want no part of Nordheim."

"All right, who is this crazy son of a bitch?" Costello coarsely hissed.

"That's an interesting comment, Frank," Doug chimed in. "Why do you say crazy?"

"Because that's what this maniac is."

"Frank, it is patently clear that you know something about this bastard," Bart asserted.

"Yes, I do. What do you want from me?"

"I want to talk with Luciano. He was helpful to us in the invasion of Sicily. Maybe he will help us track this bastard down."

"Uncle Sam didn't treat Lucky very well. They showed no appreciation for what he had done in greasing the way for our troops in Sicily. They still kept him in exile. Anyway, he loves this country. I can arrange a meet with him, but I have a piece of startling information from him."

"Frank, I knew it. I'm beginning to read you. Let's have it," Doug interjected.

"Nice and easy now, my friends. I had a call from Luciano over the weekend. There is very little that shocks me. But Lucky told me an incredible story, which he wanted me to pass on to someone with connections to Washington. I've been thinking about it. I was going to get the word to J. Edgar Hoover. I haven't done so yet. Now, along comes you, Barton Milburn. Do you have White House contacts?"

"Yes, I do. Right to the top."

"All right. Doug tells me you are a lawyer. Here's one dollar, and I am retaining you for this one purpose. Savvy?"

"Okay, let's play it that way."

"I do not want to be dragged into this. I'll tell you what Luciano wanted conveyed to Washington. I'll take the Fifth if anyone official questions me, understood?"

Tension pervaded the atmosphere. Beads of perspiration formed on Bart's upper lip. Doug puffed heavily on a cigarette. The seconds pounded Bart's temple in rhythm with his throbbing veins.

Costello took a deep drag on his cigarette and propelled rings of smoke skyward. "This maniac, this weirdo, proposed two hits at a price of two hundred million per hit. The targets, he said, were the head man in England and the headman in France."

Bart and Doug stared at Costello, both in a state of disbelief.

"Churchill and de Gaulle," Doug snapped.

"Why? Why?" Bart mused loudly.

"Lucky said it had something to do with a French investigation of corruption in their police department being instigated by Churchill and de Gaulle."

Bart pounded the table. "That's it!" he exclaimed.

"That's what?" Doug queried.

"I know about the probe going on in Paris, but I'll not discuss it."

"Bart, you will pass this on to the President."

"Most certainly, Frank. I hope he believes this wild scenario."

"He'd better. A maniac like Nordheim is capable of anything. If you need a meet with Luciano, Doug can reach me any time."

"I'll be in touch."

On arrival at National Airport, Milburn called Steelman at the White House. "John, I must see the President as soon as possible. There's been a development."

"Hold it one minute, Bart. Come directly. He'll squeeze you in."

At the White House, after a wait of ten minutes, with Steelman hovering over him, curiosity abounding, Bart was ushered into the Oval Office.

"What's the urgency, Colonel?" Truman asked.

Bart relayed the latest intelligence garnered on his trip to New York.

"Can this be authentic information? This is so incredible that it defies all rational thinking," Truman said.

"Mr. President, it is so preposterous that we have to accept it. We must alert the Prime Minister and the general. I would also like to discuss an immediate strike in Cuba."

Truman placed calls to Churchill and de Gaulle, alerting them to Nordheim's planned assassinations. "We're going after him immediately, Winston, so just be cautious," Truman urged.

That night, Barton Milburn entered the Pentagon, showed his credentials and was escorted to the Defense Secretary's office. Present were five-star General Omar Nelson Bradley, chairman of the Joint Chiefs of Staff; five-star General (retired) Walter Bedell Smith, director of the CIA; Secretary of Defense Robert M. Lovett, and officers representing Defense Intelligence, Army Intelligence, Air Force Intelligence, Naval Intelligence, and the National Security Agency.

"Forgive me, gentlemen, for cutting it so close," Milburn apologized, looking at his wristwatch.

"You're just on the button, Colonel," Lovett declared. "Gentlemen, most of you know Colonel Barton Milburn."

Acknowledgments were murmured, and a few hands waved at the late arrival.

"Colonel Milburn, I haven't seen you since the Germans signed the unconditional surrender on May 7, 1945, in Reims," General Bradley announced.

"Sir, that's a day I'll never forget."

"Nor will we all," General Smith echoed.

"Colonel Milburn has been appointed by President Truman to head up an operation to capture this maniac who we believe may be a Nazi war criminal," Lovett said. "Brief us, Colonel Milburn."

Bart did a thumbnail sketch of the activities leading up to the moment.

"Working with the authority of the President under the aegis of the CIA, we have tracked the movements of Nordheim from Genoa to Palermo, Sicily. He is leaving there soon for a rendezvous with his associate in Havana, Cuba."

"What is your plan, Colonel?" Bradley asked.

"I have dispatched two agents, a pseudo Countess de Cordoba and her bogus husband, Anthony Fuentes, to the Nacional Hotel in Havana. I have arranged for a member of the gambling interests in Cuba, who shall be nameless here, to make further contact with Nordheim. He is the man he met with in Palermo and a..."

Lovett cut in, "Are we dealing with Mafia elements, Colonel Milburn?"

"Hold it, Bob," Smith snapped. "That question wasn't asked when we invaded Sicily and the mainland of Italy. I strongly suggest we not dissect the elements of this mini-war we are about to engage in."

"You're quite right, General. I'm sorry I brought it up," Lovett said. "My apologies for the interruption, Colonel. Proceed."

"The gambling interests have a strong hold on Fulgencio Batista, the de facto ruler who became president a few months ago in Cuba. Two associates of the man from Palermo will be meeting with Batista to ensure his tacit cooperation with whatever operation we launch in Havana. They are also arranging for our Countess to be introduced to Nordheim's associate. She will act as an emissary of Eva Peron. Her mission is to bait and distract him from Nordheim, who we assume will have bodyguards. We don't think the associate will be guarded."

"What do you need from us?" Bradley inquired.

"Not having scouted the terrain, so to speak, I have to be prepared for any contingency. We need a team of at least eight to ten, possibly twelve, well-trained men in civilian clothes to join me in a clandestine military, or rather paramilitary, operation. Handguns only, on an if-required basis. I doubt there will be any gunplay. I'll try to avoid it at all costs. Manacles and anesthetics if our quarry becomes rambunctious. An aircraft is needed, and that's it."

"Mr. Secretary, I would recommend a dozen Rangers and a Fairchild Friendship F-27, unmarked," Bradley said.

"That sounds good, General. How soon can that be arranged?" Smith queried.

"By noon tomorrow, ready for takeoff," Bradley replied.

"Excellent. Gentlemen, this show is ready for Act One," Lovett declared.

CHAPTER TWELVE

Friday, April 4, 1952 - 9 a.m. - Palermo, Italy

Lucky Luciano, in his posh apartment, had just finished a lengthy telephone conversation with Frank Costello. Then he dialed the Grand Hotel Iglea.

"Nordheim, meet me at your yacht in one hour. I may have an answer for you."

"That is good. Come."

Nordheim and Luciano sipped fresh coffee on the aft deck.

Luciano said, "I'll join you on your flight to Cuba. I believe there is someone there who'll handle the hits for you. I'll bring you together with this person or persons. For that, if they come to terms with you, I'll receive ten percent from you. In other words, you'll pay me forty million for the intro."

"What means *intro*?"

"Introduction. Yes or no?"

"How you figure forty million? For what?"

"For arranging the hit. Don't be cute with me. Do you want it or don't you?"

"You want me to pay two hundred million for each hit and forty million on top of that, just for arranging it?"

"Listen to me, tough guy, either you pay or forget it. With the kind of money you've got, this is pennies to you. Shit or get off the pot. Why don't you have your man Mayfield do it?"

"You're the tough guy, Luciano. Suppose they fail, then I'm out forty million American dollars."

"That's life, Herr Nordheim, or better, that's the name of the game. Yes or no? If they take the job, I'm to be paid on the spot in Havana. What will it be?"

"I can see why the Mafia is so successful."

"What Mafia? This is strictly business. I am a businessman. Personally, I think you're crazy to try this hit. It's going to rock the world."

"That's exactly right. It is only the beginning. You have a deal. We leave Saturday morning at 10 a.m."

Nordheim then sent his yacht ahead to Havana.

☆ ☆ ☆ ☆

Friday, April 4, 1952 - 2 a.m. - Washington
Barton Milburn was fast asleep when the phone stridently jarred him awake. He hoarsely answered, "Yes?"

"Luciano here."

"Hold it. I'll go downstairs to my den."

"Okay."

He splashed water on his face, dried quickly, lit a cigarette and plopped into his leather swivel desk chair. "To what do I owe this honor?"

"In line with our earlier conversation, I've enticed this sick bastard to fly with me to Havana aboard his plane. I've worked out a deal to introduce him to the hit lady you suggested. We'll be there quite late tomorrow or in the early hours Sunday morning."

"That's fine, Charlie."

"Oh, how many people are you bringing, Colonel?"

"Fifteen, plus a crew of four. We leave in the next few hours."

"Okay, get this now. Costello will arrange accommodations at the Riviera Hotel. Dandy Phil Kastel runs the place. He'll put you on a floor by yourselves. You're Costello's guests."

"No, no, we'll pay our way."

"Costello wants to be a patriot. Oblige him."

"Thanks. I'll see you there. 'Night."

Two hours later, the phone rang, destroying any further attempts at sleep. "Yeah, what now?" Milburn rasped.

"Sorry to awaken you, Colonel. This is Sophia."

"Hold it," he said, getting out of bed and walking to the den. "What's up, Sophia?"

"Bird number two arrived sporting a mustache and beard. He's registered here at the Nacional Hotel under the name of Dov Schwartz. Cute, eh? I matched him to file pictures. He's ripe for picking."

"Play it cool."

"What other way is there? I'll engage him in conversation regarding Eva's plaint. When is number one coming?"

"He won't be there until late tomorrow night or Sunday morning. So, hit lady, you won't meet with him and Luciano until sometime Sunday. By that time, we should have Dov on ice. I'm coming in with our troops late tonight. We'll be quartered at the Riviera Hotel, about ten minutes away from you. I'll contact you when we arrive."

☆ ☆ ☆ ☆

Friday, April 11, 1952, same day - Andrews Air Force Base, Maryland
   Twelve tall, sturdy and formidable men in casual civilian clothes were stowing their gear aboard a Friendship F-27.
   Barton Milburn, Jacques Laurent and Lloyd Sedgwick approached the plane.
   "Attention, men," Captain Wallace Devereaux snapped. All twelve stood at attention and saluted. Barton and his team returned the salute.
   "Colonel Milburn, we are at your service and yours to command. I am Captain Devereaux."
   "At ease, men. Thank you, Captain. These men are from the CIA," he announced, introducing them individually. "When we become airborne to Havana, I will brief you on our mission and will answer any questions you may have. Everybody got his passport?"
   "Handled an hour ago, sir," the captain confirmed.
   A uniformed major joined the group, smartly saluting Milburn. "I am Major John Flaherty, your pilot for this flight. I have a crew of four: two attendants and two in-flight crew members. We will be treating all of you to first-class flight service."
   The men broke out in unexpected applause.
   Bart laughed, "That's very kind of you, Major Flaherty. We are on a historic mission. Let us wish ourselves good luck."
   The flight took off uneventfully, then, leveling at 25,000 feet, it followed the American coastline over the Atlantic Ocean.
   Bart stood up in front of the plane and outlined their mission. "When we check into the Hotel Riviera and settle down, you will be issued firearms to be concealed under your jackets. All of you are to wear suits, dress shirts and ties. You will look more FBI than Rangers. You are allegedly here, on this covert operation, as members of a trade commission. Try to act the part of politicians."
   "Sleazy, sir?" a voice from the back jested.
   Laughter followed.
   "Not that bad," Milburn rejoined with a smile. "Any questions?"
   "Sir, who are these two jokers?" Captain Devereaux said.
   "For this purpose, I can only describe our quarries as Nazi war criminals. That will suffice for the nonce. Let's do this surgically. A clean-cut snatch of each man, no fireworks and no run-ins with the local policia. No rough stuff unless necessary. However, we will brook no interference. If that occurs, we will do what is necessary. No gunplay, except in self-defense."
   "Will you be armed, Colonel?" Devereaux asked.
   "Yes, just like you. Colt .45's or Berettas. Do this within the parameters outlined, and we might squeeze a couple of days of R & R in this pearl of the Antilles. Sunshine, beaches and pretty *señoritas.*"
   Applause and a couple of loud *Oles* and *Bravos* followed.

A State Department officer, accompanied by two uniformed U.S. Marines, greeted Milburn and the entourage in Havana.

"Colonel, I am Hervey Shaw, commerce attaché to our embassy. I am here to facilitate your party through customs and immigration. Welcome to Havana, sir."

"Your efforts are appreciated. Lead on."

The processing was cursory. The airport was crowded with weekend arrivals in this capital of gambling, lavish shows and revelry. Havana was an open city, and the economy was booming. Tony Fuentes met the arriving party as they cleared immigration and customs.

"Colonel, I've got a bus out front to take you to the Riviera Hotel."

"Great, Tony. How's it going?"

"Two hours ago, Sophia sent a note to Dov Schwartz. I watched his face in the lobby. He was startled. He looked around and spotted our gorgeous lady. He cautiously approached her after she waved her dainty hand at him. They are having cocktails as we speak."

"I hope she doesn't scare him off. You had better take a cab and get back there pronto. I'm sending Jacques Laurent with you. Don't let this bum out of your sight."

Bart beckoned Jacques, whispered in his ear and waved the two of them off with parting advice, "Don't let him leave the hotel. I'll join you soon."

At the Riviera, the aptly named Dandy Phil Kastel welcomed the arrivals. "Colonel, Mr. Costello has arranged the whole sixth floor for your party. Your wish is our command. If I personally can be of help to you, just let me know. I am at your service."

"That's very kind of you, Mr. Kastel. I'll remember that."

Kastel snapped his fingers, and a well-dressed, middle-aged, gray-haired man stepped forward. "This is Emilio Ramirez, our manager. He will escort your party to the sixth floor. Your people can sign the registration cards in your rooms.

"*Bienvenido*, Colonel. *Mucho gusto.* Please follow me."

As soon as the men were ensconced in their rooms, Bart pulled Captain Devereaux aside. "Come into my suite."

He pointed at two large leather bags. After setting the numbers on the combination locks, he opened both bags. One contained .45 Colt automatics, the other was filled with Berettas. Boxes of ammunition shells were in each leather bag.

Bart took a Colt and shells for himself. "Your choice, Captain."

Devereaux opted for a Colt.

"All right," Bart declared. "Let's go get him."

At the Nacional Hotel, the captain and three Rangers entered the lobby observing the arriving tourists, mostly Americans.

"This joint is jumping," Devereaux observed.

Bart proceeded to the cocktail lounge, spotting Sophia and Bormann in a back booth. He fixed his eyes on Martin Bormann, verifying for himself the existence of the infamous right-hand man of Adolf Hitler. On the other side of the room, he joined Jacques and Tony.

"That guy can really guzzle the juice," Fuentes stated.

"What's he drinking?" Bart asked.

"He's almost finished a bottle of rum. She's been nursing a couple of banana daiquiris. Those are native specials."

"If Sophia can lure him to her room or his, I believe we can take him without too much fuss. This might be easier than I thought," Bart presupposed. "I've got four Rangers in the lobby, in case he's got some buddies here."

"I've cased the joint and haven't spotted any possible cohorts," Tony ventured.

"Go to a house phone and call the Riviera Hotel. Ask for a Major John Flaherty. Tell him to get out to the airport with his crew and to be ready for a quick takeoff for Guantanamo in the next hour or two. I want him to be on the ready," Bart ordered.

Ten minutes later, Bormann staggered to the men's room. Jacques followed.

Bart sidled up to Sophia's booth. "How goes it?"

"At first he was very antagonistic. I told him that Eva wanted me to talk to him about her share of the Nazi loot. He denied its existence, insisting that his name was not Martin Bormann. However, after a few drinks he was holding my hand. After a few more, he told me he loves me. He wanted to know if I married him, would he become a count. I told him it was possible. He then admitted his true identity, the plunder, and said he might be willing to share it with me."

"Get him up to his suite. We'll be right with you. We might be able to take him while he's drunk. I'll hit him with an anesthetic. I've got four Army Rangers in the lobby. They can carry him to my car. We'll rush him to the airport and fly to Guantanamo, where he'll disappear for a while."

"I want to go with you."

"No way, Sophia. You stay for the arrival of the big man. See you upstairs." Bart returned to his table. Bormann staggered back to the booth.

"Oh, Martin let's go up to your room. You could use a rest."

He threw a handful of bills on the table."That's a very good idea, *Meine liebchen*," he replied.

She held his arm in support as they made their way to the elevator. Bart and Jacques crowded into the lift with them.

Bormann, Sophia and Bart exited on the fourth floor. The captain went to the fifth floor and raced down the stairway to the fourth.

Bormann fumbled with his keys to suite 410. The door opened and suddenly Bart grabbed him from behind, pushing the stocky man into the room. Two tall, muscular men rushed out of the bedroom.

Bart leveled his Colt at them. At that moment, Jacques, Tony and the four Rangers entered. One of the men jumped at Bart, who instinctively slammed him across the jaw with his gun. He fell in a heap. The other began flailing his arms at Bart. Jacques zapped him with his gun. Bormann grabbed at Bart's feet, but a kick knocked him cold. Sophia held onto Tony with a look of satisfaction.

"Lock the door, Jacques," Bart coolly ordered. "Put the *Do Not Disturb* sign on."

For a moment, the group sat and stared at the prone men.

"We've got a problem, men. We hadn't counted on these two guys. We've got to cart this trio to the airport."

He removed a leather case from his inside jacket pocket, then zipped it open, taking out three hypodermic injections.

"Roll their sleeves up so I can put these bums to beddy-bye. This will hold them for at least three hours."

With professional acumen, he administered the anesthetics. "Now, search these rooms for any papers or items of interest. Jacques, search these bodies and relieve them of anything of interest. Pack their clothes. We will take everything with us. Leave nothing. Put all papers in a pillowcase."

Passports, credit cards, file papers and several thousand dollars were stripped from the pockets of the comatose prisoners. A Ranger presented a locked leather bag, found under the bed.

"Pry it open," Bart commanded.

Captain Devereaux produced a hunting knife. Bart gave him a quizzical look. He nodded. The captain snapped the lock open. The case contained a bounteous cache of hundred-dollar bills.

"Men, I want that counted," Bart declared.

Jacques studiously oversaw the tally.

"Tony, come here please."

"What's the plan, Colonel?"

"Tony, you are now Doctor Sanchez. Look in the phone book for a private ambulance service. Tell them you have three men suffering from food poisoning and they are to be flown to Miami for special treatment. Have them come to the back of the hotel at the freight dock. No report is necessary; you've already handled that. Ask for three gurneys, which you will lead up here. Here's tipping money."

"Good plan, sir."

"Get with it."

Tony scoured the Havana Yellow Pages. He called Havana Ciudad Emergencia Servicio. In crisp Castilian Spanish, he ordered an ambulance with three gurneys.

"They'll be here in fifteen minutes," Tony announced.

"Fine. Sophia, you are the distraught sister of our special guest," Bart ordered. "Hover over Herr Martin, applying a handkerchief to your teary eyes."

The money count revealed a stash of five hundred thousand dollars.

"Just pocket money," Bart mused.

Tony, now Doctor Sanchez, took two Rangers with him down the freight elevator. Captain Devereaux and the two other Rangers carried Bormann and one of his henchmen into the bedroom and placed each one on a twin bed. The other sleeping giant was placed on the couch with a pillow behind him and covered with a blanket. The capacious ambulance, red lights flashing, backed up to the freight dock of the Hotel Nacional. Two attendants in white jackets took three collapsed gurneys and placed them on the dock.

"I am Doctor Sanchez," Tony declared. "These men will stay here. They are members of the family. Come with me."

"*Si*, Doctor."

Upon reaching Bormann's room, the gurneys were unfolded and wheeled into the suite. The three heavy men were lifted by Rangers and attendants and rolled to the freight elevator. Sophia sobbed audibly, dabbing her eyes with her kerchief. "Doctor Sanchez" comforted her in Spanish.

Sophia sat in the front seat next to the driver. Tony and two Rangers joined the attendant alongside the somnolent prisoners with sirens wailing and red lights flashing, the ambulance headed for the Havana airport. Tony directed the driver to the far end of the tarmac. Major Flaherty supervised the attendants and the assisting Rangers in pushing the gurneys up a ramp into the body of the Fairchild Friendship F-27. They were tortuously lifted into the last row of seats. Blankets were spread over the snoring patients.

The driver, Pedro Ramirez, approached Tony at the foot of the ramp.

"Doctor, I have to fill out this form. What are the names of the patients?"

Tony flashed ten one hundred-dollar bills. Pedro's eyes rolled.

"Listen, Ramirez, these men are very important American politicians. I am sure they do not want any publicity. They drank too much and ate some poisoned food. Here's five hundred for you and five hundred for your *compañero*. Forget this ever happened. Tell your boss this was a false alarm. *Comprendo?*"

"*Si, si*, Doctor. *Muchos gracias.*"

Ramirez held a whispered conversation with his associate, who nodded acquiescence. The red lights were dimmed and the sirens muted as the ambulance silently left the airport.

A Cadillac rolled up to the F-27. Bart and Jacques alighted.

"Captain Devereaux, take your Rangers and drive this car back to the Riviera Hotel," Bart instructed. "You and your men are free for this evening. Enjoy yourselves. I'll be back late tonight or first thing in the morning. Check the desk for any of my messages. If I need you, I'll leave a message. If I'm needed, call Admiral Wayne Thomas at the Guantanamo Naval Base. Here's his number."

Bart and Jacques entered the plane cabin, and Bart produced three sets of handcuffs, with which he quickly manacled the drugged prisoners.

"Captain Flaherty, let's go."

The engines were revved, the plane taxied, cleared the tower and sailed off into the dusk. Thirty-five minutes later they flew over the Guantanamo Naval Base.

"Colonel Milburn and party request Admiral Thomas's permission to land. We need three gurneys," Flaherty advised the naval controller.

"Circle at two thousand. Stand by for clearance."

Five minutes later the plane was cleared, and it touched down in a perfect landing. A Jeep rolled up to the F-27. A handsome, suntanned, uniformed officer agilely leaped out of the vehicle and approached the mobile staircase. Bart skipped down the steps. "Colonel Milburn here, sir," he said, smartly saluting the admiral.

"Greetings, Colonel. What have we here this lovely evening?"

He removed his scrambled, egg-visored cap, revealing a full head of tousled blond hair, his blue eyes sparkling in welcome.

Bart updated the admiral.

"You're kidding. You've captured Martin Bormann? Holy Toledo, what a catch!" the admiral marveled. "We have a little history going here. What about this Nordheim person, where is he?"

"He is due on Sunday. Sir, our prisoners will need a special band of watchdogs for 24-hour surveillance. They are to be stripped naked, orifices checked, photographs and fingerprints, please. The cells must be fully lighted 24 hours a day for constant observation. All prisoners separated, with no communication."

"Understood, Colonel."

Three Marines pushing gurneys pulled up to the plane. They saluted the admiral and stood at attention.

"At ease, men," Thomas said, saluting.

Jacques stood at the top of the stairs, awaiting a signal from Bart.

"Sir, there are three men up there. Bormann and two others, bodyguards, I think. They are in a state of stupor for at least another two hours, courtesy of anesthetics. They are quite hefty. My men on board will assist these Marines in getting them down. We need a ramp for the gurneys."

The admiral snapped his fingers and ordered the ramp. It was rolled out in short order. The gurneys were collapsed and carried aboard. The rollaway stairs were temporarily removed. On board, all helped load the inert bodies strapped onto the gurneys. The rollers were carefully lowered down the ramp.

The staircase replaced the ramp, and the Rangers and Jacques debarked. Bart introduced Jacques and the Rangers. A parade of gurneys, Marines and Rangers followed the admiral's Jeep containing Bart and Jacques.

High gates and barbed-wire fences surrounded the naval stockade. Thomas and Milburn watched as two Marines rolled the gurney bearing the limp 200-pound body of Martin Bormann into an isolation cell in the basement of the naval prison. Two prison guards removed his handcuffs and stripped him bare. He began to moan. His eyes fluttered, trying to adjust to the overhead light. He blinked incessantly.

"*Was ist los?*" Bormann cried, patting his naked body.

"*Dov Schwartz, achtung! Du bist ein prisoner,*" Bart snapped.

Bormann sat up, suddenly noting the two Marines, the two prison guards, the admiral and Milburn surrounding his cot in the center of the bare cell. He tried to rise, and fell back.

A white-jacketed medic joined the group. He applied a stethoscope to Bormann's chest and back.

"Bring him back to the infirmary," the doctor ordered. "Strip him!"

A hospital gown was thrown over Bormann's broad shoulders and he was shuffled barefoot across the hall into the dispensary. There, he was thoroughly examined-all orifices, between his toes, beneath his tongue and all his teeth.

"Haul him into the shower," Thomas ordered.

The two guards hauled the stocky prisoner to his wobbly feet, and with the help of the two Marines dragged him into a shower room. A guard handed him a bar of sodium hydroxide hard soap and turned on the cold water.

"*Schweinhund!*" he screamed, stepping away from the frigid spray.

The guard adjusted the cold spray to lukewarm temperature.

"Wash yourself, you pig! And don't forget your asshole. Wash!" the admiral angrily ordered.

The bewildered man feebly rubbed the bar of soap into lather.

"Wash!" a Marine commanded.

Bormann complied meekly.

Five minutes later he was handed a large bath towel. He stared at his audience. "*Ach, Amerikaners,*" he uttered.

The admiral noted the tattooed numbers on Bormann's right arm.

"Where did you get those numbers on your arm?"

"I was in Dachau concentration camp. I am Jew," he replied in English.

"How come you weren't circumcised?"

"My father was Catholic. My mother was Jew. So my father didn't believe in it. I was raised as Jew, when my father died in first war," he craftily countered.

A guard handed him a set of undergarments, a jumpsuit and a pair of slippers. He was fingerprinted and photographed, then his hands were manacled and leg irons were applied.

"Why am I your prisoner?" Bormann whined. "By what authority you do this to me?"

"I'll explain that to you later. Back to his cell," Thomas ordered.

The other two prisoners got the same treatment separately, under the observation of Jacques and the Rangers. They were placed in cells on floors one and two, isolated from the general prison population. Two guards were assigned to each cell, with instructions for complete silence.

The Rangers and Jacques were invited to the officers' mess hall. Hot leek-and-potato soup and a spread of luncheon meats, cheeses, fruit and hot coffee were well received.

On the way to the mess hall, Admiral Thomas asked Bart, "Why did you call Bormann Dov Schwartz?"

"Sir, that's the pseudonym he used on his passport. I used that so that your personnel won't know who we have here. In fact, if Bormann should reveal his true identity to your guards, I would appreciate you advising your guards that any information he imparts be immediately forwarded to you. Stamp it out, if you will, by advising your men that whatever identity he assumes other than Schwartz is strictly bullshit."

"I'll do that, but why the secrecy?"

"Admiral, I was put in charge of this operation directly by President

Truman. He wants it kept top secret for the present."

"Colonel, in my book, orders are orders. We will abide."

"Thank you, sir."

"Let's grab a bite of chow."

"Suits me fine. After that, sir, I want a very private session with Herr Bormann, with Jacques Laurent on guard during that period. Is that okay with you?"

"Milburn, he's your prisoner. Set the rules and we'll comply."

"Admiral, I appreciate your cooperation. This base is your domain and I am conscious of that."

"Listen to me, brother. We both went through that hellish war. If I can assist in finalizing that chapter, I'll be a happy warrior."

"Well said, sir."

The admiral shed his tunic. Bart was in shirtsleeves. They joined the hungry group in the mess hall. A casual camaraderie was soon established, with talk of the upcoming baseball season and the final days of football. No mention was made of the new prisoners.

The Navy chef appeared and said, "Sir, I can whip up some hot food, if you like."

"Sergeant Wolf, your repasts are legendary. However, this spread is fine. This Marine is a culinary artist, gentlemen," the Admiral complimented.

"Admiral, sir, you made my day."

"So be it, Eddie, as always. We've been together since Okinawa, haven't we?"

"Sir, it's been my honor and pleasure," the robust, ruddy-faced Marine said.

Turning to Bart, the admiral said, "This Marine is a highly decorated fighting machine. He was severely wounded on Okinawa. He was transferred to my battleship, the Virginia. We got to know each other. My medics took good care of him. I asked him what he would do when the war ended. He said he would open a restaurant, because he liked to cook. When he recovered, I had him transferred to me. He's been cooking ever since, and mighty good, I would say."

Bart and Jacques were excused for their meeting at Bormann's cell.

"How's he behaving?" Milburn asked the guards.

"He rattles off in German most of the time. We just fed him some soup and a ham-and-cheese sandwich. We heard he was Jewish, so we offered something besides ham. He didn't mind, and gulped it down."

"You two are relieved now. Captain Laurent will stand guard while I question him."

"May I ask, sir, who is this prisoner?"

"You may not ask anything. Those are the rules. Play by them. Understood? This is top secret. That goes for all the personnel at this base," Milburn snapped.

"Sorry, sir. It won't happen again," the man apologized, saluting.

The two guards departed through an outer iron door.

Jacques turned the key and slid the massive bolt with a loud metallic clang.

Bart pulled a chair into the cell. He set a tape recorder on the floor. Jacques placed his gun on the lamp table outside the cell and plopped into an armchair.

Bormann sat on the jail cot, handcuffed and feet in chains. "Why you treat me like a criminal?" he plaintively pleaded.

"Because that's what you are."

"You record what I say because you think I am a thief or a gangster?"

"Worse."

"How so?"

"Let's stop playing games. Do you know where you are?"

"This is American jail."

"Right, but what kind of jail?"

"You tell me."

"Okay, smart ass. This is an American military jail. Does that tell you something?"

"No, that tells me nothing. You have falsely arrested the wrong man. By what law do you hold me?"

"You are the right man. You are a prisoner of war."

"The war is over."

"Not for you. That associate of yours led us right to you. He told us the time and place to find you," Bart disingenuously said.

Bormann leaned back momentarily, stunned by the assertion.

Bart let him ponder the revelation.

"Who is this associate?" Bormann hoarsely asked.

"Would you like to guess?"

"No, I do not believe what you say."

Bart switched into perfect German. "Don't be a fool. You are really a clever man with a good mind. Face reality. You're in a military jail, held by Americans. Why would we do that, if you were not a rotten, filthy murderer and thief? You sit here thinking we are stupid. Come clean."

"Clean like what?"

"You're not Dov Schwartz. You're not a Jew. You are a no-good Nazi son of a bitch."

"You call me a murderer, a thief, a Nazi and a son of a bitch. Why? Are you a Jew?"

"No, I'm not. People of all faiths despise Nazis. The whole world hates you. Wake up - the Third Reich is dead. *Kaput*. Open up, pal, or we'll open you up in ways you Nazi bastards haven't thought of. No suicides like Goering and Goebbels. You know those names, don't you?"

Bart stood up, his six-foot-three height and his military posture appearing menacing to Bormann.

"Don't stand over me like that."

"Why not, *mein herr*?"

"It makes me nervous."

"Like Himmler?"

"He was *dreck*."

"Hmm, that's a nice Yiddish word. It means shit."

"See, I told you. I'm Jew."

Bart laughed. "You're a sly heel. You traduced all of your Nazi associates while you rose to high power in the Third Reich."

"What is *traduce?*"

"In simple language, you destroyed their reputations. You said evil things about them. You charged them with being disloyal to your Führer. That way you became the number two man of Nazi Germany. You were appointed minister of the Nazi party by him."

"That's a lie."

"What's a lie? Himmler, Goering, Hess, Goebbels and other Nazi degenerates, or that you were not number two man in the Third Reich?"

"You are making a fairytale."

"How come you have suddenly lost interest in who was the associate who let us know where to find you?"

"I haven't forgot. I've been thinking about that. Maybe it is...Franz Schwerin...or..."

"Oh, cut the crap. You mean those two storm troopers we arrested in your rooms at the Hotel Nacional. Franz Schwerin and Ernst Krueger."

"Ja, how you know these names?"

"Listen, schmuck, their passports gave us their names. They are ex-Gestapo agents working for you."

"Then who is this associate?"

"You know damn well who. Frederick Avram Nordheim, or, should I say Adolf Hitler? That is who."

Bormann covered his face with his huge hands, in shock. "*Nein, nein*, this cannot be," he cried through his twitching fingers. "Never, never in one hundred years. Impossible."

"What's impossible, Martin? Your Führer wouldn't cross you?"

"Never, he could not..." Bormann stopped himself. His eyes were wide and frozen. Bart bore his eyes into the prisoner, and his heart was pounding at the slip-up and ensuing revelation. The air was filled with tension. After a moment, Bormann raised his eyes and spoke. "I will say no more. You call me a murderer. I never killed anyone. You call me a thief. I never robbed anyone. You call me a Nazi. Prove it. I do not want to talk any more."

"Well, well, well, *Martin Bormann*," Bart sneered. "Maybe you ought to sleep on a few things. Here are a few items for you to think about, Martin Bormann. One, it was indeed Adolf Hitler from whom we learned you were to meet him at the Hotel Nacional in Havana. He is coming here Sunday from Palermo, Sicily. Two, he had you transfer the loot, Nazi gold, from Buenos Aires to Barcelona, Spain, where he stashed it on his new luxury yacht, the Flying Eagle, which he unloaded in Portofino and placed in a Genoa bank. Three, in 1945 you supervised the unloading of gold, currencies, jewelry, and fillings from the teeth of six million Jews off two Nazi submarines. Think about it. Your Führer doesn't love you, he *uses* you. The only one he ever loved was Geli Raubal, who committed suicide because of him and his sexual perversions. Think hard, Martin Bormann - you are a born scheming survivor.

Maybe I can help you survive some more. Think, think, think."

Bart took the recorder and walked out of the sterile cell with its slab cot, seatless toilet and wash basin. The bright light shone down on the subdued and forlorn figure in manacles and leg chains. Bart slammed the steel gate to the windowless cell and turned the large key forcefully. Lifting the phone on the desk, he asked the guard to return.

Jacques, in a state of shock, addressed Bart.

"Colonel, his reaction to the name Adolf Hitler…it has to be true."

"I know, Jacques. If I had any doubt as to the true identity of Frederick Nordheim, it was just eliminated."

Not another word was spoken as they walked to the hangar for their flight back to Havana. Bart looked at his watch. It was 10:30 p.m. The night would be long and sleepless.

CHAPTER THIRTEEN

Saturday, April 5, 1952- 9 a.m. - Havana, Cuba

Barton Milburn and Jacques Laurent had finished their continental breakfasts and were sipping coffee in their suite at the Riviera Hotel.

"Bart, I was thinking about your answer to Bormann when he asked you under what law you were holding him. Do you have to supply him with a lawyer?"

"Jacques, I'll be frank with you. We can hold war criminals until we are ready to prosecute. Ask Berger and Sedgwick to come here."

Phillip Berger and Lloyd Sedgwick had just finished their breakfasts. There was a knock at the door. Phil answered.

"Morning, Jacques. Come in and have some coffee," Berger said.

"No, the colonel wishes you gentlemen to join him."

When they reached Bart's suite, he advised them to sort out the materials in the pillowcase taken from Bormann and the two storm troopers.

"Check out everything. I'm going to the lobby to make a phone call on one of the public phones. I'll be back shortly. Jacques, take the pillowcase out of that canvas bag. Don't touch that other leather bag with the hundred-dollar bills."

In a closed booth, Bart called the White House.

"How may I help you, Colonel," the White House operator inquired.

"This is urgent. What's your name?"

"Grace, sir."

"Please, Grace, I must speak to Dr. John Steelman."

"What is your number, sir, in case we're disconnected?"

He supplied it.

"Hold on, I'll track him."

Steelman was puttering in his garden at his home in Alexandria, Virginia. "Colonel, I've just planted some roses. It's that time of the year, you know. How are things going?"

"Good luck with your horticultural endeavors, sir. I am pleased to report that *our plants have blossomed.*"

"Come again?"

"We have in custody our number two quarry."

"No kidding. Martin?"

"In the flesh, sir, manacled and caged."

"Bingo. That is exciting news. Where are you?"

"In Havana. And we've stashed him in our naval base just northeast of here."

"Guantanamo?"

"You said it."

"Who knows this?"

"None of the personnel here, with the exception of Admiral Wayne Thomas, commander of the base, and my team."

"I won't ask for details. I must relay this to the President immediately. What about number one?"

"He is expected to arrive tomorrow morning. Keep your fingers crossed. This may be a bit dicey."

"You've got the Rangers with you?"

"Yes, plus three of my men."

"There was no public flurry when Martin was detained?"

"None at all, clandestine all the way."

"Where can you be reached?"

"Here at the Hotel Riviera for the next couple of hours and later at Admiral Thomas's headquarters."

"Barton, my friend, you've exceeded all expectations. The President's intuition about you was right on target. Bravo!"

Bart smiled, then hung up and joined the team. They were examining credit cards, passports, letters, wallets and assorted items. Berger held up a bottle. A label on the small, blue bottle had a red X on it. Bart took the vial, opened the cap, gingerly smelled the contents and quickly withdrew. "Well, look what we have here. Cyanide pills, a coward's best friend."

"Goebbels and Goering pass from the hangman's noose," Sedgwick noted.

"I'll have this devil's brew tested at Guantanamo," Bart declared. "What have we come up with so far?"

"In the lining of the money bag we found two of Bormann's passports. Here is one for Dov Schwartz, issued in Malmo, Sweden, in January 1946, with some strange ports visited. Here's another one with a Swiss diplomat jacket issued to Gustav Leifler, with his photograph, face shaved. He used it for trips to Argentina, Monaco, Paraguay, and Bermuda. The first one took him to Geneva, Zurich, Liechtenstein, and Vancouver, Canada."

"Let me have those," Bart requested. He placed them in the inside pocket of his jacket hanging on the back of his chair. He directed Jacques to call Sophia and Tony. "Have them come here."

"Colonel, you've seen the passports for the two storm troopers, Herren Ernst Krueger and Franz Schwerin, issued in Malmo, Sweden, January 1946, the same day as Dov Schwartz's," Sedgwick said, passing the documents to Bart.

"Here are some letters written in German. Two addressed to Schwerin at Lohengrin Ranch, Mar del Plata, Argentina. Three letters to Krueger at the same address. They are obviously from their wives," Berger said, handing them to Bart. "Ilsa Schwerin is living in Munich and Leni Krueger resides in Stuttgart about 120 miles from Munich," Berger said.

Bart glanced at the contents of the missiles and said, "These are indeed two lonesome ladies, whose children miss their daddies."

Sophia and Tony joined the group.

"How is my future husband doing?" Sophia gibed. Tony rolled his eyes.

Bart laughed. "He doth languish in yonder jail, pining for thee, fair lady."

The Shakespearean aura was infectious. "'Tis my sword which must be applied to your knave," Tony articulated with an attempt at an English accent.

The phone rang. Jacques answered, then handed the phone to Bart. "Someone says he's your uncle."

"I'll take it. Hi, where are you?"

"I'm here at the Riviera in room 743."

"See you in fifteen minutes."

No one asked who the caller was, and Bart didn't say.

"We'll all be leaving for Guantanamo in about two hours. I have an appointment, Jacques, so notify Major Flaherty to have the plane ready. See you all back here," Bart declared.

Frank Costello, often referred to as the Prime Minister of the Underworld, opened the door of room 743, the presidential suite. The hotel was one of the many properties in Havana owned by Costello, Luciano, and Meyer Lansky, financial genius of the mob. "I've ordered lunch, Barton. How would you like some Chicken Paella? It's very good here."

"That's fine, Frank."

"I have a bar here. Martini, scotch, rum, whatever."

"Vodka martini."

The dapper Prime Minister of the Underworld quickly mixed the chilled drinks, dropping an olive into each glass. Room service delivered Caesar salads and two Chicken Paellas. During the meal, they chatted sports and politics.

"Truman was smart to quit when he was way ahead, a good man," Costello said.

"What's your guess as to his successor?"

"Eisenhower will be a shoo-in. I think Governor Stevenson of Illinois will be his opponent. But he doesn't have a chance against the war hero."

"Would you bet on that?"

Costello, the gambling king, laughed. "I'm not a gambling man, Bart, despite my business. I furnish the means to the average gambler. I never gamble personally."

"Thanks for coming, Frank."

"Well, it's for a good cause. Chasing Nazis is good sport. Besides, I will use this trip to visit our hotels here."

"Luciano says Nordheim is due here tomorrow, or very late tonight."

"Yeah, and I hope we can pull off this sting for you. I understand you have a hit lady to play the part."

"Yes, she's quite an actress, not as a profession, but adept at playing a part," Bart replied. "She's with the CIA."

"Who is this Nazi, really?"

"Frank, I am under orders of secrecy. As much as I would like to take you into our confidence, my hands are tied. We can't even discuss it with high officials in any branch of government."

"Hey, Milburn, I understand. I'll not press you. But, I have to tell you he must be a madman to want to knock off Churchill and de Gaulle for two hundred mil per carcass. Wild, wild."

"What's the plan, Frank?"

"Lucky will meet us and your hit lady here in this suite to work out the details. He'll then take her to his yacht."

"Frank, actually it is a husband-and-wife team."

"That's okay. I'll let Lucky spell out the terms. We're going to strip him of a small bundle in advance. You won't object to that, will you? After all, it's just business."

"No problem. The more you take from him the better. Don't be surprised if he seems upset about an associate of his missing. We have him."

"Good deal. The less we know and the sooner you grab the bum, the better."

"Frank, I've got to go now. I'll be back in my room late tonight. Leave a message saying *Your uncle called*, if you need me. Thanks for lunch."

Costello smiled. They shook hands.

Sophia, Tony, Sedgwick, Berger and Jacques joined Bart on the flight to Guantanamo. They were briefed on the Bormann interrogation and prepped on the planned hit sting on Nordheim. The six of them were escorted to Admiral Thomas' office, where he effusively welcomed the group.

"Admiral, this lady has acted as the Countess de Cordoba. She had cocktails with our prisoner yesterday. He was quite enamored with her. Depending on my further interrogation of this man, I might want to let her talk about him. Any objection?" Jacques asked.

"Normally we don't allow women into the cells. However, she's a CIA agent, so there is no objection."

"Thank you, sir."

"Lieutenant McKay will ride over with you in the minibus. Good luck. Call if you need anything."

Chairs were set up in the darkened area outside Bormann's cell. The two guards joined Bart outside the iron door.

"How has the prisoner behaved?" Bart asked.

"Sir, this guy has a Jekyll-and-Hyde personality. He whimpers, cries, and then roars like a lion in English and German. He threw his rations at us and then pleaded for food. He went berserk when we clipped his beard and mustache off. We gave him a close shave on his face and head. Then he went into a crying, moaning jag," they reported.

"Par for the course, men. Thanks. Take a break. We'll call you or your relief when we're through here."

Jacques put his gun on the table. The rest sat back in their chairs. Milburn opened the cell door. The shorn prisoner sat up on his small cot. Bart placed the recorder on the floor.

"So, you see what they have done to me. They shave my head and face."

"Just like you did to the Jews."

"I was not a part of that."

"Oh, so you finally admit you are a Nazi."

"I am not a Nazi, and I never shaved anybody's head," he whined.

At the top of his lungs, Milburn shouted, "You are a liar!"

Bormann fell back on his cot, startled by the change in Bart's demeanor. "I will say no more to you. I want a lawyer."

"Since when do prisoners of war get lawyers, you sniveling Nazi bastard? How long do you think you can keep up this game? Didn't you think about what I told you last night? Do you want to spend the rest of your life here in an American boot camp or at the end of a hangman's rope?"

"I am Jew. Why you torture me?"

"Torture you? We haven't even begun. Maybe we will pull your fingernails out one at a time and then your toenails and then cut off a finger, one at a time, and then your toes, and then your left ear, and then your right ear. *That's* torture."

"*You* are a Nazi. That's what they do to prisoners."

"You should know. You were Hitler's right-hand man. You helped him escape from the bunker. Listen carefully, Martin Bormann," Bart said, modulating his voice to a soothing, sincere whisper. "You have been betrayed by your Führer. That is how we were able to capture you. I have a lady here we arrested. I am going to let her talk with you."

"What lady?"

"You'll see."

He walked to the bars of the cell.

"Bring that prisoner in here. Come on, Madame, talk to your friend, you Nazi sympathizer."

The cell door was opened and Tony gently shoved her past Bart, who clanged the bars behind her. She dabbed a handkerchief to her eyes.

"Martin, what have these beasts done to you? They shaved your head and beard. Why are you in handcuffs and leg irons? Oh, dear man, this is *awful*."

"*Ach, meine liebchen*, they say I am a Nazi."

"Martin, be practical. The Third Reich is dead. They know all about you and Nordheim. They say they have captured him."

"Is he being held here in this place?"

"I heard something about Palermo. Maybe that's where they got him."

"*Ach, Gott!* That's where he was coming from to Havana," he hoarsely whispered.

"So, you see, you are all alone. Talk to the colonel, he can help you."

"He is very tough, like the Gestapo."

"If you cooperate, he won't be so hard."

"Why they arrest you?"

"They think I'm a Nazi associated with you. I didn't tell them anything. I have important friends in Washington," she said.

"Maybe you can help me. I have plenty of money."

"I know that. What about the Nazi gold you promised Eva Peron and then me?"

"Get me out and I'll give you a share of that money and more."

"It will take a little time, but I think I can make life a little better for you."

"Where are we?" he asked.

"I don't know. They blindfolded me and put me on a plane. All my things are still in Havana," she said.

"Are we in America?"

"I don't know. I think so. I called my lawyers before we got on a plane. They don't know where I am now. But when they protest to the State Department that the Countess de Cordoba is being held by the American Army, there will be hell to pay."

"Countess, if we marry, I will be a count, with diplomatic immunity."

"We'll see," she replied, musing to herself, *Dream on, you fool!*

"Are they putting you in a cell?"

"No, so far they kept me in an office."

"Tell the colonel to come in. Don't leave me if they release you. I'll tell you where some money is for lawyers."

"What about your wife? Is she still in Germany?"

"No, she died in Austria seven years ago."

Sophia rattled the gate. When it was opened, she stepped out and whispered in Bart's ear, "The bird is ready to be cooked. Pluck him."

The recorder had been running during the colloquy between Bormann and Sophia. Bart entered, asking, "That lady is one of your people?"

"*Nein*, she is a countess. She is a very important lady. She is not a Nazi. She is a friend of the Perons. Why you arrest her?"

"Because of her connection to you. Tell us the truth and maybe we'll let her go."

"I just meet this lady. She brings me message from Eva Peron. You make mistake when you arrest her."

"We will check her out. Now, are you ready for the truth?" Bart asked.

"If you take off the handcuffs and chains, I will be better to talk. It is even hard for me to go to the toilet. And your food is terrible. Your water, it smells. Treat me like I deserve."

"Who are you to say you deserve better treatment?"

"Remove the chains and cuffs and I will tell you. No remove, no tell."

"All right, they'll be removed. But if you hold back, I'll personally clamp them back on you."

Bart sent for a guard. The chains and manacles were removed.

"Sir, do you want us to stand by?" the guard cautioned.

"Not necessary. Leave the restraints and the keys with me."

Bart ordered Jacques to join him. "Bring a chair, and some fresh water."

A vacuum pitcher and a plastic cup were forthcoming.

Jacques poured the ice water and handed the cup to the forlorn prisoner. He swallowed the contents in one gulp and held the cup up for a repeat. He sipped the second cup slowly, slobbering between drafts.

Jacques seated himself behind the prisoner, patting his gun.

Bart stood over Bormann, who was resting on the cot.

"Who are you?"

"I am Martin Bormann, Minister of the National Socialist Party, second in command to the Führer, Adolf Hitler. I demand the courtesy and respect under the rules of the Geneva Convention."

"The rules do not apply in your case, Martin. You were not a soldier. You are classified as a Nazi war criminal. So there are *special* rules for you."

"I am not a criminal. I have served my Führer, like you are serving your government. I took orders, but I never approved of Himmler's methods."

"You stood by while six million Jews were murdered and robbed. And millions of Christians, Gypsies, dissenters and prisoners of war were tortured and annihilated, you misbegotten turd."

"I was not part of that. Many times I tell Adolf we should not waste those Jews. Their brains could be used in this war. It was stupid, but it was Reinhard Heydrich, Goering, Goebbels, and then that snake Himmler who went all they way in killing those Jews. Hitler was too busy running the war."

"Are you saying that Hitler didn't want to exterminate the Jews?" Bart snapped in German.

"*Nein*, he was merely using them as scapegoats to arouse the German people. That is how he came to power."

"Were all the German people in favor of sending all the Jews to concentration camps to be slaughtered?"

"Not for murder. Just to be detained."

"Are you a good Christian?"

"Maybe not so good. But I could not stop Himmler. He was the master butcher. Even Hitler couldn't stop him. The war was going badly and Himmler controlled the Waffen SS and the Gestapo. On the last day in the bunker, he stripped the Reichsführer of the SS and the Minister of the Interior from the party and all offices of state, and stripped Reichsmarshall Hermann Goering of all rights and power."

"How did you and Hitler escape from under the chancellery, and who was placed in that funeral pyre in his place?"

"I will tell you no more, until you tell me what will happen to me. Another Nuremberg trial and hanging? Another Spandau like Hess? At least they were treated better than me before hanging."

"Bormann, you are not the real target. If you cooperate, we can work out a deal with you. Be smart and answer all questions put to you."

"Colonel, I wish to say something to you privately. Turn off that recorder."

"You can trust this man, he is like my brother."

"No, just you alone."

Bart waved Jacques out.

"Don't do anything foolish," Jacques hissed at Bormann, waving his gun in his face.

He cupped his hands and whispered in Bart's ear. "I am a very rich man. I am worth three billion dollars. Help me to get to Argentina and I will put one billion dollars in your hands. Now, you be smart. You're a young man. Think of the life you could have with a fortune like that."

"That's a very generous offer, Martin. I'll think about it. Now talk."

Bart turned the machine on again. Jacques was waved back into the cell.

"Now, how did the escape take place? The Russians confirm Hitler's death. That was pretty clever how you fooled the world."

Bormann chuckled hoarsely. "Pretty smart is right. Before I tell you, how about a little schnapps and some decent food? A steak or a wiener schnitzel?"

"You are an arrogant bastard."

"My stomach is arrogant, not me."

"You're an alcoholic as well."

"*Nein*, I hold my liquor."

"That's not what your record shows."

"Only my enemies say that about me. Cooperate with me and I'll answer all your questions, Herr Colonel."

"All right, we'll take a break now. I'm putting your manacles on for now. I don't want you to injure yourself. I'll see if I can get you some food and a little schnapps. Relax now."

The guards resumed their vigil. Bart called Admiral Thomas for a meeting.

"How is the interrogation going, Colonel?" Thomas asked.

"Better than I had hoped. I need a favor. I am at a point with him where, with some softer treatment, he will be ready to spill his guts."

"How can I help?"

"A shot or two of whiskey or, better, I think a couple of beers and a hearty meal. He asked for a steak or a wiener schnitzel."

The admiral laughed, "The gall of this crud." But he rang for Marine Sergeant Eddie Wolf. "This is ironic, Colonel. I am going to request Sergeant Wolf, who is Jewish, to prepare a repast for this Nazi bastard."

"For heavens 'sake, sir, don't let him poison our prisoner. At this point he is very valuable. We may be making history here."

"Not to worry, Colonel; he is quite sensible."

Sergeant Wolf arrived at the door.

"Yes, sir, Admiral," Wolf said as he saluted both men.

"Eddie, sit down and relax. Colonel Milburn has a request."

"Sergeant, I would like to have you prepare a good hot dinner for our Nazi prisoner."

Wolf recoiled. His ruddy complexion blanched. "With due respect, sirs, is this some kind of joke?"

"No, Eddie, listen to me carefully. First, what I tell you now is top secret. We're still at war chasing Nazi criminals. This guy in tow is a high-up kraut who is cooperating. Prepare a good, sumptuous meal for him. This is part of a battle plan. This will help loosen his tongue. Bottle your natural hatred and treat the meal as another weapon against the Nazis. Okay? Don't poison our prize."

"That being the case, I'll kill the mother with culinary kindness. What should I make for him?"

"How about a wiener schnitzel?" Bart suggested, chuckling.

"Can do with a couple of sunny-side eggs on the veal cutlet with garlic potatoes, assorted vegetables. How's that?"

"Excellent, plus two bottles of beer."

"I have a request, Admiral."

"What's that, Sergeant?"

"I'd like to serve it. I want to see what this bastard looks like. Please excuse the language."

Admiral Thomas looked at Milburn.

"That's okay, but no questions; just serve him," Bart barked.

"Understood, sir." Wolf saluted and retired to his chores.

Forty minutes later, Wolf pushed a room-service cart to the door of Bormann's cell. "Dinner is served," he announced.

Bormann looked up, noticed the tablecloth, and bucket of ice, housing two bottles of beer. "That is good," Bormann asserted.

The manacles were removed, and Jacques sat behind Bormann, watching him down the food and slurp the beer. Wolf, arms folded, contemptuously observed the prisoner. As soon as he finished, Wolf took all the utensils off the table and simultaneously removed the rolling cart.

"*Wunderbar!*" Bormann exclaimed. "Tell your chef this food is excellent."

"I'm the chef," Wolf snapped.

"Well then, my compliments to you."

Wolf saluted and rolled the table past the cell door. Under his breath, he muttered, "Kiss my ass, you rat bastard."

Bormann turned to Jacques. "Do you have a cigarette?" He was handed a Marlboro, then Jacques' Army lighter lit up Bormann's perspiring face.

Bart returned. Two guards handcuffed the satiated prisoner, who up to that point had undergone a moment of euphoria.

"*Was ist los*? Why you do this again?"

"This is just routine, Martin. I am going to take you to an interrogation room. I'll take them off there," Bart said.

Bormann was blindfolded and hustled to an interrogation room above the basement. Seated at a bare oak table were Phillip Berger, Lloyd Sedgwick, Anthony Fuentes and Jacques Laurent. Behind that room, separated by a one-way glass, sat Sophia Carrera, who was able to hear and see all that transpired.

The guards removed the manacles and the blindfold, then they were excused. Bormann rubbed his eyes, scanned the room and asked, "Is this a trial?"

"No, it's time for the truth. No more bullshit."

"Du willst mich wohl veraschen."

"Nobody's trying to pull your leg, Bormann. Now, we're getting down to the nitty-gritty. The truth, the hard truth, *verstehen?*" Bart rasped.

"Ja, genug."

Bart placed the recorder in front of him.

"Martin Bormann, this is April 5, 1952, 2 p.m., Eastern Standard Time. You are being interrogated at a United States military base by Colonel Barton Milburn, Phillip Berger, Lloyd Sedgwick and Jacques Laurent. The questions and your answers are being recorded. Do you understand that?"

"Yes."

"What is your name?"

"Martin Bormann."

"You do understand English?"

"Yes."

"Are you aware that you were tried in absentia in Nuremberg and convicted?"

"I was not there for a trial, so how can they convict me? And for what?"

"For crimes of barbarism, murder and the death of six million Jews, plus millions of others and every heinous crime that man's inhumanity to man can conceive."

"You think that I, one man, am guilty of all that?"

"You were the Machiavelli behind Hitler. You climbed over Goering, Himmler, Goebbels, Hess, Speer, and the whole hierarchy of the evil Third Reich. You were Hitler's right arm. He trusted you more than anyone in your government. Do you claim you are innocent?"

"Yes, I am innocent. I kill no one. I follow orders. Himmler, that *schweinhund*, he is the killer. I got nothing against Jews. Hitler used his attack on the Jews to arouse the German people so he would become Chancellor. Blame him for killing Jews. He wanted to drive them out of Germany, but no country would take them. He was too busy running the war, while Himmler, the chicken farmer, ordered them killed. Such a waste of manpower. I would never do that. I would put them in the army and the factories and use their scientists in the war. So why blame me? I wasn't involved in the SS, the Gestapo or the Wehrmacht. I was concerned with domestic affairs. I took care of Hitler's finances and personal affairs."

"Mr. Bormann, next to Hitler, you became the most powerful man in Nazi Germany."

"Only near the end of the war."

"I'm going to have one of these men here read you some excerpts from our file on you."

"Before you do that, I want to know something for sure."

"What is that?"

"Did Hitler really tell you where I could be arrested, Colonel? I must know this for sure."

"I told you that we learned of your trip to Havana from the lips of your Führer," Bart evasively replied.

"*Unverzeihlich, undankbar bedauerlich, der himlose ochse, der hat nicht alle Tassen im Schrank.* I saved his life, I collected his billions, I made him the richest man in the world. Are you sure you not trick me? Why he sell me?"

"You tell us."

Bormann paused for a moment. His face hardened. "Well, I tell you something. If he is arrested by you Americans, watch out. He has plans to destroy the world. He is a very dangerous man. I say no more now. Go on, read my file. I want a cigarette, or better yet, a cigar and a drink."

His anger and distress were palpable. Bart threw a pack of Marlboros on the table. Jacques lit his cigarette. Bormann reached for the Kleenex box and mopped his sweaty brow.

"Lloyd, let's have a few tidbits of this gentleman's background. Maybe that will refresh his memory."

Sedgwick wiped his reading glasses, slowly adjusting them to his face, then deliberately read from the file: "Martin Bormann, born June 17, 1900, in Halberstadt, a German city in Lower Saxony, with a population of 40,000. His father was a sergeant major who played the trumpet in a military band. Theodor Bormann owned a stone quarry. Died when Martin was four years old. His mother remarried a director of a small bank. Education went as far as trade school studying agriculture. Went into army as a gunner in field artillery. He saw no action. In 1920 he worked as manager of a good-sized farm owned by the von Truenfel family in the province of Meckzenburg. He joined an anti-Semitic union for agricultural professional training."

Bormann cut in, "I was not anti-Semitic. After the Versailles Peace Treaty, Germany was in a very bad depression. The smart, educated Jews were getting the best jobs. This union tried to get equal treatment. That's why I joined. They didn't hate Jews. We were jealous. The Jews are too smart, well-educated."

Sedgwick continued, "Bormann hooked up with Gebhard Rossbach, a former lieutenant in the First World War, who led the union of street bums, misfits and veterans. Martin became section leader and treasurer. A Walter Kadow tapped the till, got caught with his dukes in the tambourine. Twenty-three-year-old Martin was the treasurer, so he reported the theft. On 31 May, 1922, Kadow got drunk with members of the Rossbach group. He was dragged from the bar to an inn. He was severely beaten and two bullets to the head were administered, execution style. In July 1925 Bormann was arrested, along with the other members of the Rossbach group. On 12 March, 1924, they were tried. In the three-day trial, there was no direct evidence involving Bormann, so he was sentenced to one year. The others received sentences up to 10 years. When he was released at the end of his sentence, times were tough for the ex-convict. He joined Hitler's National Socialist Party, known as the Nazis, on February 17, 1927. In November he was appointed to the staff of the Supreme Command of the Sturmabteilung or SA, better known as storm troopers, or street fighters, who cowed the German populace."

Bormann interrupted again, "I got out of that, the SA, because they were a bunch of street gangsters, bums, the rabble, the worst dregs of society. I was not of that class. *Eine lunte riechen.*"

"*Lunte?*" Sedgwick queried.

"Rats," Berger translated.

Sedgwick continued, "Bormann married Gerda Buch on 2 September, 1929. Her father was Walter Buch, a major in World War I. He was chairman of the Nazi Party Court for Party Discipline. He was powerful in the upper echelons of the Nazi power structure. Hitler attended the wedding. Their first child, born 14 April, 1930, was named Adolf, after his godfather Hitler. He fathered nine children.

"On 25 April, 1930, Bormann became *Leiter der Hilfskasse*, which was leader of the aid fund of the Nazi party, compensating families of the men killed or injured in street fighting for the Nazis. He ingratiated himself with hundreds of officials.

"In July 1933, Bormann was appointed Reichleiter and chief of staff to Rudolf Hess. Bormann was a powerfully built man, five feet, seven inches in height, and was nicknamed *The Bull* because of his thick neck, broad shoulders and muscular arms. He was soon wearing fitted military uniforms. As time went on, he came closer and closer to the Führer, but he played it low-key. Bormann was in charge of all Nazi affairs. He took control of the office of Deputy Führer. Hitler noticed Bormann's efficiency with every detail.

"The convincing maneuver for Hitler's favor was Bormann's analysis of the SA and its chief of staff, Ernst Röhm, a homosexual," Sedgwick continued. "The storm troopers, he reported to the Führer, were a public concern and a threat to the hierarchy. The brown shirts were the scum of Germany. Their elimination was set in motion on 30 June, 1934. It became known as *The Night of the Long Knives.* It lasted three days. Röhm and his band of degenerates were slain by SS hit men. Bormann was not involved in the executions.

"Later, Himmler decided that Bormann was a rising star, so he commissioned him as an SS-Gruppenführer, which is a major general. It was an attenuated relationship, and Bormann called him Uncle Heinrich. Himmler became godfather to Bormann's fourth child, Heinrich Ingo. He did not become servile to this chinless wanton executioner. Privately, Bormann despised the chicken farmer.

"After Rudolf Hess's ill-fated flight to Scotland in 1941, Bormann moved into full power. He became Hitler's right arm and his most trusted lieutenant. He not only handled Hitler's finances, he was the guardian of the door. No one reached Hitler without being screened by Bormann. Only those Hitler summoned had access. Others who sought audiences with the Führer had to be cleared by Martin. He also served as purveyor of gossip and often demeaned the top officers of the Third Reich to suit his own ambitious rise to power. In fact, in his own way, Bormann manipulated Der Führer. And behind the scenes he was the most powerful man in the Nazi hierarchy."

Bormann exploded, "*Quatsch. Bist du verrückt?* Bullshit! Bullshit!"

"What is wrong, Martin?" Bart asked.

"I not manipulated. I help him, that's all."

"Well, this report isn't necessarily perfect."

"Go on, finish your fairytale."

Sedgwick continued, "Bormann supervised the building of Hitler's house, known as the Berghof, above Berchtesgaden. He also built one for himself close by."

Heavy banging on the door halted the interrogation, and Jacques opened the door slightly.

"An urgent note, sir, for the colonel, sir."

"Thank you."

The missive was passed to Bart. It read, *Washington on line, holding.* Signed, *Thomas.* Bart excused himself, asking Berger and Laurent to continue the questioning. He retired to the connecting soundproofed room behind the one-way window facing the interrogation. Sophia handed him the phone.

"Milburn here."

"This is Smith. A couple of urgent items, Bart. The Flying Eagle has been spotted by Air Force reconnaissance twenty miles out, heading to Havana. A couple of Israeli agents have been observed snooping around the Nacional Hotel. Are they aware of your catch?"

"Hell no, General. I don't want them anywhere near here."

"Do what you think necessary. That's all. Call me at any time."

Bormann was hustled back to his cell, then Bart and team hastened to the Guantanamo base airstrip. On board, Bart briefed the entourage on the news imparted by General Smith. "Nordheim should be flying in late tonight. Sophia and Tony, your turn at bat is imminent," he said.

A message awaited Bart at the Riviera desk. It read, *Uncle expects you and guests for dinner at eight.* He glanced at his watch. It was 7:05 p.m.

"Sophia and Tony, meet me at my suite in half an hour. Phil and Lloyd, stake out the Nacional for the Israeli agents. No contact, just observe. Also, watch for Nordheim and Mayfield. Jacques, go down to the harbor off the Malecon to watch for the Flying Eagle. Call Captain Devereaux to have as many of his Rangers as are available to cover the waterfront with you. If anything important arises, I'll be in Costello's suite, room 743 here, or back in my rooms."

At eight o'clock Bart, Sophia and Tony arrived at the President's Suite, where Costello greeted them warmly. Lucky Luciano was there, to the surprise of Bart, who had expected him to arrive on Nordheim's plane later or in the morning. After the introductions, Bart raised the question of Luciano's early arrival.

"We got in two hours ago. The man didn't go to the Hotel Nacional. He had a car meet us at the airport. He dropped me off here at the Riviera and took off. He will meet us at his yacht at noon tomorrow for lunch. I don't know where he is now. He's a close-mouthed bastard," the Mafia chief related.

"So, this beautiful Countess is our hit lady," Costello joked, laughing.

"Thank you, Mr. Costello, and this handsome gentleman, Tony, is my husband and partner for this sting," Sophia noted.

Costello popped open a bottle of Dom Perignon. He poured the choice champagne into five chilled flute glasses.

"Here's to success for your mission," the underworld prime minister toasted.

"Hear, hear," Tony cheered.

Two waiters arrived with two rolling tables laden with epicurean delights caviar, shrimp, oysters and *pâté* for appetizers, also roast duckling, sweet potato and assorted vegetables. The dinner was a jovial affair. The two Mafiosi regaled their guests with anecdotes about the news media, Sinatra and political diatribes hitting at Thomas E. Dewey, the man who prosecuted Luciano.

The waiters returned with steaming cappuccinos, then Napoleon brandy was poured into snifters for the group. Havana cigars were passed around to the men, and with Sophia's approval, they lit up. She smoked a Sherman cigarette in an ivory holder.

"Gentlemen, your hospitality is deeply appreciated by all," Bart toasted with his brandy glass.

"You see, Countess, despite what you have heard about us, we are quite civilized," Costello laughed.

"Okay, let's talk business," Luciano said. "The name of the game is to treat this maniac seriously. He is willing to pay two hundred million dollars for a hit on Churchill and an additional two hundred million for the death of de Gaulle, plus a ten percent finder fee for me, payable up front, plus twenty-five mil as a down payment and one million to you for the conference, in advance."

"Is this man totally out of his skull?" Tony challenged. "Who the hell does he think he is?"

"That's what we want to know," Costello queried.

Bart avoided any comment.

"Countess, do you and Tony have a plan you can lay on this nut?" Lucky asked.

"Try this on for size. As for my identity as the Countess de Cordoba, Tony and I plan a world tour on behalf of World War II orphans. We will be able to visit Churchill, de Gaulle and other world leaders to enlist their support. We can assure him that Truman will receive us first, to give our charity drive credibility."

"Details of the hit is what Nordheim will demand," Lucky insisted.

"I'm coming to that. Churchill is sixty-seven years old. He drinks a lot of brandy. There is a drug called Tersac, which cannot be detected in an autopsy. It accelerates the heartbeat causing instant death. We'll present him with a vintage Napoleon Brandy."

"Okay, that's for Churchill. What about DeGaulle?"

"I will take that. I have a ring, which I show you now," Tony declared, displaying a circular band with four rows of diamonds. "The middle diamond on the bottom has a hole in it, and when pressed into a handshake it barely scratches the skin and emits an undetectable deadly poison called Bersol, which takes twelve hours to kill."

"Hey, you two, are these poisons for real?" Costello challenged.

Bart laughed, "They are fictitious, but Nordheim won't know that. He'll be told that they are recent discoveries in Hotan, China."

"Is there such a place?" Luciano asked.

"Absolutely, but he won't be able to check it," Bart assured him.

"What if he wants a demonstration?" Lucky asked.

"I'll challenge him to shake hands. He'll decline. I'll press my hand on the table and a dot of sulfuric acid will show. That'll scare him," Tony averred.

"Okay, now if he waffles, tell him to take it or leave it. Get up and start to leave. He'll buy the deal," Lucky advised. "I'll be meeting him at eleven to collect my fee and your million for the conference."

☆ ☆ ☆ ☆

Later that evening

Darren Mayfield met with Jorge Aguilar, manager of the Hotel Nacional, who said, "*Señor* Mayfield, I am very distressed. Dov Schwartz and the two other gentlemen with him left without paying their bill of $4,655.60. This is very embarrassing."

"Didn't anyone see them leave?" Mayfield angrily demanded.

"No, I have checked with all my people. *Señor* Schwartz entertained a very beautiful lady in the lounge. They drank a good deal. Lots of caviar. He seemed a little drunk. They went up to his suite. That's the last time he was seen. Maybe they went to another hotel or to her home."

"What did she look like? Was she a *puta*?"

"No, no, *Señor*. This was not a whore. She looked and acted like high society. Very classy lady. The waiter said she spoke Castilian Spanish."

The telephone rang in the manager's office, and a young secretary entered the room.

"*Señor* Aguilar, Antonio, the *Cajero*, is on the phone. *Importante*," she declared.

"*Hola*, Antonio, *que pasa?*"

"*Señor* Schwartz's bill has just been paid."

"By whom?"

"A black man."

"A Cuban?"

"*Si.*"

"Is he still there?"

"No, he just left."

Mayfield and Aguilar raced out of his office on the mezzanine. They ran down the steps to the front door. The manager questioned the doorman.

"The black man was a taxi driver I've never seen before. He left about five minutes ago. It was a red and white cab. He was in and out in less than five minutes. I let him park for a couple of minutes after he said he was delivering an envelope for a *Señor* Schwartz."

The two men returned to the cashier's cage.

"Antonio, how did the man pay for Schwartz's bill?" Aguilar asked.

"All cash, sir."

"Let's look at Dov Schwartz's suite," Mayfield suggested.

The rooms were spotless. Mayfield checked each room, looked under the beds, inspected the carpets carefully and looked into each of the bathrooms. There was no evidence of foul play. He handed a hundred-dollar bill to Aguilar and departed. A cab delivered him to the luxurious home of dictator Fulgencio Batista, who was entertaining Frederick Avram Nordheim.

"So, where is Dov?" the Führer inquired.

"He was last seen with a beautiful lady."

"Was he drinking?"

"Quite a bit, according to his bill, which was just paid by a taxi driver."

"A woman, *ach. Der Pimpel und der Muschi*. You think that's what happen? He go with her some place? Her house? He make *bumsen* maybe?"

"Yeah, sir, but what happened to the two men with him?"

"That bothers me. Your excellency, *Señor* Batista, I need your *policia* to find him and that lady."

"Herr Nordheim, I'll have our best men check it out." The Cuban strongman picked up the phone, pressed a button and rattled off instructions for the search of Dov Schwartz.

"As I was saying, Fulgencio, do you trust Costello and his partner Luciano?"

"Oh yes, I have done business with them and their partner Meyer Lansky for a long time. They are strictly business and always honor their word."

"What about the Jew, Lansky?"

"A very good, very smart man. I would trust him. He is a fine gentleman."

"Do they pay you as much as I do?"

"They don't pay me. We collect taxes from their gambling interests. The returns are very substantial. Our economy is thriving."

"More taxes than I pay you?"

"Much, much more."

"You think I should buy an interest in their hotels and casinos?"

"That's up to you, Herr Nordheim."

"We'll see. I will stay aboard my yacht tonight. Call me if you locate Schwartz."

"My driver will take you to your boat," Batista offered, and Nordheim accepted with a nod.

Bart and Jacques focused their infrared binoculars on the Flying Eagle, moored at the marina. Batista's bulletproof Cadillac limousine pulled up to the gangplank of the yacht.

"There they are, Colonel!" Jacques exclaimed, pointing at Mayfield and Nordheim.

"We've got to set up a round-the-clock surveillance," Bart declared. "Let's find Captain Devereaux."

"He's down to the left, near the bow of the yacht. I'll get him."

"No, no, Jacques. With Mayfield aboard, I don't want to chance his seeing you."

Two Rangers strolled by their vantage point. Bart whistled. They turned in recognition.

"Come here, men," Bart beckoned.

They saluted.

"One of you, go slowly toward the bow of the boat. Have Captain Devereaux join me here."

Devereaux joined them on the incline where they were stationed. They sat on the stone balustrade overlooking the Malecon, then Bart outlined a plan for a twenty-four-hour observation of the yacht.

"Captain, our target just boarded the ship. Did you see him?"

"Sir, he's the one with the beard?"

"Right you are."

"Work out a plan for your Rangers to take shifts watching that yacht. Have them make note of everyone boarding or leaving it. There is a public phone about fifty yards to the right of the bow. I'm to be called, no matter what the time, if Nordheim debarks. Under no circumstances are you to lose track of him. I'll be back early in the a.m."

"Right, sir, I'll have it set up shortly. These two men will be on watch while I round up the rest of my men."

"Thank you, Captain."

They exchanged salutes and parted in opposite directions, each devoted to setting up the best possible sting.

CHAPTER FOURTEEN

Sunday morning, April 6, 1952 - Havana

Jacques and Bart took positions on the stone balustrade facing the marina, observing Luciano's arrival. Shortly thereafter, a taxi delivered a gangly young man in a nondescript khaki uniform and leather boots to the yacht. Mayfield and the khaki-clad visitor were on the aft deck examining the helicopter. The young man entered the cockpit of the aircraft. In short order, the engines purred and the rotors fanned the air. The test lasted five minutes before the engines were silenced.

Mayfield and the pilot left the yacht and sauntered along the Malecon. Two crew members set up a table on the aft deck in the shadow of the rotorcraft. A white-vested waiter appeared with a pitcher of freshly squeezed orange juice and glasses.

"So, Herr Nordheim, you really want to go through with the hits?" Luciano gently inquired.

"That's what we are here for."

"The two will be here for lunch at twelve. Let's settle our business now."

"I wondered when you would get around to money."

"Listen carefully, Frederick Nordheim, I'm strictly business and I don't fuck around. I didn't fly here with you for the weather. Pay me now or fuck off!"

"You know, my Mafia friend, if you spoke to me like this ten years ago, you would be dead in thirty seconds."

"Are you really a Jew, or an important Nazi?"

"Wouldn't you like to know?" Nordheim laughed hoarsely and slapped his knee. "Here is your *verdammtes geld*. How you say, *dough*?" He handed over a cashier's check for forty million dollars drawn on the Banque de Lorraine in Geneva.

"How good is this?"

"Take it to any bank here in Havana. They can verify it, and the funds can be wired here."

"For your sake, I hope you're right."

"Is that a Mafia threat? I don't like that. If you don't trust me, how can I trust you?"

"Herr Nordheim, don't get your dander up. How about the one million for the conference with the hit lady and her husband?"

"Here is another check for one million dollars, tough guy."

"And if you agree to hire these people, there is twenty-five mil due as a down payment."

"If they convince me they can do the job, I have a bearer check for them." He waved it under Luciano's nose.

"It smells good. Now, let me look at it." Charlie perused the check. "Satisfied?"

"Herr Nordheim, I have to ask you one more time...do you really want to go through with these hits? The world will be up in arms. These are very important people you want erased."

"They are *scheisse* to me. I have a score to settle. After this, I might have some more business for you."

"Does Mayfield know about this?"

"I never let one hand know what the other is doing. I am sixty-two years old and for fifty-one years of my life that is the way I always operated. I can change the world if I like."

"A man with all the money you have could do many good things, too. You are the richest man in the world, so why don't you try?"

"You run your own business and I'll run mine."

A catering truck pulled up to the yacht. A liveried crew of three boarded and began setting up the table on the aft deck. Then a limo arrived.

Sophia was dressed in a black shift dress with a string of pearls around her neck. Tony wore a blue blazer with brass buttons, white trousers and shoes to match.

"This is Mr. and Mrs. Carter," Luciano said, introducing the couple. "Herr Nordheim."

They shook hands.

"You are a very striking woman."

"Thank you, Mr. Nordheim," Sophia coolly replied.

"Let us have lunch and we'll talk after I dismiss the servants."

Chilled *vichyssoise* and crab cakes for the trio, a vegetable salad for Nordheim, and the conversation was limited to the beauties of the West Indies. Sophia kept silent, playing her icy part. The table was cleared and the caterers were dismissed.

"How do you propose to accomplish your assignment?" Nordheim asked.

"Before I get into that, Herr Nordheim, there is a little matter that has to be taken care of," Sophia coldly countered.

Charlie laughed.

"Excuse me, here is your check. It will be honored at any Cuban bank," Nordheim said.

She glanced at it, folded it carefully and handed it to Tony. He slipped it into a side pocket.

"Tony, give the details to Mr. Nordheim."

"By the way, I recommend the Antilles International Bank for immediate clearance of your checks," Nordheim suggested, his eyes fixed on Sophia's inscrutable mien.

"Why are you staring at me that way, Herr Nordheim?"

"You are a very cold woman."

"I am in a very cold business."

Tony outlined the same scenario he had presented to Luciano and Costello the day before.

"These are new drugs?"

"Very new," Tony said.

"You have that ring with you?"

Tony produced it, warning Nordheim to be careful touching it.

"How does it work?"

"Why don't we shake hands and find out?" Tony asked as he adjusted the diamond and flattened his hand on the table. A droplet of moisture appeared.

"*Wunderbar*. That small amount kills?"

"In twelve hours, and it can't be detected in an autopsy," Tony ventured.

Sophia extracted a tissue from her purse, leaned over, wiped the moisture and walked to the rail, tossing the paper into the water.

"How will you get to visit Churchill and de Gaulle?"

Sophia detailed her role as a countess plugging for her war orphans' charity.

"And you think you can first meet publicly with Truman?"

"Certainly."

"How you arrange to see him?"

"That's my business. That's what you are paying for."

"What if I ask you to kill Truman?"

"Don't ask," she snapped.

"I was hoping to have these killings done in a spectacular way. Like shooting them before a crowd with the press and their cameras there."

"Then you want a few street gangsters or druggies for that kind of a job. We're a class act with a fine clientele," Sophia indignantly asserted.

"Countess, you have a deal. I expect to see two highly spectacular funerals in England and France on my television."

☆ ☆ ☆ ☆

From a distance, Bart and Jacques observed the action.

"Colonel, look over to the right. Isn't that Sean Briscoe of the Mossad? He is walking toward the gangplank."

"What in the hell is he doing here?"

Mayfield stood at the entry of the yacht and shook hands with Briscoe when he reached the top of the staircase. "Welcome aboard, Fitzgerald. Glad you accepted the job of first mate. Your predecessor disappeared with a Cuban Señorita. You wouldn't do something like that, would you?"

"Mr. Mayfield, I am happy for the job and you can depend on me. Besides, I like the three-thousand-a-month salary," Briscoe said in a thickened version of his Irish brogue.

"The maritime union here recommends you very highly. Come, meet your boss." Mayfield steered Briscoe to the saloon.

"Herr Nordheim, meet Mr. Fitzgerald. He is applying for the job of first mate."

"Pleased to meet you, sir," Sean said.

"Sit down, young man. You are Irish?"

"Aye, sir."

"Do you have your passport with you?"

Briscoe produced it.

"Sean Fitzgerald, Belfast, Northern Ireland. Hmm, what are you doing in Havana?"

"To be quite frank with you, sir, I am here on an enforced vacation. I came here on a Dutch freighter. I had a bit of trouble with the British police."

"You're a Catholic, are you?"

"Aye, sir."

"You are part of the IRA, I can tell."

"Does that mean you won't hire me?"

Nordheim chuckled. Mayfield echoed.

"What say you, Darren?"

"I like the cut of his jib."

"You're hired. Be a good boy, and some day you'll be promoted to captain on one of my ships."

"You won't be sorry, sir. I'd like to pick up my belongings. I'll be right back."

"One moment, I'll introduce you to our captain," Mayfield said. He pressed a button on the phone.

"Leif, join us in the saloon."

The captain entered.

"Leif, this is Sean Fitzgerald, your new first mate."

Briscoe stuck out his hand. Sandstrom, not too pleased, stared at the outstretched hand for a few seconds, then sullenly offered a limp hand in resigned recognition.

"Pleased to meet you, captain."

"Ja."

"He'll take Conrad's cabin," Mayfield directed.

"Ja, come. I show you."

After seeing his new quarters, Sean left the boat to pick up his luggage.

Bart and Jacques spotted him looking for a taxi. Bart raced to the rented Cadillac. Jacques maintained the watch. Briscoe hailed a cab. Bart followed. The cab stopped at Sloppy Joe's, one of Havana's famous tourist watering holes.

Briscoe went to the bar, where he was joined by a stocky, sandy-haired man in Bermuda shorts and a short-sleeved polo shirt. Bart looked up and down the street to see if he had been followed. He parked the car and ambled into the crowded bar, then sidled up to Briscoe and calmly ordered a drink.

Startled, Briscoe looked up at Milburn, his mouth agape.

"What the hell are you doing here?" Bart hissed.

"Meet me up the street at the Casa Miguel, room 21. It's a fleabag, but a front for me. I'll explain," Briscoe whispered.

He and his companion left. Bart gulped his drink and followed. In the seedy, darkly lit hotel, Bart found room 21 and knocked at the door. The furnishings were sparse, consisting of twin beds, a single chair and a flickering lamp on a rickety bedside table. The single window faced an alley loaded with clotheslines and assorted laundry. A discomfited Briscoe introduced Simcha Cohen.

"We met," Bart crisply averred.

"Oh, yes, at our meeting in Tel Aviv," Sean acknowledged.

"Come on, what are you up to?"

"I've just been hired as first mate on Nordheim's toy."

"Why? You're going to louse up my mission here," Bart angrily said.

"Hey, Colonel, cool it. We're on the same side. I might be of great help to you. We're leaving Nordheim to you. Simcha and I are tracking a son of a bitch named Adolf Eichmann, who, next to Himmler, was the number one killer of Jews. We heard that Nordheim was going to his ranch in Argentina. Eichmann was there. Maybe still is. But, for sure, he is headed for Buenos Aires. We hoped Nordheim would lead us to Eichmann."

"What if we bag Nordheim here in Havana?"

"Well then, we'll help you."

Bart relaxed. He was convinced of Briscoe's sincerity.

"Sean, what are you going to do if the yacht takes off with Nordheim aboard?"

"I'll play out the hand as first mate. At least you'll have an insider in me tracking him."

"Can I count on your reporting to me if we don't snag him here?"

"Absolutely, Colonel. I am under orders from Prime Minister Ben-Gurion to cooperate with you to the fullest extent. You can count on me."

"How did you get the job of first mate?"

"We kidnapped Conrad Pfeiffer, his first mate. He is now on a Russian freighter en route to Vladivostok. I then greased a palm at the maritime union hiring hall, specifying the Flying Eagle. Simple, eh?"

"Not bad."

"Simcha is going to Buenos Aires to check on Eichmann there."

"Okay, Sean, contact Katherine Wharton at the CIA; here's the number, memorize it. Just say *Lucy calling* and she'll find me anywhere I might be. *Shalom*, gentlemen."

"*Shalom*," they chorused.

Berger and Sedgwick relieved Jacques at his observation post. Bart and Jacques headed back to the Hotel Riviera.

A message awaited Milburn. It read *Call Uncle Allen, signed Lucy.* He called Allen Dulles, asking, "What's up?"

"I'm joining you for a daiquiri. I'll be there at 2200 hours, Flight 52, Eastern Airlines. Reserve a pad."

"I'll pick you up."

Sophia and Tony were in the Riviera Casino at the crap table. Jacques traced them. They returned to Bart's suite.

"I was on a winning streak when Jacques pulled us away," Sophia complained.

"Yeah, she was doing real good," Tony chimed.

"How good?" Bart asked.

"We were ahead a hundred and twenty-five dollars," she declared.

"Very impressive," Bart observed. "Fill me in on your Nordheim *tête-à-tête.*"

"First, let me hand you checks totaling twenty-six million dollars. A mil for the conference and 25 mil for a down payment," Tony stated.

"Why didn't you shoot crap with it?" Bart snickered.

"If we did, the way Sophia was tossing the cubes, we'd have owned this hotel."

The two took turns reviewing their session with Nordheim.

"Luciano stopped at the bank to validate his forty-million-dollar finder's fee for introducing the hit lady and me. Not a bad day's pay. What are you going to do with these checks?"

"I'll turn them over to Allen Dulles, who's arriving here tonight. They will be held as evidence."

"What do we do now?" Sophia asked.

"You two, take a couple of days of R & R here or fly back home."

"We would like to wait a day or two to be part of Nordheim's capture."

"Okay, enjoy yourselves. See some of the spectacular shows and tour the sights. If you're needed, we'll leave a Lucy message for you."

Eastern Airlines Flight 52 from Washington touched down at the Havana Airport at 9:55 p.m. Allen Dulles, using a diplomatic passport, quickly passed through customs and immigration. Bart caught his eye and waved him to the baggage area. They met. Dulles retrieved one garment bag and followed Bart wordlessly to the Cadillac.

En route to the Hotel Riviera, Milburn briefed Dulles on all that had transpired to date.

"When is the next session with Bormann?"

"First thing in the a.m."

"Fine, I want to see this creep. I will participate in the cross-exam."

"Allen, a word of caution. This is a wily S.O.B. I have him convinced that Nordheim sold him down the river. Bormann is a survivor. He will open up under certain conditions. He could be a precious font of information, giving us enough detail for a six-million-count indictment. What we really want is a trial of the Third Reich *in toto*. Nazi Germany and its truckled, complacent, yielding population."

"Hold it, Colonel. You're not making this a personal vendetta against the German people?"

"Haven't these mass murders by a well-educated Christian nation been glossed over by revisionists? Where are the *mea culpas* from Germany and the thirty-two other countries that refused Hitler's offer to sell them at one hundred and fifty dollars per Jew at Evian-Les-Bains, at the Hotel Royal on the French side of Lake Geneva, on July 6, 1938? That date is seared in my mind, Allen. Nothing personal, just plain, honest outrage."

"I can understand now why Truman picked you to head up this operation. But, for heaven's sake, let's have some cold, calculated objectivity here," Dulles said.

A queasiness hit Bart's stomach. A cold chill raced down his spine as he recalled the Mossad's warnings about the Dulles Brothers. He concentrated on his driving and remained silent, then prudently decided to shift mental gears. "Allen, I guess I was on the podium for a B'nai B'rith rally, and I'm sorry I got carried away. You're right."

"Understood. I agree, though, we have to milk Bormann. Nordheim is the prime target. When will you move on snaring him?"

"Hopefully in the next day or two. I've got the Army Rangers, along with Berger and Sedgwick, surveilling the yacht round the clock. If he leaves the boat, he'll be snatched. Storming the yacht could be sticky. It is a big vessel and someone on board could sound the alarm system or radio a mayday call. We don't want the Cubans involved. We were lucky with Bormann."

"So far, so good, Bart. How long we can keep these prizes under cover is moot. Either Truman and the Attorney General or Eisenhower will have to decide whether these tyrants will be given a secret military trial or a wide-open circus-type jury trial, which I would personally dread."

"Eisenhower? You figure him to be elected?"

"In a landslide, friend. Bet on it."

"Well, Election Day is seven months hence. A lot can happen before that."

"Colonel, the political conventions are only three months from now. I think Eisenhower will ask Truman to put this matter on hiatus until he takes office. He doesn't want this affair to detract from the election campaign."

Bart took note of the present tense used by Dulles. Apparently, he mused, there has been communication with Ike. Dulles seemed to be reading his mind.

"Truman will probably brief both candidates."

"I hope we can keep them on ice that long," Bart said.

At the Riviera Hotel, Bart steered Dulles to an unoccupied suite. "I arranged these rooms for you, Allen, on the assumption that you would prefer to be here incognito."

"You are so right. You think like a CIA man. That's your forte. Love to have you aboard."

"I'm doing this on a *pro bono* basis. Besides, you can't afford me. How about breakfast at 0700 hours in my suite right next door?"

"Suits me. Goodnight."

☆ ☆ ☆ ☆

Monday, April 7, 1952 - 10 a.m. - U.S. Naval Station, Guantanamo
Admiral Thomas, Allen Dulles and Bart Milburn were huddled in the executive office.

"Mr. Dulles, we're honored by your visit."

"My pleasure, Admiral. How is our Nazi guest faring?"

"He's a cantankerous prisoner. He's having a very hard time adjusting to his incarceration. He keeps ranting that he is entitled to better quarters and better food. He keeps asking for the colonel. Apparently he has developed an affinity for Milburn. He also asks if the countess is a prisoner. He wants to talk with her."

"Allen, that bare cell is stark in every aspect. It might prove fruitful if we were to upgrade his quarters without risking chances for a possible suicide. We might hold out a deal for him. He's an inveterate survivor. If we hold out an olive branch of a future for him, he'll grasp onto that like a drowning man."

"That has merit, Bart. Maybe the admiral can suggest something."

"We have a room with adjoining bath used for officers in house arrest awaiting court-martial."

"Does it have a cell door so that he can be observed?" Bart asked.

"No, but we can arrange that."

"We'll see how he behaves this morning before we decide to upgrade our guest," Milburn declared. "I assume we can arrange for better cuisine, Admiral."

"Call the shot, Colonel, and it will be done."

Bormann was pacing his meager cell. Bart excused the two guards and brought two chairs into the barren cell. He took the key, locked the cell door and greeted the unshaven prisoner.

"*Ach*, Colonel, at last you visit me in this *gestunken* jail. I deserve better than this. *Und* who is this you bring?"

"Martin, this is Allen. He is my associate."

Bormann came closer and stared at Dulles. Bart detected a flicker of recognition. Martin's irritable demeanor changed.

"Mr. Allen, it is my pleasure to meet you."

"Herr Bormann, how are you being treated?" Dulles inquired.

"Terrible, except when the colonel is here."

"Okay, Martin, I'm turning on the recorder. We have some more questions," Bart said.

"I will cooperate if you can get me better quarters. Also, I want some decent food, Colonel."

"It can be arranged depending on your answers. Don't hold back, and your request will be granted."

"By the way, Herr Bormann, where and when did you learn to speak English?" Dulles asked.

"I learned a little English in school. Later, Hitler wanted us to study English to be prepared for the occupation of Britain. All the top officers and men were tutored before the war. During that time, I spoke in English with the Duke of Windsor and his wife when they visited Hitler in the Berghof at Berchtesgaden in October, 1939. He told me I speak good English."

"What was the Duke doing there? The war was on," Bart snapped.

"The Duke and his wife supported Hitler. He wanted to make peace. That Swedish fellow, Axel Werner-Gren, arranged the meeting. He told us that there were a lot of important English people who believed in Hitler. Hitler wanted to put Windsor back on the British throne. The Duke promised to help a peace agreement. Churchill was to be assassinated."

"Did the duke know that?" Dulles cut in.

"No, but they were going to have those pro-peace people in the Cliveden Set try to arouse the English people to start a peace movement. Hitler wanted peace with England because he was going to launch Operation Barbarossa, the stupid invasion of Russia. Big mistake."

"Who else was there?" Dulles pressed.

"Foreign Minister von Ribbentrop and Walter Schellenberg, the SS chief. Hitler promised to put the duke back on the throne. The duchess loved that idea. The duke said the English constitution wouldn't allow it, because he had abdicated. Hitler said, we will control that. Just make peace and the British Empire will remain intact and Germany will rule Europe. The duke was very interested. He promised to cooperate."

"Did you or Hitler think he was a traitor to his country?"

"*Ach*, yes, but *our* traitor."

"Maybe he was, in his own mind, a patriot trying to save his country," Dulles said.

"Some patriot," Bart scoffed.

"Just a thought," Dulles murmured.

"Did the Duke of Windsor cooperate with Hitler during the war?" Bart pressed.

"Plenty, but when Churchill ordered him to the Bahamas, we had a plan to kidnap him in Spain. Before that, when we occupied Paris, the duke and duchess fled to the French Riviera. While they were there, they sent a message to Hitler, which I handled. The duchess wanted her jewels and wardrobe in Paris sent to her. I arranged it. So, you see, we were on friendly terms. She sent me a note of thanks. She addressed me as General Bormann. I had the title of major general."

"Aren't you smearing them?" Dulles queried.

"*Nein*, that's the truth," Bormann protested.

"I believe you, Martin. You have no reason to lie," Bart asserted in a gentle remonstrance to Dulles.

"Where did Nordheim get all his money?" Dulles asked.

"Like I told the colonel, I helped open numbered bank accounts in Geneva and Zurich. The Swiss banks did a lot of business with Germany during the war. The Swiss government was pro-Hitler. In 1944, I realized that the war was lost when the Americans got a foothold in France after the Normandy invasion. I called a meeting of all the big manufacturers to move their money and assets to safe places. Hitler had collected art, jewelry and other priceless objects. I turned them into cash. We also got lots of money from our suppliers. You know, like an override."

"Most of that money came from six million dead Jews. Their possessions, their homes, their furniture, their art, their jewelry, their bank accounts, and even the gold dental fillings from their dead mouths, Martin Bormann. You know that," Bart snarled.

"Colonel, everyone in high places grabbed what they could. That fat lecherous Hermann Goering stole most of the art from every country we invaded. That chinless murdering chicken farmer Heinrich Himmler collected gold from the Jews' mouths. Hitler's money came mostly from the treasuries of the countries we conquered. We collected some of the gold from Himmler. He was a thief who tried to cheat Hitler out of the loot. I caught him and threatened to destroy him. He was weak *scheisse*. Even our generals were hiding loot they collected. Even the street bums in the SA stole from their victims. The property of the Jews brought in a lot of money. The country was ravaging the victims. We stripped the Jews of everything, even their clothes. You know, to the victor belongs the spoils."

"Bormann, you and Hitler got very rich that way. Aren't you ashamed of what was the greatest mass murder and robbery in the history of the world?" Bart angrily roared.

"Why should I be ashamed? Everyone was grabbing what they could. I had no hand in killing or robbing. But, as the war went on, we realized that we shouldn't let Goering, Himmler, Heydrich, Eichmann, Mengele and all the SA, SS and concentration-camp commandants stuff their pockets. Hitler told me to collect all I could for a rainy day. I followed orders. I made him the richest man in the world."

The bile had risen in Milburn's throat during Bormann's amoral rationale of the Nazi psyche in their conscienceless ravage of their victims.

"Where is all this money, Martin?" Dulles coolly pressed on.

"Hitler's money is all over the world. Mostly in Switzerland, but also in American treasury bonds, Vancouver banks, Paris banks, American stock-brokers, Sweden, Belgium, Argentina, Liechtenstein, in Winston General holdings, ships, cattle, real estate and gold. He is worth over forty-three billion American dollars."

"How about you, Bormann?" Bart icily demanded.

"I have maybe three billion in assets. I send money to my children. My wife, before she died, was running a Jewish orphans' charity. I sent her money. I am not ashamed. But now my money means nothing. I am a prisoner. If you two are interested, I would gladly split what I have with you if you let me go."

"Go where?" Bart snapped.

"To Argentina for a quiet life for my remaining years, and you men would be very rich."

"Where is your money?" Dulles queried.

"Oh no, I'm not stupid. I not tell you so you can seize my funds. You make a deal with me and I will transfer money to your accounts. I am a business-man. I ran all the Nazi business."

"We'll think about your offer, Martin. Now, tell us how you and Hitler escaped from the bunker under the chancellery."

"Hitler? Escape?"

"Cut the shit, Martin. The cat's out of the bag."

Bormann stared at Milburn, then smirked, "Not now. Maybe later. First, I have some questions."

"Fine. Ask," Bart agreed.

"Like your Judge Roy Bean, I get a trial and then you hang me? Is that what you plan for me?"

"If you testify against Hitler, you will have a deal. You will not be hanged, I guarantee that," Bart declared.

"But I'll be a prisoner for the rest of my life, not so?"

"We have a law in America. It is called the Witness Protection Program. We give a new identity and secret location for witnesses who cooperate with our Justice Department and testify against known criminals. I will try to arrange that for you if you voluntarily testify against Hitler and other Nazi war criminals," Bart said.

"My life would be worth nothing. There are Nazis all over the world. They will come after me. I'll be killed in no time."

"No, you'll be hidden and protected."

"Colonel, get me out of this rat hole...give me decent treatment and let me think on that. Are you sure that Nordheim told you where I was?"

"You mean *Hitler*. I told you it came from his own lips," Bart evasively reiterated.

"It is so hard to believe. That ungrateful *schweinhund*. I dedicated my life to him."

"Anything further, Allen?"

"No, not right now."

"Martin, I am going to have you moved into a room with your own toilet and shower. Don't do anything foolish there like trying suicide, or anything to antagonize the guards. You'll get three good meals a day. You will be allowed to shave and bathe. You'll get books to read. Promise me you'll behave," Bart said. "If you don't, it's back to this cell for you."

"Thank you, Colonel, I promise, and I don't believe in suicide. That's for *scheisse* like Goering, Goebbels and Himmler. Not me."

"Aren't we lucky," Bart uttered in a parting shot.

☆ ☆ ☆ ☆

Monday, April 7, 1952, same day - 11 a.m. - Havana

Darren Mayfield, Havana's Police Captain Juan Escobar and Detective Lieutenant Jorge Flores entered the lobby of the Capri Hotel and approached the front desk.

"We wish to talk with Señor Raft," the captain imperiously addressed the desk clerk.

"Mr. Raft is having his breakfast now," she replied, referring to the Capri's front as owner, the actor George Raft. "Who shall I say is calling?"

"Who do I look like? I am Police Captain Escobar. *Prisa.* Now!"

"Si, Señor," the flustered clerk muttered, then reached for a phone. "The police wish to see Señor Raft."

He held the phone and waited. A moment went by, and the clerk hung up. "Señor Raft is in the coffee shop. He said for you to join him."

The taciturn actor was seated at a table, sipping on a cup of steaming coffee. Without a word he pointed to chairs at his table, inviting them to sit. He continued to sip his coffee. Not a word of recognition crossed his lips. He continued to read his newspaper.

"We are here, Señor Raft, about the taxi that was reported stolen yesterday."

"Mmm," he mumbled as he worked on his coffee.

"How was it stolen?"

The consummate actor, reprising the gangster role he had played so many times in the movies, lit a cigarette, vented a spiral of smoke, coolly stared at the trio and cryptically stated, "The driver went for a piss. Some joker took the cab for a joyride. End of script."

"Cut the crap, Raft. There's more to it than that," Mayfield snarled.

"Who the fuck are you?" Raft hissed back.

"I'm Darren Mayfield, formerly with the FBI. I represent Frederick Nordheim and am searching for his associate, Dov Schwartz, who disappeared from the Hotel Nacional."

Raft spewed a cloud of smoke directly in Mayfield's face.

"J. Edgar didn't teach manners to you pricks. I don't give a shit if you were the maharajah from the Black Hole of Calcutta. Don't come in here telling me to cut the crap!" Raft contemptuously retorted.

"Listen, pal, you may have been a big shot in Hollywood, but you don't mean a fart to me. I'm here to investigate a kidnapping. I think you know something about it."

"Why, you cocksucker, someone must have boiled your brains in a tub of shit. Get your ass out of here or I'll have you thrown out, you ex-FBI asshole," he coldly hissed.

Mayfield was thoroughly upset and at a loss for a quick riposte. Captain Escobar stepped in and attempted to placate the cold, unruffled actor.

"Sir, may I ask you for a little more detail on the cab driver whose taxi was stolen?"

"Sure."

"Has anyone confirmed that he went to the toilet when the car was taken?"

"Yeah, one of your detectives talked with him. Actually, he had a case of diarrhea."

Lieutenant Flores looked at the captain and nodded his head in affirmation. "So that's it?"

"Captain, the poor bastard was crying up a storm. He came to me, and that's when I reported it stolen to your police. That's all I know. What's all that got to do with a kidnapping? If they used the cab to hustle him away from the Nacional, then why the fuck aren't you checking *that* hotel?"

"The person came in that cab to pay Schwartz's bill," Escobar said.

"Maybe the guy wasn't kidnapped. Maybe he ran off with some pussy."

"Mr. Raft, I want to apologize for my manner in speaking to you the way I did," Mayfield said.

"Okay."

"You see, Mr. Nordheim is the richest man in the world, and he values the life of his associate Schwartz. Nordheim is a friend of Luciano."

"Who is that?" Raft craftily asked.

"You don't know Luciano?"

"Never heard of him."

"Isn't he a partner of Meyer Lansky?"

"If he is, he is a mighty silent one."

"This is a farce, Captain, let's go."

The trio rose to leave. Raft ordered more coffee and went on reading the New York Daily News. Ten minutes after Mayfield and the police left, Raft called Costello's room at the Riviera.

"Can you spare a few minutes, Chich?"

"Yes."

"I'll be right there."

Luciano and Costello were sitting on the terrace of the suite eating breakfast. Raft joined them for more coffee. He recounted the scene at the Capri.

"Forget it, George. Yeah, I know that prick Nordheim. Don't think about it any more. That Mayfield is a bad, stupid hombre."

The Nacional Hotel was under siege. Captain Escobar, Lieutenant Flores and Darren Mayfield scoured each floor, questioned every maid, room-service personnel, bellhops, bell captains, the concierge, doormen and managers. Finally they went to the freight dock at the back of the hotel. Trucks were backed up to the dock unloading food supplies. Several men were rolling loaded carts into the kitchen elevator.

The detectives followed along, questioning the laborers as they toiled with the heavy loads. A detective detached one Javier Mendoza from his chores. He rushed him up back to the dock and onto the macadam lip of the cargo entry. He beckoned Escobar. "Javier, tell the captain about the sick men and the ambulance."

"The three men were unconscious and the lady was crying. I couldn't see her face, because she was crying and had a handkerchief over her eyes and her head was down in her hands."

"Where did the ambulance take them?" the captain demanded.

"I don't know. The doctor chased us away."

"Who is *us*?"

"Emilio, that hombre there," he answered, pointing. "Hey, Emilio! Come here!"

Emilio walked over to the men.

"Tell us what you saw."

He repeated Javier's version of the events. The captain and Mayfield were frustrated as they made their way to the lobby. Lieutenant Flores was in the cocktail lounge questioning the bartender. A detective hailed the captain and directed him to the bar. The bartender, José Sanchez, was quite voluble. The captain pulled him away from the bar and sat him at a table with Mayfield and Flores.

"That man can drink like a thirsty elephant. He had champagne, rum and coke, daiquiris, and the lady just sipped on two banana daiquiris. He was staggering, and the lady helped him walk out. She held his arm."

"How much was the bill?" Mayfield asked.

"Two hundred and ten dollars. He left three hundred on the table. The waiter, Tony, split the 90-dollar tip with me."

Tony repeated the bartender's version with one interesting embellishment.

"Señor Schwartz was a lover. He was kissing the lady's hand all the time. She was liking it. Then they leave. I think maybe they go upstairs to make love."

"Have you seen the lady before?"

"No."

"A *puta*?"

"Oh, no, *fina dama*, classy."

The captain called off the sweep and returned to headquarters. Mayfield returned to the Flying Eagle. Nordheim was in a state of agitation. He was pacing the aft deck, then joined Mayfield in the lounge. "You learn something?"

"A little...they were taken away in an ambulance."

Nordheim cut him off. "Look at this!" he barked, handing a coffee-stained sheet of paper to Mayfield.

A badly typed ransom note in a mixture of English and Spanish stated: *Señor Schwartz is okay. Urgente. Two milion Amerikan dolar. He be safe. No pay, totalmente. No policia. Call policia, Schwartz muerte. If pay, fly Cuban flag on boat. Then we contact with orderes. Viva, Revolucion.*

Mayfield exploded, "Communist bastards! They're in the Oriente mountains. A prick named Castro and an Argentinian, Ernesto 'Che' Guevara, are running a guerrilla rebellion against Batista."

"You think this is real, Darren?"

"We can't ignore it."

"Raise the Cuban flag and we will talk with Batista."

Mayfield ordered the flag hoisted alongside the Liberian flag.

"They will be watching the yacht. How do we contact Batista?"

"Darren, I will call him and tell him it is important he come here alone after dark in a private car with no escort."

Back at the Riviera Hotel, Costello reached Jacques Laurent in Bart's suite. "Have Milburn call me right away. Do you know where to reach him?"

At Guantanamo, an operator buzzed Admiral Thomas.

"Sir, there is someone calling Colonel Milburn. He said it is urgent. Lucy calling."

"Put him on hold."

He relayed the message to Bart, who was in the officers' mess with Dulles. Bart was summoned to the phone. Jacques relayed Costello's message and immediately called.

"Uncle, what's up?"

Costello cryptically told of the day's developments, from the encounter with George Raft to the police sweep at the Nacional Hotel. All was outlined. He then detailed the ransom scam.

"How did you do that?"

"Colonel, you know better than that. Don't ask."

"You're so right. That's wonderful. Thanks for your help."

"Remember, we're patriots too."

"In my eyes, yes. *Ciao.*"

That night a rickety pickup truck arrived at the gangplank of the Flying Eagle. A slight drizzle dotted the landscape under a heavy cloud cover. In the misty night, Fulgencio Batista, wearing a baseball cap and covered by a poncho, ascended the gangplank.

Mayfield stood back from the dim overhead light and escorted the Cuban dictator to the saloon.

"My deep gratitude, Your Excellency. This is most serious," Nordheim exclaimed, handing him the ransom note.

Batista donned reading glasses and studiously perused the kidnap note.

"*Bolla de idiotas pendefos maldito ay milida. Que pendejo es* Castro, he is the son of a dog!" Batista exploded.

"Can we do business with this rebel?" Nordheim asked.

"No, he needs the money for his revolt. I don't want him to have that money to buy arms."

"Your excellency, I want Schwartz back alive. So, please, don't do anything in attacking Castro. He'll kill my man."

"Then, what will you have me do, Herr Nordheim?"

"I will pay him with counterfeit money, then you notify the Americans he has the illegal bills."

"I will hold back. Keep me advised of his next instructions. We will keep a quiet watch. *Adios, Señores.*"

Later that night, Batista returned home. Waiting for him in his ornate living room was Meyer Lansky, the chancellor of the exchequer for the Mafia operations in Cuba.

"Meyer, what an honor. Have you been waiting long? This must be important. How about some brandy?"

Lansky accepted, and the two men toasted each other. "Fulgencio, my dear friend, I am here on a delicate matter."

"I am at your service, *amigo*."

"This man Nordheim is a very evil man. He is a Nazi criminal. Don't do anything to help him."

"I have suspicions of him. He just advised me of the kidnapping of a Dov Schwartz, an associate of his. He has a ransom note from Fidel Castro."

"Don't pay any attention to that. Castro has nothing to do with that."

Batista, totally taken aback, gasped, "Then who?"

"My friend, this is far above us. It is political, not criminal. We have nothing to do with it. Fulgencio, we are partners and you are doing very well with us. Cuba is thriving. We will consider your hands off on this matter as a personal favor."

"Meyer, I know you are a loyal Jew. I respect the Jews. I will do nothing to help this Nazi bastard, *hijo de puta*."

"Good enough. Now, if he gets a note to pay the ransom, I want him to bring the money in person. If he asks for protection, give it to him, but have your men fumble so that Nordheim can be snatched. If he asks your advice, tell him to do it, but have Mayfield carry the money."

"I will cooperate. I meant to tell you that the money he will pay is counterfeit."

"We figured that. American Secret Service men will grab him with the money. They'll put Mayfield away for a long time."

"Where will the payoff take place?"

"At the last hangar at the airport. Clear all personnel away, except the crew at the Fairchild 7-27. No gunplay unless Mayfield draws a gun. *Comprendo?*"

"Keep me informed and I'll work closely with you, Meyer. You know that I'll be losing some income from Nordheim."

"We'll make it up to you."

"*Gracias, amigo.*"

"*Hasta luego.*"

☆ ☆ ☆ ☆

Tuesday, April 8, 1952 - 10 a.m. - Havana

The big three of the Mafia were gathered over a late breakfast in Frank Costello's suite. Meyer Lansky and Luciano were briefing Barton Milburn on the kidnapping plot. Dulles opted not to attend the conference. It was just as well, because the conferees had objected to his presence.

"A note will be delivered to the yacht in the next couple of hours. And, as you advised, Colonel, Nordheim must deliver the payment in person to the last hangar at the airport. Mayfield can come with him. No one else. Is that right?" Costello asked.

"Perfect, if it works."

"Batista will advise him to do it. He will promise him protection, but will have his men go to the wrong hangar. An honest mistake," Costello laughed.

"If Mayfield is with him, I'll have our Secret Service grab him and shuttle him to Key West aboard another plane, which will be ready for an immediate takeoff," Bart declared.

The close-mouthed Lansky looked at Bart intensely. "Son, this is a very personal thing to me. I want this Nazi bastard put away," he passionately declared.

"Mr. Lansky, your help in this matter is most deeply appreciated. I am sure our government will share my views."

"I doubt that, Colonel, but I feel *your* sincerity."

The meeting was over. Bart joined Dulles and went to the American Embassy. After clearing with the ambassador, they were granted a private office with a safe telephone. The White House operator put Bart straight through to John Steelman.

"How goes the campaign, Bart?"

"Quite well, to this point, John. This could be D-Day II. We're set to go if our quarry bites at the cheese tonight or tomorrow night. We're planning for the Secret Service to snatch the ex-FBI sleazeball."

"Details?"

"In short, a kidnap scam of number two for a two-million ransom note. I believe it will be paid in funny money. That's as far as I'm willing to go. Mayfield should be put on ice, maybe by the military, for aiding and abetting Nazi criminals to escape. It's up to the Prez. We have to keep this worm away from the press."

"That's a hot potato."

"Yes, but he's hotter on the loose. We have to tuck him away."

"Agreed. I'll brief the boss. Good luck, Barton. This could be a grand slam."

"Mum's the word, John."

Dulles cabbed to the hotel. Bart drove toward the Malecon. He observed Jacques at his vantage point surveilling the yacht. He whistled sharply. Jacques, recognizing the shrill sound, turned to the Cadillac, then raced up the incline.

"Where is Captain Devereaux?"

"Bart, he's at my left at the fore end of the boat."

"Send one of the Rangers to get him here. I don't want you too close to the yacht. Mayfield may spot you."

The captain duly appeared.

"Captain, I want you and Jacques to come with me back to the hotel. Where are Sedgwick and Berger?"

"They were relieved. They were on duty all night," Jacques answered.

"Okay, let's go."

Jacques awakened Berger and Sedgwick. Fifteen minutes later they appeared at Bart's quarters. Hot coffee and croissants were quickly delivered. Bart outlined the plan for the planned midnight rendezvous with Nordheim.

"I want you, Captain, and all the Rangers at the back of the hangar. When

I whistle, you and your men, guns drawn, are to surround Nordheim and Mayfield. Don't interfere with the Secret Service. You'll meet them and be prepared to help them, if necessary."

"Colonel, how do you propose to subdue them?"

"I want you and your men to seize him. I will chloroform the bastard and apply the manacles. Once we carry him on board, I'll give him a shot of anesthetic. If the Secret Service requires help with Mayfield, assign four of your men to assist. He will be chloroformed as well, and I'll supply the anesthetic for the Secret Service to use if required."

"What do you have in mind for us?" Berger queried.

"Phillip, you're a master of disguise in these covert operations. You're nominated to be the ransom collector. Black jumpsuit and black knitted head mask. Take a Colt .45 with you. Don't shoot unless they draw on you. Then, fast, shoot them in the legs. I doubt that will be necessary. We want them alive. That goes for you too, Captain Devereaux."

Sedgwick raised his hand.

"Lloyd, you are to be the driver in the car with our facsimile body of Schwartz-Bormann. Captain Devereaux, have you a man who could play the part of Schwartz? He will be manacled, blindfolded and his mouth taped, slouching in the back of the car. I realize your men are taller than Bormann, so he will have to slouch down in the car. Nordheim will want to see if Schwartz is still alive. So your man can groan and move. It'll be dark. The visibility will be poor. The whole thing should be over in minutes."

"I've just the man for the job," Devereaux said.

☆ ☆ ☆ ☆

The Flying Eagle - 3 p.m. - Havana

A motorcycle noisily arrived at the Flying Eagle gangplank. The cyclist ran up the steps to the entry. He handed a manila envelope to a crew member. It was addressed to Señor Nordheim, marked *Personal*. The messenger left. The crewmember knocked on the door of Nordheim's master suite. It took several taps on the door before an answer was elicited.

"*Ja*, come in," Nordheim sleepily said.

The young man presented the envelope to Nordheim, who was clad in his pajamas. Rubbing his eyes, he hoarsely questioned, "How did this come?"

"By motorcycle messenger, sir."

"Where is he?"

"He's gone."

"*Scheisse*. Find Mayfield and send him here, *schnell*."

He tore open the large envelope and removed a soiled yellow paper. The message was sloppily typed. Nordheim adjusted his bifocals and read:

Midnight tonight, Schwartz exchange for two million dollars. No policia. Only you come and Meyerfiel, nobody else. No fuck with us. No games. Quick exchange you take Schwartz we take money. No deal. We blow up your ship

next. If okay take down Cuba flag. Make clean deal. At Hangar 13.
Viva, Revolucion

Mayfield entered. He studied the missive intently while Nordheim paced the room.

"I'll go alone," Mayfield volunteered.

"*Bist du Verrückt.*"

"Why?"

"Because they want me to come."

"We better talk with Batista."

"Tell him to come now. Dressed like last night. Same car."

"Is that wise?"

"Do it now. Don't question me. All they want is the money. I understand these things," Nordheim assured him.

An hour later the dictator arrived, wearing overalls and a wide-brimmed straw sombrero. "What you think, Your Excellency?"

"I would go if I were you. They are hungry for money. You will be protected. This will give me time to place our forces at the hangar, looking like mechanics and plane crews. Make the exchange and then we will arrest them. I want to teach Castro a lesson. Their car or cars will be surrounded. Once you complete the transaction, put Schwartz in your car and leave. I want you away, in case there is any shooting. The airport exits will be closed off."

"This smells bad to me. Suppose they try to snatch Herr Nordheim," Mayfield asked.

"That is not their game. They need money now. I know how they think. Besides, I'll have more people there than they can handle. They know better than to come with a lot of people. I'll bet you there will be only two men there. One in a car with Schwartz, and the other will approach you for the money. Don't take any guns with you. He will put you down."

"Let's do it. I have the money all ready in a suitcase," Nordheim declared.

"Good, lower the Cuban flag now, in case they are observing the boat," Batista suggested.

"Darren, order a car."

"Not necessary. I'll send one with one of our detectives as your driver."

"*Nein*, they will be suspicious. Mayfield will drive."

"You are right, Señor."

The phone rang in Milburn's suite. Jacques answered. "It's for you, Captain Devereaux."

"Hello. Yes, Bob. Tell the men to come here now and go to their rooms. We'll have a little powwow."

"What was that about?" Bart inquired.

"They lowered the Cuban flag. The exchange is on for midnight. A guy in a sombrero and overalls entered the yacht. He just left. I wonder who that was? A motorcycle messenger delivered the ransom note earlier."

"Gentlemen, this is a mini-D-Day II. Let's make a little history at 2400 hours. Everyone should be in place in and around the back of the hangar at thirty minutes before that. Mechanic work smocks will be distributed to your men at that time, Captain."

Dulles was silent during Milburn's assignments.

"Allen, any flaws in our plan? Or any suggestions?"

"No, it's your show and it sounds good. I'll be there as an observer."

At 8 p.m., two men knocked on the door of Bart's suite. Each was slightly over six feet tall. Beneath their business suits there was a hint of sinew. "Colonel Milburn, I am Adam Watkins and this is my partner, Samuel Collins." He flashed their Secret Service credentials.

"Welcome, gentlemen. Thanks for coming on such short notice. Meet my associate, Jacques Laurent."

A knock on the door and Bart opened it.

"Gentlemen, I am sure you know Allen Dulles."

"Indeed we do, and we're impressed by his presence," Watkins said.

"Flattery will get you everywhere," Dulles snickered.

"Jacques, would you bring that bag under the bed?"

It was produced. Bart snapped it open. He pointed to the five hundred thousand dollars. "Is that stuff real?"

The two men picked up a couple of packets of hundred-dollar bills. Collins pulled a magnifying glass from his pocket. Watkins had a strange object that looked like a fountain pen. Collins thumbed his packet, rippling the stack, with the magnifying glass passing over each bill. Watkins ran a blue marking over several bills with his pen-like object. They looked at each other, both nodding in acquiescence.

"This is one of the best pieces of counterfeit we have encountered in a long time. Where did you get it?"

"We seized it here in Havana from a Nazi war criminal, who shall remain nameless."

"We have a right to know. He belongs to us, Colonel Milburn."

"I'm afraid not, my friends. This matter is top secret, under the jurisdiction of the President of the United States. Secretary of the Treasury Snyder is fully aware of the matter at hand."

That statement appeased the two men. Bart filled them in on the upcoming midnight exercise.

"You will be picking up one gentleman tonight with two million more of this funny money. You came in an Army plane. Put him on board and jail him in a federal pen. Don't charge him until we at the CIA meet with Secretary Snyder. I'll be back tomorrow," Dulles instructed.

"Which penitentiary do you suggest?"

"Homestead brig. This affair is a very delicate one. The entire Cabinet has been briefed, with instructions of total secrecy. Don't question this ex-FBI bum, whose name is Darren Mayfield. No leaks to the media. Have your boss call General Smith, director of the CIA, who arranged for you two to come here," Bart sternly advised.

"We got it. We'll play," Watkins acknowledged.

"Our Army Rangers will join us here shortly so that you can eye each other. They will assist you in nailing Mayfield. There is another man whom we will take to parts unknown. I don't like being mysterious, but this is literally a cloak-and-dagger operation. We'll work with the Secret Service in tracing the origin of the counterfeit, and hopefully locate the plates and place of manufacture," Milburn assured.

"That's of most interest to us," Collins asserted.

"Any more questions?"

"No."

The Rangers were invited to join the group.

CHAPTER FIFTEEN

Tuesday, April 8, 1952 - 7:30 p.m. - New York City

Doug Milburn was about to leave for a date with his special lady, the star of the Broadway hit musical *California,* a Hollywood spoof.

He had just finished shaving and was approaching his desk in the seventh floor city room of the New York Daily News when Neil Toomey alerted him that there was a woman in the reception area asking to see him.

"She seems distraught and says she has an important story."

"Hell no, Neil. Let her talk to one of the night guys."

"She's crying and says it's very important. She knows you're here. The receptionist told her. She insists it be you and no one else."

Doug was donning his jacket and adjusting his tie as he exploded, "Balls of fire! Why me at this hour?"

Neil shrugged, "Don't the big ones always happen this way, Doug?"

"Take her into the interview room next to Shand's office. I'll be right there." Doug called Sardi's.

"This is Frank, May I help you?"

"Frank, this is Douglas Milburn..."

"Oh, yes, Mr. Milburn, how are you?"

"Fine. Listen, Frank, I'm to meet Miss Constance Luce at 7:45, but I'll be late, so be sure to have her call me here at Murray Hill 2-8585 as soon as she arrives. Be on the watch for her."

"Yes, sir, Mr. Milburn. We have your reservation. I'll get her to call right away."

"Thanks, Frank."

In the interview room, a well dressed, beautifully coiffured redhead in her middle thirties was seated, sipping water out of a plastic cup. It was obvious that she had been crying. She tried to stand, but Milburn motioned her back into her chair.

Angry as he was, he politely said, "Miss, or is it Mrs., why couldn't this wait until tomorrow?"

"Oh," she began to blubber, "I am frightened. I am afraid someone will want to kill me."

He stared at her for a long few seconds, then planted his huge hulk in the chair behind the desk.

"Who would want to kill you?" he asked, hoping she wasn't one of those paranoid psychopaths he came in with weird delusions at least once or twice a week.

"I don't know," she replied.

"What makes you think someone wants to kill you?"

"If you'll listen for a minute, you'll understand."

He sized her up. She was well spoken. Definitely not a New York accent. "Where are you from?"

"Beverly Hills, California. I arrived here this morning on the American Airlines red-eye flight. Please let me explain why I'm here and asked to see you. I'm sorry it's so late, but I just came into some information that's frightened me out of my skin. I've been walking the streets for the past three hours trying to figure out what to do."

"Well, if it was so bad, why didn't you go to the police?"

"Oh, no, that's the last thing I would want to do under the circumstances."

"What circumstances?"

"I have to begin at the beginning, if you don't mind. I've read some of your syndicated columns and I've read two of your books. I figured you could help me sort out my problem."

"What's your name? Who are you? I want to see some ID," Doug snapped.

She was taken aback by his tone, but began fumbling in her purse, finally dumping the contents on Doug's desk. Keys, wallet, lipsticks, a large wad of cash, mostly hundred-dollar bills, two folded legal-sized envelopes, airline tickets, a perfume sprayer, a small bottle of pills, a fountain pen and small pad, and a hotel key littered the desk blotter. Doug stared at the array of mysteries in a woman's handbag.

"Here's my driver's license," she said as she handed her wallet to him. "As you can see, my name is Christina Lyons. I live on Wallace Ridge in Beverly Hills. I am 34 years of age. I am a widow. My husband was an Air Force officer, Captain Thomas Lyons, shot down over Inchon, Korea, almost two years ago. I have two children, a boy aged seven and a girl aged five."

"My maiden name may mean something to you. It was Christina LaVelle."

The phone rang. Doug held up his right hand to the lady in front of him.

"Hello, honey, what time do you go on?"

"Doug, if you're stuck, I'll understand. Can you meet me after the show?" Constance Luce suggested.

"Connie, you're a doll. I'll be backstage as soon as I can, but certainly by curtain time."

"I love you," she kissed him over the phone.

"Love you, too, sweetheart."

Christina Lyons said, "Mr. Milburn, I'm so sorry. Please forgive me." She rose to leave.

"Sit down, Mrs. Lyons. I didn't mean to be so curt with you. My fiancée is a very understanding lady. Now, let me see if my memory serves me. Are you the daughter of that famous plastic surgeon Phillip LaVelle who disappeared in Geneva about seven or eight years ago?"

"Yes, yes, yes," she mumbled. "Oh, yes, you remembered. I have..."

"Wait one minute, Mrs. Lyons," Doug stopped her. He picked up the phone receiver and said, "Give me the morgue, please." Noticing a look of horror on the face of his guest, he said to her, "No, no, *morgue* is the name we use for the library. Hello, Fred, Doug here."

"What's up, pal?" was the reply.

"Need the file on Phillip LaVelle, pronto. I'm in the interview room next to Shand's office."

"You got it."

Turning to Mrs. Lyons, Doug said, "Please continue, and I'll not interrupt."

"Thank you, Mr. Milburn. As you may know, my father left home on June 10, 1945, for New York. He stayed at the Plaza in New York and on June 11 he retained a New York law firm, Curtis, Grogan & Lange. He had a will drawn and left a letter for me. Both were placed in a safe-deposit box at the Hudson National Bank on the ground floor of their building at 52 Broad Street. He left the key in an envelope addressed to me and noted on the face of it, *Not to be opened by anyone other than my daughter, Christina LaVelle Lyons.* He instructed Mr. Gordon Curtis, who handled the matter, to contact me immediately if anything happened to him during his trip to Europe. He had told my mother that he was going to do some plastic surgery in Europe for a very important person, but didn't know his name. Arrangements were to be made with a New York attorney named Waldo Heiser."

Doug stopped her at this point. A copy girl dropped four elongated envelopes of news clips on his desk, and he quickly glanced through some of them. "Christina, mind if I call you by your first name?"

She nodded assent.

"Call me Douglas," he continued. "According to these clips, you filed a missing-persons report with the Beverly Hills police two weeks after he left for Paris. They brought the matter to the FBI, Interpol, and the Swiss and French police. The report states here that Phillip LaVelle was last seen getting into a limousine outside of the Hotel Le Richmonde in Geneva, Switzerland."

"I know all that," Christina cried.

"Let me go on for a minute or so, and then I have some questions," he said.

"The limousine had been hired from the Depot Limousine Service, a very reputable company and a family business for over 30 years, for a Louise

Bancroft from London. She had checked in that morning, several hours before your father arrived. The reception-desk man, Walter Bregman, described her as a scholarly woman, about 45 years of age, who spoke with a slight Irish brogue. She checked out of the hotel about 15 minutes after your father left."

"Mr. Milburn, I am well aware of those facts," she said. "I've been to Geneva several times and talked with the authorities there. I also spoke with the hotel personnel. They all told the same story. I went to Scotland Yard in London. They could not find a Louise Bancroft in London, nor was there a passport issued to anyone by that name. Both the Swiss and the British police checked the airlines and there was no record of a Louise Bancroft having flown into Geneva. Swiss Customs had no record of her. The consensus of Interpol, Scotland Yard and the Swiss is that she came into Switzerland illegally."

"All right, Christina," Douglas said, "but now the reports indicate that your father never returned to his hotel. A wide search over all of Europe was conducted. The attorney, Waldo Heiser, with whom your father met, also vanished. The authorities suspected foul play. So, tell me, what suddenly shook you up today and brought you here?"

"My father's attorney, Mr. Gordon Curtis, has been trying through the courts to have my father declared deceased so that we could have access to his safety-deposit box at the Hudson National Bank. This morning, Judge Frederick Bryant ruled on Mr. Curtis' petition to the court and declared my father, Phillip LaVelle, legally deceased. He granted a court order to the Hudson National Bank to give me access and possession of all items in my father's safety-deposit box. Mr. Curtis gave me an envelope with a safety-box key in it. We went to the bank, presented the court order, and the box was given to me and carried by a bank guard to a private room. Mr. Curtis said he would wait in the lobby for me, and I was left alone to go through the box. It was a large box. There was a tremendous amount of money and a large package in a leather briefcase. I tore the paper wrapping off the package-at least one million dollars in that case. In two manila envelopes were stacks of one-hundred-dollar bills. I was so shocked that I didn't bother to count any of it. There were three envelopes addressed to me."

Doug, momentarily spellbound by the revelations, cut into her narrative. "What did you do with the money?"

"Bear with me, Mr. Milburn, or Douglas, if you prefer."

"Sorry, go on."

"The three envelopes are what terrified me. I have two of them with me. The third one contained a key to a safety-deposit box in the United California Bank at 9601 Wilshire Boulevard, Beverly Hills. As per his instructions, I rented another box at the Hudson National Bank in my own name, Christina Lyons, and transferred everything from my father's box into my own new box. As a precaution, I put the United California Bank box key in an envelope and left it in the new box of mine."

"Okay," Doug said. "I presume these two envelopes on the desk are the ones you are referring to, right?"

"Yes. One contains his notarized and witnessed will, which leaves all his worldly possessions and wealth to me, with instructions for setting up trusts for my two children. It's what's in this second envelope that I'll let you read."

She reached over the desk and handed the folded envelope to Doug, at the same moment shoveling into her handbag all the items previously spilled on the blotter in front of him.

Doug lit a cigarette and pushed the pack and lighter to her. As he began reading the contents of the letter contained in the folded envelope, she took a cigarette from the pack. Doug, continuing to read, leaned over, picked up the lighter and put the flame to her cigarette. He noticed that her hand was shaking nervously.

After a silence of three minutes, he looked up at her, shook his head, and in a measured, low tone, almost a whisper, said, "Christina, I am going to read these contents aloud so that both of us can gauge the impact of this warning."

"Go on," she replied.

"The letter reads:

June 11, 1945

My Darling Christina,

Should you be permitted to open this safety-deposit box, you may properly assume that I am dead. If I have not returned from my trip to Switzerland, that will be the case and it will be the result of foul play. Let me explain. I have been retained by an attorney, Waldo Heiser. His card is attached to this letter. He has given me a retainer of one million, two hundred and fifty thousand dollars in cash plus three million dollars deposited to a numbered account 1124079 for me at the Banque Lorraine in Geneva. I confirmed it by telephone from a private line in Mr. Curtis' office. He doesn't know about that call unless he's looked at his bills.

This is payment for me to perform a complicated plastic surgery on a man who was described by Mr. Heiser as being a very important man. He said the man was a high Russian official who has escaped from the Soviet Union with many millions of dollars. He said that Joseph Stalin would try to track him down everywhere in the world. He believes the man would like to begin a new life in the United States. He said he hates communism and the entire hierarchy in the Soviet Union. He doesn't want the KGB to find him. Therefore he wants a completely new face, and he felt I was the best doctor to do it for him.

The fee was so munificent that my greed overcame my caution. But I felt I was in too far, because when Mr. Heiser first called me at my office in Beverly Hills he said he wanted me to come to New York for a consultation only, and would pay me $100,000 plus my fare, hotel, and other expenses. And after the consultation, he was prepared to pay me a seven-figure sum if I agreed to fly to Paris to participate in an operation. That's what brought me to New York and prepared me for a possible trip to Paris. However, after my meeting with Heiser, he upped the ante and told me the story about the Russian official.

Now, sweetheart, I don't want to alarm you, yet I can do naught but alert you to some danger that may result from this adventure.

At the time you read this letter, I may be speaking to you from the grave.

Heiser told me that if I revealed anything about the 'High Russian Official' and his face change, not only would I be killed but also my entire family would be wiped out. He said that if everything went well and I forgot about the man and the operation, I would never be bothered again.

Whatever you do, don't go to the police. Find someone you trust. Talk it over with your husband, Tom. He has some high connections in the Air Force. As to the money, talk to someone at Price Waterhouse and arrange to pay estate taxes. You don't have to reveal any of this except to declare it as part of my estate. Don't discuss this with Mr. Curtis. He's a good man, but it's best he doesn't know about it. I am not sure that Heiser was speaking for a Russian official, because my evaluation of him is that he is of German heritage, and God forbid that the patient might be an escaped Nazi.

Forgive me for causing you this stress. I love you with all my heart.

> *Your loving father,*
> *Phillip La Velle"*

Christina Lyons sobbed audibly as Doug finished reading the sensational document.

Still crying, she said, "I'm sorry I came in here. I shouldn't have shared that letter with anyone, especially a newspaperman. You can't or wouldn't dare write a story about this, would you?"

"Mrs. Lyons, the sleazy tabloids would have a field day with this story. Fortunately for you, this newspaperman functions with a moral conscience. I wouldn't think of endangering your life, or that of your children. Rest assured, I have no intention of putting you at risk."

"Oh, please, thank you."

"Mrs. Lyons, my brother is a fairly prominent lawyer in Washington. I'd like your permission to discuss this with him. He was a colonel in Army Intelligence and is very well versed in international affairs. He can be trusted implicitly."

"Mr. Milburn, on one condition. No story unless I say so."

"My word on that, unless it breaks elsewhere. Then I have no control over it. Now, stop crying and let's plan what you do next. Where are you staying?"

"At the Sherry-Netherland Hotel."

Doug looked at his watch, "It's 9:45 p.m. and I have to be at the theatre by eleven. Have you unpacked your things at the hotel?"

"No, I have only one piece of luggage, a garment bag."

"I'm going to take you to another hotel, register you under another name and have someone check you out of the Sherry, okay?"

"Yes, yes."

He picked up the phone and dialed the Sherry-Netherland Hotel. He asked to be connected to the front desk.

"What's your room number?" he whispered to Christina, holding his hand over the mouthpiece.

She whispered it.

"Hello, may I help you?" the deskman asked.

"What is your name, sir?" Doug said.

"My name is Harris, how may I serve you?"

"This is Frank Lyons, brother-in-law to Mrs. Christina Lyons in room 1202. She has been in an auto accident. Nothing serious, except a slight concussion. My wife and I have taken her to our home in Stamford, Connecticut. I'd like to have one of my associates pay her bill now and pick up her one bag. He'll bring her room key. Will that be all right?"

"Oh, yes indeed, sir. I hope Mrs. Lyons will be all right. Give her our very best."

"Indeed I will. The man coming over is Mr. Neil Toomey. Thank you for your courtesy, Mr. Harris."

"My pleasure, sir."

Doug saw a slight smile on Christina's tear-stained face as he called Toomey.

He explained the scenario to the freckled Irishman, who chuckled and shook hands with Mrs. Lyons.

"Mrs. Lyons, what is the room rate?"

"Seventy-five dollars," she replied.

"All right, give Toomey, here, one-hundred and he'll see that you get the change."

She handed Toomey two one hundred-dollar bills and a twenty for cab fare.

"Neil, bring the bag to the Beaux Arts Hotel for Mrs. Charlene Leslie of 150 Marlboro Street, Seattle, Washington. I'll have her checked in by then. Scoot, now. If this guy Harris questions you, hand him a twenty-dollar bill and tell him you're in a hurry to drive up to Stamford."

"I'll have one of the photographers drive me over," Toomey said.

"Hell, no!" Doug exclaimed. "The doorman would spot that car in a minute with the Daily News logo on its doors. Here are the keys to my car. You know it, the blue Buick parked on the apron in back of the building. We'll cab it to the Beaux Arts. Leave the car in my hotel garage, the keys at the desk, and walk back to the office. Let's go now, Mrs. Lyons. I don't want to be late for my date."

"Your lady is a very lucky person," Christina said. "I can't thank you enough."

They scurried to the seventh-floor elevators of the news building at 220 East 42nd Street, just a few blocks away from the Beaux Arts Hotel on East 44th. Luckily, an empty cab responded to Doug's whistle and they were off to the hotel. He explained to Christina that he lived at the same place.

Doug told the cabbie to wait, and handed him a ten-dollar bill as good-faith money. The cab driver responded, "You have style, man."

A quick conference with the night manager and the new "Mrs. Leslie" signed in and was given a suite for the price of a single room.

"Ms. Leslie's luggage will be here shortly. Neil Toomey is bringing it over. Oh, and Mrs. Leslie will be calling room service shortly. Won't you, Charlene?"

"Yes, I could stand some nourishment. I haven't eaten a thing today."

The manager showed her to her room, and Doug hastened to his waiting cab. Traffic was snarled, and the cabbie, at Doug's urging, weaved his way to

Park Avenue South, then cut down 34th Street, west to Eighth Avenue and north to 45th Street, where Doug alighted and briskly walked toward the Shubert Theatre. He went into Shubert Alley and was greeted by the stage manager: "Mr. Milburn, you're just in time for the finale. Go right through and you can watch it this side of the stage. Miss Luce is fabulous."

"Thank you, Jack. Take care."

Constance Luce and the ensemble were dressed in "Roaring Twenties" costumes, the women in short, pleated skirts, the men in sweaters and bell-bottom trousers. They had just finished a Jerome Robbins dance routine with a Charleston motif.

Constance sang the hit number, "Hollywood Is Just a Dream," with the chorus backing her and the pit orchestra blasting a crescendo of brass with the tympani drums pounding the finale.

The audience of twelve hundred rose as one in a standing ovation.

After six curtain calls, Constance took her final bow and the curtain came down. She removed her platinum-blonde wig, revealing her beautiful natural-brown tresses, which she unpinned, letting them fall to her shoulders. She ran directly into Douglas' arms and planted a loving kiss on his hungry lips. Constance pulled back and laughed, "Doug, you're ready to go on stage with all my lipstick on your lips and my makeup all over your face."

"I'm ready," he rejoined, smiling at her beauty and using his handkerchief to remove the evidence of the affectionate buss.

"Come into my dressing room and we'll clean you up, my leading man," she said.

She changed her stage outfit behind a wardrobe screen while Doug washed his face.

"Where are we going for supper, Douglas?"

"How about El Morocco, good food and a little close dancing?"

"That's a nice and naughty suggestion."

☆ ☆ ☆ ☆

Wednesday, April 9, 1952 - 12:05 a.m. - Havana

The José Martí Airport was unusually quiet. Air traffic was periodic and planes arrived infrequently. Takeoffs were in intervals of an hour.

Captain Devereaux and his Rangers loitered behind the specified hangar. The Fairchild F-27 was inside the hangar. The doors were closed. Major Flaherty and his crew were aboard the fully fueled plane, ready for a quick takeoff. An improvised bed had been prepared at the rear of the plane.

Guantanamo Naval Station had been alerted for a late arrival.

Milburn and Dulles were behind a side door entry to the hangar. Lloyd Sedgwick drove the rented Cadillac. The Schwartz-Bormann pretender slouched in the back seat, with the masked Phillip Berger next to him. They pulled up to the hangar slowly. The headlights were extinguished.

There was no sign of any other vehicles. A helicopter, flying low, hovered briefly over the hangar, focusing a searchlight on the Cadillac. It then turned skyward and circled the scene below.

The light had not extended across the rear of the hangar. Bart raced to the back door and hustled the Rangers stationed outside into the interior. The aircraft returned, and the powerful light scanned the hangar's front and back as well as both sides of the mammoth building.

Sedgwick wisely flashed his headlights in an attempt to signal an all-clear to the hovering copter.

Dulles, peeking through a slightly open door, saw the flashing lights and swore, "What the hell is Sedge doing?"

"He's giving him an 'all clear.' He is right," Bart said.

Suddenly, the copter stopped its flight and hovered momentarily, then descended slowly to within ten feet of the Cadillac. The searchlight pierced the interior of the waiting car. The light revealed the driver, Sedgwick, the masked Berger and the slouching form of the phony Bormann, who waved his manacled hands over his head.

"*Ach*, Bormann is waving his handcuffs. *Schweinhund*."

"Let me go and I'll blow their heads off," Mayfield yelled in defiance of the roaring rotors.

"*Halt's maul*, stupid. You want to get us killed? Leave your pistol here," Nordheim angrily rasped. "Let me down."

The steps were lowered as the blades were feathered, and Nordheim cautiously descended.

He defiantly put his hands on his hips and stared at the Cadillac. Sedgwick turned on the headlights. The masked Berger got out of the car and slowly approached Nordheim.

In a simulated Spanish accent, Phil demanded, "Where is money? *Que pasa, Señor* Nordheim?"

"Where is Schwartz?" the man countered.

"Look over there."

Nordheim arrogantly strode closer to the vehicle. Two feet away from the open window, he heard the muffled moans and groans. He stared intently at the pseudo Bormann with the cap on his head, blindfolded and with duct tape across his mouth.

"*Confencer? Satisfactorio*? Now you pay. He go with you, *Señor*," Berger hissed.

Nordheim shouted to the copter, "Bring the money," and frantically beckoned with his extended arms.

Berger moved quickly to Nordheim and patted him down.

"I have no weapons, *Señor*," Nordheim growled.

"But I do." Berger flashed his Colt .45.

"You will not need it," Nordheim rejoined.

"We'll see."

Mayfield joined them with the suitcase. He placed it at Nordheim's feet and opened it. The two Secret Service agents were poised outside the hangar. Berger pointed a flashlight at the neatly stacked money. He nodded his head and shouted, *"Bueno!"*

Suddenly, the Cadillac lights were doused. In a split second, a choreographed tableau was enacted. Bart led Captain Devereaux and four Rangers silently in an attack on Nordheim. His hands were instantly manacled behind him. Bart quickly applied chloroform with a gauze pad and duct tape over Nordheim's mouth. He sank to the ground.

At the same time, Jacques and the Secret Service agents, assisted by four Rangers, were giving the same treatment to Mayfield, who pulled a gun, which Jacques viciously snapped out of his hand. The Walther-37 clanged to the ground. Jacques delivered a chop across his neck, rendering him unconscious.

Two Rangers, guns drawn, raced up the steps of the helicopter. A Ranger zapped the pilot and carried his inert body to the tarmac. The other Ranger turned off the copter's engine. Mayfield was left lying prone alongside a hedge. Nordheim was hauled into the hangar and lifted into the 727. He was dumped on the specially fashioned bed. Two Rangers guarded the passive figure.

Secret Service agent Collins pointed a searchlight to an adjoining hangar. He dotted the darkness with four flashes of light. A conveyor cargo plane taxied toward the intermittent beams of light. Mayfield's unconscious body was lifted aboard, with the help of the Rangers. Watkins and Collins each carried bags containing the counterfeit $500,000 of Bormann's and the yet-to-be examined two million dollars of Nordheim's.

Dulles and Bart were huddled in the hangar at the rear of the F-27, discussing what to do with the helicopter pilot, who had been chloroformed and manacled.

"No doubt he's excess baggage, but we can't let him loose," Bart said.

"If he's just a temporary hired hand, we'll have to let him go sooner or later," Dulles speculated.

"Yes, but he can be a walking leak if we set him free. We have to take him to the base. After interrogation, we can decide his future," Bart declared.

Captain Devereaux, Berger, Sedgwick and Jacques waited for the colloquy to end. They felt the flush of victory and were speculating about the next steps to be taken.

Adam Watkins entered the hangar and walked toward Bart and Dulles.

"Gentlemen, I congratulate you on one of the smoothest takedowns I've ever witnessed," he complimented.

"Thank you, sir."

Bart turned to the Secret Service agents and said, "It was a pleasure working with you. Here's a couple of hypodermics, which will put Mayfield to sleep for at least three hours."

"Colonel, the pleasure is ours. Here is your receipt for the two packages of money."

"Thank you. Some of that loot will have to be saved for trial evidence. You can always reach me through Langley. Ask for Katherine Wharton and tell her it's a *Lucy call* for the colonel. She'll track me."

"Lucy?"

"Yeah, it's a code word."

"Good luck, and thanks."

Dulles and Bart walked over to the four men waiting for instructions.

"Men, your execution was superb. My congratulations to all of you and your Rangers, Captain Devereaux."

"Colonel, it was your planning that made it work. We are thrilled to be part of this exercise. It was smooth."

"As an immediate reward, your group can stay at the Riviera for the next couple of days for some well-earned R & R."

He reached into a briefcase and handed the captain $7,500.

"What's this for?"

"Captain, that's five hundred for each of your men and yourself. This is real money for expenses. Don't let your boys blow it at the crap tables or on naughty *señoritas*."

"That's mighty generous, sir. We'll remember you for a long time."

"Please, take the Cadillac back to the hotel. The doorman will hold it for me."

Devereaux saluted and departed. Jacques, Berger and Sedgwick were ordered to spend the night at Guantanamo.

"Men, pick up that copter pilot and put him aboard."

"Allen, I assume you want to be there when Herr Nordheim-Schickelgruber arises from his idyllic siesta."

"I'm not looking forward to sleeping in a bunk. But what the hell, it's for a good cause, so let's go."

Bart anesthetized the helicopter pilot. The hangar doors were opened, and Captain Flaherty taxied to runway two. He revved the motors, obtained clearance, and flew southeast over the Caribbean along the Cuban coast to Guantanamo.

☆ ☆ ☆ ☆

Guantanamo Base, Cuba

A cadre of naval servicemen was working with two gurneys as the F-27 came to a halt. Admiral Thomas greeted Bart and Dulles as they debarked.

"Colonel, you radioed for two gurneys. Who is the second guest?"

"We don't know yet. He's a helicopter pilot who flew Nordheim into our hands. We'll have to shake him down when he comes to."

"We have Schwartz in a room. He's behaving himself, although he keeps pestering our guards, asking for you."

"Would you order your men to bring our sleeping beauties down to these gurneys? My three men aboard will wait until they're removed."

Six stalwart gobs raced up the portable staircase and gingerly brought the passive bodies down. They were quickly strapped on the gurneys. Jacques, Phillip and Lloyd descended. Captain Flaherty taxied the F-27 to an assigned hangar.

"Admiral, will you have enough available beds for me, Mr. Dulles, these three men and the plane crew?"

"Yes, indeed, Colonel. It's all been anticipated. Now, we have Schwartz in a room, we have his two cronies in separate cells in the brig on different floors. Nordheim will go into the basement cell previously occupied by Schwartz, and this unexpected guest will be put in a similar cell, removed from the others. None of them will be in earshot of the others. We'll be a little taxed for guards on round-the-clock security."

"Actually, Admiral, the only ones requiring close surveillance are Schwartz and Nordheim - who incidentally needs a body search for suicide pills. These men must be kept alive. As for Schwartz's two buddies and this helicopter pilot, let's keep them manacled and chained. We'll interrogate them immediately. If necessary, I can send for some Rangers, who are still in Havana."

"Under these circumstances, we can handle the situation."

"We have to wait for word from the White House as to how long these guests will be honoring you with their stay," Dulles said.

Bart and Jacques accompanied the gurneys to the stockade. The sonorous chorus emitted by the slumbering prisoners added to the cadence of the sailors.

Petty Officer Frank Romero led Dulles, Sedgwick and Berger to the officers' mess to await the return of Bart and Jacques. In the infirmary office, Nordheim and the copter pilot were stripped naked and their orifices were checked. The unconscious men were put in prison clothing, manacled, leg-chained, photographed and fingerprinted. They were then dumped into their respective cells. Guards were assigned to Nordheim. Bart and Jacques thanked the sailors and the medics, then joined the others at the officers' mess.

"Our babies have been put to bed," Bart announced.

Admiral Thomas regaled the gathering with war stories. Dulles added a few of his own. Bart joined them in a spread of ham-and-cheese sandwiches and soft drinks. Captain Flaherty and the crew entered and were promptly served.

"Our hotel is doing a fine business," Admiral Thomas bantered. "When you're finished here, Chief Petty Officer Romero will lead you to your assigned quarters. You'll find toothbrushes, toothpaste, shaving cream and razors, plus pajamas for all of you."

"Very thoughtful, admiral. Accept our deep appreciation for your hospitality."

"My pleasure, Colonel."

An ensign appeared and saluted. "I have a message for Colonel Milburn, sir."

Bart reached for it and quickly opened the envelope, then withdrew a folded paper. He read it and quickly asked the Admiral for the use of a telephone.

The message read, *Call Lucy, urgent.*

At the far end of the dining area, he reached Langley, asking for Katherine Wharton.

"I've been waiting for your call, Colonel. You are to call your wife. She said it was urgent."

"Was she distraught?"

"No, sir. She said not to alarm you, but she has some vital information. That was it. She was quite calm."

"Thank you, Katherine. Sorry it's so late."

"No problem. I'm a night bird hooked on a TV mystery," she replied.

Bart dialed home. "Did I awaken you, sweetheart?"

"No, I was reading. How's my missing husband? My bed is very cold."

"We'll have to do something about that. What's so urgent?"

"Doug called an hour ago. He and Constance were at El Morocco. He was calling from a phone booth asking for your whereabouts. He said it's urgent and that he has vital information for you. Call him in the morning at his hotel or office."

"Will do. How are you, Elizabeth, and the children?"

"We're fine, dear, but lonesome. The kids miss you. When will you be home?"

"Two or three days. All I can tell you, my love, is that we hit the jackpot. Now, mum's the word. Don't call Dad. I'll do that after I report to the head man."

"Not to worry, darling. I know better. Congratulations, my loving hero."

"Love you. Be patient."

CHAPTER SIXTEEN

Thursday, April 10, 1952 - Guantanamo Naval Base, Cuba

Nordheim's rage had reached a crescendo. The night in the cell had all the aspects of an insane asylum. He spewed epithets, foamed at the mouth, banged his head against the wall, and in a mixture of German and English yelled for a lawyer. The guards finally strapped him to his cot, immobilizing him. They covered his mouth with duct tape. A medic injected him with a tranquilizer.

"This guy is out of his gourd. He keeps screaming in German and English. He keeps saying *bumsen, ficken* and lots of German swear words," a guard said.

"*Bumsen* means fuck. So you got his message."

"We had to strap him down. He's a wild animal. I brought some food and he tried to kick me in the groin. I had to slap him down. It was self-protection. I hope you won't report me, sir."

"You did right. Don't worry about it. Get some rest, fellow."

Jacques positioned himself at the guards' table.

Bart Milburn and Allen Dulles entered the cell and looked down at the recumbent figure. The Van Dyke beard and flowing mustache were gone. His head was shaven clean.

Nordheim's eyes revolved erratically. He blinked spasmodically. He tried to raise his head. Moans were heard behind the duct tape.

Bart, in perfect German, bellowed, "If I remove the tape from your mouth, will you behave yourself?"

The prisoner nodded his head several times.

"Here goes," Bart declared as he roughly pulled the tape off in one jerk.
"Die bist verrückt!" he screamed.

"I'll tape you again."

The stricken Führer nodded. Bart placed his tape recorder on a chair brought in by Dulles.

"Adolf Hitler, you are under arrest by the United States military forces as a prisoner of war, and you are in an American prison; do you understand that?"

"Nein. No, I am *not* Adolf Hitler. I am a Jewish survivor of the Nazi concentration camps. Look at the numbers tattooed on my arm. Look at my penis. It is circumcised. My name is Frederick Avram Nordheim, a Swedish citizen."

"Cut the bullshit. You've had an excellent job of plastic surgery. Were you charged extra for the circumcision? Or did you have a *mohel* do it?"

"Geh zum Teufel."

"All right, my *gestunken Führer.* Your hell has just begun."

"Why you shave my head and face?"

"Isn't that what you did to those Jews in your death camps?"

"No, that's what the Nazis did to me. You are not a Jew. You are of English-Irish descent. Catholic, *ja?"*

"No, Protestant, with a few drops of Jewish blood in me. I would be eligible for Dachau, Auschwitz or Ohrdruf," Bart hissed, turning off the recorder. "Listen, you miserable perverted demon. I've been to your concentration camps, and you're nothing but a filthy diseased piece of *scheisse!"*

"Who are you to talk to me like this? You will pay for this. You put me in handcuffs and leg irons and strap me to this bed. Is that American justice? I want a lawyer, now!"

"Herr Hitler, did you give lawyers to your prisoners of war? Did you give lawyers to those poor innocent Jews you robbed and slaughtered? You craven megalomaniac, you make Genghis Khan and Torquemada look like saints. You're the most evil despot in the history of civilization. We'll get the truth out of your foul lips if we have to pull every nail off your fingers and toes before we chop them off one at a time. After that, we'll give you a full circumcision, removing your penis and your one testicle. That is what we learned from you, Himmler, Heydrich, Goering, Goebbels, Eichmann and all the rest of the Nazi scum. You son of a bitch, *Schickelgruber,* are a blight on humanity, which can never be erased. You put the mark of Cain on every German."

Hitler yelled, *"Schtop it, schtop!* No one ever talk to me like that!'

"Of course not, because you, the Führer, put the fear of the devil over everyone in Germany, France, Czechoslovakia, Poland, Holland, Belgium, Denmark, Norway, and most of Europe. You and Stalin caused the deaths of fifty million people, Jews and Christians alike, as well as sending the cream of your youth into battle. What kind of an amoral cretin are you?"

"No more. *Du kannst mich mal am arsch lecken,"* he swore.

"The same to you, slimeball. You belong in a padded cell. Enjoy your stay."

"Who are you?"

"I am Colonel Barton Quentin Milburn, your worst enemy. Enjoy yourself, *asshole.*"

"Wait one minute. What about the Geneva Convention rules?"

"We'll abide by it just the way you Nazi bastards did."

Bart slapped a thick strip of duct tape over the distraught prisoner's mouth. Dulles followed him out as the colonel slammed the cell door shut with a clang that resonated throughout the basement. Jacques phoned the guards to return.

"Don't favor this verminous bastard in any way," Bart advised the security detail. "And don't let him try to kill himself. We need him alive. If he starts to choke, remove the tape from his mouth, but keep him miserable. I want to break his spirit."

"Yes sir, it'll be a pleasure, Colonel," the Navy men responded.

"If he has to eat, spoon-feed the cretin."

On the way up the circular iron staircase, Dulles remarked, "I couldn't believe my ears, the foul argot you pitched at him. I didn't think you had it in you."

"Allen, I have trampled through muck and mire throughout Europe with our GIs, and those wonderful, heroic dogfaces taught me every word in the slang dictionary. I railed at this overrated imbecile in an effort to demean him. He won't be an easy egg to crack. We have to wear him down, strip him of his dignity and make him realize the futility of his impersonation. It will take days."

"Bart, I'm not chiding you for your venomous attack. In fact, I was fascinated. I'm inclined to agree with your bad-cop approach, which will have its desired effect. It obviously worked with Bormann. When you get him to the pussycat stage, you can stroke him, good-cop style. I'm impressed and a little shocked. You're good at your tactics."

"Thanks, Allen. The venom I spit at him was purely embedded instinct implanted during my tour of the death camps."

Admiral Thomas waved Bart into his office and asked, "How is our guest?"

"I just gave him a going-over. He has a lot to think about. Sir, do you have any padded cells in the brig?"

"Yes, we do. Two of them for loonies, which we use every once in a while."

"Do they have observation openings in them?"

"Of course."

"I'd like to move number one. He's been hitting his head against the walls. I don't want this baby to cheat us with a suicide. Besides, I want to give him harsh treatment until we wear him down. He's a tough nut to crack."

"Colonel, if you approve, let's put him in a padded cell encased in a straitjacket for a day or two and spoon-feed him."

"Great idea. With around-the-clock watch."

"How about keeping him naked with meager rations?"

"Perfect. He's a vegetarian. Watery soups, just for a couple of days. Take the duct tape off his mouth. Let him rant and rave to his evil heart's content."

"Done."

"How about the use of a safe phone?"

"The one next door has a scrambler on it. Go to it."

Bart called Steelman, who patched him into the Oval Office. "Mr. President,

I am pleased to report the incarceration of targets one and two plus two henchmen, a helicopter pilot and an ex-FBI traitor."

"Barton, you have exceeded my wildest expectations. I'll not press you for details. When can I expect you here?"

"Sir, I need about two days to wear them down. Number two is about ready to spill his guts. I just gave number one some severe treatment. He's tough. Two days of misery and he'll soften up."

"Keep at it."

Bart called his brother at the Beaux Arts Hotel, but he was not there. He dialed the direct newsroom number, Murray Hill 2-8585. Neil Toomey answered.

"Douglas Milburn, please. This is his brother, Bart."

"One second, I'll have him take you in a booth."

"How is my kid brother?" Doug chimed when he came on.

"Fine, Doug. How are you and your lady, Constance?"

"Couldn't be better."

"Do I hear wedding bells?"

"They're getting clearer every day."

"Who's your best man?"

"Begging the question? *You*, you ninny," Doug joked.

"What's so urgent?"

"Pay dirt."

"How so?"

"Not on this phone, except this: I have the daughter of a famous plastic surgeon who disappeared in Switzerland in 1945."

"No kidding. Is she under wraps?" Bart asked.

"Oh, yes."

"Can she hold for two or three days?"

"I think so. Where are you?"

"Out of the country. Can you bring her to Washington when I get back?"

"Is it that important?"

"Very much so. This is a stroke of luck. I'm up to my hips in intrigue. If you could oblige me by bringing her to D.C., it would be extremely helpful."

"For you, Barton, anything. Call me when to come."

"Doug, give my love to the folks, and Bunny and Constance."

Dulles asked Bart if he could make some calls.

"It's all yours, Allen. Jacques and I are going to check out those Gestapo boys, or storm troopers, or whatever they are. After that, we'll have a bit of lunch and fly back to Havana."

Back at the cells, Bart asked, "How's Krueger behaving?"

"He's been very quiet, Colonel."

"Okay, your men are excused. We'll call you when we are through. Let's have the key."

"He might get rough, sir," the guard warned as he passed the key to Jacques.

"We can handle him," Jacques said, displaying his Colt .45.

The guards exited. Jacques opened the cell door and locked it after they entered. The prisoner sullenly stared at Bart and Jacques.

"*Sprechen sie* English?" Colonel Milburn asked.

"*Ja.*"

"Good. Herr Krueger, you are a prisoner of the United States military."

"On what charge?"

"You're an escaped Nazi war criminal."

"*Nein, Ich bin* a Swedish citizen, who works for *Herr* Schwartz."

"You mean Martin Bormann."

For a brief moment, a look of surprise was evident.

"Martin who?"

"Cut the bullshit, storm trooper!" Bart ordered. "Do you want a firing squad or a hanging?"

The suddenness of the question stunned Krueger. He began to dissemble. "Hey, I work for salary. I'm not Nazi. I'm not politician. I am working man. Hang me for what?"

"For lying to me. You are a Nazi Gestapo agent working for Martin Bormann and Adolf Hitler."

The large man rose to his full height, almost as tall as Milburn, and raised his manacled hands in an effort to strike Bart. Without hesitation, Jacques drove his right hand in a smashing blow at the prisoner's solar plexus. With an explosive whoosh, Krueger fell onto the cot. His Cuban-acquired suntan turned greenish yellow as he pulled himself into a fetal position.

"Listen, dog, if you want some more, stand up!" Jacques yelled at him. After a few minutes of respite, Laurent jerked him into a sitting position.

"Krueger, try that once more and you'll be put in chains," Bart warned. "Now, answer my questions truthfully and maybe we can help you. Bormann has already confessed to everything, so don't be a fool. The Nazi movement is kaput. Finished. Dead. Don't be an idiot, *dummkopf!*"

"What Bormann tell you?" Krueger whined.

Without missing a beat, the colonel took a long shot. "Bormann said that Franz Schwerin and you, Ernst Krueger, were officers in the Wehrmacht assigned to the Waffen SS as Hitler's guards. You did duty at the Chancellery bunker during the last days of the war."

Krueger fell back onto the cot. He closed his eyes and bit his lips. His body heaved convulsively. Jacques moved to lift him. Bart held up his right hand as a stop sign and put his other hand to his lips for silence.

"*Der* informant?" Krueger cried.

"No, Ernst, he knows that Nordheim is *kaput*, so he is cooperating. He wants to help you."

"Help me?"

"Yes, he wants you to cooperate."

Krueger wheeled around, sitting on the cot with both feet on the floor.

"In order, what you want to know?"

"What was your rank in the war?"

"I was major and Franz Schwerin was hauptmann."

"In what service?"

"We was assigned to SS and then as special guards."

"Guards to Bormann or Hitler?"

"To both."

"How did that happen?"

"We were in Gestapo under Himmler. Bormann picked us after the Americans invaded France and later occupied Paris. We were operating there and left when the Allied troops came in. Bormann had a big argument with Himmler because of us. He ordered Himmler to send us to the Berghof in Berchtesgaden."

"So, you really were bodyguards for Hitler?"

"But Bormann was our boss."

"Were you in Berlin with them?"

"*Ja.*"

"Did you help Bormann and Hitler to escape?"

"Hitler is dead."

"Bullshit."

"I say no more. I want lawyer. The war is over."

"Not for you. If you want better treatment, you'll have to tell the whole truth. Think on it. Remember what happened to your leaders at Nuremberg. I'll leave you now, Ernst."

✫ ✫ ✫ ✫

Franz Schwerin was snoring loudly when Bart and Jacques entered his cell. The door was slammed shut forcefully. Schwerin, startled, sat up abruptly.

"Captain Schwerin, you are a prisoner of war in a United States military prison, *verstehen sie?*"

"There is no war. It's over."

"Not for Nazis. You are an escaped war criminal."

"You have illegally captured me in Cuban territory. This is out of your jurisdiction."

"Are you a lawyer, Franz? You are now in American territory."

"So, you hijack us illegally. I know the law. I want a lawyer."

"*Armleuchter!*" Bart said.

"No, I am not stupid. You speak German?"

"Not now, Hauptmann Schwerin. Be smart."

"How you know I was captain?"

"I know you and Ernst were in the SS with Himmler. Bormann had you assigned to Hitler after Paris fell to the Americans. You were at the Berghof guarding Hitler and later in the bunker with him in April, 1945."

"How you know that?"

"You Nazis underestimated the Americans. We know everything about you Nazi lice."

"I was doing my duty. Just like you. I took orders and obeyed."

"You killed Jews!"

"*Nein*. Himmler killed Jews. Himmler killed everybody. He was an animal. I got nothing against Jews."

"Nobody in Germany killed Jews. Is that your position?"

"No, I know what Himmler and Heydrich and Eichmann were doing. How could I stop that? I am a loyal German, but I did not approve everything. Yes, I studied law, but there was no law in Germany during the Third Reich. So, I followed orders and stayed alive for my family. I played the Nazi game."

"Then how come you are now working for Bormann and Hitler?"

Schwerin rose to his feet and then dropped to his knees. "I work for them because I am *eine Hure*, a rotten whore. They pay me big money, which I send to my family. I am good Catholic. I say *mea culpa* a thousand times."

"How many Jews did you arrest?"

"None. I was part of an intelligence unit chasing spies and Nazi defectors. I hated Himmler and his killers. Bormann was not a killer."

"What about Hitler?"

"He was too busy with the war. I know he was anti-Semite, but he was slightly *verrucht* toward the end."

"Are you for real?"

"What you mean?"

"Did Bormann or Hitler know your true feelings?"

"No, I played the game like a good whore. Even when I go to confession, I don't tell everything to the priest. Some priests weren't real, but they dressed and acted like priests. They were Gestapo agents placed in the churches. I know this."

"Did you help Bormann and Hitler escape from the bunker?"

"I stop here. Who are you, sir?"

"I am Colonel Barton Quentin Milburn. I could be your worst enemy or a good friend. Think. Tell the truth and life will be easier for you. *Auf wiedersehen*," he said, exiting.

On the way to Bormann's new quarters, Jacques stopped in the hallway and confronted Bart. "You believe that guy Schwerin?"

"Jacques, we have to keep an open mind. This guy might be on the level. That's why I didn't press him about the escape. Let him stew for a while."

The Navy guards outside the gated door of Bormann's room stood at attention and saluted Bart and Jacques. The salutes were returned, then Bart asked, "How's our guest behaving?"

"Big change in that man. He's a real pussycat. He acts like a top executive. The admiral has ordered top-drawer treatment for him. Three meals a day. Lots of reading material and a radio-music only, no news stations on it."

"Take a break, men. We're going to visit the man."

Bormann was seated in a reclining chair, puffing on a Havana special cigar, perusing a magazine. A stubble of hair was evident on his face and head.

"*Willkommen, Herren*. How you like my quarters?" he asked, waving his cigar toward the pleasantly furnished bedroom with separate bath. Cuban music played softly.

"How is Herr Bormann today?" Milburn asked.

"Colonel, you are a man of your word, a gentleman. You see, you catch more flies with honey than you do with vinegar. This is the treatment I deserve. I appreciate it."

"If the Nazis captured me, would they treat me this way?" Bart said.

"Sorry to say, the answer is *nein*."

"Tell me, is the food good?"

"It is not a Deutsche rathskeller, but good American food. The chef is *sehr gut*."

"Where did you get the cigar?"

"It came with the meal."

"Martin, am I your friend?"

"*Jawohl*, Colonel."

"Then why don't you tell me about the escape from the bunker in Berlin?"

"I will in due time, Colonel. I have to figure out a few things. I have lots of money in Swiss banks. I told you I would share it with you if you arrange for me to go to Argentina. You don't want to hang me, do you?"

"No, I promised that won't happen if you come clean."

"I am clean. I showered today."

"No, no, come clean means open up and tell me everything. If you hope to be free some day, you'll have to testify against Hitler in court. If you don't, then I can't arrange a deal for you to be free."

"I am a very organized person. Let me weigh all the possibilities and we'll talk about a lot of things. So, give me a little time to think."

Playing along with the game, Bart offered a half grin to the prisoner and walked out. The next stop was a visit to the mystery helicopter pilot who had no identification in his clothing.

The guards were excused. The cell was the same barren, no-windows confinement similar to the earlier one occupied by Bormann. The prisoner was stretched out on his cot, manacled and in leg irons. The lanky pilot ignored the presence of Milburn and Laurent.

"Sit up," Milburn barked.

He didn't budge.

"Sit up or I'll pull you up."

His gangling body turned toward the wall.

Jacques delivered a vicious kick to his extended bony buttocks. The prisoner screamed in pain. He rose from the cot, rubbing his backside. "You broke my bone, you son of a bitch!"

"Nobody broke your bone. If it was broken you wouldn't be able to stand," Bart rasped.

"What the hell is going on here? Who the hell are you?" he wailed. "I want out of here."

Bart detected a mix of a German accent with a touch of Brooklynese and New York vernacular.

"Do you know why you're here?"

"No, and who the hell are you?"

"My name is Colonel Barton Quentin Milburn. You are in a United States military jail. Now, who the fuck are you?"

"Never mind my name. What right do you have to arrest me? I want a lawyer."

"You are a prisoner of war. So, no lawyer."

"What war?"

"Very cute. Let me make it crystal clear. If you think that bony ass of yours hurts now, you ain't seen nothing yet. Yours is in a sling from here on. You are being charged as an accessory to a number of crimes. For starters, obstruction of justice, accessory to helping war criminals escape, aiding and abetting a kidnapping, possibly being a war criminal yourself, then we would throw in accessory to murder, just for starters. If that be the case, you'll hang with the others. Have I got your attention now?"

He plopped on his cot and stared at the two men. His manacled hands began to tremble. In a quivering voice he finally mumbled, "You got the wrong man. I am a pilot. That's all. I work for Mr. Nordheim. He is a very rich man. He'll get me out of here."

"Nordheim can't get himself out of here. He's a miserable escaped Nazi war criminal, and he'll take you down with the rest of you cretins. Now, what is your name?"

"I'll say nothing until I talk to a lawyer. I know my rights."

"Jacques, I think this cutie pie's a seasoned jailbird. Watch this bum, while I make a call. If he gets violent, shoot him in the legs. I want him alive for a while."

Jacques brandished his Colt .45.

Bart went to the guard's table on the other side of the cell door, dialed, then waited.

"Admiral Thomas's office."

"Is the admiral there? This is Colonel Milburn."

"No sir, can I help? This is Lieutenant McKay."

"Who does the fingerprinting here at the brig?"

"That would be Petty Officer Davis. Do you need him?"

"Yes, is he available? I want to print and photograph a prisoner. What number cell is this?"

"I know where you are. I'll send a couple of MPs to escort the prisoner to our I.D. room. It's right down the hall from where you are."

Five minutes later two burly MPs came to the cell. They lifted the surly pilot in a no-nonsense manner and helped him shuffle into the identification room. Petty Officer Noah Davis, a black man standing a formidable six feet, five inches of pure muscle, displayed a cheerful, beguiling smile. He saluted the colonel and beckoned to the prisoner.

"Come to me, my melancholy baby," he sang. "I'm going to take your pretty picture." He clamped his ponderous hand on the bony shoulder of the prisoner and pushed him against a wall opposite a large camera. "Hold this number plate in front of you. Drop it and I'll drop you."

He took a frontal shot and two shots of his left and right profiles. And in short order, he roughly fingerprinted the recalcitrant pilot.

"Now, what's his name, Colonel?"

"That's the problem, Mr. Davis. Slim here is traveling incognito."

"How about marking his file *Slim Jones, alias incognito*," Davis chuckled.

"Fucking nigger bastard," Slim muttered.

In a millisecond Davis backhanded the pilot's face, sending him ten feet into a semiconscious state, blood spurting from his mouth.

"That poor fellow slipped, Colonel."

"I'm afraid he did," Bart echoed.

The petty officer handed the MPs a couple of paper towels. "Clean him up," he ordered. "And take the piece of shit back to his cell."

"How soon can I have those photos and fingerprints, Mr. Davis?" Bart asked.

"I'll have them in about a half hour or less, Colonel."

"I want to thank you for your cooperation, Noah. Send them up to the admiral's office."

"My pleasure, sir," he responded, then saluted with an infectious grin.

The guards took up their post at Slim's cell, relieving Jacques. The prisoner was back on his cot moaning.

"I have a hunch, Jacques. Come with me. I want to see Bormann again."

They were back in Bormann's cell.

"Colonel, you must like me. *Was ist los?*

"Martin, I may have to stop all your privileges and put you back in a cell."

"Why would you do this to me? I think you my friend. Now you play with me?"

"This is over my jurisdiction. The American Secret Service wants you. I don't want to turn you over to them. I am holding you as a war criminal."

"What do your Secret Service want with me? Are they like the SS?"

"Worse."

"Tell me why."

"There was five hundred thousand American dollars found in your bedroom at the Hotel Nacional. It was counterfeit, imitation money. Phony. *Falsches geld. Verstehen?*"

"*Das Arschloch. Verflucht!*"

"Who is the asshole, Martin?"

"Nordheim sent me that money because I have no time to withdraw money from my bank."

"Who brought it to you?"

"That *dummkopf* Joachim."

"Who is Joachim?"

"He is pilot for the big plane, also flies the helicopter. He deliver the bag of money."

"What's his full name?"

"Joachim Heydrich. He was *hauptmann* in the Luftwaffe flying a bomber. He was shot down and captured over an American base in England in 1942.

He is the nephew of Reinhard Heydrich."

"What happened then?"

"With other prisoners he was shipped to America. He escaped from a camp in Kansas. Got to New York City. He spoke good English. The German-American Bund gave him shelter. The Bund gives him new identity."

"What kind?"

"They change his name to James Martin, give him driver's license, Social Security card and apartment in Yorkville in New York City. They have lots of Germans there."

"What did he do in New York during the war?"

"They get him job as longshoreman. He becomes spy and sends messages of ships and cargo leaving from Hudson River, through Swiss Consulate to Bank Lorraine in Geneva. The bank gives code message to German ambassador. Hitler send work for Heydrich in America and send more reports. Lots of your ships were sunk in the North Atlantic. In June 1945, Hitler tells me to send letter to him to come to our mansion in Malmo, Sweden. I ask Banque Lorraine to wire him ten thousand dollars. So he comes and works for Nordheim as pilot for Lockheed plane. Also, for helicopter we have there. He becomes courier all over Europe and South America. So, you see, he was Hitler's boy because he was Reinhard Heydrich's nephew."

"Why did Hitler send you false money?"

"I don't know. But, maybe this *Scheisse* switched the real money for this, how you say, counterfeit?"

"Martin, where does all this *falsche geld* come from?"

"During the war, we had very good plates made of American dollars, English pounds and Swiss francs. We turned billions of that money into purchases of arms, gold, diamonds, and art collections. That's how Nordheim became so rich. The money was manufactured in Munich. Later, the printing was moved to Berlin."

"Where are the plates now? And how do they launder this phony money?"

"Are you going to turn me over to the Secret Service?"

"No, not if you tell me everything."

"I want your word as an officer and a gentleman."

"You have my word, if you tell all."

"The plates and the printing press are in the mansion at Malmo. Also, we have other sets of plates in Hamburg on the Reeperbahn. They make dollars, pounds and some deutschemarks. The Swiss banks launder the money and ship it to South America."

"The Reeperbahn? Why print there?" he asked, referring to the widely known Mile of Sin, where prostitutes sit behind store windows hustling the tourists, and "dog and pony" shows are rampant.

"Because nobody will bother the operation. It's in a safe house near Konigstrasse. There are former SS officers living there."

"Okay, Martin, you're being a very good boy. Are you ready to talk about your escape?"

"Not yet, Colonel. I am thinking about it."

Bart squelched his impulse to beat the truth out of Bormann, and opted instead to pay a visit to Nordheim's cell in the basement. "How is he behaving?" Bart asked the guards.

"He was screaming and yelling in German and English. Look at him now...he's exhausted and half asleep."

"Take a break, I'll call you when I'm finished with him."

Bart peered into the padded cell. He opened the cell door and walked over to the passive Nazi in his straitjacket.

"*Herr* Nordheim, are you ready to behave yourself?"

"*Ja, Schweinhund*. You will be sorry you did this to me."

"Listen carefully. If you promise to calm down, I'll have the jacket removed. If you start to hit your head against the wall or get violent in any way, it will be put back on. If you behave in the next day or two, I'll have you moved to a cell. Cooperate and things will get better for you."

"I will be better. Please take this jacket off."

Bart sent for the guards. "Remove the jacket. If he gets disorderly, slap it on again. He stays in this cell until I change it."

☆ ☆ ☆ ☆

Same Day - Havana

Captain Flaherty set the F-27 down at the José Martí Airport.

Dulles, Jacques and the colonel deplaned at Hangar 13. Nordheim's helicopter had been rolled inside the hangar. They took a look inside the aircraft, and inspected the six-seater thoroughly, hoping to find something. A square bag opening widely at the top contained myriad maps. A briefcase with a combination lock was under the pilot's seat. It was locked. The two bags were removed.

The three men took another tour of the copter's interior, cutting open the backs, fronts and seats, searching for hidden contraband. They found nothing. Jacques pulled the back off the pilot's seat and found two drawstring suede packets. He opened them to discover hundreds of cut diamonds. "Bingo," he chortled. "Look at what I found."

Dulles examined the bounty. "If this is real, it's worth millions," he whistled.

Jacques tore up the carpet. He tapped the plywood flooring and hammered a hole in the glued pieces of wood. He flashed a light through the opening. "There's something down there," he exclaimed.

The three men ripped open the false plywood flooring.

Jacques reached in and arduously pulled up a very large, heavy leather bag, which Bart and Dulles took from him. Two more bags followed suit. Bart went up front and found a large lever. He jacked the combination locks open on the three pieces of luggage.

The three stared at the find, awed by its contents. Each bag contained varying quantities of thousand-dollar bills, five-hundred-dollar bills and hundred-dollar bills.

"There has to be at least a hundred million dollars here," Dulles ventured. *Could it all be funny money?* Bart mused to himself.

The heavy bags were transferred to the F-27. Captain Flaherty and his crew were aboard. Bart went up to the cockpit. "Any of your men capable of flying that helicopter?"

"Just me, I guess," Flaherty responded. "What do you want to do with it?"

"I want to move it to Guantanamo as evidence."

"I have a suggestion, Colonel. I'll fly it to the base. My co-pilot, Lieutenant Frank Moretti, is an excellent pilot, so he can take the F-27 to the base. We can leave from there to D.C. The whole operation will be done in forty-five minutes."

"Allen, what do you think?"

"Sounds good to me, Bart."

"Captain, let's do it," Bart declared.

The helicopter arrived fifteen minutes after the F-27 landed. The rotorcraft was stored in a hangar.

Bart placed a call to the White House. "John, I'm coming in tonight. Can the Prez see me in the morning?"

Steelman advised the President.

"He'll see you at 11 a.m."

☆ ☆ ☆ ☆

Rock Creek Park, Washington - Later that morning

Bart and Jacques' arrival was unexpected. Stanley, the white-haired English butler, greeted them as they walked into the house.

"Colonel Milburn, Mr. Laurent, welcome home."

"Thank you, Stanley," Bart replied. "Where's Mrs. Milburn and the children?"

"They are in the children's playroom, sir."

Jacques retired to the study. Bart tapped gently on the playroom door. Mrs. Bishop's English aplomb was jolted. "Colonel Milburn, what a surprise!"

Elizabeth, Michael and Jenny tackled Bart. The children whooped, "Daddy! Daddy!"

Elizabeth planted a hungry kiss on Bart's lips. Michael and Jenny ran to Jacques and he lifted one in each arm, receiving kisses on each cheek. The raucous welcome, filled with a warm manifestation of love and joy, finally subsided. Bart and Jacques were peppered with *non sequitur* questions from the children. The session with Michael and Jenny had a therapeutic effect on the two men, momentarily erasing the dramatic events of the last few days.

After the children were put to bed, Elizabeth, Bart and Jacques sat down to dinner, which was prepared and served by Stanley. Elizabeth waited patiently for some word about their activities during their absence.

After the table was cleared and the coffee served, she lit a cigarette and casually said, "I trust you enjoyed your vacation, gentlemen."

"Jacques, that's her subtle way of asking what we've been up to."

"You are both tanned and healthy, so I assume it was a pleasant sojourn in warm climates."

"Honey, we've been extremely fortunate in our mission. We've captured and imprisoned two very important members of the Nazi hierarchy. This was a historic coup. Jacques was magnificent."

"The colonel planned and executed the whole mission," Jacques countered.

"Elizabeth, as I told you on the phone, I will phone your father after I see the President in the morning. In due time I'll tell you more."

"All right, how long do you plan to stay?"

"Honey, after our meetings here, we'll have to return."

"Return where, Barton Milburn?"

"How would you like to spend the Easter holidays in Havana?"

"With you?"

"Of course."

"With the children and Mrs. Bishop?"

"Yes, I'll rent a villa on the beach."

She leaped out of her chair and planted a loving kiss on Bart's lips.

"I knew there was something I liked about you," she giggled. "For being so nice, I have a little surprise for you." She sat smugly back in her chair, a big grin on her beautiful face, and quietly announced, "Another Milburn is going to be added to this family."

Bart was momentarily nonplussed. The news slowly sank in as he stared at his wife, who kept smiling.

"You mean..."

"Yes, yes. My doctor confirmed it yesterday. I am pregnant."

Bart pulled Elizabeth out of her seat and her, planting kisses all over her beautiful face. Jacques applauded.

CHAPTER SEVENTEEN

Friday, April 11, 1952 - 10:30 a.m. - The White House

The cherry blossoms were in full bloom on a lovely day, so Bart lowered the top of his Cadillac convertible and drove to 1600 Pennsylvania Avenue. Jacques sat alongside him, enjoying the view of the Potomac. The sky was solid blue, with a gentle sun bathing the nation's capital. At the West Gate, Tom Reilly greeted Bart.

"Colonel, this is a beautiful day. Good to see you. You're on for eleven. Nice to see you again, Mr. Laurent."

"You too, Tom."

Reilly noted the names on his clipboard and waved them through. Steelman met them at the entrance.

"Gentlemen, you are ten minutes early. Come into my office."

Bart gave Steelman a summary of Jacques' role in the mission.

"Mr. Laurent, I am impressed. You men had quite an exciting and successful venture. The President will be most interested in the details."

The door of the Oval Office opened into Steelman's office, and Truman, glasses on his forehead and a big smile on his face, summoned the group with a hand gesture. "All right, Colonel, lay it out for me."

Bart delineated a full report, without embellishment. He forthrightly detailed the role of the Mafiosi participation.

"I'll consider this a military operation. There can be no rewards for their assistance," Truman said forcefully.

"Mr. President, none was offered and none requested. By the way, these patriotic rascals conned Nordheim out of forty million dollars for introducing our hit lady to him. We netted twenty-six million dollars - one million for the conference and twenty-five million for a down payment to her. The cashier's checks made out to bearer are in the hands of the CIA, to be used as evidence."

Truman leaned back and laughed uproariously. Steelman joined him. "The perfect sting. A real con job on this scummy bastard. Those hoods are sharp," Truman chuckled.

"Colonel Milburn, you have exceeded my expectations. This is historic. Now, we have a few problems to sort out."

"I believe so, sir."

The President punched his intercom. "Hold my calls."

Jacques leaned over and placed a package of Monte Carlo photographs in one envelope. He placed a second one, marked *Prisoners*, which contained photos of Nordheim, Bormann, the chopper pilot, Joachim, and the two Gestapo men. Truman pored over them silently.

"I don't think I've enjoyed anything as much as the sight of these bums in durance vile," he said, slapping his desk for emphasis. "I am tempted to personally visit these depraved bastards. I would like to see him on his knees begging for mercy. I'm sure Churchill, de Gaulle and Ben-Gurion would pay any price for admission. At any rate, I'm obligated to notify Ben-Gurion for confiding in me and Churchill and de Gaulle for their cooperation."

"Sir, you mentioned that we have a few problems to sort out. I assume you are alluding to procedure with some sort of judicial solution for Hitler and Bormann. Before you tackle that problem, may I allude to something that requires immediate attention?"

"What might that be, Colonel?"

"The half million in counterfeit money we found under Bormann's bed at the Nacional Hotel in Havana. The multi-millions that Jacques here found in the Nordheim-Hitler chopper. And more important, the revelation by Bormann that all of the bogus bucks that were flooding Europe during the war are still being printed. Some in Hitler's mansion in Malmo, Sweden, and some in Hamburg. In the latter, of all places, on the Reeperbahn."

"Reeperbahn? Why in the hell there? Maybe we ought to put our two prime whores, Nordheim and Bormann, behind the windows of the Mile of Sin. Think of what that would do for the German economy," Truman said.

"That hypothesis, sir, if put into effect, would last less than a day. The Israelis or some locals would blow them to smithereens."

"Right, right, the wish was the father to the thought, Bart. Go on."

"In addition to that, we found possibly a hundred million dollars in thousand, five hundred, and hundred-dollar bills under the flooring of the helicopter. All of this loot is presently at Langley, taken there by Allen Dulles. We also found two packets of diamonds hidden in the back of the pilot's seat. The hundred million, more or less, has not been tested for validity."

"What do you propose?"

"First, we have to bring the Secret Service in on our recent find. They took the $500,000 counterfeit when we helped them arrest Hitler's point man, ex-FBI agent Darren Mayfield."

"Yes, I ordered him temporarily parked in isolation at Leavenworth."

"Sir, we have to raid Hamburg and Malmo to get those plates. They are turning out dollars, pounds, francs and deutschemarks."

"You don't mean for us to do this without the cooperation of Chancellor Konrad Adenauer and our occupation forces in Germany and the Prime Minister of Sweden?"

"Of course not. The word *raid* is a figure of speech encompassing those details, sir."

"Steelman, what open time do we have for tomorrow?"

"Sir, it's a Saturday and it's wide open."

"That's fine. We have to spoil a few weekends. Have Secretary Snyder, Attorney General McGranery and those Secret Service men who arrested Mayfield, also Chief of Staff Bradley, here at 10am. Colonel, you and CIA agent Laurent be here at that time. Also, Smith or Dulles."

"Yes sir," Steelman answered.

"Now, I'll place calls to Ben-Gurion, Churchill and de Gaulle. Goodbye, gentlemen."

"Sir, one item, if you don't mind...please ask the Israeli Prime Minister what his Mossad man Sean Briscoe is doing in Havana. He's got himself a job on Hitler's yacht as first mate."

"Sean Briscoe, an Irish Mossad agent?" the astonished Truman queried.

"Oh, he's Jewish, sir. His uncle was the first Jewish Lord Mayor of Dublin."

"Oh, yes, I remember. He marched at the head of a St. Patrick's parade in New York. He has a brogue thicker than a Guinness stout. I'll make a note of it. Fascinating."

Bart, at his office, checked in with partners Martha Arnold and Austin Graybeal. Miss Arnold bussed him on the cheek and Graybeal gave him a brotherly hug. Pledging them to silence, he told them his mission had been successful and that they had captured two prominent Nazi war criminals. He let it end there. They didn't press for more.

Back in his own office, he kissed Miss Telford, who blushed to her roots. After signing a stack of papers and checks, he placed a call to his brother Douglas and invited him to bring Christina Lyons to the house on Saturday afternoon. His next call was to Dandy Phil Kastel at the Hotel Riviera in Havana.

"Colonel, how are you sir?' We are still holding your rooms."

"Please do that, Mr. Kastel. I expect to be back there in a couple of days. We'll pay for all the time it's held."

"No problem."

"I need a personal favor. I know you're well connected locally."

"How can I help?"

"I want to rent a villa for me and my family. Will you recommend a real estate agency?"

"How many rooms do you need?"

"Well, sir, there's my wife, two children, a governess and an associate. I need to retain a cook and a maid to live in. I need a secure house on the beach or close by."

"For how long?"

"A month or two, with options."

"You don't need a real estate agent. I know of a perfect place for you. There is a large, beautifully furnished estate on three acres, fenced and gated, at Playas del Este, just a couple of miles south of Havana. It has a tennis court, a large pool, two guesthouses, a security system and all the modern goodies. A small bridge over the road leads to the beach. There are two servants, husband and wife, that go with the house. They reside in the smaller guesthouse. The villa has ten bedrooms. It belongs to a banker by the name of Irwin Gullen, who is in Switzerland now and won't be back until the end of the year. He intends to travel through Europe and Russia. I'll call his associate, Harry Branlow, in New York. I think it will go for four or five thousand a month, plus salaries for the servants. The gardener and general maintenance are included in the rent. I can put the arm on Gullen's man and maybe get it for four thousand. How does that sound?"

"Knowing your taste and the accoutrements at your hotel, I would say that's fine. I would be very grateful."

"How soon do you want to move in?" Kastel asked.

"As soon as possible. A couple of days would do."

"Where can I reach you?"

"In Washington, and here's two numbers, one for my office and the other for my home," Bart replied, and passed on the phone numbers. "I am much obliged for your assistance."

"My pleasure, sir."

☆ ☆ ☆ ☆

Saturday, April 12, 1952 - 10 a.m. - Washington

General Bradley, chairman of the Joint Chiefs of Staff; General Smith, Allen Dulles, Attorney General James McGranery, Secretary of the Treasury Snyder and President Truman were seated in the Cabinet room when Bart Milburn was ushered in by John Steelman. Secret Service agents were in a waiting room. They waved at Bart as he passed through. Bart looked at his wristwatch.

"You're not late, Colonel. I've moved this meeting up so that I could brief these men on your mission and the problems facing us now. Come, sit over here next to me," Truman said.

Milburn placed his briefcase on the giant-sized conference table. Bradley raised his hand. Truman nodded.

"Mr. President, I believe I speak for all members present. Colonel, your planning and execution in capturing these two most wanted Nazi war criminals deserves this nation's gratitude. You handled this mission with superb efficiency. You did it quietly, with no fanfare and not a single bullet fired. My deepest congratulations," Bradley said.

Applause followed around the table.

A palpably embarrassed Milburn muttered, "Thank you, sir. May I point out, this was a *team* effort."

"Modesty will get you nowhere," Truman quipped.

McGranery, Snyder, Smith and Dulles added their plaudits to the colonel, then Truman began. "The first order of business, gentlemen, is the problem of the counterfeit money and its continuing manufacture in two countries, specifically in Hamburg, Germany, and Malmo, Sweden. We have occupying forces in West Germany, but it is now a constitutionally organized sovereign state. Therefore, we have to coordinate cooperation with Chancellor Konrad Adenauer in West Germany and with King Gustav in Sweden for joint action simultaneously. Once we set a plan, we'll bring Secretary of State Acheson into the act," Truman said.

"Mr. President, we have the two Secret Service agents in charge of the case standing by. May we bring them in at this point?" Snyder requested.

Truman nodded at Steelman, who quickly summoned agents Adam Watkins and Samuel Collins. The men were introduced.

"Go ahead, John," Truman said.

"Mr. Watkins," said Snyder, "quickly update us on the monies captured."

"The half million dollars taken from ex-FBI agent Darren Mayfield is almost perfect in counterfeit money. It is about the closest to perfection we've ever seen. The one hundred and three million shown to us by the CIA is perfectly legal American currency."

"In that case, one hundred odd million should be held as evidence to determine its intended use," Attorney General McGranery said.

"Who will hold it?" Snyder asked.

"That's up to the final decision as to whether there will be a military trial, a Justice Department criminal trial pending a grand jury indictment, or a trial in Nuremberg or The Hague. There are legal arguments favoring any of those alternatives," McGranery said. "At the moment, I would place those bags of good money as contraband with the Federal Reserve for safekeeping. The Justice Department will hold the counterfeit for the grand jury and subsequent trial."

"Colonel, you've been in charge of this mission. I believe you should continue with this operation as an ancillary adjunct to the Hitler corollary," Truman advised.

"Isn't that stretching the colonel's efforts to the max?" General Smith said.

"Maybe so," McGranery said. "But I would posit the following. Colonel Milburn broke the case, therefore it holds that his follow-through of dotting the I's and crossing the T's becomes necessary. He speaks perfect German, which will serve in good stead in Germany and Sweden. Plus, to finish the escape factor of Hitler and Bormann, I would think he has to go to Malmo. He will have ample help from our armed forces, the Secret Service, the CIA, the

Justice Department and the State Department, plus your help, Mr. President, in securing German and Swedish cooperation."

"Well stated, Jim," Truman said. "What say you, Colonel?"

"At the moment, sir, I am yours to command," he replied with a grimace.

"Looks like you swallowed a sour pill, Bart," Truman observed.

"Unfortunately, sir, the task may be sour, but the anticipation is sweet. The name of the game is success; I'm ready."

"General Smith and Mr. Dulles, do you have any objections?"

"Not at all," Smith replied. "I would like Allen Dulles to assist the colonel. It holds that the colonel can't be in two places at once. I would suggest that Dulles take on the strike on Hamburg simultaneously with Milburn's strike in Malmo."

"Good suggestion, Beedle," Truman agreed.

"Then I would suggest, gentlemen, that agent Watkins go with Milburn to Malmo and agent Collins accompany Dulles," Snyder said. "We want those plates desperately, besides breaking up their operation."

"May I point something out, Mr. President?" Watkins asked.

"Speak up, son," Truman said.

"These counterfeiters have and are printing phony British pounds, French and Swiss francs, and deutschemarks. Are these other countries being invited to the party, sir?"

"You have raised a monumental quandary, dammit," Truman said.

There was a moment of silence as each man pondered the question.

"I will speak with Prime Minister Churchill and de Gaulle. I will ask them to assign no more than two men from MI6 and no more than two from the French DGSE. They are to report to you, Colonel Milburn, at a place and time to be designated. With regard to operations in Hamburg, and Malmo, I will speak with Chancellor Adenauer to assign two policemen to our military, the office to be named by General Bradley. Further, I will ask King Gustav in Sweden to cooperate with you, Barton. The exact purpose will not be revealed. Bizarre as that sounds, they either buy my scenario or we fly alone and embarrass all concerned," Truman said.

"Mr. President, isn't that a bit high-handed in the milieu of the delicate sphere of diplomacy?" Attorney General McGranery said.

"Frig the striped-pants routine. In matters such as this, things usually get fouled up. I'll get Acheson to brief our ambassadors on a need-to-know basis, but with no specifics."

"Mr. President, we are an occupying force in West Germany," said Bradley. "We haven't yet signed our peace contract, which is due on May 26 this year. Therefore, with your approval, we can handle Adenauer and the local police on our terms. I'd like General Lyden Walsh to handle the matter on the scene. He's a sharp and smooth operator. I think Colonel Milburn knows him. He will not mind working subordinately to the colonel. They were good friends during the war, right, Bart?"

"Perfect, General," Milburn agreed.

"All right, Omar, that takes care of Hamburg. I'll handle King Gustav and the Prime Minister of Sweden. And that's that. How soon, Colonel Milburn, can you mount this operation?" Truman asked.

"After coordinating our team in the next few days, I would make C-Day Tuesday, April 22, sir."

"So be it."

"Agents Watkins and Collins, thank you for your efforts. You may leave now."

"Mr. President," said Bradley, "before they leave, I would like to ask Colonel Milburn a question pertaining to his designation of C-Day, which I guess he has tagged as Counterfeit Day…"

Bart interjected, "General, that's what it stands for."

"We Army men understand each other," he replied. "What I want to suggest, if it fits Barton's schedule, is that we meet in the morning at my office in the Pentagon. The Secret Service will join us, while we map out a plan and I can put our pieces in place."

"How about that, Colonel?" Truman said.

"That's fine, if it's an early meeting. I have to get back to Guantanamo tomorrow to visit my nervous Nazis."

"How about 0900 hours, Colonel? We should be finished by 1100 hours."

"Suits me. How about you, Collins and Watkins?"

"Can do," they chorused.

"Settled," General Bradley declared.

The two Secret Service men left.

"The ponderous problem, gentlemen, is a legal dilemma," said Truman. "What do we do with this misbegotten Luciferian beast we think is Hitler? Our Constitution, our Bill of Rights and our Declaration of Independence makes no provision for this devil incarnate, as Colonel Milburn described him."

"There are alternatives to our putting the bastard on trial," said McGranery. "We can turn him over to the Israelis, to the British, the French, the Dutch or The Hague and a host of others, or to Germany for a real *mea culpa*. But, Mr. President, none of that will fly with you because of that sign on your desk saying *The Buck Stops Here*. The problem is procedure."

"We could always let the son of a bitch commit suicide like his accessories Goebbels and Goering, among others," General Smith noted.

Brief laughter erupted among the men.

"That would be too easy a way out," Truman declared. "Any other suggestions, gentlemen?"

"I'm inclined, sir, to let Colonel Milburn proceed with his efforts to milk Bormann as a potential witness against Hitler. And, further to that, I agree with the colonel's attempts to break Hitler down to where he admits he is the Führer and does away with his masquerade as Nordheim," Smith said.

"And what after that?" McGranery queried.

Bart broke in quickly. "Let us set up a military tribunal for what we will euphemistically call a preliminary hearing. At that point in time, after the hearing, the panel can order a full military trial, a civil trial, or refer it to the

Nuremberg or The Hague. Out of that procedure, we will be able to solicit enough material from survivor witnesses for a major first-rate trial, media-circus type, here in the U.S. or elsewhere."

"Mr. Attorney General, how does Colonel Milburn's scenario strike you?" Truman questioned.

"I buy it, sir. It gives us time to quietly test our judicial options."

"That's it, colonel, so get on with your mission," Truman said, then quipped, "But enjoy the rest of your weekend."

As the group was leaving the West Wing of the White House, Milburn whispered to Smith, "A little problem I wanted to avoid involving the President, I need to discuss with you and Dulles."

They walked over to Smith's town car.

"The yacht must be removed from Havana," Bart declared. "With Nordheim missing, the yacht's captain will notify Froelich and Fenwick. In fact, they may be on their way to Havana. In that case, we'd be obliged to arrest them on any one of a dozen charges."

"As I recall, Fenwick served as ambassador to Germany and later became an advisor to Neville Chamberlain, and Froelich was Nazi ambassador to England. A slimy pair," Smith recalled.

"What's the captain of the Flying Eagle like? Is he a Nazi?" Dulles asked.

"Hell no, Allen. He believes that Nordheim killed his fiancée in Malmo. He kept his job in hopes of finding info as to how she disappeared. He has been supporting the mother of his girl. It's in your early file."

"A suggestion, then, Colonel: Get him off the yacht. Make him see the light. Put him on our payroll and take him to Malmo with you. He can be an asset."

"Not bad, Allen," Smith interjected.

"If we snatch Fenwick and Froelich, we will be crowding the facilities at Guantanamo," Dulles observed.

"Admiral Thomas is an old friend of mine," Smith added. "He is delighted to be part of history. Bart, they have lots of room on that base. When I get back to the office, I'll call him. He'll cooperate. Believe me, I know the man. Where can I reach you later?" Smith asked.

"I'll be home. I'm expecting a witness who could be vital in unmasking Nordheim."

☆ ☆ ☆ ☆

Saturday, April 12, 1952 - 2 p.m. - Washington

Bart and Jacques were headed for the Milburn home, Jacques driving now while Bart scribbled some notes. The convertible top was up as they drove along the Potomac toward Rock Creek Park.

Stanley greeted them at the door. "Mrs. Bishop and Madame have taken the children out for lunch and a visit to the zoo, sir."

"Yes, that was planned, Stanley. Have you set the table for four? I'm expecting my brother and a lady."

"Yes, sir, everything is in order. A Mr. Kastel called. He said the villa is yours, as of now."

"Thank you, Stanley."

Douglas Milburn and Christina Lyons arrived by taxi. Jacques opened the door before they had a chance to ring the bell.

Doug hugged Jacques and introduced Mrs. Lyons. Bart bounded down the plushly carpeted staircase, embraced his brother and warmly welcomed Christina, who excused herself to go to the powder room. They gathered in the den.

"Mrs. Lyons, would you like a drink?" Bart offered.

"Indeed I would. How about a vodka martini?"

"We're noted for that." Bart smiled.

Jacques carefully prepared a pitcher of the libation. He took a bottle of chilled vodka from the refrigerator behind the bar, gently poured a few drops of vermouth and dropped an olive into each frozen glass.

"Mrs. Lyons, you are here with trusted friends. Please relax and feel at home," Bart said in a soothing manner.

"I know. I've just been nervous these last few days. My life has been threatened."

"You are quite safe, and this problem will be resolved shortly," Bart assured her.

"How can you be sure?" she cried, tears welling up in her eyes.

Jacques handed her a small box of tissues, then attentively sat next to her.

"May I have a cigarette?"

Jacques handed her a long filtered Kent and lit it.

The beautiful woman looked at Jacques appreciatively and asked for a refill of her glass. He quickly filled it. In a strange move for the usually impassive Laurent, he patted her delicate hand and whispered, "We are your protectors."

Through her teary eyes, she rewarded him with a warm smile. Doug and Bart exchanged intellectual nods.

Stanley appeared and in a crisp English accent announced, "Luncheon is being served."

The group entered the dining room. Jacques held Mrs. Lyons' arm. As they were being seated, he held her chair. She glanced at him, whispering, "Thank you."

Stanley served a finely chopped Caesar salad, then announced, "We have a choice of broiled salmon, teriyaki chicken or filet mignon."

"I'm ravenously hungry," Christina Lyons asserted. "I'll try the filet, charred and medium, please."

"The same for me, Stanley," Jacques said. Doug and Bart opted for the salmon.

"How about some wine, Mrs. Lyons?" Jacques said.

"That would be delightful." She smiled. "Please call me Christina."

He looked at Bart, who nodded. Behind the bar, Jacques extracted a bottle of 1947 Bordeaux. He opened it, sniffed the cork and poured her a small amount for tasting. She sipped and nodded approval. Bart filled the other glasses and raised his glass, "To Christina."

A couple of *hear hears* from Bart and Doug followed.

"Jacques, do you live here?"

Before he could reply, Bart interjected, "Jacques Laurent is our adopted brother. He lives here and works very closely with me. He is a very dear and loyal friend. He is also head of the Nazi desk at the CIA."

Elizabeth looked at Jacques with a smile and a nod of admiration. Noting the harmonious relationship between Christina and Jacques, Bart launched into a biographical sketch of Jacques' background. He added quite a few accolades to his outline, stressing his bachelorhood.

"Quite impressive, Jacques," she observed.

They adjourned to the den, where coffee was served. Douglas had prepared a *précis* on the disappearance of the world-famous plastic surgeon Phillip La Velle, father of Christina Lyons, so he handed copies to Bart, Doug and Jacques. She quietly sipped her coffee and smoked a cigarette while the men intently read the documents.

"Christina, this document ties in with a matter I am pursuing for our government. I don't want to get your hopes up, but I believe I know who your father's patient was. I want your word of honor that you will not reveal my interest in your case. What I am engaged in is of the highest priority and is top secret."

"Oh no, I want secrecy, too."

"Jacques and I are working on a situation to which the disappearance of your father has been a missing link. In the next few days, I believe I can solve the mystery of your father's fate. Now, don't press me for more information. I would like you to look at some photographs."

Jacques placed a briefcase on the mahogany coffee table. Bart opened it and withdrew a legal-sized manila envelope. He thumbed through a package of pictures. One at a time, he placed single pictures before Christina.

She passed on the first two. On the third she exclaimed, "I think this man was shown to me by the French police. In their picture, he had a mustache."

"Look at it real hard. Study the features carefully," Bart implored.

She reached into her purse and withdrew a pair of designer reading glasses. Placing the glasses on the bridge of her nose, she peered intently at the picture. She placed the forefinger of her right hand over the upper lip of the subject.

"I am sure this is the man they showed me."

"When they showed him to you, did they indicate what connection he might have had with your father?"

"They believe he was one of the men who had lunch with my father at the Plaza Athenee. Do you know who he is, Mr. Milburn?"

"I believe so, Christina, but I'd rather not identify him at this point in time. I don't mean to be mysterious, but for your sake it's better that you not know. In due time we'll reveal everything to you. Please bear with me. Also, you may call me Bart, Barton, or Colonel. We're going to be close friends."

"Christina, my brother Bart knows exactly what he's doing. I can't even touch this story with a hot poker," Doug declared.

"I understand."

"Christina, look at this picture."

She replaced her glasses. Jacques was entranced. She studied the photograph for thirty seconds. "Yes, they showed me this man as the other person who lunched with my father."

"Are you certain?"

"Without question, Colonel. Those faces have been etched in my mind."

"You have been very helpful. Now, what are your plans? Where do you go from here?"

"That's just the point. I don't know. I am afraid. I feel like there is a contract out on me."

"Forgive me. I've been so callous in overlooking your plight while I questioned you. We can't have you living in a state of fear."

"Where are your children?" Jacques solicitously queried.

"They are with a friend of mine in Holmby Hills, which is contiguous to Beverly Hills, but I am afraid to leave them there too long."

Jacques beckoned Bart to join him outside the den. They made their apologies and excused themselves. "Colonel, I have a wild suggestion. If Elizabeth will approve, how about taking this important witness to Havana with us. You've got this villa now. How about some Rangers for security?"

Bart eyed him silently, then said, "I believe you're smitten."

"She is a very fine woman," he blushed.

"I think Cupid just hit you."

"I like her, if that's what you mean."

"It's not a bad thought, if Elizabeth will take to her. Let's go back in."

Christina and Douglas were discussing various solutions to the dilemma of her safety.

"Christina and Douglas, can you folks stay for dinner?"

Mrs. Lyons looked at Douglas for an answer.

"Constance is expecting me. We're driving up to Fairfield, Connecticut late tonight after the show. We're house guests of Zanuck. He wants to talk Connie into making a film of her current show *California*. It's a big hit, you know.

"You certainly can't miss that. How about leaving Mrs. Lyons in our care? That is, if she accepts. We can put her up here in our guesthouse."

"That's fine with me. How about you, Christina?" Douglas asked.

"I have no place to go except my quiet room at the Beaux Arts. My bag is at the airport."

"Give me the key to the locker and I'll have a cab bring it here," Doug volunteered.

"Now that we've settled that, I have an important question to ask. Did you take any of the money from the safe-deposit box?" he inquired.

Christina was flustered by the question. She stammered, "I took two thousand dollars for extra spending money while I was here. Did I do wrong?"

"No, not at all. Do you have any of it with you?"

"Yes, I have about fifteen hundred with me."

"May I see it?"

She reached into her purse and produced a wallet, which she handed to Bart. He extracted two hundred-dollar bills and held them up.

"Are these the bills from the safe-deposit box?"

"Yes."

He reached into his pants pocket and peeled off two hundred-dollar bills. "Here, I am swapping these bills in place of these two."

He handed the wallet and the two bills from his pocket back to her.

"Is there something wrong with my money?" she querulously demanded.

"I hope not," Bart replied. "There has been some counterfeit floating around, so I want to make sure that these rascals didn't cheat your father."

Bart placed the two bills in an envelope and sealed it. The outside door opened and closed with a loud noise.

"Daddy's home!" Michael shouted as he ran into the den and jumped into his father's lap.

"Uncle Douglas!" squealed Jenny, jumping into his lap.

Both children scampered to Jacques, hugging and kissing him.

Christina, smiling, watched the joyous scene. Elizabeth and Mrs. Bishop tried to get the children to leave. Bart stood up, kissed his wife and introduced Christina to Elizabeth and Mrs. Bishop. Douglas embraced Elizabeth and pecked her on the cheek, then bussed Mrs. Bishop. Bart excused himself for a moment and left the den with the children, Elizabeth and the nanny.

"Come on, children, it's bath time," Mrs. Bishop coaxed.

Bart followed Elizabeth into their bedroom. He clasped her in his arms and planted a loving kiss on her lips. She responded with a hungry mouth.

"If we keep this up, you'll not return to your guests," she giggled.

"Honey, this lady, Mrs. Lyons, is a vital key to what I am working on. She is also a very troubled woman. With your permission, I'd like to put her up here tonight in the guesthouse. And further to that, I would like her and her two children, six and five years old, to stay at the guesthouse of the villa in Havana. If you have the slightest objection, I'll make other arrangements."

"Barton, dear, who is she?"

"She's the daughter of that famous Beverly Hills plastic surgeon, Phillip LaVelle, who disappeared in Switzerland seven years ago. She is a very cultured and educated woman. I'm sure you'll like her."

"Darling, if you feel it's necessary, that's fine with me."

"Tell you what - reserve your decision until after dinner. Size her up and then give me a thumbs-up or down."

"That's a deal. Now scoot, I have to shower. The zoo is a very smelly place."

Back in the den, Jacques was regaling Christina and Douglas with funny episodes during the war. He had them laughing when Bart returned.

"Have I missed something?"

"Bart, our brother here ought to be in show business. He tells some hilarious stories. I'm not sure they're all true, but humorous nevertheless," Doug said.

"Oh, I know that side of Jacques. He reserves his humor for special guests," Bart added.

"Folks, I have to leave. I'll have Christina's bag here by cab. My love to the kids and Liz. You're in good hands, Christina."

She thanked Doug profusely.

"Wait a minute, Doug," Jacques interjected. "Christina, how would you like to ride with me while I drive Douglas to the airport? I'll take the station wagon."

"I would like that."

"Bart, I will bring Christina directly to the guesthouse. Would Stanley check out everything there?"

"Good idea. I have some calls to make. Give our love to Constance. I'll keep you updated, brother."

Bart placed a call to Dandy Phil in Havana.

"Colonel, good to hear from you," Kastel said.

"Is the house ready for occupation?"

"Yes, you can move in any time."

"By the way, how big is the guesthouse?"

"It's a beauty. It has four bedrooms, four baths, and two servants' rooms with two baths. It is beautifully furnished, immaculate. Gullen uses it for his *politicos*. He's a real wheeler-dealer."

"How are the security systems in the main house and the guesthouse?"

"*Perfecto*. The state of the art and then some, with direct connections to the *policia*. If you need round-the-clock guards, that can be arranged for a thousand dollars per week. The place is gated, fully fenced and electrically connected to the security system. Any breach turns on floodlights and sirens."

"Phil, I'm very grateful. I'll be there sometime tomorrow."

"Colonel, I forgot to mention, a new Cadillac and a Ford station wagon go with the house. No extra charge."

"Very generous, sir. Hold our rooms at the hotel. I have some of our people coming back."

"The floor is yours."

The next call reached General Smith at Langley. Bart briefed Smith on the LaVelle affair.

"Now, if you can get Martin to reveal the details of the escape and the plastic surgery, we're in business," the general said.

"How did we do with General Bradley?"

"Gung ho, Colonel. You'll have Captain Devereaux and six Rangers, who were with you in Havana. They will be at Andrews at 1200 hours awaiting you. Berger, Sophia and Tony will be there, as well. You're meeting with Brad at 0900, right?"

"Yes, sir."

"Good luck."

Stanley was advised to prepare the guesthouse for Mrs. Lyons. "We'll be dining out this evening. Just prepare dinner for the children, Mrs. Bishop and yourself."

Bart's next call was for a dinner reservation at the Shoreham Hotel. Later that evening, Elizabeth, Christina, Jacques and Bart were warmly greeted by the Maitre d', Nino. "Nice to see you again, Mr. Milburn. I have your favorite table. Not too close to the orchestra."

Bart had a ten-dollar bill in his hand as he shook Nino's hand. The dinner went along smoothly. Elizabeth and Christina chatted about Beverly Hills, Hollywood, London, children, and some of the current scandals. Jacques was enamored, a sight that Barton had never observed in his friend. It was a heart-warming sight for Bart, who loved him as a brother.

The soft musical renderings of Cole Porter, Irving Berlin, Hoagy Carmichael, Rodgers and Hammerstein, and Johnny Mercer enticed Bart and Elizabeth to the dance floor. They were soon followed by Christina and Jacques.

Elizabeth nuzzled against Bart's ear and whispered, "She's a charming woman. I think Jacques is moonstruck. Look at the way she's nestled on his shoulder. He's in dreamland."

"I hope he takes it slow," Bart ventured.

"Bart, I wouldn't mind her joining us in Havana."

"Thank you, my love. I'm leaving for Havana tomorrow. Jacques will fly with you on Monday morning. Have Stanley lock up the house and come along with the entourage. He will be helpful there."

They returned to the table, where Christina and Jacques were heavily engaged in conversation. Bart disclosed his plans for Mrs. Lyons.

"I'll have to return to California to bring my children. I'm rather fearful of showing up there."

"Suppose Jacques accompanied you as your bodyguard? I assure you, he's the best."

Jacques looked at Bart, a look of pleased surprise crossing his face.

"Oh, I'm sure of that," Christina responded, "but, I can't impose on this dear man."

"It will be *mon plaisir*."

"*Vous êtes très gallant*."

In seconds the two were chattering away in French.

"All settled, Colonel."

"Fine. Leave in the morning, then come directly to Havana. You'll change planes in Miami. See you there on Monday. Bring your children's nanny with you."

CHAPTER EIGHTEEN

Sunday, April 13, 1952 - 9 a.m. - the Pentagon

In the conference room of the chairman of the Joint Chiefs of Staff, Omar Bradley sat at the head of a long oak table, ready to speak. "This is not a prayer meeting, gentlemen. I hope you've all been to church this morning," the five-star general said drolly.

Suppressed laughter followed from the officers, Secret Service men and CIA agents at the table.

"I'll forgo introductions. As I call your names, raise your hands, and that will suffice for identities," he continued. "Colonel Milburn, who is in charge of this double-pronged 'Operation C-Day,' which stands for 'Counterfeit'. Secret Service agents Adam Watkins and Samuel Collins, who will make the official arrests of the counterfeiters we are after. Agent Collins will be assisted by the Army in Hamburg. The colonel will personally lead the strike in Malmo, Sweden. Agent Watkins will make the arrests in Malmo. Milburn will determine who is to be held."

The four names mentioned raised their hands.

"Major General William Barclay, here on my right, will act as liaison officer between this team and General Lyden Walsh, in charge of our troops in the Hamburg area, who will furnish the manpower needed there. Captain Louis Edigio will be aide to General Barclay. Allen Dulles, deputy director of the CIA, will have final authority as to which prisoners are to be held for Colonel Milburn's interrogation team."

The four men for Hamburg raised their hands.

Bradley continued, "Major General Paul Donovan will act as liaison to

Swedish troops or police, as the case may be. His aide will be Major Daniel Goldstone. To repeat, Colonel Milburn, under the direct authority of our Commander-in-Chief, President Truman, is in full charge of these simultaneous raids. Jacques Laurent of the CIA will be his deputy. Now, we will hear the plan. Colonel, the floor is yours."

Milburn detailed the plan of operation. "All assigned personnel will be in Hamburg and Malmo two days before the raid on Tuesday, April 22nd. The raid will occur at 2100 hours, Hamburg time, synchronized with Malmo time. Allen Dulles will coordinate all personnel involved in Hamburg. The movements and attack will be organized in accordance with the terrain and the activity occurring at the scene. I will do likewise in Malmo. You will have two days to scout the targets, or in the parlance of cops and robbers, we'll have two days to case the joints."

"Remember, Germany is occupied by our troops," Bradley observed. "General Walsh is expecting you men. He has arranged quarters for you on arrival. The local *polizei* will be called into the operation fifteen minutes before the strike. We can't afford any leaks. The criminals we're after have bribed officials all over Europe. The same holds true in Malmo."

"Further planning will be implemented at the two locations," Bart interjected. "Act like tourists and dress accordingly. In Sweden, people will be housed in the city of Lund, which is 30 kilometers from Malmo. It's more touristy than Malmo. Allen Dulles has arranged a safe house for us. It's a small bed and breakfast inn on the outskirts of Lund, closer to Malmo. We're a Chamber of Commerce group from Alexandria, Virginia, on holiday. Weapons will be supplied in Hamburg and Lund."

"Gentlemen, we've chartered a Pan American plane to deliver both teams from Andrews. Our first stop will be Hamburg. You'll be met by an Army chartered bus. Have your passports ready. The flight will take you to Copenhagen, and a ferry will take you to Malmo in forty-five minutes. You will be met at the ferry and will be transported by chartered bus to our inn."

Questions were asked and answered, then the meeting was adjourned.

A sergeant drove Bart to Andrews Air Force Base. Jacques drove the station wagon back to the house to pick up Christina Lyons for their trip to Los Angeles.

☆ ☆ ☆ ☆

Later that same day - Havana

The four-engined plane taxied to Hangar 13 at the José Martí Airport, then a shuttle bus drove Milburn, "Countess" Sophia, Tony Fuentes, Phillip Berger, Captain Devereaux, his Rangers, Major Flaherty and his flight crew to the Hotel Riviera.

"Get settled, folks, and have a nice evening. We leave for Guantanamo at 0900 hours. The bus will be leaving the hotel half an hour earlier," Bart said. "The Rangers will do a twenty-four-hour watch on the Flying Eagle."

"Colonel, the flight crew will leave here an hour earlier, sir. We'll taxi there," Flaherty said.

Bart found Kastel in the hotel casino, and they adjourned to the hotel manager's office. The lease was signed and the check was paid.

Then Dandy Phil offered to show him the mansion.

A short distance from the hotel, they stopped at a gated driveway, where Phil pressed a remote control and the electric gates were opened to a bricked driveway. The villa was everything Kastel had described, and then some. But while Bart had expected a Cuban or South American architectural motif. Instead, the mansion was of Mediterranean design.

Emilio and Maria Garcia, the two domestics, opened the door and in slightly accented English exclaimed, "Welcome, Mr. Kastel!"

"This is Colonel Milburn. His family will arrive tomorrow."

"*Bienvenida*, Colonel. *Mucho gusto*."

"Thank you, Emilio and Maria. My Spanish is not too good."

"That's okay, Colonel, we speak good English and we teach you some Spanish," Maria said.

A quick tour of the lavishly furnished home and the guesthouse revealed a fastidiously maintained dwelling.

"There will be my wife and two children, a governess, butler, my adopted brother and myself staying in the house. Our friend, Mrs. Lyons, her two children and a governess will occupy the guesthouse. If you need an extra day maid, hire one," Bart said.

"Colonel, I think an extra day maid is needed," Kastel suggested. " I'll send over Sylvia, an excellent hotel day maid. She speaks perfect English, has worked here before and is a friend of the Garcias. Same pay."

"*Bueno!*" Maria exclaimed.

"Good deal, Phil," Bart agreed.

"You sleep here tonight, Colonel?" Emilio asked.

"No, tonight I'll stay at the hotel. Tomorrow night I'll be here when my family arrives."

On the way back to the Riviera, Bart expressed his appreciation to Kastel. "Phil, this villa exceeds my expectations. The price is more than reasonable."

"Costello is your friend. I'm his partner. Nothing is too good for our friends. Besides, Gullen owes us a lot."

"I'm going to take you up on arranging round-the-clock security, and I have one other favor to ask, Phil. Could I have your hotel shuttle bus pick up my family at the airport? I'll pay for it."

"No pay is necessary, Colonel. Let me know the flight number, and just tip the driver."

"Your hospitality is deeply appreciated."

That night Bart called Elizabeth, described the mansion and obtained her flight number.

Later, at dinner with Sophia, Tony and Phillip, he detailed the procedure of examining Bormann and Hitler. "Sophia, when you are allowed a visit with

Bormann, tell him you're out on bail as a material witness. Explain that you have a very smart lawyer who is well connected to the White House."

☆ ☆ ☆ ☆

Monday, April 14, 1952 - Guantanamo Naval Base

Martin Bormann was asleep in his comfortable quarters. The radio was playing classical music softly. The guards were relieved, and Bart took their place. He placed his Colt .45 next to the phone on the table and took a hard, curious look at Bormann, who awakened with the clang of the gate that had replaced the door of that room.

"Colonel, I thought you had abandoned me," Bormann groaned in German.

"English only, Martin," Bart insisted as he placed the tape recorder on the lamp table next to his cot.

"How long you keep me here?"

"As long as you refuse to tell me everything I want to know, starting with the details of your escape."

"Where is Nordheim?"

"See, you are still playing with me!" Bart roared. "You mean Hitler or Führer, don't you? Why the hell don't you say so?"

"Don't be angry, Colonel. Where is the Führer?"

"He is in a padded cell. Why are you protecting him, after he sold you down the river?"

"I told you a lot so far, haven't I?"

"Now you listen to me, Martin Bormann. The time is up for games. I want facts, true ones, or I'll wash my hands of you and send you to Alcatraz or Leavenworth. Have you heard about those prisons?"

"*Ja, ja.* I want to make a deal with you. I will testify against Hitler, if you help me go to Argentina."

"No promises now, except we won't hang you if you tell everything and testify against Hitler."

Bormann moaned and buried his head in his pillow.

"Come on, Martin Bormann, *Reichsleiter*, lieutenant general, and most powerful Nazi, sit up like the great man you were."

"I will answer your questions, but sooner or later I want a lawyer."

"Maybe that can be arranged. Your friend, the countess, is out on bail. She has a smart, well connected lawyer. She promised to cooperate."

"How can she cooperate? She knows nothing."

"Yes, she knows plenty about Eva Peron, President Peron and all you Nazi bastards' connections with Argentina, their banks and the Swiss banks. She likes you and says you're not a real Nazi. She says you're a good politician who had nothing to do with the Holocaust."

"She say that? Good woman."

"Let's get down to business. You and Hitler escaped to Malmo, Sweden. You bought a mansion there, turned part of it into an operating room and hospital. A prominent American plastic surgeon operated on Hitler and changed his face. Both of you bought your way into Swedish citizenship, taking the names of Nordheim and Schwartz from a Jewish cemetery."

"Who told you this? Hitler?"

"Bormann, I will warn you for the last time. I do not have the patience to play cat-and-mouse games with you. Don't ask questions. Just answer mine," Bart heatedly demanded.

Bormann winced at Bart's corrosive tone and grim mien. "Tough American."

Bart turned off the recorder.

"Don't play with me, Bormann. I've treated you far better than any Nazi rat deserves. If you really want to know how tough I am, keep stalling. I know you're a smart-ass. That's how you became so powerful. You're a cunning cutie pie. But, play your Machiavellian games with me and I'll break your balls. I'll give you a taste of Auschwitz and turn you over to the Israelis or the Russkies. Death will be a merciful and charitable gift before I'm finished with you. Now, start talking, *hochstapler!*"

The change in demeanor and character turned Bormann's faded tan complexion to a yellowish green. During the war he had observed Hitler's rages against Nazi vassals. Bormann had delivered diatribes of his own. But nothing as vehement and vitriolic as Milburn's tirade had ever been leveled *at* Bormann. Bart's contrived histrionics obviously produced the desired result.

"I'll answer your questions. But you shouldn't insult me like this. I told Hitler the Americans were a hard people. I warned him not to get them involved in the war. He laughed at me. He said they were hedonists, flabby, self-indulgent, weak and cowardly. *Sie sind Flaschen und warschlappen.* We learn different."

"Your Führer was a lucky piece of dog turd. He was a *hochstapler*, a con man, and the pied piper of a dissolute, leaderless rabble. You were part of them, groping your way to the top as an ingenious ass-kisser. He was a sociopathic megalomaniac. I hope you understand what I have said."

"*Ich habe gehört. Verstehen sie.* I read a lot."

"Right now your Führer is *ein Trottel.* A whimpering half wit."

"*Ja,* that's where you are wrong. He's a very dangerous man. Psychotic. He has people all over the world and has plans to create *verwustung.* How you say in English?"

"Havoc."

"*Ja, ja.*"

"How did you escape from the bunker under the chancellery on April 30, 1945? A straight answer now." Bart turned on the recorder.

"All right. Hitler married Evan Braun. He told everyone that he would die with Eva. Goebbels and his wife agreed to kill their children and themselves. A few days before, a General Ritter von Greim and Hanna Reitsch, a great woman test pilot, flew into Berlin and came into the bunker. She pleaded with Hitler not to stay. She said the German people needed him. The Russian artillery was getting closer every day. Goering sent him a wire asking if he should take over. Hitler went wild. He screamed that his generals were deserting him. He named von Greim a marshal to take over Goering's position as head of the Luftwaffe."

"Most of that is history," Bart interjected. "How did you get out?"

"I'm coming to that, Colonel. Himmler, he heard, was trying to make peace. He went crazy. SS Gruppenführer Hermann Fegelein, who was married to Eva Braun's sister, was Himmler's representative in the bunker. Hitler demanded to see Fegelein. He wasn't there any more. They found him in his apartment in Berlin. He was brought back to the underground of the chancellery. In spite of his relationship to Eva Braun, the Führer ordered his execution. That's when I noticed he was the same size as Hitler."

"So what happened?"

"*Ach*, okay, Colonel, you said you would hang me. Do you mean that?"

"Only if you don't tell me the real truth. A straight answer, Bormann. Now."

"Okay, here's the real truth. Hitler never intended to kill himself. He planned to keep Nazism alive. The suicide was a cruel, how you say, charade. Hitler's a born coward. He had planned the escape two months before, on April 30, 1945. I lied to you in my previous story. As I mentioned, Fegelein was exactly Hitler's size and build. He didn't tell me of his plan to execute Fegelein. He told Fegy to go home the night before. Then the bastard had him arrested for leaving the bunker. They took Gruppenführer Fegelein to the garden of the chancellery and executed him. I was shocked when Hitler ordered the execution. Personally, I didn't think he deserved it. Hitler was wild. He told me to bring the body to the back door and stuff him in the maid's broom closet in the basement. Elsa Kinder, the maid, was told to go home in Berlin."

"Go on."

"The Goebbelses went to their room and poisoned their children and themselves. Hanna Reitsch, the pilot, said there was a plane in the back of the chancellery. I rushed into Hitler's room, with Schwerin and Krueger standing guard. Eva Braun was dead from a cyanide pill. Hitler ordered Schwerin and Krueger to bring Fegelein's body from the closet down the rear steps of the bunker. They brought him in. We changed his uniform with Hitler's clothes. Hitler then ordered me to fire a shot into Fegelein's head. I did it. Hanna Reitsch, Schwerin and Krueger were in on the plot. I couldn't interfere."

"Then what?"

"We wrapped Fegelein's body in a blanket and we did the same to Eva. We let Fegelein's foot hang out of the blanket. He was wearing Hitler's pants. A phonograph was playing, people were joking, and I smelled cigarette smoke. Everyone thought Hitler was dead. They had heard the gunshot. We had the bodies placed on a Viking pyre outside the chancellery, and we poured on more gasoline. There was a strong wind and the flames burned quickly, so we had to keep pouring on more gasoline.

Schwerin and Krueger helped me pick up all the papers in Hitler's room. General Heinrich Müller and his SS men helped us work out the switch. Hanna had the twin engines of a Junker passenger plane, belonging to Albert Speer, warmed up. We all crammed in, slammed the doors, and she raced due north over the Baltic Sea, flying low to avoid radar, then landed on a farm near Malmo, Sweden."

"Why Malmo?"

"Because Hitler owned a house there. He had ordered me to purchase it a year before, in 1944. I had meetings with industrialists there planning to move our industries out of Germany. There are hundreds of corporations I helped establish all over the world with money, bonds, patents, and stocks in big American companies."

"You know, Martin, if you are lying to me, I will throw you back in your cell. I have Krueger and Schwerin locked up, and they'd better confirm your story."

"I know. But you will have to make them tell the truth."

"Tell me about the house in Malmo. Describe all of it."

"It has three floors, fifteen bedrooms and baths, an operating room and a sterile recovery room. There is a large cellar with an entry in the back and an entry from a closet in the kitchen just behind the pantry."

"Is that where the fake money is being made?"

Bormann hesitated and poured water from a plastic container into his cup. He sipped slowly, thoughtfully framing his answer.

"Come on, Martin. Hold back and you'll pay the price."

"*Ja*, that's where it is being done."

"Who launders the money?"

"You mean, wash it?"

"Don't be cute. You know what that means."

"Through the Banque Lorraine by Konrad Fliegel, treasurer of Winston General."

"I'm going to show you some pictures. Tell me if you recognize these men. Who is this man?"

"That's Darren Mayfield."

"Good. Who is this?"

"Gunther Froelich."

"Okay, those are the two men who had lunch with Dr. Phillip LaVelle at the Plaza Athenee in Paris. He is the surgeon who changed Hitler's face."

"*Ja*."

"What happened to the doctor?"

"I do not know."

"Bullshit."

"Honest, I don't know. When the operation was over, Hitler had to stay in bed for a week. The doctor stayed with him and so did the nurse. While Hitler was recuperating, he sent me to Buenos Aires. The operation was in May, 1945. I stayed in Argentina for two months, June and July, 1945."

"Why did you go there?"

"I bought him the ranch in Mar del Plata. I also consolidated the funds we have in the banks in Buenos Aires. I also waited for the German submarines to come. We unloaded over one hundred million in gold, currency and diamonds. Then I flew back to Geneva to the Banque Lorraine. From there, I go to Liechtenstein to establish Winston General. I come back to Malmo and almost couldn't recognize the Führer. He had a new face, with a beard and a large mustache. The doctor and the nurse were gone. That's all I know."

"You met the doctor and the nurse?"

"Yes, he is Dr. LaVelle, very famous. And the nurse, Joan Bauman, a very nice girl."

"Who paid them?"

"Froelich took care of everything. Mayfield recommended Dr. LaVelle. He said LaVelle was best plastic surgeon in America. He arranged to hire him. From Geneva, they fly him to Malmo. They didn't tell him where they were taking him. That's all I know."

"You became a good friend with President Peron and his wife, Eva."

"*Ja*, very good friends. I set up joint accounts with them."

"Then you crossed them by taking all the money and gold out of Buenos Aires on Hitler's Lockheed plane."

"No, I didn't cross them, Hitler did. But later I meet Eva in Monte Carlo and I promise to give her share back. Then you arrest me, and what can I do?"

"All right for now. Are you good at drawing?"

"You mean, like pictures or plans?"

"Plans?"

"*Ja*, I do that for the Führer all the time. He draws good, too. He was artist."

"Draw me a sketch of the Malmo house and roads leading to it, and it better be accurate or you'll find yourself in a Siberian igloo. I also want a detailed map of the Ranch in La Plata, the main house, other buildings, gates, fences and all the roads to it." Bart handed a legal pad and a pencil to Bormann.

"Why you want this?"

"No questions. Do it."

Bormann's sketching skills were above par. The rendering of both houses was almost pictorially graphic. It showed two roads of approach to the front and back. A third road coming from an incline circled the house to a wrought-iron gate at Malmo.

"What is this road up here leading to the La Plata ranch house?" Bart asked.

"That is a secret road we use if we're being followed."

"Now you're doing good. Sketch the layout inside both houses. Show the windows on each floor. Are the gates electric?"

"*Ja.*"

He quickly sketched the interiors, room by room. Proud of his handiwork, he handed the legal pad and pencil to Bart, then sat back with a self-satisfied look on his round face. "How you like that, Colonel?"

"If this is correct, you did very well, Martin. I'll arrange a good dinner for you. I will leave you now."

"How about movie magazine with all those ladies?"

"I'll try to find one for you."

☆ ☆ ☆ ☆

Milburn's next stop was Schwerin's cell. Phillip Berger stood guard. The Gestapo agent was defiant.

"I have a few questions, Franz."

"*Geh zum Teufel.*"

"Hell, eh? That's where you're going, *du Trottel*. Hitler and Bormann are *kaput*, finished. You have a choice - cooperate, or we'll break every bone in your body before we hang you. Listen carefully, *scheisskerl*, answer my questions or you'll be a dead Nazi in the next half-hour. You Gestapo roughnecks don't know what rough is. You got ten seconds to say yes or no. In English only. Make up your mind, *die muschi*."

Bart raised his arm and looked intently at his wristwatch. The seconds ticked to five, and the Gestapo bully succumbed. "Yes."

"Smart boy, Franz. You don't like the handcuffs and the chains. Well, give me honest answers and I'll make life a little more bearable."

"What questions?"

Bart turned on the recorder.

"Were you Hitler's bodyguard?"

"Yes."

"Is Nordheim Hitler?"

Franz hesitated.

"Last chance, or I turn you over to our mechanics."

"What is mechanics?"

"They take engines apart. They do piecework. A finger at a time, then your toes, and then one eye at a time until they get tired. Is that what you want? Answer my question."

"Ja, Nordheim is Hitler."

"Look at these sketches and tell me what this is."

"That is the house in Malmo."

"Now you're cooking."

"Who is this man?"

"That is Darren Mayfield."

"Who is this?"

"That is Gunther Froelich."

"Were you at the Malmo house when the doctor operated on Hitler?"

"We were on guard duty outside the house."

"When did you see Hitler after the operation?"

"Not for a month. Nobody could see him except the Doctor and the nurse. Then, Mayfield and Froelich after the first week."

"What happened to the doctor and the nurse?"

"I don't know."

"Bullshit, you scumbag. You and Ernst Krueger killed them."

Franz tried to stand, and yelled, "*Nein, nein*, not us! It was Schultz. We were not there at that time. We were with Bormann in Argentina."

Bart knocked him back onto the cot.

"How do you know Schultz did it?"

"He told us when we came back from Buenos Aires."

"What's Schultz's first name?"

"Hugo."

A bleak memory flitted through Milburn's mind. Without losing either a beat nor a change in tone, he calmly asked, "Who is Hugo Schultz?"

"He was a commandant at a concentration camp. He later was captured by the Americans. Someone had shot him and he claimed he was a wounded soldier. They put him in an American hospital, as a POW, and he escaped when he was recovered."

"At which camp was he the commandant?"

"Ohrdruf."

"Where is he now?"

"He works at the house in Malmo. He is now a colonel. General Heinrich Müller, head of the Gestapo, promoted him."

"That's all for now."

The guards replaced Phillip.

"Where are Sophia and Tony?"

"They're in the MP office up front, Colonel."

"Get them to join me in the yard. You too, Phillip."

Bart was outside the brig smoking a cigarette. An MP was guarding the entry door to the jailhouse.

"Let's take a little walk," he said, as Sophia, Phil and Tony joined him.

The sun was bright in an azure, cloudless sky.

"Tony, Bormann couldn't see you outside his quarters, could he?"

"No way. The table I sat at in the dark is at an oblique angle. In fact, you couldn't see me either."

"Good. Here's the next move. The countess is going to visit Bormann. You are her attorney. You just got her out of jail on a bond of two-hundred-fifty-thousand dollars."

"Sophia, I want him to open up about his money, where it is, and so forth. Also, he might reveal where some of his cronies are. He might want you to contact them to help spring him. He'll ask you what this place is. Tell him this is a military base in Key West, Florida. He obviously knows this is in a tropical area. Let him bribe the hell out of both of you. Keep it short and sweet. Tell him they will only allow a visit of thirty minutes. Phil, you will occupy the guard post that Tony had. Take his gun, in case he gets rambunctious. Excuse the guards and tell them to stand by. When the thirty minutes are up, knock at the gate door and yell, 'Time's up.' I'm going to visit Der Führer. Meet me at Admiral Thomas's office when finished here," Bart ordered.

The steel door was opened to the glaring ceiling light focused on the motionless, debilitated prisoner in a fetal position on an iron cot. The padded, windowless cell had a foul smell of urine and feces. Bart stared at the shackled body. Musing, he recalled the biblical aphorism *How are the mighty fallen,* epitomized by the sight of the helpless wretch before him.

The stench was unbearable. He applied a handkerchief over his nostrils, walked to the cell door and pulled it open. Coughing, he directed Phillip to ask the guards to bring a disinfectant spray or deodorant quickly. It was not an unusual request, the guards said, as they handed a couple of cans of Lysol to Phillip. With one container in each hand, Bart more than generously sprayed the compartment and the prisoner.

"Phillip, come here. Look at this...it's a picture you'll never forget. This is the misbegotten dictator who caused the death of fifty million human beings and almost conquered all of Europe. Now he's lying in the fetal position."

Phillip could hardly believe his eyes. Bart startled him and the prisoner by shouting, "*Achtung, achtung! Heil* Hitler!"

Hitler heaved himself off the cot and fell to the stone floor.

"Nordheim, get up and sit on the cot!" Bart ordered.

The obviously weakened prisoner struggled to his feet, lifting himself laboriously to a sitting position. He suddenly vented a loud flatulent discharge.

Bart laughed, "Well, I guess it's true. In some of the books and reports I've read about this guy, he had a stomach problem, which caused him to fart like that. That's when he decided to become a vegetarian. Apparently that hasn't helped."

Bart pointed the deodorant at the prisoner and sprayed. Hitler brought his manacled hands to his face and rubbed his blinking eyes.

"*Was ist los?*"

"Adolf, the time has come for the truth."

"*Was?* Adolf?"

"Listen carefully. Keep up your stupid denials and you will get a hundred times worse treatment than your pratt boy, Mussolini. When we get through with you, Stalin might want you, or the Israelis, or a forced march through Poland. *Verstehen?*"

"I am sick man. Why you do this to me? I am Jew. Why you do to me like Himmler? I am Nordheim, Swedish citizen."

Bart walked over to the whimpering prisoner. He stood over him menacingly, his full height of six feet three inches and broad shoulders casting a shrouded shadow over the craven figure.

Hitler looked up at the giant posture, searching Milburn's steely blue eyes. "What you want from me?"

The colonel's interrogation techniques, honed during the war, came full circle. The histrionics necessary to collapse recalcitrant captives came forth when Bart bellowed vehemently, "Adolf Hitler, this is my last warning! Answer me truthfully or you will be subjected to the worst torture known to man. You know what your SS did to the Jews? Well, we learned from you how to let our mechanics work on you. A fingernail, then a finger at a time, one by one, will be cut off. Then your arms. Then your toes. Then your ankles. Then an eye at a time. Then every tooth in your mouth. But we won't let you die, because death is too merciful a release for a devil like you. I'll give you thirty seconds to make up your mind. Either say yes or no."

Bart lifted his left arm and looked intently at his wristwatch. Twenty-five seconds of silence ensued. He turned to the cell door and shouted, "Guards!"

The cowering führer softly said, "*Ja.*"

Emulating a drillmaster, Bart roared, "I can't hear you!"

"*Ja, ja,*" Hitler shrieked.

Deliberately, the colonel placed the tape recorder on the floor in front of Hitler.

"Adolf, when I turn on this machine, I want you to speak loudly in response to my questions."

"I am hungry. I cannot eat those meat sandwiches."

"In a little while. First, answer some preliminary questions. If you don't understand any word I'll explain it in German."

"Preliminary?"

"*Vorlaüfig. Einleitend.* Understand?"

"*Ja.*"

The recorder was turned on. "This is Colonel Barton Quentin Milburn. The date is 14 April 1952. The time is 11:05 a.m., Eastern Daylight Time. I am in a cell with a prisoner of war. I will now address the prisoner. What is your true name?"

The defeated prisoner reluctantly looked up at Bart and slowly confessed, "Adolf Hitler."

"What was your position in Germany?"

"I was Chancellor, der Führer. And I want respect by your army. The Geneva Convention rules must be observed."

"You are an escaped war criminal and a prisoner of war. I am going to leave you now to think over your answers." Bart shut off the recorder, then roared, "Adolf Hitler, you are going to answer a lot more questions. You come here as a Jew named Nordheim. You lied to me. You are also the richest man in the world, with money you stole from the six million Jews you murdered. I want you to think about your position here."

"*Ja,* I think you better think about some surprises I have for your country."

"Is that a threat?"

"No, no, just a fact. I have a lot of friends in this world. I am not without power."

"You can fart that power out of your dirty ass. By the way, look at this picture. Do you know this lady?"

Hitler stared at the photograph and his lips quivered. "Put that away."
"That is your sweetheart, Angela Raubal, your niece, with whom you had an incestuous affair for two years. She committed suicide because of your kinky, perverted sex games. You're a sick son of a bitch, *mein* Führer. How would you like for the German people and the rest of the world to know about your weird sexual perversions? We know about her suicide letter."

"Bormann tell you that? He is a liar. He wants to protect himself. Her letter was destroyed."

"How could you call your most loyal friend a liar?"

"No, they are all traitors. Goering, Himmler, my generals, and now

Bormann."

"Maybe when I see you again you'll tell me the truth."

"*Ja,* I tell you plenty. Now, get me some decent food. Also remove these chains."

"Later, Adolf," Bart said going away, then he returned to Admiral Thomas's office and asked, "Could you have Nordheim showered and sprayed? Sir, he smells awful."

There were two messages awaiting his return.

He placed a call to the White House responding to his first message.

Without any preliminaries, John Steelman put him through directly to President Truman.

"Colonel, what have you got?"

"Both prisoners have confirmed their identities."

"No doubt as to who they are?"

"None whatsoever."

"How is the interrogation going?"

"Number two is more forthcoming, and at this point in time has turned against his colleague. With regard to the head honcho, I just broke him about twenty minutes ago. He's in shackles in a padded cell. No windows, and a glaring light over him twenty-four hours a day. He threatens that his friends around the world will retaliate."

"That's what I want to talk to you about. I've spoken to Churchill, de Gaulle and Ben-Gurion. They are pledged to secrecy. Ben-Gurion warned me to be on the alert for some terrorist action by Hitler's cohorts against the Allies. He has acquired some very sophisticated state-of-the-art explosives. I beg you to press both of these bastards on that subject. Also, work on those lesser bums you have in custody. Ariel Rubin of the Mossad is the source of this information."

"Yes, sir. Has Ben-Gurion said anything about Sean Briscoe's presence in Havana?"

"Yes, Colonel. They are searching for another Nazi executioner named Adolf Eichmann. Briscoe has been ordered not to interfere with your efforts. Ben-Gurion knows he's planted himself as first mate on the yacht."

"Mr. President, in that regard, I want to get that yacht out of Havana or hijack it for storage in Guantanamo. The associates of Nordheim will be curious about his disappearance. I also want to search that vessel from stem to stern. I have a hunch there is more hidden in that hull besides the gold we discovered."

"Don't take it to Guantanamo. It may become a problem. If Briscoe wants to take it to Argentina or Israel, let him do it. Although I don't think at this stage of Israel's problems that they want that boat as an eyesore."

"How about getting it back to Malmo? Let the Swedes impound it as a courier for the counterfeit money, which it probably was."

"Good thought, Barton. Work it out. So, April 22 still is your C-Day?"

"Right, sir."

"Good luck. Keep me updated," Truman concluded, and he hung up.

Bart was about to answer his second message when a midshipman knocked on the conference door of Admiral Thomas's office. "There is a Captain Devereaux on the line, sir."

"Put him through."

"Colonel, there is a development," Devereaux began.

"What is it, Captain?"

"The Flying Eagle captain and a distinguished man left the yacht and we tailed them to police headquarters. I've been using your Cadillac. I hope you don't mind."

"Not at all."

"There's more. They left police headquarters and went to Batista's office. They stayed about a half-hour and returned to the yacht. That's why I left a message for you. When I got back to the dock here, one of my men who had been on duty here all night just taxied back from the hotel with a message from Mr. Kastel at the Riviera Hotel. He said it was urgent for us to locate you to call him at the hotel."

"What phone are you using, Captain?"

"The public phone near the bow end of the boat."

"Good. What's that number?"

He supplied it.

"Have one of your men stand by it for the next hour, in case I want you."

"Yes sir."

Bart then called Kastel. "What's up, Phil?"

"Meyer Lansky wants you. I'll connect you."

"Mr. Lansky, this is Colonel Milburn."

"Good. I had a call from the head man. He had a visit from a Sir Clive Fenwick and a Captain Leif Sandstrom. They want an all-out search for Mr. Nordheim. They say he and a Mr. Schwartz have disappeared. They believe that the two men have been kidnapped. They've been to police headquarters, and Sir Clive, who is executive vice president of Winston General, is prepared to offer five hundred thousand dollars for the return of Nordheim and another half a mil for Schwartz. The head man told them to hold off on the reward until he can make some discreet inquiries. That kind of money can cause a panic search by the local police."

"That's bad news, sir. Can you persuade the head man to stall the reward offer for three or four hours? I'm not in Havana now. I'll be there in about ninety minutes to two hours. I think I can handle it when I get there. I am very grateful to you."

"I told you I want to help. If you need me, call Phil; he'll know where I am. *Gey gesunderheit*, if you know what that means."

"Yes, it means *go in good health* in Yiddish. You, too, sir."

Bart summoned Sophia, Tony and Berger into the conference room. "Where is Major Flaherty and crew?" he asked.

"They are all at the officers' mess," Phil said.

"Call them and tell them we're leaving for Havana, pronto."

Bart called the public phone at the marina dock. Captain Devereaux answered.

"Stand by, I'm on my way."

"Yes, sir."

On the flight back to Havana, Bart briefed Tony and Sophia on his sessions with Bormann and Hitler, plus the problem in Havana.

"How did your session with Bormann go?"

"Very well," Sophia replied. "He was very cautious at the outset. He was uncomfortable with Tony's presence, so I excused Tony. I was alone with him. After a great deal of questioning me about being held as a material witness and being bailed out by Tony, he seemed satisfied with my explanation. I told him Tony was very well connected with Truman. That got his attention. He asked to bring Tony back into the room."

"Did he reveal anything important?"

"Here goes. General Heinrich Müller, head of the Gestapo, heads-up fifty trained ex-Gestapo agents living on the ranch in La Plata. They are fully armed and trained in commando tactics. The idiot wanted me to have them attack this prison and release him. I told him it would take a whole division to get near the prison in Key West. His next suggestion was to retain Tony as his lawyer. Tony said no because of a conflict of interest with my case. He asked Tony to find another lawyer. He'll give him a million-dollar retainer, and five million if he is bailed out."

Tony cut in. "I said I would try. But I advised him to cooperate with the colonel, who is a very tough, but honest man. If he wants to make a deal, I said, the colonel is very powerful and can do more for him than a dozen lawyers. Get on the good side of the Colonel and he can do wonders for you, I pounded into him. He asked if you can be bribed. I impressed him with one thing: Testify against Hitler fully and then maybe you can bribe him. It will have to be a very large amount of money. He offered five hundred million dollars for you to exile him to Argentina. I promised to feel you out."

"Tony, you're a scoundrel. A well-trained one at that," Bart said. "He offered *me* a *billion*," Bart laughed.

"Here's the choice piece of the pie; the man linked to all of his money and Hitler's money is the treasurer of Winston General, Herr Konrad Fliegel, with offices in Liechtenstein and Geneva," Sophia added. "The banks are the Banque Lorraine in Geneva and the Banque Royale in Zurich. The other two key men are Gunther Froelich, president, and Sir Clive Fenwick, executive vice president of Winston General. Tony, tell Bart the important thing he revealed about Hitler."

"He said that Nordheim, a.k.a. Hitler, has plans to wreak havoc around the Western world if he is ever apprehended," Tony said.

"I've heard that from other important sources," Bart asserted. "Now listen carefully, Sophia...you've been aboard the Flying Eagle for lunch with Nordheim, and Captain Sandstrom saw you on that occasion, am I right?"

"He saw me when I came on board with Luciano."

"Okay. When we set down at the airport, I want you to take a taxi directly to the Flying Eagle. Ask for Captain Sandstrom. Tell him you have a message from the gentleman who was with you at that luncheon with Mr. Nordheim. That person says he can help locate Nordheim. Stress that you are only the messenger and that you don't know anything more than that. Tell Sandstrom he must come alone with you immediately."

Tony quickly spoke up. "Colonel, aren't you putting her at risk?"

"I'll have six Rangers, fully armed, ready to storm the boat, with me leading them, if she isn't off that yacht in twenty minutes. The Cadillac is at the dock now. Sophia, are you comfortable doing this?"

"Absolutely, Colonel. Tony, I can handle it. They want Nordheim back more than holding me."

"If Sir Clive or Froelich is on board and one of them insists, demur, but not too adamantly. If one of them is with you, we'll snatch both of them. If Briscoe appears - he's that red-headed, freckled guy from Mossad - give him the eye or a signal of some kind. He'll understand. If he is the one who greets you first, whisper *Sloppy Joe's Saloon, 8 a.m. tomorrow,* and be careful that you're not observed. Should Sandstrom come with or without anyone else, tell him *a Cadillac is waiting.*"

Two cabs were engaged at the airport.

"Sophia, we will go ahead for a five-minute head start. Lay a twenty-dollar bill on your cabbie and take a roundabout route to the dock."

Bart and Tony found Captain Devereaux at the public phone. The plan was quickly and succinctly described. The captain whistled, and six of his men gathered a hundred yards away from the bow of the yacht. All the men were armed.

"If we don't have to board the boat to rescue the lady, one or two men will come down off the yacht with her. One of you open the car door for them to enter. Captain, you drive. One other man will join us. The lady and one man in back with me; the other man, if there is one, will sit next to you, Captain, and one of your men will flank him. Now, I need a gun."

Captain Devereaux smiled. "Take your choice. I've a Colt .45 and a Beretta."

Bart took the Colt, then continued, "Tony, if Sophia and Sandstrom are alone, there will be no problem. I just want to have a heart-to-heart with the captain. If it's either Sir Clive or Froelich, follow us in a cab with a few Rangers. I'll go back to the airport to Hangar 13. We'll manacle and chain the unlucky son of a bitch for the night aboard our plane for a trip to the base in the morning. That guy will be your prisoner."

"On what charge?"

"Counterfeiting money."

☆ ☆ ☆ ☆

The countess arrived, alighted elegantly and dismissed the cab. She walked up the gangplank slowly. A young Oriental crew member met her at the entry.

"I wish to see Captain Sandstrom."

As fate would have it, the first mate, Sean Briscoe, came forward. "That's okay, Chan, I'll handle it."

Sophia rewarded him with a warm smile. She waited for Chan to depart. "How may I help you?"

She looked in all directions and whispered, "Briscoe, Sloppy Joe's Saloon, Colonel, 8 a.m." Then she loudly proclaimed, "I am the Countess de Cordoba here with an important message for Captain Sandstrom."

"Yes ma'am, would you care to have a seat right through this door, and I'll find the captain for you," he said deferentially, winking at Sophia. Sandstrom arrived in two minutes.

"Do you remember me, Captain?"

"Yes, Countess, you had lunch with Mr. Nordheim and another gentleman on the aft deck."

"Well, that other gentleman asked me to bring you a message. He wants you to come with me now. He says he can locate Mr. Nordheim. That is all I know. I have a car waiting."

"This is very unusual. I must tell this to another gentleman."

"I'd rather you wouldn't. He just wants you."

"I'm sorry, but this is too important for me to handle alone."

"Well, hurry; I must be out of here in the next ten minutes."

Sandstrom pressed a button on the phone. "Sir Clive, come to the salon. It's urgent," he implored.

Fenwick entered and asked, "Who is this lady?"

"This is Countess de Cordoba. She had lunch with Herr Nordheim a few days ago here on the aft deck. She has a message of importance. This is Sir Clive Fenwick."

Sophia repeated the message. Fenwick poured question after question at the countess, but she maintained her lack of any knowledge other than the message itself.

"Sir, I must leave. If you do not comply, the problem is yours, not mine. I am doing this as a favor. From this point on, I'll wash my hands of the whole affair," she said.

"Please forgive me, Countess. Our concern for Mr. Nordheim's welfare is paramount. Perhaps I've been a little testy. However, I must insist that I accompany you and Captain Sandstrom for this rendezvous. Where are we going?"

"That's just it, Sir Clive, I do not know. His chauffeur is at the pier and will take us to him."

"Very well, let's go."

Sean Briscoe watched the trio descend the gangplank. The door of the Cadillac was opened. Fenwick and Sandstrom were quickly patted down for weapons. Clive was blindfolded and pushed into the front seat next to Captain Devereaux at the wheel, flanked by a Ranger. Sandstrom silently sat between Sophia and Bart in the back.

The Cadillac sped away toward the José Martí airport.

"What is the meaning of this?" Fenwick demanded.

"Be quiet, sir. If you want to see Mr. Nordheim, you'll behave yourself. Now, shut up!" Bart ordered.

Major Flaherty and his crew were in the hangar doing their routine checkup on the F-27. Bart knocked on the side door. When it was opened, he directed that the front doors be opened. He waved Devereaux to drive in. Devereaux, on signal, pulled Fenwick out of the car.

"Come aboard, sir, and everything will become clear," Bart gently invited.

He was marched to the rear of the cabin. Handcuffs were quickly applied. Fenwick's scream was quickly muffled with duct tape slapped to his mouth. Devereaux rolled up Sir Clive's sleeve, then Bart administered a dose of anesthetic.

"Captain, I'll need two of your men to spend the night here with our distinguished guest. Have them pick up some sandwiches and soda pop for themselves."

Soon Fenwick was snoring gently through his nose. Bart removed the tape.

"I'll be flying him to Guantanamo in the morning. Have your man in the car come here on watch until your other men relieve him. I still want surveillance maintained at the yacht. Now, I want to have a private talk with Mr. Sandstrom. Stick around; I don't think I'll be too long."

Bart opened the Cadillac door and said, "Sergeant, go into the hangar. Your captain will give you orders."

"Yes, sir."

Sandstrom sat silently alongside the countess. Bart asked Sophia to sit in the front of the car with Tony. He joined the yacht captain in the rear.

"Leif Sandstrom, you have nothing to fear. As you may have gathered, we are American military people. Understand?"

"Yes, sir, but I am confused."

"First, do you know who Mr. Nordheim is?"

"No, except he is a very wealthy man. He is a Jewish survivor of the Nazi concentration camps."

"Let me set you straight. Nordheim is not Jewish. He's a Nazi war criminal who escaped the Allied troops at the end of the war."

"I am not surprised, sir. I have been suspicious of him and his associates. I didn't think he was a Nazi, but he's a bad man in many respects."

"You had a fiancée named Joan Bauman. Is that right?"

A moment of silence and Sandstrom gulped audibly. "How you know that?"

"We have investigated Herr Nordheim. We know all about his plastic surgery. Joan Bauman was his nurse in Malmo."

"That is so. Nordheim was badly injured in an automobile accident. She was hired after the operation."

"He was not injured. He had his face changed."

"Where is Joan?"

"I am very sorry to tell you this, Captain. Your fiancée was murdered, on Herr Nordheim's instructions. She was killed by Hugo Schultz."

"I know that dirty rotten rat. I will kill him," Leif hissed. "Oh, those bastards. She was going to be my wife," he whimpered. "That swine was and still is in charge of security at the Malmo mansion. He told me she ran away with another fellow."

"How much does Nordheim pay you?"

"Three thousand a month plus my keep."

"I want you to work for America. We'll pay you four thousand dollars a month for at least one year. Nordheim is *kaput*. Finished. Understand that?"

"Yes. He's dead?"

"No. He's very much alive, but you won't see him for quite a while. Now, I'm in a hurry. I don't have much time. Do we have a deal?"

"Yes. What do you want me to do?"

"First, don't tell anyone what happened here tonight. We've arrested Sir Clive Fenwick. You'll receive a telegram when you get back to your yacht. It will be from Nordheim telling you to bring the yacht to Malmo. How does he sign his wires to you?"

"He signs it *Avram* and says *Come now* to whatever port he wants."

"How soon can you leave?"

"I am fully provisioned and fueled for a trip to Argentina. I only need a few things more."

"That's about the same distance as Malmo."

"Close."

"Who's on board besides the crew?"

"No one."

"If you leave about ten tomorrow morning, how long will it take you to get to Malmo?"

"I can make it in six days if the weather remains calm. That would be Monday, April 21."

Bart reached into his ever-present briefcase and pulled out an envelope. "Here's five thousand dollars advance pay. Raise your right hand and repeat after me. 'I swear I will be true and loyal to the American Army. However, I will do nothing against the interests of my country, Sweden. I promise not to reveal this to anyone.'"

Sandstrom repeated the oath, contrived by Bart.

"Countess, you are a witness to Captain Sandstrom's oath of loyalty."

"Yes, sir, Colonel."

"One last thing, Leif. You don't mind if I call you by your first name?"

"No, sir."

"All right, one thing - I will be in Malmo waiting for you. Where do I find you? We have work to do there."

"I'll be living on the boat."

"Stay away from the mansion in Malmo."

"Yes, sir."

"Countess, drop me at the Eastern Airlines entry, then drive Sandstrom back to the yacht. You and Tony enjoy your evening. Meet me here at the hangar for takeoff at ten. Stop at Western Union. Fake a telegram from Miami to the Flying Eagle, signed *Avram*. Remember the text. Lay one hundred dollars on the Western Union clerk."

At the Eastern counter, Bart checked the Estimated Time of Arrival of two flights, one from Washington and a connecting TWA flight from Los Angeles. They were due within twenty minutes of each other at 6:45 p.m. He had less than an hour to kill, so he called Kastel at the Riviera. "Phil, this is Milburn. Two things. Is your courtesy bus ready to roll?"

"I can have it there when you give the word."

"How about 6:30 p.m.? I'll be out front looking for him."

"The bus is clearly marked Hotel Riviera. The driver's name is Chico."

"The other item. Where can I reach Meyer Lansky?"

"He just came in. What's your number there, in case we're disconnected?"

Bart gave it to him.

"Hold on now."

"Hello, Colonel, this is Meyer."

"Okay, Meyer, this is Barton calling."

"What's up, Barton?"

"Tell the head man, Mr. Batista. I presume, that Mr. Nordheim is on his way to Geneva. He left from Miami early today. Sir Clive Fenwick is on his way to catch a flight out of Miami to join him. Schwartz left for Buenos Aires two days ago."

"Is this the *emmess*?"

"No, Meyer, but if you think of a better story, that's okay, too."

"I'll tell him that's the party line. He'll play it. Good work, Barton. Thanks for the call. Best to your family. If you need anything, let me know. Enjoy your new villa."

Bart called the house, and Emilio answered. "Ah, *Señor* Colonel, we are waiting for your family."

"There will be ten people arriving, plus me, at 6:45 p.m. We should be there before eight. Can you feed all of us? My butler will help."

"Yes, we have prepared a fine Cuban dinner. You'll be surprised. The new girl Sylvia is here to work. You have your remote for the gate?"

"Yes. See you soon."

The first group to arrive consisted of Jacques, Christina, and two very well-mannered, well-dressed children. The boy was holding Jacques' hand. Christina had the girl. A nanny carried two bags.

Jacques, assuming a fatherly attitude, said, "Matthew and Katherine, say hello to Uncle Bart."

The youngster stuck out his hand and declared, "Nice to meet you, sir."

The little girl came forward and shyly said, "Hello, sir."

Bart shook their hands, pecked a kiss on Christina's cheek and hugged Jacques. "Good trip?"

"Fine," Christina replied.

A porter was there. Jacques handed him the baggage tickets.

"I'll meet you all at the baggage area. Elizabeth's flight is due in minutes."

Ten minutes later the Milburn party arrived. Hugs and kisses all around, then Elizabeth handed Bart their baggage tickets.

"I have two new little friends waiting to meet you, children," Bart announced.

"Where are they, Daddy?"

"Follow me."

Bart had two porters and their luggage carts standing by. The entourage followed.

Michael and Jenny spotted Jacques. They whooped, "Uncle Jacques!" and ran into his arms. He introduced them to Matthew and Katherine.

"Mrs. Bishop, meet Elsie, the children's nanny."

The ladies shook hands. Elsie was middle-aged, pleasingly plump, with an infectious grin. "'Tis my pleasure, mum." The accent had a bit of Cockney inflection.

"British, are you?" Mrs. Bishop asked pleasantly.

"Yes, mum."

"You needn't 'mum' me. Where from?"

"Knightsbridge."

"Oh my, we have a lot to talk about, Elsie. My name is Nora." A rapport was in the making. "Say hello to Stanley, our butler."

In a courtly manner and in precise, stilted English, after shaking her hand, Stanley said, "It is indeed my pleasure, Elsie."

The courtesy bus was at the door. The three porters struggled with the excessive amount of luggage.

Chico helped the eleven passengers aboard the bus.

Elizabeth noted the lighted Hotel Riviera sign on the bus. "This is a hotel bus. Where are we going, Barton?"

"To our villa, sweetheart. The bus is a gesture by the owners of the hotel I was staying at previously. I hope you'll like this cozy house I've rented."

"Cozy?"

"You'll see." He winked, she arched a brow, then they boarded the noisy bus and departed.

CHAPTER NINETEEN

Monday, April 14, 1952 - Havana

Bart and Elizabeth had a private early breakfast in the den. Jacques and Christina dined in the breakfast room with the four children and their nannies.

"Liz, there is a Caddy and a Ford station wagon in the garage. Which one do you want?"

"I'll take the station wagon."

"Jacques and I will be back for dinner."

"You haven't said a word about why we're here. Anything you want to tell me?"

"Honey, you know I can't go into details, but...are you ready for this? We've captured two top Nazi war criminals. That's as far as I can go."

"Oh my God!" she cried out, holding her hand to her mouth.

"Now, this is absolutely top secret, honey. Not a word, even in your sleep."

"No, no, of course not."

"Jacques and I nabbed them with the help of Army Rangers. I have them in cells at the Guantanamo Naval Base. That's where we're going now."

"Oh, Barton. Thank you for confiding in me. I'm so proud of you." She hugged and kissed him.

"Have a good day, honey."

"There's a lot for us to see and do, Bart, so don't fret about us. We may even take a dip in the sea. The kids will love the beach."

Bart and Jacques drove to Sloppy Joe's saloon. Sean Briscoe, carrying a suitcase, was at the door of the saloon, which hadn't yet opened for business. He spotted the car.

"Get in," Jacques called.

Sean jumped into the back of the car and Bart pulled away quickly.

"That delicious countess is a beautiful piece of work," Sean commented.

"She's one of our top agents," Bart explained.

"I eavesdropped on her session with the captain and Sir Clive. She was magnificent. They ate out of her hand. The captain returned to the boat. I assume you lads have Clive boy in custody?"

"Right you are, Sean. Now, down to business. Prime Minister Ben-Gurion has been briefed by President Truman. We've got Nordheim and a few of his henchmen in detention."

"Fabulous."

"It is urgent that the Flying Eagle get the hell out of Havana."

"That explains everything. Sandstrom told the crew we are heading for Malmo, Sweden, this morning. You did a number on the captain."

"Yes, he's working for us now."

"Can you trust him?"

"Yes, he has a score to settle. Nordheim had his fiancée killed. A Nazi death-camp commandant murdered her. The captain's on our payroll now. He saw us snatch Fenwick. I had a long talk with him. He's a good man. Now, the choice is yours. Stay on board to Malmo or jump ship now."

"I'm trying to get leads on Adolf Eichmann's whereabouts. You've got me in a bind. What's your advice?"

"Sean, we are running an operation in Malmo. I'll be there a couple of days before the yacht arrives. This is top secret. Don't even let your home office know this until its conclusion. We're going to raid Nordheim's mansion. Chances are we are going to nab a few interesting Nazis. When that happens I'll let you have a shot at squeezing them for the information you're seeking. If Froelich is there, he might be the best source of information. Sandstrom knows I'll be there, but he doesn't know that I am going to use him as a guide."

"I'll go, but I'll hate that boat ride."

"Good, we don't have much time. Do you want me to tell Sandstrom you're one of our men? No mention of Mossad."

"He's a bit resentful of my being chosen as first mate. It might be a good idea. I can also keep my eye on him."

Bart wheeled the car in the direction of the dock. "I'll drop you at the gangway, Sean. Tell the captain that the colonel is in the car and that I want to talk to him and you. Hey, take your bag with you, Sean."

"Damn, I almost forgot. This bag is for you, Colonel. It contains four reels of 16-millimeter film of the concentration camps in countries across Europe. The footage is a compilation of American, German and Russian pictures of the most horrific carnage in history. It will not be released for some time."

"This is fantastic, Sean. I've been through these camps, and those atrocities gave me nightmares."

"The Prime Minister sent this for your use. It will ice your spine and sear your senses." Sean raced up the steps and headed for the yacht's bridge. The two men soon emerged and approached the Cadillac.

"Get in the car for a minute, men."

"Leif, this man, your first mate, is one of my men..."

The captain stared at Jacques. "You are the French customs superintendent in Monte Carlo. What are you doing here?"

"*Monsieur Capitaine*, I, too, am truly a deputy to Colonel Milburn. I meant you no harm." Jacques put his hand out to Sandstrom and they shook hands. Both men laughed. The captain patted Sean on the back and said, "And you? I think I like you better now."

"Me, too," Sean replied.

Captain Devereaux and his Rangers observed the proceedings from their vantagepoints.

"Are you all set to take off, Leif?" Bart asked.

"In about two hours."

"Captain, I believe there are some things hidden in the hold of your yacht or behind some of the walls. I'd like to search your boat before you leave. Any objections?"

"None at all."

"I have some Army men who will join me."

"Fine, come right ahead."

Bart got out of the car, looked in the direction of the public phone and whistled a high-pitched, piercing call. Devereaux and his Rangers came running. Holding his hand up as a peaceful sign, Bart explained the object of the search. "Captain Sandstrom, this is Captain Devereaux and his troops. He will assist us in the search."

Sandstrom saluted and Devereaux and his men returned the recognition. Jacques' familiarity with the vessel came in handy. He briefed the men on what and how to look for money, gold, papers and contraband of any kind. The search resulted in a bonanza of a wide variety of items.

Jacques opened the false flooring beneath the carpet where the gold had been stored in Nordheim's suite. He found four heavy suitcases, which contained vast sums of assorted currencies. They contained one hundred, five hundred and one-thousand-dollar American bills, French francs, Swiss francs, English pounds, deutschemarks, gold and jewelry.

In Nordheim's office, Devereaux found a button under a teakwood desk. He pressed it and a wall panel slid open. The shelves were loaded with Nazi propaganda circulars, correspondence in German and Spanish, maps of American military installations, and a detailed rendering of the Panama Canal. There were also maps of British military and naval bases; maps of Israel and the Suez Canal; letters in Arabic to Nordheim and Froelich; and a map of Paris with circles drawn around the Arc de Triomphe, the Eiffel tower and the palace at Versailles.

Bart found a cache of German weapons, machine guns, automatic rifles, grenades, land mines and large boxes of dynamite, all under the floor of the salon.

"Captain Devereaux, bring my car here; we'll have to load the two cars with this booty. We'll put it on the plane."

A shocked Sandstrom assisted in loading Bart's Cadillac and Gullen's car. After the F-27 was freighted, Bart handed Devereaux an envelope.

"What's this for, sir?"

"It contains twenty-five hundred dollars of spending money for you and your men. Have a nice evening. I'll see you in the morning. Check your messages, in case I need you."

'Thank you, sir."

☆ ☆ ☆ ☆

Same day - noon - Guantanamo Naval Base

"Admiral Thomas, do you have a 16-millimeter projector on the base?"

"Certainly. We receive new movies every week in 16-millimeter directly from Hollywood to entertain our men."

"Well, I've just received some real dirty pictures which I'd like to screen. Will you join us?"

"Sorry, dirty films are not my bag, Colonel," Thomas declared in a strange tone.

Bart laughed, "I don't mean porno films. These are dirty, rotten scenes of the death camps confiscated from the Germans and Russians, and some American footage."

"Oh, I misunderstood. I'll have Ensign Fulton set it up in our auditorium."

"Fine, sir, but before that I have a distinguished prisoner who needs a little privacy. Is Bormann's former cell in the basement available?"

"Yes, indeed. May I inquire as to his identity?"

"He is Sir Clive Fenwick, executive vice-president of Winston General, Nordheim's holding company. He's the former ambassador to Nazi Germany before the war. He was an advisor to Neville Chamberlain during the appeasement period of cutting up parts of Europe."

"Colonel, I met that sleazy ass-kissing son of a bitch when I was a captain assigned to liaison with the British Admiralty, just before the war. His dungeon suite is ready. Where is he?"

"He's aboard our plane. A wheelchair will do the job."

The admiral buzzed the infirmary and ordered two men to bring the wheelchair to the hangar. He ordered Noah Davis to photograph and fingerprint him and then have the medics search and shower him.

Bart stepped out and ordered Phil to deplane the new prisoner. "Phil, he'll be put in the basement cell. If he gets vocal, have the guards slap some duct tape over his mouth. A taste of shackles and handcuffs is in order." Then he turned to the admiral and said, "Admiral, I need to use a safe phone."

"Colonel, sit at my desk, and take the red phone from the bottom drawer on the left side of my desk. The office is yours."

Bart reached Steelman at the White House. "John, I am in possession of some very disturbing material, and my suspicions lead me to believe it indicates a possible clear and present danger to the United States and parts of the rest of the world."

"What's the source?"

"We ransacked Nordheim's yacht and discovered maps, weapons, explosives and a huge amount of currencies and jewelry. I'm inclined to believe that Herr Hitler has planned an all-out terrorist world explosion in the event of his capture. In fact, Bormann hinted at it and the man himself threatened me with the same, but more cryptically."

"Have you advised General Smith or Dulles?"

"Once again, John, my first duty is to the President," he replied testily.

"Okay, Bart, cool it. I won't press you for more detail. The President is tied up at the moment in a Cabinet meeting reviewing the NATO agreement. The session will wind up in about ten minutes. We'll call you then."

"I'm in Admiral Thomas's office. Call me on the red line. You might consider making this a conference call with General Smith and Dulles, or both."

"Stand by, Colonel."

Bart stepped into the conference room. "Admiral, I am waiting on a call from the President. We'd better hold off reviewing those concentration-camp reels."

"No problem, Colonel."

A tortuously nervous half-hour passed. Bart chain-smoked during the wait, then the phone rang. "Yes, this is Colonel Barton Milburn."

"You're on with the President, General Smith and Allen Dulles, Colonel," Steelman announced.

Bart proceeded to outline in detail the materials confiscated from the Flying Eagle. The three men listened silently to every word. At the conclusion of the report the President observed, "On the surface, this sounds rather ominous, Colonel. Care to venture a gut opinion?"

"Sir, this maniac is capable of anything. I would not treat this lightly."

"I'm inclined to agree, Mr. President," Smith concurred.

"Where are those materials, Bart?" Dulles asked.

"Aboard the F-27 in a hangar here."

"Colonel, I think you had better bring that stuff here for analysis," Truman declared. "General Smith, where should this material go?"

"Sir, I believe this should be a joint examination by the CIA and the Joint Chiefs. I recommend we have a truck meet the colonel's plane at Andrews and deliver the material to the Pentagon. I would recommend, Mr. President, that General Bradley preside. We'll leave the explosives here."

"Colonel, hold on," the President urged.

Bart could hear Truman talking to Bradley.

"Okay, Colonel, Bradley wants everyone there at 0900 tomorrow. Can you make it?"

"Yes, sir. Please have the truck there at 0800, sir."

Bart entered the admiral's conference room, where Tony, Sophia and Jacques were chatting with Thomas. "We are meeting with the Joint Chiefs of Staff and the CIA brass at 0900. You are all aware of the contraband appropriated from the Flying Eagle. Those maps and other materials indicate the possibility of some very serious terrorist activity planned by Hitler in the event of his capture or disappearance. We have to lean very hard on each of our prisoners to get some leads as to how and what is planned. Particularly, who is the outside man who will set it in motion."

"Colonel, if I can help I'd be more than obliged to break one of these bastards," Admiral Thomas volunteered. "I think my war record will attest to my abilities."

"Glad to have you, sir. We'll store the explosives here in a safe place."

"You're in charge, Colonel. Call the shots."

"Tony and Sophia, take Bormann through the routine. Tell him if he doesn't come clean with me, all bets are off. He knows what that means. If he levels, I'll follow your visit. I'll take Hitler," Bart added, then turned to the Navy man. "Admiral, I'm giving you a choice cut of meat. Chew up Sir Clive Fenwick. Get rough. Tell him we have mechanics that pull fingernails, toenails and then cut off fingers one by one, as well as toes, one leg at a time. We don't let our tortured prisoners die, just suffer. Then one eye at a time. This pussycat should fold quickly."

"You're a tough man, Colonel."

"Comedians Jack Healy and Jackie Gleason at the Club 18 in New York say, *We cut the taffy to fit the kisser.* I follow that philosophy. Questions?"

"How do we explain our sudden visit to Bormann?" Sophia asked.

"You tell him the Flying Eagle has been raided and they found some plans of Hitler's attempt to blow up the world. Your lawyer, Tony, learned all this from his friend Truman."

"Neat," Tony said.

"As much as you remember, make notes immediately after," Bart instructed. "Now, press hard, all of you, and pull no punches. We'll gather here in the conference room to exchange notes. Admiral, have your guards stand outside the doors of the cell corridors, in case they're needed. I don't want them to hear the interrogations."

Tony and Sophia went directly to Bormann's quarters. He was lying in bed smoking one of Havana's special cigars and was buried in a girlie magazine. The radio was blaring Cuban rumba music. Tony turned off the radio and ripped the magazine from his hands.

"*Was ist los?*"

"Sit up, Herr Bormann, we have trouble," Tony snapped.

The countess, in a grief-stricken mode, bemoaned the latest developments.

"Where you learn all this?" Bormann nervously asked.

"Direct from my friend, President Truman," said Tony.

"Martin, dear, don't be foolish," said Sophia. "If this is true and Hitler's terrorism begins, all of you will be thrown in dungeons - you know, solitary confinement. No food, no water, no light. Tony, tell him what you told the President about Bormann."

"Martin, I told Truman you are a nice fellow, that you are cooperating, that you had nothing to do with the Holocaust. He said, *Well, we'll soon find out. Go see him. If he cooperates and tells all and will testify against Hitler, we can make a deal.* I asked the President if we could exile you to Argentina.

He said, *It depends on how Bormann cooperates with the Colonel.*"

"Hitler is *verrückt*, crazy," said Bormann. "Here is the richest man in the world. He's worth forty-three billion dollars. He could live like a king. The *arschloch*. Like you say, the war is *kaput*, over, finished, and he wants to get vengeance. *Der schwanz, der pimmell.* Excuse my words."

"You mean he's a *schmuck*," Tony offered.

"That's what I said."

"Martin, dear, the President has dismissed my case. I am not on bail anymore," Sophia interjected. "I am a free woman. I came here to help you. I like you, Martin. When you get out, I want you to pay my lawyer two hundred thousand for helping us. Now, when the colonel comes to see you, tell him everything you know about Hitler's revenge."

"I'll do that. I will also pay your bill. Countess, I love you," he said, kissing her hand.

☆ ☆ ☆ ☆

Franz Schwerin was in a nasty mood when Jacques entered his cell. In guttural English, he stared at his visitor and said, "Who the fuck are you?"

"Your worst enemy, asshole."

"Take these handcuffs and chains off and we'll find out whether you are *die muschi* that I think you are."

Both men were six feet two, about 195 pounds, and evenly matched. "Pussy, am I? All right, pal. I'm gonna give you a shot at me. I want to see how tough you Nazi Gestapo really are." Jacques summoned the guards, "Take the manacles and chains off this prick. You can watch this asshole in action."

"Sir, I don't think we should do that."

"That's an order, man."

Jacques removed his jacket and rolled up his sleeves while the restraints were being removed.

"Now, lock the cell door," he ordered. His peripheral vision alerted him to Franz rushing at his half-turned back. In a split second Jacques turned and kicked him in the groin. Schwerin dropped like a sack of potatoes.

"Come, come, you Nazi piece of shit, we haven't started yet."

Schwerin groaned and staggered to his feet, assuming a boxing stance.

Jacques backhanded him, slapping both cheeks. "Is that the best the Gestapo taught you, tough guy? Come, show me what you've got."

Schwerin swung wildly, missing his target. He rushed Jacques again, attempting a clinch, but he was hit with a left to the jaw and a crunching right to the solar plexus. With a loud swoosh he sank to the floor.

"All right, that was round one. Take a rest and we'll see if you can do better," Jacques taunted.

Schwerin crawled to his bed. Jacques handed him a plastic cup of water and threw some in his face. The guards at the cell door applauded. Two minutes later Jacques pounded the wall and call out, "Round two! Time's up, you Gestapo prick."

Franz crouched in an attempt to tackle Jacques. He received a left, then a right smash to each eye. A right cross broke his nose and the claret spurted over his shirt and onto the floor. As a parting shot Jacques threw an upper-cut, which split the lips of the thoroughly defeated Gestapo agent.

Schwerin fell back on his cot, a bloody mess, whispering, "You broke my nose and cut my lip."

"That's exactly what you wanted. You asked me to take off your shackles so you could see what kind of a *pussy* I am. Are you convinced or do you want more, *muschi*?"

"No more, no more."

"Guards, get some towels and help me get this tough guy cleaned up. We have some talking to do."

The guards brought towels, water and some bandages. Pieces of cotton were stuffed into his nostrils to stem the flow of blood. "Captain Jacques, that was about the best professional fight I've ever seen," one guard said.

"Are you a pro, sir?" the other guard asked.

"No, I taught my troops in that art," Jacques replied. "Now, men, thank you. Herr Schwerin and I have some things to discuss. Stand by behind the corridor door, please."

"Here, Franz, have a cigarette," Jacques offered, then lit it.

"I want to lay down."

"No, sit on your cot and listen to me. Your Führer is *kaput*. Bormann is cooperating. Now it's your turn. If you think the Gestapo was tough, you're going to learn that Americans are a hundred times tougher. They have a unit called the mechanics. Are you listening?"

"Yes," he moaned through the towel over his mouth.

"When a prisoner doesn't cooperate, we turn them over to this unit."

"What is mechanics?"

"They pull fingernails and toenails, then they cut off one finger at a time. The same with toes. After that, they cut off one arm, then the other. After that, they pluck one eye, then the other. They make sure you don't die, just suffer. So, you see, you fucking Nazis, who killed six million Jews, at least put them out of their misery. But with scum like you, we want you to beg us to die. Death is too good for scum like you and your crazy *schweinhund* Adolf Hitler. Do you hear me?"

"*Ja*, I hear you. What you want from me?"

"Are you ready to answer my questions honestly? Hitler has plans to blow up certain installations around the world. Before you say you don't know anything about it, think carefully, or I'll send for the mechanics."

"Listen, I took an oath of loyalty to Der Führer. I'm a soldier like you. Do you want me to violate my oath?"

"*Dummkopf*, get it through your *arschloch*! Hitler is no longer Der Führer. He is in a nuthouse, a padded cell, nothing but a lunatic. So your oath doesn't mean a fucking thing."

"Yes. He has plans to blow up the world if he is ever caught. You will be sorry."

"Sorry about what?"

"About the damage his people will do."

"Which people?"

Silence.

"Okay, jerk, I'll turn you over to the mechanics."

Jacques walked to the cell door.

"Wait, one minute, let me think. Give me some water."

He was handed the plastic cup. After swallowing the water, he began to talk. "General Heinrich Müller, the head of the Gestapo and Gunther Froelich are in charge of the *Revanche Plan*."

"You mean *Revenge Plan?*"

"*Ja*, that's what I say."

"What are they planning to destroy?"

"I don't know exactly. Bridges, buildings, canals, Israel, stuff like that."

"Name one thing."

"The White House in Washington."

"If you are lying to me, the mechanics will call on you."

"I have told you the truth. I swear by Jesus Christ."

"You swear by a Jew like Jesus?"

"Jesus Christ was not a Jew. That is *Juden* propaganda."

"Have you ever read the Bible, you atheistic bastard?"

"Not the Old Testament written by *Juden* liars."

"You're an ignorant sick piece of dung."

Jacques slammed the cell door shut and called the guards to take over.

☆ ☆ ☆ ☆

Admiral Thomas, in full uniform, made an authoritative entrance to the cell holding Sir Clive Fenwick.

He ordered the guards to go to the other side of the doors leading to the cell corridor. Fenwick, manacled and shackled, sat up on his slab cot.

"Sir, I am glad to see you. I need someone in authority to release me from this terrible ordeal. I am unlawfully imprisoned here. I would like to have my ambassador notified of this outrage. By the way, you look familiar. Have we met before?"

"Sir Clive, you are in a great deal of trouble. Your association with Adolf Hitler has made you an accessory to a myriad of crimes. Before and after the fact."

"You're an admiral, are you not?"

"That I am."

"This is a military base, and I have not been a party to any war crimes."

"Do you admit that your associate, Herr Nordheim, is indeed Adolf Hitler himself?"

Fenwick was startled by the assertion. He fell back on the cot, bewildered, then began dissembling. "I was an ambassador, and I have been knighted.

I am a prominent British citizen. Nordheim is a Jew I protected. I want my solicitor. The United Nations will hear of this. I will..."

The admiral cut him off with a roar, "Sit up, you pathetic traitor! Now stand up!"

Shocked by the outburst, Fenwick struggled to comply with the order.

Thomas stood nose to nose with the former diplomat. "Listen carefully, you traitor! I want you to answer my questions truthfully. Lie just once and I'll turn you loose to the worst hell on earth, far worse than the Nazi Gestapo ever dreamed of in their Nazi orgy of death. Think about that for a minute," he hissed, pushing the prisoner back on the cot.

The admiral placed a tape recorder on the stone floor in front of Sir Clive. Fenwick's palsied tremors seemed uncontrollable. Thomas administered two sharp slaps to Fenwick's face. The trembling stopped, and he began to cry loudly.

"Try to be a man. Let's start over. What is your name?"

"Sir Clive Fenwick."

"What is your current occupation?"

"I am executive vice president of Winston General, Ltd."

"Who owns Winston?"

"Frederick Avram Nordheim."

"What is his real name?"

A long pause delayed his reply.

"What is his name!" Thomas screamed at the prisoner.

"He is Adolf Hitler," he whispered.

The drillmaster technique came into play.

"I can't hear you!" the admiral bellowed.

"*Hitler*, Adolf *Hitler*."

"That's better. Do you know that Adolf Hitler has been arrested and is in a padded cell?"

"No, I do not."

"Do you owe loyalty to this contemptible bastard who sold Martin Bormann and the rest of you down the river? He squealed like the stuck pig he is."

"I owe loyalty to myself."

"That's a good answer. Now, if you want your conditions here improved, answer the rest of my questions truthfully. Tell me, what do you know of his master plan of revenge?"

"A little bit."

"What's *a little bit?*"

"He has a Revenge Plan, which will be activated if he is apprehended by the Allies."

"Fenwick, pay close attention to what I am going to say. You are still in your fifties. You're obviously a well-educated man. Although I question your intelligence, I believe you will observe with clarity the position you are in."

"I am fifty-six years old and I am very intelligent. Let me hear your bloody lecture."

"On the contrary, this is not to be a lecture. Let me state some facts, with which in your alleged infinite wisdom you'll have the opportunity to evaluate your future."

"Am I being held here illegally?"

"The answer is a firm no. Do you want to brazenly avoid the wrath of the Führer, or subject yourself to torture and an eventual tryst with the hangman in the Tower of London?"

Fenwick resumed his sobbing.

"Stop your whimpering and listen to these facts."

"Yes, yes," he cried.

"You are obviously a rich man. Cooperate with us and you may live long enough to enjoy your ill-gotten wealth. The choice is yours. What is the Revenge Plan?"

"If I cooperate, can we make a deal?"

"That depends on the full, unabridged disclosures by you. There is one more caveat - you must be willing to testify against Hitler and his minions."

"If I do, will I be protected? He has killers all over the world."

"You'll be protected. Now talk. What is the Revenge Plan?"

Sir Clive wiped his eyes and drank some water from the plastic cup.

"Admiral, he has put the plan in the hands of Gunther Froelich, the president of Winston General, and General Heinrich Müller, head of the Gestapo."

"Don't hold back now. What is the agenda of the Revenge Plan?"

"It is a wild, crazy plan, which I opposed vehemently. When I heard what they were devising, I objected. Froelich threw me out of the room and Hitler called me *Die Flasche,* a wimp. He went crazy, screaming at the top of his lungs."

"Where did this take place?"

"At Hitler's ranch in La Plata, Argentina. Müller has over fifty well-trained Gestapo men there in training. All of them served in the Wehrmacht and were hand-picked to be in the Waffen SS, the fighting arm of the Gestapo."

"The agenda, Clive."

"Everything from blowing up the Panama Canal, the Eiffel Tower, the Versailles Palace, the Knesset in Israel, the English Parliament building, Buckingham Palace, and the Suez Canal, and the assassination of Allied leaders. I'm sure there is more."

"When is this going to take place?"

"Within thirty days of the confirmed knowledge of Hitler's detention."

"Sir Clive, that is all for now. You've made the right decision. I'll have the manacles and the chains on your legs temporarily removed. Your fare will be upgraded. What would you like for dinner, as a reward for your cooperation?"

"You're not twitting me?"

"No. What would you like?"

"A steak, potatoes and vegetables, please, sir, and some cigarettes," he pleaded.

"Okay. Behave yourself now. The guards will remove your restraints."

☆ ☆ ☆ ☆

The conference room was closed off and phone calls were put on hold, with the exception of those from Washington.

"Bart, sit up here at the head of the table. This meeting is yours," Admiral Thomas said.

The colonel polled the room. Tony and Sophia reported on Bormann's statement regarding revenge. They reiterated their cooperation. They displayed his $200,000 note. Jacques recounted the events in Schwerin's cell. He encapsulated what Schwerin called the *Revanche Plan* to destroy bridges, buildings, canals, Israel, etc. The other Gestapo agent, Krueger, was more pliable, but knew no more than his confederate. The most specific and startling report was delivered by Admiral Thomas's interrogation of Sir Clive Fenwick. He briefly sketched the encounter. "This tape recording speaks for itself," he said, and turned on the machine.

The cultured English accent captured the rapt attention of the group. The enormity of the revenge bloodbath allegedly planned by Hitler and his henchmen sent a chill through the room. After a moment of silence, Bart pounded the table, focusing the group's attention to the matters at hand.

"We have an added element to our plans for Hamburg and Malmo. It appears now, subject to the will of the President and the Joint Chiefs of Staff, that we'll have to take out Hitler's compound in La Plata, Argentina."

"That calls for a full-scale military operation, Colonel," Thomas observed. "That might be an act of war."

"Do we have a choice, Admiral? It's not my call. You know where the buck stops."

"Who will you bet on?" the admiral pressed.

"My money is on President Truman and General Bradley," Bart replied. "Admiral, I believe your presence at the Pentagon meeting would be valuable."

"I'll have to clear that with Admiral Prince. I would very much like to be there, so I'll make that call now."

"Admiral, no details to him, please. Just urgency. I'll back you up on that call, if he wants to talk to me."

"Come ahead, Colonel."

In the admiral's office, the red phone was extricated from the bottom drawer of his desk. Admiral Edward Prince, Chief of Staff of the Navy Department, answered.

"Ed, this is Wayne Thomas. I have Colonel Barton Milburn on the line with me."

Bart joined in on the conversation, and the request to have Thomas attend the meeting at the Pentagon was forthcoming. The response was affirmative.

"Thanks, Admiral Prince," Bart replied.

CHAPTER TWENTY

Wednesday, April 16, 1952 - 9:00 a.m.- The Pentagon - Arlington, Virginia
The chairman of the Joint Chiefs of Staff, General Omar Bradley, presided over the meeting involving the Joint Chiefs and the secretaries of the Army, Navy and Air Force. Also present among the American military hierarchy were the Secretary of Defense and the top echelon of its intelligence forces of the Army, Navy and Air Force, as well as the director of the Central Intelligence Agency and his deputy.

Facing the group around a huge conference table were Colonel Milburn, Admiral Wayne Thomas, Sophia Carr, Tony Fuentes, Lloyd Sedgwick, Phillip Berger and Jacques Laurent. Bradley called the meeting to order, then introduced Milburn and his team. "Colonel Milburn, this is your show, so raise the curtain."

Several large bags were placed up against a wall. Bart opened the first bag and placed a stack of maps in front of Bradley.

"General, sir, we haven't had an opportunity to photocopy these maps in time for this meeting, so my apologies, sir."

"No problem, Bart. Pass them around. I'll have copies made during the discussion."

A few minutes passed as the originals were passed around. Bradley buzzed his intercom. "Captain Esta Arnold, come in." She entered and saluted. "Captain Arnold, I want twenty-five copies of these maps made immediately. Make certain no extra copies are made or left behind. They're top secret."

"Yes, sir, General." She saluted, and the burden was placed in her outstretched arms. Lloyd Sedgwick's eyes followed the attractive redhead clear across the room as she exited. Tony jabbed Lloyd back to attention. Lloyd winked at him, indicating his approval of the lady. Bart glanced at her, noticing a marked resemblance to his law partner, Martha Arnold. He wondered if there was a relationship.

The next hour was spent in a review of events to date. Captain Arnold returned with the stacks of map copies carried by two sergeants. She had them piled on a long credenza parallel to the conference table. Sedgwick continued to stare at the captain. She met his eyes and marched out of the room.

Bradley said, "All right, Bart, we've got Hitler, Bormann, Sir Clive Fenwick, the two Gestapo bums and the pilot, the loot consisting of the guns, the currencies, the gold and jewelry. The explosives are stored in Guantanamo. These maps are, in and of themselves, indicative of evil intent. We are fully prepared for our raids on Hamburg and Malmo on 22 April. The currencies should be examined today by the Secret Service. You will handle that."

"Yes sir."

"All right, now let's have the bombshell," Bradley ordered.

"We have taped our interrogations. I'd like to play a few excerpts," Bart announced.

The tapes of Bormann, Hitler, Franz Schwerin, Ernst Krueger, the pilot, and finally the interview by Admiral Thomas of Sir Clive Fenwick were played, and the tension in the room grew as the words of Sir Clive Fenwick responded to Admiral Thomas's questions. The detailed agenda of Hitler's *Revenge Plan* stunned the war-toughened audience.

Epithets were shouted at random. Bradley gaveled the meeting to order. All were silenced.

"The gutter language expressed emanates from GI experience in the front lines of war. It also highlights the effect of the invidious nature of the beast we're dealing with. We are faced with a tactical enigma," said Bradley.

"General, we must nip this in the bud," Defense Secretary Lovett asserted.

"Mr. Secretary, we have just been through a diplomatic exercise clearing the way for our proposed raid on Hamburg, Germany and Malmo, Sweden. The President and Secretary of State did some fancy dancing with Chancellor Adenauer in Germany and Sweden's King Gustav. Major General Paul Donovan, our liaison in Sweden, has been tiptoeing on thin ice over there. It seems that Nordheim, a.k.a. Hitler, has bribed half of Sweden's officialdom. Now we are faced with Nazi-lover Peron in Argentina," Bradley said.

The chiefs of the Army, Navy and Air Force voiced a consensus. In tandem, they stated a single course of action. "We have to strike the ranch at La Plata and capture as many of the Waffen SS as remain alive. We have to search and destroy the ranch."

"General Bradley, may I express an opinion?" Bart cut in.

"Go right ahead, Colonel Milburn."

"The key villains, not in our hands at the moment, are Gunther Froelich and General Heinrich Müller, the head of the Gestapo, who escaped our forces. They are the ones who have their fingers on the button, to use the atom-bomb analogy."

"Colonel Milburn is right on target," General Smith of the CIA interjected.

"Time is of the essence, Beedle. What do you propose?" Bradley asked.

"We must locate these men in an all-out worldwide search in the next twenty-four hours. We'll turn loose every available CIA agent to find their current location. We are all aware that any attack on Argentina is an act of war. Under the war act, only the President, our Commander-in-Chief, can authorize that. Further, an all-out attack will become fodder for the United Nations. The Soviets and their Arab cronies will give us worldwide media attention. Our so far secret capture of Hitler and Bormann will trigger organized political chaos."

"A fine summation, Beedle, but what are the alternatives?" Bradley asked.

Bart looked at Allen Dulles, who nodded. "General Bradley, I assume you and Secretary Lovett will discuss this matter with the President."

"Bart, my friend, you'd better believe it. We'll be at the White House at the conclusion of this meeting."

"Therefore, General, I'd like to voice an opinion, presumptuously, in the presence of this august and knowledgeable body of men. And follow that with a suggestion."

"Go right ahead, Colonel Milburn."

"My opinion, sir, from what we've learned about the Perons recently indicates that Peron has too many skeletons in his closets. A propaganda barrage from us about his Nazi connections, his share of stolen Nazi money, his Swiss bank account and his sexual peccadilloes will depose him. He certainly isn't foolhardy enough to declare war on the U.S."

"What are you getting at, Colonel?" Bradley snapped.

"We have an agent here in this meeting who could help pave the way for a diplomatic solution to this problem and at the same time keep the matter under wraps for the good of all concerned."

"You've got our attention, Colonel. Spell it out."

"Sophia Carrera is known to the Perons as the Countess de Cordoba, which in fact, by lineage, is authentic. She and Tony Fuentes, here, have built a rapport with Eva Peron and were entertained by the Perons recently. Eva is bitter at the Nazis for having deprived her of her share of the loot unloaded there by German submarines in July of '45. I propose sending them down to Buenos Aires forthwith to pave the way for the assault. They will have to spell out propaganda threats if he doesn't want to cooperate. Our ambassador to Argentina, Franklin Withers, will cooperate. He helped us considerably when Tony and Sophia were there."

"General, this plan has been discussed with Colonel Milburn," Dulles said. "General Smith and I see a lot of merit in the plan. If a full-scale assault is to be made, we can do it in the guise of joint military maneuvers between two friendly countries. Send an aircraft carrier, battleships and destroyers on a friendly visit. One hundred or two hundred Marines deposited up the Rio de la Plata could do the job surgically, with Peron assigning some trusted troops."

"Our Secretary of State was very finicky about Hamburg and Malmo, so I visualize his mustache bristling in the breeze and his body twitching when briefed on the contemplated action," Bradley said.

Bradley stepped to the rear of the room and held a side conference with the chiefs of the Army, Navy and Air Force. He beckoned to General Smith, Dulles and Bart Milburn. After a fifteen-minute deliberation, he returned to his seat at the head of the table. "Gentlemen and dear lady, plans are to be implemented forthwith for a full-scale attack on the La Plata ranch. Of course, we will have alternate plans if Peron succumbs to a diplomatic solution as outlined by Colonel Milburn. All contingencies are to be considered. The Navy and two hundred Marines will work with Colonel Milburn. Should the President approve, we will dispatch an aircraft carrier and ships now in the Caribbean area to pay a courtesy call at Montevideo, Uruguay, which is in close striking distance to the Rio de La Plata, outside Buenos Aires. An attempt will be made to get President Peron aboard an Essex-class aircraft carrier for an inspection trip. His ego should be the lure like cheese in a mousetrap. That's it, so start your planning now. Be on the ready. I am off to see the President. I would like Secretary Lovett, General Smith, Mr. Dulles and Colonel Milburn to come with me."

☆ ☆ ☆ ☆

The president was awaiting the Bradley group, so Steelman led them to the Cabinet room. President Truman and Secretary of State Dean Acheson entered shortly thereafter.

General Smith summarized the problem.

The usually reserved Secretary of State pounded the table, exclaiming, "This defies all sanity!"

"That's not all, Dean. This maniac has put out an assassination contract on Churchill and de Gaulle," Truman added.

"This is a nightmare, Mr. President," Acheson declared.

"There's more. May I play this tape recorder with some of the interviews?" Smith asked.

"Turn it on," Truman said.

At the conclusion of the taped interrogations, Acheson was speechless.

Bradley asked Bart to lay out his plan of sending the countess and Fuentes to work on Eva and Juan Peron.

Bradley put the question to Truman. "We would like to send a small fleet to Buenos Aires for a friendly visit and joint exercises with his navy. With his forehand knowledge and approval, our two hundred-Marine task force will surround the one hundred-acre ranch and launch a commando raid on the mansion and outbuildings. If our threats work, he will comply. I think a call from you to Peron would set the start for our joint maneuvers. His fear and his ego would merge in acquiescence. Secretary Acheson would talk with their Foreign Minister. All this would happen after the Countess de Cordoba and Tony Fuentes have had their little threatening chat with them."

"If he refuses, this will be an outright act of war," Acheson fumed.

"Dean, relax. There are other contingency plans. What say you, Secretary Lovett?" the President asked.

"A call to Uruguay's President would make him happy for the courtesy call," Lovett agreed. "Peron will be aware of our visit there and he'll be jealous. I'm in favor of a go-ahead today,"

"All right, men, put all this in motion. I'll do my part. Keep me fully advised. I will sign an executive order to that effect," said Truman.

Bradley took Bart by the arm and marched out of the building.

"Son, you should have made the Army your career. We need men like you. I'm sure you would be a general in very little time."

"Thank you for the compliment, General Bradley. I'm in the reserve and will be ready if ever needed."

"Bart, I'm very proud of you."

"Thank you, sir. Coming from you, there is no higher praise."

"How's your schedule for today, Bart?"

"Wide open, sir."

"I think it would be fruitful for you to come to the Pentagon. Review your assault on Hamburg and Malmo. Then sit in on the contingency plans for Argentina."

"Good idea, sir. I think Phillip Berger and Jacques Laurent should join us for the Hamburg raid. Phil is heading that one for the CIA, in concert with the Secret Service. I would like, in order to save time, to have those Secret Service agents examine the currencies in your office."

"Ride with me, Colonel, and call them from my car. Jacques can drive your car."

Bart asked Jacques to drive his convertible to follow Bradley's car to the Pentagon. He advised Tony and Sophia to pack and arrange a flight to Buenos Aires. Sedgwick was sent to Andrews Air Force Base to have the F-27 ready for a trip to Havana. Bart called to Phillip Berger to ride with him and General Bradley, then phoned Secret Service agent Adam Watkins, inviting him and Sam Collins to join him at the Pentagon to examine the Nordheim money.

The day at the Pentagon was fruitful. The Malmo and Hamburg plans were completed and detailed. The big drill took several hours. Truman's call to General Bradley advised him that the fleet visit to Uruguay was received enthusiastically. Word was passed to the Navy. The fleet was off the coast of Brazil, heading north. The ships made a U-turn and headed south for Montevideo, Uruguay. A special team of two hundred commando-trained Marines was preparing a flight to Montevideo to join the fleet. Dulles and Milburn briefed Army Rangers and commanders in two groups for the Hamburg-Malmo sorties.

Milburn met with Secret Service agents Watkins and Collins. Bradley let them do the examination of the currencies in his office. He showed a keen interest as they used their paraphernalia to check the bills. Soon the arduous task was completed.

Watkins reported, "Under the hundred-dollar bills are stacks of five hundred and one thousand dollar bills. It sums up to two hundred and seventy-five million dollars of counterfeit money. The French francs, the deutsche-marks, the Swiss francs total in American exchange about seventy-five million dollars. The foreign bills appear to be legitimate. We will check with their embassies for confirmation."

"Good Lord, I bet they were going to flood Cuba with the phony bills," Bradley conjectured. "They would probably float that stuff at the gambling casinos."

"They would also do a lot of bribing throughout South America," Bart said.

"Here's a receipt for this loot, Colonel," Collins said. "We'll take it all to our labs. I hope you find those plates."

"You'll be with us when we raid," Bart said.

Admiral Thomas, Bart, Jacques and Sedgwick headed for the F-27 at Andrews Air Force Base. The flight was smooth and uneventful, landing at José Martí Airport in Havana. Bart and Jacques deplaned. Admiral Thomas and Sedgwick continued on to Guantanamo.

☆ ☆ ☆ ☆

Havana

At the villa, Elizabeth and the family gave the returning warriors a royal welcome. Christina and her children joyously greeted Jacques, who on impulse hugged and kissed Christina. She instinctively returned the kiss. Bart and Elizabeth, momentarily surprised by the sign of affection, averted their glances. The four children surrounded Jacques, seeking attention. Christina, blushing and embarrassed, led Matthew and Katherine into the playroom. Mrs. Bishop and Jacques followed with Michael and Jenny, leaving Bart and Elizabeth alone in the foyer and in each other's arms.

That evening, the children and the two nannies dined in the breakfast room. Elizabeth, Bart, Christina and Jacques enjoyed cocktails in the den. The usually reserved Jacques regaled the group with an endless variety of amusing stories, many of which were new to Bart and Elizabeth. The laughter was spontaneous. This was a side of Jacques the Milburns had never seen before, and they were delighted. Christina laughed so heartily that tears rolled down her tanned cheeks.

"Your German, French, Italian, Spanish and Russian accents are perfect, Jacques. You ought to be on the stage," she said.

"I have an ear for voices. I picked them up during the war."

Stanley entered, announcing, "Dinner is served."

After the meal, Bart and Elizabeth went upstairs to kiss the children goodnight. Christina tucked her children into bed at the guesthouse and told them their usual nightly story. Bart and Elizabeth retired to the den, inviting Jacques and Christina to join them. They politely declined, with the excuse that they were going for a stroll on the beach.

A moonlit starry sky sparkled in the sea. Jacques held Christina's hand as they slowly walked on the sand in their bare feet. The lifeguard's watchtower was unoccupied. They sat on its bare bench and shared their life stories.

"The Nazis affected both our lives," Jacques said.

"I am so proud of the work you are doing, Jacques."

"I won't rest until I finish. I'm sorry I can't tell you more about this mission. But so far we've been very successful."

"I'll not press you for more."

"Christina, please forgive me. I want to say something to you. If I'm out of order, just say so."

"What is it?"

He stared directly into her beautiful bluish-gray eyes. "I believe I have fallen in love with you."

"Jacques, I am very fond of you. In fact, I believe I love you too. But hadn't we better let time decide that for us? You're the first man I've been interested in since I was widowed."

She leaned over to Jacques, pursing her lips. He put his arm around her, pulled her close to him and planted his lips on hers in a long, lingering kiss.

They held hands while walking silently back to the villa, each absorbed in their own thoughts and euphoria.

CHAPTER TWENTY-ONE

Thursday, April 17, 1952 - Guantanamo Naval Base

Bart entered Hitler's cell. The guards were dismissed. *"Achtung!"* he shouted at the figure in the fetal position on the slab cot. Hitler struggled to a sitting position. His eyes were focused on Milburn, who continued to converse in German.

"Adolf Hitler, you have been identified by Bormann, Sir Clive Fenwick, your bodyguards, Schwerin and Krueger. I also have all the information about your *Revanche Plan.* So let's be open with each other. Cooperate and I'll make life easier for you here. Refuse and you will stay in this stinking padded cell, shackled and manacled. It's your choice," Bart said, handing the prisoner a plastic cup of water.

The prisoner sipped slowly, then, in measured tones, with a sense of authority, said, "I *am* Adolf Hitler, the *Führer.* I demand respect and the treatment accorded to a head of state."

He raised his manacled hands, attempting a Nazi salute.

"Heil Hitler," Bart mocked. "Listen to me...you don't have a state. Germany is not yours any more. Got it? You're stateless. You're a man without a country. With all your stolen billions, you don't even have a pot to piss in. Once again, you're a derelict."

Hitler glared at Milburn. "All right, *scheisse meister.* Make with the questions."

"Never mind the insults. How did you escape from the bunker?"

"I suppose you already know. Bormann and his slippery mouth. He drugged me before I could shoot myself. They put me on a plane and flew me to Malmo, Sweden."

"Very good, *Herr* Hitler. That's the truth. Now, what did you do to Doctor La Velle, who gave you a new face?"

"I didn't do anything to him. I paid him a lot of money."

"He was murdered at Malmo."

"I didn't do it."

"Did you order him to be killed?"

"No, no. *Der Holzkopf* Schultz killed him and the nurse, Joan Bauman. I found out about that later. He said Mayfield told him to do it. Mayfield does not deny it. He said the doctor was a Jew. Why should I care if he's a Jew? My mother had a Jewish doctor. LaVelle was a good surgeon."

"Then tell me, Adolf, why did you have six million Jews killed?"

Hitler flew into a rage. He tried to get up from his slab bed, but Bart pushed him back.

"Now, be careful; you wouldn't want to fall again."

"I didn't kill the Jews! I was busy as commander-in-chief of the war! I wanted the Jews out of Germany and to go to Palestine."

"Come on, Hitler, you warned the world, but they didn't pay attention to your book, *Mein Kampf.*"

"The Jews were too smart, too well-educated. They had the best jobs. Doctors, lawyers, bankers, businessmen, scientists and teachers. So I used them to arouse the German people who were jobless and suffering in a depression that was a result of the Versailles Treaty. It was a political move."

"Hitler, your rationale is a crock of *scheisse*. You blame everyone but yourself. You triggered *Kristallnacht*, you opened Dachau, invaded Poland, slaughtered all the Jews there and in Holland, Belgium, Czechoslovakia, Norway and France. You're a maniac and a murderer. History will show you as the most evil megalomaniac that ever existed."

"*Was ist* megalomaniac?"

"A syphilitic asshole who believes, like a child, that he has unlimited power."

"Your insults mean nothing. I had all the power. I don't have syphilis. *Nein*. It is a lie."

"You had it, and the English discovery of penicillin helped you. Tell me, do you believe in Jesus Christ?"

"No, he was a Jew bastard who fooled the whole world."

"You sick prick, your father was a bastard, wasn't he, Mr. *Schickelgruber*? Did you think you were the new messiah?"

"I was like a messiah, wasn't I?"

"Do you really believe that?"

"I didn't walk on water. I walked on land and saved our German people from hunger, inflation and homelessness. Isn't that a messiah? I'm even suffering now, like Jesus."

"Except you ended up causing the death of millions of people in Germany and throughout Europe. Jesus Christ was a gentle, kind man who healed and loved his followers. It took a lunatic like you to kill, rob and destroy."

"Lunatic, am I? Jesus Christ was a Jewish rabbi who preached against the orthodox Jews. So they formed a new religion called Christianity. There have been more wars in the name of Christ over the last two thousand years. Look at Charlemagne. He invaded Italy in support of the Pope. He took Spain from the Muslim Moors. He Christianized the Saxons. In the year 700 he put Leo III back as Pope, who crowned him Emperor on Christmas day and started the Holy Roman Empire. Catholics and Protestants have been killing each other ever since, even now in Northern Ireland."

"You surprise me, Adolf. Have you read the Bible, or just history books?"

"The Old Testament is Jewish propaganda. The New Testament is Christian propaganda. *Mein Kampf* tells the truth."

"So, that's the new Bible?" Bart smirked.

"Why not? The people believed in it."

"You didn't believe in the Ten Commandments."

"That Jew, Moses, chiseled those tablets by himself. It sounds good, but nobody lives by it."

"Do you believe in God?"

"What God? Which God? Whose God? People hold onto that myth because they are too weak to do things for themselves. People are like sheep. Where was God for those Jews who went to Himmler's and Eichmann's gas chambers like lemmings crawling into the sea? Where was Christ when Jehovah's Witnesses were slaughtered by Reinhard Heydrich? Where was God when the Moors became Muslims in the eighth century and invaded Spain, then moved on France? How many Christians did the Muslim Moors kill in the name of their God? And what about Torquemada and the Inquisition? He killed his share of Protestant Christians and Jews. Where was the Catholic God then? I think he was responsible for much of the Jewish diaspora to the rest of Europe."

"Hitler, for someone who seems to know so much history, you obviously learned nothing from it. Here you sit, the richest man in the world. From 1933 to 1945 you were the most powerful man in Europe. Now, by the hand of God, you are in a padded cell, manacled and tied up in chains. You have a Revenge Plan to blow up the world. God said *No.* He put you in our hands. Messiah, you call yourself? You're the Devil incarnate, or one of his demons, at least."

"Stop the insults."

"You're no genius; you've got the mind and the heart of a guttersnipe. You began your manhood as a derelict and you're ending it as a derelict."

"You'll be sorry for this!" Hitler screamed.

"I've had enough of your threats," Bart said as he turned toward the door.

"Wait one minute."

"What for?"

"I have important friends - Joseph Kennedy, the Duke of Windsor, President Peron of Argentina, Franco of Spain, and Father Coughlin. When they find out what you do to me, you'll be put in jail. You think about that."

"No, you think about this. You decided to wipe out all the Jews and you almost did. You conquered France, Belgium, Holland, and most of Europe. You were still at war with England. You learned nothing from Napoleon. You took command of your troops and concentrated on killing Jews, Christians, Gypsies, Jehovah's Witnesses, and all your dissidents. You didn't have brains enough to try to effect a peace with England, knowing you couldn't defeat them after the Battle of Britain. You could have consolidated your gains and rebuilt your somewhat decimated Luftwaffe and built up your manufacture of more planes, tanks and armaments. But you believed you were invincible. So, against the advice of your general staff and even your loyal friend, Bormann, you came up with the plan called Barbarossa and invaded Russia. The Russians outsmarted you. They retreated while fighting your troops, waiting for their most powerful weapon, winter. Your ill-clad soldiers froze to death while the U.S. helped the Russians to build up their armaments and their Air Force. Like you, they cared less for humanity and threw millions of soldiers at your troops. Your defeat at Stalingrad proved you incompetent. Your general staff lost respect for you. You wanted to be like Frederick the Great, but you became Hitler the Half-pint."

"Stop it!" Hitler sobbed for the first time.

Bart bore in with his analysis, still in German. "Instead of going into Moscow, you forced your staff to besiege Stalingrad. You were a wanton child playing with your toy soldiers, and you got your ass kicked. So, with your warped mind and your propaganda genius Goebbels, you formed your axis with Japan and Italy. Japan attacks America on December 7, 1941, at Pearl Harbor, the Philippines and Guam. The U.S. and Britain declare war on Japan on December 8. You couldn't stay out of it, could you? You and Italy declare war on the United States. Just exactly what Churchill wanted. Military genius? Military maniac! You took all your victories and spoils of war, threw the dice and came up with craps. But, unlike most losing gamblers, you stole forty billion dollars for taxi money and escaped to Malmo, Sweden, with a new face. Think of what the German people, who are wearing the mark of Cain, will think of you when history analyzes you as a crazed charlatan."

Hitler threw a tantrum. He rose, shouting vile language in German, and began banging his head against the seatless toilet. His flatulence was audible and he became incontinent.

Bart whistled for the guards. "Get the straitjacket. Don't take it off him unless I or Admiral Thomas directs you."

"Yes, sir."

"Give him a cold shower. When he's clean, put him back in the straitjacket. Stale bread and water only."

"Sir, yes sir."

Bart returned to Admiral Thomas's office and advised him of the progress.

"Sir, we have to cut him down to servility. However, I want the medics to check his heart regularly. Also, if the doctor approves, I want to keep duct tape over his mouth. I don't want him to choke to death by self-induced vomiting. He should be carefully watched."

"I hear you loud and clear," Thomas replied. "I'm all for it."

The admiral picked up the phone and ordered the treatment of Hitler as described by Milburn.

☆ ☆ ☆ ☆

In another cell nearby, Jacques and Lloyd Sedgwick took turns interrogating Joachim Heydrich, Hitler's pilot. His cantankerous attitude was pacified by Jacques' martial-arts techniques. Once convinced that he was in for some serious treatment, he relented.

"Now, tell us, you were the nephew of Reinhard Heydrich, the man with the *iron heart*," Jacques said.

"He was my uncle. I know nothing about an *iron heart*."

"Your Uncle Reinhard was a very important man to Hitler and Himmler."

"He was more important than chicken shit Himmler. My uncle taught him everything. How to run the SS, the Waffen SS, the whole fucking Gestapo."

"How did you escape as a prisoner of war?"

Joachim evaded the question and asked Jacques, "When did you get your English accent? You're an American."

"In English schools. Where did you get your New York accent?"

"In New York and Brooklyn."

"How did you escape? Last time I'll ask."

"It was easy. I was transferred to a POW hospital. I told them I was a captain fighter pilot. I caught some flak in my back and they patched me up. We were transferred to a POW camp outside Kansas City. We were loading Red Cross trucks with food and clothing for flood victims in Missouri. I was on the truck loading, and hid behind some boxes and blankets. I found some clothing, a shirt, overalls and rubber boots. When we arrived outside St. Louis, they started to unload the truck. I helped. Nobody paid attention to me. It was raining very hard. I was soaking wet and shivering. A Red Cross lady took me by my arm and led me into a shelter.

"*You poor thing,* she said, *sit down here. I'll get you some coffee and dry clothes.* I spoke English, which I studied for the invasion of England. I thanked her. She brought me a flannel shirt, fresh underwear, a sweater, a jacket and pants and a pair of sneakers.

"She said, *Go into the men's room and change your clothes now. I'll have some food for you.* I changed clothes. She brought me a hamburger, french fries and more coffee.

"*Now, after you eat, lie down on one of those cots and try to sleep.*

"Next morning, I got up before daylight and walked out to the road. It stopped raining. I thumbed a ride on a big truck going to Chicago. The driver asked me who I was. I told him I was a Jew who came from a concentration camp looking for relatives. He was Italian-American. He cursed the Nazis. When we got to the freight yard in Chicago, he took up a collection from the other drivers and handed me two hundred dollars. They all slapped me on the back and wished me luck. I said I had relatives in New York. One of the truckers, a Jew, drove me to the railroad station and bought me a ticket to New York. You Americans are such suckers," Heydrich concluded, sneering.

Jacques looked Joachim in the eye with a menacing stare. There was total silence. Lloyd began pacing the cell. He expected Jacques to explode. However, Jacques kept his cool. "That was very nice of those people to treat you like that, especially the Jew who drove you to the railroad station and bought you a seat on the train to New York."

"Yeah, I was surprised. They were a bunch of jerks."

"Don't you appreciate kindness?"

"Not from my enemies."

"What did you do next in New York?"

"I went to Yorkville in New York City, where there were a lot of members of the German-American Bund. Fritz Kuhn, the head man, knew my Uncle Reinhard before the war when he visited Germany. He took his orders from Herr Goebbels. There are a lot of Nazi supporters in America."

"So what did you do?"

"I went to a *rathskeller* on 86th Street. Everybody there spoke German. I asked the bartender where Fritz Kuhn was. He got suspicious of me. Two big men, like storm troopers, took me into a back room. They questioned me until I convinced them who I was. Fritz Kuhn was missing."

"Then what?"

"They examined my scars from the wounds on my back. They bought me some drinks and dinner. Other men joined the table. They asked a lot of questions about how the war was going. I told them we were winning. The next day, they got me a nice room and bath on 87th Street near Lexington Avenue."

"Nice people, eh?"

"Sure, they were Nazis. I was taken to a warehouse on 23rd Street by the East River. It was a German intelligence office underground. Five men questioned me for six hours. Everybody spoke German. They made me swear my loyalty oath to Hitler. Then they arranged a job for me at the Brooklyn shipyard. The pay was good. I reported to them every day. They liked my reports. I stayed at the job for six months."

"Then what."

"They verified me with my fingerprints to Himmler. My Uncle Reinhard had been assassinated. The Abwehr, the German Secret Service, ordered me to join the longshoreman's union in New York. The Bund bought my way into the union. I worked on West Street. I loaded ships bound for the Allies in the North Atlantic."

"So you became a spy."

"Yes, for my country. We sank a lot of ships."

"Why didn't you go back to Germany when the war was over?" Sedgwick asked.

"The American troops occupying Germany would have arrested me. Besides, I couldn't get an American passport."

"So how did you finally get out?" Lloyd persisted.

"Wouldn't you like to know?" Joachim smirked.

Suddenly Jacques slapped his face with a resounding blow. Joachim fell back on his slab cot, dazed.

"Sit up, shithead!" Jacques ordered. "We know, but I want to hear you tell us how you got out."

Quietly and with a whimper, he replied, "Darren Mayfield brought me out. He changed my name to Jacob Gross, had a concentration camp number tattooed on my arm and handed me a Swedish passport. I even learned some Yiddish, which is like German."

"Then what?"

"I got a job working for Herr Nordheim, a very rich man. I was his pilot on a Lockheed Constellation. I also fly his helicopter. They took me to Malmo on a Swedish freighter."

"Who is Nordheim?" Jacques demanded.

"He is a rich Jew."

"You're a lying bastard. We know who he is. Your last chance to tell the truth, or the mechanics will go to work on you," Jacques shouted.

A twenty-second silence ensued. With more force than before, Jacques delivered another blow to Joachim's face. He reeled back on the cot, semi-conscious. Laurent scooped water out of the toilet and poured it over his eyes and nose. "Sit up now," Jacques snarled, grabbing Heydrich's chin and lifting him into a sitting position. "Who is Nordheim?"

"*Der Führer*," Joachim barely whispered.

"Louder."

"*Der Führer*," he hoarsely answered.

"Adolf Hitler?"

"*Ja, ja.*"

"Why didn't you say so the first time?"

"I am a soldier under oath."

"How many times have you stayed at Nordheim's apartment in Paris next door to the Plaza Athenee on the Avenue Montaigne?"

"Five, maybe six times," Heydrich replied.

"Nice apartment?"

"*Ja.*"

"Two floors?"

"*Ja*, two floors and a basement for storage."

"Two elevators, one for guests, and a private elevator which goes direct from the basement to the penthouse," Jacques added.

"That's right."

"Herr Froelich and Konrad Fliegel bring beautiful ladies there to make a little bumsen?"

"Only when Herr Nordheim is not there," Joachim said weakly.

"Why not?"

"Herr Nordheim likes privacy with women. He likes different sex than bumsen."

"How different?"

"I don't know. I never see it. I only hear Froelich and Fliegel laugh about it."

"Laugh about what?"

Sedgwick paced the cell again, wondering why Jacques was delving into Hitler's sexual practices.

"I only heard something about young girls urinating on Herr Nordheim, and other crazy things, but I don't believe it."

"Did you know that the truck driver was Jewish when he took you to the railroad station and bought you a ticket to New York?"

"No, not right away. But, when he said *Gey Gesundheit* and *Zul zein mit glick,* I knew that was Yiddish. Then he said *Shalom* and I realized he was Jewish."

"If he hadn't wished you good health and good luck in Yiddish, you wouldn't have known he was Jewish, isn't that right?"

"I guess so."

"Can you tell a Jew when you see one?"

"*Ja,* the ones with the wide fur hats, long beards and curls of hair down to their ears. Also, the ones that wear those round caps on their heads."

"That's all?" Jacques pressed. "How about the doctor that examined you when you were brought in?"

"No, he's no Jew."

"How about me?"

"You're English and you're no Jew."

"Well, you stupid, uneducated Nazi asshole, this man," he said, pointing at Lloyd, "is *not* a Jew; the doctor who examined you *is* a Jew, and now look into my beautiful blue eyes...are you ready, you motherfucker, what do you see?"

"I see a Christian."

"Wrong, *schwanz, Ich bin ein Yid.* How does that grab you, *scheisskerl?*"

"*Du willst mich wohl verarschen.*"

"I'm not pulling your leg, *arschloch.*"

"I don't believe you, because you don't look Jewish."

"Well, stupid, you don't look like a Nazi, but you are." Thoroughly disgusted, Jacques headed for the door, with Lloyd following behind. As he exited, Jacques muttered, "Enjoy your stay here, *asshole.*"

Sedgwick and Laurent headed for the admiral's office.

"What was with the sex stuff?" Sedgwick asked.

"Lloyd, we've read reports about Hitler's kinky sex. This guy practically confirmed it. Bart knows about that."

"Did you see anything in our files on that subject?"

"No, but other sources have written about it. There is stuff in our files unconfirmed that Hitler's father, Alois Schickelgruber, was the bastard son of a Jew named Frankenberger. That would make Hitler's grandfather the reason he attacked the Jews. He was trying to hide his lineage, if the story is true."

"I've read reports to that effect, Jacques."

The admiral's door was open, and Bart gestured them to come in.

"How'd it go with the pilot, men?" Admiral Thomas asked.

"Well, we have another ingredient in our potpourri of events to come. In short, we have to raid Nordheim's Paris penthouse apartment."

"Why, Jacques?" Bart asked.

"Froelich and Krieger stay there and entertain ladies when *Der Führer's* not around. They might be hiding out there, along with Fliegel. Also, the apartment has a large basement used for storage. Need I say more? Besides, it's not too far from the Eiffel Tower."

"Bingo, Jacques. Right on," Bart agreed.

"Potpourri is right, Jacques," Thomas said. "You're spread thin. Hamburg, Malmo, Buenos Aires, and now Paris. Hit one, you have to hit them all."

"My buddy, Captain Gaumont, could handle that raid with one of our CIA men and one of the Secret Service's men there. We could make it a counterfeit raid, " Jacques suggested. "That is, if de Gaulle will cooperate."

"Oh, he'll cooperate," Bart responded. "May I use your red phone, sir?" he asked.

"Certainly, use my chair. Do you want privacy?"

"No, stay right here."

Bart reached the President's aide. Steelman ordered a standby. Ten minutes later the President, General Smith and Dulles were on the line.

"Mr. President, we have another raid to be made in Paris."

"What's there?"

Bart explained Jacques' plan, adding, "Remember, sir, three things. Hitler's planned hit on de Gaulle and, in the Revenge Plan, his goal of blowing up the Eiffel Tower and the Versailles Palace."

Smith chimed in, "Right on target, Bart. That apartment and storage room have to be ransacked. All prisoners taken must be turned over to us, except the counterfeiters found there, if any."

"Mr. President, what about de Gaulle?" Bart asked.

"Don't worry, I'll handle Charlie," Truman replied. "By the way, how's Schickelgruber?"

"Sir, he's close to a full break. I put him back in a straitjacket. Sir Clive is in hand, Herr Martin is a pussycat, and the others are broken. A few more days of bread-and-water treatment and number one will fold."

"Good deal."

Dulles broke in, "Mr. President, the extremely harsh treatment of Hitler could backfire."

Bart stiffened. Jacques tensed.

"Do I hear a note of compassion?" Truman caustically queried. "Explain that, Dulles."

"Not compassion, sir, just prudence and pragmatism."

"Nice alliteration, but no expressive explanation," Truman countered.

"Trial lawyers, particularly those representing the ACLU, will make much of our oppressive tactics."

"Counselor Milburn, what say you for the prosecution?" Truman gibed.

"Mr. President, in this instance, I am inclined to reply with gutter language. However, I will repress the urge and cite the following. I am trying, sir, to give this monster a taste of Auschwitz. Let the defense counter that," Bart passionately declared.

A few *hear, hears* followed, including some by General Smith.

"Case dismissed," Truman said, ending the conversation.

After the President hung up, Jacques uttered, "Son of a bitch."

Bart, quietly steaming after Dulles' remarks, silently pondered the Mossad's warnings about Dulles.

"Jacques, I don't want Dulles involved in these raids."

"Who will you send to Hamburg in his place?"

"The perfect man for that job is our in-house Lon Chaney."

"Right - you mean Phil Berger, master of disguise."

"When we get to the house, Jacques, call him and tell him he's my man to head up the Hamburg raid. He speaks perfect German."

"Bart, what will you suggest for Dulles?"

"I just got an inspiration. Our distinguished deputy director should be sent to London to brief MI6. We owe it to them and Churchill. I'll call Beedle and set it up. You take care of Phil."

"Brilliant. They can't refuse."

The calls were made that evening. Smith agreed. Phil was delighted. He left for Hamburg on a Pan Am flight that evening.

☆ ☆ ☆ ☆

Later that day - 5 p.m., Havana

Bart and Jacques arrived at the villa gate. A moonlighting police guard advised them that the family was at the beach.

"*Señor* Colonel, my partner is watching them from the bridge," he said, pointing to a man viewing the beach with binoculars.

"*Muchas gracias*, Sergeant," Bart replied, and pointed his remote control at the gate.

Stanley greeted the two men and repeated the guard's information.

"I have three messages for you, Colonel, and one for you, Mr. Laurent. I placed the slips on your desk, Colonel, and one on the desk in your room, Mr. Laurent."

Bart went directly to his den.

One message was from Miss Telford, advising that Colonel George Spota would be in Washington until Sunday at the Mayflower Hotel. *He would like to hear from you.* The second message was from Katherine Wharton: *Lucy is at the B.A. Hotel. Has made contact. Meeting her aunt and uncle for lunch tomorrow. Love to the children.* The third message was signed, *Allen. 0700. Omar office Sunday.*

Jacques read his message, *Call me at home any time tonight. Felix.*

He placed the call. "Felix, how are you?"

"Fine, I called to set a time and place for Sunday."

"I'll be staying at the Plaza Athenee. A suite has been reserved. Let's make it 8 p.m."

"I'll see you then, Jacques."

Jacques went directly to Bart's den.

George Spota and Bart were chatting on the phone.

"When did you intend to leave for Paris?" Bart asked.

"Any time after we have lunch," George said.

"Let's pass up the lunch. There are three flights non-stop, two by Pan Am and TWA, and one by Air France. Are you flying first class?"

"What else is there?" George laughed.

"Reserve four seats, first class, Air France, on their 9:30 flight for you, me, Richard Maybrook and my adopted brother, Jacques Laurent. I'll see you at National Airport. Surprised? I have to go to Paris on business."

"Wonderful, Bart. I'll call back with the confirmation."

Bart fixed two martinis and handed one to Jacques. They clinked glasses. "News, Jacques. Katherine Wharton relayed a message that our countess has set up a lunch with the Perons for tomorrow."

"My fingers are crossed, Bart."

"Let me call Maybrook now." He picked up the phone, dialed, and waited. "Richard, Bart Milburn here."

"What's up, buddy?"

"Change of plans, Rick. Forget our luncheon date. Meet me at 0700 at the Pentagon. General Omar Bradley's office. I'll clear you at the front desk. From there, my friend, we have a noon flight to Paris. Passport and pack accordingly."

"Gotcha."

"'Bye."

Spota called back. The four first-class seats on Air France were confirmed.

Shortly thereafter, the troops whooped their way into the house, with four children, two nannies, Elizabeth and Christina bringing up the rear. Bart and Jacques took turns kissing and hugging the youngsters. Bart embraced Elizabeth and planted a resounding kiss on her lips. Jacques tentatively approached Christina, so she stepped forward, hugged him and impulsively kissed him on the lips.

Mrs. Bishop and Elizabeth took Michael and Jenny to their baths. Elsie and Christina did likewise with Matthew and Katherine at the guesthouse. Bart and Jacques swam a few lengths in the pool. After quick showers, they changed clothes and joined the ladies and the children in the spacious living room. The men lay flat on the thick carpet and, in an old Army routine, bounced and passed the kids high over themselves and back and forth to each other. The ladies laughed and the children giggled.

To the relief of the men, Elizabeth declared, "Game is over. Dinner time, kiddies."

"Once more, Mommy," Jenny pleaded.

The high jinks got a last turn, and Mrs. Bishop and Elsie brought the elated youngsters into the breakfast room for their nightly repast. Jacques mixed the dry martinis at the den bar. The suntanned ladies lifted their glasses to a toast by a pregnant Elizabeth, who opted for ginger ale. "To our heroes. Welcome home."

Jacques raised his glass to Christina and whispered, *"Je vous aime."*

She understood and blushed as she raised her glass in acknowledgment of *amour*. Bart winked at Elizabeth. A couple of drinks, a few jokes and small talk followed.

After dinner, Jacques and Christina bid the kids goodnight. Matthew and Katherine kissed Uncle Jacques goodnight. The couple walked along the beach again and found their appointed bench at the lifeguard tower available. They talked for hours, interspersed with a few passionate kisses.

On the way back to the guesthouse, Christina said, "It is amazing how Matthew and Katherine have taken to you, dear Jacques. They called you Uncle tonight."

"They are delightful children."

He kissed her goodnight and tiptoed to his room in the quiet house.

The next two days were filled for the four children and the two couples. Days at the beach, tours of Havana and a carnival of merry-go-rounds and assorted rides for the kids.

The two couples spent the evenings at nightclubs, enjoying their spectacular outdoor floor shows, with special reservations and red-carpet treatment arranged by Dandy Phil Kastel. The checks were complimentary, despite Bart's protestations, so he tipped everyone generously.

CHAPTER TWENTY-TWO

Sunday, April 20, 1952 - 7 a.m. - the Pentagon, Arlington, Virginia

General Bradley, chairing the meeting, opened it with a quip. "Another Sunday to keep you heathens out of church."

Laughter.

"I turn the floor over to Colonel Milburn. Colonel?"

"Thank you, sir. Gentlemen, as we all know, these operations are top secret. Any leaks will be pursued intensively. This is not a warning; this is a fact. Now, with regard to the Paris operation, Jacques Laurent, who heads the Nazi desk at the CIA, and I are leaving for Paris at noon. We will be meeting this evening with French authorities of the DGSE, their counterpart to our CIA and British MI6. Our attack on an apartment building will be fully planned tonight to coordinate with the timing of the Malmo and Hamburg sorties. Secret Service agents Samuel Collins and Adam Watkins will be on a Pan American charter flight with six Army Rangers, in civilian clothing, leaving Andrews Air Force Base for Paris when this meeting is over."

Bradley said, "Not the least, but vitally important, is a fourth and dangerous event. First, I will introduce General Lucas Whitney of the U.S. Marine Corps. Raise your hand, Luke."

The stone-faced officer saluted.

"His aide, Colonel Joseph Metcalf. Hands up, Joe."

He waved his hand and smiled.

Bradley outlined the giant-sized caper to be executed at the La Plata ranch. He explained the joint exercises of American and Argentine fleets as a cover for two hundred Marines to surround and attack the main house and other buildings and seize-and-search actions, but no destruction, if possible. "Though fully armed, we will not fire unless attacked. Colonel Milburn and Agent Laurent will be joining General Whitney and Colonel Metcalf for the raid on Thursday, 24 April. Time of attack to be determined at the scene. All prisoners captured are to be immediately deposited in tenders to the Enterprise aircraft carrier in the custody of Colonel Milburn. General Whitney will pick a detail to guard prisoners. A Pan Am charter plane will be at the Montevideo, Uruguay, airport to transport the prisoners to a special destination. I turn over to you now, General, one hundred photographic copies of the ranch, its buildings, its roads, gates, fences, and so forth. Any questions?"

"No questions, sir, just a comment. I assume that General Whitney has arranged transportation to join the fleet."

"Our plane is standing by, Colonel, with two hundred hand-picked Marine commandos."

☆ ☆ ☆ ☆

Same day - 9:30 a.m.

The Air France flight taxied down the runway at National Airport, roaring its four engines to a takeoff and climbing to 20,000 feet over the Atlantic Ocean en route to its Paris destination.

George Spota and Barton Milburn sat next to each other and unbuckled their seat belts. Across the aisle of the first-class section, Jacques Laurent was briefing Richard Maybrook on the Paris objective and backgrounding him on the previous events in Havana and Guantanamo.

George and Bart were animatedly talking about old times and Spota's current film project. "What kind of a cast have you got?" Bart asked.

"Charles Boyer, David Niven, Gig Young, Robert Coote and Gladys Cooper. We've already shot about a third of the script in Hollywood. We've got a major scene to shoot in Paris."

"Where are you shooting?"

"Our location scouts are looking for a building on which we'll put up a brass plate with the legend *Hotel Ascoteur* for a close-up."

"Day or night filming?"

"Bart, why are you so interested? Knowing you as I do, you're up to something. Level with me."

"Just tell me, day or night?" Bart laughed.

"Okay, it's a night shot, sometime after dark. Now, what's up?"

"I've got a weird idea lurking in the back of my mind, and I'll open up with you, if you'll answer a few more questions."

"Go ahead, ask."

"How long will the scene take?"

"Ten minutes or less. We want to show a stretch limo pulling up to the fake hotel. The doorman opens the car door. Four tall men and a lady get out of the limo. The other men open the trunk and remove three objects, which are packages containing paintings. Charles Boyer, David Niven and Gig Young enter the hotel single file, following the carriers. They enter the elevator and ride to a penthouse. The camera follows the ascent on the lighted numbers above the elevator doors. That's it. We shoot the other scenes in a suite setup in the studio. Satisfied?"

"Great. If necessary, could you shoot that scene at 2300 hours, 11 p.m. civilian time?"

"How necessary, Colonel Milburn?" Spota asked with a smile.

"All right, George, I'll level with you as far as I can, but what I tell you is top secret."

"You've got my attention."

"I am back in temporary service heading up a team for a raid on Nazi headquarters here in Paris. Is that enough for you to know at this point?"

"Say no more, Bart. You're my best friend. How can I help? You know how I feel about Nazis."

"I'll supply your building, but I want to use your rehearsal as a cover for our raid on a particular building. I assume the guys carrying wooden packages of the paintings will be extras?"

"Yes, we haven't even hired them yet."

"Well, I'll supply those four men that get out of the limo and open the trunk. They'll carry wood-covered packages into the elevator to the penthouse. Tell your actors to push the down button and get the hell out of there and the building. Wrap up your crew and go back to the Plaza Athenee."

"What happens next?" Spota asked.

"All hell may break loose, or we'll tackle those bastards in the penthouse by surprise without any shots being fired."

"What about the French police?"

"Okay, smart ass, dear friend, the French police will be part of my act."

"I know Jacques over there. Who's the other guy?"

"Dammit, George, you know I love you. Jacques is head of the Nazi Desk at the CIA, and the other guy is Richard Maybrook, a deputy to the director. How does that grab you?"

"Hey, you've got my pulse going. I want to put on my helmet and go sniping with you, old buddy."

"Listen carefully, George. I am meeting with the French officials as soon as I get to the hotel. I have to review this cockeyed idea of mine with them. Will you be in your suite this evening?"

"Yes."

"I may call you to join us, if they approve. And, most important, if it is a go, can you get set up to shoot on Tuesday at eleven that night? I won't be here for the fun. Maybrook will be in charge."

"I'll need word tonight at the latest, Bart, to prepare. Where is this building?"

"Next door to the Plaza Athenee," Bart answered, chuckling.

"You're the same old Bart - full of surprises. How do I get permission to film at that building and to tack up our *Hotel Ascoteur* brass plaque? We usually have to pay or bribe someone for the privilege."

"That'll be my job, and we'll recompense you for the costs of your crew."

"Not necessary, I'll charge that to rehearsal."

"One more item, George - the men acting as extras carrying the art will be tall, tough-looking men in civilian garb. They are Army Rangers."

"Tell them not to look at the camera. Just keep walking, looking tough."

"You're the director. You'll tell them what you expect them to do. Are you laying cable or lines in the lobby leading to the elevators?"

"Yes."

"Tell your union crew that other men will help with that," Bart said. "Actually, they'll walk along as observers, thus doing no work to violate union rules. Jacques, with his perfect French, will act as supervisor of our so-called trainees. They might be French detectives and a few of our Army Rangers. Jacques will appease any union officials." Bart paused, then added, "Now, I'll sit with Maybrook, whom you met coming on the plane. Jacques will sit with you as you explain the scenario to him. Then we'll get together again and talk of old and new times, George."

Seats were exchanged, and Bart briefed Richard on the improvised plan. He approved. Jacques listened intently to Spota's version of the planned scenario. Jacques smiled in acquiescence. Seats were exchanged again.

Lunch was served. Paté, lobster bisque and a juicy filet mignon with vegetables. *Café au lait* followed.

☆ ☆ ☆ ☆

Sunday, April 20, 1952 - same day - Buenos Aires, Argentina

The change of seasons was manifesting a precursor to winter, with strong autumn winds driving a slashing rain off the Atlantic Ocean. An official limousine drove into the circular driveway of Eva Peron's house. Autumn leaves bedecked the Mercedes Benz. The dying floral display in front of the house was being pelted with a hailstorm. The driver, a uniformed sergeant, opened the door of the luxurious sedan and held a large umbrella over the exiting passengers.

A dark-skinned maid in black uniform and white apron held the house door open as a beautiful young woman and a man carrying a doctor's bag scurried away from the vicious elements into the warm house.

Eva Peron, her face sallow and free of makeup, was ensconced in a huge leather chair with her feet on the leather hassock. She wore a silk quilted robe over flannel pajamas. She was facing a huge stone floor-to-ceiling roaring fireplace. The crackling logs serenaded the glowing embers, lending a cozy and homey ambience to the luxuriously furnished room.

"Countess, take off that hideous trenchcoat," Eva ordered.

"Eva, this is Dr. Mordecai Reznikoff, the foremost cancer specialist in New York, or in America, as a matter of fact. He is the physician we spoke about, " Sophia said.

"Doctor, I am grateful for your presence. However, for you to fly all the way down here seems like an exercise in futility. I am a dying woman. Science is baffled by cancer. It is a scourge on humanity," Eva said in Spanish.

"*Verdadero*," he replied in perfect Spanish. "But there is always a possibility of remission. We can also make life more bearable during stressful periods. Let us talk in English."

"I have ups and downs, Doctor. I don't want to suffer."

"That's why I am here at the behest of your friend, the Countess de Cordoba. Your doctor let me look at your medical file this morning. He knows I'm here."

Dr. Reznikoff, a tall man in his early fifties, exhibited a droll bedside manner. With a twinkle in his eyes and a dazzling smile, he impishly said, "*Señora*, may we adjourn to your bedroom. I am sure the countess will excuse us."

"That's the best offer I've had this year, Doctor," she beamed, springing to her feet with surprising dexterity. She called, "Olivia, come here and bring some coffee and things for the Countess."

Eva undressed. Naked except for her pink panties, she lay back on the bed. Over a half-hour period, the doctor examined her thoroughly and professionally, then asked, "Why have you refused therapy?"

"Because it makes me feel awful, and I don't want to lose my hair."

"Apart from your cervical cancer, I detect chronic leukemia, which I think is causing most of your distress. I recommend a nitrogen mustard treatment. It will take one day. You will feel revitalized for months at a time. I am going to give you a shot of B1 and a small dose of morphine. Here is a bottle of pills. Take one every four hours and you'll feel fine."

"What are these pills?"

"They are a concoction of mine. It's a combination of B1, lots of vitamins and a painkiller. You'll feel stronger and it'll help keep you active. Your doctor will give you morphine when needed. I'll discuss the nitrogen mustard treatment with him. You're a fighter. Think positive and keep fighting," Dr. Reznikoff urged, then he administered the B1 shot to her left hip as she demurely lowered her panty. He injected the morphine into her left arm.

"Thank you, Doctor. Now join the countess while I dress. I'll be with you shortly."

The countess was engrossed in a Life magazine. She was staring at a reprised collection of Margaret Bourke-White's pictures of the Nazi concentration camps. Reznikoff poured a cup of coffee for himself from the electric percolator.

"How is she, Doctor?" Sophia asked.

"A very sick woman. She has a few months at best. I've recommended some treatments to make life more tolerable."

"I'm sorry for her."

"So am I."

"Have you ever seen these pictures, Doctor?" She handed him the magazine.

"Oh, my Lord, yes. Why are they reprinting that stuff?"

"So people won't forget."

A beautiful woman entered the room. It was Eva, in a dark gray double-breasted jacket, a royal blue blouse and pleated black skirt with high-heeled satin pumps. Her complexion was no longer sallow, and makeup brightened her face. Her lipstick was a bright red. "I feel wonderful. This man is a genius. I feel like dancing."

The transformation was arresting.

"You look wonderful, Eva," Sophia said.

"What are you two looking at?"

"Margaret Bourke-White's pictures of the Holocaust in Life magazine."

"Disgusting, aren't they?" Eva asserted. "Those Nazi bastards. At first I didn't believe in those stories of the Holocaust. In fact, the first time I saw some of those kinds of pictures was in 1948 or 1949 when I was in Paris, and Suzanne Bedault, the wife of the French Foreign Minister, took me through the Federation of Resistance Deportees. I donated one hundred and fifty thousand francs."

"But your husband let so many Nazis escape into your country?"

"I would like to throw every one of them out. They are arrogant thieves. You know what I am talking about, Sophia," she angrily responded.

"*Señora* Peron, I am very pleased to have met you. I will talk with your doctor. I must leave now," Reznikoff said.

"Thank you for everything, Doctor. Send me your bill. My driver will take you wherever you like, then send him back here. The countess and I are going to have lunch."

"There is no bill. It's all been handled by the countess. *Adios*."

Olivia served lunch.

"Where is your butler, Emilio?"

"I fired that snake. He was on the Nazi payroll. That's why you had trouble at the airport when you left here last time. Olivia heard him calling someone before you left here. He listened to our conversation about Bormann."

"That's what I'm worried about now. Will your husband really cooperate with President Truman during the fleet exercises? He, or one of his aides, may tip off the people at the La Plata ranch."

"If there is the slightest leak, Sophia, I will personally shoot that whistle-blower. I want the Americans to clean out that Nazi ranch. Some of my money may be in that mansion."

"Eva, please talk to your husband to make sure there are no leaks. If something goes wrong at the ranch, relations with the U.S. will be very bad."

"Is that a threat?"

"Yes, but it's not my threat. It is President Truman's intention to cause a great deal of harm to President Peron's administration. I tell this to you as a friend. American Intelligence has plenty of information about his dealing with the Nazis and the corrupt members of his staff. Also, lots about his womanizing. Eva, I don't want to hurt you or your husband. I am very sincere. I am trying to help you."

A shaken Eva poured herself a large glass of vodka. Her hand trembled as she sipped the drink.

"I believe you, Sophia. I can tell you are sincere. I wish I had known you a long time ago. I love Juan Peron, but sometimes he's a fool and plays both sides of the street. I must rush over to see him now," she declared, reaching for the vodka bottle.

Sophia snatched the bottle from her hand, admonishing her, "Eva, no more drinks. You're feeling good and strong right now. See him while your head is clear. Convince him to be careful with whom he confides. America can do so much more for Argentina than a defeated, struggling Germany can."

"You are so sensible. You'll be staying for a few days, won't you, Sophia?"

"Yes, Tony and I will be at the hotel. By the way, you and your husband are going to be honored on board the aircraft carrier. Don't tell anyone, but Ambassador Withers will escort you that day. Medals will be pinned on both of you. Act surprised. Call me at the hotel after your talk with President Peron."

Later that evening, Tony and Sophia were having dinner in their suite, and there was a gentle knock on the door. With a Colt .45 in his right hand at his side, Tony cautiously approached the double doors. "Who is there?" he asked.

A gentle female voice whispered in broken English, "I am Olivia."

Tony was about to ask, "Who the hell is Olivia…" when Sophia waved him off. "Open the door," she demanded.

Evita's maid hesitantly entered. She had a rain-soaked babushka on her head and a dripping rubber poncho over her body. She reached under the poncho and produced a legal-sized manila envelope, handing it to the countess.

"*Por favor*, Countess."

"Come, Olivia, take that scarf off your head and stand by the fireplace," Sophia said in Spanish.

"Gracias. I must leave now." Olivia opened the door and left.

Sophia used a steak knife to slit open the wax-sealed flap. She removed a letter envelope and four diagrams on large folded sheets of blueprint paper.

Sophia opened the envelope and read the letter, written in Spanish:

Dear Countess,

I write you because I don't trust the telephones. Juan Peron has sworn on a Bible to cooperate. He wants you to be sure of his silence and joint efforts with the Americans. He gave me the architect's drawings of the main house, two guesthouses, a storage house and an underground leading to the Rio de la Plata. There are three large launches, powerfully motorized.

You must get these drawings to Colonel Milburn. They lay out the roads, the secret passages, the tunnels and every detail of the ranch. The gates, the fences and the electrical system, from which power can be cut off just outside the ranch in an iron-covered switchbox marked with two XX's in the map on the fourth page.

Juan wants you to realize his sincerity by furnishing you these renderings. Thank you for your friendship, dear Sophia.

With great affection, Eva.

Tony erupted, "Bingo! This is too good to believe."

"Oh, it's true all right," Sophia replied. "Bart will be delighted."

Monday morning, April 21, 1952 - Paris

The Avenue Montaigne was a beehive of activity. Workmen were checking phone lines, and the gas company had trucks digging holes along the sidewalks. In the center of the street, a mobile gate surrounded a manhole leading to the underground, where workmen in yellow overalls were feeding cable lines into the opening. The Oxford Manor next to the Plaza Athenee was being serenaded by jackhammers. In reality, all of the working personnel were police observers.

Captain Felix Gaumont escorted George Spota into the lobby of Oxford Manor. They approached the manager's office. The lettering on the door in gold leaf read, *François Marmel.*

Felix knocked. A high-pitched voice replied, "Enter." A short, middle-aged man in a crimson velvet jacket spoke in French.

"How may I help you, gentlemen?" he asked.

Gaumont produced his credentials.

"This gentleman is the famous Hollywood director-producer, George Spota."

"Oh, how delightful! Please, please, sit down," François squealed joyously. "How may I help you?"

"Please, speak English," Gaumont requested.

"Of course. Welcome, Mr. Spota," he replied, extending a limp handshake.

"Monsieur Marmel, I would like to shoot a short ten-minute scene tomorrow night, about 11 p.m., outside your beautiful building, and a small bit in this luxurious lobby. Here is an envelope of one thousand American dollars for your cooperation."

"This is for me?"

"Yes, just for your help."

"Will I be in the movie?"

"If you want to. You could play the concierge. We'll pretend this is a hotel," Spota said.

"Oh, lovely! Oh, no! What should I wear?"

"Stand back a moment, please," George said.

Spota held up both his hands, thumbs joined, forefingers straight up simulating a camera lens, and viewed François up and down. The manager posed stiffly.

"I love that velvet jacket. Do you have a pair of grey trousers?"

"Indeed I have."

"That outfit, with a white shirt and a solid-colored blue tie with kerchief to match."

"I have just the right tie and kerchief!"

"All right, sign this waiver. Here's a thousand dollars. Before we shoot the scene, I'll pay you another thousand," George said.

"Wonderful. Oh, do tell, who are the other actors?"

"Charles Boyer, David Niven, Gig Young and Gladys Cooper."

François fell into his chair and mumbled, "Boyer, Niven, Young, Cooper and *Marmel?* Mon Dieu, this is heavenly!"

He breathed heavily and rolled his eyes back into his head.

"We'll put a brass plate over the Oxford sign. It will read *Hotel Ascoteur.*"

"*Magnifique!*"

"We'll start to set up in the street about two hours before we film. I'll go over your part with you at that time."

"What will I say?"

"Say in English, *Good evening, go right up. His Majesty is waiting for you.*"

"Oh…yes…I'll study that tonight!"

"Do you want me to write it out for you?" George asked.

"Please."

Spota scribbled the lines. Gaumont was having trouble containing his laughter.

François signed the waiver and asked, "What about those barbaric workmen out there?"

"I'll take care of that. They'll be gone. This picture is very important for Paris," Captain Gaumont declared. "Now, don't tell anybody about this, or we'll have a big crowd, which will spoil everything."

"Mum's the word. Oh, I'm so happy!"

Gaumont and Spota joined Bart, Jacques and Maybrook in the suite. Gaumont laughed so hard that he fell onto the couch holding his side. Spota laughed quietly. The others stared at them in amazement.

"What in the hell is so funny?" Maybrook asked.

Gaumont began to explain, and exploded into guffaws between words. Spota took over and reenacted the scene at the Oxford apartments. All five men laughed.

The chimes at the door halted the hilarity. Maybrook opened the door. Colonel Marchaud, Major Duval, and Secret Service agents Zach Huston and Troy Gardner entered.

"We heard you guys laughing the minute we got off the elevator," Marchaud said.

Gaumont overcame his laughing jag and reprised the cause of the mirth with appropriate gestures.

"Felix, you play that part very well," Jacques quipped.

Over coffee and croissants, the group got down to the serious business of the raid during the mock motion-picture filming scheduled for the following night.

"Maybrook is in charge of the apprehensions. If Herr Froelich, General Heinrich Müller, Konrad Fliegel or any important Nazis are captured, plus those DSGE men you don't want, they are to be rushed to Orly Airport. Also, the Secret Service people may arrest those involved for holding counterfeit money. Hustle them to Orly Airport, Hangar 11, where we have a Pan Am charter waiting. There will be twenty U.S. Army Rangers aboard ready to take over. Any objections, Colonel Marchaud?"

"None at all. As you Americans say, it's your ball game. We're here to assist. All our hand-picked men will be on hand," the colonel continued. "We have a legal warrant. De Gaulle spoke to us personally. We're all in accord."

"With all my thanks for your friendship and hospitality, gentlemen, Jacques and I are off to Copenhagen," Bart said as he and Jacques began to exit.

"Copenhagen?" Duval questioned.

"Oh, yes, for the 45-minute ferry connection to Malmo."

"Good luck," Maybrook said, waving.

☆ ☆ ☆ ☆

Monday, April 21, 1952 - 3 p.m. - Leipzig, East Germany
Students at the University of Leipzig were walking to a change of classrooms for other courses. This citadel of communist education in the Saxony section of East Germany maintained a broader curriculum than most of the Soviet-controlled state.

A young woman with auburn hair and blue eyes, carrying books by Guy de Maupassant, Emile Zola and Alexandre Dumas, walked up to the information desk. In her hand was a pamphlet of the school curriculum. She wore a red sweater with a gold chain dangling a gold crucifix and a long black skirt with a pair of sneakers over short white socks.

In perfect German, she asked an elderly white-haired lady, bespectacled with rimless glasses, "Is it possible to take just one course?"

"Have you graduated secondary school?"

"Yes."

"I see you are carrying French books."

"Yes, that's why I'm here. I want to learn French. I speak Russian and English."

"Quite good. Why French?"

"Because I'm going to apply for a job at the foreign office. I want to serve in government."

"Smart girl. You usually have to sign up for four subjects for each term. Why not take all the courses, with French as one of them?"

"I might do that. Is the French professor a good teacher?"

"Oh yes, the best."

"May I talk to him?" the student asked.

"It's a lady professor. Her class is over at 4 p.m. She's in room 405. Go up there and wait until the class is dismissed. Her name is Professor Joyce Laurent."

"Oh, thank you very much."

"You're quite welcome."

The young woman bounded up two flights of stairs, found room 405, then sat down on her books outside the French class. Half an hour later the four o'clock bell rang, and the French class emptied the room quickly.

Professor Laurent was behind her desk gathering exam papers. The young woman walked up to her desk. Joyce Laurent was a beautiful woman in her late twenties. She wore no makeup, and her brown hair was long and gathered in a bun at the nape of her neck.

"Professor, may I talk with you?" she said in German.

Without looking up, the professor said, "I don't have the time now. I have to score these papers."

The young girl said one word, "Jacques."

Joyce dropped her stack of papers, startled, and looked up suddenly at her uninvited visitor.

The girl put two fingers over her lips for silence. She ran back to the classroom door and locked it. She came back to Joyce, walked around the desk and whispered in her left ear in perfect French, "I am Lisa Haber, with the Israeli underground. Your brother Jacques has been searching for you since the war ended."

"He's alive and well?"

"Very much so, Joyce. He is an American citizen now. He wants to get you out of here."

Joyce fell into her chair, sobbing, and Lisa patted her back in sympathy.

"You are not trying to trick me? You are wearing a cross. Are you Jewish?"

"Of course. This is part of my cover. Where can we go to talk, Joyce?"

"Not to my apartment. The neighbors are very nosy. The communist police are all over the place. Do you have a car?"

"No, I came by bus."

"I have a Volkswagen outside. We can ride around and talk freely."

"That's fine."

"Go, now, to the parking lot. I'll be right behind you. We shouldn't walk out together."

They met at the secondhand VW Beetle and quickly entered it. Joyce drove slowly away from the home-going traffic. She kept looking at her rearview mirror, but no one was following.

"Lisa, tell me about Jacques."

"Your brother is in a very important job with the U.S. government. He is living well in Washington with an adopted brother and his family. That man's name is Colonel Barton Milburn. They are very close. Milburn is well connected with the Israeli intelligence, the Mossad. He asked them to find you."

"It is very dangerous to leave this country. They kill escapees."

"We know that, but we have ways. Have patience. I must get word back to the Mossad and to your brother. Don't do anything foolish. Don't change your lifestyle, and don't confide in *anybody*."

"I feel like this is a dream," Joyce cried.

"Are you married, or involved with a man?"

"No, I trust no one. Some of these German commies try to date me. I decline. They call me a lesbian. I want you to know I am all woman, and I pray to get out."

"Do you want to go to Israel?"

"Anywhere that's free. But I must see my brother. I thought he died in the war. My parents were killed, and Jacques' wife and two children were gassed at Auschwitz. I was in the Gross-Rosen concentration camp when the Russians came in. That's how I got stuck here."

"Who sent you to the concentration camps?" Lisa Haber asked.

"When France surrendered to the Nazis, Hitler and his troops marched into Paris without a fight. That doddering old fool, Marshal Petain, formed the Vichy government and the anti-Semites came out of the woodwork. They helped the Nazis round up the Jews. It was chaos. I tried to escape. I was caught. I was moved from Dachau to Flossenburg, then Buchenwald, Ohrdruf, and finally to Gross-Rosen. I managed to stay alive as a seamstress and also as an interpreter. The Russians came and liberated Gross-Rosen. They kept a lot of us. Those communist bastards are just as bad as the Nazis. I've been stuck here ever since."

"We need a plan to stay in touch, Joyce."

"What do you suggest?"

"I can't give you my address or personal telephone number, in case you get picked up by the *polizei* or the KGB. They'd squeeze that information out of you, and our whole underground operation here would be endangered. I'll give you another telephone number, if it is urgent for you to reach me. It's at a men's clothing factory. If you call that number, say, *This is Gross clothing, tell Klauber we need two dozen size 42s right away.* Give me your home address and phone number."

"Lisa, do you have a daytime job?"

"Yes, why do you ask?"

"I have two night classes a week for people who work during the day. Why don't you enroll in those classes? They are held on Tuesdays and Thursdays from 7 to 9 p.m. We can keep track of each other that way and build up an open friendship. Sometimes I have late coffee with some of those students, who are a bit older than you."

"That's a wonderful idea. I can do that. But I don't want my French knowledge to give me away," Lisa said.

"Fake it and improve as we go along," Joyce improvised. "Here is my address and phone number. If you call, just say this is your language student, Rose, and you want to see me whenever you decide to discuss my test papers."

"All right, Joyce, we have a plan."

"Lisa, remember to come to class every Tuesday and Thursday night. The course is free. If you don't show at any time, I'll worry."

"Be patient; it may take some time to get you out. Your brother will be notified in the next twenty-four hours. Now, drop me off at that bus stop two streets ahead."

☆ ☆ ☆ ☆

Monday, April 21, 1952 - 7 p.m - Malmo, Sweden

The ferry from Copenhagen docked in Malmo as scheduled, and Ranger Captain Devereaux and Sean Briscoe were at the dock when Bart and Jacques stepped ashore.

"What an unlikely pair," Bart joked, greeting them.

Jacques whispered a *shalom* to Sean.

"We have a Volvo station wagon rental over there," Briscoe said, pointing.

Captain Devereaux drove, while Bart rapidly fired questions at the captain and Sean. "What's happening on the Flying Eagle?"

"We've had a most interesting visitor," Sean answered. "Konrad Fliegel came aboard with two heavyweight Nazi bodyguards. We guessed they were part of the Waffen SS. He questioned Captain Sandstrom and me."

"Well, what happened?"

"Sandstrom was perfect. He was very matter-of-fact. He showed the telegram signed *Avram,* ordering the yacht to Malmo. Fliegel insisted on knowing where Nordheim had gone. We both guessed he had left for Buenos Aires and would be here in Malmo in a couple of weeks."

"Did he inspect the yacht?"

"No, strangely enough, he left two numbers to reach him at the house, then he and his hoods left," Sean replied.

"What's going on around the house?"

"We've got Rangers dressed in tourist clothes, occasionally driving by in rented cars. We have long-range cameras focused on the front of the house. The local Swedish special police assigned to us have been very cooperative. We took one helicopter tour of the house and the grounds. We filmed the whole layout with a 16mm camera. A guy named Mike Paterno said you sent him to wiretap the lines at the house and the Flying Eagle."

"Yes, he's our man."

"Sandstrom recognized him and confirmed his identity. He saw him in Monte Carlo with your guys," Briscoe acknowledged.

"Our guys have counted at least fifteen men coming and going," Devereaux continued. "About six floozies in night visits have been observed entering and leaving in the early pre-dawn hours."

"How many vehicles parked there?"

"Two Daimler limos, two Mercury minibuses, three Volvo station wagons and five Mercedes Benz luxury sedans," Devereaux counted. "At least those twelve."

"Any sign of Froelich? You have pictures of him."

"No, not a sign."

"How about General Müller?"

"No, not so far."

"Are we set for tomorrow night?" Bart asked.

"Yes. The place is quietly being surveilled round the clock. Troops and police are undercover at half a mile from the grounds," the captain answered. "They are stationed at the bed-and-breakfast hotel between Malmo and Lund."

Secret Service agents were in the coffee shop. They rose and greeted Bart and company.

Milburn said, "Sean, go back to the Flying Eagle and relieve Sandstrom. Send him here right away in the Volvo. You take command of the yacht. We need Leif here to act as our hound dog. He knows the terrain. He'll sniff out trouble fast."

"I hope I don't miss the fireworks tomorrow," Briscoe said, then took off. Bart and Jacques settled into a special suite with connecting bedrooms. The Lundmal bed-and-breakfast inn was more capacious than most hostels, due to the beaches for tourism and the fact that Lund was the home of Sweden's second largest university.

The coffee shop served as a large conference room for Bart, who called all personnel together for a briefing and exchange of ideas. Captain Sandstrom arrived in time for the meeting. Present were Major General Paul Donovan and his Swedish counterpart, General Sven Coplen. Bart explained Leif's role as the lead bird dog. Captain Devereaux and his Rangers would head the attack. Rope grapples would be shot to the roof for the commandos to smash the windows and climb in. The front and back doors were to be blown open with explosives. Sandstrom would deliver a truckload of champagne, beer and wines, doctored with sedatives, to the house on April 22 at 2100 hours. Leif presented a teletype message in German, saying *My birthday was April 20, but I was traveling and couldn't arrange this gift. Celebrate now. Heil, Avram.* A huge birthday cake with a large swastika in the center would be carried by two men through the double doors. The cake contained a fair amount of phenobarbital.

☆ ☆ ☆ ☆

Monday, April 21, 1952 - same day - Hamburg, Germany

That same evening, Phillip Berger and group of Army Rangers, looking like tourists, cruised the notorious Reeperbahn, known as the "Mile of Sin" all over Europe. Sex was for sale behind the windows of prostitutes, scantily clad and hawking their wares. Berger led them to the adjoining streets of Grosse Freiheit and Herberstrasse, where the raunchiest action took place behind those windows. They surveyed the entire area, with scant attention to the harlots. They were searching for the building sketched by Bormann, strolling from the Sankt Pauli U-Bahn station going west to the end, which is Königstrasse. Berger spotted the building before the end of the mile and pointed at the target, conveniently using his middle finger as a pointer.

They reversed their march for a quarter of a mile, then returned to their objective for one more look. The general consensus of the Rangers when they returned to their lodgings at the Prem Hotel was voiced by Sergeant Timothy O'Brien. "Anyone who would spend money on those ugly, dirty whores has to be desperate. My right hand makes better love to me, and the price is right."

A burst of laughter followed.

Berger held a briefing meeting with the key officers in his rooms. He outlined a course of action, which called for two of the men to enter the lower windowed floor for ostensible sex action with the whores. They were to draw the shades and, showing their guns, duct-tape the whores' mouths, manacle their hands and tape their feet together.

"When accomplished, tap the windows," Berger ordered.

Other soldiers supplied by Major General William Barclay and led by his aide, Captain Louis Edigio, would follow the Rangers to storm the building from roof to ground. Berger outlined the moves of his tactical team. They would be in a large bus on Königstrasse at a time coinciding with 2200 hours in Paris and Malmo. The time zone in Hamburg, Paris and Malmo were exactly the same. 2300 hours was exactly strike time. It would be 1700 hours in Washington.

☆ ☆ ☆ ☆

Monday, April 21, 1952 - 6 a.m. - Atlantic Ocean, en route to Argentina

A part of the Atlantic fleet of the U.S. Navy was slowly cruising from Montevideo, Uruguay, to Rio de la Plata, Argentina. The contingent of ships consisted of the aircraft carrier Enterprise, escorted by two cruisers and four destroyers. Two hundred battle-ready Marines were on board the cruisers. General Lucas Whitney commanded the Marines. His aide was Colonel Joseph Metcalf. Admiral Cornelius Putnam commanded the fleet.

Two Argentine cruisers, a destroyer and a frigate were maneuvering in the Buenos Aires port. Argentine and American flags fluttered over the city.

Ambassador Withers entertained the Perons, the countess and Tony Fuentes at a quiet dinner at the American Embassy. Mrs. Withers handed a bouquet of orchids to Eva and a bouquet of roses to the countess. A bottle of 1935 Dom Perignon champagne was poured into the six flute glasses.

Withers stood up and toasted, "To a permanent friendship between Argentina and the United States."

"*Olé, olé*," the Perons echoed.

Withers continued, "To the noble President Peron, our best wishes, and to his beautiful wife, Eva Peron, our blessings."

Tony, Sophia, Mrs. Withers and the ambassador raised their glasses and cheered. Sophia blew a soft kiss to Eva, who returned the gesture.

After dinner, Peron joined Tony and the ambassador in his den to partake of brandy and cigars. Withers and Tony expressed President Truman's gratitude for the fleet exercises and his cooperation in the raid on Wednesday, 24 April.

The duplicitous Peron assumed a mantle of sincerity and declared, "I am more than pleased to get rid of those Nazi *putas*."

"There will be no leaks?"

"I gave my oath and assigned a special trusted squad to help. Count on secrecy," Peron said passionately.

"Will the roads to La Plata detour traffic?"

"Already planned."

They continued their planning of the ceremonies to be held aboard the aircraft carrier.

Eva and Sophia stayed at the dinner table, while Mrs. Withers discreetly excused herself.

"Where is Bormann?" Eva asked.

"Please, Eva, don't press me on that. He promised to share the money with you. It will take time."

"But, my darling Sophia, I don't have too much time. If I suddenly leave this Earth, you know what I want done with that money. My sisters will help."

"Don't talk of death. Think positive. How are the medicines working?"

"Your doctor friend is a genius. Between the morphine, his pills and the B1s I'm able to function. But I know how sick I really am."

"Eva, please make sure that the fleet exercises and the raid go well. It is vital."

"You have my word. I will not die with a lie on my lips."

CHAPTER TWENTY-THREE

Tuesday, April 22, 1952 - Malmo and Lund, Sweden

Colonel Milburn asked Jacques to round up the key officers of the Rangers, the U.S. Army liaison and the Swedish contingent. They met in the coffee shop of the Lundmal Inn and cleared the lobby and kitchen of all personnel.

Bart opened his briefcase and unrolled two maps. The first one was spread on two tables that had been pushed together. It was an aerial view of the Nordheim compound. Using a ruler, he pointed to a building cater-cornered, three hundred feet behind the main house on the right side, as viewed from the front. It was standing under a knoll obliquely so the roof could be observed from the flat ground of the mansion.

Jacques rolled out the second map, which was a rendering of the environs of the entire area, displaying a guesthouse, a number of outbuildings on the left of the mansion, a servants' building, and a barracks-type building a hundred feet in back of the main building.

Copies of the two maps were distributed to the gathering.

Bart said, "Gentlemen, here is an addendum to our planned scenario. Three minutes before 2300 hours, cordite will be lined around the back of the barn, which I just pointed out to you. It's marked with a red X. Several gallons of gasoline will be splashed at the wooden structure. The building's rear cannot be observed from the house or the flats. This will cause quite a blaze. Any questions?"

"Who will set the fire?" Devereaux asked.

"You'll know that after the event," Bart said. "By the way, Captain, has everyone acquired their camouflage outfits?"

"Yes sir, Colonel."

"I will ask all personnel to wear camouflage outfits, including all officers. We have an ample supply in room 2. All arms will be distributed here at 2100 hours. Our bus and cars will depart here at 2130 hours promptly. The Swedish police will lead us to a secret detaining point as we reach the outskirts of Malmo. Two police motorcycles will head the convoy."

"What time do you want us back here, Colonel?" General Coplen inquired.

"Sir, please join us here at 1900 hours for dinner. We're serving a light meal."

☆ ☆ ☆ ☆

Same day - Hamburg

The Reeperbahn was not crowded with tourists. Rangers and other Army men in civilian clothes strolled casually in the Mile of Sin, shrugging off the whores' sexual taunts.

Clad in tourist garb, Phillip Berger and Secret Service agent Larry Witten strolled the Mile of Sin after sundown. They seemed to be interested in the blandishments of the licentious ladies. They stopped at either side of the target building. Both men went through the process of gesticulating, as though they were trying to establish the price for the whores' services.

Berger gestured with a thumbs-down and moved on to the window of their objective. Witten entered the door contiguous to their objective. In each instance, the prostitutes led their johns behind a velvet curtain.

Berger argued price as he examined the surroundings. Acting hesitant, he walked to a door next to a cheap metal bed.

"Why you look there?" the middle-aged whore asked.

"I'm nervous. I don't like people looking in here," Berger slyly replied.

"That is my apartment up there. My husband is at work," she lied. "Come now, you make *bumsen* for ten dollars, *blasen* fifteen dollars. Which you like? My name is Helga."

"What is *blasen*?"

"Americans call it *blow job*."

"Thank you, but no. I will give you twenty dollars if I can go out the back way. I don't want my friends to see me."

"No fucky?"

"No, just let me out back and I'll give you fifty dollars."

"Come, *du tollpatsch*."

She opened the back door and led him into a dimly lit, clammy basement fouled by a rancid mildewed odor. Phillip covered his face with a handkerchief. Facing a wooden staircase with five rickety steps, she pressed a button and an iron cover opened to an alley. He handed her fifty dollars and ran into the night air. The alley was gloomy black. There were street lights at the end of the narrow passage. He headed straight toward a street light and found himself on Königstrasse, where the Mile of Sin ended.

Pedestrian and automobile traffic was thin. He stood under a street light, took out a pad and pencil from his side pocket and sketched Helga's quarters, the doors, the basement and the steps to the alley, showing its exit to the street. He walked back to the target building in search of Witten, but avoided being sighted by Helga, who was at her window hustling customers.

Agent Witten was being wooed by Lilly, a younger version of Helga. The agent had a droll sense of humor. Lilly spoke guttural English.

"*Bumsen* or *blasen*, Yankee?" she asked.

"What is that?"

"You stupid?"

"Not stupid, no speak German."

"Okay, *bumsen* is fucky, *blasen* is sucky."

"Oh no, I am a married man."

"So, why you come in here?"

"I thought you were selling ice cream."

Lilly snickered, "*Was ist los? Dummkopf.* You come to *Hurenhaus* for ice cream, *der Trottel.* You pay me for my time, now."

She reached for a whip, a tool of her trade, in a threatening gesture.

"Hold it, Lilly, I will pay you. Let me out the back way. My wife and friends are out there. I'll give you twenty dollars."

She dropped the whip and glared at him.

"*Das Arschloch*, you make fun of me."

"No, look, here's the money. Get me out back, please," Larry pleaded.

"Out back is thirty dollars, *der Hochstapler.*"

"Okay, it's a deal," he said, handing her three tens.

She opened the back door and put him through the same routine as Helga had done for Berger.

He finally caught up to Phil, pacing toward Königstrasse.

They matched notes. Phil waved his right arm. A Mercedes limo pulled up to the two men. They drove to Hamburg *polizei* headquarters. General Barclay was conferring with Chief of Detectives Berndt Werner.

Drawings and photographs of the alleged counterfeit site were spread over a long table. A blown-up photo of an aerial shot was tacked to a wall.

Berger and Witten recounted their experience at the building and the one next to it. Both men drew sketches of the interior, the back door and the alley.

Chief Werner had been an avowed anti-Nazi since Hitler rose to power as leader of the National Socialist Party. His father was a surgeon, his mother a prominent Protestant leader in the church. General Barclay and Berndt were old friends. There was a deep rapport between the thirty-two-year-old chief and the general of the American occupying forces.

While they went over the maps and drawings with Berger and Witten, Werner related, "Herr Berger, while we're not proud of the Reeperbahn, it has been a historical tourist attraction for decades. Recently we landed a helicopter on the roof of the building, next to the one you are raiding. We did that as part of a fire drill."

Berger, on the uptake, asked, "Are you trying to suggest something, Chief?"

Werner chuckled, "I took the liberty yesterday of having our building department check that roof. It is very sturdy and supported by iron beams, which will hold thirty tons of pressure. Does that suggest something to you?"

"It certainly does. Now, where do I get a helicopter large enough to hold, say, twenty men or fifteen men or ten men..."

"I can supply that, Mr. Berger, if you want to go that route," Barclay said. "I have an HH-53C Sikorsky with 3,400-horsepower engines and a maximum takeoff weight of 40,000 pounds, speed 175 mph. Do your own math and decide how many men you want to carry. The copter has a crew of five."

"Dammit, though, those rotors make a helluva noise. It might scare those bastards we're after," Berger said.

Barclay laughed.

"What's funny about that, General?"

"Try this for size. I assume this whole caper should be over in fifteen minutes or less. With Chief Werner's approval, how would you like our very talented Army band to parade this 'Mile of Sin' with "Stars and Stripes Forever" blaring, flags waving and a German police contingent following behind. We'll play some loud German tunes as well."

The four men in the car laughed hilariously.

"It will be an unusual occurrence in this district, but I'll go along with it," Werner agreed. "One more thing. Agent Witten, you may only take prisoners caught making American counterfeit money. If we find false *deutschemarks*, they belong to me," Werner declared.

"Understood."

"One minute now," Berger interjected. "We will hold any of Nordheim's associates. That's what we are here for. That was the understanding reached with your ambassador."

"Gentlemen, no need to fight over the captives. If there are one or two counterfeiters making *deutschemarks*, that will suffice for me after this giant charade. That's not asking too much. We have media here, too, that we have to throw a sop to."

"Well stated, Chief," Berger conceded. "Where'd you get the word *sop*?"

"In America. We have bribes here too."

☆ ☆ ☆ ☆

Tuesday, April 22, 1952 - same day - CIA headquarters, Langley, Virginia

On a direct line to the White House, General Walter Bedell Smith, director of the CIA, and President Truman were discussing the coordinated triple assault that were to take place at 5 p.m. (1700 hours) Washington time in Malmo, Hamburg, and Paris.

"Beedle, I don't want to set up a situation room here at the White House. If the press room detects unusual traffic here, they'll speculate."

"We are preparing one here, Mr. President. I can keep you advised on a minute-by-minute report if you so desire," the General suggested.

"The French DGSE are carrying the heavy load in Paris," Truman said. "Dulles, I assume, will brief MI6 in London. Colonel Milburn updated me on all the action. The planning in each raid is unique. I hope the execution occurs without incident and a minimum of notice. Now, mind you, General, should anything untoward become public, we will classify this as a raid on counterfeiters. Nothing more. All right, gentlemen, let's go get 'em."

CHAPTER TWENTY-FOUR

Tuesday, April 22, 1952 - 2100 hours, C-Day - Malmo, Sweden

Captain Leif Sandstrom drove a loaded station wagon into the circular driveway of the Nordheim mansion. A fog was rolling in from the restless Baltic Sea. He pressed the doorbell, and chimes resounded through the house. Hugo Schultz peeped through the aperture in the massive door, then he opened it. "*Herr* Sandstrom, what brings you here?"

"Colonel Schultz, Herr Nordheim has sent you some nice presents to celebrate his birthday of two days ago. I have a load in my station wagon and a message for Herr Fliegel. I need some of your friends to unload the station wagon. We'll need two men to carry his birthday cake. It's very big."

"Wait one minute, Sandstrom."

Hugo returned with four husky men. The front floodlights were turned on. Konrad Fliegel came through the door and shook hands with the yacht captain. Leif handed him the teletype message signed *Avram*.

"*Ach*, this is good news. *Ja*, we missed his 63rd birthday, but it's never too late to celebrate," he proclaimed as he watched the potables being carried into the house.

Two men lifted the birthday cake and carefully carried it to the dining room.

"Captain, you are welcome to have a drink with us."

"Herr Fliegel, I appreciate that, but I have to get back to the boat. We are repairing our pure-water pump, and I want to be sure it's properly done."

"Is it serious, Captain?"

"Oh, no, it will be perfect in the next hour."

All the activity in the driveway was being observed by Bart and his cadre, and then the floodlights were doused as Leif drove away.

An hour later, singing emanated from Nordheim's mansion. Soon a loud chorus of the Nazi hymn, the *Horst Wessel* Lied, pierced the fog-shrouded atmosphere. *Deutschland über alles* followed. A record player rendered Wagner's "The Ride of the Valkyries" blasting the area. Party time was in full swing. Boisterous revelry reached a fever pitch, with loud "Heil Hitlers!" resonating in the environs.

"Stick the *Horst* up your Nazi *Wessel*," Bart whispered.

Captain Sandstrom shut off his headlights and pulled up to Bart's vantage point.

"Was that Hugo Schultz who met you at the door?" Milburn asked.

"Yes, and he was happy to receive Nordheim's message."

"Good. Now, I want you to drive up to the house again. The floodlights are out. I've placed some men face down in the back of the station wagon. Ring the bell. Our men will jump out. I'll hit Schultz, or whoever answers the door, with a tranquilizer. That way we won't have to blast the door open. I'll be with you."

"Sure, Colonel, let's do it."

The troops' watches were synchronized. The crescendo at the house had peaked. Some interior lights were extinguished, then heavy fog blanketed a sudden silence.

Jacques and two other men rolled a Jeep to the knoll in front of the barn. The cordite was quickly spread in the back of the barn. Two gallons of gasoline was poured along the rear of the barn. An ignited gasoline-soaked rag impaled on a small branch was tossed at the flammables. The Jeep took off. Flames spread quickly. The location of the blaze's crackling, muted by the heavy fog, was not easily detectable until the flames reached the roof. The troops quietly crawled to the edge of the house.

At precisely 2300 hours, the station wagon, loaded with ten men in the rear and Bart crouching in the front seat, drove into the driveway. Ropes were clamped to the roof. Everyone was in place. Sandstrom punched the doorbell. The chimes rang. A staggering Hugo Schultz opened the door.

"So, you came back for the party, Captain?" he slurred. "Hey, there's a fire..."

Bart fired the tranquilizer shot, hitting Schultz, who folded like an accordion. The bus unloaded twenty men. Schultz's mouth was duct-taped, his hands cuffed, and his limp body thrown into the bus.

The building was stormed. The guesthouse and the outbuildings were raided. The main house was a mess. Sleeping bodies were sprawled in chairs, on couches, the plush carpets and the staircase. Fifteen comatose men were quickly handcuffed and their feet bound, then were carried to the bus. A second bus pulled into the driveway.

Secret Service agents Watkins and Collins, assisted by Army men, crashed into a locked door on the third floor. They tackled two slightly drunken men who were loading a steamer trunk. Both men drew Lugers, but were quickly disarmed with rifle butts to the head. Both sank to the floor. They were duct-taped and manacled.

Servants fighting the fire were captured. Malmo fire trucks arrived on the scene.

The Secret Service men noted the counterfeit printing machine, partly dismantled. Bart watched as they searched the drawers in the huge trunk. A zippered black leather case was found hidden inside two freshly starched shirts. Unzipping the case, they discovered printing plates for hundred-dollar, five-hundred-dollar, and thousand-dollar American bills. Loads of currencies were discovered.

"Bingo!" Collins yelled.

At that moment, Magic Mike Paterno ran into the room.

Breathlessly he gasped, "Colonel, Konrad Fliegel is somewhere in this house or on the grounds somewhere. He was trying to make a call to Geneva, Switzerland. I had all the lines tapped. I cut the main telephone lines. He was talking to an overseas operator when I broke his line."

Bart rushed out of the room. Mike followed. He ordered an instant search for Fliegel. Donovan's troops and the Rangers searched every inch of the house. The Malmo firefighters had contained the fire. Jacques found the tunnel leading from the house to a back road. He stationed two men at the tunnel's road exit. Jacques used his war training and lay flat on the cold concrete as he crawled along the tunnel. He held a high-powered searchlight high above his head. He noticed a door halfway through the underground pass and kicked it open. Konrad Fliegel was crouching in the dark. The light bathed him. He reached inside his jacket. Instinctively, Jacques kicked him, and Fliegel was knocked cold. Jacques reached into Fliegel's jacket. His hand, smashed by the kick, was holding a Beretta automatic gun. Jacques whistled loudly and waved his searchlight. Two Rangers ran to him.

"Take him to Colonel Milburn."

Word was passed that Fliegel had been found. Bart had him manacled and placed in the station wagon as he regained consciousness.

"Herr Fliegel, make one false move or open your mouth and I'll break you in two," Bart warned.

Fliegel apparently hadn't partaken of the drinks or the cake, as he was cold sober.

"Is this a kidnapping?" he whispered in a British accent.

"I told you to shut up! Sergeant, tape his mouth," Bart ordered. "And tie his feet."

The grounds and buildings were searched thoroughly once more. The counterfeit equipment was placed in a pickup truck and covered with a tarpaulin. Twenty-two people were taken into custody, plus five servants. A large cache of weapons was loaded into an Army truck.

Not a shot had been fired. Twenty minutes later the operation was completed successfully. General Donovan had arranged for the temporary use of a Malmo stockade.

The servants were questioned and released into the custody of the Swedish police, who expropriated the mansion. The other seventeen prisoners were prepared for transport to Guantanamo for further investigation.

☆ ☆ ☆ ☆

Tuesday, April 22, 1952 - same time - Hamburg, Germany
At 2200 hours, pedestrian traffic increased on the Mile of Sin. Tourist-dressed Rangers and soldiers, simulating inebriated college students, reveled along the Reeperbahn, bargaining for sex. So far, no sales. The frustrated ladies behind their windows shouted epithets at the strollers.
"*Das Saufgelage!*"
"*Geh zum Teufel!*"
"*Der Nichtsnutz!*"
An hour of boisterous horseplay brought a few police who politely toned down the pseudo-tourists. At 2300 hours a U.S. Army band marched along the Reeperbahn stridently playing "Stars and Stripes Forever." A helicopter gently, but loudly, landed on the target building. One Ranger agreed to visit the prostitute in that building. As she opened her door, ten Rangers followed. Her window shade was drawn. Her mouth was taped and her hands cuffed, her feet tied with nylon rope. Six men raced up to the stairs to the second level. Commandos jumped from the copter and entered the fire door on the roof.
Six men were sitting at a round table stacking American one-hundred, five-hundred, andd one-thousand-dollar bills. Secret Service agents Witten and Parker raced to the printing press.
"Here they are!" Parker yelled.
He held up two plates for one-hundred-dollar bills.
"Where the hell are the others?" Witten shouted.
The six men, numbed by the surprise attack, were being put in restraints, while others of the marauders searched every inch of the premises. The men were shackled. Witten grabbed one of the counterfeiters by the throat.
"Where are the other plates?"
"*Was ist los?*"
"Bullshit," he hissed, holding the one-hundred-dollar plate under his nose. "*Was ist?*"
"*No sprechen* English."
Captain Werner entered. In German, he said, "They will break every bone in your body. Where are the plates?"
"Under *der* carpet," a short little man with thick eyeglasses whined.
The table was moved, the carpet was ripped and the plates for all denominations were retrieved, then wrapped in tissue paper.
"*Wohin gehen die Deutschemarken?*"
The little man pointed to the next building where Helga plied her trade.
"How do you get there from here? Who's the boss here?"
A stocky barrel-bellied man stood up. "We are just employees," he said in slightly accented English. "We are printers by trade."
"Where is the boss?" Chief Werner demanded.

"In the first building on Königstrasse, top floor."

"What's your name?" Witten demanded.

"Karl Sturner. This is only my second day on this job."

"And where do they make the marks?" Werner queried.

"Through that secret door in back of you," Karl pointed. "Remove the big picture of Frederick the Great and you'll see a button. Push it and the door will open."

With guns drawn, the Rangers, led by Colonel Floyd Davis and Hamburg police, cautiously entered a darkened room. A flashlight revealed another door to the right. The raiders backed against the wall as Werner kicked the door down. A stray shot was fired at the Rangers. Bursts of shots were aimed at the ceiling.

A raspy voice yelled, "*Dummkopf!*"

A second voice said, "Don't shoot, we give up!"

"Drop your guns," Werner repeated in German and English.

A flashlight revealed four well-dressed men huddled on the floor of a well-furnished anteroom. The gunshots brought a dozen more Rangers, holding automatic rifles. The four men in the anteroom were removed roughly, their guns seized, and were taken to the engraving room to be manacled.

The armed soldiers stood ready as they slammed through the door past the anteroom. A large living room revealed six men in tuxedos and four women in evening gowns huddled behind a grand piano. No one was armed. The fright on the women's faces was obvious. The men stood up in a military stance.

"What's the meaning of this?" a tall man arrogantly demanded in German.

Berger, arriving at the scene, snapped, "Speak English!"

A second man, apparently a former military officer, declared in perfect English, "Who the hell are you?"

"The U.S. Army, the German army and the Hamburg police. Now, who the hell are you?" Berger bellowed.

"Sir, I don't know you. I am Admiral Horst von Ludwig, retired. I am also executive vice-president of Eagle Shipping Corporation. You have illegally and mistakenly raided a private party."

"Retired from what, the Nazi army?"

"How dare you call me a Nazi?"

"Which army are you retired from?"

"The army of the Third Reich."

"Then you are retired from *Der Führer* Adolf Hitler's army," Berger said. "Those are two dead entities, the Third Reich and the Nazi Army. You are under arrest, all of you. Chief of Detectives Werner, show him the warrant and take them away. I'm going upstairs."

The chief ordered his men, with the assistance of the Rangers, to place handcuffs on the six men and four ladies. A short struggle ensued, with the ladies hysterically crying and asserting that they were invited guests to the soiree.

An attack was in progress at the top floor of the apartment house next door on the corner of Königstrasse. Berger found two distinguished men in tuxedos absorbed in a game of chess. Assuming a tough-guy stance, he pointed a Colt .45 and demanded, "Put your hands up and don't move!"

Two Rangers, backing up Phil, charged in with two automatic rifles pointing at the shocked chess players. With Berger still pointing his gun, the Rangers quickly manacled the two men. They identified themselves as Richard von Leute, president of the Banque Lorraine in Geneva, and Peter Weber, Banque Royale executive, Zurich.

A complete sweep of the Reeperbahn alleys' secret apartments hidden over the windowed sex-for-sale district resulted in the capture of the counterfeiters, the counterfeit plates and millions of dollars of fraudulent money, plus plates and millions of fake French francs. Slightly over a hundred AK-47s, two hundred assorted handguns, cocaine, heroin, and fifty pounds of marijuana were confiscated. The total of detainees was six women and thirty-four men. They were bused in two military vans to an outlying army stockade for interrogation.

After twenty-four hours of questioning, they held Hermann Horstmann, boss of the counterfeiters of the American money. A close-mouthed Nazi, he was a former major in the Waffen SS who reported directly to Gunther Froelich. Berger tagged him for a trip to Guantanamo. His six employees were turned over to Chief Werner. The two bankers, von Leute and Weber, were ticketed for the U.S. Naval Base in Cuba, as was Admiral von Ludwig. The six ladies were one-night dates and were detained locally. The rest of the men were being held pending fingerprint checks, rap sheets, and CIA, Interpol, MI6, DGSE and German *polizei* checkups.

☆ ☆ ☆ ☆

Tuesday, April 22, 1952 - same day - Paris
Shortly after twilight, George Spota and his crew prepared for the filming of *The Rogues* movie sequence. Police lined up yellow traffic cones, and detour signs were placed at each end of the Avenue Montaigne. A lane was provided for cars headed in and out of the Plaza Athenee Hotel and the Oxford Manor. French police and U.S. Army Rangers wore work clothes matching those of the film crew. Richard Maybrook, standing in for Bart Milburn, played the role of assistant director. He wandered into the Oxford Manor building at will. Mobile dressing-room vans lined the street opposite the Oxford.

François Marmel, manager of the Oxford, nervously watched the machinations of the film crew, soundmen, electricians, best boy, and all the men and women plying their trade in the mysteries of making a motion picture. George Spota was in his suite dining with the film's stars and the writers of the film. Present were David Niven, Charles Boyer, Gig Young, Robert Coote and Gladys Cooper, plus screenwriters Ivan Goff and Ben Roberts. Spota explained that this would be a rehearsal with a caveat. All agreed to participate in the charade.

After dinner, Spota went down to the location to check out the crew. He walked up and down the street, thanking the police for their cooperation. The first assistant director, Lorna Neal, a real no-nonsense professional with a deceivingly amiable personality, had the full respect of the crew and the actors, and she had everything set up to perfection. Spota had briefed her on the caper, and her abiding hatred for the Nazis ensured her full attention to detail. She walked over to Captain Felix Gaumont, who was standing next to the cameraman.

"Captain, I'm Lorna Neal, the first AD, or assistant director. Mr. Spota suggested I handle a delicate matter with you."

"I am at your service, *Mademoiselle*," he gallantly replied.

"We usually have a gratuity for the police who help with the crowds and traffic. I understand there are ten uniformed police on duty here tonight. I have ten envelopes, each containing five hundred francs, which is equal to one hundred dollars. May I give you these for distribution to your men, sir?"

"Very considerate. You are most charming, and I'll handle it for you. Please keep your crew away from the Oxford Manor once the filming is completed. That is for their safety, Miss Neal."

"I'll attend to that," she assured him with a warm smile.

Spota waved her to join him at the Oxford entrance.

"I've briefed all the actors, Lorna. Now, take our budding star and give him a quick touch of makeup. He's a nervous wreck in there."

Spota and Neal went to François' office. The little man, dressed for the occasion, was repeating his lines in front of a hand mirror.

"Monsieur Marmel, this is Lorna Neal, our assistant director."

"*Mon plaisir*," he gushed, bowing.

"It is makeup time, sir; come with me," she ordered in a professional manner. She escorted him out of the building, passing Richard Maybrook on his way in. Marmel was taken to a van where the makeup artists were at work. Spota left.

Maybrook connected a hidden microphone to the lobby switchboard. He attached it to Nordheim's penthouse telephone and strung some twisted wires to the cables planted there by the sound crew. Spota had advised them to cooperate. Crewmen reeled the wire out to the street alongside the Plaza Athenee. One of Captain Gaumont's men, dressed as a hall porter, took his position at the switchboard. François Marmel returned, noticing the man at the switchboard.

"I usually answer the calls from a table switchboard in my office."

"He's only an extra. He has no lines to speak. You sit at this desk I've moved over here. See, I've put a brass plaque here, which says *Concierge*. The camera will sweep the lobby and come to rest, focusing on you. This makes it look more like a hotel," Spota explained.

"Oh, yes, you picture people think of everything," Marmel giggled.

"One more thing - as soon as you do your scene, rush across the street to the van behind the makeup truck, where you'll repeat your lines into a tape recorder six or seven times as an audio backup. You must run over immediately. We do the same with the stars."

"I understand. Oh, please tell me now, how do I look?"

"Superb."

Like a peacock, Marmel sucked up his posture, raised his eyebrows and, gushing with narcissism, turned and strutted away on his light little feet.

Everyone was in place as the five actors entered the building. The limousine was parked in front of the Oxford Manor, which now sported the new brass sign *Hotel Ascoteur.* The interior and exterior were appropriately lighted.

Marmel sat at his concierge desk. Niven walked up to François, who greeted him with a nervous smile. A hand-held camera recorded the scene. Niven said, "The king is expecting us."

Marmel shook his hand and, halting, delivered his lines, then pointed to the elevator. "His Majesty is in the penthouse, waiting for you," he ad-libbed.

Niven, Boyer, Young, Coote and Cooper turned and entered the elevator. The cameras shot the entire scene. Marmel rushed out of the building.

The elevator descended. The actors exited quickly into the street. Half of the oversized crew rushed into the Oxford Manor. The fifteen men were led by Felix Gaumont and Colonel Marchaud. In the basement, Major Duval and a cadre of fifteen took their positions. The special direct elevator to the penthouse had been rendered inoperative. The power had been shut off. A moment before 2300 hours, the telephone in the lobby rang.

The police "porter" answered.

"Allo."

"Who is this? Where is François?" a guttural voice demanded.

"This is Pierre. Monsieur Marmel is not well."

"What is going on? I heard the elevator come up here and then go down."

"A motion picture was being made. It's all over now, Monsieur."

The phone clicked off.

The time was precisely 2300 hours. All floor doors to the stairway were manned by police. Gaumont and his men took the lobby elevator to the penthouse. Marchaud activated the private elevator in the basement and pressed the button, which took it directly into the penthouse. The police in the basement rounded up a butler, two maids and a cook. All were German, speaking a smattering of French and English. They were handcuffed and rushed out of a delivery door to a side street and placed in a police van.

Allen Dulles suddenly appeared. Maybrook had not expected him in Paris. "What the hell are you doing here?" he asked.

"I was in London, briefing MI6, and I caught a flight to Paris just to observe the action."

Maybrook was obviously discomfited. "Please don't interfere."

"Don't worry, Richard."

The storage door was solid steel. A sergeant sent for an acetylene torch.

Four men in their shirtsleeves were startled. They had been seated at a card table. Chips and cards were scattered as they rose in fright.

Marchaud opened the front door, then Gaumont and his crew entered the luxurious penthouse. Guns were leveled at the four men. Gaumont ordered his men to do a thorough search of the premises.

He immediately focused his eyes on one of the four, who declared in fractured French, "What the hell is this?"

He made a move to a telephone, but Gaumont recognized him from his photographs, and bellowed, "Herr Froelich, touch that phone and I'll blow your hand off! Hands up, all of you."

Quickly the four men were manacled. Captain Gaumont took the lead on the top floor of the duplex. He sent part of his cadre to the floor below. Simultaneously, the two floors were scoured thoroughly. Baggage, trunks, correspondence, ledgers and packets of miscellany were delivered to a special Army truck to transport evidence.

Maybrook and Gaumont huddled in the kitchen of the lavish apartment. Secret Service agents Zach Huston and Troy Gardner went to the basement.

"These bankers should be held on a variety of charges and shipped pronto to our special brig," Maybrook asserted.

However, Dulles suddenly appeared and said, "Listen carefully, Richard. These men are important bankers, very well connected with the Swiss government. I'm inclined to let them go."

Maybrook flushed, and his eyes coldly stared at his superior. "Sir, may we caucus for a moment? I'm sure these gentlemen will forgive us," Maybrook apologized.

Dulles and Maybrook walked into the oversized pantry. Maybrook slammed the door shut resoundingly.

"What's up your craw, Maybrook?"

"Mr. Dulles, hear me out. What I am about to say will probably end my career at the CIA. At this moment, I'm in charge of this operation."

"What in hell are you talking about?" Dulles testily demanded.

"First of all, you don't belong here."

"Well, I am here and I will participate."

"Mr. Dulles," Maybrook declared, "you are the deputy director of the CIA and my senior at Langley. But I am here in command under the orders of Colonel Barton Milburn. He is operating on the authority of President Truman. Therefore, in this instance, sir, my authority supersedes yours. Do you challenge that?"

Dulles, red-faced, angrily replied, "My political training is far superior to yours. Taking these Swiss bankers into custody will lead to an international scandal for the United States. Your ignorance of these nuances will cost us dearly. I'm warning you right now that if you use your temporary authority, the repercussions will not only destroy your career, but you'll be responsible for the downfall of your pristine hero, Colonel Milburn."

"Do I hear you correctly? Are you using the word pristine as a sarcastic pejorative to your alleged friend, Colonel Milburn?"

"Wait one minute. I have a high regard for Bart. That wasn't sarcasm. Pristine, in this instance, was meant to be a compliment," Dulles equivocated.

"Allen, despite your harsh words, I'll attempt to ameliorate our differences with a rationale that might convince you of the motivational imperatives for taking these bankers into custody," Maybrook said calmly.

"Okay, Richard, convince me," Dulles challenged. "And don't forget, I was stationed in Switzerland during the war; I understand these people."

"Think of what is confronting us: the Revenge Plan. If tipped off by one of them to Froelich or General Müller, the atrocities will begin. Other than that vital caution, let me point out a major mystery to be solved. The Swiss were the best allies the Nazis had during the war. They are illegally holding money stolen from the pockets and mouths of the Holocaust victims. Those two bastards know where the plunder is hidden. They are also Hitler's bankers. This, if brought to light, would make bounteous grist for the media mills. Need I say more?" Maybrook said.

"Your argument has questionable validity, but I'll play along," Dulles responded.

Reluctantly they shook hands, and Maybrook mused over Bart's report from the Mossad regarding the Dulles brothers. They returned to the kitchen and advised Colonel Marchaud that the bankers would be shipped to the U.S. Shortly thereafter, agent Huston entered the room, short of breath.

"Gentlemen, we have finally cut through the steel door in the storage room," he panted.

"What did you find, Zach?" Marchaud asked.

"Sir, this is something you gentlemen will have to see for yourselves. There are several compartments built like a bank vault. I can only describe it as a combination of a King Midas treasure and a Nazi arsenal, plus a mass of currencies," Huston said.

The five men used the direct elevator to the basement. Eight soldiers, fully armed, stood guard at the storage room. The steel door, similar to a bank-vault safety mechanism, minus the timing device, was lying askew. Soldiers guarded both ends of the corridor.

Gingerly, the colonel, the chief, Dulles, Maybrook and Huston climbed over the slanted steel door. The interior was composed of a maze of compartments. Each had required keys. They were torched open with acetylene.

Compartments one and two were large, about fifteen by twenty feet, and contained shelves of gold bars on the walls. Compartment three was stacked with American, British, German, Dutch and French currencies. Compartment four contained safe-deposit boxes loaded with cut diamonds, jewelry, emeralds and assorted expensive men and women's watches. Compartment five, a very large chamber, contained approximately 40 paintings of Impressionist artists such as Van Gogh, Gauguin, Renoir, Monet, Pissarro, Cezanne and Degas among others. Classics included Rubens, Leonardo da Vinci, Raphael, Titian, Bellini and Tintoretto. A sharp turn to the left revealed a wide-open double door. This was the arsenal, with cases of hand guns, boxes of automatic AK47s and ammo, grenades, flame throwers, light anti-tank bazookas, large containers of poison gas, dynamite, TNT, nitroglycerin and some other items that had to be analyzed.

Secret Service agent Troy Gardner remained at compartment three, photographing the shelves of currencies and plucking samples from each of the assorted legal or illegal tender.

The discoveries in the storage room of the Oxford Manor presented a political dilemma to the combined forces. The first order of business was the allocation of prisoners. The authorities used the Nordheim penthouse as temporary headquarters. The dining room served as a conference room. Soldiers and police were assigned to guard all exits and entrances to the Oxford Manor. The building took on the ambiance of a military stockade. Tenants exiting and entering were required to produce identification.

Colonel Marchaud, in charge of the French DGSE, presided over the meeting. Seated around the huge mahogany dining room table were Marchaud, Captain Gaumont, Secret Service agent Zach Huston, Allen Dulles, and an irritated Richard Maybrook.

"We are going to be here for several hours, say two or three, to allow for the streets to be cleared of onlookers before we move anything from this building," Maybrook announced. "We must do this in the quiet of the night. I have arranged for a mobile commissary to feed coffee and sandwiches to all of the men on duty. We'll partake of the same fare."

"Very thoughtful, sir," Marchaud said.

"Now, as to dispositions, under the terms of our agreement the U.S. Army has the right to seize and possess all arms and weapons of destruction. Therefore that arsenal in the storage room is herewith confiscated by our forces. Any objections?"

The consensus was unanimous.

"Item two: Who wishes to speak of the retention of the assortment of prisoners?"

A babble of voices was hushed by Colonel Marchaud.

"One at a time, please, gentlemen. Let's go round the table, starting with Captain Gaumont. We are here under instructions to cooperate with the CIA. Gaumont wears two hats. He works with us at the DGSE and he is also captain of detectives for the city of Paris. Any local laws broken here, Felix?"

"I have a comment directed at the Americans. French Intelligence, to which I have been assigned in a dual role, is aware of the Nazi Revenge Plan. We are aware of planned assassinations, as well as the destruction of the Eiffel Tower and the Palace of Versailles. As outrageous as this information may be, we cannot ignore it," Gaumont declared.

Dulles and Maybrook looked at each other in surprise. Others in the room were startled. Dulles exploded. "That information was and is top secret! How did you come into possession of the so-called Revenge Plan?"

Marchaud broke in, "Mr. Dulles, we have great respect for the CIA. But, please, do not denigrate the talents of the DGSE."

"I have great respect for your intelligence service, Colonel Marchaud, but I suspect the answer is simpler than that. I believe that the leak came from one of our agents, Jacques Laurent, to his wartime buddy, Captain Gaumont,"

Dulles huffed.

Felix jumped out of his chair and stood belligerently over the seated Dulles. "That is a fucking lie! You have maligned one of your best and most loyal agents. Such a canard cannot go unchallenged!"

Marchaud interjected, "Felix, please sit down."

"No, Colonel, not until I wipe the slate clean of Mr. Dulles' filthy accusation."

Dulles rose and faced the taller, rugged and enraged captain. Gaumont met him eye-to-eye. "If you must know the source of that information, Mr. Deputy Director of the CIA, I refer you to your immediate superior, General Walter Smith. Jacques Laurent wouldn't even give me the time of day, if it was top secret, with a clock right in front of my face."

A flushed Dulles melted into his chair. Maybrook winked at Gaumont in approval. During the silence that followed the outburst, sandwiches and coffee arrived, defusing the tension that filled the room.

The conferees were ravenously hungry. Few words were spoken as they devoured their bland edibles. Hot coffee was quickly consumed, and additional pots were placed on the kitchen stoves. The military food couriers were dismissed with thanks from all. Colonel Marchaud broke the silence. "Mr. Dulles, I am forced to confirm Captain Gaumont's statements."

"That being the case, I am obliged to humbly apologize to Captain Gaumont and in turn to our loyal Jacques Laurent," the abashed Dulles said.

Colonel Marchaud resumed control of the meeting. "It is my sworn duty to question those suspects who may be involved in this dastardly plan," Gaumont said.

Maybrook whispered in Dulles' ear, and he nodded assent.

"General Marchaud, we are inclined to agree with Captain Gaumont's position. We are caught in a myriad of responsibilities. Yes, we are a team with one objective: to capture war criminals and protect our allies from any of their machinations," Maybrook said.

"What's the solution, Maybrook?"

"I suggest that the DGSE, with your approval, permit Captain Gaumont to join us on our trip back to the U.S. with only the current detainees to be at his disposal jointly with our interrogators."

Marchaud declared, "That sounds fine."

Dulles added, "We'll share all the information we have up to now affecting France with the captain."

Colonel Marchaud whispered to Gaumont, then, turning to the others, said, "I have to get approval from headquarters and obtain a budget for his expenses."

"His expenses, including food and lodging plus a return-flight ticket, will be paid by us," Maybrook replied.

"It's pretty late, but I'll venture a phone call for approval," the colonel said.

"There is a bank of private phones in Nordheim's den. Go to it," Maybrook directed.

"If this is approved, I can have a bag of clothes and other items, including my passport, delivered here by my son within the hour."

"Go into the den, Captain. If the colonel gets the okay, call your son to rush your bag and passport here right away," Maybrook advised.

Marchaud rose and stretched. "It's time for a break. There are three posh latrines on this floor. Relieve yourselves, men."

Maybrook returned with a silver tray loaded with six snifter glasses and a bottle of unopened Napoleon brandy. He placed it on the sideboard, as smiles prevailed.

"A little of that will make a long day shorter," Dulles observed.

Each of the six glasses contained a moderate amount of the precious liqueur. Cigarettes and cigars were lit, and the room was soon bathed in a cloud of smoke. Marchaud and Gaumont returned with approval for Gaumont's trip to the U.S.

"I interrupted a moment of *amour*. My son was entertaining a lady. My bag and passport are on their way. I notified the front door to let him come up."

"Now that we have resolved the dilemma of the arms cache, we will leave the explosives to your people to analyze, Colonel Marchaud. Dispose of it as you like," Dulles said.

"We'd appreciate a memo of the analysis, Paul," Maybrook requested.

"No problem, Richard."

"The prisoner problem is solved," Marchaud declared.

"Next is the matter of currencies," Maybrook said.

Before Marchaud could speak, Secret Service agent Zach Huston asserted, "The American currency goes with me and my partner, Gardner, who is watching the loot in the basement. The French francs go to you, Colonel Marchaud. We'll take a few samples and give you some of ours. We'll take all the rest for examination."

"That's fair enough, Mr. Huston," the colonel agreed.

"Any comment about the gold, precious stones, assorted jewelry, watches, ecetera?" Gaumont asked.

"That goes with us," Maybrook quickly asserted. "Let me explain why. It has been agreed by de Gaulle, Churchill, Truman, and Ben-Gurion that these Nazi criminals be put on trial by the Americans. All this contraband is evidence."

"Understood," Marchaud agreed.

"Now comes the art collection," Gaumont said.

Those pieces are evidence, as well. After the trial, the true owners will be tracked down and they will be returned. Stuff like this was stolen by those degenerates, Goering, Hitler, Himmler, and other German vermin. And, by the way, that gold was probably extracted from the mouths of the gassed victims, melted and turned into bars," Maybrook said passionately.

"Any objections, men?" Marchaud asked.

The chimes pealed. Gaumont went to the door. A tall, handsome young man handed a large suitcase and an envelope to his father. They hugged each other.

"Gentlemen, this is my son, Armand, who will graduate from the Sorbonne this June," Gaumont said proudly.

He was greeted with a round of applause.

"*Merci beaucoup, Messieurs,*" Armand responded.

On the way out, Gaumont told his son to advise his mother that he was leaving for America on urgent business.

"As to the ledgers, correspondence and other papers gathered here, I assume that goes to the CIA?" Marchaud conjectured.

All agreed.

"Sir, I have one caveat," Maybrook said.

"Let's hear it."

"I want the word of honor of Colonel Marchaud and Captain Gaumont that the locale of our destination and incarceration of the prisoners will not be revealed to anyone by Gaumont, even to you, Colonel. This, for the present, is the highest priority. One inadvertent leak and our entire strategy will be destroyed," Maybrook cautioned.

Gaumont and Marchaud whispered to each other.

"Agreed," the colonel affirmed. "What about the servants?"

"I recommend that the DGSE thoroughly interrogate them about visitors and other activity in this penthouse. They might pluck a few nuggets of value from them," Dulles suggested.

"Will do," Marchaud agreed.

The process of boxing and packaging the loot took over an hour to complete. The prisoners were blindfolded and hustled into buses stationed at the rear of the Oxford Manor. The buses and the loaded truck, followed by a busful of Army Rangers, convoyed to Orly Airport. The prisoners, Army personnel and the two Secret Service agents, Huston and Gardner, boarded the chartered Pan Am.

Dulles and Maybrook took turns on the telephone. Dulles called General Smith at his home and briefed him in telegraphic terms. Maybrook reached Katherine Wharton and, in *Lucy* code, advised her to contact Bart for a quick briefing on the Paris raid, as well as the surprise arrival of Dulles. He asked her to reach Sedgwick at Guantanamo to advise him that the captives and the contraband would be en route to Cuba. Also, she should inform him that Captain Gaumont was coming to Guantanamo to investigate France's endangerment in the Revenge Plan. This would be necessary to avoid a diplomatic snarl.

"Congratulations," she replied.

The charter flight took to the skies.

CHAPTER TWENTY-FIVE

Tuesday, April 22, 1952 - same day - Lund, Sweden

Katherine Wharton reached Bart Milburn in Malmo at the Lundmal Bed and Breakfast Inn, as he was about to leave. "Lucy, we had a very successful visit with the family. They are coming back with us. Pass that on to Beetle. Delighted with Uncle Gunther and his piggybankers."

Bart and his caravan raced to their rendezvous with the Flying Eagle. The Rangers and other Army personnel struggled with the difficult task of unloading the truck carrying the contraband found aboard the yacht.

Sean Briscoe and Leif Sandstrom stayed out of the bloodless coup. They observed with admiration the Americans' surgical strike, then both helped in loading the spoils aboard the Flying Eagle. There was one untoward incident during the crossing of the channel between Malmo and Copenhagen. Leif left Briscoe at the helm, with the excuse that he had a stomach cramp and needed to go to the head.

Sandstrom casually walked aft, pleasantly advising the Rangers that the yacht would make the crossing in about thirty minutes. He looked at the collection of prisoners, including Gunther Froelich.

"*Der Kotzbrocken*, traitor, Sandstrom. *Der Schweinhund, arschloch*, double-crosser!" Froelich screamed at the captain.

Sandstrom leaned over him and spat directly in his face. "Drop dead, Herr Froelich, Nazi bastard!"

Two Rangers slapped the tape back onto Froelich's mouth. Leif then found his prey, Hugo Schultz, and while the Rangers were busy, he grasped the manacled murderer of his fiancée by the neck and lifted him to his feet.

He smashed his ham-sized fist into Schultz's mouth, delivering a resounding punch and loosening several teeth. "Murdering Nazi scum!"

The former Ohrdruf commandant collapsed. One of the Rangers looked at the comatose figure and opined, "That's a fine sleeping pill, Captain."

Sandstrom returned to the bridge and relieved Briscoe.

"Steady as she goes, Captain, I want to talk to Colonel Milburn."

Briscoe located Bart in the salon. "Colonel, can you spare a second?"

"Sure, Sean, sit down. What's on your mind?"

"You're heading for Argentina. With your permission, I'd like to fly with you to Buenos Aires."

"Sean, you've been very helpful, but I don't want you involved in our mission there. You've performed very well here in Malmo, but that's as far as it goes."

"Colonel, hear me out. I have no intention of being anywhere near you in Argentina. I'm chasing Adolf Eichmann. We've had leads to three places there - Rosario, Santa Fe and Parona. The minute you land in Buenos Aires, I'll be heading north, scouting those towns. I've been of help to you with this friggin' yacht, so how about a little *quid pro quo*?"

"You're a charming rapscallion and a good friend; yes, welcome aboard."

"Thanks, Bart."

Captain Sandstrom calmly steered away from Malmo into the Øresund, part of the Kattegat strait shared by Denmark and Sweden, heading toward Copenhagen. Two miles offshore, the Flying Eagle followed the guidance of Copenhagen's flashlight signals.

Sandstorm anchored a quarter-mile from shore. A flotilla of large tenders sidled up to the yacht. The prisoners were the last to be transferred to these big motorboats. The packages, trunk, boxes and miscellaneous materials seized were transferred to the launches, then to trucks. The prisoners, Rangers, Jacques and Bart boarded a large bus and headed for the Copenhagen airport. By pre-arrangement, they drove onto the tarmac, where the BOAC De Havilland jet-liner was in a specially assigned hangar. The loot and prisoners, with their captors, were finally on board, and the jetliner took off for Argentina.

It was a new experience for the passengers as the jetliner roared down the runway, speedily rising to 30,000 feet and leveling off.

Captain Derek Campbell came out of the cockpit and introduced himself to Bart.

"Welcome aboard, Colonel Milburn. Prime Minister Churchill sends his compliments and wishes you Godspeed, sir."

"That's very kind of you. Thanks for the message," Bart said.

"May I sit next to you for a moment, Colonel?"

"Please do."

"I want to assure you that my crew and I have been sworn to complete secrecy by General Lloyd Forsythe concerning this flight and its destination. All we know is that you have captured some Nazi war criminals. Under British secrecy laws, our lips are sealed. It is a felony offense to violate that law. I am a retired colonel. I was a fighter pilot in the big mess. I despise Nazis. We are at your disposal, sir."

"That's very reassuring, Colonel Campbell. We are kindred souls. We've been through it all," Bart replied. "This plane made history in its maiden flight to Rome."

"Jet planes will make this planet a lot smaller," Campbell said. "By the way, I am referred to as Captain these days. That's the title conferred on pilots in civil aviation."

"Very well, Captain. Thank you for your hospitality."

"Our stewards will be serving supper shortly. What do you want us to do about your prisoners in the rear?"

"Nothing. Let them stew in their own Nazi juices."

"Colonel, I share your sentiments."

"By the way, where do you intend to refuel?"

"This is going to be a very long flight, Colonel. I understand that our final destination is Buenos Aires, so our first stop will be the Azores. I understand from your associate, Mr. Laurent, that you wish to deposit your prisoners at your naval base in Guantanamo Bay."

"That's correct, Captain."

Campbell smiled mischievously, "I could fuel up again in Miami, or even, say, Havana, if you prefer."

"Oh, that little bird, Jacques Laurent, whispered in your ear," Bart laughed.

"We have our own intelligence system. Your wife and children are vacationing there. We could lay over about ninety minutes or more for a quick visit. We need that time for fueling and checkup. We also need to pick up food supplies. Give me a phone number and we'll radio ahead with an ETA for your family to meet you at the José Martí Airport restaurant. How does that sound?"

"That is music to my ears."

"It's only a twenty-minute flight to Guantanamo from Havana on this bird. My pleasure, Colonel. The *No Smoking* sign is off. Relax, have a drink. See you later."

Jacques had been checking on the prisoners, then he joined Bart.

"Froelich has been screaming bloody murder."

After the food service, Captain Campbell dimmed the cabin lights. Bart, Jacques and the Army men took a much-needed nap.

They refueled at the Azores islands eight hundred miles off the coast of Portugal, where Bart placed a collect call to the villa in Havana. Elizabeth answered and accepted the call. "Liz, my love, we are en route. We'll stop for refueling at José Martí Airport. You'll receive a call from the BOAC people giving you an estimated time of arrival. Meet us in the coffee shop of the airport."

"Oh, Bart, that's wonderful. Hurry."

"Bring Christina and all the kids."

"We'll be there, my hero. I love you."

"I love you, too."

The flight continued to its stopover in Havana, and a few hours later, the De Havilland comet landed at the José Martí Airport's extended runway.

384 ☆ DAVID B. CHARNAY

Campbell advised Bart that they would be servicing the plane for approximately two hours.

"Your wife should be in the coffee shop now. Our BOAC desk here notified her of our ETA. Enjoy," Campbell said with a smile.

Bart, Jacques and Briscoe exited the jetliner. Captain Devereaux told his Rangers to split up in units to stretch their legs and have a snack at the coffee shop.

Briscoe headed for a public phone at the coffee shop. Four children raced to the door at the sight of Bart and Jacques. Jenny and Michael grasped Bart's legs with a chorus of *Daddy!* Matthew and Katherine jumped into Jacques' arms. Kisses were bestowed on both men. The children were carried to a table in the rear. The two ladies planted kisses on the lips of their men.

Elizabeth and Bart mumbled love talk to each other. Mrs. Bishop and Elsie tried to contain the four children. Jacques and Christina observed the hackneyed aphorism *Absence makes the heart grow fonder.* Their eyes met.

"Jacques, I can't believe how much I missed you," she whispered, kissing his ear.

His moistened eyes focused on her adoring face. Shamelessly, he took her in his arms and planted a loving kiss on her welcoming lips.

The kids chortled, "Kissy, kissy!"

The talk was fast and furious. The subject of the raids was quickly disposed of, with Bart declaring that all three missions had been flawless in execution.

As the food was being served, Sean Briscoe approached the table, and was invited to join the family reunion. He declined politely, saying he wished to talk with Jacques privately.

Apprehensively, Jacques rose and excused himself. Sean led him to a quiet corner of the restaurant. The Milburn family stared at the two men.

"What is the problem, Sean?" Jacques asked.

"No problem, but very good news for you."

"What is it?"

"Jacques, I have just reported to the Mossad. Ariel Rubin sends his love and wished me to tell you that your sister, Joyce, is alive and well. She has been located and spoken to."

Tears flooded Jacques' eyes and began to roll down his face. He embraced Sean so tightly that Sean pleaded for air. "Where is she?"

"She's a professor of French at Leipzig University. Our underground lady agent is now in full contact with her. This agent has enrolled in two night classes taught by your sister. This is so they will keep in touch with each other."

"I have to see her."

"No, you don't dare make a move. Any strange contact will endanger your sister and destroy our underground operation. Leave it to us, we have moved lots of Jews out of East Germany. We have our ways. Promise to do nothing. Don't let this news go farther than Bart and family. That's an order from Ariel."

"God bless you, Sean. I promise. Please have your people keep me advised."

Briscoe went to the counter for his lunch. Jacques returned to the table, dabbing his teary eyes.

"What's wrong, Jacques?" Bart said.

"It's wonderful news. My sister is alive and well. She has been contacted by the Mossad in Leipzig, East Germany. These are tears of happiness."

A joyous atmosphere bathed the table. Water glasses clinked in toasts to the good news. Christina hugged Jacques and kissed his cheek. Elizabeth rose and walked around the table. She kissed Jacques' forehead and declared, "I am so happy for you, dear brother. Now we have to get her out." She embraced him.

Two hours later the jetliner took off for Guantanamo. After twenty minutes the jet plane roared down a long runway and taxied back to a designated hangar. Admiral Thomas and Lloyd Sedgwick, flanked by a cordon of Marines and naval shore patrol, greeted Bart as he debarked.

Bart briefed the two men with details of his cargo of prisoners, plunder and troops. Admiral Thomas described his annex brig in anticipation of captives from Malmo, Hamburg, and Paris.

"Colonel, with regard to the Argentine expedition, some other arrangements will have to be made. Assuming some fifty or more detainees are to be incarcerated, have you planned to bring them here?"

"Admiral, I admit I've been remiss in that respect. As you know, my plate has been quite full these past few days. My deepest interest is in Hitler and Bormann, and now we have Herr Froelich here as well. He should be kept here. En route here is Konrad Fliegel, also to be kept here, plus some bankers on board the jet. The flights from Paris and Hamburg are several hours behind us."

"Colonel, I have a suggestion, if you can clear it with the President."

"I welcome any help."

"Homestead Air Force Base in Florida is about an hour flight from here. They have a large stockade."

"Lloyd, supervise the unloading. Prisoners and troops off first, loot after that. Froelich and bankers in the main brig - separated."

"Gotcha."

"Admiral, I have to make a quick call to D.C. and then take off for Argentina as soon as the plane is fueled."

"Come to my office, Bart."

The call was placed to the White House, where John Steelman answered.

"Colonel, you've hit three home runs."

"John, we have a tactical problem. We have three planeloads of Nazis and contraband due here at Guantanamo. Admiral Thomas has built an annex to the brig. That will max out capacity at this base. What do we do with the Nazi bastards captured in Argentina?"

"That is a conundrum, Bart."

"A nice word for our problem," Bart said. "The admiral suggests the stockade at Homestead Air Base."

"I'll go over it with the Prez and General Smith. You're on your way to the Argentine festivities. We'll have an answer for you in the morning."

"Thanks, John."

"Fabulous job so far, Bart. Good luck."

Bart returned to the jet plane.

Laurent and Sedgwick directed the troops to take each prisoner to assigned cells, separated from one another. The plunder was stored in a stone warehouse arsenal, which was to be guarded around the clock. Sedgwick was assigned to prepare a written inventory. He was instructed to advise Maybrook and Berger to do likewise. Jacques and Bart boarded the jetliner. Briscoe was already on board, fast asleep.

In minutes they were airborne, en route to Buenos Aires.

The flight was uneventful, giving Bart and Jacques the opportunity to follow Briscoe's lead and catch up on some much-needed sleep.

One hour out of Buenos Aires, they awoke. They had coffee and sandwiches, then Jacques informed Bart of the actions of Captain Sandstrom aboard the Flying Eagle. "He lifted Hugo Schultz out of his seat and knocked him cold with one punch. The Rangers acted as though they saw nothing. One guy called it a *sleeping pill!*"

"It's a wonder he didn't kill him. I'm glad he didn't. I want a few minutes with that bastard myself."

"Bart, what do I do about my sister?"

"You do nothing, Jacques. I'll talk to Ariel Rubin at the Mossad. I will also take it up with the President. Maybe he'll arrange an exchange of prisoners with those commie bums."

The *No Smoking* sign lit up, then Campbell announced, "All seat belts fastened, please."

As they circled the approach, they looked out of the windows and discerned the American fleet lined up in the Rio de la Plata. The plane touched down gently and roared its way to an elongated runway. The jet made a U-turn and came to a halt at the Buenos Aires airport entrance.

Bart and Jacques alighted and were greeted by Ambassador Franklin Withers, Sophia, Tony, Marine Colonel Joseph Metcalf and General Lucas Whitney, the Marine commander. Salutes and handshakes were exchanged. Sean Briscoe, carrying his suitcase, stealthily alighted from the plane and disappeared on the tarmac, avoiding immigration and customs.

"We've arranged a two-bedroom suite for you and Jacques at the Phoenix Hotel where Tony and I are staying," Sophia announced.

"Ambassador Withers, General Lucas Whitney and his aide, Colonel Joseph Metcalf, are joining us there for a talk over supper," Tony declared.

"That's a super idea," Withers replied. "Colonel, just a walk through customs and immigration. It'll take two minutes. I have cleared it for you, gentlemen."

"Very thoughtful, sir. Thank you," Bart said.

Campbell came over to Bart. After introductions to his greeters, Milburn thanked Campbell profusely for his trip and courtesies. The group entered Withers' limousine.

At the hotel, they adjourned to an elegant suite. A table had been attractively set for the seven. Two waiters and a busboy were at attention. Wine bottles were being chilled in standing ice buckets.

"Who arranged this?" Bart asked.

"This is courtesy of Ambassador Withers in the interests of secrecy," Sophia whispered.

Wine was poured, toasts exchanged, and a superb dinner was served, highlighted by charcoal-broiled Argentine Beef Wellington, with coffee, brandy and cigars for the men. Sophia lit a Sherman cigarette in a pearl holder. The table was cleared and the service crew discreetly departed.

Before the briefing session began, Sophia addressed Bart. "Colonel, you will notice, hanging in your closet, your full dress uniform. Steelman, at the request of President Truman, insisted that you wear it for the ceremonies tomorrow. It has all your medals and fruit-salad ribbons in place. It was shipped here on General Whitney's plane in a garment bag - hat, shoes and all!"

Bart flushed. "How in the world did they get it?"

"Steelman spoke to your wife. She arranged with your houseman, Stanley, to have it cleaned and pressed."

"I saw my wife when we refueled in Havana, and she never said a word about it."

"Steelman asked her not to mention it, because you would balk at it."

"Talk about covert actions, this tops it all," Bart joked.

The group laughed.

"Mr. Ambassador, may I suggest that you bring us up to date as to the diplomatic phase of our arrangements with President Peron for tomorrow's festivities?" Sophia suggested.

"My pleasure, dear Countess," Withers responded, smiling. "The scenario, as succinctly as possible, is as follows. The U.S. fleet and the Argentine flotilla will be at the mouth of the Rio de la Plata. Two hundred Marines will be forming a phalanx of one hundred on each side, forming an aisle with General Whitney and Colonel Metcalf up front to lead the Perons through this honor guard. My wife and I will act as escorts for President Peron. The countess and Tony Fuentes, at the request of the First Lady, will escort Eva Peron to the launch, which will take us to the Enterprise. Colonel Milburn will be at the launch as President Truman's personal emissary. He will introduce himself to the Perons. He will then hand him a personal letter from Truman, conveying his best wishes. Here is the letter, Colonel."

The White House letter with the presidential seal was passed along to Bart.

"The festivities aboard the carrier will be long and drawn-out until dark," the ambassador contined. "We'll sail along with the Argentine ships for awhile. We'll put on a display of six fighter planes taking off from the carrier and show them some fancy flying. Admiral Putnam will have a late reception of food and drinks in the officers' mess. We'll pin some medals on Peron.

"A Marine band will play the national anthems of our two countries, then a short concert of American and Argentine music will follow," Withers went on. "Chairs will be set up for the Perons and all the Argentine officers and notables. We'll stall until dusk. Admiral Putnam will feign some mechanical problem, so that when he drops anchor for the launches to take them ashore it will be real dark. The second act of this show is yours, General - and Colonel Milburn."

"We have a dozen well-armed Marines hidden in the woods on the outskirts of the ranch with two-way radios," GeneralWhitney said. "Our main contingent of Marines will stage a formal parade with a band of music marching to the ranch area. Up the road and away will be thirty of Peron's special platoon of handpicked men to join us. Flags, drums, and all the bullshit. Excuse me, Countess."

She smiled.

"According to our instructions, Colonel Milburn will call the play from there on."

"Thank you, General Whitney. You have been given renderings and photographs of this outpost. There are at least fifty well-armed Nazi Waffen SS men at this so-called ranch. The main man we are seeking is a Nazi General Heinrich Müller, the former head of the fighting unit of the Gestapo. So, we are trying a trick that worked well for us in Malmo, Sweden. April 20th was Hitler's birthday, and we sent a station wagon loaded with doctored liquor and a huge birthday cake loaded with phenobarbital to the house two hours before the attack. It worked. They were half conscious when we hit them."

"What's the plan this time?" Metcalf asked.

"Tony Fuentes can answer that."

"Under orders from Colonel Milburn," Tony said, "I had a load of booze prepared in the States, along with a huge cake with a swastika in the center. A phony telegram from Miami has been prepared for General Müller. It reads, *Sorry I couldn't be with you on my birthday, 20 April. Will see you in two weeks. Celebrate now. Avram.* It was written in German and prepared by Colonel Milburn."

General Whitney, a battle-hardened vet, pounded on the table. "I won't count on booze as a weapon. I want my men battle-ready and prepared for the worst, then hope for the best."

"Sir, I could ask for no more than that. Just one caution: I want as many of our targets alive as possible. It is vital that Heinrich Müller be taken alive. In all cases, I want all of your men back alive and unharmed," Bart said.

"Amen," Whitney said. "Who will deliver the load?"

"One of our agents. He'll deliver it with the note and will return in two hours with the ruse of picking up the empty bottles and the used beer cases. When the door opens, we storm in. A fire will have been started on one of the barn structures as a diversion," Bart explained.

"Who'll set the fire?" Metcalf asked.

"I'll take care of that," Jacques answered.

Bart continued, "We have arranged to have a special tank truck arrive with the Argentine firefighters. That tanker will contain a combination of tear gas and tranquilizer gas. At 2000 hours, attack time, with masks on and windows broken, the hose of the tank truck will pour this gas combo through every window. A second tanker will hose the stuff into the back of the house,"

Bart explained. "For the surrounding buildings, we have boxes full of tear gas and grenades, extra weapons, duct tape, manacles and chains. All will be delivered to you and your men when the parade moves toward the ranch."

"Okay, I'll have a further briefing for my men. We'll strike hard and fast. Manacle all prisoners. Here's to success, and my compliments to all," the general toasted, holding up his glass.

☆ ☆ ☆ ☆

Thursday, April 24, 1952 - 2:57 p.m. - Rio de la Plata, Argentina
The sun was high in the azure sky with white flecks of scattered clouds. A light breeze gently fluttered the array of Argentine and American flags adorning the landscape. The Atlantic waters were placid.

At 3 p.m., the ambassador's limousine pulled up to the dock as scheduled. The Perons and their escorts, Ambassador Withers and his wife, Countess de Cordoba and Tony Fuentes, marched through the aisle of Marines. The Marines stood at attention and saluted the Perons and escorts. Bart Milburn, in full dress uniform, medals and ribbons prominently displayed, delivered a sharp salute. Peron returned it.

Withers said, "Colonel Milburn is President Truman's personal emissary to you, Mr. President."

Bart took two steps forward and kissed the hand of Eva Peron. She turned to Sophia and whispered, "He's so handsome."

Sophia smiled and nodded.

"I can see from those ribbons, Colonel Milburn, you've been through the war all over Europe," Peron said.

"Yes sir, Mr. President, and I have here a personal letter for you from President Truman." Bart saluted.

The party approached the launches en route to the aircraft carrier Enterprise. General Whitney and Colonel Metcalf helped them board the tenders. Several other launches carried notables to the famous carrier, renowned for its activity in the Midway and Coral Sea battles.

The Marines were directed to a picnic area for chow time. Jacques and Bart sat with General Whitney. His aide, Colonel Metcalf, was directing the mobile catering vans in the distribution of food to the two-hundred-odd people seated at the long wooden tables.

They observed the fleet slowly sailing in the tranquil waters. It was a perfect autumn day south of the Equator. After two hours of dining and R & R, they observed the squadron of six fighter planes flying in a V sequence. The sun was sinking in the west.

Colonel Metcalf called, "Attention! Right face! Column of fours! Follow the Jeeps!"

Six large buses followed the marchers. At the outskirts on the banks of the Rio de la Plata, the men were ordered onto the buses. Twenty Marine musicians and their instruments were in the back of one of the buses.

A small truck passed the buses en route to the Nordheim ranch. Three miles past the Marines, the truck followed the macadam road to a wrought-iron gate. The driver, a short, stocky man with sandy hair and freckles, got out of his vehicle, adjusted his overalls and pressed the button of a two-way loudspeaker.

A voice in guttural Spanish responded, "Who's there?"

"Package delivery."

The gate opened to a brick driveway. In the twilight darkness, the truck pulled up to the door of the large two-story building. Lights were turned on and a tall, heavy man opened the door.

"What do you have?"

The silent driver handed the telegram addressed to Heinrich Müller.

In Spanish, the tall man repeated, "What's in there?"

The driver opened the back doors of the truck and affected a stutter in Spanish. "There is m-much liquor and a l-large cake."

"Wait a minute."

Two other large men in vaquero outfits came out and pointed flashlights at the interior of the truck.

A tall, trim, grey-haired man, in a black double-breasted suit, military in stance, holding the opened telegram in his hand, shouted in German, "*Bringen sie mit!*"

Six men helped unload the fully packed truck. Two men carried the huge birthday cake. The man in the black suit approached the stocky driver. Struggling with his Spanish, he asked "Who sent you?"

Stuttering, the driver said, "A *Señor* Schultz. He s-say he g-go to Rosario. He pay m-me with American dollars. He also s-say you t-tip me."

The tall man laughed and, reaching into his pants pocket, pulled out a large roll of bills. He peeled off five twenty-dollar bills and handed them to the stocky man. He patted the driver on the head and making fun of his speech, uttered, "*Buenos n-n-n-noches, s-s-s-s-Señor*. Ha ha ha!"

The driver backed the truck up, turned around and slowly headed for the gate, which opened automatically by an electric eye, saying to himself, "Ha ha *this*, loser."

He passed the Marine units and smartly saluted Colonel Metcalf. They smiled at each other.

Jacques, hiding in the woods about fifty feet away from the main house, observed the activity in the unloading of the truck. His long-range binoculars focused on the tall man in the double-breasted black suit.

He whispered into his transceiver, "Bart, Müller is here."

"Roger," he replied.

Ninety minutes later the Argentine contingent lined up, with the Marine band behind them. The two hundred helmeted Marines in two columns stood at attention. Argentine and American flags were carried in the lead. The band struck up military marching music and the parade began down the dark road, lit up by torchlights carried by the Argentine special unit.

Jacques and two Rangers in camouflage outfits, carrying cans of kerosene, ran through the woods to a large barn-like structure. They unraveled a roll of cordite, tied it around the structure and splashed the kerosene over the exterior wood.

Music and singing emanated from the house. The barn was torched. Jacques and the two Rangers disappeared into the woods. Tongues of flame licked their way up to the roof of the building, lighting up the area. For the first ten minutes of the expanding fire, no one from the main house noticed.

The Marine band music was coming closer to the ranch. At 2000 hours, a Marine scaled the front gate and passed in front of the electric eye used for egress. The gate swung open and the Marines raced through. Mobile equipment followed. A device on the fire truck catapulted heavy rocks at the house, smashing windows. A pair of hoses poured tear gas mixed with sedation liquid into the main house.

Marines surrounded the building. Men came running out of the house and were hit with rifle butts. Most of the Waffen SS troops were either drunk or slightly sedated.

Machine-gun fire spurted from a second-floor window, which was quickly deactivated by the hose of liquid tear gas and tranquilizers. The Marines, with their gas masks in place, poured into the house through the front door, back doors, windows, and the basement.

The occupants were not as pliant as the drugged captives in Malmo had been. However, the spray from the tear gas was effective. A few hand-to-hand struggles were quickly ended with rifle butts from behind. The guesthouse and other buildings yielded a total of twelve compliant prisoners.

The main house had forty of the Waffen SS troops manacled. Bart entered the office on the second floor and found Heinrich Müller standing with his hands in the air. Bart removed his gas mask and pointed his Colt .45 at Müller, who was being prodded from behind by a masked figure in camouflage clothes. The figure had an automatic rifle buried into Müller's back, while the other hand carried a machine gun with its ammo belt dragging over the carpeted steps.

"Jacques, is that you?" Bart coughed.

The machine gun was rested on the landing. The mask was removed and Jacques said, "Herr General was busy on a dead telephone."

"How did you get into the house?"

"I climbed up on the ropes and looked in the window on the second floor. *Voila!* There was our prize, General Heinrich Müller, at his office desk trying to reach *Der Führer*, or who knows."

Bart pulled Müller's hands behind his back and quickly applied handcuffs.

In slightly accented English, the general demanded, "Who are you and what are you doing here?"

Marines were hauling manacled prisoners out the front door.

Bart pointed at the proceedings and replied, "You Nazi rat bastard, what does this look like? Take a guess."

The Nazi general rattled off in German, "American swine, you are out of your jurisdiction. The Argentine government will deal with you. America will pay a heavy price for your actions today."

In his meticulous German, Bart snapped back, "*Heil Scheisshitler, du arschloch*, your gory, murderous days are over!"

Taken aback by Bart's linguistic expertise, Müller reverted to English and said, "Why you handcuff me?"

"Let me make it very clear, Gestapo general, you are a Nazi war criminal who escaped from our troops. You are under arrest by the U.S. Government, with the help of the Argentine authorities."

Through the open windows and doors, the night breeze was clearing the residue of tear gas. Jacques pushed Müller into the well-lighted dining room. In the center of the table was the half-devoured birthday cake. The swastika was intact in the center of the sugar-encrusted batter.

"Take a good look at your swastika, the last tribute to your *Führer's* birthday," Jacques said, pointing.

He lifted the platter holding the cake and smashed the swastika portion into Müller's face. The cake splattered the Nazi's double-breasted jacket. Bart's surprise was evident. "Jacques, why?" he queried.

"Bart, I want a little personal time with this son of a bitch. He was the one who ordered my family to Auschwitz. I've waited almost ten years for this moment. It took all my strength to keep from blowing his brains out when I had him upstairs," Jacques answered bitterly.

Taking him aside, Bart calmly said, "My friend, contain yourself. We have a lot of work to do with him and the others. You'll get time with the pig."

The fifty-two captives were manacled and chained. All were sitting in the wet grass two hundred yards away from the main house. Müller, escorted by Bart and Jacques, was placed in the rear of a bus.

General Whitney asked, "What the hell is that on his face?"

"Jacques dumped the cake in his kisser," Bart said, explaining the motive.

After hearing the explanation, the general declared, "It's a wonder he didn't kill him on the spot."

"Luke, we now have to sweep each building and basement for arms, evidence, and any Nazi goodies we can find. Would you assign some details for the search?"

At that moment a loud explosion jarred the complacency that had pervaded the scene. The barn blew burning wood skyward. The scene had been evacuated, with everyone assuming that the fire had been contained.

"Everyone stay put!" Metcalf shouted.

Whitney, Milburn and Laurent ran to the barn and soon learned the cause of the eruption. Fifteen high-priced cars were shattered and burning. Fire hoses quickly contained the fires. A count revealed that four Daimlers, three Rolls Royces, five Cadillacs, two Jaguars, and a Bentley had been destroyed.

Five Jeeps with four armed Marines fanned out on the hundred-acre ranch to check the outbuildings. Twenty Marines entered the main house for a thorough search from the attic to the basement. Jacques and Bart went to the second floor and probed the desks, closets, and false walls.

Ten men, five at each end of the tunnel, crawled through the underground passage, exploring the walls for hidden entries, and reconnoitered the walls for movable barriers leading to stairways. They found two repositories of two large aluminum-lined arsenals, containing arms and ammunition, ten machine guns, one hundred Soviet Kalashnikov automatic AK-47s, boxes of hand grenades, hundreds of Walther 7.65 handguns, flame throwers, explosives of various types, dynamite fuses, fourteen armor-piercing bazookas and fifty rockets. A lieutenant, Terence Corrigan, crawled rapidly out of the tunnel and ran to General Lucas Whitney. He saluted smartly and anxiously described a find in the tunnel.

"Lieutenant, do you see that second truck? Take twenty men and very carefully remove everything in those two arsenals. There has to be a latched door in the ceilings. It's probably covered by grass. They didn't count on moving that stuff through the tunnel. Wait, I'll go with you. Get the truck and the men. Bring plenty of flashlights. I'll try to activate the electric system."

Müller's desk contained maps of Paris, with the Eiffel Tower photographs, architectural drawings of its structure, and photos of the Versailles palace. Jacques found a strong metal lockbox. "Shall I shoot the lock open, Bart?"

"Can't you pry it open?"

"I'll try."

He found a screwdriver. After prying and pounding, the lock sprang open. Inside was a stack of official Nazi envelopes sealed with wax swastikas.

"We'll take the box and examine those documents later," Bart ordered.

In the guesthouse, Captain Kirk La Follette unearthed a tall safe hidden behind a door. It was covered with a tapestry depicting pirate Norsemen plundering the coast of Europe in the 8th century. Captain La Follette found Colonel Metcalf and disclosed the discovery of the safe. "Find Colonel Milburn, and tell him of your find. Tell him I want to see him. He's somewhere in the main house."

Bart and Jacques exited the building, lugging their spoils. Captain La Follette saluted Bart, and informed him that Metcalf wished to discuss the safe he found.

The temperature was falling to the middle 40s. The prisoners sitting on the wet grass were moaning, groaning and shivering. Bart passed them and yelled, "*Schweigert!*" He approached Metcalf. "I think we ought to put these SS tough guys in those buses with the wire-gated windows. I don't want any pneumonia cases among these bums."

Metcalf issued the order, and the prisoners shuffled their way onto the paddy wagon-type buses. Armed Marines were assigned to guard them.

"Now, what do you want to do with that safe, Bart?"

"Joe, do you have a talented safe burglar among your men?" he asked jocularly.

"No, but I have a former banker who might have that talent."

"Let's try him. If we fail, we'll blast it open."

"Major Kyle Carlton, up front."

A tall, rugged redhead saluted both men, then said, "Sir, if one of the medics will lend me his stethoscope, I'll try to click it open. I assume it has a standard combination lock on it."

The medics were going through the prison bus, patching head wounds on the SS troopers.

The major borrowed the listening device and followed Bart and Jacques. He sprawled on the floor, applied the stethoscope to his ears and placed the rubber listening device against the locking mechanism. He twirled the numbered-disk combination lock. He heard a click, raised a finger and wrote a number on a pad. Fifteen minutes later the taciturn major's personality changed. He turned the safe handle and with an infectious smile, exclaimed, "Tah-dah!"

Jacques echoed, "*Fantastique!*"

"Good job, Major," Metcalf said, tapping his back.

The safe was laden with assorted currencies, a pile of twenty-dollar gold coins, diamonds, rubies, emeralds, and plain gold wedding bands. The jewelry was obviously loot taken from the hapless victims of the Holocaust.

Files of correspondence, pre- and post war, as well as wartime, were in specific manila files. All were addressed to Adolf Hitler. A quick glance at the voluminous files encased in open manila jackets, where each had an identification tag at the top, revealed some astounding names. Among them were Lady Astor, Lord Halifax, Neville Chamberlain, Joseph P. Kennedy, the Reverend Charles Coughlin, Fritz Kuhn, the Duke and the Duchess of Windsor, Juan & Eva Peron, Ernest Bevin, and Charles Lindbergh."

A large briefcase with a combination lock was pried open by Jacques. It contained maps of the Panama Canal, Washington, D.C., Tel Aviv, Paris, London, Holland, Belgium, and Moscow, a detailed layout of the Kremlin, photos of all four sides of the White House, plus an architectural rendering of the interior, and 10 Downing Street and an aerial photo of Chequers, Churchill's retreat.

They searched the house for luggage. They found five suitcases and filled them with the contents of the safe. Four Marines carried the cases to the bus containing the other plunder.

A Jeep with an American flag attached to the fender raced into the razed Nordheim enclave. A helmeted Marine brought the vehicle to a stop at the bus where Bart was directing the placement of the confiscated material. Seated next to the driver was Tony Fuentes.

"Hey, boss, I bring news!" Tony shouted. "General Smith called and asked me to relay a message to you."

"Let's have it."

"All important prisoners and contraband go with you to Guantanamo. The Gestapo prisoners and whoever else you decide go to the stockade at Homestead Air Base. Secretary of Defense Lovett has arranged a secluded military jail there. General Alton Gregory expects the load."

"Excellent. How did the *fandango* go with the Perons?"

"*Perfecto*. The Navy guys treated him like an emperor. Ambassador Withers was fabulous. Eva and Sophia were as close as sisters. Long speeches by all. Medals for Peron, a special medal for Eva and a red, white and blue sash. A long concert by the Marine band, a full-swing inspection of the Enterprise. The admiral gave Peron a history of the battles of Midway and the Coral Sea. We watched the Argentine navy maneuvers in sync with ours. We stalled on the way back, claiming mechanical problems. We dropped them off less than forty-five minutes ago. They're thoroughly exhausted."

"Time for us to get the hell out of here. Sophia and you are coming with us to Guantanamo," Bart said.

"She's at the hangar with our bags, waiting on you."

"Come with me. I want to get this show on the road."

General Whitney and Metcalf worked with Jacques, sorting out the prisoners for the buses allocated for the chartered planes to Cuba and for the newly designated trip to Homestead Air Force Base in Florida. The Rangers and a detachment of Marines would act as guards en route to Guantanamo. Metcalf called the Marines to attention.

"At ease, men. Colonel Milburn has a few words for you."

"My deepest appreciation and highest praise to you men for your excellent execution of this operation. You did your jobs with skill and courage. Not one of you was injured. We have been the beneficiary of a perfectly executed surgical attack. Your mission here will be recorded in history. My compliments to each and every one of you. My highest praise to General Whitney, Colonel Metcalf and your entire corps. I speak in behalf of your Commander in Chief, President Truman. Thank you, all."

"In behalf of our men," Colonel Metcalf said, "It has been an honor to serve with you, Colonel Milburn, in such a worthy cause. This is undoubtedly an exclamation point to the end of World War II. Down with these Nazis and up with the Stars and Stripes forever! You and your deputy, Jacques Laurent, have earned our highest admiration. Three cheers for both of you."

The hurrahs blasted through the quiet of the starry night.

☆ ☆ ☆ ☆

Friday, April 25, 1952 - 8 a.m. - Washington

President Truman, his counsel Clark Clifford, Attorney General McGranery, Secretary of the Treasury Snyder, Secretary of Defense Lovett, General Omar Bradley and General Walter Bedell Smith were having an early breakfast in the White House dining room. Then the table was cleared, hot coffee was served, and the butler departed, closing the doors.

"All right, Omar, let's have it," Truman requested.

Bradley delivered a terse report on the four sorties in Malmo, Hamburg, Paris, and Rio de la Plata.

"A clean sweep. Not one man injured. The raids were surgically performed.

Colonel Milburn planned this with precision and succeeded. He is a man of unquestionable talent. If he had stayed in active service, he'd be a general by now."

"Why don't you recommend a star for him?" Truman suggested.

"You said it first, Mr. President. I'll follow through."

"Now comes the hard part, gentlemen," Truman said. "We have all the big ones in the Revenge Plan. We also have the entire Waffen SS Gestapo gang, at least over fifty of them. We have the counterfeiters and the plates. We have the whole enchilada, including Bormann and the Führer. How long can we keep this under wraps?"

"From a legal standpoint, Mr. President, the Department of Justice should get into the act. Colonel Milburn and the CIA haven't enough legal personnel to interrogate this gang. Then, we must plan for trials," McGranery declared.

"I agree. What do you have in mind?" General Smith responded.

"I can furnish up to ten assistant U.S. attorneys, highly qualified interrogators whose lips will be sealed, to assist Milburn."

Clifford, the President's counsel, having been briefed, spoke up, with his habitual gesture of putting his hands together with his fingers tapping one another. "Mr. President, we are fully aware of this earth-shaking news," he slowly and methodically summed up the problem. "Hitler, Bormann and General Müller are clearly war criminals. After a preliminary hearing, there is no doubt that a judge or a court *en banc* will order a trial. Do we turn them over to The Hague, try them here in the United States, or set up a repeat of Nuremberg? Here, of course, we will have a media circus, with every country in the world watching it on television. A very serious problem is, who would be willing to defend them?"

Snyder quipped, "At best, three outstanding Jewish lawyers."

After the laughter, Truman addressed the Attorney General. "Jim, I like the idea of using assistant U.S. attorneys. Let me discuss it with General-to-be Milburn."

☆ ☆ ☆ ☆

Friday, April 25, 1952 - noon, same day - Guantanamo

Bart Milburn and his team had returned to Guantanamo Naval Base and were preparing to interrogate the new arrivals. First, however, Bart decided to pay a visit to his prize catch, and Richard Maybrook accompanied him. From the doorway of the padded cell, it was impossible to equate the craven figure in a fetal position on the slab bed as the strutting Nazi Führer who had almost conquered all of Europe.

"Take a break, fellows," Bart said, excusing the guards. "I'll whistle for you when we're through here."

"I can't believe this is the man," Maybrook whispered.

"Now, watch this, Rick."

Bart noisily opened the cell door and in a very loud command, yelled,

"*Achtung, Heil* Hitler!"

The body stirred, his hands rubbing his eyes, trying to adjust his sight to the glaring overhead light. In a gratingly hoarse voice, Hitler said, "*Heil, was ist los?*"

Maybrook stared at the man, shorn of his beard and mustache, with his shaven head and face showing stubble, trying to sit up on his slab bed.

"Are you sure this is the *Führer*?" Maybrook asked.

"Ask him."

"*Du bist der Führer?*" Maybrook struggled with his German.

"*Du Dummkopf. Ich bin der Führer.*"

"What did he say?"

"He called you an *idiot* and said he's the *Führer*. Talk English, Adolf," Bart commanded.

"Oh, it's you again. You're trying to starve me to death," he uttered weakly.

"No, we won't let you off that easy. You remember the people you starved in Auschwitz, Dachau, Nordhausen, Buchenwald and Ohrdruf?" Bart reminded him. "Well, now you've had a slight taste of their suffering."

Hitler's thin, emaciated, pallid face quivered. His hands trembled as if palsied, and his lips had turned blue. Bart whistled loudly and the guards rushed to the cell door.

"Call the medics to come immediately. Hurry!" Bart ordered.

Maybrook grabbed Hitler's bony wrist and attempted to feel his pulse. Bart sprinkled water on his forehead. Hitler's murmuring was unintelligible.

Lieutenant Golden and another medic came in. The doctor checked his pulse, took his blood pressure, and reached into his bag for a hypodermic syringe, then injected it into Hitler's buttocks. He squeezed Hitler's cheeks to open his mouth and slipped a pill under his tongue. Within minutes his trembling stopped. "Hold him up, please," the lieutenant ordered.

Maybrook balanced him in a sitting position. The medic gently gave him some water. After a few sips, Hitler grabbed the plastic cup and guzzled the cupful in one swallow.

"What's wrong with him, Doc?" Bart asked.

"Two things. He's dehydrated and suffering what I would call a hunger spasm. He is in a state of fright, as well. His heart's okay. This is something that occurred frequently at the concentration camps. If you want him alive, better start feeding him some regular food, Colonel."

"Thanks, Lieutenant."

"Don't thank me. If I had my way, I'd kill the son of a bitch," he muttered softly. "But, as a Doctor under orders, I did my duty here today."

"I understand your emotions, but what is your professional advice as to food?"

"Feed him some chicken soup with matzo balls," the lieutenant snickered. "All right, vegetable soup, soft bread and some fruit. A banana would be good - that is, if you want to keep him alive. He's lost quite a bit of weight."

"Would you oblige me, Lieutenant, and ask that Marine chef to send that food down as soon as possible?"

"Is that an order, sir?"

"If that's required, the answer is yes."

The lieutenant saluted, and so did Bart. The medics left and the guards were excused.

"That lieutenant is Jewish, isn't he?" Maybrook asked.

"Yes, and has quite a record. They called him *Golden Hands* during the war in the Pacific. Much decorated and, according to the admiral, he saved more arms and legs during Midway and Coral Sea. He's here for another year as a favor to Thomas."

Hitler silently sipped on another cup of water.

"Listen, Adolf, your Revenge Plan has fallen apart. Froelich, General Müller, Fliegel, and your whole Waffen SS Corps have been captured. Your counterfeit operation has been seized. Your bankers are in prison. Your show is over," Bart said.

"You lie to me," the crestfallen Nazi leader moaned.

"No, it's the truth."

"I trust no one. I want proof."

"You'll get proof," Bart replied, and headed for the door.

The next stop was a visit with Konrad Fliegel. The little man, head shaved, was sitting on his bed, mumbling to himself. He barely noticed Milburn and Maybrook enter. Bart ordered the guards to bring two chairs into the newly prepared cell in the annex brig. The guards left for a much-desired break.

The two men sat close to the prisoner, who continued with his mumbling.

"Herr Fliegel, how are you today?" Bart asked in German.

The hapless man strained his eyes in an attempt to focus on his visitors.

"Not very good. Do you have my eyeglasses? I cannot see you too well."

"Speak English and I will look for your glasses," Bart offered.

Maybrook found a pair of gold rimmed, dust-covered bifocals on the guard's desk outside the cell. He handed the spectacles to Fliegel, who used the sleeve of his prison garb to clean the lenses. He adjusted the glasses with his two manacled hands.

"Who are you?" he asked.

"We are officers of the United States government," Bart replied.

"Why am I here?"

"You are under arrest on a number of charges. Conspiracy to aid and abet the escape of Nazi war criminals, also murder, attempted murder, planned assassinations, money laundering, counterfeiting, treason, and..."

"Enough, enough. Stop that litany of nonsense," Fliegel said in perfect English. "This has gone too far. I've had enough of this Nazi business. I wish to see a priest."

"A *priest* and not a *rabbi*?" Bart sneered.

"No, I am no longer going to pretend to be a Jew. That was Nordheim's idea. I am Catholic. I want to confess my sins and go on to my maker."

"You wish to commit suicide. Is that what you're saying?"

"Hell no, it's a sin to do away with oneself."

"Let's start with the truth," Bart urged, turning on the tape recorder.

"My name is not Konrad Fliegel. It is Keith Reynolds. I was a British citizen before the war. I served as a comptroller in the office of the Chancellor of the Exchequer during Prime Minister Neville Chamberlain's administration. Ambassador Joseph P. Kennedy, America's envoy to England, was a very good friend of the Prime Minister. I met him at a dinner at 10 Downing Street. He was very interested in my position. The ambassador had me to lunch a few times, always probing me about world financial affairs. He was vehemently against the possibility of war with Germany. He liked Hitler and said he was building Germany into a great power. He wanted the U.S. to come to Hitler's side."

Milburn and Maybrook were enthralled with Fliegel/Reynolds' sudden admission. The prisoner reached for a plastic cup. Maybrook poured water into it.

"Go on, Keith," Bart gently urged.

"Keith - ah, it is a long time since I've been addressed by my true name. I was invited to a dinner at the Court of St. James's by Ambassador Kennedy. I had just been promoted to Assistant to the Chancellor of the Exchequer. It was at that dinner that I met Charles Lindbergh, Lady Astor and other members of the Cliveden Set, rich people supporting Hitler. Lindbergh told the guests that evening that he had been to Germany several times and that Goering's Luftwaffe was the most powerful in the world. He had no doubt that his Nazi air force could bomb England and France into submission. Kennedy and the rest of them were very anti-Semitic and blamed the Jews for all the world's ills. All of them approved of Hitler's treatment of the Jews. I knew a number of Jews in the British government and industry. I respected them and met with them socially, so I was confused by Kennedy's hatred of Jews."

"What made you change your citizenship?" Maybrook asked.

"My wife died of cancer on July 30th, 1939. This was quite a blow to me. I had to raise two young daughters. Kennedy is a Catholic and so am I. He came to the services for my wife and sent a tremendous amount of flowers to the funeral. Prior to that, he helped me invest in a number of American stocks and some English shares. I made quite a bit of money. He had me place my funds in a Swiss bank."

"Which one?" Bart asked.

"The Banque Lorraine in Geneva. A few weeks after the funeral, he invited me to his office. He questioned me about Chamberlain's weakness with the English voters and Churchill's popularity. Then, like a bolt out of the blue, he advised me to leave the country because there was going to be a terrible war. Where would I go, I asked him. Then, he said something very strange."

"What was that?" Maybrook pressed.

"He said he could get me a job at the Banque Lorraine. He had a good friend there, the president of the bank. I could be of great help to him over there, he said. I could become a very rich man and be able to protect my children before the war broke out. I thought about it for two days before I got back to him. He called von Leute. I flew to Geneva, met with the bank president. He offered me a munificent salary, a contract and a beautiful house at a ridiculously low price that the bank would carry on one hundred percent mort-gage at three percent interest. There was one catch - I had to become a Swiss citizen. He recommended a prestigious school for my two teenage daughters. I promised to let him know my answer in a few days. He was very charming. We chatted in German for awhile. He was impressed with my knowledge and pronunciation of German. I also spoke French with him."

"What happened after that?" a mesmerized Bart asked.

"I flew back to London and left a message for Ambassador Kennedy to call me. I talked it over with my two children. They thought it was a great adven-ture. Two days later, Kennedy's office called and told me to come to his office for lunch that day. He told me that Hitler was going to invade Poland. I agreed that I would resign my position that day and would accept von Leute's offer. On August 28th, 1939, I had my sister put my house up for sale or lease and, with my two daughters, we flew to Geneva. Kennedy was right. Hitler invaded Poland three days later."

He stopped at that point and begged Bart to remove his handcuffs, which was promptly done. He also said, "I'm famished, sir. May I please have some food?"

They removed his shackles and took him to the admiral's office. Then they moved into the conference room for a repast of freshly squeezed orange juice, scrambled eggs and crisp bacon, croissants, fresh butter, and large pots of coffee and cream.

Fliegel-Reynolds had a ravenous appetite, so he was served a second por-tion of eggs and bacon. Bart replaced the tape in his recorder. The admiral quietly joined the trio and partook of coffee.

"May I have one of your American cigarettes?" the surfeited prisoner asked.

Bart handed him a pack of Marlboros and lit it for him. Keith inhaled deeply.

Over the next two hours, Fliegel-Reynolds poured out a huge amount of amazing information about Hitler, Bormann, Goering, Goebbels and Himmler; the large amounts of Jewish accounts in Swiss banks, the laundering of bona fide currencies and counterfeits; the vaults filled with gold, jewels, cut dia-monds, and loot seized from conquered countries. He told of Kennedy's ma-nipulations in his bank accounts, as well as Hitler's accounts and transactions in the name of Nordheim and Winston General Ltd. He divulged information about I.G. Farben, the Perons, and art collections and valuables stored in vaults in Geneva and Zurich. He outlined Switzerland's role in helping Nazi Ger-many finance its war effort, and he decried the Holocaust and the world's inaction to the Nazis' bestiality.

He painted a macabre portrait of the excruciating torture of Jews: the maniacal and methodical execution of millions in gas chambers, the starva-tion method of death, outright machine-gun mass murders by firing squads and grave digging by victims for their own burial in large pits. Himmler, he related, thought bullets were too expensive, so they devised gas executions in the guise of showers. Vultures flew over the death camps.

"How did you know all that?"

"I was sent into Germany during the war to pick up money from these evil, licentious, murdering bastards for deposit in our bank. I met Goering, a fat drug addict, in the midst of an orgy of men and women at the Four Seasons Hotel in Munich. Another time I met Himmler and he took me to Dachau, nine miles outside Munich. Later he showed me pictures of his gas showers, boasting how he had saved money by putting large numbers of men, women and children in his death chambers. The people were naked. Soft music played. It was ghastly. I have nightmares of dead, emaciated bodies stacked up on top of each other."

He came to a sudden stop, then cried out, convulsively sobbing, "Oh, my God, why was I a part of all this? May God forgive my transgressions," he prayed. "Killing all those Jews. Why?"

"That's enough for today," Bart declared.

They had Fliegel-Reynolds moved to a bedroom with bath, but under observation. The shock of his disclosures was evident on every face.

Admiral Thomas advised Bart that the plane from Hamburg had arrived an hour before. Berger supervised the placement of Admiral Horst von Ludwig, vice president of Eagle Shipping, and the two bankers, Ricardo von Leute and Peter Weber, into special cells far apart from each other. The rest were placed in the brig annex.

Sophia and Tony were asked to write a report on their talk with Bormann. The admiral had already prepared a memo of his session with Sir Clive Fenwick.

"This being a Friday, and a fruitful one at that, I declare the weekend be devoted to a little R & R, while our miscreants stew in their Nazi juices."

A chorus of "amens" followed. A forlorn Jacques and his partner Gaumont joined the gathering in the conference room.

"Bart, those three unidentified companions were hard-nosed bastards," Jacques declared. "They wouldn't answer any questions. We decided to turn them over to the medics for examination, cold showers, shaved heads and whatever. Noah fingerprinted them and got mug shots before and after the treatment."

"Good. Richard, call Flaherty at the hangar and tell him to prepare for a flight to Havana," Bart told Maybrook.

Admiral Thomas pulled Bart aside. "Mind if I fly to Havana for a little R & R over this weekend? I've been stuck in this outpost of civilization too long. I need a break. My excuse is to confer with you." He grinned and winked.

"Be my guest, and you are welcome to stay at my house."

"Oh, no, I want to stay at a hotel, wear my civvies and explore that haven of iniquity."

"You can stay at the Hotel Riviera in a suite at no cost. We have the sixth floor for our people."

With what sounded like a *non sequitur*, Bart asked, "How do you like Maybrook?"

"I like him very much. He's a bright lad with a good sense of humor. Why do you ask?"

"You'll need a companion to wander this wide-open city. He's a bachelor and would enjoy your company."

"Colonel, for a tough hombre, you are a kind, thoughtful and gracious friend. I accept. Let me change into plain clothes and notify Captain McMahon to take charge of this store."

Bart called the villa, advising Elizabeth that her wandering lover would be returning home.

CHAPTER TWENTY-SIX

Friday, April 25, 1952 - 5 p.m. - Havana

The cadre of heroes, consisting of the admiral, Maybrook, Sophia, Tony, Jacques, Gaumont and Bart landed at the José Martí Airport. A shuttle bus took them to the villa. Bart had called ahead to have Stanley prepare drinks and hors d'oeuvres and to prepare Elizabeth for the shock of unexpected guests. Bart insisted they come in. After a few demurrals, they were persuaded.

The police guards at the gate saluted. Elizabeth pecked a kiss at Bart and graciously greeted the guests. She ushered them into the capacious den.

Jacques nervously looked around for Christina. Gaumont stared at him. Bart asked, "Where's Christina, Liz?"

"She wasn't certain that you wanted her here. She's in the playroom with the children, Mrs. Bishop and Elsie."

"Jacques, drag her out here."

He returned shortly with Christina and a telltale mark of lipstick on his mouth. She shook hands all around and opted for a dry vodka martini. Gaumont kissed her hand.

Bart explained to Christina that they were all associates in his endeavors. "They are friends, as well."

He then went on to explain who Christina was. All expressed their sympathies.

"Now, before you all leave for the hotel, I want you to meet our special troops. Brace yourselves for the onslaught. Stanley, have the squad come in."

In short order, Michael and Jenny jumped into Bart's lap, whooping, "Daddy, I missed you!"

Matthew and Katherine raced into Jacques' arms. "Uncle Jacques!" they squealed.

The children switched their attacks from Bart to Jacques and vice versa.

"Colonel, I see another side of you. I am impressed by your beautiful family. And you, too, Jacques," Admiral Thomas remarked.

A Dalmatian puppy named Squire appeared on the scene, sniffing for friend, foe or food. The admiral lifted the dog into his lap and petted him.

"Mrs. Milburn, I have come to admire and respect your husband as a very tough military man, and I must admit he is a man of exquisite taste to be fortunate enough to have you as his wife. He also strikes me in this atmosphere as a thoroughly domesticated man."

"Thank you for your kind words," Elizabeth replied in her English accent. "You've mentioned the military and the domestic, but I assure you that there are many more personas to my dear husband, each of them evident in specific areas, war or peace."

"Admiral, the history of the Milburns is legend," Sophia interjected.

"I am familiar with their war experience, the romance and this beautiful result," Thomas said.

"We've got to be off, Bart," Maybrook prudently suggested, so Jacques and Bart saw them to the waiting shuttle bus.

Gaumont whispered to Jacques, "You love that Christina, n'est-ce pas? She is magnifique."

"Dear friend, she makes life worth living. I am going to ask her to marry me."

"I am happy for you."

The shuttle left for the Riviera Hotel.

Later that evening, Bart and Elizabeth engaged in pillow talk. Bart expressed his feelings of guilt for not having spent much time with his family.

"Darling, Bart, you're such a good man. I understand the scope of your undertaking. I'm so proud of you. Keep at it, my love, and I'll back you all the way," She declared emotionally. "I love you."

"Elizabeth, you are a pillar of strength for me and our children. I love you, too," Bart replied as he doused the bedroom lights.

The weekend was a joyous one for Bart, Elizabeth, Jacques, Christina and the children. On Sunday evening, a splash of cold water came through the phone.

"General Milburn, your President would like to see you tomorrow at 3 p.m.," John Steelman said.

"John, this is not a propitious time for me to leave Cuba. We struck a treasure trove of information. The head man's treasurer is doing a mea culpa and has opened the Pandora's Box of Nazi evil."

"Bart, this is an order. Be here."

The next sound Bart heard was a buzzing dial tone.

Jacques was at the guesthouse with Christina. Bart advised him of his trip to Washington and ordered him to have Maybrook, Tony, Sophia, the admiral and himself return to Guantanamo to continue probing Fliegel-Reynolds.

"Take charge, Jacques, and be sure he's treated with empathy. Get him to spill everything. We need a lot of detail. Be sure he's well fed. He's a ripe banana, so peel him carefully. Let Sophia provide the feminine touch and compassion."

"I understand, Bart. It will be handled your way," Jacques assured.

☆ ☆ ☆ ☆

Monday, April 28, 1952 - 3 p.m. - Washington, the White House

Steelman met Bart at the West Gate entrance. He was returning from a luncheon meeting. After leaving his cab, Bart walked into the West Wing and halted Steelman before entering his office.

"What's this *General* crap you threw at me last night, John?"

"Just a little joke," Steelman slyly replied. "Come on, he's waiting for you."

The door to the Oval Office was open. Truman was at his desk, talking into a speakerphone.

"That's fine. I'll see you here at four," he concluded, waving Milburn into his office.

"Have a cup of coffee and light one of your infernal cigarettes, if you like, then listen carefully without interruption to what I have to say," the president said.

Bart did just that, realizing that Truman's mien indicated that a matter of importance was about to be divulged. During the fifteen-minute recitation by Truman, the colonel drank two cups of coffee and smoked three cigarettes.

"Well, Colonel, can we drag this tangled web in silence through the next seven months without a leak?"

An irritated Milburn, very much in control of his emotions, coolly and in clipped tones, said, "It hasn't leaked up to now, has it, Mr. President?"

"I'm afraid so. The Dulles brothers, no doubt."

"A secret shared is no longer a secret," Bart philosophized.

"Exactly. Well stated."

The subject was set aside momentarily while Bart detailed the bonanza of information revealed by Fliegel-Reynolds.

"Barton, my boy, you're either a very lucky man or a genius. You've struck the mother lode of the machinations of Hitler's Third Reich. You're in position to perform an autopsy on the body politic of Nazism. I am very impressed and congratulate myself for having chosen you for this assignment."

"Thank you for the praise, Mr. President, but one correction, sir - I was not chosen. I was drafted." Bart smiled.

Truman laughed, "This is more fun that that Korean mess. You would have been miserable with that pompous press hound MacArthur. I'm glad I removed him."

"Where do we hide Fliegel?" Bart queried.

"I've got it," the President uttered, slapping his desk. "What better place than Blair House? It's guarded by my Secret Service. For the present, it's the last place Dulles would think of looking."

"How do I get access?"

"There is a back door for service deliveries. I'll clear you with the Secret Service so that you and Jacques can get at him at any time."

"I would like to place a couple of men to live with him and keep him under constant surveillance and away from telephones."

"We'll put him on the third floor. We'll cut off the phones. Your people can have access to the second floor for phones. How does that sound?"

"That's a plan, Mr. President. The two men I have in mind are Army Rangers I trust fully."

The red light blinked, and Truman picked up the phone. "One minute more, John."

"It's fortuitous that you mention the Rangers. Just the man to arrange that is coming in here now."

Truman buzzed the intercom. "Send them in, John."

General Omar Bradley and his aide, Colonel Drew Croll, entered the Oval Office, escorted by John Steelman, with a broad grin on his scholarly face. Bart stood up and saluted the general and his aide.

"I guess it's time for me to leave, Mr. President," Bart said.

The four men laughed. Bart was perplexed. Truman was quietly gloating, a self-satisfied smile on his face. General Bradley and Colonel Croll suddenly turned stone-faced. Bart had a fleeting thought that he was about to be activated out of retirement.

"Barton Milburn, stand at attention," Bradley ordered.

He assumed the posture.

"You are hereby promoted to brigadier general in the Army of the United States Reserves. We are proud to present you with these stars. Further, you have been awarded the Medal of Freedom for services rendered above and beyond the call of duty."

Croll stepped up and pinned the medal on Bart's lapel, then handed him the stars. Bart was nonplussed, standing at attention.

"I guess now, General, we ought to call him out of retirement," Truman laughed.

"Congratulations, General Milburn," Steelman said, shaking his hand.

Bradley, Croll, and the President followed suit. At Truman's request, the five men relaxed and sat down.

"I have some special bourbon here, so how about a toast?"

Steelman filled the glasses and poured a little branch water with it.

"To our new general," Truman toasted.

"To you, gentlemen, I can only offer my profound thanks for the honor conferred upon me today. Here's to your health, sirs," Bart returned the toast.

"You earned it, son," the President declared.

☆ ☆ ☆ ☆

Same day - Guantanamo Naval Base

Phillip Berger entered Admiral von Ludwig's cell, prepared to interrogate him.

The arrogant prisoner had lost none of his cavalier demeanor, despite the restraints and his bleak confines. "Who the hell are you people, and where are we?" he shouted.

Berger ignored his question. Adopting an attitude of utter disdain for his prisoner, he removed a Colt .45, casually examined it, and set the safety catch. He deliberately put it back in his jacket's side pocket. He stared at the admiral eye to eye for a minute without a blink. Von Ludwig turned away and pretended to adjust his handcuffs. Berger continued his stare.

"Why are you looking at me like that?" the admiral asked in a quieter tone.

Berger shook his head from side to side, indicating a momentary sympathy for the prisoner. "You're in a barrelful of trouble, Herr Nazi," he said snidely.

"I am *not* a Nazi."

"Horst von Ludwig, vice president of Eagle Shipping, which is owned by Adolf Hitler, is not a Nazi? Surely you're not a communist?" Berger twitted.

Von Ludwig expressed a look of surprise. He asked, "Why am I here like a common prisoner?"

"Von Ludwig, you're not a stupid man. Your English is perfect. Stop playing the innocent fool. You're facing a hangman's noose for a myriad of crimes."

"What crimes?"

"Escaped Nazi war criminal, obstruction of justice, accessory to murder, counterfeiter, war crimes against humanity, Hitler's associate, ecetera."

"I don't know Hitler."

"Bullshit. Nordheim is Hitler. You know it and we know it. We have him locked up. He confessed. So stop playing games with us."

"What do you want from me?"

"The truth. The absolute truth, and maybe I can help you."

"How?"

"Tell us everything and I can make life a little more bearable for you. Once the trial starts, it will be too late to make a deal with you."

"What kind of a deal?"

"Maybe a suspended sentence. Maybe a release, if you testify against your Nazi friends. Full cooperation, no lies, and go all the way for us."

Von Ludwig sat on his cot, his head cupped in his manacled hands, his elbows on his knees. There was a long silence. Berger sat stock-still. Suddenly the admiral's arrogant demeanor collapsed, and tears began to run down his cheeks.

"I am not a Nazi, nor was I ever. I was in the German navy when Hitler became chancellor. I worked my way up to admiral in the high command. We didn't like Hitler. He was a maniac when he declared himself the Führer."

Phil turned on his tape recorder.

"I have a wife and four beautiful children," the admiral continued. "They are now living in Copenhagen, Denmark. We escaped in early April, 1945. There was no doubt that the war was lost. There was an order received by naval headquarters in Bremen for a ship to deliver a load of gold and other valuables to Buenos Aires, Argentina. We knew that the British and American armies were moving fast in our direction. I was in charge of assignments for the German fleet. Our days in Bremen were numbered."

"So how did you and your family escape?" Berger gently said.

"There was a U-boat, an *unterseeboot*, a submarine, as you call them, just off the coast of Holland. I ordered it to Bremen. My family lived in our home in Hannover. I drove there and took our valuables, necessities and family to my headquarters in Bremen."

"Who ordered the boat to take the gold and stuff to Argentina?"

"The message came from Martin Bormann."

"All right, go on."

"An army truck arrived. Soldiers and some of our naval personnel helped load the U-boat with large wooden boxes. The captain of the submarine was Lieutenant Commander Otto Vermouth, an old friend of mine. I had promoted him to the command of that U-boat. He was very grateful to me. I called him into the office and told him that my wife and four children were in a room upstairs. My wife's family lived in Copenhagen."

Berger broke in, "Was your wife a Dane?"

"Yes. Her parents were very important people in Denmark. They came to Germany in 1939 on a diplomatic mission; her father was an emissary of King Christian X, to sign a ten-year pact with Hitler. I met her then at a reception. We danced and fell in love at first sight. Two weeks later we were engaged, and a month later we married. She spoke perfect German. Later, Hitler invaded Denmark."

"How old was she then?"

"Nineteen. I was twenty-seven and a lieutenant commander assigned to naval intelligence, headquartered in Bremen. I bought a home in Hannover. So I was close to home."

"You really produced four children in a hurry. How old were they when you escaped?"

"Eight, six, five and three." Von Ludwig laughed weakly, managing a sickly smile.

"So, what happened then?"

"I pleaded with my old friend Otto to take us on board the U-boat. I wanted him to drop us off on the coast of Denmark. It was still occupied by the German Army. He finally agreed and I brought my wife and children to the U-boat. They were placed in Otto Vermouth's cabin. I wore my admiral's uniform. He radioed the German command in Copenhagen to have a motorboat meet the sub and to have a car ready for the admiral. It was close to midnight and we were quickly transferred ashore. The U-boat headed into the North Sea and immediately submerged for its journey to Argentina."

"There is something that smells about this story."

"What do you mean, smells?"

"Where did you go in Copenhagen?"

"Very simple. The German command and the Gestapo were ordered not to mistreat or bother my wife's family, on orders of Hitler relayed by Martin Bormann. I drove directly to their farm estate on the outskirts of Copenhagen.

The Daimler was mine to use. When I knocked on the door of the main house, my father-in-law almost fainted when he saw me in my uniform. My wife ran up to him with the baby in her arms and the other children behind her. He quickly pulled us into the house and bolted the door."

"Didn't Hitler try to find you?"

"No, Bormann covered up for me. He knew later where I was. He was good to me. He never told Hitler I left my post in Bremen."

"You're telling me all this of your free will?"

"Yes. I am sick of the Nazis, and I'm ashamed of the stain they left on Germany by killing all those Jews."

"You're not an anti-Semite?"

"Hell, no. Before the war, I went to school with Jews. I ate at their homes. They came to my home. My family had close Jewish friends and got them out of Germany in the middle of the Thirties."

"You're not making this up?"

"In the name of God, I swear it's true. You know how the Danish people protected Jews during the occupation of Denmark?"

"Yes, but what has that to do with you?"

"My father-in-law, Christopher Salmar, was hiding twenty Jews on the farm. They worked in the fields. He clothed them, fed them and even paid them all through the war. I worked on the farm with them."

"What did you do with your uniform?"

"I burned it."

"How did you get connected with Nordheim's Eagle Shipping Company? Also, did you know he was Hitler?"

"May I have some water, please?" Von Ludwig asked.

Berger filled the plastic cup. He removed the handcuffs and handed him the water. He drank it slowly.

"In December 1946, the day after Christmas, a Mr. Darren Mayfield showed up at the farm, which I was managing."

"What did Mayfield want?"

"I was in downtown Copenhagen, buying supplies. He spoke to my father-in-law and told him he had a very important business proposal for me. When I got home, they were having coffee and talking about farming."

Berger was getting impatient.

"Well?"

"All right. Mayfield handed me his calling card. He was a vice president of administration for a company called Winston General Ltd., of Vaduz, Liechtenstein. My father-in-law excused himself. Mayfield whispered to me that Martin Bormann sends his regards and thinks very highly of me. He recommended me for an important job running a fleet of ships for Eagle Shipping, a subsidiary of Winston General. I told him I was doing very well managing this farm. He asked how much I was earning. I said six figures in American dollars. A hundred thousand, he said. I said a little more. Two hundred thousand, he said. I said no, not quite. Then he threw a number that staggered me."

"What was that?"

"Five hundred thousand a year plus bonuses of ten percent of the profits annually. A five-year contract, and we'll let you carry your meat and dairy products for export at half the price of any competitor. I asked if it was a public company. He replied that it was owned entirely by the richest man in the world, a Jew by the name of Fredrick Avram Nordheim, who escaped from a concentration camp."

"What happened next?"

"I talked it over with my father-in-law and my wife. They all agreed I should check it out. I went back to the dining room and asked, where is Mr. Nordheim, and where would I be operating? He said forty-five minutes away from Copenhagen by ferry in Malmo, Sweden. He also added that they would buy me a new house in Copenhagen as an inducement to signing a five-year contract with options of five years each term, and a million-dollar bonus if I sign for each option period."

"Pretty handsome offer."

"He invited me to Malmo to meet Nordheim the next day. Nordheim had a Van Dyke beard, large mustache, wearing Western cowboy boots, dungarees, and a Stetson hat like they wear in the American movies. He was very charming and explained that his fleet was growing fast and he needed my talents. He handed me a prepared contract. I took it home and showed it to a lawyer in Copenhagen. He said it was a fine contract. Two days later I signed it. They paid for a house on twenty-five acres near the ranch. They agreed I could commute to Malmo five days a week. Weekends free. I might have to travel to various ports of interest."

"When did you suspect or find out..."

"About six months before you arrested me, I met with Bormann at the ranch in Rio de la Plata. There was a strange meeting there of some Nazi faces I recognized from the Waffen SS. I wasn't invited to the meeting. I saw a lot of guns. Some of these men were dressed like *vaqueros* - you know, Argentine cowboys. I couldn't believe what was going on there. It looked like the old Nazi military stuff. Then I recognized General Heinrich Müller. He recognized me. He called me Admiral, shook hands and said welcome to the good old days. My suspicions grew."

"Did you think that Nordheim was Hitler at that time?"

"No, Nordheim's face didn't look a bit like Hitler. He was at least three inches taller than the *Führer*. After that, I learned we were shipping arms to North Korea. This fellow Mayfield bribed one of my men to reroute two ships bound for Israel to North Korea. They disappeared. There was some talk that the Americans bombed them during an air raid on Chongjin."

"Now listen to me, carefully, Horst. I am recording everything you say, so tell everything you know about Hitler, Bormann, Goering, Goebbels and Himmler and all the other degenerate Nazis," Berger ordered. "I expect you to testify in court. If you lie about anything, your life is *kaput, fini*, done, finished, over and out. *Verstehen?*"

"Yes, yes, I understand. This may shock you, but please believe me, while I was suspicious of the whole bunch, I actually learned that Nordheim, who pretended to be a Jew, was *Der Führer* early that evening before your raid."

"You're right, that is hard to believe. You've been working for this man for six years and now you say that you just found out he is Hitler?"

"Please, I swear on a Bible, this is the truth. I had very little personal contact with Herr Nordheim. I would hear from Bormann sometimes, but never directly from Nordheim. Until April 22nd, I thought Hitler was dead."

"Then how did you learn that Nordheim was Hitler?"

"After dinner that night. One of the men was Eric Volberg, a vice president of the Banque Royale in Zurich. He was a very rude, uncouth boor of an alcoholic. He wanted me to go with him to the Reeperbahn to make a little *bumsen*."

"Yeah," Berger cut in. "This was a strange location for a gathering."

"I was amazed when I first saw that street full of whores. Anyway, I said no. *We better stay here*, I told him. He was very drunk and talkative. *Why don't you drink?* he asked me at the bar. The other men and women were at the piano. One of the ladies played it and they kept singing. I took a beer. Eric raised his glass and whispered, *Heil Hitler*. I said *Hitler's dead* and told him to stop that Nazi *scheisse*. *Du trottel, arschloch*, he called me. *You're working for Hitler and he's not dead. He owns you*, he said. *You're crazy*, I said. *Nordheim is Hitler, holzkopf*, he insisted. He continued with *Heil Hitler*. In short, he told me Hitler escaped, had plastic surgery, grabbed billions and will rise again. Then he said something shocking to me. He said, *One of these days he's going to blow up the Panama Canal and you're the man picked to arrange it, Admiral von Ludwig. Heil von Ludwig*."

"An amazing story, Horst. I hope you are telling the whole truth. I have one more question, and I want a straight answer."

"What is it?"

"If you truly despise the Nazis, then why did you stay on?"

"My country was at war. I was sworn into the navy to serve my country. Was that any different than what your soldiers did to the American Indians, or the Spanish-American War, or what happened in your Civil War, brother against brother? What about General Pershing's war against Mexico? What are you doing in Korea now? I'm sure that lots of soldiers in those actions fought valiantly in wars they didn't agree with. Besides, look how the Negroes are treated in your South."

"That's a specious argument. Apples and oranges."

"Specious? Apples and oranges...?"

Berger cut him off. "Specious means inaccurate and untrue. Apples and oranges are two different items; you can't compare them to each other. You and all the Germans allow a Christian, cultured country to turn demonic. Is that patriotism?"

"I am ashamed of Nazi Germany. The Holocaust will be an albatross around its neck for hundreds of years. Hitler and his gang of street thugs took over our government by brute force. They executed anyone who opposed the Nazis.

But I was in the naval part of the war and was isolated from all this. I learned of the atrocities like the Allies did, after the war. What more can I say? I'm Christian, with full belief in God. I beg forgiveness for me and all of Germany."

"We'll talk some more, Horst. I'm going to remove you from this cell and put you in some decent quarters with better food."

"Thank you; you won't be sorry. I'd like my family to know I'm still alive."

"We'll try to do something about that later. Now, behave. You'll be moved within the hour."

Berger took his tape recorder and hastened to the admiral's office.

Maybrook, Sophia and Tony were in the conference room. The admiral was on the phone in his office. Berger waved at him and pointed to the conference room. The admiral joined them. Berger recounted his session with von Ludwig. The admiral used the intercom to move von Ludwig into a room with a bath and regular meals, at Berger's request.

"Those three unidentified men from Paris, what have we got so far?" Berger asked.

"Captain Gaumont has been working on them in regard to counterfeiting," Maybrook answered.

"Wrong track," Berger snapped. "Get Gaumont in here."

Gaumont was summoned from the brig and joined the group.

"How goes it with those three?" Maybrook asked.

"They are tough and tight-lipped. The Arab pretends he speaks no English, French or German. He..."

Berger almost jumped out of his chair. He half rose, fell back and exclaimed, "Arab! Oh, shit. This guy is one of the three guys that Froelich was bringing to Hamburg. They're not part of the counterfeiting. Felix, you were in the Paris raid. Besides the phony money, there was an arsenal of explosives, grenades, flame-throwers, bazookas and AK47s. In Hamburg we found one hundred or more AK47s and two hundred handguns. Were Froelich and his three companions bringing the contents of the Paris arsenal to Hamburg? They were all going to meet on board the Bald Eagle ship. Ponder that, my friends."

"You're obviously referring to the Revenge Plan and that last statement by von Ludwig about the Panama Canal," Tony concluded.

"Right on, Tony."

"I've got an idea," Maybrook said. "We have mug shots of those three. How about having the countess show them to Bormann? We'll see how cooperative he will be with his *amour*."

"Great suggestion," Sophia assented. Tony cut her a jealous look.

Maybrook opened his briefcase and handed the countess pictures of the three unidentified prisoners. Then she left, with Tony following.

The admiral ordered sandwiches and coffee for the conference room.

☆ ☆ ☆ ☆

Jacques and Noah Davis were in the dark room on the floor below. The telephoto machine slowly spun three photos and a memo over the revolving rollers. Davis stood back against the door as Jacques hovered over the machine. A red light cast an eerie glow on the two men. Noah removed the telephoto material and handed it face down to Jacques.

"Sergeant, thank you very much."

"My pleasure, sir."

Jacques went upstairs and looked at the photos in the light. The names of the three intransigent prisoners were clearly printed under their pictures. They were Hans Langsdorff, Herman Klaus and Abdul Ahmed-al-Said.

The memo described the men, reading:

Hans Langsdorff, former captain of the Graf Spee, scuttled his hunted battleship off the coast of Uruguay after being surrounded by three British cruisers in December, 1940.

Herman Klaus, captain of an Eagle oil tanker, running oil from Iraq, Saudi Arabia and the Arab Emirates.

Abdul Ahmed-al-Said, also known as El Cobra, lives in Libya and is desperately wanted by the Israelis. He's responsible for three bombings in Tel Aviv, killing a total of 46 innocents, some of them tourists, and injuring over 125 men, women and children. Speaks English, German, Arabic and Aramaic. Dangerous and slick.

Love, Lucy

Jacques went to the conference room, where Maybrook, Berger and the admiral were finishing up lunch. He laid the photos and the message before Maybrook, who read it aloud. Sophia returned with Tony.

"Bormann recognized two of the three," she said.

As the telephotos were passed around, they reached Sophia.

"He gave us the two Nazis, but didn't know the Arab," Sophia said.

Berger seized the pictures of Langsdorff and Klaus.

"Admiral, where have you put von Ludwig? I want to show him these two photos."

"He's on the floor above Bormann's quarters. An MP will direct you."

"I'll be right back."

Phil found Horst von Ludwig stretched out on a comfortable bed in a neat room.

He stood up. "Thank you, Phillip. You kept your word."

"Horst, look at these pictures and identify these men."

"Oh, that's Herman Klaus, captain of an Eagle oil tanker. This other man is familiar...let me think for a minute."

Berger paced the room impatiently. Von Ludwig reached for a pack of cigarettes. He asked Phil for a light. Phil threw his lighter to von Ludwig, who casually lit his cigarette while staring at the picture. He handed the lighter to Berger's outstretched hand without looking up, absorbed in his study of the photo. "Yes, yes, I know him," he exclaimed. "He was a hero in 1940. This is Hans Langsdorff, the captain of the Graf Spee who scuttled his battleship so the British navy couldn't capture it. You must know that story, Phillip."

"I sure do, Horst."

"Why do you ask about these men?"

"These are two of the three men that Froelich was bringing from Paris."

"I don't understand Klaus being in Paris. He's supposed to be in the Pacific as captain of the Gold Eagle, delivering oil to Japan. Langsdorff is also a surprise. I thought he was retired."

"Thanks, Horst." Berger raced back to the conference room.

When he entered the room, Jacques was just getting off the phone. "That was Bart," he said. "I've been ordered to D.C."

Same day - Washington

John Steelman walked with Bart to the west exit of the White House. Secret Service agent Gary Farmer met them at the door.

"General Milburn, this is Gary Farmer, one of our best Secret Service agents. He will drive you to your destination and will stay with you until his services are not required."

"My pleasure, General," Farmer said with a smile.

"I'll call you with an ETA, Bart, and don't forget to call me at eleven tomorrow." He turned and said, "Thanks, John."

Gary Farmer brought a Lincoln Town Car to the door.

"First stop, Gary, is the Cafritz Building. Drive right up the ramp to the fifth floor."

"Yes, sir."

Ten minutes later Bart invited Farmer into the reception room of Graybeal, Arnold & Milburn, where Miss Telford greeted him effusively.

"What a wonderful surprise," she gushed.

"Hello, Nancy. Coffee for that gentleman in the waiting room, please."

She called Luigi for the coffee.

Bart placed the silver stars and the Medal of Freedom on his desk blotter. Miss Telford was about to place some checks to be signed on the desk when she noticed the items.

"Oh my God, you've been promoted! And that medal! Oh, I am so *happy*," she sang. "Congratulations!"

Bart busily signed checks as Miss Telford ran to tell Austin Graybeal and Martha Arnold the good news. The two partners entered the room. Bart stood up to greet them.

"Is it really *General* Milburn?" Martha asked.

"I'm afraid so," he replied.

Austin walked around Bart's desk and hugged him.

"Look at his medal!" Telford giggled.

Martha picked it up.

"Medal of Freedom, *my, my*. You must have done something spectacular.

Can you tell us?" she queried.

"All I can say is that the mission has exceeded all expectations."

"Congratulations, and no more questions, General," Austin said.

"Dear partners, I regret I haven't been carrying my load here. But, I'm sure when you learn the facts of my errant behavior, you'll approve of my activities," Bart said.

"Rest assured, you're carrying your load, Bart," Austin replied.

"I may or may not be in town for a few days. I'll keep in touch through Miss Telford. I have to leave now. Thank you both for your support."

"Good luck, General," Austin said.

Gary Farmer drove through the heavy homeward-bound traffic to Clinton, Maryland, the site of Andrews Air Force Base. After identification, they drove on the tarmac to Hangar 11. They sat in the Town Car and listened to the radio news. Due to Daylight Saving Time, the sun was slowly dipping in the west. At 8:10 p.m., the Fairchild F-27 taxied to the hangar.

"That's us, Gary," Bart exclaimed.

The plane came to a stop. Major Flaherty lowered the automatic ramp. Jacques and Fliegel-Reynolds debarked without a word. The prisoner, dressed in civilian clothes, was hustled into the back seat of the Lincoln. Farmer sat quietly at the wheel of the car. Jacques embraced Bart. "Colonel, good to see you."

"Jacques," Bart laughed, "it's *General* now."

"No kidding."

"It's true."

Jacques, in a mocking gesture, stood at attention and saluted.

"But to you, my brother, I am still Bart. How's Keith?"

"Excellent. Cooperative and grateful. Take a minute here I have something to tell you. Who is that driving the car?"

"That's Gary Farmer, a Secret Service agent stationed at the White House. Truman assigned him to us. He knows nothing about us."

Jacques recited the developments before his call summoning him and Fliegel to Washington. He revealed the names of the three recalcitrant, formerly unidentified prisoners captured in Paris. Bart was mulling over the startling information when Major Flaherty approached the duo. He saluted Bart and asked, "Will we be needed any more this evening, Colonel?"

Jacques couldn't resist. "Major, it is *General* Milburn from now on."

Flaherty saluted again, "Congratulations, General Milburn."

"Thank you, Major. No, the evening is yours. Give Jacques a phone number where you can be reached. I'm not sure at this point whether we'll be here for a couple of days or flying back sometime tomorrow."

"General, the plane will be fueled, stocked and checked out for flight at any time."

"Thank you and your crew. Have a nice evening, Major."

Agent Farmer drove them to the service entrance of Blair House. There was total silence during the trip. On arrival, Farmer whispered to Jacques, "If you need me, the general should call Dr. Steelman."

Edward Hopkins, the chief butler, greeted the three arrivals and escorted them to their quarters on the third floor, then said, "Choose your own rooms, General. We've set up a dining table in the drawing room. When ready for supper, dial the front desk."

All the rooms were tastefully furnished. Bart took the suite. For security reasons, Jacques and Keith were assigned to connecting rooms. After their ablutions, the three men joined at the supper table in the drawing room. Bart dialed the front desk.

A waiter appeared. "Something to drink, gentlemen?"

"Keith, what would you like?" Bart asked.

"A dry gin martini, if possible."

"Yes, indeed, sir," the waiter replied.

"Two vodka martinis for us."

Keith was awed by the surroundings and the attention. "I am very grateful to you, gentlemen, for your treatment of me," he said.

"If you want to get back to your daughters, just be honest with us," Bart reminded. "Cooperate and you'll be treated well."

"Sir, I am glad to cooperate and to purge my soul of the despicable connections with these Nazi vermin. I have been praying to God for forgiveness for my sins."

"Good for you, Keith. God will help you if you are sincere," Jacques said.

The three men ordered small salads, sirloin steaks, baked potatoes and assorted vegetables. After dining, they sat on leather chairs in the corner of the spacious room. Napoleon brandy was poured into snifters. Jacques and Keith lit cigars. Bart smoked a cigarette.

"This is more like my days in London," Keith declared.

"Would you return to England if you could?" Bart asked.

"If they would take me back, I would love it. With all I have to reveal about the Swiss banks, I can't go back to Switzerland. Maybe, if free, I could stay in America."

"We have a relocation program for people who testify for the government. That might be the answer for your problem. You'd better get your daughters out of Switzerland. Who is looking after your daughters?"

"My sister, who was widowed in the last month of the war. She came to live with us in Geneva in 1947. She had no children of her own. The girls-Louise is now sixteen and Gladys is seventeen-have been raised by their Aunt, Letitia Wesley, and myself. Mrs. Wesley is still a British citizen. When I'm home, she goes on holiday to England. All she knows about me is that I was a banker who later became treasurer of Winston General."

"How did you come to leave the bank?" Bart asked.

"I stayed with the Banque Lorraine until 1950. Winston General was the bank's largest depositor. Herr Froelich and Sir Clive Fenwick visited the bank in February, 1950. They were there for lunch in our dining room, and president von Leute asked me to join them. I had met Sir Clive, when he was ambassador to Germany, at dinners with Prime Minister Chamberlain."

"Well, what happened at the lunch?" Jacques impatiently inquired.

"It was a routine lunch, bankers with important customers. Over coffee and cigars, it was no longer a mundane affair once Froelich addressed von Leute. *We are looking for a new treasurer for Winston General, Ricardo, and I think we've found him,* he said. *Who would that be?* von Leute asked. *This man right here,* he said, pointing at me. I was shocked. To shorten my story, von Leute agreed to let me out of my contract and to keep the mortgage on my house. Sir Clive pitched in and said they would pick up my contract and double my salary. I had no say in the matter. That's how it happened."

"Did you ever sell your house in England?"

"No, I lease it for high rentals, mostly to Americans. During the war, a rich refugee family from France had it on a long-term lease. A broker handled the details for me."

"Is the house still occupied?" Bart asked.

"I don't know. Why do you ask?"

"I have a suggestion. Your sister, Mrs. Wesley, should take your daughters with her back to England. The children are still British citizens, are they not?"

"Now that you mention it, sir, we never changed their citizenship. I was the only one that did."

"Since the Banque Lorraine had given you a one hundred percent mortgage, let them foreclose and keep the house. Besides, I doubt that Mr. von Leute will be seeing that bank for a long time, so this would be a most propitious time for them to leave Geneva. They can do it quietly, as if they were going on holiday," Bart suggested.

"How do I get word to them, and how do I get my money out of the bank, sir?"

"Let's see, now. No one knows that you are being detained here. You haven't been gone that long. The Banque Lorraine will still take instructions from you, am I right?" Bart said.

"Yes, that's true."

"How much money have you deposited there?"

"In American dollars, I'd say about twelve million."

Jacques and Bart remained serene, despite the startling disclosure.

"Are they aware that your true name is Keith Reynolds?"

"No, they only know me as Konrad Fliegel."

"Is that the name on your passport?"

"Yes."

"All right, follow me carefully. Recently, Nordheim had the bank buy American treasury bonds."

"Yes, I arranged some of it."

"Good. Have them wire all your funds to an American bank to buy ten million treasuries and place two million in the account of Keith Reynolds. Tell them not to ask questions, that you're following Herr Nordheim's instructions. I'll have papers for you to open such an account here with a prestigious bank. Only you can draw that money. I will allow you two monitored phone calls, one to your family in Geneva and the other to the bank.

In no circumstances will you be allowed to pass a secret message. If you try, back in jail you go."

"You're asking me to trust you completely."

"Any doubts, then forget it. Your funds will be frozen here or there, no matter. At least here we'll allow you to draw sums for your family. Remember, you are still a war criminal and possibly subject to charges of fraud in connection with your service at a Swiss bank, which has been defrauding Jews out of their families' deposits."

"I'd like to think on this overnight."

"By all means, or leave everything status quo."

Bart went to his suite and placed a call to Elizabeth, engaging in small talk and endearing terms. Jacques did likewise from his room to Christina in the villa's guesthouse.

☆ ☆ ☆ ☆

Tuesday, April 29, 1952 - 8 a.m. - Guantanamo Naval Base

Phillip Berger visited Ricardo von Leute in his rancid cell. The distinguished banker, head shaven and mustache removed, presented a grotesque comparison to the fastidious banker arrested in Hamburg. His manacled hands and shackled legs added a bizarre note to the scene.

"How are you today, Herr von Leute?" Berger snidely inquired.

"You American dogs will pay for this. Do you realize who I am?"

"Of course. You're a miserable Nazi-loving thief and a counterfeiter. You are the scum of the Earth. You and your Swiss colleagues have stolen billions from dead Jews. You've helped finance the Nazi war machine. You're guilty on all counts. That's who you are. You're facing a hanging or a firing squad."

The embittered prisoner's voice fell several decibels. "You're not serious."

"I couldn't be more sincere."

"How could this be?"

"I just told you, slimeball. All those charges are true. You will never see your homeland again."

"I'm entitled to a lawyer."

"Not as a Nazi war criminal."

"I am Swiss, not German."

"You could be an Eskimo, for all I care. You're an accessory to those who committed war crimes, and war criminals don't get lawyers until their trials. Your life is over, *du Zuhalter*."

"Pimp, you call me?"

"You arrogant snake, you and your Nazis don't know what tough is. We kicked the shit out of Hitler's Nazi bastards. They lost the war, and you Swiss bloodsuckers are still helping them. We have Nordheim, who is really Hitler, in custody. We have Bormann, Peter Weber, Admiral von Ludwig, Konrad Fliegel, Gunther Froelich, General Heinrich Müller and his whole frigging Waffen SS, and we know about the conference on the Bald Eagle."

"My God, is this all true?"

"You better believe it, *du Scheissekerl.*"

"Stop insulting me."

"I've got some more good news for you, *Oberhauptmann.* We have captured your Graf Spee hero, Captain Hans Langsdorff; Herman Klaus, and your Arab explosives expert Abdul Ahmed-al-Said, a.k.a. *El Cobra.* How's that for a jackpot?"

The dignity of the prisoner was shattered. He howled, "I begged Nordheim to forget his Revenge Plan. The man is a lunatic!" His face turned beet red and his teeth chattered.

"You have one chance to avoid a death sentence, or possibly a way out of your despicable plight."

"What is that?" von Leute gasped.

"A full confession, and to testify at the trials against the whole stinking cesspool of Nazis."

Von Leute was panicking and sweating profusely. It was a pitiful sight to observe this cavalier member of the powered gentry decompose.

"Think about it, Nazi lover."

"You have a foul mouth."

"Yes, and that's a compliment compared to your foul mind, heart and soul." Berger slammed the cell door shut, satisfied that he had driven a wedge into the supercilious façade of the banker. Phillip then walked directly to the cell holding Peter Weber. The Swiss banker was fast asleep when Berger clanged the cell door back and forth. Startled by the vibrant resounding of the steel prison door, Weber sat up suddenly, a look of fright on his stubbly face.

"Confession time," Berger roared.

"Was ist los?"

Berger wasted no time and repeated his performance with von Leute. Weber remained mute during the tirade. However, the jangling of his metal restraints indicated his emotional reaction.

"Von Leute has confessed, Weber," Berger lied. "Think about it, *Scheissemeister!"* he shouted as he opened the cell door.

"Wait!" Weber screamed.

The cell door slammed closed as Berger departed, yelling, "Later, Nazi."

☆ ☆ ☆ ☆

Admiral Thomas, tape recorder in hand, visited with Sir Clive Fenwick. The session was cordial and businesslike.

The recorder was on, and Sir Clive gave his recital of Nazi horrors, duplicity among the royals and the inbreeding of the monarchs of Germany and England. Kaiser Wilhelm and King George V were first cousins, the sons respectively of Queen Victoria's eldest daughter and eldest son. He described the weakness of Prime Minister Neville Chamberlain and the influence of Ambassador Joseph P. Kennedy on Chamberlain, and the pro-Nazi role of the

Cliveden Set and Charles Lindbergh. He detailed the relationships of the former King of England, Edward VIII, who renounced the throne for a married woman and later became the Duke of Windsor, marrying the woman, Wallis Warfield Simpson, after her divorce. The duke and duchess admired Hitler and visited him several times just before the war. Hitler expected England to surrender and put the duke back on the English throne. Fenwick poured out the saga of intrigue, deceit, the wanton mass murders of Jews in the concentration camps, and the Swiss banks financing the Nazi Wehrmacht. He revealed the laundering of counterfeit money. Hitler's intent was to destroy the American and British banking system. Sir Clive then ended that session with his mea culpa: "While I was ambassador to Germany, I followed the line established by Chamberlain. I was guilty of giving him some very tainted advice. I am ashamed of myself, but I was not involved in the money matters. Froelich's domain was finance. He also helped Hitler build up a massive fortune. I admit I am a rich man."

The admiral shut off the recording machine and returned to his naval chores. In another cell, Sophia was milking more information from Bormann. Meanwhile, Tony Fuentes stopped by each of the cells of the three no-longer-unidentified mystery men. His visits were short and to the point. He showed photos to each man. All three had been given the treatment of examination and had their hirsute adornments shaved from head and face. With Herman Klaus, he showed him his picture and remarked, "You were supposed to be delivering oil to Japan."

Klaus looked discomfited.

Tony left quickly and entered Hans Langsdorff's cell.

"Here's your picture, Mr. Graf Spee. You should be ashamed of yourself to be associated with these Nazi bastards."

Langsdorff muttered, "I was never a Nazi. I was a German officer."

"Bullshit," Tony snapped, then opened the cell door and slammed it closed.

☆ ☆ ☆ ☆

Abdul Ahmed-al-Said, inhibited by his leg shackles, was attempting a lotus position. Struggling with his leg irons, he barely focused on Phillip Berger.

"Where's the Frenchman?" he snarled in German.

"He was insulted, El Cobra, when you threw the bacon to the floor," Berger snickered in English.

"El Cobra, what is that? Besides, I don't eat pig food," he said, switching to English.

"Here's your picture, Abdul."

The prisoner clumsily straightened up.

"*Ahmed* and *El Cobra*, what's that?"

"Stop the crap. You are Abdul Ahmed-al-Said, known the world over as *El Cobra*. You're wanted by Interpol, the FBI and the Israelis."

"Fuck the Israelis! We'll eventually drive them into the sea and one day we'll take over America. What Hitler started, we'll finish. We'll kill every Jew in this country. Hang me and I go to Allah."

"*Schmuck*, you'll not be hanged. First, we'll give you some lessons in torture. We have a mechanics squad to deal with you before we give you to the Israelis."

"Mechanics?"

Berger outlined Bart Milburn's concoction of the mechanics' mystical procedures.

"Americans are too soft for that," the Cobra ventured.

"Were they soft during the war? We made the Gestapo look like pussycats. We just kept it quiet. You Arabs think you invented torture; we learned a lot from the Nazis and the Arabs, we took it one hundred steps farther. We keep you alive all during the mechanics' treatment. You'll beg us to kill you, but you'll suffer a thousand times worse than the victims of the Holocaust."

"I spit on the Americans and the Israelis," Abdul hissed, then spat on the floor.

"Ahmed, you're a filthy animal, and I'm going to recommend we bathe you in a barrel of hot pig fat."

Ahmed began praying to Allah in Arabic. Berger started to leave. His hand was on the cell door when the prisoner cried out, "One minute!"

Phil turned and looked at him contemptuously, then said, "What now, asshole?"

"You wouldn't do that. It's against my religious principles."

"What's so fucking religious about you? You're an amoral sociopath. Don't talk to me about religion after you exploded bombs in Tel Aviv, killing and maiming hundreds of innocent people. Tell me where God accepts a murdering rat like you. God creates humans and you kill them, you rat bastard."

"Who are you?"

"I'm your worst fucking enemy. I am an American Jew."

El Cobra angrily shuffled toward Phillip with his manacled hands outstretched, attempting to choke him. Phillip watched Abdul approaching, then, as he got within reach, Phillip whirled and, with a football drop kick technique, delivered a boot to the stbble-faced prisoner. The inanimate body sailed head over heels onto his slab cot. Blood flowed from his nose and mouth. Phillip had been a punter on the Yale football team.

Berger whistled for the guards. "Take care of this camel dung. He tried to attack me," he said, and exited the cell.

☆ ☆ ☆ ☆

In Gunther Froelich's cell, the president of Winston General looked like a derelict in his prison garb. He looked at Maybrook with an expression of utter hopelessness. The former German ambassador to England tried his diplomatic skills on the newcomer. "Sir, may I ask who you are?"

"I am an officer of the government of the United States. You may address me as Richard, Herr Froelich," Maybrook said, matching the role being played by the prisoner.

"In that case, address me as Gunther. Are you in the diplomatic service?"

"No, something more sinister, Gunther."

"You don't look the part, sir. Sinister in what respect?"

"Sir, I must advise you that you are under arrest, charged with a large number of felonies, under the war crimes act, as well as criminal violations of American law."

"The war has been over for seven years now. How could that be?"

"There is no statue of limitations for war criminals. Besides a laundry list of war crimes to which you have been an accessory, you are being charged with a conspiracy to destroy the Panama Canal, the destruction of properties in America, England, France and Israel, and, of course, your current activity in counterfeiting. Further to that, you have a partnership with Herr Nordheim, who in reality is Adolf Hitler himself. Will that suffice as to *how that can be?*" Maybrook stressed.

"Am I entitled to legal counsel?"

"Not at this time, Mr. Ambassador. War criminals do not get lawyers until we are ready for trial."

"Mr. Richard, you and your people are making a very serious mistake. I have some very prominent friends in your government, in Britain, France and all over the world. Your unwarranted detainment of me and your treatment of me will cause a great scandal."

"For whom - you or us? Your life on the outside is finished. You can only make it easier for yourself by cooperating with us. A full confession and candid answers is the only medicine for a cure to your ailments," Maybrook said.

"I have nothing to confess."

Maybrook's demeanor took a 180-degree turn. "Gunther Froelich, let me advise you to drop that mantle of innocence. Hitler is in custody, as are Bormann, Sir Clive, Fliegel, all your counterfeiters and a host of others."

"But what has that to do with me?"

"Don't be an asshole. We have confessions from most of them. Do you want to be the ugly duckling of this scummy Nazi crowd?" Maybrook capped off the colloquy with the Milburn myth of the mechanics corps. "Think that over, Mr. Diplomat. I'm through with you."

He punctuated the visit with a forceful slamming of the cell door.

In another cell, Gaumont recorded the questioning of the counterfeiters picked up in Hamburg. Karl Sturner and the five printers were quite responsive. Gaumont also tackled Hermann Horstman and his six employees.

All roads led to Froelich, von Leute, Peter Weber and Eric Volberg, vice president of the Banque Royale. Mayfield was mentioned as a distributor and courier.

The team exchanged notes in the admiral's conference room, then retired individually to transcribe the recordings into handwritten copies.

CHAPTER TWENTY-SEVEN

Tuesday, April 29, 1952 - same day - the Blair House, Washington

At a late breakfast, Keith Reynolds, alias Konrad Fliegel, proffered three pages of notes, describing atrocities he had heard about, to Bart Milburn, who read it intently while drinking coffee and smoking a cigarette, then tacitly passed it over to Jacques.

"This is very helpful, Keith; thank you," Bart said.

"General, I have decided to pursue the plan you outlined last night."

Bart looked up in surprise at the use of the word *General*. He realized it was out of the bag when that title was inadvertently mentioned on their arrival at Blair. He decided to let the remark go.

"Very well. Do you have a bank in mind?"

"Yes, the First National City Bank and stockbrokers Merrill Lynch. They are known as the most respected banks and brokers."

"Keith, you are aware that we'll freeze those accounts, except for money drawn in amounts necessary for your family. We will monitor those accounts. All that money will earn interest. If and when you are released, the freeze will be thawed. Then the money will be freed to you. That will be the pledge of our government in writing."

"I am satisfied. I have one request. Could you allow two hundred and fifty thousand dollars to be sent to England for the care of my children and my sister."

"I'll recommend that it be done," Bart agreed.

"You're a gentleman, sir," Keith said.

"Now, I have to make some calls at eleven o'clock. Make your calls now.

Jacques and I will monitor from extension phones. Any untoward remarks and our relationship ends, understand?"

"No problem, General."

"Let's go. Which one first?"

"The Banque Lorraine, then your call in my behalf to the National City Bank in New York to set up my account, and locally here to Merrill Lynch. After that, I'll speak to Mrs. Wesley, and, please, a word of love to my daughters, sir," Reynolds pleaded.

Jacques looked at Bart and nodded in approval. Each man went to his respective room. The calls were made and the transactions completed. Keith was allowed a monitored personal phone call to his family, in which he told them to gather their things and take the first flight out to London. After hanging up, a teary-eyed Reynolds returned to Bart's suite.

"You did well, Keith," Bart commented.

Keith returned to his room. Bart's phone rang. It was Steelman. "How's the general this morning?"

"Fine, John, and thanks for your support."

"You earned it, my friend. You've got four Secret Service men arriving through the service entrance at noon. They are agents Adam Watkins, Sam Collins, Larry Witten and Ken Parker. They all assisted during the raids and have been briefed on Reynolds. They'll guard him in shifts. Mr. Hopkins has been informed to set up the accommodations."

"Thanks, John, and thank the Prez."

"One minute, Bart. The Attorney General has been trying to track you down. Call Jim as soon as you can."

"Will do, John. After I set up this Secret Service watch here, I'll leave word with them, in case you are looking for me."

Bart called the Department of Justice, and was quickly hooked up with Jim McGranery.

"General Milburn, I presume?" the Attorney General quipped.

"Definitely not Livingstone, Jim."

The jocularity ended there. "I've been trying to locate you, Bart. Where the hell are you?"

"I'm here in town."

"Great. How about lunch today here at my office?"

"Urgent or social?"

"A little of each."

"How's 1:30?"

"See you then, General."

☆ ☆ ☆ ☆

Same day - 1:30 p.m. - the Department of Justice

After a warm greeting, McGranery led Bart into a private dining room. During lunch they chatted about politics, Dwight Eisenhower's chances against

Gov. Adlai Stevenson and gossip on Capitol Hill. After coffee was served, McGranery told the waiter they were not to be disturbed.

"There's been a leak," he declared.

"I know," Bart snapped. "Dulles, I'm sure. While we're on that subject, are you aware of the Dulles brothers' pre-war German connections?"

"Bart, I've read the FBI files on them."

"What's the legal answer to our problem with these Nazi war criminals?"

"Well, let's look at it pragmatically. Hitler, Bormann, that Graf Spee guy and General Müller, plus that gang of Gestapo troops at Homestead, are fair game. I'm worried about the fringe characters."

"You were a judge before you were Attorney General, Jim. Put your robe on for a minute, and let me try my rationale."

"Go ahead."

"Your honor, the men in question have aided and abetted the Third Reich's war against humanity. They financed and connived with the Nazi war machine and their atrocities in the same way as these monsters, Hitler, Himmler, Goering and Goebbels. Those death camps were financed by Swiss banks, counterfeit money, and the gold torn from the mouths of six million Jewish cadavers. Are they not war criminals, sir?"

"Counselor, your argument, in principle, is very persuasive. However, can you cite a precedent?"

"There are many precedents, Your Honor, for ongoing investigations. There is a current conspiracy, sir, to blow up the Panama Canal, the Arc de Triomphe, the Eiffel Tower, the White House, 10 Downing Street and other targets. All these prisoners were gathering for a conference on an operation of Adolf Hitler's Revenge Plan when we took them into custody. This was an ongoing war crime, despite the unconditional surrender of Germany. The prosecution rests," Bart declared with a smile.

"Specious at worst, convincing at best, Bart. But I can't think of a precedent."

"Well, dammit, let's set a precedent. They're getting a preliminary trial with military counsel. When the regular trial is set, they can have all the lawyers they can buy. I can't visualize the Supreme Court overturning a conviction of these sleazeballs. Let's not try them on every count. We get overturned, we try them again on different counts unrelated to the first charges."

"Bart, you're emotionally involved."

"You're damn right I am, Jim."

"If they are tried in the U.S., we may have some flak. But I'm prepared to work with you, Bart."

"Good. One more item. Jim, we've hit pay dirt with a few of Hitler's cohorts."

"Such as?"

"Bormann, Sir Clive Fenwick, Fliegel, Admiral von Ludwig and others are ready to fold. All great witnesses. Now we need concentration camp survivors to depict the sordid story of murder, mayhem, torture, hard labor that led to death, rape of women and children, and all of Himmler's organized gas executions. We also have enough film footage of the camps to break a sphinx's heart."

"Bart, down to business. I have chosen ten assistant U.S. Attorneys to assist you in preparation for trial. Some are Army Reserves."

"Can they be trusted not to leak this story?"

"No doubt. These are career men vying for the top job and eventual judgeships. We'll make them take an oath of silence, if necessary."

"Will they be willing to work solely under my aegis?"

"If I order them to do so."

"Will you?"

"Of course, but I want to be briefed. You will need me, Bart."

"It's a deal. I want to meet them."

"Name your day."

"I'll be at the Blair House the 1st of May. Can you get them to the Mayflower Hotel for a meeting and extended stay?"

"Consider it done," the Attorney General promised.

☆ ☆ ☆ ☆

Same Day - 1 p.m. - Blair House

Lunch had been served in the drawing room for Jacques, Reynolds, and the four Secret Service agents.

During an intensive two-hour interrogation, a Byzantine scheme to destroy the financial structure of the western world was delineated by Keith Reynolds, a.k.a. Konrad Fliegel. Agents Watkins and Collins made copious notes. Jacques helped them record the labyrinthine conspiracy. Nazi agents and the forced labor of expert printers were recruited in conquered countries to manufacture plates for the counterfeiting of foreign currencies. The father of the plan was Gunther Froelich. The mastermind in the execution of producing the fraudulent money was Joachim von Ribbentrop, who was rewarded by Hitler with the post of Foreign Minister. He was tried at Nuremberg for his role in the war. None of his efforts in the counterfeit conspiracy were exposed at the trial. He was found guilty of all other counts and hanged in 1946.

Fritz Kuhn, the leader of the German-American Bund, recruited FBI Agent Darren Mayfield. He helped two expert American counterfeiters, who were out on bail pending trial, escape on a German freighter a few months before the attack on Pearl Harbor. They helped manufacture the printing plates for American currencies. They also located the source of the proper paper. After completing the training of Nazi craftsmen, they were executed.

As the war continued, von Leute and Weber laundered the phony money and processed the cash into the mainstream of commerce throughout the world, helping finance Hitler's war machine, the Wehrmacht.

There were agents in every country, whether belligerents or at peace. They discreetly used the false currencies to bribe officials, industrialists and politicians for the purchase of materials or aid in the Nazi war effort.

This font of information stunned the experienced crime experts. Jacques cynically took in the bizarre account. His experience with the Nazi psyche had inured him to any account of their artifices. Watkins, Collins, Witten and Parker were astonished by Reynolds' detailed account.

"Gentlemen, I had no part in any of this. When I worked at the Banque Lorraine, I handled the book work, never the cash. When I became treasurer of Winston General, all our monies were genuine," Reynolds declared.

"What about the phony money on the yacht and the stuff found in Malmo and Hamburg?" Witten demanded.

"That was Froelich's domain. They never trusted me with their chicaneries, and I am glad they didn't."

Bart returned to Blair House and joined the men in the drawing room. They gave him a short run-through on Keith's cooperative saga. Jacques informed Bart that John Steelman had called.

"All right, men, I need some privacy."

When the room cleared, Milburn called Steelman. After a wait of five minutes, he answered the call. "Bart, we've had a word from Prime Minister Ben-Gurion. He wants you to call Ariel Rubin at the Mossad."

"What's up?"

"Two things. One, Jacques Laurent's sister. The other, he asked the President if they can have two observers present for any trials to be held. The President agreed, and told him you would keep him informed."

"That's fine. What about Laurent's sister?"

Jacques ran to Bart's side.

"Nothing more. Just call Rubin."

☆ ☆ ☆ ☆

Wednesday, April 30, 1952 - 12:30 a.m., Israeli time - Tel Aviv

The Mossad headquarters' operator informed Bart that Ariel Rubin was at his home. "I'll patch you through, Mr. Milburn."

The connection was made. "Colonel, call me in half an hour at my office. I'll talk to you on a safe phone."

Jacques nervously paced the room while Bart quietly sipped a cup of hot coffee. The minutes painfully ticked away on the old-fashioned wall clock as the pendulum slowly swung back and forth. The call was put through thirty minutes later.

"Can I listen in, Bart?" Jacques pleaded.

Bart nodded, and waved at the extension phone.

"Ariel, how are you?"

"Fine, Bart. I see a note on my desk from the prime minister. You are now General Milburn. Congratulations."

"Thanks. I am still Bart to you."

"We have news of Laurent's sister, Joyce."

"He is on the line with us, Ariel."

"*Shalom*, Jacques. We have some partial good news for you."

"*Shalom*, Ariel. I can't wait to hear."

"After Miss Laurent's night class last evening, her contact, Lisa Haber, took her out for coffee. One of our rascals, just back from Argentina, showed up with two members of our underground in a truck from Prague, Czechoslovakia. You guessed it - Sean Briscoe and the two undergrounders, dressed as priests, were carrying a load of barley, hops and potatoes destined for Rostock."

"Where is she?" Jacques cut in.

"Patience, *landsman*," Rubin declared. "She is in a safe house in Rostock."

"Go on, Ariel," Bart said.

"Rostock is a port. Do you have any American ships in that area? If so, we can have them take her to Copenhagen and fly her to wherever she wants to go."

"Ariel, is she absolutely safe?" Jacques pleaded.

"The safe house is a convent and she is dressed like a nun. That's how safe she is, Jacques."

"Ariel, thanks. We'll check on ships in the Baltic Sea. Get some sleep," Bart said.

"What can we do? Should I go over there?" Jacques asked.

"Please, brother, try to look at this as a wartime covert action. Let's check our options. Your presence here at this time is more important. Those Mossad people have proved their efficiency. I'll call the White House now."

"Bart, you're so right."

The White House operator answered, "General, I believe Dr. Steelman is on his way out."

"This is urgent. Please get him at the gate. Please," Bart implored.

"What is it, Bart?" Steelman demanded when he came on the line.

"Forgive me, John. This is personal and of some gravity."

"Okay, Bart, I'll switch this to my office. Hold on." In two minutes, Steelman said one word - "Shoot."

Milburn explained the Mossad caper and the need for a ship somewhere close to Rostock, East Germany.

"Help me if you can, John. If she's caught by the East Germans or the KGB, they'll either kill her or put her into one of their *gulags*. Those commies are just as bad as the Nazis," Bart appealed with considerable emotion.

"Barton, my friend, you have my full attention and empathy. I'll cancel a dinner appointment. First, I have to get an okay from the Prez, then I'll call you back," he said and hung up.

"See, Jacques, our friends have compassion. He's canceling a dinner date. He's going to get clearance from the President. If he gets the go-ahead, the Navy can trace every ship and its location, whether it's a Navy ship or commercial," Bart said.

"Bart, I love you."

"Sorry, Jacques, I'm happily married."

They laughed. The next few hours were long and fretful as they awaited a White House call. Finally the phone rang. "Yes, John?" Bart answered as he pointed to the extension phone.

"Is Jacques on?"

"Yes, sir, I am on."

"I'm not going to give you any information on this line. Come across the street to my office through the West Gate. Hurry."

The two men ran across Pennsylvania Avenue and breathlessly approached the West gate of the White House. Both showed their picture IDs. Janis Henry, Steelman's secretary, ushered the men into the office of the President's aide.

A huge map covered Steelman's desk. His spectacles at the end of his patrician nose, Steelman stared through a magnifying glass at a geographical area that he had marked with yellow see-through crayon. He looked at the two men and motioned them to chairs.

"Admiral Prince, chief of staff of the Navy Department, has gone all-out to cooperate. I can't take chances discussing naval intelligence on an open phone."

"Understood, John. What have we got?"

"We have cruisers and subs in that area. I don't think we can bring them into the act. We don't want to tangle assholes with Walter Ulbricht, the dictator of East Germany, or Joseph Stalin's Soviets. Those commie bastards love international incidents. We armed and fed those bastards throughout the war, and now they thank us every time by pissing on our legs, like stray mongrels."

"So what have we got?" Bart asked.

"There is an American-owned freighter flying a Liberian flag loading up in Copenhagen, Denmark. Its next stop is Hamburg to pick up a load of cars. If the Mossad can move that truck southwest, close to the East-West border, the ship, named the Sea Horse, will slow down to a crawl. Now, this part is tough. You'll need a fast motorboat."

"When is the Sea Horse due in Hamburg?"

"Wednesday, May 2, docking at 8 a.m. She can even come to a stop at any time in the Baltic between the Warnow River mouth to Rostock and the mouth of the Elbe River, leading to Hamburg."

"What assurance do we have that the Sea Horse captain will cooperate?"

"Bart, we don't, until you and the Mossad underground can get your ducks in a row. They have to get that truck to the waterfront without being detected. The transfer of the lady has to be done in minutes. The closer to the East-West German border, the better. My guess is, get as close to the Elbe River as possible, for the safety of the ship."

"Hypothetically, John, the truck finds a spot, they have a motorboat, how do we get the ship's captain to play the game?"

"That's where the buck stops," he replied, pointing to the Oval Office. He paused and looked at the map on his desk, a smirk on his lips.

"All right, John, spring it. What are you alluding to?"

"If, by happenstance, a nameless American cruiser were to be coming off the coast of Denmark toward the Elbe for a visit to Hamburg at the same time the Sea Horse is en route, they could arrange to flank the freighter and have the motorboat slip in between both ships. Then they would be shielded from the East German coast. She boards the freighter, and the motorboat seeks haven in Denmark. They can claim motor trouble, or seek fuel, or whatever excuse they come up with. The lady is en route to Hamburg and the cruiser picks up speed and passes her."

"Clever. Whose scenario is that?" Bart queried.

"An admirer of yours - Admiral Prince. Now, the ship is in your dock. Get going. To you, Jacques, and your sister, all my blessings."

"By the way, John, who owns the Sea Horse?' Bart asked at the door.

"Corisa Shipping."

"Who are they?"

"A couple of boys who grew up on the lower east side of New York. Cort Ryan and Isadore Goldberg. Cor and Isa. How's that for a quinella? Good friends of ours."

"Thanks, John," Bart said.

Jacques, who was holding back emotion, stuck his hand out and shook Steelman's hand. "God bless you, sir."

Bart and Jacques exited and walked back in silence across the street to the Blair House. Just before entering the suite, Jacques raised a question.

"Should Joyce get into Hamburg, will the authorities there hold her?"

"Good point. West Germany is still occupied by American troops. She must be presented to any American soldier and declare that she is seeking asylum in the United States of America. The West Germans don't want to tangle with communist East Germany."

"How do we get word to her to do that?"

Bart rubbed the back of his neck, pondering the question. "Jacques, let me sleep on it. We'll talk in the morning."

As the sun was rising, breakfast was served. Watkins and Collins were having breakfast with Keith. Bart and Jacques ate together. When they finished, Bart broke the silence.

"Okay, I've thought it over. I'll call General Barclay. I'll also have Phil Berger call Chief of Detectives Berndt Werner. He participated in the Hamburg raid. We'll ask them to meet the Sea Horse. Werner will instruct Joyce as to what to say and to surrender herself to the general. She has no passport. I'll get the White House to clear her for political asylum and have the general put her on an American commercial flight. We'll prepay her ticket here. All this depends on the success of the Israelis."

The phone rang. Bart answered. It was Steelman. "I think we've got it worked out."

Bart motioned for Jacques to pick up the extension. "Go ahead; Jacques just picked up."

"Oh, good morning, Jacques. I received a call from Ariel Rubin early this morning. They found a back road leading to a spot at the tip of the Baltic Sea opposite Lübeck. Now, just before the sea narrows at a cove five miles north of Lübeck, which is on the west side, there is room for the Sea Horse and the carrier to flank each other. There is a very small marina ten miles north of there. They hijacked a little outboard motorboat and lifted it on to the truck. They set fire to a few of the boats as a diversion and left by the back road to the cove."

"Now what?" Bart asked.

"Contact Admiral Prince tomorrow morning. He'll fill you in on the next move."

"Will do. Thanks, John," he said and hung up. "You heard it, Jacques."

"I know. All I can do is pray," Jacques murmured.

☆ ☆ ☆ ☆

Thursday, May 1, 1952, same day - noon - Department of Justice

Bart left word with the operators that he and Jacques could be reached at the Attorney General's office. McGranery escorted the two men into a large conference room. Ten men rose to their feet as the Attorney General and his two guests entered.

"Meet General Barton Milburn and Jacques Laurent, head of the Nazi Desk at the CIA. You men will be working under their jurisdiction, as I described to you."

The bright and knowledgeable young men were introduced. They came from the cities of New York, Chicago, Los Angeles, San Francisco, Seattle, Dallas, Phoenix, Detroit, Miami, Philadelphia, and Atlanta.

As the thirteen men dined, the Attorney General outlined a modus operandi for the interrogation process of the fifty-odd prisoners in the Homestead stockade.

The table was cleared and the doors were locked, then the Attorney General turned the meeting over to Bart.

"Gentlemen, you have been chosen to participate in a history-making juridical event. The mission is top secret. I don't think it is necessary to submit you to an oath of secrecy. When you were initially appointed, you took an oath, which covers your affiliation in this case. All of you have been given top-secret clearance. In affirmation of my statement, raise your hands and say *Aye*."

Ten hands were raised in a chorus of ayes.

McGranery spoke up. "Men, I must underscore the importance of your assignment. Not a word of your involvement in this case can be discussed outside of the group present here today. The slightest leak will be pursued to its source. The consequences of such a leak are twofold. One, the leaker will be discharged, disgraced and possibly prosecuted. Two, the leak could destroy the mission."

The ten men focused their attention on McGranery, Milburn and Laurent at the head of the table.

"Now, I am going to appoint a captain of your team. His designation as team leader is in no way a diminution of your talents. I am making this assignment for two reasons. One, to ensure an orderly and coordinated effort. Two, I know this gentleman from a previous affiliation. Please accept it in the spirit of team play. He will report to agent Laurent and me only. Will you raise your hand, please, Gideon Cartman of the Southern District in New York?" Bart requested.

The well dressed, wavy-haired man raised his hand casually. His eyes scanned the room and he smiled at Bart. "Thank you, General."

"I hope you'll feel grateful in the aftermath. In a way, I'm sorry to burden you with this task."

Jacques rolled out a huge blackboard, then pulled down a screen. The lights were dimmed and the window shades drawn. Without a word being said, a movie projector lit up the screen. The silent pictures drew gasps of horror.

The sequence of concentration camps ran five minutes, without voiceovers or graphic descriptions. Fleshless corpses with bullet holes in each skull and stacks of emaciated bodies piled as high as five feet. The first discovery of the Ohrdruf camp on April 12, 1945, by Generals Dwight Eisenhower, Omar Bradley, and George Patton and a young Colonel Barton Milburn viewing thousands of naked tortured carcasses. Vultures circled the charnel area. Open graves with nude bodies of men, women and children with parasitic insects crawling in, out and over the deceased victims. A filmed scene of a Nazi soldier throwing a baby against a stone wall with a crying mother, hands outstretched, obviously pleading for the life of her baby. The soldier, after he kicked the body of the dead baby, turned and fired a shot between the eyes of the distraught mother.

As the film continued, it showed trenches of naked men, women and children tossed on top of each other at the camp. Living and dead bodies were stacked on one another in open pits. The carnage was evident in the final episodes depicted in the screening. It ended with a scene of General Patton, he of the deserved nickname "Blood and Guts," vomiting over a fence behind Eisenhower's and Bradley's backs as they viewed a pyre of burned bodies.

The film footage flickered to its end. The lights went on and the window shades were lifted. Bart's eyes were teary. Some of the men applied handkerchiefs over their faces. Jacques wore a visage of hate, his eyes moist.

"Gentlemen," Bart said, "I believe we have captured your full attention. You are going to meet and interrogate approximately fifty of the perpetrators of these atrocities. They are members of the Waffen SS fighting troops. We captured them in a raid on an enclave in La Plata, Argentina, not far from Buenos Aires. Each one of these men is to be peeled like a ripe onion. Individually, one at a time. Some will crack and incriminate others. The interrogations are to be recorded. Although each man is manacled and shackled, they are tough and dangerous men. You will have at least twenty Army Rangers or Marines to protect you and keep them in line."

"General, what specifically are we to try and get out of them?" Cartman asked.

"Start with the day they were born, their parents, education, when they joined the Nazi Party, how and why, up to their whole career from 1932 to 1945 on to now. Did any of them serve in the death camps? What happened there in detail? Probe, probe, probe, skin every one of them."

"What about those who won't talk at all?" Forrest Sherman of Seattle asked.

Bart delineated his mythical "mechanics" unit and their methods. "If they cooperate, hold out a little hope of some relief in the future. Tell them we don't hang them, but they'll spend the rest of their lives in camps more vicious than Himmler's worst. We've already broken a few higher-ups with these tactics. If they agree to testify at trials, amnesty might be granted. Impress upon them that they are war criminals. Jacques, anything you want to add to that?"

"General, should we discuss the Revenge Plan?"

"Yes, Jacques, lay it out."

Laurent detailed the plan. The shock in the room was palpable.

"Gentlemen, there are rooms for each of you at the Mayflower Hotel," Bart said at the end of the meeting. "Mr. Cartman, call me through the White House operators and I will tell you when to leave for Homestead. Have a nice day sightseeing and whatever."

☆ ☆ ☆ ☆

Friday, May 2, 1952 - Copenhagen, Denmark

The Sea Horse sailed slowly into the Kattegat, separating Malmo, Sweden, from Copenhagen, and leading out to the Baltic Sea. In the open waters, she passed a U.S. cruiser. The captain tooted a single blast, which was returned by the cruiser.

On the trip to the rendezvous with Sean Briscoe and his precious cargo, the cruiser dawdled two nautical miles behind the Sea Horse. The sea was choppy, with a slight breeze flapping the Liberian flag. The sun was dipping into the horizon.

The truck was nestled in the cove behind a row of trees on both sides. Shortly after twilight, Briscoe helped Joyce Laurent out of her comfortable but confining area. She had been sleeping. The beautiful woman, with no cosmetic makeup, greeted him with a nervous smile.

"Hungry, are you, my lady?" he asked in his Irish brogue.

"Oh yes, father."

"What's with the father bit?" he queried.

"You are a priest, aren't you?"

"*Ich bin a Yiddish* priest."

"You're joking."

"No, I am an Israeli and a friend of your brother, Jacques. My name is Sean Briscoe."

She hugged him and planted a kiss on his cheek.

"How is Jacques?"

"He's fine, and part of this plan. Here is a chicken sandwich and a bottle of Coca-Cola. I've removed the cap."

The other two pseudo-priests were on watch, checking out the area. Joyce sat in the front of the truck and devoured the sandwich, finishing the bottle of Coke.

"Sean, where is the ladies' room around here?" she asked.

"Go to the back of the cove. Here's a flashlight. I'll stand guard out here.

Take these Kleenex tissues with you."

"How thoughtful."

One of the men came up to Briscoe and whispered, "There are two guys over to the right about two hundred yards. They're sitting on the bank fishing."

"Let them be. If they are not gone before midnight, I'll take care of them," Sean said, displaying his gun.

"No, no. You can't fire any shots."

"Of course not, Herschel. Just to frighten them. You'll tell them in German that we're *polizei* hunting some thieves. We'll remove our collars."

"Okay."

Joyce returned. They put her in the front seat and told her to relax.

☆ ☆ ☆ ☆

Same day - Guantanamo Base

Martin Bormann was snoring loudly when the cell door opened. He lifted one eyelid and glanced at his visitor.

"*Ach*, my dear Countess, I have been dreaming about you."

"Nothing naughty, I hope."

He managed a raspy laugh.

"Martin, I have some bad news for you, I'm afraid."

He sat up in his comfortable bed, planting his feet in his slippers.

"*Was ist los?*"

"Hitler has placed the blame on you and Himmler for the Holocaust. He confessed that he wanted to ship the Jews, the Romas-you know, Gypsies- and the Jehovah's Witnesses out of the country. He says he didn't want to kill them, but you and Himmler planned the genocide."

"He is a *liar*."

"The Americans want to put you back in a cell with handcuffs and leg irons."

"No, no, that is a terrible mistake. He is trying to save himself. After all I did for that bastard, he turns on me."

"Do you want to talk to the men who arrested you?"

"*Ja*, I want to make things straight. I will testify. They will really learn the whole story."

"I believe you, Martin. You must save yourself. Adolf is not your friend. He used you."

"That's what he did. He has always used me. I saved his rotten life. Tell those men I want to talk to them, now."

He rose from his bed and paced the room. Sophia looked at him, feigning sympathy.

"Go, go, call them."

She left.

In the admiral's conference room, Maybrook, Berger and Tony were in an animated conversation about the recalcitrance of Gunther Froelich and Heinrich Müller when Sophia entered the room. She held up her right hand, thumb and forefinger joined in a circle indicating an "okay."

"Bormann?" Maybrook asked.

She outlined her ploy of pitting Hitler against Bormann.

"Don't tell me he fell for that old con," Tony skeptically challenged.

"Why don't you find out for yourselves," Sophia countered. "He's ready to talk to you."

They rose and followed her to Bormann's comfortable quarters.

"Where is the top man, Countess?" the distraught prisoner demanded.

"These are the men who want to put you back in a cell," she replied.

"*Nein*, I want him here," Bormann insisted.

She turned to Maybrook, "Get the admiral in here."

Fortunately, the admiral was in full uniform when he arrived.

"Are you the boss of this place?"

"Yes, I'm in charge here. What's the problem?" Thomas asked, not fully sure of what had transpired.

Before the countess could clue the admiral, Bormann shouted, "The countess tells me that Hitler accused me and that snake Himmler of being responsible for the Holocaust. These men want to put me back in a cell. Hitler is a sick liar. He turned on me."

Thomas didn't miss a beat. "You say that's not true, Martin?"

"Of course it's not true. I want to tell the whole story. But where is that tall man who brought me here?"

"Which fellow?"

"The big tall man you call Bert."

"Oh, Bart, you mean. He's with the President now trying to decide what to do with you," Tony said. "He's the one who ordered these men to hear your side of the story. That's the American way. If what Hitler said about you is true, then they are going to put you in a cell and let the mechanics take care of you."

Sophia sobbed behind a kerchief, which she held over her mouth.

"Don't cry, Countess. I will talk to these men."

Chairs were added to the room. A tape recorder was placed on a lamp table next to Bormann's bed. Maybrook, Tony, Berger, Thomas, and Sophia sat in a semi-circle facing Bormann, allegedly the most powerful Nazi next to Hitler in the waning years of the war.

"From the beginning, Martin, every detail from the day that son of a bitch was born, when he was Adolf Schickelgruber, until now," Berger forcefully demanded in German. "But do it all in English."

"*Ja*, I'm ready."

"Say your name first," Maybrook cued.

"Martin Bormann, and Hitler is a lying lunatic!" Bormann began with a vengeance.

"No, no. Start at the beginning with everything you know about him," Berger cut in.

Over a five-hour session, with a few breaks for nourishment, Bormann unburdened himself with a detailed history of the evils committed by the

Nazis. Himmler was the chief executioner, with extraordinary power to destroy Jews, Gypsies, Jehovah's Witnesses, etc. He recounted the roles of Goering, Goebbels, Hess, Ribbentrop, Keitel, Kaltenbrunner, Rosenberg, Frank, Frick, Streicher, Seyss-Inquart, Eichmann, Sauckel, Jodl, Speer, Müller and Froelich. Also, as he continued his litany of horror, he mentioned dozens of others. His memory astounded the shocked listeners.

At the end of this day's interrogation, he exploded, "That egomaniac believed he was a military genius! So, in 1942, he ran the war and let Himmler and his street bums try to erase the Jews from the face of Europe. Now he wants to blow up the world. There are Nazi followers everywhere. You better find them because there will be some terrible things going to happen in Revenge Plan."

"You'll repeat all this in a court of law?" Maybrook asked.

"Yes, and much more. I have had enough of that *schweinhund* that I served so loyally," Bormann blubbered.

The admiral and the others left the room, satisfied that the key witness had confessed. Sophia patted the exhausted Bormann on his stubbly head.

☆ ☆ ☆ ☆

Same day - Blair House

Bart called the White House operator for a connection to Admiral Prince at the Pentagon.

"Bart, I was just about to leave. If you want to follow the action in the Baltic, come over here by 6 p.m. and Captain Clyde Ashley will track it. He's handling this end of the show. I thought you might be anxious to watch. The cruiser will relay it directly to us."

"Admiral, I am indeed grateful. May I bring Laurent with me? It's his sister who's the centerpiece of this tableau."

"Of course, he's most welcome."

The White House operator, Helen, came on, "Do you want the base now, General?"

"No, put me through to the Mossad in Tel Aviv. Ariel Rubin, please."

"*Shalom*, General," Rubin answered shortly.

"Where do we stand, Ariel?"

"The ships are sailing in tandem. In a few hours they'll be at the cove transfer point. Sean reported an incident that occurred a little while ago."

"What happened?"

"There were two men fishing about three hundred yards away from the truck. They started to wander in the direction of the cove. Sean pointed his gun at them. They went for their guns, and our other two men tackled them from behind. So no shots were fired."

"Well, who were they?"

"Haven't you guessed? They were a couple of KGB bastards. They were disarmed and tied up, with their mouths taped."

"What have they done with them?"

"They're in the back of the truck now."

"Not with Joyce Laurent?"

"No, she is in the truck cab."

"What's Sean going to do with them?"

"If everything goes according to plan, they will be left in the truck, which was stolen in the first place. Miss Laurent gets transferred to the Sea Horse, and my three men will head for the Denmark coast to refuel, or will board the ship."

"Ariel, that's a complication."

"Not to worry. In either instance, the Danes are friendly. The Hamburg *polizei* can be handled. We have undercover agents standing by in both places. That's our problem, not yours."

"Thank you, Ariel. *Shalom*." Bart hung up and briefed Jacques about the Mossad. "We have a date at six with Captain Ashley to watch the action of transferring Joyce to the Sea Horse. And yes, you can come. I have to call Maybrook now."

The call to Guantanamo was short.

"General, I have very good news for you," Maybrook chuckled.

"Let's have it, Richard."

"Bormann gave us a virtuoso operatic performance over a five-hour interrogation. He spilled everything, thanks to Sophia."

"Excellent. How'd she get him to open up?"

"She soothingly coaxed him into it by telling him that Hitler blamed the Holocaust on Bormann and Himmler. He wanted to talk to you first, but the admiral said you were with the President and ordered us to give him a chance to tell his side of the story. He flipped."

"Good deal. Congratulations to all."

☆ ☆ ☆ ☆

Same day - 5:45 p.m.

Bart and Jacques raced through the homebound traffic. Jacques was driving while Bart penned some notes on a pad. They entered Captain Clyde Ashley's office at 5:57 p.m. and received a warm welcome.

"We've got about ten minutes before we raise the curtain. Have some coffee. You may smoke, if you like. Get comfortable," said Ashley.

Jacques' excitement was obvious. Bart was reserved. Ashley appeared to be in battle mode. The coffee was passed to Jacques and Bart. Ashley poured a cupful for himself and all three lit cigarettes. A screen was brought up with an outline of the Southern Baltic Sea. Red-dotted miniature ships were portrayed in tandem.

"The first ship is the Sea Horse. A quarter-mile in back of her is the cruiser, pulling up fast. That man sitting in the corner is in telegraphic contact with the cruiser. He will recite the action. He is Lieutenant Paul Lefcourt. Now, you see, the cruiser is getting closer to the freighter. The sea is narrowing," Ashley said.

Jacques was chain-smoking. The minutes nervously ticked away.

"Paul, take it from here."

The Morse code dots and dashes took over and clacked away as Lefcourt recited the coded action. The report resembled a radio sportscaster calling a game.

"The cruiser is about to flank the freighter. Lights on the cove shore are blinking red and intermittent flashlights. The freighter flashed lights back to the cove. A small outboard motorboat is racing full speed toward the freighter. The outboard is steering behind the Sea Horse in between the two ships."

The clicking stopped suddenly.

"What's wrong?" Jacques cried out.

"Let me try to make contact," Lefcourt said.

The dots and dashes were hurriedly delivered by the lieutenant. The answers started again.

"They are entering on the starboard side of the freighter. They had to drop a rope ladder. Their gangplank is on the port side. That caused a delay. Here goes. The lady is being helped up the ladder with a security rope around her waist in case she falls. She made it. She's on *board!*"

Jacques, Bart and Ashley applauded, then began slapping each other's backs. The clacking sounds kept coming.

"Hold it, sir. Three men have just climbed up the freighter ladder. One has a bag. The Sea Horse is pulling away toward the Elbe River mouth."

The three men looked at the lighted board map. The Sea Horse was moving. The cruiser was maneuvering toward a 180-degree turn.

"That was perfect," Bart exclaimed.

Jacques was wiping away the tears.

"That'll do it," Ashley proclaimed as he prepared to shut off the lighted map.

Then the dots and dashes resumed a furious clatter.

"Hold it, sir. A barrage of floodlights is being focused on the cruiser and searching in the direction of the Sea Horse. The freighter is already out of the range of lights. The cruiser captain has halted the ship's reversal and is standing still amidstream, blocking the narrow waters. They've spotted two launches speeding toward them. Battle stations have been ordered."

"Holy Toledo!" Ashley exclaimed. "If the commies are looking for trouble, they picked the wrong ship and the wrong captain. If I know Tim Lynch, I'll bet you a hundred to one he'll blow those commies right out of the water if they try to get past him."

The tapping continued. "The cruiser has focused their floods on the cove shore and upstream on the approaching launches. They just fired flares in both directions, lighting up the cove area, with five men working the floodlights. The two large open motorboats have six men in each boat armed with rifles and what looks like machine guns."

"Do you think they are going to chase the Sea Horse?" Jacques queried.

"Not a chance, with Lynch in charge. He's a cold cookie with a hot temper."

The map showed two little boats approaching the cruiser.

"The cruiser has just fired shots above the cove. They've repeated showering bursts of machine-gun fire over the top of the approaching launches. They've stopped alongside the cruiser, which is straddled across the narrow Baltic Sea."

A long moment of silence ensued.

"What the hell is happening?" Jacques snapped.

The telegraphic dots and dashes answered. The lieutenant resumed his account.

"*Drop your guns or we'll shoot,* the captain has ordered. They have complied. One of the men is using a bullhorn. One of them is shouting in English, *Two of our citizens have been kidnapped. Are they on your ship or that freighter that just passed you?* The captain is using his bullhorn to tell them they know nothing of a kidnapping. The commie says they are East German police and would like to come aboard. The captain says, *If you try to board this ship, we'll blow you right back to Moscow.* They are now swearing at Lynch in Russian, which he understands. He is now yelling at *them* in Russian. The cruiser lights are focused on the launches, practically blinding the KGB agents."

Another lapse, as the tapping stopped.

"This is almost farcical," Bart observed.

The dots and dashes began again. "*They are going to report this to the Kremlin,* the man is shouting. *Now we want to chase after that freighter. The two missing men were fishing near that cove.* The captain is telling them, *Why don't you look there? They may be hiding from you.* They've answered, *Those men are East German polizei.* The captain's reply is, *Then what the hell are you Russians doing here? Chase that freighter and I'll drill all twelve of you some new assholes. Now get out of here!*"

Bart, Jacques, Ashley and the lieutenant roared with laughter. The long and short sounds continued transmitting.

Still laughing, the lieutenant reported, "They are heading for the cove. The cruiser is remaining in the straddle position. The ship lights are following the speeding launches. The twelve men have jumped out of the boats and have sloshed their way ashore. Two of the men tied long ropes to trees to keep the boats from floating away. The lights have focused on the truck. The men are busily unloading the cargo. The captain has his long-range binoculars peering at the scene. They've just pulled two men, tied up by ropes, from the truck. They are putting them in a launch. Stand by."

"That takes care of that," Ashley commented.

The click-clack began. The lieutenant picked up his broadcast. "The motor launches are headed north. The cruiser is completing its U-turn and will keep the KGB crowd in sight. Over and out."

"A most interesting evening, Captain Ashley. Great entertainment. Thank you and Lieutenant Lefcourt," Bart said.

"Our pleasure, General, and Mr. Laurent."

☆ ☆ ☆ ☆

Saturday, May 3, 1952 - 8 a.m. - Hamburg

The Sea Horse docked promptly at 8 a.m. Captain Alexis Sonopolous gave Joyce Laurent his cabin when she came aboard. Sean Briscoe had her bag, which had been packed for her by Mossad agent Lisa Haber. The captain arranged to have her best dress pressed for her. She slept until 6 a.m. After a shower, she donned a light blue dress and navy blue coat. She joined Sean Briscoe, Herschel Perlman, Arthur Klein and the captain for breakfast. She thanked the men profusely for their efforts. She kissed each of them and then hugged the captain.

"You are a beautiful woman," the captain declared. "Too bad I'm married."

At the dock, General Barclay, in full dress uniform, and Chief of Detectives Werner raced up the gangway. They identified themselves and were escorted to the bridge. Captain Sonopolus politely greeted them.

"There are some strange people on the dock, Captain. We would like to talk to the lady alone for a moment. We'll be taking her off the ship. Then I have a message for those three men who rescued her."

"Come with me," he said. He then turned to his first mate and ordered, "Barney, start loading the cargo aboard."

The captain knocked on the door of his cabin. Joyce opened the door and looked frightened at the sight of the general and Werner, also in full dress uniform.

"Miss Laurent, these gentleman wish to speak with you privately. I'll be across the hall in the cabin facing this one if I'm needed."

The chief closed the door behind the departing captain.

"Don't be frightened. We're friends of your brother, Jacques, and General Milburn."

She relaxed.

"You are asking for asylum in the United States, aren't you?" Werner asked persuasively, nodding his head as a cue.

Quick on the uptake, she replied, "That is true."

"You must state that to General Barclay."

"I was a political prisoner and I wish asylum in the United States, General Barclay," she complied.

"You are now in the care of the United States government."

"I can't believe this ordeal is over."

"Now, the chief has arranged for a customs officer and an immigration officer to come on board and clear you. The reason for that, Miss Laurent, is that we are going down that gangplank directly into a limousine to take us to the airport for a flight to New York and a connecting flight to Washington. I have your ticket."

"This is wonderful. I hope I'm not dreaming," she said, smiling.

He opened the door, and the customs officer, followed by the immigration officer, entered. The customs officer pointed at her bag.

"Is this all the luggage, Miss?"

"Yes."

He stamped it and left.

"Sir, this lady has given herself up to me for asylum in the United States."

"Very well, General, here, are our release papers. Have the lady sign them," the immigration officer replied.

She applied her signature. He quickly stamped it and a duplicate. She accepted the form. "Thank you, sir."

He saluted and left. Briscoe and the other two were in the hallway. They walked up to Joyce.

"We want to say goodbye and *shalom*," Sean whispered.

She kissed all three, leaving lipstick imprints on their cheeks. Minutes after the three men left, Werner escorted Joyce. A crew member carried her bag. The captain wished her well. She kissed his cheek. Teary-eyed, she went down the gangplank to a white limousine, escorted by Barclay. An American Army sergeant opened the door and she entered, followed by the general. She noted the American flag on the right front fender. Sirens wailed as they left the docks.

"I guess this isn't a dream, General."

"No, my dear lady, you are on your way to America. If the plane catches a good tailwind, it should be on time. Your brother will be notified of your arrival."

"General, you're so kind and thoughtful. Who paid for my ticket?"

"General Milburn advanced it. Your brother is with the CIA. You knew that?"

"No, I didn't. Oh my, he must be very important."

"Yes, I would say so."

At the airport, Joyce was checked into seat 1A in first class.

"Let's have a cup of coffee while we wait for your flight to be called," Barclay suggested.

They went to the coffee shop and chatted about her experiences.

"You've had a hard time, my dear girl. The best of life is ahead of you. America is a wonderful country."

"I don't know where I'll be staying."

"Now, now, that's a foolish statement. Your brother and General Milburn have that all taken care of. Don't worry about anything."

Flight 402 was called, and the general walked with her to the gate. She pecked his cheek, entered the Pan Am flight and plopped into her first-class seat. She looked out the window and spotted an El Al plane circling. Ten minutes later, the Pan Am plane raced down the runway, heading skyward. They leveled off at twenty-five thousand feet, setting a course over the Atlantic on their way to America.

CHAPTER TWENTY-EIGHT

Saturday, May 3, 1952 - same day - Washington, Blair House

The phone jangled next to Bart's bed. It was 5 a.m. Sleepily, he answered, "Milburn."

"Sorry to wake you, sir, but General Barclay is calling from Hamburg."

He leaned over to the decanter next to his bed and splashed water on his hand, applying it to his face. "Put him through, please."

"Bart, sorry to wake you. Our precious Miss Laurent is en route to New York's Idlewild Airport, flight 402, due at 1100 hours. Thought you'd like to know, especially Jacques."

"Bill, I can't thank you enough." Bart hung up, then rang Jacques' room. "Hello?"

"It's me, Jacques; come in here."

Jacques entered Bart's room and asked, "What's wrong?"

"What you mean is what's right. Joyce is in the air on Pan Am Flight 402, arriving in New York at 11 a.m. at Idlewild Airport."

Jacques stared at Bart. He was speechless. He stood there in his pajamas and cried. Bart handed him a box of Kleenex tissues and pushed him into a leather chair. Jacques sobbed silently, his shoulders shaking and his chest heaving, a ten-year sorrow ameliorated.

"All right, Jacques, she's fine and in good health. We have work to do. She has to be cleared through customs and immigration." Milburn called the White House operator and asked to be connected to Attorney General McGranery. "Did I wake you?" he asked when McGranery answered.

"Hell no, Bart, I'm due at the office for an 8 a.m. meeting. What's up?"

The developments of Joyce Laurent's escape and her imminent arrival in New York were quickly explained to McGranery. "Can you clear her through so she can take a flight to Washington? Jacques and I will be there when she arrives on Pan Am Flight 402, due at 11 a.m."

"No problem, Bart. I'll make a call from the office to our bureau in New York. She will have to come to our office tomorrow for a debriefing. After that, she will be provided with the proper documents. Have you spoken to 1600?"

"Yes. Steelman said he'll clear it with the Prez."

"That's just a formality. The jurisdiction is within the Department of Justice. Congratulations, that's a real coup. Give Jacques my best."

"Jim, I am very grateful. You're a very special friend. Thanks for your compassion."

"It's my pleasure, Bart."

The next call awakened Stanley at the Milburn home.

"Yes sir, General, nice to hear your voice."

"Stanley, prepare the guestroom next to Mr. Laurent. His sister will be occupying it for some time."

"Oh, dear Lord, has she been released from East Germany?"

"Indeed. Stock up. Order the newspapers for delivery. Mr. Laurent will be home with her later today. I'll be staying at the house as well."

"I'm delighted, sir. How's the family?"

"They're fine. 'Bye."

Bart checked flights to Idlewild. There was only one at 8 a.m. on American Airlines. The time was 7:28 a.m. Quickly they showered, shaved and dressed. They raced to National Airport and parked the convertible. Jacques and Bart boarded the American Airlines flight to Idlewild Airport in Queens, New York.

On arrival, they headed for the Pan Am check-in counter. They noted the ETA on the board behind the desks. It showed an on-time arrival at 11 a.m. Bart left word with the VIP manager that if there were any calls for a General Milburn or Jacques Laurent, they would be in the coffee shop. Over coffee, Bart pressured his nervous "brother" to eat a hearty breakfast.

"You'll need all your strength, Jacques," Bart urged.

They sat in silence, smoking cigarettes.

"How do I look?" Jacques asked nervously.

"Like a movie star," Bart joked.

"It's been ten years, you know."

"I know, brother. She'll be in your arms soon."

"Will Mr. Laurent or General Milburn please come to the Pan Am desk," the loudspeaker announced.

Bart handed a twenty-dollar bill to the waitress. "Pay our check and keep the rest," he said as they dashed out.

A tall, middle-aged, gray-haired man met them at the counter. He beckoned them away from the busy desk.

"I am Frank Buckley, immigration director of the New York district.

I assume you're General Milburn and you are Mr. Laurent?"

Jacques flashed his CIA credentials. Buckley adjusted his spectacles, looked at the ID and nodded his approval.

"So, it's *your* sister arriving on this flight?" Buckley smiled. "General Milburn, are you related to the Laurents?"

"By adoption. Jacques here is my brother," Bart declared. "It's a long story. They will be living with me and my family in Washington."

"Well, gentlemen, here's the routine. According to procedures, all arrivals from out of the U.S. are processed through customs and immigration before family and friends can make contact," Buckley said, pointing to the upper level for international flight arrivals.

"How will she be able to clear?" Jacques asked.

"Here's the scenario. I will take her in custody and maneuver her past the inspectors ahead of the debarking passengers. I must ask her if she is seeking political asylum in the U.S. It's pro forma. She must reply with one word, 'Yes.' That's it. I'll take her and her luggage, if any, into an office where she can sign an admittance paper. She'll get a copy signed by me. At that point, I deliver her to you and she's all yours."

"Where do you want us to wait?" Bart queried.

"General and Mr. Laurent, come with me now."

They followed Buckley up a flight of stairs. He took them to a small office alongside a gate. As they peered through the gate, they noticed the lineup of immigration officers' desks and the men standing and talking.

"You'll see her escorted to the office just on the other side of this gate. You may come out of this office and wave to her if you like. She'll be with me for five minutes or less."

"Sir, you are most kind."

"Listen, my friends, when word came down from the Attorney General himself, I undertook this assignment personally. I realize the emotional trauma involved here. Gentlemen, I feel a strong empathy in this situation. I am most happy to participate. We were warned not to make this a media event. There is an American flight to D.C. at 12:30 p.m. If this flight from Hamburg is on time, you can make it. If not, I can arrange a car to take you to La Guardia for an Eastern shuttle flight that leaves every half-hour."

During the wait, Bart placed a collect call to the villa in Havana.

Elizabeth answered. "Dear Bart, how are you, my love? Where are you, in New York?"

"Sweetheart, I am at Idlewild Airport. That's why I called collect."

"You're not leaving for some mysterious place, are you?"

"No, no, my love. I have wonderful news. Jacques and I are waiting for his sister Joyce's arrival from Germany."

"Oh, this is wonderful news. How did you rascals manage that?"

He gave a brief account.

"Bring her here for a lovely rest."

"We must get her a passport and all sorts of validation."

"How's Jacques?"

"He's a nervous wreck."

"What are your plans?"

"She'll have the guest room next to Jacques. I'll stay there tonight after a dinner meeting. Thanks for sending Stanley home."

"Instinct. No more questions, my love. Tell Jacques I am happy for him and welcome the new member of our family."

"Elizabeth, you're one of a kind. The very best."

Pan Am Flight 402 circled New York Harbor. Joyce Laurent gazed at the Statue of Liberty, the skyline and the approach to the runway. When the plane touched down, the captain asked the passengers to remain seated. The plane's door was opened and Frank Buckley entered. He went to seat 1A in the first-class section.

"Miss Laurent?"

"Yes?"

"Please come with me."

"Am I being arrested?"

"Not at all," he answered with a smile.

All the passengers gawked.

She rose and made a dignified exit, followed by Buckley. He took her arm and whispered, "I am the director of immigration for New York. Your brother and General Milburn are waiting for you. Welcome to America."

"Oh, my God, I can't believe it's happened."

"We have a form to fill out, and then you'll be free."

They approached the office alongside the gate. Milburn and Laurent, on the other side of the gate, spotted the woman walking with Buckley.

Jacques was speechless as she neared them.

"She's gorgeous, Jacques," Bart said softly.

"Joyce, I'm *here!*"

"Jacques, Jacques!" she screamed.

Buckley hustled her into the office. She sobbed fitfully.

On the other side of the barrier, Jacques clutched the gate, tears rolling down his face. Bart's eyes were moist.

Buckley scribbled furiously. He patted Joyce on the shoulder.

"Here, my dear, sign this line here and you can go to your brother."

She wiped her teary eyes and wrote her name. Buckley stamped the original and the duplicate. He ushered her to the gate and opened it. She ran to her brother.

Jacques clasped her to his chest. They kissed each other's cheeks over and over. Bart stood by, emotionally trapped by the scene before him. The murmuring of Joyce and Jacques stopped. Jacques held her in front of him and turned her to Bart.

"This is Barton Milburn, my brother and dearest friend."

She put her arms around Milburn. He kissed her and said, "Joyce, you are my sister now. Welcome to your new home and country."

Buckley had been watching the reunion. The hardened pro handed Joyce's bag to Bart. "General, life does have some fine moments."

"Indeed it does. Thanks for your courtesies, Mr. Buckley."

When they arrived at National Airport they drove to Rock Creek Park along the banks of the Potomac River, where they stopped for a moment to show Joyce the Lincoln Memorial.

At the Milburn house, Stanley held a bouquet of roses, which he handed to Joyce as she entered the home. Jacques escorted her to her room, which was blanketed from side to side with vases of flowers. On her bed, in Stanley's handwriting, was a sign bearing the words *Welcome home, Joyce.*

Jacques told her that it was Bart who had worked with the Israelis to get her out of Leipzig.

"Tell me about him. And how did you meet?"

"It's a long story, Joyce. We will have lots of time to talk and match notes. Freshen up and let's join Bart for lunch."

The three of them had lunch, prepared by Stanley. Bart had her laughing with his account of what took place after she boarded the ship.

The phone rang and Stanley answered it, then announced, "General, the White House wishes to speak with you."

He brought the phone to the table.

"General, Dr. Steelman is calling," the operator stated.

"Yes, John."

"Everything went well with the lady, I hear."

"Yes, it sure did."

"Is she there with you now?"

"Yes."

"Well, the President would like to have a word with her."

"That's wonderful. I'll put her on."

"Joyce, President Truman wants to talk to you," he said, grinning.

"Oh my," she gasped, taking the phone. "Hello?"

"This is President Truman, Miss Laurent. I want to personally welcome you to the United States of America."

"Thank you, Mr. President," she replied. "And I wish to thank you for the privilege."

"It is my pleasure. I'll arrange with General Milburn to have you visit with me."

"Thank you, Mr. President."

Joyce was bubbling with joy and amazement. "I can't believe that the President of this great country wanted to talk to me. He invited me to visit him," she cried out in delight.

"Jacques, take Joyce to Garfinckel's, our best department store, and buy up a storm. New clothes and all the other things that ladies need."

"Good idea!" Jacques exclaimed. "Joyce, let's go shopping."

Bart went to the den, picked up the red phone and called the White House operators to trace the Attorney General.

"He's on the line, General."

"Jim, I'm sorry to bother you at home."

"No problem, Bart."

"I know you scheduled a debriefing session in the a.m. for Joyce Laurent, so I have a double-barreled question for you."

"Shoot."

"Can you postpone that session, and may she come with me to Havana?"

"We can delay the debriefing for a few days and, frankly, since tomorrow's Sunday, I would prefer to play golf. But why Havana?"

"Two reasons. First, my family is there and I want her and Jacques to visit there. Second, she is going to be a very important witness at the trial. I would like her to go to Guantanamo and see if she recognizes some of our detainees. That's more of a rationale than a must."

"I admire your candor, General Milburn. I'll have a special document prepared, showing her as a resident of the U.S. sent to you in the morning. How soon do you need it?"

"By 8 a.m., if possible, to me at Blair House."

"Nothing comes easy for you. I'll make a call right now. It'll be there by 8 a.m. Any other problems?" McGranery asked.

"Plenty, but I'll handle those," Bart said. "Thanks for everything. 'Bye."

Bart called the villa, and after small talk and love exchanges he advised Elizabeth that the trio would arrive Sunday afternoon.

☆ ☆ ☆ ☆

Sunday, May 4, 1952 - 6:45 a.m. - Blair House

Before arriving in the drawing room, Bart had phoned ahead to wake up Keith Reynolds.

Coffee was served. Keith shuffled into the room, wearing his pajamas. His hair was disheveled. He rubbed his drowsy eyes.

"Have some coffee, Keith. I want you wide awake."

"Yes, General."

He sipped his coffee as Bart outlined his plan.

"I want you to talk to that same fellow who transferred your funds."

"René La Fleur, vice president at the Banque Lorraine."

"Yes. Tell him Mr. Nordheim wants to know if there are any funds in the name of Laurent - Joyce or Jacques or any other Laurent. Also, to check the Banque Royale and any other banks. If there are any funds, ask how much, and to transfer the funds immediately to Laurent, care of Carlton Reilly at the National City Bank, coded Douglas. If he resists, tell him to take the funds out of Nordheim's account as a guarantee, if there is a problem. Don't forget, you're Fliegel. Understand? I'll be listening."

Bart placed the call directly. He handed the phone to Reynolds and picked up the extension on the bar.

"This is Konrad Fliegel. Is La Fleur there?"

"One moment, sir."

"Konrad, good to hear from you. How are you?" La Fleur inquired.

In an authoritarian tone he answered, "Fine, René. Now, listen carefully. Herr Nordheim wants an immediate answer. Are there any funds on deposit at Lorraine and/or Royale in the name of Laurent? Also, can you make a quick check with the other banks? Hurry now; I will hold the line."

"Do you want me to call you back?"

"No, dammit, Mr. Nordheim wants the answer now. Do it!" Keith shouted.

"Yes sir, one moment."

The moment stretched to ten. Bart had his second cup of coffee and smoked several cigarettes in the interim.

La Fleur came back on the phone. "Herr Fliegel, there are two accounts. One here at Lorraine and one in Royale in the name of François Laurent for a Joyce Laurent and one in Zurich in the same name for a Jacques Laurent. There are two similar accounts at the Banque d'Orsay."

"How much is there? In American money."

"At Lorraine, we have three million seven hundred and fifty thousand dollars. At Zurich, they have four million, two hundred thousand. At the Banque d'Orsay, there is one million two hundred thousand in each name."

"That comes to ten million, three hundred and fifty thousand," Keith said. "Have the whole amount wired posthaste to the name I gave you. Mr. Nordheim will guarantee the transfer."

"Sir, can we have a written confirmation soon?" La Fleur pleaded.

"In due time, René. Make the total transfer now and do your paperwork later between Lorraine, Royale and d'Orsay. This is urgent. How soon will the wired funds be sent?"

"Within the next ten minutes."

"Don't delay, or Nordheim will skin you."

"Herr Fliegel, I'll personally wire the ten million three fifty right now. Give my regards to Herr Nordheim."

"Good man, René." He hung up.

Bart patted Keith on the back. "You were masterly, my friend. Go back to sleep."

The phone rang. It was the White House operator. "General, there is a Captain Esta Arnold on the line for you."

"Yes, Captain Arnold?" Bart answered.

"General, I apologize for calling this early. General Bradley gave me the assignment last evening. I've been trying to track you down, sir."

"What is the message?"

"A transport plane will be ready to leave Andrews for Homestead at noon or a little later, depending on those ten U.S. Attorneys' ability to get there. There will be twenty Marines on board at Hangar 14 to go with them. I will act as liaison and will report to you directly. I am under your command, sir."

Bart smiled and thought about Lloyd Sedgwick's interest in the lady.

"Captain, the team of U.S. Attorneys is headed by Gideon Cartman.

I'll call him now and get them rolling. Also, CIA agent Lloyd Sedgwick may be joining that flight if I can reach him. If not, he will arrive there separately. He's my number one man on this job. Report to him."

"Yes, sir. Thank you, General."

"You can always reach me through the White House operators. 'Bye."

Bart called Cartman at the Mayflower Hotel, and a sleepy man answered. "Gideon?"

"Yes?"

"Get your ass out of bed. Round up your men and get out to Andrews Air Force Base, Hangar 14. Your group, twenty Marines and Captain Esta Arnold will be on hand. She's been assigned as liaison to me by General Bradley. The plane is set to leave at noon."

"We'll be there, General," Cartman agreed.

Bart tried Sedgwick's home on the chance he was back from Leavenworth. Sedgwick answered, then said, "I got back here late, Bart. I was going to report to you this morning."

"How did it go with Mayfield?"

"Not good; he's a tough, smart-ass bastard. He's going to need a lot of working-over. Can we get him out of there and into Guantanamo?"

"Let me think about it. How soon can you get to Andrews for a flight to Homestead? I've got ten U.S. Attorneys and twenty Marines at Hangar 14 leaving at noon to question those SS bums we picked up in Argentina."

"I can make it."

"You'd better, if you want to fly with Captain Esta Arnold."

"You're not kidding, Bart, please."

"No, that's on the level. She's to coordinate with you. I ordered it. I told her you're my number one man."

"Bless your heart. I'm on my way, sir."

"Get dressed first," Bart jested.

Before takeoff from Andrews, Bart awakened his brother Douglas at his apartment in New York. He gave him a concise report on Joyce's escape and followed with instructions to call Carlton Reilly at the National City Bank to place the funds in new accounts respectively for Joyce and Jacques Laurent. "Doug, I coded the transfer in your name so that Reilly would know we are responsible for the wired money. I'll call him on Monday."

"Talk about a windfall! This is a bonanza. Do Jacques or his sister have any idea that their father had that kind of money?"

"I don't know. I haven't told them yet what I did this morning. I am at Andrews now on our way to Havana to spend the weekend with Liz and the kids."

"Before you leave, kid brother General, I have a bulletin for you."

"Let's have it."

"Are you ready for this?"

"Stop stalling. What's up?"

"Constance and I are going to be married, and you're my best man."

"Fabulous! When is this going to happen?"

"Sunday, July 6th. Her show closes on Friday, July 4th. Now, Bart, don't be circling the globe that day."

"I wouldn't miss this for Hitler's funeral. Congratulations, and *ciao*."

☆ ☆ ☆ ☆

Sunday, May 4, 1952 - same day - Havana

As they were about to exit the F-37, Major Flaherty approached Bart and whispered, "General, sir, I am required to log our passengers on each flight. I should have asked you about the lady. Is she officially on this flight?"

Bart laughed. "No problem, Major. First of all, she is Jacques Laurent's sister, Joyce, just rescued from East Germany. During the war she was in several concentration camps. She is here now as a witness to see if she can identify some of our prisoners."

"Thank you. I'll just log her as Miss Joyce, a witness."

"That's fine, Major. You and the crew check into the Riviera Hotel. The sixth floor is ours. Just tell the desk you're part of my team. I'm declaring this a long weekend. So enjoy the rest of today and Monday. We will be going to Guantanamo on Tuesday morning. I'll get word to you as to the time."

"We'll be ready, sir. Thank you very much."

The crew unloaded the baggage. Jacques hailed a shuttle bus and they were on their way to the villa. Joyce was fascinated with the beauty of the Caribbean, the shoreline, the tropical climate and the festive atmosphere of Havana. At the villa gate, she was impressed when the two uniformed police officers saluted their arrival.

Elizabeth was out in front of the house with Christina, the four children, Mrs. Bishop, Emilio and Maria. They each held up balloons with the legend "Welcome Joyce." A huge banner stretched across the driveway overhead, attached to a light pole from the flagpole above the door, reading "Welcome Home Joyce."

Elizabeth hugged Joyce, kissing her cheek. The children shouted in unison, "Welcome, Joyce!"

Bart and Elizabeth enjoyed a lingering kiss. Jacques and Christina did likewise. The children whooped around Bart and Jacques. Joyce shed copious tears of happiness. Elizabeth took Joyce by the arm and led her to the guest room next to Jacques.

The long weekend proved to be a joyous melding of the Milburns, the Laurents and the Lyonses into one close-knit, happy family. After dinner on Sunday night, Bart asked Jacques to join him in the office next to the den. "Jacques, I have some very good and very special news for you and Joyce."

"What would that be?"

"You and Joyce are millionaires. Money has been left to you by your father."

"How could that be? He sent all his money to those thieving Swiss banks."

Bart described his activities with Fliegel, a.k.a. Reynolds, early that morning.

"I'm phoning my brother now for confirmation."

He reached Douglas at the Beaux Arts Hotel in New York. His brother said, "Bart, I was just going out the door when you rang. Connie and I are having a late supper with Darryl Zanuck and Gene Kelly. And yes, Reilly confirmed the receipt of the Laurent funds. Give them my love. 'Bye."

"The money is there in your and Joyce's names."

"Bart, there is no one like you. I must tell this to Joyce. I must tell you, I had a problem in proposing to Christina, because she's a rich woman, but I have no qualms now."

"Hallelujah!"

"Shall I call Joyce in here to let her know?" Jacques asked.

"Why not?"

Christina and Mrs. Bishop were putting the children to bed. Joyce and Elizabeth were relaxing in the den. Jacques beckoned Bart to join the ladies for the revelation of the good news. Two brandies were poured in snifters. Jacques handed one to Bart. Both men lit cigars, toasted the ladies, and sat back in their leather lounge chairs.

"Come on, you rascals, you look like a couple of Cheshire cats," Elizabeth probed, smiling.

"Bart, you tell them," Jacques urged.

Once again, he related his maneuver that morning in having Fliegel transfer the Laurents' funds out of the Swiss banks. Joyce turned pale and her hands trembled.

"Bart, my love, aren't you the most devious one! All to the good, mind you," Elizabeth gasped, hugging the silent, teary-eyed Joyce.

"This can't be happening all at once!" Joyce cried out.

"Well, let's drink to your good fortune," Bart proposed. "To my rich relatives!"

Joyce leaped off the sofa she shared with Elizabeth and ran over to Bart, then hugged him and kissed his forehead.

"Indeed, you are my brother. Thank you, thank you."

She went back to her seat next to Elizabeth.

"I have a question. How did your father manage to accumulate that much money?" Bart asked.

"My grandfather built a tremendous business from a small machine shop just outside Paris into a giant manufacturing business making small motors and parts for the automobile industry," Jacques began to explain.

Joyce picked up the saga. "When each of us were born he set up trusts for us, which he added to each year. In 1936 he was stricken with cancer. He sold the company for ten million dollars. He died a year later and left the money to the trusts, with my father named as trustee. Knowing that war was on the horizon and that Hitler was a menace to Jews, my father sent the funds to the Swiss banks."

Jacques continued the story. "My father was well-to-do as a prominent doctor. The reason there is slightly more in my account is due to the age difference. Mine was started earlier than Joyce's. However, I'll make sure we even out the amounts to each of us."

"Oh, Jacques, please, that's not necessary," Joyce demurred.

"I'm your older brother," he asserted.

Christina entered the room, announcing that all the children were snug in their beds. The good news was imparted to her, and she joined the festivities, kissing Joyce and Jacques.

"By the way, I have some more news," Bart declared, puffing a ring of smoke skyward. "Douglas and Constance are going to be married Sunday, July 6th, two days after the show closes. I am to be the best man."

"Bart, that's wonderful," Elizabeth exclaimed. "All this good news in one day!"

Jacques looked at Christina and squeezed her hand.

Joyce rose and apologized, "These have been several hectic days. I'm overwhelmed by all that's happened, but I am a very tired lady, so may I say goodnight and love to all of you."

"Sleep well. Tomorrow we'll go to the beach and bathe you in sunshine," Elizabeth said.

Bart and Elizabeth headed for their bedroom. Jacques and Christina left for their favorite bench at the lifeguard station overlooking the moonlit Caribbean. As they reached their secluded spot on the beach, Jacques reached for Christina, pulled her close to him and kissed her lips, then lingered there.

"Jacques, I missed you and thought about you every day and night. You've changed my life. I fear nothing when you're with me."

"Christina, I love you. I want to tell you something that's been on my mind constantly. I hesitated to ask you the most important question because of the differences in our financial positions…"

Christina cut him off. "Our financial positions have nothing to do with my feelings toward you. I love you and that's it, with or without money. If you didn't have a dime, it wouldn't matter."

"Shush, let me say it now."

He dug his bended knees in the sand, and with a mock gesture earnestly proposed, "Will you be my wife, dear wonderful Christina?"

She giggled, "Rise, my knight, I accept, and promise to be a good wife."

A long kiss followed. Brushing the sand off his trousers, he reached into his pocket and pulled out a velvet box, opened it and handed it to her.

"Oh, Jacques, what a beautiful ring, and such good taste! When did you find time to buy this?"

"When I took Joyce shopping. She helped me pick it out. Let me put it on your finger."

It was a three-carat diamond encircled by rubies and emeralds.

"It's *beautiful*."

The betrothal was a *fait accompli*. Holding hands, they walked back to the house, discussing future plans. At the guesthouse, he left her with a long kiss.

✮ ✮ ✮ ✮

Monday, May 5, 1952 - 9 a.m.

Breakfast was served. As Christina raised her orange juice, Elizabeth noticed the ring and squealed, "Don't tell me he proposed, Christina?"

"Yes, he did, like a knight in shining armor!"

"What a beautiful ring! Jacques, you're a delightful rascal. My best to both of you."

Bart raised his juice glass and declared, "My very best to two wonderful people. My two brothers, Doug and Jacques, are getting married. Cheers!"

The couple blushed and thanked Liz and Bart.

"After breakfast, Jacques and I have some business to discuss, and then we'll join you and the children at the beach. It's a beautiful day," Bart said.

The two men walked to the pool and sat at a glass-topped table. Stanley brought a tray of coffee, cream and sweeteners. He placed an ashtray before them and quietly left.

"The time has come, Jacques, to prepare for preliminary trials and to set dates for the final trials. We are setting legal precedents, and I'm troubled as to our jurisdiction," Bart said.

"They are escaped war criminals. They should be tried by the Army if you intend to keep the Russkies out of it. Who decided the jurisdiction in Nuremberg?"

"The Allied powers. But I am being driven by my personal desires. Here we are, seven years after the end of the war, and a generation is growing into maturity totally oblivious to the worst crimes in history, perpetrated by the Germans before and during the war. I want the world to wake up and remember the millions of innocent people slaughtered by the Nazis, and the participation of the Romanians, Slovakians, Ukrainians, and even the Russians. I also want to highlight the Swiss thievery, as well as their pro-Nazi role in the war."

"Bart, you must put this question to Truman. And don't forget, six months from now we will elect a new president. It looks like Eisenhower to me."

"You're right, Jacques. There will be several trials, dammit. My law practice is zero right now. Are you going to stick it out after you marry Christina?"

"Of course. How could you ask that? I'll stay with this until the finish."

"Then what?"

"Bart, I have a little secret. I've been keeping a diary. I have a desire to write a book. Maybe several."

"Wonderful idea. With your experiences, it would be a real thriller, maybe make into a movie, Jacques."

Emilio brought a telephone to the table and plugged the wire into an outlet. "The White House is one the phone, sir."

"General, this is Helen, sir," the White House operator said. "I have Lloyd Sedgwick on the line."

"Put him through, please."

"General, I am sitting here at Homestead Air Base headquarters. We're on a clear line in General Watson's conference room. With me are Gideon Cartman and Captain Esta Arnold. May I put you on a speakerphone?"

"Go ahead, and I am asking Jacques Laurent to pick up an extension. Jacques, pick up the extension in the pool house."

In seconds, Jacques was on the line.

"What's up, folks?" Bart asked.

"We spent last evening looking over the highly vaunted Waffen SS'ers. They were given the Guantanamo treatment. Shaved heads, mustaches, beards, cuffed and shackled. They didn't look too ferocious."

Cartman broke in. "General, there are a few of them who look like they are ready to crack."

"Well, dammit, *crack* the bastards. Why the call?"

"General, may I say a word?" Captain Arnold requested.

"Yes, Captain, what is it?"

"That's why agent Sedgwick placed this call. As I walked down the line of cells, one of the prisoners, Herman Kraus, whispered to me in English. He said he can point out camp commandants, and named a Kurt Eimann as the SS officer in charge of executions."

"This is Lloyd, General. I want your permission to pull him out of his cell and sequester him for us to do a number on him. He may give up a few of these tough guys."

"By all means. Do the good guy/bad guy mechanics routine. Gideon, brief your guys and go to work pronto. Time is of the essence. Lloyd, have Katherine Wharton check Langley's classified files on Kurt Eimann and Herman Klaus. Then send her the list of all the Waffen SS thugs in our custody. Be sure of their right names, and see what pops out of the oven. Congratulations to all of you. Jacques and I will be in Guantanamo tomorrow. Over and out."

The rest of the beautiful day was spent at the beach under a solid blue sky and a benevolent sun, with a cool wind emanating from the placid Caribbean. Joyce, an excellent swimmer, stroked her way a half-mile out to sea until the lifeguards frantically whistled her back. Jacques and Bart raced toward her, yelling, "Sharks!" She U-turned and picked up her pace to shore.

She apologized, "I felt as though I was swimming my way to freedom. I'm sorry I worried you. I've never had a day like this."

The rays of the sun highlighted her auburn hair and hazel eyes. Her face glowed with a reddish tan. The three women, Elizabeth, Christina and Joyce, caught the attention of passersby. The children were busily building sandcastles. Joyce joined them and artistically sculpted little soldiers. The children called her Aunt Joyce.

"Those are *gendarmes* guarding the castle," she explained.

"I know a *gendarme* is a policeman!" Michael shouted.

"How did you know that?"

"Uncle Jacques told us that."

"I know how to say *Merci beaucoup*," Matthew added. "It means thank you."

"Would you children like to learn to speak French?" Joyce asked.

A chorus of "*oui's*" was the rejoinder.

"I will try to teach all of you, if you are good boys and girls."

Emilio, Maria and Sylvie appeared with all of the equipment for a picnic lunch. They spread two large blankets and covered them with tablecloths.

Plates, knives, forks and spoons were arranged for the diners, consisting of the four children, Mrs. Bishop, Elsie, Elizabeth, Christina, Joyce, Bart and Jacques.

"*Muchas gracias!*" little Katherine chirped.

"That's Spanish for thank you," Michael whooped.

That evening the children were fed an early dinner and tucked away. Bart announced reservations at the Cubanacan, one of the outstanding outdoor showplaces. The food and spectacular show were touted by entertainment critics throughout North and South America. Bart, Elizabeth, Jacques, Christina and Joyce sat at a front row table underneath the lighted trees, with palm fronds dangling overhead. A cast of a hundred dancers, singers, comics and musicians entertained in a style indigenous to Cuba, the pearl of the Antilles.

Joyce was overwhelmed by the dazzling spectacle. At the conclusion of the production, two bottles of Dom Perignon champagne were delivered to the table, compliments of Phil Kastel, who had arranged the reservations. The waiter delivered a sealed envelope to Bart. He opened the missive, glanced at the contents and excused himself. At the entrance to the cabaret, Dandy Phil greeted Bart and maneuvered him to a white Cadillac limousine. A uniformed chauffeur opened the rear door and walked twenty feet away from the front of the luxurious automobile. The air-conditioning was cooling the interior. Kastel poured two snifters of brandy from the mini-bar.

"What's this all about, Phil?" Bart asked.

"General, when we spoke about the reservations here earlier today, I didn't want to talk on the phone about a message I received from the Uncle in New York. He contacted your brother Douglas, who told him you were in Havana. I was about to call you at the villa for a meet, but you surprised me with your call."

"This must be really important," Bart said as he calmly lit a cigarette and took a sip of the brandy.

"Judge for yourself. Have you heard of a mouthpiece by the name of Alden Gaines?"

"Yes, he's a hotshot lawyer and politico from Chicago. What about him?"

"A prison guard sent a man who had done some time at Leavenworth to tell Gaines that Darren Mayfield was tucked away at that institution. He was being held incommunicado in solitary confinement. Gaines trusted his client sufficiently to put ten grand in an envelope for the guard."

"How the hell did Costello find out about this, and when did he get the feed?" Bart snapped.

"The client of Gaines, who shall remain anonymous, worked for Joe Kennedy and Costello when they were partners during Prohibition. He had called Frank this afternoon for another matter and casually mentioned he was coming to New York to pick up a large sum of money for Mayfield from a Wall Street brokerage house."

"Which broker?" Bart asked.

Kastel produced a notebook from his sports jacket, adjusted his bifocals and read, "Thornton & Wiley. Frank pressed him and got the whole story out of him."

"I'm very grateful to you, Phil, and to Frank. Thanks for everything. I've got to go now."

"General, we're patriots, too," was Kastel's parting shot.

Bart returned to his table and asked for his check. It was complimentary, courtesy of Kastel. He rushed his party into the Cadillac and raced back to the villa. All in the party were aware of Bart's tension, and engaged in small talk. Bart and Jacques hastened to the office next to the den. A call was placed to the White House operators, who on request patched him through to the Attorney General's home.

"What now, friend?" McGranery said.

Bart relayed the information gleaned from Kastel.

"The Bureau of Prisons is under your jurisdiction, Jim. Fortunately, it's after hours. I doubt that Gaines can get a habeas corpus signed before morning."

"Don't kid yourself, Bart. Alden Gaines is well connected in the Windy City. He has judges on his payroll. He can roll one out of bed any time," McGranery cautioned.

"At least it's worth a try. Can you get Mayfield out of there, pronto?" Bart entreated. "Once he's free, our whole secret will be unraveled. It's urgent, Jim. I expect to press for a preliminary trial in the next couple of weeks."

Jacques paced the room, nervously puffing on a Havana cigar.

"Where the hell do we stash him? It's 10:30 here now. That would be 9:30 Central time in Kansas," McGranery said. "I appointed the warden at Leavenworth. He's a solid guy, a former Marine Corps colonel, Clyde Wilson. I repeat, where to?"

"There's a National Guard Airport just outside of Kansas City, Missouri. I'll try to get a plane to pick him up. I'll call Steelman," said Bart.

"Better yet, Bart. I'll call the warden right now. If the habeas corpus hasn't been served, I'll have him start the removal. He may be very interested in who the guard was that passed the message from Mayfield. He should lock that son of a bitch up. I'd like to stop those funds being handed over to the anonymous client of Gaines. You call the operators at the White House and track Steelman down for a conference call with us. 'Bye."

Bart called the White House. The operators reached Steelman at home, and he agreed to stand by for the conference call.

☆ ☆ ☆ ☆

Leavenworth, Kansas - same night

Warden Clyde Wilson was in his office catching up on his paperwork. He answered the phone.

"Sir, I have Attorney General McGranery on the line," the operator said.

"Put him through."

"Sir, this is quite an honor, Mr. McGranery."

"Cut the *Mr.* bullshit, Clyde. This is Jim."

"Yes sir, Jim."

"You have a prisoner there named Mayfield."

"Well, I know who you mean. He's a snide prick, you know, smart ass ex-FBI and all that bullshit. He wouldn't give us his name, rank, serial number or any means of identification. So we booked him as John Doe."

"Perfect. I want him out of Leavenworth as quickly as possible. You may be served with a habeas corpus by that sleazeball lawyer, Alden Gaines. You can honestly avow that you don't have anyone on your roster of prisoners by that name."

McGranery filled him in on a guard using a former prisoner to line up Alden Gaines for ten thousand dollars. "Put that guard in chains and I'll have Mr. Anonymous in custody at the Wall Street broker's office. Your John Doe is being held on counterfeit charges, plus many others."

"When do you want him?"

"Have you got a couple of trustworthy men to take him for a merry-go-round ride for several hours, winding up at the National Guard airport outside Kansas City? That is, after they confirm the location with you. They are not to question him. This may be an all-night assignment. I'm checking with the White House and will call you back. But, by all means, move him out quietly and immediately, Clyde. This is vital and top secret. I'll brief you one of these days."

The warden summoned two of his former Marines, now serving as prison guards - Mike Donnelly and Morgan Winslow. The warden outlined the plan.

Mayfield, fast asleep in solitary confinement, was yanked out of his foul-smelling, unlit cell and hauled to his feet. The smell of his prison garb, as well as his body odor. was unbearable. Mike and Morgan rushed him into the shower room. He was stripped naked and thrust under a lukewarm shower. He was handed a bar of soap. "Wash up quickly," one guard ordered.

"Fuck you," Mayfield said.

Mike struck him across his buttocks with a club. "Wash your mouth, too, John Doe."

The shower was turned off. Winslow handed him a coarse towel. He was provided with clean underwear and nondescript shirt and trousers. His head had been shaved and showed a little stubble. After donning a pair of brown socks, he was handed a pair of low-cut shoes. The warden led them to the exit gate and handed Mayfield a pea jacket. The temperature outdoors was in the low forties. A sedan with wire-netted windows and mesh between the front and back seats was parked at the exit. Mayfield was handcuffed and his legs shackled. The two ex-Marines sat in the front and drove off into the misty night.

"Where the hell are you taking me?"

"To meet your maker, if you don't shut up," Mike snapped.

"Take me to New York and I'll make you both rich men," Mayfield pleaded.

"How rich, dickhead?" Morgan asked.

"One million dollars to each of you."

"Counterfeit?"

"No, real money."

"Shut your trap, sleazeball! We know all about you," Mike bellowed.

The car crossed the bridge over the Missouri River from Kansas City, Kansas, into Kansas City, Missouri, then circled the outskirts of the city and located the National Guard airfield. They drove past it toward St. Louis.

"Where the hell are we going?" Mayfield rasped.

"To your very private hell, you traitorous bastard," Winslow replied.

☆ ☆ ☆ ☆

Washington - same time

Steelman, McGranery, and Bart Milburn were hooked up in a conference call by the White House operators. Bart explained the Mayfield problem.

"I've asked the operators to cut into this call if there is a report from Warden Clyde Wilson from Leavenworth," McGranery said.

"Bart, isn't John Doe Mayfield being held initially on counterfeit charges?" Steelman queried.

"Yes, but there are a multitude of felonies on which he could be indicted, including possibly murder and treason. He's a very bad boy with an astutely guileful mind, FBI-trained. Bailing this cretin out would destroy our whole operation," Bart declared.

"Can't the Secret Service tuck him away?"

"I'm worried about that legal louse Alden Gaines. He's tricky and well connected. We've got to shut him up," Bart said, ignoring Steelman's question about the Secret Service.

The operator cut in. "I have Warden Wilson on line."

"Put him through," McGranery ordered.

"Jim, John Doe is out of here on a tour of the Missouri countryside," the warden said.

"Thanks, Clyde. I'll be in touch. Call me if Gaines or one of his partners shows up with a habeas corpus."

"Will do," the warden replied, then clicked off.

"Bart, I see only one way to deal with John Doe. Have him brought to your country club in Guantanamo. You're the only one who can break him," Steelman said.

"I agree," the Attorney General said.

"How do we get him there?" Bart asked.

"We have a couple of Army transport planes at the Kansas City airport for emergency use of the President or his family. I'll make a call and see if we can turn one loose. Those ex-Marine prison guards will have to accompany John Doe to the base, drop the prisoner, and return to Kansas City for their drive back to Leavenworth. Let me check it out now."

"One more thing, John. I don't want to use the FBI to pick up Gaines' anonymous client at the Wall Street brokerage house," McGranery said.

"Have your U.S. Attorney use a couple of U.S. Marshals to pick him up," Steelman suggested.

"Good idea, John."

Steelman called the Air Force office. McGranery reached the U.S. Attorney in the Southern District of New York. All the pieces of the legal jigsaw puzzle were put in place. Jacques called the Riviera Hotel. Major Flaherty was out exploring Havana's nightspots. A Lieutenant Marvin Green answered the phone.

"Yes sir, may I take a message?"

"Are you a member of Flaherty's crew?"

"Yes, sir."

"This is General Milburn's aide, Jacques Laurent. He wants the F-27 ready in the morning for flight to the naval base at 0900 hours."

"Yes, sir. I know you, Agent Laurent, and we'll be ready, sir."

CHAPTER TWENTY-NINE

Tuesday, May 6, 1952 - Guantanamo Naval Base

Bart called the admiral before takeoff from Havana, and the team gathered in the conference room forty-five minutes later. Bart briefed the admiral, Maybrook, Sophia, Tony and Berger on the previous evening's developments. "John Doe, a.k.a. Mayfield, should be arriving here shortly. Admiral, I would like to isolate this bastard."

"We'll place him in solitary in the basement. He's been through the routine in Leavenworth, so we'll repeat it here with the John Doe mug shot by Noah," Admiral Thomas.

"Now, before you update me, I wish to advise you that we should prepare for preliminary trials in the next few weeks to be held here at the base. I assume you have a courtroom for this purpose, Admiral?"

"Indeed we do, and we'll dress it up a little."

"Admiral, each defendant will need counsel. Can you pick a few good men for that dirty job?" Bart asked.

"I may have to request help from the Navy Department, General."

"Let me point out the fact that we have ten assistant U.S. Attorneys in Homestead quizzing that Gestapo gang we captured in Argentina. They will be part of the prosecutorial team. I will consult with the President and the Attorney General about making these prelim trials a joint armed-forces affair. Also, the choice of judges will obviously require the input of the Joint Chiefs. There is no doubt in my mind that the prelim judiciary will bind these men over for full trials, with the defendants choosing their own attorneys," Bart said.

"In the interim, I'll be checking our lists for possible defense attorneys, General. Where will the major trial take place?" Thomas asked.

"That's the major conundrum challenging us at this time. Nuremberg or The Hague, where the trials will be buried by the media, or here in the good old U.S.A., where the whole thing will become a media circus - TV, radio, and the printed press," Bart answered. "Another factor is to keep the Soviets out of the show."

"Why not in the U.S.?" Maybrook asked.

"Off the record, now, I've been told that Eisenhower suggested Independence, Missouri, Truman's home town. The President demurred, but said he would consider Kansas City, the heartland of America. However, mind you, there will be a new President when the major trials are held," Bart said.

"Yes, and it will probably be Eisenhower," Maybrook ventured.

"Truman will brief both candidates, and hopefully I'll be meeting with them after the conventions in July," Bart said. "We have to synthesize the evidence we've collected from the cooperative witnesses. We have to collect evidence from survivors of the concentration camps. My wife is one of them, and Jacques Laurent's sister is another. Witnesses are scattered all over the world, as are the Nazis who escaped the Allies' net. We may get some from those Gestapos at Homestead. Maybrook, Sophia and Tony put together a list of highlights from those who have confessed. I'll take on Hitler today. Jacques, try your hand on Abdul the Cobra. Berger, take on Hans Langsdorff."

"General, I'd like to take a crack at Herman Klaus," Admiral Thomas volunteered.

"Go to it, and don't forget the mechanics ruse," Bart replied. Then he ended the meeting and briskly walked to Hitler's cell. He told the guards on watch duty outside the padded cell to take a break, then asked, "How is he behaving?"

"He's been walking around ever since the medical officer told us to remove his leg irons. He's much calmer now with his three meals a day, General. At first he would only eat vegetables, but now he is eating chicken and fish," one guard answered.

Hitler stopped pacing, as Milburn stared at the revitalized prisoner.

"So, it is *General* they call you," Hitler snapped in German. His complexion was no longer pallid and his stance was imperious, despite his manacled hands. There was a hint of his former arrogance in his demeanor.

"Adolf, speak English."

"*Nein, sprechen Deutsch* only."

"*Setzen!*" Bart barked, as he turned and pulled a chair into the cell.

Hitler stood obstinately, watching Bart set the chair down facing the slab cot. "*Setzen sie sich!*"

At six feet three, Milburn towered over the five-foot-eight former Führer. Bart's icy blue eyes glared at the stubborn Nazi leader. Suddenly he grasped Hitler's shoulders, wheeled him around and thrust him onto the cot. He placed his recorder on the table next to the bed. In perfect German, the general addressed the startled prisoner.

"We'll talk in your language. And stop playing the *Führer* with *me*."

Hitler sat up on his bed, planting his feet on the concrete floor.

"I hear the guards call you *General*. You are in charge here?"

"Yes."

"I am entitled to the Geneva Convention rules of war."

"There are no rules in your kind of war. You not only killed millions of innocent people, your Nazi soldiers executed American prisoners of war at Malmedy and all over Europe. I saw the bodies."

"I did not order that."

"No, and you didn't order the execution of six million non-combatant Jews, plus millions of Christian dissenters, Gypsies, Jehovah's Witnesses, homosexuals, and the sick and infirm. You're history's worst monster."

"Herr General, listen to me...why don't you execute me, if that's what you think?"

"Because, as I told you before, death is too merciful for an ogre like you."

"We are in America now, not so?"

"Yes."

"Then by your rules I'm entitled to a lawyer and a trial. I am not guilty of killing those Jews. I just wanted to remove them from Germany. Himmler went crazy and killed them while I was running the war."

"You are a lying bastard, *Schickelgruber*."

"Do not insult me."

"Well, you will have a preliminary military trial, and legal representation *will* be appointed for you. That court will probably bind you over for a formal trial. At that time you'll be able to retain your own lawyers. That's the American way."

"When are these preliminary trials going to take place? Will I be permitted to speak at this trial?"

"It will be in two or three weeks, and you'll be allowed to speak."

"I need a pencil and paper to prepare for my trial."

"We'll see about that," Bart huffed, then slammed the cell door, taking the chair and the recorder with him.

☆ ☆ ☆ ☆

Meanwhile, in another cell, Hans Langsdorff, a heavy-set man with a rugged countenance weathered by years at sea, spoke to Berger in English. He had a guttural Germanic accent.

"Why am I being treated as a common criminal, sir? How do I address you?" he asked into the recorder.

"You are being charged as a war criminal. My name is Phillip. Answer my questions and maybe we can remove those shackles and handcuffs." He paused briefly, then asked, "You are the former captain of the Admiral Graf Spee, which was blown up and scuttled on December 17, 1939, off the coast at Montevideo, Uruguay, on the orders of Adolf Hitler?"

"Yes, I followed orders."

"Now you are still following Hitler."

"No, I work for a Jew, Herr Nordheim."

"Come on, Captain, let's have the truth."

"That is the truth."

"Do you know who Nordheim is?"

"Sure, he's the richest man in the world."

"You don't mind working for a Jew?"

"No, I have never been a Nazi. I was a naval officer in the service of my country."

"Are you so naïve that you don't know who Nordheim really is?"

"I haven't met him personally. I was hired by Herr Froelich to work for Eagle Shipping."

"Why were you at that planned meeting when you were captured?"

"We were to have a corporate meeting the next day, that's all I know. I was told that I was going to be assigned as captain of a new ship."

"Captain, the Führer and Martin Bormann are in custody. They are alive and well."

"I can't believe that."

"Nordheim is Hitler."

"That is not true."

"Believe me, it is a fact. What was that Arab, Abdul 'The Cobra' doing there with you?" Berger asked, boring in.

"I was not sure who he was. I don't know the name Abdul or the Cobra."

"Where were you going to take this new ship?"

"It was to go to Ecuador," Langsdorff answered.

"Through the Panama Canal?"

"Of course."

"What was the cargo?"

"I don't know."

"Was Ahmed to go on that ship with you?"

"Yes, but they called him Armand, not Ahmed. He spoke German and English."

"Didn't you know that he is one of the most dangerous explosives experts? He is wanted all over the world. Interpol has him as the number one most wanted man. He's killed lots of Israelis."

Langsdorff looked genuinely surprised.

"Captain, you are either a great actor or a dummkopf," Phillip chided. "Have you heard of the *Revanche Plan*?"

"No, what's that?"

"Hitler's revenge plan to blow up the Panama Canal, the Versailles Palace and a lot of other things in this world."

"I swear I never heard such a ridiculous thing."

"Your new ship was to be used to blow up the canal. That's why Abdul the Cobra was to go with you. The cargo was probably explosives. That's enough for now, Captain."

☆ ☆ ☆ ☆

Down the hall, in another cell

Abdul the Cobra snarled at Jacques. "You are a Jew. I spit on you." He spat, ejecting a mouthful of saliva, which Laurent sidestepped. He walked up to the prisoner and kicked him in the groin. The Cobra sank to the cold floor, groaning as he assumed a fetal position, his manacled hands covering his testicles.

Jacques calmly opened the cell door, pulled a chair into the cubicle, placed it against the wall and lit a cigarette. Abdul stopped moaning. The recorder was turned on. The prisoner straightened out of his coiled position and lifted himself to his cot, sitting with his head bowed. "Give me a cigarette," he muttered.

"Go fuck yourself, animal," Jacques casually responded, lighting a second cigarette. He blew the smoke at the Cobra.

"You're a tough guy. If I didn't have my hands and feet chained, I'd kick the shit out of you," the Cobra hissed.

"Not now, pigmeat. Later, before we get through with you, I'll give you a chance. I'd love to tear you to pieces. Now, answer my questions."

"Go to hell, you Jew bastard!"

"This is going to be your last chance. After today, you'll be turned over to the mechanics unit. The first thing they'll do to you is put you in a barrel full of hot pork fat."

"You can't do that, it's against my religion."

"Why should we respect your religion when you don't respect anyone else's?"

"What do you want?" Abdul asked.

"Tell me how you were going to blow up that ship in the Panama Canal."

Abdul showed his dismay by pounding on the cot with his manacled hands. "Who told you that?"

"*Schmuck*, we know the whole Revenge Plan. Talk or I'll leave here now. After the mechanics get through with you, we'll turn what's left of you over to the Israelis. They want you *real bad*."

"Just tell me who ratted on me and I'll talk."

Jacques lit a third cigarette and silently mulled over a likely candidate. After a moment of silence, he said, "Froelich."

"That son of a bitch. It was *his* plan."

Continuing the lie, Jacques said, "He was going to pay you two million dollars for the job."

"He's a liar. The job was to cost five million for me and two million each for my two brothers."

"You don't have any brothers."

"Not by blood, but we are all brothers in the *jihad*. Even without me, they'll do the job."

"Why are you working for that Jew Nordheim?"

"He's no Jew. He's an important Nazi."

"Adolf Hitler, maybe?"

"That's all I have to say, Jew dog."

Jacques flipped the lit cigarette, hitting him in the face. The sparks flew as Abdul scrambled to pick the burning butt off his prison uniform. He put it to his lips and took a deep drag on it.

Exhaling, he yelled, "They'll blow up the canal, Tel Aviv, Paris and a lot more, without me, Jew *Arschloch!*"

"*Bon jour, vous bicot, le chat.*"

☆ ☆ ☆ ☆

Tuesday, May 6, 1952 - 10 a.m. - Leavenworth Penitentiary, Kansas

A black Lincoln limousine stopped at the driveway to the entrance of the foreboding gray stone federal prison, which housed the most vicious criminals in America. A portly, ruddy-faced man of medium height, wearing a black double-breasted jacket, pinstriped trousers, a starched white shirt and a red bow tie and kerchief to match in his outside pocket, got out, then adjusted his pince-nez to his nose.

"I am attorney Alden Gaines, and I wish to see Warden Clyde Wilson," he said to the guard at the entrance.

"Is he expecting you, sir?"

"Tell him I have a habeas corpus writ with me for one of your prisoners."

"Please take a seat on that bench and I'll advise him of your presence."

"I prefer to stand," Gaines said arrogantly.

The guard called the warden's office, and shortly another guard appeared, telling the Chicago attorney, "Follow me, sir."

He was ushered into a waiting room outside the warden's quarters.

"Please have a seat, sir. The warden will see you shortly," the guard said.

"I prefer to stand," Gaines huffed again.

"As you like, sir."

After a twenty-minute wait, a middle-aged, gray-haired woman wearing a blue serge pantsuit and a tie beckoned the restless lawyer into the warden's office.

The tall, heavy-set man stood up, towering over the notorious counselor. "Come in, Mr. Gaines. How may I help you?"

Gaines removed his pince-nez, polished the glasses deliberately, adjusted them back on his nose, reached into his expensive gilt-initialed briefcase and withdrew his writ of mandamus, signed by federal Judge Craig Nelson, then presented it to the warden.

"Mmm, Habeas Corpus for Darren Mayfield. That name isn't familiar to me. Let me check it out," he said as he buzzed his intercom. The grey-haired lady opened the door. "Miss Barnes, please look at our inmate roster for a Darren Mayfield and bring me his file."

"What's he in here for, Counselor?" the warden asked.

"That's what I want to know."

The ex-Marine decided to play with the pompous visitor, so he buttered him up with compliments. "You are quite famous, Mr. Gaines. You have won some very important cases in Chicago and elsewhere. I've read about you in the newspapers."

"That's very kind of you, Warden. I just try to do my job for my clients."

"I think we've had a few of your clients in here."

"Well, you win some, make deals on others, and occasionally lose some."

"We recently released an Anthony Cardona. He was sentenced to five years for a bank-fraud conviction."

Gaines flushed and nervously polished his lenses. "Oh, yes. The U.S. Attorney offered him a deal as an accessory to a bank swindle. He pleaded guilty, and as I recall, he only served three of the five-year sentence."

"That's correct, Mr. Gaines. He behaved himself here. He's a smooth cookie." The door opened. Mrs. Barnes entered.

"Well, Gladys, what have we got on Darren Mayfield?"

"Sir, there is no Darren Mayfield in this institution."

"Are you sure?" the warden queried.

Gaines' florid complexion paled slightly. "Warden, I am sure there is a mistake being made here," he asserted.

"There is no mistake, Counselor. We keep very meticulous records of our prison population. Where did you get that information that Darren Mayfield is here?"

"From a very reliable source. It is very confidential."

"Well, it might be another prison, sir. There is no Mayfield here. Check with the Bureau of Prisons. They keep duplicate records of all federal detention centers," Wilson said.

"Do you mind checking again, sir? I have a valid writ."

"Gladys, send the PK in here."

She harrumphed her way out. Five minutes later, a tall, muscular man in uniform appeared.

"This is Liam Mahoney, our principal keeper. He is a walking index of every inmate."

"Pleased to meet you, sir. I am Alden Gaines, attorney at law. I have a habeas corpus writ for a Darren Mayfield. Is he here?"

"There is no one by that name in Leavenworth. Does he have an alias?"

"Not that I know of."

"That's it, then."

"This is very strange," Gaines said as he departed in a huff.

The two ex-Marines snickered softly as Gaines slammed the door.

☆ ☆ ☆ ☆

Tuesday, May 6, 1952 - same day - New York City

The Wall Street offices of Thornton & Wiley were unusually busy. The New York Stock Exchange market had started off with a selling spree. The Dow was down 42 points, based on rumors that China was pouring troops across the Yalu River into South Korea.

Two U.S. Marshals had just left the office of Ernest Thornton. They briefed him on the potential arrival of a man representing Darren Mayfield. The harried stockbroker agreed to cooperate, and advised them to sit at a desk outside his office. A well dressed, swarthy, dark-complected man was ushered into Thornton's office.

"I am Anthony Cardona. I have a letter from Darren Mayfield," he said to Thornton.

The marshals listened at the door, then entered. "Mr. Cardona, you are under arrest."

They read him his rights. The marshal rushed Cardona out of the organized chaos of buying and selling stocks. At the elevator, they pinioned his hands behind his back.

"What's the charge?" he pleaded.

"Obstruction of justice, conspiracy, et cetera. Now, shut up!"

They rushed him to the Federal House of Detention in lower Manhattan, where he disrobed and changed into prison garb. Among his possessions was an envelope with ten thousand dollars, a Rolex watch, a gold ring bearing a large ruby, car keys, a Madison Hotel key, an address book, and a scrawled letter to Thornton & Wiley signed by Darren Mayfield.

"I'll take that letter," the marshal said to the prison clerk.

He signed the requested receipt *Joseph Doyle, U.S. Marshal*, then he and his partner, Aaron Ward, were directed to a private room where they placed a call to Attorney General McGranery.

"Sir, this is U.S. Marshal Doyle. We've arrested Anthony Cardona. He is in the Federal House of Detention here in Manhattan. He had ten thousand in cash on him, plus the letter signed by Mayfield."

"Good job, Doyle. Where are you now?"

"At the detention center, sir."

"You're close to the Federal Courthouse on Foley Square. Hustle over there and ask for U.S. Attorney Aldrich. Give him that letter. He'll take it from there."

"Yes, sir."

At the U.S. Attorney's office, a secretary handed a note to Aldrich, who was in a plea-bargaining session. He glanced at the message and abruptly excused himself, then picked up the phone in his office to speak with the Attorney General.

"Aldrich here, sir."

"Mort, that matter I spoke to you about has been accomplished. The prisoner, Anthony Cardona, is residing at your favorite housing facility. U.S. Marshals Doyle and Ward are on their way to you with a letter signed by a Darren Mayfield. Cardona is not a U.S. citizen. He just finished a stay at Leavenworth. Do not make a record of the name of Darren Mayfield. He's a John Doe. Got it? That's top secret."

"Yes, sir. What do you want me to do with Cardona?"

"Take him before a friendly U.S. Commissioner and charge him with conspiracy to obstruct justice, planning the escape of a John Doe prisoner in a federal prison, bribery of a prison official, and treason. Call your pal, the warden, and tell him no phone calls for Cardona until you give the word."

"Are we going to try this guy?"

"No, Mort, eventually I'd like to have him deported, on one condition."

"What's that?"

"No jail time if he agrees to plead guilty and doesn't fight deportation."

"You think he'll accept that?"

"Well, I think his friends might convince him."

"Jim, isn't this Tony 'The Peach' Cardona who worked for Joseph Kennedy and Frank Costello in the booze business?"

"The very same. Mort, we've known each other a long time. This is on the fringe of a very high-priority matter. Extremely top secret. Handle this personally. Don't share it with staff. I want him on ice for a few days. He may try to bribe a guard to get a message out. Cut him off at the pass, buddy. No bail. Some day soon I'll brief you."

"I'll take care of it," Aldrich agreed.

The U.S. Attorney poked his head into the conference room, whispered to an assistant to take over the plea-bargaining negotiations, then left and hailed a cab to the Federal House of Detention. In short order he was in an interrogation room, where Cardona was delivered to him.

"Sit down, Tony."

"Who are you?"

"I'm Morton Aldrich, the U.S. Attorney for the Southern District. You're in a lot of trouble, son, and so soon after leaving Leavenworth."

"I want a lawyer."

"In due time, my friend. But first, let me spell it out for you." Aldrich, a former captain with the 101st Airborne in Europe during the war, was a tough veteran and a sharpened student of human nature, so he came on strong. "Don't try to smart-ass your way out of here. You're facing at least twenty years without parole, possibly a life sentence for treason."

"Treason? You're crazy. I'm a good American!" Tony screamed.

"Don't raise your voice. Yes, treason."

"How?"

"You helped a Darren Mayfield, who is really John Doe, a German spy. There is no Darren Mayfield. Where did you get that ten thousand dollars? Not only that, you're not an American citizen. Perhaps you're a spy, too."

"Hey, hold it for a minute. This is getting too heavy for me. I'm no spy. I've been in this country since I was ten years old."

"How come you never became a citizen?"

"I forgot."

Aldrich laughed loudly. "You forgot? That's the dumbest excuse I've *ever* heard. You ran booze from Canada for Joseph Kennedy and Frank Costello. You've got to be smarter than that. Come clean with me and I'll try to help you. Con me and you're on your own. Which is it going to be?"

"I want a lawyer."

Aldrich rose and said, "Okay, pal. I'm taking you before a U.S. Commissioner to file charges, then you're on your own."

"Hey, sir, wait. Please, sit for a minute. What do you want to know?"

"What were you doing with that money, and why were you at that stockbroker's office?"

"Look, I don't know any Mayfield. I never saw the guy. There is this prison guard, Al Wirtz, at Leavenworth. He knew I was being released, so he sent me to a Chicago lawyer, Alden Gaines, with two notes. One was for ten grand for me. I was to take one hundred G's from Thornton & Wiley to the mouthpiece in Chicago. That's all I had to do with the whole friggin' thing. I don't know any spies or anything about that treason crap. That's the whole *schmear*, so help me," Cardona wailed, crossing himself.

"If that's the truth, I'll try to help you. You're from Naples, aren't you?"

"Yeah, why?"

"How would you like to visit your relatives, or do a long stretch?"

"Is that an offer?"

"Not yet. I won't arraign you for forty-eight hours. No phone calls. Make one, and you've lost me as a friend. I'm inclined to believe you. Don't cross me. That phony Mayfield is a Nazi spy. So be cool. Rest up for a couple of days at this lush hotel. Talk to no one, and I'll try to get you off the hook."

"Thanks, Mr. Aldrich. I told you the truth."

The U.S. Attorney turned him over to a guard. He stopped at the warden's office and asked that the prisoner be removed from the other denizens of the House of Detention.

Back at his office, he phoned Jim McGranery and reported the confession. The Attorney General called Leavenworth and relayed the Cardona version to the warden, Clyde Wilson.

"Al Wirtz, you say. Why, that son of a bitch! He's the last guy I would suspect. I'll crucify that two-faced bastard!"

"Hold it a minute, Clyde. Don't blow your top yet. We've got to put a clamp on this whole affair."

"I can't sit still for this double-crossing holier-than-thou-ratfink."

"Come on, Clyde, cool it and listen. In due time you can do what you like. For now, if you charge him with a felony, he'll have a lawyer, and the whole story will ruin a very delicate, top-secret operation. As an old Marine, make believe we're still at war. Call the guy in. Suspend him for thirty days on condition that he never discusses this affair with anyone. Tell him that the prisoner using the name of Mayfield is just a John Doe, who is really a Nazi spy. Any leaks from him and he'll be charged with treason, besides all that aiding and abetting crap. Put the fear of hell in him. He's in deep water."

"Okay, okay," Wilson fumed. "What about that sleazeball lawyer Gaines?"

"Ah, that's going to be handled by someone else. Now, Clyde, please hold that temper."

"Don't worry, Jim, I'm a team player."

"Gotcha."

The Attorney General reached Bart Milburn at Guantanamo, and outlined the developments in Leavenworth with the visit of Alden Gaines after the removal of Mayfield, renamed John Doe, and the apprehension of Cardona. The guard was identified, he was told, and would be silenced by Warden Wilson.

"Bart, we have to deal with the Attorney," McGranery warned.

"Let me think for a minute. You say Cardona worked for Costello and Kennedy in the booze business?"

"Oh yeah, he ran motorboats from Windsor, Ontario, across the river into Detroit during Prohibition."

"Jim, I think I know how to zip the lip of this Mafia mouthpiece. Don't ask me, because you don't want to hear it."

"It's your ball, carry it. 'Bye."

Bart remembered Frank Costello's daily ritual at the Terminal Barber Shop in the Waldorf Astoria Hotel in New York. He placed a call on the admiral's red phone. Costello was about to leave and was in the process of tipping the barber, manicurist, and shoeshine man when the call came in. Bart easily recognized his hoarse voice.

"This is Bart Milburn, Frank. Is there a phone booth outside the barber shop I can call you on?"

"Yes, friend, I use it often. It's Murray Hill 2-9654. Call me in five minutes," he whispered.

Costello finished dispensing his largesse, then casually walked out to the phone booth on the hotel mezzanine. The booth was not occupied, and he entered just as the phone rang.

"I'm here, Bart. What's up?"

"Do you know a Chicago lawyer by the name of Alden Gaines?"

"Yeah, a slimy shyster. What's wrong?"

Bart explained the scenario.

"Rest easy. His mouth will be zipped. What's going to happen to Tony Cardona? He's not too bright, but not a bad guy. I'd vouch for him to keep his mouth shut."

"Frank, he won't have to do time. However, he will be deported. He's not a citizen."

"Where is he now?"

"They've got him on ice at the Federal House of Detention in New York."

"If you could put in a good word for him, I'd appreciate it. I'll take care of the Chicago matter."

"I'll do my best."

"If you can avoid deportation for him, I'll guarantee his silence. He will be a good witness later on against the shyster, the guard, and your John Doe. You've got my word on that."

"Okay, I'll try. Is that a *quid pro quo*?"

"No, I'll follow through on the counselor, but the Cardona matter will be considered a favor."

"Fair enough, Frank. You'll hear from me. Thanks," Bart said.

☆ ☆ ☆ ☆

Chicago - same day

In the late afternoon, a limousine stopped in front of the First National Bank on La Salle Street. Two nattily dressed men alighted and entered the office building. They entered the offices of Gaines, Leslie & Morgan.

A blonde receptionist asked, "Is Mr. Gaines expecting you, gentlemen?"

"My name is John Fischetti. This is August Santori. I phoned earlier."

A smartly dressed, middle-aged woman appeared.

"Come this way, gentlemen," she said, smiling thinly.

The attorney rose and greeted both men, then said, "Please, sit. Do you have a problem, John?" Gaines asked.

"No, Alden, you do."

"What does that mean?" the florid-faced man demanded.

"Let me make it simple for you, counselor. You got a habeas corpus for a Mayfield at Leavenworth. There is no such person. Drop it. Forget it and the name of Mayfield. You never heard of him, understood?"

"Don't push that Mafia crap at me. Who the hell do you hoods think you are?"

Santori, better known as Big Augie, rose from his chair, pulled a .38 caliber Smith & Wesson from his inside jacket and held it to the temple of the terrorized attorney.

"Mr. Gaines, you just insulted Mr. Fischetti and me. You called us *hoods*. We would appreciate an apology. Now," he calmly and quietly whispered, pressing the gun into the man's flesh.

"Hey, I didn't mean that in a pejorative sense."

"Cut the per...whatever that means. Say you're sorry," Augie snarled.

"I'm sorry, okay?"

Santori pocketed the weapon.

"Maybe you didn't understand me, Alden," Fischetti said softly. "We're here to do you a favor, and you get on your high horse and berate us? You're in deep shit, my friend. If you don't take our friendly advice, it will be at your own risk."

"Wait a minute, John. I'm entitled to an explanation."

"Get this into that smart-ass legal head of yours. You got Tony Cardona arrested today. You got a prison guard facing jail. On top of all that, you're looking for a Mayfield who is a Nazi spy. Now, *schmuck*, the big boys want you to forget that name and to never talk about it. Besides, look how much business you stand to lose if you don't play ball. In fact, you might have an accident."

Gaines' hands trembled. Sweat dotted his brow. His lips quivered, and his complexion was several shades lighter. He mopped his face with a light blue silk handkerchief.

"Why didn't you tell me that this message comes from the top?" Gaines whimpered. "You have my word as a lawyer that the matter is closed. From here on, I know nothing of this situation."

"Have a good day, Alden," Fischetti mocked, then they left.

☆ ☆ ☆ ☆

Guantanamo, Cuba - later that day

The White House operator reached Bart Milburn in the admiral's office. "General, I have Douglas Milburn on the line."

"Fine."

"Bart, I just had a call from the Uncle. He was very cryptic. The message is as follows: *Chicago matter has been put to rest.*"

"Great, Doug - don't ask me what that means."

"This gumshoe business of yours has my mind doing cartwheels."

"Douglas, this little message is but a pimple on the ass of a dinosaur. Scratch it and the infection kills the Tyrannosaurus rex."

"What in hell are you rambling about, Bart?"

"In simple terms, Douglas, we had a glitch, and your buddy helped. You know I'm involved in a heavy-duty top-secret operation. It's so damned important that any leak will destroy a vital mission. When we're together again, I'll give you a hint of the magnitude of this venture. Bear with me, dear brother. My best to the family and to Constance."

"Barton, first I ask you about two ships that disappeared off the coast of North Korea, and you tell me to forget about it. Now comes this message from the Uncle about a Chicago matter. How long is this conspiracy of silence going to last?"

"We're lucky so far. All I can say, Doug, is that this is high-priority top secret. When you know what we are doing, you'll approve one hundred percent. Here's a teaser for you to keep confidential. We don't want the commies privy to our activities. Enough said?"

"That's a helluva teaser, kid brother General," Doug laughed. *"Ciao."*

Bart returned to the admiral's conference room just as Jacques came in from his visit with Ahmed the Cobra. The admiral was visiting Herman Klaus. Berger had finished his session with Hans Langsdorff. Sophia, Tony and Maybrook were preparing a compendium of declarations from the key prisoners.

"Bart, Ahmed got nasty," Jacques began. "I roughed him up a little. He finally let a few things out of his filthy mouth. Froelich, he said, planned the Panama Canal blow-up. He further stated that the Revenge Plan would be executed without him. His last words were, *They'll blow up the canal, Tel Aviv, Paris and a lot more.* We have to put our allies on the alert, as well as our CIA and combined military forces. There are others out there on the loose as backups." Jacques played the tape of his session with the Cobra.

The admiral returned in time to hear the recording. "That's a threat we can't ignore," Thomas declared. "I just left Hermann Klaus. He practically confirms what the Arab's tape indicates. It all ties in with my previous session with Sir Clive."

"Let's get all the interrogations and tapes ready. How are you coming along, Richard, Sophia and Tony?"

"We should have them blended in an hour or so," Maybrook replied.

"You three keep at it. Admiral, would you care to join Jacques and me at the compound? This is the time to intimidate those fifteen prisoners we picked up in Malmo."

"My pleasure, General." They exited quickly and headed for the compound, where six redoubtable Marines were on guard. The prisoners were in the yard in front of the prison barracks enjoying the tropical Cuban sun. The Marine guard at the gate saluted the three men as they entered the paved surface of the fenced confines. At a signal from the admiral, a Marine sergeant blew a shrill whistle. Four other Marines, rifles in hand, marshaled the fifteen prisoners into the barracks.

"Sit on the floor!" the sergeant shouted, and repeated the order in German, "*Setzen sie sich!*"

"How many of you understand English?" Bart asked.

Ten raised their hands.

"Do all of you speak German? *Sprechen sie Deutsch?*"

All raised their hands.

Bart turned to the admiral. "I'll give it to them in German, and you and Jacques can reiterate my remarks in English. Stress the mechanics routine and the possibility of hanging."

Bart delivered a short message in German. "*Stillgestanden* (Attention)! You men are in very serious trouble. You are war criminals and face a sentence of hanging. You will be questioned one at a time. Those of you Nazis who cooperate and answer honestly will get consideration. We know you are Gestapo, or better yet, Waffen SS soldiers. You may think you are tough, but you haven't met the Americans' mechanics squad."

There was a nervous shifting and whispering among the group, then Bart spun the yarn of what the mechanics do to recalcitrant prisoners.

"After they get through with you, we let you suffer until the court finds you guilty. Then we hang you right away. *Das ist alles.*"

The admiral compassionately advised them to talk honestly to the interrogators then he repeated Bart's dire predictions. Jacques laid it on thick. He repeated Bart's warning in English, French and German.

"Don't be heroic, *Arschlochs*. Your bosses are singing canaries. Tell the truth and maybe you'll be sent home some day."

The three men abruptly turned and exited the barracks. One of the prisoners stood up and shouted, "We are not Nazis!"

The four Marines guarding the door, rifles in hand, slammed the door behind them. The men were terrified by the admonitions. One of the men, who seemed to be in charge, possibly an officer, addressed the group in German.

"This is America. They don't do things like that. They were trying to frighten us. Give them nothing…"

He was cut off by expletives. The group of fifteen broke up into animated meetings of twos, threes and fours. The session with Bart, Jacques and the admiral had had its effect. The result was a complete fracture of their previous solidarity. Bart used the red phone in the admiral's office, and the White

House operator put him through to John Steelman.

"How are you doing, General?"

"Too good, my friend. Is he available? If so, maybe he'll allow you to listen in."

"Urgent?"

"Extremely."

"Hold on."

A minute passed.

"General Milburn, what's the crisis now?" President Truman said.

"Sir, the word *crisis* aptly describes the problem, and calls for a full answer."

"Let's have it."

Bart repeated the Revenge Plan. "We have enough confessions to warrant an alert to our allies whose territories are likely to be targets of the worst possible acts of terrorism. While we have captured the top men and what would seem to be their first team of potential perpetrators, there are indications that there is a backup team prepared to carry out the head maniac's orders, such as blowing up the Panama Canal, the Versailles Palace, Westminster Abbey, Tel Aviv, and possibly the Capitol in Washington, or the White House, for that matter. Caution is the operative word, sir."

"Do you find those threats credible?" Truman asked coolly.

Bart bit his lip angrily. After a few seconds he responded. "Sir, with the deepest of respect, may I recall how the world ignored Hitler's threats in the Thirties. We ignored *Mein Kampf.* Chamberlain placated this maniac, and our isolationist policy bathed us in complacency. France stood by and…"

Truman cut Bart off. "I don't need a history lesson, young man. Your point is well taken. Bring your evidence here tomorrow at 5 p.m. I will have the necessary Cabinet members present."

"Mr. President, should I convey this information to General Smith?"

"Not necessary, Barton; he'll be in attendance at the meeting. I appreciate your dedication."

"Sir, one other point, if I may."

"Go ahead."

"We are close to starting preliminary trials under the aegis of the military, unless you have orders to the contrary."

"I am glad you brought that up. Hold on for a minute while I check my calendar."

Bart lit a cigarette, then reached for the electric percolator and poured hot coffee in a mug. Five minutes later Truman was back on the phone.

"I've cleared my calendar. Can you be here for a buffet lunch at 1 p.m.? This may be a long session."

"I'll be there, Mr. President."

Admiral Thomas came into his office. Bart was ruminating about his conversation with Truman.

"Our newest guest has arrived, blindfolded. He doesn't know where he is."

"Mayfield?"

"Yes, I assumed you wanted him to have our special welcoming treatment shaved head, orifices checked, cold shower, mug shot, full restraints, and placement in one of our pricey dungeons."

"Exactly."

"What's next?"

"Sir, I've been ordered to the White House for a conference at 1300 hours tomorrow. Let's check the conference room and see how they're doing with those confessions."

Jacques and Berger had returned to the conference room. The admiral and Bart were there.

"I was curious about Mayfield," Jacques said. "He didn't see me. I watched the boys put him through the welcoming routine. He looked like a dirty old dishrag. His mouth worked like an old harlot behind bars. When he refused to stand still for his photo session, Noah's forehand served some aces across his pale face. The bruises put color back in his cheeks. He threatened to have everyone fired when his lawyer shows up with his habeas corpus."

"Noah told him to stick his habeas up his corpus," Phil laughed.

The team sitting around the conference table joined in the hilarity.

"Jacques, I am appointing you as chief executioner of Mayfield. Not his corpus, just his spirit," Bart quipped.

"We finished the compilation of the confessions," Maybrook declared.

"I'm leaving for D.C. late tonight. Jacques will take over for me. I'll be taking the material and recordings you folks have prepared," Bart said. "Here's the drill from here on in. All of you are to go for a full-court press on all of our detainees. Record everything. The Waffen SS should be taken one at a time. Give them the mechanics or the hanging threat, as the reaction indicates."

"I'd like a crack at that Swiss banker, Peter Weber," Admiral Thomas volunteered.

"He's yours, sir," Bart replied. "Jacques, besides Mayfield, take on General Heinrich Müller. He should be ripe by now. Maybrook, try your hand on Hugo Schultz, but no mention of my name. Leave the *coup de grace* for me. He's the son of a bitch I shot at the Ohrdruf concentration camp. Work out a rotation on those SS punks. Turn the young ones over to Sophia. She can do the hearts-and-flowers routine. Play on their anxiety to see their parents, family, girlfriends or wives. Any questions?"

"General, I assume that we can get as rough as necessary," Maybrook said.

"Full-court press says it all. Just don't kill anyone," Bart joked. "By the way, if Gideon Cartman, Sedgwick or anyone from Homestead calls, route them to the White House operators. That's it. Jacques, call Major Flaherty at the hangar. Tell him I'm going to Havana. The plane should be on standby there for any emergency use by one of you, or for my return from D.C. I'll be flying out on the Eastern red-eye. Call Elizabeth and have her meet me at the coffee shop."

Ninety minutes later Bart joined Elizabeth at the terminal coffee shop. They had a light snack at a corner table. He briefed her on his journey to Washington without revealing the purpose of the trip.

"Honey, when I return, I'm going to take you and Joyce for a look-see at some of the prisoners. Maybe you'll recognize some of the commandants at the death camps, or Gestapo bums. You and Joyce have been shuffled through some of those concentration stockades. Would you mind doing that?"

"Barton, dear, I've been looking forward to that tour. Those Nazi scars are lodged in my subconscious, and they come to mind quite often."

"Maybe this visit and their trials will be the catharsis to erase those scars."

"Barton, I'm so proud of you."

"Likewise. I'll be back in a day or two at the most. Love to the kids and all at the house. Tell Joyce that her brother is at the base. Come now, I'll see you to your car."

☆ ☆ ☆ ☆

Wednesday, May 7, 1952 - 1 p.m. - Washington

Bart arrived at the White House West Gate at 12:50, and went directly to Steelman's office.

"Welcome, General. You've ignited a firestorm here," the President's aide declared.

"I hope so, John. When you have experienced a bit of the Nazi virus, you can't treat it with aspirin. Remember *Mein Kampf*, my friend. Don't ever forget the prophecies contained therein. The world paid a helluva price by ignoring the contents," Bart said.

"I'm your friend, Bart. Before you walk into the Cabinet room, I want to caution you not to exaggerate this incredible scenario of the so-called Revenge Plan. Pardon the cliché, but you have a tiger by the tail. That's a tough audience in there. I don't want you to destroy your credibility by yelling fire in this particular theatre," Steelman said.

"You are my friend. I am your friend. Remember Irish patriot John Philpot Curran's statement during the Right of Election of the Lord Mayor of Dublin on July 10, 1970? I'll quote you part of it. *The condition upon which God hath given liberty to man is eternal vigilance.* Now, if this fucking citadel of democracy is going to be ruled by a bunch of striped-pants Pollyannas, then beware of the incipient clones of Hitler that will rise again," Bart said. "My gut instincts, plus empirical knowledge, have driven me to this moment. I sincerely hope I'm mistaken. I'd rather err on the side of caution than stupidity."

"I'm on your side, pal. Go to it."

Steelman led him into the Cabinet room. The assemblage awaited the arrival of the President. Attendees were in groups of twos, threes and fours. Bart quickly appraised the gathering of Cabinet members and military leaders, indicating in his mind's eye the effect of his warning to Truman. He placed a flexible oversized briefcase against the wall opposite the buffet credenza, saluted the Joint Chiefs and their chairman, General Omar Bradley. They waved back at him.

Attorney General McGranery took Bart by the arm and steered him into a corner of the vast room. "Bart, we've two very important subjects to discuss here today. Stick with the Revenge Plan until that one is resolved. After that, we can try to resolve the trial procedures. I've tentatively arranged for us to meet with Supreme Court Justice Robert Jackson, the former U.S. Chief counsel at the Nuremberg trial."

"That's terrific. I admire that man. I've read some of the excerpts of his prosecution."

"Let's have a drink," McGranery suggested.

Bart chose iced tea. McGranery poured a short glass of wine. Huddled at the end of the buffet were General Walter Bedell Smith, Allen Dulles, Secretary of Defense Robert Lovett and Secretary of State Dean Acheson. The President arrived, and the conversational hum was muted.

"Come on, gentlemen, hit the chow line. We have a lot to discuss," Truman said jocularly.

A queue was quickly formed. The group dined and exchanged small talk, gossip and some media bashing, a Beltway sport. The President was flanked by the Attorney General and the Secretary of Defense. Bart sat to the right of McGranery and to the left of Bradley. The table was quickly cleared and the service staff left the room. Truman tapped a spoon against a crystal water glass, bringing the meeting to order.

"All present are aware of General Milburn's exploits resulting in the capture of Adolf Hitler and a large number of his Nazi minions. Thus far, it is the best kept secret in this sieving town and the world, for that matter. We are about to hear some details of a very sinister plot to disrupt the current peace. If the presentation of General Milburn is in fact accurate, our country and our NATO allies are facing a clear and present danger. General Milburn, the floor is all yours," Truman said.

Bart rose, picked up his oversized briefcase and placed it alongside his chair.

"Gentlemen, in brief, our team, generously supplied by General Smith, is composed of CIA agents, assisted by Admiral Thomas and a French captain of detectives, Felix Gaumont. The roundup of our prisoners was facilitated by General Bradley and the Joint Chiefs. We have Hitler, Bormann, Joachim Heydrich and General Müller, head of the Waffen SS, the fighting arm of the Gestapo, and others in Guantanamo. Fifty-odd are in Homestead, seventeen at the naval base. Here is the crux of the problem. Avram Nordheim, now exposed as Adolf Hitler himself, has devised what he calls the Revenge Plan. He intends, among other things, to blow up the Panama Canal, the Capitol building and possibly the White House, the Versailles Palace, the Eiffel Tower, the British Houses of Parliament, Westminster Abbey and possibly Buckingham Palace, Tel Aviv, and a myriad of locales."

"This is positive lunacy or an idle threat to ruffle our feathers," Allen Dulles roared.

Milburn ignored Dulles' outburst, then calmly placed his tape recorder on the Cabinet table. "May I play some confessions for you, gentlemen?" he asked as he looked at Truman for approval. The President nodded.

In succession, they heard Sir Clive Fenwick, Martin Bormann, Konrad

Fliegel a.k.a. Keith Reynolds, Admiral Ludwig, and Ahmed the Cobra. Hitler's voice was last. The room was stock-still. Bart removed the recorder and sat quietly awaiting a reaction.

General Smith broke the silence. "When does this maniac expect this plan to become operative?"

"Within thirty days, if he doesn't surface," Bart replied.

"Bart, you've had him since April 22nd," Truman said. "Today is the 7th of May. That would suggest fifteen days from now or sooner. How much credence do you lend to these confessions?"

"Mr. President, while we have most of Hitler's team in custody, the one statement I'm inclined to take at face value is the ranting of the Cobra. He more than hints that there is a backup team spread around the world ready to implement the devil's handiwork," Bart replied.

"What we have heard so far is indeed a somber scenario. I'd like to hear some comments from you, gentlemen," Truman requested.

General Bradley raised his hand.

"Go ahead, Omar."

"Mr. President, those of us who have had first-hand knowledge of the apocalypse unleashed by this megalomaniac can attest to the wildest machinations of this verminous bastard. There are no rules in this demon's book. I take General Milburn's concerns most seriously."

"There is more interrogation to be done," Dulles asserted. "A few more days of pressure of these SS guys might make the difference. We'd be rushing to judgment if we were to put our NATO numbers into a tizzy by what they would consider our paranoia."

Bart's knee-jerk reaction was anticipated by McGranery, who placed his hand on Milburn's arm, holding back an explosive retort.

"The confessions heard here today are indeed sinister. We would be well served to alert our allies quietly about a potential cataclysmic outbreak of terrorism," Secretary of State Acheson slowly and decisively asserted.

McGranery jabbed a surprised Milburn. "The most cautious man in this room has just spoken," he whispered to Bart.

Acheson's remarks set the tone for the rest of the meeting.

"Mr. President, an ocean of blood flowed in World War II," General Bradley said emotionally. "I was in it from day one. The carnage concocted by this monster was highlighted in early April, 1945. That was the day when Eisenhower, Patton and I entered the Ohrdruf concentration camp. Young Colonel Barton Milburn was there with us. We had no idea of the horrific sight we were encountering. Naked bodies of men, women and children in pits dug by the deceased, stacked by the hundreds on top of each other. Bullet holes in their skulls. Blood and Guts Patton, our tough guy, pulled away and vomited. I cite this as a small example of the kind of bestiality this monster, Hitler, can wreak. Havoc is one of his prime tools."

Secretary of Defense Lovett raised his hand.

"Yes, Robert?" Truman nodded.

"Mr. President, I agree with Dean's remarks. The Joint Chiefs, the CIA and the State Department have to come up with a coordinated plan to deal with this threat, with your guidance, sir. Yet, we have to handle this very discreetly or our best kept secret, so far, will become porous. The media will go berserk," Lovett said.

"General Milburn, what do you envision as the first steps of this Revenge Plan?" Truman asked.

"Sir, based on two specifics, I would venture that the meeting planned for April 23 was designed to parcel out assignments of terror. I believe that the presence of Hans Langsdorff, the captain who scuttled the Graf Spee, and Hermann Klaus indicate to me that two Eagle ships, one on the Pacific side of the canal and the other on the Atlantic side, were to be loaded with explosives placed there by Ahmed the Cobra."

Admiral Edward Prince, Chief of Staff of the Navy Department, who had been sketching an outline of the Panama Canal, put his pen down on his pad and raised his hand. The President nodded. "General, assuming that this cabal of jackanapes comes within proximity of either end of the canal, how do they propose to safeguard the crews of each ship? I realize that it would take just a few men to head vessels into the entrances."

"Admiral, when Captain Langsdorff scuttled the Graf Spee, he had his crew abandon ship and open the cocks to draw water and set off explosives, sinking the vessel. In this instance, I would surmise that they would lower a lifeboat launch and head for the Panama jungles. They would use timing devices to set the explosives within the vessels designed to damage the canal locks," Bart speculated.

"Being aware of Hitler's perverted mentality, I would not discount this barbarous scenario," Prince declared. "For one, Mr. President, I would recommend a worldwide track of every one of Eagle Shipping's vessels in cooperation with NATO and all available intelligence sources."

A chorus of "amens" filled the room. Truman slapped the table for attention. "Gentlemen, apparently we have a concurrence of opinion to take whatever measures are necessary to thwart Hitler and his jackanapes, as Admiral Prince described them. *Jackanapes,* a word I haven't heard in years," Truman said with a muffled laugh.

"Mr. President, how do you propose to alert our NATO partners without causing a media leak?" Acheson queried.

Before the President could ponder a reply, Bart asserted, "Mr. President, with your permission, sir, I have a suggestion."

"What is it, Barton?"

"All of this began when the Israelis asked us to check on Nordheim. It wouldn't be that big a white lie, sir, if the warning was relayed to us by Prime Minister Ben-Gurion. He would assume the responsibility for the alert and blame the Jihad. In return, eventually we will repay him for the favor by turning Ahmed-al-Said, the Cobra, over to Israel."

All eyes in the room focused on Bart. The Cabinet room was silent. Truman spun his pen on the table top, weighing Bart's suggestion. The dignified and always reserved Dean Acheson pierced the silence with a guffaw, totally out of character. The gathering turned their surprised gaze to Acheson, who smugly twirled his mustache.

"What's so funny, Dean?" Truman asked.

"Mr. President, that suggestion from General Milburn has all the earmarks of a diplomat's verbal pirouette at a UN assembly. Not bad, not bad," Acheson commented.

"I take it, Dean, that you are complimenting General Milburn?" Truman asked.

"Yes, indeed I am. In my experience, sir, I've heard of stranger ploys in the diplomatic arena."

Lovett raised his hand.

"Bob?"

"Mr. President, if General Milburn's suggestion is ascribed to the Israelis after their approval, then the military committee of NATO, which headquarters here, should be called into session quickly."

"Do I hear any objections before I speak with Prime Minister Ben-Gurion?" No one disagreed.

"Mr. President, if Ben-Gurion approves, I'd suggest, as a matter of form, that we invite their ambassador here for a briefing on the necessity to maintain a tight clamp on this world alert and its sources," Acheson suggested.

"Good idea, Dean. However, the Israelis are uniquely qualified to prevent leaks," Truman said. "Gentlemen, I'll try to reach the Prime Minister now from my office. The Attorney General will take up phase two of this session: the question of trials for these vermin, as far as where, when and how. Go to it, Jim. I'll be back after my talk with Ben-Gurion."

Truman and Steelman left the room.

"Gentlemen, I'll try to answer any legal questions," McGranery began. "General Milburn will outline the scope of the adjudications contemplated."

Bart delineated the progress to date - the potential witnesses, the interrogation process and the locales of the prisoners.

"How soon do you expect to start the wheels of justice rolling?" General Bradley asked.

"Sir, the current objective is to arraign the prisoners at an evidentiary hearing under the jurisdiction of the Department of the Army within the next thirty days, more or less."

"Hold it right there, Barton," Bradley said. "Are you *au courant* with the inquiry concerning violations of the Geneva Conventions of 1949?"

"Yes, sir, as well as pre-'49 back to the Nuremberg trials, which began on October 20, 1945, against twenty-three high Nazi war criminals."

"Let's take a ten-minute break. I want to confer with the Joint Chiefs," Bradley said.

Bart stood up, stretched, poured a cup of coffee from the electric percolator and lit a cigarette. The Attorney General joined him.

"What's going on, Jim?" Bart asked.

"Brad and I have been communicating on the legal proprieties to be observed in the conduct of these trials. He was concerned about the Supreme Court's position if the adjudication were to take place in the United States or its territories. I refreshed my memory. In *Ex parte Quirin,* the court upheld the jurisdiction of an American military commission because they considered the charges against the defendant to be a war crime."

"Dammit, I had read that. There were two other such cases brought before the court," Bart responded. "You handed me photocopies of those cases weeks ago. I just skimmed through them."

"Yes, my friend, there was the Yamashita case, where they granted the petitioner a hearing because the commission sat in the Philippines, which was then under U.S. jurisdiction. It was denied. Also, in *Johnson v. Eisenkrager,* they refused a petition because the commission sat in China, and sentenced the German accused to prison in Germany. So you are on solid ground with a military tribunal in the good old U.S. of A.," McGranery said.

"What is Bradley conferring about with the Joint Chiefs?"

"Time, place and participants. Look over there. Lovett's in the huddle."

Bart glanced at the ad hoc conference at the other end of the room. The conclave then was terminated, and the group resumed their places at the huge Cabinet table. The Attorney General tapped a crystal glass, and the meeting came to order.

"General Bradley?"

"The Joint Chiefs, with the concurrence of Secretary Lovett, recommend the following. Heretofore, war crimes were under the jurisdiction of the Army Judge Advocate General. It is the consensus that the three departments, Army, Navy and Air Force, sit on the tribunals. Anyone care to comment?"

"General Bradley, do you have any suggestions as to where these trials should be held?" McGranery asked, playing the straight man, aware of what was coming.

"It is further recommended that all war crime prisoners be incarcerated at the U.S. Disciplinary Barracks at Fort Leavenworth, Kansas. The prison there is large and more than adequate to house a large group of detainees. An Executive Order from the President is required. Any objections?"

"Sir, are there facilities there for housing cooperating prisoners who will testify for the prosecution? Should they be housed separate from the accused?" Bart asked.

"Lots of quarters to accommodate the segregation," Bradley assured him. "Now, there is one more recommendation. For the purpose of continuity of effort, it is the unanimous opinion of the Joint Chiefs that you, General Milburn, be called up from your reserve status to head up the prosecution team. You will be promoted to major general, subject to President Truman's approval."

Bart was taken aback by the sudden change in the prevailing current of events. He was totally unprepared for what Bradley had said. He looked at McGranery, who shrugged his shoulders and smiled.

"Do I have a choice in this matter, General Bradley?" Bart's discomfiture was apparent.

"General Milburn, we've known each other for ten years, just shortly after your graduation from West Point. I was very proud of your war record, as was Ike. Now you are in a position to receive world recognition. I cite the example of Supreme Court Justice Robert Jackson, who took a hiatus to become U.S. chief counsel at Nuremberg. The same opportunity is now yours. You have displayed a knowledge and experience beyond your years. I realize that this would be a great personal sacrifice. Yet, if I were your father or mentor, I'd say go for it," Bradley said.

Before he could reply, Truman and Steelman returned to the conference.

"Gentlemen, I've had a very satisfactory conversation with Prime Minister Ben-Gurion," said Truman. "He accepted General Milburn's report that the Mossad had learned of a campaign of terrorism about to be launched against the NATO powers and Israel. In fact, he was grateful for the information. While I was out, I called Prime Minister Churchill and alerted him. I've got a call into de Gaulle. Let us set up a briefing for the NATO military committee forthwith. Bob Lovett, will you arrange that? Now, what about the trials, gentlemen?"

Bradley repeated the consensus of the Joint Chiefs and the appointment of Bart Milburn as chief counsel. He asked for an Executive Order to activate the Joint Chiefs' recommendations. Truman polled the room for comments on a name-by-name basis before putting forth the question.

Bart whispered to the Attorney General, "You knew this was coming."

McGranery shrugged his shoulders, smiled and responded "Aye" to the President's poll.

"There is unanimity of affirmation to the Joint Chiefs' proposal. What say you, General Milburn?"

"Mr. President, while I am quite honored by the honors conferred upon me today, I am also in a state of ambivalence beset by personal considerations. However, it is obvious that I have little choice. My reserve status precludes any demurral on my part. I accept the honor and pledge an unstinting effort to the challenge ahead."

"That's fine, Major General. You can have your two stars as soon as the Secretary of Defense hands you notice of your call-up to active duty," Truman said as he noticed Lovett shoving an envelope to Bart.

"Talk of conspiracies!" Bart whispered *sotto voce* to McGranery, who joined the laughter.

"What was that remark, Barton?" Truman asked.

"I'll answer that, Mr. President. He has charged us all with a conspiracy," McGranery said.

The room exploded in a burst of laughter, then Truman tapped the crystal glass. "General Milburn, now that we've settled that matter, tell us what your plan is for the trials."

"Sir, I realize that there is a worldwide complacency settling in among the democratic nations. The Nuremberg trials never received the attention they deserved. The horrors of the Third Reich are becoming a fading memory. Therefore, after the evidentiary hearings at Fort Leavenworth and the full trials begin early next year, I would recommend that the media be permitted to cover the trials of these monsters. Cameras in the courtroom, television aired the world over..."

Allen Dulles banged on the table and in a sudden outburst declared, "This is absolute lunacy! We'll be embarrassing our allies and people here in the U.S. I see no reason to air..."

Bart angrily cut him off: "If this effort is to be a cover-up for the royals, the Cliveden Set in England, the America Firsters here at home, and the misbegotten anti-Semites and hatemongers the world over, then you've chosen the wrong man as chief prosecutor. Remember what Woodrow Wilson said in January, 1917, before the Senate, and I quote: *I am seeking only to face realities and to face them without soft concealments.* Those words are worth repeating," Bart heatedly declared.

"Let's hold it a minute," Truman interjected. "Why this acrimony, Mr. Dulles and General Milburn? Do I detect a feud here?"

General Smith, who had replaced Averell Harriman as ambassador to Moscow, had the complete confidence of Truman. He had earned his stripes as a warrior, a diplomat and now headed the CIA, a key position reporting to no one but the President, so he spoke up.

"Sir, there is no split in our ranks. What we have heard here from Mr. Dulles and General Milburn is an honest difference of opinion. Dulles and Milburn worked side by side conscientiously in the apprehension of these Nazis. I believe I speak for both men when I say there is a mutual respect between them. The question of what may come out of these trials is moot. I believe that Dulles fears a media circus, and Milburn righteously wants to awaken the world's conscience and heat the flames of outrage. We've been sitting on the biggest postwar secret, and there is a point in time, as guaranteed by the First Amendment, when the media will have the right to the full story. I believe that General Milburn is correct in desiring an open trial fully reported by the press and the electronic media. He will handle it with decorum, rubric and dedication. Mr. Dulles can speak for himself, but I am certain he will cooperate."

"Beedle, you are a born diplomat," Truman declared. "Allen Dulles, speak your piece."

"Mr. President, I wish to apologize to General Milburn. He's carried a heavy load with a magnificent performance and result. He has my fullest support. General Smith quite correctly summed up our difference of opinion. I yield to the powers that be. I am a loyal soldier," Dulles said.

"We're agreed on a plan. Now, what else do you need, General Milburn?" Truman inquired.

"We need the fullest cooperation of the Judge Advocate Generals of the Army, Navy and Air Force. We need judges and a defense counsel."

He paused and whispered to McGranery, who nodded assent.

"Sir, I have just asked the Attorney General's permission to mention the fact that Supreme Court Justice Jackson has agreed to meet with me and give me the benefit of his experience as chief counsel at Nuremberg."

"That's excellent," Truman said, then nodded to Bradley. "Yes, Brad, go ahead."

"I've observed this little flareup with great interest. I agree that the story of the carnage in Europe has to be fully aired. I've reported to you, Mr. President, a good deal of the intrigue that occurred prior to the war inside England as well as here in the U.S. There's lots of dirty linen in high places. I'm certain that Allen Dulles doesn't want the hysteria that might result from certain revelations to carry various individual reputations down the gutter streams into sewage," Bradley said.

"Precisely," said Dulles.

"With due respect to all present, and to maintain clarity, it is not our intention to commence a witch hunt," Bart explained. "The apocalyptic firestorm launched by the Nazis, terminating in Germany's Armageddon, resulted in the greatest carnage in history. Our goal is to do an autopsy on the body politic and the psyche of those who engendered and participated in the outrage. The operative question, Mr. President, is, *Where the hell is the world's outrage?* Forgive my language," he said passionately.

The impassioned declaration caused a moment of silence. Dean Acheson pierced the quiet with loud hand-clapping. All eyes turned to the distinguished Secretary of State.

"*Quo vadis? Whither goest thou?* General Milburn has aired the answer that's been lurking in our subconscious these many years," Acheson said. "Congratulations."

"Meeting adjourned, *sine die*," Truman jibed.

Steelman advised the President that de Gaulle was returning his call.

Dulles approached Bart, stuck his hand out and said, "We're on the same team, pal. I'll be there for you."

Bart thanked him and shuffled his papers into his briefcase. Bradley beckoned Bart and McGranery.

"Barton, when do you want to come to my office to plan the transfer of your prisoners to Fort Leavenworth? Attorney General McGranery has offered to give us his input. I recommended to the President the appointment of Judge Advocate General Wilford Ross as senior military officer to preside over the preliminary evidentiary hearings. I hand you now his Executive Order to form a commission to arraign and conduct a preliminary investigation to elicit sufficient evidence."

"General Bradley, as always, you are way ahead of me. Wilford Ross is perfect. He is a no-nonsense, strict, but very fair judge. We have somewhere between eighty to ninety prisoners for the hearings. May I assume, sir, that Judge Ross will, under the President's order, appoint one, two or more judges to facilitate the procedure?"

"Barton, that's something you'll take up with Ross."

"Yes, sir."

"Jim, could you entice Justice Jackson to the huddle?" Bradley asked.

McGranery agreed.

"Sir, please set the time to suit you," Bart said.

"How about 0900 tomorrow?" said Bradley.

Bart and McGranery assented.

"I'll try to woo Jackson to the meeting," McGranery added.

"Congratulations, Major General Milburn. I'll have your stars and official call-up to active duty finalized by then. I'm proud of you, son," Bradley said.

McGranery and Bart departed together. Steelman flagged them at the West Wing exit.

"The boss spoke to de Gaulle. He was very grateful."

On the way to their parked cars, McGranery embraced Bart. "You had a lot of support going for you. Bradley and Acheson are confidants of Truman. All three are rooting for you, as I am. I'm sure that Clark Clifford is aware of all this. He's caught up in other matters for the President. I'm sure the Prez has consulted with him on the whole situation. See you in the a.m. *Ciao.*"

Bart drove directly to the Cafritz Building, where Miss Telford greeted him. "Welcome, stranger."

He acknowledged her with a tentative smile.

"Something wrong, sir?"

"I'm not sure, Nancy. Are Graybeal and Arnold here?"

"Yes."

"Ask them if they are available."

Bart started to sign some checks and papers on his desk when the intercom squawked. "Bart, join me in my office. Martha's on her way," Austin Graybeal said.

Bart entered the office, furnished in early American antiques. Martha Arnold and Graybeal welcomed him warmly.

"How goes your private war, Barton?" Graybeal jested.

"Too damn well."

"What does that mean?" Martha asked.

"In the strictest of confidence, we have captured some high-ranking Nazi war criminals."

"That's good," Austin gibed.

"What I have just revealed is top secret. Not a word to anyone."

"Of course," the two partners chorused.

"Here's the good or bad news for me. I have just been called up from my reserve status."

"Oh, my Lord, what does that mean? Are you being sent to Korea?" a worried Martha asked.

"No, I have been appointed chief counsel and prosecutor for these trials and promoted to major general. I had no say in the matter. I just learned of it at a meeting with the President and the Joint Chiefs."

"Barton, why the hangdog expression? We're mighty proud of you," Graybeal declared.

"That's a very high honor," Martha added.

"Yes, but what does that do to my career as an attorney and my partnership in this firm?"

"Barton, our business is booming. Your appointment will lend added prestige to this firm," Graybeal asserted. "Justice Jackson took leave from the high court for Nuremberg. There is no reason to be concerned."

"Austin, I should be taken off the payroll during my hiatus."

"Nonsense," Martha declared.

Graybeal agreed, "We will continue your compensation as a partner in this firm. We pay you or pay it in taxes. Better if *you* pay the income tax on that money," he laughed softly.

"That's very generous."

"Whenever your secret mission and the trials become public, your service to the government will add to our prestige immeasurably," Graybeal added.

"Austin, besides being a very astute lawyer and diplomat, you think like the CEO of a conglomerate. Thank you both. I'll keep in close touch, and you can always reach me at anytime through the White House telephone operators."

"If either one of us can be of help to you, Bart, don't hesitate to ask," Martha said.

"Thank you. Now, what about Miss Telford? Can I take her with me?"

"We'd prefer she stay with us. There is much she can do here, as well as follow through on your caseload for us to handle."

"Well, I'll go back to my office. I have to tie up some loose ends."

"Godspeed, partner," Graybeal said.

"Go get 'em, tiger," Martha cheered.

Bart finished his chores, briefed Miss Telford and kissed her tear-stained cheek.

CHAPTER THIRTY

Thursday, May 8, 1952 - the Pentagon - 0900 hours

Bart appeared at the office of the Chairman of the Joint Chiefs of Staff in full dress uniform. His trim figure, bedecked with service ribbons, was impressive to the personnel he encountered upon entering the massive citadel housing the nerve center of America's military might. He was quickly ushered into the Chairman's conference room. General Bradley returned Milburn's salute.

"I see the uniform still fits. How do you manage to keep your weight down?"

"Fortunately, I don't have a sweet tooth, sir."

"I wish I could say the same."

Bart greeted Secretary Lovett, Attorney General McGranery, and the Chiefs of Staff: the Chief of Naval Operations, Admiral Prince; General Paul Forley for the Marines, General Maxwell Taylor for the Air Force and General Smith of the CIA. McGranery took Bart by the arm and moved him to the center of the large conference table.

"Justice Jackson, may I present General Barton Milburn."

The distinguished 60-year-old jurist cordially greeted the young general. Despite his pallid countenance, Jackson displayed a sparkling smile. "General, I've looked forward to meeting you. I have been briefed on your exploits and your upcoming assignment."

"Justice Jackson, I'm honored, sir. I've read your statements and interrogations at Nuremberg. You were magnificent."

"Thank you. I hope I can be of some help to you. Jim here told me of your goal to air the vile machinations of the Nazis. The world needs to be reminded of their bestialities and the condoning conduct of the German people during the Third Reich. Nuremberg didn't get the media coverage it deserved."

Bradley pounded the table with his knuckles.

"I have a quick chore to perform, and then we'll get down to business. General Milburn, please stand. I hand you notice of your activation in the U.S. Army from your reserve status. I take pleasure in pinning on your second star, giving you the rank of major general."

Applause followed. Congratulations echoed through the room.

"Now to the business at hand. General Milburn, how soon can the prisoners at Guantanamo and Homestead be transported to Fort Leavenworth?"

"Sir, the CIA staff loaned to me are at the naval base finishing up some key interrogations. The same holds true at Homestead for the ten U.S. Attorneys, a CIA agent, and your Captain Esta Arnold. Incidentally, she's quite a sharp officer. She hit pay dirt with an important prisoner. This is Thursday, the 8th, so could we set the transfer to next Monday, May 12th?"

"That sounds right. I've spoken to General Warren Fielding, commanding officer at the fort. That should give him sufficient time to provide quarters for your cooperative prisoners and jail cells for the rest. Your staff, the judges, prosecutors and defense personnel will be housed at Fort Leavenworth. There is ample room at the Command and General Staff College for all. The students and faculty will be provided quarters elsewhere. There are officers' quarters and barracks there for the legal entourage. Best done this way for security. The MPs will take care of that. Army, Navy and Marine personnel will be housed in barracks at the fort. The Air Force will arrange transports from Guantanamo and Homestead. Any questions, men?"

"General Bradley, the Judge Advocates General of the three departments are standing by for a planning session with General Milburn. I presume that once the judges, prosecutors and defense teams are appointed, they'll be provided with a plane from Andrews Air Force Base?" Admiral Prince asked.

"That's correct, Admiral."

Jackson raised his hand.

"Justice, go right ahead," Bradley said.

"I have cleared my calendar for this day, and if General Milburn would care to have me sit in with the Judge Advocate General, I am available."

"Sir, I would be honored," Bart said.

"General Milburn, the floor is yours. Lay out your plan and timetable," Bradley ordered.

Bart delineated the objective of having a series of evidentiary hearings before a judge, hoping that all prisoners, based on *prima facie* evidence, would be bound over for trial early the following year.

"Why next year?" several of the men queried.

"Gentlemen, this is a rather delicate question. I'll try to answer it cryptically, at best. I ask your indulgence in reading between the lines. Were it up to me solely, I would move for a speedy trial. However, there will be a new administration elected in six months. The national party conventions will take place between now and then. There's been a request to not have these explosive trials brought to world attention and overshadow the campaigns. My hands are tied by Executive Order."

A wave of muttering crisscrossed the huge conference table. Jackson came to Bart's rescue. "Gentlemen, as a jurist I deplore trial delays. However, in this case we are dealing with war criminals. The Supreme Court has found that trials of this sort are not subject to the dictums of our civil laws. It is not indecorous for a judge in criminal courts to set trial dates for murders or other high-crime cases six to eight months after a preliminary hearing. Most times it is beneficial to the defense, sometimes to the prosecution, or both sides, in preparing their cases."

Bradley stepped in. "Let us not question Milburn's position in this matter. I am certain that the nominees of both parties would prefer it this way. The new administration, I am sure, will cooperate in the efforts to prosecute these vermin."

"Just an added fillip to this discussion," Jackson interjected, "these trials, mind you, are historical in nature. The fewer diversions for the news-hungry media, the stronger will be the blow against complacency and fading memories."

"General Bradley, it just occurred to me that in transferring prisoners we have a problem," Bart declared.

"What's that?"

"We have to separate those who will testify for the prosecution from the others. In addition, we can not commingle the top Nazis so they can exchange information. Expedience would dictate a shuttle arrangement of flights from Guantanamo to Fort Leavenworth. At this point in time, we have some of them informing against each other."

General Maxwell Taylor, who had been doodling on a legal-sized pad, raised his hand.

"Yes, General?"

"Brad, I have a suggestion. General Milburn has an F-27 at his disposal now. Let's do this in two stages. Homestead would be the launching pad for a selective shuttle operation. Move the main body of detainees out of Homestead first in a large transport plane, leaving prosecution witnesses behind. Have the F-27 carry selected prisoners to Homestead in a series of flights and incarcerated there. Those not subject to segregation can be dumped en masse at Homestead. We'll have that class of prisoners shipped on a large transport to Fort Leavenworth. General Milburn can sort the traffic as he sees fit. From Guantanamo to Homestead is a short flight. How does that sound?"

"Barton, any comments?"

"Yes, sir, General Bradley, that is an excellent plan."

"Very well. Who will coordinate flight availabilities with General Milburn?"

"Brad, I am assigning Colonel Tyler Ashby and his staff to work and supply the planes necessary. General Milburn will call the shots. All personnel assigned must be advised that this operation is classified as top secret. This matter is settled."

Bradley next opened discussions on the tribunals to the main trials to be held in 1953. Unanimous agreement was reached for the Army, Navy and Air

Force to appoint judges to sit on all tribunals needed for the eighty to ninety defendants.

Bradley said, "Gentlemen, prepare your list of candidates from career officers only. The preliminary hearings will be tried before Judge Advocate General Wilford Ross, chosen by the President. The main trial tribunals will be put on hold, because the next President will have the final say. Your lists will be held in abeyance until after the upcoming election."

"Sir, may I ask what charges General Milburn will present to the evidentiary hearings?" Jackson queried.

"Barton?" Bradley said.

"The very same as those charged at Nuremberg. Four counts: conspiracy to wage aggressive war, war crimes, crimes against peace, and crimes against humanity. That would cover all the defendants who will be bound over for the full trials in, say, early 1953," Bart replied.

"I understand, General Milburn, that you were assigned by General Eisenhower to visit most of the concentration camps. You wrote a full report on your findings, and the report has been classified top secret. Why?" Jackson asked.

"That's a question I've been asking, sir."

"I asked for that report when I was preparing for Nuremberg. All I got was the usual Washington merry-go-round. I wanted to use your material at the trials," Jackson said.

"I was recruited for this current job by the President. I hope to convince him to pry it loose for the major trials in '53 before he leaves office. If we open these trials to the public, it is my intention to air every atrocity in an attempt to shock the world with the gravity of these crimes. Let the world hear live on radio and television the outrageously monstrous deviation of human behavior by the Nazis. There are no words that can truly depict the orgy of torture and death practiced by Hitler, Himmler, Goering and the rest. And they haven't stopped their crime spree yet," Bart declared passionately.

"What do you mean by *yet*?" Jackson asked.

Bart looked at Bradley.

"That's the next order of business," the chairman said. "Go ahead, Barton. Justice Jackson knows this is highly classified."

General Milburn spelled out the Revenge Plan of Nordheim, a.k.a. Hitler. When Bart concluded, Jackson excused himself from the meeting.

"Gentlemen, this is now a high-security matter, which without doubt presents our government and others with a clear and present danger. This is in your domain. I am certain you are prepared to deal with it now," General Smith said.

Bradley advised the gathering of the nation's military leaders that President Truman had spoken with Prime Minister Ben-Gurion of Israel, who agreed to be the source of the information about the Revenge Plan, thus ensuring the secrecy of the American capture of the Nazi leaders. He further said that Prime Minister Churchill and French President de Gaulle had been alerted.

"Secretary Lovett, do you have any comments?"

"Yes, General Bradley, I spoke with Lieutenant General Whitley Gardner, the British representative at NATO. He is chairing the military committee. He is convening a secret special session at 1100 hours tomorrow."

"Fast world, Mr. Secretary. Who will attend from the U.S. team?" Bradley asked.

"I realize this is short notice. However, I would expect you, Mr. Chairman, and the Chiefs, plus General Smith of the CIA. I would like General Milburn to attend as the President's personal representative without revealing his full role in this matter. Let us cover that by using him as special liaison to the Mossad. That's my personal recommendation."

"Bob, will the President approve of this pretense? We would be ill-advised to have this deception come to light when the full story is aired next year. Our relationship with our NATO partners must be pristine. I don't think we should chance an eruption at that time," Bradley cautioned.

"Brad, we have ample coverage for that. Churchill and de Gaulle have been briefed by President Truman. I'll have a sidebar with General Gardner, asking him to have the members not press Milburn for specific answers. We have to protect our secret, yet Barton can stress the danger factor. The President, I am sure, will approve," said Lovett.

"That sounds reasonable. Now, we have to go on the alert, effective immediately. The Air Force and the Navy should be tracking the location of every Eagle ship in Nordheim-Hitler's fleet. Army, Navy and Air Force intelligence should be alerted and, in cooperation with the CIA, should be checking into Nordheim's Winston General's operations the world over." Bradley turned to Bart and said, "General Milburn, these two days are extremely important and busy ones for you. Upon the completion of your work tomorrow, you'll be free to return to Guantanamo to finish your chores there and organize the shuttling of prisoners to Homestead and finally to Fort Leavenworth," Bradley said.

Admiral Prince raised his hand.

"Yes, Ed?"

"General Bradley, will you be available to meet with us later today after we establish the alert mechanisms with our respective forces?"

"Yes, how about 1700 hours back in this room?"

Prince turned to his counterparts. They nodded.

"That's fine, Brad."

"Meeting adjourned," Bradley said, then beckoned Bart. He whispered, "Join me and General Smith for a quick bite of lunch. After that, you and Justice Jackson are to meet with Judge Advocate General Ross."

In the private dining room of the Chairman of the Joint Chiefs of Staff, the walls were decorated with pictures spanning the career of the five-star general. A large window overlooked Arlington, Virginia. Bart looked at the trophies and other awards of the famous General.

Bradley put a paternal arm around Milburn's shoulder. "Come on, Beedle, sit there, and Bart, you sit here," he invited. "This is a long way, men, from our days in Europe."

Bart nodded, remembering the days with Bradley and Smith during the war. The day at the Ohrdruf concentration camp loomed large in his mind's eye.

"I find it difficult, Brad, to imagine that we are dealing with the Führer and his gang in the flesh. I am anxious to take a look at this degenerate bastard," Smith said. "Bart, tell us a little bit about Adolf at Guantanamo and how you got him there."

Milburn sketched the capture of Nordheim-Hitler and his conduct in the brig at the Naval base. "He's somewhat schizoid in his behavior. Off the record, I had him strait-jacketed for several days in a padded cell. This was primarily to cut him down to size. At first he kept insisting he was Frederick Nordheim, a Jew, who went from a concentration camp to being the richest man in the world. The plastic surgery was a masterpiece of human sculpturing. The face was changed completely, and he sported a new visage with a Van Dyke beard and a flowing mustache when he was captured. When we had his head and face shaved, he temporarily lost his arrogance."

"What caused that?" Bradley asked.

"You've heard the recording, sir. I admit I struck him the first time. Twice after that, he switched from being Nordheim, the oppressed Jew, to the arrogant Führer. The last time, I did a reprise of his stupid military tactics. He folded then. You should really play the recording of my last session with him," Bart suggested.

"I'll do that, Bart."

"I listened to all of it, Bart," General Smith said. "My friend, it was, and is, a classic masterpiece. I expect you will repeat that at the trial."

"If there is a trial," Bart muttered.

"What do you mean by that?" Bradley asked.

"It's a personal reservation of mine, sir."

"Barton Milburn, if something's bugging you, speak up. You are sitting here with two of your staunchest supporters. Let's have it, friend."

"I think I know his concerns," Smith said.

"Sir, I beg that what I say is strictly off the record and respectfully not to be repeated."

"Shoot, and what you say dies here," Bradley assured him.

"It's the Dulles brothers. Ike's going to be elected. Allen will replace General Smith as CIA director, and John will probably become Secretary of State. They are very concerned that their German connections, pre-war, will come to light in an open trial. Both brothers were up to their hips representing interests that contributed to Hitler's rise to power. I'm not accusing them of being pro-Nazi. I think they are loyal Americans, but they would try to divert their earlier money-grubbing careers from being publicized in open court, which would make it privileged material for the press."

"Beedle, are you aware of this background information?"

"Yes, Brad. I learned a good deal of this when I was Ambassador to Moscow. Stalin bent my ear with this mess of porridge. Also, Laurenti Beria, head of the NKVD, the Soviet secret police, and a member of the Politburo, told me that the Dulles boys represented I.G. Farben, the holders of the patent for the poison gas at Auschwitz that Himmler used to kill millions of Jews. They had a large file on Allen and John. I did a little secret checking of my own. It's true enough. Yet Allen's war record in the OSS was good when he served in Switzerland."

"I'm somewhat disturbed by these revelations. Bart's misgivings are not without merit. Now, in retrospect, Allen's remarks about open trials loom in my mind as a precursor to obstacles confronting Bart's efforts for wide-open trials, especially Hitler's," Bradley mused openly.

"General Bradley, forgive my presumptuousness for gazing into my crystal ball, but I believe that if Ike is elected, he will replace you as Chairman of the Joint Chiefs," Bart said.

"I am aware of that, Barton, and I look forward to it. Next year I'll be sixty years old. It's time my military career came to an end. However, if there is any attempt to bury these trials I'll be in the vanguard of those crying foul. If Ike becomes President, I don't think he'll want me ranting and raving on Capitol Hill and to the National Press Club about open trials," the usually low-keyed Bradley declared as he pounded the luncheon table, rattling the glasses, plates and utensils. "Besides all that, my term as Chairman expires in August of '53."

Smith laughed heartily. Bart coolly observed the demonstration.

Bradley continued, "Beedle, this is no laughing matter. I didn't lead the First Army at Normandy on D-day to find us at this stage of affairs covering up a trial of the worst monster in the history of man. Complacency and apathy almost destroyed civilization and allowed that megalomaniacal sociopath Schickelgruber to kill at least twenty million civilians and combatants, wiping out two generations. And look at the millions Stalin killed. Between them, fifty million died. This century has been infernally blighted, and we're only halfway through it."

"Bart, move ahead. We're both behind you," Smith declared.

"Right on, Bart. Go full tilt at your windmills. We'll be riding with you. Don't worry about Ike. I'll have a chat with him. I'm sure *Give-'em-hell Harry* will do likewise," Bradley added.

Bart left the luncheon for his meeting with Judge Advocate General Ross, buoyed by the send-off by Bradley and Smith. Sergeant Kovac met him as he entered the offices of the legal branch of the Army, and he saluted the two-star general.

"Sergeant, I'll wait for the arrival of Supreme Court Justice Jackson. He should be here momentarily."

He sat, thumbing through a magazine. Five minutes later, Justice Robert Jackson arrived and Bart rose.

"Sorry to be late, General Milburn. I had lunch with Secretary Lovett and Attorney General McGranery. We talked about Nuremberg, and mostly about the magnitude of the task confronting you."

"No problem, sir," Bart said.

"On a personal level, Barton, refer to me as Bob. I know we are going to be good friends. Here is a booklet on the Nuremberg military trials. It's titled on the inside cover page, *Nazi Conspiracy and Aggression - Opinion and Judgment.*"

"I am very grateful. I hadn't seen this particular publication."

"It was published by the U.S. Government Printing Office in 1947. It has the imprimaturs of the State Department, the former War Department and the Nuremberg trials. Actually, it is a compendium with excerpts of the prosecution and the defense."

Bart beckoned Sergeant Kovac. "This is Justice Jackson, and we await General Ross' pleasure."

"I am honored, sir. I'll tell Judge Ross you are here, gentlemen," the sergeant replied.

Wilfred Ross, a young brigadier general with a pleasant mien, greeted the two men, pointing to a round conference table. "Welcome to my humble quarters, gentlemen. I am honored by the presence of both of you. Justice Jackson, I read everything available about the Nuremberg trials. Your opening address was a masterpiece. And you, sir, General Milburn, your exploits to date are prodigious and extremely impressive," he declared.

"You've made two friends with your generous accolades," Jackson said.

"Yes, indeed," Bart echoed.

"Our staff is preparing a list of legal officers for the prosecution and the defense," Ross began. "This is being done in collaboration with our counterparts in the Navy and Air Force. The reason I will not be involved in those choices is to avoid a conflict of interest, inasmuch I've been assigned as presiding commissioner for the evidentiary hearings. I'll choose three or four Judge Advocates to assist in the plethora of cases to be investigated."

"Very wise decision, General Ross," Jackson said.

"General Ross, it is imperative that all participants be cleared for this highly classified assignment," Bart said. "It's top secret. So far we are quite fortunate. There have been no leaks."

"I am well aware of the necessity for top secret clearance, General Milburn," Ross replied. "I've stressed that to the team working up a list of candidates."

"Excellent," Bart said. "Please brief us on your normal evidentiary hearings."

Ross outlined the rules of the average hearings. "Let me stress that this situation is unique for a stateside proceeding. In my opinion, sirs, the format should be very much akin to a wartime arraignment. A presentation of charges, backed up with *prima facie* evidence, is required. We know that the major defendants are going to be bound over for trial. That will be *pro forma.* Of the eighty or ninety defendants who will appear, if it is determined that any one of them does not fit the mold of a war criminal and *prima facie* evidence is not produced, as a trier of fact I would be compelled to dismiss the charges."

"General Ross, I am very pleased to hear you state that," Jackson said.

"I have no problem with your position, General Ross," Bart said. "I don't want some miserable wretch to be subjected to a *West-of-the-Pecos, Judge Roy Bean* type of trial. It is conceivable that in our four raids, someone was in the wrong place at the right time. I doubt it. But, fairness, yes. Forgiveness, no,"

Bart said. "I might state now that we may tangle in the courtroom. Please don't take it personally."

Ross laughed. "That won't be the first time that's happened to me."

Jackson revealed some of the doubts about the Nuremberg tribunal's decisions. "Franz von Papen was found not guilty. That was outrageous. This slick politician helped Hitler form the coalition cabinet. He stepped back from sharing the power, became Vice Chancellor, and solidified the Führer's control. Further to that, after his supporters were murdered he became minister to Austria, after Engelbert Dollfuss, the Chancellor, was assassinated. Von Papen was the mastermind of the fall of Austria into Hitler's *anschluss*. In my opinion, he should have been sentenced to at least ten years. Later, a German de-Nazification court tried him, found him guilty and sentenced him to eight years at hard labor. He maintained he had no knowledge of the atrocities. They could have found him guilty of *mopery,* to coin a word."

The intercom in Ross' office advised that the Judge Advocates General had gathered in the conference room.

"We'll be there in a few minutes," Ross replied.

Jackson rose. "I don't think I'm needed in that meeting," he said.

"Sir, it would be a distinct honor if you could spare a few minutes to meet these men. They are cognizant of your efforts at Nuremberg and your position on the high court," Ross said.

Bart looked at the distinguished jurist, smiled and nodded his head in assent.

"Very well, but not for more than a few minutes. This is a working session for you two," Jackson said.

The three officers rose when the trio entered. Ross introduced Jackson and Bart. The surprise was palpable. They all shook hands with the jurist and Bart.

"Please sit, gentlemen. I'll spend a few minutes with you and then you can get to work," Jackson said.

Questions about Nuremberg abounded, and Jackson graciously answered the queries. Ross thanked him and escorted him to the elevator. Bart waved at him as he departed.

Ross returned, and the meeting was under way. Bart repeated his cautionary statement of top secrecy. A two-hour planning session ensued. Ross explained that he would have no hand in choosing names for the prosecution or defense. Ross outlined the parameters of the legal procedure and advised that a firm date had not been set. Bart ventured two to three weeks for the hearings.

"General Milburn, would you care to set a date for the law officers to arrive at Fort Leavenworth?" Ross asked.

Bart reached into his briefcase and withdrew a calendar.

"Let me see, today's the 8th. We should have all the prisoners shuttled to the disciplinary barracks at Fort Leavenworth by the evening of Monday, the 12th of May. No later than the following day. How about Monday, May 19th, for the law officers and the judges? I'll arrange an Army transport plane from Andrews Air Force Base to fly you to the base."

Ross looked at his confreres. They nodded. "That's good, General. Would you guess the hearings to start within two weeks after that?"

"Let's shoot for the hearings to begin on Monday, June 2nd, at 0900 hours."

"That's great. It will give both sides time to prepare," Navy Judge Advocate General Walter Bering said.

"General Milburn, you will be prosecuting the heavies, I assume?" Air Force Advocate General Leslie Horgan queried.

"You assume correctly. I'll assign the additional prosecutors at the scene. Colonel Grogan will assign the defense lawyers to their clients. He's familiar with all of them. There will be ten U.S. Attorneys there who have been interrogating fifty-two Waffen SS prisoners. We'll be ready with a plan when your people arrive. For security reasons, all of us will be housed at Fort Leavenworth."

"You've just answered my question," Army Judge Advocate General Robert Souza said. "I was curious about our quarters."

"By the way, I'll be choosing the three or four judges to assist," General Ross adjured. "The average hearing should take no longer than 30 minutes, except for large groups, maybe an hour. You all know of me, I conduct an orderly court. No theatrics." Ross held up a purple-colored book titled *Manual for Courts-Martial United States*. "Look at pages 14 and 15. It covers war crimes. It's dated 1951."

A short while later the meeting was adjourned. Bart then drove to 1601 Pennsylvania Avenue, Blair House, where Secret Service agents Larry Witten and Ken Parker were playing gin rummy. Keith Reynolds was reading Martin Gilbert's biography of Winston Churchill, and he seemed rested and composed. The sight of Bart in full uniform got the attention of the three men. All stood up.

"General, is that a *second* star I see?" Witten inquired, smiling.

"I hadn't noticed," Bart joked.

"Congratulations, sir," Parker exclaimed.

Reynolds shook his hand.

"Gentlemen, Keith Reynolds' last evening here should be special. Let's order a nice dinner. Keith and I will be leaving here tomorrow afternoon."

"General, where are you taking me?" Keith nervously inquired. "Back to jail, sir?"

"No, no, Keith. It's just a stopover at another location. Top secret. Not to worry."

Bart went to his quarters and placed a series of phone calls. He briefed John Steelman on the day's progress and the upcoming meeting with the military committee at NATO.

"If the President wants me, I am at Blair House. I'll be leaving after the NATO session for Guantanamo, taking our prize prisoner here with me."

"Bart, do you need guards for his protection?"

"John, that's not a bad idea."

"Why don't you take two of those Secret Service men with you? Play it safe."

"Glad you mentioned it. Can you clear a plane for me, John?"

"When?"

"Our meeting is at 1100 hours and a NATO meeting after that. How about 5pm out of Andrews, Hangar 14?"

"I'll confirm at Blair, Major General Milburn," Steelman said.

Bart then reached Jacques at the naval base.

"The full-court press is working," Jacques reported. "The sleazeballs are ratting on each other."

"Great. How's *Der Führer*?" Bart snickered.

"Arrogant as hell."

"I'm coming into Havana tomorrow night with Fliegel-Reynolds. I'll keep him at the Riviera with two Secret Service guys guarding him. Meet me at the airport. We'll spend the evening at the villa before going back to the base on Thursday."

"See you then, brother. Give me an ETA before takeoff."

The next call went to the villa in Havana. "Stanley, is Mrs. Milburn there?"

"Oh yes, sir, General. Nice to hear your voice."

Elizabeth came on line. "Oh Bart, darling…"

He cut her off and pompously declared, "This is *Major General* Milburn. May I speak with the lady of the house?"

"Barton Milburn, that's wonderful, but what does that mean? Are you being called to active service? Not Korea?" she gasped.

"Yes and no."

"What does that mean?"

"Yes, I've been activated. No, not for Korea."

"Dearest Bart, I'm worried."

"Don't worry. I've been promoted, put on active duty to act as chief prosecutor of these aberrant bastards."

"Barton, my love, I am so proud of you. When will I see you? The children miss you."

"Liz, baby, that plaintive appeal impels me to come home tomorrow night. Jacques will be there to meet me at the airport."

"I'll be there, too."

"Not necessary. I am bringing a prisoner and two Secret Service men. They'll be dropped at the Riviera Hotel. I'll fill you in on the rest. Are you and Joyce prepared to go to Guantanamo on Saturday or Sunday to take a peek at some of the prisoners? Maybe you and Joyce may spot some familiar faces."

Her pristine British voice sharpened and reverted to the vernacular. "You're bloody well right, sir. That's a high priority for me, and I'm sure it would be for Joyce. After all these years, with my subconscious memories of those camps, that would be a welcome catharsis for me to see them behind bars," she said passionately.

"Love you, miss you and be prepared…your husband's coming home."

"Naughty boy."

Bart opened his briefcase and removed a pad, a pen, and a sheet listing the members of the military committee of NATO. The countries involved were noted. They were Belgium, Canada, Denmark, France, Great Britain, Iceland, Italy, Luxembourg, the Netherlands, Norway, Portugal, and the U.S. Greece and Turkey had recently been added.

"Fourteen members," he mused. "I hope they won't all be there."

The phone rang, and the White House operator announced, "Dr. Steelman is calling, General."

"Yes, John?"

"You've got a plane. Hangar 14. It's a turbojet. Should be a faster flight. They'll be ready at 4 p.m., or 1600 hours, as you Army people say."

"Thanks, John."

"Wait a minute, that's not all. The President wants you to stop by here at 9:30 a.m. A short visit prior to your eleven o'clock NATO session."

"I'll be there. Thanks for the turbo."

Bart returned to his perusal of the NATO sheet. He scribbled some reminder notes for the upcoming meeting. He noted that the Brussels NATO conference, on February 20 last, had set a goal of fifty divisions and four thousand planes by the end of 1952. He put his notes back in his briefcase. After a shower, he joined the men in the drawing room. Keith was listening to the news. Witten and Parker were deeply involved in their gin rummy game.

Reynolds looked up at Bart and commented, "I see that your General Eisenhower is seeking the Presidency. He is being challenged by a fellow Republican, Senator Robert Taft. America is a great country."

"You'd better believe it. Nothing like the stupidity of Nazified Germany, Keith," Bart said.

"Are you going to stay for dinner?" Keith asked.

"I may as well. Let's order," Bart declared.

He picked up the phone, and Hopkins answered.

"We'd like to order dinner for four, please."

"A waiter will be right up, sir."

Witten acted as bartender. Keith opted for a glass of Zinfandel wine. The others took dry vodka martinis. Bart lit a cigarette, rested his feet on a leather hassock and relaxed for the first time that day. A waiter appeared, suggesting, "The chef recommends Southern fried chicken. He says it is very special."

All three agreed. Keith said, "I've never had chicken that way."

"Try it, or you'll never know what you've missed," Witten prodded.

He reluctantly consented.

"Salads for all, gentlemen?" Fred asked.

They agreed, and ordered cold beer with it. Sports and politics were discussed. Keith listened. After the repast, brandy was poured into snifters. The phone rang. Witten answered. "It's for you, sir," he said.

Bart went to his rooms and answered. "I have a Douglas Milburn calling, sir."

"Doug, how are you?"

"Fine, Bart, fine. The reason I'm calling, I just had dinner at Toots Shor's;

you know, at the back table with Bob Considine; Jack O'Brian, the Journal American columnist; Meyer Berger of the Times, Leo Durocher and Dan Topping, owner of the New York Yankees."

"That's nice. So what?"

"O'Brian said you've been promoted to major general and have been called back to active duty. Is that true?"

"Yes. But, dammit, it only happened yesterday. It wasn't official until today. Where the hell did he get that?"

"I don't know, Bart. Are you being sent to Korea? That's what O'Brian thinks."

"Good, let him believe that. Between us, it's not true. I'm back in the Army on intelligence duty here. That's it, and *strictly* confidential."

"Congratulations, kid brother. I won't pry."

"Tell the folks and give them my love. It's too late to call now."

"No, it's not. They're at the theater. Should be home in the next hour. By the way, you remember that story I wrote a few years ago about Jimmy Rutkin, the ex-bootlegger who filed suit against Joseph P. Kennedy for twenty million dollars at the Supreme Court here? The story died after that because old Joe reached Joe Patterson, our publisher; Bertie McCormick, publisher of the Chicago Tribune; old man Hearst, Scripps-Howard, and everybody else. I was furious then because I wasn't permitted to follow through. Well, I'm twice as mad now."

"How come? What happened?"

"If you recall, not long after I wrote the piece, exclusively, two intelligence agents from the IRS came to the office and insisted on seeing my safety-deposit box in our building at the National City Bank. So I called Tom Cavanagh of the Daily News legal department to join us. Cavanagh and these two guys came with me when I opened the box. Out popped a stack of War Bonds. One of the guys, named Guthrie, turned to me and said he was sorry to have bothered me."

"Well, I knew all that. What's got you in an uproar now?"

"As you know, that was in 1948. Well, last night I was in Shubert Alley, waiting for Constance to finish her show. There was Guthrie smoking a cigar. He sidled up to me and asked if I remembered him. I told him I sure as hell did. He then told me he had retired. I said, so what? He told me to cool it. *I am on your side*, he said. *What does that mean?* I snidely replied. *You know who dropped the dime on you?* he said."

"Come on, what's got you riled?"

"He let loose. Joseph P. Kennedy used some muscle with the story that Costello was paying me off with laundered money. Guthrie swears it's true."

"I believe it is true. Joe Kennedy has the clout. Don't stew, Doug. Wait 'til you hear about his connections with Hitler and the Nazi hierarchy. But watch your back - Old Joe is a powerful and devious SOB. His son John is running for the Senate in Massachusetts. That state belongs to the Kennedys, so John will be a shoo-in. The kid brother, Bobby, is working as counsel for that screwball Senator McCarthy."

"I'm aware of his power. They are a get-even family, especially that kid

Bobby. Interesting to watch him and that other co-counsel Roy Cohn tangle assholes."

"Cool it for a while. They're grooming John for President. Watch out."

"Okay, brother, and good luck. *Ciao.*"

Bart returned to the drawing room, picked up his brandy snifter, lit a cigarette and watched the nightly news until the signoff. He went back to his room, called his parents and filled them in on his promotion. His sister Beatrice was out for the evening.

"Who is she out with?" Bart asked.

"She's been dating a very nice young man," his mother, Jeannette Milburn, replied.

"Is it serious, Mom?"

"Could be."

"What does he do, and has Douglas checked him out?"

"Now, Barton, I don't want you or Douglas to interfere. He's a vice president at Smith Barney, a prestigious Wall Street firm."

"What's his name?"

"Jeffrey Rothschild."

"Has Douglas checked him out?"

"Yes, and he has a very fine family. He graduated summa cum laude from Harvard."

"Is he related to the Rothschilds, the bankers and vintners?"

"Distantly, I believe. I'm not sure."

"I hope she doesn't rush into marriage."

"Shush, Barton. Bunny has her two feet on the ground."

"Okay, Mom, I love you. Best to Dad and Beatrice."

"Stay out of Korea if you can, Barton. Love you."

He returned to the drawing room and advised agents Witten and Parker that they were to accompany him and the prisoner to Havana for a one-night stopover prior to the following day's flight to Guantanamo.

☆ ☆ ☆ ☆

Friday, May 9, 1952 - 8:30 a.m. - Washington

Bart slept late that morning, then shaved and showered quickly. He wolfed his breakfast of orange juice, toasted English muffin and coffee, glancing through the Washington Post. *Senator Robert Taft, at a Republican fundraiser, railed at Eisenhower's lack of political experience,* the front page headlines noted.

"He's a fine general, but has never held elective office. I have legislative experience, he has military experience. The war's over. We need a steady hand at the nation's tiller. We don't have time for on-the-job training," he was quoted.

Other stories read: *Stalin's Health Deteriorating. West Germany Preparing for Peace Contract with Western Allies on May 26 in Bonn. Josef Mengele, notorious nazi who viciously tortured, experimented on and murdered hundreds of thousands of Jews, Christians and others, has been traced to Para-*

guay, and has also been seen in Argentina, according to reports from Tel Aviv. The sports page indicated that the Yankees and the Brooklyn Dodgers were leading their respective leagues. Bart noticed the time. It was 9 a.m. He tossed the papers, picked up his briefcase and hastened across the street to the White House. The morning sun shone out of a solid blue sky and highlighted the lingering days of the cherry blossoms. He felt the warmth of the sun's rays and the gentle breeze at his back. He strode vigorously across Pennsylvania Avenue to the West Gate of the White House, where he was greeted at the gate by guard Tom Reilly. "Morning, General Milburn. It's a beautiful day."

"That it is, Tom. How's the family?"

"Good. My daughter got a scholarship at Wellesley and my son is studying at Yale. My wife says she's lonely."

"Congrats on the kids, and take your lady out to dinner, Tom," Bart advised, then headed for Steelman's office, resplendent in his uniform. The two stars glistened.

"Well, if it isn't Major General Milburn. I'll bet you're one of the youngest two-starrers in the service," Steelman said.

"Jealous, John?"

"You're not kidding. I wish I was your age."

"Were you ever?" Bart riposted.

"Smart-ass. Go right in, he's waiting for you."

Entering the Oval Office, Bart noticed President Truman staring out of his window, looking toward the Washington monument. "Morning, Mr. President."

"Morning, General," Truman replied without turning. "Come here. Look at that obelisk. It looks like an obscene finger pointing at the Capitol."

Bart laughed, and Truman snickered.

"I don't think old George would appreciate that description of his monument," Bart said.

"I think he would. He had his troubles with Congress, as I did," Truman replied. "Yet I was once a member of that august body. Be seated. You make quite a figure in your uniform."

"Thank you, sir."

"Bring me up to date."

Bart gave him a concise report.

"You've got quite a busy day and a busy month ahead of you. By the way, your friends on the hill, Senators Clements and Bridges, got your appointments to brigadier and now two-star general confirmed quickly by the Armed Services Committee without an appearance by you. *Pro forma.* They are good friends of yours."

"Yes, they are. Styles and Earle are personal friends. They have been to my house for dinner several times."

"That's good, Barton. You'll need them when the word gets out about the capture of Hitler, Bormann et al."

"After the hearings and these lice are bound over for trial, Mr. President, I would like to set the major trials for early February, 1953, rather than May.

How does that suit you?"

"Fine with me. I'll be a civilian by then. It's up to the next President. We'll talk about that after the conventions. Now, there are two things that I wanted to talk to you about. First, at the meeting with the military committee of NATO, be sure to stress the Mossad's role in alerting us to Hitler's Revenge Plan."

"Mr. President, I assure you I'll be very cautious as to the source of our information."

"Remember, you're there as my representative."

"Thank you, sir."

"Now, item two. Watch your back with Allen Dulles. He's very concerned about his and his brother's pre-war roles in Germany becoming public knowledge. If Ike wins the election, they'll be very powerful."

"Sir, if these trials move ahead on a wide-open public basis, I will not protect them, or any member of the Royal family, or Lindbergh, Kennedy, and all the other pro-Hitlerites."

"Good. I've spoken to Bradley about this. His voice and mine will be in sync behind you. Churchill doesn't give a damn about the Duke of Windsor or his wife. He thinks she was a Nazi spy. Also, watch out for that Mafia-connected, bootlegging Joe Kennedy. He's grooming his kid, Jack, for the Presidency, you know. They've got Massachusetts set to elect Jack Kennedy to the Senate."

"How does he rate with J. Edgar?"

"He has quite a file on Joe, a notorious womanizer and a Wall Street buccaneer."

"Thanks for the warning, sir."

"Barton, I am very proud of you. If I had a son, I would want him to be like you."

"That's high praise, sir."

"All right, now go to work," the President said.

CHAPTER THIRTY-ONE

Friday, May 9, 1952 same day - 11 a.m.
Military Committee of the North Atlantic Treaty Organization, Washington
   The members of NATO sat at a huge conference table, where British Lieutenant General Whitley Gardner called the meeting to order: "I note, with gratitude, the presence of all members of the Military Committee of NATO. Secretary of Defense Robert Lovett; General Omar Bradley, the Chairman of the Joint Chiefs of Staff; General Maxwell Taylor, Admiral Prince, General Fosley; and Major General Milburn, representing President Truman. Welcome."
   "Thank you, General Gardner. We are here to brief this committee on a most serious matter," Lovett said.
   "Please proceed."
   Lovett detailed the Revenge Plan. There were gasps of horror and dismay. Gardner banged his gavel for order.
   Rene LeClaire, military attaché at the French Embassy, was recognized. "Mr. Chairman, I've been encouraged by President de Gaulle to pay strict attention to this warning by our American partners. Yet I must admit this is the most ludicrous delusion that I have ever heard."
   "I would be inclined to treat this matter most seriously," Denmark's representative, Colonel Henrik Toomer, declared. "Nothing the Nazis concoct would surprise me."
   Over the next hour, the fourteen countries represented engaged in a discussion over the validity of the bizarre prophecy by the Americans. The free-for-all came to a halt when Canada's representative, General George Craig, coolly suggested, "Wouldn't it be advisable, gentlemen, to ask for the source of

this mind-boggling plan?"

Gardner said, "Gentlemen, before I call on the next speaker, I ask you not to press him too deeply for specific answers beyond that which he will outline for you. General Milburn, the floor is yours, sir."

Bart slowly and carefully described the Revenge Plan's alleged plan to terrorize the world with the destruction of monuments, icons, government buildings, and the Panama Canal.

"We have been following information supplied to us by the Israeli government. Let me assure you that, based on our intelligence apparatus investigations, this plan was conceived by none other than Adolf Hitler, before the end of the war. That's his legacy to the Nazi movement. The world complacently ignored his threats and he almost conquered all of Europe. His minions are prepared to create chaos in a world at peace. I beg you all to be on guard," Bart cautioned. "Their new weapons are terrorism."

The momentary silence indicated a somber evaluation of Bart's remarks.

"I withdraw my previous remarks, and I apologize for the use of the word 'ludicrous.' This is a most serious and disturbing revelation," LeClaire said.

"Do we have unanimity of opinion?" Gardner asked.

All hands were raised.

"That being the case, NATO, as well as its individual members, must be in a state of alert. We must do it covertly and without any leaks to the media. Such leaks would only strengthen the evil hands of these Nazi scoundrels who are lodged in countries the world over," Gardner declared.

"I would add that we need a coordinated intelligence operation to be put in place," General Bradley advised. "Each country should notify the military committee of any untoward or suspicious action which comes to their attention. Feed it in here to our chairman, General Gardner."

"I will keep close touch with the Israeli Mossad and feed any information that would be meaningful to you, General Gardner," Bart said.

"Thank you, General Milburn. Now, let's get down to the business of how to ferret out these bloody bastards," Gardner said. "I might point out that Prime Minister Churchill has quietly ordered an alert for Great Britain."

"The United States of America, at the order of President Truman, has done likewise. We have reason to believe that the Eagle Shipping company might use their ships to blow up the Panama Canal. Watch for those ships in your ports or at sea," Bradley warned.

As the meeting was about to plan a worldwide operation, Bart asked to be excused.

"Thank you for your presentation, General Milburn," Gardner said.

Bart hurried to the Pentagon for his meeting with the intelligence officers of the Army, Navy and Air Force. Rear Admiral Willard Fleming, Air Force Brigadier General Clifford Grayson, and Army General Franklin Corletti were at the conference table when Bart arrived.

"Sorry I'm late. I've just finished a briefing at the military committee of NATO," Bart apologized. "That's what I am here to do for you men now.

I admit, I can afford to be more candid than I was there. You are all aware of this matter being classified top secret?"

"General Bradley spelled it out," Corletti said.

Over the next hour, Bart painted the full picture. "We're kindred souls here, men. We are all intelligence officers and know what's required," he said.

"General Bradley enlightened us on your war record and what you've accomplished in this mission. It's an honor to work with you, General Milburn," Fleming said.

"How do we reach you, General Milburn?" Grayson asked.

"For the time being, the White House operators will hook you up with me. After Monday, May 12th, I'll be at Fort Leavenworth. I'll be leaving for Guantanamo when I leave here. When I finish my job at the Fort, I'll be asking General Bradley for an office here at the Pentagon."

"We'll be happy to be working with you," Fleming said with a smile.

Bart shook hands all around and departed. Bart was driven to Blair House to pick up his prisoner and the two Secret Service agents. Keith Reynolds was hustled down the back way into a Lincoln Town Car. At Andrews Air Force Base, they drove onto the tarmac to Hangar 14. A new Lockheed Air Force turboprop plane was parked there. Captain Oliver Lawson saluted Bart. "Welcome aboard, sir," the lanky pilot said.

"Thank you, Captain. How long will this flight be?"

"Three hours, sir, to Havana."

He ordered Witten and Parker to board the plane with Reynolds.

"Rev her up, Captain. I want to make a quick phone call."

He used the hangar phone to call the White House operator and was connected with Jacques Laurent at the naval base.

"Three hours or so. See you at the Havana airport coffee shop. Bring the Cadillac."

"Only three?"

"Jacques, it's a turboprop jet."

Later that day - Havana

Jacques stared at Bart in full uniform as he entered the restaurant at the terminal, then embraced him. "They hooked you with the two stars," he said. "You're back in the Army."

"I'm afraid so, brother."

"Do you want some coffee or something?" he asked.

"Just a Coke, and we can talk for a few minutes."

Bart motioned Witten and Parker to a table in the rear of the dining area. "I see Reynolds-Fliegel. Has he been behaving?"

"Jacques, he's a born-again Christian. He should be a very powerful witness."

The two men updated each other on the events of the last few days in their respective spheres and their plans for the future.

Bart waved at the Secret Service agents to bring Reynolds to the car. Jacques drove the Cadillac at high speed to the Riviera Hotel.

"Why so fast, Jacques?" Bart asked.

"A car is tailing us," he whispered.

"Slow down and see what they do. Fellows, don't look back," Bart ordered.

A taxi raced past them. Jacques relaxed. He slowed down. They noticed the cab leaving the Riviera circular driveway as they pulled up to the entrance. Witten, Parker and Reynolds were hustled by Jacques and Bart to the sixth floor. Two bellboys carried their luggage behind them. Bart showed them to a two-bedroom suite.

"This was my suite. You'll be comfortable here. Order dinner and sign my name to the check," Bart explained.

"This is perfect," Witten declared.

Reynolds went to his bedroom. Parker carried his suitcase behind him, then returned, saying, "He's all set. Very pleased with the accommodations. He's a nice little guy. I can't believe he was the same person mixed up with those Nazi creeps."

"Come here, you two. Don't leave these rooms until either Jacques or I come for you in the morning. Are you armed?" Bart said.

"Yes, we both are," Witten replied.

"Fine. Don't let the waiters see Reynolds. Keep all doors bolt-locked at all times."

Witten and Parker stiffened, and patted their holsters.

"Why all the caution, General?" Parker asked.

"These Nazi bastards have some Cubans on their payroll. Caution is the watchword, men. See you in the a.m."

Jacques checked the locks and chains on all the doors of the suite before they departed. When the elevator reached the lobby, a smiling Phil Kastel greeted them.

"General, you look mighty fine in that uniform. Two stars, eh? I'm impressed. Congratulations."

"Thank you, Phil."

Jacques nudged Bart and grabbed Kastel's arm.

"Keep talking and don't turn," he hissed. "That man and woman in winter clothes sitting to the right of the elevators reading newspapers - do you know who they are, Mr. Kastel?"

"No, they just checked in right before you arrived. I'll go to the desk and look at the names. I'll be right back."

"What's bothering you, Jacques?" Bart asked as he took a peripheral look at the couple.

"I've seen his picture in the Nazi files. His name will come to me. As to the woman, I don't know."

"Jacques, are you sure? You were jittery in the car about being followed, and now this?"

Kastel, acting out his part, returned with a big smile.

"They are registered as Mr. and Mrs. Walter Bancroft. The clerk said the lady did all the talking with an Irish brogue. They have a suite on the third floor."

"Walter, Walter, that's it," Jacques whispered, feeling in his jacket for his gun.

Bart noticed Jacques' reaction.

"That's *what*?" Bart demanded.

Kastel was taken aback. He nervously glanced about in search of his security men.

"Bart, that's Walter Schellenberg, the SS chief."

"Are you absolutely sure? Do you have your gun with you?"

"Yes, yes. But why is he here? Smile, smile, Bart. They're looking at us over the top of their newspapers. They're going to the elevators now. A man just joined them. He looks Cuban, dressed in white slacks and a light blue jacket."

"Phil, I want to move our people out of my suite. Where can they go? Quick now, please."

"To the fifth floor. Then have them take the service elevator from there to the penthouse. The door is open. I just left there."

Bart rushed to the house phones. Witten answered. "Get your asses out of there, *now*."

He advised them to follow Kastel's directions.

"What's up?"

"Move. I'll be up there in minutes."

Kastel clicked a metal toy cricket, and two burly men in tuxedos appeared suddenly. He pointed toward the elevators. Bart and Jacques followed through the crowded lobby.

"General, this is Jim and Frank, my best boys from Covington, Kentucky. They are armed."

In the elevator, Bart said, "I think these people are here to execute a hit on my people."

"God, I don't want any fireworks in this hotel," Kastel begged.

"There won't be any if we do this right," Bart said.

"Sir, tell us what you want us to do," Frank asked.

Jacques punched the third-floor button. He had his Colt .45 in hand.

"What room are they in?" Bart asked.

"328, just to our right." Kastel pointed as he punched the hold button on the elevator panel.

"Stay here," Jacques hissed. "I'll check them out."

He walked down the hall and knocked on the door of 328. There was no response. Jim, the security man, approached and held up a passkey. Jacques nodded. The door was opened and the two men, guns in hand, entered the suite. It was unoccupied.

The five men took the elevator to the sixth floor. As they exited the elevator, the two men and the woman were heading to the elevator. Jacques and the two security men pointed their guns at the surprised trio coming toward them. The Cuban man reached for his gun. Jacques smashed him across the cheek with his Colt .45, and he sank to the floor, blood splattering his shirt and white slacks.

"Hands up!" Bart shouted.

They complied as Bart patted the man down. Jacques snatched the lady's handbag. Bart extracted a semi-automatic from the man's pocket. Jacques found a Beretta in the lady's bag. Kastel was used to violence, but he admired Jacques' professionalism. Jim and Frank lifted the semi-conscious Cuban man, dragging him toward the sixth-floor suite. The man and woman, hands in the air, were prodded through the open door of the rooms. A dinner table with untouched food stood in the center of the living room.

"*Setzen sie,*" Bart roared.

"*Was ist los?*" the man asked.

Bart whispered to Jacques, "Call Major Flaherty's room. If he's there, ask him to come here with his crew pronto. Tell him to come armed."

The woman, red-haired with spots of gray, wearing bifocals, rasped in a heavy Irish brogue, "What do you thieves want?"

"Don't play stupid, Madame. Your husband is a Nazi war criminal wanted by the Allied governments," Bart snapped.

"You're a fucking nut, soldier boy!" she shot back.

The Cuban was moaning. Jim threw a wet towel at him. There was a knock at the door.

"Who is it?" Jacques answered.

"Major Flaherty."

The door was opened, and four uniformed American Air Force men entered. They saluted Bart, nodded to Jacques and quickly surveyed the scene.

"Phil, thanks for your help. We've got the situation under control now. We'll be out of your hair in the morning. Sorry for the theatrics."

"No problem. I enjoyed every minute."

"General, may I have a private word with you?" Frank, Kastel's aide, asked.

Bart walked over to the window facing the Caribbean.

"Sir, that man on the couch is a dangerous hood. His name is Pablo Munoz. He's a killer. Be careful. He has police connections," Frank whispered.

"Thanks for the information."

Kastel joined them at the window and said, "If you need help taking them out in the morning, let me know. I'll clear the service area and you can remove them from the freight elevator to the loading dock."

"I appreciate that, Phil. We could use your shuttle bus to the airport."

"You've got it."

Kastel and his men left. Bart whispered to Jacques, who left the room and went to the lobby. The doorman pointed at the Cadillac. Jacques opened the trunk and removed three sets of handcuffs and two rolls of duct tape. He hastened back to the suite. The woman was shouting obscenities at Bart, while the man was imploring her in guttural English to keep quiet. The Cuban was swearing in Spanish.

Major Flaherty and his flight crew sat quietly, their guns drawn and pointed at the three prisoners. With Bart's help, Jacques handcuffed the German and the Cuban. Flaherty handcuffed the woman. Jacques taped the mouth of the woman and the Cuban. Bart told him to tape their eyes. He left and proceeded to the penthouse. He explained the events of the last hour to Reynolds and the Secret Service men.

"Come with me, gentlemen. I want you to see our latest catch. Keith, maybe you can identify these people. They are manacled and blindfolded. Don't talk in front of them. Just whisper to me."

Bart tapped on the door to the suite. Flaherty turned the bolt lock and opened the door. He placed two fingers to his lips for silence. Flaherty recognized Reynolds and the two Secret Service agents as previous passengers on his F-27. He nodded to them.

Reynolds took a long look at the three blindfolded and handcuffed prisoners. He pointed at the man and woman, nodding his head as a sign of recognition. He looked at the bloodied Cuban on the couch and shrugged his shoulders.

Jacques was searching the prisoners, and patted them down. He noticed the lack of a cleavage outline on the woman's breasts. He placed his hand on the center of her blouse, buttoned high to her neck. He ripped the blouse open, put his hands inside the open garment and withdrew a .22 caliber gun. He found a snub-nosed revolver attached to the right foot of the Cuban. Bart led Reynolds to the bedroom.

"Did you recognize those two? You nodded your head."

"Yes, General Milburn, the man is Walter Schellenberg, chief of the SS. The woman goes under the name of Louise Bancroft. She works for Nordheim. She lives in Belfast. I saw her once in Malmo and once on the yacht, Flying Eagle. I think it was in Monte Carlo. I believe she is connected with the IRA. I don't think her true name is Bancroft."

"What about the Cuban?"

"I've never seen him before."

Bart picked up the phone. "Could you connect me with Mr. Kastel, please?"

"One minute sir, I'll page him."

"Yes?" Kastel finally answered.

"Phil, Bart Milburn. I'm sorry to disturb you. Where are you?"

"You're not disturbing me. I'm in the casino."

"Can I pull you out of there? It's rather important. Would you oblige me and meet me at the fourth-floor elevator?"

"I'll be right there, General."

At the elevator, Dandy Phil asked, "A problem, General?"

"I need to reach Meyer Lansky right away."

"What's the problem?"

"I need to get that killer, Pablo Munoz, and those two extradited out of Havana. Meyer Lansky has the clout with President Batista. I need that paper tonight. Is it possible?"

"With Meyer, anything is possible on this island," Kastel said, looking at his Rolex watch. "Yes, he's having dinner with George Raft at the Capri. Let's go to your room and I'll call him."

They walked back to the suite. Bart knocked on the door. Jacques opened the living-room door.

"Open the door on the right and lock up this one," Bart directed. Phil nodded to Jacques and entered the bedroom, then went to the phone directly. Jacques whispered to Bart, "That woman had two passports in her bag. One in the name of Bancroft, resident in London. The other one is Louise Maloney. The man's passport is Swiss, with the name of Walter Bancroft."

"Meyer, General Milburn is anxious to talk with you." Phil handed the phone to Bart.

"I am very sorry to disturb you, sir."

"No problem. What is it, Barton?"

"Meyer, I have a Pablo Munoz, who was here to put a hit on one of my people. We've captured him and need an extradition writ to take him to U.S. territory. Am I pressuring too much in believing you can help us?"

"That's a very dangerous man in your custody. He's a professional hit man, considered tops in his trade. How soon do you need it?"

"Now," Bart replied.

"You're in the same rooms at the Riviera?"

"Yes."

"Stand by, and I'll call you right back."

"Phil, I am grateful for your help," Bart said.

"I told you we're patriots too," Kastel replied as he left.

Bart went back to the living room. The woman was struggling with her restraints. The man was motionless. The Cuban was stretched out on the sofa, pretending to be asleep. Major Flaherty and his men were seated, guns in their laps, watching the prisoners.

"*Achtung!*" Bart shouted.

Schellenberg sat up straight in his chair, jangling his foot chains. The woman tried to stand up. Flaherty pushed her back in her chair.

"General Schellenberg, I'm going to remove the tape from your mouth."

Bart less than gently ripped the tape from his face.

"*Schweinhund!*" he screamed.

Bart addressed him in German.

"Who did you come here to kill?"

"*Bumsen!*"

Bart slapped him hard across his face.

"Listen, you Nazi prick, you are a war criminal in custody of the United States Army. Your days are numbered. Is this Irish lady really your wife?"

"*Scheisse* the Yankee Army!"

Bart backhanded him, drawing blood from his mouth. He applied the tape over the crimson flow. He turned to the lady and ripped the tape from her mouth.

"You son of a bitch!" she cried.

"Louise Maloney, do you miss Herr Nordheim?"

"That's none of your fucking business," she muttered.

"We'll see about that. Aren't you the lady who followed Dr. LaVelle and helped hustle him to Malmo, Sweden, from Geneva, Miss *Bancroft*? Alias *Maloney*, or is it vice versa?" Bart snickered.

She stiffened. There was no reply. He replaced the tape on her mouth. The phone rang and Jacques answered. "It's you know who," he said to Bart.

"I'll take it in the bedroom.

"Hello?"

"It's me - Meyer."

"A Lieutenant Lopez will be there in a half hour with your writ. Good luck."

"Meyer, you're a genius."

"Is that killer involved with the Nazis?"

"That's why I want him out of here."

"Good deal. Hang the bastard."

"Thanks again, and *ciao*."

Bart returned to the living room and called Major Flaherty aside.

"John, I hate to do this to you and your crew, but I'd like to move these three to the naval base tonight. Do you mind making the round trip? Dump them there and come right back. I'll call ahead."

"Glad to do it, General."

"Have you and your men had dinner?"

"Yes sir, we had just finished when you sent for us."

"Two things, John. When you get back, fuel up so that we can leave for the base at 1100 hours. Second, tie these prisoners up as soon as they get on board. Don't take any chances. I'll borrow the hotel shuttle bus to run you and your crew to the airport. Jacques will go with you to the airport and assist tying them up. I'll call down for the shuttle."

He went into the other connecting bedroom, where Witten, Parker and Reynolds were biding their time. Bart reached Kastel by phone in the casino. He asked for the use of the hotel shuttle bus.

"It'll be at the receiving dock in a few minutes. The driver can be trusted. He's Rico, the same one your men used before."

"Thanks, Phil. I hope the house is doing well."

"Yeah, we have some high rollers, and they're leaving a lot of loot tonight."

There was a knock on the living-room door. Bart heard it and ran back to the big room. Jacques opened the door. A tall Cuban police officer announced, "I am Captain Julio Lopez. I have some papers for the General."

Bart came to the door. Lopez saluted. Milburn returned the gesture.

"I am required to see the prisoner before I release these documents."

"Very well, go to the bedroom door on your right. I must ask you for your gun, Captain, and will return it to you when you leave," Bart politely requested.

Lopez smiled, unsnapped his holster and handed his .357 magnum to Bart. Jacques dragged the reclining Pablo Munoz to his feet and helped him shuffle into the empty bedroom. He threw him on the bed. Bart opened the bedroom door and the tall, husky captain came in. The prisoner had his face buried in a pillow. Lopez leaned over and turned him face up. "Sit up, *puta*."

Bart peeled the tape off his eyes and mouth. Munoz strained his eyes to adjust for the light. He looked at the captain and snarled, *"Chingate. Mierda."*

Lopez slapped him resoundingly. "They finally got you, *hijo de puta.*"

Bart and Jacques watched the two exchange insults.

"He's all yours," Lopez said, handing the large envelope to Bart.

Bart walked out with him, and handed the gun to Lopez.

"Thanks, Captain."

"My pleasure. That scumbag has killed a lot of people, including two cops. He got off by bribing judges. Lucky for him, you took my gun. I was tempted to kill that scumbag."

Jacques, at Bart's request, called the villa to advise Elizabeth that they were in Havana and would be home soon. She answered the call.

"Jacques, you and Bart had better come here immediately. Something terrible has happened."

"My God, Liz, what is it?"

"There's been a shooting."

"Who's been shot?"

"No one in the family. Hurry. Hurry!"

Jacques rushed out to the corridor and excitedly hailed Bart and the captain at the elevator.

"Come back quick!"

Bart and Lopez ran back to the bedroom door.

"What's wrong?" Bart demanded.

"There's been a shooting at the house."

"Anybody hurt?"

"Not in the family. That's all Elizabeth told me."

Bart shouted for Major Flaherty. "John, hold everything. Tie up the prisoners and keep them under surveillance. Jacques and I have an emergency. Lieutenant, you'd better come with us to my house."

They raced to the front door of the hotel. Bart advised the doorman to hold the shuttle bus until later.

"Yes, sir. Do you want your car?"

"No," the captain advised Bart, "we'll use my car."

Bart and Jacques entered the captain's police car. Lopez turned on the flashing red lights and the tires squealed as he pressed his foot to the gas pedal. At eighty miles an hour, they were at the villa in minutes. Police cars were at the open gate and in front of the house. A paramedic ambulance was parked in the circular driveway. A dozen police officers were scattered over the grounds. A few members of the press were at the gate. Captain Lopez maneuvered his car alongside the ambulance. There was blood on the driveway.

Bart and Jacques ran through the open door. Elizabeth embraced Bart. Joyce and Christina hugged Jacques. Although the women seemed surprisingly contained, nervousness was reflected in their eyes. The children were in the guesthouse with Mrs. Bishop and Elsie. Emilio and Maria were not at the house. The captain beckoned police Lieutenant Juan Garcia, who appeared to be in charge. Bart ordered Elizabeth, Joyce, and Christina to the den. "I'll be with you soon. Relax," he said.

He joined the captain and the lieutenant. "Before you two go over this affair, it is vital that the press be told this was an attempted robbery," Bart whispered to the captain. "That's a high priority. President Batista will agree, I assure you."

"I understand, General Milburn," he said, waving to a sergeant.

In Spanish, he instructed the sergeant to follow the script.

"Now, what happened here?" Bart asked.

"Lieutenant Garcia, tell us what happened. Speak English," the captain ordered.

"Two men have been shot by your two security men, who are members of our police force. They are not critically wounded and are being tended by the paramedics in the ambulance. One is wounded in his right arm. The other one was shot in the leg. They fired shots at the security police, who quickly overcame the two and disarmed them. The two men had scaled the fence and were trying to break into the house while a woman was passed through and was talking to your lady at the front door. After the shots, she ran to a Buick sedan driven by another man and disappeared. Your security officers called headquarters to report the shooting. After all, they are Havana police officers moonlighting for you, General. A trace is on for the Buick," Garcia summed up.

"Who are these men?" Jacques asked.

"They are not Cubans."

"Have you talked to them?" Bart queried.

"They will not talk."

"When did all this happen?"

"About two hours ago. The paramedics arrived thirty minutes ago."

"May I look at them?" Bart asked.

"Go right ahead."

Bart, Jacques, and Lopez walked over to the ambulance. Lopez ordered the paramedics to step aside. Bart and the captain stepped into the large van. Jacques stood on the steps of the vehicle. After a long minute, Bart took a long shot and yelled, "*Achtung!*"

There was a visible reaction by both men, who sat up on the gurneys.

"General Schellenberg is waiting for you men," he said in German.

"*Scheisse*," the leg-injured man swore.

"Nordheim is concerned about you," Bart persisted.

"*Scheisse, scheisse*," both men shouted.

"Captain, have they been searched?"

"Let me check them now."

Both men's jackets were on the floor. Bart reached for them and ran his hands through the pockets. Two Argentine passports, for Horst Lamen and Johann Weist, two round-trip Eastern Airlines tickets from Miami and room keys of the Hotel Nacional were extracted. Lopez ran his hand along the linings of the jacket. He felt something sewed behind the linings. He ripped the satin and found envelopes in each jacket. Each contained large amounts of American hundred-dollar bills. Bart looked at the envelopes, which contained sheets of notepaper.

"Let's look at the paper," Bart suggested.

The notes on the paper carried the name of Harry Branlow, room 206, Hotel Nacional; a sketch of the villa grounds, a full description of the main house and the guesthouse. The name of Christina Lyons was scribbled on her photograph. Bart asked the captain to stop outside with him. Jacques went inside the house to talk with the women. Bart persuaded the captain to handcuff the prisoners.

"Captain, this Harry Branlow is obviously involved as an accomplice in a conspiracy to commit murder," Bart declared.

"How do you arrive at that conclusion, sir?"

"These men were here to murder Christina Lyons. She is a very important witness in a military trial in the United States. I wish I could tell you more. Please send some men to the Nacional Hotel and detain him. Please do that right away. Hold him there until you and I can confront him. Now, I want to arrange a meeting with your President. I represent President Truman. Let's keep this from becoming an international incident."

"Do you think that President Batista will see you?"

"Yes, I have to make a phone call. I'll be right out."

The captain ordered Lieutenant Garcia to detain Harry Branlow at the Nacional Hotel, pending his arrival. Bart called the Capri and reached Meyer Lansky.

"Meyer, this is urgent. Call me at this number from a phone booth. Something has happened."

"Gotcha."

The phone rang in the office next to the den, where Jacques was talking with Elizabeth, Christina, and Joyce. Bart spelled out to Lansky the events that had taken place at his house.

"It was an attempted hit on a very important witness against the Nazis."

"Nazis? That's my meat. What do you need?"

"I want a meeting with Batista. It's vital."

"Stand by. I'll call you right back."

Bart entered the den. He kissed the three women on their foreheads. "How are you all?"

Elizabeth replied, "We're fine."

They seemed relaxed. All were sipping glasses of wine.

"Bart, the lady who came here today asked for Christina Lyons. She said she represented Lloyds of London and wanted to settle an insurance policy in which Phillip LaVelle had Christina as the beneficiary," Jacques said.

"What did she look like, Elizabeth?"

"Barton, she was middle-aged. Maybe no more than fifty years of age. She had red hair with sprinkles of gray. She was tall and wore a double-breasted jacket and pleated skirt. She wore thick bifocal glasses with black rims. She showed me her card. Her name was Barclay. I don't remember her first name. She had a thick Irish brogue. I was suspicious of her and told her no one by that name lived here. Then we heard the shots and she ran."

"Liz, did you see the car and who was driving?"

"Yes, he was an older man, maybe sixty, dignified, with gray hair under a Homburg hat. Her clothes and his were winter type, peculiar for this climate."

"They were after me," Christina said. "Those security guards saved us."

"Yes, they might have killed all of us," Elizabeth ventured.

"Well, I think you can relax. We're closing this house Monday morning. Christina will be living with us in Washington. We'll have full security," Bart assured them. "Tomorrow we are going to Guantanamo."

"Oh, I can't impose on your generosity," Christina said.

"We won't take no for an answer," Elizabeth declared, hugging her.

The phone rang in the office, and Bart answered.

"General, I spoke to Mr. B. He's at a reception now. He can see us at 11:30 at his house. That's an hour and a half from now."

"What do you mean by *us*, Meyer?"

"Barton, my boy, I usually go to bed early, but in a situation like this, you're going to need some clout. Come directly to Batista's house at eleven and we can talk."

"See you then."

Jacques came into the office.

"Bart, I don't believe Emilio and Maria's story about a sick sister. Their absence is too coincidental."

"Good point. I'll have the captain send two men to their house and bring them here. Let's go see Mr. Branlow at the Nacional."

Bart told the ladies that the house would be fully protected and that Emilio and Maria were going to be brought back to the house.

"Don't ask them any questions. I'll do that when I return," he said. On the way out, he saw Captain Lopez talking to the two security policemen who had shot the intruders. "Gentlemen, I owe you a great deal for your heroic work in protecting my family," Bart said, shaking their hands. "I'll be seeing you later. You're heroes." He pressed a handful of money into their hands. Both men beamed. Bart asked Captain Lopez to leave some extra men to augment security. He gave him Emilio's address and asked to have them brought back to the house.

"What shall we do with these two men in the ambulance?" Lopez asked.

"Are they patched up all right, or do they need further medical attention?" The captain checked with the paramedics.

"They think we should try to have the bullets removed and to receive tetanus shots. I'll send them to an emergency room and bring them back here," Lopez said.

"Fine. Send a couple of tough officers with them."

"Don't worry."

On the way to the Nacional Hotel, Bart advised the captain of his upcoming meeting with President Batista. At the hotel, they knocked on the door of

Harry Branlow's suite 206. A police officer opened the door, saluted his captain and instinctively saluted Milburn in his general's uniform. Bart and Jacques acknowledged the salute.

In the luxurious living room, another police officer was guarding Branlow, who was manacled. A slight man, Branlow was sallow-complected under his tropical tan, probably due to fear. His hands were shaking.

He looked at Bart and tremulously asked, "What is the meaning of all this? These men will tell me nothing."

"You damn well know by now why you are being detained," Bart roared.

"Hey, I am an American citizen and demand to see my ambassador."

Jacques sat down next to him on the couch.

"You're nothing but an accessory to attempted murder, you rotten bastard! I have a good mind to blow your brains out," Jacques hissed into his ear.

Captain Lopez lit a Havana special cigar and sat in a comfortable lounge chair, observing the scene. Bart stood over Branlow, lifted his chin and stared into his eyes, which were blinking nervously.

"Well, well, look at what we have here. It is none other than the dishonorably discharged Colonel Branlow. You're the son of a bitch who was peddling ten million dollars worth of Russian bonds stolen from German headquarters when we occupied Paris," Bart exclaimed.

"I heard about him," Jacques grumbled.

"Listen, rat, you're a traitor tied up with Herr Nordheim and his whole Nazi contingent. You've got a date with the scaffold," Bart snarled.

"Let me take him into the bathroom and have him commit suicide," Jacques quipped.

"No, that's too easy a way out. Maybe he'll tell us how he masterminded the hit on Mrs. Lyons."

"Hey, do you realize who I am?" Branlow asked.

"Yes, you're a partner of Irwin Gullen, the banker. Does he know you're a traitor?"

"What do you want?" Branlow pleaded.

"Give us the total unvarnished truth about this stupid caper and you might save your life."

"I can't talk in front of these police. They'll kill me."

Lopez jumped out of his chair, blew a cloud of smoke into Branlow's face and bellowed, "What are you trying to say? You think we're corrupt like you?"

Branlow coughed. "One of your men is part of this."

Lopez grabbed him by the throat and shouted, "Who? Tell me or I will kill you."

Branlow was choking. His face color was darkening. Bart pulled the captain away. "Give him a chance to talk."

Branlow had a coughing spell. Jacques handed him a glass of water.

"You almost killed me," he croaked.

"Who?" the captain persisted.

"Captain Juan Escobar had a picture of Mrs. Lyons. He recognized her on the beach and followed her to Irwin Gullen's villa," Branlow stammered.

"Quick now, I don't have much time. What's the whole story?" Bart demanded.

Branlow fell apart and described the sequence of events. "Nordheim placed a million-dollar bounty on Christina Lyons. Escobar called Darren Mayfield's apartment in Chicago. His brother, Paul Mayfield, answered the phone and said his brother was in Argentina. He called the number in Buenos Aires and it was disconnected. He called Paul, who passed the message on. Paul reached Walter Bancroft in Belfast. Bancroft and his wife came to New York and reached me by happenstance because Gullen was in Europe. I met with them at the Waldorf Astoria. They paid me two hundred thousand dollars to come with them to Havana. They told me that Mrs. Lyons was a Nazi spy and that they had been hired by the Israelis to bring her to Tel Aviv. They asked who rented the house and I told them that a Colonel Milburn did. They said Milburn was a double agent. I drew a map of the home, because they wanted to capture Milburn, too. When we got here, Escobar came to this suite and met with Bancroft and his wife. He told them that Milburn's plane was expected soon. So they went to the airport to follow Milburn. Where is this Milburn?"

"That's me, you sleazeball bastard!" Bart growled.

"You? You're a two-star general. Milburn is a colonel."

"He was. Now he's a general. And you are in deep doo-doo, ex-Colonel Branlow."

"Hey, I was trying to help Israel."

"Yes, with the aid of a Nazi, General Schellenberg, former chief of the SS, you worthless cretin. His wife is a hit lady for the IRA. Fine company you keep, you money-grubbing bastard! You can count your money from the end of a hangman's noose."

Bart, Jacques and the captain huddled in the suite bedroom.

"Can you keep Branlow here until after our meeting with your President? No phone calls for him, in or out!"

"Si, I'll order my men to hold him."

They drove to Batista's mansion. Security police waved them through. Meyer Lansky and Batista were savoring snifters of brandy and puffing long Havana cigars. Captain Lopez saluted the President and whispered in his ear. Batista shook hands with Milburn and Laurent. He excused himself to Lansky and the two visitors. Captain Lopez and Batista left the den and conferred in the dining room. Lopez related Branlow's implication of Captain Juan Escobar in the attempted assault at Gullen's villa.

"Escobar? I don't believe it," Batista muttered.

"What should we do, Mr. President?"

"Have him brought here now and disarm him."

"I'll have to do it myself with a couple of your most trusted officers."

"Take Lieutenant Esteban Galvano and Sergeant Enrique Vasquez. They are in the kitchen. Hurry."

Returning to his oak-paneled den, he sat in his leather chair, picked up his cigar and lit it. The snifter of brandy in his left hand was lifted in a toast.

"To Cuban and American friendship," he saluted with a smile.

Lansky and Milburn returned the toast.

"What is the problem, General Milburn?"

Bart detailed the events of the evening, then said, "Mr. President, I know that you are aware of President Truman's orders for our roundup of escaped Nazi war criminals. Our mutual friend, Mr. Lansky, has been helping us."

"Yes, I know a little something about it."

"We have kept Cuba's name out of our reports thus far. Tonight we have this assassination attempt at my rented villa against an important witness. A lady."

"Come, come, General, what do you want from me?"

Lansky laughed. "Fulgencio, you always get to the point. I admire you for that. It's a very simple matter. I would personally appreciate your granting the general's request."

"In straightforward terms, Mr. President, our government would be grateful if you would sign an extradition order for the immediate release of Walter Schellenberg, alias Bancroft, and his alleged wife Louise Bancroft, alias Maloney," Bart said. "Schellenberg was the general who headed the Nazi SS. Also, we have Pablo Munoz, a Cuban hit man. We also want Horst Lomen and Johann Weist, as well as Harry Branlow."

"General, I don't want Nazis in my country. However, I am concerned about Harry Branlow. He is a vice president in Mr. Gullen's bank. We do business with them. I respect Gullen. I don't know much about Branlow, but he's an American citizen," Batista said.

"Mr. President, all the more reason to extradite him. First, he's a dishonorably discharged American officer who is an accomplice to a conspiracy to commit murder. You don't want to try him in your courts and open a scandal involving one of your police officers, Captain Escobar."

Batista flinched. Lansky recognized the implications set forth by Bart. "Fulgencio, take my advice. Clean up the whole thing by turning them all over to the Americans. Things are going well here in Cuba - lots of American tourists. We don't need this kind of publicity."

"As always, Meyer, you are a practical man. Very well, I'll draw up an order and you will repeat all those names," Batista agreed and went to his desk. He pulled out a long form and shouted, "Olivia, come here!"

A young woman appeared.

"Sit here and type up this document."

"*Si, Señor Presidente.* You signed one for three people earlier. Shall I put all six names in this one?"

"Yes. General, list those names for my secretary. And also have her type up your request for extradition, which you will sign. She speaks perfect English."

She smiled at Bart as he stood over her. She rapidly typed the extradition form and swiftly completed Milburn's dictation, which formally requested the order. She brought the two documents to the cocktail table and handed a pen to Bart. He signed the request and passed the pen to Batista, who quickly scrawled his name on the extradition form. The secretary applied a seal to the documents. Olivia bowed, smiled at Bart and departed. The front door opened. The butler led Captains Lopez and Escobar into the den. Escobar was dressed in tan slacks, an open-collared shirt and a pair of sneakers.

He saluted the President and asked in Spanish, "Why am I here, sir?"

"General, tell him. He speaks good English."

Bart crisply detailed the charge made by Branlow.

"Is that true, Juan?" Batista asked.

"Yes, it's true. That lady's picture has been circulated by Mr. Nordheim, that Jewish millionaire. She's a Nazi spy. I saw her on the beach near Irwin Gullen's villa. I called Nordheim's assistant, Darren Mayfield. He is in Europe somewhere, so I gave the information to his brother, Paul. There is a million-dollar reward to the person who finds her. She is wanted by Israel. Mayfield called Harry Branlow, Gullen's vice president. That's the whole story, Mr. President."

"Did you know that there was an attempt to kill someone at the villa, which I am renting?"

"No, Captain Lopez told me nothing."

"Where were you all day, Juan?" Batista asked.

"Do you want me to tell you in front of these people?"

"You know Mr. Lansky. These two men are General Milburn of the U.S. Army and Jacques Laurent of the CIA. We have no secrets from them. Dammit, speak up!"

"Sir, I've been in the Oriente mountains for the last two days tracking that rebel bastard, Fidel Castro. You sent me up there Tuesday morning. I just got back when Captain Lopez came to my house. He pulled up behind me just as I arrived. What's wrong here?"

"That's true, Señor Presidente," Lopez confirmed. He was wearing a one-piece camouflage outfit and was covered with dried mud. I let him change clothes."

"Well, I believe your story, Captain Escobar. But you foolishly got involved with a bunch of Nazis. General Milburn will explain."

Bart detailed the fast-moving events.

"I'm inclined to believe your story, Captain," he declared.

"Sir, I hate all Nazis. In fact, I detest them. I am married to a Jewish lady and have three children with her who are being raised in the Hebrew faith. Besides, General, I served in the 101st Airborne during the war. I met my wife, who is a Belgian Jew, when we freed Belgium. She's from Brussels. I wouldn't dirty my hands on those Nazi bastards. I don't understand a Jew like Nordheim being involved," Escobar passionately declared.

"Captain, take my word for it, Nordheim is *not* a Jew. He is an escaped Nazi official. I'm glad to learn that you were not involved in this criminal plot. Your background is impressive. I was there with Patton when we relieved the Bulge. What was your rank?"

"I was a master sergeant, sir. I have a Bronze Star. My mother and two sisters live in Miami. They are American citizens. I am a loyal Cuban and I love America."

"Captain Escobar, I am relieved to know you are in the clear," Bart said.

"Thank you, sir."

"Mr. President, I ask that none of this be discussed by your officers," Bart requested. "This should be treated as an attempted robbery."

"I assure you it will be treated as such."

On the way out, Bart thanked Lansky profusely.

"Come here, Bart. I want to whisper something to you," Lansky said.

Bart lit a cigarette and moved to the back of the car as Jacques, Lopez and Escobar entered the vehicle.

"This is a secret, and I'll deny it if you repeat it. I have two sons, and one is a spastic, who is under therapy by Dr. Howard Rusk. That was arranged by your brother Douglas. The secret is my other son's career. He's now a high-ranking officer in the U.S. Army. Because of my notoriety, his name was changed legally at a very early age. Now, forget I told you that."

"Meyer, you're an amazing man, and I'll not judge you by newspaper accounts," Bart said. "You've been very helpful."

After dropping Escobar at his home a mile away, Lopez drove Jacques and Bart to the villa. The ambulance was at the exit lip of the driveway apron. The two men were on gurneys inside the van. A police officer advised that the two wounded prisoners had been treated at the hospital. The bullets were removed from their wounds. The doctors said their conditions were stable. Both men were manacled and shackled. Inside the house, they found a frightened Emilio and a crying Maria.

"Why did you lie about your sick sister?" Bart snapped at them.

"*Señor*, a lady gave us two thousand American dollars and told us to go home. There was going to be a big surprise party for *Señora* Lyons by her father, who had been missing for years. She was a nice Irish lady."

"When did she tell you this?"

"Last night when we had the night off and were going home. She stopped our car just outside the gate. She wanted to know if you were home. I told her you would be flying in early this evening," Emilio haltingly explained

Elizabeth spoke up. "Bart, I think they're telling the truth. They were stupidly naive. Don't be hard on them."

"If I find out that they were lying, I'll hang them," he retorted.

Elizabeth sent the two servants to their rooms.

"Liz, you may as well go to bed. I have to make a couple of calls and I'll be gone for awhile. I have to deposit some prisoners in our bastille," he said.

"Okay, darling," she said as she kissed him.

"Captain Lopez, you'll find some sandwiches and coffee in the kitchen. Jacques will show you," Bart said.

He went to the office and called Major Flaherty at the Riviera Hotel.

"John, I hate to do this to you after a long night. Can you handle those three prisoners and get them aboard the plane? If you need help, ask Secret Service agent Witten to assist. Leave Parker with Keith Reynolds."

"Yes, sir, General, can do."

"Further to that, I have an additional load, which Jacques and I will deliver to the hangar. I want you to fly them all to the base and return here for a flight back there at 1100 hours tomorrow for me and two ladies. I'll have the hotel shuttle bus waiting for you at the loading dock in back of the hotel. The driver's name is Rico. Now, flash the operator to transfer me to the doorman."

After a short wait, the doorman answered. "This is Pedro."

"This is General Milburn. Is Chico still waiting for me?"

"Yes, sir, the shuttle bus is parked out front."

"Let me talk with him."

After a minute's wait, Chico answered, "Yes, sir, General?"

"Major Flaherty is bringing some people down to the loading dock. Take them to the José Martí Airport. I'll see you there."

"Yes, sir."

A second call was placed to the Naval base. Sergeant Alan Wilcox answered the call.

"This is General Milburn. Who is the duty officer, Sergeant?"

"Sir, Lieutenant Tom Martin. Do you wish to speak to him?"

"Yes, that is, if the Admiral has gone to bed."

"No, as matter of fact, they are together in the Officers Club."

"Great, let me talk to the Admiral."

"Barton, we've missed you," the Admiral greeted when he came on. "Your whole team is here with me. What's up?"

Milburn gave the Admiral a summary of the evening's events.

"Major Flaherty is about to take off with six prisoners. One requires a gurney. He was shot in the leg. Will you give them the treatment and stash them in separate cells? After Monday then, we'll be out of your hair."

"How come?"

"I'll explain tomorrow. I'm coming down with my wife and Jacques' sister to try and identify some of those Nazi bastards."

"We'll take care of it."

Lopez and Jacques were munching chicken sandwiches and slurping Coca-Cola.

"Come on, fellas. Bring the food and drinks with you," Bart ordered as he snatched a sandwich and Coke for himself.

"Where to?" Lopez asked.

"Jacques and I will ride in the ambulance with our two beauties. You lead the way to the Nacional Hotel, where we will pick up Branlow. We'll put him in your car, and Jacques will ride with you to the airport. I'll follow you in the ambulance. We'll need a policeman to ride with you two, and I'll need one in the ambulance with me."

Lopez turned on the red lights and activated the sirens. The ambulance turned on its flashing red lights and squealed its way behind Lopez's car. Eight minutes later they were in front of the Nacional Hotel.

Lopez raced through the lobby to Branlow's suite. Two policemen, with the manacled Branlow, followed the lieutenant out to his car. The prisoner was unceremoniously dumped into the back seat, surrounded by Jacques and a policeman. The other police officer joined Bart in the ambulance.

With lights flashing and sirens screaming, the two vehicles raced to the airport. Jacques directed Lopez onto the tarmac to the last hangar. The shuttle had not yet arrived. The prisoners in the van remained mute, ignoring Bart's questions. Ten minutes later the shuttle bus arrived.

"Major, you and your crew get the plane ready. Jacques and these cops will help get the prisoners on board," said Bart.

Flaherty and crew went to work. Jacques entered the shuttle, Colt .45 in hand. Lopez led Branlow aboard the plane and seated him in the rear, as directed by Sergeant Moss, who applied shackles to his feet and quickly slapped duct tape over his eyes.

The two men and the woman were taken from the bus by Jacques and the policeman. The reluctant prisoners were prodded by guns. Jacques quickly shackled the three and blindfolded them with duct tape. The two wounded men were helped aboard by Lopez, two policemen and Bart. They were shackled and blindfolded. Branlow yelled obscenities, so his mouth was quickly duct-taped. The lady screamed, and soon all the prisoners were muted by tape. Each member of the crew was armed. The engines were revved up, and the plane taxied for takeoff.

Bart, Lopez, Jacques, the policemen and the ambulance driver watched the plane lift to the starlit tropical skies. Bart reached into his pocket and withdrew a wad of hundred-dollar bills. He delivered his largesse to the police officers and the ambulance drivers and forced five hundred dollars into Lopez's reluctant hands.

"Not necessary, General," Lopez protested.

"Don't insult me, Captain. Please put it away."

"*Muchas gracias*, General."

"*De Nada*, Captain. Take me home, please."

CHAPTER THIRTY-TWO

Saturday, May 10, 1952 - noon - Guantanamo Naval Base

Bart, Elizabeth, Jacques and Joyce deplaned from the F-27, and a welcoming committee led by Admiral Thomas and the CIA team greeted them. Richard Maybrook hugged Elizabeth, shook hands with Jacques and was introduced to his sister Joyce. Sophia pushed Maybrook aside, interrupting his lengthy attention to Joyce. Berger, Fuentes and the admiral congratulated Joyce on her fortuitous escape from East Germany. The admiral invoked personal privilege in kissing Elizabeth and Joyce. Both ladies were pleased by the warmth of their reception. The sun was high in a royal blue sky. A cool sea breeze fanned the base.

"General, before we get on with the business of the day, we've prepared a special lunch. Please follow me, folks," the admiral requested.

A Navy bus carried the party to the Officers Club, and when they entered the club the officers rose and the noncom attendants applauded the group. A banner behind an elongated table bore the legend *Welcome to Elizabeth and Joyce.* The ladies, somewhat embarrassed, threw kisses at the men.

"Admiral, you're a special friend," Bart said gratefully.

The table was set for a high-ranking reception. Tropical flowers were in vases in the center of the dining area.

Lunch was served. The festive air was filled with small talk and anecdotes, delivered mostly by their host. Compliments for Bart abounded. Toasts to the ladies and a heartfelt welcoming speech to Joyce brought tears to her eyes. The party then adjourned to the conference room, and Bart announced the plan of moving all the prisoners to Homestead Air Force Base, where they would be sorted and shuttled to Fort Leavenworth.

"I wish I could join you, General," Admiral Thomas said. "I feel as though my family is leaving me."

"We'll be missing you, too, sir. You've been an immense pillar of support," Bart replied.

"I have prepared a sixteen-millimeter film of our prisoners before we line them up in the interrogation room. It has a one-way glass through which you can view them without them seeing you, ladies," Thomas said.

"Wayne, that was very thoughtful of you," Bart replied.

Thomas spoke into his intercom. "Okay, men, come in."

Petty Officers Noah Davis and Frank Romero appeared. Davis, a big grin on his face, walked over to Bart, saluted and shook his hand.

"General, I haven't had so much fun dealing with these creeps since the war ended. Thanks for the experience."

"Noah, you're a good man and I thank you for your help."

Romero wheeled in a projector. Davis turned on the lights and pulled down the shades. A screen was lowered at the opposite end of the room.

"If you will turn your chairs to face the screen, I'll douse the lights and our feature film will start," Davis joked.

The lights were extinguished, and the film flickered intermittently. Romero adjusted the focus and a clear picture emerged, showing shackled prisoners arriving at the base. The faces were indistinguishable. A few frames later, there were close-up shots of each individual captive.

Next came the mug shots, made by Davis, with the captives holding prison numbers and their names stenciled beneath the photos. One after the other showed Bormann, Ricardo von Leute, Peter Weber, Heinrich Müller, Gunther Froelich, Hugo Schultz. At this point Elizabeth screamed, "Stop! That is Hugo Schultz. He was the commandant at Ohrdruf. He beat me. Bart, that's the man you shot. Is he here?"

"Yes, Liz, he's here all right."

"Oh, dear God," she sobbed fitfully.

The film stopped and the lights came on.

Bart patted her back, "Come now, sweetheart, these are bad memories."

The admiral handed her a glass of wine.

"Sip this. The worst is over," he said.

"I'm sorry. The sight of that beast shocked me," she said.

The lights were doused and the film continued. Pictures of Nordheim with his Van Dyke beard and mustache followed, with the ignominious transformation to his convict stance before the camera, holding his number and the name *Nordheim*. His head and face pictured him shaven of his hirsute adornments.

"Who is that?" Elizabeth murmured.

Bart, standing behind her, whispered, "That, my dear, is Adolf Hitler himself. In the flesh."

"Oh, no, is that possible?" she cried.

"Believe me, honey."

Joyce leaned over to the admiral and asked if the film could be rolled back to the beginning.

"There is a face there I'd like to see again."

Thomas ordered Davis to roll it back. When it came to Heinrich Müller, she loudly exclaimed, "Stop!"

"What is it, Joyce?" Jacques asked excitedly.

"He is the man who was in charge of the Gestapo men in Paris who rounded up the Jews. He was on the train when I was taken to Dachau. Later, when we were moved to Chelmno, he was there watching the execution of thousands of prisoners. I was hiding in the forest when the Russians came. The Nazis fled like rats. The Russians shipped the rest of us to Leipzig. I'm sure he's the one."

"He was head of the Gestapo that carried out the organized mass murders of Jews. He escaped from the bunker under the chancellery, as the Russian Army was about to overrun Berlin," Bart explained.

The footage continued with Abdul-al-Said, a.k.a. The Cobra; Herman Klauss, Hans Langsdorff, and the newest prisoners, Harry Branlow, Louise Bancroft; Walter Bancroft, a.k.a. Schellenberg; Pablo Munoz, Horst Leman, and Johann Weist.

"Admiral, tell them to hold it there," Joyce begged.

The film was making a flapping noise, indicating the end of the reel. Romero quickly rewound the reel and put it on fast forward. He stopped and rolled the clips again past Pablo Munoz and Horst Leman when Joyce yelled, "Stop!"

Weist's picture slowly moved to a close-up. Davis brought it to a stop. Joyce stared at Weist's face. The room was silent.

"I am sure he was an officer at the Chelmno death camps. He was using a machine gun to slaughter men, women and children. Oh, my God, it was *awful*. I was a young girl who felt very old watching those beasts," she cried.

"Well, well, look at what we got here today," Jacques exclaimed.

"Let's go now to our special interrogation room," Admiral Thomas suggested.

The group settled in armchairs facing a large one-way window. The lights in the viewing room were dimmed. On the other side of the window there was a stage resembling a police lineup room. The procedure was winnowed down to one prisoner at a time. Davis' huge frame and two heavyweight MPs awaited the appearance of the first prisoner.

Hitler shuffled onto the stage, his small frame contrasted with the giant-sized trio. He tried to adjust his eyes to the glaring lights. The backdrop contained a huge measuring board lined with size indicators. Hitler showed his height to be five feet, eight inches in his shoes. Davis had him face front, staring at the blank window. He was turned right and left to show his profiles.

"*Was ist los? Verdammen noch mal. Schwarzer. Der arschloch.*"

"What is your name?" Davis snapped.

"*Schwarzer, ich bin der Führer, sieg heil!*" he declared as he held his arm out straight in the Nazi salute with his middle finger obscenely pointing at the one-way mirror. Davis lifted him by the scruff of his neck and unceremoniously propelled him out the door.

"Dear God, Barton, this is your top dog Nazi catch?" Elizabeth asked in shock.

"That's him. Our other catch is Martin Bormann."

"Oh my," she awed. Then, observing Hitler holding his arm up in the Nazi salute, she remarked, "That arrogant filthy animal."

"He has highs and lows. He must have realized that there was an audience behind that glass," Admiral Thomas observed.

The parade of prisoners continued without further incident. The last one on view was Martin Bormann. The stocky man behaved well and executed a salute to the one-way window. The lights were turned on.

Joyce, misty-eyed, in a muted voice, said, "It is difficult to match these derelicts with the Nazis who almost conquered all of Europe and killed millions of innocent people. I hope you hang these bastards, Barton."

"No, Joyce, that's the easy way out for these vermin," Bart countered. "I'm recommending boot camps at hard labor for the rest of their lives. If I have my way, they'll experience what a concentration camp was like."

"I don't have a bit of compassion for these evil bloody animals," Elizabeth declaimed.

"I am completely empathetic with you ladies. You were there and experienced the horror of their inhumanity," Admiral Thomas said.

Bart placed his arm around Elizabeth. "Sweetheart, I have a meeting with the admiral and the team to arrange for the orderly transfer of these prisoners. Would you and Joyce like a tour of the base?"

"That's fine, Bart. Do what you have to do."

The admiral arranged for Captain McMahon to escort the ladies on the tour. In the conference room, Bart spelled out the schematics for the transfer of the prisoners.

"Colonel Ashby will supply the planes as needed. However, I don't want Hitler or Bormann to be seen by any of the other prisoners. I want to keep those two separated," Bart said.

"We have our own fleet of planes here. Why don't we blindfold, mute and shackle each of those swine and add a few prisoners to each plane in the same condition, plus a half dozen Marines to guard them and fly all directly to Fort Leavenworth?" Admiral Thomas speculated.

"Wayne, that's a helluva plan. I didn't have the nerve to impose this on you. General Fielding is all set to receive these bums. I would recommend that Maybrook and Berger accompany the Führer. Sophia and Tony should ride with Bormann," Bart said.

"I have a surprise for you, Bart. Two turbo jet transports were delivered to us a few days ago. This will be a good test for their maiden runs," Thomas said.

"That being the case, Wayne, I'll send the F-27 with Major Flaherty back here to pick up the balance of the crud. Give him some Marines as escorts. He'll drop the rest of the contemptible bastards at Homestead," Bart added.

"That's a plan, Bart."

"Wayne, hold the flights in readiness for a go-ahead from me on Monday morning. I want to touch base with General Bradley and Colonel Ashby before we make the move."

"That's fine, Bart. It's been a profound pleasure to work with you. I am available for the hearings or the major trials."

"The pleasure is mine, sir."

☆ ☆ ☆ ☆

Saturday, May 10, 1952, same day - Havana

With the family reunited, the children and Christina spent the day at the pool. Security around the house was tight. The rest of the weekend was devoted to quality time with the four little ones. Bart settled his account for the villa rental with Phil Kastel, who refused payment for the rooms and charges at the Hotel Riviera.

"Listen, General, Meyer Lansky and I are Jews," Kastel said. "No matter what the press's conception of us gambling people is, we are loyal Americans. And when it comes to capturing Nazis, we have a strong desire to help the effort. You and your guys deserve our deepest appreciation. Costello is behind you all the way. This is our small contribution to your efforts. *Gey gesunter heit*, pal."

"Thanks for everything, Phil. *Zul sein mit glick*," Bart replied, and departed.

On Sunday afternoon, Bart tipped all the police on duty at the villa, then Captain Lopez and a motorcycle escort led the family in the Hotel Riviera shuttle to José Martí Airport. Lopez and the police helped carry the luggage to the F-27.

On arrival at National Airport in Washington, a shuttle bus brought the family to the Rock Creek home.

☆ ☆ ☆ ☆

Monday, May 12, 1952 - Washington

Bart spoke with General Bradley and outlined the plan to send Hitler and Bormann, plus select prisoners, directly to Fort Leavenworth. He approved. Bart's next call went to Colonel Ashby, and the operation was put in motion. The last call was put through to Admiral Thomas.

"All systems go, Wayne. Jacques and I are leaving now for Homestead."

"Smooth sailing, Bart."

Stanley drove Bart and Jacques to Andrews Air Force Base. The flight was uneventful. At Homestead, Brigadier General Alton Gregory, commander of the base, greeted Bart and Jacques. He saluted and the two men responded. Salutes were exchanged.

"Welcome to Homestead Air Base, gentlemen," Gregory said.

They drove to Gregory's headquarters, where a master sergeant poured coffee for Bart, Jacques and the General.

"We are all set for the transfer operation to Fort Leavenworth. Colonel Ashby has sent us two C-121 Lockheeds. We have extra planes on the base if needed," Gregory said.

"Has Gideon Cartman given you a list of the prisoners to be separated from the mass?" Bart asked.

"Yes, I have it right here. Forty-seven can be commingled. Five are to be detached. Shall I send for Cartman?"

"Please do. Mind if I smoke?"

"Not at all, General. I have the same bad habit." He picked up the phone. "Sergeant, ask Cartman to come here, please."

"Yes, sir."

Bart, Jacques and Gregory lit up. More coffee was poured. Cartman arrived, saying, "Howdy, gentlemen."

"By the way, General, I understand that Mr. Cartman is a reserve officer with the rank of major," Gregory said.

"Interesting. Where did you serve, Gideon?" Bart asked.

"You know that, Barton," he said, smiling.

"Yes, you were with General Mark Clark in Italy at Cassino."

"That's right." Cartman paused to shift gears, then said, "We've got five former concentration-camp commandants so far. I told you about the one that Captain Esta Arnold reported. Lloyd Sedgwick of the CIA has worked with us, ferreting out the other four."

"Where are Sedgwick and Arnold now?" Bart asked.

"In the outer office."

"Can we have them join us, General?"

Gregory punched his intercom, asking them to enter.

Captain Arnold saluted, and Sedgwick shook hands with Milburn.

"At ease, Captain. Sit down, please."

Gregory asked, "Have you divided the fifty two into groups?"

"So far, the five commandants should be flown in a separate plane, possibly two or three more that we are not sure of," Sedgwick replied. "As a whole, these Waffen SS bastards are a mean-spirited, well-trained gang of thugs. Each one has the killer instinct. Dyed-in-the-wool Nazi pit bulls."

"The five and the three possibles go in one plane. Divide the other forty-four into two groups. We have ten attorneys, Captain Arnold, Agents Laurent and Sedgwick, and me. That totals eighty-nine passengers, plus plane crews," Bart said.

"I have a new turbojet. How about the eight in that plane?"

"That sounds good, General Gregory."

"Bart, please call me Alton."

"Fine. I think six Marines should be on each of the other planes. Jacques, Captain Arnold and Sedgwick will go with me and the five commandants and the suspected three on the turbo. We could use four armed soldiers on board, if you can spare them."

"I've got some tough MPs for you, Bart."

"Alton, our procedure to date has been to blindfold the prisoners and tape their eyes and mouths. Can we round up the Marines, the MPs and the U.S. Attorneys? I'd like to address them. Gideon, are all your men packed and ready to go?" Bart asked.

The responses were affirmative.

"Let them gather outside these headquarters," Gregory ordered as he pressed his intercom. "Sergeant Clements, round up those Marines and send those four MPs here."

Cartman left to gather the U.S. Attorneys. The men summoned were outside the commander's office ten minutes later. The uniformed men stood at attention as the two generals emerged.

"At ease, men. General Milburn, who is in charge of this operation, has a few words for you," Gregory announced.

"Men, first to the Marines and the MPs. You will be guarding some of the most evil, dangerous, heartless and inhumane criminals ever in the history of mankind. This is not an exaggeration. All prisoners are to be handcuffed, feet shackled once they are on board, blindfolded and muted with duct tape. Be careful that none of them vomit and choke to death. If it starts to happen, just rip the tape off their mouths. Keep your eyes on them constantly. At Fort Leavenworth, their foot shackles will be removed sequentially as they are hustled to their cells. MPs will meet the planes at Fort Leavenworth."

"Understood, men?" General Gregory shouted.

"Yes, sir," they roared.

"Now, to the U.S. Attorneys, five of you are to be in each plane. Major Cartman will make the assignments and split the Waffen SS guys into two groups. To all of you, do not tolerate any misbehavior from the prisoners. Any questions?" Bart asked.

None were posed.

"Let's move them out. Dismissed!" Gregory snapped.

Jacques pulled Bart aside. "Barton, as soon as we get the planes loaded, I will stick around until the F-27 arrives with our prisoners and they are transferred to a plane for Leavenworth. What I would like to do is go back to Washington to help Joyce do her debriefing and then fly her to New York to sign our new accounts at the National City Bank. Can you spare me?"

"How thoughtless of me. Of course, Jacques, do that. Why didn't you stay in Washington?"

"I wanted to help."

"Fine. Fly back with Major Flaherty."

"I'll come to Kansas City on a commercial flight and rent a car for the trip to Fort Leavenworth," Jacques said.

"No, call me with an ETA and I'll have you picked up at the Kansas City airport."

They joined Gregory and walked out to the tarmac, then watched the loading of the blindfolded and handcuffed prisoners onto the Lockheed C-121s. Six Marines and five U.S. Attorneys entered each plane. Bart entered one of the planes and Jacques boarded the other. They observed the shackling of the detainees. Everything was in order. Gregory, Bart and Jacques waved at the pilots as the transports roared down the runway, en route to Fort Leavenworth. "How about lunch, Barton?" Gregory said.

"That's fine, Alton. We haven't had breakfast."

They went directly to the Officers Mess. The General's table, against a window facing the airfield, gave them a view of the two planes flying skyward. "How about a few Bloody Marys and Eggs Benedict, gentlemen? They are very good here."

Both men approved. Sedgwick and Captain Arnold dined at the other side of the room. Bart and Jacques noted the rapport between the two and exchanged intellectual nods. Sergeant Clements approached Gregory and saluted.

"What is it, Todd?"

"Sir, an F-27 is making its approach."

"Thank you, Sergeant."

The three, having finished their repast, made their way to the airstrip. A turbo jet was parked at the terminal. Four MPs saluted the generals as they approached. A box containing shackles was at their feet.

Major Flaherty brought his plane to a parallel position alongside the turbojet. A mobile staircase was quickly brought to the exit of the F-27. Bart waved at Flaherty, who saluted back. Two MPs ran up the steps. A Marine opened the door. The two wounded men were quickly helped down the stairs and transferred to the turbojet. Branlow and the rest were hustled on board. All were blindfolded, shackled and handcuffed. Four Marines left the turbojet. The MPs replaced them. Bart and Jacques entered the F-27. Jacques advised Flaherty that he was flying back to Washington with him.

Bart and Jacques hugged each other, then Bart saluted the crew. He joined Sedgwick and Captain Arnold, and they profusely thanked Gregory for his courtesies. They boarded the turbojet and were off to Fort Leavenworth.

☆ ☆ ☆ ☆

Monday, May 12, 1952 - later that day - Fort Leavenworth, Kansas

Phalanxes of military police and armed soldiers awaited the incoming planes at Sherman Army Airfield. Jeeps and buses were lined up to drive the prisoners to the disciplinary barracks. General Warren Fielding was surrounded by his staff.

The first plane to arrive was the turbojet from Guantanamo carrying Hitler and gang. Maybrook and Berger were the first to deplane. They approached Fielding and flashed their CIA ID's. Fielding, a tall, battle-hardened figure, greeted them warmly. "Call the shots, gentlemen, and we'll dump your garbage accordingly."

"The number one man for complete isolation will be brought down first. In fact, here he comes."

Two Marines hustled Hitler down the steps. His shackles had been removed. Fielding snapped his fingers, and two MPs stepped forward. "Take this bag of shit to the dungeon, cell 15, and shackle him," he ordered.

The others were treated accordingly. The second turbo arrived. Sophia and Tony deplaned. They displayed their CIA credentials, and Fielding told them to sort out their prisoners.

"Sir, this first one coming down now is to be treated a little better than the others. He's a very important cooperating high Nazi. Do you have a room and bath for him? Also, we have two very special prisoners to be housed separately in special quarters with room and bath," Tony requested.

"What the hell do you think this is? We're not a hotel or a country club!" Fielding barked.

"Sir, General Milburn will explain and identify these prisoners. He should be arriving momentarily," Sophia said.

"Madame, there is nothing I hate more than a Nazi. I had enough of them during the war. By the way, is that the Colonel Barton Milburn who was an intelligence officer on Ike's staff?"

"Yes, sir, the very same," she smiled.

"Well, I'll be an SOB. He rode with us when the Third Army blasted into Bastogne," the general said. "He and Patton were buddy-buddy. We were friends. He's quite a guy, my kind of guy."

Bart's turbo taxied in ahead of the other two transports. Bart bounded down the steps and hastened to Fielding and his staff. The two generals, both in full uniform, looked at each other. Fielding held out his arms and the two men clinched.

"This is a helluva long time since Reims, when those Nazi bastards signed their surrender, Barton," Fielding said.

"Warren, you haven't changed a bit."

"Neither have you, except for those two stars."

"Once two colonels, now two generals."

"I've only got one star," Fielding joked.

"The other should be along soon."

Sophia stood there, while the MPs were waiting for orders.

"Oh, Barton, this lovely lady is asking for a room and bath for that creep prisoner over there, and her partner here is requesting special housing for two other prisoners. I told them this is not a hotel," Fielding said.

"Warren, come over here for a minute," Bart whispered in his ear.

"This must be a joke. Martin Bormann? Come on. Who are you kidding? Bradley said they were big-shot Nazis, but not *that* big."

"Warren, are you ready for this? That first one you got for solitary is none other than *Der Führer*. Of the other two prisoners, one is the former British ambassador to Germany. He's been working for Hitler. The other one is Konrad Fliegel, alias Keith Reynolds, who was the treasurer of Winston General, owned by Nordheim, alias Hitler."

"If that's true, why the hell didn't you kill these fiends? Why are we babying them?"

"Come on, Warren," Bart asserted. "You were told to prepare this place for a series of important trials."

"Yeah, but I had no idea of the magnitude of your catch. Bradley was so matter-of-fact when he called me, but, hey, it's your show, Bart, and I'm with you all the way."

"One caution, Warren. The identities of these men are classified top secret. Your guards have to be sworn to utmost secrecy. One leak and there will be a feeding frenzy. If there is a leak, Truman has sworn to track down the source with every available means. I'll spell the whole thing out to you later. Let's get these prisoners parked. Give Bormann a room and bath. Sir Clive Fenwick and Reynolds also get private rooms. Two guards to watch them."

"You got it, friend." Fielding returned to Sophia. "Madame, my apologies. I am aware of the situation."

She smiled warmly, looking at him. He turned, then bellowed orders. The prisoners were quickly consigned to their cells. Bormann and the others got their rooms and baths.

The two other C-121 Lockheed transports arrived in tandem. They were unloaded first, with the U.S. Attorneys. The prisoners were quickly led to their cells.

Bart was shown to his quarters, a Victorian house adjacent to the commanding general's quarters near South Colt Avenue. Fielding and Bart met for dinner at the Truesdell Hall dining facility. They dined in a quiet secure area. Over a three-hour period, Bart outlined the events over the last four months. He held Fielding spellbound with his recital.

"Barton, this is a most incredible series of events. Does the President fully appreciate what you've accomplished?"

"I guess these two stars attest to that."

"What's going to happen to your legal career?" Fielding asked.

"That's anybody's guess."

"I wish I had been involved with you in this assignment."

"Well, you're part of it now," Bart said.

"If Ike's elected, and I think he will be, will he allow you to hold wide-open public trials here?"

"I hope so."

"I do, too, even though this base will become a madhouse."

☆ ☆ ☆ ☆

Tuesday, May 13, 1952 - 10 a.m. - Department of Justice, Washington

Attorney General McGranery led Jacques and his sister Joyce into a small conference room. He introduced them to Deputy Attorney General Daniel Greenberg and his assistant, Martin Richards.

"Joyce, relax and tell these gentlemen the full story of your life to date. This is routine for political refugees. We are your friends and are happy to have you reside in this country. When you are through, come into my office. Will you be comfortable if I borrow Jacques for a little while?" McGranery asked.

"Of course," she replied, smiling.

Greenberg and Richards offered her coffee. They listened intently to her saga. A series of questions followed. Richards made copious notes. After two hours, the session concluded, and both men were deeply touched by her experiences during the war and later behind the Iron Curtain. They escorted her back to McGranery's office. "Here is your lovely sister, Mr. Laurent. She is quite a woman," Greenberg declared with great admiration.

"Jim, thanks for your courtesy," Jacques said.

"My pleasure. Good luck to both of you."

Jacques and Joyce drove to National Airport, parked the car and hurried to the Eastern Airlines counter. He purchased two round-trip tickets to New York. He stopped at a pay phone and called Douglas Milburn at the New York Daily News, advising them of their ETA at La Guardia Airport. Ten minutes later they were en route to the big city.

Upon arrival, Douglas hugged Joyce and planted a big kiss on her cheek. He then hugged Jacques. They drove to the Wall Street headquarters of the National City Bank. Carlton Reilly, executive vice president of the giant bank, greeted them. He shook hands with Douglas.

"You've brought us some fine clients, Douglas. I suppose you expect a commission."

"That'll be the day," he smirked.

He escorted them to his office, where they signed the required forms.

"Now, you don't want to keep all this money in checking accounts. What do you propose to do with these funds? How can I help you?"

Jacques was well prepared for the question.

"The bulk of the money, for the present, should be placed in short term U.S. T-bills," he declared. "And I'll roll them over as I follow the yield."

"Very wise decision. We can handle that for you."

"I have a checking account at the Columbia National Bank in Washington, and Joyce will open an account at that bank. We would like to transfer $250,000 to each of our accounts at that bank."

"Easily done, Mr. Laurent. Please sign these transfer slips, and I recommend that you keep no more than $100,000 in an FDIC bank."

"What is FDIC?" Joyce asked.

"Federal Deposit Insurance Corporation. It's a government agency which protects depositors up to $100,000 if the bank fails."

"Well, we'll open an account at a second FDIC bank," Jacques said.

They thanked Reilly for his efforts. Douglas invited Joyce and Jacques to join him for a late lunch at the Colony restaurant.

"Constance will meet us there. She's anxious to meet Joyce," he said.

"My pleasure," Joyce agreed.

En route uptown on East River Drive, Joyce was getting a first-hand look at the skyline. During the drive, Douglas raised the question of Joyce's plans.

"Two things I'd like to do. First, I'd like to teach French at a university.

Second, I'd like to write a book about my experiences in the concentration camps and the evils the Nazis committed, also the evils committed by Stalin's Russia and communist East Germany. The atrocities I saw defy the devil's imagination."

"I think you'll have no problem landing a professorship. Your book could be a blockbuster. I'd love to collaborate with you."

"I'd be happy to work with you, Douglas," she responded, smiling.

"Both of you will have to clear the timing of a book with Barton," Jacques observed.

"Of course," Douglas assented.

At the posh Colony, Constance Luce had arranged a surprise for Douglas, Joyce and Jacques. She had invited Dr. and Mrs. Milburn and Beatrice Milburn to join them for lunch. The Milburns hugged and kissed Joyce and Jacques. Constance followed suit.

"What a beautiful new member of our family," Jeannette proclaimed. She followed with a French accolade, "*Vous êtes très jolie.*"

"*Merci beaucoup*, Madame Jeannette," Joyce replied, blushing.

"I'll have to brush up on my French, Joyce," Bart's sister "Bunny" asserted.

"Beatrice, come to Washington and we'll spend the days speaking French."

"Call me Bunny, everyone does."

"*Oui*, Bunny."

Constance asked Joyce to relate her escape from East Germany. Joyce captivated her new family with the saga. There were tears and laughter throughout her account.

"That will be a great scene in your book that Doug mentioned. I think your whole story would make a great movie," Constance said.

The lunch was capped by Dr. Milburn's comment, "Joyce, you now have a full family. Douglas and Barton are your brothers. Bunny is your sister. We can't replace your parents, but treat Jeannette and me as your aunt and uncle."

"Thank you all so much," Joyce said.

"Don't forget me. Come July I'll be your sister," Constance declared.

Douglas drove the two to La Guardia Airport, and Jacques and Joyce returned to Washington. Elizabeth met them and drove Joyce to the house. Jacques took a flight to Kansas City.

Wednesday, May 14, 1952 - Fort Leavenworth

Bart met Jacques' flight and drove the twenty miles from the Kansas City airport to Sherman Army Airfield. He filled him in on the arrangements being made for the evidentiary hearings.

"Jacques, we've got ninety-four prisoners to bring before the court. The law officers and presiding Judge Advocate, General Ross, will be here in five days, on Monday, May 19. Our work is cut out for us to get our evidence and charges prepared against each prisoner."

"Bart, thanks for picking me up at the airport, but you should have remained here with the legal eagles."

"They're in session now. Let's join them, and I'll get you settled later in a house assigned to us."

They entered the conference room in Fuller Hall. The men rose. Bart ordered them to sit and continue their discussion.

"General, we were at the point of classifying the death-camp commandants," Gideon Cartman advised.

"What do we have now?"

"There are six commandants we have identified."

"Let's hear it."

"There's Hugo Schultz of Ohrdruf, and I think you have more than a nodding acquaintance with that specimen," Cartman began. "The rest are Colonel Wolfgang Schreiber of Buchenwald, Major Franz Sauckel of Mauthausen, Lieutenant General Hans Krause of Auschwitz, Colonel Joachim Schmidt of Gross-Rosen, and Colonel Johann Weist of Chelmno. There's one guy here we haven't broken. A couple of informers say he was the commandant at Drancy camp. He has a strange name for a German, Colonel René Soltere, and..."

Jacques cut him off. "Let me talk to that son of a bitch. Drancy is a suburb of Paris. That's where my sister was sent at first, after the Germans took Paris. I'll bet he's a Vichy Nazi."

Bart noticed Jacques' ire. "In due time, Jacques. Let's finish here first."

The U.S. Attorneys stared at Jacques and experienced an emotional surge, in contrast with their systematical appraisal of evidence. Their empathy was apparent, and it brought them closer to the job at hand.

"Among the others are some vicious animals who participated in the actual methodical slaughter of the Holocaust victims. There is more than a conspiracy of silence among them. Their lips are zipped in concert. A hard bunch," Cartman declared. "The commandants have been placed in separate cells away from the others."

"Fellows, I realize that you lawyers will not resort to our methods of unzipping lips. Jacques and I are considered experts in that art. Yes, I am a fellow attorney, but in our previous careers during the great conflagration we improved our skills beyond the Nazis' expertise," Bart said vehemently.

"General Milburn, were this a matter before a civilian tribunal, some of us would take umbrage from a legal standpoint at that statement. On the other hand, in this instance the gravamen of these monstrous crimes requires extraordinary measures," Cartman said.

"That's very assuring, Gideon," Bart replied snidely.

"Having said what I did, Bart, most of us were there, dropping our juridical robes and wigs. We would love to join you in kicking the shit out of these depraved bastards," Cartman shot back.

The laughter was spontaneous.

"Gid, you had me there for a minute," Bart said, laughing. "Keep at it, men. Brigadier General Ross, the Presiding Commissioner, and the team of Advocates General, comprising defense and prosecutors, arrive here tomorrow. Be prepared for them. The evidentiary hearings are set for this Monday. Good luck."

Master Sergeant Wilbur Jackson, who had been assigned as an aide to General Milburn, was standing by his Jeep when Bart and Jacques emerged from CAG headquarters. He saluted the men.

"Where to, sir?"

"Sergeant, to the Disciplinary Barracks," Bart directed.

He wheeled to Scott Avenue past the memorial chapel and the vast complex, then onto Riverside Avenue to the huge detention facility.

"Sarge, we'll be here for at least an hour. Find yourself a cup of coffee or whatever," Bart ordered.

"Thank you, sir."

At the office of the Military Police, Bart was cordially received by Major Whitney Holt.

"We would like to have prisoner René Soltere brought to an interrogation room. We'd prefer one that is not readily discernible by passersby."

Holt smiled knowingly. "I have just the place for you, sir. It's called our TGR, or *tough guy room.*"

They were escorted to the end of a long corridor into a stark, windowless room, with a solid metal door and stone walls, containing a table and three chairs. Facing the table was a single chair under an overhead light. A green-shaded gooseneck lamp stood on the table.

"Perfect," Bart said.

"Will you need an MP to stand by? He's on the way with the prisoner," the major said.

"We can handle him without the MP."

The major appraised the two tall, muscular figures and smiled. "I'm sure of that, sir."

A knock at the door sounding like a thud caused the major to turn and pull it open. A tall, heavy MP shoved a stocky, manacled, head-shorn prisoner into the room and propelled him to the chair facing the table, then saluted the trio.

"Am I to stay, sir?" the MP asked.

"No, Sergeant, let's take a walk. The general will buzz you when needed."

They left, and Jacques locked the steel door.

"René, do you speak English, German or French?" Bart snapped.

The prisoner remained silent.

Jacques stood over him, held his face up to the light and in French shouted in his ear, *"Piger!"*

Rene had a knee-jerk reaction.

"Sprechen sie deutsch?" Bart yelled.

Silence.

A resounding backhanded slap across Soltere's right cheek brought a groan and the expletive *"Arschloch."*

"In English," Bart advised, and he warned the recalcitrant Waffen SS member to answer questions, or the mechanics routine would decide his fate. Jacques repeated the admonition in French. Bart followed with the German version.

They peppered him with the questions, "*Parlez-vous français?*" "*Sprechen sie deutsch?*" "Do you speak English?"

He replied in obscenities, "*Merde, scheisse, bullshit.*"

Jacques applied his thumb to a nerve behind the man's ear. Soltere screamed in pain. "Now, speak!" Jacques demanded.

"You are animals!" Soltere cried in English. "What do you want?"

"Answer our questions and you'll be treated better."

"I don't know anything," he replied.

"Rene Soltere, you're in a lot of trouble. You are facing treatment by our mechanics squad, worse than any Nazi torture, a firing squad or a hanging. If you cooperate, life will be a lot easier for you. Make up your mind. Answer our questions or else."

"If I answer, the SS will kill me. If I don't, you'll kill me."

"We'll protect you and segregate you from them," Bart assured him.

Soltere was silent. He contemplated the issue. Bart nudged Jacques to refrain from any further questions. They lit cigarettes. Soltere waved his manacled hands, mutely requesting a smoke. Jacques placed one in his mouth and lit it. Soltere took a deep draft of the cigarette and exhaled spirals of smoke. After a few more puffs, he spoke. "How do I know that you will protect me?"

"I am a lawyer and a general. I give you my word."

"I don't trust lawyers, but I'll trust you as a general, if you give me your word of honor."

Bart laughed. "Okay, if you will agree to testify at the trial, I'll give you my word of honor."

"Testify to what?"

"The truth of your experiences."

"All right, what do you want to know?"

Bart asked Jacques to remove the manacles, and then Soltere was handed a hot cup of coffee.

"Who is the officer who has ordered your Waffen SS prisoners to remain silent?"

"General, there is a state of fear imposed by Colonel Erich Müller. He is the nephew of Heinrich Müller, the SS *Gruppenführer* and general of the Gestapo. He was the senior officer, under his uncle, who disappeared after your men captured us on Nordheim's ranch in Argentina."

"He didn't disappear. We have him," Jacques snarled.

"Can't be," Soltere said. "The colonel told us that General Müller was going to attack this place and get us released."

Bart and Jacques laughed derisively.

"*Etre dans la merde,*" Jacques chortled.

"How did you become commandant at the Drancy concentration camp?" Bart coldly demanded.

"Well, first I have to tell you what led to that," he said.

"Okay, keep going."

"I was promoted to major when Petain formed the Vichy government. I became an aide in his office, mostly because I spoke fluent German. When Hitler came to Paris on June 23, I was assigned to his sightseeing staff. That's when he spoke to me. I told him my mother was German. He told Himmler to use me in rounding up the Jews. I went to Vichy to work as an aide in the office of Petain…"

Bart interrupted angrily, "I asked you how did you, at such a young age, become commandant of Drancy?"

"General Müller came to Petain's office one day and asked Petain to send me to Paris to act as liaison between the Gestapo and the French police. He told me Hitler liked me. After that, I was working with the Gestapo, arresting Jews. I didn't like it, but I was afraid to say so. In 1942 I was sent with a train carrying Jews from Drancy to Auschwitz, where I was put into the Gestapo in a German uniform. They made me swear allegiance to the Third Reich. After six months at Auschwitz, I was sent back to Drancy."

"Commandant? Commandant? *Merde!*" Jacques shouted.

"In late 1943, the Drancy commandant, August Schwemer, was shipped to the Russian front. I was his assistant. That's when they made me commandant, by order of Heinrich Müller. Drancy was a small camp at the beginning. When I took over, it was the transit camp to deport French Jews to Auschwitz."

"Then what happened?" Bart asked.

"When the Americans were almost at Paris, we were flown to Berlin. Because I spoke French, English, German and Italian, I was transferred to the Waffen SS, the *Schutzstaffel.*"

"Explain why they would take a Frenchman into the SS," Jacques said.

"Because I was an Aryan. My hair is blond and my eyes are blue. I could fight; you can see my muscles."

"That's a crock of crap, you pig. You sent my family to Auschwitz! I ought to kill you right now. You and I are going to have a private session, you murdering bastard!" Jacques bellowed.

He leaped out of his chair, eyes ablaze, jaw jutted, and, out of control, tried to choke Soltere. Bart wrestled him away. Soltere, in an effort to avoid the attack, fell back on his chair, which tumbled and sent him sprawling. Jacques managed a vicious kick in the man's ribs.

"Jacques, dammit, control yourself!" Bart angrily demanded. "What the hell is wrong with you? I promised to protect him. Now, look what you've done. Pull yourself together. He'll be a helluva witness and informant. Cool it now, brother."

There were tears in Jacques' eyes. He leaned over the table and cradled his head in his arms. Bart lifted Soltere off the floor, and reset his chair. Jacques whispered in his ear, "I'm sorry. It won't happen again."

Soltere was shaking, terrified. His lips were chattering and uttering sibilant sounds. Bart rubbed Jacques' back and neck, conveying his empathy.

He bent down and whispered, "Go outside, Jacques, and leave me alone with this creep. I'll be out shortly."

He led him to the door and locked it behind him. After twenty minutes of placating Soltere, he elicited a description of the other prisoners. The final series of questions dealt with the Revenge Plan. Soltere revealed that they were all trained at the La Plata Ranch in a variety of terrorist actions. Bart shut down his recorder and patted the prisoner's head.

"I'll keep my word. You will be separated from the rest of your gang. I want you to try to make a list of as many names as you can and what their assignments are. If you do good, I'll make life much easier for you."

He buzzed for the MP. "This prisoner is to be put in a separate cell, Sergeant. I'll clear it with Major Whitney on my way out. Treat him well."

"Yes, sir."

Jacques was in the jeep talking with Sergeant Jackson. Bart hopped in and put his arm around Jacques' shoulders.

"I'm sorry, Bart. He brought back some bad memories."

The next two days, Thursday and Friday, were devoted to intensive sessions with the U.S. Attorneys to catalogue witnesses and defendants. Bart made it manifestly clear that all prisoners were defendants, despite the fact that some were willing to testify against a codefendant.

CHAPTER THIRTY-THREE

Thursday, May 15, 1952 - 0900 hours - Andrews Air Force Base, Maryland

Brigadier General Wilford Ross, Judge Advocate General, and sixteen uniformed Judge Advocates General gathered at the café at the Andrews terminal prior to their flight to Fort Leavenworth. Milburn and CIA agent Jacques Laurent joined them. Ross introduced to Bart ten of the men who would act as defense lawyers and three as assistant prosecutors. The remaining three would act as judges, assisting the presiding judge in processing the trials of the ninety-four defendants.

"Wilford, should we need additional prosecutors, if the process drags? I have a thought, which I'd like to run by you," Bart said.

"Go right ahead, General."

"Among our ten U.S. Attorneys, five of them are in the Army Reserves. Any or all of them could be pressed into temporary active service as prosecutors if the trials get bogged down or too cumbersome for us. What do you think?"

Ross laughed. "With due respect, sir, I'd describe you as a wily opponent to your adversaries."

Bart and Jacques joined in the laughter.

"Not a bad idea, if necessary," Ross continued. "However, let us decide that question if the occasion requires such relief. I assume that your role in representing the President and your relationship with General Bradley would facilitate their activation on short notice.

"So far they've granted every request."

"Time will tell. Shall we board our flight?"

The nineteen men walked through the terminal. Other than Jacques and

Bart, the presiding judge and the other men carried two bags, one of which held law books. At the new turbojet Air Force transport plane, the pilot saluted the generals and their entourage. Thirty Marines assigned to the legal team were on board.

The flight was smooth and uneventful. The captain radioed the tower at Sherman Army Airfield, advising the controller of his cargo and requesting an Army shuttle bus for the legal team. On clearance, he made a smooth landing.

Two shuttle buses drove the forty-nine men to Headquarters Command Personnel and Administration Center at the corner of McPherson and McClellan avenues. The group signed in and was processed. The Marines were assigned to a section of the Disciplinary Barracks, which had been cleared for their arrival. Judge Ross was lodged in a townhouse. Bart and Jacques were sharing the Victorian dwelling. All were given appropriate IDs for access to the commissary, a huge supermarket, and the Post Exchange, serving as a post office and department store. Conference rooms and courtrooms were set up at the Disciplinary Barracks.

The next few days were devoted to assigning defense counsels to the prisoners. The U.S. Attorneys briefed the prosecutors. Bart and Ross discussed procedures and what evidence should be shared with the defense.

Jacques spent his time interrogating Walter Schellenberg, alias Bancroft; Louise Bancroft, alias Maloney; Harry Branlow, Pablo Munoz, Horst Leman and Johann Weist. The attempted assassination at the Havana villa perplexed him, so he told Bart that he wanted to unravel the source of the contract on the lives of Christina and Bart himself.

"Go to it. I've little time to prepare for the hearings."

Hour by hour, day by day, he tried to untangle the skeins of the mystery of the perpetrators who had sought to kill Bart. *What did they know about Bart? Did they know about Nordheim's disappearance?* Schellenberg and Maloney, alias Bancroft, maintained their fractiousness. After a physical exercise with Jacques, Munoz admitted he was a paid hit man recruited by Branlow. Munoz sustained three fractured ribs; the barracks infirmary taped his torso and sewed a cut over his right eye. Leman and Weist each required treatment for assorted bruises and cuts. Branlow took four hours of Jacques' punitive tactics before he succumbed. "No more, no more, I'll tell you! When I met with the Bancrofts, Paul Mayfield, Darren Mayfield's brother, was there. He was the one who gave me the $200,000 to come to Havana with them. Mayfield came to Havana with us. They told me the story about Mrs. Lyons being a Nazi spy and that Colonel Milburn was a Nazi agent."

"I've heard that bullshit. Who hired Munoz?"

"I recommended him. Mayfield hired him. He spoke to me alone before we got to Havana."

"Was he staying at the Nacional?"

"Yes."

"Where?"

"Right next door to me," Branlow answered.

"You rotten prick, why didn't you tell us?" Jacques raged.

"He would have killed me!"

"Why was he after Milburn?"

"He had a note from his brother Darren, who was in Leavenworth prison. The note told him that he should contact a Chicago lawyer, Alden Gaines, to get him out of prison. He also wrote that Colonel Milburn kidnapped Nordheim."

"Were they going to kill Milburn?"

"No. When I told them Milburn had rented Gullen's villa, he flipped. He wanted to capture Milburn and find out where he had stashed Nordheim."

"What was Munoz, the hit man, going to do?"

"He was to hit Mrs. Lyons. I don't know why."

"What about the Bancrofts and the two other Nazis, Leman and Weist?"

"They were to capture Milburn. That's why they trailed him from the airport."

"Was Escobar part of all this?"

"No, he wanted his piece of the million-dollar bounty. A greedy, stupid *schmuck*."

"Where is Mayfield now?"

"I don't know where we are now, but I'll bet he followed us here," Branlow speculated.

"What else do you know about Nordheim, Schellenberg and Maloney?"

"What I originally told you. They said they were working for the Israelis. They also told me that Nordheim, the Jew, financed the search for Mrs. Lyons, a Nazi spy."

"So that cockeyed story you told us in Havana left out a major ingredient. Paul Mayfield."

"I was afraid. He's a killer."

"Branlow, if you have left anything out of your story, tell it now or you'll not leave this place alive."

Jacques rushed back to the house on the base. He quickly briefed Bart with the information derived from Branlow.

"Holy Toledo, Jacques. We need a photograph of Paul Mayfield and we have to find out how that Alden Gaines or Anthony Cardona sent that letter to Paul Mayfield."

Bart placed a call to Katherine Wharton at her home in Alexandria, Virginia.

"Katherine, this is your lover, Lucifer."

"General Milburn, I wish that was true. How can I help you?"

"This is urgent, Katherine. I need a photograph and a file on a Paul Mayfield, the brother of Darren Mayfield."

"I'll get it first thing in the morning. You're at Fort Leavenworth, I know. I'll telephoto what I find to General Fielding's office."

"Katherine, if necessary, call Attorney General McGranery. He can tap into FBI files. Tell him it's for me."

"Will do."

Bart looked at his list of phone numbers on the base for Maybrook,

Berger, Sophia, Tony, and Captain Arnold, then dialed them, summoning all to his quarters.

After a rundown of Jacques' session with Branlow, he said, "The possibility that Paul Mayfield is in the vicinity of this fort can not be overlooked. When the pictures arrive, I want you to fan out and check all the local hotels. We've got to find him."

☆ ☆ ☆ ☆

Friday, May 16, 1952 - Washington

Attorney General McGranery answered his private phone.

"Jim, this is J. Edgar. Do you have a moment for me? I have a file you requested."

"Come ahead." McGranery mused, *That son of a bitch. I asked for that damn file from a file clerk and he winds up with it. Damn, damn. Truman called him a snake. What's he up to now?*

The intercom box announced the arrival of J. Edgar Hoover, director of the FBI. The stocky director entered with a supercilious smile. "Enjoying your new job, Judge?"

"Not as much as you enjoy yours."

"*Touché.*"

"What's on your mind?" McGranery asked.

"First, here's the file on Paul Mayfield. Interesting. He's the brother of Darren Mayfield, a former agent of ours."

"Why would you go out of your way to personally deliver this file? I routinely requested it from a file clerk."

"Well, that leads me to another, more interesting question."

"And that would be?"

"We have had a request to investigate the disappearance of Frederick Avram Nordheim. It's been alleged that this Jew, who is the richest man in the world, has been kidnapped."

"Here in the United States?"

"No, that's why it's not in our jurisdiction. We've had a query from Interpol. We've also had strange anonymous tips that the CIA has illegally arrested some Nazi war criminals. Do you know anything about this?"

"Mr. Hoover, you are poking your sniffing nose into a cesspool of danger. Have you tipped your sleazehound buddy, Walter Winchell, with these unfounded tidbits?" McGranery said.

"Hey, Jim, why the animus?"

"Hold it, J. Edgar. You can throw your weight around here in the beltway, but not in this office."

McGranery picked up his direct line to the White House. Hoover, confused and discomfited, stared malevolently at the Attorney General.

"Mr. President, I urgently request a meeting with the director of the FBI and me."

"Is he with you?"

"Yes."

"Come right over."

"Why, what is this all about?" Hoover said.

"Never mind, let's go."

In the Attorney General's chauffeured car, McGranery told Hoover not to discuss the matter on the trip to 1600. John Steelman quickly ushered the two men into the Oval Office.

Truman's innate loathing of the FBI director manifested itself in his lack of cordiality, but he did say, "Be seated, gentlemen."

McGranery repeated Hoover's remarks. Truman's mien depicted his anger. "Listen to me, Hoover, touch this matter just slightly and I personally, *Harry S. Truman, President of the United States*, will destroy you. I'll charge you with every crime I can conjure."

Hoover was shocked by the President's outburst. "What the hell is going on here?" he shot back. No one had ever challenged him with such acidity.

"Don't give me that *What the hell* bullshit. I am warning you to zip your lip. If you or your pal, Clyde Tolson, leak anything about Nordheim, Mayfield, or Nazi war criminals, I'll bring you before a closed session of the Senate Judiciary Committee. I'll ask for your dismissal as director of the FBI. You're treading on a classified top-secret matter. If you leak it to Winchell or any other member of the media, I'll crucify you. And if you're looking at me as a lame-duck President, be advised that whoever is elected will follow through on my threats."

"Threats?"

"Yes, dammit, *threats*. Now, get the hell out of my office!" Truman roared.

"Mr. President, I assure..."

"*Out! Out!*" Truman cut him off.

En route back to the Justice Department, Hoover mumbled epithets. "That fucking haberdasher..."

"Shut up, Hoover!" McGranery shot back, pointing at the driver.

Back at his office, McGranery quickly thumbed through the file on Paul Mayfield. He studied his photograph in a police uniform. The file indicated that Mayfield had been a lieutenant in the Palm Beach, Florida, Police Department and resigned under fire on a bribery allegation. His present occupation was his operation of Allied Detective Services, with offices on La Salle Street in Chicago. In FBI jargon, it was alleged that he had Mafia clients, and Swiss bank and Nazi connections. The report read, "Resides in Forest Park, Illinois, in a two-story Tudor home with Greta Schlosser, a German national. She has a Swedish passport, issued in Malmo, Sweden. Schlosser is active in the International Society of Aryans in Chicago. Also had a pad on East 63rd Street in New York City."

McGranery had the file copied and rushed to Katherine Wharton at the CIA. She immediately sent the material by telephoto to the office of General Warren Fielding for the attention of Bart Milburn. She also asked General

Smith to have a CIA agent check out Paul Mayfield's office in Chicago, home in Forest Park, and New York apartment.

Bart had copies made of the photograph and handed one to each of his CIA operatives. Phillip Berger drove to the Kansas City airport to check passenger lists and car rentals to Mayfield. Maybrook, Sophia, Tony and Sedgwick checked hotels in the city of Leavenworth. On a hunch, Milburn called Warden Clyde Wilson at the Leavenworth Federal Prison.

"General, what can I do for you?" Wilson asked.

"Sir, I am checking on a Paul Mayfield. Has he been looking for a Darren Mayfield?"

"Interesting that you called. He was here yesterday. We do not have a Darren Mayfield in our prison population."

"I know that, Warden. I've been working with Attorney General McGranery, sir, and I am aware of your cooperation."

"Just to make sure as to who you are, I'd like to call you back."

"Call me at General Fielding's office at Fort Leavenworth. Here's the number."

The call was quickly returned. "General Milburn, I was just being cautious."

"I understand."

"Well, here is the license number of a Hertz rental car he is using. He left his phone number- it's at the Commander's Inn, across from the Fort Leavenworth gate, room 502."

"Much obliged, Warden. You've been very helpful."

No sooner had he hung up than the phone rang, and Sophia breathlessly reported that their target was at the inn opposite the gate of the base.

"He just pulled in, driving a Ford."

"Yes, I know he's staying there. Don't leave, but stay out of his sight. Where are you now?"

"I'm in a phone booth near the gate."

"I'll have two MPs join you, but don't go after him."

Bart called McGranery. "What's my legal option, Jim? Do I use MPs to grab him?"

"Well, you've got him on a conspiracy to capture you, to kill Christina Lyons, aiding and abetting Nazi war criminals, and obstructing justice. He's in your purview of authority. Grab him now. The CIA is checking on his mistress, Greta Schlosser. Miss Wharton advised me of that."

"Good deal. *Ciao.*"

Berger called.

"Come back, we've located him."

Jacques, Bart and two hefty MPs got into a Jeep. All carried arms. They raced to the Metropolitan Avenue gate. Bart spotted Sophia at the phone booth.

"He's still in there," she said. "That light blue Ford over there is his. I let the air out of his left front tire."

"Good. Now, everyone, let's wait a while for him to come out. Sergeant, stand at the gate, as though you're on duty. Keep your eye on me."

Forty-five minutes later a tall, mustached, well-dressed six-footer approached his Ford. He noticed the flat tire. As he went to his trunk, Bart, Jacques and the MPs raced toward him. He reached for his gun when Jacques turned the corner and dived at him, throwing him face down. Bart disarmed him. The MPs pulled his arms behind his back and handcuffed him. He was rudely raised to his feet. Drops of blood flowed down his face from a cut on his forehead. His chin was sprinkled with pavement dirt. "Who are you clowns?" he rasped.

"Paul Mayfield, you're under arrest for aiding and abetting Nazi war criminals, attempted murder and kidnapping, obstruction of justice, and possibly treason."

"You're out of your fucking skull, *soldier boy*! I'm a private eye searching for a kidnapped man. You're interfering with my investigation. I want my lawyer."

"Mr. Alden Gaines is not available. Mr. Nordheim sends his regards. They'll see you in court," Bart snickered, then turned to Jacques. "Jacques, go with the boys while they process this scumbag into a cozy cell. I'll send the paperwork to the provost marshal."

Bart joined the prosecution team in the conference room at the Disciplinary Barracks. Books were stacked on recently constructed shelves. Among the treatises were volumes of G.M. Gilbert's 1947 Nuremberg Diary. Gilbert had been the prison psychologist at the trials. A host of other books lined the shelves. A mass of government documents copied from the National Archive dealing with Nazi atrocities, the lurid account of the Holocaust, and individual records and biographies of thousands of Nazi war criminals. The history of the Nazi orgy of terror during the reign of the Third Reich from 1933 to 1945 in loose-leaf books were being studied by the assembled group. The U.S. Attorneys were briefing the military defense lawyers when Bart entered.

"No saluting, gentlemen. Let's work as lawyers and do away with the military amenities," Bart declared.

"General, it has occurred to us that we should have as many survivors as possible, as witnesses," Judge Advocate Captain Liam Kelly suggested.

"I don't think that would be necessary at these evidentiary hearings. However, they would be vital for the official trials. We got these bastards testifying against each other. Let me talk to Presiding Judge Ross. I value his opinion."

"Sir, these materials are so far beyond the pale of a civilized mind to contemplate," Gideon Cartman agonized. "The German atrocities defy the imagination. The archival material speaks for itself. The accounts of bestiality haven't been fully conveyed to the world, let alone the American public."

"Men, I've been there. General Eisenhower assigned me to visit these death camps. I wrote a full report, which has been classified top secret. I am attempting to have that report declassified for the major trials. You will be viewing shocking footage of these atrocities in the next few days. These pictures will sear unforgettable images in your hearts and minds of the savage orgy of torture and death inflicted upon millions of innocent Jews, Christians, the old, young and feeble victims," Bart said coldly.

In another conference, defense lawyers were dividing lists of prisoners into specific categories. The major war criminals, consisting of Hitler, Bormann, Müller, Schwerin, Krueger, Heydrich, Langsdorff, von Leute, Weber, Horstmann, Froelich, Maloney, Schellenberg, Leman and Weist, were to be arraigned, as well as the eight camp commandants. The bulk of the Waffen SS prisoners were divided into groups. The problem facing the defense was the legal representation for the cooperating prisoners who would testify. The representation of Branlow, the Mayfield brothers and Pablo Munoz remained moot for the moment. The Waffen SS men were to be tried in two separate courts.

☆ ☆ ☆ ☆

Sunday, May 18, 1952 - 1930 hours - Andrews Air Force Base
Tight security was in force at the terminal, and a press blackout had been imposed. MPs surrounded Hangar 18, where a brand-new Air Force turbojet was preparing for flight. Two black limousines were cleared onto the tarmac as they raced to and entered the hangar. A squad of twelve Marines stood at attention and saluted the distinguished passengers.

Secretary of Defense Lovett, Attorney General McGranery, Chairman of the Joint Chiefs of Staff General Omar Bradley, CIA Director General Walter Smith and his deputy, Allen Dulles, quickly boarded the plane. The Marine squad followed. The doors of the hangar were opened and the turbojet taxied in the twilight onto Runway 2. The tower cleared the big plane for takeoff. It roared its way skyward toward a starlit sky and a full moon, then turned west at twenty thousand feet en route to Kansas. Later, they circled over the Missouri River on the border between Kansas and Missouri, then the tower at Sherman Army Airfield cleared the plane for landing at 2200 hours Central Time.

☆ ☆ ☆ ☆

Fort Leavenworth
General Warren Fielding, base commander, and a phalanx of MPs greeted the arrivals. Two Cadillac sedans and a military bus were lined up. The Marines gathered the baggage, boarded the bus and followed the entourage to CSGC, the Command and General Staff College. They signed in and were taken to a private dining room in the Officers Club for a late supper. After the light repast, Fielding escorted them to special quarters.

"Breakfast at 0800, gentlemen, and court begins at 0930 hours. Transportation will be here to drive you to the courts at the Disciplinary Barracks. Good night, sirs," Fielding said, then saluted.

☆ ☆ ☆ ☆

Monday, May 19, 1952 - 0930 hours - Disciplinary Barracks, Court No. 1
The Cabinet men, the Joint Chiefs and the Marine squad were seated as spectators in the specially prepared courtroom. The U.S. Attorneys and the CIA team sat behind the Chief Prosecutor, General Barton Milburn. Defense attorneys were at a table separated by five feet from the prosecution team. MPs acted as clerks and bailiffs. Interpreters were placed beneath the judge's bench. Earphones were distributed to counsel and the distinguished guests of the court.

"All rise," said an MP.

Brigadier General Wilford Ross, in full dress uniform, walked to his bench and signaled to those who rose to be seated.

"Before the prisoner is brought before the court, I would like to note the presence of the distinguished members of our government. Their presence will not be inscribed in the record. I will instead attach a memorandum expressing the honor of their presence."

Two MPs escorted the prisoner to the defense table. He was not handcuffed or shackled. Bart rose and handed an MP copies of the charges against Adolf Hitler, alias Frederick Avram Nordheim, former Chancellor of the Third Reich of Germany in the years 1933 to 1945. Copies of the indictment in the German language had been presented to the prisoner two weeks before the hearings.

He was charged with crimes against peace by planning, preparation, initiation and waging wars of aggression, which were also wars in violation of international treaties, agreements and assurances; and with war crimes against humanity. He was also charged with participating in the formulation or execution of a common plan or conspiracy to commit all these crimes. Copies of the charter provisions were duplicated from the Nuremberg manual and distributed to all participants in the trial.

In an opening statement, Judge Ross declared: "We are about to begin a series of evidentiary hearings. Let me make it manifestly clear to the prosecution, the defense, and for the record that these proceedings are not being held for the purpose of determining the guilt or innocence of the defendants. Rather, it is my duty to decide whether there is sufficient credible evidence to bind the defendants over for trial by a military tribunal.

"I have before me motions challenging the authority of our commission. Motions in behalf of defendant Hitler, a.k.a. Nordheim, in which he contends that he was illegally apprehended out of the continental U.S., incarcerated, manacled, shackled, placed in solitary confinement, restrained in a straitjacket and treated inhumanely. I have incorporated all the motions in the foregoing statement. I note that the prisoner is present with his counsel. I also note that the prosecution is present. The court recognizes Major Horace Chapin, defense counsel for Hitler, a.k.a. Nordheim."

"Your Honor, I represent Mr. Nordheim. In his behalf we challenge the jurisdiction of this court to hear the charges against the defendant."

"Counsel, let's proceed before this commission appointed by the President of the United States, which constitutes the supreme authority of this court."

"But, sir…"

"Never mind the *but, sir,* and allow me to finish my statement. I'll tolerate no further interruptions."

"My apologies, sir."

"Noted. Now, the pretense in reference, Counsel, is very simple. Who is your client? Nordheim or Hitler or both?"

"Sir, may I confer with my client?"

"Go to it."

Major Chapin, with two members of his staff, Lieutenants Louis Happenie and Virgil Woods, conferred with their client. A heated discussion ensued, with the defendant pounding the table. Judge Ross banged his gavel repeatedly.

"Major Chapin, I've clocked your conference. It has taken you eleven minutes and fifty-two seconds to determine the defendant's identity. You have had two weeks to study the indictments and to determine his true identity. You are aware, Counselor, that these proceedings are governed by the *Manual for Courts-Martial United States 1951?*" he said, holding up the purple hardcover book bearing the legend described.

"Yes, sir, Your Honor."

"Then you are familiar with the section dealing with war crimes?"

"Yes, sir."

"Proceed. Who is your defendant?"

"He wishes to identify himself, sir. We've advised him to let us do so."

"Come now, I will not turn these hearings into a farcical travesty of justice. I will allow him to state his name."

The defendant stood up. His head and face were shaved. He was dressed in a prisoner's khaki jumpsuit. The judge and all the participants wore earphones to hear the translations in anticipation of the German language. His stance and gestures were classic Hitleresque.

"To this kangaroo court, I announce I am Chancellor, the *Führer* of the Third Reich. I am Adolf Hitler and I demand-"

Ross cut him off. "You are entitled to nothing and can demand nothing, Mr. Hitler. Be seated and allow your counsel to defend you."

Hitler shouted in German. "*Arschloch!* Who the *bumsen* do you think you are? This is a *bullscheisse* court!"

Ross angrily pounded his gavel. "Counsel, sit the defendant down and shut him up or I'll have him shackled and muted by the Military Police." Hitler continued his tirade, which was peppered with invectives. Two MPs, at a gesture from the judge, slammed Hitler into his chair.

"Let the record show that the defendant's disruptive conduct has caused the court to place him in restraints in order to suppress his abusive outbursts," Ross declared.

"Your Honor, I beg the court's indulgence to continue my argument contained in the motions before you," Major Chapin continued. "I have a plea for a writ of habeas corpus on the grounds that the alleged crimes took place outside the United States."

"Before you go any further, Major Chapin, I cite to you, and for the record, the Supreme Court's decision on your specific request on the grounds you state. In *ex parte Quirin*, the court upheld the jurisdiction of the military commission, similar to this court, despite the fact that the civil courts were functioning, because the charges against the defendants involved were what the court considered to be a war crime. Therefore, your motion challenging this court's jurisdiction is herewith denied. Let's move on," Ross said.

Bart Milburn rose.

Major Chapin raised his voice. "Your Honor, I am not finished addressing the motions before you."

"You'll have the full opportunity to argue your motions, Counselor. General Milburn, for what purpose do you rise?"

"Sir, with due respect to defense counsel and this court, in the interest of saving the court's time, I would like to state for the record that these motions are specious at best. The answers, as stated in your denial of motion one, are fully covered by the *Manual for Courts-Martial United States*, effective 31 May, 1951. I beg the court's indulgence to let us get on with evidentiary hearings and do away with motions fully intended to cloud the most serious issues to be presented to the trier of fact."

"Mr. Prosecutor, I note your well-intended statements. However, in the interests of fairness, as well as the gravity of the crimes alleged in your indictments, I'm inclined to grant the defense the widest latitude permissible under military law."

"Thank you, Your Honor," Bart replied.

"Counsel for the defense, Major Chapin, you may continue."

"Your Honor, my client vehemently declares he is not guilty of the particular offenses stated in section II, detailing crimes under International Law, listed as *(A) Crimes Against Peace, (B) Crimes Against Humanity, and (C) War Crimes.*"

"Are you prepared, Counselor, to argue mitigation on those three charges?"

"That's the problem here. Our client has refused to accept me and the two members of our defense team as his counsel. He demands that he be allowed to defend himself."

"Approach the bench, gentlemen."

Chapin and Milburn went into a sidebar conference with Ross.

"Major Chapin, is he trying to make a mockery of this tribunal?" Ross asked.

"I don't think so, sir. Here is a note he scribbled to me."

Ross read the note and whispered its contents to Bart. *"Tell the judge I will behave. I must defend myself. Only I can answer those charges. They are false. If this is true American justice, prove it. I am perfectly sane. A. Hitler.* General Milburn, how say you?"

"Judge Ross, remove his restraints and allow me to present the prosecution's case. He can rebut my statements with the help of his counsel. I believe he'll be digging his own grave. After all, this is a preliminary hearing analogous to a civil court."

"I'll allow it, providing he doesn't disrupt the decorum of this court. One outburst and he'll be curbed again. Let's move on."

Ross asked the MP to have the tape and handcuffs removed. Hitler stood up and addressed the court in German. Everyone, except Bart, adjusted their earphones.

"Excuse me, Your Honor. I will answer the charges when my turn comes."

"Be seated, Mr. Hitler. We will now hear the opening statement by the prosecution."

Horace Chapin immediately rose and addressed General Ross.

"Sir, I wish to call the court's attention to a very serious charge against the prosecution."

"Major Chapin, does this provacative statement pertain to this defendant?"

"Sir, it is broad in scope covering witnesses against my client. My complaint is based on section 140 of the 1951 Manual for Courts-Martial covering Confessions and Admissions; Acts and statements of Conspirators and Accomplices as delineated on pages 248 and 249."

Ross gaveled.

"Hold it right there, Major Chapin. Defense and prosecution into my chambers now."

In chambers, Ross read a motion presented by Chapin as Bart lit a cigarette. Ross removed his glasses and glared at the two men.

"General Milburn, is there any substance to Chapin's charge that you have threatened some of these prisoners with a firing squad or this peculiar mechanics fable?"

"Yes, it's true in some instances. However, those were intended to break a conspiracy of silence on the part of these evil bastards."

"Well, whatever the intent I am inclined to disallow the use of any cnfessions so obtained."

"General Ross," Bart said, "on page 249 of the Manual it is clearly stated *A confession or admission of the accused is not rendered inadmissible by a promise or threat which was not an efffective cause of obtaining the statement.*"

Chapin cut in. "Sir, General Milburn is..."

"Hold it," Ross snapped. "I'm not running a kindergarten here. If voluntary, I'll allow it. If not, then it is not admissible."

"General Ross," Bart said, "I have all the evidence apart from these confessions. However, each prisoner can speak for himself. If they say it was induced by threats, I'll rely on our evidence. If they say it's voluntary, so be it."

"Major Chapin, what say you?" Ross asked.

"I'll abide by your rulings, sir."

"Very well. Let's get back to court, gentlemen."

Over the course of the next two days, hearings were held in two separate courtrooms. Bart delivered a searing opening statement and an ample supply of evidence was presented. On Wednesday, May 21st, in Courtroom 1, Judge Ross declared that the prisoners would be bound over for trial on Tuesday, February 3rd, 1953. Judge Farnsworth did likewise in Courtroom 2.

CHAPTER THIRTY-FOUR

Thursday, May 22, 1952 - 10 a.m. - Fort Leavenworth, Kansas
Secretary of Defense Lovett arranged for a meeting in General Fielding's conference room. Bart, Jacques and his CIA team met with General Bradley, General Smith, Allen Dulles and the Joint Chiefs.

Lovett said, "On behalf of the President, whom I spoke to an hour ago, and all present here, I wish to congratulate General Barton Milburn for the magnificent job he and his staff have accomplished in rounding up these war criminals and in organizing these evidentiary hearings. He put his career as a successful lawyer on hold to undertake this assignment."

There was a prolonged round of applause. Bart, though embarrassed, maintained a solemn mien as all eyes turned to him.

"Gentlemen, I thank you for your compliments. I cannot let this moment pass without acknowledging the help of everyone present, plus the full support of General Bradley, the Joint Chiefs, the assistance of General Smith and the CIA staff loaned to me, and the efforts of Allen Dulles. And, of course, President Truman."

Bart noticed Dulles' grin of appreciation. Little did Dulles realize that Bart had deviously mentioned him in an effort to offset any negative comments that might be forthcoming from him as the deputy director of the CIA.

"General Milburn, assuming that there will be no leaks before the elections, when will the news of the capture of Hitler and his minions be made public?" Dulles asked.

"Mr. Dulles, you are much more politically astute than most. However, I'll try my hand at political analysis. As of this moment, General Eisenhower was recalled to active duty by President Truman to command NATO forces in Europe. I would venture an opinion. Now that he's a candidate for the presidency, he will resign that post by the end of this month. The conventions in Chicago for both parties are two months away in July. Election Day this year will be November 4th. Shortly thereafter, the winning candidate will confer with outgoing President Truman, who will occupy the White House until January 20th, 1953. Truman can make the announcement unilaterally any time he sees fit. However, being the class act that he is, he will consult with the President-elect before any statement will be issued concerning this explosive piece of news. The nominated candidates will be briefed before the election. It is out of courtesy to these men that Truman agreed to keep this top secret, so as not to blanket the campaigns. If this story breaks prematurely, it will dominate the news. In short, sir, my curbstone opinion in answer to your question would be an announcement sometime between, say, November 15th and December 15th," Bart concluded.

"General Milburn, that's as fine a piece of political analysis as I have heard from any of our media mavens on the airwaves," Smith said.

"Beedle, I agree. Milburn is right on the button," Bradley commented.

"I am going to voice an unpopular opinion," Dulles uttered. "I am personally opposed to holding public, broadcast trials for these beasts."

A cold wind chilled the room. Total silence ensued. Bart coolly reached into his tunic, extracted a silver cigarette case, deliberately snapped it open, plucked a cigarette and lit it calmly with his Dunhill lighter. He expelled a cloud of smoke. Bradley stared at Dulles with a malevolent look. Smith gritted his teeth. The Joint Chiefs were appalled and kept silent. General Fielding nudged Bart. Lovett made eye contact with Milburn, who, in return, nodded. Bart took a long drag on his cigarette, expelling rings of smoke to the ceiling. Very softly, in a voice tinged with contempt, he broke the silence. "Mr. Dulles, would you indulge us with a cogent reason to cover up the monstrous evil perpetrated by these infrahuman species?"

The icy tone got the full attention of the participants. Dulles was taken aback by Bart's soft delivery, and all eyes focused on him. "These trials will embarrass some very important people the world over. The Nuremberg trials told the story. Need we embellish it to appease certain lobbies?" Dulles said.

The lawyer in Bart took over. "Mr. Dulles, in your reference to lobbies, are you euphemistically referring to a Jewish lobby, a British lobby, a French lobby, a German lobby, or even an unspecified American lobby?"

"Oh, come now, Bart, you're putting me in an awkward position. I meant no harm. I just voiced an opinion. Let's drop it," Dulles said.

"Allen, your war effort in the OSS was excellent. Your cooperation with me has been first class. Please don't besmirch your reputation with the inference of a cover-up," Bart implored. "Besides, I thought we settled that at the White House."

"Okay, forget I mentioned it."

"We're leaving in the morning." General Bradley declared. "General Fielding and you are old buddies. He knows you're running the show, and he's running Fort Leavenworth, so I'm sure you two will make for a harmonious pair."

"Count on it, sir," Fielding said.

"Amen," Bart echoed.

Dulles offered no response. The meeting was adjourned. As the group dispersed, Bart was surprised by the presence of Richard Maybrook, who was in conversation with an MP in the corridor.

"What the hell are you doing here, Rick?"

"Cool it, Bart. Let's go somewhere private. I've run into a bombshell, and a sticky one at that. We have to sort it out."

They strolled along Riverside Avenue in the cool spring twilight.

"What's the bombshell?"

"Bart, this Colonel Helmut Wasser was commandant at Auschwitz for the last forty-five days after Colonel Arthur Liebehenschel deserted the camp. He wants to talk with you and will act as a witness."

"Rick, he's represented by Lieutenant Lillian North. I can't talk with him now."

"Bart, she is the one who made the request for him."

"Is he looking for a deal?"

"I don't know. Lieutenant North is waiting to hear from you. Says it's urgent. Wants him removed from the rest of the prisoners."

They returned to the disciplinary barracks. A master sergeant MP drove Bart to his Victorian house quarters and continued on with Maybrook to pick up Lieutenant North. The blonde, blue-eyed Judge Advocate jumped into the jeep. The sergeant saluted and turned to his wheel, displaying a smile of approval. At the house, Jacques and Bart were sipping vodka martinis and smoking long brown Sherman cigarettes.

"Shall I wait, sir?" the sergeant asked.

"Not necessary; we'll call the Provost Marshal's office," Maybrook said.

Bart and Jacques stood up when Lillian North and Maybrook entered the house.

She saluted General Milburn. He returned the gesture and said, "Let's cut the formalities, Lieutenant. How about a drink?"

"I'd love one, sir."

She opted for a scotch and water. Maybrook poured it for her and fixed himself a vodka martini.

"All right, Lillian, what is the problem?" Bart asked.

"Colonel Wasser says he can produce a diary written by his predecessor, Rudolf Höss, which chronicles the atrocities during his regime as commandant. He is very secretive and wishes to testify for the prosecution."

"Is he asking for a deal?" Bart inquired.

"No, but as his counsel I'm impelled to ask for one," she said with a smile.

"No deals. Depending on what he has to offer, we might consider leniency."

"General, the man's in danger. Get him into a cell removed from the rest of the population."

A call to the Provost Marshal arranged for a Jeep, the removal of Colonel

Wasser to an interrogation room, and the assignment of two MPs to escort the prisoner.

☆ ☆ ☆ ☆

One hour later - Disciplinary Barracks, Fort Leavenworth

Despite his manacles and shackles, the head-shorn commandant stood up when Bart, Jacques, Maybrook and Lieutenant North entered the interrogation room. The MPs produced extra chairs and left the room.

"We'll be just outside the door, General," one of them said.

"*Sprechen sie* English, Colonel?" Bart asked.

"Yes, sir."

Bart turned on the recorder, then, for the record, said, "Your lawyer, Lieutenant Lillian North, is here. Please state your name."

"I am Helmut Wasser, a former colonel in the Gestapo Waffen SS and commandant at Auschwitz concentration camp from late November, 1944, until January 1, 1945, when I escaped the oncoming Russian army."

"The Russians came into Auschwitz almost twenty days later," Bart observed. "How did you get out of Poland?"

"I speak Polish, Russian, English and German. I took the clothes of a partisan and his rifle. I was captured. I convinced a Russian colonel I was a Polish partisan. He put me on a troop train heading for Stettin. The train stopped for water. I jumped off and hid out on a farm. I knew the war was almost over. A nice Polish lady gave me work on the farm. Excuse me, Ma'am...she was very horny, so I serviced her."

Lieutenant North did not react.

"After Germany surrendered," Wasser continued, "I stowed away on a Swedish ship for Malmo. I saw Martin Bormann on May 12 in a car parked outside of a drug store. I knocked on the window, identified myself, and he gave me a job in a house owned by a rich Jew, named Nordheim. Later, I learned he was Hitler. General Müller came to the house. He recognized me and sent me to the Waffen SS in Argentina."

"A likely story," Jacques snapped.

"Cut the bullshit. What about Höss's diary?" Bart demanded.

"I swear by the Bible my story is true. I took the diary when I escaped from Auschwitz. It's buried by the third tree back of the barn at Nordheim's ranch in Rio de la Plata. It is a full account of Höss's atrocities at Auschwitz. It's wrapped in pliofilm, a rubbery substance. I let all of the Jews escape. I stopped all the beatings there. I saved a lot of Jews from the gas showers. You can check it out. If you hang me, at least I can make peace with God. I am not a monster," he cried, and tears rolled down his cheeks.

"All right, Helmut, we'll put you in a separate cell. We'll check your story out. If you have lied to us, heaven help you."

Sobbing, he tried to wipe his eyes with his handcuffed hands. "I will also tell you about Hitler's stupid Revenge Plan. He's a maniac," he wept. "I will testify for you. I am forty years old with a wife and two young children in Canada. I am not a Nazi. I never was. I hid it. I was in the German army. What could I do?"

Bart beckoned Lieutenant North, Jacques and Maybrook to a corner. "Do you believe this guy?" he asked them.

Lillian North spoke first: "I do."

The other two agreed.

"I'll take a shot at him tomorrow."

The MPs were called. "Put this man in a cell removed from the others. Take off the restraints. See that he is fed properly. I'll clear it with the Provost Marshal."

"Yes sir, General." They removed the restraints and led him out.

For Bart and Jacques, the next few days were devoted to intense questioning of Erich and Heinrich Müller, Abdul Ahmed-al-Said (the Cobra), Langsdorff, Klauss, and Hugo Schultz. The CIA team interrogated the rest of the Waffen SS group. The ten U.S. Attorneys assisted. Bart's number one target was Erich Müller. The heavyset prisoner was seated on his slab bed. He took note of the general's two stars, then, in colloquial English, he said, "The boss is here."

"That's right, I'm here, and we're not going to play games. I want some answers or I'll break every evil bone in your body, *verstehen sie?*"

Müller's knee-jerk reaction was telltale. "*Was ist los?*"

"Listen, slimeball, you killed American prisoners of war at Malmedy. I saw their bodies."

"That's a lie," Müller countered as he stood up.

Bart angrily drove his fist into the prisoner's abdomen. He fell back on the cot with a loud "whoosh."

An MP rushed in. "Trouble, sir?"

"No, the prisoner's a little clumsy."

The MP smiled knowingly and saluted. "I'll be right outside the door, sir."

Bart removed his tunic, shirt and undershirt. Müller, still breathless, observed the bare-chested, muscular general.

"What the hell are you going to do?"

"Just what I said. I'm going to break every fucking bone in your body."

"Why me?"

"Don't play cute with me, *arschloch*. I'm going to refresh your memory, Colonel Erich Müller. You were in charge of the SS brigade, as part of the first Panzer division in the Ardennes. Hitler's last stand - operation *Wacht am Rhein*. We called it the Battle of the Bulge."

"So what? I was a soldier like you."

"Listen, shithead, you speak perfect English. You trained with those Nazi bastards who wore American uniforms and tried to mislead our troops. Your *schmucks* spoke like Americans, but they couldn't answer questions about baseball, Hollywood, and the little things that unmasked you."

"You were there?" Müller gasped.

"You can bet your Iron Cross I was there. I counted seventy-one dead

American prisoners of war that you and your men lined up and mercilessly executed. You call yourself a soldier. Only the Nazis would be so heartless as to slaughter unarmed soldiers. Get up on your feet, motherfucker. I've waited seven years for this moment!" Bart roared.

"Hey, hold it. You got the wrong man. Those were Field Marshal Model's orders."

"You lying bastard. Stand up, you gutless rat!"

The prisoner didn't move. Bart backhanded him across his right cheek. Müller rose and threw a right jab, barely touching Bart's chin. The combative stance by Müller satisfied Bart's plan. He furiously battered him relentlessly into total submission.

"Tell me what happened at Malmedy, you spineless snake! Talk or I'll work you over some more!"

The semi-conscious SS colonel, bleeding from his nose and mouth, muttered, "Enough, enough. You're trying to kill me."

"Just answer my questions, *scheissemeister*. Here's a wet towel; wipe your face."

"You're going to hang me or put me before a firing squad. Why should I answer? You won't believe me," Müller replied as he dabbed his bleeding face.

"Tell me the truth and your chances of living will improve. Now talk, no bullshit. This is a very personal issue with me. Do you understand? Talk or I'll put you in front of a firing squad in the next thirty minutes."

"You can't do that."

"I can and I will. Now, it's your choice, *schmuck*. A firing squad, or the truth about Malmedy? I'll give you five minutes to tell the truth," Bart threatened.

Bart looked at his wristwatch and noted the minutes ticking. He reached for his undershirt, shirt and tunic, and donned his garments. Five minutes passed. Müller nervously watched Bart's movements, but he remained mute. The general rapped on the steel door. MP Staff Sergeant Wesley Austin appeared and saluted smartly, "Yes sir, General?"

Bart turned his back to Müller, winked at the sergeant and ordered, "Tell the Provost Marshal to order a firing squad for the execution of Colonel Erich Müller."

A second MP appeared.

"Manacle the prisoner," Bart ordered.

Müller struggled to avoid the handcuffs. Both MPs pinned him down on the cot, turned him face down and applied the restraints. Another sergeant, Ashley, saluted the general, who was calmly adjusting his tie. He noticed the bloodied prisoner.

"I'll report back, sir, as soon as the firing squad is assembled," the MP declared loudly.

The MPs started to close the steel door when Müller screamed, "No! No! I'll will tell you everything."

"Too late, *arschloch*," Bart snapped.

"I will tell you everything. Please hear me out," Müller pleaded.

The MPs were halfway out the door, playing along with the charade.

Bart turned to them, his back to the shivering prisoner. Winking again, he said, "Set it up." He took a key from his pants pocket and unlocked the handcuffs.

"Is there something you wanted to tell me, Müller?"

"SS General Josef Dietrich. He commanded the Sixth Panzer Army. He wasn't a very good general. Lieutenant Colonel Joachim Peiper commanded the 1st Panzer Regiment. He was young, very well educated, well trained and very tough. He and General Dietrich didn't get along with each other."

"Cut the Nazi politics. Who killed the American prisoners of war?"

"You want the truth? I'm trying to tell you what happened!"

"Fine. Talk."

"I was part of Lieutenant Colonel Otto Skorzeny's special troops. There were two thousand, dressed in American uniforms. We were trained to confuse the oncoming Patton's Third Army. I thought it was stupid. Skorzeny knew I was Heinrich Müller's nephew. I asked to be transferred to the Sixth Panzer Army. I was assigned to the 1st Panzer Regiment as a captain under Colonel Peiper."

"So what happened?"

"I was directed to a café in Lanzerath. I found Colonel Peiper briefing some officers and Luftwaffe men. He had a map tacked to the wall with daggers. When I came in, he said to me, *Who the hell are you?* I handed him my transfer orders. He was very sarcastic. He called me *Heinrich's little boy.* He told me to sit down and listen to his instructions."

"Come on, Müller, I don't have all day."

"Peiper's tanks needed fuel. He assigned me to a tank in the middle of the column. On the way to Bullingen, the tanks stopped. I stood on top of my tank. I saw six Americans with their hands up. Suddenly, an SS Sergeant had the men shot down in a burst of fire. Later, in Bullingen, thirty more American POWs were killed. About twelve more were shot while their hands were in the air. We drove on to Baugnez, two miles south of Malmedy."

"Did you participate in shooting Americans?"

"Honest to God, no. I told Peiper about the slaughter of the American prisoners. He called me an *arschloch* and said that Hitler's orders were to show no mercy, to forget the rules of war. *Kill and destroy* was the battle cry. Later, trucks carrying one hundred fifty American soldiers from your Battery B reached the crossroads. We attacked with cannons and machine guns. We captured one hundred twenty men. I was ten tanks back. Colonel Peiper ordered the Americans to drop their guns and put their hands up. They were stripped of their possessions - watches, cigarettes, gloves, and whatever they had. Then they were marched to an open field and the machine guns, handguns and rifles poured bullets into the group. You say seventy-one. I say more than that were shot. Maybe some survived. I didn't fire one shot."

"What happened after that?"

"Well, you know, Patton and his Third Army pushed us back. The Americans got very tough after the Malmedy massacre. That was the beginning of the end of the Third Reich."

"How did you get away?"

"I followed Peiper's tank. He dumped the tank. We had begun our attack at Bastogne on December 16, with five thousand men in our regiment. By Christmas Eve, we had eight hundred men. Our column was scattered. Peiper regrouped them and headed toward Lienne Creek at the crossroads of Habiemont."

"How did you get away?"

"Believe it or not, you can check this out, but an American Jewish lieutenant, Alvin Edelstein, commanded a squad that wired the Habiemont bridge and placed mines on the roads leading to the bridge. We heard them yell, *Blow! Blow!* There was only one way out as the Americans blasted us. We retreated to La Gleize and occupied the town. We captured a Major Hal McGowan."

"So, what then?"

"Peiper spoke fluent English. McGowan knew about the Malmedy massacre. We had one hundred and fifty-three American prisoners. Peiper tried to make a deal to exchange the prisoners, if McGowan would guarantee that the American commander would free the German wounded. During Christmas Eve, McGowan escaped. We got lucky. The Americans were singing Christmas carols. We swam across the freezing Salm River and made contact with German troops. That son of a bitch, in cold blood, killed at least three hundred and fifty American prisoners of war and over one hundred and twenty-five civilians, then he was decorated by Hitler."

"What happened to you?"

"I was assigned back to my uncle, General Heinrich Müller. As you know, we escaped to Argentina."

"So, you and your uncle are part of the Revenge Plan?" Bart snapped.

"I can help you with my uncle. I think the plan is stupid. He can give you all the details. I know some of them. Hitler is insane, with billions of dollars."

"Do you think General Müller will listen to you?"

"Yes, he may want to make a deal."

"We'll see about that. First, he has to agree to talk to me."

"How can I talk to him?"

"I'll arrange it. Now, one more very important question. Forty-three of your murderous troops were found guilty and hanged. Thirty of them are in jail. Joachim Peiper disappeared. Where is he now?"

Müller began to fidget. He nervously wiped droplets of saliva from his chin. In a split second, Bart's visceral reaction caused him to pounce on the prisoner and haul him to his feet. "Don't fuck around with me. My condition was the *whole* truth. Let's have it. You obviously know where he is."

"You're hurting me."

Bart released his chokehold on Müller's throat. "Talk!"

Müller sat back on his cot. "General, if word gets out that I talked, my life wouldn't be worth a *pfennig*. I'll need protection."

"You and your uncle will be protected if you testify at the trials next year."

"Do I have your word on that?"

"Absolutely."

"Joachim Peiper has changed his name to Luther Jockler and is now executive vice president of BEC Ltd. in Munich."

"What is BEC?"

"Bavarian Electronics Corporation. A very big company. He is Hitler's man there, and very rich."

"Okay, Erich, if this is all true, you have saved your life. If your uncle wants to live, tell him to talk."

Bart knocked on the steel door, and the two MPs entered. "Sergeant, cancel the firing squad."

Müller's sigh of relief was audible.

"Yes, sir. Does he go back to his cell?"

"No, I want him in a decent cell, removed from the others. I removed his cuffs. Treat him well. I'll be back soon, and I want this prisoner and General Heinrich Müller brought to that special interrogation room. I'll notify the Provost Marshal."

"Will do, sir," they responded, saluting.

Bart was driven to General Fielding's office. He waited for the general to finish a phone conversation, then Fielding came out of his office and invited Bart to join him.

"Warren, I need a safe phone to call the White House. It's urgent, and if you want a quick thrill, you can listen to my end of the conversation. I think you'll enjoy this," Bart said.

"Come in here and use my red phone," Fielding said.

Bart lit a cigarette; Fielding a cigar. John Steelman answered the call.

"Has the boss got a minute, John? We have a hot potato."

"Hold on."

"What's up, Barton?"

"Mr. President, I hope you and Dr. Steelman are the only ones in the oval office?"

"Hold it."

Bart heard the President say goodbye to someone.

"Okay, General, shoot."

"Mr. President, you are well aware of the massacre at Malmedy in December 1944?"

"Very much so."

"Well, I broke a prisoner twenty minutes ago. He revealed the perpetrator of that mass assassination of our POWs. Is Steelman listening to us?"

"No."

"Do you want him on the speaker to make notes? This becomes an international matter."

"He's here, and the speaker is on."

"The man who killed those seventy-one POWs at Malmedy killed over three hundred fifity POWs in all, plus one hundred twenty-five civilians. His name was Lieutenant Colonel Joachim Peiper. We hanged forty-three of his men and jailed thirty of them. Here's the problem. Peiper escaped and is living the high life in Munich under another name. He is now Luther Jockler, vice president of BEC Ltd., Bavarian Electronics Corporation. He is Hitler's man."

"Barton, you continue to amaze me. This is a real coup. What do you suggest?"

"Mr. President, you are about to sign a peace contract with Germany next Monday, May 26. I am sure that Chancellor Adenauer is quite anxious to seal that historic document. I strongly recommend that he cooperate in the immediate detention of Peiper, alias Jockler. Of course, we'll have to verify Peiper's true identity. There are photographs of him in the CIA files."

"Barton, hold on, I'm going to patch General Smith into this conversation."

"That's fine, Mr. President. I have another goodie for him to get busy on which might intrigue you, sir."

Bart lit another cigarette and whispered to Fielding that General Smith of the CIA was being hooked up. Fielding was spellbound. He was puffing his cigar in spurts.

"Smith is on, Bart," Truman said.

"Hi, Barton. I just got a fast briefing from Steelman's notes. What do you suggest?"

"You've got a couple of top men in Munich?"

"That's right. Paul Tompkins and Elliot Goodman."

"There are pictures of Peiper in your Nazi files. Do you want me to send Jacques Laurent to Munich to work with your guys? Jacques is their senior man in charge of the Nazi desk," Bart said.

"Good idea. I'll have a plane to fly him over. They'll meet Jacques at the Four Seasons Hotel. I'll have the photos delivered to him at Andrews. Give Katherine Wharton an ETA. Once he's identified, what's the plan?" Smith asked.

"Mr. President, I've thought this out. May I make a suggestion, sir?"

"Shoot."

"This could make momentous news. If you can pressure Adenauer to work with our military occupying forces, have him okay a public arrest with lots of media attention. Then, have a military tribunal, with full German cooperation, try him as a war criminal, which he is, and let the cameras in the court," Bart said.

"What about witnesses?" Truman asked.

"We have thirty of them in jail there, and I have one dynamite eyewitness here. He rode with Peiper and saw the massacre."

"Barton, my boy, I love your plan. I'll need quick confirmation of his identity. Have Laurent call me directly as soon as they identify that animal. This is a bonanza. What's the other goodie you mentioned?"

"Sir, may I hold you for one second?"

"Hurry."

Bart whispered to Fielding, "Get Laurent here pronto. He's at the Disciplinary Barracks."

"Mr. President and General Smith, the last commandant at Auschwitz is here. He was in that position for the last thirty days or so before the Russkies came in. He escaped and stole the diary of that bastard Rudolf Höss…"

Truman gasped, "Rudolf Hess?"

"Höss with an 'o,' sir."

"Okay…go on."

"General, you better make a note of what I am going to tell you. Rudolf Höss was Himmler's man at Auschwitz and personally handled the extermination of two and a half million Jews, plus others. Höss was tried and hanged by a Polish tribunal. His successor was Arthur Liebehenschel. The Poles hanged him. Colonel Helmut Wasser was commandant in late November 1944. The Russians are at the doorstep. He frees the Jews and disappears with Höss's diary containing all the gory details in it."

"Where is the diary now?" Smith asked.

"That's why I suggest you note this. It's buried at Nordheim's ranch in La Plata. It's at the third tree just behind the barn. Your man, the lawyer Ernesto Nogales, is the perfect man to retrieve it. That diary would be devastating to those Nazi bastards at the main trial. It's wrapped in heavy-duty pliofilm."

"I'll take care of it, Bart," Smith said. "Get Laurent to Munich tonight. I'll have a turbojet at hangar 14 at Andrews. When will he leave there?"

"In the next hour."

"Good work, Barton."

"Thank you, Mr. President."

Jacques arrived at Fielding's office, winded and with blood spattered on his shirt and hands.

"What the hell happened to you?" Bart said.

Breathlessly he explained, "I just beat the hell out of Hermann Klauss."

"All right, catch your breath."

Fielding handed him a glass of water.

"First, let me talk, and then you can tell us about Klauss."

Bart outlined the assignment to Munich. Fielding told him that a turbojet was standing by to fly him to Andrews Air Force Base, where another turbo would be ready to fly him to Munich.

"Travel light. Check into the Four Seasons Hotel. One of your CIAs, Paul Tompkins, will meet your plane. Another agent, Elliot Goodman, will meet up with you at the hotel."

"Good men," Laurent exclaimed.

"Now, what happened with Klauss?"

"I sat him down in the interrogation room. When I turned my back to put a chair at the desk and to place the recorder on the table, he blindsided me with a chop on the back of my neck. He's a strong son of a bitch and almost knocked me cold. I rolled over and kicked him in the balls. That doubled him up and I gathered my senses."

"What happened then?"

"I lost my temper and worked him over. Finally, he broke down and admitted that he and Hans Langsdorff were going to blow up and sink ships on both ends of the Panama Canal. Nordheim - I mean Hitler - has advanced them one million dollars each and deposited four million dollars more for each of them at the Banque Lorraine, to be released by von Leute when the job was done."

"That maniac!" Fielding exclaimed.

"Get going, Jacques. Clean up, change your clothes and get out to Sherman Airfield," Bart ordered. "You've got your instructions. Good luck. Call Katharine Wharton with an ETA from Andrews."

"I'll order a Jeep for you," Fielding said.

"Not necessary, sir. Sergeant Adams is waiting out front for me."

"I've got two labyrinthine messes to pump out of this Nazi cesspool of evil," Bart said.

"Can I help?" Fielding offered.

"Warren, you've got enough on your plate, managing this complex."

"What's the problem?"

"Quoting Lewis Carroll's *Alice's Adventures in Wonderland,* things are getting 'curiouser and curiouser'. We've got the Müllers and their role in this maniacal Revenge Plan. The other problem is this latest piece of intelligence by Laurent-the preposterous attempt to destroy the Panama Canal. The Holocaust defies comprehension in a civilized society. Now we have more horrors from this Nazi's grotesque mentality."

"Bart, this has been an education for me."

"There is a question lurking in my mind, Warren. Will there be a Holocaust II? Not necessarily against Jews, but who is next? 'What is past is prologue,' Shakespeare said in, of all things, *The Tempest.* We had it in World War II. When will the tempest end?"

"Quite philosophical, Bart."

"Yes, I'd better go after these bastards now."

Bart brought Maybrook and Sedgwick into an interrogation room, where four MPs also delivered General Müller and his nephew Erich.

"Herr Müller, you and your nephew had an opportunity to talk. I arranged that so that we can have a frank discussion with both of you. We are fully aware of the Revenge Plan," Bart said in German. "And you are aware of the Nuremberg trials and the results."

"Let us speak in English, General. You threatened Colonel Müller with a firing squad. That's very clever, but not the American way. I know all about you, General Milburn. I had a file on you during the war. You were an intelligence officer and the youngest colonel on Eisenhower's staff. When we had Sir Alfred Lipton's daughter as a Jewish prisoner at Ohrdruf, whom we wanted to exchange for Rudolf Hess, you shot the commandant who was trying to escape with her. You have since married her. You are well educated, a lawyer by profession and a very tough, hard young man, so I consider you a worthy opponent."

"Well, General, I want you to understand that I know everything about you, too. I am not surprised by your short biography of me. I'll not waste time on your biography. We are aware that you were the SS *Gruppenführer* and chief of the Gestapo. They called you *Gestapo Müller,* a brutal martinet who captured most of Hitler's enemies and helped orchestrate mass murders of Jews. You escaped from Hitler's bunker the day after Bormann helped Hitler to escape. And, yes, I would use the firing squad. We're tougher than you Nazis."

"Not bad, General. Not bad."

"We have enough on you to hang you or put you before a firing squad."

"Well, what's holding you up, young General?"

"I also know you're a born survivor - apolitical. You are rich and want to live a long, luxurious life."

"Is that an offer?"

"No, just an analysis."

"Then what do you want?" Müller asked.

"I'll make this short. This meeting will be our last one, unless you agree to cooperate."

"Who are these two men?"

"They are intelligence agents on my staff."

"CIA, I bet. Okay, cooperate in what way?"

"Were you really going to carry out the Revenge Plan?"

"You're a master at your job. You captured *Der Führer,* you captured Bormann, and you got me and my whole Waffen SS. Yet, there are others out there, sort of a back-up team, to execute that idiot's scheme. So your answer is no, because it's stupid."

"Did you say *idiot?*"

"Yes, Hitler, with all his billions, is *kaput.* He lost the war fucking around with that so-called Jewish problem. He was crazy to invade Russia before he could have consolidated his control of Europe. Then the *schmuck* declares war on America. He's a mental case."

"Then why did you round up his enemies and Jews?"

"Himmler did that. That chickenshit farmer would have arranged to assassinate me. To be quite frank, I wanted Hitler and Himmler dead, so that I could make peace and take control over Germany."

Musing to himself, *What a crock of shit,* Bart played along with the scenario. "In other words, you didn't round up the Jews for slaughter?"

"No, it was Himmler, that pious Christian. I just did my job. I knew we were losing the war. I was just biding my time. I'm not a true Nazi. I'm not an anti-Semite. I fought alongside some very brave Jews in the first war. The Jews were no threat to Germany. Hitler used them as political pawns. Himmler just went too far."

"General Müller, you're a pragmatist. Open up with me. Testify for the prosecution and I'll make life easier for you and your nephew."

"We want protection, three meals a day and decent quarters."

"That can be arranged."

"You word of honor from one general to another?"

"Only if you tell us the full truth about everything."

"That's a deal. Let's shake hands on it."

Bart froze, but forced himself to comply. The recorder was put on. Over the next two hours, Müller and his nephew spilled a horrific tale in answer to questions by Milburn, Maybrook and Sedgwick. Bart arranged a round-the-clock guard over the two in their bedroom-and-bath quarters in the Disciplinary Barracks.

On the way out, Bart said, "I've got to wash my hands after touching that slimy bastard."

"You were great," Maybrook declared.

"At least you got what you wanted, Bart," Sedgwick said.

"All right, fellows, we got two more cuties to work on now, so let's have a quick bite before we send for them."

"Who are they?" Sedgwick asked.

"Hans Langsdorff, the Graf Spee captain, and Herman Klauss, whom Jacques beat the hell out of. He confessed. Langsdorff needs the urge to purge."

The trio dined on hamburgers, french fries and colas, then returned to the interrogation room. The two prisoners were at odds with each other. However, after an harangue by Milburn on the futility of their ability to collect their bounty offered by Hitler, Langsdorff capitulated. One hour passed, and he validated Klauss's version of the scheme to destroy the Panama Canal.

A tired Bart Milburn returned to his quarters, stripped, and stayed in the shower for fifteen minutes. He donned his pajamas, fixed himself a Rusty Nail, a combination of scotch and Drambuie. Munching on potato chips, he listened to the late-night news on the radio. CBS repeated an earlier report by Ed Murrow about the impending peace contract to be signed in Bonn the next Monday, May 26th by West Germany, the U.S., Great Britain and France.

The story brought his brother to mind, and he wrestled with his conscience. Musing about Douglas playing along to ignore certain stories impinging upon his Nazi spoor, he wondered if his brother was going to cover the peace signing at Bonn, Germany. Instinctively, he picked up the phone and called Douglas at the Beaux Arts Hotel.

Constance answered the call. "Barton, dear, how nice to hear from you."

"Connie, how are you?"

"Just wonderful. Douglas is still at the office."

"What time is it?"

"Just midnight here."

"I'll call him there. If I miss him, I'll call you back."

Bart reached Douglas at the New York Daily News. "What the hell are you doing at the office while your fiancée is pining away at your pad?"

"Bart, I'm finishing a long Sunday feature on the events leading up to the peace contract to be signed at Bonn on Monday. Why the call at this hour? Something wrong?"

"No, Doug, everything's fine. How soon will you finish your article?"

"One more paragraph and I'll put a thirty on it," he said, referring to the newspaper term for "the end."

"Are you going to cover it in Bonn?"

"Haven't made up my mind. Why?"

"Finish your piece and call me at this number from your private line at home. I've something to tell you, against my better judgment, or rather, my conscience."

"Will do. My appetite is whetted."

Forty minutes later Bart's private phone rang.

"What's up, General Milburn?" Doug laughed.

"Smart-ass, this is a plum I'm going to hand you. In heaven's name, forget the source."

"You got my attention. I have pencil and paper ready."

"Get the assignment to Bonn by way of Munich. Catch the very next flight to Munich. Go to the Four Seasons Hotel and connect with Jacques there. It's a blockbuster."

"What's up?"

"I'm going to be very cryptic. The perpetrator of the Malmedy massacre is the target. He's the former Joachim Peiper, now a.k.a. Luther Jockler, executive VP of BEC Ltd., the Bavarian Electronics Corporation."

"Holy Toledo, Bart, this is a fabulous story!"

"Now, listen carefully, Douglas. No story until this fiend is apprehended. You're just an accidental observer on his way to Bonn. Make up a cover story for your stopover at Munich. Jacques is in charge, assisted by CIA agents Paul Tompkins and Elliot Goodman. The U.S. Army commander of our occupying forces in Bavaria will assist. He's a good friend of myself and Jacques."

"I love you, brother."

"Doug, tell it to Constance," he laughed.

Bart called the Four Seasons Hotel in Munich and left word for Jacques Laurent to call Bart on arrival. Mulling over what he had done, he justified it as a self-serving distraction to the media against any leaks of activities at Fort Leavenworth.

.

CHAPTER THIRTY-FIVE

Thursday, May 22, 1952 - Munich, Germany

Jacques Laurent studied the file on Joachim Peiper and the 1944 Malmedy massacre during the flight over the Atlantic. He slept throughout the trip, catching up on some much-needed rest. He arrived at the Munich airport refreshed and ready for the assignment of capturing the shrewd and heartless villain. He reviewed the files again, etching in his mind's eye a living portrait of his prey.

As the plane taxied to the hangar, Jacques spotted Paul Tompkins and a familiar face in a full-dress general's uniform. He deplaned and shook hands with Tompkins. He turned to Major General Paul Donovan, who had worked with him in the Malmo, Sweden, raid. With a broad smile on his face, the general embraced Jacques.

"General, what are you doing here in Munich?"

"Jacques, my friend, I happen to be the commander of our occupying forces in Bavaria. When these men called our headquarters asking for assistance and mentioned your name, I couldn't resist joining you in tracking down this mass murderer. Welcome to Munich, and let's find this son of a bitch Peiper-Jockler."

The general's Mercedes took the two men over the fifteen miles non-stop to the Four Seasons Hotel. They went directly to a suite reserved for Laurent, where Jacques answered Bart's message. Over their room-service lunch, the men planned their surveillance of Luther Jockler, whose office was just five blocks from the hotel.

"This creep has a mansion in the suburb of Schwaben. He lunches regularly at the Aubergine on Maxmiliam Platz," Elliot Goodman said.

"Jacques, Chancellor Adenauer spoke with President Truman," Donovan said. "The Chancellor reached me at home and advised me that Chief of Detectives Kurt Ludwig has been assigned to work with us. He's at a charity luncheon fundraiser for the widows of police killed in action. He'll join us here shortly."

Jacques passed out photographs of Lieutenant Joachim Peiper.

"He's a handsome son of a bitch," Tompkins observed.

"Behind that façade is a steely, cold-blooded, murderous animal," Jacques declared. He outlined Peiper's ruthless execution of unarmed American prisoners of war.

Donovan amplified the description of the events at Malmedy. "I was with General Patton when we got the word. He refused to stop. We kept chasing the krauts, but the word went through the ranks and it pumped their adrenaline as we destroyed those Nazi bastards."

A knock at the door signaled the arrival of Chief Ludwig. The general opened the door and greeted the youngish, six-foot chief. His sparkling smile lit up the room.

In perfect English, he said, "Sorry I'm late...glad to meet you men." Donovan made the introductions.

"How was your luncheon?" Jacques asked.

"Wonderful; we raised two hundred and five thousand marks," he replied, sipping a soft drink.

The next two hours consisted of creating a plan for capturing Joachim Peiper, alias Luther Jockler.

"I have two trusted men outside his building and two more surveilling his mansion. They will make no moves without my presence."

"Kurt, I have a special squad standing by to assist," Donovan noted.

"Do you have proof, Chief Ludwig, that Jockler is Peiper?" Jacques asked.

"We have only one man's testimony. Detective Lorenz Holzer visited the BCE office, acting as a buyer. He was taken to the showroom. He saw Jockler, who has a moustache. He's fairly sure he resembles the very early pictures we have. It's not a positive ID."

Jacques passed out sets of pictures of Peiper. "Can you stay for dinner, Chief?" he asked.

"Let me call home. In my house, my wife is the boss. No, let me correct that - my two children boss *her*," he added, laughing.

He made his call from the adjoining bedroom of the suite. The men commented favorably about Ludwig. When he returned to the table fifteen minutes later, he said, "Sorry I took so long. My wife told me that Detective Holzer was anxious to talk to me. I called Holzer, and he's on the way over here with a series of pictures of Jockler shot from a TV truck parked across from his building as he was leaving. The pictures have been developed."

Dinner for six was ordered, to include the expected Detective Holzer. Jacques excused himself, showered and changed into casual clothes. Room service removed the table and replaced it with two tables, joined and covered with new linen and place settings. Holzer, a tall, bespectacled, neatly dressed man, arrived. He spoke English with a slight German accent. The chief made the introductions, then passed his pictures around after the waiters left. Over coffee, they matched the recent films to the military photos furnished by Jacques.

"Holzer is also a sketch artist. Lorenz, could you draw a picture of this man without the mustache?"

He studied the new pictures, took sheets of hotel stationery from the suite desk and began sketching. When he finished, they matched his drawing with a frontal shot of Jacques' file picture.

"That's the same man," Donovan affirmed.

"Lorenz, when he left his office, did our men follow him home?" Chief Ludwig asked.

"Yes. He entered his Mercedes limo and headed straight home. Detective Schwerin called me at the office while I was waiting for the pictures to be developed."

"Who's watching the house now?"

"Detectives Franz Lieber and Otto Klein. They'll be there all night."

"Gentlemen, Jockler's schedule is very routine. He leaves home promptly at 8:15 a.m. His chauffeur, Hugo Clausenberg, is his bodyguard as well. We believe he's a Nazi who served as a sergeant in the 3rd Panzer Division on the Russian front," Ludwig said. "The limo is there promptly at 7:45 a.m. He brings a stack of newspapers with him. He places some at the front door and leaves the rest on the back seat."

"He lives just outside Munich. Is that correct, Chief?" Jacques queried.

"Just outside Schwaben, only a few miles from here. By the way, sometimes he stops at the famous 19th century inn called the Gasthaus Englischer Garten, where they serve breakfast in the garden alongside a stream. At that time, he leaves at 8 a.m."

"Is there a quiet stretch of road between his house and the inn?" Jacques continued.

"Yes, his house is two miles from the inn, which is another two miles from downtown Munich. Call the play, Mr. Laurent."

"While we want his capture to be a highly publicized event, we don't want to endanger innocent civilians. Therefore, I suggest we take him about a half-mile from his residence, not in front of any homes," Jacques said.

"I agree," Donovan concurred. "Let me stress, Chief Ludwig, that this man is a war criminal. We will take possession of him. As to the trial, Chancellor Adenauer and our President can decide when, where and how he'll be tried - an American military tribunal or your courts."

"We're not politicians, General, so that decision is theirs. Let's capture this bastard. I suggest we take him to Munich police headquarters and notify the media. From there, we will turn him over to you in front of the cameras."

"One point, Chief. We'll be fully engaged in the capture, but Tompkins, Goodman and I will not appear in any photographs, nor is the CIA to be mentioned."

"Understood."

"Okay, here's the plan. We'll have a police car stop the limo a half-mile from the house. There will be two unmarked cars at the point where the limo is stopped. Four motorcycles will be parked near the inn. A radio call will bring them to the scene. General Donovan advises that he'll have a U.S. Army bus with twelve American Military Police close by in radio contact. Peiper, alias Jockler, and his chauffeur will be manacled and placed on the bus. The cycles will lead the convoy to police headquarters, with sirens and flashing lights in operation. I'll have a detective drive the limo to headquarters."

"Under military procedure, he can't have a lawyer right away," Donovan emphasized.

Jacques, suffering from jet lag, bid them goodnight, and they all departed amiably.

☆ ☆ ☆ ☆

Friday, May 23, 1952 - 0700 hours - Schwabing, Germany

All units were in place as planned. The Mercedes Benz sped to the Jockler mansion at 7:40 a.m. Twenty minutes later, the tall, well-dressed man in a Savile Row suit, entered the limousine. Chauffeur Hugo Clausenberg held the door and saluted his patron. Joachim Peiper, alias Luther Jockler, leaned back and perused his newspaper.

A rented BMW sedan drove slowly from the inn, with Douglas Milburn at the wheel. A Daily News photographer, Bill Wallace, was busy in the back seat adjusting several cameras, a long-range one called Big Bertha, usually used at baseball games for close-ups of 2nd base action, and two regular flash-bulb units. Using binoculars, Doug spotted the limo moving in his direction. A police car, siren wailing, was moving up to the Mercedes.

Jacques, gun drawn, focused on his objective, which came to a halt. Wallace, helped by the morning sun rising in the east, pointed his long-range camera toward the open-windowed rear door, snapping shots of a police officer talking to the driver of the limo. The driver got out of the car and showed his license to the officer.

Doug stopped his car and walked toward the scene. Suddenly there was a flurry of action. Eight Munich detectives surrounded the car, led by Chief Ludwig. Twelve American MPs came out of the woods with semi-automatic rifles. The chauffeur foolishly pulled out a gun and shot the police officer in the shoulder. A fusillade of bullets from the MPs and the detectives riddled the body of Hugo Clausberg. Laurent opened the rear door of the limo and pointed his gun close to the face of the startled Joachim Peiper.

"Don't shoot, I'll give you all my money!" he yelled in German, his hands high in the air.

"*Heraus damit!*" Jacques replied in kind.

As Peiper complied, Jacques poked his Beretta into Peiper's mouth. He quickly patted him down, assisted by Ludwig. Detectives searched the interior of the limo and produced two guns, a Walther and a Luger. Peiper, his eyes bulging, his mouth filled with the barrel of Jacques' gun, noticed the American Military Police. He was quickly manacled, his hands behind his back. Jacques removed the gun. While intent on his prisoner, he peripherally noticed Doug Milburn and his photographer being hassled by the MPs.

General Donovan checked Peiper's pockets. Jacques tapped the general on the shoulder and whispered in his ear, "Please tell your MPs to let that reporter and his photographer alone. I'll go over there and get rid of him. I'll send him to police headquarters."

Donovan snapped his fingers and caught their attention. He held his right arm up to a halt position and then pointed at Jacques, who was striding toward Doug, Wallace and the MPs.

"Sir, who are you?" he snapped at Doug.

"I'm from the New York Daily News, sir."

"Fine. There is no press allowed here. If you and your photographer want to get the story and more pictures, I advise you to hasten to Munich police headquarters. We will be there shortly with the prisoner. Now get out of here!"

"Yes, sir," Doug politely agreed.

At that moment Peiper was shouting in English, "You've made a big mistake! You've killed my chauffeur and you got me handcuffed. Do you realize who I am?"

Jacques joined Donovan and said, "Listen, Nazi, I know who you are. Finally we got you, Lieutenant Colonel Joachim Peiper. Now shut your murdering mouth or I'll shut it for you!"

An ambulance, sirens screaming, arrived at the scene. Chief Ludwig pointed at the dead body and snapped one word, "Morgue."

The wounded policeman was rushed to a hospital in a police car. A shouting Peiper was hustled aboard the MP bus. Jacques followed. On board, he threw the prisoner into a seat at the back of the vehicle, then instructed the MPs to duct tape his mouth and shackle his feet.

Donovan sat next to Jacques and ordered the driver to head for the Munich police headquarters. Four motorcycle police led the way, with all the other cars following, sirens screaming.

The headquarters building was surrounded with a potpourri of media - TV trucks, hand-held cameras, sound trucks, soundmen for radio and TV transmission, and a melange of male and female reporters. Doug and Bill were comfortably stationed at the double-door entrance. Chief Ludwig waited until the cameras were surfeited with their shots of the prisoner being slowly helped up the steps. The clamoring reporters, with or without microphones, kept shouting questions. Ludwig held his hand up to quiet the news-hungry press, and the shouting stopped.

"General Donovan and I will be out here in thirty minutes to give you a full statement. Now, be patient, folks, and behave yourself," he said in German, and repeated it in English and French.

In the interrogation room, Peiper remained silent, refusing to answer questions. General Donovan took over. "Lieutenant Colonel Joachim Peiper, you are a war criminal under arrest by the United States Army. You are charged with the heinous crime of slaughtering hundreds of unarmed American prisoners of war at Malmedy, Belgium."

"Fuck you and your whole American Army! You got the wrong man."

Jacques delivered a resounding slap across his face. "You ruthless piece of crap, you'll be a pussycat when we get through with you!" he yelled.

"Chief Ludwig, let's show this piece of dung to the press, then haul him off to our stockade," Donovan suggested.

They dragged the prisoner out front. The MPs took him to the Army's penitentiary on the outskirts of Munich. As promised, Ludwig and Donovan patiently fed the story to the voracious news media. Laurent, Tompkins and Goodman disappeared through the back door of the police headquarters, then headed for the stockade in a police car.

Jacques phoned President Truman, who expressed his appreciation. He placed a second call to Bart at Fort Leavenworth and cryptically declared, "The bird is in the cage. I've advised 1600. What do you want me to do now?"

"Where are you?"

"At the stockade."

"Has he cracked?"

"Not yet."

"All right, spend an hour or so with him, then leave him to Tompkins and Goodman."

"I'll take a whack at him and fly back. I've got a turbojet waiting at the airport."

"Have them fly you to Andrews. We'll spend the weekend with the family."

"Good deal."

"Congratulations," Bart said.

Donovan arrived at the prison, and Jacques asked him for an hour with the prisoner.

"For God's sake, Jacques, don't kill him."

Following the "mechanics" lecture, the prisoner remained stolidly obdurate. Suddenly, he began berating Jacques with every vile epithet he could muster. "I know you're a Jew."

"So, you're a tough Nazi, eh?" Jacques asked snidely.

"Tougher than you."

"How would you like a shot at me?" Jacques goaded.

"You don't have the guts, you American piece of shit."

"Sit still, while I take off your restraints."

Jacques removed his jacket, shirt and undershirt. He unlocked the shackles and turned Peiper over to remove his handcuffs. Peiper removed his jacket and rolled up his sleeves.

"Come on, Jew bastard!" the prisoner shouted as he rushed at Jacques.

With one punch Jacques knocked him sprawling.

Peiper rose and said, "A lucky punch, *schweinhund*."

This time he circled Jacques, looking for an opening. Jacques watched him, his hands at his sides. Peiper attempted to pummel Jacques, who side-stepped the onslaught. Within five minutes, Jacques had beaten the arrogant, muscular Nazi to a broken, bloody, semi-conscious state.

"Had enough, tough Nazi?"

"*Ja, ja*, enough. Who are you?"

"I am a French-American Jew. Tell that to your crazy *Führer*. Now, one last chance before I start over again. Why did you kill those unarmed POWs?"

"I was ordered to because we couldn't move ahead with them."

Jacques replaced the restraints.

"Now, tell me the whole story - or I'll kill you."

Peiper spilled his horror story, and the recorder caught all of it.

"I was under the command of SS General Joseph Dietrich, commander of the Sixth Panzer Army. I commanded the spearhead of the attack. Dietrich was a former bellboy and street bum. He had no military training. So I moved ahead in my Royal Tiger tank. On our way into Bullingen for fuel, we captured sixty-two prisoners. An SS sergeant ordered the first twelve POWs mowed down with machine guns. I stopped him, so the remaining prisoners were forced to help us fuel the tanks. After that, I realized we couldn't carry the prisoners. I ordered thirty of them shot. We ran into your Battery B of your 285th Field Artillery, which came out of the Hurtgen Forest. There were one hundred forty men in Battery B rolling into Baugnez. We fired on them, and your GIs jumped out of their trucks. We captured one hundred twenty of them and took carbines, watches, wallets and gloves, then marched them into a field and mowed them down. Those were *Der Führer's* orders. No mercy. I just did my job."

Jacques left, and told Donovan he had it all on tape.

"I'll have a copy made for you, General."

"Jacques, you'd better put your shirt back on."

Jacques assigned Tompkins and Goodman to stay on top of the Peiper case. When the press scattered, they returned to headquarters to transcribe copies of the tape, one each for them, Donovan and Ludwig.

Jacques rushed back to the Four Seasons Hotel to pick up his bag. The door to his suite was not locked. He pulled out his Beretta and slowly entered the luxurious living room. Seated at the desk was Douglas Milburn, dictating the Peiper story to the New York Daily News. Bill Wallace was using the bedroom phone to telephoto his exclusive pictures. When Doug finished his report, he hugged Jacques.

"This is one of the best news beats I've had in years, thanks to you and Bart."

"For heaven's sake, Douglas, don't use any pictures of me or use my name in the story."

"We know better than that, Jacques."

"I'm flying back now. Do you want a ride to Washington?"

"No, we're staying a couple of days and then we're off to Bonn. Thanks."

"Keep the suite - it's paid for," Jacques said, then he left.

☆ ☆ ☆ ☆

Saturday, May 24, 1952 - Washington

When Jacques arrived in Washington, the newspapers and radio stations were in a feeding frenzy.

Spring in the nation's capital was in full bloom. The lawns were deep green. The tree's boughs were laden with a variety of leaves. Flowers of every hue were in abundance on lawns and in gardens. The vernal sun was benignly shining through a gentle warm breeze, fluttering flags and awnings intermittently.

Jacques, Christina and Joyce took the children to the zoo on Saturday. Bart and Elizabeth put the top down on the Cadillac convertible and drove to Chesapeake Bay, where they dined on the famous soft-shell crabs at a waterfront restaurant. It was a day devoted to romance. There was no discussion of Bart's mission, other than the disclosure of his imminent return to Washington.

"How did you arrange that?" Elizabeth asked breathlessly.

"I'll be doing a nine-to-five at the Pentagon. Bradley is setting up offices for me. Monday morning I have a session with the President, after which I fly to Fort Leavenworth to wind up affairs there."

"Bart, I'm thrilled, and the children will be happy."

☆ ☆ ☆ ☆

Monday, May 26, 1952 - 1700 hours - Fort Leavenworth

Soon after arrival, Bart and Jacques convened a meeting of the U.S. Attorneys, the CIA staff and the prosecution team in a large conference room at the Disciplinary Barracks. After Bart updated the gathering on Jacques' exploits in Munich, they got down to business.

"Now, listen up," Bart said. "Here are my plans. I'll be moving into the Pentagon on Monday, June 3rd. General Bradley is setting up a secure section close to his offices. Our prosecution team and the CIA group here will operate from there, preparing for the major trials in February, 1953. While Nuremberg took eight months to prosecute the Nazi leaders, I am going to try for several trials to be held simultaneously. I'd like to conclude this whole process in three to no more than four months."

"That's quite a target, Bart," Gideon Cartman said.

"Gideon, we can try. We are going to have a camera in the court, plus pool coverage. I want to get this horror story across to the younger generations as dramatically as we can. Most youngsters don't know anything about these Nazi beasts. The attention span of today's kids is that of a gnat. Our education system from high school through college doesn't carry it in the history curriculum. It's our job to inform them and never let them forget. Where the hell is the outrage in our complacent society?" Bart heatedly declared. "In fact, as an afterthought, I'll prod the press to survey and poll these youngsters about such names as Hitler, Bormann, Goering, Goebbels, Himmler, to name a few."

"A lot of dirt will come out during these trials," Jacques interjected.

"You better believe it. I'll bet Kennedy's, Lindberghs and the royals' gold-plated asses will be tarnished," Bart snapped. "Plus a few other high-and-mighties. Yes, the brave British people fought and died to protect their 'realm'!"

"What about our prisoners?" Tony Fuentes asked.

"Glad you mentioned it."

"We'll rotate you each week to be here checking on them. Maybrook, Sedgwick, Tony, Berger, Sophia and, if Bradley approves, Captain Esta Arnold. I'll prepare an assignment sheet after I pull your names out of a hat to set the order of rotation. Any questions?"

"Sir, I'd like a minute alone with you," Cartman said.

"Okay. Now, the rest of you can meet here at 2200 hours this evening for affirmation of our plan by Judge Will Ross."

The group gathered around Jacques, peppering him with questions about his Munich trip. Cartman and Bart retired to the opposite end of the large room.

"What's on your mind, Counselor?"

"Bart, three of our guys and I realize that our terms as assistant U.S. Attorneys will end when the new president takes office in January, '53. The four of us are reserve officers. Is there a chance that we can be activated as participants in the trials? You could use the help. We're all pros."

"You'd be giving up a wide spread in salaries," Bart countered.

"That doesn't matter. We've talked it over. However, by doing this, we don't want to wind up in Korea," Cartman laughed.

"What's your rationale, Gid?"

"Two of us are Jews and were shaken by what we learned here. On the self-serving side of the request, we realize that the exposure would immeasurably enhance our futures in the private sector."

"Gideon, I had no idea you were Jewish. Not that it matters."

"So is Morton Aldrich. Neither of us is temporal. But we are aware of our roots."

"What was your rank, Gideon?"

"Major."

"And Aldrich?"

"Major."

"How about the other two?" Bart asked.

"Dwight Seagrave, a captain, and Justin Palmer, a major. The four of us have good records as prosecutors."

"For the nonce, Gideon, your team will report to me at the Pentagon to continue your current tasks. First, I want to clear it with Attorney General McGranery. After that, I'll have to ask General Bradley to effect the activation. Do you guys still fit in your uniforms?" Bart laughed as he scribbled the four names on his legal pad.

☆ ☆ ☆ ☆

Friday, May 30, 1952, Memorial Day - 10am - Fairfield, Connecticut
Plans had been made for the family to spend the holiday at the Milburns'

sixteen-acre enclave in exurban Connecticut.

A deep blue sky and a warm sun brought an 85-degree temperature, as Dr. and Mrs. Milburn greeted the two carloads when they pulled off Merwin's Lane into Jennie Lane, a private road to the compound. Bunny Milburn and a tall stranger waved at the arrivals from the front steps of the tri-level house. Michael and Jenny ran to their grandparents. Douglas and Constance suddenly appeared from the huge garage. They greeted Bart, Elizabeth, Jacques, Christina and the four children, Jenny, Michael, Matthew and Katherine. He gave Joyce Laurent a special hug. Mrs. Bishop and Elsie ran after the children. Constance Luce walked down the driveway, joining the hugging and kissing. Harris, the family butler, and two maids brought the luggage into the house. Bart and Elizabeth ran up the five steps to the front door, then both kissed Bunny.

"Say hello to Jeffrey Rothschild, my dear friend," Bunny said.

Elizabeth shook his hand with a big smile on her beautiful face. Bart reached out and felt a strong handclasp. "Jeffrey, nice to meet you," he said.

"I've been looking forward to meeting the legendary General Milburn," Rothschild declared. His social charm was immediately apparent. His physique was athletic.

Bart, at first glance, liked what he observed. He hugged Bunny again and kissed her cheek, then he noticed a diamond ring dangling on her necklace, so he whispered in her ear, "Does that ring mean what I think it does, Bunny?"

"I'll tell you all about it later. Let's take a swim."

Jeannette and Norris Milburn - Bart's parents - were seated at the pool house facing the huge pool, delightedly watching their grandchildren. The four children were splashing Jacques, while Christina sat on the steps watching the byplay. One at a time, Jacques lifted Michael, then Jenny, followed by Matthew and Katharine, throwing each of them into a diving mode. All four were excellent swimmers, but were not allowed to go into the deep end. Bart, Elizabeth, Christina, Constance, and Joyce joined in the aquatic fun.

Harris and the maids, Molly and Agnes, were busy at the pool house kitchen preparing lunch. Bart lit the barbecue. A buffet table was set up in front of the pool house. Salads, shrimp, smoked salmon, baked salmon, cold duck, chicken, potato salad, cole slaw, pickles and chili were generously spread on the table. Bart took charge of the hot dogs and hamburgers at the barbecue. An assortment of soft drinks were in the refrigerator. A large urn contained iced tea.

The children surrounded Bart, who dispensed the charcoal-broiled hot dogs. The men opted for hamburgers. The ladies chose the buffet. Dr. Milburn had built an ideal children's playground of swings, slides and a mini-merry-go-round, electrically operated. Doug and Jacques teamed in a tennis doubles match with Bart and Jeffrey on the professionally built court. They were evenly matched. However, Jeff Rothschild and Bart proved to be a notch better than the others, so three sets were enough.

"Jeff, where did you learn how to play like that?" Bart asked as he toweled himself.

"At Phillips Exeter, and after the war at Harvard."

"After the war? Were you in it?"

Rothschild smiled. "Yes, much to my parents' dismay."

"How come?"

"I graduated Exeter in 1944 at seventeen years of age. A friend of mine and I lied about our ages and joined the Marines. After training at Parris Island, I was sent to the Pacific."

"See any action?"

"A little at the Solomon Islands and Iwo Jima in February of 1945."

"Don't be modest. Medals and rank?"

"Purple Heart, Bronze Star, and field promotion from sergeant to lieutenant."

"Quite impressive. Where's the wound?"

Rothschild lifted his tennis trunks and exposed a scar on his hip.

"I got hit on the last day of the battle on March 17, 1945, St. Patrick's Day and my mother's birthday," he laughed. "I was laid up for six weeks. They removed the bullet, but I had a bad infection."

"Was that the end of it for you?"

"No, I was back in island-hopping action. In late July I was assigned to the USS Missouri, and on August 14th I saw MacArthur accept the Japanese surrender."

"Fabulous experience. When did you get out?"

"That's a story in itself. I was on guard duty at his Tokyo headquarters. MacArthur was coming out of his office and I saluted. He stopped and asked how old I was. I told him the truth - eighteen. He asked me about my education and I admitted I was seventeen when I joined. *You graduated Exeter?* he asked. *Well, I'm giving you your honorable discharge, if you promise to finish your education in college.* I was shipped out. Visited my parents and was accepted at Harvard in late September of 1945. So here I am, sir."

"Good gad, don't call me sir."

"Okay."

"How do you feel about my sister Beatrice?"

"I love her."

"How does she feel about you?"

"I'm waiting. I proposed, gave her a ring. She said she'll wear it on a necklace for a while and will wear it on her finger if the answer is yes."

"I calculate your age as twenty-five or twenty-six - am I right?"

"I'll be twenty-six on July 10th."

"Well, if you truly love her, remember the old saying, *Faint heart ne'er won fair lady.* By the way, are you related to the famous Rothschilds?"

"Yes, distantly."

"You are of the Jewish faith?"

"Would that make a difference?"

"Hell no, I'm on your side, friend."

Bunny, Joyce, Constance and Christina were chatting with Jeannette Milburn at poolside. The svelte, youngish matriarch was regaling the girls with anecdotes about the foibles of her clientele at Maison Jeannette.

She cautiously left out their names, spanning Hollywood stars, society doyennes and the *wannabes*.

Peals of laughter rang out. Douglas, Dr. Milburn and Jacques were drinking cold beers and laughed in reaction to the musicality of the ladies' hilarity. Bunny noticed Bart and Jeffrey in deep conversation at the bench alongside the tennis court. She nervously toyed with the ring on her necklace.

The weekend proved to be a joyous bonding of the Milburns. They visited the Pequot Yacht Club and were treated to a tour of Long Island Sound on a friend's yacht. Joyce was entranced with the beauty of the shoreline. Douglas pointed across the sound.

"That's Long Island - New York just across the sound. This side of the water just south of here is Westport. There were battles fought here during the Revolutionary War with England. See, there's a statue of a Minuteman in Westport."

"What's a Minuteman?" Joyce asked.

"Our armed men were called that because they were ready to fight on a minute's notice."

Bunny and Jeffrey were in deep conversation at the aft deck of the yacht. She removed the ring from her necklace and handed it to him. She extended the ring finger on her left hand. He carefully slipped it on. They kissed.

☆ ☆ ☆ ☆

Sunday evening

The decision to avoid the holiday traffic was unanimous, so they all agreed to leave early Monday morning. During dinner, Bunny, wearing Jeffrey's ring, held it up and announced her engagement. Bart raised his wine glass and toasted the couple. Dr. and Mrs. Milburn beamed. Douglas, Jacques, Christina, and Joyce joined in the tributes.

Two other announcements followed. Jacques rose, and with a wide grin, declared, "I am proud to inform my family here this evening that Christina has consented to become my wife."

An uproar of approval filled the room. When the joviality subsided, Joyce rose.

"I have a bit of news to share with my new family."

All faces turned to her in anticipation. Jacques, an expression of concern on his face, mused, *I hope she's not hooked by some guy.* After a short pause and a few *hear, hears*, she declared, "I was not going to mention this until Wednesday, but in the spirit of all the good news here, I'll let the cat out of the bag."

"Come on, don't hold us in suspense," Bart urged.

"Well, it's not final yet, but I'm not flying back to Washington with all of you. I'm booked on a flight to Boston for an interview at Harvard Tuesday morning."

"What for, Joyce?" Jacques asked.

"Thanks to Dr. Steelman, or possibly President Truman, I've been recommended for a professorship to teach French there, as well as to lecture on

Behind the Iron Curtain conditions in East Germany."

"Fabulous!" Bart exclaimed.

"When did this happen?" Douglas intervened.

Elizabeth answered, "I knew about it. While you men were at Fort Leavenworth, I answered the phone and it was Steelman calling for Joyce. After she spoke to him, we decided to keep it a secret."

☆ ☆ ☆ ☆

Monday, June 2, 1953 - Arlington, Virginia

Bart and his team settled in their new quarters at the Pentagon, across the Potomac River from the nation's capital. The U.S. Attorneys marveled at the five-story building, set on thirty-four acres. They were awed by the magnitude of the nation's defense nerve center. General Bradley visited the prosecution section and welcomed the group. Bart walked back to the general's office and proposed the activation of U.S. Attorneys Gideon Cartman, Morton Aldrich, Dwight Seagrave and Justin Palmer.

"Have you cleared this with McGranery?"

"Yes, he figured they were lost to his department through the trials in 1953."

"Fine, I'll put it through today."

Bart handed him a sheet detailing all the names and necessary information.

"I'll recommend their return to reserves on request," Bradley said. "By the way, Bart, the capture of Peiper has the media in a delirium. Ed Murrow called me. He's doing a two-hour reprise on the Battle of the Bulge. He wanted me to comment on the capture of Peiper and appear on his show. I declined, but allowed him to record some of my remarks. I won't ask you how your brother happened to scoop his colleagues."

Bart started to answer, but Bradley smiled and held his hand up as a stop sign.

"Thank you, General."

"Incidentally, both you and Jacques deserve medals for that coup, which was brilliant. I'll mention it to the President. Now get to work."

Bart saluted and returned to his new office. He sent for the four U.S. Attorneys.

"Men, I hope your uniforms still fit. Also, you'd better start practicing your salutes. You'll be activated shortly."

They laughed.

"It's *Bart* for the present, though?" one asked.

He nodded.

"We've got to find living quarters, Bart," Cartman noted.

"On that subject, men, a little advice. Rents in Arlington and environs are much lower than D.C. You will get an allowance out of my budget for quarterage."

Captain Arnold handed him a note, indicating that the CIA director, General Smith, had called.

"All right, men, scoot. I need privacy," Bart ordered.

As soon as the room was cleared, he picked up his private phone and dialed directly to General Smith. "Milburn here, Beedle."

"Bart, we've hit a jackpot. Nogales found the Höss diary. It arrived here about an hour ago. I've been perusing it. Fascinating reading about Auschwitz. In part, it's self-serving. He was a devious, lying bastard, but there's enough in there for the trial. The savagery of those Nazi animals is almost incomprehensible. They killed two and a half million there. Seems like a contest between death camps as to who could kill the most," he added, sighing disgustedly.

"How soon can I have it?"

"I am having copies made for safety's sake and will have it over to you within the hour."

When it arrived, Bart closed his door and asked his assistant, Sergeant Louis Harding, to hold all calls, except for the White House and high brass. He read the Höss diary and scribbled notes on a legal pad. His visceral reaction brought a kaleidoscopic reel of depressing memories to mind. He sent for the prosecuting team and discussed the highlights, then asked that the Waffen SS prisoners be combed for Auschwitz personnel.

☆ ☆ ☆ ☆

Sunday, July 6, 1952 - New York City

The wedding of Constance Luce to Douglas Milburn was held in the ballroom of the Waldorf Astoria. It was reported as one of the most glittering social events of the year. The two hundred invitees consisted of a melange of socialites, actors, directors, producers, newspaper reporters and editors, politicos, and the entire cast of the recently closed hit show *California*. Marine General Lloyd Campbell and a cadre of Douglas' war buddies were lined up. The bridegroom and his best man, Bart Milburn, in full dress uniform, awaited the bride. Peter Duchin's orchestra played the wedding march.

Constance, beautiful as ever, and wearing a wedding gown designed by Jeannette Milburn, was escorted by her father, Millard Luce, slowly through the Marine phalanx, with Michael and Jenny holding the train of her gown. Federal Judge Frederick Van Pelt Bryant performed the wedding ritual and delivered a serious message on the sanctity of marriage.

Douglas kissed the bride and led her to the dance floor for a waltz. Bart tapped his shoulder and danced away with Connie. Elizabeth, the maid of honor, joined Douglas and whirled away. The guests reveled to the sweet melodies of the Duchin Orchestra, playing classics of Cole Porter, Irving Berlin and show tunes of Rodgers and Hammerstein, who also were present.

After a sumptuous lunch, the bride and groom, flanked by the Luce and Milburn families, formed the nuptial's receiving line. After hugging and kissing the family, the newlyweds ran through the double doors. They changed clothes in their suite and made their way to the Waldorf garage. A limo rushed them to Idlewild Airport for their honeymoon flight to Paris and on to Cap d'Antibes in the south of France.

☆ ☆ ☆ ☆

Wednesday, July 23, 1952 - Arlington, Virginia

The next two months were devoted to intensive preparation for the prosecution of the Nazis. The team was collecting archival material from over twenty European countries. Research was being conducted by an expanded team from the CIA, Army Intelligence, the British MI6, the French GDSE, and West Germany's anti-Nazi intelligence team set up by Chancellor Konrad Adenauer. Poland, Denmark, Belgium, Norway, and others were combed for atrocity details.

Bart addressed a meeting of over one hundred and twenty-five men and women from the CIA and all the armed-forces intelligence units. All of them had received security clearances. He stressed the necessity of maintaining secrecy about their mission. "I have met with the leaders of the American Jewish Joint Distribution Committee, known as the JDC. It was founded in 1914. All through the period 1933 through 1945, they worked underground helping Jews escape the Nazi hordes. As of this time, they are helping displaced Jews and those who seek to get to Israel. They will give us the fullest cooperation. Questions?"

"General, what about the Israelis?" Major Jordan Coxe asked.

"Glad you asked. The Mossad, which is the counterpart of our CIA, has been very cooperative to date, and will work hand and glove with us all the way. However, the reason I haven't assigned any of you to Israel is the fact that agent Jacques Laurent, head of the Nazi desk, and I have a close personal relationship with them and Prime Minister Ben-Gurion. By the way, in your travels, if you pick up any leads on Adolf Eichmann, report to me or Jacques Laurent here immediately. The Israelis are searching for him, and it becomes *quid pro quo*. They help us, we help them. Understood?"

Bart invited Jacques, Maybrook, Sophia Carrera, Berger, Fuentes, Sedgwick, Majors Cartman, Aldrich, and Palmer, and Captain Seagrave to join him at the podium.

"These people are our front-line team in preparation for the trials. The CIA people here will collect the information you send us. Now, let me stress a few points. You have been chosen because we believe you're dedicated to this cause. Anyone who has any qualms about your role in this cause, and I emphasize *cause,* get the hell out. There won't be any recriminations on my part. This has to be an all-out effort. I want every detailed atrocity committed by these Nazi vermin reported. If there is a drop of anti-Semitism in your skulls, quit now. I don't want you. There are two kinds of anti-Semites - the uneducated ne'er-do-wells and the snobby closet kind. Meld them and you have a Nazi. We are not just preparing for the usual pro-forma type of trial. There is more than enough evidence on hand to convict these dissolute sociopaths who wear the mark of Cain. Nuremberg tried a handful. We've got the most evil murderers in the history of civilization. This is a crusade. We want the world to see and hear the most monstrous crimes that challenge the hallucinations of madmen. You will be shown films of these atrocities that will affect your minds, hearts and stomachs. I've been to these camps. Words cannot describe the heinousness and horrors of the crimes committed by these sociopathic scum. Are you with me?" Bart asked.

The audience rose as one and applauded.

"Thank you, and go get 'em," Bart said. His front-line team joined him in the conference room.

"General, if I may say so, that was the best locker-room sendoff I've ever heard," Major Aldrich commented.

"All right, folks, we have some pragmatic political problems to sort out," Bart said.

"Shall we take notes, sir?" Captain Esta Arnold asked.

"No, not necessary. Here's what we're facing. The political conventions in Chicago are over. It's Eisenhower vs. Stevenson. I've met with both of them to brief them on the trials. In my opinion, Stevenson doesn't have a chance. Our next Prez will be Ike. The question is, *Will he back us the way Truman has?*"

☆ ☆ ☆ ☆

Friday, July 25, 1952 - 1 p.m. - the White House
Truman arranged a lunch meeting of CIA Director General Smith, Bart Milburn, Attorney General McGranery, General Bradley, and Speaker of the House Sam Rayburn. Bart was momentarily surprised and disturbed by the presence of Rayburn.

"General Milburn, rest easy," Truman began. "Speaker Rayburn has been fully briefed by me about your Nazi coup. His lips are sealed. Sam, a close friend of mine, is the most savvy and highly respected politician by both sides of the aisle. This luncheon was requested by General Smith, the subject being Eisenhower and Stevenson with relation to the Nazi trials."

"General Milburn, your accomplishments deserve our nation's thanks. I personally congratulate you," Rayburn said.

"Thank you, sir."

"Bart, feel free to voice your apprehensions over your planned trials and any possible interference by a new administration," Truman said.

"Though I'm not political, nor am I a pollster, having observed the two candidates, it is my firm belief that Ike will be our next President."

"Regretfully, the President and I share your prediction," Rayburn agreed.

"The trouble, Sam, is that Stevenson doesn't have the fire in his belly, and Ike is a war hero," Truman observed.

"The Dulles brothers will be important members of Ike's administration," Bart said. "They have much to hide about their pre-war activities. In an open series of trials, revealing their German clients could be very embarrassing. Others will try to cover up Joe Kennedy's, Lindbergh's, the royals', and other Nazi supporters' roles relating to the Third Reich. The prosecution won't bring it out. It will emanate from Hitler's defense."

"That's a point well taken," General Smith said.

"Mr. President, I want to repeat my intent. If there is an attempt by the Dulles brothers to smother these trials, I'll condemn it publicly. I'll appear on every talk show to expose a cover-up," General Bradley heatedly declared. "Personally, I don't think Ike will hinder the wide-open trials. I know the man."

The subject was discussed and analyzed. After an hour of dissection, Speaker Rayburn suggested that Bart proceed full tilt with his trial preparation.

"The campaign will get under way on Labor Day," Rayburn said. "Let's keep track of it. By October, the polls will indicate which way the wind blows. If they show Ike in a big lead, I recommend an off-the-record meeting, Mr. President, with Eisenhower. He asked you to keep the capture of Hitler and his minions off the record. He now owes you a forthright position on these trials."

"At this point, Mr. President, may I delineate our plans? A full and open trial, microphones in the court, for the world to hear Hitler and his gang of murderous thugs in person," Bart explained. "We want the fullest coverage by the media. This is a crusade to educate the postwar generations. Nuremberg didn't get the coverage it deserved, according to Justice Jackson."

The discussion turned to the method and the day of the announcement of Hitler's capture. Finally, Truman addressed the question.

"Inauguration Day is January 20th. I will suggest a joint announcement with the President-elect on Thursday, December 11."

☆ ☆ ☆ ☆

Saturday, July 26, 1952 - Buenos Aires

Ambassador Franklin Withers traced Bart Milburn from the State Department to the White House operators. They rang the Rock Creek Park home, where Stanley, the butler, answered, "Milburn residence."

"We have Ambassador Withers on line, calling for General Milburn."

"One moment, ma'am."

Stanley scurried to the pool house. Bart and Jacques were playing with the children in the pool. Stanley put an extension phone on a glass table. Bart, aware that the call was important, lifted himself out of the water, donned a terrycloth robe, reached for a cigarette and lighter on the table, and said, "Milburn here."

"General, I have Ambassador Withers calling from Buenos Aires."

"Put him on, please."

"Franklin, this must be important to call on a Saturday."

"Yes, I think it is. Two things, General. Eva Peron died this morning. I'm sure you'll hear it on the news, but that is not the reason I'm calling."

"I've gathered that. What's up?"

"The first I heard of it was a phone call from Eva's sister Elisa Duarte. She told me she was delivering a sealed message for the Countess de Cordoba on instructions from Eva before she died. It was to be sent in the event of her death. Eva's personal maid, Olivia, brought it to me here at the embassy."

"Most interesting. Is it marked *Confidential*?"

"Yes, *Personal and Confidential*. I'm sorry to disturb you, but I don't know where to reach Sophia. I know she's on your staff, and I thought it might be important, so can you help?"

"By all means. It was very proper of you to call me. I appreciate it. As you know, I have been activated and we are working at the Pentagon. She's there with me. Could you pouch it to my attention at the Pentagon and I'll give it to her?"

"I'll do just that. It should be there sometime Monday. Congratulations on your second star, General."

"Much obliged. How's the weather?"

"It's our winter here, so it's cold and overcast."

☆ ☆ ☆ ☆

Monday, July 28, 1952 - 2 p.m. - the Pentagon

A State Department messenger delivered a legal-sized manila envelope to the attention of General Milburn, and Bart buzzed Sophia Carrera. "The envelope just arrived."

She breathlessly knocked and entered the general's office.

"Do you want to open it here?" he asked.

"Of course."

He handed her the wax-sealed missive. She reached over his desk and picked up a miniature sword-shaped letter opener. She slashed the top of the packet and withdrew a thick, legal-sized white envelope. It was hand-addressed to the Countess de Cordoba with the legend, *Not to be opened until after my death,* and signed *Eva Peron.*

"Go ahead and read it by yourself. If it concerns our project, highlight it for me," Bart said.

Sophia walked to the large window overlooking the Potomac River and silently absorbed the contents of Eva Peron's letter. Bart was deep in classifying defendants and specific crimes committed. Sophia returned to her chair, waiting to capture his attention. He looked up at her and noticed her somber expression.

"Barton, this is quite a document. In short, she details the Argentine-Nazi connection. She describes almost everything in my report of her statements to me about the Nazi submarines surrendering to Argentina. Bormann was there when all that gold, currencies and jewelry were unloaded. She reveals the duplicity of the Swiss banks in laundering the plunder. She wants me to find Bormann and have him send her half of the loot to a priest, Father Benitez, for an Eva Peron foundation to help the *descamisados*, the shirtless ones. She admits helping the Nazis in the early days, but she turned on them because of their atrocities and their lies to her. That sums it up."

"What do you think caused her to put that confession in writing?"

"Perhaps her guilt and her attempt to make peace with God. You'll see in the letter that she has begged Peron to help the Jews and deport the Nazis from Argentina. It's a *mea culpa*."

The intercom in Bart's office announced a call from General Bradley. "Bart, drop whatever you're doing and come to my conference room on the double."

"Sophia, make a dozen copies of Eva's letter. We'll discuss it later," he said as he ran out of the room.

A group of stone-faced officers sat around the oval conference table, maps spread in front of them. The Joint Chiefs of Staff grimly looked up at Bart.

"General Milburn, that damned Revenge Plan may become a living nightmare," Bradley said.

"Which element, sir?"

"We've been tracking two Eagle ships heading in the direction of the Panama Canal - one on the Pacific side and the other on the Atlantic. Since the alert's been on, we've had the Eagle Shipping fleet under surveillance. The one in the Atlantic is an old cargo freighter, the Eagle Lady, which picked up a load of fruit and coffee in Santo Domingo in the Dominican Republic. It's slowly en route toward the canal."

"How close is it?" Bart asked.

"About one hundred miles from the first lock of the canal," Admiral Prince estimated. "She's plowing along at eight knots."

Bradley turned to Air Force Chief of Staff General Maxwell Taylor and asked, "What's the story on the other ship?"

"This is an old cargo ship, which picked up a load in China. She's the Eagle King. She's been at sea almost a month. Her course took her from the South China Sea for a stop at Mindanao, Philippines. She is now three hundred miles out, headed toward the Pacific lock. She is riding low, which means she's loaded with cargo or explosives."

"We've got four destroyers, two on each side of the canal," Prince said. "The Coast Guard is out there as well. There are cruisers for backup."

"Just on the side of caution, we've got to stop them within no less than thirty miles from canal entrances and board the vessels," Bradley said.

"What happens if they don't comply?" Bart asked.

"We deep-six them," Prince said vehemently.

"What about the crew?" Bradley asked.

"We'll give them sufficient warning to lower their lifeboats or jump ship," the admiral replied.

"The next few days should be very interesting," Maxwell Taylor observed.

"General Bradley, if this pans out as contemplated, I hope we can save a few members of the crew. I would like to question them. One of our prisoners mentioned that Hitler-Nordheim had a backup gang to do his derring-do," Bart said.

"We'll ask our destroyers to pull some out of the water or to capture the whole bunch," Prince said.

"Well, Barton, my boy, it appears that your warnings were not in vain. This madman Hitler and his Revenge Plan may do some damage elsewhere," Bradley declared.

"Sir, I appreciate being apprised of this piece of intelligence. I respectfully request permission to follow day-to-day developments and, at the moments of truth, be permitted to follow the action."

"That's precisely why I sent for you, Bart. We've set up a situation room, and Admiral Prince will brief you."

Prince said, "General Milburn, the room is next door to my office. We are all set up now to track both ships. By the way, your friend Admiral Thomas has left Guantanamo and is aboard the cruiser Knoxville. He is commanding the Atlantic operation. Admiral Cornelius Putnam will command the Pacific side. There is an odd twist to this. There has been communication to both ships in Arabic, German, and Spanish. We've assigned six interpreters in relays for twelve-hour duty to monitor their radio messages. So far, we've not yet pinpointed a Morse code operator in Colon, Panama, in contact with the ships. We haven't decoded the languages yet. We've flown a mobile scanner to Colon to work with the local police in the search of the dot-dasher. You are welcome at any time, day or night, to the situation room."

"No use wasting your valuable time, Bart, until that thirty-mile limit we've set up. When they get close, you'll be notified. Just leave your whereabouts with the duty officer," Bradley advised.

"We've got twelve fighter planes and four bombers standing by at Guantanamo Naval Base. We've got spotter planes flying high, tracking them," Taylor announced.

"Go on, Bart, take a look at the situation room," Bradley suggested.

☆ ☆ ☆ ☆

Tuesday, July 29, 1952 - Mossad headquarters, Tel Aviv, Israel

Ariel Rabin, director of Israeli intelligence, placed a call to Bart at his home. Bart, fast asleep, opened one eye and glanced at his luminous digital clock. It registered 5:16 a.m. Elizabeth turned her back to him and dug her head deep into her pillow. Bart answered, "Yes?"

"Sorry to wake you, General; this is Ariel Rabin."

"Hold it - I'll take it in my den."

He stopped at the bathroom, splashed water on his sleepy face and went downstairs to his den.

"What the hell time is it there?"

"It's 3:19 p.m. our time."

"What's so important that you had to wake me?"

"I waited as long as I could. Your alert paid off. About two hours ago, we spotted a vegetable truck carrying tomatoes, underneath which was a ton of ammonium nitrate. It was being driven by a kamikaze Arab on his way to join Allah. He was headed at high speed toward the Knesset, our parliament, which was in session in the opera house at Allenby Square near the waterfront."

"My God, what happened?" a suddenly wide-awake Bart exclaimed.

"I'll let Colonel Yitzhak Rabin and Sean Briscoe give you the details. I'm putting you on the speakerphone."

"General Milburn, this is Colonel Rabin. Briscoe and I were walking from

Moghrabi Square at Allenby Road when we saw this wild-eyed idiot come racing and weaving through traffic. We yelled at security police in front of the building, *Shoot at his tires!* Sean and I had sidearms. We stopped traffic and fired at the truck's tires simultaneously with the police. All the tires went flat, and the truck turned over on its side, tomatoes rolling all over the area. Fortunately, there was no explosion."

"Bart, this is Sean."

"Who else would it be with that accent?"

"After grabbing the stunned driver, we very carefully searched under the load of remaining tomatoes. We found the dynamite intact. We had the area cleared and had the Knesset evacuated. Our explosives unit carefully took the load away."

Rabin cut in. "Bart, we've just finished our *polite* interrogation of the driver. After we threatened to boil him in pork fat, he postponed his appointment with Allah. Here comes the jackpot."

"I'm listening."

"We have reason to believe that his brother is in your possession," Rabin chuckled.

"Not Ahmed the Cobra?"

"Bull's-eye, the very same," Rabin confirmed.

"What are you going to do with him?"

"A firing squad or a life sentence."

"How old is he?"

"Just a young squirt. Twenty-two or twenty-three."

"Fine. I know it won't be a firing squad. But hold him incommunicado. He would be an excellent pawn in our dealings with the Cobra."

"To be quite frank with you, Barton," Rabin said in a serious tone. "We would like very much to have Ahmed in our hands. Any chance of that?"

"It's possible, Ariel, after we milk him dry. Extradition, officially requested, might do the trick. Hold off until I give you the word."

"It's a deal. One more item that may be of interest. For the moment, this has to be between us."

"Agreed."

"We've got a KGB defector. Brought us photos of all the cadavers in Hitler's Viking funeral pyre, plus the copies of all the findings of a half-dozen medical examiners - coroners, as you call them. In short, they calculate that the body is not Hitler's. The carcass had bullet wounds in two ribs and bullet holes in the back of the skull and one in his right shinbone. The right arm - Hitler's arm - was injured in Count von Stauffenberg's assassination attempt on July 20, 1944 - shows no dents or signs of injury. We're doing some more research. I'll keep you informed."

☆ ☆ ☆ ☆

Thursday, July 31, 1952 - Arlington, Virginia
Berger and Jacques had made trips intermittently to Fort Leavenworth.

They were able to identify eight more of the prisoners who served in the execution camps, naming Treblinka, Majdanek, Sobibor, Chelmno, Belzec, Auschwitz, Birkenau, Janoweska, and Buchenwald, as well as two at the Vilma ghettos.

Jacques returned to the office late that afternoon. Berger and Sedgwick remained at Fort Leavenworth, continuing their interrogations. Bart thumbed through a pile of reports on the prisoners. Then the intercom squawk box erupted. "General Milburn, are you there?" Bradley said.

"Yes, sir."

"Showtime, Bart."

"Jacques is with me; may I bring him?"

"Of course. Hurry."

They raced over to the situation room. Bradley and the Joint Chiefs were there. Vice Admiral Leslie Fulton stood at the lighted screen in the darkened room. Two lieutenants handled the telegraphic communications.

On the screen was a mapped outline of the Panama Canal environs, with the Caribbean Sea on the west and the Pacific on the east, due to the strange configuration of Panama. Miniatures of the destroyers and the two Eagle ships were depicted with red-light dots on the targets and green lights on the stalking vessels. Bradley and the Chiefs stood over a table, which was also mapped. Two ensigns moved model ships as called for by the telegraphers.

Bart and Jacques sat alongside three interpreters - Commander Lucas Wagner, fluent in German; Lieutenant George Siegal, expert in Arabic, Aramaic and Hebrew; and Chief Warrant Officer Peter Sanchez, expert in Spanish and Portuguese. At that time, the Eagle Lady was thirty-five miles from the Caribbean entrance to the canal. Admiral Thomas was aboard the cruiser Lincoln, ten miles behind two destroyers closing in on the freighter. Two U.S. Coast Guard cutters were cruising on each side of the western entrance.

On the eastern approach, thirty-two miles back, Captain Terence Grogan was directing operations aboard the cruiser Taft. Admiral Thomas ordered the destroyers to flank the Eagle Lady. At the thirty-two-mile range, the destroyers reached the targeted ship.

"This is the United States destroyer Falcon. Stop. We want to board your ship!" a loudspeaker bellowed.

The Eagle Lady ignored the order and picked up speed. The Falcon fired two warning shots across her bow. Machine-gun fire was directed in return. The cruiser was half a mile away, speeding to the scene.

"Back off fast," Admiral Thomas ordered.

The destroyers did a 180-degree turn and raced away from the freighter. On the Pacific approach to the canal, a similar set of circumstances occurred. Captain Grogan learned that two of his men on one of the destroyers were wounded.

Almost simultaneously, Thomas on his side, and Grogan on the other, ordered, "Battle stations!"

Messages in Arabic and Spanish emanated from the two ships. Within seconds, the cruisers let loose with barrages of cannon fire. The destroyers were speeding away from the firestorm lighting up the night sky. Crews were jumping off the tanker and the freighter. Both ships exploded thirty miles from the approaches to the canal and began to sink. The destroyers were ordered to return to the sinking ships for survivors. Searchlights explored the waters. On the Caribbean side, three men in life jackets were hauled aboard a destroyer and transferred to Admiral Prince's cruiser. Captain Grogan had two survivors brought to his cruiser. In the situation room at the Pentagon, a roar went up.

"That was fast action," Bradley observed.

The telegraphic messages were busily clicking away. All the actions were shown on the screen as the ships were maneuvered on the table map by the ensigns. The same was displayed by the red and green lights on the screen. Lieutenant Paul Wyan began reciting Admiral Thomas's report.

"The freighter fired at us. No injuries. We were forced to attack. The ship was obviously being scuttled as we fired two rounds. It sank fast and exploded on its way down. Three Libyan survivors. Returning to Guantanamo. Any orders to the contrary?"

Bradley dictated, "Great job, Admiral. Wait for Coast Guard to pick up survivors. Head home after that."

Lieutenant Frank Polk said, " I have Captain Grogan reporting."

"Tanker sunk. Two men on destroyer shot. Nothing serious. One barrage and she was listing. Delayed explosion. Only two survivors; believe they are Latinos. Possibly Argentinians. Orders, please?"

Admiral Prince replied, "Do your wounded need hospital care? If so, leave them at Panama Hospital."

"Not necessary. They're in sick bay being attended now. Flesh wounds. Medics report no danger."

"Congratulations, job well done. Have destroyer deliver two survivors to Coast Guard cutter coming your way from Panama. Air Force will fly them to Fort Leavenworth."

"Well, gentlemen, that was a good night's work," Bradley declared.

CHAPTER THIRTY-SIX

Tuesday, September 2, 1952 - Washington

The day after Labor Day marked the end of the summer dog days in the nation's capital. The summer heat emptied the city during August. Bart and the others all returned from the long weekend refreshed and prepared for the arduous task of sorting out key elements of the interrogatories of two incidents that had occurred during August in London and Paris. They were both related to the Revenge Plan. Neither event was fully reported by the media, as Bart related the occurrences to the staff.

General Lloyd Forsythe, director of the MI6, reached Bart in Connecticut on Sunday, August 15, through the White House operators. He detailed a raid that morning in London's Soho section, based on a tip, and rounded up four Nazis and three members of the Aryan Swords from Liverpool. They discovered a cache of AK47s, Walther and Luger handguns, grenades, and two tons of explosives. The Nazis were former low-ranked SS officers. They confessed that the targets were Westminster Abbey, Buckingham Palace, and 10 Downing Street. Prime Minister Churchill insisted that Forsythe notify General Milburn immediately.

Ten days later, on August 25th, the chief of Paris detectives, Felix Gaumont reached Jacques Laurent at home shortly after midnight. Bart, Elizabeth, Christina, Joyce and Jacques were in the den enjoying a nightcap when the phone rang. Bart answered.

"I have a call from Paris for a Mr. Jacques Laurent," the operator announced.

"It's for you, Jacques. Take it in the office."

Jacques entered the office and picked up the phone. "This is Jacques," he said.

"Jacques, are you watching your television?" Felix Gaumont blurted breathlessly.

"No, no. What's up, mon frére?"

"A disaster. Go turn on the t.v."

Jacques raced to the den, flipped the television set to channel four and reached for the extension phone.

"Oh, my," Elizabeth said.

A telephoto showed an explosion in Paris. Edwin Newman was reporting the news from NBC's London desk.

"The tremendous explosion occurred just before dawn," he said. "NBC correspondent Henri Barron is at the scene. He is on the phone. Go ahead, Henri."

"So far we have twenty-six fatalities and eighty-six seriously injured. The explosion occurred on the Champs Elysée two streets this side of the Arc de Triomphe in the center of the Place de l'etoile, which forms the intersection of twelve avenues."

"Hold on, Felix," Jacques said," we are looking at the warzone and listening to a report from the scene. Here, talk to Bart," Jacques said.

Barron continued his report. "Apparently, a large truck and a bus collided leaving traffic snarled. Police were trying to clear the tieup when suddenly the truck exploded. It was a violent blast. The bus was blown to pieces when the gas tank exploded. Earlier, Paris' chief of detectives Felix Gaumont spoke to the press. Here is his statement."

Gaumont appeared on the screen. "This accident was caused by a truckload containing dynamite, nitroglycerin, gunpowder and assorted weapons. Four men in that truck are deceased. We have identified one of the bodies as Ahmed Mali, an Algerian dissident. This is a sad day for France. There will be no further reports while our investigation continues."

Bart advised Gaumont, "Your statement to the press just came through."

"General," he replied," this was a Revenge Plan operation. There is no such person as Ahmed Mali. I called De Gaulle. He approved the coverup."

"My regrets, Felix," Bart said. Here's Jacques."

"Felix, how many prisoners?" Jacques asked.

"We've got two former SS men, wounded but able to talk. Two more Nazis - they're being questioned - and two Arabs for a total of six live ones. There are five more dead, yet unidentified. The worst of it is that twenty-six civilians are dead, eighty-six are seriously injured and maybe a hundred people have minor injuries. I'd love to come to Leavenworth and kill Hitler and everyone of those Nazi SS bastards."

"Mon frére, in due time they'll get their just diserts. Calm down and go back to work. We'll talk tomorrow. Keep us informed. Adieu."

✩ ✩ ✩ ✩

Next day

General Bradley sent for Bart. They discussed the Paris tragedy.

"No doubt about Hitler's Revenge Plan now, Bart. He and his minions are animals," Bradley said.

"I disagree, sir."

"Oh? How so?"

"Animals only forage for food."

"Touché. Okay, let's discuss your report. Bart, I know how hard you worked in covering the concentration camps. You didn't manage to keep a copy of your report, did you?"

"No, I wish I had. After I completed it, I turned it over to General Eisenhower."

"I remember Ike telling me how grim it was. However, he never let me read it. Don't ask me how I know. It wasn't Ike's idea to classify it top secret. If you recall, in '47 Truman appointed that banker, James Forrestal, the first Secretary of Defense, when the department was created. Well, hold on to your hat, son - John Foster Dulles and brother Allen convinced Forrestal to have that report classified. Truman had too much on his presidential plate. So he never saw the report."

"Why, why, why, sir? What were they trying to cover up?"

"Barton, you're a hell of an Intelligence officer, now a two-star general, and above all, a topnotch lawyer. You saw the I.G. Farben operations that were set up at Auschwitz I, Auschwitz II, Birkenau, and Auschwitz III at Monowitz."

"Yes, I saw all three, but they were trying to dismantle them when I was there."

"Well, those plants were built there to use the Jewish slave labor to feed the war machine, their Wehrmacht. It had its factory at Auschwitz III - Birkenau. Those bastards also produced the Zyklon B for the gas chambers where they killed millions of Jews and others."

"General Bradley, I know that. In fact, those Nazi monsters cleared the entire population out of Oswiecim for a fifty-square-mile area to accommodate I.G. Farben."

"Now, Bart, you have to do a little research on how Standard Oil partnered with Farben over the protests of the Du Pont company. Our expertise in the manufacture of tetraethyl lead was vital for the military buildup before we got into the war. It was the Ethyl Corporation, which was owned fifty percent each by Standard Oil and General Motors, and developed tetraethyl lead. It was vital for the Luftwaffe," Bradley added.

"That's scandalous!" Bart exclaimed. "But how does that tie into the classification of my death-camps report?"

"I don't know if the Dulles brothers were involved initially in that intrigue. But, at the behest of someone, or for themselves, they didn't want the I.G. Farben story exploited. I don't know the full reason for Forrestal's suicide. I won't speculate."

"Damn, I never made the connection of Farben to the Auschwitz part of my report. I recall now that General Telford Taylor took over the prosecution of Farben and some twenty-odd defendants at Nuremberg in 1947. I have to talk with Justice Jackson and General Taylor."

"Bart, he might put you together with his deputy Josiah Dubois, who prosecuted the case. He's retired. When ready, we'll talk to the President in an effort to have your report declassified. Also, try to get your hands on the Farben trial. It was nasty."

☆ ☆ ☆ ☆

Friday, October 17, 1952 - Washington
The Supreme Court had been back in session for two weeks when Justice Jackson returned Milburn's call and asked, "How may I help you, General?"

"Mr. Justice, we're very interested in the I.G. Farben trial at Nuremberg."

"Well, as you know, I returned to the bench after my stint with those Nazi lice at Nuremberg. General Taylor succeeded me as chief counsel. He assigned Josiah Dubois to prosecute twenty-four defendants in the I.G. Farben case. One was excused because of illness. He convicted twelve. The sentences by the tribunal were outrageously mild considering the gravity of the crimes. The case, with its pre-war underpinning, is a national disgrace," Jackson said.

"Sir, can we meet?"

"I'll see you in the Shoreham Hotel cocktail lounge at 6:30."

"Looking forward to it, sir."

Nino, the maitre d' at the Shoreham, greeted Bart and led him to a booth at the back of the lounge.

Five minutes later, Nino escorted the jurist to the booth.

"Sorry I'm late, Barton."

"No problem, sir."

"Let's drop the sirs and keep it to Bob and Bart."

Both ordered Harvey's Bristol Cream on the rocks. A clink of the glasses, and they got down to the question at hand.

"Bart, there are three experts on the I.G. Farben scandal, and I emphasize scandal. Those men are, of course, General Taylor, his deputy Dubois, and a man named Joseph Borkin."

"Who is Borkin?"

"He was a former investigator and researcher for the Senate Special Committee to investigate the munitions industry, headed by Senator Gerald Nye. During his stint with the committee, he checked into I.G. Farben Industrie Aktiengesellschaft, and he became obsessed with their machinations. In 1938 he was a technical counsel to the Committee on Patents in the House of Representatives. He always referred to I.G. Farben as his Moby Dick. Later, he headed the patent and cartel section. He wrote a book called *Germany's Master Plan* and, carefully, to this day is monitoring the Farben/Standard Oil/Ethyl deal. He covered every detail of Taylor's Nuremberg prosecution."

"Bob, this IG Farben story has been kept under wraps, or maybe the enormity of the Nazi atrocities became a convenient cloud for the Farben crimes at Auschwitz here in the good old USA," Bart said.

"Had I been privy to the Farben facts twelve years ago when I was Attorney

General, there would have been a special grand jury here in D.C., and quite a number of indictments. I would have asked President Roosevelt to recall Ambassador Kennedy. I would have had Kennedy and John Foster Dulles before that grand jury."

"Do you think they were culpable?"

"The whole deal smells to this day."

"Well, I'll try to find Dubois or Borkin."

"I wish you luck. How goes your investigation and preparation for the trials?"

"Quite well. My present plan is to try Hitler first. However, I am ambivalent about the efficacy of that idea. My reason for the single trial was to destroy his psyche and strip his persona to shreds."

"Barton, that's one way to go. A little advice, though - putting him on trial with some of the heavyweights you have in tow will have the effect of their turning on each other as they did at Nuremberg. As I understand your objective, you are desirous of exposing the atrocities to a complacent society."

"Bob, I have a greater goal than that. I want to ignite the world's sense of outrage that has been lacking pre-war, throughout the war and the present. On top of all that, I want to educate a postwar generation and sear the souls of those who looked the other way. I also want to erase the revisionist prose of those paid jackals who are pushing this anti-Semitic bullshit. The Aryan societies and the pro-Nazi idiots in high places and the gutters. I want to pour the multi-million gallons of blood shed by these hate-filled monsters down the throats of their closet supporters," Bart declaimed passionately.

The jurist sipped his drink and studied the young general for a moment. "I am almost twice your age and not in the best of health, but I wish I had the vigor, the drive and the passion you evince so that I could be alongside you during these trials. Give them hell."

"I'm not going to allow their civilian lawyers to drag out the trials or make a mockery of our justice system," Bart vowed. "I've studied your work at Nuremberg. You were fair, patient and tough. I have the advantage of your prosecution, plus the mountain of evidence that has been gathered over these seven years since the war. I will sublimate your fairness and patience. Toughness is my watchword."

"Oh, to be young again," Jackson sighed.

☆ ☆ ☆ ☆

Tuesday, October 21, 1952 - New York Daily News, 220 East 42nd Street, New York

Douglas Milburn and managing editor Bob Shand were discussing the upcoming trial of Joachim Peiper, to be held in Munich. The Malmedy massacre of the American POWs had gripped the country's attention. The Daily News kept the story alive with daily stories and Sunday features.

"Our circulation has jumped over a hundred thousand readers since you broke the story of Peiper's capture," Shand said.

"What's a hundred thousand to the Daily News? We've got the largest circulation in the country now," Doug laughed.

"Every little bit helps," Shand chuckled.

"Bob, the Peiper trial is set before a military tribunal on Monday, November 10th. I'll be here through Election Day, November 4th. Constance and I will leave two days after that for Paris, where we'll spend the weekend, and then on to Munich."

"How long will this trial take?"

"The word I get is two to three weeks, at the most. My brother, Bart, will be testifying."

"How come?"

"He was an intelligence colonel on Ike's staff, as you know. He discovered the first bodies of seventy-one Americans executed by Peiper."

"Doug, he's a two-star general now. How come he's back in service? I spoke with him at your wedding, but I never asked what happened to his successful legal career."

"Bob, I've never held back on you. We've been close friends. He's been activated from his reserve status by Truman for a top-secret assignment. I expect a sensational announcement from the White House soon. My lips are sealed."

"Doug, I won't press you, but what was this survey or polling you talked Harry Nichols into yesterday? Is that something for publication, or did you take advantage of our city editor?"

"The result of that poll is not for immediate use, but it could fit as a sidebar for my Munich stories or later."

Shand, an Annapolis graduate, coolly lit his pipe, thoughtfully leaned back in his swivel armchair and stared out the window behind his desk. He turned back and lifted several sheets of paper out of his top drawer. "Doug, I have here a strange poll. Let me read the questions to you."

"I know what it says."

"Nevertheless, I am going to air it with you. The following poll was conducted at a major high school in each of New York's five boroughs. *Who is Adolf Hitler?* The same questions followed for Hermann Goering, Rudolf Hess, Heinrich Himmler, Joseph Goebbels, Joachim von Ribbentrop, Alfred Rosenberg, Martin Bormann, and so on. The results are shocking. We used five reporters to gather these answers: Guy Richards, Jack Turcott, Martin Kivel, Kay Gardella, and yourself. That's a lot of talent, Doug, for a sidebar. What's up?"

"Bob, bear with me. Each of us used two hours of the early morning before they were due in for their regular time at 11 a.m. The results will eventually be a shocker to our mature readers and to veterans. I assure you that when the right time comes, you'll be pleased."

"I notice that not one student knew all the names. Eighty-two percent knew none. It's incredible that here we are, seven years after the war's end and the Nuremberg trials, and the ignorance of our youth is appalling," Shand declared. "We ought to do a big feature on this," he added. *"The Holocaust Is Fading Away. Don't We Teach History Any More?"*

"For a moment, Bob, I thought you had me on the griddle."

"Here's one kid saying, *Himmler pitches for the Boston Red Sox.* Another says, *Hitler is a U.S. senator.* A third kid describes von Ribbentrop as a Dutch artist. My Lord, this is *unbelievable!* What possessed you to conduct this poll?"

"Strictly off the record, and I want your word on that."

"You've got it. Go ahead."

"My brother asked me to do it and said it would be very newsworthy soon. This ties in with his secret assignment. After all, Bob, he tipped me to the Peiper story. Enough said?"

"Doug, I had a hunch it was something like that."

☆ ☆ ☆ ☆

Tuesday, November 4, 1952 - Washington - election night

The Milburn family prepared a buffet dinner and invited special guests to join them to listen to the election returns on the radio. Sets were placed in the living room, dining room, and den. Invitees included General Bradley, Senators Styles Bridges and Earle Clements, law partners Austin Graybeal and Martha Arnold; the CIA director, General Smith; and Bart's key staff.

The polls in the East closed at 8 p.m. NBC, CBS and ABC were competing in calling the winning states for the candidates before the full counts were declared. By 11 p.m., long before the West Coast polls had closed, Eisenhower was declared the winner in a landslide by the three networks.

Senator Clements, the Democratic whip, turned to his Republican friend Bridges and said, "Congratulations, Styles. The Senate and the House vote will not be decided until the West Coast returns are in. Right now it's nip and tuck."

"Earle, the Gallup Poll called it right on the button. We'll know our respective fates in the morning."

The guests departed at midnight. Bart and Jacques retired to the den and continued to watch the returns. Elizabeth and Christina retired for the evening. Joyce was in Cambridge, Massachusetts, watching the election results. The phone rang. Jacques answered. "Joyce, what are you doing up so late?"

"The same as you. I have never seen an American election. Is Eisenhower going to be a good President?"

"Time will tell, honey. How does it feel to be a professor at Harvard?"

"I love it. They treat me like a queen here. I'm so happy. Let me say hello to Bart."

"Hi, Joyce. How's everything?" Bart asked.

"Wonderful, thanks to you."

"Will you be home for Thanksgiving?"

"I'll try."

"We're expecting you."

"I'll be there."

Jacques and Bart stayed up very late. The returns showed a winning margin of 6,621,000 for Eisenhower and an electoral landslide of 442 to 89. The Republicans won the Senate by 48 to 47 and one Independent. They also won the House by 221 to 211, with one Independent.

"Jacques, Styles Bridges will be president pro tem of the Senate, and majority leader if he wants it. He's got a bum ticker. He might pass up the leadership. Joe Martin is sure to be the new Speaker of the House," Bart said.

"How will that affect us?"

"Time will tell. Truman had better meet with Eisenhower regarding the announcement of our prisoners and the trials."

☆ ☆ ☆ ☆

Wednesday, November 12, 1952 - Dachau, Federal Republic of Germany

The American military court in Dachau, just outside Munich, was heavily guarded. Security was extremely tight. Media from all over the world were camped outside the confines. The trial of Lieutenant Colonel Joachim Peiper was about to begin in the austere courtroom. Metal detectors were installed at the entry.

The print and electronic press were given special passes. They occupied all the interior rows, with the overflow accommodated in a huge tent in back of the makeshift judicial forum. Only one camera in the courtroom projected sound and video of the proceedings to the overflow media. There was no television transmission by the networks.

White-helmeted, armed Military Police lined the interior and exterior of the court. A line of armed troops surrounded the perimeters of the outer gates of the compound. TV trucks were broadcasting the comings and goings of witnesses. At the press tables, the American contingent consisted of Douglas Milburn of the New York Daily News, Bob Considine of the New York Daily Mirror, Ed Murrow for CBS, Meyer Berger of the New York Times, David Brinkley, syndicated columnist Drew Pearson, Quentin Reynolds for the Scripps Howard syndicate, William L. Shirer, Howard K. Smith, Winston Burdett, Charles Collingwood, Eric Sevareid, Daniel Schorr, David Schoenbrun, Lowell Thomas, Dorothy Thompson, Dorothy Kilgallen of the New York Journal, Westbrook Pegler of the New York World-Telegram, and a host of other journalistic luminaries.

At the defense table was the 37-year-old prisoner, a fashion plate in his made to order double-breasted blue suit, white shirt, red and blue striped tie and red pocket handkerchief. He looked more like a movie actor than the cold-blooded perpetrator of the Malmedy massacre. He was flanked by four high-priced civilian lawyers: two from Zurich, former Judge Karl Wyman and Felix Stamler; and two from Frankfurt am Main, Wolfgang Brumer and Luther Gangfried. Alongside that table, the prosecution team was headed by Judge Advocate General Samuel Le Beau.

The Provost Marshal barked, "Court will come to order. The tribunal is now in session."

Presiding Judge General Lucius Clay and Associate Judges Colonel Winston Andrews and Colonel Donald Lewis, in full dress uniforms, beribboned and bemedaled, entered and seated themselves.

"This is a war-crimes trial and will be conducted under the rules of the *Manual for Courts-Martial, United States, 1951*. This manual has been distributed to counsel for the defense. Is that understood?" Clay declared.

"Yes sir," Karl Wyman replied.

The language of choice was German, and earphones were worn by all participants as well as the media. Interpreters sat beneath the judicial bench.

"The defendant is accused of grave breaches of the Geneva Conventions of 1949, specifically the commission of any acts if committed against persons or property protected by the convention. The issue here, as defined by section 602A: Willful Killing, Torture, or Inhumane Treatment. I will skip the rest and refer to the latter part of that paragraph: Willfully causing great suffering or serious injury to body or not justified by military necessity and carried out unlawfully and wantonly," General Clay said emphatically.

"Your Honor, I wish to object on the grounds that Joachim Peiper is the wrong defendant and should not be on trial here."

"Objection overruled. We'll soon determine his status. How does he plead?"

"Not guilty!" Peiper shouted.

Clay called on the prosecution to present the United States Army's case against Lieutenant Colonel Joachim Peiper, alias Luther Jockler. The tension in the humid makeshift courtroom was evident. The packed room was motionless. Judge Advocate General Samuel Le Beau, fifty-five years old and a former assistant district attorney in Brooklyn, New York, approached the center of the room and faced the tribunal. His scholarly appearance belied his incisive legal skills in attacking the jugular.

"Your Honors, members of the American military: The defendant, Joachim Peiper, is on trial here for one of the most heinous war crimes committed on the field of battle. As a regimental commander of the 1st SS Panzer Regiment and participant, he cold-bloodedly executed three hundred and fifty-three American prisoners of war and one hundred and eleven civilians. This was one of the worst possible abuses of the Geneva Convention. This disgraceful, heartless mass murder occurred during the Battle of the Bulge, deceivingly named by the Nazis as the *Wacht am Rhein*. This despicable form of the human species is responsible for the infamous Malmedy massacre. The prosecution is prepared to prove Peiper's guilt far beyond a reasonable doubt."

"Objection. Members of the tribunal, we ask that the prosecutor's prejudicial descriptions of Mr. Peiper be stricken from the record," Wolfgang Brumer declared.

"Overruled," Clay snapped. "You'll get your own turn, Counselor."

The first witness called was a tall man dressed in civilian garb, with a military bearing. He took the oath and faced Le Beau.

"State your name for the record."

"Kenneth F. Ahrens."

"Did you serve in the American Army during the Battle of the Bulge?"

"Yes, sir. I was a sergeant in Battery B of the 285th Field Artillery Observation Battalion."

"Tell the tribunal what you personally observed in that battle."

Ahrens delivered a detailed account of how his unit rolled into Banguez when they were attacked by Peiper's Tiger Tank regiment. He surmised that over a hundred and twenty-five men of his battery had been forced to surrender to greater forces.

"What happened then?"

"They disarmed us and marched us into a half-frozen field. Tanks, half-tracks and soldiers with machine guns began a mass execution of us while our hands were in the air. Bodies fell all around me and I was shot in the back. I lay still and saw that man firing a machine gun," he said, pointing at Peiper. "He ordered his troops to make sure we were all dead by putting a final shot in the heads of all the bodies. He was laughing, and so were his troops, as they fired shots into the dead and live ones' heads as they lay there."

"How did you manage to survive?"

"Suddenly that Peiper bastard ordered his men to get out of there. They heard General Patton's Third Army tanks approaching. Another guy alongside me yelled, *Let's get out of here!* He, another soldier and I, all three of us wounded, hurried out of there. They fired a few shots at us. We hit the ground. They were gone. We were all bleeding. A Jeep was coming our way. We dove into the bushes. We saw it was an American driving it. We yelled for help. It was Captain Mark Nelson. He took us to the 291st Engineer Combat Battalion. There were a few other survivors. They rushed us to the medics.

"Mr. Ahrens, please remove your jacket and roll up the back of your shirt."

The witness exposed his bare back to the tribunal and turned to the press tables. A long scar indicated that an operation had been performed.

"Please explain that scar, Mr. Ahrens."

"The bullet was in the thoracic area. I had lost a lot of blood. I was injected with penicillin and lots of plasma. A Lieutenant Charles Kivowitz operated on me in the field and saved my life."

"Your witness," Le Beau announced to the defense.

Donning his jacket, Wolfgang Brumer arrogantly approached the witness, who was readjusting his shirt.

"Shall I help you?" he asked in slightly accented English.

"Step back, Counselor," General Clay ordered. "Get no closer than ten feet."

"Sorry, Your Honor. I was only trying to be helpful," he softly apologized, and turned his back to the witness. After a few seconds' pause, he wheeled around and demanded, "Mr. Witness, how can you be so certain that the defendant is the man you described as the man who ordered and participated in the killing of these alleged prisoners of war?"

In a split second, Ahrens pointed his finger at Peiper and, in a cold, measured voice that cut through the courtroom, declared, "That face is deeply etched in my mind. There isn't a day that I don't envision that murdering son of a bitch firing his gun at us. I'd know that face…"

Brumer shouted, "Stop! I object!"

General Clay shouted, "Object to what? You asked the question. Let him finish his answer."

"As I was saying, I would know that face even if I was dead. I'll go to my grave with his evil Nazi face in my mind."

Peiper casually looked at his highly polished, manicured fingernails.

"No further questions," Brumer snarled.

"Call your next witness," Clay ordered.

"The prosecution calls Otto Klausner."

The defense table went into a huddle. The serene posture of Joachim Peiper turned into an excited verbal exchange with his lawyers. All heads turned to the double entry doors. A tall, sallow-faced man, slightly bent over, walked very slowly to the witness stand. He stood long enough to take the oath and wearily plopped into his chair. Obviously he was a sick man. After he had given his name, the questioning went back to German. The interpreters took over.

"Mr. Klausner, did you serve in the Wehrmacht?" Le Beau asked.

"Yes, sir."

"What rank and where?"

"I was a captain in Lieutenant Colonel Peiper's regiment."

"Did you shoot any prisoners of war?"

"No, I did not."

"Did you observe any American prisoners being executed?"

"Yes. I was standing on top of my tiger tank and I was shocked to see Lieutenant Colonel Peiper ordering our men to shoot the Americans. In fact, *he* was shooting, too."

There was a loud gasp from the press and other observers.

Peiper stood up and shouted, "Traitor, liar, you are a dead man!"

Two MPs pushed him back into his seat. The witness pointed his finger at Peiper. "You are a mad dog! If you want to kill me, you'll have to do it before my cancer does."

"How well did you know Joachim Peiper?"

"Not on a personal level. I despised that animal. Everyone knew that he was a favorite of *Der Führer* Hitler. They were two of a kind. Born killers. I am not a Nazi. I was never a Nazi. I was a loyal German drafted into the army. I am a religious man and I go to God to confess my sins," he said as tears rolled down his face.

"*Schweinhund, arschloch!*" Peiper screamed.

"One more outburst and your client will be muted and shackled," Clay roared.

Captain Klausner continued to describe in more detail the horrors that had occurred in the Malmedy massacre. Three more American survivors of the slaughter backed up Ahrens' account.

☆ ☆ ☆ ☆

Thursday, November 13, 1952 - second day - Joachim Peiper trial

The media were absorbed with the trial. The news was broadcast around the world. Reuters, the Associated Press, United Press, International News Service, and all the print media and broadcast networks were reporting all the Q & A of the first day's startling testimony. Newspapers around the world headlined the story. Chief Counsel Le Beau made it clear that he was moving at a fast pace for a short trial. His first witness of this day was another startling surprise.

"The prosecution calls former Major General Erich von Heiser."

After the oath, von Heiser gave his name and former status as a member of the high command under Field Marshal General Gerd von Rundstedt, Supreme Commander of the German Army. The witness preferred to testify in English, in which he proved to be quite fluent.

"General von Heiser, did you participate in the so-called Watch on the Rhine, or Battle of the Bulge, as we Americans call it?"

"Yes, I did until I was captured by the Americans."

"Was Marshal von Rundstedt the commanding officer in this surprise attack at the Ardennes?"

"No, not at all. Tactically, it had all the elements of what your history calls Custer's last stand. Hitler was desperate. We were being slaughtered in the east by the Soviets and in the west by the Americans, British, Canadians, and some French. He pulled forces from the Russian front for this assault. We had lost the air war, the war at sea, and then came this last futile effort."

"You did not approve?"

"Absolutely not."

"Did Rundstedt approve?"

"No, he was a decent but weak man. Eventually he was captured by the British."

"Did any of the top officers order the killing of prisoners of war?"

"Hell, no. We fought by the rules. But Hitler addressed the troops and told them to show no mercy, whatever that meant."

"Did you know the defendant Peiper?"

"Yes, he was an ambitious scoundrel who wormed his way into Hitler's good graces. Hitler promised to make him a general. Von Rundstedt held up his promotion. I heard of his heartless execution of those prisoners only after I was captured."

"Tell the court how that came about."

Von Heiser described how Patton's juggernaut had caught them by surprise. The Third Army had captured thousands of German troops. In detail, he revealed how he had tried to pass himself off as a private.

"I was tricked by a very clever young American intelligence officer by the name of Colonel Barton Milburn. He pulled me and three other German prisoners out of the marching line of POWs. It was a very cold night. He told his sergeant and some of his men to take the three men out back, but he was using this to question me."

"Yes, and what happened then?"

"I made believe I didn't speak English. He told the sergeant to shoot one man at a time if they didn't reveal who I was. I heard a shot, and in English called him cruel and inhuman. One of his men ran in to tell him something, but he wouldn't listen. Then I stood up and announced myself as Major General von Heiser. The soldier who rushed in said that was what he had wanted to tell the colonel. The colonel smiled at me and announced that none of my men had been shot. That was a ruse, very clever. He treated us very well after that. He told me about your American POWs being slaughtered. I was shocked."

"What happened after that?"

"I was a POW for the rest of the war."

"What is your present occupation?"

"Three things. I operate a large dairy farm, which has been in our family for generations; I write books on the meaning of democracy and the evils of communism, and I'm an unpaid advisor to Chancellor Adenauer."

"Did you know that Peiper was using the pseudonym of Luther Jockler?"

"No."

"No further questions."

The defense grilled the general for thirty minutes with little success. The next witness called was Bart Milburn. The six-foot-three figure, in full dress uniform, made an impressive entrance. Prosecutor Le Beau led Bart through von Heiser's account and a validation of his military career.

"General Milburn, please tell the court your role at the Ardennes."

"As an intelligence officer on the staff of the Allied Supreme Commander, General Eisenhower, now President-elect of the United States, I was assigned to ride with General Patton's Third Army. I was there to observe and interrogate prisoners of war."

"You rode in a tank?"

"Yes."

"Tell the court what you observed at Malmedy."

"I stopped my tank at a wooded area. In an icy, muddy field I encountered one of the most shocking, heartrending, gruesome sights I saw throughout the entire war. There were seventy-one dead American soldiers, unarmed, lying face down in the partly frozen mud. I inspected each corpse. There were multiple bullet wounds in their backs and heads. It was obvious that they had been ruthlessly murdered in an unexpectedly heinous execution. I found out later that there were other bodies carted to the woods when Lieutenant Colonel Peiper heard our tanks coming. His murderous gang fled. That cowardly animal wantonly murdered our young soldiers," Bart charged, pointing at the defendant. "Here are pictures of the cadavers."

"We enter these pictures as evidence. No further questions."

The defense declined cross-examination.

"The prosecution calls Jacques Laurent."

The tall, impeccably dressed witness marched quickly to the dock. He was given the oath.

"Tell the court your occupation."

"I am the officer in charge of the Nazi desk of the United States Central Intelligence Agency."

"You were present at the capture of Joachim Peiper, alias Luther Jockler? How was he captured?"

"We had him under surveillance at his office and his home for several days, with the help of General Donovan, the Munich chief of detectives, and two CIA agents. The morning we stopped his limousine, his chauffeur and bodyguard shot a Munich police officer. The police returned fire and killed the chauffeur. Peiper tried to resist, but was subdued."

"That's the Jew bastard that beat the hell out of me!" Peiper screamed.

The press corps scribbled frantically.

"No further questions. Your witness," Le Beau said.

"Once again, I am warning the defense, if your client disrupts this Court, we will take necessary measures to keep him under control," General Clay warned.

Wolfgang Brumer angrily shouted at Laurent, "Did you attack the defendant while he was handcuffed and shackled?"

"Objection," Le Beau loudly declared. "No evidence has been adduced here today indicating such an attack."

"Counsel will join the tribunal in chambers," Clay ordered.

In a specially prepared office in back of the chapel, the three judges, four defense lawyers, and the prosecutor gathered.

"Sam, in spite of no foundation being established, I'm inclined to allow the witness to answer. In the light of the serious implication contained in the question, it is a serious charge that can only be erased with proper mitigation, if the charge is valid," Clay explained.

Judges Andrews and Clay concurred.

"That being the ruling, sirs, this opens a can of worms. The attack referred to by learned Counsel Brumer is on a taped version of the incident. I ask the tribunal's permission to have the witness defend himself by playing that tape. It's an integral part of the record," Le Beau said.

The four defense lawyers were taken by surprise, and argued vehemently with the tribunal in an effort to forestall the tape recording from being played.

"You opened the door, Counselor Brumer," Judge Lewis said, smiling.

Back in the courtroom, Judge Clay ordered Laurent to answer. The question was read back by a stenotypist.

"I went into his cell to interrogate him. He was handcuffed and shackled. He tried to attack me. My recorder was operating, and the entire incident is fully recorded and speaks for itself."

"I move that the recording be turned on and be considered part of the witness's answer," Le Beau said.

"Motion granted," Clay declared.

The courtroom was still. Jacques set the tape recorder on a chair placed in front of him by an MP. The silence in the room signaled the upcoming drama. He turned it to the loud mode. Jacques pressed the "on" button of the recording device. First heard was the sound of the cell door being opened and slammed shut. The clang resounded throughout the chapel courtroom. The handcuffs and shackles rattled when Peiper attempted to attack Jacques. The thud of his punch to the prisoner's solar plexus was followed by Peiper's whooshing and moaning. *So, you want a piece of me?* Jacques' voice penetrated the room. Peiper's assent was clearly audible. *Let me remove your shackles and turn over while I take off your handcuffs,* Jacques' voice said, causing Peiper to hold his ears. The ensuing sounds of the one-sided fight in the cell and the dialogue that ensued had all the elements of a radio melodrama. It became obvious that Jacques had given Peiper a boxing lesson.

The prisoner's plaintive attempt at blaming it all on Hitler's *No mercy* directive rolled on, plainly incriminating the no longer arrogant Peiper. The enormity of the Malmedy massacre was manifest. The press dashed to the doors in an effort to file their stories.

The afternoon session was highlighted by the testimony of the American commanding officer, David Pergrin, of the 291st Engineer Combat Battalion. He repeated his report to headquarters of the horrible, cold-blooded slaughter of eighty-six American prisoners of war. The full count came to three hundred and fifty-three POWs and one hundred and eleven civilians.

Le Beau dramatically announced, "The prosecution rests."

The defense, shocked by the prosecution's abruptly truncated case, asked for a one-day recess to round up defense witnesses. It was granted for a Saturday session. An hour later, Jacques and Bart were in Douglas Milburn's suite at the Four Seasons Hotel enjoying cocktails with Constance Milburn.

"That was quite a show. What do you think will happen to that snake?" Connie asked.

"A hanging," Bart tersely replied.

An hour later, Douglas, with journalists Ed Murrow and Quentin Reynolds, arrived. Doug made the introductions and poured drinks for all.

"So, we meet the beautiful bride and the hero brother," Reynolds toasted.

"Correction. Two brothers. Jacques is our adopted brother."

"Cheers to all," Murrow toasted, raising his glass and holding the ever-present cigarette in his left hand.

"When are you guys leaving?" Douglas asked.

"Jacques and I are flying back to Washington at 1900 hours," Bart said.

"Quentin, that's 7 p.m. for you civilians," Murrow gibed, laughing.

"Don't forget, Ed, I've been there too," Reynolds countered.

"How about a few words for CBS from you, General, and your brother Jacques," Murrow requested.

"My censor, Douglas here, might object on the grounds that he doesn't want to be scooped," Bart chuckled.

"What about me?" Reynolds said.

"You'll write a column, I'll have it in print shortly, and Ed will have it live on the air. It's okay," Doug agreed.

Murrow produced his recorder. Bart made a short denunciation of the Third Reich and the merciless slaughter of the Jews. Jacques embellished the capture of Peiper. Doug and Connie were at the window smooching.

☆ ☆ ☆ ☆

Saturday, November 15, 1952 - Washington
After a full day with Elizabeth and Christina entertaining the children, Bart and Jacques watched TV and caught up to the two-day finish of the Dachau trial. The best the defense could do was to call five character witnesses - two businessmen and three women. Personal friends of Peiper's family testified to his good character in civilian life. The defense rested. The tribunal was back in one hour. Peiper was found guilty on all counts. The mandatory sentence was death by hanging.

☆ ☆ ☆ ☆

Monday, November 17, 1952 - 10:15 a.m. - the Pentagon
Bart was summoned to General Bradley's office.
"Morning, Barton. Be seated."
"Morning, sir."
"We have a date with the President at 1100 hours. He spoke with Ike."
"Anything forthcoming?"
"No, he was cryptic."
Bart looked at his wristwatch, "We had better leave soon."
On the way over the 14th Street Bridge, Bart highlighted the Dachau trial.
"Sam Le Beau wrapped it up fast," Bradley said.
"He was great. General Clay ran a tight legal ship. No nonsense," Bart observed.
The two men were quickly ushered into the Oval Office. Truman stood up and shook their hands. After they were seated, he said, "I invited Ike to join me in a press conference here at the White House to announce the capture of Hitler and his gang. He demurred on the grounds that he and Mamie were going to take a long rest and said it was my show. He won't return until the middle of December."
"Have you made a decision, Mr. President?" Bradley asked.
"Yes, we're going to put on a great show," Truman snickered.
"May I ask what you have up your sleeve, sir?" Bart asked, smiling.
"Yes, yes. On Monday, December 1st, we'll announce a very important press conference at 2 p.m. Present will be you two men, General Smith, Jacques Laurent, and key participants in the four raids that resulted in the roundup of these Nazi bastards."
"Mr. President, I guess Jacques, because he heads the Nazi desk, General Donovan for the Malmo raid, General Barclay for the Hamburg sortie, the Paris raid should include Richard Maybrook of the CIA, and General Whitney for the Argentine roundup," Bart summed up.
"You left out a few people, Barton," Truman added.

"Who, sir?"

"Your whole CIA team."

"That does make quite a show. Shouldn't we clear the exposure of my team, all CIA people, with General Smith?"

"Of course."

Bradley laughed.

"What's so funny, Brad?"

"Mr. President, Ike might be sorry he missed the show."

"He put more than his toe into the political arena. Our press conference will be a course in Politics and Public Relations 101. There will be worldwide coverage and a few repercussions from comrade Stalin."

"Sir, the fact that there have been no leaks to date is very heartening. Now that the election is over, it has occurred to me that it would be advisable to have full concurrence for the open trials. We need congressional support on a bipartisan basis."

Truman removed his glasses and, with a tissue, polished the lenses. Bradley was silent, a hint of a smile on his usually stoic face. Adjusting his metal-rimmed glasses, Truman quizzically stared at the young general. After a short pause, he expressed his musings. "Politics, General? Or is that the lawyer in you talking?"

"Sir, in my present posture I am apolitical. The combination of the military and the legal side in me has made me a pragmatist."

"Spell it out."

"There are forces here and abroad who would be aversely opposed to a wide-open trial of Hitler et al. For example, the Dulles brothers; the British royal family, to protect the Windsors; Lindbergh, old Joe Kennedy, and the closet Nazi supporters."

"As the chief counsel, is it your intent to focus on those people? Not that I want them protected."

"That's just the point, sir. The exposure of them will not emanate from me. The explosive comments will come from the serpent's mouth, *Der Führer* himself. He's a voluble snake with sharp fangs, spewing copious amounts of venom when threatened or agitated."

Bradley chuckled.

"What's so funny, Brad?" Truman asked.

"I think I know where Barton is going."

"Clue me."

"The foregoing, sir, is a prelude to a presumptuous suggestion."

"Let's have it."

"Mr. President, as a little icing on the cake for your press conference, may I suggest you invite Sam Rayburn and Joe Martin, his successor as House Speaker, and Senators Styles Bridges, Everett Dirksen, Earle Clements and Lyndon Johnson. With them in tow, the naysayers in both aisles will be harnessed."

"Do I detect a political career in your future, General Milburn?"

"No, sir. No desire. Law is my game."

"That's pretty sharp thinking, son. Tell me why you named Republican Senator Dirksen and Democratic Senator Johnson."

"I'll let you in on a little secret, Mr. President. Bridges is going to hand Dirksen the majority leadership. Johnson, as you know, being the minority whip, is the upcoming power among the Democrats."

Bradley broke in. "Mr. President, Barton is right on the money. Ike is going to be pressured to curb these trials. If we get these six men in lockstep, Ike won't be dissuaded from supporting the open trials. I know Ike well from working with him through the war. He listened to the top staff."

"How do we prevent a leak from them?" Truman asked.

"Simple - they are politicians who love the limelight and won't risk their careers with a brazen leak," Bart said.

"All right, General Milburn. I know of your friendship with Bridges and Clements. I want you here to brief these men when I call them together. I'll set it up for next week just before they break for the Thanksgiving holidays and their winter vacation," Truman said.

On the way out, Truman whispered to Bradley, "That young man is brilliant."

"I know. If he stays in the military, he could one day be Chairman of the Joint Chiefs."

☆ ☆ ☆ ☆

Tuesday, November 25, 1952 - the White House

Senators Bridges, Dirksen, Clements and Johnson and Representatives Martin and Rayburn joined the President for a command luncheon. Also present were Generals Bradley, Milburn and Smith. The gathering was festive, with accolades to Truman for his successful presidency. The camaraderie was sincere, despite their political differences. After the coffee was served and the waiters left the room, Senator Dirksen raised a question in his velvety voice. "Mr. President, the presence of these two generals and the CIA director indicates an international problem. Is that not so?"

"Gentlemen, there is no problem other than that Korean fracas. However, I have some startling news to impart. First, I want the word of honor from each of you that not a word of what will be revealed is to be leaked or discussed, even with your families. This is top secret," Truman said.

There were unanimous assurances.

"I will be holding an important press conference, and I want all of you present. You'll be pleased to drop whatever you're doing to attend on Monday, December 1st at 2 p.m. General Milburn will brief you now."

In concise and measured tones, Bart revealed the capture of Adolf Hitler and his minions. The shock on the officials' faces was evident. Spellbound, they listened to the forty-minute summary of events that had occurred since Bart's Valentine's Day call to duty by the President. General Bradley followed with a short commentary on the role played by the Army, Navy, Marines and Air Force in Operation Lucifer. General Smith reported on the CIA team assigned to Bart.

"Mr. President, how, in this sieving town, were you able to keep this secret?" Senator Bridges queried.

"May I answer that, sir?" Bart interjected.

"Go ahead."

Bart said, "The President promised to track down leakers with all means at his disposal."

"You better believe he would," Speaker Rayburn said.

"Okay, gentlemen, we need your full bipartisan support for wide-open trials. Ike has been briefed," Truman announced.

Unanimous agreement followed.

"See you all here at noon, December 1, for a buffet lunch and then the press conference. Happy Thanksgiving to all," Truman said.

☆ ☆ ☆ ☆

Monday, December 1, 1952 - 0900 hours - the Pentagon

Gathered in General Bradley's conference room were the Joint Chiefs and Generals Smith and Milburn. The speakerphone was in the center of the large table. An operator's voice announced, "General Bradley, I have General Fielding on the line."

"Put him through."

Bradley advised him of the men present, then added, "Warren, how is it shaping up?"

"Gentlemen, Fort Leavenworth has been turned into a veritable fortress."

Bart raised his hand. Bradley nodded.

"General Fielding, this is Barton Milburn. The President's press conference, as you know, starts at 1400 hours. You can bet that minutes after he announces that Hitler and all the prisoners are at Fort Leavenworth, all hell will break loose. Your local press, as well as all the media, national and worldwide, will jam your phones and pound your gates. Frankly, you'll be under siege."

"When should I deploy my guard units?"

"Warren, two hundred Marines should be arriving there in the next hour. Settle them in and assign them in concert with your other personnel to their posts at 1350 hours," Bradley replied.

"With regard to telephones, radio, and television camera hookups, our public-affairs people will answer their questions, but the media will have to make their own arrangements with the phone and electric companies," Fielding said.

"How is the court construction proceeding?" Bart asked.

"We've expanded the major court and the other three."

"Warren, this is Beedle. Your public-affairs people will be swamped by their regular duties and the firestorm coming your way."

"Point well taken," Bradley cut in. "General Milburn, the public relations should be in your domain throughout the trials. You've got Captain Esta Arnold on your staff. She's very savvy in dealing with the press. Let's set up a PR team and relieve Fielding's general operations."

"Sir, I would much prefer it be handled that way," Bart responded. "I would suggest two persons from each of the services who have the professional expertise." Air Force Chief Maxwell Taylor spoke up. "I have two excellent men."

"We do, too," Marine Chief Forley said.

The Navy and Army chiefs concurred.

"Bart, you have a staff of nine, which includes Captain Arnold. How does that suit you?" Bradley asked.

"That's perfect. I would ask General Fielding to set up a press office for them close to the prosecution's headquarters. Please place the defense office as far away from us as possible. The big Nazis will be hiring a slew of civilian lawyers. And while I'm on that subject, it has occurred to me that everyone tied to these Nazis has to be screened," Bart observed.

"General Bradley, we need to have service intelligence officers, plus some of our CIA agents to double-check Hitler's, a.k.a. Nordheim's, operatives. They might try to come in the guise of legal assistants or press people. Fingerprint and photograph everyone," General Smith said.

"Sir, with due deference, we can't do that to the legitimate media," Bart countered.

"We'll have video pictures of everyone entering through a metal detector at the gate. Those people whose credentials are suspect, legal or press, can then be subject to fingerprinting. Once validated, they'll be given a special pass," General Fielding announced.

"Why not advise the media that photographs will be required, due to security reasons? They would understand that," Smith said.

"Not bad, sir. I think that will play," Bart concurred.

They spent the next hour hammering out the final details.

☆ ☆ ☆ ☆

Later that day - 1:30 p.m. - the White House

The press room was packed to standing room only, and an air of anticipation pervaded the room. Promptly at 2 p.m., President Truman led an impressive array of men into the room. The government's power structure was aligned behind him at the podium. He introduced the four senators, the Chiefs of Staff, Secretaries Lovett, McGranery and Acheson, the director of the CIA, and Bart Milburn.

Truman said, "Members of the press and other media, I have an important statement and then will open this press conference to questions. The matter I will report to you will be startling in nature. It has worldwide implications. Item number one is as follows...."

He paused. Full attention was focused on the jaunty President. He removed his glasses and rubbed his eyes. Being the consummate tease, he looked around the room and delivered his news bombshell.

"Adolf Hitler is not dead, nor is Martin Bormann, as reported. They are alive and in the custody of the United States."

The announcement stunned the audience. Seconds passed, and then the room erupted in a roar of mingled reactions. Truman waited for the din to subside. He continued slowly in his narration of the capture of Hitler, Bormann and ninety-six or more Nazis and affiliates.

"They will be brought to a war-crimes trial before a military tribunal on Tuesday, February 3, 1953. The man who headed this spectacular roundup is Major General Barton Milburn. He will also act as chief counsel to prosecute Hitler, Bormann and the others."

Truman beckoned Bart and General Bradley to the podium.

"Before we take any questions, I want to point out that the Joint Chiefs and their chairman, General Omar Bradley, cooperated worldwide, as did the director of the CIA, General Smith, and Jacques Laurent, head of the CIA's Nazi desk. President-elect Eisenhower was fully aware of the operation. We have a bipartisan effort going here, as evidenced by the presence of our four distinguished senators. Now for your questions," Truman concluded.

The usual clamor for recognition subsided when the President pointed at Mae Craig of the Copley News Service.

"Mr. President, I have a double-barreled question."

"I'm not surprised, Mae."

"First, why has this been kept secret these many months? Second, has the United States conducted this manhunt unilaterally?"

"A good question deserves a good answer. Two questions are entitled to better answers." After a wave of nervous chuckles from the press, Truman answered, "It was a matter of top-secret intelligence efforts to track down these Nazi monsters. A leak of any kind and our prey would have scattered to their ferret holes. The word unilateral doesn't apply in this instance. Our first lead came to me from Prime Minister Ben-Gurion of Israel. I conscripted this young reserve officer, who was practicing law, into heading the search. I consulted with Prime Minister Churchill and President de Gaulle. British, French, and Israeli intelligence cooperated fully."

Hands went up, and he recognized Ed Murrow of CBS.

"Sir, would you explain why the Soviet Union was not involved?"

"Simple, Ed - we didn't need them."

Loud laughter ensued.

"Follow up, Mr. President," Murrow pressed. "Won't the exclusion of the Russians exacerbate tensions in this Cold War?"

"On the contrary, Ed, they are welcome to attend the trials. I think they should applaud our achievements. Maybe, after they hear the news from you folks, they would be pleased to lift the Iron Curtain."

More laughter followed, then Truman pointed at Meyer Berger of the New York Times.

"Mr. President, my question is directed to General Milburn."

"Go right ahead."

"General, could we have some details of the capture of Hitler and Bormann, and the names of some of the others?"

"I'll give you a quick answer to the last part of your question. We have prepared a list of most of the prisoners for distribution at the conclusion of this press conference. We conducted four raids and a couple of minor sorties, and hit the jackpot."

"Could you elaborate, sir?"

Bart described the Malmo, Hamburg, Paris, and La Plata, Argentina, raids. He gave credit to Sweden, Germany, France, Cuba, the CIA, the Joint Chiefs, General Bradley, Jacques Laurent, and, above all, the support of President Truman.

Bob Considine of the New York Daily Mirror, was acknowledged. "General Milburn, you and Mr. Laurent recently testified in Munich in the case against Joachim Peiper, the Nazi officer who perpetrated the Malmedy massacre. In fact, you testified that Laurent captured him, is that not so?"

"Mr. Considine, that's true."

"Quite an achievement. Would you describe how that came about?"

"With the President's permission, I'd like Mr. Laurent to detail it for you. However, the source of that information will become manifest in the upcoming trials. Mr. Laurent, step up here."

Laurent delivered a brief account of the surveillance and capture of Peiper, alias Luther Jockler.

"General, when will the regular trials begin?" Mae Craig asked.

"I wish to emphasize that the trials in February are military evidentiary hearings. The procedure is somewhat analogous to civil criminal-court procedures. A Judge Advocate will decide on *prima facie* evidence to be presented by the prosecution as to whether the defendants should be bound over for a formal trial before a tribunal," Bart explained.

"General, is there any legal doubt about Hitler's guilt?" Quentin Reynolds asked, smiling.

The press corps laughed.

"Quent, I am sure your question is facetious. However, we have more than ninety-odd defendants. Under the jurisdiction of general courts-martial for violations of war crimes, each defendant shall be accorded a fair hearing."

"When will the full trials begin?" Considine asked.

"That's speculative. The defendants will be hiring attorneys and the prosecution has much investigation and preparation ahead of them. A ballpark guess on my part is possibly six to nine months after the trial hearings. Please don't hold me to that," Bart evasively replied.

The conference went on for another hour. The senators, congressmen, Bradley, the Joint Chiefs, Secretary of State Acheson, Secretary of Defense Lovett and Attorney General McGranery answered a myriad of queries. Truman called on Bart to lay out the rules for the media at Fort Leavenworth. Bart explained the necessity of having proper credentials with photographs of the bearer. He laid out the area and the arrangements to help them. A murmur of protest erupted.

"Please, we are trying a mob of evil men, so *security* is vital. There are escaped Nazi war criminals and supporters extant, all over the world. These precautions are for *your* protection as well as ours. Please cooperate," Bart said.

Drew Pearson, the world-famed syndicated columnist, rose.

Truman said, "This is the last question."

"Mr. President, could General Milburn tell us about Hitler's Revenge Plan?"

A hush blanketed the room. Bart looked at Truman, who wearily shrugged assent. Bart spelled out the Revenge Plan devised by *Der Führer*. He advised that a worldwide alert was ongoing. He depicted the aborted terrorist attacks in Tel Aviv, London, and Paris.

"Now, hold it for one minute," he suddenly declared as he huddled with Truman and General Smith.

The media tensely awaited the results. Truman and Smith concurred. Bart returned to the podium.

"Ahmed the Cobra, wanted worldwide, is in our custody and his brother is being held by an unnamed country. He is not on the list to be distributed. Coincidentally, his brother is in the custody of one of the aforementioned countries, where he participated in a bombing plot. That's all I have to say."

A barrage of questions erupted in the wake of the President's departure. The room resounded with applause. The White House press corps raced to their cubicles in the White House pressroom. Within fifteen minutes, the wire services' bulletin bells rang in newsrooms around the world. The networks cut into daytime shows, game shows, and other programming. The timing of the President's news conference was a bonanza for the print and electronic media.

On the East Coast of America, the time element helped the afternoon papers print a final edition with the story. In New York, papers such as the Daily News and Daily Mirror had it in their bulldog editions, hitting the streets at 8 p.m. The Times and Herald Tribune would follow an hour later. The major Midwestern and West Coast papers would print extras within an hour. For London and Paris, the news was perfectly timed for their radio and TV news hours at 10 p.m., Greenwich time. Homebound traffic drivers were honking their horns in consonance with automobile radios. Both ends of Checkpoint Charlie in Berlin were agog with the news.

Banner headlines were on the street throughout the world. World leaders were on the airwaves in North and South America, Europe, Asia, and Australia, being interviewed. London's Fleet Street, England's press center, was in a state of organized chaos. Le Monde put out a special extra on the streets in Paris. Church bells rang all over Europe. The streets of Tel Aviv were packed with cheering, joyous crowds. Leaders of NATO member countries were clogging the telephone lines in an attempt to congratulate Truman. Soviet leader Stalin was awakened. The Politburo members were rousted from their beds for a meeting at the Kremlin. The world was astir.

☆ ☆ ☆ ☆

𝔅𝔬𝔬𝔨 𝔗𝔴𝔬

The Trial of Adolf Hitler

CHAPTER ONE

Monday, December 1, 1952 - Fort Leavenworth, Kansas
The hundred-and-twenty-year-old Army installation was under siege. Local reporters were soon joined by batches of newspeople. Buses from the Kansas City airport, twenty miles southeast of the fort, were delivering cadres of media personnel. Local hotels, motels, and bed-and-breakfast inns were getting reservations by the minute. Throughout the night, TV vans, radio units and mobile homes were flowing into the beautiful bucolic area overlooking the Missouri River on the border between Kansas and Missouri. The surrounding rustic area was quickly becoming a beehive of activity.

General Fielding had set up a special gate away from the main entry to the fort. The combination of Marines and Army guards kept the press under control and routed their inquiries to the improvised press gates. However, the first evening was one of frustration for the media. The Public Affairs Office posted a notice on the gate with the information that there would be no statements that evening.

☆ ☆ ☆ ☆

Tuesday, December 2, 1952 - 2 a.m. - Zurich, Switzerland
An executive committee meeting of the Banque Royale had been hastily convened. Switzerland's largest city, the hub of international banking, was aglow with lights shining through the windows from its dozens of banking edifices. Majority stockholder Waldo Schlicht, a short, portly man, adjusted his gold-rimmed, tinted glasses and declared, "This is a crisis of immense proportions."

He pointed to a stack of newspapers with glaring headlines: *HITLER, BORMANN CAPTURED.*

"Herr Schlicht, undoubtedly this is a threat to the entire Swiss banking system," the chairman of the executive committee, Werner Sturtmann, said. Schlicht cleared his throat. "That is why we're here. Let's proceed with a plan. First, we have to call off the search for our president, Peter Weber. He is either dead or is in the custody of the Americans. Victor, call the Pinkertons and cancel their investigation."

"Yes, Herr Schlicht," corporate secretary Victor Lieber replied.

"Now, we must put Nordheim's and Bormann's accounts in the control of one person, who will report to me. That will be you, Johann."

The executive vice president and acting CEO, Johann Klauber, answered, "I have put those accounts on hold, Waldo. Do you want them activated?"

"Yes, we must retain lawyers for them immediately. Control of their testimony must be maintained insofar as our banks are concerned."

A similar scene was transpiring in banks throughout Switzerland. The roiling effect of the explosive news of the American coup was manifested by the frenetic activity of the secret Nazi benefactors. The sordid story of Switzerland's role in World War II had to be suppressed. The country's quasi-neutrality was on the verge of being exposed.

The Banque Royale initiated a conference call to six other banks in Zurich and Geneva. Rene La Fleur, executive vice president and CEO of the Banque Royale, got into a shouting match over procedure. The heated dichotomy was ameliorated by Georges Tyman, head of the Banque Internationale in Geneva. Agreement on a plan was reached at 4:30 a.m. A review meeting was set for Monday, December 22nd, at the Bellevue Palace Hotel in the capital city, Bern.

☆ ☆ ☆ ☆

December 2, 1952 - the same day - Washington

Bart Milburn spent the day preparing his legal team for the transition of the prosecution to Fort Leavenworth on Tuesday, January 6, 1953. Major Brent Watson, public relations officer was fending off a barrage of pleas from the press for interviews with General Milburn. He adroitly parried the repeated requests. That afternoon, General Fielding called.

"Bart, you can't visualize the circus surrounding this place, but we've got it under control. I addressed the media outside a special press gate we've assigned for them. When they pressed me about the prisoners, I either gave them a *No comment* or an *I don't know.*"

The two generals laughed.

"By the way, Captain Esta Arnold has been very helpful. She's a real pro in dealing with the press. She took quite a load off me. The public-affairs men arrived a little while ago. Captain Arnold is organizing a press information office now."

"That's fine, Warren."

☆ ☆ ☆ ☆

Same day - 9 p.m. - Milburn home, Rock Creek Park

After the children were put to bed, Jacques and Christina joined the Milburns in the den.

As Elizabeth entered, nine months pregnant, Bart laughed, "That's a beautiful lady waddling in here."

"*That's* a new dance," she giggled, patting her bulging abdomen.

Bart helped her into his large leather chair and lifted her tired feet onto the hassock. Suddenly, Jacques and Christina made a surprise announcement.

"We would like to get married in a simple wedding on Sunday, December 14th," Jacques announced, smiling while holding Christina's hand. "If it's okay with you, Bart, we'll go on a short honeymoon and be back in time for Elizabeth's delivery."

"That's wonderful. I'm not due until the last week of this month," Elizabeth said.

"That calls for a drink, and a little Perrier for you, Liz," Bart said.

"Joyce will be here tomorrow. She'll stay until after New Year's, and will help with the children and assist Elizabeth," Jacques said.

The following day, in a flurry of activity, the room for the wedding was booked at the Shoreham by Christina and Jacques. Elizabeth worked the telephones, ordering invitations and calling the Milburn family in New York, her father in London, and a select group on a list prepared by Bart.

☆ ☆ ☆ ☆

Sunday, December 14, 1952 - 2 p.m.

Forty guests attended the wedding of Jacques Laurent and Christina Lyons. Among the guests were the Milburn family from New York; Sir Alfred Lipton, accompanied by Barbara Courtney, a 45-year-old aide to Winston Churchill, a pleasant surprise to Bart and Elizabeth; Senators Bridges and Clements, Generals Bradley and Smith, and the CIA staff assigned to Bart.

The marriage ritual was performed by Supreme Court Justice Robert Jackson. Bart acted as best man and Joyce Laurent was the maid of honor. Soft music and a lavish lunch followed. The bride and groom left, with the bride's bouquet being tossed at Joyce. Jacques and Christina left for the airport in a limousine. They were bound for Los Angeles, with two days at the Beverly Hills Hotel and a flight to Acapulco, Mexico.

The Milburns, Sir Alfred, Barbara Courtney and Joyce Laurent returned to the Rock Creek Park home, where Bunny and Jeffrey Rothschild announced their engagement. The family reacted joyously. Michael and Jenny expressed their happiness by alternately climbing on the laps of their grandparents Jeanette, Dr. Milburn and Sir Alfred. The other two children, Katharine and Matthew, reveled in their acquisition of an expanded family.

For Bart and Elizabeth, it was quality time, as she whispered to him, "I believe Dad has more than a romance going with his lady friend."

"Do you approve?"

"Very much so."

The gathering was a mind-clearing event for Bart Milburn.

☆ ☆ ☆ ☆

Monday, December 22, 1952 - Bern, Switzerland

The giants of the Swiss banking industry assembled in a closely guarded conference room, where an atmosphere of crisis prevailed. Waldo Schlicht chaired the tension-fraught meeting. In deference to Zurich's German-speaking members and the French-speaking Genevans, they compromised on the English language.

"We are all aware of the dangers confronting Switzerland's banking system," Schlicht gravely asserted.

"*Ja*, yes, *oui*," the group chorused.

"The capture of Frederick Avram Nordheim and his exposure as Adolf Hitler could spell total disaster for us. Of course, we all believed *Der Führer* was dead."

Everyone nodded assent.

"Let's stop wringing our hands and get down to business," René La Fleur heatedly interrupted.

"Very well, let me spell out what we must do. Since our phone conference, Georges Tyman, René La Fleur and I have drawn up a plan of action. The floor is yours, Herr Tyman," said Schlicht.

"Gentlemen, we must transfer a portion of the trouble accounts to the Cayman Islands. So we'll be able to draw funds from there, non-traceable to us, for the defense of our clients."

"Lawyers must be hand-picked to keep Nordheim, Bormann and others from disclosing anything about our banks," La Fleur said.

"Yes, yes, René, I am coming to that. There is much more that has to be contained!" Tyman shouted.

"Well, dammit, say it!" La Fleur roared back.

"Let me say it very plainly. The Swiss role in the war should not be aired at these trials," Tyman replied.

"Why don't you put it on the table, Georges?" La Fleur challenged. "Which of the banks here helped the damned Nazis?" La Fleur pounded the marble top.

"*Um Gottes willen. Bist du verrückt!*" Schlicht roared. "Do you mean to say your bank's hands are clean, *Monsieur* La Fleur?"

"No, and God won't help us. I am not crazy, just facing the facts," La Fleur shot back. "How about all that Jewish money we have, and the gold from their teeth? The Americans will be all over us, then the British and the French. Besides lawyers for them, we need lawyers for ourselves. A unified defense for the banks. The Jews around the world will be claiming the money for survivors and the families that were murdered."

"Murdered? That's Jew propaganda. Are you a *Jew*, La Fleur?" Schlicht sneered.

"Listen, you Nazi pig. I am *not* a Jew. I am also not a *Nazi*. But, like you and everyone else in this room, I *am* a thief. That's one thing we all have in common. We're a bunch of greedy thieves who consorted with those Nazi murderers. Greed, greed, greed. Our *mea culpas* won't help, so let us put up the barricades and protect ourselves," La Fleur said.

"Who murdered who? Nobody was murdered," Schlicht persisted.

"No? Then why are we concerned about survivors? Dead people. Six million of them, and you shut your eyes and hear nothing. Schlicht, you love those misbegotten Nazis because you're one of them. You're not even true Swiss. You're like our cheese, full of holes."

"René, enough. Let's plan and agree on what has to be done," Tyman pleaded.

Over the next two hours, a plan was agreed upon for a bold, united front. Help would be sought from high officials. A legal team would be put together to thwart an onslaught of demands by Jews for their rightful inheritance. Death certificates would be demanded from claimants. A wall of denial would be erected. Lawyers for all.

☆ ☆ ☆ ☆

Wednesday, December 24, 1952 - Christmas Eve - Washington

That morning, a limousine, followed by a taxi laden with gift-wrapped packages, drove into the Milburn driveway. Jacques and Christina, tanned and smiling, opened the front door. The drivers, with the help of Stanley, carried the many of gifts into the house, placing the presents at the base of a huge decorated Christmas tree. Bart and Elizabeth were awakened by the whooping delight of the four children. Mrs. Bishop tried to shush them, to no avail. The Milburns stood at the head of the stairs, sleepily observing the scene below.

"Mr. and Mrs. Laurent, I presume?" Bart bellowed hoarsely.

"Wake up, sleepyheads!" Jacques laughed.

Joyce ran down the stairs and hugged the newlyweds. The day was devoted to wrapping other packages and adding a few finishing touches to the tree. As twilight faded into the night, the twinkling, decorative lights on the exterior of the house came on. Bart turned on the tree lights as the children were outside marveling at a lit-up Santa Claus on the roof. When they returned to the house, the tree's rotating lights caught their attention. A tired Elizabeth leaned back in Bart's huge leather chair.

"Daddy, look! It's snowing!" Michael yelped.

All joined to view the gentle snow, which was spreading a carpet of white over the nation's capital. Rock Creek Park became a rustic fairyland, far removed from the steel and stone structures of government in the downtown section of Northwest Washington. It was a Dickensian setting on Christmas Eve, minus the Scrooge laments. The fireplace was aglow with tongues of flame, warming the room. Elizabeth decreed that the presents would not be opened until after breakfast in the morning.

A light repast, and all retired to the quietude of the snow-muted area.

The next morning, the snow had abated. After a hurried breakfast, the children scampered to the Christmas tree. Jacques, Christina, Joyce and Bart helped open the gifts as a restless Elizabeth watched from her comfortable lounge. Two hours later, Elizabeth softly called Bart to her side. She whispered, "Barton, darling, it's showtime."

For a moment he tried to decipher her remark, when suddenly it struck him. Wide-eyed and with excitement, he whispered, "I'll get your things, darling."

"Not necessary, sweetheart. Everything is in the car. Just get my coat and purse."

"Shall I call the doctor?"

"Bart, please relax. I called him while you were fussing with the presents and the kids."

Christina caught the tenor of their conversation. "We'll come with you to the hospital," she offered.

"No, you and Jacques stay here with the kids," Elizabeth calmly ordered.

Joyce had her coat on and was holding Elizabeth's mink coat. "I'm coming with you, whether you like it or not."

Bart drove carefully, and in less than twenty minutes they arrived at University Hospital on 23rd Street. Two hours later Joyce called the house.

"Jacques, it's a healthy baby boy. He weighs seven pounds, five ounces and has a *very* loud voice."

☆ ☆ ☆ ☆

Monday, January 5, 1953 - Bethesda, Maryland
Bart Milburn drove into the driveway of a colonial mansion. He was greeted at the door by a liveried butler and escorted to a large library room. President-elect Dwight David Eisenhower rose from behind an antique early American desk, exhibiting a warm smile. Bart saluted and smiled back.

"Not necessary," Ike said, but instinctively returned the gesture. "Good of you to come on such short notice." He pointed to a high-backed armchair.

"Sir, had the call come from anyone else, I might have declined. I had just brought my wife back from the hospital."

"Nothing serious, I hope?"

"Sir, on the contrary. Ten days ago, she presented me a healthy son, Quentin Norris Milburn. I'm spending as much time with her as possible before leaving for Fort Leavenworth."

"Congratulations. How is Elizabeth?"

"She's fine, sir. Sends her love to you."

"Thank you, Bart. First, you are to be commended for your magnificent job in rounding up Hitler, Bormann and the rest of those Nazi cretins."

"Thank you, sir."

The general sat alongside Bart and offered him a cigarette. Bart opted for one of his special long brown Shermans. He struck his Dunhill lighter and lit Ike's cigarette and his own.

"We're a long way from the surrender of those bastards seven years ago," Eisenhower said.

"Mr. President, we certainly…"

"Hold it, Barton, I am fifteen days away from that title. General or Ike will do until then."

"Very well, sir."

"All right, General Milburn, let's get to the reason for your presence here today. This house, incidentally, has been loaned to us for my transition team. I am going to summon Herbert Brownell and John Foster Dulles to join us. The subject matter is your open trials of Hitler and company."

The former supreme commander of the Allied forces blew a few smoke rings. Bart tensed at the mention of Dulles. Ike stood up, walked to his desk and pressed twice on the intercom button of a beige phone. Two men entered the library. Bart rose. One was a trim, Ivy League type. The other, taller, bespectacled, with a salt-and-pepper mustache and scholarly in mien, forced a smile at Bart.

"General Milburn, this is Herbert Brownell Jr., my choice for Attorney General, and John Foster Dulles, our next Secretary of State."

They shook hands.

"Your fame and exploits precede you, General," Dulles said.

"Quite an accomplishment," Brownell echoed.

Ike casually tinkered at a rolling cart containing assorted alcoholic drinks. "What will you have, Barton?"

"I noticed the Bristol Cream. That's fine on the rocks for me."

"Good, I'll try that. Scotch on the rocks for you two?"

They agreed. Bart sipped his drink and anxiously waited for a bombshell. He stared at Dulles.

"Bart, we've got a dissension in our ranks on the political feasibility of your open trials. John here will explain," Eisenhower opened the subject.

Dulles polished his glasses in a studied manner. Bart, a keen observer of human deportment honed by his years as an intelligence officer, realized that the Wall Street lawyer was nervous. He noticed Ike's casual air in contrast to Brownell's repression of a smile. The scene added up to the fact that Ike was noncommittal, Brownell was in favor of the trials, and Dulles was deeply concerned. That mental observation was confirmed by Dulles' opening remarks.

"General, you're quite a young man to be caught up in such an international political maelstrom. These trials could evoke explosive testimony that might tarnish the reputations of some of America's friends and allies."

"That's quite possible, Mr. Dulles. However, I doubt that any true friends of our country will suffer at my hands."

"Milburn, why this media circus? One Nuremberg is enough, wouldn't you agree? Based on the results in that trial, you should be able to get a conviction in a truncated hearing. Do away with a rehash of the so-called Holocaust. In fact, hang them now or put them before a firing squad. Get it over with. Besides, it's cost-effective."

Bart, realizing he was up against one of the most brilliant lawyers in Washington, contained his temper and, in a tone slightly above a whisper, baited his adversary with a question. "Mr. Dulles, did I hear you correctly say, 'the *so-called* Holocaust'? Are you implying that it never happened? If so, sir, you have two witnesses in this room who were there. General Eisenhower and I were at Ohrdruf with the media. General Bradley and Patton were there as well. Old Blood and Guts spilled his cookies when he saw the horrors of the Nazi murder orgy."

Eisenhower winked at Brownell, who was absorbed with Bart's courtroom style. Brownell, a distinguished attorney, shook his head, affirming Ike's reaction.

"Young man, I had…"

Bart interrupted Dulles' reply. "Sir, please don't patronize me. The appellation of *young man* is pejorative and offensive."

Dulles bit his lip and took a long look at Bart. Eisenhower turned to the window to cover a muted chuckle. Brownell noted Dulles' discomfort. Dulles realized that Milburn's youthful appearance was deceiving. He shuffled his legal cards and tried a new approach.

"General Milburn, if I have offended you, I humbly apologize. You are a lawyer and so am I. Sometimes in an interesting dichotomy, our courtroom manners are perverted in making a point. I'm truly sorry."

"Please continue, sir."

"My choice of the phrase *so-called* was inappropriate. The horrors perpetrated by the Nazis cannot be depreciated. I am concerned about our relationship with the British, West Germany, France, Switzerland, the Vatican, and some major American industries."

"Mr. President, Mr. Brownell and Mr. Dulles, the upcoming trials of Hitler, et al., have been broadcast throughout the world. The purpose of having open trials is to put the spotlight on the bestiality of Hitler's Third Reich. This will be a stark warning to new generations and a complacent society that it can happen again if we are not vigilant. If there is any attempt at a cover-up, then I'm not the man for the job," Bart said.

"Barton, there will be no cover-ups in my administration," Eisenhower quickly assured him.

"John, the way I see it, General Milburn intends to focus on the atrocities," Brownell interjected. "If anything is revealed that is embarrassing, it will come from the mouths of the defendants."

"I went over this whole situation with Jim Hagerty, who left the New York Times to be my press secretary. The media, he told me, feels that this is a bonanza for the United States image the world over," said Eisenhower.

Dulles sulked.

"By the way, sir, Prime Minister Churchill and President de Gaulle have been most cooperative in this operation. I have personally briefed them," Bart related, boring in.

Dulles was not through. "General Milburn, you have been working with my brother Allen at the CIA?"

"Yes?" the hackles were rising on his neck. His thought processes battled the question. *Do I take on the next Secretary of State, who's covering his ass and that of his brother? Or do I put Ike on the spot? I have to live in D.C. with this duplicitous front for I.G. Farben and Standard Oil, et al.*

"He tells me you are an excellent soldier, as well as a lawyer. Which career do you intend to pursue?"

"Sir," Bart replied, "I do not believe that question is germane to the subject at hand."

"Obviously you've missed the point of my question. If it's military, your mentor will be President in two weeks. That could augur well for your future. If it is as an attorney, a friendly administration would enhance the fortunes of your law firm. Should this dog-and-pony show of yours discomfit certain interests, you might inherit some formidable enemies."

The last shred of equivocation fled from Bart's mind. He coldly calculated his reply to the less-than-subtle threat. The gauntlet had been thrown. Eisenhower and Brownell exchanged glances. The President-elect shook his head negatively. Brownell followed suit.

"Mr. Dulles, your inference is quite clear. However, I am impelled to pierce shadow for substance. Monsters, carnivorous at that, will be in the dock. Hardly a place for dogs and ponies. Now, if you are concerned about the Duke of Windsor, Charles Lindbergh, Joseph Kennedy, Pope Pius and his Concordat with Nazis, I.G. Farben, Standard Oil, Vichy France, the Cliveden Set, the Swiss government and their corrupt banks, then your point is well taken," Barton said icily.

Dulles was obviously fazed. Eisenhower's casual attitude was replaced by a sincere effort to ameliorate the simmering feud. "Barton, I am certain that your intent in these trials is to expose the bestiality of the Hitlerites. As you stated, we were witnesses to the results of this inferno. We lost a lot of precious American lives in destroying the infamous Third Reich, so I don't think your goal is to conduct a witch hunt in the course of these trials."

"Of course not, Mr. President, but to use a cliché, let the devil take the hindmost; if someone gets besmirched by the defense, so be it. I can't mute these bastards."

"That's just the point," Dulles interjected. "As Secretary of State, I'll be subject to a backlash from some of the aforementioned sources."

Eisenhower said, "Do your job as you see fit. Keep me informed if anything untoward arises. By the way, Barton, I spoke with Truman this morning. He asked me if I knew of any reason why your concentration-camp report to me should not be declassified."

Bart waited for the punch line. He looked directly at Ike. Smiling, Eisenhower declared, "I told him I didn't know why it hadn't been opened before now."

Bart returned the smile. "It will be very useful in the trials, sir."

"General Milburn, I trust you understand my concerns. I wish you the best. Call me if you need help," Dulles said, forcing a smile.

"Indeed I do."

"Jim McGranery briefed me. He thinks very highly of you. If you need my help, don't hesitate to call," Brownell said.

Eisenhower placed his arm around Bart's shoulder and walked him to the door.

"Don't let Dulles get under your skin. He may have a few skeletons in his closet, but I assure you he's a loyal American and will make an excellent Secretary of State."

"I wish I were as sanguine as you are, sir."

"That's one thing I always admired about you, Bart. You never pulled a punch," Ike said, chuckling.

On the drive back to D.C., he pondered Eisenhower's choice of the Dulles brothers. He mused, *Allen in the CIA and John for Secretary of State. What a quinella! Ike's such a nice guy, why would he want those two with their Nazi and Swiss bank records?* At a gas station, while his convertible was being fueled and checked, he called his office at the Pentagon. Advised of a call from John Steelman, he dialed the White House. "John, what's up?"

"As you are undoubtedly aware, we are in the process of tying up loose ends and cleaning house before evacuating the premises for the next tenant two weeks from now. The President would like to see you before you leave for Fort Leavenworth."

"How's he fixed now? I can be there in about thirty minutes or so."

"I'll check."

After a lapse of a minute, Steelman said, "Come ahead."

Thirty-five minutes later Bart pulled up to the West Gate. A little banter with the guard, Frank Murphy, was exchanged. "There will be a change here in the next couple of weeks, General."

"That's true, Frank, but you'll be here for the new occupants, won't you?"

"I hope so."

Truman was in a jovial mood. This was a side of the President Bart hadn't encountered in his previous visits. Steelman seemed to be slightly harried, which Bart surmised was due to all the housecleaning.

"Barton, my friend, good to see you," said Truman.

"The pleasure is mine, sir."

"You're looking at a happy man. In two weeks I will be a civilian. My wife and daughter can't wait to get out of this bastille," he laughed.

"Sir, you have had a very successful and history-making tenure here."

"Thank you. I did my best and my conscience is clear. Let's get updated."

"Sir, I just came from a command performance with your successor."

"Oh, was it confidential, or can you speak freely?"

Bart described the visit to Bethesda that morning. In detail he related his verbal duel with Dulles.

"I can't understand Ike being taken in by that rascal and his brother. A couple of money-grubbing legal sharks, I would say. They've got a lot to hide," Truman commented.

"I'll not be party to any cover-ups."

"Barton, I'm proud of you. Very proud. You've more than justified my faith in you, at great expense to yourself. General Bradley will be staying on as Chairman of the Joint Chiefs until August. I hope he recommends you for a medal. You deserve it."

"That's very kind of you, sir."

"All right, now, let me check off some final notes. I am declassifying your report on the death camps, forthwith."

"Great."

"Now, while the Russians are upset about our unilateral trials, they are playing it low key. Andrei Gromyko is coming as an observer, Churchill is sending Anthony Eden, and de Gaulle is sending Pierre Mendes-France. Ben-Gurion is sending Abba Eban. I suppose Ike or Dulles will send someone to patronize them. A little advice: If any one of these observers want a *tête à tête* with you, oblige them. It helps our international rapport."

"Certainly, Mr. President."

"By the way, how's Elizabeth and the new baby?"

"Just fine, sir. Thank you and Mrs. Truman for the flowers."

"How's that Miss Laurent doing?"

"Just fine. She's a professor at Harvard."

"So I heard. I promised to have her over for tea. Is she here in town?"

"Until Wednesday."

Truman looked at his calendar. "Well, if she's available, have her join me here at 5 p.m. tomorrow. Is Elizabeth strong enough to get around?"

"Oh, she's up and about. And quite capable of running me ragged."

"Good. Present my invitation to Jacques, his new wife and sister. You bring Elizabeth. I am sure Bess and Margaret will be happy to see all of you."

"Very kind, Mr. President."

The next day, in the President's private quarters, the group was being entertained by the Truman family. A bit more than tea was served. The President's anecdotes had them laughing. Joyce told her escape story. Jacques related the Paris raid. Truman played the piano. He fumbled through Edith Piaf's hit song "La Vie en Rose." Compliments flowed back and forth. The two hours were enjoyed by all.

Upon leaving, Truman whispered, "Give 'em hell, Bart."

"I've heard those words applied to you, sir."

They laughed. On the way out, Truman again whispered to Bart, "I forgot to tell you - I signed an executive order adding ten million dollars to General Bradley's budget for your trials."

☆ ☆ ☆ ☆

Tuesday, February 3, 1953 - Fort Leavenworth

The morning's dawning sun hid behind cumulus crowds with temperatures hovering at the freezing point. The fort was a beehive of activity. The exterior was lined with armed Marines. They maintained order, circling from McPherson Avenue to the other end of the military installation on Metropolitan Avenue. Pedestrian and vehicular traffic were checked by Military Police. Sightseekers were detoured.

While the normal function of the hundred-and-twenty-year-old garrison was being maintained, wartime atmosphere prevailed. Security was at its peak. The environs of Fort Leavenworth, which comprised the heartland of America, were being scouted by unmarked cars containing security personnel from all branches of the military, the CIA and the FBI. The area being surveilled encompassed a radius of forty miles, including Kansas, to the Missouri towns and cities of Parkville, Weston and St. Joseph. It covered both Kansas City, Kansas, and Kansas City, Missouri, on both sides of the Missouri River. The alert was invoked as a result of Hitler's Revenge Plan.

At their Victorian officer's quarters, Jacques was in the kitchen preparing breakfast. Bart was at a desk in the living room making some final notes for his opening statement to the tribunal.

Alicia Lawrence, wife of MP Master Sergeant Louis Lawrence, had signed on as a day housekeeper. She set the table and was squeezing fresh orange juice. The lady was in her early forties and had been a nurse during the war. She was the mother of two teenage boys. General Warren Fielding had recommended her to Bart as a very trustworthy woman, who did various chores to augment the family income. The Lawrences were saving their money to send their boys to college. She was a handsome, buxom, red-haired woman of Welsh descent, a motherly type with a fine sense of humor. Bart and Jacques took to her immediately, and hired her for their pseudo-bachelor life at a generous salary, much more than she had requested. Jacques' culinary talents had earned her respect.

"Mr. Laurent, usually I don't allow men in my kitchen, but I am making an exception for you. My husband can't even boil an egg," she laughed.

"Alicia, when these trials are over, I'll teach him."

"Please don't. I don't want him or my boys messing up my kitchen."

Jacques placed ham and eggs, toasted English muffins and some fried potatoes on the waiting tray.

"Come on, General, breakfast is served," she said.

Preoccupied, Bart sat down and silently attacked the food. Alicia poured steaming hot coffee for the two men.

"Enjoy. This is the big day at last. I'll make the beds and tidy up the house right quick. I'm going to listen to the big show on the radio. My husband's on duty in the court. Lucky stiff."

Bart looked up at her. "Alicia, wish us luck."

"More than that, I hope you destroy those bastards. I was overseas and saw a bit of their evil deeds."

"Bless your heart, Alicia. You're a fine woman. That husband of yours is a lucky man."

"That's what I've been telling him for the last twenty years."

"You must have been a child bride," Jacques said.

"Not really. I was eighteen and he was nineteen. He was a private in the regular Army. I was studying to become a nurse. He's a good man and a good husband and father."

A sergeant knocked at the door. An Army sedan was there. Alicia had their coats and hats ready.

"The clouds have darkened, and there is a hint of snow. Keep warm," she warned.

En route to the Disciplinary Barracks, they stopped at a townhouse for General Wilford Ross, who had been recommended by General Bradley to act as a courts-martial advisor to the prosecution staff.

"Will, as I've told you several times, your presence here is deeply appreciated," Bart said. "I relished your analysis last night to our team."

"My pleasure, Bart. I wouldn't have missed this big show for a promotion in rank."

"I think that will come after these trials."

"If I know Bart, he'll be recommending a promotion for you, Will," Jacques added.

The three men went through the metal detector as they entered the Disciplinary Barracks. They stopped at their offices. The three former assistant U.S. Attorneys, who were activated from their retired status to Judge Advocates General, were loading two carts with a large quantity of evidentiary material. Gideon Cartman, Dwight Seagrave and Justin Palmer halted their activity, turned and smartly saluted Bart, who looked at his wristwatch.

"All right, gentlemen, showtime."

Next door, the CIA team composed of Philip Berger, Lloyd Sedgwick, Tony Fuentes, Sophia Carrera and Richard Maybrook, joined by Jacques, followed the prosecutor to the courtroom. Routinely, all passed through another metal detector.

The courtroom was filled to capacity. The room was surrounded by a cordon of white-helmeted Military Police with guns in their holsters. Two large American flags were posted on either side of the tribunal bench. The defense and prosecution tables were directly in front, two yards apart. Translators and court reporters were stationed beneath the bench. The defendants sat in rows, ten feet behind the legal teams. All were dressed in business suits with white shirts and a variety of colored ties and kerchiefs in their front jacket pockets.

The media were seated in a bleacher arrangement against the walls of the court. A VIP section to the right of the prosecution, with armchairs, accommodated Andrei Gromyko, of the Soviet Union; Anthony Eden, Great Britain; France's Pierre Mendes-France, and Abba Eban, of Israel. Sean Briscoe and Ariel Rabin of the Mossad sat in the bottom row of the bleachers, with press badges of the Tel Aviv Times and the Jewish Daily Forward. All were provided with earphones.

Six defense attorneys were at their tables. Two of the six were there primarily for Hitler's defense. Four microphones were in front and one was in the back of the courtroom. Two on opposite sides of the courtroom were set to feed all networks, foreign and domestic. Their cables stretched out of the building to a myriad of vans parked on Riverside Avenue. Anchormen would be broadcasting from those vehicles. Auditoriums at Park College and St. Mary College accommodated the overload of the media.

The tribunal, chosen by the Chairman of the Joint Chiefs, General Bradley, consisted of Admiral Chester W. Nimitz, five-star commander of the Pacific Fleet; General Claire Chennault, organizer of the famed Flying Tigers and commander of the World War II U.S. task force in China, and General Holland M. Smith, World War II commander of the U.S. Marines in the Pacific theater of war.

A provost marshal loudly ordered, "All rise!"

The tribunal, in full dress uniforms, entered the hushed courtroom.

"The court is called to order. Be seated," Nimitz said.

The distinguished admiral's sparse white hair, in contrast to his tanned face, shone under the overhead lights. His piercing blue eyes scanned the crowded room. His battle-hardened face, and those of Chennault and Holland, conveyed a no-nonsense message.

Nimitz said, "Good morning. This tribunal, duly appointed by the government of the United States, is now in session. A caution to counsel and the defendants: These proceedings will be orderly. No outbursts will be permitted. A message to the media and observers. The dignity of this tribunal shall not be assailed by improper conduct. Appropriate measures will be taken to deal with any infractions disturbing the decorum of this court."

The indictments were read. They duplicated the charges in the Nuremberg trials. *Count One*: The common plan of conspiracy involved in acquiring totalitarian control of Germany; utilization of Nazi control for aggressive war. *Count Two*: Crimes against peace; violations of international treaties, agreements and assurances. *Count Three*: War crimes - murder and ill treatment of civilian populations and prisoners of war; deportation of civilians for slave labor, and killing of hostages. *Count Four*: Crimes against humanity - murder, extermination, enslavement; persecution on political and racial grounds.

"On the four counts of the indictments, how do you plead?"

A round of "*Nicht schuldig*" was routinely delivered.

"The prosecution may present its case," Nimitz said.

Bart was mindful of a last minute missive to him, which stated,

Dear Barton,

You are not subject to the constraints put upon me by a four-nation tribunal in Nuremberg. Therefore, my friend, forgo the legal erudition and the sententious prose for stark, incisive terms and, in the parlance of the theatrical, go for the jugular.

Godspeed,
Robert Jackson

Bart rose to his full height of six feet three. In full dress uniform, he was a handsome and imposing figure. His icy blue eyes stared for a long second at Hitler and the other defendants. Facing the bench, he addressed the tribunal and began his opening statement:

"Your Honors, distinguished members of this war-crimes tribunal, for the record, my name is Major General Barton Q. Milburn, chief counsel for the prosecution. We are here today to pursue a corollary to the Nuremberg trials. We have presented to this court the full records of those trials, prosecuted by Supreme Court Justice Robert Jackson and General Telford Taylor.

"Members of the tribunal, the key word in this trial is *outrage*. The most egregious, horrific crimes in the history of mankind have been perpetrated by these defendants over a period of twelve years, from 1933 to 1945. The seeds of these barbaric iniquities were sown in the body politic of Germany, a cultured, Christian country, by a duplicitous derelict, who migrated there as a stateless person. Adolf Hitler was ineligible for public office because he was not a German citizen, having been born in Austria. This conniving Pied Piper of Death got around the law and bought his way into an appointment as a councilor in Brunswick, a state controlled by the Nazis. Thus, three weeks before the election, he automatically became a German citizen. Twice he was defeated for the presidency of Germany by General Paul von Hindenburg.

"Encompassed in the indictments are the horrors committed by these defendants. When detailed by witnesses, and with the presentation of overwhelming evidence, we will hear and see the abysmal atrocities committed in contravention of any law ever devised by man. As a matter of fact, there was total violation of the Ten Commandments, recognized by all religious orders and secular society as the basis-in fact, the foundation- of law in all of civilization. We have here, in the dock, the monstrous perpetrators of the most heinous crimes in the history of mankind."

Bart paused. The translator's words, delivered in German, evoked an outburst of invectives from the prisoners. Admiral Nimitz furiously pounded his gavel. "Defense counsel, restrain your clients or this court will take drastic measures to do it for you."

A gangly, nattily dressed, bespectacled lawyer stood up. "Members of the tribunal, I am Baron Edward von Wolf, counsel for Herr Hitler and others. I beg to apologize for the interruption. However, the defendants can hardly be blamed for their reaction to the scurrilous remarks by the prosecutor. Therefore, I protest and object and ask that General Milburn's statements be stricken from the record," he demanded in perfect English.

"Your apology is accepted, your objection is denied. Now, sit down and do not interrupt again," Nimitz said sharply.

Bart continued, "These proceedings are conducted in compliance with the Manual for Courts-Martial, United States, 1951, dealing with war crimes, sections 498 through 508. Herr Hitler and his minions, plus thousands of John and Jane Does, plus unindicted co-conspirators, are on trial here on four counts: aggressive war, crimes against peace, crimes against humanity, and war crimes. Were this a civil court, the indictments would specify six million counts of murder, millions of counts of rape, mayhem, robbery, slavery and genocide, as described in section 502: Grave breaches of the Geneva Convention 1949. War crimes: willful killing, torture or inhuman treatment, including biological, willfully causing great suffering or serious injury to body or health and extensive destruction and appropriation not justified by military necessity and carried out unlawfully and wantonly."

"General Milburn, I trust you are not going to cite the entire manual dealing with war crimes," Chennault said.

"No, sir, Your Honor. Let me get to the gravamen of the charges. We are here in this courtroom to judge the perpetrators of the greatest carnage in the history of civilization. The defendants are the demonic leaders of this outrage. However, what else will come to light is another crime not inscribed in our laws, yet a crime which cannot be overlooked. That crime, sirs, is complacency and apathy throughout the world, then and now. Indifference to genocide."

"Mr. Prosecutor, please get on with the specifics of your case," General Smith requested.

"Yes, sir. I start with this most evil of men, Adolf Schickelgruber Hitler, *Der Führer* of the Third Reich, the Pied Piper of Death and the leader of the Four Horsemen of the Apocalypse who brought war, famine, pestilence and death to all of Europe."

Bart strode dramatically to the defense table and pointed his finger directly between the eyes of Adolf Hitler, who whispered, "*Arschloch.*"

"Germane to the litany of crimes committed by this prime figure and his co-conspirators is an overview of the background of this fiend, Adolf Schickelgruber Hitler."

Hitler jumped out of his chair, his attorneys trying to restrain him, his hands shaking and shouted, "*Was ist Schickelgruber? Ich bin Hitler*, Chancellor of the Third Reich, *du Quatschkopf!*"

Bart fixed his eyes on Hitler's blinking orbs, his forefinger steadily pointed at him. Nimitz gaveled intently to stifle the loud vocal reaction of the prisoners and observers. Defense lawyers quickly pulled Hitler back into his seat before the MPs could reach him.

"Any more antics, Mr. Hitler, and your mouth will be taped and you'll be put in restraints. Any disturbances by observers and this tribunal will clear the court," Nimitz coldly declared. "Continue, General Milburn."

"Who is Hitler? Born April 30, 1889, in the Austrian town of Braunau. His father was Alois Hitler, a name changed from Hiedler. Without delving into his ancestral heritage, there is evidence that Hitler believed that he was one-fourth Jewish, based on the illegitimate birth of his grandfather, Alois Schickelgruber. This was and is Adolf Hitler's fixation. He tried to hide the records of his grandfather, Alois Schickelgruber, illegitimate son of Maria Anna Schickelgruber. A wealthy Jew named Frankenberger was believed to be the real father of his grandfather Alois. This is contained in Nuremberg trial records. Hans Frank, former Reichsminister, testified that this devil incarnate asked him in 1930 to check on these whispered allegations of Hitler's possible Jewish ancestry. Maria Anna was a servant in the Frankenberger home. Unwed, she was pregnant with Hitler's father. Frank's testimony alleged that Marcus Frankenberger paid for the upkeep of her son until his fourteenth birthday.

"Hitler's years from the age of nineteen to twenty-four were desperate years. He had failed in his studies. He was a failed artist. He was a derelict, consorting with the dregs of society. At age twenty-five, he was in Munich, still a derelict, still failing as an artist. In early 1914 he was arrested as a draft dodger. At the Austrian consulate, he looked like a street bum and cried his way out of a jail sentence. He was told to report in two weeks. After examination, they found him physically unfit for military service.

"However, when Germany went to war in August 1914 he was found fit enough for the German army. He became a courier and was slightly injured by a piece of shrapnel in his derriere. He was sent to a hospital when the war ended. He received medals in 1914 and 1918. Whether he earned them or not, the decorations were suspect. He learned of the public's disillusion with the Weimar Republic's acceptance of the draconian terms of the Versailles Treaty.

"This homeless derelict discovered fertile ground for his gutter-smart ambitions on the soapbox circuit. He honed his silver-tongued forensics in beer halls. His loud, disputatious harangues among the dissolute ne'er-do-wells, street bums and thugs attained the notoriety he sought. He joined the *Deutsche Arbeiterpartei*, the German Workers Party, in 1919. Two years later, the party name was changed to *Nationalsozialistische Deutsche Arbeiterpartei*, or NSDAP, the National Socialist German Workers' Party, later known as the Nazi Party, with Hitler as party chairman.

"In 1923, his evil intent was manifest with his invasion of a nationalist meeting at a beer hall, the Bürgerbräukeller, where he announced, *The national revolution has started.* The following day, he led a march which was dispersed by Bavarian police," Bart continued.

"On April 1, Hitler was found guilty of treason and sentenced to five years in prison at the Landsberg fortress. He was released in November 1924. Nevertheless, this ex-convict, this corporal, this Austrian immigrant, put out a book called *Mein Kampf.* His ideas were written by four men - Rudolf Hess, Emil Maurice, Gottfried Feder, and Alfred Rosenberg. In this Nazi bible, his mantra was expressed. *Get rid of the Jews. Aryanize Germany and give us lebensraum. More room. All of Europe, possibly the world.* This came out in 1925. In 1928 his Nazi party elected twelve deputies to the Reichstag, their parliament. This was two percent of the vote.

"Joseph Goebbels became his propaganda chief. He was a master of mob psychology. The art of panoply was his forte. Parades of uniformed men, beating drums and monarchical pomp were the prime tools for gathering a combination of dissolute mobs meshed with a disconsolate citizenry and their impressionable children. Hitler's haranguing whetted the appetite of a disillusioned populace. The mobs succumbed to Hitler's artifices. The beat went on.

"On September 14, 1930, the Nazi party elected 107 deputies - 18 percent - to the Reichstag. Money poured into the coffers of the Nazi party from dues and secret contributions from industries in and outside Germany. Swiss banks, I.G. Farben, and Krupp, plus closet fascist sympathizers, poured funds into Hitler's drive for power.

"Goebbels, Goering, Hess, von Ribbentrop and Himmler rounded up the dregs of humanity. They marshaled street bums, thugs, thieves, ex-convicts and derelicts into ranks of uniformed storm troopers. This was the SA, the *Sturmabteilung*, wearing brown shirts and Nazi armbands, and with their elongated searchlights used as clubs, striking fear into the hearts and minds of the German people.

"In 1932, on February 25, Hitler became a German citizen, several weeks before election day. On April 10, von Hindenburg was re-elected President. Hitler lost with thirty-seven percent of the vote. Then, on November 6, the Nazi party polled thirty-three and a half percent of the vote, electing one hundred ninety-six deputies to the Reichstag.

"January 30, 1933, was the crucial turning point in the iniquitous history of Germany's Third Reich. Hitler was named Chancellor. Von Papen stepped aside from sharing the office with Hitler, after his secret meeting with Hitler, Hess and Himmler in the home of Kurt von Schröder, a banker in Cologne. Von Papen was warned by Himmler that if he didn't accept the post of Vice Chancellor, his life would be forfeit within days.

"On March 5, 1933, the Nazis elected 288 deputies, still not a majority. Sixteen days later, the Reichstag met. Goering excluded the communists, and the Nazis had an overwhelming majority. Power ran apace from that point. Hitler ordered a boycott against Jewish doctors, lawyers, and commercial enterprises. Later, a Concordat between Germany and the Vatican was signed by von Papen and Cardinal Eugenio Pacelli, who became Pope Pius XII in 1939. Hitler checked out of the League of Nations, as did Japan a few months earlier.

"The momentous day was August 2, 1934, when President Hindenburg died. Hitler announced his total control of the German government. *Der Führer* had become the dictator of the Third Reich. The tyrant flexed his muscles with his uncontested power. This duplicitous, gutter-smart, funny little man with a Charlie Chaplin mustache was not to be laughed at.

"He was full of bombast to the German people," Milburn went on. "Quietly, he was building his army and putting Nazi industry on a war footing. A complacent world did not heed his warnings in *Mein Kampf,* nor did they protest his treatment of Jews. Closet anti-Semites in and out of Germany supported him.

"The Reichstag passed the Nuremberg Law, outlawing all those with Jewish blood, ignoring the a hundred thousand German Jews who fought heroically in World War I. Hitler was caught up in his own mantra of *Get the Jews*. It was a political battle cry which infected all of Germany and was the precursor of the greatest carnage in the history of mankind. Every one of the defendants here participated in the genocide of the Jewish people all over Europe. The Holocaust has put the mark of Cain on all of Germany. Megalomania was growing in the mind of this subhuman, as power took him beyond his ken. His preoccupation with the so-called Jewish question cost this presumed genius a possible victory in his maniacal quest to control all of Europe. Let's quickly trace his plans to ravage every country in Europe.

"He violated every line, every word, and finally the entire Treaty of Versailles.

"The world looked away.

"March 7, 1936 - Hitler sends his troops into the Rhineland. No power objected.

"July 11 - Germany recognizes the sovereignty of Austria. He signs a pact not to interfere in Austrian affairs. He next announces the Italo-German axis. The axis then recognizes the Franco junta as the legal government of Spain. Following that is an anti-Comintern pact with Japan.

"September 7, 1937 - Hitler disavows the Versailles Treaty.

"October 13 - Hitler agrees to respect the sovereign territory of Belgium.

"November 5 - Hitler has a secret meeting with Goering, von Fritsch, Raeder and von Neurath and reveals his plans of aggression for the domination of Europe.

"February 4, 1938 - Hitler shakes up the German High Command. Reichswehr Minister von Blomberg and Commander-in-Chief von Fritsch and thirteen generals are removed. Keitel is named Chief of Staff. Von Ribbentrop becomes Foreign Minister, replacing von Neurath.

"February 12 - Hitler gives an ultimatum to Austrian Chancellor Schuschnigg. Three days later, the Austrians yield to Hitler's demands. Seyss-Inquart is appointed Austrian Minister of the Interior.

"March 9 - The Austrian Chancellor declares a plebiscite for March 13.

"The German threats worked. Schuschnigg resigns two days later. President Miklas names Seyss-Inquart as Chancellor. Hitler's troops march into Austria the following day. Not a shot is fired. Prime Minister Chamberlain flies to Hitler's home in Berchtesgaden to discuss Hitler's demand for the Sudetenland in Czechoslovakia. Roosevelt appeals to Hitler for negotiation. He ignores him.

"October 1 - Hitler's troops enter the Sudetenland.

"November 7 - Ernst von Rath, a secretary in the German Embassy in Paris, is shot by Herschel Grynzspan, a Polish seventeen-year-old. Von Rath dies two days later. Hitler uses this as an excuse to let the SA storm troopers stage a pogrom throughout Germany. Jews were killed, thousands were arrested and sent to concentration camps. Synagogues were burned and Jewish property was destroyed. Hitler demands a fine of one billion marks on German Jews. Half of the four hundred and eighty thousand Jews began fleeing the country," Bart added, pausing for effect.

"January 20, 1939 - Nazi troops enter Prague.

"April 14, 1939 - Hitler reads a letter from President Roosevelt asking Hitler and Mussolini to promise that the independent nations will not be invaded. The Reichstag laughs.

"August 23 - A Soviet-German pact is signed in Moscow, greasing the wheels of war.

"August 25 - President Roosevelt of America, President Daladier of France and Pope Pius XII appeal to Hitler to avert war.

"September 1 - Germany invades Poland.

"September 3 - England and France declare war against Germany.

"April 9, 1940 - Hitler's blitzkrieg invades Norway and Denmark.

"May 10 - Hitler invades the Netherlands, Belgium and Luxembourg.

"May 14 - Holland surrenders.

"May 28 - King Leopold surrenders for Belgium.

"June 14 - Paris falls to the Nazis.

"June 22 - Germany and France sign a peace treaty.

"August 8 - The Battle of Britain results in heavy destruction in London.

"September 17 - Hitler's *Luftwaffe* sustains heavy losses and pulls back from an invasion of Britain.

"October 6 - The Nazis enter Romania.

"October 28 - Italy invades Greece.

"March 11, 1941 - Hitler invades Yugoslavia and Greece.

"June 22, 1941 - Germany invades Russia.

"December 7, 1941 - Japan delivers a sneak attack on Pearl Harbor, and Japan declares war on the United States and Britain. Four days later, this genius, Hitler, prepares for the beginning of the end by declaring war on the United States.

"This chronology was contained in the Nuremberg Diary by prison psychologist G.M. Gilbert, who had access to Goering, Hess, Ribbentrop, Keitel, Kaltenbrunner, Rosenberg, Frank, Frick, Streicher, Funk, Doenitz, Raeder, Sauckel, Jodl, Seyss-Inquart, Speer, and von Neurath. All were found guilty, hanged or imprisoned. Fritsche, von Papen and Schacht were found not guilty.

"These men were just part of the criminal organization which controlled Germany for twelve years and wreaked havoc on the world. Fifty million people died as a result of the machinations of this Pied Piper of Death and his cohorts. However, the fiery cauldron of hate, plunder and devastation was quenched by the armed might of the Allied forces.

"In its wake came the unveiling of Nazi bestiality unparalleled in the history of mankind. Corrupt, despicable, contemptible, degrading, blood-curdling crimes exceeded the devil's handiwork and defied human hallucinations.

"Revisionists are at work at this moment and for generations to come. They are fully financed by these minions of hate and their closet supporters, who will try to erase this stain of the century from our history books.

"There he sits, the richest man in the world, who escaped the Allies and, with a facelift, pretends to be Frederick Avram Nordheim, a Jew," Bart said.

"While the foregoing would have been a full plate for any tyrant, this unbridled, power-mad monster unleashed a death campaign against Jews, Seventh Day Adventists, Gypsies, the lame, the elderly, and children. Only the fit were dragged into forced slave labor at concentration camps all over the conquered lands of Europe.

"At Auschwitz, I.G. Farben built factories there for these enslaved Jews to work for the Nazi war machine. While two and a half million Jews were being gassed to death, babies were tossed alive into crematoriums. We have eight concentration-camp commandants in the dock here.

"With permission of the tribunal, we would like to screen films that have recently come into the prosecution's possession. The footage, which was made by the Germans, the Russians, the British, and the Americans, graphically depicts the bestiality of the Nazi carnage."

"Objection!" an attorney roared in English. On his feet and fastidiously dressed was a familiar figure.

"On what grounds?" Nimitz asked. "Identify yourself."

"I am Alden Gaines, a member of the Illinois Bar and accredited to practice in federal courts."

"State your objection rationale, Counselor."

"The footage mentioned by the prosecutor has not been properly introduced as evidence. I represent the eight alleged commandants of the alleged concentration camps and am co-counsel for Mr. Hitler. Presentation of prejudicial and inflammatory evidence in an opening statement doesn't meet the standards of evidentiary material. No foundation has yet been established for its introduction, nor is there any proof of the validity of these films."

"Would the prosecution care to respond?" Nimitz asked.

"This footage was screened at the evidentiary hearings, when these defendants were bound over for trial," Bart countered. "We have ample evidence to produce to this tribunal to validate the authenticity of the footage, which was obtained from the archives in the United States Army war-crimes office. I have an array of witnesses who can attest to the veracity of these pictures, which were photographed by the Nazis, the Russians, British, French, and Americans. With regard to the material on the liberation of these camps and the results of the atrocities, I personally visited most of the camps and wrote a full report on what I observed, which was classified top secret. This material was declassified six weeks ago. I am prepared to testify as to its accuracy."

"I will object to that as well," Gaines said.

Nimitz excused Bart and Gaines, then huddled with Smith and Chennault. The tribunal returned to the bench. After the court came to order, Nimitz announced their decision.

"The objection of the defense is sustained. The films may be introduced at the proper time when evidence of atrocities is presented, based on testimony by witnesses for the prosecution. Does the defense wish to present its opening statement?" he asked.

Four lawyers rose.

"Come on, Counsel, we're not going to have a Tower of Babel. Who speaks first?"

After a short huddle, Gaines took the floor. "With deep respect for this tribunal, this court does not have the jurisdiction to try these defendants, on the grounds that they were illegally taken into custody in foreign sovereign states. Accordingly, I ask for a dismissal of all charges contained in these specious indictments. That is my objection to these proceedings."

"Counselor Gaines, you are an American member of the bar. Are you accredited to argue before the United States Supreme Court?" Nimitz asked.

"Yes, sir."

"Then this tribunal assumes you are familiar with the high court's decision in *ex parte Quirin*? If you need a refresher, the clerk will hand you a copy."

"Your Honors, I am familiar with *Quirin*. However, the circumstances in this case require an examination of the methods used to capture these men and the treatment accorded them during their confinement."

"All that you have stated was reviewed during the evidentiary hearings. Presiding Judge General Ross heard the same argument. These men have been remanded here for trial properly. Your objection is overruled."

"Exception."

"So noted. Let's proceed."

"The defense reserves the right to make our statement at the conclusion of the prosecution's case," Gaines declared.

"We've run a bit late this morning., It is now 1300 hours, 1 p.m. There will be a recess until 1500, 3 p.m., and we'll sit a bit longer this afternoon."

Bart and his team retired to a specially prepared conference room in the Disciplinary Barracks. They dined on lentil soup, assorted sandwiches and coffee.

"That sleazeball Gaines must have been on Hitler-Nordheim's payroll for a long time. It'll be interesting to see if he defends Darren Mayfield and his brother Paul," Jacques mumbled through his sandwich.

"He's either incredibly brave or incredibly stupid. After all, his Mafia clients must be watching this trial. Their reaction to his presence here should prove interesting," Bart replied.

"Who's our first witness, General?" Major Cartman inquired.

"Sir Clive Fenwick. That'll make *Der Führer* sit up," Bart said.

"Here's Fenwick's file," Jacques said.

"General Milburn, I've reread Fenwick's confessions. May I suggest that you advise him to keep his answers solely on the inculpatory facts and leave out the self-serving *mea culpas*. Let him save that for his own defense," General Ross said.

"You're right, Will. In fact, I'd like to grant immunity or a suspended sentence for him and Keith Reynolds."

"Discuss it with Nimitz," Ross said.

Back in the courtroom, on his desk, Bart found an envelope with a short comment from Ed Murrow on its face. *Great job so far. The note inside should please you.* He opened it and found a note from Fred Friendly, producer at CBS. *General Milburn, my congratulations. Our nation and the world are glued to this historic trial. It is a turning point in the true meaning of the first amendment. A watershed event in the freedom of the press.* Bart turned, caught Murrow's eye and winked. The tribunal entered.

"The prosecution calls Sir Clive Fenwick," Bart began.

The dignified man entered, took the oath and sat attentively, staring at Bart. An agitated Hitler hissed loudly at Fenwick. Baron Wolf placed his hand over Hitler's mouth.

Bart approached the witness. "State your name for the record."

"Sir Clive Fenwick."

"What was your occupation before the war?"

"I was British ambassador to Germany."

"You were an advisor to Prime Minister Chamberlain, is that so?"

"Yes, sir."

"You were friendly with *Der Führer* Hitler at that time?"

"Yes, sir."

"Objection. The prosecution is leading the witness!" Baron Wolf shouted.

Before Nimitz could respond, Bart declared, "Question withdrawn. Sir Clive, in your own words, please describe as succinctly as possible your pre-war role in Nazi Germany and in England."

"Objection."

"On what grounds?" Nimitz snapped.

"This witness's role as an ambassador is not germane to indictments in these proceedings."

"Your objection is overruled. We haven't heard his testimony. Should the tribunal find your objection meritorious, his testimony will be stricken from the record."

In measured tones, his British accent slow and deliberate, Fenwick delivered an absorbing tale of behind-the-scenes activity in Germany and England prior to the outbreak of World War II. He repeated the substance of his confession to Admiral Wayne Thomas. "With 20/20 hindsight, I have concluded that my errors, crimes of omission and commission were egregious."

"Specifics, please."

"Yes, I was Chamberlain's advisor. I felt that Hitler was trying to rehabilitate Germany's weakened economy. I also tried to help prevent a war. There was some strong support on the home front to appease Hitler. Chamberlain was a weak man. He succumbed to pro-Nazi, anti-Semitic supporters. He meant well. He was trying to preserve the peace. So was I."

"Who were his supporters?"

The press section adjusted their chairs. The anticipatory rustling of the media caused a pregnant pause.

"Answer the question," Bart demanded.

"Some members of the royal family, because of their inbreeding of English and German monarchs, plus the Duke of Windsor, formerly King Edward VIII, were all pro-Hitler."

"Who else?"

"American Ambassador Joseph P. Kennedy and Colonel Charles Lindbergh wanted the U.S. to support Hitler. The Cliveden Set, headed by Lady Astor, wanted to put the Duke of Windsor back on the throne."

"Objection on the grounds that this is purely hearsay," Alden Gaines challenged.

"Your Honors, this is not hearsay. If Sir Clive may continue, he will give first-hand knowledge of these facts," Bart said.

"Overruled. Continue, General Milburn."

The dramatic disclosures caused the wire-service members of the press corps to rush to the exit. Bulletins were to be wired around the world.

"Tell the court how you learned these facts," Bart said.

"Sir, I was a participant in meetings with the Duke of Windsor, when he and his duchess met with Hitler at Berghof, his lair in at Berchtesgaden. I was there when Hitler met with Chamberlain. I was at several dinners at the Cliveden estate of Lady Astor, when Lindbergh told us the German Luftwaffe could flatten London and Paris, conquering both France and England. I heard Joseph P. Kennedy use foul anti-Semitic remarks, accusing President Roosevelt of being a pawn of the Jews."

"Are you, or were you, anti-Semitic?"

"Absolutely not. I inveighed strongly with Chamberlain to protest Hitler's treatment of the Jews. I even argued with Hitler on that subject. He told me to talk to Goering and Himmler. I had lots of Jewish friends."

Bart moved closer to the witness. He sharply asked, "How do you justify your employment as executive vice president of Winston General Ltd., Hitler's company?"

"I was recalled from my post when Germany invaded Poland. At the war's end, I believed Hitler committed suicide in his bunker on April 30, 1945. In July of that year, Darren Mayfield came to my home at the behest of Frederick Avram Nordheim, allegedly the richest man in the world. He lured me to Malmo, Sweden, with an offer of one million dollars a year plus bonuses. I could hardly refuse. With his plastic surgery, Van Dyke beard and broad mustache, he didn't look a bit like Hitler."

"Have you any knowledge of the *Revanche Plan*, better known in English as the Revenge Plan?"

"Yes," Fenwick answered firmly.

"Tell the court how you learned of that plan."

"The plan was put in the hands of Gunther Froelich, the president of Winston General, and General Heinrich Müller, head of the Waffen SS."

"What is the Revenge Plan?"

"In case of Hitler's apprehension or death, a maniacal effort is to be activated creating chaos all over the world."

Hitler screamed, "*Lügner*, liar, *Arschloch!*"

All of his lawyers stood up and roared, "Objection! Objection!" Nimitz hammered his gavel. "All of you be seated. We'll hear from you one at a time."

Baron Wolf adjusted his pince-nez glasses. "Sirs, this mythical plan does not come within the scope of these indictments. We strongly object to extraneous alleged crimes being added ad hoc."

"Nonsense. These men are war criminals," Bart shot back. "Their insidious actions, particularly of *Der Führer*, are pertinent to all crimes committed in the past, present or future. We will provide the evidence necessary to substantiate our contention."

"Objection overruled. Continue, General."

"Sir Clive, when you first heard the plan, what happened?"

"When I heard what was being devised, I opposed it vehemently. It was a few days before we were captured. It was then that I heard this was Adolf

Hitler's orders."

"Where was this?"

"At Nordheim's, I mean Hitler's, ranch in La Plata, Argentina. There were fifty well-trained Waffen SS officers there. General Müller was in charge. I objected, saying it was crazy. Froelich threw me out of the room. He called me *a Flasche*, a wimp. He screamed at me."

"Sir Clive, once again, what was the plan?"

"They were prepared to blow up the Panama Canal, the Eiffel Tower, the Versailles palace, the Arc de Triomphe, the Suez Canal, the Israeli parliament in Tel Aviv, and the British Parliament, and assassinate Allied leaders. There is more, I'm sure."

The courtroom observers were in a state of shock. The media were abuzz. They scrambled for the door. Bart turned his back and declared, "No further questions. Your witness."

A heavy-set man, immaculately dressed in a black jacket, striped grey trousers, double-breasted gray vest and flowing red tie, approached the witness. "Members of the tribunal, for the record, my name is Erich von Maunder. I am co-counsel for Adolf Hitler," he announced in guttural English.

The cross-examination began on a strange note. "Sir Clive Fenwick, we have met before. Is that correct?"

"Yes."

"Our relationship was quite cordial?"

"Yes."

"I have always believed that you were a man of impeccable integrity. Why have you turned into a consummate liar?" he rasped.

Bart jumped to his feet. "Objection! This question is a self-serving statement, utterly and despicably out of order. Counsel should be sanctioned for his unseemly statement. If he wishes to impeach this witness, he has all the means at his disposal with proper cross-examination of the witness's truthfulness."

Von Maunder quickly replied, "I withdraw my question and apologize to the court."

Nimitz tapped his gavel. "Counselor, be advised that this tribunal will not tolerate any deviation from proper cross-examination. Do not frame your questions in the guise of a statement. You have ample opportunity to make declaratory remarks in your summation, predicated on testimony adduced in proper cross. Accept this warning. Proceed."

"Mr. Fenwick, how long have you been employed by Herr Hitler?"

"Two weeks."

"You have testified that you were hired by Adolf Hitler in July 1945. Now you are telling this court that you were employed for just two weeks. That proves your credibility is at stake here. *Yes or no?*"

"Not so. I was not hired…"

Von Maunder shouted, "Yes or no!"

Bart rose. "Sirs, direct counsel to allow the witness to answer."

"I am entitled to a yes or no answer to a patent lie. Unless the witness has been suddenly stricken with amnesia, he is lying."

General Smith looked at the witness and asked, "Mr. Fenwick, are you all right?"

"Yes, sir."

"There seems to be an inconsistency in your testimony. Your answer to counsel's question was *two weeks*. Did you mean to state that?"

"Yes sir. I was hired by Frederick Avram Nordheim, a wealthy Jew..."

"Objection!" von Maunder yelled.

Nimitz banged his gavel. "Sir Clive Fenwick will be permitted to answer your question."

"Yes or no," von Maunder pressed.

"I'll explain."

"No, you won't, *yes or no?*"

"I only learned that Nordheim was Hitler..."

"No, no, no! Answer my question *yes or no?*"

"Stop that, Counselor. I've ruled that he can answer in full," Nimitz snapped.

"I object."

"Overruled."

"Exception."

"Noted. Go ahead, Sir Clive."

"Nordheim hired me. I worked for him for seven years. But it was at La Plata, Argentina, just two weeks before we were captured, that I realized Adolf Hitler was still alive."

"If you were so shocked to learn he was Adolf Hitler, why didn't you leave?"

"Because my life was at stake. Any attempt to leave that compound would have meant my death. The raid on that ranch was my liberation. That madman, with his Revenge Plan, is enough proof that he is a born killer."

"Objection."

"Overruled. You opened that door, Counselor," Nimitz declared.

"Herr Fenwick, you handled some finances for Winston General."

"Correct."

"Did any of those transactions indicate any Nazi connections? In fact, they did business with Israel, is that true?"

"Some token transactions, such as carrying oranges in some of the Eagle ships. But I was suspicious of two Swiss banks, one in Zurich and the other in Geneva. You may recall..."

"I didn't ask you that," von Maunder angrily uttered.

"Let him finish his reply," Bart demanded.

"Yes," Nimitz said.

"In fact, I took the matter up with you in Zurich. There were withdrawals from our accounts at the Banque Royale and the Banque Lorraine for Josef Mengele and Martin Bormann in Argentina. You said it was a mistake and that someone was playing tricks on the Swiss banks. You quickly cleaned that up for us. Now I don't think it was a mistake."

"It was a mistake!" von Maunder yelled.

"No, it wasn't. You represent the Swiss Bankers Association. You know

now how those banks are cheating the Jewish depositors."

"Objection, objection!" Baron Wolf and the other lawyers shouted.

Nimitz pounded his gavel.

"Liar!" Maunder yelled.

Bart sat back and smiled at the chaos.

"I demand an apology," Maunder implored.

"You're out of order," Nimitz declared.

"Sir Clive has insulted the Swiss banking system."

"Do you wish to ask any further questions?"

"Yes. Sir Clive, your statement about Swiss banks is not based upon personal knowledge, is it?"

"One has to be deaf and blind, while all the media are reporting on the lawsuits against the Swiss banks and their support of Nazi Germany during the war. Also, their refusal to release funds to the heirs of those Holocaust Jews asking for death certificates."

"No further questions."

Von Maunder threw his hands skyward. Nimitz, Smith and Chennault conferred. Bart looked at his wristwatch. Nimitz addressed counsel. "Gentlemen, it is late. There is no point in calling another witness at this hour. Court is adjourned until 0900 hours, 9 a.m., tomorrow."

The courtroom emptied quickly. A heavy snowstorm, wind-driven, had layered Fort Leavenworth with a foot of snow. The prosecution team adjourned to their conference room. The atmosphere was euphoric. The MPs brought fresh coffee and freshly baked biscuits.

"It's coming down heavy out there, General," a master sergeant noted.

"It's cozy in here," Bart replied. "Thanks for the goodies, Sergeant."

When they left, Gideon Cartman clapped his hands. "Fenwick put it right through the wicket," he laughed.

"Apropos, Gid. But, you have to admit that von Maunder is guilty of several counts of *schmuckery*. You'd think a high-priced lawyer would know better."

"He's not a criminal lawyer," Jacques stated. "Those Swiss banks will have his hide. They must have been watching it on TV."

Sophia asked, "Bart, who's our next witness?"

"I'm going to put on one of our death-camp survivors. We've lodged them at the Lincoln Inn, which we took over. They are comfortable there. On second thought, I'll save them for later. I think Keith Reynolds, alias Konrad Fliegel, will be a real shocker. He'll not only validate Fenwick's testimony, but he'll lead us into the death-camp atrocities. That should set the stage for the Holocaust, as well as the Swiss's not-so-neutral role in the war."

"Perfect, Bart," Berger declared. "That should entice Hitler to the stand."

Assent was unanimous.

"Just a note, Bart. Nimitz, Smith and Chennault are excellent. They are running a tight ship and giving us latitude."

"Couldn't be better. Nimitz knows his law," Bart agreed, then he addressed the group. "Sedgwick and Captain Arnold, collate the files on Reynolds-Fliegel.

This stuff will throw the defense into a tizzy and will be grist for the media mill. Maybrook, Laurent and I will review Keith's confession over dinner tonight. The rest of you get a good night's rest. Let's brave the elements."

At their Victorian house, Alicia was preparing a shepherd's pie, consisting of mashed potatoes, a variety of vegetables and chunks of lamb. Her husband, MP Master Sergeant Louis Lawrence, sat at the kitchen table, drinking coffee and smoking a cigarette. The front door opened. Bart, Jacques, Richard and Sergeant Alex Greenberg, their driver, entered. All were shaking snowflakes off their fleece-lined mackinaws. Alicia met them in the hallway.

"Mean night, gentlemen. I've got a hot dinner in the works for you."

"Alicia, you're a doll," Bart said, smiling.

"I hope you don't mind, sir. My husband's here in the kitchen. You can tell *him* I'm a doll," she chuckled.

"I'll do that. How about some coffee for the sergeant here?"

"Oh, I know him. He's a friend of ours. Come with me, Alex."

They heard Alex and Louis exchange greetings. Bart entered the kitchen. The two MPs jumped to their feet and saluted.

"Never mind the salutes. You're guests here. Alicia, I hope you've made enough food to feed these rascals."

"More than enough, sir."

"General, if I may, I was in court today. You were magnificent, sir," Louis said.

"Thank you, Louis. You've made my day. Enjoy your dinners."

A roaring fire countered the howling winds of the snowstorm. Laurent, Maybrook and Bart enjoyed the homemade cooking. They sipped a fruity Burgundy wine. They spent two hours parsing Fliegel-Reynolds' confessions.

"You were right, Bart, in keeping Bormann and Reynolds out of the courtroom. I saw Hitler haranguing the other defendants. He still thinks he's *Der Führer*," Maybrook said.

"I have a call to make. Rick, you can camp here tonight, or Sergeant Greenberg will drive you to your quarters."

"Thanks, but I need a change of clothes. I'll leave with him."

Bart phoned home. Stanley answered, saying, "General, I watched you all day. You were wonderful."

"Thank you."

"Here's Mrs. Milburn."

"Barton, my Galahad, I'm so proud of you."

"Just don't forget it when I come home."

"Naughty boy."

"How's Quentin and the other imps?"

"All doing well. When are you coming home?"

"This upcoming weekend, depending on the weather. We're having a mean snowstorm."

"I pray for good weather. We miss you."

"Me, too. I love you."

"Ditto."

CHAPTER TWO

Wednesday, February 4, 1953 - Fort Leavenworth
The storm had abated, but two feet of snow blanketed the fort. Army engineers had snowplows clearing the roads in and around the installation. The sky was clear blue and the winter sun shone brightly. The temperature was in the low forties.

The courtroom was full. An MP bellowed, "All rise." The tribunal was seated.

Nimitz motioned to the standees to be seated, then said, "For the record, the prosecution and defense are all present. Call your first witness, General Milburn."

"We call Keith Reynolds."

The little man marched down the center of the courtroom. He was dressed in a navy blue serge suit with a solid light blue tie in a Windsor knot, with a matching handkerchief. He adjusted his gold-rimmed bifocals and faced Bart.

"Good morning, Mr. Reynolds."

"His name is Fliegel!" Hitler shouted.

"That's your correct name, Mr. Reynolds?"

"Yes, sir, I was born in England and my surname was Reynolds. I used the name of Konrad Fliegel when I went to work for Frederick Nordheim."

"Why did you use the name of Fliegel?"

"It was a prerequisite that I become a Swiss citizen and change my name if I wanted the job at the Banque Lorraine."

"Back up a little, Mr. Reynolds. Give us the background leading up to your job at the bank."

He repeated the essentials of his confession to Bart and Maybrook, reiterating his decision to stop pretending to be a Jew. He served as a comptroller in the office of the Chancellor of the Exchequer during Prime Minister Chamberlain's administration. Bart then led him to his promotion as assistant and advisor to Chamberlain.

"I met Ambassador Joseph P. Kennedy, America's envoy to England and a good friend of the Prime Minister. He took a great interest in me. We lunched a few times. He kept asking me about financial matters. He was very much against war with Germany. He admired Hitler. He wanted the U.S. to join up with Hitler."

"Your Honor, this is fascinating, but is hardly pertinent to the issues before this court," Wolf argued.

"*Schweig*, you fool," Hitler whispered. "He is saying good things about me."

"I withdraw my remarks."

"Continue," Bart urged.

"One night, I was invited to a dinner at the court of St. James's by Kennedy. At that dinner, I met Charles Lindbergh, Lady Astor and members of the Cliveden Set, rich English people supporting Hitler."

Hitler whispered to his lawyers, "See, I had important support in England."

"Kennedy was very anti-Semitic. So were the others at that dinner. Kennedy told Lindbergh to tell us what he saw in Germany."

"What did Lindbergh say?"

"Hearsay!" Baron Wolf shouted.

"*Setzen sie*," Hitler ordered.

Embarrassed, Baron Wolf sank in his chair.

"Go on," Bart said.

"Lindbergh said Goering's Luftwaffe was the most powerful in the world and could bomb England and France into a quick surrender."

"Hitler's Luftwaffe!" Der Führer shouted.

"Mr. Hitler, if you want to testify, you'll get your chance. Now, sit down and shut up," Nimitz angrily ordered.

"Mr. Reynolds, were you, or are you, anti-Semitic?" Bart asked.

"Definitely not. I was very disturbed by the anti-Semitism expressed by Kennedy and the others."

"Why did you change your citizenship?"

"My wife died on July 30, 1939. Kennedy is a Catholic and so am I. He sent a lot of flowers to the church. He attended the services. He had helped me make lots of money in American stocks and English shares. He advised me to place my money in the Banque Lorraine in Geneva. I had two young daughters to raise. A few weeks later he invited me to lunch. He was curious about Chamberlain's weakness and Churchill's popularity. Then, suddenly, he told me to leave the country. He said there would be a terrible war."

"What did you do?"

"Kennedy said I could be of great help to him if I took a job with the Banque Lorraine. He said I would become a very rich man and would be able to protect my daughters if I made the move. Two days later I called him. He called von Leute, president of the bank. I met with him in Geneva. Von Leute offered me a bounteous salary and a beautiful house. The bank would give me a mortgage for 100 percent of the cost of the house at three percent interest. I had to become a citizen. He liked my fluency in German and French."

"Well, what happened next?"

"Two days after I returned to talk it over with my children and my sister, Kennedy invited me to lunch. He told me to leave London quickly because Hitler was going to invade Poland. I resigned my position and on August 28, 1939, I put my house up for sale or lease and took my two daughters to Geneva. Kennedy was right. The Nazis invaded Poland four days later."

"Tell the court about your job at the Banque Lorraine."

"I kept the ledgers of deposits for Hitler, later Nordheim."

"Were there bank accounts for the Nazis and their supporters?"

Objections from four lawyers halted the Q & A. Nimitz ordered the attorneys into chambers.

Jacques whispered to Bart, "Allen Dulles is at the door talking with Baron Wolf and Alden Gaines. Don't look now, but they're coming this way."

In chambers, there was a verbal free-for-all. General Smith, a hardened, no-nonsense Marine, lit a cigarette and eyed the four defense lawyers, who were gesticulating and stepping on each other's lines while objecting to references to Swiss banks. Nimitz and Chennault chatted with Bart and Cartman.

At the crescendo of Alden Gaines' citation of several Supreme Court decisions, Smith released a large cloud of smoke and in military style yelled, "Shut the hell up! Shysterism will not be tolerated here. You're yammering like a bunch of fishwives. One at a time may speak."

The outburst produced a shroud of silence. Nimitz and Chennault maintained a quiet dignity. Bart forced himself to cover a chuckle. Cartman was open-mouthed in shock. The four defense lawyers were visibly abashed.

"I've heard your objections, gentlemen. Now I'd like to hear the prosecution's response," Nimitz ordered.

"Members of the tribunal, apparently my learned opponents have overlooked the bill of particulars attached to the list of indictments," Bart interjected. "It is clearly stated that the Banque Lorraine, the Banque Royale, a group of other banks and the Swiss Bankers Association are named as unindicted co-conspirators."

Confusion reigned supreme. The four defense attorneys shouted at each other, then Nimitz slapped his desk. "Your objections are overruled. Take your arguments out of this chamber, now!"

Cartman handed the section dealing with the unindicted co-conspirators to Nimitz. He smiled at Cartman and Bart. The dismayed defense lawyers sheepishly returned to the courtroom.

"Mr. Reynolds, do you recall my last question?" Bart continued.

"Yes, sir." He recounted his confession with details of Hitler-Nordheim, Bormann, Goering, Goebbels and Himmler's banking business with the Swiss banks. A startling account was rendered of the thousands of Jewish accounts frozen and the laundering of bona fide currencies and counterfeits. He said that the vaults were filled with gold, jewels, cut diamonds and loot plundered from conquered countries.

Reynolds paused in his recital and slowly drank a full glass of water.

"Please continue," Bart said.

"Kennedy used the banks to manipulate his accounts during the war. I.G. Farben received large sums from the Wehrmacht and acted as a conduit to funnel large sums into Hitler's, Goering's and Himmler's accounts. Billions of marks, dollars, francs and counterfeit currencies were laundered in exchange for war materials. Frozen Jewish accounts were pilfered to finance the Nazi war effort."

"*Lügner*, liar!" Hitler yelled.

"That's the last time for you, Mr. Hitler. Your mouth will be taped," Nimitz angrily exploded. "Stand up and face me. You are *not Der Führer*. Do you understand me?"

The interpreters repeated the excoriation in German. Hitler remained standing, stuck his arm up in the Nazi salute and silently plopped arrogantly into his chair.

"Let the record show that Herr Hitler just exhibited his Nazi salute. His disrespect for this court is herewith noted," Nimitz declared.

Hitler's lawyers huddled with him, warning him of the consequences if he continued his tirades.

Bart urged Reynolds to detail his saga. "Did you have knowledge of Nazi atrocities?"

"Objection on the grounds of hearsay!" Wolf roared.

"Your objection will be sustained unless the witness can furnish first-hand knowledge," Nimitz ruled.

"Do you have personal knowledge of Nazi atrocities?" Bart pressed.

"Yes, I do. The Swiss were helping finance Nazi Germany. A consortium of a few banks transferred funds to them. The world stood still while the Holocaust was slaughtering thousands of Jews every twenty-four hours. There were two wars going on: the Nazis versus the Allies, and the despicable, horrible, monstrous killing of unarmed Jews, Christian dissenters, Gypsies, Jehovah's Witnesses, the lame, halt, babies, children, old people, Russians, Poles, Belgians, Dutch, French, and prisoners of war all over Europe."

Another flurry of objections was denied. Murmurs of shock swept the courtroom as the wire-service reporters raced to the doors to file more material from the startling testimony. A verbal battle took place among the eight concentration-camp commandants. The MPs raced to the second row behind the defense table. Nimitz, Smith and Chennault rose. "This court will take a fifteen-minute recess."

Two MPs escorted Reynolds to the men's room. Bart lit a cigarette and relaxed at his table. Douglas Milburn and Ed Murrow walked over to Bart.

"Dynamite, brother," Doug patted him on the shoulder.

"General, it's about time that the filth in Pandora's box was exposed. I've been a lone voice in recent days. This airing is not only therapeutic, it's a very much needed education," Murrow said.

"Ed, I deeply appreciate your kind remarks."

Bart stood up, looked at them and said, "Off the record, agreed?" They nodded. "Remember Al Jolson's remark?"

"Yeah," Doug whispered. "You ain't heard nothin' yet."

"You said it, I didn't. No quotes out of context."

They laughed.

"Scat now, fellas, I've got work to do."

Jacques walked toward the door with Douglas. Out of earshot of the media, he whispered, "When you're through with your reports, brother, join us for dinner at our house. Here's a slip with the address."

"I'll be there, Jacques."

When the court came to order again, Reynolds was back on the stand. He continued a horrific account of the torture of the Jews, slave labor, emaciated, starved, skeletal cadavers, methodical assembly-line executions of millions in gas chambers, machine-gun murders by firing squads, and grave-digging by victims for their own burials in large pits.

"Himmler said bullets were too expensive, so he devised gas chambers in the guise of showers," Reynolds testified. Although the account was a reprise of his confessions, its effect on the millions listening to the broadcast had the world in a state of shock. Revisionists were baffled, and were meeting to plan contradictory answers to the lurid testimony.

"How did you know all that at first hand?" Bart asked.

A dramatic pause ensued as Reynolds slowly drank another glass of water. The tribunal, stone-faced, scanned the courtroom. The press were intently scribbling their notes, and some were whispering their reports into tape recorders. The prisoner's agitation was manifest, but he repeated his confession. "I was sent into Germany at Himmler's request to gather money from these evil, licentious, murdering bastards for deposit in our bank. In Munich, at the Four Seasons Hotel, I was sent to Goering's room. This fat drug addict was in a large bed having an orgy with men and women. He asked me to join in. I refused. His reputed satyriasis was evident. He said, *Take that bag on the dresser and get out.*"

"Satyriasis? I know the word, but please explain it for the record," Bart requested.

"Excessive sexual craving in men, like nymphomania is for women. Although I heard he was a bisexual."

Nervous laughter exploded in the courtroom. Nimitz grimly gaveled for order. "This is hardly the place for jocularity," he declaimed. "The issues before this court are deadly serious. Go on, Mr. Reynolds."

"Later, I met with Heinrich Himmler. This chinless chicken farmer, with his concave stance in a Nazi uniform, surprised me. He looked like a circus clown. Yet he was the coldest murderer of them all, even though he could have been a waiter in a Rathskeller. He took me to Dachau, just nine miles outside Munich. He showed me pictures of his gas showers. Music was playing. It was sickening, and he gloated, showing me photos of naked men and women being put in these charnel houses. There were cadavers of men, women and children stacked on top of each other. This monster laughed, telling me how efficient he was. At Auschwitz, in Poland, he said, *We've exterminated two and a half million Jews. When we're through, there won't be a Jew left alive in Europe. In Russia, we've already killed one million. Next comes England and then America. Germany will rule the world. When Hitler is gone, I'll be the next Führer.*"

Tears rolled down Reynolds' cheeks. Not a sound could be heard in the aghast audience.

"What else?" Bart gently asked.

"Sir, I can't believe I was part of this monstrous cabal. *Mea culpa.* I still have nightmares over the beastliness of this formerly Christian country. If this court finds me guilty for my small part in this and sentences me to hang, I'll go with a prayer of forgiveness. I can't go on any more."

"No further questions," Bart said.

"Court is adjourned and will convene at 1400 hours, 2 p.m.," Nimitz announced.

☆ ☆ ☆ ☆

Court was in session promptly at 1400 hours. The tribunal called for order, and Reynolds was back on the stand.

"The defense may cross-examine," Nimitz decreed.

Alden Gaines stepped forward, as Reynolds nervously clasped his rosary beads.

"Mr. Konrad Fliegel, are you a rich man?"

Bart jumped up. "Your Honors, this man's name is Keith Reynolds. I ask the court to instruct counsel to address the witness by his proper name."

"Members of the tribunal, he legally changed his name to Fliegel and gave up his British citizenship," Gaines countered.

"If it please the court, I have a document here, which I offer in evidence. Mr. Reynolds' name and citizenship in England have been restored. He has rejected his Swiss citizenship." Bart handed the provost marshal a set of British citizenship papers and a British passport dated December 24, 1952. The tribunal examined the documents and instructed the provost marshal to let Gaines examine them. Jacques and the defense team smiled. Gaines, nonplussed for the moment, studiously perused the papers in an effort to get his thoughts organized. Behind him, the defendants were muttering expletives. "Slick," Gaines murmured.

"Did you say something, Counsel?" Nimitz asked.

"No, sir."

"Proceed."

"Mr. Reynolds, are you a rich man?"

"Not at the present time."

"That's a vague reply. Let me help you. Isn't it a fact that a considerable sum of money was transferred to your account here in the United States?"

"Yes."

"Then you are a rich man."

"No, sir, I'm not at the moment."

"What does that mean? Have you lost it?"

"No."

"What happened to those funds?"

"The United States government froze those funds."

"All of it?"

"Except two-hundred-thousand dollars for my children to use. Personally, I have no money. I am a prisoner of this government."

"You are under indictment?"

"Yes, sir."

"Have you been promised freedom or some consideration to testify against your fellow defendants?"

"No, sir."

"You are under oath. American courts deal severely with perjurers."

"I am not a perjurer."

"Then why did you tell such monstrous lies against your fellow defendants?"

"I told the truth about these evil monsters. Adolf Hitler is the most evil man in history. He orchestrated..."

"Objection. Stop now!"

Bart was on his feet.

"Not necessary, General. Please be seated. I'll handle this," Nimitz said testily.

"Now, Counselor Gaines, if you cut off a witness because you don't like his answer, I'll hold you in contempt. In a military court, that means instant incarceration in the brig. Do you understand me?" Nimitz said.

"Yes, sir."

"Finish your answer, Mr. Reynolds."

"Hitler orchestrated the worst crimes in the history of man. He was financed by some Swiss banks and the stolen Jewish money, possessions and gold fillings from their dead bodies. He is a monster and so are his cohorts."

"Objection. I ask that all of Mr. Reynolds' remarks be stricken from the record."

"Mr. Gaines, do you recall your question?"

"Yes."

"Well, let me read it back to you. *Then why did you tell such monstrous lies against your fellow defendants?* With such a question, what in the name of common sense did you expect for an answer? You opened the door wide enough for tons of truth to drive through. You asked for it and you got it. Objection overruled," Nimitz declared.

Gaines, discomfited and angry, lost control of himself, attempting to cover his embarrassment with his client and fellow attorneys, shouting, "Do I detect a biased judiciary? This court is making a mockery of our justice system!"

"Are you through, Mr. Gaines?" Nimitz calmly asked.

"You're damn right I am."

"Well, I'm not. You are herewith being held in contempt of court. You are fined ten thousand dollars and given ten days in detention. Provost marshal, have two Military Police escort Mr. Gaines to his cell."

"This is an outrage! I demand bail!"

"Your offense is not bailable."

The MPs quickly manacled Gaines and rudely escorted him out. The press ran to the doors. The observers were buzzing. The TV cameras focused on the struggling exit of Gaines. The rat-a-tat-tat of the gavel resounded throughout the courtroom. Hitler stood up.

"What is it, Mr. Hitler?"

"I wish to defend myself."

"Sit down. Mr. Wolf, do you wish to continue the cross-examination?"

"I would like to, but Mr. Hitler has discharged his attorneys. I believe, sir, he has the right to defend himself, *pro per*."

"General Milburn, do you wish to comment?"

"Under Section 48 of the Manual for Courts-Martial United States 1951, page 67I, titled Counsel for the Accused, Section 48A titled Statutory Right to Counsel of Choice - broadly interpreted, there is no restriction stated for a *pro per* defense. Further, he would be assisted by co-counsel appointed by the court. He may have civilian co-counsel, at his own expense."

"Very well, Mr. Hitler, would you accept co-counsel appointed by the court, or have Baron Wolf guide you on the rules of the court?" Nimitz asked.

"Baron Wolf *er ist genug*."

"Enough, you say? Baron Wolf, will you assist?"

"Yes, sir."

"Mr. Hitler, you may cross-examine, at your own risk, within the rules of this court."

"*Entschuldigung*. I will speak in Deutsch."

"Mr. Reynolds, do you speak German, or do you prefer to use the earphones for translation?"

"German is fine, sir."

"Herr Fliegel, I have..."

"Now, now, it's been established that the name of the witness is Keith Reynolds, so let's get off on the right foot," Nimitz said.

"*Was* means *foot*?" Hitler asked.

Baron Wolf whispered the explanation.

"Ah. So, Mr. Reynolds, you work for me, Adolf Hitler, for two years. Not so?"

"No. I worked for you when you were Frederick Avram Nordheim, a Jewish philanthropist and survivor of Auschwitz."

"You never suspected I was *Der Führer*, Chancellor of Germany's Third Reich?"

"Oh, I never met you when I worked at the Banque Lorraine. I handled deposits of millions in your secret account when you were Hitler. When you hired me, you had a new face with plastic surgery. Even your voice was changed from what I saw and heard on the newsreels."

"Herr Reynolds, you testified here that you realized I was *Der Führer* a few days before your capture. I wasn't there, was I? How did you know?"

"When Heinrich 'Gestapo' Müller referred to you, Nordheim, as Hitler,

Der Führer."

"Yet when you worked for the bank, you met with Goering and Himmler and took their money for deposit. You were also handling my deposits."

"Yes, you were Hitler then, and Nordheim when I worked for you," Reynolds replied.

"Weren't you, in fact, working for me when you handled deposits in my name as Hitler?"

"Technically, yes. When the war ended, you were announced as a suicide with your wife Eva Braun. Your atrocities as Adolf Hitler came to light when you and Nazi Germany were defeated. You are a despicable monster."

Although Hitler's right hand was palsied, he controlled the tremors by placing his hands on his hips. Now he assumed a typical Hitleresque stance. "You are a religious man. A Catholic, yes? You believe in Jesus as the Messiah?"

"Objection. The witness's religious beliefs are not pertinent to the issues in this case," Bart protested.

"Hear me, hear me," Hitler pleaded.

"Objection overruled. We'll see where the deponent is going."

"Yes, I do believe."

"You know that Jesus was a Jewish rabbi?"

"Yes."

"Did you know his name was Yeshua Ben Joseph?"

"No."

"Have you read the Bible?"

"Yes. All the time."

"Do you believe in the Bible?" Hitler asked.

"Very much so."

"Yet you don't know that Yeshua means Joshua. The Greeks changed it to Jesus and called him the Christos, the anointed one. Thus he is now known as Jesus Christ, the Messiah."

"Maybe."

"Jesus had a mission. He preached against the Orthodox Jews, chased the money changers out of their temple. Did you know that he had a calling?"

"Yes."

"Is it possible another Messiah came to Germany with a calling?" Hitler pressed.

"No, no, not you."

"Yes, me. My bible for my people is *Mein Kampf.* That's the real bible, and I am to be crucified for my mission. Do you know that?"

"You're a filthy, rotten atheist. You call yourself the Messiah for the German people?"

"Yes, yes, I am the Messiah. The German people follow me." Hitler now seemed his old arrogant self.

"General Milburn, aren't you going to object to this self-serving heretic litany?" Nimitz asked.

"Your Honor, the defendant's cross-examination, while going far afield of the issues, is digging his own grave. No objection."

"Very well."

"I think you are a megalomaniac who corrupted a whole nation," Reynolds said.

"That is Jewish propaganda, just like the Old and New Testaments. The English word for those books is apocrypha. All the so-called scribes for the New Testament, the propaganda for Christianity, were Jews except Luke. Did you know that?"

"Yes."

"Well, Nazism was the true religion. The Jews caused World War I and World War II. I led the crusade to destroy them and you call me names. Why? Are you being paid by the Jews?"

"Adolf Hitler, you are and were suffering from delusions. You are Satan personified. Messiah of Hell, that's who you are. A messenger from hell. Mephistopheles. Your religion is paganism. All you Nazis are pagans. Lucifers!"

"*Schweigen, Arschloch!*" Hitler roared. "Holocaust One came, Holocaust Two will come soon. *Mein Kampf* is the true bible!"

"Enough, Hitler. Sit down," Nimitz ordered.

General Smith spoke up. "On a matter of personal privilege, I would like to express my outrage at Hitler's blasphemous cross-examination of Mr. Reynolds."

"Members of the tribunal, may I be heard?" Baron Wolf requested.

"Who are you representing now?" Nimitz asked.

"I am co-counsel for the eight alleged commandants, and I have been re-hired by Mr. Hitler. However, I rise in behalf of Counselor Gaines. I have a note here from him asking for permission to appear before you for the purpose of expressing his sincere apologies for his outrageous conduct before this Court. *Outrageous* is his word."

"We will hear your argument in his behalf in the morning. The tribunal will take your appeal under advisement, Counsel." Nimitz looked at his watch, then added, "I have been advised that another storm is expected within the hour. Court is now adjourned until 0900, 9 a.m., tomorrow."

He rapped his gavel. Bart busily gathered his files, then felt a tap on his shoulders. He looked up and in surprise stood up when he recognized the man standing behind him.

"General, I'd like a word to congratulate you."

Bart smiled at the usually dour former ambassador to the United States. The smile was returned.

"*Spassiba*, Mr. Gromyko."

They conversed in Russian. "I remember you as a young colonel when you met with our general staff in Moscow in the summer of 1941 after the Soviet Union was invaded by these Nazi bastards."

"Yes, Mr. Gomyko, you were very cordial to me. In fact, I remember our dinner in the Kremlin with Marshal Zhukov."

"Your fluency in Russian surprised us all."

"I remember the lecture you delivered to Zhukov on the proper way to make Russian borscht. You said a cold potato should be put in the soup. He argued it should be hot."

Both men laughed. Abba Eban and Jacques watched the sight of the Cold War warriors exchanging pleasantries.

"Well, General, you were very helpful in getting Roosevelt to ship arms to us," Gromyko continued.

"I was curious as to how cool you people were during the invasion."

"Our main secret weapon, as you know, was to let this *schmuck* drive his Wehrmacht deep into the steppes of Russia for the Russian winter to destroy him. When they got to Stalingrad, we were ready for them. This would-be military genius learned nothing from Karl von Clausewitz, or from the failures of Napoleon. We showed them up. Winter is always a great weapon for us."

"I hope our countries thaw this Cold War, Andrei."

"Well, maybe. Stalin is not well. Maybe there will be a change. However, Barton, we are not too happy that the Soviet Union didn't participate in your raids, and our exclusion from this tribunal. We haven't made too much noise about our displeasure, as I've convinced Stalin not to sound sour grapes."

"Andrei Andreyevich, I know you to be a decent, well-educated man with a great future in your country. You're not an anti-Semite, are you?"

"No, of course not. What can one man do in an oligarchy with a dictator at the helm? I could be hanged for saying this, but I'm loyal to my country. Better days are coming."

"*Dos vedanya*, Andrei."

Abba Eban caught Bart's eye. The media were gone. Gromyko left. Jacques pointed at Eban, indicating a meeting. Bart nodded toward the door. They met in the corridor leading to the conference room. In the dimly lit hallway, Bart greeted Eban. "Abba, how are you?"

"A bit disturbed, General," he declared in his clipped British accent. "I don't mean to pry. Correct that, I *do* mean to pry. What was that *tête á tête* with that commie bastard?"

"Small talk - a few words of Soviet displeasure with their exclusion from these proceedings. He urged me to bring out Nazi atrocities in Russia. That's about it. He mentioned Stalin is not well."

"Yes, our Mossad says his days are numbered. However, that's not what disturbs me. When are you going to get into the hard core of the Holocaust?"

"Abba, you anticipate me. I started with two insiders, Sir Clive Fenwick and Keith Reynolds, as a lead-in for the anatomy of the atrocities. I've got eight commandants of these death camps in the dock. I'll strip them to the bone. Intermittently, I intend to put on survivors as eyewitnesses to the assembly-line slaughter of millions of Jews. During all that, we will be able to run those ghastly films of the carnage. Satisfied?"

"Thank you, Barton. I guess I am impatient. You've been magnificent so far. I just want to update Prime Minister Ben-Gurion."

At that moment, Sean Briscoe stuck his head in the corridor through a partly opened door. An MP was restraining him. "Bart, this is urgent," Briscoe begged.

"Okay, Sergeant, let him come here."

"General, Bart, I just saw one of Hitler's legal eagles hand him a vial. I think you ought to check it out now. Suppose it's cyanide. There goes your trial," Briscoe breathlessly urged in his heavy Irish brogue.

Bart ran into the conference room. The prosecution team was startled by the urgency displayed at Bart's entry, followed by Jacques, Eban and Briscoe. He picked up the phone. "Give me the cell block pronto. This is General Milburn."

"Yes sir," the duty officer, Master Sergeant Coniff, replied.

"Hitler's been handed a vial of something. If it's not too late, handcuffs and shackles. Strip him naked. Hurry, I'll be right there."

"Thanks, Sean. Now, you and Mr. Eban must leave. Come on, Jacques."

At full speed, they ran toward the detention cells. A struggle was taking place in Hitler's cell. Invectives were heard in German from Hitler and in English from the MPs.

As Bart and Jacques entered the brightly lit cell, Hitler was in the process of being disrobed. His wild-eyed look focused on Milburn. "*Ach, das Arschloch* is here."

The MPs finally stripped him naked. The provost marshal searched his clothes. An MP had a power grip on Hitler's face, forcing his mouth open. He stuck his left hand into his open mouth. Hitler bit down. The MP pulled his hand out, a white pill in his hand, blood dripping from his knuckles. The MP handed the white capsule to Bart and then instinctively smashed a knockout punch to Hitler's jaw, sending him to the cement floor.

"He had it under his tongue," the MP sighed.

"Get a medic here with a tetanus shot for this sergeant. Also, have him bring rubber gloves. Check his anus and all of his orifices and between his toes."

"General, I'm sorry I punched him cold. It was a reaction to the bite."

"Sergeant, the only thing I'm sorry about is that bite on your hand. You've got my full support."

The sergeant shouted, "Bingo!" He pulled a vial out of Hitler's pants pocket. Bart took the cap off the small bottle. He smelled it gingerly.

"I don't think it's cyanide."

Two medics arrived. One cleaned up the sergeant's wounds and gave him a tetanus shot and an antibiotic pill. The other medic probed Hitler's anus, checked between his toes and peered into his ears with a pen light. Hitler opened his eyes.

"General, as a precaution, I'm going to give him an oral wash and a speed enema. He shows no signs of ingestion."

"Go to it."

"Sergeant, this man is to be put on a suicide watch from now on. Jacques, we've got to get Sean to point out the person who gave him this vial. Now, doctors, I want your lab to analyze these capsules. Have the answer delivered to me in the morning by 0800 in the prosecution conference room. Also, let me know how the sergeant's hand is healing."

On the way out, they checked René Soltere on the upper floor, advising him that he would be testifying in the morning. Soltere was a former member of the Gestapo in Vichy France, and a Nazi camp commandant.

CHAPTER THREE

Thursday, February 5, 1953 - Day Three

At 0800, the prosecution staff and the CIA backup team were in the conference room, where pitchers of fresh-squeezed orange juice were on the table. Bart was discussing the testimony of René Soltere when an MP approached him. "Sir, Captain Wallace, our medical officer, has a report for you."

"Send him in, Sergeant."

The captain, prematurely gray at the temples, tall and professional, saluted, then said, "Sir, I have the analysis you requested."

The lab report was a short paragraph: *The ingredients in the vial are mild amounts of Permethrin, normally used as insecticide. Contains Phenoxypheny Methyl 2.2 icis-transdichloralthenyl and 2.2 dimethylpropenecarbolate. Analyzed by Major Ernest Palmer, 1345 hours 2/5/52.*

"Sit down and have a cup of coffee," Bart said.

Jacques placed a cup in front of him and poured the hot beverage.

"What's the answer, Captain?"

Wallace sipped the hot brew and looked speculatively at Bart. "Sir, something strange is going on here. At first we expected to find pure cyanide in those capsules. There were twelve in all - the one taken from the mouth of the prisoner and eleven others in the vial. All twelve were carefully analyzed. There was a combination of Permethrin in each one, ingredients used as insecticides. These are mild and cause vomiting and severe cramps, not sufficient to cause instant death, like the one Goering used in his suicide at Nuremberg."

"Are you certain?"

"Absolutely, sir. It could have killed him if he took large amounts without proper medical attention, lots of water orally and enemas, plus antidotes."

"What do you make of it?"

"Whoever provided it is either an amateur chemist or someone who wanted him to suffer if more than one is ingested."

"Baffling."

The captain handed the analysis report to Bart. "By the way, sir, here's the vial. Strange, the label on that bottle had been removed. It looks exactly like ones usually containing nitroglycerin."

"Hell, that's for heart conditions, usually placed under the tongue for heart pains or flutters," Bart said.

"Exactly, sir."

"Captain, thank you for your efforts. Please, don't let your lab boys discuss this outside your domain."

"We never do. Our medics are under orders to keep infirmary matters confidential. By the way, sir, our entire staff has been catching the trial on the radio with our patients each day. Forgive my language, sir, but you're doing a hell of a job. We're right proud of you."

Bart laughed. "Thank you, Captain."

The captain saluted and left. Jacques and Bart discussed the analysis, then Bart said, "Find Sean Briscoe. He'll probably be in the courtroom shortly. Ask him to point out the person who handed the pills to Hitler."

Bart beckoned Gideon Cartman and Lloyd Sedgwick, saying, "Fellows, I am going to look in on Hitler. You two, bring René Soltere to the witness room. Check his attitude and willingness to testify fully. I'll meet you in court. We have half an hour. Hurry."

The cellblock duty officer, Master Sergeant Brian Coniff, was in the last few hours of his shift. He saluted Bart.

"How's Herr Hitler this morning?"

"He slept through most of the night. Woke up two hours ago, yelling, *Mein herz arslochs* or something like that."

"Get a medic in here now."

"Yes, sir."

Bart took the cell-door key and opened the steel door.

"*Du bist verrückt*, General. Why you do this to me?" Hitler shouted, waving his handcuffed hands. I was taking pill for my heart."

"What's wrong with your heart?"

"When I get excited, it pounds too fast."

The medic arrived and saluted. "Lieutenant Martin Gould, sir."

"Check his heart."

The young medic opened his bag and removed a stethoscope. He listened to Hitler's heart, chest and back. Applying the pads of a blood-pressure instrument, he said, "The heartbeat is a little fast." Squeezing the rubber bulb, he studied the register. "Sir, his blood pressure is unusually high. With your permission, sir, I'll give him a tranquilizer. Diazepam. That should calm him down."

"Go ahead."

Hitler took the pill and, with a glass of water, swallowed it.

"Get dressed, Adolf. You're going back to court."

"Sergeant, have you got some food for this contemptible soul?"

Coffee and a roll were supplied. Hitler wolfed down the roll and slurped his coffee. Bart lit a cigarette and quietly observed the *Führer* staining his Van Dyke beard with the drink.

"You think I was committing suicide. That's for *muschi*, like Goering. Unless you hang me, I'll be around for a long time. Maybe *Der Führer* again."

"Hitler, not *Der Führer*. You'll be the number one *arschloch* of all time."

Sergeant Coniff was called back into the cell.

"Have two of your men bring the prisoner to the court," Bart ordered, then left.

In the corridor leading to the courtroom, Jacques and Sean Briscoe had a young man up against the wall. Two MPs flanked him. Bart recognized him as one of the paralegals assisting the defense team. He was well dressed, in his middle twenties, with blond hair and a fair complexion. At the moment he was pale, and, in a German accent, he kept repeating, "Not me, not me."

Bart intruded and coldly asked, "Not me what?"

"He insists that a lawyer gave him the vial to hand to Hitler," Jacques answered. "Which lawyer, he wouldn't say."

"*Sprechen sie Deutsch?*" Bart asked.

"*Jawohl.*"

Bart took him away from the group. In German, he advised the frightened young man to name the lawyer. "What's your name?"

"I am Adolf Kliest."

"Are you German?"

"*Nein*, I am Swiss."

"Do you have a family?"

"Yes. In Zurich. A father, mother, two sisters and a fiancée."

"Too bad. They'll miss you, because you'll be facing a firing squad this morning. It's a shame for a young man like you to die so early in life."

He began slobbering, saliva running down his chin and cried loudly, "*Nein, nein*, I tell you!"

Jacques, Sean, and the MPs smiled.

"I told you he'd break him," Jacques said.

"Who gave you the pills?"

"Erich Stolz. He's the lawyer the bankers hired for Hitler."

"Take this boy to a holding cell," Bart ordered the MPs. "And then come back to your posts in the courtroom."

Sean went back to his seat in the press section. Bart and Jacques entered the courtroom. Ten minutes before the time for the court session to begin, Bart huddled with Judge Advocate General Wilford Ross, Gideon Cartman, Morton Aldrich, and Jacques. He posed the question of putting Ricardo von Leute on as his first witness, also as a hostile witness to flush out his lawyer, Erich Stolz. The alternative was to go ahead with René Soltere, as scheduled.

Ross adamantly insisted that the prosecution should proceed with Soltere and thus bring the atrocities to the fore. Cartman agreed. Aldrich and Laurent urged that the von Leute interrogation reveal the passage of pills by his counsel, Stolz. The short conference ended in a decision to have a session in chambers with defense counsel after Soltere's appearance.

An MP, acting as bailiff, loudly called, "All rise."

The military tribunal appeared. Admiral Nimitz routinely motioned with down-turned hands the signal to be seated. "The first order of business deals with the appearance of attorney Alden Gaines," he began.

Two MPs escorted the disheveled, unshaven attorney before the bar. He apparently had slept in his expensive, now wrinkled, suit.

"You wish to appeal your contempt citation, Mr. Gaines?"

"Honorable members of this tribunal, I wish to humbly apologize for my unseemly conduct in this court. I freely admit it was an aberration on my part. My excuse, while foolhardy on my part, at least, is tendered to explain my totally despicable conduct, which possibly compounds my flagrant violation. Sirs, I had imbibed too much alcohol before yesterday's session. I ask for forgiveness and to be permitted to continue representing my clients."

Nimitz, Smith and Chennault adjourned to a corner of the bench. Five minutes later they returned to their seats.

"Mr. Gaines, your ten-day jail sentence is temporarily suspended and will be taken under advisement. Your fine of ten thousand dollars will stand. Your apology is noted in the record. You may return to your place as defense counsel," said Nimitz.

"Thank you, sirs...I am most grateful."

"Call your first witness, General Milburn."

"The prosecution calls René Soltere."

Two MPs escorted the witness to the stand. He appeared composed. He was neatly dressed in a blue serge suit, a light blue tie and black loafers. The oath was administered.

"Please state your name for the record," Bart opened.

"René Soltere."

"What is your age?"

"I am thirty years old."

"What was your profession prior to your arrest?"

"I was a member of the Waffen SS."

"You are French by birth, are you not?"

"Yes, General, but my father was French and my mother was German."

"You worked for the Vichy government after France surrendered to Germany, after June 22, 1940?"

"Yes, sir."

"Are you a French or German citizen?"

"General Milburn, as I testified at the earlier hearings I didn't know. But I can answer that now. I have never lost my French citizenship. Of course, I prefer to belong to my native country."

"How do you know that you are a French citizen?"

"Your Major Cartman, who was very kind to me, checked it out through the French embassy in Washington. They told him they have no record of my, how you say in American, *disenfranchisement*. There was a general amnesty for all the French people who lived under the Petain government."

"Explain how you became commandant of the Drancy concentration camp."

"Objection. Counsel is leading the witness," Baron von Wolf interrupted, standing.

"How so, Counsel?" Nimitz asked.

"General Milburn brings up Drancy and establishes the witness as the commandant. In other words, sir, he has testified to two facts not brought out in proper interrogation."

Bart said, "Your Honor, if counsel is attempting to slow down testimony, I will oblige him, with permission of the court. The matter contained in my question is part of the record of the evidentiary hearings. I was trying to save the court's time by moving along to the core of the prosecution's case."

"General Milburn, I think one or two quick questions will bring forth the answers you seek. Therefore, the objection will be sustained. However, I advise defense counsel not to nitpick with niggling objections. Let's move on," Nimitz ruled.

"Mr. Soltere, after the surrender of France, what was your occupation?"

"I was an aide to Marshal Petain."

"After that position, what was your next job?"

"I was sent to the Drancy concentration camp outside of Paris."

"What was your job there?"

"I supervised the transfer of French Jews to Auschwitz camp."

"What was your rank?"

"I was a captain in the Vichy government and then promoted to major. Because I spoke fluent German, I was assigned to escort Hitler when he toured Paris. I answered all his questions in German. He asked how I learned to speak perfect German. I told him my mother was German. He told Himmler to use me to round up Jews."

"How did you become a member of the SS?"

"In 1942 I was sent on a train carrying Jews to Auschwitz. I was put into an SS uniform there."

"What did you see and learn at Auschwitz?" Bart asked.

"Rudolf Höss, the commandant, met me at the train. He told me to speak French and tell the Jews to undress completely right there at the station. Men, women, old and young, as well as all the children. He told me to tell them they were going to showers as a matter of hygiene. But first, General Höss picked young and middle-aged men for forced labor. He chose some pretty young and middle-aged women and sent them to the barracks. The majority marched quietly to the gas chambers. An orchestra played soft music."

"Did you see what happened?"

Soltere repeated his evidentiary-hearings testimony. The commandant defendants repeated their booing, as they had done previously. This time Soltere snapped and added a few gory details. He stood up and shouted, "See those four men in the last row on the left? They were the worst rapists in the camp."

"Sit down," Nimitz ordered.

"Be specific. Identify them and tell us what they did," Bart ordered.

"Hans Klepper, Barnard Werner, Gunther Frommer and Hugo Baumer, they took four virgin Jewish girls from ages twelve to fourteen and kept them in a shack near the I.G. Farben plant. They killed their families, fathers, mothers, brothers and sisters."

"In the gas chambers?"

"No, late at night they executed the twelve relatives of the girls in execution style by shooting them in the head as they made them fall on their knees, and threw them in the ditch where piles of other bodies were lying on top of each other."

"How do you know that?"

"I watched it with my own eyes."

"Did you report it to Commandant Höss?"

"No."

"How did you know about the young virgins?"

"I spied on them."

"What happened to those children?"

"Over a period of a month they took turns having sex with these young girls. Children, they were. They fed the kids to keep them from starving."

"What happened after a month?"

"They brought other soldiers over and made a whorehouse out of the shack. They charged each soldier five marks for each rape. They also sold whiskey to the soldiers. One night there was a wild orgy going on. I was looking through the window and saw one of the soldiers trying to have anal intercourse with a 12-year-old. She screamed very loud. Two officers were coming out of the I.G. Farben plant. They broke into the shack. They pulled their guns and Klepper and Frommer shot the two officers dead. They were lieutenants."

"You watched this take place?" Bart asked in awe.

The courtroom was silent and tense. The media were scribbling away furiously. The tribunal grimly listened to the account.

"I watched one of the worst scenes other than the gas murders. They quickly undressed the officers and carried their naked bodies to the ditch and jumped in, standing on the pile of dead bodies, lifted some of the carcasses and stuffed the naked lieutenants underneath the bodies they lifted. I couldn't move. I was frozen in fear and shock."

"What happened next?"

"The twelve-year-old girl by that time had bled to death. They took her naked body and threw it into the ditch."

"Where were the sentries?"

"There were none in that area near the I.G. Farben plant. There were four other soldiers who were drunk and wanted more sex with the three other girls, who were half conscious."

"What happened then?"

"In the shack, there were four cots. The three soldiers, two sergeants and a corporal, were on top of these girls having sexual intercourse. Werner, Frommer and Baumer tiptoed to the beds and put their guns to each soldier's head. They fired one shot in back of their skulls, killing them instantly. Then they fired shots in the upturned faces of these pitiful half-conscious girls," Soltere added grimly.

"Then what?"

"I figured I better get out of there, and crawled to the Farben plant. No one was in sight, so I got on the paved road and walked back to my quarters. On the way, I looked back at the shack and it was on fire. I fell on my bed and pretended I was asleep. I heard the siren of our fire truck."

"Well, what happened after that?"

"I stayed in bed. I couldn't sleep at all. Next morning, Commandant Höss called a meeting of all the officers. He said he wanted to find the Jews responsible for the deaths of the soldiers and the fire. Klepper, Werner, Frommer and Baumer were at the meeting. They said, *We'll find the bastards that did this.* I said nothing. That afternoon, they took ten innocent slave laborers and forced all the Jews in camp to watch their execution by a firing squad."

"Why didn't you speak up?"

"They would have killed me on the spot. Höss always believed his men. He was an animal."

"How long did you remain at Auschwitz?"

"The next day I was sent back to Drancy."

"No further questions. Your witness," Bart snapped.

Handkerchiefs and tissues were in evidence drying teary eyes. The wire-service people ran to the doors. A stocky, swarthy man rose and menacingly walked slowly toward Soltere.

"That's far enough, Counsel."

The man stopped, and in German announced to the tribunal, "I am Klaus Brackmann, representing the alleged commandants and the four men mentioned by Herr Soltere."

"Proceed."

"Herr Soltere, *verstehen sie Deutsch?*"

"*Jawohl.*"

"Very well, tell the court, are you a writer by profession?"

"No."

"You know what I mean, an author."

"No."

"Well, you should be. You are very good at fiction."

"Objection. Counsel is testifying," Bart interjected.

"Sustained. Get on with it, Mr. Brackmann."

"You didn't see what you described in a mythical shack?"

"Mythical? All you have to do, Counsel, is to refer to the archives obtained by the American military. It is also recorded in the German war-crimes office."

"Does it mention the names of Klepper, Werner, Frommer and Baumer?"

"No, but it has the burning of the shack and the dead bodies found there."

"Then it's your word against theirs, isn't that so?" Brackmann challenged.

"Maybe not so. There were a lot of SS men who visited that children's whorehouse run by those animals. The Americans or the Germans can find some corroboration of what I say. They might have some of them in custody now. I am not a liar."

"You're a Frenchman who wants to get even with the Germans. Is that why you made up this fantasy?"

Bart shouted, "Objection!"

"I withdraw my last question."

Brackmann spent the next hour trying to break Soltere's story, to no avail. Nimitz banged his gavel. The tribunal requested defense attorneys and the prosecution to join them in chambers. Added to the conference was attorney Erich Stolz, who had not appeared before the court in the first two days of the trial. Present for the defense were Baron von Wolf and Alden Gaines; for the prosecution, Bart, Gideon Cartman and Morton Aldrich.

"Gentlemen, we have a delicate situation to resolve here. As a matter of fact, if this is not resolved to the satisfaction of this tribunal, criminal charges will be leveled. Who will speak for the prosecution?" said Nimitz.

"I defer to Major Cartman," Bart said.

"Your Honors, a vial of insecticide was handed to defendant Hitler at the conclusion of yesterday's court session. A paralegal on the staff of counsel Erich Stolz was observed passing the vial to the defendant. Fortunately, our Military Police prevented an ingestion of a capsule from that vial."

"What was in those capsules?" General Smith asked.

"It was analyzed, and contained an insecticide. While one pill would not be lethal, several could cause severe internal pains if not treated quickly."

"Mr. Stolz, would you care to reply? You are not required to incriminate yourself," Nimitz said.

"Your Honor, there is no reason for me not to reply. The answer is quite simple as to my role in this matter. Yet there is something strange here which does require investigation."

"Very well, please explain."

"My client, Hitler, when excited, experiences fibrillation and places a nitroglycerin pill under his tongue. I obtained a prescription for the medication by using the name of Nordheim for myself with Doctor Armand McKinney in Lansing, a town near here. Only twelve pills. I had it filled at the Heartland Pharmacy in Lansing. It was close to the inn I am staying at."

"Sir, may I ask Mr. Stolz why the label on the bottle was removed?" Bart asked.

"Believe it or not, General, when I was shaving yesterday morning the small bottle fell into the running water in the sink. The label came loose. I didn't think it mattered, so I took it off."

"Why did you pretend you were Nordheim?"

"Because it was for him."

"A likely story."

"Strange as it sounds, check it out."

"You can bet we will."

"This matter will be put on hold, gentlemen, pending General Milburn's investigation. That's it. Good evening," Nimitz said.

That night, Bart assigned Phillip Berger and Sophia Carrera to check out Dr. McKinney and the Heartland Pharmacy in Lansing.

☆ ☆ ☆ ☆

Friday, February 6, 1953 - Heartland Pharmacy, Lansing

The waiting room of Dr. McKinney's office in the town of Lansing, just south of Leavenworth, was filled with mothers and their children, elderly men and women. Phillip and Sophia quietly flashed their CIA credentials. A pleasant, gray-haired receptionist said, "You'll have to wait, he's treating an accident victim. It might be half an hour."

"We'll only need a few minutes. We realize he's busy," Sophia said, pointing at the waiting patients.

Dr. McKinney, a tall, low-keyed elderly man, greeted them with a broad smile. "How can I help you?"

They asked him if he remembered issuing a prescription for nitroglycerin to a Mr. Nordheim. "Yes, here's the duplicate," he said, reaching across his neat desk.

"May we borrow that, sir?" Berger asked.

"No, but here's a carbon copy."

"That'll do. Thank you, sir."

"What's the problem?" the doctor asked.

"This is a preliminary investigation. We'll let you know."

They hurried across the street to the Heartland Pharmacy. A large overhead sign hung over the modernized shop in a two-story building displaying a mortar and pestle underneath its name in gilt letters and the legend *Serving the Heartland Since 1895*. At the counter, a gray-haired elderly man, wearing a white smock, greeted them. "Morning, folks, how may I help you?"

Sophia and Philip flashed their IDs.

"CIA? My, my. I've read about you folks. What is the problem? I am the proprietor, Lucas Adams."

Sophia showed the carbon copy of the prescription for nitroglycerin prescribed for Frederick Nordheim.

"Yes, we filled that. What's wrong with it?"

"Did you personally fill the vial with twelve capsules?" Berger asked.

"First of all, they're not capsules. They are very small white pills. Second, my pharmacist handled it."

"What's his name and where is he?"

"Marcus Feingold, and he's back in our lab right now."

"May we talk with him?"

"What's wrong?"

"We won't know until we talk with Mr. Feingold."

"This sounds serious."

"Mr. Adams, it *is* serious," Berger emphasized.

"Let me assure you that Marcus is a very fine and talented man."

"Please send for him," Sophia insisted.

The elderly man spoke into an intercom. "Marcus, come up front, please."

"Coming, sir."

A tall young man, prematurely gray, with a salt-and-pepper mustache, emerged from behind a pleated curtain.

"Marcus, these people are from the CIA. They want to talk with you about the Nordheim nitroglycerin prescription."

With a perfect British accent and a sickly smile on his face, he replied, "I am not surprised."

"What does that mean?" Sophia asked.

"Yes, I prepared that insecticide for *Der Führer*. I hope he was real sick. Am I under arrest?"

"My God, Marcus, what have you done?" said Adams.

"Mr. Adams, you have been very good to me. I am sorry. I could have killed that monster, but I just wanted him to suffer a little."

"Why, why, Marcus? You are a good man. Why would you do such a thing?"

Two customers entered at that moment.

"Is there some place we can talk to Mr. Feingold privately?" Berger asked.

"Go up those stairs to my office."

"Elsa is in the back, Mr. Adams. She can handle everything you need," Feingold said.

The office was furnished in early American, with a rolltop desk and high wooden armchairs.

"Mr. Feingold, why did you change the nitroglycerin to insecticide?" Berger asked.

Tears rolled down Feingold's cheeks. Silently he took off his white smock and rolled up his sleeves. Tattooed on his left arm were five numbers, obviously concentration-camp numbers. It was mute testimony to his motive. Sophia and Phillip softened their approach to the suspected miscreant.

"Tell us, where and how did you get those numbers?" Sophia gently asked.

"My father was a professor of medicine at Heidelberg University. He was the famous Dr. Abraham Feingold, author of the book *Filterable Virus,* also *The Radium Effect on Cancer.* He was decorated at the university for his work. My mother was a teacher of languages at the Heidelberg high school. I had two sisters and a brother. They were younger than me. We were having breakfast at our house in Heidelberg on September 1, 1939, the day the Nazis broke into our home. We were planning to leave Germany that day."

"What happened then?" Sophia said.

Feingold sobbed loudly, his chest heaving convulsively. His words were inaudible, drowned by his cries. Sophia and Phillip waited. She patted Feingold on his back, trying to soothe him. Phillip handed him some tissues from a box on the desk.

"I'm sorry," Feingold mumbled. He blew his nose, wiped his tears and continued. "They ransacked our house, stole everything-jewelry, silverware, a wedding ring off my mother's fingers, dumped all the loot and money in pillowcases and bags. Then they arrested us. We were sent to Dachau. I was seventeen years old. They beat me and my father and mother. They slapped my young sisters and punched my fifteen-year-old brother unconscious." He stopped and stared out the window. "What more do you want?" he sighed.

"Did you all stay at Dachau?" Phillip pressed.

"No, we were held there under horrible conditions for nine months. One day they put us on a train with thousands of others in cattle cars, with no food for three days, to Auschwitz in Poland. We didn't realize it was a death camp. I was put to work at the I.G. Farben plant they were building. My father worked in the infirmary. My mother became a seamstress. My sisters were thirteen and fourteen and were used to shine soldiers' boots and to clean their quarters."

He began sobbing again. They waited.

Finally, he shouted, "Those filthy, rotten bastards raped my two sisters; gang rapes, you call it. Six men to my thirteen-year-old sister Freda and nine men to Helga. Two of the slave laborers carried them to the infirmary. Helga died that night. Two nights later Freda died. My father and mother were so distraught they went to the assistant commandant, Hugo Klemmer. He had them shot on the spot that night. I was hiding outside his office. I saw Klemmer kill them. He ordered four men to carry their bodies to the crematorium. I watched as their bodies burned."

"How did you stay alive?"

"I waited underneath his office until midnight. While the guards were changing, I crawled away and somehow was able to get to the Farben construction site. Materials were being unloaded from trains at the siding. I joined the rest of the slave labor in unloading the cars. Shortly before daylight I climbed on top of one of the freight cars. I knew they were going to leave to pick up more materials for the Farben factory."

"What happened then?" Sophia tearfully asked.

"Germany had been at war with Russia since June, 1940. I knew they needed plenty of arms. I hoped the train would go to a seaport. It was late December, 1941, when I was on top of that train. I almost froze to death. I was asleep one night when a German officer walked on top of the next car. I heard him coming and slid between cars." He paused again, wiped his tears and blew his nose.

"What happened?" Phil asked.

"Even though I hadn't eaten for days, I was still strong enough to grab his legs as he tried to cross over to the next cars. I pulled him down and smashed his head against the connecting locks between cars. He was unconscious. He had a heavy coat on. I stripped him to his underwear, took his rifle and revolver. I hit him over the head with his gun and threw him off the train. It wasn't going too fast."

"Was he dead?" Sophia asked.

"I don't know. I took his clothes, boots, the rifle and his Luger and climbed back up to the top of the train. The train moved slowly. I was finally able to change into his smelly clothes. He was a *Hauptmann*, a captain. I put on his hat and coat. I felt through his pockets. There were four bars of chocolate in his tunic. I carefully ate pieces of them. The train was going north across Germany. I got rid of my striped clothes with the star of David on it. Except I tore the Star off it and stuffed it in my coat pocket."

"How did you manage to escape the Gestapo?" Phillip asked.

"The train arrived at the Hamburg dock three days later. I jumped off the train before it stopped at the waterfront. It was before daybreak. I walked toward the docks and the soldiers kept saluting me all the way. There was lots of money in the wallet, as well as *Hauptmann* Hermann Krausmeier's ID. He was a Gestapo officer."

"How did you get out of Hamburg?" Sophia asked.

"There was one of those all-night restaurants facing the docks. They weren't too busy. I walked in. A couple of soldiers saluted. I returned the salute and sat at the counter. I ordered three scrambled eggs, lots of coffee and rolls. My appetite was ravenous. I controlled myself and ate slowly. A seaman from an Argentinian freighter sat at the counter next to me. He couldn't speak German and had trouble ordering. I speak several languages taught to me by my mother."

"What languages?" Berger inquired.

"English, Spanish, Italian, French, and my native German. I also understand Yiddish, which is very much like German. So I interpreted for the Argentine fellow. He was very grateful."

"So the plot thickens. I can guess what happened," Phillip chuckled.

"You can?"

"Go ahead."

"He told me the name of his ship was the Queen Evita, with a Liberian flag. They had just unloaded meat, flour, and textiles. The ship was sailing at 5 p.m. for Stockholm, Sweden, to pick up a load of automobiles to be delivered in Buenos Aires. He said the captain was an alcoholic and that the first mate, his cousin, really ran the ship. I told him I was here to inspect his ship. He believed me. I treated him to breakfast. We went to the ship."

"Didn't anyone stop you?" Phillip asked.

"No, a few soldiers saluted me and I boarded the *Queen Evita*. The captain's name was Pedro Juarez. I was introduced to his cousin Raul Juarez, the first mate. He took me on a tour of the ship. He opened the captain's door. The captain was snoring, obviously drunk. He invited me to the galley and we had some Argentine wine."

"This is quite a story," Sophia said.

"Well, it's true."

"I don't doubt you. Go on."

"Well, to shorten the story, I told him I was ordered to go as far as Stockholm with him. He said he'd give me a cabin. It would be an overnight trip. The ship took off at 5 p.m. During the night, Pedro and I played chess. We drank quite a bit. At least he drank more than me. I finally took a chance and told him I was deserting the Nazi army. That pleased him; he hated Nazis. I offered him some German marks to give me a change of clothes. He got me the clothes, but refused to take the money."

"How did you get past Swedish immigration?" Sophia interrupted.

"Raul, the first mate, gave me seaman's papers so I could leave the ship. Getting by immigration was routine. I left with most of the sailors and headed straight to the American embassy to apply for political asylum in America."

"Who did you talk to there?" Berger questioned.

"It seems like I was questioned by everyone, until finally Ambassador Leslie took me in his office. One of your CIA people questioned me for two hours. I told him I wanted to join the American Army after he told me about Pearl Harbor. I didn't know that America was at war with Germany."

"What happened then?" Sophia asked.

"He called a Captain Arthur Klein into his office. He was the military attaché to the embassy. He took me into another interrogation room. He was Jewish and wanted to make sure I wasn't pretending to be a Jew. After an hour, he was convinced. To make a long story short, I was flown to New York. The immigration people questioned me some more. Two weeks later, I was sworn into the United States Army as a private and was shipped to Camp Dix in New Jersey for training. I applied later for OCS, Officer Candidate School. I became a lieutenant assigned to the First Army back in Europe. I became a captain and interpreter in General Bradley's army. After the war, I wound up at Fort Leavenworth. I was honorably discharged and then attended the University of Kansas on the GI Bill. I studied medicine, which I am still doing while I work as a pharmacist. I expect to graduate in June. I am an American citizen now."

"Okay, Marcus, relax. You are not in trouble. We'll see to that," Sophia assured him. "But we have one more question. Would you be a witness at the trial, if you are asked?"

"Don't ask. I beg for the privilege to testify against those Nazi rats."

"Go back to work. We'll tell your boss there is no problem. We'll be in touch."

"Here's my address and home number."

Driving back to the fort, Sophia said, "What an amazing story. He'll make a fine witness."

"I'll bet many survivors will come forward," Phillip said. "Wait until Bart hears Feingold's story."

CHAPTER FOUR

Earlier that same day - Gold Star Deli, Delancey Street, lower Manhattan
Diners were glued to the radio set. Itzhak Paplowsky was carving corned beef behind the counter. He dropped his huge knife and yelled at the top of his lungs, "That Frenchman is telling the truth!"

"Itzhak, are you crazy? Make those sandwiches!" Sam Goldstein, the boss, shouted at him, as the customers looked up in amazement.

"No, I was at Auschwitz! I know the story. I was there. I was a *Kapo* and I saw the bodies of those children. I also saw their parents killed. Most of the *landsmen* there and the soldiers knew that those four animals were responsible."

The clientele urged him to call his rabbi. The boss yelled for him to prepare the sandwiches. The deli was in an uproar. The boss went behind the counter and took over Itzhak's chores. Itzhak undid his apron and ran to his temple. He found Rabbi Martin Golden, a young man more Conservative than Orthodox, so Itzhak poured out his story.

"Calm down, Itzhak. Do you want to testify in that trial?"

"Yes, I must. I'm a survivor of Auschwitz. I owe it to the dead to testify."

"Okay, I was a chaplain in the war. Let me call some friends. Go back to work, and I'll call you at home tonight. *Gey gesunter heit.*"

Rabbi Golden placed a call to the Pentagon. "Colonel Robert Duncan, please." He identified himself to the sergeant who answered.

Duncan came on. "Colonel Duncan here. Martin, you son of a gun, how are you?"

"Just fine, Bob. Have you been listening to the trials?"

"You betcha. My buddy, General Milburn, is doing a helluva job."

"Your buddy?"

"Yeah, we worked together on Ike's staff."

"Perfect." Golden related Itzhak Paplowsky's story.

"Holy Toledo. Where are you now?"

Golden gave him his phone numbers at the temple and at home.

"Sit tight, I'll get right back to you."

☆ ☆ ☆ ☆

Fort Leavenworth

Bart and the team were having lunch in their conference room. Sophia and Berger related the results of their investigation. However, the saga of Marcus Feingold struck a nerve with Bart.

"This guy, if for real, will make a great witness. Get him here after court tonight. Let's talk with him."

"No charges against him?" Berger queried.

"That's up to the U.S. Attorney," Bart replied.

An MP entered. "Sir, there's a Colonel Robert Duncan calling from the Pentagon."

"Switch it in here, Sergeant," Bart instructed, then picked up. "Bob Duncan, what trouble are you in now?"

"Found a terrific witness for you."

"Explain."

Duncan relayed the events of the last hour.

"Bob, that's fabulous. How would you like to fly him out here?"

"How do I manage that?"

"Switch me to General Bradley and stand by. I want Itzhak Paplowsky here in the a.m."

"You don't kid around. I'm for it."

"What's up, Barton?" Bradley asked.

Bart explained.

"That's a piece of luck. I was listening to that Soltere testimony and that shyster trying to break him. I'll see to it that Colonel Duncan brings him to you tonight," Bradley confirmed. "I'll have a turbo at Andrews take him to New York to pick up his witness at Idlewild. I'll switch you back to Duncan. Tell him to come to my office. I'll arrange a plane now. You're doing great, my boy. Keep at it. Oh, wait a minute - I meant to tell you the White House is being besieged with calls and letters from Aryan groups and on the other side with complaints about that blasphemous stuff about *Mein Kampf* being that guy's bible and Jesus being a Jew. You might hear from Ike on that. Be prepared."

Another MP, out of breath, entered the room. "General Milburn, sir, the whole town's buzzing. There's trouble headed this way."

Bart turned toward Sophia and calmly stated, "Flip it on."

Sophia turned on the radio. A news report was in progress.

"Chief of Police John Anderson has notified Kansas State Police of the neo-Nazi march toward Fort Leavenworth. Provost Marshal Major John Drake, according to the public-affairs office, is in conference with General Warren Fielding, commander of the installation. Our reporter, Sarah Fox, is at the Seventh Street main gate. What do you see, Sarah?"

"Fred, there are at least one hundred Ku Kluxers, skinheads and neo-Nazis carrying signs. They are about two hundred yards from where I'm standing and are approaching here at the main gate. They are carrying banners and signs. I'll have to wait until they get closer to read the signs. Our photographer, Willy Jones, is up there taking pictures for our sister TV station, Channel 3."

"Stand by, Sarah. We have a report coming in. We turn you over to Alex Thompson, anchorman for Channel 3, who has been covering the trial. This will be a simulcast. He is at the press gate at Fort Leavenworth."

Thompson said, "We are here outside the U.S. Disciplinary Barracks at the special press gate off Riverside Avenue. We have just learned from Provost Marshal Major John Drake that two hundred Army MPs and two hundred Marines have been activated to prevent any attempts by protesters from entering the grounds either through the press gate or the main gate at Seventh Street."

At that point Bart stood up, quickly gathered his things and headed for the door.

"Phil, track down Fielding and have him meet me in the provost marshal's office."

"You got it," Berger replied.

Alex Thompson's radio report continued: "I have just been handed a note. Another group of marchers is approaching the press gate. Oh my, they have been identified as the Christian Crusaders. Yes, I see them now. Our TV cameras are focused on them. Our viewers can see their signs, *Jesus Saves, Down with Mein Kampf, Hang the Pagans, Stop the Nazi Propaganda,* and so on. Sarah, do you hear me?"

"Yes, Alex."

"What's happening at the main gate?"

"The marchers are throwing rocks and, oh my Lord, they've thrown stink bombs and tear gas over the gate. The state police just arrived. Your TV people are here. There is a scuffle..."

Thompson broke in, "There you have it. The state police are wielding clubs. They are charging the main gate. Hold it, there is a battle going on at the press gate. Another group of Nazi sympathizers is using clubs, attacking the police. The Ku Klux Klan has broken through the press gate. MPs and Marines are using their rifle butts to subdue the invaders. This is a bloody scene. As a CBS affiliate, we are now on a national hookup. Ed Murrow will pick up from here."

Murrow said, "We are broadcasting on a CBS simulcast while the trial is in temporary recess. We have left the courtroom drama for one taking place at the gates of this venerable Fort Leavenworth, where the historic war-crimes trial is taking place.

"What we have here is a street war between religious forces, the Christian Crusade, and the Aryan Swords, skinheads, neo-Nazis and ruffians of all stripes. A bloody battle, as you can see on TV, is in progress at both ends of the fort. Hundreds of Military Police, Marines, Kansas state troopers and local police are attempting to quell the battle. Stink bombs and tear gas have been hurled over the fences at the main gate and this improvised press gate outside the U.S. Disciplinary Barracks where the trial is taking place. Those sirens you hear are ambulances arriving at both ends of the fort. Nazism apparently is not dead. I turn you over now to the main gate, where reporter Sarah Fox, of our affiliate, KKLO, is standing by."

Bart and General Fielding were in the provost marshal's office observing events on a TV monitor. Captain John Drake was on the phone with Colonel Jeremiah Brown, commander of the security troops, who was directing operations.

"General Fielding, sir, Colonel Brown wishes a word with you," Drake said, handing him the phone.

"Something strange here at the front gate. The Christian Crusade and the Nazis are not really hitting each other. They are going through the motions of wrestling with each other and knocking down their signs. The Aryan Swords are wearing swastika bands. The Ku Klux Klan have removed their white robes and are storming the gate."

"Where are you, Colonel Brown?"

"At the main gatehouse."

"Stand by for a moment." Fielding repeated the message to Bart, who was staring intently at the TV monitor.

"Warren, this is a phony demonstration," Bart said. "I've looked at the Christian Crusade and the Aryan Swords. Come over here. Look at this monitor, over there in the upper left corner. Those two guys with the swastika armbands and the two men they are talking to are Christian Crusaders."

"My God, what's going on?"

"Look, they are checking their watches, as though they are expecting something. They keep looking up and down Metropolitan Avenue. Holy Toledo, Warren! This is part of the Revenge Plan. The whole area around the fort must be cleared immediately. Arrest as many as possible of the phony protesters, even if they are outside the fort."

"What the hell are you talking about, Bart? Have you blown your cork?"

"Warren, stop wasting time. I'm warning you. There may be one or more suicide bomb trucks headed here. This is what they did in Tel Aviv. In fact, this building may be blown to bits. All traffic within a mile from here must be stopped and searched. Get the National Guard, your own troops, the State Police and the local police on the alert. Anyone interfering should be shot."

"Barton, here goes. If I'm wrong, they'll have my ass."

"No, they won't. I'll move the tribunal to the Officers Club. What do we do to protect the media?"

"Warn them and get them to the artillery barracks. The MPs will lead them."

"Get on the horn, Warren. I know I am right. Don't let anyone leave the grounds," Bart ordered.

"Major Drake, call the State Police. Stop all traffic. Erect roadblocks one mile from any road leading here. I'll call the governor. First, I want to speak to Colonel Brown."

Bart hastened to the conference room at the Disciplinary Barracks, where Fielding had Colonel Brown on the phone.

"Arrest all the protesters, Christian Crusaders, Ku Klux Klan, Aryan Swords, skinheads and any son of a bitch you suspect in or outside those gates. Shoot those who resist. Now, at the corner of Seventh Street just outside the gate facing the information building, there are two Crusaders and two Nazis in a huddle. Have your MPs or Marines grab them instantly. Do you see them?" Bart asked.

"Yes."

"No one is to leave the grounds. No one. Now, I am ordering a general alert that Fort Leavenworth be surrounded by our personnel fully armed. If a truck attempts to crash our grounds, shoot at the tires and machine-gun the trucks. We believe suicide-bomb trucks are headed here. Get going on your two-way radio," Bart ordered.

Major Drake passed the message on to the State Police. Fielding reached Lieutenant Malcolm Teague and passed the same orders to him at the press gate. "Major Peter Troy of Public Affairs should be there now to lead the press to the artillery barracks."

Major Drake reached Major Leonard Cross at the garrison headquarters and relayed the message to the commander. General Fielding arranged for the MPs to get all women and children into their houses or the gymnasium. Fort Leavenworth was put on a siege basis, following the rules normally imposed for tornado alerts.

Radio and television stations were beehives of activity, with full staffs reporting the startling events. Ed Murrow, David Brinkley, Eric Sevareid, Daniel Schorr, Mike Wallace, Richard Hottelet and others kept broadcasting. James Reston of the New York Times, Douglas Milburn of the New York Daily News, and Quentin Reynolds operated from the Commander's Inn at Sixth Street and Metropolitan Avenue, across from the Fort Leavenworth gate. They were dictating their stories from public phones.

The MPs and Marines, using semi-automatic rifles and bayonets, were busy rounding up all protesters. During the scuffles, dozens of protesters and militia were injured. The four men at the corner of Seventh Street were quickly apprehended. Within an hour, all traffic had been stopped and searched before all the barricades were set up in the one-mile perimeter leading to the fort.

Bart had advised Admiral Nimitz and Generals Smith and Chennault, plus his staff, and had them transported to the Officers Club. He spoke to the duty officer in charge of the cellblocks and ordered a complete lockdown and a doubling of guards, fully armed. The defense lawyers and staff were moved to the chapel center. Baron von Wolf was missing.

The fort was surrounded by two thousand armed men. One hundred eighty-five protesters were arrested and taken to a football field. All were handcuffed, leg-shackled and seated on the turf. St. John's Hospital on South Fourth Street was under great stress. The emergency room was packed. Many others were waiting for treatment. MPs and prisoners waited their turns for cuts and bruises to be attended. Overhead, State Police helicopters were surveying the area.

"An airport shuttle bus is leaving Sherman Army Airfield," a police pilot radioed from his copter. "Heading toward Disciplinary Barracks."

The shuttle bus came barreling down the road from Sherman Airfield, heading toward the Disciplinary Barracks. For some inexplicable reason, there were no barriers in front of it. Lieutenant Colonel Malcolm Teague and his men tried to stop the oncoming vehicle; then, without hesitation, he yelled, "Shoot the bastard!"

He and his men let loose simultaneously with a fusillade of bullets. The volley of fire hit the tires, windshield and engine of the bus. Fortunately, it rolled over to the left, flipping twice and exploded with a giant roar, flames rising twenty feet or more. The impact threw a dozen soldiers to the ground. Pieces of shrapnel wounded eight men, including Teague.

Ambulances raced to the scene as other MPs ran to the assistance of the wounded. Two men were unconscious, and were later determined to be suffering from concussions. As they were being tended to by paramedics and raced off to St. John's Hospital, another incident was in the making at the opposite end of the fort.

A moving van raced from the town of Lansing, just south of the fort, heading for the back gate. Two State Police cars faced each other, forming a roadblock. MPs and State Police flashed blinking red lights in an attempt to stop the huge semi-trailer. It scattered the two blocking police cars.

Colonel Brown ordered a barrage of firearms and machine guns, causing an immediate explosion that lit up the sky. The van crashed into the back gate close to Shawnee Village. Twenty-two men - State Police, MPs and Marines - were injured. Seven bystanders inside the gate - five women and two children - were unconscious, struck by the shrapnel. Colonel Brown, his chin bleeding, went to the rescue of the injured. The Fort Leavenworth medical team joined him.

By nightfall, a nervous peace descended on the fort. None of the injuries were life-threatening. Full order had been restored.

☆ ☆ ☆ ☆

Washington - 9 p.m.

President Eisenhower, General Bradley, Secretary of Defense Charles Wilson, Attorney General Herbert Brownell and press secretary James Hagerty were in the Oval Office. Ike was behind his desk. A speakerphone was in use. Bart, General Fielding, Colonel Lyman Trask and Provost Marshal John Drake were in the CAC conference room briefing the White House group.

"So far, Mr. President, no fatalities. We have a hundred eighty-five prisoners sitting on the turf of our football field, manacled and in leg irons. The

Kansas State Police picked up another twenty-two, who are in their custody. The U.S. Attorney for the Kansas District and the FBI have been very helpful," Bart reported.

"Where in the hell did they come from?" Ike snapped.

"So far, we learned they came from all over the U.S. and convened in Kansas City, Missouri," Fielding answered. "According to the FBI, they had a convention there in the name of the Christian Crusaders. According to U.S. Attorney Washburn, there is no such organization as that, to date."

"Warren, what alerted you to the possibility of the suicide bombers?" Bradley asked.

"If it wasn't for General Milburn, this fort would have been devastated. Several thousand would have been killed and injured. He spotted two neo-Nazis in conversation with two Christian Crusaders, and forced me into battle action," Fielding replied.

"Bart, are you there?" Eisenhower said, raising his voice.

"Yes, sir."

"What do you make of it?"

"Plain and simple, Mr. President. It's part of Hitler's legacy. It's his Revenge Plan, of which you are well aware. We have probably captured a good portion of escaped Nazi war criminals and their American closet Nazis."

"Gentlemen, this is Attorney General Brownell. I am sending fifty FBI agents to help question and identify these men. Let's see...you have a hundred eighty-five and the State Police have twenty-two. That totals two-hundred seven in all."

"Mr. Attorney General, we appreciate all the help we can get. At the moment, we are photographing and fingerprinting the men in our custody. The State Police are doing the same," Fielding said.

"Sirs, this is Milburn. We need an all-points bulletin for one of Hitler's attorneys, Baron von Wolf, a Swiss national."

"On what grounds, General Milburn?"

"He disappeared during the lunch break. I believe, sir, he was Hitler's conduit to this gang. We've checked his hotel. His clothes are still there, but he's gone. None of the defense lawyers have any knowledge of his whereabouts."

"General Milburn, he may have been among the injured. However, we have no proof of his involvement in this attack."

"With due respect, sir, my visceral reaction is based on two things. One, he was seen by an MP entering a Cadillac driven by a uniformed chauffeur. Two, my dealings with these Nazi bastards over the past ten years have polished my crystal ball. If not an APB, how about checking international flights? I'll bet his swastika he's on his way to Switzerland."

"Herb, I'm inclined to agree with Barton. In all the years I've worked with him, I've learned that he has an uncanny sixth sense about these bastards," Eisenhower said.

"I'll issue an order immediately," Brownell said.

"One more thing, Mr. Brownell. He may be carrying a diplomatic passport," Bart interjected. "It could be a phony. If he is spotted, tell your people to ignore the passport. It may not be a Swiss passport, but possibly a Liechtenstein one. That's where Hitler, a.k.a. Nordheim, has his headquarters."

"Got it, General."

"What about the trial, Barton?" Eisenhower asked.

"We are proceeding as usual. Court will start at 0900 Monday."

"General Fielding, advise the press there that I'll be making a national address in our pressroom in the next forty-five minutes. I want to assure the nation that everything is under control."

"Yes, sir, Mr. President."

"Congratulations to all of you and your entire personnel for a job well done. Goodnight."

☆ ☆ ☆ ☆

Monday, February 9, 1953 - 0700 hours - Fort Leavenworth

General Fielding and Bart had called an early meeting in the conference room with Provost Marshal Major Drake, Lieutenant Colonel Teague and Colonel Lyman Trask, MP commander. Present were Philip Berger, Richard Maybrook and Jacques Laurent. A sparse breakfast was on the buffet credenza.

"Bart, kick it off," Fielding said.

"First, the trial will begin at 0900. Tempted as I am to give Hitler a going-over, prudence prevents me from doing so. General Fielding and I will cooperate in the investigation of the who, why, when, where and how the assault on this fort was planned. Jacques Laurent, head of the CIA Nazi desk, will coordinate the interrogation with the FBI, State Police, Colonel Trask, Lieutenant Colonel Teague and Major Drake. Maybrook and Berger are part of Laurent's team. There are a hundred and eighty-five prisoners freezing their butts off at the football field, guarded by MPs and Marines. At police headquarters, there are twenty-two more being held by the State Police. We want each one thoroughly checked. Their pictures and fingerprints were taken on an assembly-line basis Friday night at the Disciplinary Barracks. Warren?"

"This is a military base. We don't play by civilian rules. This is our jurisdiction. We don't want any bullshit from the FBI, the State Police or the local authorities. Squeeze the hell out of these bastards. They attacked an American military installation. They are, as far as I am concerned, prisoners of war. At the moment, my outrage is such that I have no recollection of the Geneva Convention. They are technically war criminals, part and parcel of Hitler's Revenge Plan," Fielding vehemently declared.

"The FBI people will be here momentarily, and they will be taken to Courtroom Two, where we'll join them," Bart said.

"Despite the fact I am commander of this base and am outranked by one star below Major General Milburn, that is not the reason he will be in charge of this continuation of his Operation Lucifer. He's headed this operation since the beginning in February 1952. Make it clear to all that he is operating under a presidential directive. I will be working with him as a team," Fielding asserted. "Understood?"

"Yes, sir," they chorused.

Gideon Cartman poked his head into the room.

"Come in, Gid," Bart ordered.

"We've got several witnesses out there. Who are you putting on first, General?"

"Is Greta Fischer here yet?"

"I picked her up at the hotel," Jacques said.

"Who is she?" Cartman asked.

"She's a very special surprise witness, Gideon. I haven't had a chance to brief any of you, due to Friday's diversion. She flew into the Kansas City airport last night at her own expense. Jacques met her plane late last night. Don't question her. I'll put her right on the stand first. Sit and have a cup of coffee," Bart added.

"General, you have long sleeves," Cartman quipped.

"What does that mean?"

"You have a lot of surprises up there."

Bart laughed. Ten minutes later an MP knocked on the door.

Fielding shouted, "Come in!"

The MP saluted and announced, "I've led the FBI men into Courtroom Two, sir."

"Thanks, Sergeant. We'll be right there."

The group followed the two generals to the courtroom. Fifty men stood up. One man met them at the door. "I am Assistant Attorney General Thomas Wayne. These FBI agents are handpicked at your service."

Bart and Fielding waved them to be seated.

"I am General Warren Fielding, Commander of this base. This is General Barton Milburn, chief prosecutor and head of Operation Lucifer. Mr. Wayne, have you informed your people of this operation?"

"Yes, sir, Attorney General Brownell briefed us."

Bart stood up. "All of you are aware that Operation Lucifer is top secret. In classified communication, we use the word *Lucy* in secret reporting verbally on the telephone or in writing. Use your initials with it. For example, *This is AZ Lucy,* or whatever your initials are. Please give me a list of your names. If there is a duplication of initials, insert your middle one, such as ATZ. Got it?"

"Yes, sir," they chorused.

"General Milburn, here are two lists of our FBI agents, one for you and one for General Fielding," Wayne said.

Bart introduced Jacques and the rest of the team.

"One last word, men," Fielding cut in. "This is purely a military matter. An Army installation has been attacked. This operation is strictly under our jurisdiction. That goes for the FBI, the State Police, local authorities and anyone else. General Milburn is in command of this operation. Any questions?"

"I'll have to clear that with the Attorney General," his assistant, Thomas

Wayne, advised.

"Oh, yes, well, you can clear it with the Chairman of the Joint Chiefs, General Bradley, and the President if you like, but do it pronto," Fielding snapped.

Bart said, "While you are in the business of clearing, how about getting our men to take these FBI agents out to the football field? Use the locker room out there for your not-so-gentle chats with these Nazi creeps. I'll wager Hitler's new mustache that there are a few escaped Nazi war criminals among the hundred and eighty-five prisoners and the twenty-two at police headquarters. I want the four men picked up at the corners separated in isolation cells. I want to chat with them."

"General Fielding, is there equipment available to telephoto pictures and fingerprints to D.C.?" Assistant Attorney Wayne asked.

"Yes, we have it right in this building. Major Drake here will handle it for you right next door to his office. He'll be working with you, as will Colonel Trask, Lieutenant Teague and CIA agents Laurent, Maybrook and Berger. Go to it. You, Mr. Wayne, may use the phone in our conference room down the hall. The MP at the door will direct you. I'll be at my office if needed. General Milburn will be in Courtroom One prosecuting those vermin."

Cartman and Milburn headed for the court.

"Any hint as to who Greta Fischer is?" Cartman asked.

"She's a survivor. She is not a Jew. Her husband was. She was freed by the Americans at Dachau. A great, heartrending story. Simon Wiesenthal got her for us."

The courtroom was packed, as usual. The tribunal asked for the first witness.

"Mrs. Greta Fischer, please," Bart called out.

Two MPs led a smartly dressed, svelte, middle-aged blonde to the stand. She had beautiful blue eyes, which bore signs of deep sadness as she took the oath. She sat in the chair and peered intently at the defendants.

"Do you wish to speak English or German?" Bart asked.

"I speak English, but prefer to testify in German."

"State your name, please."

"Greta Fischer."

"Where do you live?"

"Stuttgart, Germany."

"What is your occupation?"

"I am a teacher at the Stuttgart gymnasium, you call it high school, secondary school preparing for college."

"What do you teach?"

"Two things, English language and German history."

"How long have you lived in Germany?"

"I was born in Stuttgart on December 5, 1908. I lived there until August 1942."

"Where did you live after that?"

"Dachau."

"The concentration camp?"

"Yes," she answered sharply.

"How did that come about?"

"It's a long story."

"Try to tell it in your own words, as succinctly as possible, please."

"My maiden name is Greta Fischer. I am a widow. I was married to Wolfgang von Schreiber. He was an eminent surgeon. He wrote five books on modern surgical techniques. People from all over Europe were his patients. We have two sons and a daughter."

"Where are your children now?" Bart asked.

She remained mute. Her lips quivered. Her eyes were moist. She reached in her purse and removed a handkerchief and a pair of bifocal glasses. She carefully polished the lenses and adjusted them to her eyes and stared intently at the defendants. Her calm demeanor turned into a display of wrath.

"Is that *Schweinehund* with the phony beard and mustache Adolf Hitler?"

The courtroom spectators turned as one to face *Der Führer*.

"*Jawohl, Frau Fischer. Das bin ich.*" Hitler stood and bowed.

"Sit down," Nimitz ordered.

"He is the animal that ordered the execution of my husband and two sons at Dachau right before my eyes. They were so brave. I fainted and woke up in the infirmary."

"Why? Are you Jewish? Was your husband Jewish?"

"No," she answered, then sobbed for two minutes. Bart handed her a glass of water.

"Do you wish to be excused to compose yourself?" Nimitz asked.

Angrily, she said in English, "Hell, no. I will testify in English now, if I may."

"Go right ahead, Mrs. Fischer," Nimitz gently replied.

Her English had a British accent.

"Where did you learn English?" Bart queried.

"In London, when my father, Heinrich Fischer, was ambassador to England in 1924 for the Weimar Republic. I was sixteen years old then. That's when I first met my husband. He operated on King George V to remove his infected gall bladder. The king was of German heritage. He changed the royal house name from Saxe-Coburg-Gotha to Windsor during World War I. When the King recovered, he invited my father, the ambassador, and Wolfgang von Schreiber to dinner at Buckingham Palace. My father took me to that royal evening."

"Did you finish your studies in London?"

"Yes, when I was twenty years old, and a year later I married Dr. Schreiber. I then studied to become a nurse. After I was accredited as a registered nurse, I worked at the Stuttgart Hospital. Soon I was helping him in his surgery."

"Let me bring you to the birth of your children."

"In 1929 I became pregnant with my first son Gunther, and two years later my daughter Lisa was born. In 1933 my son Frederick was born. I became a full-time mother. Hitler became Chancellor of Germany, and our country was going through a metamorphosis from a decent cultural nation into a sick society ruled by gangsters."

"Explain that, please," Bart urged.

"To put it in a medical analogy, a virus of hate became epidemic. Goebbels' propaganda, Hitler's hate-mongering speeches, our teachers were teaching the Nazi criminal doctrines to our children, and the brown-shirted SA hoodlums were spreading fear throughout Germany. From a religious, cultural country, the majority of our population unwittingly became pagans like Adolf Hitler."

"Please move on, Frau Fischer."

"During the war, the British discovered penicillin. My husband got samples of it and had it manufactured for all of Germany. Hitler sent for him to come to his chalet called Berghof, Berchtesgaden. He was covered with lesions on his back. After a blood test, plus a full examination of *Der Führer*, he knew the answer."

"Did he find anything wrong?"

"Yes. Hitler had syphilis."

"That's a lie!" Hitler yelled.

"Quiet!" Nimitz ordered.

"Madame Fischer, what did your husband do for him?"

"He injected penicillin and advised his incompetent doctor, Theodor Morrell, to give him a second shot one week later. My husband cured his syphilis."

"It was for my pneumonia!" Hitler screamed.

"Was Hitler grateful?"

"At the time, yes. He sent him an Iron Cross and had him promoted to lieutenant general in charge of medical operations."

"What got you into Dachau?"

"Himmler wanted my husband to work with Josef Mengele experimenting on Jewish children. My husband refused."

"What happened next?"

"Himmler had the Gestapo investigate my husband. We were followed everywhere. One day we were at home with the children. The Gestapo broke into the house. They ransacked the place. Took every picture and record they found in the house. They dragged me, my husband and our three children out of the house."

"Where did they take you?"

"To Gestapo headquarters, and accused my husband of hiding his Jewish background and called him a traitor."

"I thought you said he was not a Jew?"

"They had proof that my husband's grandfather on his mother's side had married a Jew. My husband swore he didn't know that."

"So he sent all of you to Dachau."

"Yes, he said it was Hitler's orders."

"That's a lie. This is all new to me!" Hitler screamed.

"You'll get your chance, Mr. Hitler," Nimitz said. "Sit down."

"Is that all?"

"No, that's not all!" the lady screamed. "There they are! Those two in the back row. They shot my husband and children!"

The courtroom was in an uproar. Nimitz restored order. Bart approached the bench.

"Your Honor, with the permission of the court, I would like Madame Fischer to place her hands on the two men to whom she pointed."

"Objection," Alden Gaines roared.

"Overruled."

Two MPs escorted Mrs. Fischer down the aisle past the press rows. She strode purposely and, upon reaching the rear row, she delivered two loud slaps to the faces of the two startled defendants. She scratched the faces of both men with her two hands before the MPs could pull her away. Blood was on her hands and trickled down the cheeks of the victims of her attack.

"There will be a fifteen-minute recess," Nimitz ordered.

It was great theater. Gaines, Bart and Greta Fischer were called into chambers when court resumed. Gaines demanded that charges be brought against the lady.

She apologized to the judges. "I just lost my head," she cried.

"Let's go back to court," Nimitz declared after he lectured the lady on her conduct.

Back on the stand, she appeared calm. "After Dachau, I was sent to Auschwitz to act as a nurse. Himmler would have killed me if Marshal Kesselring had not intervened.

"What did you do and see at Auschwitz?"

"I saw the most horrors that men can conceive. They were gassing Jews by the thousands every day. I saw Commandant Höss put five men and five women naked on their hands and knees on the dirt and ordered them to race like frogs to the crematorium. Halfway there, he and two soldiers shot them first in their buttocks. Then they stood over them and fired shots into their heads. They forced other Jews to lift the bodies and put them in the flames of the crematory. I saw live babies thrown into those flames. Germany had gone berserk. This was not just Hitler, Goering, Goebbels, Himmler, Müller and a few others; it was a whole country addicted to paganism."

"Do you really believe all of Germany was involved?"

"Not all, but most. I was finally released from Auschwitz by Marshal Kesselring. I worked at a hospital in Munich. Before the war, there were fewer than 500,000 Jews in the German population. Less than one percent. By wartime, half of them were gone. By war's end, there were fewer than thirty-six Jews left in Berlin. Some came back. This is a stain that will be on Germany for a long, long time, all because of that maniac Hitler, who hypnotized a country into becoming pagans. Germany is striving to live down their sins."

"Are they doing well?" Bart asked.

"Adenauer is a good man, trying hard. But there are lots of Nazis still there, and lots of them are scattered around the world. Look at how they tried to blow this place up. Hang those bastards!"

"Objection."

"Sustained. Strike that last sentence," Nimitz ordered.

"Your witness," Bart said.

Luther Krieger approached the witness.

"Counselor, I think it would be well to take our lunch recess now, rather than interrupt your cross-examination," Nimitz offered.

"I agree, sir."

"Court will resume at 1400 hours, 2 p.m. for civilians," Nimitz said, smiling.

The prosecution team retired to the conference room. During the lunch break, Sophia, Berger and Bart reviewed the full details of Marcus Feingold's story.

"He's a perfect witness. Did you tape him?"

"I had the machine going, but he didn't know it," Berger admitted.

"It doesn't matter. If he's who he says he is, we'll use him. However, transcribe the tape. It'll help me in the interrogation."

"We've also got that guy from the New York deli coming in," Cartman said. "He'll back up Soltere's story."

An MP knocked at the door. "General, the Attorney General is on line two for you, sir."

Bart picked up the receiver of the blinking phone. "Milburn here."

"General, I've got some good news for you," Brownell said.

"Mr. Attorney General, I could use good news at all times."

"First, let's cut the formalities - my name is Herb and yours is Bart. Let's keep it on that basis. Bart, your visceral reaction, as you stated it, was quite good, with one slight exception. Baron von Wolf is in our custody, as of an hour ago."

"That's good news. How and where?"

"He was nabbed at Idlewild Airport. The exception is, he was *not* heading for Liechtenstein. He was using a phony diplomatic passport and was booked on a flight to Buenos Aires, home of the free Nazis and the depraved," Brownell said.

"What now?"

"Your call, Bart. We can bring him here to D.C. for interrogation, or deliver him to our U.S. Attorney in Kansas, where the two of you can take a whack at him. You guys decide the charges."

"I prefer to have him here. We might get him to turn canary, which should be worth the price of the trip."

"You've got it. Good luck, Bart."

The MP returned. "General, the provost marshal's office asked me to advise you that we have been receiving thousands of letters for you. And our switchboard has been jammed with all sorts of calls."

"What kind of calls?"

"Hate messages, congratulatory messages, and some so-called survivor messages."

"Have the operators note the survivor messages."

"They've noted all of them. The provost marshal knows you are quite busy with the trial. He wants to know if someone on your staff could go through them."

"Is Major Drake in his office now?"

"Yes, sir."

"Thank you, Sergeant. I'll call him now. Stand by, or rather, sit down."

Bart lifted the phone and was quickly connected with John Drake. "Major, I'm sorry your switchboard is tied up."

"No problem, General."

"Is there an office available close to our conference room?"

"Yes, several across the hall from you. What's the problem?"

"In the light of the response we're receiving from the media coverage, it might be advisable to set up a mailroom and some extra phones to route some of the calls that have a bearing on the trial. For example, we should screen the calls and sift through the mail."

"General, there are two connecting offices opposite the conference room. We could put a bank of phones in one of them and install a large table in the other one for those who will read the mail. Do you have the personnel to handle it?"

"That's my second request. My staff is tied up with the trial and with the new arrivals of the neo-Nazis. I could use about six fairly savvy men to handle these messages. The pertinent phone messages should be taped."

"Give me five minutes and I'll call you back on line three. I want to clear this with General Fielding."

"I'm due in court in about fifteen minutes. Thanks for trying," Bart said, then turned to the MP. Sergeant Winslow, your first name is Kyle, am I right?"

"Yes, sir," he he answered.

"You heard my conversation. Now, this is voluntary. Would you like to be part of the screening staff?"

"I certainly would, sir."

"What is your educational background?"

"I am a graduate of Yale University with a B.A."

"How come you're not an officer?"

"By choice, sir. I enlisted as a private and served in Korea, where I became an MP. I am a master sergeant now. I went through OCS and expect word any day now on promotion to lieutenant. I have been studying criminology."

"I'm impressed."

Major Drake called. "General, it's all cleared. General Fielding said to give you all the help you need. He thinks you need at least eight people, four for each chore."

"John, I've got one man here I'd like to impress into service, provided it's okay with you."

"Who would that be?"

"Sergeant Winslow."

"You couldn't have picked a better man. Is he there with you?"

"Yes."

"Well, sir, if you don't mind, tell him he is no longer a master sergeant. His graduation papers from Officer Candidate School are on my desk. He is now Lieutenant Winslow."

"That's great."

"Your phone bank will be finished by the time court adjourns this afternoon. I'll have a list of eligibles for you by that time. Please have the new shavetail report to me right away. I'll have him supervise the phone installations and the furnishings for those offices. We've got huge bags of mail which we'll send along."

"Thanks for everything, John." Bart again turned to the MP. "Lieutenant Winslow, report to Major Drake forthwith," Bart ordered.

"Sir, it's sergeant."

"Not any more. Your OCS diploma is on Major Drake's desk," Bart said.

Winslow stood up and saluted. "Yes, sir!"

"You're on my staff now."

"Good move, General," Cartman said. "Time."

"Yes, let's go."

They arrived minutes before 1400 hours. The rest of the staff were seated. The tribunal took their places, and Greta Fischer was in the witness chair.

"Proceed, Counselor," Nimitz ordered.

Luther Krieger, young, tall, sandy-haired, neatly dressed in a black jacket, gray trousers, a white shirt and a red knit tie, walked slowly toward the witness. "Why did you change back to your maiden name?" he asked Greta.

"Because Himmler's excuse for killing my husband was treason. He told the press he was a traitor. And that syphilic bastard Hitler, who pretended to be a Jew…"

Krieger cut her off and shouted, "Objection! I ask the court to strike her vituperative remarks from the record."

Bart jumped to his feet. "Your Honor, I'll not contend the pejoratives being stricken. But I'd like to hear her full answer."

"The objection is sustained," Nimitz declared. "Madame, you may finish your answer without those descriptive words. They are to be stricken from the record. Take it from the word 'traitor.' "

"They called my husband a traitor. It was in all the papers. They also killed my little children. And that monster Hitler did nothing to clear his name. My husband cured his syphilis."

"Objection."

"Overruled."

"Was your husband a traitor?" Krieger asked.

"He was a loyal German, but he wasn't a Nazi. He saved hundreds of arms and legs of those poor young men Hitler threw at the Red Army and the Allied forces. He destroyed a whole generation of our youth."

"Are you an Aryan?"

"Do you mean, am I descended from Indo-Iranian stock? The answer is no."

"That is not what I asked you."

Bart was on his feet. "Her answer was very proper. The word Aryan, as Hitler used it, is a malaprop. Aryan in any dictionary or encyclopedia will confirm her answer. It has no Nordic connotation. Learned counsel can look it up."

"Do you wish to rephrase your question?" Nimitz asked.

"Malaprop or not, are you of pure German blood?"

"Yes, my eyes are blue and my hair is natural blonde. My blood is red like yours, his, and every Jew in the world."

Laughter pealed through the courtroom. The tribunal smothered their smiles.

"What was your parents' religion?"

"Catholic."

"Were you baptized?"

"When I was a baby."

"What was your husband's family's religion?"

"They were Lutherans."

"What are you?"

"A Godist."

"What kind of a religion is that?"

"A pure religion of our Creator, called Godism. There is only one God for all of mankind. Can you dispute that?"

"I'm asking the questions here. You don't believe in Jesus Christ?"

"Jesus Christ was a wonderful, pure messenger from God. He was born a Jew, and if he had been in Germany Hitler would have sent him to a death camp."

"Your Honor, please advise the witness to give specific answers."

"Counselor, you have opened this theological discourse a mile wide. In this country, we have freedom of religion. She has a right to her own beliefs."

"Your husband had Jewish blood, isn't that so?"

"What does Jewish blood look like? Is it blue, green, white, purple..."

"Objection," Krieger huffed.

More laughter.

"Answer my question."

"I don't know and I don't care. I loved him with all my heart. He didn't have pagan blood, yellow, like all your Nazi hate-ridden vermin."

"Do you believe that all the German people were pagans?"

"No, but millions of them were. One man didn't kill all those Jews, Jehovah's Witnesses, Gypsies, Christian Germans, and all the millions in all those other countries in Europe. Nazi Germany had an army of millions, and they had families. All followed this Austrian corporal in his Nazi paganism. He believed he was the Messiah. Three and a half million German boys died, seven million were casualties."

"Madame Fischer, you are a bitter woman."

"Yes, I am."

"Why do you still live in Germany?"

"Because I want to help my country extract the evils of Nazism. I want to help our youth know the truth about the atrocities."

"Are you an expert on atrocities?"

"Yes, I am. I saw the wanton slaughtering of all kinds of people. I saw babies bayoneted, burned alive in roaring fires in crematoria. I saw Jews by the thousands lured into showers, which were really gas chambers. I saw soldiers laughing as they shot Jews for no reason at all. I saw emaciated slave laborers die at their jobs. I saw them starve to death. Atrocities? This was Hitler's hell. May he roast in it."

"Madame Fischer, you have a vivid imagination. None of that happened. You are a bitter woman repeating Jewish propaganda."

Bart roared, "Objection! Counsel is testifying. The prosecution will present stark evidence supporting every word spoken by the witness. His remarks are part of the revisionist lie propagated by the Nazi vermin."

"No further questions," Krieger huffed, waving his hands as he retreated to his chair.

"Rebuttal, Your Honor," Bart requested. "Madame Fischer, this trial could clear your husband's name. Would you change your name back to von Schreiber if that were to happen?"

"Gladly and proudly."

"When you were at Auschwitz, you saw Jews digging their own graves into large pits?"

"Yes."

"You saw dead Jews being removed from gas chambers?"

"Yes."

"You saw gold fillings taken from the mouths of the deceased and dropped in buckets?"

"Yes, and I saw soldiers sneaking some of those gold fillings into their pockets."

"Frau Fischer, you are a liar!" Hitler yelled, jumping up.

In a split second, Greta Fischer reached into her oversized handbag, removed a book and hurled it with unerring accuracy, striking Hitler on the forehead.

"There is Rudolf Höss's diary of his confessions, translated by Andrew Pollinger. He was the commandant at Auschwitz and admits killing two and a half million Jews. Read that, you bastard! He wrote that before a Polish court had him hanged."

The court was startled by her reaction and outburst. There was an uproar of approval and applause. The tribunal allowed a few minutes to pass before the gavel restored order. The wire-service reporters and TV commentators ran to the doors.

"You were baptized as a Catholic and your husband was a Lutheran. When and why did you convert to Godism?"

"I'll answer the why first. Because of our different religious heritage, we were married by a judge. We both had an abiding belief in God Almighty, the Creator of all things. We both believed in the teachings of Jesus Christ, as well as Moses and the Ten Commandments. We explored Catholicism and Martin Luther's teachings. When we found out about Martin Luther's anti-Semitism, my husband, an educated man, was revolted. So was I. We turned to Godism, to us the purest worship of God. We became Godists and we pray in the Temple of God, the God of all living things."

"Objection. Is the witness delivering a personalized sermon?" Krieger bellowed.

"General, haven't we gone far enough with this theological business?" Nimitz said.

"Bear with me, Your Honor. One or two more questions and we'll connect this lady's testimony to our prime defendant, Adolf Hitler."

"General, don't test the patience of this court. Keep it short. Objection overruled, Mr. Krieger."

"What did you learn about Martin Luther?"

"In his early years, he campaigned to have all Jews convert to Christianity. In the early part of the 16th Century, he became rabid. His writings then advocated that all synagogues be destroyed, all Jewish homes be burned down and all Jews be driven out of the country. Hitler picked up that despicable advice and used it as a political tool. Jews in Germany were only one percent of the population."

"But why did you reject Catholicism?"

"I didn't reject Catholicism per se. We were displeased with Cardinal Pacelli's Concordat with Hitler. Pacelli became Pope Pius XII. Yet look at this. Is this a protest?"

Greta reached into her blouse and revealed a gold necklace with a crucifix, a Star of David, a miniature gold piece in the form of a temple, and a gold minaret.

"Explain those pieces, please," Bart requested.

"The crucifix is for Christianity, the Star of David is for Judaism, the temple is for the Temple of God, and the minaret is for Islam, all monotheistic. Therefore, there is only one God for all of humanity. Yet there have been wars and killing in the name of religion for thousands of years. Along comes this Austrian demon, Hitler, and for twelve years he tried to turn Germany into a pagan nation. Never in history have there been monsters like him and his Nazi ideologies of murder, mayhem and malevolence."

"Sir, I ask this tribunal to strike all of this witness's rantings from the record," Krieger objected.

"Counselor, this is a military tribunal," Nimitz replied. "But even in a civil court, when an attorney opens the floodgates of a reservoir of information, the flow cannot be stopped. You opened the gates, and you'll get your chance to rebut any statements with the same latitude allowed with this witness. Now, let's go on. Do you want to rebut at this time?"

"No, no further questions of this witness."

"Court is adjourned. We will convene at 0900 hours, 9 a.m. tomorrow," Nimitz said.

Bart returned to the prosecution conference room. The mail and telephone rooms across the hall were furnished with the phone banks and mail files. Small conference tables were placed in each room. Kyle Winslow, still in his master sergeant's uniform, reported that everything was in order for the mail and phone operation.

"Aren't you Lieutenant Winslow now?" Bart asked, smiling.

"Yes, sir, General. I'll change uniforms later with my new bar. I've been busy getting those rooms set up. Here's the list of eligibles provided by Major Drake."

"All right, Kyle. Do you recognize some of these names?"

"Yes, sir."

"I'll rely on your judgment. Pick four to sort the mail. They are to read the ones from those who claim to be survivors, separate those and attach a brief comment on the pertinent ones. Have you arranged to tape the calls?"

"Yes, sir."

"Tape those accordingly, with brief comments on them. Anything really urgent, talk to Gideon Cartman or Jacques Laurent. You are now my aide. Supervise the operation."

"Sir, there are at least two thousand letters in those bags and more at the post office."

"Have everything operational by 0800 hours."

"General Milburn, thank you for the opportunity."

"You're welcome. Good luck. Go change into your officer's uniform."

The phone rang, and Cartman answered. "Yes, he's here. Okay."

"Who was that?"

"Jacques is on his way here."

"Fine!"

Phil Berger and Sophia Carrera entered. A discussion ensued as to who would be the next witness. Bart looked at his watch. "I'm inclined to put Itzhak Paplowsky on first to confirm Soltere's version of the children's whorehouse set up by those four degenerates."

The phone rang again, and Sophia answered. "It's Colonel Duncan."

Bart grabbed the receiver. "Where the hell are you, Bob?"

"I'm right here with our witness."

"Where?"

"In the provost marshal's office."

"Well, dammit, get your asses over to our conference room in this building. Ask for an MP to guide you."

"En route, sir."

Jacques arrived, and breathlessly declared, "Barton, we've got a bonanza."

"Such as?"

"So far, of the hundred and eighty-five prisoners, at least seventy-three have been identified as Waffen SS here in this country illegally. They are in the CIA Nazi desk's list, wanted by Interpol and confirmed by the FBI with the German War Crimes Office in Munich."

"Bingo. How about the rest of these bastards?"

"There is a meeting in one hour in the Townsend Gymnasium with the Assistant Attorney General and the FBI, the State Police and the U.S. Attorney. Can you make it?"

"You better believe it."

An MP knocked on the door. Jacques opened it. "Colonel Duncan for General Milburn."

"Come in, Bob," Milburn called, then greeted the colonel with a hug.

"General, this is Itzhak Paplowsky."

The middle-aged man was prematurely gray, neatly dressed and tall, but slightly hunched over as he extended his hand.

"General, it is a great privilege to meet you," Itzhak Paplowsky said in a Polish accent. "I listened to you on the radio."

"My pleasure, Mr. Paplowsky," Bart replied.

"Call me Pap. Everybody does."

"Okay, Pap."

Bart introduced him to the staff, then said, "Sit down, please. I'm going to put you on the stand in the morning. Did you hear René Soltere on the radio?"

"That's why I'm here. He told the truth about those little girls."

"We're going to ask you questions here. If we sound tough, don't mind it. We're just preparing you for the cross-examination."

"General, after what I've been through with those Nazi *momsers*, nothing scares me any more. Every day I live now is a bonus. I'm lucky to be alive."

The next thirty minutes encapsulated six years of torture, horror and grief. His eyes reflected the pain he was trying to hide in his narration, but he calmly answered a barrage of questions.

"Pap, you'll do fine. Just tell it like you told us. I'll guide you through it."

Colonel Duncan asked, "What's a *momser*?"

Bart laughed. "It means bastard."

"*Du vast Yiddish*, General?"

"*A bissel.*"

"*Du bist a landsman?*"

"He's a *landsman*," Bart said, pointing at Jacques.

"A *Français landsman*," Jacques quipped.

"*Shalom.*"

"He is another one." Jacque pointed at Berger, who immediately engaged him in some Yiddish repartee.

"*Du bist a hamischer mensch.*"

"That's enough now. Phil, have you a bedroom for Pap here?"

"Yes, he and Marcus Feingold will stay with me. They'll be company for each other. Feingold's there now. An MP will take Pap there."

"Jacques, Colonel Duncan will be billeted with us. He can repay us by going to work."

"General, if that's on the level, it would be a privilege."

"Okay, Bob, come on with us to this meeting with the FBI, for openers."

Bart, Laurent, Cartman, Sophia, Berger, Sedgwick, Fuentes, Ross, and Duncan made their way to the Townsend Gym. A flurry of snow greeted them on their trek. A cadre of MPs were stationed at the entrance to the gymnasium. They saluted Bart and his group. Bart looked at the MPs, helmeted, armed, wearing fleece-lined short coats covered with snowflakes.

"Men, I would advise you to move your posts to the vestibule. Security wouldn't be breached. There are eight of you. Take turns at the interior windows and there won't be any frostbite cases."

A master sergeant spoke up. "Sir, General Fielding is in there. We're here on his instructions. We appreciate your suggestion, sir."

"Okay, I'll clear it with him. Stand by."

Seventy-five men were seated on folding chairs in the center of the basketball court. They faced a conference table with General Fielding, Assistant Attorney General Thomas Wayne, U.S. Attorney Farley Washburn, FBI Deputy Director William Bledsoe, Colonel Jeremiah Brown, Kansas State Police Superintendent Kermit Garner, Leavenworth Chief of Police John Anderson, and Provost Marshal Drake.

Bart waved at the gathering and whispered in Fielding's ear. Fielding beckoned one of the MPs standing against the wall. He ordered him to bring the MPs guarding the front doors to come into the vestibule. The MPs arranged chairs for his entourage at the long table. Bart sat next to Fielding, who called the session to order.

"Gentlemen, we have full representation here of the FBI, State Police, local police, Military Police, Fort Leavenworth's command, and Major General Barton Milburn, chief prosecutor and head of Operation Lucifer. I'm turning this meeting over to General Milburn."

"Gentlemen, as previously explained to you, the attack on this fort is undoubtedly part of Adolf Hitler's *Revanche Plan*, or, in English, the Revenge Plan. He operated under the name of Frederick Avram Nordheim, pretending to be a Jewish survivor of the death camps. At the time of his apprehension, he was the richest man in the world. Most of you have profiles on him. Copies are available to the rest of you. One note - Attorney General Brownell advised me a few hours ago that Baron von Wolf, one of Hitler's lawyers, has been apprehended at Idlewild Airport in New York. He was booked on a flight to Buenos Aires. Wolf is en route here to be delivered to the U.S. Attorney by the FBI. In my opinion, he was Hitler's man who triggered the suicide bombing, phony demonstration and general attack on this installation. I turn the floor over to Assistant Attorney General Thomas Wayne."

"Gentlemen, as of the moment, of the two hundred and seven in custody, a hundred and eighty-five are here on the base, twenty-two in State Police detention quarters, a hundred and twenty-seven have been identified as illegal aliens, and all of them are believed to be escaped war criminals. Fifteen of them are part of the twenty-two held by the State Police. Of the hundred and eighty-five here at the Fort, a hundred and twelve are illegal. We are waiting for further IDs for the other eighty."

"By the way, Mr. Wayne, due to the snowstorm, the hundred and eighty-five have been moved to canvas cots in the basement of the disciplinary barracks. Your FBI agents, in concert with our CIA team, can use the interrogation rooms on the floor above. MPs will help," Fielding said.

"General Milburn, I hand you this file of the hundred and twenty-seven identified," Wayne said. "We are waiting word of their wartime affiliations. The four men who seemed to be the leaders have not been identified as of yet. We'll keep you advised."

"Fine. I scanned this file and noticed you've attached the photos of the hundred and twenty-seven. We have a few cooperating witnesses. They may identify them and fill in their backgrounds. Richard Maybrook, Lloyd Sedgwick, Tony Fuentes, Sophia Carrera and Phillip Berger here will undertake that chore. Raise your hands, please."

They complied.

"General, I'll be glad to move the fifteen who are known illegals over here," Chief Anderson volunteered. "We're a little crowded."

Bart laughed, "So are we, Chief. Hold them until tomorrow. However, we'll interrogate them at your headquarters tonight. Berger and Fuentes will question them."

"What about Baron von Wolf?" Wayne asked.

"If you have no objection, we have a nice isolation cell here for him. Our tactics here may be more suitable for our purposes. Your people won't be bound by civil rules of justice. This is a wartime matter."

Muffled laughter followed. Wayne replied, "All I heard, General, is that you have a cell available. The U.S. Attorney and I agree to house him here. When changes are decided upon, the decision will be made as to who has custody of this bounder and who will prosecute him."

"Fine. Go to work, gentlemen. Keep warm. This meeting's adjourned."

CHAPTER FIVE

Tuesday, February 10, 1953 - Fort Leavenworth

The tribunal called for the next witness. Itzhak Paplowsky held his head high, overcoming his normal tendency to hunch over. He took the oath with a loud "I do."

"Please state your name, sir," Bart said.

"I am Itzhak Paplowsky. Everybody calls me Pap."

"Are you a survivor of the Holocaust?"

"Yes, we call it the *Shoah*."

"That's the Hebrew word for Holocaust?"

"Yes, sir."

"Where were you born?"

"Warsaw."

"What was your profession?"

"I was a lawyer."

"Where were you educated?"

"After graduating from the gymnasium, my father sent me to the University of Berlin. After two years, I had to leave because anti-Semitism was on the rise in Germany. I finished my studies in Warsaw. After college, I studied law, built up a fine practice representing Jews and Gentiles. My father had a department store. He was a very successful man."

"Tell us about your family."

"I had two brothers, two sisters and two wonderful parents."

"Are you married?"

"I was, and had two children, a boy and a girl."

"Where is your family now?"

"They are all in heaven now," he cried, tears rolling down his cheeks.

"All of them?"

"Yes. Those dirty, filthy, Nazi bastards tortured my father and mother, raped my two sisters and then shot them when they moved us all out of our homes. Robbed us of everything we had. They searched our houses, ransacked everything, and took our money, jewelry, paintings and anything valuable. I saw soldiers and Gestapo agents pocket things for themselves. Thieves, every one of them."

"What happened then?"

"We were all moved to what they established as the ghetto. All of the family was intact. A Star of David was sewn on our clothes. We also wore armbands with the Jewish insignia. As a family, we were secular Jews, but observed the holidays, especially Yom Kippur."

"What happened at the ghetto?"

"A Jewish council was formed. My father, brothers and I refused to serve on that committee. They had to pick from the Jewish population men to do the most menial, dirty tasks for these German lice. They shoveled snow, washed streets, cleaned stables, packed manure, and all kinds of personal jobs for the Nazi officers."

"What happened to your family?"

"One night my brothers, Adam and Aaron, were with me cleaning toilets in the soldiers' barracks. When we finished, we walked back to the barracks. There was a lot of screaming and yelling. A soldier was beating a horse and a young woman's hair was tied to the horse's tail. As the horse ran past us, we saw it was my sister, Molly. We ran after the horse. Shots were fired at us. My brother Adam dropped. His brains spilled in the street. Aaron and I ran down an alley and circled around a warehouse. The horse was there chewing on some garbage containing spoiled apples. We quickly untied my sister from the horse's tail. She was half alive. We carried her to the back of the warehouse."

"What happened after that?"

"She was bleeding from her face, arms, and profusely from her vagina."

"Was she able to talk?"

"Yes, but she was dying. With her last words, she told us she had been raped by three soldiers. My other sister, Talia, was taken by two other soldiers. Those were Molly's last words. She died right there." Tears ran down his face, and there were many watery eyes in the courtroom. Silence prevailed.

Bart stood back and sympathetically suggested, "Pap, would you like a recess?"

"No, dammit, no!" he screamed. He wiped his face with his jacket pocket handkerchief.

"What happened then?"

"We carried her body down the dark street. A soldier stopped us. He pointed his rifle at us. We gently lowered my sister's body and raised our hands. I speak good German. He said, *Was ist los?* I told him we found her body tied to a horse's tail. He laughed. I was taller and heavier than him. I was in a fury and suddenly I dived at him, knocking him to the ground. My brother Aaron grabbed his rifle and beat him to death with the butt. I took his pistol, a Luger, from his holster. He had a pocketful of bullets. I took them too.

We put his body behind the bushes along the road. We picked up my sister with the rifle underneath her body. There was a crowd in front of our building in the ghetto. There were a few soldiers trying to move the gathering. We sneaked around to the back of the building and went to our flat. No one saw us. My wife Elsa saw us and began to scream. I laid my sister on a bed and clamped my hand over Elsa's mouth."

"Then what?"

"She quieted down and cried. I asked, *Where are the children?* She said, *They are next door with the neighbors.* I demanded, *Where's Mama and Poppa?* She couldn't talk, and just pointed out the window to the street." He stopped his narration, struggling to mouth the words.

Bart handed him a glass of water. The media, spectators, and the tribunal were spellbound. A nervous rustling was heard in the defendant's section.

"Pap, shall we stop?" Bart asked, genuinely sympathetic.

"No, no, General," he said, wiping his eyes. "I ran down to the street. The crowd was being dispersed. In the center of the street were my father and mother, dead with bullet wounds in their heads and bodies. Maybe twenty bullet wounds in each."

"What did you do?"

"A *Hauptmann*, captain, asked me who I was. I told him, *They are my parents.* He seemed sympathetic. He wasn't Gestapo. He said, *Take them away and bury them. Schnell, before the SS comes back.* I was young and strong, so I carried them one at a time to our flat. Aaron helped. Before daylight, we put them in a supply cart and took them to a ghetto cemetery. Neighbors helped us dig the graves. A young rabbi performed the *Kaddish* for my parents and my sister. Talia didn't come. Later, we found her."

"Explain *Kaddish*, for the record."

"That is the Hebrew word of the prayer for the dead."

"Go on."

"Later that day, a woman brought my sister Talia to our flat. She was disheveled, with dirt and blood on her face and dress. She looked like a ghost. She kept mumbling, *No more, no more.* My wife and I cleaned her up. Her vagina was bloody. My sister stuffed cotton in her. She had a high fever. Two days later she said, *Sergeant Otto Krause killed me.* She died that night. We buried her in the early hours. The next day, I was trying to find this Otto Krause, but all of us were put on a train to Auschwitz."

"What did you do with the gun and the rifle?"

"The Jewish council was preparing to fight the Nazis, so Aaron gave them the weapons."

"Who went to Auschwitz with you?"

"My wife, two children and my brother, plus twenty thousand other Jews were stuffed into cattle cars. We could hardly breathe; we were so crowded in those smelly trains. No food, no water, no toilets. It was death on wheels. Dozens of elderly died. It was torture."

"What happened when you got to Auschwitz?"

"Half the crowd was stripped naked and sent to the showers, which were really the gas chambers. We were lucky. We were sent to barracks. The next day my brother Aaron and I went to work with other slave laborers to help build the I.G. Farben plant, where they were going to make that Zyklon B gas. My wife became a housemaid for a colonel. My children were put behind a fence with other kids."

"How did they survive?"

"They didn't. That colonel turned out to be Rudolph Höss. He killed my wife and two children."

"Why?"

"He tried to rape my wife. She scratched his face and ran out of his quarters screaming as she fled through the camp."

"What happened after that?"

"I was working at the I.G. Farben site. After the Gestapo caught my wife, they made all the Jews watch. They brought my children to stand alongside her. In front of everyone, he shot her between her eyes and then fired a full round at my children. All three lay there all day. I saw the bodies when I came from my job. Other people told me what had happened. I was in a state of total shock. Chaim Herzog pulled me away. I fainted."

"What happened after that?"

"When I came to, I looked out of the barracks and saw my wife and two children being thrown into the flames of the crematorium. I had to be restrained from running out after them. Several men held me down. I'm not the suicide type. I am the get-even type."

"What do you mean by that?"

"All of my family were gone. Most people would have killed themselves in those camps after that. Not me. Chaim talked me into going back to my job in the morning. They told me that if I didn't, Höss would find out about me and send me to the gas chambers."

"Didn't Höss know about you?"

"He was too busy trying to meet his quota of killing at least ten thousand a day. So I went back to the I.G. Farben job the next day. I convinced the civilian architect that I could make things go faster if I could live in one of those shacks on the site."

"Did he agree?"

"Only after he wanted to know how to speed things up. I proved to him that the delays were due to the slow arrivals of particular parts, which were holding up production."

"What was his name?"

"Albert Speer, a close confidante of Hitler, who was on an inspection tour. He ordered the Gestapo major to make me a foreman and to move me into a shack. He asked my name. I said I was Isaiah Papp. He made out a card appointing me foreman with my new name on it. He signed it."

"Did you save that card?"

"Yes, I have it here in my wallet." He extracted it and showed it to Bart.

"Pap, I would like to submit this card as evidence. It will be returned to you."

"Okay."

Bart presented it and it was marked. Then he asked, "Do you remember another shack near the one assigned to you?"

"Yes."

"Tell the court about that other shack."

"It became a whorehouse run by SS men."

"How long did it operate?"

"About a month."

"Who were the men operating that whorehouse?"

"Those four men in the back row."

"Mr. President of this tribunal, please allow the witness to tap each suspect on the shoulder."

"So ordered."

Two MPs escorted Paplowsky to the rear of the courtroom. He placed his hand on Hans Klepper, Bernard Werner, Gunther Frommer and Hugo Baumer.

A few of the defendants yelled, "Jew bastard, you'll be dead soon!"

"Not before you, *scum*," Paplowsky sneered.

The MPs pulled him back into the aisle and marched him to the witness stand.

"Did you know that they were abusing children in that shack?" Bart asked.

"No, not until the fire was put out. I went in there and saw the bodies of these burned children."

"What else did you see these men do?"

"I saw them carrying bodies and hiding them in the pit with all the Jews that were gassed that day."

"No further questions."

Klaus Brackmann moved to cross-examine the witness. "What is your real name, sir?"

"Itzhak Paplowsky."

"Why are you called Pap?"

"It's a nickname."

"Not Isaiah Papp?"

"No."

"Will the real Itzhak Paplowsky stand up?"

Milburn roared, "Objection. Counsel is playing games."

"Sustained."

"We're trying to show that this man is not who he says he is."

"Then what the hell is this?" Paplowsky cried out as he rolled up the sleeve on his left arm and showed five tattooed numbers.

"Mr. Paplowsky, do you wear glasses?"

"No."

"How is your eyesight?"

"Better than yours."

"Objection; the witness is not responsive."

"Answer the question," Nimitz ordered.

"My eyes are 20/20."

"Let's test that."

Brackmann deliberately strode back to the rear of the court. He stood next to a towering staff sergeant, then pointed to stripes on his sleeve.

"How many stripes are there on this sleeve?"

"Three."

"Very good. What's the color of his eyes?"

"They are hazel colored."

"Very good."

"How many fingers am I holding up?"

"Two."

"Wrong."

"No, I'm right. You quickly raised a third finger."

"Sergeant, come up here," Nimitz ordered. "For the record, your name, please?" Nimitz ordered.

"Sergeant Alfred Towne."

"How many fingers did counsel raise?"

"Two, and when the witness answered, he raised a third finger."

"Excused."

Brackmann stood before the witness.

"Trickster!" Paplowsky shouted, and held up his right hand middle finger in an obscene gesture. Chuckles were heard in the courtroom. The tribunal ignored the display.

"Mr. Paplowsky, are you a citizen of the United States?"

"Yes, since 1950. That was my proudest day."

"What is your present occupation?"

"I am a counterman in the Gold Star Delicatessen on Delancey Street in New York City."

"Isn't that beneath the potential of a former lawyer?"

"Oh yes, but I am studying law at NYU. I expect to graduate this June. Then I take the bar exam. I'm still a young man."

"Thank you. No further questions."

Nimitz ordered a recess, then said, "Court will resume at 1400 hours."

During the recess, Bart and Jacques decided to forego lunch. Baron von Wolf was in an isolation cell. He was brought to the special interrogation room, isolated from all traffic in the area. The handcuffed lawyer in leg chains, his clothes badly wrinkled, stubble on his face, stared forlornly at the threatening men. Bart lit a cigarette. Jacques followed. Both disgorged clouds of smoke at the discomfited figure seated on a rickety chair.

"Baron von Wolf, you are in the worst possible trouble. Why have you put your life at risk?" Bart said.

"You're a dead man," Jacques declared.

"I am a Swiss citizen and I wish to see my ambassador."

"He'll see you, but you won't see him. He will come to identify your body."

Wolf's sallow complexion turned white. A trickle of saliva ran down his chin. "What does that mean?"

"Come, come, my man, you're an intelligent person. You've committed an offense punishable by death at a military installation. No trial is required under our rules. Within the next two hours you'll be facing a firing squad," Bart said.

"This is impossible. I should have a trial. Why will you kill me?"

"I'm sorry for you. How stupid can a man like you be? The attack on this fort was an act of war. You triggered the demonstration as a diversion for two suicide-bombing attempts on this fortress. Your Nazi life is *kaput*. Do you want a priest for your last two hours?" Bart said.

"I was only acting as Hitler's lawyer!" von Wolf blubbered.

"Don't bullshit me, you money-hungry shyster! You left the court before the riots and were headed out of the country. You are as culpable as those two suicide drivers, hired Arabs on their way to see Allah. I don't think God will accept you. Where do you want your body sent? Argentina or Switzerland?"

"Oh, dear God, help me."

"Help you for what? You're a lawyer. You know what a deal is. Do you want to make a deal? This is a one-time offer."

"What kind of deal?"

"A full confession. Every detail, and you can save your life."

Von Wolf was silent. Bart took a small pad from his pocket and handed it to the weeping attorney.

"Here's a pen. Make out your will. I'll find the chaplain and send him in." Bart and Jacques rose to leave.

"Wait, wait. Is your offer that of an attorney or a general?"

"Both."

"I'll talk. I'm not going to take the fall for *that* maniac."

Jacques produced the tape recorder and turned it on. "This is Tuesday, February 10, 1953, 1300 hours. I am General Barton Milburn. CIA agent Jacques Laurent, head of the Nazi desk, is with me in Detention Room Five in the United States Disciplinary Barracks at Fort Leavenworth, Kansas. We are interrogating one Baron Edward von Wolf, a Swiss attorney and co-conspirator in the attack on this fort on Friday, February 6, 1953. He voluntarily wishes to make a statement. Prior to that, I will now address him. Baron von Wolf, you have the right to remain silent. Is the statement you are about to make being given of your own free will and desire? If so, state your name and repeat what I have just stated."

Jacques stood over him menacingly.

"My name is Baron Edward von Wolf, of Zurich, Switzerland. I make the following statement of my own free will."

He spoke for thirty-five minutes, the essence of which was that on Saturday, January 23, he called an Erich Koch in Skokie, Illinois. "We told him that Nordheim ordered plan *Sieben X* be put into operation as soon as possible. Two million dollars would be deposited into Alden Gaines' account for the expenses and an additional two million for Koch. I had the money wired from a special account in the Cayman Islands."

In the continuing account, von Wolf said they had been preparing for the assault ever since Nordheim was captured. A convention in the name of the Christian Crusade, a fictitious organization of Nazis, would be held at the Muehlebach Hotel in Kansas City, Missouri, scheduled for Sunday, February 1, just one day after the call. Hitler had authorized five million dollars each for Gaines and von Wolf.

Bart shut off the machine. "Baron, you have been given a reprieve. I assume that Mr. Koch is in our custody?"

"Yes, he is."

"Relax. We'll check out your story. I've got to get back to court."

The tribunal met with prosecution and defense lawyers. Alden Gaines was brought into the chambers. U.S. Attorney Farley Washburn was present. Bart succinctly advised the tribunal that Alden Gaines' role in the attack on the fort had not been fully determined.

"This is a total farce. General Milburn's prejudice toward me is patently clear. This is a frame-up," Gaines declared, solely for the ears of his fellow lawyers and defendants.

"Members of this tribunal, Baron von Wolf is undoubtedly a co-conspirator. I will be presenting our case against him before a grand jury tomorrow morning. I'd appreciate his being held here in your jail facilities temporarily," Washburn said.

"Mr. Gaines, you are permitted to continue as counsel in von Wolf's place, pending the U.S. Attorney's investigation," Nimitz agreed.

"Thank you, sir," Washburn said.

The defense lawyers remained mute.

"Clear out, gentlemen. See you in court," Nimitz said.

The tribunal called the court to order.

"Let the record note that counselor Baron Edward von Wolf will not be representing Adolf Hitler and other co-defendants before this bar. He has been arrested on charges of conspiracy to attack and destroy Fort Leavenworth," Nimitz said.

A loud roar of shock reverberated throughout the courtroom. Wire-service reporters raced for the doors.

"Call your next witness, General."

"The prosecution calls Marcus Feingold."

The tall man marched in military lockstep with two MPs to the witness stand. After taking the oath and stating his name, he sat in the witness chair and stared stone-faced at the defendants.

Bart asked, "Mr. Feingold, where were you born?"

"Heidelberg, Germany," he answered in unaccented English.

Bart led him through the details of his family history and experiences with the Nazis. He cried through the parts of the Gestapo raid on the house, the capture of his parents, his two sisters, his brother and himself. Angrily, he detailed their nine months at Dachau, followed by their harrowing transfer in stuffed, smelly cattle cars to Auschwitz with thousands of other hapless Jews. He repeated his story of his two sisters being gang-raped and killed by soldiers, and the murder of his parents for protesting to Lieutenant Colonel Erich Müller.

"Before you go any further, tell the court of the atrocities you observed at Dachau."

"It was during our nine months there that we saw the bestiality of German soldiers and the Gestapo officers increase in intensity. They tore beards off the Orthodox Jews, stripped their wives naked and painted swastikas on the breasts of these women. They used riding crops to whip any Jew in their way, or for no reason at all. If they found a Bible or a Torah, they tortured those who had them and then tore page after page out of the Bibles and threw them in fires. Once I saw them take a hidden Torah, put it out in front of the barracks and piss on it. Then they fired shots into it and finally threw it on a bonfire. Young soldiers, with hardly any fuzz on their faces, and older soldiers were participating and laughing."

"What did you see at Auschwitz?"

"They were monsters. I saw a former schoolmate, a German no more than twenty-one years old, who used to be a friend of mine. He was a Christian boy, and we played on the same soccer team, yet there he was at Auschwitz, wild-eyed, hate in his cherubic face, bayoneting a mother carrying a baby. When she dropped, he lifted the baby with his bayonet and hurled it onto a barbed-wire fence. The bleeding mother tried to crawl toward her baby, which was hanging on the barbed wire. He watched her progress, and the slave laborers watched her intently. None of us were able to move. Soldiers stood around with their rifles, waiting for one of us to try to help. My schoolmate, Christopher Engel, looked at his compatriots for approval, then he took steady aim and shot this bleeding, desperate young mother, with two bullets in her head. Then he kept firing into her dead body. The other soldiers whistled and applauded, then the miserable punk turned around and performed an exaggerated curtain bow."

The courtroom spectators were frozen in disgust.

"Mr. Feingold, that is certainly a revolting incident."

"Objection," Erich von Maunder shouted. "That story by Feingold is more fiction. Further, counsel has testified in his last statement."

"Mr. President, I will present witnesses who will validate the atrocities that occurred at those death camps. Some of our witnesses are Nazis in our custody," Bart said.

"Objection overruled."

Jacques walked over to Gideon Cartman, who was in a discussion with General Wilford Ross at the defense table. "Excuse me, gentlemen. Here is the list of prisoners arrested in Friday's attack. Look at this name."

Ross and Cartman stared at the sheet while Bart continued his direct examination.

"Holy Toledo," Cartman said.

"Yes, it's Christopher Engel. Let's hope it's the same man Feingold named."

"Tell Bart I'm going to visit this guy right now," Jacques said, then left.

Bart pressed for more detail from Feingold. "What was the worst you saw at Auschwitz?"

"Everything, sir. This large inferno became the biggest mass-murdering machine in history. Trains with twenty boxcars of men, women, children, the old and young, kept arriving almost daily with Jews from all walks of life. Most were secular Jews. Orthodox Jews make up only about ten percent of the Jewish population. Scientists, doctors, educators, authors, historians, shop-keepers, housewives, the upper class, middle class, the poverty-stricken, rab-bis, and some Jehovah's Witnesses, Christian dissenters, Gypsies, the lame and the halt kept pouring in. They were stripped naked. Some were sent to the barracks to work as slave laborers like myself. Then, in an organized assembly line, they were sent to the gas chambers, which were disguised as showers. Like lemmings going into a sea of death. Soldiers and medics pulled gold fillings from the mouths of the dead, who were then hurled into common graves and later put into crematoriums. All children under twelve were killed."

"You observed this personally?"

"Almost everyone of us saw it at one time or another. The worst of it was, soldiers joked and laughed while they made the inmates carry dead bodies away from the gas chambers to clear them for the next batch of victims."

"Would you recognize any of the Nazis you saw at Dachau and Auschwitz?"

"General, there isn't one of them that isn't etched in my mind forever. I have a talent for faces. However, that piece of shit sitting there with his Van Dyke beard doesn't look like that clown Hitler, with his funny mustache. He had plastic surgery and pretended to be a Jew."

Three lawyers stood up at once and shouted, "Objection!"

"He's lying and using foul language," von Maunder declared.

"Okay, the court reporter will eliminate the 'S' word describing Herr Hitler," Nimitz, deeply touched by Feingold's account, said testily.

The three lawyers kept chattering at the tribunal. General Smith, flushed and angry, roared, "Sit down! One at a time. This isn't a circus. This is deadly serious business. Behave yourselves. Sit."

Nimitz glanced at Smith and nodded approval.

"Mr. Feingold, you've described your escape from Auschwitz and your trip into Stockholm, Sweden. You were granted U.S. political asylum and joined the American Army. What was your rank?"

"Captain, finally with General Omar Bradley's First Army as an inter-preter on D-Day. I went through the invasion of France with him. I inter-preted for intelligence officers who questioned POWs. Some of their Nazi POWs were fourteen, fifteen and sixteen years old. That *schmuck* Hitler sent these babies to their deaths. He is a desperate maniac."

"No further questions."

Objections rang out.

"Overruled. Court is adjourned until tomorrow at 0900 hours."

"Your Honor," Bart declared, "The prosecution requests that we recess until Monday. We have a delay in witnesses coming in and need time to prepare to bring them into court."

"Any objections from the defense counsel?" Nimitz asked.

"None. However, Your Honors, may I have a word?" the Swiss bank lawyer, Stolz, requested.

"What's on your mind, Mr. Stolz?" Nimitz asked.

"We need to have a very short conference with our client Herr Hitler privately."

Nimitz waved to an MP. "Have all the prisoners removed to their cells. The court is to be cleared. MPs are to guard all exits from the outside. The defense lawyers will confer here. When they finish, return Hitler to his cell. How long will it be, gentlemen?"

"Less than an hour, sir."

"Very well, then. Court is adjourned until Monday, February 16, at 0900 hours."

Bart gathered his things and led Feingold into the corridor.

"My friend," Bart said, "your testimony was very good. However, you're not off the hook for tampering with Hitler's pills. I spoke with Farley Washburn, the U.S. Attorney, who will go easy on you and only charge you with battery with a suspended sentence. We'll try to keep it off your record, but there are no guarantees."

"I know I was wrong and I regret it, but I just couldn't forget the past," Feingold replied.

The court was cleared, then Hitler let loose in one of his typical wartime tirades. "*Arschlöcher!* Why do you let those witnesses lie and tear me apart? You're like my generals. You're *muschies!*"

"Listen, Hitler, you are no longer *Der Führer*. You made big mistakes in the war and now you are compounding your stupidity with more errors of judgment," Stolz yelled.

"What are you talking about?"

"Gaines and Baron Wolf followed your orders to attack this fort, and they are in jail. You are a mad, rotten idiot!" Stolz shot back.

"Von Maunder, are you going to let him talk to me like that?"

"He's right. Stop this revenge *Scheisse*. There is very little need to cross-examine these witnesses. They're telling the truth."

"Then why are you here defending me?"

"Because the Swiss banks want to protect themselves."

"Then I'll fire you both."

"That leaves you with no defense," Stolz replied.

"I'll defend myself. I'll take the stand and tell my story."

"Don't be a windbag, *du Quatschkopf*. You bullshitted the German people with speeches. This is America, and the whole world is watching this trial. Don't make a fool of yourself," von Maunder pleaded.

"Eight years ago I would have you two shot for talking to me like this."

"Listen, ex-*Führer*, that was then and this is now. We'll do the best we can for you, and if you like, I'll call Zurich and ask them to hire two more lawyers to assist."

"Send for Otto Meissner. He was a judge. He lives in Germany. He's a free man. They never tried him at Nuremberg. Also, find Gertrud Scholtz-Klink. She is very smart. She's in Germany. Pay them whatever they want from my account."

"We'll do our best."

"Not good enough. Tell your Swiss Bank Association I'll put them in the gutter if they let me down. Get them here by Monday. Now get out of here!"

The lawyers knocked on the locked doors, and two MPs took Hitler to his cell. Stolz and von Maunder braved the elements to their car.

"I hope they hang this sick dog," Stolz said.

In the prosecution conference room, Bart and the prosecution team were listening to reports from Lieutenant Winslow and Lieutenant Grace Larsen, who was in charge of the phone bank.

"Sir, the phones were going all day. Hate calls mostly. We've heard foul language that hasn't been invented yet."

Bart, Cartman and General Ross laughed.

"All right, Lieutenant, what do we have of prime interest?"

"We have a Polish lady in Allentown, Pennsylvania, who survived in Chelmno. Her husband and three children were killed. It's a heartrending story. She's willing to testify. No money to come here. Working as a domestic for a rich Christian family. I have their names and phone number. Another call is from a Russian lady in Encino, California. That's part of L.A. If her story is true, it's a biggie. She lost five children, a husband, two brothers, two sisters, her father and mother. She and a brother survived at Buchenwald. Rescued by American troops. A Belgian Jewish man from Skokie, Illinois, was in the death march from Dachau to Tegernsee. He's feisty and full of hate for the Nazis. Well spoken. Lost his wife, three children, parents and grandparents. Says he is still fighting Nazis in Skokie. I don't know what he means. A young girl, a student at Harvard, lost two sisters, two brothers and both parents at Treblinka. She speaks good English. Says she is studying French with Professor Joyce Laurent. She said you know her teacher."

"I sure do. She's Jacques Laurent's sister and my adopted sister. I'll let Mr. Laurent handle that call. You'll meet him soon. He's head of the CIA Nazi desk," Bart responded.

"One more call to report."

"Go on, Lieutenant."

"A man, claiming to be a Catholic priest in St. Louis, says he can give you a lot of atrocities on Jews, pre-war and postwar. That's all he would say."

"All right, type it all up and we'll follow through," Bart said, then turned to the new lieutenant. "Kyle, how's the mail going?"

"Slow, but sure, sir. The hate mail is not that heavy. We are putting those in separate files, along with the hate calls that have been taped. I figured, sir, that you might want the FBI or the CIA to track down these neo-Nazis."

"Good thinking."

"So far we have twenty letters from survivors. All of them qualify as potential witnesses. Two are from Paris, five from Israel, one Toronto, two Montreal, one Philadelphia, two Holland, one Belgium, one Chicago, one Geneva, one Denmark, one Czechoslovakia and two Rome. Here is one from

Vienna addressed to you, General, marked *Personal and Confidential.*"

"What we have so far are five phone calls and twenty letters, plus this personal letter to me."

At that point Jacques entered. There was blood on his tie and shirt. He looked grim.

"Jacques, meet Lieutenant Grace Larsen, and you know our new lieutenant, Kyle Winslow. So far we have twenty letters and five callers volunteering as witnesses. One of the letters is from a student of Joyce's at Harvard."

His face lit up. "I'd like to see that letter."

Jacques stood there reading the letter. All eyes in the room stared at his bloodstains. Bart lit a cigarette and tossed the pack on the table. Both lieutenants lit up.

"This is a very pathetic letter. When Joyce and Elizabeth come to testify, they should bring this girl, Tevyah Klein, with them."

"Okay, Jacques, now where did that blood on your tie and shirt come from?"

Jacques angrily tore open his shirt. A taped gauze covering a six-inch cut was bloodstained. "Do you want to hear it now in front of these lieutenants?"

Sophia stood up and touched the bandage on his chest. "Did a medic look at this?" she asked.

"Yes, he wanted to stitch it, but I told him I'd be back."

"Sure, they can stay and learn something," Bart said.

"I don't want to use language that might shock Grace here."

"Mr. Laurent, I've heard it all and more. Go to it," Grace Larsen said.

"Well, I went down to the cell that Christopher Engel was in. You know, the guy that Feingold testified about, who bayoneted the baby and killed the mother. He looked like a choir boy. So, I was relaxed and figured I could get him to talk about his role at Auschwitz. As I was adjusting my chair, this Nazi prick had a knife and stabbed me. My chair went over backwards with me on top of it. He jumped on me. I went berserk and beat the shit out of him. His ribs are broken, his nose is smashed and he was unconscious by the time I was through pounding him. He's a big guy, about six-foot-two. I bet he weighs two hundred and forty pounds."

"Did you get to talk to him?"

"You can bet Hitler's ass I did. The MPs came in. We washed his face and brought him to. Then I dismissed the MPs."

Jacques reached into his pocket and withdrew an ivory-handled dagger and threw it on the table.

"Where the hell did he get that?" Bart demanded.

"That's what's got me so fucking angry. Pardon me, Lieutenant," he said to Larsen, apologizing for his language. She nodded. "He was not given the routine search before he was put in the cell. He hid the piece in his mattress. They checked him out later. Before that, he had the blade in a sheath tied around his bare skin."

"What did you get out of him?" Cartman asked.

"In short, he says he's Adolf Eichmann's nephew. He's a captain in the Waffen

SS. At first he said he wasn't Christopher Engel. I slapped him-not too hard-I didn't want to knock him out again. Then, I showed him his mug shot and a picture of him in his black Gestapo uniform. *Lie once more and I'll put you in front of a firing squad,* I said. I had already told him about the mechanics squad. The firing-squad threat did it, and he poured forth like diarrhea of the mouth."

Larsen and Winslow were enthralled by Jacques' recitation.

"Did you ask him about that bayonet killing of the woman and her baby?" Bart asked.

"Finally, in passing, we got around to that. Heinrich Müller had lectured the senior officers. He told them that every soldier and Gestapo agent stationed at Auschwitz must earn his *cherry* by killing at least one inmate personally. *Once they kill, they are no longer boys,* he quoted Müller. *Send those who show signs of weakness to the Eastern Front.* For weeks after that, Jews were shot for no reason at all, except it conformed to the Final Solution. This miserable rich kid's grandfather is Joachim von Ribbentrop, the Foreign Minister, who was tried and hanged at Nuremberg. His father, Kurt Engel, was a bank president who later was Deputy Foreign Minister under von Ribbentrop. He's a pussycat now. When I got through with him, he pissed in his pants. Here's the tape of this inhumane little bastard. Bart, let's hang them all."

"We'll talk about that. Go have that wound stitched. That's an order, Jacques, now," Bart ordered.

The phone rang. Winslow answered, then handed the phone to Bart. "One moment, sir. General, J. Edgar Hoover is calling."

"General Milburn here," he replied.

"This is Clyde Tolson, sir. Mr. Hoover is on another phone and will be with you in a moment."

"Mr. Tolson, I'll put Lieutenant Winslow on hold until Mr. Hoover is ready to talk. I'm very busy at the moment."

Bart winked at the group and handed the phone to the lieutenant. He punched a button on the extension phone and was connected with Provost Marshal Drake.

"John, I need Interrogation Room Five and, one at a time, I want to question those four that we have in isolation. You know, the ones we nabbed at the corner of Seventh Street."

"General, I'll have it set up in ten minutes. Two of my strongest MPs will deliver and guard."

Winslow was on the phone with Hoover. "He'll be with you shortly, Mr. Hoover. The general is just finishing an important call."

After Bart hung up with Drake, he casually lit a cigarette, put his feet on the conference table, took a sip of hot coffee, emitted a few rings of smoke and nodded to the lieutenant.

"Here's the general now, sir."

"Milburn here."

"This is J. Edgar Hoover, General."

"Nice to hear from you, sir," Bart smirked.

"You must be mighty busy, General. Sorry to intrude."

"Mr. Director, you're always welcome," Bart said, turning on the charm.

"Kind of you to say so, General. I've been listening to you on the radio; you're very impressive and I wish to congratulate you. Sorry I wasn't part of your Operation Lucifer."

"Apparently you are now, sir."

"Just want you to know that we are bending every effort to identify all of your recently acquired prisoners. If you need any special help, I am at your service. We have been tracking Nazis for some time. Let's drop the formality and call me Edgar."

"That's very kind of you, Edgar. I appreciate your cooperation. Your men out here are really very helpful."

"By the way, General, there is a personal friend of mine, a nationally syndicated columnist and broadcaster who has been trying to be accredited for the press section there and has been running into roadblocks. That's Walter Winchell. He's anxious to attend the trial and to do his regular Sunday radio broadcast from there. It would be a personal favor for me if you could expedite his press credentials."

"I am surprised to hear this. I thought it was routine for the media to receive their credentials upon request."

"General, he was told that only daily reporters, and not columnists, were being accredited."

"Edgar, I am chief prosecutor and am running these trials. But, as a special favor for you, I will personally ask General Fielding, commander of Fort Leavenworth and an old war buddy of mine, to make an exception for Mr. Winchell. It will be expedited in the next hour. Where do I reach him?"

"General, you have made a good friend today. I am most appreciative. I am on your team. Godspeed. He's at the New York Daily Mirror, Murray Hill 2-1000."

"Thank you, Edgar."

The team looked at Bart, who said, "Ass-kissing sleezeball and his press agent, *Anus-sniffer Winchell*. Kyle, get Captain Esta Arnold in Public Affairs on the line, please."

"Captain Arnold here, sir," she answered.

"Esta, call the Daily Mirror in New York, Murray Hill 2-1000, and ask for Walter Winchell. Tell him or his secretary that he is fully accredited to attend the trial, courtesy of General Barton Milburn and J. Edgar Hoover. Tell him to have a photograph of himself, as part of the security rules here. Tell him to ask for you when he arrives. As to his broadcasts, tell him he'll have to make arrangements with radio station KKLO here in Leavenworth, or with WDAF, WHB or KCMO in Kansas City. Wait about twenty minutes before making your call. Also, prepare his credentials. Have you got it?"

"Yes, sir. I took it in shorthand."

"Good work, Captain. Call me in an hour or so at my house. I'm curious about the reaction."

Jacques returned and said, "Come on, buddy, we are going to meet one of the leaders of the riots."

Jacques and Bart entered the special sound-proofed interrogation room. Two MP's stood on either side of a stocky man, stubble-bearded, head shorn and eyes bloodshot. The trio stood against a stone wall, the MPs dwarfing the handcuffed and leg-shackled prisoner. After exchanging salutes, the MP's pushed the prisoner into a chair.

"General, we'll be just outside the door. Knock and we'll come in," one of the guards said, then the steel door was slammed shut.

"Who are you?" Bart asked one of the three men.

"None of your fucking business."

"So, it's like that?"

"Why the fuck am I in here?"

"Maybe it was a charge of loitering?"

"Yeah, that's it."

"You call yourself Nathan Bedford Forrest, plus a few aliases."

"Bullshit."

"Is that your alias or a swear word?"

"Very funny, soldier boy."

"Nothing is funny here, smart ass," Bart countered sharply. "You don't look like you're one hundred and thirty one years old. Your record, which I have here, indicates you're only fifty-two."

"What the hell does that mean?"

"All right, Grand Dragon, you call yourself Nathan Bedford Forrest. That was the name of the Confederate general who founded the Ku Klux Klan in 1866 when he was forty-five years old. He died in 1877. Are you his great-grandson?"

"Okay, soldier boy, I legally changed my name."

"From William Ramsay to Earle Watkins to Joseph Mayo."

"Hey, I want a lawyer."

"Listen, loser, your real name is Hugo Kuhn, and you're the brother of Fritz, former head of the German American Bund. You're a felon, an ex-con who has done time in jail half of your rotten life. From age fourteen to twenty-one you were in reform school for stabbing a teacher. Two years later you moved from Chicago to New York to live with your Nazi brother Fritz. Soon you were caught robbing a restaurant and convicted. You did eight years at Sing Sing. Next you moved to Los Angeles and tried to set fire to a Negro church in L.A. and spent five years at Chino. Through a Ku Kluxer there, you got a job as a security guard, and with your new name you joined the Ku Klux Klan and worked your way up to grand dragon. Somehow, you got to be a rich man, supported by a Jew named Nordheim, except you didn't know that. You were paid by Winston General Ltd. How do you like that?"

"Bullshit."

"Here are some facts for your short remaining years, tough guy, and this is not bullshit. You are going to face a firing squad in the morning. Your associates will keep you company."

"What associates?"

"Those two phony Christian Crusaders and the other Nazi bastard who helped run the attack."

"What's this crap about a firing squad?"

"This is not funny, smart ass. Do you want to write a will for your wife and two sons that you left in Chicago when you moved to Skokie?" Bart asked.

"You're not kidding."

"No, this is a military base. You attacked it. Technically, that's an act of war. Some call it treason. No court is necessary. Make out your will. We don't serve a last meal to the condemned. Here is a pad and pen. Your body will be shipped to your wife. Let's go, Jacques."

They went to the door and tapped it. The two MPs entered.

"This prisoner is going to make out his will. He goes before a firing squad at 0700 hours," Bart said, winking.

"Yes, sir. We'll take him to death row as soon as he's finished with his will, sir," the MP said as he closed the door behind Bart and Jacques.

The stocky man stood up and yelled, "Come back!"

There was no reply.

"Come on, Hugo, start writing or we'll pull you out of here," an MP ordered him.

"Hey, get them back. I got a lot to tell them," he cried, his handcuffed hands pleading.

"They're probably gone."

"Well, call them. I have a lot to tell them."

"Man, you're dealing with a tough general and the chief Nazi hunter."

"Don't stand there; try to get them."

"Sit down. Sit or I'll knock you down. Joe, see if you can reach the General or Mr. L.," the MP told his partner.

Outside the door, Jacques and Bart were waiting.

"Jacques, wait ten minutes and go in. I'll be in Major Drake's office. If he really lets loose, call me. Tell him the firing squad has been ordered."

The MP and Jacques finally approached the tense prisoner, and in a quivering voice he asked them, "Where's the general?"

"He's busy. What do you want?"

"I'll tell him the whole story if he'll cancel that firing squad."

"Like what?"

"Who hired me, who those other guys are, who planned this whole caper."

"If this is a con job, it won't help."

"Please, sir, I'm leveling. I won't play any games."

"I'll try to get the general, but God help you if you make a fool of me. You won't have an unbroken bone in your body when I get through with you."

Jacques picked up the phone and reached Bart. "General, sir, I know how busy you are, but Kuhn wishes to make a full confession to you."

"Tell him I'm busy. Think he's ready?"

"Please, General, I think he's for real."

"Okay, I'll be right there. Tell him he better be ready to start talking. Do you have the recorder?"

"Yes, thank you, sir."

Bart entered shortly and the MPs retreated.

"Jacques, put the recorder on the table."

Bart pressed it into operation. He repeated the ritual introduction and advice of free-will confession, then said, "Go ahead, Forrest."

"I was hired by Baron von Wolf to put this convention together at the Muehlebach Hotel in Kansas City, Missouri. It was planned a few months ago by a Mr. Darren Mayfield, who is Mr. Nordheim's aide-de-camp. It was his idea to form the Christian Crusade. I'm not Forrest. I'm Hugo Kuhn, alias Joseph Mayo. I lied about being Forrest."

"Keep going."

Kuhn named Mike Fitzgerald, an ex-pugilist who fought as a light-heavyweight under the name of Mike Fitz. He had a whack at the title until a Jew named Maxie Rosenbloom, light-heavyweight champ, knocked him out in the first round in Madison Square Garden. Another Jewish guy named Bob Olin took the title from Rosenbloom. Fitz got a shot at the new champ. Olin put him away in the third round. Fitz became a Jew hater after that. He joined the Aryan Swords, who have branches all over the world. He beat the draft because his eyesight was impaired.

"What's his profession now?" Bart asked.

"He got himself one of those correspondence diplomas from one of those phony divinity schools in Red Water, Mississippi. He soon became known as the Reverend Fitz Maguire of the Christian Crusade, which was a front for the Aryan Swords. He left his wife and kids and moved to Skokie, Illinois, a town of about 45,000. It became a center of anti-Semitism. My brother helped finance him during the war."

"Your brother Fritz Kuhn was head of the German-American Bund in the Yorkville section of New York. Hitler financed him, am I right?"

"Yes. But at that time I wasn't involved with him or my brother. I was in the can."

"Are you an anti-Semite?"

"Hell no, I don't even know what that's all about. I'm a mercenary. I'll work for anybody that pays me. If the Jews pay, I'll fight the Nazis. If the Arabs pay me, I'll fight the Jews. If the niggers pay me, I'll fight the whites."

"You're an amoral whore," Bart snapped.

"Yes, there's nothing moral about me, A or B," Kuhn agreed.

"You're funny or stupid. Who are the other two men who planned to blow up this fort?"

"Hey, General, I had no idea about those suicide-bomb trucks. They lied to me."

"How did they lie to you?"

"They told me we were waiting for two truckloads of more protesters. We were supposed to try to disrupt the trials."

"One little lie from you and you know what you'll be facing?"

"I know."

"Come on, who are these other two men?"

"Frederick Glasser and Herman Tuller. That's the names they used at the convention in the Muehlebach Hotel. They told us to split up in two or more factions. The Christian Crusaders were to be run by Reverend Maguire and I was to head up the Aryan Swords, the skinheads and other neo-Nazis. Alden Gaines and Baron von Wolf met with Maguire, Glasser, Tuller and me in a private suite. Maguire and I were paid $250,000 apiece in certified checks from the Banque Lorraine in Geneva. Gaines said he would help us cash them at the La Salle Bank in Chicago after the caper. Von Wolf spoke to Glasser and Tuller in German. I figured they were Nordheim's guys. I now know he is Adolf Hitler. All I did was carry on this phony demonstration. I swear I had nothing to do with the bombing," Kuhn added.

"Okay, Forrest, Hugo or whoever you are. Back to your cell. Pray you've told me the truth."

"Cross my heart."

"What heart?"

Bart sent for the MPs, then said, "Hold off on the firing squad. Put this bum back in isolation."

Sergeant Alex Greenberg, assigned driver for Bart, met Jacques and Bart at the exit door.

"Sir, there's a nasty snowstorm. You'll need your heavy coats to go out there. I've brought galoshes for you and Mr. Laurent."

"Very thoughtful, Sergeant." Bart ran to the conference room and brought two fleece-lined short coats and a plastic cover for his brimmed hat. A forty-mile-an-hour windstorm was pelting the fort with a combination of sleet and snow. Greenberg nursed the sedan through the storm at a speed of five miles per hour, stopping intermittently to wipe the windshield, which was not responding to the wipers. When they arrived at the Victorian house, Bart invited the sergeant to come in.

Mrs. Lawrence greeted them. "I was concerned you weren't going to make it here. I have a number of phone messages for you. I also have a hot dinner on the stove. Alex, go in the kitchen; Louis is in there. I'll feed both of you. General, your messages are on your desk. Dinner in half an hour," she directed in a motherly manner.

Jacques poured two glasses of Chivas Regal scotch and handed one to Bart, who was screening his messages. The first message came from Simon Wiesenthal in Vienna:

Four survivors will arrive Sunday at Kansas City Airport on TWA Flight 214 from New York at 2 p.m., your time. They will make powerful witnesses. They are: Auguste Masten - Re: Treblinka; Dr. Arthur Glosberg - Re: Sobibor; Rebecca Claubert - Re: Mauthausen; and Beth Lowen - Buchenwald and Mauthausen. They will be accompanied by Paul Stone and Amalia Levin, two associates of mine. This is what I promised in my letter to you. Have them met at the airport. Treat them well. They suffered greatly. Shalom.

Message two was from Sophia:

Reached survivor Natasha Orlovsky, the Russian lady from Encino, California. She will be here on Wednesday, February 11, with her brother. She's the one who lost five children, her husband, both parents and two brothers at Buchenwald. Rescued by Americans. She will pay her own way. I promised to reimburse her. She said it was not important.

The next message was from Captain Esta Arnold:

A Miss Rose Bigman, Winchell's secretary, spoke to me. She said to tell you how grateful Mr. Winchell is. He thinks you are wonderful. He has been listening to you on the radio and TV. He wants you to listen to his broadcast Sunday night. He is going to say some 'laudatory things about you.' Those are her words. Would like to meet you when he arrives on Monday.

"Yes, Mr. and Mrs. America and all the ships at sea, look at me, I'm here at the big trial," Bart mimicked the famous gossipmonger.

"What's that about?"

"It's a message from Hoover's press agent, Walter Winchell, who is coming here Monday. Mr. Ego himself. There are more important items on our agenda. Kyle and Grace, thank you. Back to work."

They saluted and left.

"Sophia, the time has come to visit your admirer, Martin Bormann. He's living the life of a potentate. He's in a room-and-bath quarters here in the barracks with three meals a day, cigars and cigarettes, a radio, and round-the-clock guards. Test him. See if he's ready to testify. You and Tony should tell him the truth about yourselves-you're CIA. Watch his reaction. The reason for this is simple: Both of you are potential witnesses. Also, I have two photographs here of a Frederick Glasser and Herman Tuller. They were they key men at the convention planning the attack on this fort. I have a hunch they are bigtime Nazis who escaped the Allied net."

"Come on, Tony, let's do it now," Sophia said.

Martin Bormann had just finished his dinner and was in a reclining chair puffing on a Havana special, listening to the nightly news. As soon as the MP opened the door to Bormann's detention quarters, Tony loudly yelled, "*Achtung!*"

Bormann instinctively jumped out of his relaxed position.

"*Ach*, you fool me. *Meine liebe*, Countess. I have not seen you in quite a while. Why you not bring me *Schnapps?*"

"Sorry, Martin, I'll try to get permission," Tony replied.

"Sit, we'll talk. The trial is very revealing. Germany is on trial, not just Hitler. His crazy Revenge Plan attack on this fort makes the world hate us more."

"Martin, that's true. Is it possible that you didn't know what was going on in these death camps?" Sophia asked.

"Countess, I swear that I begged Hitler to get rid of Himmler. But I never realized the horrible treatment and killing of those Jews. Hitler was busy being the military commander-in-chief of the Wehrmacht. I'm sick from what I heard on the radio. Why are you two at the trial?"

"The truth, Martin...Tony and I are with the CIA," Sophia admitted.

He leaned back in his reclining chair and puffed on his cigar, not surprised by the revelation.

"I suspected that long ago. But, tell me, Sophia, are you a real countess?"

"Yes, Martin. I am the Countess de Cordoba, niece of King Alphonso XIII of Spain."

"*Jawohl.* I knew you were part of a royal family, and I still love you."

"Martin Bormann, for a nice fellow, how could you be a Nazi?" she asked.

"You want the truth? I'll tell you. I was young and ambitious. I saw Hitler take power. I wanted money and power. So I decided, how you say in America, I hitched my wagon to a star. I had no part of killing Jews and others."

"Are you an anti-Semite?"

"I told you before, I urged Hitler to use those Jewish scientists, industrialists, doctors, lawyers, bankers, educators, and their military heroes in the first war. He had used the Jewish attacks as a political battle cry to gain power. It was those degenerates like Goering, Himmler, Heydrich, Roehm, Streicher, Rosenberg, Eichmann, Höss, Kaltenbrunner, Ley, and, of course, that intellectual Goebbels. He was a genius at propaganda and staging big rallies and military marches. They scared the *Scheisse* out of the average German."

"Don't tell me the Germans *suddenly* became anti-Semites?"

"No, maybe they hid their feelings, but they went berserk with the drumbeats of hate."

"Martin, I warn you to testify truly, or you'll either be hanged or spend your life in a boot camp at hard labor."

"That General Milburn is really very smart and very tough. I won't cross him," Bormann promised.

Sophia put two photos in front of Bormann.

"This one is Hermann Esser, a good friend of Hitler," he said.

"That's not Hermann Tuller?" Sophia asked.

Bormann was amused by the question.

"No." He smiled. "This man is Herman Esser. He was one of the organizers of the NSDAP, you know, the National Socialist Party, now called the Nazis. He was almost as good as Hitler with his rabble-rousing anti-Semite speeches. But he had one problem. He liked to make *bumsen* with any woman he met. Your American word for that, excuse me, is *fuck*. In 1938, Hitler was embarrassed by his conduct. He appointed him Secretary of State for tourist traffic. He was not caught by the Allies. The Munich Court sentenced him to five years at hard labor. Gunther Froelich bailed him out on appeal last year. Last I heard of him, he was in Canada."

"Who is this other one?"

"That's Hans Gunther, alias Frederick Glasser. He wrote books on ethnic studies. He was a professor at the University of Freiburg. During the war, he wrote propaganda for Goebbels. The Allies never touched him. He travels freely around the world and makes speeches on racial purity. Both of these men are on the payroll of Winston General."

"Very good, Martin," Sophia said with a smile.

"Why you want to know about them?"

"Because we have them in jail here."

"Why?"

"They helped organize the attack on this fort. They're facing a firing squad."

"*Dummkopf.* That maniac Hitler will get everyone who works for him killed. Don't forget the *Schnapps*, please?"

"You earned it, Martin."

Tony taunted him with a parting remark, "*Heil* Hitler."

"*Heil Scheisse*," Bormann responded as they left the room.

The rest of the week and the weekend were devoted to trial preparation for the following Monday. Jacques, Berger, Sedgwick, Sophia and Tony worked on interrogations. Jacques and Berger concentrated on the four planners of the bomb plot, Erich Koch; Hans Gunther, a.k.a. Frederick Glasser; Herman Esser, a.k.a. Hermann Tuller, and Hugo Kuhn, a.k.a. Reverend Forrest, a.k.a. Joseph Mayo.

On Saturday and Sunday, in twelve-hour sessions each day, the prosecution staff, consisting of Bart, trial consultant General Ross, and Judge Advocates Major Cartman, Major Seagrave, Major Palmer, Lieutenant Colonel Robert Souza and Captain David Prescott drew up a chart of witnesses.

"Before we put on the next batch of atrocities from the survivors, let's call Admiral Horst von Ludwig," said Bart. "You've heard his taped confession. He was not a Nazi. He deserted and was protected by Martin Bormann. I want that stuff about moving gold and money to Argentina."

The team concurred.

CHAPTER SIX

Sunday, February 15, 1953 - 2 p.m. - Kansas City airport, Missouri

A Sherman Army Airfield shuttle bus transported Jewish Chaplain Major Adam Gordon, Phillip Berger, Sophia Carrera, Colonel Jeremiah Brown, four MPs and Jacques Laurent to the tarmac awaiting the arrival of TWA Flight 214. Arrangements had been made with TWA management to allow Simon Wiesenthal's four survivors and their escorts, Amalia Levin and Paul Stone, to debark first.

The flight was on time. As the ramp was lowered, Major Gordon and Colonel Brown raced up the steps and led the party off the plane. Two MPs on each side formed a mini-phalanx as the survivors and their escorts alighted. Auguste Masten, Dr. Arthur Glosberg, Rebecca Claubert, Beth Lowen, Paul Stone and Amalia Levin expressed their thanks. Colonel Brown introduced the welcoming party.

Jacques, Phil and Chaplain Gordon greeted them with "*Shalom*."

Paul Stone, of the Jewish Relocation Agency, spoke up. "Gentlemen and lady, your reception is deeply appreciated. *Shalom* to all of you."

Jacques reeled off a few words of welcome in Yiddish, putting all at ease.

"All speak English," Stone replied.

Gordon asked if they required kosher food. "If so, there are refrigerators and microwaves in your rooms. We've arranged accommodations at the Commanders Inn just across from the Fort Leavenworth gate. Six bedrooms and baths."

The group boarded the Army bus, followed by the MPs. Gordon explained on the bus that kosher food could be served in his special dining room. The survivors and escorts were pleased and impressed.

☆ ☆ ☆ ☆

Monday, February 16, 1953 - 0900 hours - Fort Leavenworth
The tribunal was on the bench.

"Call your next witness, General," Nimitz ordered.

"Admiral Horst von Ludwig."

The tall, distinguished naval officer marched to the witness stand, where the oath was administered. Nimitz beckoned to an MP clerk and whispered to him. The MP turned and walked to the press section. He was heard addressing Walter Winchell. "Sir, please remove your hat."

The columnist reluctantly complied, exposing his shiny bald pate. A few snickers were heard behind him. Bart peripherally noticed the distraction and smiled at Nimitz.

"Admiral, you were in charge of German fleet assignments in Bremen on the coast of the North Sea?"

"Yes, sir."

"In your own words, tell us why and how you escaped."

"The British and Americans were closing in on us. I gathered my wife and four children in Hanover and brought them to my headquarters."

"Then what occurred?"

Von Ludwig repeated the confession he had given to Berger. He told of the submarine off the coast of Holland, which had been ordered to Bremen by Martin Bormann.

Hitler shouted, "Traitors, Bormann and you!"

The admiral rose suddenly to his full six-foot-two-inch height, face flushed, pointed his finger at Hitler and in German, roared, "Traitor? You miserable Austrian corporal, *you* are the traitor! You brought shame around the world to Germany. You're a disgrace to the whole human race!"

"Objection! Objection!" Krieger shouted.

Nimitz pounded his gavel.

"Admiral, sit down. You, too, Mr. Krieger. I'll handle the decorum of this court. Court reporter, strike the admiral's outburst. Counselor, tell your Mr. Hitler to zip his lip or I'll do it for him," Nimitz angrily declared.

"Continue, Admiral," Bart said.

"I asked Captain Vermouth to come to my office on the second floor of my headquarters. He saw my wife and four children. I convinced him to take us on board his vessel and drop us off on the coast of Denmark, close to Copenhagen. It was still occupied by the Wehrmacht. He radioed the German command to have a motorboat meet the submarine."

"Why Denmark?"

"My wife was Danish and her family owned a farm on the outskirts of Copenhagen. The Gestapo had orders from Martin Bormann not to mistreat my wife's family. We lived on the farm until the end of the war. My father-in-law was hiding twenty Jews. He clothed them, fed them and paid them to work on the farm. I worked on the farm with them. You know how the Danish people protected Jews during the Nazi occupation?"

"You are not an anti-Semite?"

"Never. They are a fine people. I went to school with them. I ate at their houses. They came to my home. My family helped lots of Jews to get out of Germany before the war. The stupid Nazis destroyed some of the best brains in Germany when they slaughtered all those Jews, who could have been valuable to that maniac Hitler and his executioner Himmler."

"Objection."

"Sustained. Strike the word *maniac*."

The admiral repeated his confession, detailing Admiral Wilhelm Canaris's relationship to his father as a distant cousin and dear friend. Canaris was the head of the Abwehr, the German Secret Service, who turned against Hitler, but never went public.

"He told my father on his dying bed that Hitler was destroying Germany and would lose the war."

"Admiral, have you heard the Shakespearean phrase from 'Hamlet,' *Something is rotten in the state of Denmark?*"

"Yes, sir."

"Well, can you tell the court why you left your lucrative business in Denmark to work for Adolf Hitler?"

"Sir, I didn't know that Frederick Nordheim was Adolf Hitler until the night before we were captured in Hamburg. Eric Volberg, a vice president of the Banque Royale in Zurich, was drunk. He was a boorish slob. He was the one that told me Nordheim was really Hitler, with a new face by plastic surgery."

"Before we get to your employment with Winston General, Nordheim-Hitler's company, describe what was in those crates aboard the submarine headed for Argentina."

"Besides large quantities of gold bars, currencies of every country occupied by the Nazis, plus American one hundred and one thousand-dollar bills, Otto showed me some of the valuable art plundered. He said there were two hundred such classic paintings stolen from Jews, Christians and Muslims. Bormann was to meet the submarine off Rio de la Plata."

"Okay, now tell the court how you came to be in charge of Eagle Shipping."

"A Mr. Darren Mayfield came to the farm. He said Martin Bormann recommended me for a job running a big fleet of ships. It was a subsidiary of Winston General, owned by the richest man in the world, a Jew named Frederick Avram Nordheim, who escaped from a concentration camp."

He related his meeting with Nordheim in Malmo, Sweden, never guessing he was Hitler. Nevertheless, his suspicions of the Nazis gathered in Hamburg bothered him. When Erich Volberg disclosed Hitler's identity, the revelation jolted von Ludwig.

"Just before the raid, Volberg told me that two Eagle ships were going to be blown up in the Panama Canal, destroying the locks."

Defense lawyers Stoltz, Krieger and von Maunder yelled, "Objection!" Hitler pounded his table with both hands in a drumbeat of protest.

The courtroom was in an uproar, with the media heading for the doors. Prisoners waved their handcuffs noisily. Nimitz stood up and gaveled angrily. MPs hastened to the prisoners' bench and roughly forced the defendants to lower their hands.

"Counsel will join us in chambers," Nimitz ordered.

The media appreciated the break and left the courtroom en masse to file the lead story of the day: "HITLER'S REVENGE PLAN."

Nimitz, Chennault and Smith were furious. Von Maunder, Krieger and Stoltz hadn't expected the outburst that followed. Bart and Cartman were well aware of the tribunal's anger.

Smith was the first one to speak. "Where the hell do you people think you are? If anything like that outburst occurred during the Third Reich, all of the defendants and their lawyers would be taken to the courtyard, lined up and shot! Damn you, if you can't control your sleazeball clients we could call these proceedings to a halt and sentence those bastards to hang in one spectacular execution."

Nimitz and Chennault remained silent. The shocked defense lawyers began a trio of protests to the heated excoriation.

"One at a time," Nimitz harshly demanded.

"Gentlemen, we have lost control of Herr Hitler and his co-defendants. However, we strongly object to Admiral Ludwig's hearsay testimony about the fictitious plan to destroy the Panama Canal," Stolz pressed.

Bart controlled his ire. "Sirs, may I respond?"

"Go ahead, General," Nimitz said.

"Counsel is treading on very thin ice. His use of the word *fictitious* is ill chosen. He would do well to drop that subject. We have more than the necessary evidence to substantiate von Ludwig's so-called hearsay testimony. In fact, I'd prefer not to reveal facts in the presence of the defense attorneys. Their silence cannot be monitored."

"General Milburn, unfortunately, this statement by von Ludwig will have to be confirmed beyond hearsay. Are you prepared to present factual evidence to establish the validity of his testimony?"

"Gentlemen, besides producing other witnesses to testify to Herr Hitler's Revenge Plan, I propose, with the consent of defense counsel, to give you eyewitness confirmation, if it can be done *in camera* at the conclusion of today's session."

"What say you, Mr. von Maunder? Mr. Stolz?"

"What does *in camera* mean?" Stolz asked.

"Secretly, here in chambers," Nimitz replied.

While Stoltz, von Maunder and Krieger huddled in conference, Bart advised the tribunal that he would have to clear the showing of his special evidence with General Bradley.

"That being the case, General Milburn, put that on hold for the present. Get on with the rest of the testimony and cross-examination."

The defense team returned to the center of the room, and Luther Krieger addressed the tribunal.

"Your Honors, without advance knowledge of the evidence that General

Milburn offers to present *in camera*, we cannot agree to the arrangement."

"Counsel, it seems that at this point in time the issue is moot. Therefore, your objection will be put on hold. We'll take it under advisement and will rule on it before the end of today's proceedings. Return to the courtroom. We'll adjourn for lunch. When we convene, leave von Ludwig's testimony and get on to other aspects of today's direct and cross examinations until we rule on your objection."

Back in court, the tribunal adjourned until 1430 hours. The prosecution team gathered for a buffet lunch in the conference room. Bart placed a call to General Bradley.

"Barton, I think I know why you're calling."

"I guess you were listening to the trial?"

"Yes, that business about the Panama Canal. Is that why you went into chambers?"

"Yes, sir. I need your approval to show the film of the attempted destruction of the canal in camera or let the whole world see it if I produce it in open court."

"My personal reaction, Barton, is to show it to the world. That would be a statement to the Soviets, the North Koreans and any of the Commie bastards who want to play hardball with us. However, I owe it to Ike for concurrence. You're on a lunch break. What time does court reconvene?"

"1430 hours, Central Time."

"I'll call you as soon as I can."

"Thank you, General Bradley."

Bart's next call was on the base to Chaplain Major Gordon. "Major, how are the survivors doing?"

"Just fine, sir. We've given them the red-carpet treatment. Your people have been questioning them and preparing them as witnesses."

"I'd like the group to be my guests for dinner tonight, Major. Any problem with the kosher food aspect?"

"General, strangely enough, the survivors are temporal. However, I believe that Amalia and Paul would opt for kosher food."

"How do we deal with that, Major?"

"Where did you want to have the dinner, General?"

"At my place. I have one of those Victorian houses."

"May I make a suggestion, sir? Let's have a private room at Truesdell Hall. I have a Jewish sergeant chef. How would you like to host a typical kosher meal, sir?"

"Why not?" Bart laughed.

"How many, besides the six of them and me?"

"Let me see - Jacques Laurent, Phillip Berger, Major Cartman and yours truly."

"That adds up to eleven. I'll have the wine, beer and some brandy, General. What time?"

"How's 1900 hours?"

"See you then."

Jacques prepared a plate for Bart. As Bart quietly consumed his lunch, the team briefed him on the four Wiesenthal witnesses.

"Among the prime slaughterhouses are Chelmno, Belzec, Sobibor, Treblinka, Auschwitz and Majdanek. Other concentration camps killed by slave labor, starvation, beastly treatment and other methods of murder," Bart said. "Shootings, beatings, rape, mayhem, and work to the point of exhaustion and death."

"General, we have four of the charnel houses covered with these witnesses. May I suggest the order in which they should be called?" Major Cartman asked.

"Let's have it, Gid."

"First, Rebecca Claubert on Belzec. Second, Auguste Masten on Treblinka. Third, Arthur Glosberg on Sobibor, and, for a clincher, Beth Lowen on Buchenwald. After her, there won't be a dry eye in the court."

"Are the outline sheets prepared for me?"

"General, they'll be completed by the end of court today."

"Fine. Now, Jacques, Phillip, Gideon, you are all joining me for a kosher dinner with the Wiesenthal group at Truesdell Hall at 1900 hours. Major Gordon is handling the setup."

"General Bradley is on the phone," Jacques announced.

"Get Lieutenants Winslow and Larsen in here," Bart ordered, then he took the receiver from Jacques. "Yes, sir, General?"

"Barton, to hell with that *in camera* routine. At the proper point in your direct examination, ask Nimitz to let you run the film of the sinking of those two Eagle ships. You can do the voice-over, Ike and the Chiefs agreed with me."

"General Bradley, you've made my day."

A loud guffaw sounded through the receiver.

"I'll be listening to the show from here. Go to it, impresario."

Bart sent a note to the tribunal chambers advising them that he wished to forgo the *in camera* hearing. He also informed the defense attorneys through Major Cartman. Bart's message indicated that he would answer the defense's objections to von Ludwig's testimony pertaining to the plot to destroy the Panama Canal. Court convened at 1430 hours.

"General Milburn, we have an objection to Admiral Ludwig's testimony about the Panama Canal, so you may respond," Nimitz said.

"Members of the tribunal, we have had testimony about Herr Hitler's Revenge Plan. This madman has concocted the attack on Fort Leavenworth last week and planned attacks on France, Israel and England. I am prepared now to give you visual…"

"Objection! Objection! Counsel is testifying to acts not in evidence," von Maunder shouted.

"Objection sustained," Nimitz ruled, then said, "General, confine your argument to the particular issue at hand - the Panama Canal."

"Very well, sir. I would like to have a film projector wheeled in here. The prosecution wishes to place this footage in evidence of an actual attempted attack on the Panama Canal."

"Objection."

"Overruled."

The projector was placed in the center aisle. The tribunal moved to the right side of the court. A mobile screen was placed before the court. The action on both sides of the canal was photographed in 16mm film by aerial shots from two different Navy planes.

Bart did a voice-over, describing the two Eagle ships being tracked to the Pacific and Caribbean Sea entrances thirty miles away on each side. The shots across the bows of each ship and the accelerated speed of the vessels were apparent. Finally, the shooting from Eagle ships and the naval response was graphically depicted. The ships' explosions testified to their cargo. Bart finished his meticulous delineation of the events, and the courtroom was spellbound.

"We will present more witnesses, including crew members of those Eagle ships who were rescued by our Navy."

Hitler shouted, "That is a Hollywood production!"

His lawyers pushed him back into his chair. The lights came on. Admiral von Ludwig returned to the witness chair.

"Your Honors, the prosecution has no more questions for this witness," Bart concluded.

"Your witness, Counsel," Nimitz declared, looking at the defense team.

"No further questions," von Maunder replied.

Hitler was berating his lawyers. Nimitz gaveled for quiet.

Luther Krieger rose. "This motion picture, sirs, is herewith contested as not being authentic evidence of an attack on the Panama Canal. We respectfully ask that it not be placed in evidence without absolute authentication. This film could have been excerpted from a Hollywood war film, despite General Milburn's dramatic vocalization delivered quite theatrically. Talented counsel exhibits the gifts of a thespian."

Before Nimitz could speak, Bart quickly rose to the challenge and addressed the tribunal. "Your Honors, counsel for the defense is quite complimentary. May we have a short recess to produce witnesses to the events depicted in this recent event?"

Nimitz, Smith and Chennault smothered their smiles. "Will a twenty-minute recess suffice, General?" Nimitz asked.

"Yes, sir." Bart beckoned Jacques and whispered to him. Jacques hastened out of the court. A short while later, court resumed.

"The prosecution calls Ibrahim Malaka," Bart announced.

All eyes turned to the double doors at the rear of the court. A swarthy, stocky man in an orange prisoner's jumpsuit, flanked by two MPs, manacles removed, walked down the center aisle. When the oath was about to be administered, he angrily refused to comply. Jacques handed Bart a manila envelope, which held a thick book.

"Your Honors, this should solve the problem. It is the Koran."

The witness kissed the book and took the oath.

"What is your name?" Bart asked.

In a heavy Middle Eastern accent, he replied, "I am Ibrahim Malaka."

"Were you a member of the crew of the Eagle?"

"Yes."

"What happened to your ship?"

"It sank in the Pacific Ocean."

"Tell the court what happened."

In halting English, he described the approach to the Panama Canal when the American ships challenged them. Bart led him through all of the action, including the Eagle opening fire on the American ships.

"What was the cargo of your ship?"

"Dynamite."

"What happened to the ship?"

"The American ship sank us with their cannons."

"How did you manage to survive?"

"Survive?"

"Why didn't you drown?"

"The Americans pulled me out of the water."

"My last question. Why was the Eagle heading for the Panama Canal?"

"When we got into the locks, we were going to jump ship, head for the shore, and by remote control they would blow up the ship."

Bart started to walk toward the prosecution's table, then, suddenly, he strode back to the witness. "Who hired you for that job, Mr. Malaka?"

The witness nervously answered, "It was the Cobra."

"Who?"

"You know, the Cobra."

"What is the Cobra's name?" Bart demanded.

"Abdul Ahmed-al-Said."

Bart pulled a rap sheet and a photo out of his pocket. He showed the picture to Malaka and said, "Is this the Cobra, who hired you?"

"Yes, and a Mr. Froelich."

"I hand this to the court to be marked in evidence."

"So ordered," Nimitz said.

"No further questions," Bart declared.

The Cobra's name was familiar to the media. Abdul Ahmed-al-Said was on the wanted list throughout the Western world, so the wire-service reporters headed for the doors.

Attorney Krieger approached the witness. "Where is your home?" the defense attorney asked.

"Beirut, Lebanon."

"You mention a Mr. Froelich. Who is he?"

"Abdul introduced him as *the Boss.*"

"And where did this introduction take place?"

"In Paris."

"No further questions for now. We reserve the right to call him back."

"Why you shtop?" Hitler shouted.

Krieger whispered to Hitler, "*Schweigen;* I don't want him to talk about Froelich."

Bart, in rapid order, called up Mohammed Massaud, a Palestinian crew member who repeated Malaka's version of the events. The next witness was Max Shoner, a tall, brawny man. Sandwiched between two MPs, he goose-stepped his way to the stand. He took the oath and saluted the tribunal before sitting down.

"English or *Deutsch*?" Bart asked.

"*Deutsch.*"

"State your name for the record."

"I am Colonel Max Shoner."

"You were a member of the Eagle crew?"

"*Jawohl.*"

"Your ship sank on its way to the Panama Canal and you were plucked from the sea by the U.S. Navy."

"The Americans attacked us."

"That was after you fired at them."

"*Jawohl*, they tried to stop us."

"Stop you for what reason?"

"Because we were going to blow up the locks of the canal at the Caribbean entrance. It was about thirty miles from our goal."

"Why did you want to destroy the canal?"

"Because *Der Führer* ordered it. *Heil* Hitler, *Sieg heil!*" he shouted, and stood up, sticking his arm out in the Nazi salute. "*Deutschland über alles.*"

The strange spectacle stunned the court. Bart declared, "Your witness, Counsel."

Krieger said, "No questions."

Hitler's face was red. He rolled his eyes, hit his fist on the table and exploded at the witness, "*Der Dummkopf, Arschloch!*"

"Step down, Mr. Shoner," Nimitz ordered, and in a deliberately slow and stern tone of voice warned, "and Mr. Krieger, *control your client.*"

The colonel, escorted by MPs, goose-stepped back up the aisle, stopped at Hitler's row and repeated, "*Heil* Hitler." He was hauled to the exit.

Nimitz said, "Court's adjourned to 0900 hours tomorrow."

The prosecution withheld its pent-up laughter until they reached their conference room. The hilarity was spontaneous. Jacques hadn't laughed that hard since his early youth. The mirth was infectious. "Bart - excuse me, General - you set that up. Hitler must be chewing his cud right now. Did you expect that clown to pull that Nazi crap?"

"Honestly, not that far."

☆ ☆ ☆ ☆

Later that evening - Truesdell Hall

Chaplain Major Adam Gordon arranged an elongated table covered with a light blue tablecloth. Silver settings adorned eleven places. The center of the table contained a menorah, a candelabrum with seven candles used in Jewish worship. A large American flag adorned one end of the room and an Israeli flag with its Star of David graced the other end. Silver buckets held bottles of champagne.

Bart, Jacques Laurent, Major Gideon Cartman and Phillip Berger arrived ten minutes early.

"This is quite a setup, Major," Bart remarked.

"General, I went all out in an effort to relax these folks before their ordeal tomorrow."

"Very considerate, Chaplain. I brought these three *landsmen* to ease any apprehensions they might have."

"Welcome, gentlemen."

"*Shalom*," Jacques responded.

A knock at the door was answered by Major Gordon. The party of six was escorted by a lieutenant and two sergeants. Gordon greeted the arrivals, "Meet our host, General Barton Milburn."

"*Shalom*, welcome to all of you," Bart declared, and shook hands with the six guests.

All in the group spoke English, and they expressed their gratitude for the warm welcome. Berger, Cartman and Laurent shook hands with their guests.

Rebecca Claubert exclaimed, "How nice, look at the menorah!"

Amalia Levin, Wiesenthal's librarian, declared, "Your staff is very thoughtful."

"Would you like to light the menorah, Amalia?" Gordon asked.

"I think it would be appropriate if each of our survivors would light one candle. Paul, Major Gordon and I will light each of the other three."

The candles were lit, then Jacques declared, "*Mazeltov!*"

The sergeants popped the champagne bottles and poured the bubbly drinks.

"God bless America," Dr. Arthur Glosberg toasted.

"Hear, hear!" Bart followed.

Gordon arranged the seating. Bart sat at the head of the table. Paul Stone occupied the other end. Bart explained that there would be no discussion of the trial that night. Two middle-aged ladies, in black dresses and white aprons, entered with trays of hors d'oeuvres. A sergeant placed a selection of wines, both white and red, in buckets.

The fare consisted of salads, vegetable soup and Middle Eastern-style chicken breasts combined with stuffing of prunes, vegetables and crumbled matzo flavored with curry powder and diced onions, celery and carrots. Dessert was a chocolate soufflé and espresso. Bart looked at file cards containing biographies of the witnesses. The survivors were indeed a diverse group:

Rebecca Claubert - 45 years of age, a Mauthausen prisoner, now living in New York City. She is employed as a designer by a Seventh Avenue dress manufacturer. She was born in Moscow, Russia.

Auguste Masten - 52 years of age, escaped from Treblinka. He resides in Sherman Oaks, California. He is a violinist and composer in the music department at Paramount Pictures. A member of the Los Angeles Philharmonic. Born in Vienna.

Doctor Arthur Glosburg - 49 years of age, survived Sobibor. Currently living in Atlanta, Georgia. Researcher for the CDC (Communicable Disease

Center). Born in Berlin, Germany.

Beth Lowen - 21 years of age, survived Buchenwald and Mauthausen. Resides in New York City. She is studying at the Juilliard School of Music. Born in Amsterdam, Holland.

In his mind's eye, Bart pictured the ordeal of each of his witnesses. His compassion for the group was obvious. He noticed a small upright piano at the far end of the room. In an effort to maintain the light-hearted ambience of the evening, he addressed Miss Lowen. "I note here from your background card that you are a pianist and a singer as well. Would you play something for us?"

Amalia Levin spoke up. "She has a magnificent voice as well. She sang for us on the shuttle bus coming here."

"Oh, yes, I haven't heard any professional with a better voice," Arthur Glosberg exclaimed. "I talked to her about coming to Hollywood. With that face and voice, she has a great future."

Beth Lowen, a blonde with deep blue eyes, blushed and had to be prodded to the piano. Jacques led her to the instrument. She sat on the piano stool, whirled around and said in a British accent, "What would you like to hear?"

"Start with 'Hatikvah,'" Rebecca Claubert urged.

Beth ran a few scales and played the Jewish anthem, which translated into the word *Hope.* The survivors were enthralled with her classical rendition. Their eyes welled up with tears. She immediately segued into 'God Bless America.'

Jacques whispered in her ear. She ran the scales again and played Edith Piaf's 'La Vie En Rose,' singing it softly. The applause was enthusiastic. She sang a medley of Cole Porter tunes and dazzled her audience with Gershwin's 'Rhapsody in Blue.' She finished with melodies from Mozart, Brahms, and Tchaikovsky. Her musical renditions, both vocal and on the piano, were of professional caliber. She returned to her chair.

Auguste Masten, with his musical background, enthusiastically declared, "I know talent when I hear it. This girl is a natural. I believe her voice is one of the best extant. Her talent for the piano is fabulous. How did she manage to reach these heights after what she's been through?"

Bart, Jacques, Berger and the others were entranced with her impromptu recital.

"By the way, Mr. Masten, in your position at Paramount Pictures, have you ever run across a producer by the name of George Spota?" Bart asked.

"Oh, yes, General. A fine man and a very successful filmmaker. I scored his film 'The Rough Riders,' the story of Theodore Roosevelt's exploits in the Spanish American War. I had the honor of composing the theme song, 'We Can Do It.'"

"That's very interesting. He is one of my dearest friends. He served with me in the invasion of France."

"General, I do not mean to be too bold, but I would recommend this talented young lady to him. If not, I'll see what I can do at Paramount."

"I'll try," Bart responded.

The evening was a mind-clearing, therapeutic session for Bart and his associates.

"My gratitude to all of you for a wonderful evening. Major Gordon will bring you to court in the morning," Bart said.

☆ ☆ ☆ ☆

Tuesday, February 17 - 0900 hours

In its first order of business, the tribunal noted the presence of Otto Meissner, a well known German jurist under Hindenburg, and Gertrud Scholtz-Klink, a Nazi women's leader, sometimes called "the Lady Führer."

"Herr Hitler has sent for Herr Meissner and Frau Scholtz-Klink to augment his defense team. I now introduce them to the court," Erich Stoltz said.

"Fine, welcome, Counsels. Let's get on with it," Nimitz acerbically declared. "General Milburn, proceed. Call your witness."

"The prosecution calls Rebecca Claubert."

The lady with wavy, hennaed hair, smartly dressed in a blue serge double-breasted jacket, gray skirt, ruffled white blouse and patent-leather shoes, walked to the stand between two MPs. After the oath was given, she faced Bart.

"Please state your name for the record."

"Rebecca Claubert."

"What is your place of birth?"

"Moscow, Russia."

"Do you wish to speak in Russian?"

"No, English or French will do."

"Is Claubert your maiden name?"

"No, I was married to a French officer. My maiden name was Lebov."

"Tell the court, in your own words, a brief history of your life."

Otto Meissner stood up. "Objection."

"On what grounds, Mr. Meissner?"

"I prefer to be addressed as Judge Meissner."

"In what court *are* or *were* you a judge?" Nimitz snapped.

"In the Weimar Republic and the Third Reich."

"Neither of those regimes are recognized here. Overruled. Mr. Meissner, this is a military trial. She can recount her past and save the time of the court. Miss Claubert, your background, please."

"As I said before, I was born in Moscow, Russia. My father was a prominent surgeon, as well as a thoracic specialist. He was a general in charge of the medical corps of the Russian army in the first world war. My mother was a *modiste* with her own shop in Moscow. I had two sisters and two brothers. I was the youngest."

"You say *had*. Are any of them alive today?"

"One brother is a doctor living in Paris, France."

"What happened to the rest of your family?"

"May I go back a little before I get to that?"

"Please."

"When the communist revolution occurred, my father, mother, two sisters and two brothers left Russia. My family was strongly against communism. We had French relatives in the wine business. They were well-connected and we were able to settle in Paris in April, 1919."

"What happened then?"

"My father spoke fluent French, as did all of us. He took the medical tests and was once again a licensed physician. My mother became a designer for a prominent Paris couturier and later opened her own shop. My brothers, sisters and I continued our education in Paris"

"How old were your brothers and sisters when you left Moscow?"

"Molly was thirteen, Sascha was fifteen, Michael was seventeen and Anna was eighteen. Michael is a doctor in Paris now. We were a very close family. Everything was fine until the Nazis occupied Paris in June 1940."

"Then what happened?"

"My two sisters were married. Molly married a French lawyer, who was Jewish. They had three children, two boys and a girl. Anna married a French Jew, a manufacturer of shoes. My two brothers became doctors. Sascha was an intern at a hospital. I married a French colonel who was not Jewish. We had two children, a boy and a girl."

"France signed an armistice on June 22, 1940. What happened to your family after that?"

"The Vichy government collaborated with the Nazis and there was a roundup of the Jews. Our whole family, including my parents, brothers, sisters, nieces, nephews, me and my husband and children were captured. The Gestapo and Vichy police broke into our homes, stole all our possessions, money, jewels, art, silverware, clothing, everything, and shipped us to Drancy concentration camp, just outside Paris."

She stopped long enough to wipe the tears from her eyes, then her calm recital changed suddenly. "There he is, that dirty rotten son of a bitch, a traitor to France - René Soltere!"

She stood up and pointed at him. The other commandant prisoners, who were seated in the aisle, separating them from Soltere, shook their handcuffs and laughed and hissed at him.

Nimitz angrily gaveled the court to order. "Madame, please be seated," he urged.

She remained standing and yelled at Soltere, "May you burn in hell! You sent us to Auschwitz, you rat!" she screamed and fell back in her chair.

"Would you like a recess?" Bart asked.

"No, I have more to say."

"Madame, I'll have to ask you not to do that again," Nimitz cautioned.

"I apologize, sir," she whispered.

"At Drancy, did you see the rest of your family?"

"Yes, we were kept there for a month. Then, one day they told us to take our things, what little we had, and stuffed us like garbage into cattle cars. Thousands of us for three or four days, I don't remember, but it was a terrible ordeal. We could hardly breathe. No food, no water, no sanitary facilities. We were pressed up against each other. The men kept the children on their shoulders as long as they could. Forgive me, but we lived in our own urine and feces. It was the devil's caravan on its way to hell. Our dignity was destroyed. We were fighting for our lives. Three elderly people died the first night. The second night, a mother fell asleep on her baby. The baby was dead in the morning. The mother became hysterical and banged her head on the wall of the car and bled to death. The third night, two more bodies, a man and his wife, were found dead."

She sobbed loudly. The court took a ten-minute recess, then Mrs. Claubert, still shaken, returned to the stand.

"At Auschwitz, what happened?" Bart asked.

"We were pulled out of the cattle car, and that French traitor Soltere yelled at us in French to take off all our clothes. He said it was for hygienic purposes. We were going to the showers. A colonel stood alongside him and with his forefinger pointed at the lineup, set some of us to the right and some of us to the left. We knew that the showers were gas chambers. I was on the right side. They tried to put my children on the left. I held on to them," she sobbed hysterically.

After another short recess, she composed herself. Some of the spectators were crying.

"Mrs. Claubert, please continue."

"I was standing there naked with both children clasped to my breasts. Then the colonel whispered to me, asking what my profession was. I told him I was a designer and maker of clothes. He pulled me and my children to the right. I told him there were three doctors there and other seamstresses. I pointed out my father, mother, sisters, brothers and my husband. He pointed his finger at them and they all went to the right. But that was only a temporary reprieve."

"What did they do next?"

"We were taken to outdoor showers where we were hosed down and given those hideous striped clothes to wear. We were put in barracks. Each of us got a stale piece of bread and watery soup that night. The next morning, that mass murderer Rudolph Höss lined us up in front of the barracks. He ordered all of our children to what he called the playground. We never saw our children again. We learned that night that the children, my father and mother were gassed to death."

"What happened to your brother, sisters and your husband?"

"My brothers and my husband, George, worked in the infirmary. My husband pretended to be a doctor. My sisters and I made and repaired Gestapo uniforms. Over a year went by and we learned that the Nazis were suffering huge losses in the war against the Russians. My brothers were sent to hospitals in Germany to tend to the wounded. My sister Anna's husband, who was making and repairing shoes, was put to work at the I.G. Farben plant. Molly's husband, Pierre, was gassed to death. Two days later, Molly was gang-raped by five soldiers. She died that night in a captain's quarters. They threw her body into the crematorium. I see that captain sitting there," she pointed.

"With the court's permission, please walk up there and point him out," Bart asked.

Nimitz signaled two MPs to escort her. She marched between them to the last row. A prisoner bowed his head with his manacled hands, covering his face. She reached over the bench and firmly grasped his hair, pulling his head upright. He yelled in pain.

"This is the rapist animal," she hissed.

The MPs gently drew her away and tried to walk her back to the witness chair. She stopped at the third bench.

"Let the record show that the witness, Mrs. Claubert, has identified Fritz Wagner of the Waffen SS," Bart declared.

At that moment a scream rent the courtroom. Bart turned suddenly. Mrs. Claubert was pounding on another prisoner, poking his eyes.

"This dog killed my husband and my sister!"

The courtroom was in an uproar. The MPs jostled her back to her seat. Order was restored.

"Describe what happened to your husband," Bart urged.

Breathlessly, she continued, "George was a big man, very strong. One night, my sister Anna and I were pulled out of the barracks by two soldiers and were told we were needed at the infirmary. My husband followed us in the dark. Instead of the infirmary, we were taken to his quarters."

"Whose quarters?"

"That filthy rotten animal."

"I ask the court to have that prisoner rise."

Nimitz gestured to the MPs. They roughly jerked him to his feet.

"Let the record show that Mrs. Claubert has identified Lieutenant Colonel Werner Braumer, Waffen SS."

"Yes, that's him."

"Please tell the court what happened."

"There were four men there and they were drunk and naked. The two soldiers pushed us in there and left. They tore off our clothes and undergarments. At that moment, my husband, George, crashed through the door. In minutes, he broke the necks of two of the men. He knocked the third man senseless and was about to go after the captain, who you now call a lieutenant colonel. Braummer fired two shots. One struck my husband between the eyes. He shot my sister in the heart. I was lying on top of her when I heard a voice shout, *Stop it!* Colonel Walther Baer and two soldiers pointed their guns at Captain Braummer. Colonel Baer was the same man that met us when we arrived at Auschwitz."

She wiped her eyes and pointed to the right side of the rows. Bart handed her a glass of water. She kept her finger out straight.

"Who are you pointing at?"

"There is Colonel Baer, who saved my life."

"Stand up, Colonel Baer," Nimitz ordered.

"Yes, yes, that's him," she cried.

"Let the record show that the witness has identified Walther Baer," Bart said.

A fifteen-minute recess was ordered, and the media scrambled for the exit. When the tribunal returned, Mrs. Claubert was back in the witness chair. "What occurred after Colonel Baer entered Werner Braummer's quarters?" Bart asked.

"He allowed me to dress and ordered the soldiers to take me outside. I was numb and almost faint. I heard a scuffle in the building. Colonel Baer came out. He ordered the soldiers to remove the bodies to the crematorium. He said that Braummer was unconscious and drunk. I knew better. He must have knocked him out. The colonel put his arm around me and walked me one hundred feet away from the scene. I was crying."

"What then?"

"He told me that he was moving some of the prisoners to Mauthausen and if I wanted to stay alive, I better go with him the following afternoon. He hid me in a private room in the infirmary. He put a *Do Not Disturb* sign on the door. He told me not to open it for anyone and handed me the key to lock the door."

"That left you and Anna's husband, Arthur, as the only survivors. Is that correct?"

"No. The next day, Braummer sent him to the gas chambers."

"So you alone survived?"

"That's right. Late in the afternoon of that day, Colonel Baer brought me some food and a dress. He handed me a small valise with some extra clothes, underpants, a toothbrush and toothpaste. He told me I was no longer a Jew. *You speak good German,* he said. At Mauthausen, he was going to get me a job. He had two soldiers take me to the train and put me in the, how you say, the caboose, with some other women and crew members. He warned me not to talk. I pretended I had a sore throat."

"What happened at Mauthausen?"

"I worked in the clothing department. It was awful. We sorted and repaired the clothes of thousands of Jews who were gassed to death in mobile gas vans and others killed by their euthanasia program. I saw all of it. Colonel Baer checked up on me quite often. I thought he was going to try to make me his mistress, but he never touched me."

"Did you keep working in the clothing department?"

"No. One day I was ordered to the Hartheim euthanasia killing center. The camp was overcrowded. They used every excuse to bring Jews in there for experiments. Those Nazi doctors were the coldest, cruelest bastards ever put on Earth. They did surgeries when none were required. They infected prisoners with every conceivable medicine designed to kill them. Phenol injections were given to the starved, skeletonized walking cadavers. This was a scene from one of those horror movies. Soon the word was out that the Americans were coming."

She blew her nose and wiped tears from her cheeks.

"Can you continue?"

"Yes. Colonel Baer pulled me back into the Mauthausen camp. He handed me one of those striped prisoner dresses with the Star of David on it. The next day the American Army liberated the camp. That was May, 1945. I was thirty-seven years old and my hair was turning gray."

"When the American forces arrived, what did you do?"

"A Major Eugene Singer and a Sergeant John Fitzgerald saw me standing in front of the medical building. They approached me. I weighed about a hundred and ten pounds then. Major Singer began talking to me in Yiddish. I answered him in English. I took them on a tour of the camp. First I showed them the inside of the Hartheim euthanasia killing center. Five of the experimenting doctors were dressed in prisoners' uniforms. They were lying on beds, acting as though they were sick prisoners. They were crying for help. I took the major and sergeant aside and identified them as Nazi doctors."

She stopped, and sipped more water.

"Go on."

"They pulled out their guns and lined them up. *Strip them,* I said, *they may have hypodermic needles as weapons.* They stood there naked. Fitzgerald stepped out the door and blew a whistle. Six American soldiers, carrying rifles, came running. One of the soldiers had a camera. He photographed the doctors, who kept pretending they were Jews. I don't know if I should repeat what the major said."

"Go ahead."

"He yelled at them, *You Nazi bastards! You forgot to get circumcised!*"

Nervous laughter rippled through the court.

"I then took them through the building. There were fifteen men and women, emaciated and sick, huddled in one room. They had not yet been experimented on. The sergeant blew his whistle again and I heard him yell for medics. Two Army doctors arrived and started to tend to those people. A Red Cross Army ambulance pulled up to the building. After that, I got in a jeep with Major Singer and Sergeant Fitzgerald. On our way back to the main camp, I saw Colonel Baer with his hands in the air. Two Americans with rifles were pushing him along. I told the sergeant to pull up to the colonel."

"Why did you do that?" Bart asked, knowing the answer.

Nimitz broke in, "General Milburn, how much longer will this interrogation continue? It's time for our lunch recess. Do you want to break now?"

"Sir, this is ready to wind down. Five or ten minutes more and I'll be finished with this witness."

"Proceed."

"I quickly explained that Colonel Baer had been very helpful and that he had cooperated with me in hiding twenty-two children. He knew where these children were hidden. The major and I got out of the Jeep. I spoke to Colonel Baer in German. *Where are the children?* I asked him. He told us to follow him. The major told the two soldiers to come along and that there was no need for Baer to keep his hands up. Baer led us to a shack about one hundred feet away from his quarters. He put his two fingers to his lips for silence. He tapped on the door with two taps followed by three fast ones. The door was opened slightly by two Jewish men in striped prisoners' uniforms with the Star of David on them. He pushed the door wide open. Each of them had a rifle. The Americans raised their guns. *Drop the guns,* he said. *The Americans are here.*

They complied. The major called the sergeant to bring a flashlight..."

Nimitz broke in. "Can't we move this along, General?"

"Tell us what you found," Bart prodded.

"I walked in first, followed by the major, the sergeant, Colonel Baer and the two soldiers. The two Jewish men discovered a false door by sliding it open. The smell was overpowering, but nothing as bad as what happened next. There was a table standing on a dirty rug. It was removed and a piece of the floor was lifted. The smell was shockingly vile. We put handkerchiefs to our faces. It was pitch dark down there. The sergeant's flashlight showed a makeshift staircase leading to a cellar. The light revealed the emaciated faces of twenty-two children, ages from six to twelve. Boys and girls. A man and a woman were with them. There was not a sound from any of them. Two soldiers went down there and handed each child to Sergeant Fitzgerald. The man and woman who helped these little ones were Jehovah's Witnesses. Colonel Baer and I had managed to steal food every day for them. The sight of these children was heartbreaking. An Army truck took the twenty-two children, the two Jewish men and the Jehovah's Witnesses away to be cared for."

"How did you get out of there?"

"I was introduced to a General William Hartley. He had Major Singer arrange to send me to the Jewish Refugee Center in Vienna several days later. Eventually I got to Paris. I found my brother, Michael. Sascha had been shot to death by a Nazi officer. Later, I made my way to America. Michael stayed in Paris. He's a successful doctor, married, with two children."

"No further questions."

The court recessed. The prosecution team returned to their conference room for a buffet lunch.

"That Mrs. Claubert is quite a woman. Her story will be carried around the world," Major Cartman said.

Lieutenant Grace Larsen entered the room without knocking. She seemed excited. "General, sir! Turn on the radio; there are riots all over the world!"

Jacques turned it on. NBC, CBS and ABC were describing riots in West Berlin, Frankfurt, Munich, Paris, Marseilles, London, Liverpool, Amsterdam, Brussels, New York, Chicago and Skokie, Illinois, Los Angeles, Montreal, and Warsaw. Skinheads, Ku Kluxers and neo-Nazis the world over were under attack. Swastikas were evident everywhere. Nazi signs bore the legend, *Stop the Jew Trial, Heil Hitler, Holocaust is a Lie, General Milburn is a Jew, Export Jews*, and *Kill the Jews* in native languages throughout Europe, the U.S. and Canada.

Ed Murrow was on CBS radio outside Fort Leavenworth.

"From all we can gather at this moment from reliable sources at home and internationally, this eruption throughout the world and here in the United States is being characterized as an organized protest by Nazi factions. According to a highly placed intelligence officer, the riots are part of Hitler's Revenge Plan. Hazel Norris and Reginald Chancey with the BBC in London now join us with the latest events."

"Thank you, Ed," they chorused.

"Hazel, can you update us on what's happening?"

"Certainly, Ed. According to the special branch at Scotland Yard, eighty of the Nazis have been arrested. An attempt to bomb a synagogue in the Whitechapel district in London has been aborted. A lorry containing a ton of dynamite was seized in a traffic tieup. Reginald Chancey is at Scotland Yard. Reggie, what can you tell us?"

"Hazel, one of the arrested men is a member of the Aryan Swords and they have a confession. Hold it...here comes General Lloyd Forsythe, director of MI6, and Superintendent Lawton Ashton. They are going to make a statement."

"This will be brief," General Forsythe announced. "These worldwide riots are all part of an orchestrated event planned weeks ago. This outbreak has been financed by an outfit called WWS, which stands for World Wide Supremacists, a recently organized group. Their alleged headquarters is in Liechtenstein. However, the authorities in Vaduz deny its existence. That's all from me. Superintendent Ashton will brief you now."

"Folks, the riots have been contained. Nine police officers have sustained minor injuries. The participants have twenty-one men in hospitals, eight with critical injuries inflicted by outraged citizens, thirteen with cuts and bruises, none of which were inflicted by police. We await a report from Liverpool. Our investigation will go on. No questions, please."

"That's it from here, Ed Murrow," Hazel Norris said, and signed off.

Bart changed the station to the NBC affiliate. At that moment in New York City, Mayor Vincent Impellitteri was being awaited by the media. David Brinkley was reporting from the top steps of City Hall.

"Momentarily, we are expecting Mayor Impellitteri for a briefing on the riots, which began in the Yorkville section of New York. This city is literally the melting pot of the world, with a population of two and a quarter million Jews. Here is the mayor."

"Ladies and gentlemen of the press," the mayor said, "at my side here today is Chief of Detectives Henry Whalen. The riots, which began in Yorkville, have spread to Brooklyn, Queens, and the Bronx. One thousand police officers were engaged in quelling this Nazi-orchestrated attack on synagogues, Jewish-owned businesses and a Jehovah's Witnesses church. We have arrested two hundred skinheads, Nazis, former Bund members and paid thugs. The fire is out, thanks to the immediate action by our police department to stamp out this hooliganism. Activity of this kind will not be tolerated in New York City."

Brinkley asked, "Mr. Mayor, you used the word *orchestrated*. Would you expand on that, please?"

"Chief Whalen will answer that," the mayor replied.

"Thank you, Mr. Mayor," Whalen said. "Our special investigative squad, led by Lieutenants Barney Ruditsky, and John Cordes and Detective Sergeant John Broderick, immediately fanned out to known havens of hate groups. We have confessions indicating that these riots were planned a month ago in connection with the war-crimes trials taking place at Fort Leavenworth, Kansas. As the mayor stated, this is an orchestrated event. As you well know, riots are going on all over Europe and in Montreal, Canada. Our investigation will be ongoing. That's all I have to say at this time."

Further commentaries on every station were in progress. John Cameron Swayze of NBC, Elmo Roper of ABC, Gabriel Heatter of the Mutual Broadcasting System, and Lowell Thomas and Eric Sevareid, all from New York. Peter McClintock of the Canadian Broadcasting System and Howard K. Smith from London all reported on events. Bart and the team listened as Jacques twisted the dials. They ate their lunch as the commentaries poured forth.

Heatter, in his usual editorializing style, declared, "Just eight short years ago, millions were slaughtered by the Nazis. The Holocaust and the most violent war in history came to an end at the horrendous cost of many more millions of civilian and military lives. Has racism reared its ugly head again? The war-crimes trials at Fort Leavenworth have so far revealed the monstrous apocalypse launched by these Nazi vermin. The atrocities testified to by survivors, under the brilliant prosecution of General Barton Milburn, should remind us that these scum are still with us. We must stamp them out."

Howard Smith's broadcast from London was short and to the point. "Hitler is alive and so are his minions. The riots here in London and Liverpool are over. Prime Minister Churchill issued a very strong statement an hour ago. Here is it now as he spoke from his desk at 10 Downing Street."

Winston Churchill's voice came on. "This brazen display of Nazi violence should be viewed as a wake-up call to the free world. Not one man, nor did a *few* men, commit the most dastardly havoc in Europe during the second World War. It took thousands upon thousands of willing participants to execute the Holocaust. What's more, millions stood by in that evil death spree, infected by what General Barton Milburn so aptly expressed as the 'three monkeys' syndrome of hear, speak and see no evil. The attack on Fort Leavenworth, Kansas and the explosion in Paris last September were just precursors to these riots. I am calling for a meeting of the UN General Assembly to ask for the world leaders to join me in launching a worldwide search for these Nazis. I cite the aphorism first stated by John Philpot Curran: *The condition upon which God hath given liberty to men is eternal vigilance.* Our realm paid its price for its indifference from 1939 to 1945, in our lives and fortunes. We are in a recovery period now. Despots must be deposed. A vigilant democracy is the bastion of freedom. The virus of hate must be abolished."

The networks switched to Bonn, Germany. Chancellor Konrad Adenauer addressed the world in German, with an interpreter translating to English.

"The riots have been crushed. The German Federal Republic will not tolerate racism in any form. The mark of Cain is still with us. We are a democratic nation, trying to recover from the atrocities committed by the Third Reich. We have much to atone for. We will join with all democratic nations to crush Nazism wherever it shows its ugly face. I ask my people to go to their places of worship and beg for forgiveness and mercy," he pleaded, wiping the tears from his eyes.

"Enough," Bart declared. "Turn it off."

CHAPTER SEVEN

Thursday, February 19, 1953 - Fort Leavenworth

The riots apparently had their effect on the morning session of the court. There was a grim look on the countenances of the tribunal. Admiral Nimitz and Generals Smith and Chennault each addressed the defense. The sum of their remarks was a warning that no comments or outbursts by the defendant would be tolerated. Rebecca Claubert returned to the witness chair.

"The defense may begin their cross-examination," Nimitz declared.

Otto Meissner approached the witness.

"Back up, Mr. Meissner. Ten feet will suffice," Nimitz ordered.

"Mrs. Claubert, are you, or were you, a communist?"

Bart shouted, "Objection!"

She answered, "I am not, and never was, a communist, fascist, or a Nazi like you."

"Objection withdrawn," Bart smirked.

"Well, I object to her personalized answer."

"Overruled."

"Mrs. Claubert, isn't it true that you had an easy time at Mauthausen because of your sexual relationship with Colonel Baer?"

"Objection!"

Nimitz hammered for silence.

Mrs. Claubert screamed, "You are a Nazi liar like the rest of those degenerates you represent!"

Nimitz allowed her to continue.

"If you call it *easy* at Mauthausen, then you and all of you will find hell a vacation resort compared to Auschwitz and Mauthausen, where dead bodies laid on top of each other in open piles waiting to be put in crematoriums. You filthy, rotten old man. Colonel Baer never touched me. He was a Nazi who apparently became sick of your murders. Yes, he helped save those children and possibly soothed his conscience."

Meissner tried to stop her tirade, yelling, "Objection, objection, objection!" Nimitz ignored him.

"There is bias in this court!" Meissner roared as he pounded on the defense table. Books and papers fell to the floor.

"Mr. Meissner, you are herewith held in contempt of court. You are fined ten thousand dollars. One more disruption and you'll be jailed. In deference to your age, I forgo that, for the nonce."

Bart rose. "Your Honors, if it pleases the court, I ask that Counsel Meissner's despicable question, which was more in the sense, of testimony, be stricken from the record."

"One moment, General." The tribunal huddled. "Counsel, in the opinion of the court, Mrs. Claubert's strong response to that unjustifiable question would also be excised. Do you insist on striking the question?"

"Withdrawn, with thanks to the court."

"Your Honor, may I address the court?" Alden Gaines unctuously asked.

"Yes, Counsel."

"Herr Meissner is not feeling well. Gertrud Scholz-Klink asks the court's permission to finish the cross."

"Madame Scholz-Klink may proceed."

The tall, buxom woman, in a tweed jacket and skirt, approached. She adjusted a tie to her man's shirt and donned a pair of black-rimmed spectacles, which were attached to a gold chain hanging around her neck.

She stared at Nimitz and said in German, "I am not a *Madame,* please address me as *Frau.*"

"Very well, *Frau* Scholz-Klink, you may proceed."

"I have just one question, Frau Claubert. Did you bestow any favors on Colonel Baer in exchange for your getting out of Auschwitz?"

Mrs. Claubert shook her head negatively at Bart, who rose to object. With a smile of contempt, she replied, "Do you mean from the gas chambers, where they were killing Jews by the thousands?"

A snicker swept the courtroom.

"*Nein, nein,* you know what I mean. When Colonel Baer removed you from Auschwitz to Mauthausen."

"Oh, you mean from one death camp to another?"

"*Nein,* I did not say death camp."

"That's what they were. The Nazis were killing people at both places."

"Stop your propaganda and answer my question," Frau Scholz-Klink demanded. "Any favors?"

"Sexual? No. Compassion? Yes."

Frau Scholz-Klink's glasses dropped to her ample bosom and she raised her hands, shrugging her shoulders in frustration, then shouted, "No further questions."

"I call Walther Baer," Bart ordered.

"Objection! He is a defendant," Luther Krieger snapped.

"Your Honors, for the record, I submit that he could be characterized as a hostile witness, or put him on for a short *voir dire,*" Bart said.

"Granted."

The broad-shouldered, six-foot-tall colonel marched to the stand. The oath was administered.

"State your name."

"Walther Baer."

"Are you a Nazi?"

"Not now."

"Were you a Nazi?"

"Reluctantly."

"Explain."

"I was a career soldier before Hitler became Chancellor. My country was at war. I was forced to take the oath of allegiance. Heinrich Himmler forced me into the Waffen SS."

"When did that happen?"

"I was wounded during the Allied invasion of France. I was awarded an Iron Cross. My shoulder was fractured. I was sent to Berlin for an operation. Hitler, Himmler and Goebbels were coming to the hospitals in a publicity visit with photographers. Himmler recruited me for the Gestapo and sent me to Auschwitz two days before the arrival of Frau Claubert."

"Why didn't you send her to the gas chambers?"

"I was sick of the heartless killing of those Jews. I was ashamed of the way they stripped those people naked and sent them to those false showers, the gas chambers. She and her family stood there naked with great dignity. I asked what their skills were and assigned them to work jobs."

"Eventually her parents and the others were either killed or raped to death. That was Commandant Höss's doing."

"You heard Mrs. Claubert's testimony here today. Has she told the truth?"

"Absolutely," he replied as he looked at her. A quality of nostalgia and sincerity, mixed with shame and regret, was reflected in his countenance.

"Now, I'm going to ask you a very serious and troubling question. What were you doing with the Waffen SS at Hitler's ranch in La Plata, Argentina?"

"Sir, believe it or not, I arrived the afternoon of the attack on the Nordheim ranch."

"You will have to explain the why and how of that."

"Permit me to explain how I happened to be there. I must tell you first that I was captured at Mauthausen by the American troops. I was a prisoner of war for six months. When I was released, I could not go back to Germany. They were holding war trials there. I got a job in Zurich through a distant relative that lives there. I promised not to reveal his name."

"What kind of job?"

"As a clerk at the Banque Royale in Zurich. I worked my way up to the accounting department and became a vice president. I married a Swiss lady and have two children with her."

"Are you now a Swiss citizen?"

"Yes, sir."

"How did it come about that you were in La Plata when our troops captured you?"

"That's the worst coincidence in my life. A Mr. Waldo Schlicht, who is the major stockholder of that bank, sent for me about a week before your raid."

"For what purpose?"

"He wanted me to deliver some money to Mr. Nordheim, a Jewish customer of the bank, who was believed to be the richest man in the world."

"You know now who Mr. Nordheim is?"

"Yes, he's Adolf Hitler."

"You did not suspect that?"

"No. He gave me a picture of Nordheim, which certainly didn't look like Hitler. He looked like that man sitting back there that you have identified as Hitler and who admits he is Hitler. That's fantastic plastic surgery."

"How much money did he give you to deliver to Nordheim?"

"He didn't give it to me. He sent me to the Banco Caribe Antille in the Cayman Islands. He told me they would give me ten million American dollars in four suitcases. He said he trusted me, but if I failed to deliver the money, he would kill my wife and two children and track me down all over the world."

"Did you deliver the money?"

"Yes."

"How?"

"I was sent in a private plane to the Cayman Islands, to Grand Cayman, landing in Georgetown. A Mr. Ricardo Ramirez greeted me at the Banco Caribe Antille, known as the BCA. He opened the four bags and showed me the money. He took me to the airport with two other men who carried the bags."

"Did he make you identify yourself?"

"Yes. I handed him a letter from Waldo Schlicht, which was sealed with wax and a stamp of the Banque Royale. He had a full description of me, and when he opened the sealed letter there was a picture of me in it. He called Zurich and spoke to Schlicht. He was satisfied I was the courier."

"Then what did you do?"

"They carried the bags on board the plane. Ramirez spoke to the pilot privately, then we took off for Buenos Aires. When we arrived, three men met the plane. They carried the bags off into a Daimler limousine. Not a word was spoken. They looked suspiciously like Waffen SS men. I kept silent as we drove to the Nordheim ranch. That was about three hours before the Americans attacked the building."

"Was Nordheim there?"

"No, but Heinrich Müller, whom we called *Gestapo Müller,* took the bags and said Nordheim was on his way. I was sick to my stomach. The place was full of Gestapo men. I said nothing. I was scared."

"What happened after that?"

"A little while later a huge birthday cake was delivered to the house to celebrate Nordheim's birthday. The cake had a big swastika in the center of it. A message was read, saying he was sorry he was delayed and would be there soon, signed Adolf. That's when I realized that Nordheim was Hitler and still alive. I wanted to vomit."

"Just one more question. Tell the court what took place next."

"Everyone got drunk and ate the cake. Except me. There was no way in hell I was going to partake in that vile celebration. There must have been some kind of drug in the cake, because men were passing out. Suddenly we were under attack. I tried to jump out of a window when that man struck me with his gun and I was knocked unconscious."

"Which man are you pointing at?"

"That man behind the prosecution table. His name is Jacques Laurent."

"How did you learn his name?"

"Because he told me who he was when he interrogated me in my cell here."

"No further questions."

"We reserve the right to call this witness later," Erich von Maunder declared.

"Granted," Nimitz agreed.

"The prosecution calls Auguste Masten."

The witness, one of the four new Wiesenthal arrivals, wearing a blue blazer, red sweater vest and gray flannel trousers, marched between two burly MPs to the witness stand. After the oath, he sat in the chair and crossed his legs. He was completely at ease and stated his name.

"Your place of birth, sir."

"Vienna, Austria," he replied in a pleasant Viennese accent.

"Your education, sir?"

"A complete education, through a master's degree at the University of Vienna. I was a professor at the University of Vienna, teaching music and the history of Austrian music. I also conducted the Vienna Symphony Orchestra. I composed music as well."

"Vienna was a great cultural center and had a history of great composers, is that correct?" Bart asked.

"Yes, until the *Anschluss*, the takeover by Nazi Germany. Vienna produced such musical giants as Mozart, Schubert and Strauss."

"Very impressive. What occurred after the Nazis occupied Austria on March 12, 1938?"

"That was the beginning of the end for the Jews in Austria. Our national population was almost six point seven million people and only two hundred and fifty thousand Jews, about four percent of the population. About a hundred and seventy-eight thousand Jews lived in Vienna and made a tremendous cultural contribution to the arts, academia, medicine, literature, music, and the economy of the country."

"Please give the court your observations of the changes that took place."

"Overnight, we became a police state. The Jews had enough warning of Germany's policy towards Jews. We were quickly barred from what Americans prize so much. Our civil rights went right into the Nazi pipeline of hate. All Jews in government service were stripped of their jobs. After that, the Gestapo forced Jews to sell their business holdings for pennies. Those of us that had money in Austrian banks had long since transferred our savings to Swiss banks. Half the Jewish population left Austria for France, Belgium, Holland, Great Britain, America and South America."

"Why did you stay?"

"Besides my wife and four children, I had a large family, including my father, mother, two grandparents, three aunts and uncles and ten cousins. I was thirty-seven years old at that time. All of us were gainfully employed until the Nazis took over our country. We were not Orthodox Jews, but were members of a Reform synagogue. We were Austrians with an ancestry in Austria of over one thousand years. Most of my relatives served in the Austrian Army in World War I. For some reason or another, I was allowed to teach music at the university. I think Franz von Papen, Germany's ambassador to Austria, had something to do with that."

"How did that come about?"

"Chancellor Kurt von Schuschnigg, Ambassador von Papen and Arthur Seyss-Inquart had attended a concert of the Vienna Symphony Orchestra, which I conducted a few months before the *Anschluss*. Chancellor Schuschnigg invited me and my wife, Greta, to join them for a late supper at the Hotel Imperial, two streets away from the opera house. Greta was a very beautiful, blue-eyed, blonde lady. She was a former history teacher who quit to become a full-time mother to our children. That evening I was asked to play the violin. My wife accompanied me on the piano. They had us play for over an hour with lots of requests. The fact that we were Jews never came up."

"Isn't that the hotel where the Nazis established their headquarters?"

"Ironically, yes. It was built in 1869. It has been beautifully refurbished after the Nazi scum were driven out of Austria."

"Seyss-Inquart became the *Reichstatthalter*, the Reich governor of Austria."

"That's correct. All my family was without employment. Von Papen came to the university one day after the *Anschluss* and told me he had convinced Seyss-Inquart to let me stay at my professorship and to continue as conductor of the symphony. He told me to add a lot of Richard Wagner's music to our repertoire. I supported our whole family as best I could."

"When did that change come?"

"On November 8, that year of 1938, came the outbreak of *Kristallnacht* in Germany, and it spread to Austria. The derelicts and street bums threw rocks at Jewish homes, businesses and synagogues in Vienna. I knew it was time to make plans to leave. We emigrated to Paris. But there is one thing that was manifest. Anti-Semitism was like a dormant virus. It showed its ugliness in Austria and was in the closet in France."

"How did you survive in France?"

"My musical reputation was known in Paris. I got a job playing first violin in the Paris Symphony, and on weekends I played in different cafés in Montmartre."

"Let's move on to the time the Nazis occupied Paris."

"The Parisians were heartbroken that day on June 14 as the Nazi troops marched under the Arc de Triomphe, straight down the Champs-Elysées. On June 23 I saw Hitler inspecting Paris. I was in the street when he stamped his foot and jumped up and down in joy. Look at that phony plastic face of *Der Führer*. Derelict *Führer* is what I call him."

"Objection. Move to strike those pejorative words!" Luther Krieger shouted.

"You needn't raise your voice, Counselor. Objection sustained," Nimitz ruled.

"Tell the Court what followed."

"Christmas Eve, 1941. A jealous member of the symphony led the Gestapo to our apartment just off the Place de la Concorde. We were having dinner. They arrested my family - me, my wife, my children and my father and mother. They stole everything we had and pocketed jewelry, money, my wife's wedding ring and my children's coin collection. For some reason, the head Gestapo agent said to the others, *Let him keep his violin*. He seemed to know who I was. We ended up at the Drancy concentration camp outside Paris."

"Why did you stay in Paris?"

"It was very hard to leave. The Gestapo was everywhere. I had paid ten thousand francs to a Vichy France captain, Marcel Tellier, to put us on a midnight train to Geneva, Switzerland. He was going to put us on a freight car carrying a collection of paintings consigned to Herr Goering. That was to happen two nights after we were sent to Drancy. That sealed our fate."

"What followed?"

"Drancy was a police barracks before the war. It was a large six-story U-shaped building. There was no escaping from there. The area was closed in by barbed wire and guarded by French police. We stayed there for a week and then moved to a warehouse in one of the end camps at the Austerlitz train station. Drancy was a transit camp to the concentration camp in Poland. Some of the French police would give us information about the war and the Jewish question. We learned that the Americans had been attacked by the Japanese at Pearl Harbor and that Hitler had declared war on America. The French policemen said things didn't look good for the Jews."

"What did he mean by that, specifically?"

"He said that we were all being transferred to death camps. We had already learned that the Nazis had built six of what they called *extermination camps*. They were Auschwitz, Belzec, Treblinka, Sobibor, Chelmno and Majdanek. Birkenau was part of Auschwitz. Drancy held five thousand at a time for shipment. In the middle of the night, we were awakened, put on trucks and delivered to the rail station. We were literally stuffed into a foul-smelling cattle car. It was filthy, with dried feces, vomit and dried blood on the splintered floor of the car. Most of the people in that car were French, plus a few refugees from Holland, Luxembourg, Denmark, Belgium, and Norway. There was no air, no toilets, no water and no food. We could hardly move. It was a nightmare, with people dying, others defecating and urinating in their clothes and some on the floor. We arrived three days later at a place called Lodz. It was the most degrading torture that only heartless monsters could concoct."

"Lodz was not a death camp?"

"No, it was a ghetto that the Nazis had set up. We were taken there and given one room. Both my parents were deathly ill. My children had colds, so my wife and I tended to them. A Polish Jew knocked on the door. He spoke in Yiddish, which is very much like German. He had two pails of water and a stack of clean but tattered towels. He handed me a large block of borax soap. He said, *Clean up and I'll bring you some soup.* He was just a young man in his twenties. We were freezing. He came back with a stack of clean blankets. He asked me to give him our clothes so that they could be washed. We did bring some extra clothes with us. We undressed quickly and handed him our stained clothing. He smiled and said he and his family went through the ordeal. My wife and I washed all of us with the water from the pails and changed into clean clothes in our valises."

"That was quite an ordeal in that frigid weather, wasn't it?"

"It was indescribable. There was another knock on the door. It was the young man's father, mother and a teenage sister. Each was carrying something. The father brought bread and a pot of hot potato soup with pieces of chicken in it. The mother carried pillows and blankets for my parents. The young girl had a bottle of Polish vodka and six bowls and spoons. The family name was Mazewski. They came from Krakow. The father's name was Jacob. He was a doctor."

Tears rolled down Masten's cheeks. Bart handed him a glass of water and a handful of tissues, then asked, "Do you want to stop?"

"No, I'll continue. The doctor checked my mother and father. He reached in his pocket and handed them two aspirins each. *They have fevers,* he told us. My wife fed them the soup. I fed the children. Everyone was wrapped in a blanket. The doctor explained that he was the captain of that section of the ghetto. He warned us that we might be shipped out at any time."

"And did that happen?"

"Yes."

"When?"

"Two weeks later. The doctor helped me nurse my parents. They were much better. The doctor and his family became good friends with us. Then came the day when fifty Gestapo agents emptied the building of its occupants. Once again, we were stuffed into cattle cars. Soon we arrived at Chelmno, a death camp. The horror had only just begun."

"Please explain."

"My parents and my children were put in vans. My wife screamed. Two guards took her away. I stood there in shock. People behind me kept repeating, *Gas vans, gas vans!* I ran after the van. Smoke was pouring out an exhaust pipe on top of the vehicle. Shortly thereafter, my father, mother and children were thrown out of the van. They were dead," Masten sobbed. "I went berserk and jumped on the guard that threw the bodies out. I was hit from behind and knocked unconscious."

"How do you explain that you are still alive?"

"When I came to, after they dumped a bucket of water on my face, I heard music playing. For a few moments, I didn't know where I was. I thought I was dead. The camp commandant, Johann Weisst, was standing over me. There he is, in the back row."

The court ordered Masten to put his hand on the commandant's shoulder. Two MPs led him down the aisle. Weisst had a nasty smirk on his face. He snarled, "Austrian Jew maestro, fuck you."

Masten clasped his hands together and delivered a side-swiping smash to the commandant's nose, which bled profusely. In German, Masten yelled, "I will piss on all your graves, you miserable *Scheisse meisters!*"

The MPs gently pulled him back and led him back to his chair. A smattering of applause rippled through the court.

Erich von Maunder furiously shouted, "What the hell kind of court is this?"

"Watch your language and your manner of addressing this court, Mr. Maunder," Nimitz angrily replied. "I will deal with Mr. Masten."

"Somebody better," von Maunder hissed.

General Smith, in a drillmaster's tone, roared, "I can't hear you!"

Silence.

"Mr. von Maunder, stand up and repeat loud and clear your last remark," Smith ordered.

"Somebody better," von Maunder meekly whispered.

"I can't hear you."

Von Maunder shouted, "Somebody better!"

"Are you attempting to question the authority of this court?" Smith pressed.

"Indeed I am."

"Counselor, you are now in contempt of court. You are fined ten thousand American dollars, payable within the hour, or you can spend ten days in jail. Which will it be?" Nimitz angrily slammed his gavel on the bench.

"Very well, sir. I will pay that right now." He reached into his briefcase and took out two packets of bank-wrapped hundred-dollar bills, which he tried to hand to an MP.

"No, no, Counselor. Bring that money up here and hand it to the clerk," Nimitz ordered.

Von Maunder marched down the aisle, threw the money on the clerk's desk and turned back up the aisle.

"Now, as to Mr. Masten," Nimitz continued, "while our sympathy for your plight is shared by all, we cannot permit your egregious conduct of striking a defendant. Therefore we must hold you in contempt of court for disrupting the decorum of this court."

Bart jumped to his feet. Nimitz held his hand up in a gesture for silence.

"This court fines you ten dollars."

Bart quickly sat down. Masten took a ten-dollar bill from his pocket and handed it to the clerk.

"I apologize to the court, sir."

"Accepted. Continue, General Milburn."

At Bart's request, the stenotypist read his last question back.

"Commandant Weisst told me they could kill me for a attacking a guard. *Why don't you? I asked.* He said, *I'm sending you to Treblinka. They need musicians. We have plenty here, maestro.* I asked him, *Where is my wife?* He said, *You'll see her when I'm through with her.* His remark was clear enough, and I realized that she was going to be raped. I have never wanted to kill somebody, but that slimy animal was someone I could kill without a shred of conscience."

"Did you see your wife again?"

"Yes, she was on the train with me to Treblinka. However, she could not talk and was what we say in American slang, a *basket case.*"

"At Treblinka, how did you manage to survive?"

"When we arrived, we were asked to strip naked. I figured that we were going to the gas chambers. A woman guard tore the clothes off my wife. She was stark naked, with blood on her legs and pelvis. She stood there, eyes staring to the sky. I put my arm around her, assuming we were going to the showers, which were really gas chambers. I noticed a pit with hundreds of skeletonized bodies piled on each other. People started to march to the showers. Music was playing. Halfway to those deadly showers, Commandant Kurt Franz pulled Greta and me out of the line. We were both naked and cold. He asked me, *You are Maestro Masten?* I nodded my head yes. He snapped his fingers, and soon two blankets were put over us."

"Why?"

"I learned that after he let us have a warm shower and some warm clothes. He took us to his office. There, he explained that he wanted me to form an orchestra like the one at Chelmno. I thought about it for a minute and wanted to live long enough to avenge the evil inflicted upon me and my family by those rotten German bastards."

"Objection to the words *German bastards.* I ask that they be stricken from the record," von Maunder said.

Nimitz thought for a moment. "All right, strike *German bastards.*"

Bart asked Masten, "Do you have any words to replace those two?"

"Nazi killers."

"Objection."

"Overruled."

"I agreed to Commandant Franz's request. My wife and I were given a room in a shack. It had a toilet and a shower. I felt guilty. We were being fed twice a day. I looked after her while I formed the orchestra, and I watched thousands die every day."

"How long were you there?"

"Until August 2, 1943."

"Why until 1943?"

"Several things happened before that."

"Explain that to the court, please."

"As I met the trains every day seeking musicians, I found some who were not musicians. There were some Russian and Polish soldiers scheduled for the gas chambers. There were six of them. I whispered to each one. *You're a drummer, you're a violinist,* etc. They understood me. Fortunately, two of them could play the trumpet and saxophone. One Russian spoke Yiddish and one Polish man spoke Yiddish. They explained everything to the others."

"What was the purpose of having an orchestra?"

"Two things. One, to have concerts for the Gestapo, the soldiers and the guards. The other was a disgustingly evil purpose. We would have quartets play music as thousands marched to the death chambers every day. I tried to save as many as possible."

"How many?"

"Over sixty. I told the Nazis they were backups."

"Didn't Franz notice or suspect what you were doing?"

"Commandant Franz was so busy killing people that he paid little attention to me. He liked our concerts and occasionally sent me a list of musical requests. One important thing - he let me go to a warehouse where they had almost every instrument I would need. I also used the warehouse for rehearsals. One day I spotted a room where the door was slightly open. Someone had left the key in the door. I peeked in and saw a small arsenal loaded with all sorts of weapons. I closed the door, locked it and kept the key."

"How was your wife all this time?"

"Physically, fine. Mentally, gone. She didn't know who I was, but I kept caring for her and hoping for her recovery."

"What did you do about the arsenal?"

"During rehearsals, I had the Russian and Polish soldiers take guns and ammunition and put them in the music cases. At my shack, we dug a hole under a small kitchen and stored the arms there."

"Were you and your sixty orchestra people planning an escape?"

"More than that. There were several thousand slave laborers working at Treblinka. We handpicked one thousand men who we felt could be trusted for a revolt. Some of them were hiding axes, saws, picks, shovels and planks of wood to be used as bludgeons. During rehearsals, we were trained by the Russian and Polish soldiers on how to use those weapons. I learned how to use a machine gun, as well as other guns."

"What finally triggered the actual revolt?"

"I triggered it, because of what happened to my wife."

"What was that?"

"A Gestapo major came to me and told me Commandant Franz said that a new doctor had arrived. He was a German trauma specialist and could cure my wife. I was so happy. He said he would take her to the infirmary and would bring her back. I let him take her. That same day, I saw the mass murderer Heinrich Himmler inspect the killing process. Our orchestra was serenading. I was playing the violin. He complimented us on our music. If I had had a gun at that moment, I would have killed him. Franz was showing him around. Finally, he left with his other officers in a Mercedes Benz open car. It was July 31, 1943, a day I'll never forget."

"Why is that?"

"When Himmler left, Commandant Franz asked me what Himmler said to us. I told him he complimented us on our music. I then thanked Franz for sending my wife to the new doctor. He looked at me as though I was crazy. *What doctor?* he asked. I told him that a Major Krieg told me that the commandant wanted the doctor to help my wife. All he said was *Der Trottel,* which means halfwit. He turned and ran and I ran after him. He stopped at Major Krieg's quarters. He had his Luger gun in his hand and smashed the door down. The major and five other men were drinking schnapps. A naked man was on top of my naked wife. Her eyes were staring at the ceiling. The soldier jumped up and saluted the commandant. Franz went to the bed, touched her neck and yelled, *She is dead, you idiots!* He shouted at me, *Get out of here!* I ran. I knew they would kill me."

"What happened after that?"

"That night I told our men that the time had come for the revolt. I hid that night in the barracks with the men who were going to join in the attack. The Russian Jewish soldier said that Franz was looking for me. *I told him you were sick and crying a lot,* he said. Franz told the Russian to send me to him when I felt better. The night of August 1, we armed almost five hundred men. The others were going to use their axes, picks, clubs and whatever they could find. At daybreak on August 2, 1943, we attacked. We set fire to the camp. A real battle took place. I killed the major and two of his men with my machine gun. The Nazis were professionals and we were amateurs. But we killed quite a few of them. They killed more of us. Two hundred of us escaped. About one hundred were caught and killed. The rest of us, still armed, jumped on an empty train going west toward the Baltic Sea. The two Russians were fighting each other verbally. The Jew wanted to go west to the Americans, the other Russian wanted to get back to the Russian army. The Jew said, *Jump off if you want to, I'm not going back to that communist, anti-Semite Stalin. He's as bad as Hitler and Himmler combined.*"

The defendants applauded.

Nimitz pounded with his gavel.

Bart asked, "Where did you go?"

"We met up with the Jewish resistance near Kovno. Lots of them came from Bialystok, Riga and Vilna. There were over fifteen hundred men, some of them non-Jews, French, Yugoslavs, Belgians, Dutch and Italians. We fought the Nazis on a hit-and-run basis. We killed hundreds of Nazis. I finally shaped up as a good soldier. A real partisan. The Russians were coming from the east and the Allies were coming from the west. Don't let anybody tell you that Jews can't fight. Look at Israel today. Most of their veterans were partisans. We hid in the forests and, as the Nazis retreated, we picked them off. Look at that scum sitting out there waiting to be hanged. I'll pull the lever on those cowardly sons of bitches that killed millions of women and children. *Heil* Shitler."

"Objection."

"Overruled."

Even the press applauded.

"A few more questions, Mr. Masten, please."

"Go ahead."

"Where did you end up?"

"There was a barge being towed west on the Baltic Sea toward Neungamme. One hundred and fifty of us, fully armed, got on board. We knew the Americans were coming. We kept picking off retreating Nazis. We picked up their weapons and grenades. By late March 1945, we were on the eastern side of Buchenwald and Ohrdruf. We wanted to help the Americans capture the fleeing commandants and guards. We got some of them. Killed them all. The others panicked and ran back to the camps."

"Did you join up with the Americans or the British?"

"General Milburn, you don't remember me, because I had a beard and moustache at that time. I saw you at Ohrdruf that day with Eisenhower, Patton and Bradley. We came in as the generals were leaving. You were escorting an injured girl in a wheelchair. We helped round up a few of the guards."

Bart scratched his head, musing, *I'll be damned*, then asked, "What is your profession now?"

"I am head of the music department at the MGM studios in Hollywood. I also conduct the Los Angeles Philharmonic. I am a composer and I score movies."

"Thank you, Mr. Masten. No further questions."

Luther Krieger stood to cross examine Masten. He tried a surgical approach. "Sir, are you Jewish?"

"Yes, I am of that faith."

"Mr. Masten, you testified that you became a partisan and killed many German soldiers. Doesn't that run counter to your faith as a Jew?"

"Mr. von Maunder, I didn't kill Germans; I killed Nazis, faithless pagans. My answer is no. I believe the Bible states *An eye for an eye and a tooth for a tooth.* But my shooting was defensive, because we were trying to stop your Nazi hordes from killing innocent women, children, the elderly and others. We were fighting to stop those raping, plundering degenerates. God propelled me to defend our people."

"Bull *Scheisse*," von Maunder uttered. "No further questions."

"That little comment, Mr. von Maunder, just cost you another ten-thousand-dollar fine," said Nimitz.

Hitler shouted in German, "This is a bullshit kangaroo court! Why not double the fine?"

"That is more contempt, Herr Hitler," Chennault bellowed.

"That sounds reasonable, General," Nimitz agreed.

"For Herr Hitler, the fine is fifty thousand dollars, and ten thousand for von Maunder. Next time, your mouth will be taped and your counsel will be confined to jail. There will be no more nonsense in this court. This is not Nazi Germany!" Nimitz exploded. "There will be a fifteen-minute recess."

Counsel on both sides were called into chambers. Von Maunder, Erich Stolz, Luther Krieger and Otto Meissner attended for the defense. Bart, Cartman and Ross were present for the prosecution.

Nimitz, with contained anger, declared, "You men are testing the patience of this court. We are aware you were hired by the Swiss Banking Association to defend Adolf Hitler. We are not fooled that your actual presence here is to primarily protect the Swiss banks. You are making fools of yourselves and trying to demean this military tribunal. We are trying to be objective. Don't attempt to tamper with the decorum of this court. The world is watching you."

General Smith was not as temperate as Nimitz. The battle-hardened Marine exploded vituperatively. "This is the United States of America! Fool around with this tribunal and all of you become candidates for our jails. Some of our prisons are hellholes of iniquity. Mr. Meissner, I am surprised that you, a former judge, would countenance this behavior."

"Members of this tribunal, I am shocked at General Smith's language. However, I wish to apologize for the behavior of our clients and our conduct as well. I assure you, I promise a change in our representation before your court," Meissner said.

An MP knocked on the door. "Come in," Nimitz said. The MP whispered to Nimitz. "Send them in," the admiral replied, nodding.

Jacques Laurent and Secret Service agents Larry Witten and Kenneth Parker, the latter carrying a paper bag, entered.

"May we leave?" Meissner asked.

Before Nimitz could answer, Laurent snapped, "No, stay the hell where you are."

"What's the meaning of this?" Nimitz queried.

Jacques nodded to Witten and pointed to Nimitz's desk. Parker threw the paper bag onto the desk.

"Sir, I am Kenneth Parker with the Secret Service," he said, flashing his ID. "There is seventy thousand dollars of counterfeit money in that bag, paid to the clerk of the court by Mr. von Maunder for fines of contempt you imposed on him and Hitler. Von Maunder removed this fake money from his briefcase. I am obliged to arrest Mr. von Maunder."

The defense attorney turned pale and began to shake in a palsied manner.

"In addition, you'll notice that the money wrappers on each stack state the name Merchants International Bank & Trust. We've been investigating this bank and its vice president, Harry Branlow, ever since you arrested him, General. It turns out he is closely connected with Nordheim/Hitler. We believe that the two have been working together in a plot to infiltrate counterfeit money into the American currency. We don't yet know how much of the bank's money is real and how much is fake, but we have good reason to suspect that the bank has been used as a conduit for laundering the phony money.

Of course, we'll need to arrest Harry Branlow and take him into our custody."

"Fine. We don't need that scumbag anyway," Bart responded. "Jacques, take Parker with you to Branlow's cell and turn him over to the custody of the Secret Service."

"Gladly," Jacques replied, and they departed.

"I had no idea that this money was counterfeit. It was delivered by courier from the Cayman Islands. I assure you gentlemen that I am not a party to this crime," von Maunder said.

"This is a federal crime, beyond our jurisdiction," Nimitz said.

Witten quickly pulled von Maunder's arms behind his back and applied handcuffs.

"I will take him before the U.S. Attorney in this district. The case will be fully investigated," Parker declared, then took von Maunder out the back.

Court convened thiryt minutes later, and Auguste Masten was back on the stand.

"Is the defense through with Mr. Masten?"

"Yes, Your Honor."

"Rebuttal, Your Honor, for clarification."

"Granted."

"Mr. Masten, prior to your imprisonment by the Nazis and the war, did you ever own or shoot a gun?" Bart asked.

"No, sir. I didn't own a gun, nor did I ever know how to shoot one."

"Before the revolt at the Treblinka death camp, did you ever fire a gun?"

"No, sir. But just prior to our revolt, I was trained by a Russian Jewish soldier on how to handle guns."

"When the revolt occurred, you became a partisan soldier against the Nazis?"

"Yes, that was part of the war."

"Do you own a gun now?"

"Yes, sir, I am licensed. I have it for protection against thieves and Nazis."

"Do you expect a reprisal by the Nazi party?"

"Well, it's possible. Take that commandant back there, Kurt Franz."

"Of Treblinka?"

"Yes. He's here under another name."

"Your Honor, I'm not asking this man to touch his shoulder. But may I ask the court to ask Kurt Franz to stand up and come forward?"

"Kurt Franz, rise," Nimitz said.

No one stood up.

"Mr. Masten, two MPs will escort you to the man you say is Kurt Franz. Don't attempt any violence," Nimitz cautioned.

"No, sir, I promise."

Masten said to the MPs, "Let's not go down the center aisle. Walk me down the one near the right wall."

They marched to the last row. The target cringed low in his seat, head between his hands.

"Make him stand up," Masten said.

The MPs lifted the man to his six-foot height and forced him to face Masten.

"Well, Commandant Franz, we meet again, you slimy Nazi bastard! Why are you hiding from me?"

"Maestro, I kept you alive. Where is your appreciation?"

"While you supervised the killing of thousands upon thousands, you murdering bastard! At least *you're* getting a trial. If I had you alone, I'd kill you." Masten spit in his face.

Masten returned to the stand. "That is Kurt Franz. He admitted it in front of the MPs."

"No further questions."

"Sirs, one question of the MPs to verify Franz's admission."

Under oath, Sergeants Steven Casey and Lionel Perkins affirmed the admission by Franz.

"The court is adjourned until 0900 hours tomorrow morning," Nimitz said.

Radio producers competed frantically in trying to snare Rebecca Claubert and Masten for interviews. In the conference room, Bart and his staff were listening to a report from Lieutenants Grace Larsen and Kyle Winslow.

"That's quite a report. Let's review it by starting at the bottom line and work our way back to the most impressive potential witnesses. You first, Lieutenant Larsen," Bart said, "Sum it up."

"The hate calls have fallen off. Out of three hundred calls, twenty were hates. We have heard from almost every country in the world."

"For example, Grace?"

"General, I'll name cities and towns that have the most poignant stories. Warsaw, Krakow, Poland; Prague, Czechoslovakia; Milan, Italy; Paris and Marseilles, France; Tel Aviv, Israel; Kharkov, Moscow, Smolensk and Rostov, Russia…"

"Hold it there, Grace. Kyle, I assume you have quite a few letters."

"Hundreds, sir."

"Both of you meet with Richard Maybrook and Phillip Berger. Synthesize your lists with the most graphic accounts. Over the weekend, we'll review and decide which witnesses are pertinent to our objectives in exposing the bestiality of Nazi Germany. I doubt we can get witnesses from behind the Iron Curtain. The Nuremberg trials took eight months. I would like to truncate these trials to half or a third of that. Get to it."

They saluted and left.

"Let's call it a day," Bart suggested. "We can all use a quiet evening. See you all for breakfast at 0800, here."

The team emitted a few *amens*. Bart and Jacques enjoyed a quiet dinner, served by Mrs. Lawrence at the Victorian house. Both men called their wives in Washington. A knock at the door broke their reveries in the den, where they were sipping snifters of Courvoisier brandy.

"Your brother Douglas is here," Mrs. Lawrence announced.

"Send him in," Bart said.

Douglas had shed his coat and hat. A few snowflakes dotted his brown-ish-red hair. "Sorry to interrupt, Barton."

"You never interrupt, brother. Have you had dinner?"

"Yes."

"Sit down, take a shot of brandy and unburden yourself."

"I'll bet you have some news, Doug," Jacques said as he poured a dram of brandy for Douglas.

"Thanks, Jacques. As usual, your crystal ball is working."

Jacques handed him a cigar.

"We were just going to listen to the gossip columnists on radio," Bart said.

"Turn it on, but keep it low. I have something to tell you," Doug said. "There's a rumor being bruited about that Erich von Maunder has been arrested for paying his and Hitler's fines with counterfeit money," he said, puffing a cloud of smoke.

Bart lit a cigarette and winked at Jacques, who covered his smile in his snifter. The only voice heard was that of Gabriel Heatter commenting on the horrors revealed at the day's trial session.

"General Milburn, the chief prosecutor, is brilliantly performing a surgical dissection of the Nazi psyche. The testimony being elicited by him is a chilling account of the monstrosities performed by the beastliness of Germany's Third Reich. No one person or a small group could have executed this carnage, while the world turned away. Milburn, a professional lawyer, is sparing no one from the crown of thorns on Hitler's head. Millions of Germans participated in the orgy of murder, mayhem, rape, and thievery. General Milburn deserves the plaudits of the civilized world for dissecting these Nazi subhumans, as well as the accessories such as the partisan Swiss, the Clivedon Set and the anti-Semites cloaking themselves in respectability. On a personal note, I would like to see Lindbergh, Joe Kennedy, the Duke of Windsor, a few members of Congress and anti-Semitic pre-war backers of Hitler subpoenaed for this history-making open trial."

"Switch the dial, Jacques," Bart said.

Douglas shifted impatiently in his chair. He rose and walked to the bar, then poured a generous amount of brandy in his snifter. Bart and Jacques smiled at each other while Doug busied himself at the bar. Lowell Thomas was on the air, focusing on the two survivors and their testimony.

"Okay, Douglas. Here's the poop, or should I say *scoop,* you're sniffing at," Bart laughed.

"Kid brother, you're a tease," Doug joked.

"Put that drink down, take out your pencil and pad. Here goes. Von Maunder was arrested in the Tribunal's chambers by two Secret Service agents. The seventy thousand dollars in fine money for Hitler and himself is allegedly counterfeit. Your next source of information is U.S. Attorney Farley Washburn. That's it."

"Where did this funny money come from?"

"It was not the money we confiscated at Rio Plata, Argentina. My guess is that it was delivered here recently. Someone stupid had to do this. Common sense would dictate that these lawyers, who are hired by the Swiss banks, would not be financed with counterfeit bills."

"Doug, if I were you, I wouldn't waste a lot of time. Reach Washburn as soon as you can. He'll probably try to arraign von Maunder the first thing in the morning," Jacques advised.

"Right on, Jacques," Bart explained. "Try his office in Kansas City. Use that phone right there."

Doug reached the U.S. Attorney's secretary. He wrestled with her for ten minutes until he finally said, "Very well, Miss Barnes, I'm breaking the story tonight. Sorry Mr. Washburn chooses not to talk to me."

"Hold it one minute, sir. I'll check to see if he is still in the meeting."

A male voice boomed through the phone receiver, loud enough for Bart and Jacques to hear. "Douglas Milburn, are you related to General Barton Milburn?"

"Yes, but I'm an independent reporter for the New York Daily News and the Chicago Tribune News Syndicate."

"If you are his brother, that's a plus, so here's the crux of the puzzle. Before you get hooked on a story with no fins, I want you to know that Mr. von Maunder is not being charged in this matter. He is cooperating. The villain in the piece, or for that matter, villains, are in the Fort Leavenworth pokey."

"Do you have any leads as to who provided the fake money?"

"Sorry, Douglas, I have to reach your brother. I need his help."

"To be quite frank with you, Mr. Washburn, I tried to question him and he told me to call you. I'm here with him at the fort."

"Thank you for your candor. Let me talk to him. I'm more interested in getting a case together than worrying about your scoop."

Doug handed the phone to Bart. "Farley, working late tonight?" Bart asked.

"Yes, Herr von Maunder is not our man. I was going to call you. Have you got two prisoners by the names of Darren Mayfield and Paul Mayfield?"

"Yes."

"Secret Service agent Witten and I want to question them. Nothing to do with your case, just the source of the money."

"We'll need their attorney present," Bart said. "How soon can you be here, Farley?"

"We will be there in forty minutes."

"Good. We'll hunt down their attorney, Alden Gaines. Question one prisoner at a time, understood? The provost marshal's office will route you to me."

"I'm very grateful, General." Washburn hung up.

"Come on, Jacques. Let's take a look at Darren Mayfield. He should be glad to see you."

☆ ☆ ☆ ☆

February 19, 1953 - Later - Fort Leavenworth Prison

Interrogation Room 5 was windowless, with stone walls, and had all the accoutrements for quizzing recalcitrant prisoners. MPs brought the handcuffed and leg-shackled prisoner, shuffling him into the dimly lit room.

"Sit down in that chair in front of this desk," Bart ordered.

He turned and thanked the MPs, one of whom returned and whispered in the general's ear. "Mr. Gaines checked out of the inn at 1830 hours, General. We'll be outside the door waiting for Mr. Washburn."

"What the fuck is going on here?" Darren Mayfield huffed.

"Listen, Mr. Mayfield, your FBI experience won't help you here."

"Why don't you put the full lights on?"

"Oblige him, Jacques."

A glaring overhead light came on. Mayfield winced and adjusted his eyes to the sudden brightness.

"You're that General Milburn and you...why you're the son-of-a-bitchin' Frenchman that tore my cheek open in Monte Carlo!" he yelled. "What the hell is this frog doing here?"

In a measured British accent, Jacques stood up to his full height and planted his legs astride, hands on his hips. "I am chief of the Nazi desk at the CIA. You were one of my targets, as was your adopted phony Jewish father, Frederick Avram Nordheim, who is really Adolf Hitler. That's what I'm doing here. Don't ever pull a gun on a pro. Didn't J. Edgar teach you that, you miserable traitor?"

Mayfield was speechless. His pallid face flushed and his cuffed hands shook.

"I am going to give you a little advice, Darren Mayfield," Bart began. "You're in plenty of trouble now, as you'll find out at your trial, so drop your smart-ass, tough-guy attitude. Hitler can't help you anymore. His Revenge Plan is in the toilet. You are about to have two visitors. Come clean with them or you'll never smell the grass, see the flowers or enjoy the sunshine for the rest of your life; that is, if they don't hang you," Bart advised.

"What the hell are you talking about?"

The door clanged open. The two men walked in. The door clanged shut.

"Mr. Mayfield, this is United States Attorney Farley Washburn, for the Kansas District. The other gentleman is Lawrence Witten of the United States Secret Service from Washington, D.C."

"What have they to do with me?"

"His attorney, Alden Gaines, has checked out of his hotel," Bart revealed.

"The son of a bitch!" Mayfield cried out. "He skipped with all the loot, that sleazy bastard."

"What loot?" Washburn asked.

"Our defense money."

"Where did that money come from?"

"A safe-deposit box at the Midwest Fidelity National Bank right here in Leavenworth, in my brother's name."

"You mean Paul Mayfield?"

"Yes, he knew I was taken from the Leavenworth prison to this shithouse, so he placed it there the day I was moved."

"How did he know that you had been moved?"

"That screw at Leavenworth called my lawyer, Alden Gaines, and told him where I was."

"How much money is in that vault?"

"I don't really know. But it has to be several million dollars."

"Where did you and your brother get that much money?"

"From who else? Mr. Nordheim had me put it away for a rainy day. Well, this is more than a rainy day. The sky has been pissing on me since I was kidnapped in Havana."

"You weren't kidnapped; you were arrested as an accessory to a Nazi war criminal, plus other charges," Bart roared. "That's why you are incarcerated here awaiting trial."

"Mr. Mayfield, did your brother bring money for Mr. Nordheim?" Washburn asked.

"Yes, he has a safety deposit box in the name of Nordheim at the same bank."

"How much money is in that box?" Bart asked.

"Many millions."

"For what purpose?"

"For defense money."

"Or to buy his and your way out of here?"

"Maybe."

"Where is your brother now?"

"He must be in New York, or somewhere near this fort."

"Would you like to see him?" Bart asked.

"I sure would. Can you arrange it?"

"Maybe," Bart said, mimicking Mayfield's earlier reply.

"Did Alden Gaines have access to your box?" Washburn asked.

"No."

"Did he have access to Hitler's?"

"Yes."

"Well, Mr. ex-FBI agent, you and your brother are stupid assholes," Washburn said.

"Why are you calling us names, Mr. U.S. Attorney?"

"Because we have a big bulletin for you. Agent Witten will tell you the news."

"The money in Nordheim's box is counterfeit and I am sure that *moolah*, the *gelt*, the paper in your box is counterfeit, too," Witten said.

"Oh, God, no. *No*."

"God won't help you, pal," Witten quipped.

"Now I've got a little surprise for you, you traitorous bastard," Bart said, and gestured to Jacques, who walked to the steel door and tapped on it. The MP opened it. Jacques nodded to him. Another prisoner shuffled in, handcuffed and shackled. The MP dumped him in a chair ten feet away from Mayfield.

"Darren!" the new arrival exclaimed.

"My God, Paul, they've got you in here, too?"

"Go ahead, Darren, tell your brother the bad news."

His voice was choked up, almost on the verge of tears as he related the story of the counterfeit money and Alden Gaines' disappearance.

"Darren, you're a *schmuck*. I told you not to trust that fucking shyster."

Washburn interrupted the family reunion. "Paul, I am the U.S. Attorney, and this is Mr. Witten of the Secret Service. We will have your box and Adolf Hitler's box opened in the morning with a court order. Now, make it easy on yourself. Tell us how you got that money."

"Fuck you."

"That's a foolish answer!" Jacques shouted. "I've got a file on you. You are a member and an officer of the I.A.S."

"What's that?" Paul questioned.

"The International Aryan Society, you anti-Semitic dirtbag," Jacques replied. "You're a traitor, just like your brother, tough guy."

"Who is this guy?" Paul asked.

Darren shouted, "Paul, cut it out! *This guy* is chief of the Nazi desk at the CIA. He's the guy who split my cheek."

"Oh really? I'd like him to try that with me," he replied, glaring at Jacques.

"Bart, please, let me take this pussycat next door for a few minutes," Jacques urged, returning a confident glare back at Paul Mayfield.

"Come on, Jacques, cool it," Bart snapped. "As for you, Paul, pray you are never left alone with this man."

"Paul, tell him where the money came from or I will. If the money in the boxes is not counterfeit, they can't touch it. If it is, why take the rap?" Darren pleaded.

"Okay, when Darren, Dov Schwartz and Nordheim disappeared, I got that call from Harry Branlow in Havana. It sounded like a kidnapping. I called Rene La Fleur at the Banque Lorraine to send lots of money to me in New York. La Fleur said he couldn't handle it without the approval of Froelich or Fliegel. He referred me to Waldo Schlicht, the major stockholder in the Banque Royale. Schlicht said okay, he would send it in the morning by courier on a private plane. Twenty million for Nordheim and five million for Darren. That's it. All of it was put in the local bank here, plus some other goodies of mine."

"To buy your way out of here, no doubt," Jacques said.

"Not a bad idea," Paul mumbled.

"That's all for now," Washburn declared.

Darren leaned over to his brother and whispered, "We've got to make a deal. Hitler is finished."

"What kind of deal?"

"Prosecution witnesses, you jerk."

"Let me think about it," Paul snapped.

The MPs came in for the prisoners.

"General, I want to make a deal," Darren cried out as he was being hustled out of the cell in the strong grip of two MPs.

"Me, too," Paul shouted as two other MPs were lifting him out of his chair.

"Back to your cells," Bart growled. "Sleep on it and we'll talk about it later. Paul, think about the attempted hit on Christina Lyons and me. Now get the hell out of here!"

Washburn, Witten, Bart and Laurent had a short conference after the prisoners were removed.

"This counterfeit case belongs entirely to Washburn and Witten," Bart advised. "We'll help in any way we can. Jacques here will be your main contact. I've got a full plate in front of me with this trial."

"Understood. Larry and I will get a court order and go to the bank in the morning. We'll keep Jacques advised. This was a good night's work," Washburn said.

CHAPTER EIGHT

Friday, February 20, 1953 - 0800 hours - Fort Leavenworth

The breakfast meeting in the prosecution conference room was focused on analyzing the proposed testimony of Dr. Arthur Glosburg, then U.S. Attorney Washburn was on the phone for Bart. "What's up, Farley?" Bart answered.

"General, I have just arraigned von Maunder before my friend, Federal Judge Burton Moskovitz, as a material witness to a counterfeit conspiracy. You can infer from the judge's name that he was very reluctant to allow bail for Hitler's counsel. It took much cajoling, despite our longtime friendship. I had to get him out of bed to meet with us at the courthouse."

"Well, what's the bottom line?"

"He finally agreed to release him on one million dollars bail and the surrender of von Maunder's passport. The judge insisted on pure, untainted cash. Fortunately, due to the time difference, the New York banks were open. Von Maunder was permitted to make some phone calls to Zurich. The funds were wired to the Marine Midland Bank branch at 250 Park Avenue in New York. They, in turn, agreed to wire the funds to the Midwest Fidelity National Bank, which opens at 9 a.m. Central Time. I'll wait at the Judge's office until the money gets here. Von Maunder will be back in court after that. The judge signed a court order for the Secret Service to open the safety-deposit boxes. I'll go over there with agent Witten."

"You think von Maunder is clean?"

"No doubt. Besides, he has signed a full account of the affair. He can't leave the country before I put him in front of a grand jury. In fact, once we establish that Hitler's money is counterfeit, I think he will resign as *Der*

Führer's counsel."

"What about Harry Branlow?"

"The Secret Service took him to the Federal House of Detention in New York. I called Attorney General Brownell. He said, *The bank's in New York, so we'll try him in New York.* And he's to be held over for trial."

"What about Alden Gaines?"

"Oh, I've got an all-points bulletin out for him."

"A good morning's work, Farley. I have no sympathy for von Maunder."

"General, one more minute. I thought you'd like to know this. The judge praised you and then, after the official proceedings, he lit into von Maunder and called him a Nazi vassal and a few unprintable expletives. Von Maunder swore he wasn't a Nazi. The judge then called him an accessory to the Swiss bankrobbers who have stolen and hoarded the Holocaust victims' money and the gold fillings from their dead bodies."

"Good for the judge. Give him my congratulations."

"Last note. The formerly arrogant and prominent Swiss von Maunder is sitting on a bench outside my phone booth, crying like a baby."

"Pathetic. Keep me advised, Farley. *Ciao.*" Bart then gulped his coffee and briefed the team, finally asking, "Jacques, is Glosburg in the witness room?"

"Yes. So is Bessie Lowen, but that Russian lady from Encino, California, who was due here on Wednesday, sent you a telegram. She will not be able to come until next week."

"That's perfect. I'd hate to have her standing by all this time. What's her name?"

"Are you ready for this? She calls herself Countess Maria Orlov."

"Come on, I've no time for kooks."

"I checked with Lieutenant Larsen and Sophia. They said she's for real. She lived under the commies as Natasha Orlovsky and her family was wiped out. She's a Jew."

"We'll quiz her when she gets here. Let's go, gang," Bart ordered.

☆ ☆ ☆ ☆

Military Tribunal - 0900 hours

"Call your witness, General."

The MPs escorted the distinguished witness to the stand. His youthful face was crowned with a full head of fluffy white hair.

"Please state your name, sir," Bart began.

"Dr. Arthur Glosburg."

"Where and when were you born?"

""I was born September 3, 1904, in Berlin, Germany. I am forty-eight years old."

"What kind of doctor were you?"

"I specialized in pediatrics and also researched disease control."

"Were you the only doctor in your family?"

"No, my father was a doctor at the Berlin University Hospital during the Weimar Republic. He became Minister of Health in 1930. My mother was a housewife and raised six children - three brothers, two sisters and myself. My paternal grandfather owned a department store in Munich. My paternal grandmother was an author of children's books. My wife was a pathologist. My maternal grandparents owned a small dairy farm just outside Frankfurt am Main."

"Did your father serve Germany in World War I?"

"Yes, he was a Colonel in the medical corps and was the recipient of several medals, two Iron Crosses and a Medal of Valor."

"How did he earn those medals?"

"He was at the Russian front at a field hospital attacked by a Ukrainian brigade. He grabbed a machine gun and held off the attack, saving his wounded patients. The medal was pinned on him by Kaiser Wilhelm."

"Did many Jews serve in the German army during the First World War?"

"Yes, sir, over a hundred and twenty thousand Jews fought valiantly for the fatherland. Over seventeen thousand six hundred were killed in the service of their country. Many were casualties. Many won medals. Many were officers."

"What happened after the war?" Bart asked.

"We had a runaway inflation and a very severe depression. The Versailles Treaty was draconian in every aspect. It paved the way for this immigrant Austrian derelict, a street bum, to rabble-rouse a bunch of ne'er-do-wells, thugs, outcasts, ex-convicts and opportunists to join him in a social revolution. They used the Jews as scapegoats. This corporal had the mouth of a soapbox orator. The hoodlums struck fear on the general population."

"Who specifically are you describing?"

"That filthy subhuman piece of feces, Adolf Schickelgruber Hitler. Why give him a trial? Hang that son of a bitch! That piece of vermin is rich with the blood of millions of Jews and others. He..."

"Objection, objection!" Luther Krieger and Otto Meissner shouted.

Nimitz gaveled. "One of you be seated."

Meissner sat. Krieger addressed the tribunal. "This outrageous attack by the witness and his prior peroration is hardly proper testimony. I plead with the court to strike all of this witness's testimony from the record. He's done enough damage."

"Your objection to his last statement is sustained and will be stricken from the record. However, what you deem a peroration is a proper response to the question asked."

"Exception."

"Noted."

"Dr. Glosburg, please reserve your vituperation for another venue," Bart gently coaxed. "Most of the world empathizes with survivors of the Holocaust, so this courtroom is not the place to vent your emotions."

"Objection," Krieger blurted. "Counsel has disingenuously endorsed the stricken statement of this witness."

"Overruled. Nitpicking objections test the patience of this court. Proceed, General."

"In 1930, Ernst Röhm headed up an unofficial army of storm troopers," Glosburg continued. "They were called the Brownshirts. I was 26 years old then and an intern at the hospital. They were hoodlums, street bums, who struck fear in the hearts and minds of all of Germany, Christians and Jews, regardless of faith. If you didn't respect the swastika, you were beaten and robbed. I treated many of their victims in the emergency room at the hospital. Of course, Jews were their main target. But I treated priests and Protestant ministers as well."

"Did you try to leave Berlin?" Bart asked.

"We had long discussions and plans to leave Germany. In July 1933, in what they call *The Night of the Long Knives,* Ernst Röhm and all the leaders of the SA, the storm troopers, were killed. Hitler ordered them executed because he was told they were a threat to him. Strangely enough, many Germans were relieved that these thugs were no longer a threat. How wrong we were. That pious Catholic chicken-plucker, Heinrich Himmler, grew in strength with his Gestapo. Then, on August 2, 1934, Hindenburg died."

"Why didn't you leave?" Bart persisted.

"Well, in August 1936, the Olympics were held in Berlin. All doctors were on duty, in case of injuries to the athletes. Hitler was there to see his supermen dominate this ancient sporting event. When that young colored American, Jesse Owens, won the two hundred-meter race, *Der Führer* left the stadium in a huff. On the way, he stopped here at the hospital. My father, Dr. Gerhard Glosburg, happened through the emergency room. Goebbels beckoned my father. He said *Der Führer* had a severe case of heartburn and wanted something to ease the pain. Hitler also had a reflux problem that caused him a great deal of flatulence."

Bart continued, "What did your father do for him?"

"He fixed him an antacid - two wafers in a glass of seltzer. Hitler gulped it down. I came in when he was drinking it. He belched like the roar of a cannon. He then farted just as loudly."

The courtroom snickers and chuckles grew in volume. Nimitz remained silent. Bart continued his questioning without any change in demeanor. "What happened next?"

"Hitler said, *Herr Doctor, that was good, the heartburn is gone. What's in those tablets?*

"My father replied, *That's a concoction my son and I developed. It is a most recent discovery, mein Führer. It has several ingredients, calcium carbonate, magnesium and...*

"Hitler cut him off. *Tell me why you put it in seltzer water?*

"*For double carbonation, which is impregnated with carbon dioxide. It merely doubles the effervescence and loosens your gas buildup.*

"Hitler congratulated my father. Then he asked me, *Are you his son?*

"*Yes, sir,* I replied.

"*Do you have a lot on hand?*
"*No, we've just perfected it,* my father replied.
"*Can you make a few hundred for me?*
"We assured him we could.
"*Bring it to me at the chancellery.*
"Goebbels wrote our names down. We handed them our cards."
"Did you deliver it to that man?" Bart asked, pointing at Hitler.
"Yes, but he didn't have that face then."
Laughter sounded in the courtroom. The gavel followed.
"Did he know you were Jewish?"
"Not at that time."
"Did your relationship continue?"
"Over the next two years, he sent for various salves for lesions, our ant-acid tablets, laxatives and cathartic medicines. Goebbels used me for his children's pediatrician. Goering had herpes, for which there is no cure. He came to see my father. He gave him ointments to ease the spread of the blisters. The last time we saw Hitler was when he came in for a physical examination. He wanted something done to contain his flatulence. My father advised him to stay away from fatty foods. Hitler said he was a vegetarian. He gave him some double-dosed antacid pills."
"Go on."
"The next day was November 8, 1938, and that became the night of pogroms, *Kristallnacht*. The other doctors and interns were jealous of us for our high Nazi patients. The city went berserk. Someone at the hospital sent a message to Goebbels, which read, *Why do you let dirty Jews like the Glosburgs care for your children?*"
"How did you know about that note?"
"Because the next day, Goebbels sent for me. I went to his office. He pushed the letter at me and yelled, *Is this true?* I affirmed its contents. He shouted at me, *Schweinehund! You and your father don't look like Jews and don't act like Jews. Why didn't you tell us you were Jews?*
"*Because we are German doctors. Our faith doesn't matter. It is our duty to treat you.*
"He asked me, *Germans from where?*
"*From thousands of years ago,* I answered.
"*Damn it! I told the Führer and he said that because of your good services, he advises you and your family to get out of Germany. Arrangements will be made for your whole family to leave before the week is over. Your property will be purchased at fair market price. Here are your exit visas for all of you. Now go, if you want to get out alive.*
"Two Gestapo men came into the office."
"What were they going to do?"
"They were to help round up my family all over Germany, arrange for the sale of our property and make sure we left Germany. The two Gestapo men were direct from Himmler's top staff. I was in a state of shock."

"What happened next?"

"Chaos for me, my family and the city. It was November 9 and the pogrom was still going on. Synagogues were burning, books were being thrown into bonfires, Jews were being beaten in the streets, rocks were thrown at Jewish stores, breaking the windows, and thugs were stealing everything in sight."

Dr. Glosburg was choking down his emotion.

Bart handed him a glass of water, then asked, "Do you want to stop?"

"No, I'll go on. My wife, children, my brothers, sisters, grandparents, my wife's parents and two sisters were rounded up. My house was sold on the spot to a stranger for ten percent of its value. The same thing happened to my brothers, sisters and my wife's family. My father's house was sold at twelve percent of its value. My maternal grandparents got five percent of the worth of the farm."

"Did you and your family salvage any of your valuable possessions and money?"

"Fortunately, I called my grandfather in Munich at his department store and my wife's parents in Frankfurt. In both instances, they were able to wire their bank accounts to a bank in Amsterdam before the Nazis came looking for them. My father and I quickly withdrew all our funds and hid the money in our boxes of medicines and our medical instrument bags. We were allowed to take those with us. The Gestapo agents accepted our bribe."

"What about the furniture and art?"

"No, everything was included in the price of the properties. All we could take was our clothes. We arranged to meet in Essen, which was close to the Netherlands."

"How were you able to get into Holland?"

"My father had lectured on vaccines at the university in Amsterdam. Dr. Wilhelm van Werren, president of the International Medical Society, was a good friend of my father, and he had received several awards from Queen Wilhelmina, so van Werren spoke to the Queen in our behalf. Queen Wilhelmina was very sympathetic to the plight of Jews. In Essen, two Gestapo agents rode in a hired bus with us to the border of Holland. A Colonel Jan Poort, assigned by the Queen, cleared us through immigration and customs. He gave each of us identity cards for political asylum. He had a bus standing by to drive to Amsterdam."

"Where did you reside?"

"Dr. van Werren had us checked into an inexpensive, very clean inn. That night he surprised us by inviting us to a private dining room at the famous Hotel de l'Europe, built in the 1880s. It is one of the outstanding hotels in Europe to this day. This kind gentleman invited six noted doctors and the chief rabbi of Amsterdam, Hans Wilten, to the special welcoming dinner. They asked about conditions in Germany and we validated everything they heard. Then, the talk turned to us and our future. Dr. Van Werren offered my father and myself positions in their Research Center for Disease Studies. It was perfect for us. We had been working on tuberculosis and other bacterial diseases."

"What about housing and jobs for the others?"

"Rabbi Wilten suggested we rent a dairy farm, owned by a widow named Wilma Golden, in the town of Marken. It had two large houses on seventy-five acres. We worked the farm and she gave us a reduced rent and split the profits with us. All food was provided. Her husband had been Jewish and she was Dutch Reformed. She spoke German. She was a kind woman and the arrangement worked out beautifully - until May 10, 1940, when the Nazi blitzkrieg invaded Holland, Belgium, Luxembourg and France. This was the beginning of the end of our short period of euphoria."

"Explain that, Doctor."

"The Gestapo entered Amsterdam and Rotterdam by the hundreds. My father and I could no longer work at the research laboratories in Amsterdam, as Jews were being beaten and sent to labor camps. The farm was thriving. Mrs. Golden went to her church and collected a box full of crucifixes. She made us wear them. We didn't mind. We were Reform Jews, more secular in lifestyle, so, despite sporadic inspections, we continued running the farm."

"You say the euphoria was over. Was that it?"

"No, word of the farm's productivity became known, and the Gestapo came more often and stole most of our produce and dairy products. They took most of the milk and cheese as well. Then came the word on our hidden radio. On January 20, 1942, the Wannsee Conference took place, which created the Final Solution. It meant the extirpation of all the Jews in Europe."

"Where did that news come from?"

"We heard it on the regular BBC broadcasts. They said it was a conference at a villa outside Berlin on Grosser Wannsee, a very wealthy area. Representatives of all the top Nazi departments attended the meeting, which was headed by Reinhard Heydrich. Adolf Eichmann acted as secretary of that session. Present were the chief of the Gestapo, Heinrich Müller, and a list of fifteen handpicked officers. Half of them had medical degrees. They were educated men-educated, I would say, mostly in the art of murder. The report stated that Heydrich, in his address, showed charts where the mass of eleven million Jews in Europe were to be formed for slave labor and eventual execution. We knew our days were numbered."

"Were you able to hide at the farm?"

"Unfortunately not. The Dutch people tried to protect Jews, and many of them were killed for their efforts. One month after the Final Solution decree, the BBC reported that the German people were accusing their neighbors of being Jews. Further, they said that Himmler announced an intensified effort to kill every Jew in Europe before the war ended. How could a cultural Christian country become a nation of savages?"

"Objection," Otto Meissner declared.

"On what grounds?" Nimitz asked.

"This witness is condemning a whole nation."

Nimitz couldn't resist his reply. "Herr Meissner, you were a jurist, obviously well educated. Don't you understand the meaning of a rhetorical question?"

"Yes."

"Was the Third Reich a whole nation, a half-nation or just a few scalawags in a mischievous romp on a hunt for humans instead of wildlife? Or is it your contention, sir, that there was no Holocaust? Just a sportsman's holiday?" Nimitz asked acerbically.

"But, sir…"

"Never mind the *but, sir,* I invite you in a *voir dire* process to take the stand and answer my questions," Nimitz angrily declared.

"No, sir."

"Your objection is overruled. Dr. Glosburg, please continue," Nimitz ordered.

"In July 1942, Himmler came to the farm on an inspection tour with some generals and colonels in their custom-made uniforms. He told Mrs. Golden to line up all the people on the farm. She refused. There were two other autos filled with Gestapo agents. They rounded us all up. He said the farm was being confiscated for the German war effort. As he walked down the line looking at our crucifixes, he stopped and stared at my father. *I know you,* he said. *You're the Jew doctor from the Berlin hospital. I saw you at the chancellery.* As you say in America, he went bananas. *You're all under arrest, you Jew swine! You too, Frau Golden.*"

Glosburg wiped his forehead and drank some water.

"Himmler pointed at one of our produce trucks. *All of them on that truck!* He shouted, *Schnell!* The Gestapo agents hit us with clubs and pushed us onto the truck. We were driven directly to the railroad station, without any of our possessions, and crushed into cattle cars. We couldn't resist them. Guns were pointed at us at all times. Need I tell you of the hallucinations that followed, the smells, the lack of sanitary facilities, bodies crushing against wailing strangers? Three days of torture and indignity. Feces, urine, dead bodies. One woman gave birth prematurely. I helped her by climbing over other people. Another woman took off her dress to use as swaddling clothes for the baby. I had to tear the umbilical cord with my teeth. Another woman gave me her slip to clean up the mother. A man gave me his jacket to cover the baby, who cried all the time. I placed the underweight infant on the mother's chest, pulled her breast out and the baby, by nature's instinct, began suckling the mother's nipple. An hour later the mother died. Another woman, who had been separated from her own newborn baby and was still lactating, took the infant and exposed her breast to its mouth. The heat in that foul-smelling car enervated all of us. Finally we reached our destination."

"Where was that?"

"It was Sobibor, the extermination camp. The doors opened and we were being pulled out as others tried to climb over us to get out. The soldiers yelled, *Schnell, schnell,* rushing us out! They told us to undress. Soon there were several thousand men, women and children stark naked, with armed soldiers standing there making lewd remarks about the size of men's penises, women's breasts, their buttocks and the word bumsen, which means the f-word in English. The animals with the guns kept up their foul-mouthed jeering. They grabbed the premature baby and threw it in a garbage barrel. At one time in my life I was proud to be a German. No more. My family goes back more than a thousand years. My nakedness no longer bothered me as I looked at these sneering soldiers and wondered whose mother had been impregnated to produce these children of the devil. Look at them sitting back there. They know who they are."

Suddenly, there was a disturbance in the back row of the courtroom. An altercation was in progress. Commandants and soldiers were flailing away, attacking each other with their handcuffed fists. It took twenty MPs to club them into order.

Bart addressed the tribunal. "Sirs, may I respectfully suggest a recess and have the combatants separated? I believe there is a serious rift among the ranks and possibly some would like to clear their consciences by testifying their *mea culpas.*"

The defense team remained mute. Nimitz gaveled for a fifteen-minute recess. Bart caught the eyes of Sergeant Lawrence and gestured him forward. Jacques walked up the aisle to appraise the fighting prisoners. Bart put his arm around the MP.

"Sergeant, take a few of your men and see if you can sort out who was punching who. I have a feeling that some of those Waffen SS punks were belting away at the commandants. If they show a willingness to be separated, then those are the guys I want for later interrogation. Go, Laurent is scouting them now. Hurry."

The sorting-out process was completed in ten minutes, and the tribunal was back on the bench.

"What happened at the station, Dr. Glosburg?" Bart asked.

"A Colonel Johann Wolff read off some names in German. He called me, my father and three brothers. *You will go to the barracks with these soldiers. You'll shower there and will be given clothes. The rest will shower up there,* he said, pointing to a building with a metal pipe on the roof disguised as a chimney. Those were the gas chambers. *Take us all,* I told him. They pushed us with bayonets while music played. We showered and cried silently. We were given prison clothing with the Star of David on each of them. I looked out at the railroad station. They were sorting the men's clothes, separating them from the women's. They were cutting the women's hair, actually to baldness. We saw smoke, or rather, exhaust fumes like the emissions of huge trucks. It was carbon monoxide. My family was gone, with the exception of my father and three brothers."

Glosburg began to sob, his chest heaving, tears rolling down his cheeks, but he kept on talking in spurts. "They killed them all, my children, my wife, my sisters, my grandparents, all in a deceitful shower session. When we went out of the barracks, we saw a deep pit with dead bodies piled on top of each other."

Glosburg was having difficulty speaking, so Nimitz gaveled, and said, "We will recess for lunch. Court will resume at 1400 hours. That's 2 p.m."

The prosecution conference room was set up for the usual buffet lunch. U.S. Attorney Washburn and Secret Service agent Witten were there when

Barton and company entered.

"You're welcome to stay for lunch, fellows. What news do you bring us?"

"Both boxes at the bank were opened pursuant to the court order. There was twenty million of flaky paper in Nordheim's box, five million in Paul Mayfield's box, also phony paper," Washburn advised.

"This is about the best counterfeit money we've seen," Witten observed. "I had to give that stuff every possible test. The loot was nearly perfect."

"Okay, Mr. U.S. Attorney, where do you go from here?"

"I called Attorney General Brownell in D.C. Treasury and Justice are trying to sort out cases on the counterfeiters picked up in your Hamburg raid. He told me to bring this case before a grand jury. He wants indictments against Waldo Schlicht, the Swiss source of this paper; Hitler, the two Mayfields, and von Maunder as an unindicted conspirator. The indictments are to be sealed. Von Maunder is to be kept in the U.S. as a material witness. Trials to be held at the conclusion of the war-crimes trials here. Your brother should not print a story of the indictments. He can do a piece about the counterfeit money being paid for the contempt fines. Von Maunder has received enough legitimate cash to pay the fines this afternoon. He will resign as Hitler's lawyer, but will represent some of the Waffen SS bums who have turned on the commandants."

"How did he know they were going to flip-flop?"

"He was in back of the court with Witten and me when the brouhaha broke out. One of the Gestapo men whispered to him that they wanted him for representation, and he agreed. He will ask the court's permission to confer with them. I think he's in chambers now, resigning as Hitler's lawyer."

"Dammit, Forrest, I wanted a shot at that group."

"Von Maunder will willingly let you talk to them. How much longer will your afternoon session go?"

"I'm near the end of Glosburg's testimony. The court will recess early and let the defense start their cross-exam on Monday."

"Then maybe you can confer with von Maunder and his Gestapo clients later today."

"Good. Tell him we'll meet probably around 4 or 4:30 this afternoon."

Glosburg was back on the stand, composed and ready.

"Now, as you related this morning, you, your father and three brothers were spared and the rest of your family was gassed to death, Dr. Glosburg."

"Correct. My father and I were assigned to the infirmary and my three brothers were forced into the most gruesome jobs you can imagine."

"What were those tasks?"

"They were made *Sonderkommandos,* special commandos. One had to sort clothes of the victims while the other two removed the contents of their pockets, etc., tearing the seams of the clothes for hidden objects and money. Then the three of them had to hold the cadavers while men in white jackets and face masks pulled gold fillings from their mouths. One of them was my mother. They were forced to carry the dead bodies to the burial pits. There were hundreds, maybe a thousand in one pit, lying on top of each other.

Trains of forty, fifty, sixty cattle cars were coming in every day. My brothers were in forced labor as *Sonderkommandos*. At the end of July 1942, death operations were suspended for two months for repairs on the Chelmno-Lublin railway. My father and I worked around the clock caring for slave laborers from countries like Austria, the Netherlands, the Soviet Union, Belgium and France. We also had Nazi soldiers, officers and Gestapo agents as patients. I was emotionally ambivalent about keeping these Nazi vermin alive. My father was a firm believer in the Hippocratic Oath to tender to the needs of *all* who needed medical care. He lectured me to take care of everyone. We finally developed a concoction that was mixed with penicillin. It worked."

"You saved some Nazis?"

"Unfortunately, yes. The Nazis and slave-laborer patients were separated into two sections of our infirmary, or mini-hospital. Paradoxically, we cared for two disparate types of patients. One was the camp commandant, Colonel Johann Wolff, and on the other side of the wall was another patient, the chief rabbi of Amsterdam, Hans Wilten. Both were very sick men. One night I was trying to get Colonel Wolff to drink a glass of orange juice mixed with penicillin *chloramphrenical*. He grabbed my arm and said I was trying to kill him. I lost my temper and said, *Arschloch, if I wanted you dead, you'd be in your grave days ago.* He started to laugh and had a choking spell. My father and I gave him an anesthetic relaxant. His coughing stopped. He said, *Cure me and I'll get you out of here.* All I could think of was his gassing of my family. My father put the orange juice mixture to the colonel's lips. He drank it all. In minutes he was asleep from the relaxant. Two days later he was sitting up."

"What happened to Rabbi Wilten?" Bart asked.

"He was cured. In September the trains were delivering more Jews, who went into the gas chambers. A few weeks later the gassing stopped. In October there was an uprising by the Jews. The Nazi guards and those Ukrainian guard bastards opened fire, killing many Jews and preventing the rest of them from reaching the main gate. Rabbi Wilten was leading them away from the exit through the minefields. My father and I saw the colonel firing at the fleeing prisoners. My brothers were running toward the minefield. Commandant Wolff shot and killed two of my brothers. I picked up a semi-automatic gun and aimed it at the colonel. I tripped over a body and my shots struck the colonel in his legs. Despite his leg wound, he fired back and shot my father in his forehead, killing him instantly. I ran to my brothers. Both were dead. I laid on top of them and cried. A giant of a man picked me up and carried me through the minefield. He yelled, *Come on, Doctor! You can't help them.* He put me back on my feet. I still had my semi-automatic. He had one also. We were being chased. He was shooting at the guards. *Shoot!*, he shouted. I turned and sprayed a dozen Ukrainian guards. About three hundred of us escaped. My savior was a Russian Jewish soldier, whom I had treated at the infirmary. He was six feet four and strong as an ox. His name was Dimitri Orloff and he was a former colonel, captured by the Germans. He escaped from a POW camp and was later caught in civilian clothes in Bohemia, then shipped to Sobibor. The Russians were coming from the East. Orloff was bitterly anti-communist, anti-Ukrainian and anti-Lithuanian. He spoke English and fair German. He didn't want to go east to the Russian troops. Eventually we hid in the forest. I had several crucifixes in my pocket. We caught up to a hundred of the escaped prisoners. I questioned them about my one brother who escaped. They said he was slightly wounded in his shoulder, but was all right. He was somewhere ahead of us, about five miles. Some of the men had guns. They decided that Dimitri should be their leader. We moved that night and caught up with fifty more of our survivors. My brother, Phillip, two years my senior, was there, lying on the ground with a fever. I examined his wound and cleaned it up as best I could. He tried to hug me. I made him lie still. Dimitri scouted ahead. In half an hour he was back. He was carrying some towels, and pulled a bottle of aspirin out of his prisoner's uniform pocket. I forced two aspirins down Phillip's throat. He swallowed. Dimitri told us there was an unoccupied farmhouse one mile from where we were. Very quietly, we crawled to the site. Dimitri and I carried my brother."

Dr. Glosburg stopped and reached for a glass of water. The court was captivated with his account. The press was eating it up.

He continued, "Dimitri ordered the men with guns to surround the house. He found a kerosene lamp, lit it and explored the interior. There were several more lamps, which were lighted. In the basement, we found canned soups, hams, Polish salami, sausages, and hundreds of mason jars filled with fruit. There was wine, cider, Polish vodka, beer, and fifty loaves of bread, fairly fresh. A hundred and fifty men were fed. Jews were eating cheese sandwiches. Dimitri convinced the men not to get drunk on the wine and beer. We found medical supplies in one of the bathrooms. I immediately attended my brother. I washed his wound with alcohol and with a sharp kitchen knife, which I burned until it was red hot, I cut the bullet out of Phillip's shoulder. Dimitri kept his hand on Phillip's mouth. He was screaming in pain and finally passed out. I found a needle and thread, then sewed him up."

"Was he all right?"

"Perfect. Several men stayed on guard while we slept on the floor, in beds, on couches and in chairs. Just before daylight, the men on watch raced in and told us a truck was coming up the hill. Dimitri ordered us out of the house and doused all the lamps. Men grabbed knives, pitchforks, hammers, screwdrivers and sticks. We hid behind the house and the bushes around the entrance."

"Who was on that truck?"

"Ten Ukrainian soldiers. They seemed jolly and drunk. None of them were armed. When all ten of them approached the door, Dimitri shouted in Russian, *Hands up! High!* The armed men surrounded the ten men. Not a shot was fired. They were told to lie flat on the ground. One of the men said, *We are with the Russian army.* I yelled in German, *We are German!* He replied, *No, we are on the German side!* I bent over and yelled in his ear, *I thought so! You were at Sobibor, you scummy bastards!* Dimitri said to me, *That was very good, Doc.*" Glosburg stopped again, drank more water and wiped his face.

"What happened next?"

"We made them strip naked and tied them up with baling cord. Several of us discovered thirty semi-automatic rifles with lots of ammunition. We checked the house again in the daylight and found fifty pairs of overalls. Dimitri found a man's suit that fit him. We drew lots for the overalls and shirts. There were odd pairs of pants and jackets there. Dimitri took one of the men into the basement and, after a severe beating, the man told him that the owner of the farm and his fifteen employees had been lined up and shot. They were buried in a pit in the woods."

"Did he find out where they were coming from that night?"

"Yes, there was a small Polish town occupied by Waffen SS troops, about fifty of them. They all gathered in the evening at a restaurant and bar. It had a music player. Polish girls used to come in to dance with them."

"Were there any other troops nearby?"

"He said about ten miles west of there. Dimitri told him that if he was being untruthful, the ten men would be executed that night. In searching them, we found ten thousand German marks, IDs, rings, watches and other jewelry taken from dead Jews. We took the naked men and locked them up in the barn and stationed fifty of our men as guards outside the barn, with orders to kill if any attempted to escape. Dimitri picked ten of the healthiest German Jews and made them don the German uniforms. If they didn't fit right, he picked someone else. Pretty soon he had a realistic squad of German soldiers, fully armed. He trained them all afternoon on how to act, how to shoot and how to walk. All of them knew the motions from their experience as German citizens who had observed the Nazis."

"What was going to happen next?"

"At nightfall he drove the truck in his civilian suit with his ten Jewish soldiers in Nazi uniforms to the town of Osowa. On the outskirts of town, two Waffen SS officers were chatting with two Polish girls on a bench by a small park. The truck stopped. Dimitri smiled at the Gestapo officers, alighted from his truck and in German, introduced himself as General Lubov of the Ukrainian army. He said he had ten thousand Ukrainian troops in the forest this side of Sobibor. They wanted to join up with the German troops. While they were talking, the ten men got off to stretch. A Gestapo officer drew a sketch, showing them where the German troops were. They explained that Russians were on the move, heading west. They pinpointed where all units were. They saluted, anxious to woo the girls. At a small signal from Dimitri, the ten men surrounded the Gestapo officers while he pointed his Walther gun at them. They were forced onto the truck with the two girls. Quickly they drove back to the farm."

"Quite a story, Doctor."

"All of it is true. I had the job of questioning the girls, who were thoroughly frightened. The Gestapo officers were a *Hauptmann,* or captain, and a colonel. They were stripped naked. Their guns and ID came in handy. Dimitri was very tough. He took them one at a time, naked, beat the hell out of them and got all the information about Osowa, the exact location of Gestapo headquarters, the layout of the town and the details of the restaurant. He pieced their stories together and they fit."

"All right, what about the girls?" Bart asked.

"They revealed that the townspeople hated the Nazis. The Germans had beaten up a lot of their people and killed quite a few. The Gestapo officers were trying to seduce them. They wanted to take the girls to the local hotel they occupied. Both girls were decent Catholic students and were acting pleasant with the two Nazis out of fear."

"What did you do with them?"

"They told us their brothers and father were with a partisan group of one hundred men halfway south of Osowa and were waiting for the right time to attack. They were fully armed. The girls offered to lead us to them. I showed them my crucifix. They blessed me and cried with joy."

"All right, Doctor, bring us to the climax," Bart urged.

Glosburg smiled. "The colonel's Gestapo uniform fit Dimitri perfectly. The captain's fit me. We put the two naked, bloodied men in the cellar, bound and gagged, with ten men to watch them. We got back on the truck. When we got close to the forest, the two girls led us to where the partisans were. We carried white handkerchiefs to prevent any accidental shooting. The girls' father and two brothers pointed guns at us. The girls yelled, *No, no! They are partisans too!* They explained in Polish what had happened. Dimitri understood everything that was said. In short order we were embraced and became part of their partisan group. Dimitri waved his crucifix at the men. The next hour was spent planning a midnight attack. The girls were to go to the restaurant and dance with the men. To make a long story short, the partisans had three trucks. We went ahead. The first target was the Gestapo headquarters. We captured thirty-nine men without a shot. We surrounded the restaurant and broke in from the front and back and captured twelve more. All the girls were chased home."

"No further questions."

Nimitz announced, "We defer the cross-examination to Tuesday, February 24, at 0900. The court has other business in Washington. Court's adjourned."

Bart and his team hurried to the conference room. Shortly after they arrived, an MP announced, "U.S. Attorney Washburn, Secret Service agent Witten and counselor von Maunder would like to join you."

"Send them in," Bart ordered.

The trio was seated. Von Maunder advised the group that he no longer represented Hitler.

"Then why are you here, Counselor?"

"General, I assure you that my position here is not adversarial. Off the record, I will state to all of you that I am in a total state of shock from what has been adduced in this trial. Yes, I admit I was sent here not so much to defend Hitler as to protect the names of the Swiss bankers. What can I say but *mea culpa*? However, as a matter of personal conscience, I have agreed to represent six ex-soldiers who are willing to become prosecution witnesses."

"Are you seeking a deal of clemency for these men?"

"No deal. Clemency is entirely up to you and the tribunal. I believe, from what I've heard from these men, that fairness will prevail."

"Are they prepared to make statements to be recorded without any conditions being offered or accepted?" Bart asked.

"Yes, I have advised them to do so. I'm appearing for them on a *pro bono* basis. This will undoubtedly affect my legal career in Switzerland, but I am sick of the Swiss banking charade."

"In the interest of comity, I will accept your statement at face value, but..."

Von Maunder interrupted, "General, your used of the word *comedy* is disconcerting."

"No, no, Counselor, I did not say *comedy*. The word is c-o-m-i-t-y, pronounced *comity*, which means goodwill, friendliness, courtesy," Bart laughed.

"Oh, forgive me, General. Thank you. Sorry I interrupted you."

"Let me repeat. In the interest of *common courtesy*, I have to ask a difficult question to clear the atmosphere."

"What is that, sir?"

"You may or may not be fully aware of my background. In short, Mr. von Maunder, I personally have seen the results of this Nazi carnage. I visited the death camps when our troops liberated those butcher shops. Can you honestly say to me that you and your fellow Swiss citizens were unaware of the atrocities being committed by the Germans?"

There was a moment of silence. Cartman, Sophia, Tony, Maybrook, Jacques and the others focused on von Maunder's flushed countenance.

Von Maunder took a deep breath and sighed, "General Milburn, I am at least twenty-nine years your senior. While I feel I am on trial here, and deservedly so, I will give you a straightforward answer."

"That will be a breath of fresh air," Jacques snidely interpolated.

"The Swiss population was dedicated to maintaining a neutral position in this disgraceful war. In fact, actually we were not neutral in doing business with the Nazi government. Yes, we were cowardly. We heard of the Nazi *Endlösung,* or *Final Solution.* But, human nature being what it is, as a people in self-interest, we closed our eyes and mouths. I admit there are a lot of anti-Semites in our country. This is so in America also and the world over. Our leaders didn't want to incur the enmity of those madmen in Germany, especially that of Hitler. We are a small country."

"Herr von Maunder, you represent the Swiss bankers. They are hoarding the ill-gotten plunder of the Jews by holding onto their money," Bart said.

"I cannot condone their conduct in this matter. But, as you Americans proudly proclaim, a man is innocent unless proven guilty. Even murderers in your country are guaranteed legal representation. I'm not proud of my position, but I am prepared to cut my ties to these banks. My golden years are at hand. I am a religious Protestant. I'll beg God's forgiveness. The power in banking is Waldo Schlicht. He's a dangerous man."

"Not for long," Washburn declared.

"All right, Counselor, let's get on with these six potential witnesses. One at a time, or en masse," Bart said.

"Bring them all in here, sir. You'll get more coherence, plus you will be able to judge them as a group. These are not high-ranking officers," von Maunder advised.

"We've segregated them from the other slimeballs," Jacques said.

"Let's have them."

Jacques picked up the phone to the duty officer. After a few short words, he hung up. "They're on the way," he said.

While they waited for the prisoners, von Maunder said, "General, I'm too old to attempt to ingratiate myself with you and your associates here, but I am compelled to say you are one of the finest lawyers I've ever encountered, and your staff deserves my praise."

"We accept your compliments in the spirit intended," Bart replied.

The MPs knocked on the door. Jacques opened it and six cuffed and leg-chained prisoners entered. The bedraggled group was a far cry from the Nazis' halcyon days of Goebbels' propagandist panoplies and Hitler's *Sieg Heils!* All were in their thirties. Some of their faces were bruised as a result of their fisticuffs in the courtroom.

Von Maunder reached into his briefcase and passed around copies of a list of the six men. The sheets stated their ages, birthplaces, and camps to which they were assigned.

The hapless group attempted to salute with both hands manacled.

"English or Deutsch?" Bart snapped.

"*Deutsch, mein General*," their spokesman, Ulbrecht, declared.

They were aware of Bart's flawless German, having heard him in court. Bart asked Phil Berger to interpret for the group. In German, Bart asked each man to identify himself.

"I am Rudolph Kenner, thirty years old. I was stationed at Auschwitz."

"Friedrich Schultz, thirty-two, Sobibor."

"Max Klinger, thirty-four, Treblinka."

"Karl Ulbrecht, thirty-four, Chelmno and Auschwitz."

"Albert Engel, thirty-three, Mauthausen."

"Otto Schwengler, thirty, Belzec."

"All from the death camps," Bart observed. "My quick calculation indicates you were all in the regular Germany army in your teens. Were you all Nazis?"

"*Jawohl*," they answered.

Ulbrecht raised his manacled hands.

"What is it, Karl?"

Ulbrecht switched into English, "My family didn't believe in the Nazi cause. My father told me that Hitler, Himmler, Goering, Goebbels, Hess and the whole bunch of ass-kissers were going to destroy Germany. I never told anyone about that."

"How did you become a Nazi?"

"I was a student in my second year at Heidelberg University. I was drafted into the Army in 1937 at the age of eighteen. I was considered a *Wunderkind* and entered the university when I was sixteen."

"Are you still a Nazi?"

"Hell, no."

"Where did you learn English?"

"In New York City. I was there from age five to eleven, living with my uncle, my father's brother. I went to school there. I had to go back to Germany in 1930 when my uncle died of a heart attack. His wife was an American and she couldn't support me and her three children."

"Interesting. How did you wind up at Chelmno?" he asked in German.

"I was wounded at the Russian front. Shot in the leg."

He tried to show his wound by lifting his right pants leg.

"Jacques, take their handcuffs off."

Laurent reached in his pocket, produced a key and began removing their handcuffs. Ulbrecht lifted his pants and showed a two-inch scar.

"I was sent to a hospital somewhere in Poland. I'm not sure where it was. After I was discharged from the hospital, I was assigned to guard duty at Chelmno."

Bart went through the whole list. Questions were directed at each one by Berger and the others. Berger and Bart did the interpretations. Von Maunder pressed them to detail all the atrocities they had observed.

As each one talked, they became more open and graphic in their descriptions of the mass murders by gassing, firing squad killings, individual tortures, slave labor until exhaustion and death. They described how people starved to death. Gang rapes by the numbers. The horrors filled six tapes and many pages of notes. They named the commandants and the Gestapo officers. The Jews were stripped and robbed of everything, including gold fillings from their dead bodies.

"Did any of you participate in the killings?" Bart snapped.

Klinger spoke up.

"The killing was done by the commandants and the Gestapo officers. We were all privates in the army there as guards at the barracks for the Jewish laborers. But we saw everything. The Gestapo treated the soldiers like dirt at Treblinka. Sometimes they needed us to carry the dead bodies to throw them in pits. Babies, young men and women, old men and women, children."

Ulbrecht declared, "The same thing happened at Chelmno. In 1943 I was sent to Auschwitz. It was worse there. Like animals, five or six Gestapo raped one girl at a time. This happened quite often. When they were finished with the girls, they shot them and we had to put them in the crematoriums."

The soul-purging went on for hours. Honest tears flowed from the eyes of the men recanting the horrors.

"All right, now, why are you confessing all this?" Bart finally asked.

"Because we heard the witnesses tell such terrible stories, we decided that the commandants and Hitler were really the guilty ones. Why should we be classified as *war criminals*? That's how the fight started in the courtroom. We don't expect anything from you Americans. We just don't want the world to think we are all animals like them. We also realize from this trial that

Hitler, *Der Führer*, is crazy. He is a sick *Arschloch*," Schwengler cried out.

Bart lit a cigarette, stood up and looked each of the men eyeball to eyeball. He stood tall and formidable. He had their attention. They showed signs of dread. Then, in carefully phrased German, he demanded in an authoritarian tone, "Be careful how you answer this question. The truth and nothing else, understood?"

They nodded affirmatively.

"How did you wind up with the Waffen SS in Argentina?"

The question hit them with the force of a grenade. They looked at each other for a spokesman.

"Come on, boys, a truthful answer," von Maunder urged.

Ulbrecht accepted the challenge. "Herr General, I will explain and ask the indulgence of everyone here not to connect us with the information I will give you now. If the word gets out that this came from us, our families in Germany will be killed. This is one of the best kept secrets since the war."

"You can count on that," Bart growled.

"As you know, Nazi war criminals are being hunted all over the world. There are lots of Nazis in West Germany today hiding out and waiting to get to South America to avoid war crime trials. There is an enclave just outside of Dortmund, where there are over two hundred Nazi officers hiding out, waiting for a chance to leave Germany. One day, Heinrich Müller came to the place. He wanted twenty-five men to come with him to Hamburg. He said it was for a special job for a Jewish philanthropist. It would pay good money. When he mentioned a Jew, almost everyone hissed at him. *Fuck the Jew!* they yelled at him. The six of us were in the lower ranks and didn't mingle with the officers. We put our hands up. We needed money. We were trying to escape from Germany because we worked at concentration camps and would be branded war criminals. Twenty other men volunteered. We figured if we could make some money, we would find a way to escape. Heinrich Müller was the SS *Gruppenführer*, head of the Gestapo. They called him Gestapo Müller. He had a bus waiting. They drove us to the pier at Hamburg at midnight. We boarded a ship called the Lone Eagle. Little did we realize that we were going to Argentina. When we got there, we were taken to the Nordheim ranch and sworn into the Gestapo. He paid us five thousand American dollars each. Then you came and captured all of us."

"That had better be a true story. As you know, we captured Gestapo Müller," Bart said.

"Sir, that's the exact truth."

"What happened to your money?"

"We mailed it to a Swiss bank."

"Which one?"

"Banque Lorraine in Geneva."

"Lotsa luck," Jacques chortled.

"All right, back to your cells. We'll check your story, then tomorrow we'll move you to better accommodations with better food. Don't cross me, and be ready to testify. Counselor von Maunder will represent you. Goodnight," Bart finished, and waved them out.

CHAPTER NINE

Monday, February 23, 1953 - 11:45 p.m. - New York City

A northeast blizzard pummeled the city with 40-mile-an-hour winds, and two feet of snow blanketed the metropolis in six hours.

At the Rex Towers on Sutton Place, facing the East River, a bleached blonde woman, overly rouged, her lips brightly colored with Revlon's latest Fire and Ice lipstick, nervously paced the thickly carpeted living room floor of the penthouse. She puffed on a gold-tipped cigarette and took turns checking her amply applied mascara and staring out of the floor-to-ceiling double-paned window. Despite the well-heated co-op duplex apartment, she kept adjusting her fluffy furred mink scarf over a tight-fitting black gown. Wind gusts rattled the windows, and the telephone resonantly rang three times before she picked up the receiver.

"Where the hell are you?" she rasped.

"I'm in a phone booth at Fifty-ninth and First."

"What the hell are you doing there? We can't leave in this weather."

"Honey, relax and listen. Get Pete the doorman out of the lobby. I spotted him there as my cab drove by."

"How do I do that?" she asked throatily.

"Baby, it's simple. You have that extra makeup kit in the right side pocket of the Rolls Royce. Make him come up to get the car keys from you and to bring the kit to you. Wait five minutes before you call him. That will give me enough time to take the other elevator to the fifteenth floor. When I hear him leave you after he brings the kit, I'll walk up one flight on the service steps to our kitchen. Leave that door open."

"Gotcha," she said, and slammed the phone receiver down.

A man with a wide-brimmed fur hat, curls along his ears, a full mustache and a very long beard, in the guise of an Hassidic rabbi, handed the cab driver fifty dollars and ran under the canopy to the second elevator. At the fifteenth floor, he walked to the service exit door and strode briskly to the penthouse kitchen.

The woman heard the service door close, so she raced into the kitchen.

"Alden, darling - oh my God! Who the hell are you?" she screamed.

"It's me, Lilly," replied Alden Gaines, tossing the hat onto the kitchen table. Then he gently pulled the gum-pasted beard and mustache from his florid face. He discarded the long coat and hugged her. "My *cajones* are frozen. That wind is like an icicle flying through me," he groaned.

"Go take a hot shower. We can't fly out of here tonight anyway," Lilly said. "Where's the money?"

"Three bags full, my master," she retorted huskily. "What's with that masquerade costume?"

"Just caution. I don't know who the hell may be watching this place, or whether I was being followed. I wore that getup all the way from Kansas City on a TWA flight. They even served me some kosher food," he laughed.

"Alden, no one would connect you with this apartment. I only rented it a month ago, and you're never here. What's the real scam?"

"Let me shower and I'll fill you in. By the way, honey, you've got too much makeup on. Take it off."

He came out of the shower in silk pajamas, covered by a white terrycloth robe. She handed him a glass of Haig & Haig scotch and fixed one for herself. Without the heavy makeup, she was quite an attractive woman.

"Cheers, honey. Now you look like the real Lilly Darcy, the famous Academy Award-winning actress."

"Famous, my ass. Besides, *Thursday at Eleven* was over three years ago and I haven't done a film since."

"Maybe you'll do one in Europe."

"Okay, what's the scam?"

"I skipped out of the trial because those bastards, Hitler and the Mayfield brothers, were passing counterfeit money around. One of those idiot lawyers paid contempt-of-court fines with that phony money. The also are trying to connect me with the attack on the fort. They'll try to blame me for the counterfeit, too, I'm sure. That's why we're going to that villa in St. Tropez. It's a hangout for the film crowd. Directors, producers, writers, and actors all over the place. They start arriving next month."

Lilly brightened up, leaned over and kissed him. "Sweetheart, you're so thoughtful. I love you."

"Lilly, did you have any trouble picking up that money this morning?"

"None at all. I went to the warehouse, opened your locker, and a nice young man carried those three heavy bags to the Rolls. I gave him twenty dollars and made his day."

"Lilly, baby, how much money do you think is in those bags?" Gaines asked, with a Cheshire grin on his face.

"A lot, I hope?"

"Hold onto this couch, baby - are you ready for this?"

"Don't tease me."

"There is twenty million of good American dollars, plus five million in diamonds."

"You've got to be kidding!"

"No, sugar, I stashed that away after I was paid by a Swiss banker to represent Hitler and the Mayfields. It was given to me here at the Waldorf Astoria and I immediately stashed it in that warehouse. Rainy-day money. Better, I say, for a snowy day," he smirked as he pointed at a large window caked with flakes.

"Alden, dear, why are we booked on a Swissair flight if we're going to the French Riviera?"

"Honey, I've got to dump this money in a Swiss bank in Geneva. I want to open an account there so we can draw checks whenever we need money. I'm going to call Swissair now and see what they say about this storm."

He was on the phone for twenty minutes. She handed him drinks and cigarettes. Finally he hung up.

"Lilly, Swissair thinks this storm will last at least four days. I tried Air France. They have a flight out of Washington to Paris on Wednesday at 8 a.m. We can get a flight from Paris to Geneva and do our business in Geneva. We can leave that night for Nice. It's a short car ride from there to St. Tropez. I booked us first class. Are you all packed?"

"Yes."

"We'll leave in the morning in the Rolls. I'll have the Rolls shipped to us by Monarch AirFreight. How does that sound to you?"

"Great. Let's get some sleep now. No hanky-panky tonight, Alden."

"I can wait. I'm tired too."

☆ ☆ ☆ ☆

Tuesday, February 24, 1953 - 0900 hours - Fort Leavenworth

The tribunal was in place. Nimitz asked for the defense to begin their cross-examination. Dr. Arthur Glosburg was in the witness chair. Otto Meissner began the cross-examination in German. "Good morning, Dr. Glosburg."

"Morning."

Meissner's tone was deceivingly friendly. "You had a good education in Germany?"

"Yes."

"You are a successful doctor here in the United States?"

"I am not practicing medicine now, although I am licensed to do so."

"Explain, please, what you are doing now."

"I am researching medical cures for a variety of diseases."

"That is a noble endeavor."

"Thank you."

"Had you not been educated in Germany, you would not have the skills to do this work, is that correct?" Meissner asked, toying with him.

"Which Germany?"

Meissner turned his back to the witness, polished his glasses, adjusted them on the tip of his nose and stared over the rims, contemplating the minefield contained in the doctor's answer.

"The Germany you were born in, Herr Doctor."

"Yes, the same Germany you were born in, Judge Otto Meissner, the famous jurist in the Weimar Republic of Germany."

"Doctor, you are playing with me?"

"Not at all, Judge Meissner. I was educated in a cultural, religious and intellectual country until it became a jungle of savages called Nazi Germany. I was educated in the good Germany, just like you were."

"You are a bitter man, Herr Doctor."

"What would you be if the bad Germany wantonly robbed and killed your family because they did not believe in Nazi paganism?"

"Herr Hitler arranged to get your family out of Germany, did he not?" Meissner pressed.

"No, he drove us out. The Nazis stole our possessions and eventually destroyed everything in their path, killing my family and eleven million helpless individuals, six million of them Jews. How can you stand there in good conscience and call me a bitter man? I know your history."

"Enough, enough. I object, Your Honor. The witness is not responsive to my questions."

"Counselor, you let him respond to your characterization of him as a bitter man. He explained. Continue."

"You say you know my history. What has that to do with a simple answer to my first question, which dealt with your education in Germany?"

"Sir, you were born in Germany, in 1878, and rose to be a respected jurist. You became chief of the chancellery under Ebert, Hindenburg, and then came that Austrian street-bum interloper who destroyed the good Germany in which I was educated. My family goes back more than a thousand years, and that Austrian bum becomes a German citizen in 1932 and turns beautiful Germany into a slaughterhouse. Aren't you ashamed of yourself?"

The spectators applauded. Meissner stood still, silent and red-faced. He took a large handkerchief from his back pocket and mopped his face. His discomfort was obvious. He looked back at Hitler and shook his head in negation and disgust. He turned and looked at Dr. Glosburg, spread his arms, shrugged his shoulders and quickly said, "No further questions, Herr Doctor."

His shame was patently clear to all. The seventy-five-year-old man slowly walked to his table, picked up his briefcase and left the courtroom.

"*Alter Arschloch, Dummkopf!*" Hitler shouted at Meissner.

"You may step down," Nimitz told the witness.

Court was recessed for lunch. The prosecution retired to their conference room. They were strangely quiet during lunch. Meissner's dramatic exit from the courtroom had been the first sign of a conscience in the Nazi ranks.

Bart was musing the septuagenarian jurist's discomfort, weighing the question, *Does he deserve sympathy or was he just a money-hungry lawyer?* He smoked a cigarette and drank his coffee silently.

Sophia pierced the quietude with the question, "Bart, I didn't quite catch Hitler's remarks when Meissner said *No further questions.* What did he say?"

Bart looked up at her, took a drag on his cigarette, expelled the smoke and replied, "That little cretin called Meissner an *old asshole idiot.* That former street bum was reverting to type. In his best days, he couldn't shine Meissner's shoes. That old man was a legal giant in the pre-Nazi era."

"Obviously, Meissner's conscience was affected by the atrocity testimony," Berger observed.

"I am ambivalent about it all," Bart responded. "This man was one of the most revered government officials of the German Weimar Republic. He was chief of the presidential chancellery prior to the Nazi takeover. A great legal mind and a career government servant. A jurist, highly respected but ignored by the Nazis. In desperation, Hitler sends for him for this trial. But what bothers me is why the hell he stayed in Nazi Germany, and was he ignorant of the extirpation of the Jews?"

"I doubt that God will forgive him, and neither will I," Jacques growled. "Until one German walks in the shoes of a Jew, he will never understand the meaning of the atrocities and the pain of each individual victim of the Holocaust. Let him go back to Germany and make them remember the evil that was committed during the years of 1933 to 1945. And I might add, the beat still goes on. Fuck all anti-Semites, the closet types and the overt ignorant *schmucks.*"

Bart looked at his adopted brother, Jacques, with compassion and understanding. "He has said it all. Who can say it better?"

The subject was closed, and the afternoon session was called to order.

"Your next witness, General," Nimitz declared.

A blue-eyed, flaxen-haired, twenty-year-old womanl in a crimson-belted navy blue dress walked between two husky MPs to the witness stand. The audience was riveted by the beauty, personality and composure of this unusual witness. She did not have the look of a suffering Holocaust survivor. She spoke perfect English.

After the oath was administered, Bart asked, "Please state your name for the record."

"Bessie Lowen, but people call me Beth."

"Very well, Beth, where were you born?"

"In Amsterdam, the Netherlands, on December 19, 1932."

"When the war began, you were six years old, is that correct?"

"Yes, sir, but the war began September 1, 1939. We were attacked by the Germans on May 10, 1940. So, the war really began for us then. I was seven years old at that time."

Bart smiled, "I see...correct. You were seven when the Nazis invaded Holland, Belgium, Luxembourg and France."

"Objection! Counsel is testifying," Luther Krieger called out, rising.

"Are you objecting to the facts contained in that question, Mr. Krieger? Would you prefer that the information imparted by the prosecutor be elicited piece by piece from the witness?" Nimitz snidely inquired.

"Objection withdrawn."

"Do you remember my question?" Bart asked.

"Yes. I was seven years old when the Nazis invaded Holland, Belgium, Luxembourg and France."

A titter swept the courtroom.

"Are you repeating my question, or did you know that before I asked?"

"Sir, I know the entire evil history of Germany's Third Reich. It was my obsession to study the carnage committed by them on all of Europe."

"Obsession? Would you like to explain the use of that word?"

"Certainly. These Nazi savages committed such crimes against humanity that, by the age of thirteen, when they were thoroughly defeated, I began and am still studying how a civilized cultural country like Germany could have been metamorphosed into a nation of monsters. Yes, sir, it is an obsession with me. I haven't found the answer yet."

"Objection. The witness's obsession is not germane to issues before this tribunal. Her conjectures about Germany per se are pure propaganda. I move to have her remarks stricken from the record," Krieger said.

"The witness is a survivor of the Nazis' breach of every tenet, written or not, of human behavior against innocent, non-combatant civilians. Her observations validate all that has been adduced by prior witnesses. Her testimony will confirm her last statement. I ask the court to hear her out before ruling on the objection," Bart pleaded.

"Mr. Krieger, the court will hold ruling on your objection to allow the prosecution to lay a foundation for the witness's observations regarding Germany."

"No, no, we object now," Krieger persisted.

"Yes, yes, Mr. Krieger. Please be seated," Nimitz ordered.

"Miss Lowen, you are of the Jewish faith?"

"Yes."

"Are you a survivor of the Holocaust?"

"Yes."

"Objection! Counsel is leading the witness."

"Do you want a play-by-play description of what constitutes the Holocaust, Mr. Krieger?" said Nimitz.

"My client, Mr. Nordheim, contends that there never was a Holocaust. He states..."

Nimitz hammered the gavel furiously. "Stop right there, Mr. Krieger. First of all, do you have two clients, one Nordheim and the other Hitler? If so, whom do you represent? Stop this charade. Adolf Hitler, alias Frederick Nordheim, is one and the same. Are you telling this court that the Third Reich of Germany, in its reign of terror, did not commit the Holocaust?"

"Not me personally. I am repeating my client's statement."

"Which client?"

Krieger leaned over to Hitler and engaged in a heated colloquy. Nimitz waited patiently for a reply. "With apologies to the tribunal, my client, Adolf Hitler, will testify, against my advice, when the defense presents its case."

"That's his privilege, Mr. Krieger. Just don't try to slow down the progress of this case with frivolous objections. In Nazi Germany, there would be no trials. Now, let's get on with it," Nimitz caustically demanded.

"Beth, tell the court your family background," Bart said.

"My father, Dirk van Lowen, was a prominent lawyer in the Netherlands. He served on the Hague Tribunal and was a member of the upper chamber of Parliament. Just before the invasion of Poland, the Labor Party, the Catholic People's Party, and the Calvinist Party couldn't arrive at a coalition government. They finally chose my father as Premier. Holland is not an anti-Semitic country. There was no uproar over a Jew in that position. Queen Wilhelmina was a good friend of our family."

"Tell us about your whole family," Bart urged.

"My mother, Margaret, was in the art business. She collected art, antiques and other collectibles. She had a thriving shop for tourists. She also lectured on Dutch art. She raised my two brothers, Vincent and Jan, my sister Lucille and me. I was the youngest."

"How about grandparents, uncles, aunts and cousins?"

"Apart from the six of us in the immediate family, we had twenty-two other relatives. Some in The Hague, Rotterdam and Amsterdam."

"Where are they now?"

"All in Nazi crematoriums, with the exception of my brother, Vincent." Her eyes were moist, her voice soft and steady.

There was an audible gasp throughout the courtroom. Bart, in a dramatic pause, reached for some tissues and a glass of water. He silently handed the items to the young lady. She patted her eyes and carefully sipped the water. Staring at the defendant, she raised her hand and pointed to the rear of the courtroom.

"Who are you pointing at?"

"Those two men."

"Who are they?" Bart asked.

"That one on the right in the second row was the commandant at Buchenwald, Lieutenant Hermann Pister. The other one in the next row behind him was the commandant at Mauthausen, Colonel Franz Saukel."

"Will the court please order those men to stand?"

"Rise, you two men."

Both stood up.

"Yes, that's them. I'll never forget those faces. Two monsters."

"All right, sit," Nimitz ordered.

"How did you come to know those men?" Bart asked.

"I have to go back to when those Nazi hoodlums invaded our neutral country," she continued. "Our brave forces fought them off at The Hague. The Nazis were trying to capture the airfields there, but our infantry and artillery drove them away."

"You were only seven years old. How did you know what was happening?"

"I heard my father talking to our generals. I remember it as though it was happening right now. German planes were flying all over us. Parachutes were bringing troops to the ground. Their main drive then was to capture Rotterdam. My father spoke to Winston Churchill, who had become Prime Minister that day."

"Did you hear his conversation?"

"Yes. My brothers, sister and my mother were in that room. We lived in a large house, just south of Amsterdam, halfway to Hilversum. We shaded all the windows, turned off all the lights and used candlelight. My father was telling Mr. Churchill that our troops were holding off the Nazis from The Hague, which is the de facto capital of the Netherlands. The Nazis were trying to capture Queen Wilhelmina. Churchill told my father that two British destroyers would pick up the Queen and all the members of government. He told my father to leave with her, but my father refused. He said he would try to negotiate with the Germans. He then called the Queen and made arrangements for her and our officials to leave for London."

"Too bad your family didn't leave."

"The Nazis are the scum of the earth. They are the most immoral, indecent, duplicitous animals in the history of the world. What they did to Rotterdam is proof of that. History confirms that. Four days after the invasion, they…"

Krieger roared, "Objection!"

"To what?" Nimitz coolly asked.

"She wasn't old enough to tell us what happened in Rotterdam."

"Come, come, Mr. Krieger, her age isn't being contested here. I'm sure you, as well as the rest of us, have memories from our childhood that are vivid in our minds to the day of our deaths. Overruled."

Bart quickly asked, "What happened at Rotterdam?"

"A German officer, with a white flag, crossed the bridge to Rotterdam. He told our people they would bomb the city if they didn't surrender. My father told them to do so, rather than have the Luftwaffe destroy the city and kill a lot of civilians." She paused and wiped a tear away.

"What happened?"

"As our people were accepting their terms, German bombers flew over our heads and dropped bombs. They blew up most of Rotterdam, killing thousands of civilians and making one hundred thousand or more homeless. Even in wars, they are monsters. They can't be trusted. Those orders came from that filthy, syphilitic maniac who pretended to be a Jew, Adolf Schickelgruber, an Austrian alien who is too rotten to be a Jew."

Krieger and three other lawyers yelled objections. A burst of applause muted their remarks. Nimitz, Chennault and Smith rose after a fifteen-minute recess was called, leaving the open-mouthed lawyers protesting. In chambers, the three hardened warrior jurists were enjoying their first hearty laugh since the trial began.

"That young lady is very special," Smith chuckled. "Did you see the look on Hitler's face?"

"He was livid," Chennault said.

"I called the recess to let the media have a ball with her description of *Der Führer*," Nimitz added. "I'll have to sustain their objections."

"Certainly, but the damage is done," Smith agreed.

The tribunal was back on the bench, and before Krieger could address the court, Nimitz said, "Your objection is sustained. However, next time only one lawyer may rise, not the whole bunch of you. Please continue, Miss Lowen."

"By the end of the month, King Leopold of Belgium surrendered. My father had reached agreement with Arthur Seyss-Inquart, the Nazi Reich Commissioner, not to ransack the country. He turned out to be a liar. They plundered the country. On May 24th my father was distressed. The British, French and Belgian forces were locked in at Dunkirk. The Nazi tanks could have destroyed them or made them surrender. My father used a dirty word for Hitler, but he was happy."

"What did he say that made him change from being distressed to being happy?"

She hesitated and then said, "Do you want his exact words?"

"Yes, please."

"That *schmuck* Hitler ordered his troops to stop. That's how all the British, French and Belgian troops were shuttled to England. He's no genius; he's what the Americans call a *stumblebum*. I later learned what those words meant."

Laughter came from the press row.

"Now, earlier you said that Seyss-Inquart was a liar. Explain, please," Bart requested.

"He became the Nazi commissioner in charge of the German occupation of the Netherlands. He was a smooth, oily scoundrel. He ransacked every bank, art gallery, jewelry store, and exchange. He robbed the Dutch people, the Jews, Christians and whatever alike. He lied to my father. He was in charge of the Netherlands until the end of the war. In 1946 he was tried at Nuremberg. He was found guilty for sending Jews to their deaths. I'm glad they hanged the son of a bitch. I hope all of you hang!" she cried out, pointing her finger at the rows of defendants.

Krieger jumped to his feet.

Nimitz held his hand up, "Yes, Mr. Krieger, your objection is sustained. Those remarks about hanging will be stricken from the record."

Milburn smiled at Beth Lowen. "Please continue."

"There were about seventy-eight thousand Jews in Amsterdam, plus another ten thousand refugees. The first sign of trouble for the Jews came in January, 1941. Seyss-Inquart insisted that all Jews in the Netherlands report for registration. About a hundred and forty-odd thousand reported, and in 1942 he demanded that all Jews move to Amsterdam. He had lied to my father again and again. On January 20, 1942, came Himmler's Final Solution, and the Jewish deportations began. Stateless and foreign Jews were sent to Westerbork transit camp. Before they left, they were robbed of every possession."

"What happened to you and your family?"

"The Dutch churches protested to the Nazi authorities. The population was beginning to cooperate with the Nazi regime. My father's power went down the drain. The Nazis had tight control of the country. Many families tried to hide Jews. Then came the proclamation that all Jews were to be deported to Auschwitz and Birkenau camps in Poland."

"Why didn't you try to escape?" Bart asked.

"It was too late. Gestapo police were all over the place. We were home in our beds in early July. It was two in the morning. A truckload of Waffen SS pulled up to our house, smashed our front door down, and there was Arthur Seyss-Inquart and his armed thugs in their handmade black uniforms. They pulled my brothers, my sister, my parents and me out of bed. Seyss-Inquart said to my father, *Herr Jew Premier, your time has come. You and your rotten Jew family are going for a long ride. Get dressed, quickly.*"

At that point, Nimitz called a halt. "The court will recess until tomorrow, Wednesday, February 25, at 0900 hours, 9 a.m. civilian."

☆ ☆ ☆ ☆

Wednesday, February 25, 1953 - 5:30 a.m. - New York City

Alden Gaines, in his Hassidic rabbi disguise, and his mistress, Lilly Darcy, in a trenchcoat, entered the garage of the Rex Towers. They had stuffed the money bags into the trunk and the other bags in the back seat.

The blizzard maintained its fury. Gaines carefully drove onto East River Drive. Traffic was light. They drove north to 179th Street and turned left to the Cross Bronx Expressway leading to the George Washington Bridge. A black Cadillac limousine with tinted glass windows followed a quarter of a mile behind. In front of the Rolls Royce, a Ford station wagon, with two men and a woman in it, drove slowly. Now the cars were on U.S.1 in New Jersey. Snowplows had cleared the road.

The traffic was getting heavier with the usual morning workers. The Rolls Royce passed through Ridgefield Park, Palisades Park, North Bergen, over the Pulaski Skyway, Port Newark, and was approaching Port Elizabeth when the station wagon came to a skidding stop. Gaines swerved to the left and barely missed striking the car. A man jumped out of the station wagon and approached the Rolls Royce on the Bay Avenue entrance to a truck staging area.

He yelled at Gaines, "Rabbi, you were tailgating me and you hit my rear light. Let me see your license. Pull over there while I move my car off the highway."

"I don't think I struck your car," Gaines replied.

"Look at that right rear light. It's broken. Pull over while I get my car off the road," the driver snarled.

The black Cadillac limousine pulled into the Bay Avenue entrance to the port. The station wagon parked a few feet in back of the Rolls Royce. The limo pulled in front. Three men got out of the Cadillac with semi-automatics and fired at Gaines and Darcy. More than twenty rounds peppered the windshield and the open windows on the driver's side of the Rolls. The men opened the trunk and removed the money bags. They took the bags from the back seat and Lilly Darcy's purse. In less than six minutes the station wagon and the Cadillac were en route to New York City. The snowstorm intensified. All tire tracks at the scene of the double murders were quickly erased.

Thirty minutes after the gangland-type hit, a Sealand cargo container trailer truck turned into Bay Avenue. Its progress was blocked by the snow-covered Rolls Royce. Tony Scavini, a twenty-year veteran driver of tractor-trailers, surveyed the road and realized that he couldn't pull around the Rolls, for fear of getting stuck in mud on each side of the narrow two-way road. The rear of his trailer had traffic in a snarl on U.S.1. He hopped off his Mack tractor, which blocked the entrance, and stepped into the ankle-deep snow. He was cursing as he approached the stalled Rolls. In a matter of seconds he sized up the situation. He saw the bearded face leaning against the open window, covered with blood-soaked snow. A woman was lying on the lap of the man, a bloody blue bandana slightly askew.

Scavini trudged back to the cab of his tractor. He lifted the speaker of his two-way radio and reached Pat Logan, Sealand's operations manager.

"Pat, this is Tony Scavini. I..."

"Where the hell are you?" Logan shouted.

"Pat, shut up and listen. I am at the Bay Avenue entrance, blocked by a bullet-ridden Rolls Royce. There are two stiffs in there and I can't back up to U.S.1. Traffic is blowing horns at me. There is no way I can get to North Fleet Street for an approach. Call the State Police to clear up this mess."

"Sit tight, Tony. I'll make the call and join you. Don't touch anything. Ten-four."

And Tony continued to "sit tight"; he had no choice.

CHAPTER TEN

Wednesday, February 25, 1953 - 0900 hours - Fort Leavenworth

Beth Lowen was in the witness chair, patiently awaiting Bart's first question of the day. He greeted her with a warm smile, then said, "In your last answer yesterday, you were describing the raid on your home by Arthur Seyss-Inquart and the Gestapo."

"Yes, that is correct. We were brutally pulled out of our beds in the middle of the night."

"All right, tell the court what happened."

"We were given a few minutes to dress and pack a few necessities. While we did that, those hoodlums looted everything in the house. I saw them stuffing their pockets."

"Then what did they do with you and your family?"

"They beat all of us with their clubs. They hit my father on the head. He was semi-conscious. They lifted him onto a truck and pushed all of us after him. Seyss-Inquart was a sexual degenerate."

"Why do you say that?"

"I am ashamed to mention what he did to my mother."

"Miss Lowen, if it will reveal the character of these Nazis, please tell the court your reason for calling him a degenerate."

Her beautiful light complexion turned to a rose-colored blush. "That filthy man put both of his hands under her dress as he was pushing her onto the truck. He held her like that and wouldn't let go. The Gestapo men laughed. My brothers jumped on him and he let go. He took a club and beat my teenage brothers. He then made a filthy proposition to my dear, beautiful mother."

"What did he say?"

She remained silent. Bart waited patiently. "I will say it in an acceptable way."

"All right."

"He said, *I will let you stay and we will have sexual intercourse all night.* But he used dirty words, even though that isn't bad enough."

"Where did the truck take you?"

"To the railroad station, where there were maybe two thousand or more Jews standing there. Families of fathers, mothers, children, men and women and babies…"

"Go on."

"Soon a long freight train arrived at the station. Waffen SS and soldiers pushed us into filthy cattle cars. That was a nightmare. We thought we were going to Auschwitz. I heard my mother say that. However, we were taken to Westerbork, the transit camp. For some reason, the commandant there, a Colonel Berndt Holmann, came to my father and said, *You are Dirk Van Lowen and this is your family?* My father acknowledged it. He ordered a guard to take us all to barracks there. The conditions there were not so bad. It had showers and sanitary facilities."

"What happened at Westerbork?"

"Trains came every day to take a few thousand Jews to Auschwitz. We later learned that they were being gassed to death daily. One day my father was called into the commandant's office. When my father came back to the barracks, he told us of his conversation with Colonel Holmann. He said that the colonel thought a mistake had occurred. We were supposed to be sent to Buchenwald, where they had a special section for prominent persons. My father's name was on that list. He also indicated to my father that he did not approve of killing Jews. We stayed in Westerbork until January 1943. At least a half-million Jews had passed through on the way to Auschwitz and their deaths."

"What happened in January 1943?"

"Colonel Berndt Holmann came to our barracks one night. It was raining very hard. He called us together and told us we are being moved. He told us that Seyss-Inquart called him and wanted to know why we weren't sent to Auschwitz. The colonel told my father he admired him as a lawyer and for his work on the Hague court and his courage in staying in Amsterdam as Premier. *Seyss-Inquart is a very dangerous man,* he said. There is a train going to Mauthausen, where you'll have to work for the war effort and possibly get transferred to the prominent-persons section in Buchenwald. If I send you to Auschwitz, you will all be dead the day of your arrival. My father asked, *Why are you doing this for us?* He said he was a lawyer in Germany during the Weimar Republic. Many of his friends were Jews in those days. My father thanked him."

"Then what happened?"

"The next day we were put in cattle cars for the horrible journey to Mauthausen. That place was a living hell. It was a very large camp in Austria, by the Danube River, about three miles from the town of Mauthausen. We were shocked to find there was a crematorium next to a prison. It was primarily a penal camp. Every Jew there was in forced labor. We didn't see any Hollanders there; mostly Hungarians, Russian prisoners of war and lots of Polish Jews.

"Did they put your family to work?"

"Yes. My father worked in an armament factory in one of the subcamps. My brothers worked in the kitchen. My mother worked in the Hartheim euthanasia killing center. My sister, Lucille, and I did maid service for the officers. We cleaned their quarters, made their beds and did all the dirty work for them. In addition to our maid service for the officers, we had to do cleanups at the euthanasia center. There were sixty subcamps and about eighty thousand Jewish prisoners. It was a living and dying hell, minus the fire and brimstone. It was a combination work and death camp."

"Will you please expand on your last words?"

"It was divided into three sections. Camp One was the residential area. Camp Two was the work area for the Wehrmacht materials, and Camp Three was the penal camp. Punishment consisted of having to carry stone blocks up a hundred and eight-six steps from a quarry. It was called the Stairway to Death. Just look at the historical atlas of the Holocaust."

"Objection. What is this *atlas*?" Krieger challenged.

Nimitz leaned over to the witness. "Miss Lowen, can you explain your reference to an atlas?"

"Yes, sir, Your Honor. I had mentioned my obsession. I later went to the National archives establishment in Washington. A senior archivist was very helpful. He said an atlas of the Holocaust was being prepared and thay hope to someday build a United States Holocaust Memorial Museum which will show all the atrocities committed by these disciples of the devil incarnate, Adolf Schickelgruber Hitler."

"Objection, sir," Krieger wailed.

Nimitz said, "Miss Lowern, are you expressing an opinion?"

"Yes, sir."

"Overruled. Continue, General."

"Besides your opinion, your description of Mauthausen is based on your personal experiences and observation?"

"General, the facts contained at the National Archive are certainly not apocryphal," she replied. "Eyewitness observations of the atrocities performed by these hate-driven maniacs cannot be disputed by revisionists."

"Please sum up what atrocities you observed at Mauthausen."

"First, the *Stairway to Death*. This was a slow, tortuous, devilish device designed to literally work these slave laborers to death. They had to carry stone blocks up a hundred and eighty-six steps. They were underfed and eventually skeletonized. There were seven men in Block Five who didn't die fast enough for a Nazi *kapo*. They were told to die by Christmas by their Nazi guard, then he killed them, one by one. The first had his brains scattered with a pickaxe by this Nazi murderer. One after the other, including a child, were fried on the electrical gate. That's just a small part of the Nazi orgy of death. Heartless mass murderers, enjoying their contribution to the Holocaust."

At that point, copious tears flowed down her cheeks and she began sobbing convulsively. Nimitz ordered a fifteen-minute recess. Beth Lowen remained in her chair, crying. Bart gently held her right arm and slowly led her to a restroom and stood guard at the closed door. Then he walked her back to the stand.

"Are you all right? Do you wish to continue?"

"Yes, I am sorry I broke up."

"No apology necessary."

The tribunal returned.

"Miss Lowen, are you willing to go on?" Nimitz asked.

"Yes, Your Honor."

"We were on the subject of atrocities," Bart said.

"Objection to the word *atrocities*," Krieger declared.

Before Nimitz could reply, Bart said, "The prosecution will produce film, some of it captured from the surrendering Nazis, other pictures in black and white and living color, of death graphic enough to put the lie to the most skilled revisionists."

"Overruled, Mr. Krieger."

"Miss Lowen, answer my question on atrocities," Bart continued.

"One night my mother told us of the horrors in the euthanasia killing center. Experiments of all kinds were taking place. She was warning my sister and me of what we would see the next day when we were due for a cleanup."

"Objection, hearsay," said Krieger.

"Sustained."

"What did you personally see?" Bart asked.

"First, we saw a stack of twenty dead bodies. I saw a doctor have a perfectly healthy man strapped to a surgeon's table. He injected him with some fluid. The man suddenly went into spasms, violently struggling to get up. The straps burst and he fell on the floor in convulsions. A guard tried to lift him. The doctor put a hypodermic syringe to the back of the man's head. He died instantly. Two guards stacked him with the other cadavers."

"Then what?"

"Ten *Sonderkommandos* were hustled in by four Gestapo men. These hapless, emaciated Jews were ordered to take the dead bodies to the crematorium. My mother and I were in a state of shock. The doctor called them *commandos. Schnell, Juden, you're next*, he said as he lit a cigarette. Two of the Jews lifted the body and threw it straight at the doctor. His cigarette went flying, the sparks ignited alcohol, and the dead body fell on top of the doctor, who was flat on his back on the bloodstained tile floor. The Gestapo men quickly lifted the corpse and helped the doctor to his feet. He sank to his knees and gasped, *Kill them now!* The two Jews ran out of the building. The other doctors ministered to the doctor. The Gestapo gave chase. The other *Sonderkommandos* picked up surgical knives, hypodermics, saws, and a bottle of alcohol. My mother and I were told to leave. They attacked the other doctors and their assistants. Flames began licking the walls. We ran."

"What did you see outside the killing center?"

"Chaos. Jews were being shot indiscriminately. Some of the soldiers had been struck by flying bullets. The *Sonderkommandos* came running out of the burning building. Their hands and prisoner's clothing were bloody. My mother and I hid under Barracks One until nightfall. We listened to the uproar in the yard and watched the attempts to douse the fire at the euthanasia center. We finally crawled around the back to our barracks. We had a sleepless night."

"What happened the next morning?"

"All the barracks were emptied. Thousands of us were lined up in the roll-call square. We saw the killing center burned to the ground. Totally destroyed. Colonel Saukel ordered us to turn right. Hundreds of Gestapos and soldiers were lined up behind him with semi-automatic rifles. When we turned, we saw a scaffold with ten prisoners standing there with nooses dangling over them. On the gallows with them were ten Gestapo officers." She stopped, sipped some water and dried her eyes.

Nimitz asked, "Would you like to stop, Miss Lowen?"

"No, Your Honor."

"Go on, Beth," Bart gently suggested.

"He said, *Listen carefully, Jews. This is what happens to Juden criminals. These men killed our doctors and burned down our hospital. Watch,* he said and raised his hand and brought it down quickly. The nooses were applied to the necks of those men. He waved his hand and pointed to the ground. The trap was sprung. Some of the men hanged were kicking their legs, and finally all were dead."

"Was that the end of that?"

"No, the worst was yet to come. He snapped his fingers and the Gestapo lice passed the lineup and hand-picked fifty men and women, then marched them to the execution site on the right of the gallows. Ten soldiers placed machine guns on the ground. The Jewish prisoners were lined up against the wall, ten at a time. The colonel lifted his hand and shouted, *fire!* Ten dead, ten more, ten more, ten more and ten more. Innocent, decent human beings slaughtered, for what reason? They were Jews, and what is a Jew...nothing but a descendant of Abraham, Miriam-called Mary-and Joseph, parents of Yeshua Ben Joseph, now called Jesus Christ, the Greek version of his name. What price did they pay with their lives for their beliefs? May these godless Nazi bastards forever wear the mark of Cain on their foreheads, a swastika."

"Objection!" Krieger yelled.

"No need to raise your voice, Counsel. Sustained. Strike the words after *more*," Nimitz decreed. "How much longer, General Milburn?"

"Twenty to thirty minutes, sir."

"Move it along," Nimitz urged.

"Miss Lowen, as succinctly as possible, what occurred after that?" Bart asked.

"More doctors arrived, and a new euthanasia killing center was set up next to the tent camp. My mother was assigned there. My brothers, Vincent and Jan, were assigned to the quarry at the Stairway to Death. They loaded the stone blocks on trucks after the inmates brought the stones up the hundred and eighty-six steps. A British POW Jew spoke to them. My brothers spoke very good English. That was a second language in our household. They became friends. The British POW was a captain in the RAF. He managed to slip food to Jan and Vincent. As the year went by, my brothers built up their muscles handling those stone blocks. The POW told them the Allies had invaded France. Our hopes went up. Then something terrible happened." She began to cry, but insisted on continuing.

"What happened?"

"My sister, Lucille, was cleaning Captain Helmut Schroeder's quarters late one afternoon. He locked her in his bathroom and told her to get undressed. She broke the bathroom window and tried to escape. He came in and beat her unconscious. When she became conscious, the captain was in the bed with her. They were both naked. He poured her a shot glass of whiskey, which he forced down her throat."

"Objection, hearsay."

"Not necessarily. Let's hear more," Nimitz ruled.

"I was next door when I heard her scream. I pounded on the door. At that moment, the International Red Cross was making a routine inspection of the camp. Everything had been spruced up for their visit. Two men and two women wearing Red Cross bands on their arms were passing by when my sister screamed again. A Major Werner Hoffer, who was escorting the group, came to me. He asked, *What is the trouble?* I told him my sister was doing maid service and that was her screaming. One of the Red Cross visitors, a Count Folke Bernadotte, joined us. He introduced himself, then ordered the major to open the door. The major crashed the door open. There was the naked captain with his hand on my sister's mouth. He had raped her. Blood was flowing from her nose. His eye was puffed and her lip was split. She tried to cover herself with a sheet."

"Do you wish a recess?" Bart asked.

"No. The major had his gun out. My sister cried out that the captain had raped her. The two women and the other Red Cross person came in. The major ordered the captain to get dressed. One woman was attending to my sister. Count Bernadotte was making notes on a pad. He asked my name. When I told him, he inquired if I was a daughter of Premier Dirk van Lowen. I told him I was. He called the major and the three Red Cross members to join him. The count was very angry. He berated the major and the whole Nazi regime. I was anxious to go to my sister. As I looked over at her during that conference, the captain, half-naked, came out of the bathroom with a gun in his hand. He shot my sister in her right eye. I screamed, and the major fired his gun, wounding the captain. I fainted."

"How old was your sister Lucille?" Bart asked.

"She was fourteen and I was twelve at that time."

"Please continue."

"When I came to my senses, I was in the regular hospital and in a state of shock. My father, mother and two brothers were there, as well as the four International Red Cross people. Colonel Saukel and the major were there, too."

"General, we'll have to call a lunch recess now. We'll convene at 1430 hours," Nimitz ruled.

In the tribunal chambers, Nimitz, Smith and Chennault sat down to lunch. The admiral quietly sipped on a glass of sherry. The two generals stared at the light snowfall. General Smith got up and reached in the bottom drawer of a desk. He picked up a bottle of bourbon and poured it into a water glass. He took a generous swig of the Kentucky nectar and held the bottle up to Chennault, who declined.

"That kid could be our daughter," Smith said.

"Granddaughter," Nimitz wryly replied.

"What the hell kind of animals are these bastards?" Chennault said rhetorically.

"We thought the Japanese were tough," Smith said. "These Nazis make the Japs look like gentlemen. I agree with Milburn. Hanging is too merciful for these monsters!"

"Holland, you are a judge at this moment. Don't offer your opinions out loud," Nimitz counseled.

The tribunal called the afternoon session to order. Beth Lowen was again in the witness chair. Bart opened his questioning with a stark reminder of her last testimony before recess.

"Miss Lowen, you testified that Captain Helmut Schroeder shot and killed your sister Lucille. He was wounded. Did he survive?"

"Yes."

"Was he brought to justice?"

"Forgive me, General, but there was no justice in Nazi Germany. The last I heard, after he recovered from his wound he was transferred to the Waffen SS."

"How do you know that?"

"My father told me. He learned it through the grapevine at Buchenwald."

"Buchenwald? How did he get there?"

"Well, Count Bernadotte raised hell with Commandant Saukel, who acted like a pussycat in the presence of the Red Cross. *We don't have rapists like Captain Schroeder in this camp. This never happened here*, he lied through his yellow teeth," she said.

"What did the count say to that?"

"He demanded that the Lowen family be released to him."

"What did the commandant reply to that?"

"Franz said that Mauthausen was getting very crowded, due to the Russian drive. They were coming from Auschwitz, Sachsenhausen and Gross-Rosen. Therefore he would recommend sending us to Buchenwald, where they have a section for prominent personalities. Bernadotte demanded to call Himmler. He said to Saukel, *You people are losing the war. Help yourself by letting these people go.* Saukel told him, *Listen, dear Count, I would be pleased to let them go in your custody. But I have a sword over my head. Seyss-Inquart has a vendetta against the Premier. Let's call Himmler.*"

"Did they reach Himmler?"

"Yes. Bernadotte said that Himmler told him to go to Buchenwald to the prominent-personalities section and in due time we would be turned over to the Red Cross."

"When were you transferred?"

"First, I want to say we didn't believe that the miserable, rotten chief butcher Heinrich Himmler would keep his word. Bernadotte said he would check up on us. That night we were allowed to bury my sister in back of the hospital. They even gave us a wooden casket. The next morning we were put in a caboose on a train to Buchenwald."

"Was life any better there?"

"No. Buchenwald was a massive torture chamber. Life there was as miserable as you could make it."

"Go on," Bart urged.

"When we first arrived at Buchenwald, the sight was horrific."

"What did you see?"

"The Waffen SS were opening the freight cars on a train alongside us. Corpses by the hundreds were being removed and were lying in rows all the way from the station up to a bathhouse. They were skeletonized carcasses from all over Europe. That was our greeting to this *abattoir*. It was an aboveground cemetery. At first I thought we had been taken to a death camp like Auschwitz and the others. I was thirteen years old. I thought we were standing at the entrance to hell."

"What happened then?"

"I looked at those bodies and began to cry. I was thinking of my poor sister Lucille. My mother put her hand over my eyes and turned me away from the men unloading the corpses. I looked out of the window at the station. Two Gestapos were taking turns kicking a bearded man. The man on the ground was trying to shield his head. The Gestapo officers were laughing and playing soccer with his head. One of the men, still laughing, backed up and with a running start delivered a long kick, cracking the man's head open. There was blood spurting onto the Gestapo's foot. He wiped his boots against the inert body. The man was dead. They called two Jewish prisoners to haul the poor man's body away. They laughed some more. I still have those pictures in my mind."

"Beth, when you disembarked at the station, what happened?" Bart asked.

"We were ordered to line up. Satan himself, Commandant Hermann Pister, called some names and those people stepped forward. Two officers marched them to the barracks at the main camp. Then Pister called, *Lowen!* We stepped forward."

"What did the commandant do with you and your family?"

"He asked my father if he was the former Premier of the Netherlands. My father said yes. Pister then said he had a message from Commandant Saukel. He said he would talk to him later. We were then led to the special compound for prominent prisoners, just opposite the SS quarters. We were put in two sparsely furnished rooms with a bathroom. This was a lot better than the barracks."

"How so?"

"There were four cots, enough for all of us. My brothers shared a cot and I slept on the other cot in the same room. My parents slept in the next room. In the morning they lined us up and called the roll. There were some famous names there. Others, I learned, were in isolation."

"Do you remember some of the names?"

"Yes, I saw the French Prime Minister, Paul Reynaud. He knew my father and waved at him. The others were former French Prime Minister Leon Blum and his wife, and Pierre Bloch, former Justice Minister. There was Princess Majalda of Hesse, daughter of the Italian King. Paul Souden, Labor Minister of Belgium, Former Chancellor Kurt Schuschnigg of Austria, and some actors, authors, and so forth."

"What else happened at Buchenwald?"

"The gas chambers were never completed there. But Buchenwald was a death camp in another way. They tortured, worked, shot and beat people to death. It was a horror house. It was originally a prison for criminals, murderers, thieves, rapists, and felons of all kinds. When the Jews were shipped in there after Kristallnacht, the criminals became lackeys for the SS. The camp was loaded with both Jews and non-Jews. Many political prisoners suffered the same fate as the Jews. They were beaten by the SS and preyed upon by the criminals, who stole their meager rations and enjoyed torturing Jews."

"Were you and your family protected at the special compound?"

"For the first three days, everything was calm in our section. Prime Minister Reynaud and my father became close friends. He told us they had hidden radios. The Americans and British were driving the Nazis east and the Soviets were pushing them west. All this information was coming from the BBC. Reynaud said that these so-called prominent prisoners were being held for exchange for high Nazis captured by the Allies. He told us to keep a low profile and we would be liberated soon. We had a few days of euphoria, then suddenly our hopes were dashed and our temporary security was dismantled. The gates of hell opened."

"Gates of hell? Please expand on that," Bart coaxed.

"The chief Nazi king of killers, Heinrich Himmler, and his sycophants visited the camp. All the SS were in full dress uniforms. I was twelve years of age. I still have the picture of this chinless, concave-chested man, an ex-chicken farmer, strutting into our compound. I had a picture of him and his toadies sorting us out like he did with his chickens. Reynaud said, *Here comes the greatest mass murderer in history.* Commandant Pister was fawning all over him."

"Did Himmler speak to any of the special prisoners?"

"Yes. He talked to Reynaud and I heard him say *You're a good Catholic. I hope you pray. When we win this war, I'll send you back to France. You should have stayed with the Vichy government.* To my father, he said, *You're the Jew Premier of Holland. You don't look like a Jew.* Then he pointed at me. *This Aryan face must have had a Christian father. I hear she has a great singing voice. Maybe I can hear her tonight.* Then Pister spoke up, saying, *"Reichsführer, we are having a concert tonight in honor of your visit. Maybe we can have this little lady sing for us?* I cringed."

"Did you perform?"

"Most reluctantly. In front of these killers, thugs and vermin, I did two numbers, one from Bizet's *Carmen* and one from *La Boheme*. Then they yelled for *Deutschland über Alles*. I told them I didn't know the song. So the whole bunch got up, stuck their arms out and yelled, *Sieg Heil!* The orchestra struck up their anthem and sang the song. I was excused. The next day, my mother was ordered to report to the medical experiment barracks. My father was sent to the Gustloff armament factory. My brother, Victor, was sent to work dumping bodies into the crematorium. Jan was assigned to the shooting range. Commandant Pister came to my room and handed me a nurse's uniform. He insisted I try it on while he watched. I slipped into it as fast as I could. He said I was well developed. My puberty had come early and my breasts were developed beyond my years. He touched me there and I slapped his hands. He laughed. There were two sergeants with him."

"What followed?"

"The two sergeants took me to the hospital, a few yards away from the experiment barracks, where my mother was working. A Frau Klauber was the head nurse. She was a very tough woman in her fifties. The so-called doctors called her Madame Gargoyle behind her back. She showed me where the prisoner's section was, which held Jews, Christians and Muslims. In another section, the Nazi patients were being cared for. The Nazi recovery room was immaculate. The other was filthy. Both wards were crowded. That's when the gates of hell opened for me."

"Beth, please explain."

"The Nazis acting as doctors were not graduate medical men. I was given a wide variety of duties, such as emptying bedpans, cleaning messed beds, helping in surgery, and washing blood and feces wherever it was needed in both sections. One day, sixty-five Dutch soldiers were delivered to the camp. Half of them were sick or wounded. Because I spoke their language, I was assigned to help them. I took good care of them. They came from western Poland, where they were prisoners of war. The Russians were closing in on Poland. I sneaked antiseptics, bandages, medicines, clean sheets, and food to them when Frau Gargoyle was not around. A Colonel Paul Vanderhof was in charge of the Hollanders. He had a bad leg wound. I warned him not to let the Nazi doctors take him into surgery, because these amateur doctors sawed off legs with any excuse. The colonel called me *Miss Florence* after that famous nurse, Nightingale. The other Dutch soldiers called me *Nighty*."

"How much did you see in your job?" Bart asked.

"I saw these doctors kill dozens of Jews who had slight colds, bruises, coughs and low fevers. They were ceremoniously wheeled into surgery and, while I stood there, they sliced, cut, injected and just simply executed these Jews. Then they started on the Dutch contingent. Ten of them were killed in alleged operations. Frau Gargoyle chose them for the false operations. One of the patients in the prisoners' section was there after a fall at the quarry. He had no broken bones, but was merely bruised. He whispered to me that he was a Belgian doctor. Madame Gargoyle was at the shooting range. A Nazi soldier had been accidentally wounded. I got the Belgian doctor, Isaiah

Melman, out of bed and handed him his clothes. He spoke Flemish, which is a Dutch dialect. I took him to Colonel Vanderhof. None of the other nurses were there. Dr. Melman went to work on his leg. I brought him a vial of penicillin. He injected the colonel, cleaned up the wound and professionally bandaged him. I told him we must get these Dutch soldiers out of the hospital. It was dark outside. *Come with me,* he told the colonel, *I can hide you and twenty other Dutch soldiers in a special place.* We got their clothes and I watched them go down the stairs of the fire escape. The colonel kissed me. He whispered that eight of his men were Jews."

"Did you stay behind?"

"I had to. I went to the Nazi section and made myself busy. One of the spurious Nazi doctors came in and said I was wanted at the shooting range. I was told to hurry, so an SS man drove me there. I asked him what was wrong. He said, *Shut up, you'll see.* I saw the SS pushing, kicking and dragging Jews toward the shooting range. A few men and women fell to the ground. The Gestapo were kicking and beating them. Two men were being dragged by their beards. Women were screaming. When we got to the range, my father and mother were there." Beth sobbed convulsively. Then, after a ten-minute recess, she was back on the stand.

"Beth, can you continue?" Bart gently asked.

"Yes...my brother, Jan, was hanging on a hook, which was stuck in the back of his neck. Obviously he was dead. My parents were crying, holding onto each other. I grasped both of them and was shaking fitfully. More than fifty Jews were lined up against a wall. A deputy commandant, Major Horst Talner, addressed the crowd. *This rotten Jew,* he said, pointing at my dear, gentle brother, *is responsible for the wounding of Sergeant Loder, who is dying. He was asked to bring his rifle to him. When he gave it to him, the rifle exploded with a bullet in Loder's stomach. You all know the price that has to be paid for injuring an officer of the Third Reich.* Four men, at a signal from the major, fired machine guns, killing fifty men and women. I begged the major to let us take my brother down from the hook." She dabbed her eyes and continued. "That monster said, *First, all you people will carry those bodies to that truck. Then you can take your Jew brother off the hook.* There were twenty Jewish observers of this slaughter. My mother fainted. I was attending to her while those people struggled to load the dead bodies. It took quite a long time. Then we struggled to unhook Jan. When we got him down, my mother and I carried him. We were ordered to follow the truck. We got to the crematorium and there was my brother, Victor. We were surrounded by armed guards. The group was ordered to throw the bodies into the blazing furnace. Several men and my brother were forced to strip the carcasses and throw their naked bodies into the flames. Victor didn't see us holding Jan's body. After all the bodies were consumed, Major Talner ordered us to throw Jan's body into the furnace. Victor saw us and threw himself on Jan's body, crying loudly. One soldier struck Victor on the back of his head, knocking him unconscious." She paused.

"What happened then?"

"We heard artillery shells explode in the distance," Beth continued. "The sky was lighting up with flares. My father begged the major to let us bury my brother Jan. My mother was holding Victor in her arms. The major took out his pistol and shot my father between the eyes. My mother jumped up and scratched the major's eyes. Blood ran down his face. He shot my mother, killing her instantly. A shell exploded a few yards from the range. The colonel yelled, *Achtung, schnell! The Americans are coming!* I fainted after that. When I awoke, Victor was trying to lift me up. His shoulders were bloody. The Nazis were gone. My mother, father and brother Jan were lying dead on the ground. Victor and I tried to lift their bodies. I heard a noise. I looked up and there were bayoneted guns pointing at us. I heard an American voice shout, *All clear!* Two dozen soldiers climbed over the parapet and surrounded us."

"What did they do?" the general asked.

"An American said, *I am Captain Thomas Burke, United States Army. Where are the Nazis?* I told him they ran after they killed fifty Jews, my mother, father and brother lying here. He asked how old I was. I said, *Twelve.* He looked at the crematorium, then yelled, *Sergeant! I need three men to carry these bodies.* He asked me if I knew the layout of the camp. I told him I did. He called someone on his radio. Hundreds of men came across the shooting range. Tanks followed. He yelled, *All right, men, the camp is surrounded. The tanks are up front.* That was April 11, 1945. Victor and I were put on a tank and were driven to a special compound. I pointed to the SS quarters. There were thousands of American soldiers. They surrounded the SS building. Meanwhile, the walking-skeleton prisoners attacked the watchtowers. The Nazis were yelling *Kamerad* with their hands in the air."

"Do you want a recess, Beth?"

"No, I want to finish. Captain Burke was joined by a Colonel Jeremiah Brown. He had an Army doctor tend to Victor's wound. He patched him up and said he had a slight concussion, but would be all right. He gave Victor a hypodermic shot, which made him feel much better. I asked Colonel Brown if we could bury our parents and our brother, Jan. He said he would arrange a service for them in the morning with a Jewish chaplain to deliver the Kaddish. I asked him how he knew that word, which is the prayer for the dead. He patted me on the head and said, *Lady, after four years of this war, I've heard that word thousands of times. These Nazis killed lots of our Jewish boys. Chaplain Marvin Stein is an excellent rabbi.* Then he asked if my brother and I could show him and his men to every corner of the camp."

"Did you do that?"

"Yes. We first took him to the prominent prisoners' enclave. Then I found the secret place where Dr. Malmen had hidden Colonel Vanderhof and the Dutch soldiers. They were in a basement at the special compound, ironically situated next to the basement of the commandant's villa. Pister disappeared. Next, Generals Eisenhower, Bradley and Patton arrived. They had just come from Ohrdruf. They inspected the camp and then spoke with French Prime Ministers Reynaud and Blum. Chaplain Stein arranged a very dignified funeral for my parents and Jan. Colonel Brown located three caskets. He also arranged for an honor guard. After the service, they fired a volley of shots in the air."

"When we came back to the special compound, Prime Minister Reynaud called me and Victor into Pister's luxury villa. He introduced us to Eisenhower and Bradley. Both of them knew my father. They told us that Premier Lowen had set up an underground team to transit information about the Nazis to General Eisenhower's headquarters. He and General Bradley had met my father in London before Hitler invaded our country. He said my father was very helpful and brave. He asked where we would go now. I told him I wanted to go to America. My brother wanted to go back to Amsterdam. However, that was not to be that soon."

"Please expand on that."

"Prime Minister Reynaud invited us to come to Paris with him. General Eisenhower thought it was a wise thing to do. He said the British forces were driving through northern Germany toward the liberation of Holland and Denmark. *It's best that you children go to Paris with the Prime Minister,* Eisenhower advised us. We told him we had no money. Victor said Papa had transferred some funds to a bank in Geneva. Then something strange came up."

"Tell the court what that was," Bart urged.

"Reynaud said the Swiss banks were defrauding Holocaust victims of their money because they couldn't present death certificates. General Eisenhower called a major into the villa. *Prepare death certificates for those three people that were buried today. Yes, the parents and brother of these children. I'll sign it. Hurry,* he said."

"What did you do after that?"

"An American plane took most of the prominent prisoners, including the Prime Minister, with us to Paris. We landed at an American Army airfield. We were met by French and American officers. All of us were dressed in those miserable prisoners' uniforms. The French Refugee Committee was there. We were taken to the Hotel de Crillon on the Place de la Concorde. Soon we had new clothes from the Galeries Lafayette, courtesy of Mr. Reynaud. All that day, we reveled in the rooms and baths at the hotel. Two days later we were moved into a foster home by Madame Lefcourt of the Refugee Committee. It was the home of a Jewish family. They had escaped the Nazis by crossing the English Channel on a Swedish freighter. They were Colonel and Mrs. Fiedler. He was English, badly wounded and honorably discharged. He had lost his left leg. They were young people and had two little boys, four and five years old. They had a nice house in a suburb of Paris. The colonel worked at the British Intelligence office in Paris. Yvette and Richard were very kind to us."

"How long did you stay with them?"

"About six weeks. On May 4 the German High Command surrendered Holland and Denmark to Field Marshal Montgomery. Colonel Fiedler rushed home to tell us the good news. Victor wanted to go home right away. The colonel dissuaded him, saying that the war would be over in a few days and to wait until the peace was signed. The Prime Minister called us four days later. The Germans had surrendered. He gave us the name of a lawyer in Geneva that we could trust. Colonel Fiedler gave us money to fly to Geneva to try to get my father's funds."

"What did you do?" Bart asked.

"In Geneva we met with Maurice Duval, a man in his seventies but very spry. We showed him the death certificates and he laughed out loud. For a second we were shocked. He apologized and explained that he looked forward to seeing the bank's discomfort when he produced the certificates, signed by Eisenhower. Monsieur Duval was a very distinguished man.

"At the Geneva Banque Internationale, our lawyer was greeted by a vice president. He demanded to see the president, a Felix Delier. He came out and greeted Duval warmly. We went to his office. When he asked for the file on Premier Lowen's account, his attitude changed. He began to dissemble. Finally he said, *Besides, we have to have a death certificate to open files or release funds of the deceased.* Duval said, *Exactly,* and presented the three death certificates. Delier stared at the documents. There was $250,000 dollars each for my mother, Jan, Victor and me. After a threat of a lawsuit, he released certified checks of $500,000 to Victor and $500,000 to me. To make my story shorter, Victor asked me to go to Amsterdam with him. There we learned that all of our relatives had been killed in Auschwitz, except my mother's sisters, who were shipped to Dachau when the Allies were closing in on the camp. The Americans liberated her. She's alive because the Nazis used them. They are doctors."

"Where are they now?"

"Aunt Laura is living with Victor in our house there. Victor is in pre-med school. He wants to be a doctor. My Aunt Gretchen lives with me in New York. She has a good practice and is connected with the Columbia Presbyterian Hospital. She also spends time helping survivors. We have a joint fund to help those people."

"How did you manage to become so articulate in the English language?"

"I spoke English since I was a child. When I was cleared to enter the United States to join my aunt, she put me in a private school. When I graduated, I entered Columbia University. Coincidentally, General Eisenhower became President of Columbia while I was there."

"Did you ever talk to him again?"

"Yes. There was a musical at Columbia my senior year. I sang, and Mr. Eisenhower and his wife were there. The next day he sent for me. He told me how he realized I was that little girl at Buchenwald. He told me how he was impressed with my voice and maturity. I told him I was admitted to Juilliard. He was very impressed and also complimented me on my marks at the university. I was majoring in English literature. I told him I was going to write a book about the Nazi atrocities and my personal experiences during the war. I told him he would be in the book. He laughed and said, *Be kind to me.* I promised and he wished me luck. The last time I saw him was at graduation. I was the valedictorian."

"Last question, Beth. What is your present occupation?"

"I am studying music at Juilliard. Piano mostly. I am studying acting under Lee Strasberg at the Actors Studio. I'm also working on my book."

"Busy lady. No further questions," Bart concluded.

"Gentlemen of the defense, do you wish to start you cross-examination now, or wait for the morning session?" Nimitz asked.

Eric Stolz rose. "Members of the tribunal, I realize it is getting late. However, with your permission, we would like to cross-examine this lady now. It will be very short."

"Very well."

"Thank you, sir."

He walked within three feet of the witness stand.

"Oh no, Mr. Krieger, you'll have to move back," Nimitz cautioned.

"Sir, the prosecution is allowed closer proximity than the defense."

"Yes, because General Milburn is not adversarial. We don't want you to intimidate the witness by close gestures or loud inflections of your voice."

Beth looked at Bart and nodded assent.

"Your Honors, if the witness doesn't object, we'll waive ours."

"Miss Lowen, any problem with that?"

"Not at all, except if he tries to rape me."

Laughter erupted.

Nimitz gaveled and gently chided Beth, "Your remark was uncalled for."

"I apologize to the court."

"All right, Mr. Krieger, you may step forward."

"Miss Lowen, you have stated that you are studying acting. I would venture that you no longer need to study. In fact, isn't it quite clear that your performance as a witness today is a consummate piece of acting?"

Bart roared angrily, "Objection. Is counsel attempting to vitiate the harrowing truth expressed by this survivor of the Holocaust?"

"Mr. Krieger, I am sustaining the general's objection. Now, if you stick with specifics, we can move along," Nimitz said.

"You were moved from Mauthausen to Buchenwald. Was that because of your father's prestige and bribery of the commandant?"

Beth's eyes were moist. Her visage was taut. She looked at Krieger from head to toe and in a calm voice replied, "We were transferred from one hellhole to another because..."

Krieger cut her off, "Answer my question, now."

"Don't try your Nazi tactics on me. I am answering your question."

"Objection!" Krieger yelled.

"To what?" Nimitz asked.

"To *Nazi tactics*."

"I'll strike that. I warn you, however, to let her finish her answers. Cut her off once more and I'll hold you in contempt," Nimitz warned.

"Very well, sir. Go ahead, Frau Lowen."

"I'm not your *Frau*. As I was saying when you rudely interrupted me, we were moved from that death camp to a murdering torture camp because one of your Nazi officers raped my sister and then shot her between the eyes in the presence of the International Red Cross. You Nazis had a scandal on your hands, so the *bribe*, as you call it, was to cover it up and get me and my family out of there."

Krieger waved his finger at her as he moved closer, raising his voice. "Isn't it true that at Buchenwald you and your family were housed in the prominent-persons enclave with all its privileges?"

"If you keep shaking your finger at me, it will fall off or I'll break it off, you rude clown! You're not in Nazi Germany, you Swiss sycophant."

"Your Honor, can't you control this witness?"

"From what? Protecting herself? You're trying to intimidate her. Now, step back. Miss Lowen, please answer the question."

"Please have it read back."

The stenotypist obliged.

"Privileges? I worked in the hospital and watched your phony Nazi doctors saw legs off of perfectly healthy Jews and POWs. I watched them inject phenol, a killing acid, into the bodies of people who weren't sick. No gas chambers there, but phenol chambers. A different kind of charnel house."

"You personally saw that?"

"Yes."

"Yet you lived in that special compound?"

"Not for long. All the privileges I got at your beautiful house of hell was my brother being murdered by the Gestapo for a stupid accident by your Gestapo. They hung his body like a slaughtered cow on a hook, then sent for me and my parents. Then they..."

"Stop, stop!" Krieger shouted.

Nimitz gaveled.

She screamed, "I won't stop! Then they rounded up fifty Jews at random, kicking them, beating them with their truncheons, pulling men by their beards and shooting those that fell. They lined up the fifty innocent, pitiful Jews and machine-gunned them to death. Then, for good measure, they shot my mother and father. Privileges? You are scum - a hired gun by the Swiss banks to defend these rotten, filthy barbarians. May you and your godforsaken clients boil in hell!" she sobbed.

Krieger threw up his hands and announced, "Impossible. No more questions."

"You asked for it," General Smith said.

"Court is adjourned until Tuesday, March 3rd, at 0900," Nimitz declared.

☆ ☆ ☆ ☆

Wednesday, February 25, 1953 - 6:05 p.m. - the Victorian House, Fort Leavenworth

Bart and Jacques were relaxing in their quarters, sipping vodka martinis.

"I'm exhausted," Bart sighed.

"With good reason, brother."

The phone rang. "What now?" Bart fretted.

Jacques answered. "Douglas, how are you doing? Hold on, I'll ask him.

Bart, Doug wants to come over for purely social reasons, he says. He'll pick up some Chinese food."

"Tell him to skip the Chinese and come share beef stew with us."

"Doug, it's cold martinis and beef stew. Come ahead," Jacques told him.

Ten minutes later, Doug Milburn arrived. Mrs. Lawrence led him to the den and the crackling fireplace. He put his back to the fire and held his open palms to the flames. Jacques handed him the martini. "That will warm your gut, brother."

"Jacques, if you weren't already taken, I'd marry you."

"I'm sure Connie and Christina would love to hear that," Jacques laughed. "How's my tired kid brother?"

"You said it - tired," Bart retorted.

"Glad the tribunal recessed to next Tuesday. Why did they do that?"

"Something's happening in Moscow. Ike has a three-day conference set up of the Cabinet and the military. It's not a crisis. My guess is Stalin's health. Anyway, we can all stand the hiatus. We're swamped with witnesses, and believe it or not, some survivors have shown up here without notice. I've asked our staff to check them out."

"You'll not get anyone better than that Beth Lowen. She's special."

"Oh yes, Doug, that reminds me...this girl has a voice as good or better than anything I've heard in operas, pop music or radio or records. Simply stated, she's star quality. I'm not a talent scout, but I've heard the best sing. To my untrained ear, she's at the top."

"That's high praise indeed."

"Not only her singing, she handles the piano like a pro. Also, she's studying acting with Strasberg. If *he* takes you on, that's a stamp of approval. I thought you might mention her to Constance, for advice only."

"Bart, I watched her on the stand. She was magnificent. I certainly will tell Connie about her."

Dinner was served. It was an authentic homemade meat-and-potatoes meal, made especially for a freezing, stormy night. Brandy and cigars were in order in the den. At 9:30 that evening the phone rang. Mrs. Lawrence picked it up in the kitchen, and said, "Just a moment, sir." She walked into the den and said, "It's for you, Douglas."

"That has to be my office. I left word with the switchboard," he noted.

"Hi, Bob. What's up? What? No, hold it a moment. Jacques, turn on the radio, please."

John Cameron Swayze was delivering the news of the Elizabeth, New Jersey, gangland-style murder.

"*New Jersey authorities have confirmed the identity of the victims as Lilly Darcy, the motion-picture actress, and her fiancé, Chicago attorney Alden Gaines, who was most recently defending Adolf Hitler in the war-crimes trial being held at Fort Leavenworth. Both were shot to death off U.S.1 at approximately 6 a.m. today. According to reliable sources, the notorious lawyer and the famous actress were planning to leave the country. Authorities are check-*

ing mob connections and Gaines' representation of Adolf Hitler."

"Turn it off, Jacques," Bart suggested.

"What's your guess, fellows?" Doug asked.

"I don't think it was a mob hit," Jacques declared. "It's too high-profile. Besides, the mob style lately has been to put the hits in cement shoes and then dump the unlucky bastards in the East River."

Bart rolled his cigar, dipped the top of it in his brandy snifter, took a long puff, emitted circles of smoke and observed, "I agree with Jacques. My visceral reaction is that Hitler's hot hand on the Mayfield brothers arranged this execution. The question of *why* leads me to the counterfeit scam."

"Well, now that I've heard from Sherlock Holmes and Dr. Watson, I've got my speculative lead for tomorrow's commentary column. This has been a very productive evening, gentlemen," Doug said.

The banter was interrupted by Farley Washburn's call. Jacques answered and handed the receiver to Bart.

"What's up now, Farley? As if I didn't know?"

"Right on, General."

"What can I do to help?"

"I have to interrogate the Mayfield brothers with regards to the counterfeit case and its possible connection with the murders of Lilly Darcy and Alden Gaines. Brownell and Hoover don't think it was a mob hit. They smell Hitler and his Nazi Mafia. I promise not to interfere in the war-crimes trial."

"I don't know. These sleazeballs are about to flip and testify for the prosecution. I don't want them to turn on me. Let me think about it."

"General, please...I'll handle it delicately."

"Where are Maybrook and Cartman now?" Bart asked.

"They're here at the Il Cappuccino on Cherokee Street. Great Italian food."

"Never mind the commercial; Jacques and I are leaving in the morning for D.C. We're taking a four-day holiday with our families. If you want to do it tonight, I'll set it up. Bring Maybrook and Cartman with you."

"Great. I'll have Deputy Director Bill Bledsoe with me," Washburn said.

"Meet me in the prosecution conference room at the Disciplinary Barracks. You've spoiled my evening of rest, friend."

"We'll be there in twenty minutes."

"Doug, what you've just heard cannot be quoted," Bart ordered. "Speculate all you want in your column or story."

"I'm flying to New York in the morning," Doug declared. "Don't worry, Bart, I won't embarrass you."

Bart relented slightly, "If you happen to see Washburn or Bledsoe on your way out and confront them, then you are on your own."

"Thanks, brother. *Ciao.*"

"Why the hell are you letting Washburn talk to the Mayfields?" Jacques barked.

"Think about it, Jacques. If the Mayfields want a deal with us, we have to appeal to the Attorney General or the FBI for witness protection. If they are sentenced and deserve a shorter term, it's up to the U.S. Attorney to recommend it to a judge. Either way it goes, Washburn and Bledsoe are beholden to us."

"Bart, your legal mind is always in gear. I'm convinced you did the right thing."

"Come on, Jacques, change clothes. We're going to sit in for the opening session. I'm putting Cartman and Maybrook in charge to protect our interests over this long weekend. I told Liz we'll be home about 2 p.m. tomorrow and nothing's going to interfere with that."

"I agree. I told the same thing to Christina."

Interrogation room - Disciplinary Barracks

Bart, Laurent, Washburn and Bledsoe discussed the ground rules of the interrogation. The MPs delivered the Mayfield brothers, Paul and Darren, both handcuffed, to the conference room.

"There will be four of us outside this door, General," the duty officer said.

Bart addressed the two prisoners. "You men are fairly well educated. Did you study Latin?"

The others looked at him in wonderment. Darren answered, "Yes."

"Then you should know the meaning of *Dobio Switt.*"

"No, what does that mean?"

"The day of bullshit is over, so what is the truth?"

The others laughed loudly.

"Now the fun and games are over, men. You guys asked for a deal. That pertained to our case against Hitler and his Nazi vermin. We have another complication here. If you Mayfields are involved in the double homicide of Alden Gaines and Lilly Darcy, then I can't keep you out of the electric chair. Am I clear?"

The two of them looked bewildered and shocked.

"U.S. Attorney Washburn and Assistant FBI Director Bledsoe here want to question you about that. You had better level," Bart continued.

"What homicide? Who killed them? Where? When? How? This is the first we've heard about it," Darren gasped.

"Is this a con job? You guys have got to be kidding," Paul murmured.

"I'll swear on a stack of Bibles we know nothing about it," Darren professed, holding his hands up in prayer.

"Jacques, take off the manacles."

They were removed.

"Messrs. Maybrook and Cartman are here to represent the prosecution in the war crimes trial. U.S. Attorney Washburn and FBI Assistant Director Bledsoe are going to take over the interrogation relative to the murders and their connection with the counterfeit case. I assume the Secret Service will be here in the morning. They're all yours, Farley and Bill."

As Bart and Jacques were about to leave, Darren Mayfield pleaded, "We want to make a deal."

"If you're cooperative here, I'll see you next week. Now be good boys."

For three hours, Washburn and Bledsoe grilled the two brothers, with a little help from Maybrook and Cartman. The Mayfields convinced the group that they had no knowledge of the murders.

"That son of a bitch Gaines was paid to defend us and he ran out on us. It's obvious to me that he was on the lam because those fines were paid in counterfeit money," Darren speculated.

"All right, Darren, let's relax, let your hair down and talk to me, one on one, as an FBI man. You used to be pretty good at your job," Bledsoe said.

"Are you trying to con me?"

"No, Darren. We've given you the whole scenario of what happened in Elizabeth, New Jersey. Let's hear your take on this hit."

Darren looked at his brother questioningly. Washburn, in a friendly tone, gave assurance to both men. "Fellows, you are not targets in this investigation. Now we're asking for your help." Paul nodded at his brother.

"Okay, men, just remember us in your wills. I don't think the shyster Gaines knew that the moolah was phony paper."

"How do you figure that, Darren?" Bledsoe asked.

"Bill, let me give you some background on this stupid counterfeit caper. Pay attention now. Maybrook and Cartman, this will fit into your treasure trove of information. First, I'd appreciate a cigarette and a shot of that booze over there."

He had their attention as Maybrook poured the Mayfields two shot glasses of scotch. Cartman threw a pack of Chesterfields and his lighter on the table.

The Mayfields gulped the scotch and lit their cigarettes.

After a deep drag and emission of smoke through his nostrils, Darren slowly began his recitation. "Gaines had no reason to play with bootleg bucks when he was hired on for his representation of Nordheim/Hitler and me. He was called to New York to meet with my brother, Paul, at the behest of Harry Branlow. Gaines was paid $20 million in a cash advance arranged by Irwin Gullen, who was in Switzerland at that time."

"Hold it there, Darren. Was the cash wired to a bank here?"

"Yes, from the Bank Lorraine in Geneva to Gullen's bank in New York. One of Nordheim-Hitler's trusted troubleshooters is an Irish lady named Louise Maloney, alias Bancroft. She's the broad that hustled that plastic surgeon Lavelle out of Geneva to Malmo, Sweden. She handed Gaines a bag of two-carat, pear-shaped diamonds to be delivered to Hitler, to use as bribes to the guards. She is the same dame that tried to blast Christina Lyons and nab General Milburn. She's from Belfast, Ireland, formerly with the IRA. A tough dame. We had no idea she was going to pull that caper. She had a German guy with her. Isn't that right, Paul?"

"Exactly like you told it."

Maybrook and Cartman scribbled notes frantically.

"Where did you say the money was passed to Gaines?"

"At the Waldorf Astoria. By the way, now that Gaines is gone, we have no lawyers," Darren whined.

"Do you want us to appoint counsel for you?" Washburn offered.

"Not yet. Let us think about that," Paul replied.

"Paul, aren't you leaving something out of what happened at the Waldorf?"

"Darren, what the hell are you talking about?"

"The other money, that the German guy, I can't think of his name…"

"Oh, dammit, I got so caught up in this stupid hit on Gaines and the actress, it slipped my mind. That guy also called himself Bancroft. *Heil Bancroft* doesn't sound so good, does it? Anyway, this kraut hands me a large suitcase. In it were two packages wrapped in brown paper. The large one has the name Nordheim on it. The other one says Paul Mayfield. That's for Nordheim's lawyers and the other is for your brother, Darren, he says in a heavy German accent. Deposit it in a safe-deposit box for when needed. He then hands me ten grand for pocket money. Sorry, I forgot to mention it."

☆ ☆ ☆ ☆

The Victorian House

Bart and Jacques were having their last sip of brandy before retiring. The phone interrupted their relaxation. Bart reached for the phone. "Milburn,"

"This is the White House switchboard, General. We've been calling you for the past two hours."

"This sounds like Helen."

"Yes, sir, that's me."

"What's up now, Helen?"

"A Mr. Ariel Rubin, from Tel Aviv, Israel, says it's urgent that he speak with you."

"First, Helen, I'll be at my home in Washington for the next few days. Let the girls know. Is he on the line now?"

"Yes, sir, and I'll post your home number."

"Put him on, please. Ariel, I don't want to hear any bad news, I'm ready to go to bed."

"Bart, no, this is *good* news."

"Then, let's have it."

"We've been listening to the trial on radio. The Prime Minister and all of us are proud of you. We've also been getting daily reports from Sean Briscoe, who is attending the trial. We have been supporting an organization called the SOS."

"What does that stand for? Not Save Our Souls?"

"It has been a secret of ours. It stands for Society of Survivors. Jews and Christian philanthropists support it all over the world. Some of the contributors would surprise you," Rubin said.

"Well, what is on your mind?"

"It's just like you, General, to always get right to the point. Well, the Prime Minister has six survivors he wants to send you, now that you have a four-day hiatus."

"Ariel, we're getting swamped with witnesses. They have to be powerhouse witnesses. We've revealed a lot of the carnage so far."

"Yes, but what you have are survivors from the upper class of Jews. How about the poor, bottom-of-the-scale types who somehow managed to survive and tell you about the Germans, the Russians, that bastard Stalin, the Ukrainians, Lithuanians, Polish pogroms, Russian pogroms, Romanians, and the turnaround of Pope Pius XII, Pacelli."

"Okay, okay, where are these people?"

"Two are here in Israel. One is in Athens, Greece. Two are in America, one in Windsor, Canada, and one woman just out of Kharkov, Russia."

"How the hell did she get out of Russia?"

"We have our ways, just like we pulled that Laurent girl out of Leipzig. Don't ask."

"Okay, how do you round them up?" Bart asked.

"Our SOS people will take care of that, at no cost to you. Sean Briscoe will bring them to you when they arrive. He'll keep you informed. He'll arrange housing for them. Is it a deal?"

"Depending on what they tell us, we'll put them on. It's a deal."

"*Shalom*, friend."

"*Shalom.*"

"What was that all about?" Jacques asked.

"More witnesses. This time, courtesy of Prime Minister Ben-Gurion. We're getting overloaded. I'll have to cut my direct examinations and get them to the core of the atrocities. It'll have to be an assembly-line operation. Let's hit the hay," Bart suggested wearily.

CHAPTER ELEVEN

Saturday, February 28, 1953 - 11 a.m. - Washington

President Eisenhower had called for a special meeting of the Cabinet and the Joint Chiefs of Staff, and he opened with: "Gentlemen, our ambassador, George Kennan, has pouched an analysis of turbulence in the Kremlin. The Presidium is split. The question before them is Stalin's health. Secretary of State Dulles will brief you. Go ahead, Foster."

"According to our best information to date, Stalin's days are numbered. He is a very sick man."

"What do you base that on?"

"I'll let our new CIA director, my brother Allen, spell that out."

"We have been observing the comings and goings at the Kremlin rather intensively over the past few weeks. We've identified some of Moscow's most prominent physicians attending him. In the last week there has been an unusual amount of activity. We saw oxygen containers delivered," Allen Dulles summed up.

"My question, gentlemen, is which son of a bitch is going to take over? Will the Cold War turn icy?" Eisenhower posited in his question.

"According to Ambassador Kennan, the contest is between Lavrenty Pavlovich Beria, Marshal Nikolai Bulganin and Georgi Malenkov. If it turns out to be Beria, we've got problems. If it is either of the other two, no problem. That is no more than we have now," John Foster Dulles summarized.

Eisenhower turned to General Omar Bradley. "Brad, under these conditions, we can't afford complacency. With the Joint Chiefs present here with our Cabinet, I am herewith ordering a military alert. I know all about Beria.

He is a wily, opportunistic bastard. If he takes over as Premier, he'll try to outdo Stalin. He's the kind that would put his finger on the nuclear button. He was the head of the NKVD, the secret police. He's a killer. When an officer ordered a retreat during the war, his men shot him in the back of the head. Marshal Zhukov told me that Stalin used Beria to kill twenty million Russians. He also was responsible for killing Jews fleeing from the Nazis. Indeed, a very bad man."

"Mr. President, we'll be ready for every contingency. The nuclear button is in your hands, sir," Bradley said.

"Let us pray we won't ever use it."

☆ ☆ ☆ ☆

The same day - Milburn home

The return of Bart and Jacques was the beginning of four festive days. Bart got acquainted with his new son, Quentin, and reinforced the rapport with Michael and Jenny. Elizabeth and Bart, as well as Jacques and Christina, were a pair of young lovers.

The ladies reviewed the trial. Bart informed Elizabeth that she and Joyce would be the last two witnesses before he himself was to be the final witness.

"Why, Bart? You've done your job," Elizabeth protested.

"Honey, my report on the concentration camps and the Nazi death camps has been declassified. I've got to sum up what I saw at Hitler's inferno."

"I guess you're right, sweetheart," she agreed.

Jacques and Christina announced their intention to move to Beverly Hills after the end of the trials.

"Bart, your law firm should open an office there," Jacques suggested.

"That's a dandy idea," Elizabeth said.

"Are you serious, Liz?"

"Of course. This city is for politicians, and it's dull."

"Let me chew on that idea for a while."

The White House operators announced a surprise phone call.

"General Milburn, I have General Telford Taylor on the phone. Shall I put him through?"

"My Lord, yes," Bart said, picking up.

"General Milburn, this is Telford Taylor. Excuse me for disturbing you at your home during this much-needed hiatus."

"General Taylor, I'm honored."

"Please, call me Telford and, presumptuously, I'll call you Barton."

"Fine, Telford. I am pleased to hear from you. Your takeover as chief counsel at Nuremberg was the subject of many accolades by Justice Jackson and myself. I've read your recent book, *The Sword and the Swastika*."

"Thank you, Barton. While I am not an aficionado listening to trial news, I have been riveted by your performance at Fort Leavenworth. Now, here's the purpose of my call. A Holland survivor, a Jewish boy, who was a captain in the Dutch army, is now the military attaché at the Netherlands embassy in

Washington. His story, to follow the splendid testimony of that Lowen girl, will shake the roof of your courtroom. In the vernacular, it's a blockbuster!"

"Sir, you've captured my full attention."

"His name is Colonel Jan Rothleim, very well educated, speaks several languages, stands six feet four, athletic and erudite. Up to now he has not been publicized. He has medals from Queen Wilhelmina, Churchill and the French. His war record is excellent. He was captured fighting with a combination of partisans."

"Interesting. How does he fit?"

"He's been very reticent about what I am about to recount. The colonel was moved from Sobibor to Belsen with hundreds of Hollanders. The British were at the doorstep of a young woman in the throes of giving birth. She was lying on a blanket outside the barracks emitting the usual screams of labor pains when the baby was finally forced out her womb. The crowd of onlookers were yelling, *Mazeltov!* As the baby cried, a Waffen SS captain kicked the woman in the head, killing her instantly. He then picked up the newborn, which was wrapped in towels, and stomped it to death. He then picked up the inert newborn and threw it like a forward pass up against the electric fence."

"Horrible!"

"That's the crux of the sad saga. Colonel Rothleim, despite being held back by his comrades, walked over to the Gestapo Hauptmann, twisted his neck, and in a single movement killed him on the spot, then felt guilty for endangering his fellow POWs; however, the other Jewish prisoners picked up the body of the Gestapo fiend and hid it under the barracks. No other Gestapos were there. The colonel was hustled back to his troops in what was called the Star Camp, holding four thousand other Jews from the Netherlands, who were to be exchanged for German nationals. He'll also tell you about the fate of seventy Dutch Jews. That I'll leave to him."

"Where is he now?"

"In Washington. I persuaded him to testify. After reading about your trial in the papers, he yielded very quickly. I've had a rapport with him since my days at Nuremberg."

"Telford, I'll put him on the stand as my first witness Tuesday morning. Tell him to fly to Kansas City and to take a cab to Fort Leavenworth on Monday. We'll reimburse his expenses and I'll put him up at my house."

"Barton, I hope you'll forgive me for poking my legal nose into your trial."

Bart laughed, "I'm most grateful, Telford."

"When you're back in D.C., let's have lunch."

"That's a date."

✰ ✰ ✰ ✰

Monday, March 2, 1953 - Fort Leavenworth

The provost marshal called the conference room. Jacques answered.

"There's a Jan Rothleim here, sir."

"Send him in."

"Yes, sir."

A handsome, red-headed, hazel-eyed, giant of a man entered the room. He was neatly dressed in a three-button blue jacket and gray flannel trousers.

As Bart approached him, he saluted and in unaccented English, said, "General, it's my pleasure."

"Colonel Rothleim, thank you for coming. I hope you had a nice trip."

"A little bumpy, sir, but, the weather is clear here and the sun's shining."

He was introduced to the prosecution team. The buffet lunch was set up, and the colonel had a ravenous appetite. He repeated the story Telford Taylor had relayed.

"Do I get to see that Hitler bastard?"

"Oh yes, and a few more," Jacques answered.

He warmed up to the prosecution team. Pretty soon they were exchanging war stories. He had a sense of humor and soon had them laughing at some of his anecdotes, many of which were at the expense of dimwitted Nazis. Jacques took him to the house. Mrs. Lawrence showed him to his room.

"You're a big fellow. I don't know much about Dutch cooking, but I'm going to treat you to a good American meal. I hope you like a big New York cut prime steak and french fried potatoes with lots of vegetables and a salad?"

"That will be a real treat, Mrs. Lawrence."

☆ ☆ ☆ ☆

Tuesday, March 3, 1953 - 0900 hours - Fort Leavenworth

The tribunal looked rested. Court was called to order. Bart called his first witness.

The well-dressed young man, an inch taller than his MP escorts, took the oath and sat in the chair with his long legs dangling to the step below.

"Please state your name, sir."

"Colonel Jan Rothleim, Military Attaché to the Netherlands government."

"Your age, sir."

"Thirty-five."

"Where were you born?"

"Rotterdam, Holland."

"Tell us of your family."

"Family? Father, mother, a sister and two brothers. Two aunts, two uncles, four grandparents and ten cousins."

"All living?"

"No, all dead, except my sister and my father."

"How did the others die?"

"In the Nazi gas chambers."

"How did your father and sister survive?"

"My father was a fisherman and owned a small boat. My sister was sixteen years old and she loved the sea. He took her with him that day. The

North Sea was calm. He and the crew had a good catch. When the bombing started over Rotterdam, he and the crew decided to keep going toward England. They landed at Harwich. The English people were very hospitable."

"What happened after that?"

"I was off to the army with my two brothers. My father luckily got a phone call through to the house. My mother told him not to come back. They would try to get to England. A group attempted to leave Rotterdam in another fishing boat and were caught by a German destroyer. The whole family was sent to different camps with two dozen other Jewish friends."

The colonel related his story with little prodding from Bart. He and his brothers had joined the troops defending The Hague. After five days of intensive battle, holding off the blitzkrieg, the Nazis pulled back and attacked Rotterdam. The Queen and the government were protected. They boarded two British destroyers. He and his two brothers and a large number of Dutch troops retreated and joined partisan groups. In 1944, still in uniform, they were captured by the Nazis and shipped to Bergen, then to Bergen-Belsen.

"Tell the court of your experiences at Bergen-Belsen," Bart urged.

"The Allied troops were getting closer. We could hear the artillery in the distance. They moved the POWs from Bergen to the main camp at Bergen-Belsen. We were placed in what was called the Star Camp there, reserved for four thousand prisoners to be exchanged for Germans captured by the Allies. The camp mostly held Russian POWs. The Nazis knew the war was lost, so they started selling Jews for payments. Hungarian Jews and others went to Palestine and Switzerland. We were allowed to walk around the camp."

He related the story of the mother giving birth and what happened afterward. The shock in the courtroom was evident by the moans of the spectators.

"Colonel, how did you manage to evade Gestapo punishment for killing that Gestapo animal?" Bart asked.

"Since none of the Nazis saw what I did, my troops kept me under cover and none of the civilian Jews spoke of it. In fact, they spread rumors that the Nazi who killed the mother and her baby had defected and was seen crawling to the Allied lines. That rumor reached the ears of the commandant."

"How soon did the Allies reach your camp?"

"Not soon enough."

"Please explain."

"Just a few weeks before the British troops liberated the camp, the civilian prisoners and the Russian POWs were preparing an uprising. Some rifles and handguns disappeared from the Nazis' arsenal. They questioned two of the prisoners about the planned uprising and the disappearance of the arms in front of all the slave labor in the large camp."

"Did they admit anything?"

"On the contrary. Suddenly two Waffen SS officers produced long swords and, in a rehearsed movement, raised the swords and viciously cut the prisoners' heads off. I saw their heads bouncing on the ground."

A gasp resonated throughout the courtroom. Rothleim grimly stared at the defendants.

"What was the reaction of the camp prisoners?"

"Distress, disgust, fear and grief. The next morning, seventy men and women were beheaded. Then all hell broke loose. Prisoners attacked Gestapos. The prisoners lost that battle. They were machine-gunned. Bodies were spread all over the yard. My two brothers and others were ordered to carry the bodies to the crematorium. At that time I was in SS headquarters, at their request, to lead our POWs in a planned exchanged deal with the Allies. After the plan was worked out, I went back to the Star Camp to brief my men. My brothers weren't there. I went to look for them. A Russian POW, a captain, stopped me at the small camp alongside the crematorium and mass graves."

The colonel showed his first sign of emotion. His eyes teared and he wiped his face with the back of his hand. He reached for a glass of water.

"Go on, Colonel."

"The Russian and I had a language problem. I could see he was quite agitated. I asked him if he spoke German. He gasped at me and said, *Dein Bruder ist tot.* I shook him. He put his finger to his head and simulated a shooting. I ran toward the crematorium, and through the fence, I saw prisoners lifting my brother, Albert. He was being thrown into the mass grave. A minute later, I saw Aaron, my other brother, being put in the crematorium. I admit I was almost faint. At that moment, in my grief, I just lay there. It was getting dark. The prisoners were going back to their barracks. I followed them into the little camp next to the Star Camp."

"Were you able to talk to them?"

"Yes, later that night. I whistled and one of the prisoners, who spoke German, brought out the ones I followed."

The explanation, he described, indicated that his two brothers were too slow in lifting some of the headless bodies. A deputy commandant and a Waffen SS lieutenant shot the brothers in the back of their heads as an example to the rest of the prisoners.

In the stillness of the courtroom, Bart asked, "Did you ever see those men who killed your brothers?"

"Oh yes, I did. Two days later, on April 15, 1945, the British army came into the camp. They found sixty thousand prisoners sick and emaciated. Corpses by the thousands were strewn all over the camp waiting to be buried or burned. Some of the British soldiers on the tanks were Jewish. I hooked up with three of them, a Captain Samuel Garfield and two lieutenants, Arthur Blake and Adam Weimer."

"My question was, *Did you see the men who killed your brothers?*"

"I said *yes.*"

"When and how?"

The colonel remained mute.

"Why won't you answer?"

After a tense moment he spoke. "I took a page out of these heartless Nazis' book and did something I don't wish to talk about."

"Did you kill them?"

"No, I did something worse."

"What could be worse?"

"A living death."

"Explain that, please."

"The three British officers helped me find the prisoners who saw the execution of my two brothers. We took them to verify the two men who murdered Aaron and Albert. I found them hiding at the Star Camp, wearing prison clothes. I asked my Jewish prisoners to be absolutely sure these were the men, whose names were Colonel Joachim Klaus and Hauptmann Hans Kleschner. At my request, the British and the prisoners left me alone with them."

"Why?"

"I beat the hell out of them until they were unconscious. By the way, I had found my uniform and was wearing it. When people came into the Star Camp barracks, I waved them away. I threw some water on the Gestapos and asked them where they hid their uniforms. I found all their things under the mattress of one of the beds. Their Walther guns were in their holsters."

"What did you do?"

"Something that will keep them from ever hurting another Jew or any other human being again. They begged for their lives. I took their prison uniforms with the Star of David sewn on them and stuck it in their faces. I made them kiss the Star of David time and again. I had the two Walther guns, one in each hand. With each kiss I fired a shot into their kneecaps, their hands, their arms, their elbow joints, and then I castrated them with my guns."

Astonishment was evident on every face in the courtroom.

"Did they die?"

"No, I made sure they would get immediate attention. The medics came and tended to them. The doctor was a Jew, a British major. I begged him to keep them alive."

"Why?"

"Because these two vipers were the men who beheaded all those Jews. I wanted them to be paraplegics for the rest of their lives and think about their bestiality. They are alive today and are paraplegics. That's my justice for these Nazi cobras. I assure you, by nature I'm a gentle man."

"No further questions," Bart murmured.

"The defense may cross-examine," Nimitz declared.

"Colonel Rothleim, you are the military attaché to the government of the Netherlands, is that correct?" Erich Stolz asked, rising.

"Yes."

"Are you representing your government in testifying here?"

"No, I am here as an individual."

"Are you using your government's funds for your expenses coming here?"

"No, and before you ask, I expect to be recompensed by the prosecution in this case. I used my own money to come here."

"On another subject, how many men have you murdered?"

"Objection. The word *murdered* is outrageous. I demand it be stricken," Bart snapped.

"Sustained. Counselor Stolz, do you wish to rephrase?"

"You have killed men, have you not?"

"Not men, just Nazis."

"Why *just Nazis*?"

"Because they were shooting at me."

"How about the man whose neck you broke at Bergen-Belsen?"

"That was an execution for a double murder of a mother who had just given birth and the baby she produced. That's justice in a hell created by Hitler, Himmler, Goering, Goebbels and all the rest of the Third Reich of Germany."

"Colonel, can't you give me a direct answer without propaganda?"

Bart stood up to object, when the colonel raised his voice in reply.

"Propaganda? Your clients made it a new art form based on lies, deceit, robbery, murder, mayhem and calculated, premeditated murder. That's propaganda?"

"Objection - the witness has not been responsive."

"Overruled. Counselor, you used the word *propaganda*. The witness answered you in kind with his definition of the word," Nimitz ruled.

"Colonel, did you concoct those stories about the mother and the baby and the beheading of all those people?"

Rothleim leaned back in his chair, stretched his feet and jutted his jaw. "I am glad you asked that question. It so happens that your arrogant, dimwitted Waffen SS saw fit to film those outrages to send to Himmler and Hitler for their depraved mental orgasms. Those films were captured by the Allies. They are in the American, British and Holland archives. Arthur Brisbane said a picture is worth a thousand words. Those horrors are things that cannot be *concocted*, as you say. Only a demented society of savages can perform such acts."

"Have you seen those films?"

"Counselor, not only have I seen those films, I personally saw thousands and thousands of Nazi-slaughtered carcasses. Your attempt to defend these lice is an exercise in futility. The Holocaust will be remembered throughout the history of mankind. We can't let the revisionists try to erase it. We must remind the world of the greatest carnage since the beginning of civilization. Tell that to your true clients, the Swiss bankers that robbed the Jews and millions of others."

"Stop right there. I object to this witness's calumny."

Bart rose.

"Calumny? The precise word for the Nazis. Your Honors, there is nothing false or malicious in the witness's statement. Some synonyms of that choice word are deserved by the vermin being tried here. Character assassination? They have no character. Slander? Not when it's true. Defamation? How can one defame these monsters?"

"Gentlemen, hold it. You can argue these issues in your closing arguments. Let's move on," Nimitz ordered.

Hitler summoned Erich Stolz.

"Why you let him make speeches like that?"

"I couldn't stop him."

"Let me go on the stand now," Hitler requested.

"No, not until it's our turn."

"Then get him off the stand."

"No further questions," Stolz declared.

"Call your next witness, General," Nimitz declared.

Rothleim left the stand and whispered to Bart that he would like to stay to watch the proceedings. Bart beckoned Jacques. "Let him sit with you."

"Jan, you're a helluva witness," Jacques complimented him.

The next witness came through the doors in a wheelchair, propelled by two MPs. She was a thin woman with a full head of grayish white hair. She seemed to be in her sixties, her face wrought with wrinkles, and a scar was evident on her chin. She stared straight ahead, oblivious to the packed courtroom. The clerk held a bible in front of her for the oath.

"*Ich vil nicht,*" she whispered in Yiddish. Chaplain Gordon handed a Hebrew Bible to Bart, who gave it to the clerk.

"Try this," he whispered.

The woman muttered, "*Ach, das ist gut,*" and complied with the oath.

"Your Honors, with your permission, one of my assistants could ask her what language she prefers."

"Go ahead," Nimitz replied. "Identify yourself for the record."

"I am Phillip Berger, with the CIA and a member of the bar."

"Proceed."

"*Penyamya Papolski, Penyamya Russki, ober Yiddish?*"

"*Ich vill sprechen Yiddish.*"

"Your Honors, I will do my best in German, which is akin to Yiddish with some words in Yiddish, helped by Mr. Berger."

"Do we have a Yiddish interpreter?" Bart asked.

One in the group raised his hand.

"Let's proceed," Nimitz urged.

In German, Bart asked the lady to state her name.

"I am Malka Molovski."

"Where are you from?"

"Lublin, near Radom, Poland."

"Tell the court about your family."

"My father was a rabbi. My mother was a midwife. I had two sisters and one brother. I was the oldest."

"Any other relatives?"

"Two grandparents; the other two were killed in a pogrom in Kharkov, Russia. Also, two aunts and uncles were killed there."

"Was that during the war?"

"No, they were killed during a pogrom by Russian cossacks. They also burned down our synagogue in 1916. I was four years old then."

Bart stood back and took a long look at her, musing arithmetically on her current age, which belied her looks.

"That would make you forty-one years of age now. Pardon me, but you look much older."

"*Einshuldig mir*, I can't help it."

The interpreter said, "Excuse me, I can't help it."

"Then you were born in Russia."

"Yes. When the First World War was over, my father, mother, my two sisters and I left Kharkov. The communists were just as bad as the anti-Semitic cossacks. They were ruffians. Lenin and Stalin were killers too."

The Nazi defendants applauded. Nimitz angrily gaveled for order.

"So you settled in the outskirts of Lublin. You were twenty-five years old then?"

"Yes. I married a Polish man. We had two children, a boy two years old and a girl, one year old."

"You didn't mention a husband and two children."

"I was talking about relatives in Russia, not Poland. My husband worked as a garbage collector. I worked as a maid for a Christian family, nice people. The world came to an end for us when these Nazi monsters invaded Poland. My brother and husband were rushed into the Polish army. My sisters went to help at the hospital. One week after the invasion, our synagogue was burned down. The Gestapo dragged my father into the street. They were pulling him by his beard. I was hiding in a bakery store across the street. My mother was taking care of my babies. They took the Torah from the synagogue, ripped it, piece by piece, page by page, and pasted it on my papa. The Gestapo men were laughing at him. They set his beard on fire and then lit matches to the Torah pages on him, spilled kerosene on him and burned him to death."

"Did they come after you?" Bart asked.

"No, I fainted, and the baker carried me to his cellar. He was a Catholic. The Gestapo and some soldiers came into the bakery and stole all the bread. The baker came for me. He put water on my face. After it got dark, he closed the store and covered my face with a cloth so I wouldn't see my father's body, which was still in the street. I tore the cloth off and lay on my father's burned body and cried. The baker's wife showed up. They pulled me off his body and ran with me to the Catholic church. The priest, Father Paul, put me in the rectory with Sister Magda, a nice elderly woman. Mikhail Lodonovich and his wife, Elsa, and the priest were going to my house in his baker's truck to pick up my mother and sisters. They were only stopped once, but Father Paul explained they were Catholic."

"Did they bring your mother and sisters and the children to the church?"

"Yes, after they packed their clothes and small valuables, like a *menorah*. My mother was faint when they got to the church. Sister Magda prepared potato soup and home-baked bread for us."

"How long did you stay at the church?"

"One week, and a neighbor told the Gestapo we were hiding in the church. Most of the shooting was over. The Nazis occupied all of Poland. So one night over fifteen hundred Jews were put in a caravan to Majdanek, a piece of hell."

"How did you manage to survive?"

"You'll have to ask God. It would have been better if I had died. After my mother, sisters and I were stripped naked, they took all our clothes and the rings on our hands. They gave us prison uniforms with the Star of David on them. The next morning, my mother was made a cook. My sisters and I were house cleaners for the officers. Lots of Jews were sent to the gas chambers. Others were put in forced labor. But the worst came that first afternoon. They took my little boy and girl from me. I ran after the men that took the children. Someone hit me on the head. I was unconscious. I never saw my children again."

"What happened to them?"

"At first I was told that there was a children's barracks camp on the other side of the camp. It had a playground..." She began to cry fitfully.

Bart waited.

"I was cleaning Major Alfred Loehmann's quarters one day, and he said, *It is too bad about your children, Magda*. I asked him what he meant. He told me that Colonel Gunther Wachtel threw both of them into the burning furnace at the crematorium. He thought I knew. I cried. He put his arms around me and tried to comfort me. He didn't get fresh or sexual. He said, *Be careful, someday I'll tell you something*."

"How long were you at Majdanek?"

"Until the Russians came, in July 1944, but before that I saw tens of thousands of Russian prisoners of war gassed to death. I saw at least one hundred thousand Jews killed and thousands of Christians die of starvation. My mother smuggled food out of the kitchen for my sisters and me. Major Loehmann became a colonel. He had nothing to do with the killing. He was in charge of administration - ordering materials and punishing soldiers who misbehaved. He protected us."

"Why did he protect you?" Bart asked.

"I suppose he liked me."

"Did you have sexual relations with him?"

"No. Near the time of liberation, he told me he loved me and revealed he was half Jewish. His grandfather was a Jew living in America. I asked him why he didn't escape. He told me that they kill the whole families of deserters. He said he saved a lot of Jews. That night my two sisters were gang-raped. They staggered to the barracks. I went to Loehmann and he took them to the hospital."

"Did they survive?"

"Not for long. Colonel Wachtel had them removed from the hospital, but not before my sisters gave us the names and descriptions of the rapists. That night, Loehmann went to Wachtel's quarters and shot him once in his groin and once between the eyes. Then he rounded up the rapists and charged them with the murder of Colonel Wachtel. Of course they denied it. At 6 a.m., that morning, the ten of them were put before a firing squad and killed."

"That is quite a bit of justice."

"Yes, but we paid for it. A General Schellenberg came into the camp and advised that it be cleaned up so the Allies couldn't see the crematorium and the gas chambers. He ordered that all the pits filled with dead bodies be covered up. Two Gestapo men told him that Loehmann killed ten men and that it was he who shot Wachtel. He ordered Loehmann's arrest. I saw the General take out his gun and shoot Loehmann. I threw myself on top of him. They fired shots into both of my legs. At that time everyone was running. The Russians had entered the camp."

"Was Major Loehmann dead?"

"Almost. I pleaded with a Russian colonel to save him and me. My legs were badly shot up. I speak good Russian, but didn't want to do so today. I hate communists. I explained that Loehmann was a Jew and so was I. The colonel ordered his men to take us to the hospital and had his medics take care of us."

"Did Loehmann survive?"

"Yes, the bullet just missed his heart."

"How about your legs?"

She lifted the blanket and exposed one amputated leg below her left knee. The audience gasped loudly.

"What happened to Major Loehmann?"

"He married me, and we live in Israel. We have two little boys, and I'm pregnant with the third child. We're poor people. My husband drives a taxi in Tel Aviv. I've been measured for a prosthesis, a gift from the Israeli government. I'll be walking soon."

"Malka, why did you insist on testifying in Yiddish?" Bart asked in Russian.

"For my fellow survivors around the world."

"*Harashaw.* No more questions. Your witness for cross."

"In what language do you want to answer my questions, Madame?" Erich Stolz asked in German.

In classic German, she replied, "Nazi talk will do."

"Is that because you married a Nazi?"

"He was never a Nazi. He is a Jew who infiltrated your Gestapo. He was a spy in your midst. He saved hundreds of Jews from your killing machines."

"*Genug, schweigen!*" Hitler shouted.

Startled, Stolz turned and said, "No further questions."

Nimitz declared a recess for lunch, and added, "Court will resume at 1430 hours."

Malka wheeled over and raised her arms around Bart. He leaned down. She planted a kiss on his cheek and in English, whispered, "I trust you. My husband works for the Mossad. Ariel Rubin is our friend. Check with Sean Briscoe over there."

"He drives a cab too," Bart offered.

"Yes, a very special cab. But he still tracks Nazis."

"You're special, too."

"*Gey gesunterheit,*" Bart said.

During the recess, the defense team of Luther Krieger, Eric Stolz and adviser Gertrud Scholtz-Klink met with Hitler and the commandant defendants.

"This is not a Nuremberg-type trial!" Hitler angrily exploded. "That General Milburn is very sharp. He is destroying me and the whole Nazi cause like a surgeon. He's putting on a show for the whole world. This trial must stop. At this point it's obvious we will have a mass hanging," he declared in German.

"Pleading guilty won't be accepted by the tribunal," Krieger asserted.

"*Arschloch*, why should we plead guilty? I have to get on the stand and make a speech for the world to hear. With a loyal general staff, I could have won the war. It was Himmler, Heydrich, Goering, Hess, Joseph Dietrich, Eichmann, Hans Frank, Goebbels, big-mouth Schellenberg and others that killed those Jews, not me. I used them for political pawns. My tirade against them elected me. I was busy running the war. When we had control of North Africa, that was the time to export the Jews to Africa. Personally, I never killed a Jew."

Gertrud Scholtz-Klink, the Nazi women's leader, blonde, tall, and the mother of eleven children, was known as the Lady Führer. The fifty-one-year-old woman placed a cigarette in a gold holder and blew a few rings of smoke.

"What do you think, Gertrud?" Hitler asked.

"Adolf, you believe in what the Americans call bullshit. I'm tired of you passing the blame to everyone. You had Germany in your grip. You were *Der Führer*, the emperor, the tyrant, and the most feared man in all of Europe. You used the Jews as slave laborers and you knew they were being slaughtered by Himmler, Reinhardt, and animals like Höss, the commandant at Auschwitz. Did you read his diary that that lady threw at you in the court? He admitted killing two and a half million Jews."

"Stop that *now!*" Hitler screamed.

She yelled back, "No! I won't stop! I am trying to make you face the truth."

Krieger and Stolz were shocked by her attack. "This is not necessary," Stolz asserted.

"Shut up, just listen. When you were *Der Führer*, Adolf, Goebbels put on a great show for you with storm troopers, Gestapos, well trained troops and a Roman Empire style. With *Sieg Heils* and *Heil Hitlers*, you turned Germany into a military machine. With all the blitzkriegs against weak nations, you had practically all of Europe occupied."

"You shrew, what do you know? I was a leader of a disloyal staff."

"*Dog scheisse*, Adolf. Face up to it. You are a megalomaniac, like the Americans call you. Just think of what you did in your lifetime. You were born in 1889. When the war ended, you were fifty-six years old. You are now sixty-three. You stupidly attacked Russia, instead of consolidating your successes at that point. You were still fighting England, you were wasting your resources shipping Jews into a network of concentration camps in twenty countries, wasting money, men and a total national effort. So you attack the Soviet Union. Then, after the Japs got into the act, you stupidly declare war against the United States. Your war at sea was going badly. I count this as five fronts. Stupid, stupid."

Hitler put his head in his hands and covered his ears.

She continued, "You, with the help of the Swiss, became the richest man in the world. Now, instead of using your wealth properly, after you changed your face, you launched a Revenge Plan. Now the Jews have their own country, Israel, with a great air force and army. They call you a maniac. I think they are right."

Hitler rose and went into his typical tirade. *"Du bist ein hinterfotziger Verräter.* Your talent is *bumsen.* Eleven children, that's what you can do. Lay on your back and make babies."

"You are a sick man, Adolf. Pray they hang you and put you out of your misery. You sent for me. I am sick of what I have heard in this court. Germany today is ashamed of you and the whole damn Nazi *bullscheisse.* Think of the brains you put in those gas chambers. The Jews helped discover atomic energy. They stamped out infantile paralysis. You fool. Our German youth are ashamed. You and Stalin deserve each other. Go make your big speech. You learned how to be an orator in beer halls after your derelict days as an Austrian. You're not even a true German. You are an immigrant. You make me sick."

The commandants were in a state of shock.

Hitler yelled, "Gertrud, get out of here!"

She left.

In the prosecution conference room, the radio was on, and Lowell Thomas was commenting on the crisis in the Kremlin: "Despite denials from sources in the Politburo, there is every indication that Josef Stalin, communist dictator of the Soviet Union, is critically ill. Based on the flurry of activity in the Comintern and the Presidium, I would speculate that an era is about to end. Reliable sources predict the death of the Premier within twenty-four to forty-eight hours. We also have learned that there is a great deal of infighting at the Kremlin over a choice of a successor. The free world is monitoring developments here in Moscow."

Bart turned the radio off and commented, "That son of a bitch caused the death of twenty million people."

"Too bad he can't take Hitler's hand into hell's inferno with him," Jacques commented.

"Amen. Let's move on to another matter," Bart said. "We have an overwhelming response from these broadcasts. Survivors from all over the world have written and phoned their willingness to testify. If we keep this up, we'll be on trial for a year. I want to get all the atrocities I can, but, as I said before, we have to truncate the trial, yet get the full story told. The Lord only knows how long Hitler and the defense will talk."

"Bart, your idea the other day should give us the full picture. Those six soldiers at the killing camps, interspersed with our survivors, should produce the major evidence we need," Gideon Cartman suggested.

"I think they will need a little warmup to tell it all," Jacques Laurent commented.

"All right, we'll probe them tonight and tomorrow before we put them on. Let's talk to von Maunder about it. Also, we need more time before presenting our next witness. I'm going to request an adjournment until Thursday."

Back in the courtroom, the tribunal announced that court would be adjourned to Thursday, March 5th, at 0900, at the request of the prosecution. "Any objections by the defense?" Nimitz asked.

"None, sir," Krieger asserted.

Bart ordered Jacques to round up the prosecution team to convene in the conference room as soon as possible. Berger was chatting with Sean Briscoe. Maybrook, Douglas Milburn and Quentin Reynolds were huddled. Twenty minutes later Jacques ushered the team into the conference room where Bart was on the phone, smoking a cigarette. He had his long legs on the conference table and was leaning back in his chair. He held his hand up for silence. "My team is here now. Let me put this call on a speakerphone. This involves us." Attorney General Herb Brownell came on loud and clear. "Okay, Bart, give them a quick update on what we told you, so far."

"Folks," Bart said, "I have the Attorney General and the deputy director of the FBI, Sam Foxworth, on the phone. The murders of Alden Gaines and Lilly Darcy have been solved. Take it from there, Sam and Herb."

"Sam, start with the break."

"General, before I begin, am I sure that the only ones in that room are your CIA people and your prosecutors?"

"Correct. Each with top clearance. Shoot."

"We traced the license plate of the limo to Gotham Car Rentals. The nightman at Gotham found the rental slip and a copy of a young woman's driver's license, which is required by the company. In short, we found her, sweated her, and she revealed the names and locations of the three hit men and the two men and a woman in the station wagon. The hit was on February 25. On the 28th, we rounded up the gang with twenty million good American dollars and a package of two-carat, pear-shaped diamonds. They were a bunch of half-assed ex-cons who were paid twenty-five G's for the job. I stop here for Attorney General Brownell."

"Barton, the hit opens up a big can of worms. Murder is murder, and that's in the jurisdiction of the Union County DA in New Jersey. What we have here is international in scope. Hold on to your chairs, my friends. The hit was ordered by none other than Irwin Gullen, chairman and CEO of the International Merchants Bank, and his vice president, Harry Branlow."

A few whispered "wows" were expressed.

"They're a real quinella," Bart said.

"That's not all. Treasury tells us that those two were involved in the Nazi scheme to destroy the economies of the Allies by the Nazis flooding the world with counterfeit American dollars, British pounds, French francs, German marks, etcetera," Brownell continued. "The conduits for laundering involve a guy named Schlicht, who's the chief stockholder of the Banque Royale in Zurich and the International Merchants Bank in New York. To coin a word, they are all umbilically tied to *Der Führer*. You have a guy in custody who can cut the cord. Herr Martin Bormann. He may not be involved, but he knows the answers."

"Quite a story, but why the hit on Alden Gaines?"

"They figured he was on the lam and that if apprehended he would bargain his way out of the bastille by opening Pandora's Box," Foxworth declared. "Gaines was active in the money-laundering business in Las Vegas, Monte Carlo, and all over South America, particularly Argentina."

"We have Secret Service agents Witten and Parker here who have delivered Branlow into our custody," Brownell advised.

Bart laughed, "Glad you've got that rotten bastard. We don't want any part of him. One thing, Herb...the bit about destroying the economy of the world should not be made public or revealed to the press. That's part of our evidence. Don't forget, we found the phony money and the plates. Witten and Parker were part of our raids."

"No problem. We're giving very little to the media. Thanks for your cooperation, Bart."

"Happy to oblige. We can exchange notes if and when necessary, fellas. *Ciao.*"

Bart hung up the phone, then said, "I'm glad that matter's out of our hands. All right, folks, let's not dwell on this news. What I want to talk about is the direction of our trial. I want to put it in perspective. Get your pens out and make notes."

There was some mumbling about the Gaines development.

"Hey, let's stop the chatter and get down to business," Bart ordered, tapping a glass with a spoon. "I want your full attention."

His tone and attitude indicated a profound change in his normal demeanor. He looked around the table at each member of the prosecution team.

"The harrowing tales we've elicited for the eyes and ears of a world audience from our survivors barely exposes the havoc that these Nazi cretins have wrought over a period of twelve years. They have committed every crime in the history of mankind and invented new ones. Just think about it."

"Barton, what are you getting at?" Maybrook asked.

"Richard, we have the attention of the world. The war ended eight years ago, but most of our population have forgotten the bestiality of these Nazi bastards. Millions of people are trying to reconstruct their lives. Between Hitler and Stalin, forty to fifty million died. Six million Jews were wantonly slaughtered and millions of Christians died. Innocent people of all faiths were killed. Let's put this in its proper perspective. Hitler is just a showpiece in this trial. There is a subliminal coterie extant in high places throughout this world who nurtured the seeds of fascism in the two past decades. They reside in ivory towers and use all of mankind's foibles to culminate their evil crop."

"Please forgive me, general. That is an excellent philosophical statement. Is that the prelude to a specific call for a change in trial strategy?" Wilford Ross asked.

"Right on the button, General."

"One last point to my call for perspective. The civilian casualties in this war are compounded by the military youth expended in the war, which could have been averted but for the complacency and apathy of our world leaders. Here's some military numbers. Germany - 3,250,000 dead and 7,250,000 wounded, for a total of 10,500,000. Of the U.S., 300,000 dead, 700,000 wounded, for a total of one million. Great Britain - 360,000 dead and 370,000 wounded, for a total of 730,000. Add those figures to all participants and the Nazi civilian carnage, and it staggers sanity."

"What do you want to do, General?" Cartman asked.

"We're going to have a change of pace. We're going to move the trial into high gear. That's why I asked the tribunal for a one-day continuance."

"Barton, what specifically do you want us to do?" Jacques asked.

"I want a full-court press on each and every witness. No punches pulled. For example, Martin Bormann goes the alpha-omega route; either he hangs or goes to boot camp. Every nasty secret has to come out of his mouth. How the Nazis took power and turned Germany into a nation of genocidal monsters. We have six Nazi soldiers who can detail the methodical murders at the death camps with the cooperation of von Maunder. We'll use every witness to expose the Nazi supporters here in the U.S., England, France, Switzerland, and the world over. Sophia and Tony put Bormann through the grinder. Jacques, hand out the assignments on this sheet. Start at 0900 and go all day. Cartman, prepare the survivors to be interspersed between these canaries. I am working on a couple of surprise witnesses. Add to those numbers the Soviet figures. Any questions?"

A short pause ensued. "No? Well then, have a nice evening, friends."

At the house, Bart showered, donned a sweatsuit, poured a scotch on the rocks and settled into a huge leather chair in the den. He called the White House operators, asking them to locate Supreme Court Justice Jackson. Ten minutes passed and the operator rang back. "I have Justice Jackson on the phone, General."

"Bob, sorry to bother you. I hope I'm not disturbing you," Bart began.

"Not at all, Bart - I'm at home. You're doing fine. This is an excellent departure from what we did at Nuremberg. What's on your mind?"

"I've got survivors from all over the world. It would take a year to describe all the atrocities. I'm about to go for the jugular to expose how this Nazi aberration came about and expose their closet supporters."

"How are you going to do that?"

Bart explained his plan.

"Not bad, not bad. Dramatic as well, stirring up a hornet's nest in high places. You'll have a host of enemies, Bart."

"I'll balance that with the millions of friends I'll acquire. Do you see any objection to the plan?"

"No. This country and the rest of the world need that kind of catharsis."

"Bob, there are two witnesses I want to find. However, I need your advice on the efficacy of using them. And further, how do I get them? You know both witnesses."

"Don't keep me in suspense, Bart, who are they?"

"Von Papen and Schacht."

"My, my, you really are going for the jugular. Von Papen despises Hitler. He was acquitted by the Nuremberg tribunal, then found guilty by a German denazification court and sentenced to eight years of hard labor. However, he was freed for time served. I think he'd like to speak his piece to a world audience. Schacht was also acquitted at Nuremberg. He's furious at me for trying him. I can help you with von Papen, but not Schacht. Don't try to get either of them through official channels. Keep our State Department out of it."

"Any suggestions?"

"I'll call von Papen's lawyer, Johann Lister, and try him for size. I suggest you call Schacht at his office in Munich. He's the chairman of a privately held investment company called Schacht & Lieber International. He might jump at the opportunity. Both of these men are in their seventies. I'll call you directly tomorrow, Bart."

"Thanks, Bob."

Mrs. Lawrence knocked on the door.

"Come in."

"General, your dinner is ready. Is Mr. Laurent going to join you?"

"I don't know what's holding him up. But I'll go ahead without him."

Bart dined alone, studying full and partial confessions. He perused the interviews with survivors volunteering to testify, then said, "Mrs. Lawrence, it's time for you to go home. Jacques will have to warm up his dinner when he arrives. I know your husband is in the kitchen. Send him in, please."

Sergeant Lawrence saluted.

"Take your wife home now. That's an order," Bart said, smiling.

"Yes, sir."

In the den, Bart sipped a snifter of brandy, smoked a cigar and listened to the radio commentators discuss the atrocities. Snippets of eyewitness accounts of concentration camps being liberated filled out their discussions. Ed Murrow warned the audience that the stories might be too horrible for children and even shocking for some adults. Bart looked at his wristwatch. It was close to midnight. He heard Jacques open the front door. "Where the hell have you been?" he asked when Jacques poked his head in the den.

"The team decided to fan out tonight. We had some interesting talks with our special Nazi jailbirds. Your talk to us hit home. I'll be right back," he added as he went to the kitchen. Ten minutes later, he was back with a sandwich and a bottle of beer.

"What's that?"

"It's a lukewarm meatloaf sandwich. It suits me just fine."

"What was accomplished?"

Jacques was chewing his food and trying to answer. Bart held up his hand for a time-out. After a long swig on his beer, Jacques spoke up. "Bart, we screened the camp soldiers. I made a few choice remarks. They are prepared to sing the whole libretto and a few operas ad nauseam." He gulped the rest of his sandwich and emptied the beer bottle. "Mr. Bancroft, a.k.a. Walter Schellenberg, the lovely head of the foreign intelligence arm of the SS, is a pompous ass, but he'll talk. I did something I should have cleared with you."

"What's that?"

"I walked in on Bormann while Sophia and Tony were working on him."

"Why did you do that?"

"I wanted to open him up like a can of sardines."

"Were Sophia and Tony upset?"

"No, as a matter of fact, Sophia was very fast on the uptake."

"How so?"

"She told Bormann I was your right-hand man and would have a big say in his sentence, such as hanging, boot camp or a possible suspended sentence. He began to patronize me. I took a tough stand and told him that General Milburn expects him to tell the court everything about the Nazi takeover of Germany and all their secret allies. I laid it on thick. No talkie, no walkie."

"What was his reaction?"

"Well, Sophia and Tony were great. They piled it on some more. He finally said he'll go all the way. He is going to make some notes tonight for them to pick up in the morning."

"Great. Now, just between us, I am trying to get some very important surprise witnesses."

"Such as?"

"Fix us a brandy and I'll lay it out."

Jacques poured a fair amount for Bart and himself. Bart relit his cigar.

"Okay, Bart, surprise me."

"Franz von Papen and Hjalmar Schacht."

"You've got to be kidding?"

"I would like to get Martin Niemöller, Otto Strasser, Kurt Zeitzler, Franz Pfeffer, Müller, Schellenberg, and, of course, our star, Martin Bormann. With the six soldiers and our survivors, we'll have a grand finale for our extravaganza of iniquity."

"If you could pull that off, you'd be the incarnation of Merlin the Magician," Jacques said.

"It's about ten o'clock on the coast. I'm going to call George Spota in L.A."

Bart picked up the phone and dialed. Spota answered. Small talk ensued and then Bart got down to business.

"I need some help, my friend."

"Name it."

"George, I need a topnotch film editor."

"What's the project?"

"Strictly off the record, we have lots of footage on the Nazi atrocities. I want to put this stuff in order, starting with Hitler's beginning and following with whatever we can add to it. We need the Nazi bullshit Goebbels-staged propaganda panoplies right through the rise and fall to the macabre scenes of the death camps. I need two hours of footage to present to the tribunal."

"Gotcha. The perfect man for the job is Dick Reilly. He just finished a picture for me. He's the best. When do you want this done, and where?"

"Short answer - yesterday and here."

"Naturally. Do you have a moviola there?"

"What's that?"

Spota laughed, "Dear Bart, it's a machine used for editing a rough cut of a picture and synchronizing sound."

"Well, there goes my career as a producer."

"Hold it, Bart. This is easily solved, would-be producer. First, Reilly and I will go to Sherman Grinberg's film library and find all the footage on Hitler and the Nazis. Grinberg's company is the largest private collector of historical footage. After that, Reilly and a moviola and other needed equipment will come to Fort Leavenworth."

"I'll send a plane for him and the equipment. He'll be housed here at the fort. Send me a bill for his services, the extra footage and the moviola."

"Done. After this is over, come on out with Elizabeth. This is God's country."

"George, I am very grateful. I'd love to visit you."

"No problem, brother; I'll call you tomorrow evening."

CHAPTER TWELVE

Wednesday, March 4, 1953 - Fort Leavenworth - the Victorian house
At breakfast, Jacques and Bart discussed plans for putting the Nazi prisoners through a truth grinder. The red phone interrupted Bart's harangue, so he answered.

"This is Robert Jackson. I spoke with von Papen's lawyer. His client will accept a direct call from you, Barton. Here's his number. Call him now. Good luck."

"Thanks, Bob."

Milburn placed the person-to-person call.

"This is Franz von Papen."

Addressing him in German, Bart introduced himself.

"Your German is excellent, General."

"*Danke Schön, mein Herr.*"

"Let's speak English," suggested von Papen, the former Weimar chancellor and later vice chancellor under Hitler.

"Very well, sir. This is somewhat presumptuous on my part, sir, but I would like very much to have you testify at the war-crimes trial here in the United States."

"General Milburn, I have followed the trial and I am very impressed with your acumen. I've thought about it this morning after Justice Jackson's call to my attorney, with whom I've discussed this at length."

"Your conclusion, sir?"

"I will accept your invitation under certain conditions."

"You have my full attention, sir."

"All of Germany is in a state of shock and shame. I was acquitted at

Nuremberg, but found guilty by a denazification court here. Now I am delighted to see that miserable megalomaniac Hitler being exposed for the charlatan he is. Should I testify, I want your assurance that I will be permitted, within the rules of your tribunal, to tell my story in full. I'll pull no punches. As you Americans say, we are a democracy now, with half of Germany in the filthy hands of the Soviet Union. For the sake of generations to come, I must be given the opportunity to eradicate the odious stain of Nazism."

"Herr von Papen, as chief prosecutor, I pledge to you the broadest latitude to purge your soul."

"Not just my soul, but Germany's soul."

"You've got a deal, sir. May I ask another question?"

"Go on, General."

"What is your current relationship to the following men? Hjalmar Schacht, Martin Niemöller, Kurt Zeitzler, Otto Strasser and Franz Pfeffer."

"Schacht, Niemöller and Zeitzler are good men. I am friendly with them. Pfeffer disappeared. Strasser is a communist. I have no contact with him. Why do you ask?"

"I would like to have the ones you approve also to testify."

"All right, I'll help you. I'll track down Reverend Niemöller and General Zeitzler. As a matter of courtesy, call Schacht. Tell him I've agreed and will talk to him at the club tonight. Give me a number to call you back later."

"Here is the number, and by the way, I'll have an American Air Force plane bring you and the others from Munich directly here. I'll also arrange accommodations."

"Very thoughtful, General. *Auf wiedersehen*."

The person-to-person call to Schacht took five minutes.

"I am honored by your call," Schacht declared in English.

"Sir, I am aware of your anger of having been tried by the Nuremberg court and acquitted."

"I should never have been put before the tribunal with those degenerate political gangsters. I hope you hang Hitler and the whole bunch of Nazis you captured. Germany lives under a cloud of shame for their depravity."

"I spoke with Franz von Papen, and he suggested I call you. He has agreed to testify at the trial. I invite you, sir, to do likewise. Your prestige would help the world realize that not all Germans are evil. Herr von Papen expects to talk with you at your club this evening."

"Will I be allowed to describe the crimes of this immigrant Hitler and his gang of corrupt gangsters who have brought this shame to Germany?"

"Absolutely."

"I will talk with Franz and one of us will call you."

"Thank you, sir."

Bart hung up the phone and sat back in his chair. He took in a long breath and exhaled. His mind was intently focused on organizing and expediting the remaining witnesses and their testimonies. The pressure was on. His moment of thought was interrupted less than five minutes later, as the door swung open. Gideon Cartman entered the room, carrying a stack of papers. "Well, General, here we go."

Bart and Cartman poured through a voluminous file of volunteer witnesses, then whittled four hundred survivors' names down to a two-page list.

"Gideon, let's begin with Carl Bergman's saga of his family's trip on the SS St. Louis and what followed. I assume that you are satisfied with his credibility?"

"No doubts. It's as heartrending as the others."

"Okay, we follow with Rudolph Kenner, Nazi soldier at Auschwitz. Did he get the treatment last night?"

"Twice over, by Phil Berger and then by Jacques. He'll go all the way."

"Natasha Orlovsky?"

"Jacques vouched for her," Cartman declared. "She traced herself back to Count Alexei Orlov, born in 1787 and died in 1808. An interesting woman with a tragic experience, according to Sophia. I sat in for part of it. She'll make an excellent witness. A woman with a zest for life, yet bitterly cold against the Nazis and the Russians."

Most of the day was spent cataloguing witnesses for the remainder of the week. The rest of the team straggled into the conference room. Bart listened to their reports and previewed the schedule for them, then they reached a consensus.

☆ ☆ ☆ ☆

Thursday, March 5, 1953 - 0900 hours - Fort Leavenworth

The tribunal called for the next witness, and a tall, muscular man walked between two MPs to the stand. He took the oath and surveyed the courtroom.

"English or German?" Bart asked.

"I speak good English, but I prefer to answer you in *Deutsch*," he replied in a German accent.

"State your name, please."

"Carl Bergman."

"Your place of birth?"

"Hamburg, Germany."

"Is that your residence now?"

"No, I live in Israel."

"What is your current occupation?"

"I am a soldier, a colonel in the Israeli army."

"Please sketch your family background," Bart requested.

"In short, my father was a doctor, my mother ran the household. I had two brothers and one sister. My father, two brothers and I served in the German army in World War I. My mother and sister worked as nurses in military hospitals from 1914 to 1918. My brothers were killed in World War I. There were a hundred and twelve thousand Jews in the German army. Thirteen thousand Jewish soldiers were killed in that war. I was in the Prussian light cavalry at the age of eighteen and rose to captain. We were called Uhlans, after the Tatar lancers. My father was a colonel serving in the medical corps. We were both decorated with Iron Crosses and other medals," Berger said.

"After the first war, what happened?"

"I finished my education at the University of Heidelberg. There was a severe depression after a huge inflation. I got a job teaching at a middle school in Hamburg. I met a young nurse who served at the military hospital with my mother. Despite hard times, we got married and had two children, a girl and boy. To augment my income, I got a job as a longshoreman. Hamburg was, and still is, a big port."

"Did you stay, despite anti-Semitism?"

"The manager of the port had a heart attack. General Wilhelm Groener, who had power in the Weimar Republic, passed the word to the city fathers that I was the man for the manager's job. Even though the Nazis were in power, somehow I got the job. At that time, I don't think they knew I was a Jew. My hair was red and my eyes are hazel. That was in 1938. For almost a year, things went well, despite the race laws."

"Then what?"

"Kristallnacht, the night of broken glass. That was November 8 and 9, 1938, when the hoodlums, at the urging of Goebbels and the approval of that bastard Hitler, turned Germany into a horde of haters and criminals. They burned down our synagogue and hundreds of others. The country went berserk. The flames of anti-Semitism were being fanned by Goebbels, Himmler, Goering and his sycophants. I knew the time had come."

"Explain that."

"I learned that the SS St. Louis was going to take one thousand Jews to Cuba. I talked it over with my father, mother, sister and my wife. They agreed. Through my connections at the port, I booked us all on that ship. We took all our things and departed Hamburg on May 13, 1939. We hoped to get to America from Cuba. My father's sister lived in Milwaukee, Wisconsin. It was a happy crossing of the Atlantic until the captain announced that Cuba had withdrawn their permission to land. We begged and pleaded with them. All sorts of committees tried to get them to lift the embargo on human beings."

"Did anyone get off the ship?"

"A few rich people bribed their way off. We were down to the last of our money."

"Where did the ship go next?"

"After a while at Havana, some people dived off the ship. I don't know whether they died or not. The ship went to Miami, and our spirits rose. We were happy again. I had that Jewish lady's poem, "The New Colossus," which is engraved on a tablet inside the pedestal of the Statue of Liberty, written by Emma Lazurus. I read it to my family. We were sure they would admit us."

"Do you remember the poem?"

"By heart."

"Just state the two lines that gave you hope. In English, please."

"Give me your tired, your poor, your huddled masses yearning to breathe free, the wretched refuse of your teeming shore. Send these, the homeless, tempest-tost to me. I lift my lamp beside the golden door." Bergman stood and saluted the American flag behind the tribunal.

A smattering of applause emanated from the press section and spectators. Nimitz waited for half a minute and gently tapped his gavel. The witness sat down, teary-eyed. He reached into his pocket and extracted a coin.

"Here I have an American two-cent coin, dated 1864, which carries the words *In God We Trust*. It was given to me by my grandfather. That's why America is such a great country," Bergman added.

Krieger stood up. "Objection."

"Overruled. This is not a civil court. We accept a *non sequitur*, occasionally," Nimitz said, smiling.

"Did the United States admit the Jews?"

"No. We were shocked, disheartened and disbelieving. We asked ourselves, how could this open door of America suddenly be slammed shut? We believed that President Roosevelt was a friend of the Jews. We were laughed at by the German ship's officers, then we were on our way back to hell."

"What happened next?"

"On June 6, 1939, we sailed back to Europe and arrived at Antwerp, Belgium, on June 17th. Fortunately, the American Joint Distribution Committee helped us. A few of us were accepted in Belgium. The people were very warm and friendly. I spoke Flemish, which is akin to German. I also spoke French."

"Did you settle in Antwerp?"

"Yes, with my mother, father, sister, my wife and two children. I got a job as a longshoreman. My father worked at the hospital. He took the Belgian test and was allowed to practice medicine. My mother worked as a nurse. Both were getting along in years. My teenage children entered Hebrew schools. We attended the Conservative synagogue. We made a lot of friends. That was a good eleven months and then the inferno came to Belgium."

"Explain that to the Court, please."

"Those filthy, rotten, heartless Nazi swine invaded this lovely, gentle country on May 10, 1940. That derelict Austrian immigrant blitzkrieged France, Holland, and Luxembourg as well. As Jews, we were doomed."

"Did that come about soon?"

"The Gestapo, during the middle of the night, crashed into our house and robbed us of everything. We were sent to France. My son and I were slave laborers in armament factories. My father and mother worked in a hospital emptying bedpans and making beds. My wife, sister and daughter slaved in a garment factory. We all wore the yellow Star of David. The Final Solution was put into action one month after they invaded the Soviet Union, on June 22, 1941. We were moved."

"To where?" Bart asked.

"The Gurs camp, which was under the control of the Vichy government. That was a small hell. The big hell came when we were shipped to Auschwitz. We were packed like sardines in a boxcar with men, women and children. The smell there was nauseating. It was filthy from its last trip. We slept in feces, urine, vomit and blood. Our cluster added to the foul odor and the filth. No food, water or sanitary facilities. Several days of that and we arrived at the devil's domicile."

"The court has heard of the receptions there. Please tell us your experience."

"When the doors to this cattle car were opened, there was a stampede to get out. There were six people dead - two men and four women. Ten people had to be carried off that car. We were lined up and forced to undress. There we were - naked, my father, mother, sister, wife, my daughters, my son and me."

"What happened after that?"

"There was that infamous camp commandant, Rudolph Höss. I could have broken that little bastard in half. He was fingering us like cattle. He ordered me, my son and daughter to the right. Then my father and mother remained in the line. He salaciously looked at my wife and daughter. A colonel whispered in his ear and they were directed to the right. Those in line were told to march to the showers. The rest of us were sent to barracks. Fifteen minutes later my parents were gassed to death in those fake showers."

The big man reached into his back pocket, withdrew a handkerchief, blew his nose and wiped the tears from his eyes. Bart handed him a glass of water, turned his back and shuffled some papers. After a short wait to allow Bergman to compose himself, Bart faced him. "What jobs were assigned to your family?"

"General, if I may, I'm not a man who cries easily. The sudden death of my parents struck us very hard. I vowed to myself that I would exact personal justice before these Nazi animals could kill me. I advised the rest of the family to cooperate and stay out of trouble. To answer your question, they assigned me and my son, Adam, to the crematoriums. He was big and strong like me. My wife and sister, Elsa, were sent to assist nurses at the hospital. My daughter, Doris, worked as a seamstress."

"Tell the court your experiences at Auschwitz."

"My first day at the crematorium, with Gestapo bayonets at our backs, I had the choice of being killed on the spot or taking my mother's naked body from a pile of bodies and putting her into the roaring fire. My son looked at me in horror. He was struck on the head by one of the guards. It was all I could do to restrain myself. Vengeance was my custodian. My boy didn't fall. He bled a little and continued his job of pulling bodies off the pile. He found my father's body. I took Papa from my son, and with my heart breaking, threw the body in the fire. We worked all day and into the night. The guard that struck my son was a captain. He blew a whistle, indicating that was all for the night. He dismissed the other *Sonderkommandos*, but ordered me and my son to stay. All the other Gestapo men left."

"Why?"

"He wanted to quench the fire and have us shovel the ashes into metal barrels. I looked around and saw no one but the captain and my son, Adam, in the area. I stared at him and he came at me with his club, cursing me. I don't know if I want to talk about this." He stopped and his mien became bellicose as he looked at Hitler.

"Herr Bergman, I can see the anger on your face. Please tell the court what happened," Bart coaxed.

After a short pause, he spoke. "This Captain Klausmeier came at me with his club raised. I grabbed the club out of his hand and struck him across the jaw, knocking him unconscious to the ground. My son took his gun and club. I picked him up and threw him into the roaring fire. My son and I ran to the barracks. We hid the club and gun in a hole we dug in back of our building."

"Did anyone discover what happened?"

"No. The next day we kept on lifting bodies into the crematorium. Later, we volunteered to clear the ashes into the metal barrels. We found the captain's melted belt buckles and the buttons. We also found what was left of his boots and black uniform and buried everything at the bottom of the ashes in the barrel. That was the end of that. For some reason, no one ever mentioned the captain's absence."

"How long were you at that job?"

"Two weeks later they had us take bodies out of the gas chambers," Bergman continued. "We watched helplessly as these monsters waited for the trainloads of Jews. They made men, women and children strip naked in the freezing cold and walk into those shower gas chambers. Thousands and thousands marched to their deaths. I watched them pull gold fillings from the teeth of those poor, innocent people who were born Jewish. While I saw the most monstrous acts of bestiality, these Nazis outdid the devil in every aspect."

"Specifics, please."

"Specifics, you ask? First, I made a list of every one of the Aryan cream, the pure race of Germans, the supermen, the ultimate in mankind, ultimate in the crazed minds of Hitler, Himmler, Goering, Goebbels and all those Nazi scum in Germany. Specifics? Okay. I saw men and women shot in the head indiscriminately for some minor infraction, babies torn from the arms of mothers and tossed into the furnace alive, supermen tearing beards literally off the face of rabbis, women by the hundreds raped, children bayoneted, night revelries where they poured kerosene on prisoners and clocked to see how long it would take for them to die. Does the world know of the 'Black Wall' between the crematorium and the medical-experiments building, where thousands of Jews, Jehovah's Witnesses, Gypsies, the weak, women and children were executed by machine-gun fire? I've seen bayonets thrust into the vaginas of young women who wouldn't succumb to their charms. One prisoner dropped a cup of watery soup on the boots of a colonel. He was decapitated with the stroke of a sword. These conquering Aryan supermen on his staff played soccer with the head. Do you want more?"

"You saw all of this yourself?"

"Yes."

"Did you know the man who was decapitated?" Bart asked.

"Yes. It was my son, Adam," he answered, and broke down, sobbing.

The courtroom froze. There was total silence for a minute or more until Hitler stood up and yelled, "*Bullscheisse!* Hollywood fiction from a dirty Jew!"

Nimitz gaveled, and in a split second Bergman jumped out of his chair and reached Hitler, who was still standing, mouthing obscenities, and delivered a punch to Hitler's nose with a thwack which resonated throughout the court. The chaos that ensued was quickly quelled by the MPs.

Bergman was hustled back to his chair. Nimitz called for a thirty-minute recess. Hitler, unconscious and bleeding profusely, was carried out on a stretcher. In chambers, defense and prosecution lawyers met with the tribunal.

"Is this American justice?" Krieger angrily demanded.

"Don't put on that act here, Krieger!" Bart exploded. "Be sure you get paid in legitimate francs or American dollars by your Swiss bankers. You couldn't care less about what happened."

Nimitz, Smith and Chennault huddled at the window. General Smith, the Marine commander who had been through the war in the Pacific and was known as a man who was quick on the draw and never minced words, exploded, "Oh, don't come in here wheedling about justice! Your client and all the others would have been hung or put before a firing squad in other countries by now. How dare that Hitler, a piece of turd, stand up in this court and act like the Beast of Berchtesgaden? That dehorned devil can't shout in this tribunal with his filthy epithets. While we don't countenance violence in this court, it is patently clear that he provoked the witness. Both men are in contempt. This meeting is over."

Court convened, and Hitler was back in his seat with tape over his nose.

"Mr. Bergman, your conduct in this court cannot be condoned, nor can Mr. Hitler's. Therefore, you are both fined one hundred dollars," Nimitz declared.

Bart smiled at Bergman, then began, "Sir, you have given us quite a litany of atrocities committed by the Gestapo at Auschwitz. Do you wish to elaborate beyond what you have stated?"

"General, I have barely scratched the surface of the beastliness of these pure Aryan pagans."

"Proceed."

"Commandant Rudolf Höss was promoted and replaced by SS Lieutenant Arthur Liebehenschel. He was a weak man, and the Gestapo ran the place. Orderly killing was replaced with disorderly killing. Rapes and murder took place all over the camp. The Russians were getting closer. During that period, some Russian, Polish, German, French, Italian, Dutch, and Belgian prisoners with military experience joined me in stealing arms and ammunition. I wanted to live long enough to exact justice. But something happened that diverted me from joint action in our desire to attack from within. I was moved from Auschwitz I to Auschwitz II, which they called Buna or Monowitz, to work at a synthetic-rubber works. Höss returned as head of the SS garrison. Commandant Liebehenschel was transferred. SS Captain Richard Baer was made commandant of Auschwitz I. On September 13, 1944, the Americans bombed Buna. Twelve SS barracks were destroyed, fifteen SS men were killed and twenty-eight were badly injured. I was moved to Auschwitz II, or Birkenau. A German Jew came to me after I left the Buna plant, and said that my wife was going to be hanged the next day."

He stopped and drank some water.

"Why?"

"She was falsely charged with sending signals to the partisans just outside the camp. Actually, Commandant Baer had raped my sister and was attacked by my wife in the process. She struck him with a rock on the side of his face."

"Did he hang her?" Bart asked quickly.

"Publicly, with my sister and all the prisoners forced to watch. I sneaked into Auschwitz I. There was nothing I could do to stop it. Machine guns lined up everywhere. I thought of shooting Baer on the spot. My gut told me I'd be dead in seconds. Revenge could wait. She was so brave and shouted, *Rapist!* for the whole camp to hear before the cloth was put over her head. That was on October 1. Six days later another group of prisoners, not part of my group, revolted. They were the *Sonderkommando* group that worked at Crematory IV and over seven hundred of them were killed. The crematory was destroyed."

"What did you do at Auschwitz-Birkenau?"

"I lifted bodies of Hungarian Jews out of the gas chambers. Soon I began stalking all three camps with the help of some of the inside prisoner partisans. Every night we captured a Gestapo officer. We broke their necks. Thirteen in all. In late November, Himmler ordered the destruction of the crematoriums, so one hundred seventy-five of us no longer had to work there. Prisoners were being transferred. Russian planes were bombing us. I tried to find my sister. I had no luck."

"What did you do?"

"I learned we were being shipped out the day after their Christmas celebration," Bergman replied. "That night I stalked Captain Baer by myself. He spotted me near his house. With his hand on his holster, he approached me in the dark. I held my hands up and said to him, *I have information of an uprising. I don't want the other prisoners to see me talking to you.* He relaxed and joined me in back of the house. I made up a story of some outside partisans joining with a group in the Birkenau area. He took a pad out of his pocket and asked me for some names. I made up about three names, which he concentrated on writing. Then I put my arm around his neck with my hand over his mouth and twisted. He was dead instantly. I took his gun, put him over my shoulder and carried him into the woods. I found an area with a slope and I rolled his body down it."

Silence filled the courtroom. The spectators stared at the witness with mouths agape.

"No further questions. Your witness."

"Herr Bergman, are you a violent man?" Stolz asked.

"No. I love peace."

"You don't sound like a peaceful man."

"I'm sorry for your hearing problem."

"Don't get flip with me," Stolz snapped.

"You're the one that's flipped. You ask me if I am violent. I say no. You say

I don't sound peaceful."

A few laughs erupted.

"Very well, let's get to the point. You mentioned killing a lot of Germans. Do you enjoy killing human beings?"

"On the contrary, Herr Stolz, I never killed a human being, only Nazi beasts. If a beast is intent on killing a human being, you kill the beast first."

"You're very glib with your answers."

"If you call the truth glib, so be it."

"You murdered quite a few people, by your own admission."

"Herr Stolz, I never murdered anyone. There was an alien force of Nazis, the species experts call Hitlerian beasts, who warred on the human race in all of Europe and murdered six million Jews. That's what your clients are being tried for here in this court. In any civilized country, if you murder one innocent person, you are tried for murder. Should we have six million trials for each innocent person your clients maliciously slaughtered? Don't make a fool of yourself by attempting to try me. My conscience is quite clear. Examine your own. Aren't you ashamed of defending these beasts?"

"Objection."

"To what?" Nimitz asked.

"Oh, never mind, sir. No further questions."

"Court is recessed for lunch. We resume at 1430 hours," Nimitz said.

Jacques shook hands with Bergman. The network producers asked Bergman for interviews, and he looked at Jacques for approval. Jacques nodded assent.

During the prosecution team's buffet lunch in the conference room, Sophia switched on the radio. As she turned the dials, reporters were interviewing Bergman, who was excoriating the Third Reich and its willing participants in the extirpation of millions of human beings. Near the end of his harangue, bulletins were being interjected at every network. Ed Murrow broke in on the CBS affiliate, followed by Eric Sevareid, who stated:

"Joseph Stalin is dead at the age of seventy-four. The *Man of Steel* who ruled the Union of Socialist Soviet Republics for twenty-nine years succumbed at 12:57 a.m. Friday, March 6, Moscow time. This marks the end of an era of despotism, equaled only by his defeated nemesis, Adolf Hitler, who is on trial here in the U.S. for his life. We have just received word from Moscow that despite the tensions in the Politburo, a successor to Stalin will be announced tomorrow, Saturday there, on March 7. Here in Washington, President Eisenhower will convene a Cabinet meeting within the hour."

"Turn it off, Sophia," Bart ordered. "I can picture John Foster Dulles and his brother Allen trying to maneuver Eisenhower into drastic action. Ike's too cool to be stampeded. Let's get back to our job here."

"Rudolph Kenner is in the witness room having a good lunch," Jacques replied. "He's nervous. I figure a good lunch will calm him down."

"Jacques, I expect him to respond fully about his experiences at Auschwitz. That bastard insists he's not a Nazi. Give him the word, Jacques, that I expect that canary to tell every little detail of the atrocities he observed. Anything less and he'll be put away for life." He paused. "And don't let him forget that he was a member of the Waffen SS."

"I'll visit him now."

The tribunal called for the first witness in the afternoon session. Hitler yelled, "Stalin is dead! *Sieg heil!*"

Nimitz gaveled angrily. "Does Herr Hitler want his mouth taped?"

Stolz rose and apologized. Krieger had his hand over Hitler's mouth.

"Let's move on," Nimitz declared.

The former Nazi soldier was escorted to the witness stand. He hardly resembled Himmler's pompous Waffen SS soldiers. He walked slowly with his head down and shoulders hunched. He took the oath and mumbled, "*Jawohl.*" When seated, his pallid complexion indicated his nervous state, accompanied by his shaking hands.

In German, Bart asked, "State your name."

"Rudolph Kenner."

"Where were you born?"

"Stuttgart, Germany."

"When?"

"February 25, 1923."

"When did you become a Nazi?"

"In 1933, when I was ten years old."

"Did your parents make you join the Nazi youth movement?"

"No, it was my schoolteacher. All the children in my class were sworn in."

"How did your parents react to that?"

"They were scared. All of our neighbors were cheering Adolf Hitler. We used to hear Hitler, Goebbels, Goering, Hess and others on the radio."

"When Hitler became Chancellor, you were nine years old. Did you know what Nazism stood for?"

"Only that the Jews were taking over Germany and the world," Kenner answered.

"Did you know any Jews?"

"Yes. We used to play together in the schoolyard until we joined the youth movement. We played soccer and other games."

"Did you ever go to a Jewish house?"

"Yes. I ate at their house and they ate at mine."

"Were your parents Nazis?"

"Not until my two older brothers and I went into the army."

"When was that?"

"1939."

"At the age of sixteen?"

"My brothers were eighteen and nineteen, so when they were drafted into the army, I joined too."

"Did you and your brothers go on active duty?" Bart asked.

"Yes, my two brothers were killed at Stalingrad. I was in the invasion of France, Holland, Belgium and Luxembourg."

"Are you a Nazi now?"

"No."

"When did you stop being a Nazi?"

"At Auschwitz, when I saw what animals they were," Kenner responded.

"When were you assigned to Auschwitz?"

"In January 1942."

Krieger rose. "Sirs, this witness is a defendant and is being forced to testify."

"That being the case, I call him as a hostile witness," Bart shot back.

"Not necessary," von Maunder declared. "I am his counsel and he is a willing witness for the prosecution."

The commandants muttered a few epithets, such as, "*Arschloch, Schweinehund*, traitor."

Nimitz warned them that their mouths would be taped. MPs lined up in back of the protesters. The obscenities stiffened Kenner's back. He straightened up in his chair and pointed his finger at the commandants.

"Murderers, animals, thieves and barbarians! You'll cry like the babies you killed when they hang you!" he shouted. Hitler and the commandants booed.

"Tape their mouths," Nimitz ordered.

"In 1942, what were your duties at Auschwitz?"

"To maintain order among the laborers."

"You mean prisoners and slave laborers? Did you kill or beat any of the prisoners?"

"No, that was the function of the Gestapo officers."

"Please give the court an overall description of what you observed at that camp," Bart requested.

"First, we watched the trains come in every day with cattle cars filled with men, women and children. Commandant Rudolph Höss would be at the station. Thousands were ordered to strip naked. Then he separated healthy workers and sent the rest to the fake showers where they were gassed to death. It was an assembly line of executions."

"What did you do?"

"I was to lead the ones picked for labor to the barracks. The Jews went to their deaths with great dignity, while the officers joked about the naked women. I saw babies pulled from mothers and smashed to the ground. I saw live babies thrown into the crematorium."

"What else?"

"I saw gold teeth and fillings pulled from the mouths of dead bodies. I saw the Gestapo officers putting some in their pockets. I saw them take things from the men's clothes. I saw officers fondle the breasts and the vaginas of women on their way to death."

"What else?"

"Some pretty girls were pulled out of the line. They were divided up among the officers for rapes. Sometimes at night the men would be drinking and gang-raping these girls, some as young as eleven and twelve years old."

"Did you or anyone try to stop them?"

"Anyone who interfered would be shot instantly," Kenner answered.

"What happened to the girls after the rapes?"

"They were shot or strangled, and the *Sonderkommandos*, the prisoners, had to carry the bodies to the crematory."

"Did Commandant Höss permit the officers to behave this way?"

"All he cared about was the extermination of the Jews. He was the murder mechanic foreman. It got worse when Höss was promoted and Colonel Liebehenschel took over. The orderly killing turned into a madhouse of murder and ghastly games."

"Such as?"

"The Gestapo took little babies and tossed them around, swinging them by their feet and tossing them into the fire. They played soccer with decapitated heads. There were drunken orgies at night with women of all ages. Prisoners who protested were put on their knees and executed on the spot with shots to the head."

"How did you manage to survive these atrocities?"

"You become numb. Yet I have bad dreams now," Kenner admitted.

"What else did you actually see?"

"I saw people walking like living skeletons. They starved the workers to death. By the time the Russians came, two and a half million people had been killed in Auschwitz. But there was torture and hangings. When Höss left, then came the colonel and after that came Colonel Helmut Wasser. The Russians were getting close. The death marches began, and SS guards shot those who lagged behind. The ones still at Auschwitz were tortured in every way."

"For example?"

"The Gestapo officers set fire to people's beds while they were sleeping. They set fire to men with beards. Ears were chopped off if someone didn't respond to a command quickly. Men and women were forced to crawl and eat dirt. They were made to swallow it. I saw an officer urinate in the soup pot. A woman begged for a piece of bread. He threw it on the ground and told her to pick it up. She got down on her hands and knees. He stood over her and shot her in the back of the head. He yelled at two men to carry her body to the crematory. They struggled to lift her. They were too weak. He shot both of them. Then he walked away and left the three dead bodies lying there. Prisoners were too weak to commit suicide. Some tried. Colonel Wasser never left his quarters. The SS men were out of control."

"What was your rank?" Bart asked.

"Sergeant."

"How many men under you?"

"Twelve."

"What was their attitude?"

"Disgust. They stayed as far away from the barracks as they could. There were dead people in there. The smell of death was everywhere."

"Did your men see some of the things you've testified to here?"

"Yes, we saw dead people pulled out of the cattle cars when they arrived. We saw that big man who testified this morning being forced to put his gassed parents in the crematory. Captain Klausmeier disappeared. I didn't know where until I heard that man's testimony on the radio in the witness room."

"You mean Herr Bergman?"

"Yes. I didn't know whose head was being kicked around like a soccer ball until I heard Bergman say it was his son. I saw it happening."

"Did you see the hanging of his wife and sister?"

"I didn't know their names until I heard Bergman just now. We were forced to be at the hanging. Captain Baer disappeared after that. Now I know why Bergman said he broke his neck. SS Gestapo officers began to disappear. Now I know how. The Russians came on January 27, 1945. They found the bodies with broken necks. My men were forced to carry the bodies to the pits filled with hundreds of Jews like skeletons lying on top of each other. Colonel Wasser disappeared.

The Russians executed all the Gestapo officers who had remained. All the non-commissioned men and I were taken to POW camps in southern Poland. We were released three months after the war was over."

"Where did you go after that?" Bart asked.

"I went to Stuttgart. My home had been bombed out. I couldn't find my family. I had an uncle in Munich. Work was hard to find. So I went to see him. He was seventy-three years old and was operating an auto repair business and a gas station. He was glad to have me stay with him and his wife. I worked repairing autos for five years. He and his wife died in a suicide pact. I ran the repair business for a year after that. One day, Gunther Ludwig, a corporal who had worked with me at Auschwitz, pulled in to have his brakes checked. I fixed his brakes and we went to dinner. We talked over old times."

"Go on."

"Well, business wasn't too good. In fact, I was almost broke. Gunther asked me if I would mind working for a Jew. I had nothing against Jews, I told him. He said he was going to Argentina to work for a Jew named Nordheim. He said he could get me a job. Next day, Heinrich Müller interviewed me. A week later I was on my way to Argentina."

"Didn't you know who Heinrich Müller was?"

"No, not at that time. He said he was the ranch foreman working for Nordheim."

"When did you find out who he was?"

"The day you Americans raided the ranch in La Plata, Argentina," Kenner answered.

"How long were you there before that?"

"One month."

"What were you doing there?"

"We were training to go to Israel to help them against the Arab nations. That's what they were telling us, but I was very suspicious because the men were all ex-Waffen SS soldiers. I was trying to figure out how to get out of there. We were watched day and night. Security was very tight."

"This doesn't sound plausible."

"Honest, that's the truth. I admit, the pay was very good. I had enough money to get away. That day in April when that big cake arrived with the swastika on it, the picture made it clear they were a bunch of Nazis. Then the Americans came and captured all of us."

"No further questions," Bart ended.

Eric Stolz strode intently toward the witness.

"Stop there," Nimitz ordered.

"I don't mind, Your Honor," Kenner said.

Stolz moved right up for a face-to-face confrontation with the witness.

"Herr Kenner, it seems you suddenly found religion."

"I never lost it."

"Do you wish to tell this court that you observed these alleged crimes you've depicted and stayed in touch with God?"

"As a little boy, I was taught to believe in God. There were times when I wondered why a religious country like Germany turned into an atheistic society."

"What are you saying? You're accusing all the people in Germany of being anti-Christ?"

"Not all, but most did not follow the preachings of Christ. Hitler became their messiah."

Hitler's mouth was taped, but he managed to show his approval by stamping his feet on the floor.

"You are testifying here because the prosecution promised you leniency, is that not so?" Stolz challenged.

"That is a lie."

"Isn't it true that you did not really see all those atrocities that you described? You merely picked up those stories from those alleged Jewish survivors who testified here?"

Bart rose in anger and walked over to the bench, towering over Stolz.

"Objection. Counsel's question is fraught with anti-Semitism. I demand he retract those remarks and rephrase his invidiously disingenuous question."

"Sustained."

"Did you actually see the things you described?"

"Herr Stolz, I am neither deaf, dumb nor blind. Neither are you. What did you Swiss do about those atrocities, you..."

"I'm asking the questions, not you."

Nimitz cautioned Kenner.

"Your Honor, this lawyer, Stolz, is a true Nazi sympathizer and is trying to bait me," Kenner appealed.

"Objection. He called me a Nazi sympathizer. I beg the court to hold him in contempt."

Bart laughed loudly before Nimitz could reply. "Your Honors, those oxymoronic words and behavior of counsel defy common sense. Here he takes umbrage to being called a Nazi sympathizer, yet he is trying to defend the king of the Nazis and his minions. Does he not have any sympathy for his clients?"

The three members of the tribunal muffled their mirth with their hands in a simulated whispered conference. Laughter rang through the courtroom. Stolz quickly withdrew his objection, then tried to vex the witness with his next question. "Do you say now that you believe in God?"

"Yes. Hitler destroyed Germany, and God has destroyed him. He is being tried here as the demon he is. The world prayed for the destruction of the Nazis. There he sits in shackles with his evil mouth taped. The Nazis are *kaput*."

Applause resounded.

"No further questions."

When Stolz returned to his seat, Hitler struck him from behind with his handcuffed hands. Nimitz observed the assault and chose to ignore it. Stolz rose in an attempt to address the court when the gavel came down and the recess was announced.

"Court will resume at 0900 Monday, March 9."

Stolz approached Bart, looked at him long and hard, then said, "General, you made a fool out of me today. I deserved it. I am not an anti-Semite, nor am I a Nazi sympathizer. I wish to resign from this case. That maniac just struck me on the back of my head." He put his hands to the lower part of his skull, withdrew it and showed blood on his fingers.

"Come on, Stolz, let's go to the tribunal chambers."

The three judges were relaxing over glasses of bourbon. Holland Smith was puffing on a cigar between sips. After listening to Stolz's explanation and the sight of blood on his neck, Nimitz pondered his request.

"How many lawyers are going to quit *Der Führer*?" Smith said snidely.

"Well, he's got Krieger and that woman," Bart said.

"Not any more," Stolz said.

"Well, try to make amends with Hitler. Possibly he'll realize what an uphill battle you're fighting. If it doesn't work, then he'll have to find more legal talent," Nimitz gently suggested.

"I'll try, sir," Stolz agreed.

☆ ☆ ☆ ☆

Friday evening, March 6, 1953 - Leavenworth, Kansas

The March winds were doing their lion number. The car carrying Bart, Jacques and Douglas Milburn rocked on the way to the house. The shingles were slapping the building as Mrs. Lawrence opened the door and held it open for the men.

"Sergeant, Mrs. Lawrence will feed you if behave yourself."

"Oh, he's a good boy. My husband's in the kitchen, son. Join him."

"That's at least a fifty-mile-an-hour wind," Doug estimated.

The three men went right to the den, where Jacques fixed three vodka martinis. At dinner, Douglas asked Bart, "What's the story about Harry Branlow?"

"Big story, Doug. I'll background you, but your major source has to be your old buddy, Sam Foxworth. Branlow is the mastermind of the hit on Gaines and Darcy. More than that, Irwin Gullen, the banker and a Swiss major stockholder of the Banque Royale in Zurich, are co-conspirators in flooding the world with counterfeit money at Hitler's behest. Take it from there."

"That's a blockbuster."

"Keep me out of it."

"Naturally," Doug assured his brother.

Coffee was served in the den. Jacques poured three snifters of brandy. The phone rang, so Bart picked it up. "Milburn here."

"General, a Mr. von Papen for you, sir."

"Put him on."

"Mr. von Papen, nice to hear from you, *mein Herr*."

The conversation proceeded in German.

"*Danke, Herr* von Papen - Schacht *und* Niemöller. Munich, 16 March. *Auf wiedersehen.*"

"Don't tell me you've got those three to testify?" Douglas queried.

Jacques smiled.

"None of your business, Doug," Bart snapped. "No more scoopies, brother."

"I know better than that, Bart. My lips are sealed. You're going to make history. I'm proud of you."

After dinner, they were back in the den with brandy snifters and cigars. The radio was on and a bulletin declared that Georgi Malenkov had been named Premier of the Soviet Union, with Lavrenty Beria as chief of the KGB, or secret police, and Nikolai Bulganin as Defense Minister.

"Turn it off, Jacques. Ike can relax now," Bart sighed.

CHAPTER THIRTEEN

Saturday, March 7, 1953 - 1400 hours - prosecution conference room
George Spota and Dick Reilly arrived with a dozen cans of 35- and 16-millimeter film and a moviola. Jacques set them up in a workroom to process and edit the two-hour film.

During dinner that evening, Spota, Bart and Jacques reminisced, to the intense interest of film editor Reilly. Bart then focused on Spota's spectacular success in Hollywood. "We haven't missed any of your films. The whole family's proud of you, George," Bart complimented. "How is Marie?"

"Just fine. We have a beautiful little girl named Georgianna."

"Congratulations. All right, let's talk about the film."

Spota said, "We brought all the footage we could find at the Grinberg Library and added to that the material turned over to us by Jacques from the Pentagon. This should be a powerful pictorial indictment, graphically depicting the macabre orgy of murder conducted by these Nazi prehistoric barbarians."

"Your visit here is deeply appreciated," Bart said.

"I came for two reasons. First, to see you. Second, I wanted to work with Dick in editing and splicing this footage. Having watched the trial on TV, I've become overwhelmed by the tales of horror by the survivors. The stories are far more horrendous than what we saw when we liberated those camps."

"If you need anything, George, I'm at your service," Jacques volunteered.

Bart excused himself. "I'm going to call Elizabeth to let her know that I want her and Joyce Laurent here next weekend."

"Are you putting them on the stand?"

"I can't keep them off. They'll never forgive me if I do."

"When you're through, Bart, I want to talk to Christina," Jacques said.

The call was made, and Elizabeth promised to have Joyce join her on the flight. Jacques spoke with Christina. During a nightcap in the den, he revealed to Spota that he and Christina were planning a move to Beverly Hills when the trial was over.

"I intend to write a book and possibly do some writing for your industry, George."

"It's fertile territory for new ideas. If I can help, count on it."

"Thanks."

☆ ☆ ☆ ☆

Monday, March 14, 1953 - 0900 hours - Fort Leavenworth

Admiral Nimitz pounded his gavel. "The prosecution may call their next witness."

A beautiful woman in her middle forties appeared, wearing a black cashmere coat and black leather gloves. Her light auburn hair was perfectly coiffured in an upsweep hairdo. Her blue eyes sparkled over her tan complexion. Just a moderate touch of russet lipstick was the only makeup she wore under her tiny, slightly tilted nose. Her striking appearance belied her role as a Holocaust survivor. She shed her coat, revealing a taupe-colored dress and a string of pearls. Bart, in an effort to shorten the testimony, asked her to tell her story without too many questions being asked.

"My name is Natasha Orlov. I was born in Kharkov, Russia. I am forty-four years of age and am now a citizen of the United States. When I was ten years old, my parents moved to Moscow to get away from the pogroms by the cossacks. I had a musical talent. I played the piano and could sing operatic and standard tunes. When the communist revolution took place, my family fled to Germany after they killed the czar and his family."

"Why Germany?" Bart asked.

"To develop my musical career. My father was a very well educated man. He studied at the University of Heidelberg. He was a doctor and my mother was a writer. We all spoke Russian, German, French, English, and Yiddish. I studied at Berlin University. By the time I was 18, in 1927, I had completed my musical training under Maestro Gunther Obermeier, a genius in his field. He got me into the Berlin Opera. By the time I was 21, in 1930, I was recognized as a budding star and I met Count Alexis Orlov, who escaped communist Russia."

"I take it that you married the count. What was your maiden name?"

"Gordonov, but in Berlin, my family used the name of Gordon."

"Your family did very well, despite the inflation and depression in that period."

"Not really. My father worked as a doctor helping poor people, mostly Christian," she continued. "In fact, he treated anyone who needed help. He made house calls at all hours and was rarely paid for his services. I was the only one earning money singing. Hitler, Goering, Hess, Goebbels and Himmler came to the opera. Hitler handed me a bouquet of flowers. Goering kept after me, trying to get me to midnight dinners. They never realized I was Jewish.

My father felt we should leave Germany."

"And did you?"

"No."

"Why not?"

"We couldn't. Alexis Orlov and I were married in 1931. One year later, I gave birth to twin boys. The next year I had a baby girl. My husband was an excellent artist and he sold paintings in Switzerland, Holland, France, and some in Germany. When Hitler became Chancellor in 1933, we applied for passports. I had an offer from a producer named Billy Rose to come to America. For some reason, we couldn't get our passports. My husband went to Judge Hans Stoller and asked for his help. The judge checked and said that Heinrich Himmler put a hold on it. People were leaving Germany in droves. But not us. We didn't know what to do. I had two more children and couldn't work any more. So we sold our house and moved into an apartment in an area that was mostly Jewish. My parents eked out a living, he as a doctor and she as an author of children's books. Then came that horrible night."

"What night was that?"

"Kristallnacht, in 1938. I saw synagogues burned, rabbis beaten and killed. The city was in one big riot of hoodlums who were torturing and killing Jews. We were a secular family and on the first night, November 8, we were not attacked, but the following night our apartment was raided by the brownshirts, the storm troopers. My husband punched one of the hoodlums. They arrested us and our five children. They found my parents and arrested them. The Gestapo came to the police station and said Himmler had me on his list as a Jew. We were all sent to Dachau."

"How long were you there?"

"Six months, and then, for some reason, we were deported to Poland. We were penniless and hungry. Alexis spoke Polish and talked a farmer into letting us ride in his truck filled with vegetables on his way to Warsaw. There, my father volunteered to work at the hospital for food. Alexis got work painting houses and stores. We found a small apartment. My father had a patient who was a rabbi and mentioned that I was a famous singer. Soon I was singing in a synagogue. My children were enrolled in their synagogue. I did a few concerts, attended mostly by rich Christians. I began to earn some money. My father was a doctor for poor patients, Jews and Christians who paid him with foodstuffs."

"All right, Mrs. Orlov, let's move on to the Nazi invasion of Poland."

"That was the beginning of another nightmare for us. All Jews were forced to move into a ghetto. I begged Alexis to take the children and save himself as a Christian. He refused. We loved each other very much. On June 22, 1941, the Huns invaded the Soviet Union. We were forced to wear the Star of David, and the Gestapo was beginning to shoot Jews for minor infractions. On January 20, 1942, the Final Solution was put into effect. One month later, our whole family was stuffed into cattle cars and taken to the Kolo Junction. We were moved from the cattle car to another train going to the Powiercie Station. They lined us up in the courtyard of the Chelmno death camp. They told us we were going to a labor camp. They took all our possessions and made us take off all our clothes. Men, women and children were completely naked. It was shameful and degrading. They marched us to signs pointing to the washroom, down a ramp to a gas van, fifty at a time. We knew we were going to a death chamber. However, there was something wrong with the van. The Gestapo kept us waiting while they tinkered with the vehicle. A lady who was a Jehovah's Witness comforted us. She said to pray because God is waiting for us. She had two children at her side. My husband tried to comfort us. He held two of the children in his arms. I held the little one and my parents held each of the twins. The commandant, Colonel Johann Weisst, yelled, *Achtung! Everybody march!* We came to a pit or large ditch filled with dead bodies."

Mrs. Orlov's calm recital stopped at that point and she began to sob convulsively. She removed a kerchief from her purse and dabbed her teary eyes.

"Would you like a recess?" Bart asked.

"No, just a glass of water, please."

She sipped the drink and nodded her head.

"What happened at that grave?"

"Grave?" she mocked. "That was no grave; it was a garbage disposal pit. It was the most hideous sight I've ever seen. Perfectly wonderful, religious, decent, innocent people killed mercilessly and denied a decent burial. I was numb, realizing that my family and I would soon be consigned to that pile of flesh. I turned my head for a second and saw the SS lined up with machine guns. Heinrich Himmler was there, that mass murderer. He caught my eyes and walked over to me. I turned away. He tapped me on my naked shoulder and said, *So, the arrogant prima donna who ignored me at the opera is about to play her final scene.* I turned and spit in his face. The little bastard looked frightened. I said, *Your turn will come soon, in hell, you pious piece of scheisse!* Forgive my language."

"What happened after that?"

"He walked away, wiping his face, and the machine guns began their rapid fire on two hundred naked people. I was hit, and fell into a pile of dead bodies. I don't know how long it was before I realized I was alive. Bodies were on top of me. I felt pain in my shoulder, but couldn't move. It took a while for me to come to my senses. I was suddenly frantic under those bodies, hoping I could fight my way out of this sea of death. It was a living nightmare. I eventually worked my way to the top. It was dark. No living beings were around the pit. I crawled over the bodies. It was a very cold night, but I was totally oblivious to the freezing winds. I searched for my family. I saw my twins clutched in the arms of my dear husband. I was the only one alive. I climbed out of the pit of hell. I felt my left shoulder's blood-crusted skin. I explored my whole body. That was the only wound. The bullet had barely grazed the skin on my shoulder."

"How did you get out of there?" Bart asked.

"The pit was at the edge of the Rzuchowski Forest. On my naked stomach, I crawled to the forest. I found a small pile of clothes. It was just men's pants, shirts, jackets and some shoes. I sat down and picked through the assortment. I found a pair of socks, a short pair of pants and some shirts. I put three shirts on, one on top of the other. I put two jackets on. I was very weak. I managed to feel my way through the forest away from the camp. I cried and cried, then finally I stopped and went to sleep."

"How did you get out of there alive?"

"When I awoke, it was a foggy dawn. I crawled some more in the forest. Suddenly a giant of a man grabbed me by the neck. He whispered in German, *Where are you going, young man?* He stood me up and discovered I was a woman. He picked me up like I was a limp doll and ran toward the Kolo Junction. About five hundred yards from the tracks, there was a cluster of trees. There were about fifty men and four women. They were partisans of every nationality. There were Germans, French, Russians, Greeks, Danes, Dutch, Czechs, Italians and others. They questioned me. After I told my story, they patched my wound and fed me. They gave me a change of clothes. I asked what they were doing there. They were escapees from different camps and wanted to blow up the rail system to Chelmno, but it was too well guarded."

"What did they do with you?"

"They made me a partisan. They gave me a gun and taught me how to use it. A Russian Jew, Dimitri Koslov, was an escaped POW. He was a colonel and was in charge of that partisan group. He was the one that found me. I stayed with them and we fought our way west, picking off retreating Nazis. We blew up trains, captured Nazis and executed them, taking their weapons and hand grenades. We grew to over three thousand men and women. Many nights we sat around our campfires and I sang for them. I became a pretty good soldier. Dimitri made me a captain because I showed no mercy to these Nazi swine. We had a radio and followed the pincer drives by the Allies and the Russians."

"That experience caused quite a change in your character."

"Let me put it this way. I am basically the same outgoing person I always was," she went on. "However, when one's parents, five children and husband have been brutally murdered by demons, there are indelible scars on one's psyche. I love the human race, but despise alien monsters who prey on humanity. Show me a racist or an anti-Semite, no matter what strata of society they occupy, and you'll have a vacuous, insecure individual in the guise of a human being."

"Quite profound and philosophically stated. How did you finally detach yourself from the horrors of the war?"

"We fought our way west, harassing and raiding retreating Nazi troops. We got to Weimar, and finally to the rear of the Buchenwald concentration camp. The Americans had liberated the camp. It was a horrible sight of skeletonized prisoners. How could Germany, a once cultured, religious country, have spawned such monsters who perpetrated atrocities beyond the human imagination?"

"Just one or two more questions, please. What did you do after that?'

"I met a very kind, gentle American colonel, Jeremiah Brown. They had twenty thousand survivors on their hands. I volunteered to help the sick, feeble and needy prisoners. He also helped me nurse myself back to health. At his request, I enlisted other women partisans to help the Americans care for the abused prisoners. The colonel had to move on with his troops to liberate Dora-Mittelbau, Mauthausen, Flossenburg and Dachau. I asked him if he could help me emigrate to America. My only living relative was my father's sister, Molly Gordon, in California, I told him. He said he would try. I organized partisan women at Buchenwald to help nurse these prisoners, and I went to the other American liberated camps and did the same thing."

"Did you see Colonel Brown again?" Bart asked.

"Yes, at Dachau. Later, Jeremiah arranged for me to entertain the American troops in Munich. After that, the American officers had me entertaining at dozens of military bases."

"Did Colonel Brown help you come to America?"

"Yes, in January 1946 he wrote me that there was a visa waiting for me at the American consular office in Munich. The Jewish Refugee Committee bought me a ticket on Swissair to New York and a connection to Los Angeles. I live in Encino with my Aunt Molly."

"What is your profession now?"

"I am an actress in motion pictures, on television, and I tour with bands around the country."

"What is your professional name?"

"Nancy Brown."

"After Colonel Brown?"

"Correct."

"No further questions. Your witness."

Jacques whispered to Bart that Joyce and Elizabeth had arrived. A short, animated conversation at the defense table ensued.

Eric Stolz said, "No questions."

Nimitz responded, "Very well, then, General Milburn, you may call your next witness."

"The prosecution calls Karl Ulbrecht," Bart announced.

After stating his name, the tall, wiry soldier leaned back in his chair, with an air of confidence. The interrogation was conducted in German.

"Herr Ulbrecht, are you a Nazi?"

"Not any more."

"Your age?"

"Thirty-two."

"When did you stop being a Nazi?"

"At Chelmno concentration camp."

"Why?"

"Because of the Gestapo maniacs' killing, raping and inhumane treatment of the prisoners."

"What were your duties?"

"I was a soldier guard instructed to maintain order."

"Did you ever beat or abuse the prisoners?"

"No, sir. That was the Gestapo."

"Tell us of the atrocities you observed," Bart pursued.

"When that gassing van was out of order, I watched what that lady described."

"You mean Mrs. Orlov?"

"Yes, she, her whole family and two hundred naked people were machine-gunned at the death pits. I am surprised that she survived. All the others were killed, at the direction of Commandant Johann Weisst," he continued, pointing at the man in the back.

"Would the court please ask Herr Weisst to stand up?"

The colonel stood up, extended his arm and shouted, "*Sieg Heil, Heil Hitler!*"

"That's enough, Mr. Weisst," Nimitz cautioned.

"Herr Ulbrecht, would you tell the court the atrocities that turned you against the Nazis?"

"The Gestapo was composed of ignorant street bums, criminals, hoodlums, hooligans, punks and bullies. There was no moral fiber in any of them. They countenanced multiple rapes, gang rapes and outright murder. They killed babies with bayonets, throwing them live into the crematoriums. They starved the slave laborers until they died, and played games by making women race each other with their hands and knees on the dirt ground while they were completely naked. They bet on the winner and shot the loser."

"You saw all that yourself?"

"Almost every day, with every new batch of prisoners. One time, Commandant Weisst watched one of these crawling races. He took his Walther .65 and pushed it in the anus of a young girl, naked, on her hands and knees. She screamed and he fired his gun. He was drunk and laughed as she lay there dying. The other woman tried to help the wounded woman. The commandant shot her in the head. Both women were dead. This is the kind of atrocity that's been covered up."

"Are you a religious man?" Bart asked.

"I am now. I am a devout Catholic."

"You testify that what you have just described actually took place at the Chelmno death camp? Remember, you took an oath here to tell the truth."

Ulbrecht crossed himself and produced a gold crucifix. He kissed it.

"I swear in the name of Jesus Christ, the Holy Spirit and God Almighty that I have told the truth."

"No further questions. Your witness."

Eric Stolz menacingly faced the witness.

"Sergeant Ulbrecht, you were wounded by a sniper in the Polish war. Is that correct?"

"No. First, I was a corporal. Second, the so-called Polish war was not a war. It was a blitzkrieg against a defenseless nation."

"Very well, Corporal. Are you blaming *Der Führer* for all the imagined atrocities at Chelmno?"

"The fish always stinks from the head. He was an Austrian bum, not a German. You call him *Der Führer*. He destroyed Germany and let that butcher Heinrich Himmler kill six million Jews and another six million Jehovah's Witnesses, Gypsies, the lame and the halt. Who is to blame? He was responsible for the death of more than three million young German soldiers and over seven million wounded. Yes, that rotten Austrian corporal, that street bum, is to be blamed. He stinks from the head like a dead fish!" Ulbrecht spat out.

"Yet you pledged allegiance to *Der Führer* and the Nazi Party."

"*Mea culpa*, may God forgive me. He and Himmler and Goering and Goebbels and Heydrich and the whole oligarchy should rot in hell, and may God forgive you for defending these lice!" Ulbrecht yelled angrily as he crossed himself again.

"No further questions."

Nimitz ordered a recess to 1430 hours. Bart and Jacques raced to the Victorian house. Bart lifted Elizabeth and kissed her passionately. Joyce rushed into Jacques' arms, hugged him and kissed his cheek.

"I had that pleasure when I picked these dolls up at the airport," Jacques laughed.

Mrs. Lawrence set the table and prepared lunch.

"My, my, two very beautiful ladies," Mrs. Lawrence giggled. "You better keep your eyes on these ladies, General and Mr. Laurent. We have a few thousand soldiers on this base."

"Count on it," Jacques asserted.

During lunch Bart outlined the courtroom procedure to the ladies.

"Bart, we've followed every day of it and we are both prepared for your interrogation," Elizabeth chuckled.

"There is one difference for you, Elizabeth. I won't be questioning you. Gideon Cartman will be doing that chore."

"Why, Barton?"

"Because it would not be seemly for your husband to interrogate you, and it is probably a conflict of interest. But I will be looking at you lovingly," he laughed. "I'll handle you, Joyce."

"Don't handle her, just question her," Elizabeth jested.

Court resumed at 1430 hours and Nimitz ordered the next witness. Gideon Cartman rose, saying, "The prosecution calls Elizabeth Milburn."

Two hefty MPs escorted the witness to the stand. She wore a navy blue suit with a pleated skirt, white blouse, black patent leather shoes and gold chain dangling a Star of David. She focused her blue eyes on Cartman and flashed a sparkling smile. The media and the spectators were surprised and entranced. She took the oath and sat down.

"Please state your name for the record."

"Elizabeth Milburn," she replied in her perfect British accent.

"You are married to General Barton Quentin Milburn?"

"Yes, and the mother of his three children."

Laughter followed. Nimitz and his colleagues smiled.

Jacques poked Bart. "She's wearing a chain link with a Star of David."

Bart smiled. "She's making a statement."

"Mrs. Milburn, you are the daughter of Sir Alfred Lipton, former ambassador to Italy and a survivor of a Nazi German concentration camp, is that correct?"

"Yes, sir."

"Would you please tell the court how you were captured and incarcerated?"

Elizabeth detailed the events that took place the day Italy joined Nazi Germany in declaring war against Britain and the United States.

"When the Gestapo took you off the train on your way to Turin with Mother Superior and the group of nuns, how were you dressed?"

"I was clothed as a nun."

"You are wearing a gold chain with the Star of David on it. Are you Jewish?"

"Proudly. My ancestry goes back to more than five thousand years." She cast a stare of revulsion toward the defendants.

"The Gestapo tried to hold your father, who, under Geneva Convention rules, should have had diplomatic immunity and been returned to Britain forthwith."

"Yes, and it was Prime Minister Churchill who contacted Count Folke Bernadotte to effect my father's release. The Swedish Foreign Office and the Count arranged to have Himmler order his return."

"Why were you held?"

"As I described earlier, I was protected in a convent and schooled there. I learned later that the SS was searching for me, on Himmler's orders, to exchange me for Rudolph Hess or some other Nazi in British or American custody. They took the nuns and me to Gestapo headquarters in Genoa. I was questioned by General Heinrich Müller, a nasty, evil man, who said he was the SS *Gruppenführer*, the head of the Gestapo."

"What did they do with you after that?" Cartman asked.

"They threatened to kill me if I didn't answer their questions."

"What kind of questions?"

"Was I Ambassador Lipton's daughter? Was he Jewish? Was I Jewish? Why was I dressed like a nun? *You don't look Jewish*, he said. I told him he didn't look like a human. He slapped my face. An Italian woman, who was working in the Gestapo-occupied police headquarters, intervened and clutched me in her arms, then berated him for striking me. He took his pistol and struck her on her head. She collapsed. Several *carabinieri* surrounded him. They threatened him and picked up the woman. He placated them and warned his men not to resist."

"What was the next move with you?"

"I was shuttled from camp to camp until I got to Ohrdruf."

"What did you observe at these camps?"

"The most horrendous treatment of humanity… Jews, Jehovah's Witnesses, Gypsies, priests, other Christian protesters, women and children abused, starved slave laborers and humans of all creeds, ethnic and racial groups being slaughtered by gas, bullets and starvation. These Lucifers enjoyed their demonic bestiality."

"What happened at Ohrdruf?"

"I was held in seclusion for two days, then I was put in a barracks with Jews of every nationality-French, German, Italian, Greek, Russian, Polish, Czech, Dutch and Belgian. The American troops were getting close, so I was hiding with a group underneath one of the barracks. There was an intense search for me. They found us and that rotten, filthy, evil-smelling Nazi commandant, Hugo Schultz, sitting back there, grabbed me by my hair and pulled me into his office." She pointed at the defendant.

"Will the court ask Hugo Schultz to stand, please?" Cartman requested.

He was roughly propped to his feet by the MPs. "*Ja*, and that general she calls her husband shot me in the groin!" he yelled.

"Is that the man?"

"Yes, and if I may add, he was doing more than beating me. That foul-smelling pig, in trying to get me out the back way to escape the American troops, exposed himself to me in a threat of rape. It was at that point that Colonel Milburn heard my screams, knocked the door down and shot that bloody verminous bastard, who had drawn his own gun."

"Please continue."

"Other troops joined us, and I was put in a wheelchair. Colonel Milburn ordered the medics to patch me up and to take that despicable wounded man to an Army hospital for treatment. I was wheeled by this wonderful colonel, now General Milburn, my dear husband, to meet Generals Eisenhower, Bradley and Patton. The press were there. They took pictures and interviewed me. Margaret Bourke-White photographed me and the whole camp for Life magazine. General Eisenhower called Prime Minister Churchill, who sent a plane for me. Colonel Milburn accompanied me to London. End of story."

"Not quite."

"What else can I tell you?" Elizabeth asked.

"The colonel visited you frequently after the war?"

"Yes, and when I was nineteen he asked my father if he could propose to me - and I wanted to know why had he taken so long."

The courtroom rocked with laughter.

"No further questions. Your witness," Cartman declared to the defense table.

Eric Stolz addressed the lady. "Madame Milburn, did your husband coach you in preparation for this trial?"

"You may address me as Mrs. Milburn. No one prompted me. I've waited eight years to tell the world of your Nazi monstrosities. I lived through evils and observed them perpetrated on thousands, living and dead. Who needs to be coached when the scars inflicted by Nazi beasts are imbedded in the minds, hearts and souls of the living and the bodies and ashes of the dead? These monstrosities, composed of *Der Führer* and his oligarchy, outperformed the devil's imagination and hallucinations in their tortures and mass murders of the human race. How could you ask such a stupid question? There are thousands of witnesses among the German people and the rest of the world who could attest to Nazi Germany's evil without being coached."

"You are a bitter woman," Stolz said.

"Not bitter at all. I grieve for the survivors and their murdered kin. I pray the world will remember the carnage inflicted by Hitler, Himmler, Goering, Goebbels and their ignorant hooligan minions. That goes for you too, sir, and your Swiss clients who have robbed the Jews of Europe of their money."

"No further questions," Stolz huffed, and sat down.

Bart whispered to Jacques, "Tell Joyce we'll put her on in a day or two after Monsignor Pallini. We need a change of pace. Let her know she might be on tomorrow."

"Okay," Jacques agreed, nodding.

"Call your next witness," Nimitz ordered.

"The prosecution calls Monsignor Antonio Pallini."

A tall, thin man in priestly garb marched quickly between two MPs to the witness stand. He took the oath, kissed the Bible and crossed his chest. He had a set of beads in his hand.

"English or Italian, Monsignor?" Bart asked.

"I speak many languages, but let's keep it in English. I was born in New York. Father Antonio will do."

"Okay, father. You were stationed in Berlin for quite awhile. Is that correct?"

"Yes, I was a young priest on the staff of Cardinal Pacelli when he was appointed Papal Secretary of State in 1930 by Pius XI. He negotiated the concordat with Nazi Germany. I remained in Berlin as a member of the Vatican staff. In 1939 Pacelli became Pope. He was named Pius XII. I was promoted to monsignor. Being a Jesuit and outspoken, I never made it to bishop."

"Were you in favor of that covenant with the Nazis?"

"Hell no, and he knew it. But he kept me there."

"How long were you there?" Bart asked.

"Long enough to see these mad dogs turn a cultured, civilized, religious country into a pack of mad wolves, with craven cowards behind them bent on destroying Europe, and possibly world domination."

"Prior to the war, did you report the metamorphosis of the Weimar Republic to the Third Reich?"

"Yes, I bombarded Cardinal Pacelli with weekly reports of Hitler's rise to power, his verbal attacks on the Jews, his misuse of the word Aryan, which connotes Indo-Iranian languages and spread from South Russia and Turkestan through Mesopotamia and Asia Minor. Look it up in Webster's Dictionary and the encyclopedia. The word he was looking for was *Nordic*."

"Did Pacelli respond to your reports?"

"He told me to observe, report, and that's all. I met with Hitler and pleaded with him after Kristallnacht, when I saw these hoodlums of the SA burn synagogues, destroy Jewish businesses, burn books, kill Jews in the streets and arrest thousands for concentration camps. I pleaded with the cardinal to speak up, or ask Pius XI to do so. The Pope protested, to no avail. I talked with priests, monsignors and bishops in Berlin. I got a lot of lip service. I finally wrote, asking to be recalled to the Vatican. In 1939 Pius XI died and Pacelli became Pius XII. No recall for me."

"What did you do after that?"

"I helped a number of Jews to emigrate. I was friendly with a conservative rabbi, Israel Newman. We worked together, starting a pipeline of exits. Then came the invasion of Poland. I went to see Heinrich Himmler to plead with him. That pompous, phony little punk in his hand-tailored uniform professed to be a good Catholic. He asked me to pray with him for a pure Germany. He swore to me that they were not killing Jews, just resettling them in a country of their own in Africa somewhere. He got on his knees and prayed. He asked me to bless him. I prayed silently for him to stop his evil activities. He was a degenerate in a *creep's* clothing, as you Americans say. This man ordered the murder of millions every day and then would come home and pray. His piety was shameful. For a man in his early forties, he was the consummate mass murderer. Yet the sight of blood made him sick," Father Pallini added.

"What did you do when the war started?"

"I received a papal order to go into Poland and report. I got special papers from Bormann. I went to Poland after the country was conquered. I saw abuses that defied civilization and all the tenets of God. In some cases, rabbis and their flock were killed. I took off my collar and said Kaddish, the Hebrew prayer for the dead. The Gestapo was composed of dolts, uneducated street ruffians in their black uniforms. In Warsaw, an SS man struck me with the butt of his gun. As I fell, I pulled out my pass signed by Bormann. A colonel picked me up and apologized. He shot the Gestapo man on the spot. He took me to headquarters and had my head wound dressed. He begged me not to report the incident, swearing he was a good Catholic."

"Did you continue your inspection?"

"Yes. I deliberately stayed out of touch with the Vatican, for fear of being ordered to go back to Berlin. I had a car and a priest driver. We continued north and east. The cruelty of the SS hoodlums was indescribable. When we got to Lublin, we saw raids every day. They entered houses and synagogues, robbing and plundering for money, jewelry and anything valuable. The Gestapo acted like common criminals. The hoodlums beat Jews who had no money. The most outrageous sacrilegious act was the attack on the Talmudic Academy. They took the library into the street, carried the books to the center of the square and built a bonfire, burning all the books. The congregation cried, and a military band drowned out their wailing. Many Jews were whipped, to disperse them. I saw Bibles and Torahs torn to shreds and thrown into the fire. This I reported to the Vatican as a defilement of the Bible, which is the word of God in all monotheistic religions. This was a pagan rampage in a thieves' paradise."

"Did you see people killed?"

"Yes, bludgeoned to death. Rabbis' beards were set fire and doused with kerosene. It was anarchy at its worst. *Mobocracy* is the word."

"Did anyone object?" Bart asked.

"I did and they threatened to shoot me. A captain told me, *Go worship your Jew God, Christ*. I reported him to a colonel, who said that he was drunk and didn't mean it. Several shots were fired at our car, which had a cross on the doors and a flag with a cross on it. We were in a godless orgy. Yet these were German boys and men in a frenzy of debauchery. Rape was taking place in side streets and even in the synagogues before they were burned down, with people locked in there. Dante's "Inferno" was a fable. This was real. I prayed and was sick with what Father Byrne and I observed."

"What did you do?"

"We drove back to Berlin and I wrote a searing report to Pius XII. Pacelli later told me he never received my report. By the way, I had another meeting with Hitler," Pallini emphasized. "First, I spoke to Bormann, who acted shocked. He said that was Himmler's doing. He took me into Hitler's office. *Der Führer* agreed it was Himmler's doing and would tell him to stop this cruelty. He wanted these Gestapo agents punished. *This is war*, he said. *The Jews are to be relocated.* I left there feeling like I had accomplished something."

"Had you?"

"Not at all. It was lip service. Father Byrne, an Irish priest, and I got on a troop train several weeks after the invasion of Russia. There was very little resistance by the Soviet troops. The German army took town after town, city after city. Behind the troops came the *Einsatzgruppen Kommando* units. The killing machine was rounding up Jews and staging mass executions. Lithuanians and Ukrainians helped the Nazis slaughter the Jews. Russia became a massive abattoir. The Nazis collected thousands of Jews in each town and city. They made men, women and children dig giant pits, strip naked, and then they were machine-gunned to death. Father Byrne and I had binoculars and watched these pagans in their mass murders. We got as far as Kharkov and observed the *Einsatzkommando* slaughter ten thousand Jews in one afternoon. That was enough for us. We turned back. Father Byrne was driving and I was making copious notes. When we neared Warsaw, the Nazi soldiers advised us to detour around the city because there was an uprising there. We had to get petrol. We got some at a farm where a Catholic farmer was hiding some Jews. He gave us some food and begged us to take a young Jewish woman and her one-year-old baby with us. She was the widow of a Polish colonel. I asked him if there was a church close by. There was one five miles from there. We made the lady sit on the floor of the back seat. We had commandeered the car from a Nazi colonel. At the church, which was Russian Orthodox, the bishop gave us a nun's outfit to clothe the lady. He gave us some food. We got her to Hamburg, and fortunately found a Swedish captain who put her and her baby on his freighter. I got a letter from her at the Vatican six months ago. She is living in Tel Aviv with her young son and married an Israeli, a member of the Knesset. I will not mention her name."

"When you reached Berlin, did you send your report to the Pope?" Bart asked.

"Yes, and I was ordered to report to the Vatican. I thought that would mean I was relieved of my post in Germany."

"Did you leave right away?"

"I stopped at the chancellery to advise Hitler that I was going to Rome. Hitler was not there, so I saw Martin Bormann. He invited me to lunch. I saw it as an opportunity to get something off my chest. I really let him have it. I told him of all the atrocities I saw. He blamed it all on Himmler. Bormann appeared shocked, and defended Hitler. He said Hitler was now Commander-in-Chief of the Wehrmacht and too busy to pay attention to Himmler, whom he called a miserable *Schweinhund*. The big surprise was his statement that Hitler's attacks on the Jews were merely political. He needed a scapegoat and the Jews were convenient."

"Do you believe that?"

"No, but Bormann did," Father Pallini answered.

"What happened at the Vatican?"

"Pius XII called a meeting of the cardinals to hear my report of the Nazi atrocities. Father Byrne joined me. When I finished reading my report, I saw tears in the eyes of some of the cardinals. During my report, I reported what Hitler and Bormann had said about Himmler. They said he was a fanatic and that, instead of removing the Jews from Germany, he and Heydrich wanted a Final Solution. Kill all the Jews was their plan. Hitler said he would rather settle them in Madagascar or some place in Africa. According to Hitler and Bormann, Himmler recited a little history of Jesus. I made notes of this and reported it to the Pope and the cardinals."

"What was so important about the history of Jesus?"

The monsignor produced a sheet of paper from his briefcase, perused it and read from his notes. "Himmler stated: Jesus' true name was Rabbi Yeshua, in English it was Joshua, changed by the Greeks to Jesus. His mother's name was Miriam, Hellenized into Mary. Had Jesus' four brothers, Judah, Simon, James and Joseph, and their father and mother been alive in the 1930s, Himmler said he would have slaughtered them in Nazi gas chambers and burned them to ashes in their crematoriums."

"What was the reaction of the cardinals?" Milburn asked.

"They were furious, though they don't like to talk about Jesus' brothers. They were knowledgeable about Jesus and the original names of Joshua and Miriam. However, they wanted to break the *Concordat*. An argument ensued when Pacelli, Pius XII, refused to speak out publicly against Nazi atrocities, on the grounds that Hitler might seize the Vatican. As everyone knows now, he is being criticized for not challenging Nazi persecution of Jews and for not protecting them in Italy. This is all recorded in the encyclopedias and the press. But the Italian people took care of the Jews. Then, after Mussolini was killed by partisans, Italy declared war against Germany, and the British Jewish Brigade came into Italy and fought alongside the Italians against the Nazis."

"Why were you sent back to Germany?"

"Because Pius XII called me a troublemaker. What does he expect from a Jesuit? I'll probably be sent to the boondocks for what I have said here today. At least I was witness to God's wrath in the destruction of Hitler's Third Reich. He has put the mark of Cain on the German people for the most sordid twelve years in their history. There are Nazis still in Germany and all corners of the world. I pray for the countries that stood by and let this Holocaust happen.

Complacency makes them unindicted conspirators to this most evil genocide."

"No further questions. Your witness," Bart said.

"Are you a paid Jewish agent, Monsignor?" Krieger asked.

Bart angrily shouted, "Objection!"

"Please, General, allow me to answer."

"Objection withdrawn."

"Counselor, my answer is yes. I am paid by God with the gift of life to expose the devil's work whenever I accost this demon. You are a Catholic who is a paid agent of Hitler, the devil incarnate. Your compensation comes from those Swiss banks harboring money belonging to slaughtered Jews, some of which financed the Nazi war machine. May God forgive you," the monsignor sighed as he extended his hand with the sign of the crucifix.

Krieger flushed and muttered, "No further questions."

Jacques Laurent stepped forward and escorted the monsignor to the exit, saying, "Sir, I am the head of the Nazi desk at the CIA."

"Yes, I know you, Mr. Laurent."

"Would it be possible to get a copy of your report on the Nazi atrocities?"

"No problem," he said as he reached into his briefcase and extracted a printed copy. "Here, son, it's yours. You are the French Jew who fought as a partisan after France surrendered."

"How did you know that?" a surprised Jacques asked.

"I have a little intelligence organization of my own. Keep in touch with me. If you come to Rome, visit me. *Gey gesunterheit*, Jacques Laurent."

"*Zie gezundt*, Father."

They both laughed. Court was recessed to Tuesday, March 17th at 0900 hours. At Fuller Hall that evening, General Warren Fielding, commanding Fort Leavenworth, hosted a very special dinner in his private dining room. Present for the occasion were Bart and Elizabeth Milburn, Jacques and Joyce Laurent, General Wilford Ross, Colonel Jeremiah Brown, George Spota and Dick Reilly. Three sergeants assigned to dining room duty were in attendance. Two bottles of champagne were noisily popped open. The golden nectar was poured into the fluted glasses of the guests and the host.

"To the ladies who grace this table," Fielding toasted as he rose.

"Hear, hear!" the men responded.

A pianist in the corner of the room softly played a medley of Cole Porter tunes.

"To our host," Bart toasted, raising his glass.

The dinner party began. There was no mention of the trial during the lavish dinner. Jacques had them laughing with his imitations of the Nazis in German accents. Jeremiah Brown was urged by Fielding to tell a few of his stories, which were hilarious. Joyce sang *La Vie en Rose*, imitating Edith Piaf. She also rendered some American show tunes, and pretty soon had everyone singing along with her.

Following a few after-dinner drinks, Fielding coaxed the three sergeants into joining him in a version of a barbershop quartet. As the party came to an end, the pianist played "Good Night, Ladies."

"Bart, this was one of the most enjoyable evenings I've had in years," George Spota declared.

"General, thanks for inviting us," Dick Reilly added.

"How do you like your new quarters, fellows?" Bart asked.

"That townhouse is perfect and is close to where we're working on that film," Spota replied.

"Good night, y'all," Jacques said, trying a Southern accent.

CHAPTER FOURTEEN

Tuesday, March 17, 1953 - 0900 hours - Fort Leavenworth

Bart decided to hold Joyce over. The decision to put on Commandant Hugo Schultz, to be followed by the soldiers, was unanimously agreed upon by the prosecution team.

"The prosecution calls Hugo Schultz," Bart said, opening the next session of the trial.

The stocky, unshaven witness, dwarfed by the MPs, jauntily strode to the witness stand. He put his hand on the Bible, spit on the floor and answered, "*Ja.*"

Nimitz angrily snapped, "Clean that up, now!"

Schultz shrugged his shoulders, pretending he didn't understand. An interpreter repeated the order. Schultz stoically stared at Bart. Two MPs, on a signal from Nimitz, yanked the witness to his knees. They handed him a tissue, took his right hand and forced him to wipe the saliva off the floor. He was roughly lifted back into his seat. Bart came face to face with the former commandant of the Ohrdruf concentration camp. Addressing him in German, he asked him to state his name.

Schultz shouted, "Hugo Schultz, *Sieg Heil!*"

"Those days are over, Schultz. Don't play the fool. Just answer the questions."

"They make you general because you shoot me."

"You weren't worth it. Now, answer my questions or I will ask this tribunal to put you in solitary confinement. Stop playing the hero for your Nazi defendants."

"What you want?"

"Were you the commandant at Ohrdruf?"

"*Jawohl.*"

"Who appointed you to that post?"

"Heinrich Himmler."

"Did you have full authority over the camp?"

"*Ja.*"

"I am going to read ten ladies' names. Tell the court if you recognize those names." Bart read off the names of rape victims.

"I know that list."

"Who raped those women?"

"I do not know of any rapes."

"Do you realize you are lying?"

"Prove it," Schultz challenged.

Cartman handed a large manila envelope to Bart, who removed a packet of photographs. He handed one to Schultz.

"Do you recognize the man in that photograph, Herr Schultz?"

The witness was obviously disconcerted. "This is a false picture."

"What do you mean by false?"

"A manufactured photo. You know, two people put in a composite."

"The girl in that picture is Esther Goldberg, sixteen years of age, and the man lying on top of her is you, Colonel Hugo Schultz, Adolf Hitler's pure Aryan German. *Sieg Heil* and *Heil* Hitler, you liar."

"How you get this picture?"

"It was found in your desk after I captured you." Bart handed the photo to the clerk to be marked in evidence and passed to the tribunal.

"Herr Schultz, look at this second picture and the third one. They are in sequence."

Schultz looked at the two photos and his demeanor was shattered. His hands shook and his lips quavered. "No, no, no more," he muttered.

"Yes, yes, more. For the record, these two photos show a naked sixteen-year-old girl on her knees in a wooded area. Hugo Schultz, in that second picture, is standing over her with a Walther .65 gun pointed at her head. The third picture shows him standing over the dead girl. Schultz is proudly posing in both pictures." He handed the exhibits to the clerk.

"You raped that teenage girl and then executed her. Is that the Nazi formula for a pure Aryan world?"

"Enough. No more."

"You had full authority at the camp. Is this illustrative of what the Nazi word is for authority?"

"*Nein,* no, no."

"You tried to rape Elizabeth Lipton when I shot you. Isn't that true?"

"No more. I will say no more."

"No further questions. He's your witness."

Krieger declared, "No questions."

"The prosecution calls Helmut Wasser," Bart said.

A thirty-year-old man, six feet tall and military in posture, marched to the stand. After the oath, he sat confidently in the chair. He stated his name for the record.

"Helmut Wasser, you were the last commandant at Auschwitz?"

"Yes, sir," he answered in English.

"How long did you serve in that position?"

"Thirty-five days."

"Explain that."

"I was only a captain assigned to the I.G. Farben plant at Auschwitz III, Monowitz, during Rudolf Höss' reign."

"You had nothing to do with gassing Jews to death?"

"No, I never killed any Jews or others."

"What were your duties at the I.G. Farben plant?"

"I was in charge of the soldiers guarding the plant."

"Did you know what was going on at Auschwitz I and Auschwitz-Birkenau II?"

"Yes, they had killed two and a half million Jews."

"Did you protest, or try to get transferred?"

"Sir, that would have meant suicide. I would have been shot for either of those choices," Wasser muttered.

"Are you a Nazi?"

"No, sir."

"*Were* you a Nazi?"

"For a short while."

"When did you stop?"

"I was drafted at seventeen and began to see the truth of the Nazi movement. My father is a Protestant minister. After we invaded Poland, I was wounded. Nothing serious. I saw the slaughter of Jews and the burning of synagogues. I was given a two-week leave after I left the hospital. I went home to Stuttgart. I talked with my father. He was outraged when I told him what I had seen. He lectured me for hours and predicted that Germany would pay a big price for their vile deeds. He predicted the total defeat of the Third Reich and its Nazi leaders. He was so right."

"Give us an overview of what you saw and learned at Auschwitz."

"Sir, the memory of Auschwitz and Poland is etched in my mind. I have nightmares. Yes, I saw my Germany go on a rampage of hate, murder, rape, pillage, torture and hooliganism beyond anything that happened in history. I am sorry to say that I was part of the Nazi war against humanity. I have always been a good Christian, and yet all my values were shredded before my eyes. Auschwitz was the major hellhole of the world," Wasser added, genuinely embarrassed.

"Specifics, please."

"Stripping men, women and children to gas them to death. Raping ten-, twelve-, thirteen- and fourteen-year-old girls. Brutes sodomizing young boys and killing them afterward. I looked at our men and couldn't picture them as the Germans I knew as a young boy. The SS was stealing everything they could get away with. One night I was invited to a card game. When I got to a colonel's quarters, I saw them playing poker. Some of the men were betting with gold fillings from the mouths of Jews who had been gassed that day. I made an excuse and got out of there."

"When you first were assigned to Auschwitz, what was your job?"

"I was in Auschwitz II, or as they called it, Auschwitz-Birkenau, which had the largest number of prisoners. It was in nine sections, separated by electric barbed wire fences. It was guarded by the SS and ferocious dogs. I was assigned to the railroad arrival center. We had the job of opening the doors of those cattle cars loaded with Jews, Gypsies, Jehovah's Witnesses, Norwegians, Hungarians, and German Christian dissenters. Trains arrived every day. I watched them disrobe and nakedly walk to their deaths in the gas chambers. Then I saw the bodies removed, their gold fillings extracted and then dumped into the high fires of the crematoria. I had no part in that operation. The *Sonderkommando* units handled the dead bodies."

"You were in the army invading Poland. Tell the court what was the worst atrocity you saw before you were wounded," Bart urged.

"No, I was already wounded in my hip. We were in Vilna, which had been occupied by the Soviets. They had retreated. Several of us wounded men were on stretchers waiting to be taken to a field hospital. We were outside their city hall. Soon men, women and children, all Jewish, were being prodded into the square. I saw at least one thousand take off their clothes and stand naked. Trucks arrived with soldiers carrying machine guns, rifles and pistols. My hip had been causing me great pain. I soon forgot my pain. A barrage of bullets rained on these naked, innocent men, women, children and little babies, and blood was spurting in all directions. That was the first massacre I saw. I said to one of the wounded soldiers next to me, *What kind of a war is this?* And his answer was, *That's the way to get rid of the Jews. Hitler's going to wipe them off the map.* I never forgot that, and never commented to any German about it."

"Now, Helmut Wasser, please explain how you became commandant in the final days of the Nazi control of Auschwitz."

"After Colonel Liebehenschel was removed for incompetence, some of our Gestapo officers were disappearing daily. The Russians were closing in on us. A Gestapo general arrived after Baer disappeared. There were three colonels with him. They came in a big Daimler limousine. A sergeant came to me and said General von Weigen wanted to see me. I walked over to the car and saluted. I noticed the car was loaded with champagne, caviar and other foodstuffs. He asked, *Where is the commandant?* I replied, *Gone.* He said, *Very well, I now appoint you commandant.* He asked my name and scribbled on a piece of paper, appointing me. One of the colonels handed me his insignia. They were half drunk. *Now, I want two bags of ice,* the general said. I ordered two sergeants to get the ice. They opened the trunk of the car. It was loaded with meats, poultry and cheeses. The ice was placed in the trunk. He saluted and took off."

"As the new commandant, what did you do?"

"I ordered our men to start feeding the prisoners more food," Wasser answered quickly. "The Russian artillery was very close. I sent a lieutenant and a sergeant with a white flag to tell the Russians to come into the camp. Two days later, they entered the camp. We were all taken as prisoners of war. The war ended on May 8. We were released in September."

"Now, I am going to ask you a very pertinent question. No equivocation, just give the court a straightforward, unembellished answer. What were you doing at the ranch in La Plata, Argentina?"

"I had been employed by Mr. Nordheim since 1949."

"Who hired you, and in what capacity?" Bart asked.

"I was employed by Mr. Darren Mayfield as a courier to Mr. Nordheim."

"A courier of what and to where?"

"Messages and packages to his worldwide holdings, banks and brokerage houses."

"Did you ever meet Mr. Nordheim?"

"Yes, in Malmo, Sweden, and in Argentina."

"Didn't you suspect he was Hitler?"

"No, he showed me the tattooed numbers on his arm. I was convinced he was a Jewish survivor."

"Okay, tell the court how you happened to be at the Argentina ranch when you were captured."

"I was stationed in Liechtenstein. Herr Froelich sent me to Geneva to the Banque Lorraine to carry a large package to the Cayman Islands. After I delivered the package to a bank there, I was given two other packages to deliver to the ranch in La Plata. Two days later the Americans raided the ranch."

"When did you realize that Nordheim was not who he pretended to be?"

"When I arrived at the ranch and saw all those Gestapo bums there," Wasser answered emphatically. "There was no way I could escape."

"No further questions. Your witness," Bart said.

"Were you a proud German when you joined the army?" Stolz asked.

"Yes."

"You were fighting for the fatherland?"

"Yes."

"You swore allegiance to the Nazi Party and to *Der Führer*, Adolf Hitler?"

"Yes. I was seventeen years old and naïve."

"Isn't it true, once a Nazi, always a Nazi?"

"Bullshit, and you know it. That Austrian maniac succeeded in destroying Germany. When I was released as a POW and came back to the fatherland, our cities were in ruins. Hitler became a billionaire and posed as a Jew when he escaped. Look at us now...war criminals."

"No further questions," Stolz said.

Nimitz announced a lunch recess. In the conference room, during the buffet lunch, there was a phone call from Washington for Bart.

"Who's calling?" Bart asked Sophia.

"It's Allen Dulles."

"Tell him to call back in fifteen minutes."

"He'll be back in fifteen minutes, sir," Sophia politely told the caller.

"I'd like to finish my coffee before I tangle with him," Bart grumbled.

The team was impressed with Bart's attitude toward the newly appointed CIA director. After his second cup of coffee and a cigarette, the phone rang.

Sophia answered. Bart nodded. "He's right here, sir," she said.

"Milburn here," he said.

"Bart, two things. Number one, what is this request for the captured footage?"

"Evidence for the trial. How did that get in your domain? I asked the Pentagon for it."

"Just curious. Secondly, Bart, can't you ease up on the attacks on the Swiss banks? The Secretary of State is very upset. He wants us to stay friendly with Switzerland."

"Listen carefully, Allen. We've received several thousand calls and letters from survivors who want to testify. More than half of them want our help in getting their money out of the Swiss banks."

"Well, we have had official complaints to the State Department from the Swiss ambassador."

"The Secretary of State is your brother. Did he ask you to make this call?"

"As a matter of fact, he did."

Bart was icily cold. "Allen, do you know a man named Waldo Schlicht?"

"Very well. He's a powerful banker and politician."

"I have no desire to tangle assholes with you or your brother; however, hold on to your chair, my erstwhile friend. I have a bulletin for you and your brother. Schlicht is involved in the murders of Alden Gaines and Lilly Darcy."

"You've got to be kidding."

"I'm not through, buddy boy. He is the mastermind who laundered all the Nazi counterfeit money throughout the war to this day. Now, do you want to protect that slimy bastard and the Swiss banks who financed Hitler?"

There was total silence on the other end. Bart lit a cigarette and waited for a reply. The team sat in awe of this power struggle.

"Are you still there, or has the cat got your tongue, Allen?"

"Bart, that can't be true. I heard nothing about that."

"Well, the time has come for you and your brother, our illustrious Secretary of State, to check with our Attorney General, the FBI, Interpol, and the Elizabeth, New Jersey, police and the Union County district attorney. There is a sealed indictment of that powerhouse asshole banker. And for the sake of the good old U.S. of A., clean your skirts and ties with the Swiss. The battle for the Jewish funds illegally held by the Swiss will continue to the end of this century. Your pre-war Swiss connections are legend. Don't let it surface in the media, for Ike's sake as well."

Dulles' tune changed. "Sorry to have ruffled you, Bart. Thanks for the information. I am shocked."

"I thought you would be. *Ciao.*" Bart slammed down the receiver, and the team applauded.

"You're taking on some mighty powerful foes, General," Cartman declared.

"Not really. I've got the more powerful team if they want to play hardball."

"Who would that be?" Maybrook asked.

"The Congress and all of America. If they want to wash dirty linen, what better place to do it than the Senate Armed Services Committee, followed by a speech by me at the National Press Club?"

"Bravo!" Jacques exclaimed.

☆ ☆ ☆ ☆

Tuesday, March 17, 1953 - 1300 hours - Fort Leavenworth

The afternoon session began with Max Linger, a thirty-four-year-old who had served in the invasion of the Soviet Union. His record was in Bart's hand when he approached him on the stand. "Sergeant Linger, you were in the infantry assigned to guard Adolf Hitler's headquarters in the forest near Vinnitsa in the Ukraine in September 1942, is that correct?"

"Yes, sir."

"*Der Führer* was the Commander in Chief of the German army at that time. Is that true?"

"Yes, sir. The headquarters were called *Werewolf*. All the generals would meet with Hitler there. They were planning the drive against Moscow. I was assigned with other soldiers in a circle surrounding that building for his protection."

"Who were the generals there with him?"

"Besides his staff, there was *Oberkommando der Wehrmacht*, the OKW, chief of the Armed Forces High Command, Field Marshal Wilhelm Keitel, and *Generaloberst* Alfred Jodl. Also, General Franz Holder, chief of the infantry."

"How long were you there?"

"Six weeks."

"Did Hitler leave?"

"No. One night I was on guard duty at the front of the headquarters. Hitler was screaming and shouting at his generals. He was throwing things, like a lamp and some books."

"Did you hear anything he said?"

"Swear words," Linger answered.

"Try to recall the words and any names he mentioned."

"Excuse my language, but he called General Jodl an *arschloch*, an asshole, and General Keitel a *bumsen Dummkopf*. He called General Holder a *muschi*."

"What happened after that?"

"The next day, Holder was replaced by General Kurt Zeitzler. That was when our special brigade was replaced by Zeitzler's special guard. Holder ordered us back to Poland. Our unit was assigned to different concentration camps. That's how I came to Treblinka and that son of a bitch, Colonel Kurt Franz."

"Objection," Stolz said.

"Strike the words *son of a bitch*," Nimitz ruled.

"What were your initial duties?" Bart asked.

"The commandant, Colonel Franz, interviewed me and twenty other soldiers from my brigade. None of us had any experience in concentration camps. At first our troops were glad to get away from the Russian front. But the battles in the east didn't compare with the horrors at Chelmno."

"Please answer my question. What were your first duties?"

"Franz wanted to know if we had any objection to executing Jews and others. If we didn't mind, he would promote us and put us in the Gestapo. I declined. Others did too. So he assigned us to guard the *sonderkommandos* while they filled pits with the gassed dead bodies of the Jews. At first there weren't enough crematoria to keep up with the slaughter. Some of the bodies got into the pit by being shot in the head at the edge of the mass graves."

"Did you actually see the executions?"

"Oh, yes. One I remember very well," Linger replied. "A chief rabbi, Benjamin Lomonitz, refused to disrobe. The Gestapo tore his clothes off him in front of the three hundred naked men, women and children. The naked rabbi stood there with great dignity, looking straight ahead. Colonel Franz personally put his gun to the back of the rabbi's head and shouted to his men, *This is the way we get rid of Jews! Fire when I do!* He cocked his gun and fired into the rabbi's skull. All the Gestapo men fired machine guns at the same time. I saw the rabbi and three hundred bodies fall into the pit on top of hundreds of dead bodies. I vomited. There were tears in the eyes of the soldier guards. The Gestapo laughed at us. Colonel Franz slapped me in the face and called me a dirty word."

"Did he change your duties?"

"Yes, I was assigned to guard the barracks where the prison laborers were housed. I saw the arrogant Gestapo pull women out of the barracks at night. Many of the officers were drunk. They raped these ladies and killed them afterward."

"Did you see this or hear of it?"

"Both. One night, five of them took a young woman, who had been a seamstress, to the back of the barracks, and I saw five of them rape her. I was tempted to shoot them, but I was a coward. They would have killed me on the spot. They carried her to the pit and threw her in there. I think they strangled her," Max Linger concluded.

"No further questions. Your witness."

Stolz was close to the witness. "You are an admitted coward, isn't that so?"

"Yes, when it comes to killing innocent women and children."

"Isn't it true that you were removed from the Eastern Front because you were a coward?"

Linger stood up, reached into the pocket of his prisoner's jumpsuit, took out two medals and threw them directly into Stolz's face, yelling, "There are my medals! An Iron Cross and a medal for bravery. I killed two dozen Soviets in a machine gun nest. There are the cowards-Hitler, Franz, and those Gestapo *Arschlöcher!*"

Nimitz made no attempt to stop the tirade. Jacques picked up the medals and handed them to Bart. Stolz quietly went back to the defense table.

"Are you through with this witness, Mr. Stolz?" Nimitz asked.

"Yes," he murmured.

General Smith roared, "We can't hear you!"

"No further questions," Krieger answered for Stolz.

Nimitz gaveled. "General Milburn, you may call your next witness."

"We call Adolf Kleiner."

A tall, jaunty man marched in military mode between two MPs to the witness stand. He saluted Bart and the tribunal. After the oath, he sat straight up, taut, and eyed Bart.

"State your name for the record."

"Frederic Kleiner."

"I have your army photograph here, and it states your name as Adolf Kleiner."

"I no longer am called Adolf. My middle name is Frederic. I have abandoned the name of Adolf."

"Why is that?"

"Because that *Scheissemeister* Hitler bears that name, which he disgraced."

"Frederic Kleiner, you were a *Hauptmann* in the SS, is that correct?"

"Yes. Prior to that, I was a colonel on the staff of Field Marshal Erwin Rommel, commander of the Afrika Korps. I was with him at the battle of El Alamein. We were just sixty miles from Alexandria when Hitler sold us down the river with no support. So the British and American forces drove us out of Africa."

"Is that why you dropped the name of Adolf?"

"That's part of it. Rommel was like a father to me. He told me there were some brilliant German Jewish officers in World War I. Rommel and most of us didn't know how many men and how much money was being spent on concentration camps, killing camps, and clogging up our rail lines so Himmler could ship Jews to slaughterhouses. Rommel hated that clown and so did I. Germany is stained forever."

"You're an educated man. Where did you study?" Bart asked.

"I am a graduate of the University of Berlin. I majored in history and English literature. I am not, nor was I ever, an anti-Semite. I read their books and numbered them among my friends. Hitler dissipated some of Germany's great talents in all fields by killing the Jews. He's a pompous megalomaniac. Look at that creep with his plastic surgery face, here as a defendant for murder. What happened to his Charlie Chaplin mustache? He pretended to be a Jew. He is an atheistic slob!"

Hitler yelled, "You'll be shot for treason!"

"Not until you're hanged, you miserable madman!" Kleiner shouted back.

Nimitz gaveled. "Enough of that. Sit down, Hitler, or I'll mute you again."

"How did it happen that you were demoted from an Army colonel to a Gestapo captain?"

"After our defeat in Africa, Rommel's staff was disbanded. I got a notice to report to that butcher, Heinrich Himmler, another piece of turd, who told me I was now a *Hauptmann*, a captain in the Gestapo, and assigned to the Buchenwald concentration camp. He gave me a two-week leave and told me to report there."

"Did you?"

"Yes, but I went to Marshal Rommel and asked him to help me. He said he would do his best. However, he told me that Himmler was investigating *him*. I reported to the commandant, Colonel Karl Koch, in my stupid new black uniform."

"All right, tell the court your duties at Buchenwald and what you observed," Bart pressed.

"First, Koch told me he didn't like army men like me and he was assigning me to the German armament works, the DAW, which I found out was owned and run by the SS. The Jewish slave laborers worked there until they dropped. I had a desk job doing paperwork."

"Did you know what was going on in the camp?"

"I talked to some of the Jewish workers and they thought I was naïve. Finally, a couple of them told me about the starvation of prisoners, executions, torture of political prisoners, rapes, and all the terrible things you heard here in this courtroom."

"Did you see any of these atrocities yourself?"

"Yes. First of all, you have to understand that Koch and his SS officers were ignorant street bums and hooligans in uniform; an uneducated hierarchy, running the camp like it was a zoo. They shot people for no reason at all. Doctors were experimenting on healthy bodies. People were shot and thrown into mass graves. There was common depravity. Koch was replaced by a Colonel Pister and the killing stopped, but the torture continued. His method of killing was starvation. There he is, sitting back there."

"Stand up, Pister," Nimitz ordered.

A short sallow-faced man rose and shouted, "Traitor!"

"In April 1945, the Americans were close to Buchenwald," Kleiner continued. "That little bum, Pister, tried to move thirty thousand prisoners, most of them Jews, out of the camp and about eight thousand of them died. Then, on April 11, the remaining prisoners interfered with the evacuation. They formed a resistance group. Pister fled. The watchtowers were torn down. They took control of the camp. My men and I surrendered to them and handed them our guns. They controlled the camp. A lot of political prisoners remained and participated in the uprising. The prisoners were walking skeletons. A German Jew, who had been a judge in the Weimar Republic, was in charge of the organized resistance. Our lives were spared because of him. The Americans came in on April 11. There were still twenty thousand prisoners. We were taken as POWs by the Americans. During their interrogation, where I told them I had served with Rommel, I learned how Hitler forced him to commit suicide. My hatred for Hitler and his gang intensified. I thought of ways to kill him, like so many others during the war. If I had known Nordheim was Hitler, I would have shot him. I am glad to see him being tried for his war crimes."

"How do you explain your presence at Hitler's ranch in La Plata?"

"You could call me stupid or a whore, it's your choice," Kleiner replied succinctly. "After the Russians released me from the POW camp, I found it very difficult to obtain employment. I tried to get a job teaching at the University of Munich. They used me as a substitute teacher, to fill in for absentee professors. The money was hardly enough to pay my rent on a one-room apartment. I got a job as a night doorman at the Four Seasons Hotel. One night, in 1951, a dinner of the International Conference of Christians and Jews was held at the hotel. As it ended, I was busy out front calling up cars and taxis for the participants. A Sergeant Albert Engel, who had served under me when I was a colonel on Rommel's staff in the Afrika Korps, dressed in a tuxedo and accompanied by a young lady, asked me for a taxi. As I whistled for one, he said, *Colonel, don't you recognize me?* I looked at him, and sure enough, it was Engel."

"That's a long answer to my question."

"If you will allow me, I'll answer you. Engel allowed me to give the taxi to the next party leaving. He waited for me to finish my shift. Fifteen minutes later, I was through, then he, his lady and I went to a coffee shop. He told me he was working for a Jew named Nordheim at Eagle Shipping in Hamburg. The money was good and Nordheim was the richest man in the world."

"How is that related to the question?"

"I asked him what he was doing at the conference of Christians and Jews. He said that a British guy, Sir Clive Fenwick, made a speech calling for Jews and Christians to work together to stamp out anti-Semitism. He then announced a $500,000 donation from Nordheim to the conference. He was introduced as a Nordheim employee who was a member of the conference."

"Your answer is yet to come," Bart impatiently urged.

"Sir, to make a long story short, I was advised to contact Sir Clive, who was staying at the Four Seasons. I called him the first thing the next morning. He agreed to see me."

"Are you trying to tell the court he hired you?"

"Yes, and I know that Sir Clive Fenwick and Sergeant Engel, there, are in your custody. They can confirm my account."

"All right. Tell us what Sir Clive did for you."

"After my interview with him, he said he was impressed with my military career. He took my address and phone number. Two days later I was visited by Darren Mayfield. He offered me a job in Argentina to train ex-Nazis who offered to fight for the Israelis against the Arabs. I was offered two thousand American dollars a week, plus expenses and travel fare to Argentina."

"So, you accepted the job?"

"Yes, sir. I was making a little more than $200 a week, plus tips. I couldn't refuse. I left the next day for Buenos Aires with an advance of $5,000."

"Didn't you suspect those so-called ex-Nazis?"

"No, because up to the day we were captured, we always trained for war with the Arabs. But I could tell that these were the same types of uneducated street bums. However, we maintained military discipline, and I made soldiers out of those *Arschlöcher*."

"No further questions. Your witness."

Stolz took over. "Are you a whore?"

"Not in the literal sense. Maybe venal."

"You do not sound stupid."

"In spite of how I sound, I must have been stupid not to realize that that ranch was a haven for Nazis."

"Or, as you just said, you were venal."

"I'm not a corrupt man, but I was enticed by the money. So I would say the word 'whore' is more applicable."

"You wanted to kill Hitler?"

"Yes."

"Why?"

"Because this foreigner from Austria destroyed my country and killed millions of people, Jews and Christians alike. He and Himmler, Goering, Goebbels and the rest of those devils are not human. I would have been a hero if I had killed him, yet I'm glad I didn't, because then he would have become a martyr. Right now he is a derelict on trial for his murderous life."

"No further questions," Stolz said.

From that point on, the prosecution checked out Kleiner's story with Albert Engel and Sir Clive Fenwick. They substantiated his account. Sergeant Otto Schwengler, stocky, muscular and voluble, was next to take the stand. After the oath, he testified that he had been a chauffeur for Heinrich Himmler.

"Are you a Nazi?"

"I was until I was captured by you."

"How did *that* event change you?"

"As a well-educated man, I should have known better. But I was caught up in the propaganda of Hitler and Goebbels. They told us we would rule the world for the next thousand years. Then I was sitting in my cell here thinking about the atrocities I heard in this courtroom, and I asked myself, why should I die for a fool like Hitler and the Nazi leaders who killed and stole? They are billionaires."

"You were a soldier at the Belzec camp?"

"That was one of the first extermination camps designed by Dr. Christian Wirth. He was the head of the euthanasia program before that. He asked Himmler to send me to Belzec as a guard for him. I was promoted to sergeant."

"Briefly tell us what the program was at Belzec."

"It was a no-nonsense operation. It was turned from a labor camp into an execution center in southeast Poland between Zamosc and Lvov. A tube was built leading to the gas chambers. It began operating in March, 1942. Sixty to eighty freight cars would each bring eighty to a hundred Polish Jews, Gypsies, and a few Christians. Everything was done quickly. On arrival, the prisoners would undress, surrender all their valuables, march into the tube and get gassed. The bodies were removed by other prisoners, called *Sonderkommandos*, and dumped in huge pits. Fifteen thousand a day were killed. They killed six hundred thousand from March to December of 1942. In July 1943 they closed the camp. The rest of the prisoners were sent to Sobibor for extermination."

"What happened to Belzec?"

With an ugly laugh, Schwengler said, "Word came from Himmler to remove all signs of a camp there. We turned the whole area into a farm. Trees, bushes and crops were planted. When the Russians came, they found a thriving farm. All sorts of vegetables were growing over those mass graves. No one ever suspected Belzec was a graveyard."

"What were you doing at Nordheim's ranch?"

"I was training for what I learned later was Hitler's *Revanche Plan*."

"So it was no secret that Hitler was alive?"

"We didn't know he was alive until Heinrich Müller told me that Nordheim was Hitler. That was two days before you attacked us."

"No further questions."

No questions were offered by the defense. Bart and the team went into high gear and in the next two days called Albert Engel to tell his story of Mauthausen. Frederick Schultz spelled out the Sobibor atrocities. The sum total consisted of horrors inconceivable by man. It went far beyond the pale of fiction. The litany of savagery in the killing camps was so terribly heinous that the media networks kept warning their audiences that children should not be allowed to hear the testimony.

☆ ☆ ☆ ☆

Thursday, March 14, 1953 - 0900 hours - Fort Leavenworth

Joyce Laurent was called to the stand. She was a breath of fresh air to the audience after the soldiers had detailed marrow-freezing atrocities. She wore a Maison Jeannette creation, which in its simplicity added to the elegance of the svelte lady. It was a magenta wool double knit with a black belt, accentuating her statuesque figure.

"Miss Laurent, are you a survivor of the Nazi concentration camps?" Bart began.

"Yes."

"Where were you born?"

"Paris, France."

"What was your schooling?"

"My father ran a very successful bistro and was able to send me and my older brother to London to further our education at what they call public schools and are referred to as private schools here in America. I was sent over after my graduation from what you call grammar schools. After my graduation, I came back to attend the Sorbonne. My brother graduated from Oxford and took post-graduate courses at the Sorbonne."

"What happened when war was declared?"

"My brother, Jacques, to whom I was, and am, very close, was called up by the French army. He was a captain. My mother, father and I were very worried about him."

"Did you continue your schooling?"

"Yes, the first nine months after war was declared, there was no real military action. As you know, Britain and France declared war on September 3,

1939. We heard a great deal of the Nazi abuses against the Jews. My father sent our money to Swiss banks, but we lived normally, and as a teenager I continued at the Sorbonne."

"You speak perfect English. Did you learn that in London?"

"No. I studied English since I was six years old. We were a multilingual family."

"When did things change for you and your family?"

"On May 10, 1940, the German army attacked France, Holland, Belgium and Luxembourg. My father and mother wanted us to leave France. On June 14 the Nazis entered Paris. We had heard from Jacques earlier that the British and French armies were trapped at Dunkirk. The troops got to England by all kinds of boats. Jacques told us to leave, and we tried to get a flight out of Paris. Jacques joined the partisans. Nazi troops paraded down the Champs Elysées. Soon after that, Hitler and his evil sycophants came to Paris to inspect and loot the city."

"What happened to you?"

"Two nights after his visit, the Gestapo crashed into our house. They stripped everything of value in the house. They took the rings right off my mother's hands and one little ring from me. We were taken to Drancy, the transit camp outside Paris. From there, we were taken in one of those filthy, rotten cattle cars, like what has been described here. Packed like sardines in feces, blood, urine and cattle manure to a death camp called Chelmno."

Joyce's eyes were tearing. Bart handed her a small box of tissues, then asked, "Do you want to stop, Miss Laurent?"

"No, General, I wish to go on."

"Very well."

"It's the same story you've been hearing from the other survivors. The commandant, Johann Weisst, was there when the cars were emptied. There were eight dead people in our car and at least twenty people unconscious. He stood there in his black uniform, medals all over his chest and a whip in his hand. He ordered all of us to undress, men, women and children naked in the hot sun. He was ordering people to the right or the left. Those on the left were told they were going to showers. My parents went to the left. That filthy rotten mad dog sitting back there, Colonel Johann Weisst, ran his hands over my naked teenage body and ordered me to the right. Twenty minutes later my beautiful, wonderful, loving parents were gassed to death," she sobbed.

Jacques lowered his head, weeping. He covered his face with his hands and his body began to shake. Maybrook was patting his back. Bart's eyes were moist. "May we have a fifteen-minute recess, sir?" he asked.

It was granted. Jacques rushed to the stand and embraced Joyce. They held each other for more than five minutes, both weeping. She sobbed into his ear, "Jacques, look how that man is smirking at me."

"Leave it to me," he replied. "Now, calm down and finish your testimony."

"I have to go to the ladies' room."

He waved at Captain Esta Arnold. The captain approached. "Captain

Arnold, please take my sister to the restroom."

Ten minutes later, Joyce, composed, returned to the witness box, and Bart addressed the tribunal. "Sirs, would the court ask Johann Weisst to stand so that Miss Laurent can identify him as the commandant at the Chelmno death camp?"

"Johann Weisst, please rise," Nimitz ordered.

A tall, muscular man rose and arrogantly stretched his arm out in a Nazi salute, shouting, "*Sieg heil!*"

"That is the filthy pig!" Joyce declared.

"You are lucky you are alive, Fräulein Laurent!" Weisst shouted.

Jacques started to rise out of his chair. Maybrook and Sedgwick held him back.

"Later, Jacques, later," Maybrook whispered.

Bart stared at Jacques and shook his head negatively, then asked Joyce, "What happened at Chelmno?"

"They put me in the barracks, gave me one of those hideous striped prisoners' dresses with the Star of David on it. They tattooed these numbers on my arm," she said, rolling up her left sleeve and exhibiting the markings. "I wear this as a badge of honor to remember those innocent souls who lost their lives to these monsters."

Applause was scattered.

"Were you assigned to any special duty?"

"Yes, I became a maid for the Gestapo officers. There was an older officer there. He was not part of the Gestapo. He was an army general. His name was, or still is, Franz Halder. He was a general staff officer and commander in chief of the army from 1938 to 1942, when Hitler replaced him with a General Zeitzler. Halder was close to sixty years of age and had disagreed with Hitler's tactics. He was like a grandfather to me. He used to talk to me for hours."

"Did he make sexual advances to you?"

"Oh, heavens, no. He protected me from that leech Weisst, who was always trying to get me to his quarters. I told the general about the commandant's advances. He had a talk with Weisst and promised to kill him if he or any officer dared touch me. Weisst was afraid of General Halder. He was a big, strong man with a great air of authority. Weisst spread the word to his men that I was Halder's mistress. I didn't mind that gossip because, with all the raping going on there, the officers stayed away from me. The general never laid a hand on me."

"What was a general like Halder doing at a concentration camp?"

"He was very open with me. He told me about his fight with Hitler. Hitler took over as commander in chief and Halder warned him against his attack on Stalingrad. In fact, Halder helped plan the Polish, French, Balkan and Russian campaigns. He hated Hitler, the whole war, and what he called the stupid, heartless destruction of the Jews. He used a line one night that I'll never forget."

"What was that?" Bart asked.

"*This ignorant Austrian would-be painter is not only destroying millions of bodies, but he is frying some of the best brains in Germany in the crematoria.*"

"Did you continue as a maid for the Gestapo?"

"No, I was reassigned to a terrible job. I had to have the discarded clothes of the gassed victims cleaned and mended. I was handling the clothing of people who had just been killed. I worked with other women, mostly Polish Jews and Christians. I found letters and wills sewn inside the linings of men's jackets. I hid them under a carpet in General Halder's house. I couldn't hide anything in the barracks where I slept."

"What about food?"

"I was fortunate. General Halder let me have dinner with him many nights. He gave me food to take to the prisoners in my barracks."

"What did he talk about during your dinners?"

"His family, his daughters and grandchildren; philosophy, history, World War I and some of the Jewish officers in that war. He talked of their bravery. He told me that there were over a hundred and twenty thousand Jewish soldiers in that war, when Germany's population was fifty-five million people and only five hundred thousand Jews; twelve thousand were killed and thirty-five thousand were wounded. There were Jewish generals, colonels, majors and lieutenants among them. I asked him why was Hitler so stupid in killing his people like that, and his answer was simple. He said that was because Hitler was stupid. *Power in the hands of a stupid man is a most dangerous weapon. Despots are often stupid men; they don't know how to handle power.* I asked him, *Why do the German people follow him?* He said, *Fear, my dear child, fear.* He told me I was a very smart young lady. After a while I tutored him in English, some French and a little Russian, in case he had to negotiate with them."

"Did he see any atrocities?" Bart asked.

"Oh, yes. One day he took me for a walk and showed me what was going on. We stood on a hill next to the forest. He handed me binoculars and we watched the trains come in; the people disrobing, the march to the gas chambers, the bodies being tossed into the crematoria by the *Sonderkommandos*. That day when they were finished, Weisst lined up the *Sonderkommandos* and personally shot each one, twelve in all. There was a pit of dead bodies. The Gestapo threw them in there. Then they called workers out to shovel dirt over those mass graves. The Russians were getting close."

"What happened after that?"

"That was in January, 1945. On January 10th, General Zeitzler, the man who succeeded Halder, arrived in a Mercedes Benz sedan. There were two officers with him. He and Halder had dinner that night. The next morning, I came to clean his house and make his bed. He introduced me to Zeitzler. Halder was packed to leave. He said he would love to take me with them, but it was too dangerous. I pleaded. Zeitzler said, absolutely not. I asked why. They explained that Zeitzler was quitting the army and he didn't want the Russians to capture a German general like Halder. Two days later, after they left, the Russians entered the camp. That was January 17, 1945. Weisst had disappeared. The night before the Russians arrived, I hid in Halder's house. The Gestapo were shooting and killing every prisoner they could find. The next morning the Gestapo were gone. I took the pile of letters and wills I had hidden and put them in a little bag I found in the house. I went to the barracks. There were dead bodies on the ground everywhere in the camp and the barracks. I heard the Russians coming. There were forty-two people hiding in the forest. When they saw me, they came out. We found a dozen people who had been shot, but were still alive. We put them in the barracks."

"What did the Russians do?"

"They questioned us. I spoke a little Russian, as did some of the survivors," she continued. "They had doctors look at the wounded. I think they saved five of the twelve we found. Colonel Koslov took me into the commandant's office. He told me his wife was Jewish and that he had three children. He wanted to know why a French Jewish girl had been put in Chelmno. I told him it was fate. He was sympathetic and asked me to act as an interpreter with the remaining prisoners. He asked his captain to find me a dress and coat from the supply we had collected from the gas victims. He wasn't sure yet as to where the liberated prisoners were going to be sent."

"How long did you stay at Chelmno?"

"About three weeks, working with the Russians in tending to the survivors and acting as an interpreter."

"Then what?"

"Colonel Dimitri Koslov came back to Chelmno. They had just liberated Auschwitz on January 27th and found very few prisoners alive. He told me the rest were on a forced march. At Auschwitz, they found thousands of pounds of hair and clothing. The Russians were very bitter toward the Germans. Colonel Koslov said tanks were running over civilians and killing any Germans in their way as a payback for what the *Einsatzgruppen* had done to them. The colonel told me to be careful. A commissar was coming to the camp later that day to question the remaining prisoners. The colonel left, for his troops were moving into Germany."

"Did the commissar arrive?" Bart asked.

"Yes. He was an arrogant, fat little man. Very officious. His first question was, *Are you grateful that the Soviet troops have rescued you?* I answered, *Of course.* He then explained the duties of a commissar. He said their job is to be part of a military group for the purpose of teaching Communist Party objectives and to enforce party loyalty. His job at that time was to recruit liberated prisoners to the communist cause. He said he wanted me to think it over and would talk to me in the morning. He told me that they were going to serve a hot Russian dinner for the survivors."

"Did he follow through?"

"That night we gathered at what had been the Gestapo headquarters. There were thirty of us. They served hot *borscht*, also cabbage soup with a boiled potato, and *shashlik*, it's like *shish kabob*, lamb on a skewer, with onions and tomatoes. It was served flaming hot. There was lots of vodka. Hardly proper fare for the skeletonized diners. A soldier played an accordion and some of them entertained with Russian dances. The commissar, Ivan Sudanoff, then lectured us on the advantages of communism. *Capitalism will be dead after this war,* he said."

"What happened in the morning?"

"I told him I wanted to go back to France and that I preferred democracy. He got angry and said I would change my mind. That afternoon, by orders of Marshal Ivan Konev, we were shipped off to a Russian *gulag*, a labor camp outside Kiev. It was almost as bad as a Nazi concentration camp. The next three months were full of misery. We were finally shipped to what became East Germany after the war. We were brainwashed every day in Leipzig. I played along and finally got a job teaching French at the university."

Joyce wound up her testimony with the story of her escape, without mentioning the Mossad's role. The defense asked no questions, and court was adjourned.

CHAPTER FIFTEEN

Friday, March 15, 1953 - 0900 hours - Fort Leavenworth

There was an air of tension and expectancy in the courtroom that morning, as Captain Esta Arnold had been given permission the previous night to leak to the media that a high-ranking Nazi was going to testify today. The tribunal was aware of the identity and the importance of the Nazi who would be taking the stand.

"General Milburn, your next witness, please," Nimitz ordered.

"The prosecution calls Martin Bormann."

Hitler rose from his chair and stared at the double door. The stocky witness, dwarfed by two tall MPs, walked deliberately past Hitler and the defendants. A wave of murmurs swept the courtroom. The cameras focused on the witness, who had been believed to be dead and had been sentenced in absentia to hang by the Nuremberg court. To the networks, wire services and print media, this was a history-making event. Bulletins were flashed around the world.

"Your honors, I have an unusual request before I interrogate Mr. Bormann," Bart began. "I wish to introduce a prominent Tennessee attorney, who appears here today at the request of Supreme Court Justice Jackson. The tribunal is aware that Justice Jackson served as chief prosecutor at Nuremberg, where this witness was tried in absentia and sentenced to death. Attorney Abe Fortas is appearing here, *amicus curiae,* to address that issue."

"Welcome, Mr. Fortas. You may proceed," Nimitz said.

"Honorable members of this distinguished tribunal, I am here this morning somewhat reluctantly. I do not know the defendant, nor any of his associates. I am fully aware of the gravity of this trial and the tribunal's authority as a military court. I am also fully cognizant of the Supreme Court decision in *ex parte Quirin.* Therefore, it is my contention that the sentence at Nuremberg be nullified, inasmuch as he is being tried here and is appearing as a prosecution witness before this court. I might state parenthetically that I am of the Hebrew faith, but my addiction to justice under our Constitution impels me to appear before you."

"Mr. Fortas, your reputation as a constitutional lawyer precedes you," Nimitz said. "We are honored to have you here. We will take a short recess and will rule on your cogent address to this court."

Fifteen minutes later the tribunal called the court to order. "General Milburn, would you care to respond to Mr. Fortas' statements?"

"Very simply, sirs. I concur with Mr. Fortas' presentation and respect his sponsorship by Justice Jackson."

"It is the ruling of this tribunal that the question of Mr. Bormann's guilt or innocence of war crimes will be determined by triers of fact in *this* court. Therefore, the death sentence imposed at Nuremberg is herewith quashed."

"Thank you, sir," Fortas said, bowing.

Bart put his arm around Fortas and walked with him to the exit.

"I'll be a pariah in society after this," Fortas whispered.

"No, sir, you will be a hero. In my eyes, you're a legal giant with courage to match. I despise these Nazi animals, as you do."

Back at the dock, Bart's first question invited Bormann to present a brief sketch of his early life. He repeated the details of his earlier confession.

"So, you were born on June 17, 1900. You were schooled at a trade school studying agriculture. You deny that you were an anti-Semite. Yet by age twenty-seven you joined Hitler's National Socialist Party, the Nazis, on February 17, 1927. In November he appointed you to the staff of the Supreme Command of the *Sturmabteilung,* the SA, the storm troopers and hoodlums who struck fear throughout Germany."

"General, I told you and your staff that the SA was a bunch of stupid, uneducated street gangsters. They were the scum of society. *Lunte* rats. I am not one of them. I later had Hitler destroy them."

Bormann repeated his rise to party chairman for discipline. He recounted his marriage to Gerda Buch on September 2, 1929. Hitler was the godfather of Bormann's first child, named Adolf, on April 14, 1930. He ingratiated himself with party leaders. In 1933 he was promoted to Reichleiter and chief of staff to Rudolf Hess, number two man to Hitler. He explained why he was nicknamed *The Bull,* because of his thick neck, broad shoulders and height of five feet seven. After Rudolf Hess flew to Scotland, he got closer to Hitler, wore fitted military uniforms, and was promoted in charge of all Nazi affairs. Hitler became aware of his efficiency and dedication. Analysis of the SA and its chief of staff, Ernst Röhm, led to their elimination on June 30, 1934. It was known as the *Night of the Long Knives,* lasting three days. The SS executed Röhm and his degenerates. Bormann had no hand in the extermination, he said. Himmler commissioned Bormann, an SS gruppenführer, a major general. After Hess's flight to Scotland, he became number two man to Hitler. He was the keeper of the keys, handled Hitler's finances and became war guardian of the door. Only those summoned by Hitler had access. Everyone else had to be cleared by Bormann.

"So you manipulated Hitler?"

"No one could do that. I protected him."

"Let's get down to the nitty-gritty."

"What is that?"

"The facts. Where did you learn how to speak such good English?"

"I learned some English in school. Before the war, Hitler had English classes for the high command and all the commissioned officers. Soldiers were told to study English. We imported British teachers," Bormann said.

"What for?"

"In preparation for the occupation of England. I attended a dinner with the Duke and Duchess of Windsor. I spoke English with them."

"When?"

"In October 1939 at Berchtesgaden."

"That was a month after the war was on."

Bormann now startled the court and the observers. "The duke and his wife supported Hitler. They wanted to make peace. Axel Werner-Gren, the Swede, arranged the dinner meeting. He said there was a following of important English people who wanted the duke back on the throne. Hitler told them to arrange peace with the British and he would put the duke back on the throne. The duchess applauded."

"What about Churchill?" Bart asked.

"Hitler was going to have him assassinated."

"Did he tell the duke about that?"

"No, but he whispered it to the duchess."

"Who else was at that dinner?"

"Foreign Minister Ribbentrop and Walter Schellenberg, the chief of the SS."

"Did they mention their English supporters?"

"Yes, the Cliveden Set, run by Lady Astor, and Ambassador Joseph Kennedy and Charles Lindbergh," Bormann answered with curt confidence.

"Why did Hitler annihilate the Jews, and why did you stand by?"

"First of all, when Hitler started to attack the Jews verbally, that was politics. He needed to arouse the people to vote for him. The Jews were a very talented people. They were doctors, teachers, lawyers, accountants, bankers, shopkeepers, factory owners, artists, musicians, moviemakers and show producers. They are smart. So Hitler attacked them because we had a depression, and the street bums flocked to him."

"Then, as a Nazi, you approved everything that Hitler said and did. Isn't that correct?"

"No, I will tell you and the world that. Hitler, first of all, was not a German. I realized that he was a charlatan. But he was a great public speaker. During our depression and inflation, he made fiery speeches in the beer halls to the worthless, unemployed, lower-class lowlifes and drunkards. He promised jobs, a new Germany and a future for the dregs of society. He had what you call charisma. I was ambitious and worked my way into his inner circle, or at least at the beginning on the fringes of his tight group."

"Your marriage to Gerda Buch helped your career. Her father-in-law, Walter Buch, was chairman of the Nazi Party Court for Party Discipline. He got you close to Hitler, right?"

"That is true, and that's how Hitler became godfather to my first child, whom I named Adolf. I have nine children."

"Did you believe in the Nazi cause?" Bart asked.

"Not really. It was only a stepping stone to political power."

"After Hess left, you became the inside number two man. You climbed over Goering, Goebbels and Himmler."

"Not until the last days did I have the possibility of power. Goering was a fat, overstuffed drug addict. He was a bisexual degenerate. He was no problem. The first man I had to get rid of was Ernst Rohm, a homosexual who broke with Hitler in 1925. He joined the Bolivian army. Hitler, for some reason, sent for him and made him the leader of the SA, the storm troopers, who struck fear in every German household. I told Hitler that Röhm was getting too powerful. As I told you, Hitler had him and the troopers wiped out over a three day period of bloodshed."

"How about Goebbels?"

"That little club-footed bitch was disliked by most of us. However, he was the only educated man in the inner circle. He was brilliant in propaganda and at staging great parades and large gatherings for Hitler's speeches. He started that *Sieg Heil, Heil Hitler* business. Alfred Rosenberg was a stupid self-styled philosopher. He kept talking about Nordic supremacy. I paid little attention to him."

"What about Himmler?"

"That funny little chicken farmer, who looked like any man in the street, turned out to be the greatest mass murderer in the world. He pretended to be a pious Catholic and built up the Gestapo, the SS and the Waffen SS. He was a hypochondriac and my target," Bormann said.

"Target for what?"

"What I'm telling you is that I was planning to take over Hitler's job. The only reason I saved him was that he had $43 billion and I wanted him to share it with me. I had three billion, maybe four, but your capture of us spoiled my plans. Hitler is a psychopath. He was a megalomaniac when he was at his height. His *blitzkrieg* through Europe made him feel like he was the most powerful man in the world. He let Himmler continue his killing campaign, but he was too busy playing the game of a military genius on his way to conquering the world. I tried in my own way to stop the killing of Jews. I warned him that Himmler wanted to replace him as *Der Führer*. I asked him to stop the killing of Jews. He said he was too busy with the war."

"Was that the first time you tried to stop the atrocities?"

"No. Once, after the invasion of Poland, I begged him to stop the killing of Jews. Then, when Reinhard Heydrich, Heinrich Himmler, Adolf Eichmann and a group of intellectuals met at Grosser Wannsee on January 20, 1937, and decided on the Final Solution to kill Jews, I pleaded twice to stop them. The last time was after the invasion of Russia."

"What was his answer?" Bart asked.

"He had his usual temper tantrum. He said he couldn't be annoyed with trivial matters and had to run the war against the Soviet Union."

"Did you believe his answer?"

"No, because after Heydrich was assassinated in May 1942, I learned that Hitler had given Himmler personal orders to kill all Jews in Europe as punishment for the assassination of Heydrich. Hitler went wild. The assassins were from Lidice, a village in the Czech Republic in Bohemia. They killed thirteen hundred in Bohemia and Moravia, executed a hundred and seventy-two men and boys and destroyed the whole village. Hitler ordered the murder and destruction. From that point on, Himmler took over the SS and the elite Waffen SS, the fighting arm to protect Hitler. So he had control of the Gestapo and all police in Germany. Himmler, the alleged pious Catholic, conducted a war of his own. The merciless butcher became a self-appointed commander-in-chief, conducting a war against helpless, unarmed Jews, Gypsies, Jehovah's Witnesses, dissenters, lots of Christians, Muslims, colored people, homosexuals, the sick and the retarded," Bormann added.

"Are you saying that Hitler didn't know or realize the killing going on in the death camps?"

"No. He's a *Lügner*, a born liar. He was fully aware of the mass murders."

"Martin Bormann, were you a Nazi?"

"Yes, I was a Nazi because I had to be one. I was ambitious, and that was the only way to have a career."

"Do you still believe in Nazism?"

"Hell no, it is the worst thing that ever happened to this world. It got out of hand. It is a catastrophe."

"Martin Bormann, are you a con man?"

"What is a con man?"

"A cheat, mountebank, a phony, a liar and a swindler."

"Why you say such a thing?"

"Are you telling this court that you condemn Nazism?" Bart pressed.

"Yes. Look, let me make it plain for you, the court and everybody here. I am guilty by association. I am guilty for serving Hitler and I did it, not because of an ideology; I did it for three reasons. I hoped one day to replace Hitler and turn Germany into a democracy."

There was a chorus of boos, so Nimitz gaveled.

"Listen, everybody. I was born in 1900. I was in my twenties when I joined the Nazi Party. I was close to the most powerful man in Europe as things progressed. I didn't realize what Hitler was going to do with Germany. I didn't want war against Poland, which resulted in World War II. But by that

I didn't want war against Poland, which resulted in World War II. But by that time I was trapped. I became Hitler's right-hand man, but I didn't plan to kill Jews, conquer Europe or stupidly attack the Soviets."

"Why didn't you leave?" Bart asked.

"Greed. In 1944 I had a private meeting with a large group of industrialists and told them the war was lost. I said to move all holdings, stocks and interests out of Germany to America."

"You mean companies like Standard Oil and I.G. Farben?"

"Yes, lots of them."

"You are aware, Mr. Bormann, that we have taped your confession. I have your statements given to us voluntarily."

"Yes, I stated everything correctly so far."

"Not far enough. You confessed that one of the foulest secrets of the war was Hitler's attempt not only to destroy the Jews, but to brainwash the German people to get out of the Christian religion. This was a sly conspiracy, with the knowledge of Goering and Goebbels. Were you part of that?"

"No, I was true to my Catholic religion. He told Goering and Goebbels to stay with the church while they were telling their followers there was only one religion, the fatherland. He condemned the Christians because they followed the teachings of a Jewish rabbi, Jesus Christ."

"Is it not true that you carried file cards and wrote down everything Hitler said in private?"

"How did you learn that?" Bormann asked.

"Albert Speer called you the *Gray Eminence*."

"What's that? I'm not gray."

"No, that means you were Hitler's confidante, like Père Joseph was Cardinal Richelieu's confidante and called the *Red Eminence*. You had real power. Speer, who is serving a twenty-year sentence at Spandau, has been preparing his memoirs. He was close to Hitler."

"That's true, Speer was an intellect far above Hitler and his close associates. I was much smarter than Hitler, but never let him know it. Yes, he tried to get the Catholic and Protestant leaders to join him in a new religious movement called *The Fatherland*, or *Hitlerism*. He began to think he was the real messiah. He's a mentally sick man."

"You have a reputation as an alcoholic. How much of this is your drunken memory?"

"I have never been drunk on duty and I am not an alcoholic. I like to drink, but I know when to stop."

"How did you expect to replace Hitler, and why didn't you kill him?"

"I had put over $40 billion away for him," Bormann replied. "I had three or four billion. The time I should have done that was in late 1943 or sometime in 1944. But the Allied armies and the Russians had us in a pincer movement. I thought of killing Goering, the drug addict, and Himmler and Goebbels. Roosevelt called for an unconditional surrender. In 1943 there was a plot to kill Hitler. Himmler knew it. Field Marshal von Kluge was made commander of the army in Russia after the fall of France. Barbarossa was the code name for the invasion of the Soviet Union. In 1943 he was in the middle of an argument among the generals plotting to kill Hitler. Kluge was ambivalent, but he was too loyal to Hitler."

"How did you know this?"

"Himmler knew of the plot. Kluge lectured Erwin Rommel at his headquarters in France to have nothing to do with the plotters. Rommel was not involved in that plot. The attack on Russia took place in June 1941. Rommel had told Kluge the Allied invasion of France would be the beginning of the end of Hitler. Kluge later admitted that Rommel was right."

"Why didn't you take advantage of this discontent? You were in the perfect position to kill Hitler. You handled the medicines of that quack Dr. Morrell and the pills that Dr. Koester prepared for his flatulence. You could have poisoned him."

"Easy for you to say, General, but by that time Count Claus von Stauffenberg, a colonel and a hero, had attended a conference at Restenburg in East Prussia. Hitler called for an important meeting in 1944. After *heiling* the *Führer*, Stauffenberg placed a briefcase near Hitler. It was loaded with explosives. The colonel excused himself to make an important phone call. Colonel Brandt accidentally moved the bag away from Hitler as he leaned over the table. All the top generals were there in a wooden building. At about 12:45 it exploded. Hitler was slightly injured. General Beck shot himself. General Fromm, one of the plotters, immediately turned on them, had them arrested and shot in the courtyard as soon as he heard Hitler tell the world on the radio that he was alive. Hitler had a court try everyone he suspected. Then he had them tortured, hanged with wire and left dangling on meathooks. He forced Rommel to poison himself. He was wild!"

"So you had no support for a takeover?"

"No. Himmler had control of the Gestapo, the SS and the Waffen SS, which doubled their protection of Hitler. I knew we were losing the war. Our cities were being bombed every day, the Allies were coming from the west and the Soviets were driving from the east. This military clown, who considered himself a military genius, is fully responsible for the destruction of Germany. He lied to the fatherland and our troops right up to the last minute. Our cities were destroyed and our people wanted peace," Bormann said.

"Why did you save him?"

"Greed. Money. He had over $43 billion and I wanted at least half of it. After all, I was the one who put his fortune together."

At that point, Hitler rose and shouted, "Traitor! Rat! *Arschloch*! You stab me in the back!"

"Sit down, Herr Hitler. You'll get your chance," Nimitz ordered.

Bormann stood up, pointed to Hitler and exploded. "You ungrateful Austrian street bum, if it wasn't for me your enemies would have destroyed you long ago. You and your Revenge Plan fizzled like your war against the world. Today, you're plain *Scheisse*. You're the devil himself. A sociopath with no heart, no soul and lots of gas. You'll fart your way into hell, you syphilitic, one-balled, sexual pervert, murdering bastard!"

Bart and the tribunal did nothing to stop the tirade. When Bormann sat down, Krieger rose and addressed the court.

"Gentlemen, I object to this unwarranted abuse of Herr Hitler."

"Your objection is sustained. Advise your client to keep his mouth shut," Nimitz replied.

Bart coolly looked at Bormann. "Are you composed enough to continue?"

"Yes."

"Tell the court what happened on the night of April 30, 1945. Tell the court how you managed to help Hitler escape from the bunker under the chancellery in Berlin while the Russians were closing in."

Calmly, Bormann repeated his earlier confession of Hitler's wedding to Eva Braun and the execution of her brother-in-law Hermann Fegelein, whose body was placed in the Viking funeral pyre with Eva's. The Goebbelses poisoned their children and themselves. Eva had swallowed a cyanide pill. Hitler's bodyguards, Franz Schwerin and Ernst Krueger, helped him exchange Hitler's clothes with those of the dead General Fegelein. Pilot Hanna Reitsch took them to the rear of the chancellery. She loaded Speer's plane with Hitler, whom he had drugged.

Bart stopped Bormann's recital and asked, "How did you manage to fool everyone singing and dancing in the front room?"

"We cleared all of Hitler's papers and put them in the twin-engine turbo plane. All the people heard the shot and thought Hitler was dead. We had Fegelein's leg hanging out of the blanket with Hitler's pants showing. After more gasoline was poured on the fire, General Heinrich Müller and his men helped our switch. We then flew to Malmo, Sweden."

"You bought a house there. Tell the court the details of Hitler's plastic surgery."

He recounted the hiring of Dr. Phillip LaVelle, renowned Beverly Hills, California, surgeon.

"You went to Argentina during his convalescence?"

"I bought a ranch at La Plata and waited for these submarines to deliver gold bars, jewelry, currencies and other valuables. I made contact with the Perons."

Bart asked one more question. "You were to share your ill-gotten loot with Eva Peron. She never got the money?"

"No, that bastard Hitler screwed them out of their share. I have one more thing to say. I built a business empire for that sociopathic megalomaniac. I wish to warn the world that there are thousands of Nazi sympathizers. Be alert, America. Now, you can hang me, electrocute me or give me a firing squad. I was forty-five years old when the war ended. I am fifty-two years old now. I feel like I am one hundred," Bormann said.

"No further questions."

Hitler rose and menacingly approached Bormann, who was comfortably ensconced in the witness chair with his legs crossed.

"That's far enough, Herr Hitler. Stop there. You are not to crowd the witness," said Nimitz.

The dialogue continued in German, with the interpreter translating over a microphone.

"Your name is Martin Bormann?" Hitler hissed.

"Yes."

"You were my closest confidant during the Third Reich?"

"Only after Rudolf Hess flew to Scotland on May 10, 1941."

"But you were close to me before that?"

"Yes."

"I was godfather to your first-born?"

"Yes."

"I was good to you?"

"Yes."

"Then why have you turned on me?"

"Because you turned on me."

"Liar! *Arschloch!*" Hitler railed.

Nimitz gaveled. "No names and epithets, Herr Hitler. Just ask questions."

"You have testified against me. Why?"

"I know the truth. I have turned to God. You are a sick monster. A murderer. A thief. A devil. A barbarian. An egomaniac. You still want to destroy the world. You are..."

Hitler roared, "Traitor! Shut up! I made you a rich man and you bite the hand that fed you!"

"I made you the richest man in the world and you want to use that money, $43 billion, to blow up the world, you sick son of a bitch. You and your Revenge Plan," Bormann countered.

"Didn't I restore Germany to its past glory?"

"How? By killing six million Jews, millions of Germans and millions of Christians?"

"How can you lie like that?"

"I begged you not to kill the Jews. I begged you not to invade Russia. I begged you to get rid of Himmler, I..."

"Enough of your begging. All lies! You begged me to get rid of Ernst Röhm, the head of the SA."

"That's true, because they were the street bums who struck fear in the hearts of the good Christian Germans."

"Now you are a good Christian, cleansed of all your sins?" Hitler mocked.

"Yes, I am a Christian. God is my savior. I regret every minute I spent with you. I was an ass-kissing slave to you. I realize my sins. They are plenty, but you are the most evil man that was ever born! You are the devil himself. You have shamed Germany for a thousand years!"

"Martin Bormann, *du Schwein, du Arschkriecher,* how dare you talk to me like that!"

Triggered by Hitler's tantrum, Bormann reverted to English. "You call me a pig, a yes man, a wimp, an idiot, a brown-noser. Okay, I'll tell it all." He pointed his finger at Hitler and shouted in German, "Let the world know the real *Schickelgruber, Scheisse,* Hitler the coward. I wish to correct my statement that I saved him."

Hitler began mouthing epithets and pejoratives about his turncoat followers. Nimitz furiously gaveled, and an MP clamped his hand over Hitler's foaming mouth. Order was restored.

"Proceed, Herr Bormann," Bart said.

"The true story is that Hitler's escape was planned in March 1945."

"Who planned it?"

"He did, with my help. He never intended to kill himself. I was called into his den in early March during a windy snowstorm. He told me to put some more wood on the fireplace and sit down, then make some notes."

"What was the plan?"

"For the first time, he conceded that the war was lost. *The Russians will try to do to me what the Italians did to Mussolini,* he said. *I want to make the world think I killed myself. But I want to build a worldwide Nazi organization.* So the plan that I told about his escape was made in advance. All the billions were carefully sent to Switzerland. The Malmo house was purchased, at his request. This coward let Goebbels kill his wife, children and himself. He sat there smugly after his marriage to Eva Braun and let her commit suicide. It was supposed to be a death pact. After we brought Fegelein's body out of the maid's closet and Hitler changed clothes with the dead man, he told me to fire a shot into the general's head. The plan worked perfectly. The Russians believe to this day that it was Hitler's body. So you see how this false, phony *Führer* is a craven coward. I admit we cleaned out the treasury and his house in Malmo, Sweden, where he had plastic surgery to change his identity."

Hitler moaned and pounded the floor with his feet.

"How did he get the name of Nordheim?"

"He sent me to a Jewish cemetery to find a Jewish name. The tombstone indicated that it was the grave of a three-year-old boy. He agreed to use that name. Two nights later we removed the grave marker at the foot of the grave and left the headstone with the name of Nordheim only, indicating that it was a burial plot for several members of that family."

Suddenly Hitler ran to the witness chair and attempted to choke Bormann. The rugged man kicked Hitler in his stomach, sending him to the floor. MPs raced to the stricken man, who was slobbering and moaning. He muttered, "*Schweinehund.*"

Nimitz angrily banged his gavel. "There will be a thirty-minute recess."

MPs carried Hitler to the defense conference room.

Jacques laughed. "Bart, that was worth the price of admission. Look at Bormann. He's still sitting in the witness chair."

"Yes, he seems quite satisfied with himself. He probably has been wanting to do that for years. Tell him to step down."

Jacques obliged, patting Bormann on the back. After the recess, Krieger and Bart approached the tribunal.

"Your Honors, Herr Hitler is not feeling well. He has no further questions for the witness."

"Does the prosecution wish to rebut?" Nimitz asked.

"No questions," Bart said.

"Very well, General, call your next witness."

Bart raised his hand, "Sir, may we approach?"

Krieger and Stolz joined him for the sidebar.

"Your Honors, we are approaching the end of the prosecution. I would ask the indulgence of the court for a recess at this point. I would like to advise the tribunal and the defense counsel here of our contemplated schedule. At Monday's session we will be presenting two hours of footage to validate the testimonies of our witnesses. We will follow that film with one witness."

"I strongly object to the presentation of any film, Your Honors, without an opportunity for the defense to view the exhibit," Krieger declared.

"The film is not completed at this point, for one, and second, we are not required in this proceeding to present our evidence in advance," Bart replied.

"Overruled, Mr. Krieger," Nimitz said.

"On Tuesday we will have three witnesses and expect to rest our case."

"All right, gentlemen, back to your seats."

The tribunal adjourned until Monday, March 15, at 0900 hours. In the conference room, George Spota and Dick Reilly briefed Bart and the team on the progress with the film.

"We'll be finished by Saturday afternoon," Spota advised. "It's a hair-raising document. All that captured German footage will freeze their spines and shock the world. I wonder if the media should be advised of its horrible content."

"Good point, George. We'll pass a warning to them on Monday morning," Bart agreed.

☆ ☆ ☆ ☆

Sunday, March 15, 1953 - 1700 hours - Sherman Army Airfield, Fort Leavenworth

A cordon of MPs and Marines were lined up at Hangar 12 with General Willard Fleming and Colonel Jeremiah Brown. Their eyes were focused on a Lockheed four-engine turbojet Constellation making its approach to the tarmac. The plane taxied to the welcoming group.

When the exit steps were lowered, the cordon stood in lines facing each other at the plane's exit. They remained at attention as General Fleming and Colonel Brown greeted the Chairman of the Joint Chiefs of Staff, General Omar Bradley. The cordon saluted the distinguished arrival and his party of the Joint Chiefs. They entered a shuttle bus, and six motorcycles led them to two special Victorian houses. "We've provided a special dinner for you, General Bradley, and all of your officers tomorrow evening. General Milburn will brief you at that time, sirs. I trust that meets with your approval?" Fleming said.

"That's fine, Willard. Thanks for the reception."

Jacques Laurent joined Colonel Brown. Part of the cordon remained awaiting the arrival of a second Constellation, which landed forty minutes later. The Marines formed a receiving line as the plane reached the hangar. When the three men stepped down, Brown saluted them and introduced himself. Jacques, in his Brooks Brothers outfit, stepped forward.

Speaking German, he said, "Herren von Papen and Schacht and Reverend Niemöller, I am Jacques Laurent. I greet you on behalf of the United States government."

"Mr. Laurent, we speak English. Thank you for your reception. I notice that your Marine guard is fully armed. Why is that?" von Papen queried.

"Two reasons, sir. One is to honor your arrival, and two, for the security of your persons."

"Very thoughtful," Schacht said.

A shuttle, with six Marines aboard, accompanied the men, following a four-motorcycle escort. Two sergeants carried their luggage on board.

They were invited to court on Monday to view the film and were advised that they would be testifying on Tuesday. The following night, General Fleming went all out in preparing a special dinner in a private dining room at Fuller Hall. The evening was a combination of briefing by Bart, who was complimented by his guests for the handling of the trial. The Chiefs commented on Hitler and his minions, coupled with hilarity based on the turncoat testimony by Bormann and the soldiers.

After dinner, Bart addressed General Bradley. "General, I am very grateful to you for all the support you've given me. Your willingness to view these films in Court and then testify to the authenticity of the footage captured under your command of the First Army in Normandy is deeply appreciated."

"Barton, my boy, my term as chairman expires in August. I will be sixty years old at that time. I had hoped you would stay in the Army and occupy my chair some day. You are like a son to me and I am very proud of your accomplishments. However, if you go back to your law career, you'll be my attorney."

The Chiefs applauded.

"General, that is indeed very high praise. May I return the compliment? As my idol, sir, if you run for President, I will drop everything to work on your campaign."

"I'm not a politician, as you know. I don't want Eisenhower's headaches. I've paid my dues."

Everyone joined in a toast to Bradley, singing "For He's a Jolly Good Fellow."

Bart detected moisture in Bradley's eyes.

☆ ☆ ☆ ☆

Monday, March 16, 1953 - 0900 hours - Fort Leavenworth

A large silver screen was hung above the tribunal bench. The judges were seated at a small table in front of the attorneys. General Bradley and his staff sat next to them. A 16-millimeter projector was mounted on a table in the back of the court. Security had been doubled. The lights were dimmed. Dick Reilly handled the projector. Bart addressed the tribunal. "Sirs, for the record, Colonel George Spota, retired, helped coordinate this film with the assistance of Dick Reilly, who is going to operate the projector. Colonel Spota served with me in the European theater of war. We were colonels in intelligence, serving on General Eisenhower's staff. We traveled with General Bradley's First Army in the invasion of France. We were present at the liberation of the concentration camps. Colonel Spota will narrate, or as the professionals say, he will do the voice-over describing various scenes. A stop to sections of the film will be done at my direction."

Spota picked up a microphone attached to a loudspeaker, then began: "You are about to view a compilation of film photographed by the German army, the Soviet troops and the American forces. May I warn this audience and the media that this is very graphic and best described as a sea of horrors. Children most certainly should not be exposed to these scenes."

"General Milburn, let us proceed," Nimitz urged, gaveling.

The lights were dimmed. The film opened with flashes of lightning striking a huge swastika. A backdrop of stratus clouds, precursors to storms, a still photo depicting the Four Horsemen of the Apocalypse, and a score with heavy military drums added to the drama. The title "Nazi Atrocities" overlaid a segue to young boys furiously pounding giant snare drums as thousands of soldiers held framed plastic placards of swastikas, with crowds saluting with hands extended, shouting, "Heil Hitler!" A crescendo of Wagner's "Ride of the Valkyrie" played on.

A series of still photographs followed, displaying Hitler's father and mother. In mellow tones, Colonel Spota said, "This is Hitler's father, who in his third marriage married a domestic servant, Klara Pölzl, both seen here. The father, a bureaucrat, was in the Imperial Customs Service. Adolf was born on April 20, 1889. Father and son were both hot-tempered and at odds most of the time over Hitler's desire to become an artist. The father died in January 1903. Adolf was thirteen years of age and very devoted to his mother."

The camera panned the town of Linz, Austria, where Hitler's mother moved in 1905.

"Over the next two years, Adolf was a drifter. In 1907 he went to Vienna with ambitions to become a great artist. He failed his entrance exams at Vienna's Academy of Fine Arts. His spirits were low, compounded by his mother's terminal illness with cancer. She was attended by Dr. Edward Bloch, a Jewish physician who comforted Adolf. Two events began to affect Hitler's yet undefined psyche, the death of his mother in December 1907 and his failure at the academy. He returned to Vienna."

The film showed the deterioration of the eighteen-year-old Hitler from 1908 to 1910 in Vienna.

"His sister, Paula, sent him his orphan's pension of twenty-five kronen, hardly enough for food," Spota continued. "He lodged at an asylum. In the summer he slept on park benches. He panhandled, mostly from Jews. In

1910 he moved to Munich and lived at a haven for the homeless."

The film depicted him unshaven and unkempt. He was seen with vagrants, criminals and ruffians. He lived the life of a derelict. "He openly despised Christianity and socialism. Yet he was friendly with Josef Neumann, who was also penniless." Suddenly, the film kaleidoscopically reflected the cultural and social populace of Berlin, Munich and Vienna.

"At the age of twenty-four, he was still a derelict at large, begging in the streets. He rented an attic room from a tailor named Joseph Popp. The Austrian government was seeking him as a draft dodger. He wormed his way out of that when the German criminal police arrested him for failure to report for the Austrian draft. In Salzburg, he reported and was declared too weak for military service in February 1914. He returned to Munich. However, this was the turning point for this misfit. World War I had begun."

A still photo depicting Hitler was flashed on the screen, placing him next to one of the Stone Lions of the *Feldherrnhalle*, or Hall of Field Marshals. "His personal photographer, Heinrich Hoffmann, found the photo at Hitler's request years later. Hitler had written to the German government volunteering to serve. He was enrolled on August 4, 1914."

A shot of Hitler, with an elongated mustache, in a German uniform was shown next.

"His war record is murky. He was a dispatch runner. Records show that he received an Iron Cross and a wound in his buttocks. There is a further report that he was hospitalized by a poison gas attack and blinded for a short while."

Pictures of Hitler orating in beer halls flashed on the screen. A Captain Karl Mayr recommended that he join the German Workers Party.

"That was the beginning of his new career and the rise to power," the narrator continued. "Hitler honed his speaking skills in the beer cellars of Munich. The Nazi party had jelled. Three men, Anton Drexler, Karl Harrer and Gottfried Feder, formed the backbone of the nascent Nazi Party. They were anti-Semitic, anti-capitalist and anti-democracy. Hitler, the opportunist and street-smart charlatan, used his mouth to rise to the top of the movement. His mantra of anti-Semitism drew the dissolute to this Pied Piper of hate. The Nazi party grew from thousands to millions. Germany was on its way to a coalition with the minions of evil. International bad news redounded to Hitler's benefit on October 29, 1929, known as "Black Tuesday" in the United States. As you can see from these pictures, the New York Stock Exchange crashed. Billions of dollars were lost by investors, some of whom jumped to their deaths from tall buildings. This economic disaster electrified the world economy and profoundly affected Germany. A worldwide depression caused mass unemployment, resulting in a depression in the U.S., and spread throughout Europe. Germany was hit hard," Spota's voice emphasized.

"The election on September 14, 1930, showed the Nazis registering six and a half million votes, nearly twenty percent, seating a hundred and seven deputies in the five hundred and seventy-seven-member Reichstag. Despite Hitler's loss to Hindenburg in two elections, March 13 and April 10, 1932, he was second only to Hindenburg in popularity. His propaganda machine, orchestrated by Goebbels, then went into high gear. Hitler toured the country, with masses greeting him with *Sieg Heils*. Heinrich Brüning, chosen as Chancellor at the urging of the army hierarchy, outlawed the SA and the SS on April 13, 1932. He was replaced by Franz von Papen on May 30. At Hitler's urging, Chancellor von Papen lifted the ban on the SA and the SS."

Bart asked Spota to stop the film, then he interjected, "At this point in Hitler's career, he intensified his anti-Semitic rhetoric. Julius Streicher, a wild-eyed journalist and publisher of *Der Stürmer*, a vile and viciously anti-Semitic newspaper, with a circulation of six hundred thousand readers, presented apocryphal accounts of Jews raping German women, ritual murders of children, and concoctions of the most atrocious lies. He front-paged the writings of Martin Luther in 1543, which urged synagogues be set on fire, destruction of Jewish homes, calling the Jews *worms*. Hitler added these words to his repertoire, using Jews as his political scapegoats. The next scenes quickly take us to the twelve-year apocalyptic journey to Armageddon. Turn it on, Colonel."

"The film reveals Hindenburg rejecting Hitler as Chancellor on August 13, 1932," Spota continued. "This was after the July 31st new Reichstag election, when the Nazis polled 13,745,000 votes, thirty-seven percent, gaining two hundred and thirty of the six hundred and eight seats. The NSDAP, the Nazi Party, became the largest party in Germany. Another election on November 6, and the Nazi vote declined to thirty-three percent. On December 2, Hindenburg named Kurt von Schleicher as Chancellor. On January 23, 1933, von Schleicher resigned."

Bart took the microphone. "A week later, on January 30, Hindenburg, a doddering old man, appoints Hitler and von Papen as Chancellors in a coalition government. Von Papen accepts the vice chancellorship. The film shows the street bums hailing Hitler. Take it, George."

"Things happen quickly. The Reichstag burns down on February 27. On April 1 we see the boycott against Jewish businesses, doctors, lawyers, teachers and all professionals. Himmler is appointed head of the police in Bavaria. On July 20th Hitler signs a Concordat with the Vatican through Cardinal Eugenio Pacelli, who later became Pope Pius XII. The first sign of a rift between Hitler and von Papen occurs on June 17, 1934, when von Papen delivers a speech at the University of Marburg, criticizing the Nazi treatment of Jews and other power plays. Two weeks later, from June 30 to July 2, Hitler orders the end of the SA, the storm troopers. A three-day murder spree kills Ernst Röhm and his followers," Spoto added.

The pictures graphically depicted the purge.

"The SS is put under Himmler's control. On August 2, 1934, President Hindenburg dies. Hitler announces himself as Commander in Chief by combining the Presidency and the Chancellor's office. He became *Der Führer*."

Nimitz gaveled. The film stopped and the lights were turned on. "There will be a twenty-minute comfort recess," he declared.

Dick Reilly changed reels. The lavatories were crowded. The media returned from their telephone booths. The lights were dimmed and Part II of the picture opened with the now-familiar panoplies of military parades, a uniformed Hitler addressing enormous crowds in frenzied adulation in response to his rabble-rousing promises, and the denigration of Jews, Gypsies, Jehovah's Witnesses and non-Aryans. His speech was translated with closed captions graphically interpreting his remarks.

Spota picked up the voice-over: "In short order a plebiscite transferred the Saarland into Nazi possession on January 13, 1935. Two months later Hitler declared military conscription. Schools trained children starting at age six in military marching, *Sieg Heils, Heil Hitlers* and pledges of loyalty to the Nazi Party and the Fatherland.

"Here we see him visiting children at their schools. The Versailles Treaty became a mildewed document as the rest of the world battled the depression. On March 7, 1936 the treaty was scattered to the winds of world complacency. Hitler reclaimed the Rhineland and marched his neophyte troops across the bridge. The Western powers could have stopped him with a slight show of force. They opted for appeasement, a virus that consumed them for the next four years. While his hand-tailored uniforms pictorially evinced a formidable force, they were hardly ready for military defiance. A year prior to that event, his serpentine tongue had ordered the Nuremberg race laws and, also by fiat, ordered compulsory labor service for young men aged eighteen to twenty-five. All the signals were loud and clear to all of Europe and the rest of the world that war was inevitable. However, the appeasement virus had paralyzed the see-nothing, hear-nothing and do nothing powers."

Military music played loudly as photos showed Hitler and Mussolini signing an Axis treaty on October 25, 1936. One month later, Japan and Germany sign an anti-Comintern pact.

The English translations crawled across the screen.

"On November 26, 1937, Hjalmar Schacht resigns as Economics Minister. Four months later, Austria was annexed, described as Anschluss. Not one shot was fired. Hitler triumphantly led his troops into Vienna as the Austrians greeted the troops with cheers and flowers."

The film moved quickly to pictures of Neville Chamberlain and Edouard Daladier at the infamous Munich conference, showing the two men signing an appeasement agreement, handing the Sudetenland of Czechoslovakia to Germany, as Hitler, Mussolini and Goering laughed.

The clips segued into a reprise of children furiously beating large drums. Raucous, strident passages of Wagnerian music grated the ears of the audience. Violence erupted on the screen.

"The brown-shirted SA storm troopers had apparently gone berserk," Spoto resumed. "Jews were dragged by their hair and beards into the streets in Berlin, Munich, Stuttgart, Hamburg and other cities and villages. Bonfires in the streets depicted gangs burning books, with Bibles, Torahs and phylacteries being tossed into the fires. This was *Kristallnacht*, the Night of Broken Glass, November 8 and 9, 1938, instigated by Goebbels."

Spota handed the microphone to Bart, who instructed Reilly to slow the projection and, at certain atrocities, pause for stills, zeroing in on the vilest and most contemptible acts.

"What we are viewing here is the seeding of the Holocaust," Bart began. "Look closely. Here are the thugs setting fire to a synagogue; this is a montage of more than a thousand Jewish businesses being destroyed. Here is a group kicking a rabbi to death. Fires were lit all over Germany, burning synagogues, stripping their holy Torahs, hymns and prayer books for the fires. Look, here is a group of thugs tearing dresses off young girls. Turn it to normal speed, Dick. Over two nights, one hundred and fifty Jews were killed and nearly thirty thousand Jews were carted off to concentration camps. Stop the film on that shot of a rabbi's beard being set on fire by these clones of Attila the Hun. The press reported this anarchy worldwide. So far we haven't discovered evidence of world outrage at that time. I assume," Bart concluded, "that some said *Oh, it's only Jews,* while others let their subliminal anti-Semitism condone it. Our world leaders looked the other way, and a few journalists like Ed Murrow and William Shirer sounded the tocsin as the righteous cried silently. Take over, Colonel Spota."

Bart looked at von Papen, Schacht and Niemöller, who were sitting in the back of the courtroom. He detected tears in their eyes. The film continued to five days later on March 14, when Germany invaded the rest of Czechoslovakia.

"The Western powers shrug," Spota recited. "Hitler and Mussolini sign a pact of steel, which is a military alliance, on April 22. The world powers shrug. Now we come to the causal effect of World War II. On August 23, 1939, Vyacheslav Molotov and Hitler signed a Nazi-Soviet non-aggression pact and agreed to split up Poland between the two powers. Nine days later, Germany invaded Poland. Let us look at flashbacks for a moment," Spota suggested. A series of shots showed the bumbling Prime Minister Chamberlain of Great Britain and Premier Daladier of France shuttling back and forth, appeasing Hitler, and Chamberlain waving a piece of white paper on his return to England after he acceded to Hitler's demands.

"His infamous declaration of *Peace in our time* haunts millions to this day," Spota added. The flashbacks ironically showed half of Germany's Jewish population fleeing Germany.

"On September 3, Chamberlain and Daladier sheepishly declared England and France at war with Germany. The fate of Europe's nine million Jews was foretold the day of the Nazi attack on Poland, where three million Jews resided. That was one-third of Europe's nine million Jews. As we know now, six million Jews were slaughtered by the Nazis by war's end. That is two-thirds of the entire Jewish populace on the continent. Within two weeks, Poland was conquered and all the Jews were being rounded up. Murder, pillage and torture were the order of the day. In October, Hitler ordered the *mercy killing* of those not fit to live. It was a euphemism for an euthanasia program."

The film showed clips of atrocities in Warsaw, Krakow, Lublin, Breslau and throughout the country. The horrors depicted the inhumanity of man at its worst.

"All Jewish Poles still alive were moved into a ghetto," Spota went on. "Most were assigned to forced labor, while the most menial and degrading jobs were forced on Hassidic Jews. On April 9, 1940, Germany invades Denmark and Norway. Danes and Norwegians hide most Jews. This busy tyrant moves quickly, and on May 10, 1940, he invades Holland, Belgium, Luxembourg and France. The French surrender on June 10th. On August 13 he begins the air battle with Britain. His Luftwaffe takes a terrific beating and Hitler stops the battle in September. However, he kept pounding London and other English cities. Concentration camps were hurriedly being built in Poland and elsewhere. Dachau was the first one, built in 1933, nine miles outside Munich, plus six large ones in Germany. On April 6, 1941, he invades Yugoslavia and Greece. On June 22, 1941, this megalomaniac invades the Soviet Union, thinking he is omnipotent, much to the apprehension of the high command. Nine days later, he assigns Reinhard Heydrich to work out a plan for the *Final Solution* of the Jewish problem. On September 1, German Jews can no longer emigrate and are ordered to wear the emblem of the Star of David. The killing orgy began with the invasion of the Soviet Union. A unit called the *Einsatzgruppen* (the killing machine) follows the Nazi conquerors, rounding up Jews and executing them summarily. On September 3 the first gassing takes place at Auschwitz."

Bart took the microphone. "What we learned from the Nuremberg trials will be coming up on the screen shortly. Hold it now, Dick. Himmler told Rudolf Höss, the Auschwitz commandant, that the Jewish problem must be solved forthwith. Himmler directed that every Jew must be destroyed. *Do it by gassing,* he insisted. However, let's look at this most dastardly evidence of Nazi evil. Start the projector, Dick. Here we are at Babi Yar, just outside Kiev. These pictures were captured from the Germans. These craven killers photographed their own handiwork. One of the most monstrous acts of the *Einsatzgruppen*, led by the Gestapo's Heinrich Müller, who's on trial here, is to be depicted. Babi Yar is a ravine northwest of the city. The Germans entered Kiev in September 1941. The Soviet security police dynamited some buildings occupied by the Germans. As an excuse, they blamed the Jews and rounded up forty thousand Jews of the sixty thousand living there. Over a period of two days, they forced the Jewish victims to strip naked before handing over their valuables, rings, watches, gold Stars of David, and cash. Watch carefully as they take men, women, children, old men and women, and machine-gun them into the chasm. The total dead are estimated between thirty-five and forty thousand. The Nazis forced other prisoners to close the mass grave. They, as you can see, are being executed. In July 1943, with the Russian army approaching Kiev, the *Einsatzgruppen* killed the remaining prisoners of what had been a total of sixty thousand Jews."

An eruption occurred in the courtroom. Defendants were attacking each other with their manacled hands. Courtroom spectators yelled, "Murderers! Bastards! Animals!" The screaming stopped. The tribunal gaveled for silence. MPs roughly separated the combatants - soldier defendants and commandants.

The spectators yelled, "Hang them!"

Hitler screamed, "That is Hollywood Scheisse!"

Nimitz called a recess and ordered counsel into chambers. Krieger, Stolz, Bart and Cartman were ordered to sit.

"Krieger and Stolz," General Smith warned, "if you can't control your clients, we'll put every single one of them in solitary confinement. You know what that is? It's a rat hole and that's where you'll be conferring with them. That film is a searing piece of what they are capable of."

Stolz and Krieger began talking at once. Nimitz snapped, "One at a time."

Stolz raised his hand. Nimitz nodded. "Sir, after what I've seen, I have no desire to continue here. However, I'm bound to complete my distasteful job of defending these lice. What more can I do?"

Krieger promised to convey the tribunal's message to all the defendants. General Chennault suggested leg irons and duct tape for their mouths if there was another outburst. The tribunal concurred.

Bart stood up and faced the two defense lawyers. "What you have seen in those films is but a teaser to the nightmare that follows. Never in the history of civilization have we had a filmed record of a carnage of this magnitude. I warn you of what's to come."

"Why not spare us the rest of it and rest your case?" Krieger wheedled.

"No way," Bart snapped. "Not until the whole world, and especially Germany, views it."

"This is no trial. It's a horror show for propaganda purposes," Stolz declared.

"Don't pull that Nazi bullshit here, you Swiss-paid whores!" Bart railed. "You're being paid by your Swiss banks with stolen Jewish money. Trial... trial - you'll find out what kind of a trial this is when the sentences are handed down."

"Sirs, please note General Milburn's intemperate remarks," Krieger said.

"Come, come, gentlemen, everyone cool down and get back to work," Nimitz counseled.

The chatter in the courtroom simmered down to a hush when the tribunal returned to the bench.

"General, you may continue," Nimitz said.

Bart nodded to Reilly and picked up the mike. "To understand what follows, we must point out that the Nazi hierarchy, up to its hips in a two-front war, fiendishly and stupidly spent billions on rail lines, trains and concentration camps. They built six major death camps, euphemistically called extermination centers. They were Belzec, Treblinka, Chelmno, Auschwitz-Birkenau (one of the three sections of a complex), Sobibor, and Majdanek. At Madjanek and Auschwitz, there were concentration camps, forced labor camps and execution centers. Roll it, Dick."

The first camp shown was subtitled "Chelmno," and Spota began the voice-over:

"This was the first extermination camp, Chelmno, beginning the gassing of naked Jews in gas vans. Here we see the arrival of trainloads of victims. They hand over their valuables and disrobe. These heroic Nazi SS men in their custom-made uniforms, holding their bayoneted rifles to cow these help-less, unarmed victims. Look at their faces. They are jeering at the naked ladies, cat-calling the men and pushing children into the death vans."

A gasp echoed through the courtroom at the sight of an SS officer grab-bing an infant from the arms of a young mother, swinging the baby by one leg and hurling it into a flaming crematorium. The mother ran to save the baby and was shot between the eyes.

Spota commented, "That was Germany's finest, exploiting his talents. That was the Nazi special police at work."

Hitler screamed, "That was not my orders! That miserable little chicken farmer was so pious and killed babies!"

Krieger put his hand over Hitler's mouth. A dozen men and women exited hurriedly. Most had handkerchiefs covering their mouths. Two of the women sobbed loudly. Hardened reporters were evidently in shock, their faces pale.

The film kept running, showing trainloads of Jews going through the pre-death routine. The camera focused on gold fillings being extracted from the teeth of dead naked bodies. In a twilight scene, a young girl, struggling, was taken to the quarters of an officer. SS officers were shown gang-raping her.

Spota stopped the film. "This rape scene is too graphic. We'll skip a few clips, and now watch what these super Aryan supermen are going to do."

Two SS men carried the girl's naked, bleeding body, which was struggling weakly. They threw her into the blazing crematorium. The girl was fifteen years of age, a subtitle stated.

"These next scenes depict the disposal of corpses by being fed into crema-toriums and in bonfires on the grounds," Spota narrated. "In the autumn of 1944, Jewish prisoners, as you can see, are exhuming bodies from the mass graves. This is what the Nazis termed *Aktion 1005*, which is their code for doing away with evidence of their mass murders. As the Russian army gets less than ten miles from the Chelmno gate, the commandant and his SS troops line up these Jewish prisoners. He raises his left hand, holding a Walther .65 gun in his right hand. The troops train these guns on fifty prisoners. The commandant brings his right hand down and begins firing. The SS troops fire simultaneously. Watch them pick up the bodies. A few are still alive. The bodies, alive and dead, are deposited in the crematoriums. Here, the troops climb aboard trucks, the top officers run to a line of cars. The caravan abandons the camp, as the Rus-sians were half a mile from Chelmno. A total of three hundred and twenty thousand innocent humans were killed in that camp."

Reilly quickly changed reels. In the interim, scores of men and women left the courtroom, some crying, others vomiting, and men cursing. One woman, a crucifix hanging from a neck chain, passed the defense table and spat on it. The next reel was captioned "Belzec Extermination Camp."

Bart took the mike. "This is a short reel filmed by the Germans. Belzec is between Zamosc and Lwow in southeastern Poland. It was set up as a labor camp during the Nazi occupation in 1940. The Jewish slave laborers were driven to the backbreaking task of building fortifications and anti-tank ditches along the line, between the border separating the Nazis and the Soviet-occupied portion of Poland. This was the first of Reinhard Heydrich's extermination camps. As you can see, as the camera pans the countryside, the rail connections were established in the center of Lwow, Krakow and Lublin, encompassing large populations of Jews."

The camera zeroed in on the extermination area and an enclosed path leading to the gas chambers and the mass graves. "That unidentified Neanderthal in an officer's uniform is proudly showing the converted facilities to Himmler and Heydrich. Now, the next clips show the demonic activation of the Nazis' main industry-mass murder. In March 1942, trains with fifty or more freight cars, routing eighty to a hundred and twenty-five people crammed into each foul-smelling cattle car, arrive. The Nazi formula of disrobing the helpless men, women and children after taking all their valuables is evident. The next pictures speak for themselves."

Naked men, women and children marched through the tubes with arrows toward a sign labeled "Showers." Carbon monoxide was fed into the charnel house. The procession seemed endless. Bodies were thrown into pits.

Bart brought the final clips to an end by stating, "Between March and December 1942 at least six hundred thousand Jews were sent into Belzec and were murdered - carnage on an assembly-line basis. Belzec was razed in July 1943 and converted into a farm. The Soviets came in May 1944."

Nimitz ordered a recess to 1430 hours. At the conference-room lunch buffet, most of the prosecution team seemed to be in a trance. They were obviously dispirited. All suffered from a loss of appetite. Sophia's tears trickled down her face. Bart handed her a tissue. She let it fall in her lap. Tony reached for it and dabbed the moisture.

"Come on, gang, try to eat," Bart said.

☆ ☆ ☆ ☆

Monday, March 16, 1953 - 1300 hours - Fort Leavenworth

The afternoon session brought an unexpectedly large number of new faces into the courtroom, due to the emotional effect on the morning's attendees. Krieger addressed the tribunal. "Your Honors, the presentation of these films is blanket evidence against unspecified defendants. This is akin to tossing wet garbage out of a window, staining bystanders below. I object to any further presentation of these horror films."

"General Milburn, do you wish to reply?" Nimitz asked.

"Mr. Krieger's remarks are outrageously specious in every aspect. The evidence contained in these films is directly in consonance with the charges contained in the indictments. I am sure that his inadvertent choice of words was not meant to be descriptive. Tossing garbage and staining bystanders could easily be construed as analogous to tossing dead bodies into pits, or crematoriums, and splattering their blood on the perpetrators."

Spectators applauded.

"Mr. Krieger, your objection is overruled. Proceed with the films," Nimitz declared.

The lights were dimmed. The titles were superimposed over freight trains speeding toward a large sign bearing the word "Sobibor." The click-clack of the train's wheels, short toots announcing the arrivals, and large puffs of smoke emanating from the locomotive segued into a line of troops awaiting the cargo of innocents to be robbed, disrobed and executed.

Spota explained that the camp was located in the village of Sobibor, three miles west of the Bug River in central Poland. The camp was primarily an execution center. The extermination area contained gas chambers, mass graves, and barracks for the slave laborers. Housing was in another section for the SS and Ukrainian guards.

"We focus now on the barbed-wire fence and the minefield surrounding the camp. We now see the repetition of the methodically organized process of what the Nazis laughingly referred to as the *leading of the lambs to slaughter,*" Bart said.

He motioned to Spota and was handed the mike. "Let's put a stop-and-go on the film so that we can see the faces of the victims. Look at this beautiful child holding her mother's hand. Look at that five-year-old innocent little face and her naked body. Contrast her with the beast pointing his bayonet at her while she is being led to her execution. Now, look at the mother's face. She is holding an infant in her arms. The mother, a girl in her early twenties, is also naked. Now, watch what happens. A guard snatches the infant from her arms as she desperately tries to retrieve her baby. An SS officer viciously strikes her head with the butt of his rifle. She is unconscious. Her little girl lies on top of her, crying and trying to revive her. Read her lips - she's wailing *Ma, ma!* Other guards are salaciously viewing and commenting on her beautiful body. The five-year-old girl has been lifted by the SS officer, who delivers a vicious punch on the child's face as another guard takes the infant and hurls it to the ground, stamping in its howling mouth. Slow it down, Dick. The infant is instantly killed. Mother and daughter are unconscious. Both are carried to the crematorium and fed to the flames alive. The infant is tossed in after them."

The proceedings were suddenly interrupted by women in the audience screaming. One woman, crying audibly, yelled, "Kill these monsters!" A nun rose, nervously juggling her rosary beads in one hand, and held up a wooden crucifix and prayed. Another woman, sobbing fitfully, looked at the defendants and blubbered in Yiddish, "*Ver geharget* (drop dead)." Several men shouted epithets. Some members of the press exited.

Nimitz tolerated the outbursts for a few minutes and then ordered a ten-minute recess. Bart and Jacques walked out through the press exit. Ed Murrow of CBS was agitatedly pacing back and forth past his van, puffing on his ever-present cigarette. He spotted Bart and hastened over to join him.

"General, just off the record, where in hell did you get that footage?"

Jacques, puffing on his cigarette, cryptically interceded. "You said it, Ed."

"What does that mean, Jacques?" Ed queried.

"Hell - that's what you said."

Bart answered, "Ed, we've known each other a long time. Nothing I say, about this trial is for attribution."

"Agreed, General."

"This stuff was discovered among Himmler's files of horror. We had it in classified archives. The footage was declassified at my request. Use it as you will. Forget the source."

"Barton Milburn, you're a pal. When this danse macabre is over, how about a private lunch with you and Jacques?"

"It's a deal."

Back in the courtroom, order had been restored, and Nimitz announced to the guests, "Please try to subdue your emotions. Proceed, General."

The projector was activated and Spota began his narration. "The parade of death continued into the charnel houses, the gas chambers and the alleged showers. They killed two hundred thousand helpless, innocent human beings up to 1943. Aktion 1005, the cleanup - hide the evidence - was put in motion, removing all the traces of the mass murders. Jews from Austria, France, Poland, the Netherlands and Belgium were executed. In late October, Jewish prisoners revolted and attempted to escape through the main gate. The German and Ukrainian guards aborted the effort with machine-gun fire, killing one hundred men and women. The other escapees turned and ran though the minefields. One hundred were captured and executed. Three hundred miraculously escaped. Watch, now, the slaughter at the gates and the action at the minefields. At the cost of several hundred lives, the battle caused the closing of the camp and its dismantling."

A ten-minute recess was ordered. Reilly set up his next reel. When the session was resumed, the screen displayed an aerial view of a camp and, in oversized letters, the name of the village of Treblinka was overlaid on the extermination center. Bart began the narration.

"This palace of persecution, fifty miles northeast of Warsaw, has the distinction of extirpating eight hundred thousand or more Jews from Poland, Greece, Austria, Belgium, France, Germany and the Soviet Union. Of this group, two hundred fifty thousand were citizens of Warsaw. While these films are repetitive in displaying the Nazi atrocities, it is the preponderance of its monstrosities that indicates the guilt of a nation murderously berserk.

"There was a rail line from Warsaw to the village of Wolka, and the camp was two and a half miles southeast of there. A railway track was specially built, leading to the extermination camp. Within two hours of their departure from Warsaw, the victims were marching to their execution chambers, naked, robbed of their dignity, valuables and lives. Those who were too weak to walk were taken to an area where a Red Cross hospital flag was on a gate. Now, watch this scene. The SS men greet them and help them to line up with their backs to a barrage of machine-gun fire. They fall into a heap where other bodies were piled. Now, here is a horrendous, yet poignant, scene. We have a family of six, a young rabbi, beardless, a lovely young wife and four children-two girls about five and seven, and two boys of about nine and eleven years of age. They refuse to undress. They are marched to the phony Red Cross hospital. They refuse to face the pit, staring at the supermen Nazi killers. The family holds hands as the machine-gun fire rips into their bodies."

Von Papen, Schacht and Niemöller watched the rest of the film in shock. It was a depressing event for all of them. "This stain can never be erased from the annals of history," Niemöller summed up.

At the Victorian house, a quiet dinner was in session with Bart, Jacques, Douglas Milburn, Spota and Reilly. After profuse thanks to Spota and Reilly, the conversation dealt with national and international politics and sports, in an effort to cover their emotional turmoil.

CHAPTER SIXTEEN

Tuesday, March 17, 1953 - 0900 hours - Fort Leavenworth

The tribunal gaveled order. "Your next witness, General Milburn," Nimitz said.

"The prosecution calls Franz von Papen."

That announcement caused an eruption at the defense table. Hitler was furiously urging his lawyers to object. As the argument went on, an urbane, dignified figure, stately in manner and escorted by MPs, calmly approached the witness stand. He was attired in a black cutaway coat, striped pants, white shirt and a wide pearl-gray silk tie in a Windsor knot. His demeanor reflected the air of a statesman as he took the oath.

"English or German, sir?"

"I prefer English."

After stating his name for the record, Bart asked, "Please tell the court your background, sir."

"General Milburn, may I be permitted to make a short statement before I testify?"

"If your remarks are pertinent to the issues before this tribunal. Therefore, I ask the question for the record. What do you wish to say that is in consonance with your testimony?"

"My statement pertains to the Holocaust."

"Very well, proceed."

"As a result of viewing the film, I didn't sleep last night. The atrocities so graphically depicted fill me with shame for my country. The people of Germany have to confess their sins, make peace with God and the Jewish people. This stain will not be erased for another millenium. The horrendous torture, mayhem and mass murder may have been instigated by this monster, but it took millions of the German people, the Lithuanians, Ukrainians, Romanians and other monstrous accursed and detestable mad dogs, as accessories. There is much blame to be assigned - Hungary, Romania, Bulgaria, Lithuania, the Ukraine and more. *Mea culpas* will not suffice."

"All right. Now, answer my question," Bart urged.

"I was born in the Westphalia region of Germany. My ancestry goes back one thousand years. We are pure Germans. Not immigrants from Austria," he declared, looking at Hitler.

"Continue, please."

Von Papen detailed his aristocratic background, serving in the Westphalian Fifth Uhlan Regiment. After becoming a general staff officer, he was assigned as military attaché at the German embassy in Washington. He admitted his espionage duties in the United States. In 1916 the State Department had him expelled. On his way back to Germany, he landed in Southampton, England. The British seized some secret papers he had inadvertently left visible in his baggage. His diplomatic status prevented his detention during World War I.

"I was rather stupid for a thirty-seven-year-old. However, I spent the rest of the war as Chief of Staff with the Turkish Fourth Army in Palestine."

"After the First War, what did you do?"

"I resigned my commission and became a politician."

"Sir, with due respect, I have your biography here. Correct me if I'm wrong."

"By all means."

"You became a member of the Center Party, elected to represent your district in the Prussian Landtag. You were a highly respected socialite, a member of the aristocratic set and a member of the best clubs, mingling with the old aristocratic elite. You are quite a horseman and became the leader of the Herrenklub, located opposite the Reichstag. You were a passionate monarchist and editor of the Germanic Catholic newspaper."

"So far, so good, General. I just want to make it clear that I was fond of the Americans. I was serving my country while serving there. We were not at war with the U.S. at that time. I was really checking on the British embassy in America."

"Let's pass that. You were quite a popular man in Germany during the Weimar Republic," Bart went on.

"I won't be shy about it, General. I had lots of friends, and due to my education and upbringing, I moved in higher circles."

"President Paul von Hindenburg, who was Supreme Commander in 1916, was very fond of you and called you *Fränzchen*. You were a dapper figure in those days. Quite popular with the ladies."

"You said it, I didn't," von Papen said with a smile.

"Let's move along. Hitler was becoming a problem for Hindenburg."

"Yes, but he defeated that Nazi in two elections."

"Hindenburg named you Chancellor."

"That lasted for a short while. Hitler's Nazi Party grew from twelve seats in the Reichstag in 1928 to one hundred seven delegates in 1932. Hindenburg was old and sick. He named Hitler to share the chancellorship with me."

"Why did you yield to him and agree to become Vice Chancellor?"

"I have never revealed the reason for that. During a meeting with Hitler and his sycophants, Goering and Goebbels asked me to join them in the hallway of our conference room. They told me that I wouldn't be alive for another twenty-four hours if I didn't yield to Hitler. He had a mob of gangsters behind him. It was obvious that, sooner or later, I would be assassinated. I'm a practical man. I accepted their terms."

"So you became a nominal figure in his regime."

"Yes. On August 2, 1934, President Hindenburg died. Hitler merged the chancellorship and the presidency. He became *Der Führer*, the despot of Germany."

"What happened to you?" Bart asked.

"I was Vice President until 1934, when I became ambassador to Austria from 1934 to 1938. He sent that disciple of the devil Seyss-Inquart into Austria to prepare for Anschluss, the takeover of Austria in 1938. I was moved out of Germany as ambassador to Turkey from 1939 to 1944."

"What did you do after you were recalled?"

"The war was obviously lost. It is not known, but in my diminished capacity I secretly tried to send feelers to my counterparts in the diplomatic corps for a formula for peace."

"Did anyone in Hitler's circle know what you were doing?"

"Yes, Bormann knew, as did some of the generals," von Papen replied.

"Would you please name the generals?"

"For the sake of their families, I decline to answer that. There are thousands of Nazis under cover in Germany to this day."

"What was the reason your efforts failed?"

"The word from all sources was simple. Roosevelt and Churchill had firmly demanded unconditional surrender. Also, by this time, Hitler was in a state of aberration. If Hitler had been assassinated earlier, the chances of a fair peace could have been effected. The minute he faked his death, we surrendered. The war was over."

"Let's go back to 1932. Isn't it true that, as Chancellor, you were tricked by Hitler to cancel your ban on the SA and to dissolve the Reichstag?"

"Well, my own party was restless. But, to be frank, I was taken in by this alien Hitler's power. I caved in. I was worried about a revolution. Yet I regret both decisions," von Papen lamented.

"Were you a Nazi?"

"Not then and not now. I was acquitted by the Nuremberg tribunal."

"You were tried by a German denazification court and sentenced to eight years at hard labor."

"That was pure politics. It was a West German public-relations ploy and a pathetic attempt to appease the Americans and the British. We needed economic help. We wanted our piece of the Marshall Plan."

"Could you give the court a short analysis of what led to this cataclysm, which resulted in the destruction of Germany and which is now split in two parts?" Bart said.

"Sir, your question sums up the result. The birth of this heinous adventure began with the failure of America to become part of the League of Nations, which your President Wilson created. The way was paved for a degenerate immigrant to lure a dissolute lower class to take control of a defeated country suffering from depression and inflation. This Austrian alien, a draft dodger in his own country, served in the German army later. This derelict, who failed at everything in his native Austria, came to our suffering country and polished his oratorical skills, soap-boxing in beer halls. His willing audience were the scum of the Earth, the unemployed, ruffians, criminals and opportunists."

"That's history. What was the key to his political success?"

"General, I must place part of the blame on the democracies. The draconian terms of their victory in 1918 was contained in the Versailles Treaty. Germany was in the throes of an economic epileptic fit," von Papen explained.

"Neatly stated. You blame your conquerors."

"In part, sir. There was an isolationist attitude in America and indifference among the European countries. The door was wide open here for a rabble-rousing mountebank like Hitler to marshal the ne'er-do-wells to rally and take to the streets. America's Black Tuesday on October 29, 1929, with the collapse of the stock market, had a profound effect on Germany and all of Europe. A world depression was in force. This is perfect fodder for a charlatan."

"All right. Hitler becomes *Der Führer*. He violates the tenets of the Versailles Treaty. What could have been done to stop him and his anti-Semitic rhetoric?"

"The British, French and, yes, the American isolationists have to search their souls. He could have been stopped as early as March 7, 1936. That is a stain you have to acknowledge. The world closed its eyes to this scoundrel's rearmament program. A few troops standing at the border of the demilitarized Rhineland could have stopped him with a slight show of force. That would have contained him. Instead, Britain's Chamberlain appeased him. France's Daladier did the same. Roosevelt had said in 1933 that we have nothing to fear but fear itself. Hitler laughed at that, using that phrase in reverse. He used it in his soapbox orations. *That's our weapon - fear helps weaken people. Our weapon is fear - make the people of the world fear us and they will wither like dying flowers. Strength, used to subdue opposition and create fear, is our best weapon.* That was his constant mantra. He cowed the Germans into Nazism, used the Jews as the political object of hate, which got out of hand by the oligarchy he ruled, and conquered helpless, peaceful countries. This was the price the world paid for looking the other way. Millions died because of indifference."

"The oligarchy was actually the second layer of power. He ruled with a bloody fist," Bart said.

"True. Those who opposed him or displeased him were executed summarily," von Papen responded. "The slaughter of the Jews was intensified by Heydrich and Himmler. Heydrich was assassinated and Himmler, a farcical character, became the most powerful man internally. Hitler's megalomania overcame him as an imaginary military genius, while Himmler became the Sultan of Slaughter. Two-thirds of the nine million Jews in Europe were tortured, starved to death and executed. I venture to say that if the Allies and Soviets had been a little slower in their drive, Himmler would have killed Hitler in an attempt to take power. That chicken farmer didn't have the charisma to rule Germany or effect peace with the Allies. The Russians were vicious in their attempt to crush Germany. No one could make a deal with them. Nuremberg convicted and hung the oligarchy. They believed Hitler committed suicide. I am pleased to see that devil manacled, sitting here being tried for his life and exposed as the hypocrite he is. The world will remember the Third Reich for a thousand years."

"What did you do to help stop the Holocaust?"

"I spoke to all the ambassadors in Turkey when I was ambassador. It was futile. What could they do? It took the greatest war in history to stop these atrocities. To this day, I cannot fathom how a street bum like Hitler was able to turn an educated, cultured, religious country into a population of barbarians."

"Have you seen the atrocity films before?" Bart asked.

"At Nuremberg I refused to look at the atrocity films. I saw them here for the first time yesterday. Those horrors will stay with me for the rest of my life. I cry for Germany."

"No more questions."

Counsel Krieger coolly and politely stated, "Good morning, Herr Franz von Papen."

The witness, not deceived by the unctuous approach, replied, "The *mourning* is not over."

"You are a man of aristocratic background and highly respected in social circles. Is that not so?"

"I accept your compliment."

"Are you deserving of that description?"

"You've stated it. My public perception is in the eyes of the beholder."

"Your answers indicate the polish of a diplomat."

"I trust so."

"Well, it is hardly responsive," Krieger countered.

"Would you prefer that I deny your descriptions of me and demean myself?"

"Well, let us see, who is the real von Papen?"

"I hope your eyesight is 20-20."

"Let's test it. Your testimony relating to *Der Führer*, Adolf Hitler, has been very disparaging."

"*Der Führer* of what? A destroyed nation? He is *Der Führer* of devastation, murder, thievery, mayhem, and every inconceivable crime. I took the oath to tell the truth today, and that's what I have done before."

"Sir, you were once Chancellor of a Weimar Germany and later Vice Chancellor of the Third Reich. Weren't you a part of Adolf Hitler's cabinet?"

"Yes, in a nominal role. I was an outsider to his cavalry of the apocalypse

- Hitler, Goering, Goebbels, Himmler, Heydrich, von Ribbentrop, Rosenberg, Seyss-Inquart, Bormann, and thousands of others. They led us to Armageddon. The results created a heinous history for Germany by this Austrian immigrant."

"Do you deny that you played no part in Herr Hitler's regime?"

"Absolutely. I was an ambassador. As Vice Chancellor, I was excluded from his inner circle. Thank God. This man you are attempting to defend had delusions of surpassing Julius Caesar, Alexander the Great, Charlemagne and Frederick the Great. A derelict as a great warrior. A genius as commander in chief of the German army. As a tyrant, militarist and murderer, he sank to the size of a gnat," von Papen huffed.

"Yet, with this impression of Chancellor Hitler, you stayed as a servant of the government?"

"Like you and your Swiss bankers, I was afraid to leave. I was tarnished in America and Great Britain. Where else could I go? I am not proud of that, but I didn't participate in his chicanery and uncivilized behavior. It didn't take me too long to realize he was a street bum of dubious character and a sociopath. I gladly took on the ambassador's roles and was not part of his dissolute inner circle."

"Are you, or were you, a Nazi?"

"Neither. I was a German of great heritage," von Papen answered with pride.

"Are you a rich man?"

"Moderately. Nowhere in comparison to the wealth of this billionaire, Hitler, who stole every penny from the Jews and the countries he conquered. Money he managed to sequester with the help of your Swiss banks, plus counterfeit money, which some of your banks helped launder."

"Are you accusing the Swiss government of circulating counterfeit money?" Krieger challenged.

"No, just a few of your banks. However, the Swiss government was spuriously neutral in the war. I am aware of your government's cooperation with Nazi Germany. I am accusing your banks of illegally holding Jewish funds. They demand death certificates of the slaughtered Jews for the relatives and survivors of the Holocaust."

"Are you sure there was a Holocaust, Herr von Papen?"

"Herr Krieger, you're either stupid or deaf, dumb and blind. Go back to Switzerland, take a good bath and cleanse yourself of this affair. You saw those horrible scenes of what the Nazis did over a twelve-year period from 1933 to 1945. Nazi revisionism is an exercise in futility. Contrived history dies with evidentiary truth," von Papen summarized succinctly.

"No further questions," Krieger snapped as he turned away.

Hitler hissed, "Society snobs are worse than Jews. You belong in a concentration camp, von Papen."

The next witness was called. A trim, white-haired man, impeccably dressed in a three-piece suit, walked briskly between two MPs. He took the oath, seated himself comfortably, then reached into his vest pocket and withdrew his chained gold watch. He noted the time and wound the timepiece casually.

His impression and dignified appearance exuded a *laissez-faire* arrogance. He nodded to the tribunal, looked at Milburn and before being questioned, answered in German, "I am Hjalmar Horace Greeley Schacht. I wish to testify in my native language."

Bart smiled at him.

"Horace Greeley?"

"Yes, my father admired this American journalist and politician."

"Did your father give you reasons for naming you after this American?"

"Yes. He founded the New York Tribune, and his opinions were in consonance with my father's. I agree with his views."

"Could you state a few?"

"Greeley opposed slavery, believed in women's rights, favored labor unions, fought against monopolies, was opposed to war, editorialized for amnesty of the Confederates, and ran for President as both a liberal Republican and a Democrat. He was best known for his statement *Go west, young man*. That helped America grow. I am proud of my name."

"Apparently he admired America."

"Yes, except for slavery."

"Yet here you are as a witness in a case involving slavery, called *forced labor* in your country."

"Yes, with great shame," Schacht apologized. There was much good in our country until that demented immigrant turned Germany into a barbarian society, erasing all the good."

"Before we cover the ills of Nazi Germany, please give the court a brief summary of your role before and during the Hitler regime."

"During the Weimar Republic in 1923, at age forty-six, I was Currency Commissioner. During my service at the Finance Ministry, I was credited with halting and reducing inflation. As a result of my efforts at finance, I became president of the Reichsbank, our most prestigious bank. I served them for five years. Then I dabbled in politics and personal finance. I watched the growth of the Nazi Party and felt there was a chance for National Socialism to stimulate our economy."

"According to your record, which I have here, you were called back as president of the Reichsbank in 1933. You served there for two more years. You supported Hitler's rearmament program. In 1935 you were appointed Reich Finance Minister and put in charge of the Wehrmacht economy."

"That's true, but I was disturbed by Hitler's policies. Let me give you some perspective. By 1935 I perceived his duplicitous character. First of all, I didn't particularly care for him as a person. He was a low-class charlatan surrounded by amoral confidants. His followers, by and large, were an assortment of low-class hoodlums. Despite his comedic appearance, he was a provocateur with the talent of a soapbox orator."

"When did you discern the evil in him?" Bart asked.

"Well, I suspected him when he began to raise his anti-Semitism to an emotional level with the public. He named Goering, a libertine dope addict, to head his four-year plan. I resigned all my posts and criticized his stupid economic policies. How ridiculous to strip Jewish merchants of their properties, to steal their industries, to move the little storekeepers out of their properties. He was impinging on the general economy. Admittedly, the Jews are a very industrious, talented people. Doctors, lawyers, bankers, academicians, scholars, engineers, scientists, writers, musicians, producers, tailors, dressmakers, and shopkeepers. And his cadre of thugs robbed them, raped them, enslaved them and finally slaughtered two-thirds of the Jews in Europe. They destroyed ninety percent of the German Jewish population. Stupid, stupid, heartless criminals self- defeating Germany."

"What happened to you?"

"I shamefully stayed on as Minister Without Portfolio, hoping I could help get rid of Hitler and his gangsters," Schacht answered. "My connections with the dissenters resulted in my being sent to a concentration camp."

"Now, Mr. Schacht, I must ask for a frank and unambiguous answer to this question. You were a part of the Nazi government. Were you indeed a Nazi?"

Schacht flushed and angrily replied, "I was never a Nazi, then or now. Let me make myself categorically clear and precise. On my honor, I was never a member of the Nazi Party, nor beholden to Adolf Hitler. I was and am a loyal German citizen. I disagreed with Hitler and his Nazi Party. They brought Germany from its religious, cultural and intellectual state to its nadir. We are the pariahs of this world, trying very hard to restore our consciences, make peace with God and return to the family of democracies. *Mea culpas* may assuage our troubled souls, but cannot heal the tortured souls, hearts and minds of the survivors and the families of the deceased. Germany is obligated to provide spiritual and material succor to the Jews of the world. That demon Hitler defiled a great country and left a stain which cannot be erased by revisionists. Defend that if you can, Counselor."

"No further questions," Bart declared.

"Your witness, Mr. Krieger," Nimitz announced.

"No questions," Krieger dryly replied.

"Very well, General Milburn, you may call your next witness."

The next witness was called. A tall, sinewy man with salt-and-pepper-colored hair marched stride-for-stride in tempo with his MP escorts and approached the witness chair. He had a military bearing. He surprised the MP clerk by kissing the Bible before placing his hand on it to take the oath.

"State your name for the record, sir," Bart requested.

"I am the Reverend Martin Friedrich Gustav Emil Niemöller."

"Please give the court a short description of your background."

"I am fifty-one years of age. I served in the German navy as a submarine commander in the First World War. After the peace in 1918, I devoted my life to Christ. I studied theology and was ordained as a Protestant minister. I loathe war, violence and man's inhumanity to man. I became head of the Confessing Church, which opposed the practices and conduct of Hitler and his Third Reich."

"What is your present ministry?"

"I am the president of the Evangelical Church in Hesse-Nassau."

"When did you attain that position?"

"In 1947, two years after I was released from prison."

"Why were you imprisoned?"

"Adolf Hitler ordered my arrest," Niemöller answered curtly. "I was sent to a concentration camp and jailed for seven months in 1937, when the Nazi hierarchy was undermining the churches. There was a subtle undercurrent of debasing Christianity. Goebbels chose Reinhold Krause, high in the Protestant leadership in Berlin, to destroy our religion. He espoused openly the elimination of the Old Testament in church liturgy. He was discharged by Bishop Müller for having exceeded the tenets of Protestantism. A movement was about to destroy the Catholic and Lutheran religions. I spoke openly against the Nazi attempt to coordinate the Christian religious groups into a single German religion. The Nazis were brainwashing children into denying the church. As ludicrous as this must sound, Goebbels, a guileful Machiavellian propagandist, had his lackeys mount a whispering campaign among children and gullible adults that Hitler was the true Messiah. Their mantra was *Hitler will make Germany the leader of the world.* They preached Aryan supremacy. The Nazis chipped away at the Catholic Church. Religiosity was diminishing and Nazism was seeping into every household, propelled by propaganda, panoplies and militarism."

"What was the predicate of this campaign?" Bart asked.

"Firstly, they claimed that Christianity was based on the teachings of the King of the Jews, Jesus Christ, who was not an Aryan. Church attendance fell dramatically. When I was released from prison, I challenged this pagan movement. I was a lone crusader against this evil attempt to turn Germany into a godless nation."

"Did you have much support?"

"Yes, but it was a muted support. The frenzy against the Jews proved counterproductive to my efforts. Hitler exploded and wanted me executed. Wiser heads convinced him that my demise would make me a martyr. I was arrested in 1938 and served seven years in prison. I was released when Germany surrendered."

"According to prominent historians such as Professor Klaus Fischer, Martin Gilbert and William Shirer, you were revered by your following. You exposed the Nazi creation of the founding of a new religious group who called themselves the Positive Christians. Is that correct?"

"Yes. They were funded by the Nazis and insidiously spread the word that Hitler was the genuine Messiah. They demeaned Christ as a Jewish rabbi who was at odds with the orthodoxy of Judaism. They recruited spurious ministers to spread the gospel of a religion of truth, with Hitler as God's messenger. I spoke against it loudly and openly."

"While you were jailed, how did the Catholics fare?" Bart asked.

"That's history. Cardinal Eugenio Pacelli, who was appointed Papal Secretary of State, signed a concordat with Nazi Germany and the pressures eased on them. In 1939 he became Pius XII. After the war, he was severely criticized for his failure to speak out against the persecution of the Jews."

"Were you aware of the Nazi atrocities while you were in jail?"

"Only through rumors, but not to the extent of the hideous monstrosities depicted in your film."

"What was your reaction?"

"I cried and prayed to God. As a devout Christian, I cannot understand why my Christian brothers and sisters didn't revolt. As a German, I realize that Germany will bear that guilt for centuries to come. I truly believe, sir, that Chancellor Adenauer and his successors will do their best to make amends to the Jews. There are many Nazis still hidden in our country. However, the democratic government of West Germany will cooperate with the Allies in tracking them down. What you've done here with the capture of these scoundrels is hailed all over the world."

"Was Hitler the mastermind of these atrocities?"

Niemöller stared at Hitler, whose face was buried in his hands as he bent over the table. "He never visited to a concentration camp. He had delusions of becoming the second Alexander the Great, or better yet, the modern Caesar. His political power was derived from his stupid anti-Semitic diatribes. With his military victories in helpless Europe, he took over as supreme commander of the Wehrmacht. His second layer as an oligarchy took over the slaughter of Jews, Jehovah's Witnesses, Gypsies, homosexuals, the halt and the lame, with his approval. Hitler, as I judged him, is an insecure buffoon. He foolishly lost some of the best brains in executing the Jews. He is responsible for Germany being half a country. East Germany is now in the hands of the communists. If it wasn't for your Marshall Plan, we would be a bankrupt society and possibly also in the grasp of the communists. Thanks to America, West Germany is a democracy. Hopefully, we are on the road to contrition and have a sense of religious morality."

"Do you feel that the majority of the German people are in favor of reparations to the Jews?"

"I would hope so," Niemöller answered quickly.

"Would you favor your government issuing death certificates for millions of Jews slaughtered by the Nazis so that they can get their family's money as required by the Swiss banks?"

"That would be fair, but I am a man of the cloth and not a politician."

"No further questions."

Krieger took over. "Reverend Niemöller, are you a financial expert?"

"No."

"What do you know about Swiss banking?"

"I know that, in the eyes of God, the Swiss banks cooperated with Nazi Germany during the war."

"How do you know that?" Krieger challenged.

"The Allies and their intelligence agencies have validated that."

"Do you expect the Swiss banks to release monies without valid death certificates of the deceased depositors?"

"In due time, sir, you will have to release those funds. God will see to that."

"Reverend Niemöller, did the seven years you spent in jail make you a bitter man?"

"No. I had my relationship with God throughout that ordeal. Other German Christians in that jail were restored by me from the Nazi faith back to their belief in God. I am a happy man in my present occupation."

"Describe that."

"Simple. I am getting my message to the German people," he replied. "I am restoring them to faith in the Almighty and helping them with their contrition. These films will shock the good Germans back to their sanity. Is there any doubt in your mind, Counselor, that this genocide will be a catharsis for them, and you, too, if you are still a Christian. Would Christ approve the heinous crimes of Hitler's Nazis? Consult God, Mr. Krieger."

"No further questions," the Swiss lawyer said, and stalked back to his seat. Court was adjourned.

☆ ☆ ☆ ☆

Wednesday, March 18, 1953 - 0900 hours - Fort Leavenworth

Eight men and twelve women testified to their personal experiences at Chelmno, Belzec, Sobibor, Treblinka, Majdanek and Auschwitz. The survivors were composed of an eclectic group of nationalities. The only thing they had in common was their Jewish faith and heritage. Represented in the assembly line of witnesses were France, Germany, Holland, Belgium, Greece, Hungary, Czechoslovakia, Austria, Poland, Russia, Italy, English POWs, Lithuania, Latvia, Denmark, Romania, and Norway.

The horrors they described expressed personalized experiences of families being executed, raped, tortured, starved to death, hanged, and beaten to death. Each of them pointed at the commandant defendants. The defense decided not to cross-examine the witnesses. The individual heart-rending stories validated the film footage and traumatized the court - judges and spectators.

"The prosecution rests," Bart declared.

Admiral Nimitz addressed the defense. "Gentlemen, are you prepared to begin Monday morning?"

"Yes, sir," Krieger replied. "We will present Mr. Adolf Hitler, and he will defend himself."

"Are you saying that he will appear *pro per*? In other words, he will play a dual role of defendant and counsel?"

"Yes. Those are his instructions to us."

"So be it," Nimitz snapped, then gaveled adjournment.

CHAPTER SEVENTEEN

Monday, March 23, 1953 - 0900 hours - Fort Leavenworth

The media had increased in size in anticipation of the defense case and Hitler's appearance on the witness stand. There was an overflow in the courtroom. Hitler, wearing a double-breasted suit, sat at the defense table. He appeared animated. His facial color was good, and his Van Dyke beard and flowing mustache were neatly trimmed. He seemed well rested.

"Bart, I disagree with your approval of letting that monster wear that suit," Jacques bitterly muttered.

"Jacques, let the public see him the way he was. His arrogance will be destroyed when I get through with him. He's gutter-smart, despite his aberrances."

The tribunal called the court to order. "The defense may call its first witness," Nimitz directed.

Hitler marched magisterially to the witness stand. He looked at the tribunal contemptuously.

"Be advised, Mr. Hitler, that you are not obligated to appear as a witness," Nimitz declared.

"But I wish to be questioned. In German, please."

"Very well."

An MP, holding a Bible, approached the defendant in the witness stand. Speaking in German, Hitler denounced the proffered Bible for his oath. He pushed it away. The MP looked at the judges. Nimitz banged his gavel. "Listen, Mr. Hitler, don't try to make a mockery of this court."

"I prefer to be addressed as President Hitler. Also, this Bible of yours is based on the Old Testament and the New Testament, both of which are not my religions. If I don't abide by your orders, what will you do? Hold me in contempt or hang me, as you intend to do?"

"What is your religion?" Nimitz quietly asked.

"I believe my God sent me to this Earth as *Der Führer* to build a master race."

"Are you inferring that you are the true Messiah?" Nimitz asked.

Hitler, hands on hips, smiled and stated, "My followers believe that."

"All right, Herr Hitler, just raise your hand and swear to tell the truth."

He pompously sat in the witness chair, saying, "I am acting as my own *Rechtsanwalt*, lawyer, as you say. Like you say in America, Krieger tells me, I am acting *pro per*."

"All right, state your name for the record."

"President Adolf Hitler."

"President of what?" Nimitz patiently asked.

"I was the President of the Third Reich. In your country, you address former Presidents as President or former Governors and Senators by their previous titles. I demand the same respect. You may call me *Der Führer*, if you like."

"Very well, Herr Hitler, you are acting as your own lawyer, so I'll permit you to make your statement without questions being asked. Present your defense and be prepared for cross-examination after that. You will be given ample time to deliver your summation. For now, you are a defense witness."

"With permission of this court, I wish to defer my statement to my summation. At the present time I waive my right to make a statement and prefer to go directly to cross-examination by General Milburn," Hitler declared in a surprising and unprecedented turn of events. Mimicking the behavior of a king, he slowly sat down in his chair, crossed his legs, lifted his chin and arrogantly said to Bart, "You may now ask your questions, General."

Bart stood in full dress uniform with all the ribbons and medals on his broad chest. Hitler tapped his fingers on the rail of the stand. Bart decided on a pleasant approach, at odds with his instinct to viciously destroy the most evil man in the history of mankind. With great effort, he smiled at Hitler and asked if he wanted a glass of water. Hitler smiled back and nodded his head at his adversary. An MP handed a paper cup to him. The cameras were focused on the two men. The tension was palpable in the court, and was undoubtedly felt by the millions watching the trial worldwide.

"*Mein Herr*, just for the record, will you please state your true name - Nordheim, Schickelgruber, or Hitler?" Milburn queried in classic German.

"General, you cannot taunt or disconcert me with your insulting question."

"Excuse me, *mein herr*, but could you clear that up, please?"

"I am Adolf Hitler, former Chancellor, President and *Führer* of the Third Reich, the Greater German Empire, during my reign. The name Schickelgruber was my grandmother's maiden name. Nordheim was a name I used for my philanthropic activities."

"All right, we'll deal with the other two names later. But you state unequivocally that you were *Der Führer*, the leader, the dictator of the Third Reich?"

"Yes, that was the will of the people and God's will. I was sent to Germany to pull them out of the mire of despair to their deserved pride and power," he boasted.

"Are you a religious man, *Mein Herr*?"

"Not in the accepted sense of what you call Christianity or Judaism."

"You have a special God of your own?"

"Yes."

"Let's examine that. Is it not a fact that the Nazi leaders, such as Hess, Goering and that master of propaganda Goebbels, were quietly proselytizing children into a new German religion led by a specially chosen bishop? They pushed for *One Volk, one Reich, one Führer.* In other words, they recognized you as the Messiah. Isn't that true?"

"Yes, I heard that."

"Do you believe you are the German Messiah? The National Socialists are on the record as stating that Adolf Hitler was sent to them in place of Jesus Christ."

"You are misstating the facts with half-truths. Yes, there was a movement to consolidate the Catholics and the Lutherans into one church, the *Reichskirche.* But they would never compare or link me with Jesus Christ, a Jewish rabbi."

"You don't believe in the Bible, is that so?"

"General Milburn, you are an educated man. You are a lawyer. Look at the facts. The Old Testament is Jewish propaganda. The New Testament is Christian propaganda. Who was Christ? His true name was Yeshua Ben Joseph. In your language and mine, Yeshua means Joshua. The word *Christ* was a Greek word for the *anointed,* the *Messiah.* They changed the name *Joshua* into Greek, which is *Jesus.* The Christian movement began seventy years after his death, based on writings of his Jewish disciples. So Christianity was based on Judaism. My God is the real God. Not the one hatched by the Jews and their Moses, not the one devised by the Christians and their Christ, a Jewish rabbi, but the real God who sent me to reconstruct Germany and to clean up Europe."

"So, in other words, you believe you are the true Messiah?"

"Yes, and instead of a crucifixion, I will be hanged."

"Your God would make you a martyr, is that it?

Hitler jumped out of his chair and yelled, "That is the truth! My body will die, but my spirit will never leave this Earth! Maybe in the next hundred years I will be judged for the truth. I brought Germany to great heights and was betrayed by Judases for not thirty pieces of silver, but by billions in gold, by Jews, Christians, Jehovah's Witnesses, Gypsies and communists!"

"You truly believe that?"

"History will prove that. *Deutschland über alles! Sieg Heil!*"

Nimitz banged his gavel and angrily barked, "Hitler, sit down or I'll have you tied down."

"Herr Hitler, do you know the dictionary meaning of *Aryan*?" Bart asked.

"Your dictionary or mine?"

"All world dictionaries. Let me read you what it really means."

Bart went to his table and lifted a large, heavy book.

"This is Webster's Dictionary, and I quote: *Aryan - a tribal name originally*

applicable to Indo-Iranian tribes. Aryan has no validity as a racial term, al-
though it was notoriously used to mean 'a Caucasian of non-Jewish descent'. Eth-
nologists regard the use of the word in connection with race as false. If you wanted
an Aryan state, you wanted East Indians and Iranians to populate Germany."

"*Bullscheisse!*" Hitler roared.

"Your ignorance used that word instead of *Nordic.* Yet haven't you seen
Jews with blue eyes or hazel eyes and with blonde or red hair and fair com-
plexions?"

"But they are still Jews."

"Judaism is a *religion.* Christianity is a *religion.* Islam is a *religion.* None
of them are of one race. Jews are not a race. Judaism is a *religion* among
many races. Do you agree with that, Herr Hitler?"

"That is not true!"

"Why do you hate the Jews?"

"I don't hate the Jews! Edward Bloch, a Jewish doctor, cared for my mother.
They are too damned smart. They had the best jobs during our depression.
They were too educated. There were more Jews who were doctors, lawyers,
judges, and storekeepers than any segment of our population. I used my attack on them for political purposes."

"Wasn't that stupid? More than one hundred thousand of them served
with you in World War I. Twelve thousand of them were killed in that war.
Thousands of them wore Iron Crosses and other medals. They could have
been valuable to you in your Wehrmacht."

"They would have undermined my politics. They are too smart for their
own good," Hitler admitted.

"Look how Israel defeated all the Middle Eastern countries when they
were attacked."

"I don't want to talk about that."

"You were born in Braunau-am-Inn, Austria, on April 20, 1889."

"That's correct."

"You were the son of Klara Pölzl and you were the fourth child of her
marriage to Alois Hitler."

"Yes, I had a wonderful mother."

"Your father, Alois, was tough on you."

"Yes, he tried to keep me from being an artist."

"He was the illegitimate son of Maria Anna Schickelgruber, wasn't he?"

Hitler's famous gestures came into play as he roared, "You are repeating
the lies of my enemies!" He folded one arm over the other, cross-grasping his
shoulders in a defensive mode.

"He was the illegitimate son of a man named Frankenberger, a Jew, who
supported you and your mother for fourteen years. She was a cook in his house."

Hitler stood up again, hands trembling and red-faced, and angrily shook
his hands at Bart. "That is one big lie! Hans Frank wrote that book before
they hanged him at Nuremberg. I do not have Jewish blood!"

"What's wrong with Jewish blood? It's red like everybody's blood."

"Enough! No more! I do not want to talk about that!"

"All right, let's talk about your incestuous affair with your niece, Geli Raubal. She lived with you for two years before her suicide." Bart showed him her photograph inscribed, *To my dear Uncle Adolf, Geli.*

His flushed angry face faded to pale. He hung his head, staring at the picture of the beautiful girl. He remained silent. Tears rolled down the face of the notorious tyrant.

Bart obdurately pressed the witness. "She abhorred your deviant, kinky sexual practices and killed herself with your 6.5-caliber Walther pistol in a bedroom in your apartment. True or not?"

Suddenly Hitler yelled at his attorney, "Aren't you going to object to this filth?"

Krieger rose. "Members of the Tribunal, on behalf of Mr. Hitler, this nonsense about Geli Raubal is not germaine to the gravamens before this court. The defense objects to this line of questioning. I respectfully ask that all references to Miss Raubal be stricken from the record."

"Hold it one moment, counselor." The tribunal huddled.

Nimitz stated, "General Milburn, we agree with counsel's objection. The Raubal question does not pertain to the war crimes charges before this court. Please move on to another line of questioning."

Bart complied. "Adolf Hitler, when President Hindenburg named you and Franz von Papen Co-Chancellors in the coalition government on January 30, 1933, isn't it true that Goering and your gang told von Papen to yield and become Vice Chancellor or he would be killed?"

"*Nein, nein.* Papen, the aristocrat, deferred to me because he hated politics."

"On April 1 of that year, you declared a boycott on Jewish businesses and professionals. On that same day, you named Himmler commander of Bavaria's police."

"That was Goering's doing."

"Let's go to May 2, when the labor unions were destroyed and the labor leaders were arrested," Bart continued.

"Yes, they were communists."

"So on July 14, the Reichstag, which you now controlled, since the Labor Party was defunct, passed a law against all new parties being formed. That gave you all the power you needed, because on November 12, at the Reichstag elections, you garnered for the Nazi Party ninety-five percent of the votes."

"That was a popular vote," Hitler smirked.

"Going back to three days from June 30 to July 2. You ordered a purge of the SA, the storm troopers, headed by Ernst Röhm. The SS and Gestapo killed them all. You ordered Ernst Röhm killed. Why?"

"Because these street bums, under Röhm, were planning to overthrow the Nazi government. Röhm, the homosexual, wanted to kill me," Hitler huffed.

"On August 2, President Hindenburg died. You became President and Chancellor, declaring yourself the sole power by uniting both offices. In other words, that was the day you became *Der Führer*, the dictator of all Germany."

Hitler sat back in his chair and haughtily replied, "Yes, I was Germany's much-needed backbone."

"So, with total power, you began your plan to acquire all of the lands taken from Germany in the Versailles Treaty. You began campaigning for *Lebensraum,* or more territory."

"That was for land that rightfully belonged to Germany."

"Hitler, do you know what a *con man* is?"

"*Hochstapler?*"

"Right. Besides all of your so-called talents, you are a classic *Hochstapler.*"

"Are you insulting me or complimenting me?"

"You conned the world powers with your rearmament of Germany. You flexed your military muscles. So, with your threats, you got the Sudetenland into Germany. That was followed by your illegal grasp of the demilitarized Rhineland, in violation of the Versailles Treaty. The world stood still."

"General, we didn't have to fire one shot," Hitler smirked.

"On June 17th, Himmler became the most powerful man under you. He had control of the SS and became chief of all German police. Were you afraid of him?"

Hitler moved to the edge of his chair. Staring at Bart, he bared his teeth in a snarl and shouted, "Afraid? Afraid! That is a stupid question! I was *Der Führer* and the power of all Germany. I feared no one, especially not that ass-kissing, church-going *Arschloch*. He killed chickens. He raised chickens. He plucked chickens. That's how he learned how to kill Jews. I could have had him executed any time I wanted."

"That doesn't say much about your choice of hierarchies. Yet you couldn't stop him from killing Jews."

"I was too busy building Germany."

"That's a lie, Herr Hitler and you know it."

"You can *bumsen* yourself, Herr General. Reinhard Heydrich was my man, and when he was assassinated by the Jews, Himmler took over complete control."

"That's another lie," Bart said. "Heydrich, your 'protector' of Bohemia-Moravia, was killed by two Czech resistance fighters who were parachuted into Czechoslovakia by the RAF. British intelligence planned the assassination. The two men waited outside of Prague and lobbed a grenade into his Mercedes Benz convertible. He was mortally wounded and died a week later. They weren't Jews."

"What's the difference? He was one of my best men. He was to take over the SS."

"So, you admit that Heydrich was one of your best men. Were you close friends?"

"Very close."

"Hitler, you are a pathological liar and murderer."

"Stop your insults, you *Schweinehund* Yankee Boy Scout."

"That's better. I like to see the real you. Listen carefully. Heydrich and your so-called intellectuals planned the Final Solution, which was the extirpation of all the Jews in all of Europe. Himmler carried out the carnage, with your approval. You spent billions on death camps and other concentration facilities. You didn't have the guts to visit one of those camps."

"Only *you* can talk to me like that. If I had you in Germany, you would be dead in minutes for addressing me like that."

"You're an overblown street bum, a derelict who was a soapbox orator who led the scum of Germany into a band of thieves and killers. Your vaunted Nazis were *destroyed* by Boy Scouts like me. We were tougher and smarter than you. The delusion of power was a sickness of yours."

"Stop it! Stop it! I was the man who conquered all of Europe!" Hitler boasted.

"Really? England beat you in the Battle of Britain. Your invasion of Russia was stupid, and they stopped you. Then, like the idiot you are, you declared war on America, and we kicked your flatulent ass back to Berlin. Germany was in ruins."

"I was double-crossed by my high command," he whimpered.

"Your generals tried to kill you. They weren't even good assassins. You were the Commander in Chief of the Wehrmacht. You alone started the war and lost the war."

"Liar!"

"There is more. You robbed the Jews, Christians, and all the countries you invaded. You posed as Nordheim, a Jew, with $43 billion in your hands. Not bad for a street-bum émigré from Austria who took handouts from Jews in Vienna. A common street beggar who became a thug, thief, murderer, and the most evil man in the history of civilization. What say you to that?"

Hitler, foaming at the mouth, rose and shouted at the tribunal.

"I rebuilt Germany! I am *Der Führer*! Why does this court allow this general to tear me to pieces?"

Nimitz banged his gavel. Hitler kept mouthing epithets and bits and pieces of his early glories. Bart beckoned Krieger and Stolz.

"Calm him down. Tell him he'll have an opportunity to make a closing statement."

"You were very rough on him," Krieger said.

"Not as much as I would have preferred."

Krieger and Stolz escorted Hitler back to the defense table.

Jacques whispered to Bart, "Why did you stop? You were cutting him up beautifully."

"He was losing his marbles. I'm not finished with him."

Nimitz ordered a lunch break. Bart caught the eye of Sean Briscoe. He gestured with his right hand, indicating the exit door of the courtroom. Outside the courtroom, he invited Briscoe to join him for lunch in the conference room. He turned to Jacques and requested that six copies be made of the letters.

In the conference room, he introduced Sean to members of the staff who had not met him previously. He invited Sean to join him at the buffet table. Halfway through their lunch, Jacques returned with copies of the letters and handed them to Bart.

"Listen up, everyone. I have two very interesting letters here, which I do not intend to use as evidence. They are addressed to Colonel Nasser, the new head honcho in Egypt, and to Waldo Schlicht, our Swiss banking target."

All eyes peered at Briscoe, wondering why he was present.

"Oh, yes," Bart said, "I am turning the originals of these missives to our Mossad friend here for delivery to the Israeli Prime Minister."

Sean showed his surprise as he gaped at the assembly, then mumbled, "Thank you."

"Jacques, please read these letters aloud."

The contents were delivered in measured tones. Several mouths were agape, expressing shock. Others began speaking at once. They were questioning Bart for his reasons for not confronting Hitler with them at the afternoon session.

"Simply because we shouldn't let this information go public and alert Nasser, an Israeli foe, or Waldo Schlicht, whom we hope to lure out of Switzerland and have tried here for a multitude of charges-particularly for counterfeiting and possibly as an accessory in the murder of Gaines-also as a war criminal," Bart explained. "Besides, we have enough evidence of Hitler's Revenge Plan."

"General, the Mossad and all of Israel will be grateful to you."

"Sean, there is one very important caveat. Nothing in these letters or their existence can be made public until two things happen. One, not until these Nazi bums are sentenced. The other is the apprehension of Schlicht by us, your folks, the British, French, or Interpol. Savvy?"

Briscoe's brogue thickened. "I pledge my word of honor. That's the *emess*, which means *truth* in Yiddish, for you foreigners."

The tension was abated by an outburst of laughter. Bart handed the two missives to Sean, who was exhilarated by the reaction and spouted, "Israel *go Bragh*, Erin *go Bragh* and America *go Bragh!*"

More laughter.

Tony asked, "Explain?"

"That means Israel, Ireland and America forever. I am an Israeli, born and bred in Ireland and a friend of America."

The meeting was adjourned, and all returned to the court. In the defense conference room, Krieger and Stolz were in the process of mollifying an agitated Hitler.

"*Mein Führer*, the general was trying to unsettle you. He wanted you to show your temper. That's what lawyers do all the time," Krieger soothingly stated.

"Well, he's going to be surprised at how composed I'll be now that I know his game."

"*Mein Führer*, you'll have the last word in your closing speech. However, the judges will limit the time for the general's last remarks and then yours."

"That's good. I have plenty to say. I'll be my old self. I know how to play to a world audience."

☆ ☆ ☆ ☆

Monday, March 23, 1953 - 1300 hours

Hitler, escorted by MPs, jauntily marched into the courtroom, followed by his attorneys.

"He's got his second wind," Bart observed to Cartman.

"All rise," an MP clerk declared.

The tribunal entered. Hitler returned to the witness chair. His arrogant demeanor was in sharp contrast to his humiliated exit from the morning session.

Bart mused, *I'll play it his way.* It was obvious that Hitler had received a pep talk from his lawyers. *Der Führer is going to play that role,* Bart surmised, so he approached the witness with a forced smile on his face. "Herr Hitler, how are you feeling this afternoon?"

"*Wunderbar,*" was his enthusiastic answer.

"That's good. Are you prepared to clear up some open questions?"

"I have nothing to hide. I am proud of my accomplishments."

"Let us go over your record. What was the most important item on your agenda when you became *Der Führer*, the dictator of Germany?"

"Don't call me the dictator. I was the leader."

"The *all-powerful* leader, that's a fact."

"Yes, and all Germany supported me."

"The military, too?"

"Of course."

"On June 26, 1935, you ordered the conscription of all youth, ages eighteen to twenty-five," Bart continued.

"Yes, that was for labor and the military to overcome our weakened economy."

"You also quietly ordered a buildup of your armaments, such as tanks, airplanes, artillery, and assorted weapons. Why?"

"General, obviously you are not an economist. Let me explain. This created jobs and also prepared the Reich to defend itself from communist attacks. That is a simple explanation."

"Yes, very simple," Bart remarked. "In 1936, after the Olympic games, during which you removed all signs of anti-Semitism, you began putting your plans of aggression into motion."

"You have evidence of that?"

"Yes, indeed, *Mein Herr.* Let's start with your anti-communist pact with Japan on October 25. Wasn't that really a pact to get Japan to build up for a war against the United States? Japan had no desire to fight the Soviet Union."

"That's nonsense. We did that for two reasons. First, it meant trade with Japan and protection against communist Russia."

"Well, let's come back to Europe. On September 25 that year, another fascist dictator joined you for a state visit. *Il Duce*, Benito Mussolini of Italy, was wooed into what became the Axis."

"*Ja*, the Axis of Japan, Italy and Germany, purely for trade and defense. Pretty smart, eh?" Hitler gloated.

"Just a side note, how do you explain that Japan and Italy didn't join you in your anti-Semitic campaign? They were against your treatment of the Jews. Explain that."

"That was *their* choice. I told you before that I wanted the Jews to have their own country."

"Then explain why your Revenge Plan is still directed at the Israelis. You want to help the Arab nations to drive them into the sea."

Hitler's arrogance faded. He folded his arms and silently stared at Bart. After a few moments of silence, Bart said, "The Jewish people have their own country, which you just espoused. Answer my question!" he bellowed angrily.

"You shout at me? Very well, I will tell you the truth, my naïve general," Hitler responded, smirking. "The Nazi movement will grow after my body is gone from this Earth. My spirit will prevail. You believe that your capture of me and these men on trial here will stop the Nazi movement. Hitlerism will survive your onslaughts and will grow throughout the world. The seeds are planted. Communist Russia will destroy itself. Your American two-party system will disintegrate in the next hundred years. Your country is a nation of immigrants. All ethnic groups are at odds with each other. The organized so-called monotheistic religions will kill each other, like they are doing now in Northern Ireland. The Muslims, like the Sunnis and Shiites, are killing each other now. Soon there will be chaos in the Far East, with China, Japan, India, Indo-China, Pakistan, and so on. Then you'll have another big depression like we had in the Thirties. The next world war will cause revolutions the world over. Ethnic, religious, the industrial and banking set will be at each other's throats. The Israelis will try to stop the rise of the Nazi movement. So I hope the Arabs drive them into the sea. The Nazis will rise again in Germany and we'll drive the Arabs into the sea. After that, Nazi Germany will control the oil and the nuclear weapons. The Jewish *diaspora* will be hunted down throughout the world. That is my prophecy. You can write this down in your archives. *Sieg Heil!" Der Führer* shouted as his arm was extended in a Nazi salute.

"Thank you for your very frank revelations of the real *Führer*. That explains your inexorable drive to control all of Europe. Maybe the world, after that."

"Why you say that?"

"After your alliance with Mussolini, you annexed Austria on March 12, 1938. Then came the Munich conference, where you were appeased by Chamberlain and Daladier in your takeover of the Sudetenland, part of Czechoslovakia."

"Without a shot fired," Hitler boasted.

"Then came Kristallnacht, the first outright act of violence against the Jews. You winked your approval of that anti-Semitic pogrom on November 8th."

"That was Goebbels' propaganda campaign idea."

"You were *Der Führer*. You approved it. Germany went berserk killing Jews, burning synagogues, and sending thousands to concentration camps," Bart said.

"I was busy and didn't realize the extent of the riots."

"Don't lie now. Your hoodlums killed and looted all over Germany."

"Not *hoodlums;* the German *people* were venting their frustrations."

"Come on, Hitler, a minute ago you were the real *Führer* with your prophecy. Let me present you with a quick review of your actions that led us to Armageddon. You completed your military alliance with Italy on April 22nd. On August 23rd, you cut up Poland with the Russians and signed a non-aggression pact with the Soviets. Eight days later your Wehrmacht invaded

Poland. You expected France and Britain to appease you."

"Chamberlain and Daladier surprised me. I realized it was Churchill who forced them to declare war on us, two days later. I didn't want war with Britain. Their people, especially the royal family, were very much like us. The King was related to German royalty," Hitler explained.

"But, with your two-week victory over Poland, you named Reinhard Heydrich head of your terror mechanism, the SD, the Security Service, thus beginning a war on the unarmed Jews in Germany and especially against Poland's three and a half million Jews."

"*Ach*, we were only planning to move them out of Europe."

"Come on, Adolf, you killed more than two million Jews at Auschwitz alone."

"No, no, that happened after Heydrich was assassinated and Himmler took over the control of the SS, the Gestapo, and all German police."

"Why didn't you stop him?"

"Because, I told you, I was busy running the war."

"Adolf Hitler, your ego made you feel you were infallible, so on April 9, 1940, you invaded Denmark and Norway. One month later, on May 10, you invaded Holland, Belgium, Luxembourg, and France. France signed an armistice on June 22nd. Vichy France helped your SS and Gestapo round up Jews. How much *Lebensraum* did you want?"

"I was going to purify Europe," Hitler boasted sanctimoniously.

"You gave Mussolini the go-ahead on October 21st to invade Greece. He didn't do too well, so you invaded Yugoslavia and Greece on April 6, 1941."

Hitler leaned forward and pointed at Bart. "Not bad, General. This was the new greater Germany. I was the Commander-in-Chief."

"You believed you were a military genius. You had delusions of outdoing the Roman Empire."

"Not delusions - *reality*. "

"Well, let's see how great you were. What was Operation Barbarossa?"

Hitler bit his lip, sat back in his chair and asked for a glass of water. He gulped it down and stared at Bart.

"Come on, Adolf. Do you not remember the invasion of the Soviet Union on June 22, 1941? You gave orders weeks before to kill all communist leaders and their aides. *Barbarossa*, an interesting word, named after Frederick the First, a German King who became ruler of the Roman Empire."

"Just a code name."

"You created a killing machine called the *Einsatzgruppen* to follow your conquering army to kill Jews, Gypsies, the old, the weak, and children. And they slaughtered in great numbers as you rolled on to the outskirts of Moscow. Murder meant nothing to you."

"How you say, *All's fair in love and war.* I have no love for communists, and in war, I believe nothing is sacred."

"You commanded your army to turn away from Moscow and attack Stalingrad. That was the beginning of the end for you. Your 6th Army surrendered at Stalingrad in January 1943."

"My stupid generals blundered."

"Let's go back a little. Your Japanese partner made a sneak attack on Pearl Harbor on December 7, 1941. Four days later, with your troops fighting the British in North Africa and your war with the Soviets, explain why you declared war on the United States."

"Because Japan was my ally and the Americans were supplying planes, tanks and ships to Britain," Hitler answered.

"As Admiral Yamamoto said after Pearl Harbor, *We awakened a sleeping giant.* The Americans helped kick your Afrika Korps out of Africa. While all that was going on, you were spending billions, using valuable manpower, expanding the rail lines in Poland to the concentration camps and killing six million of the nine million Jews in Europe. Military men around the world called you stupid and a cold-blooded murderer."

"They'll eat those words," he vowed.

"Where? Over your grave?"

"The Nazi movement will never die!" Hitler screamed.

"Relax, we have a little more to talk about. Your friend Mussolini was defeated, so you moved into Italy. The new government in Italy declared war on Nazi Germany. The pieces were falling apart."

"Italy was not that important to us."

"Now comes something that was *very* important to you. On June 6, 1944, while you were fast asleep and your generals were afraid to wake you up, the Allied invasion took place at Normandy. You told your commander to guard Calais. You were wrong. Explain that."

"My stupid generals had been fooled."

"Meanwhile, as the Americans and British were driving your troops back from the west, the Soviets were pounding you from the east. Himmler was using your trains to transport harmless, innocent Jews to their slaughter. Where was your genius?"

"You're mocking me."

"By that time, you had to draft all men from ages sixteen to sixty. Your losses were tremendous, while you were shooting your V2 rockets at London. The Americans and British were bombing your beautiful cities, but you didn't care for the welfare of the German people."

"They were very loyal to me."

"Yes, while they died and you kept killing Jews, Christians, Gypsies, the sick, and the helpless, and you were losing the war at the same time. That's history."

"We'll rise again," Hitler asserted.

"During your last days in the bunker beneath the chancellery, you married Eva Braun, said goodbye to everyone, telling them you were going to commit suicide. The Russians were half a mile away, with their artillery pounding Berlin."

"Yes, I didn't want the communist bastards to do to me what happened to Mussolini."

"So Bormann helped you escape with your stolen billions in Swiss banks, and an American plastic surgeon changed your face in Malmo, Sweden. Then you had him killed."

"I didn't order that; Hugo Schultz did that."

A voice from the group of defendants shouted, "Hitler, you are a diseased rat! *Der Führer* is an Austrian rat!"

Two Military Policemen slapped duct tape over Hugo Schultz's mouth.

"Do you hear what your loyal commandant called you?"

"He's a piece of *Scheisse.*"

"You became the richest man in the world with the money stolen from the fillings in the mouths of Jews, their possessions, and the plunder from twenty countries in Europe. And to cap all your chicanery, you posed as Frederick Avram Nordheim, a Jew, with concentration-camp numbers tattooed on your arm. Here you are on trial for your life at the age of sixty-three in an American military base. Are you sorry you escaped from the bunker?"

"No, because I have been able to reorganize my Nazi followers all over the world."

"You are truly an insecure man, Adolf Hitler. If it were in my power, I would ship you to Israel. They would give you the royal treatment."

Before an irate Hitler could reply or Nimitz could gavel, Bart declared, "No further questions."

Nimitz gaveled. "Court is adjourned until tomorrow morning at 0900 hours."

Hitler tried to attack Bart when he rose from his chair, but an MP tripped him and he went sprawling to the floor.

☆ ☆ ☆ ☆

Tuesday, March 24, 1953 - 0900 hours - Fort Leavenworth

The courtroom was buzzing. Spectators crowded in, anticipating the closing arguments to be presented by the prosecution and the defense. At 9 a.m. the tribunal entered the courtroom and took their seats. Nimitz gaveled the court to order.

"General Milburn, you may present your closing statement."

Barton rose from his seat. He adjusted his uniform and walked directly to the open floor of the courtroom.

"Honorable members of this tribunal, I will try to be as brief as possible. This indeed is an historic moment. The accused, Adolf Hitler, has the distinction of being the most evil creature in the total history of mankind. He created the carnage of the Holocaust. Were this a civil court, he would be charged with six million counts of calculated individual murders, millions more counts of mayhem, robbery, slave labor, and torture of the most bestial savagery. His crimes defy the hallucinations of the most demented of men. His rabid behavior is somewhat of an oxymoron in that his megalomania flourished with the seeding by his Svengali propagandist, Joseph Goebbels, a calculated death spoor undertaken as a political ploy. Out of a population of fifty million Germans, there were only four hundred ninety thousand Jews in Germany. This derelict, jailbird, and draft-dodging Austrian, with the deviousness of a gutter rat, produced a book titled *Mein Kampf,* with the help of Rudolf Hess, Emil Maurice, Gottfried Feder and Alfred Rosenberg, in a jailhouse. If the world had eschewed its complacency, this outcast might have become a lowly laborer or the street bum he was originally.

"Born in 1889, he fumbled his way to Germany, which was in the throes of a depression, a defeated nation in World War I, suffering from the draconian Versailles peace treaty. Anti-Semitism was the watchword of a nascent, puny political party called the National Socialist Workers Party, NSDAP soon named the Nazi Party. Three members drafted the anti-Semitic aims of the party. Hitler, number seven in the hierarchy of the rabble of misfits, made his mark in the cellar of a Munich saloon. He silver-tongued the gathering of sluggards with the mantra *Get rid of the Jews!* It struck a chord with the dregs of German society.

"Thugs, rabble, misfits and lowlifes harkened to this Pied Piper of an imminent cosmic cataclysm. Within a year, this Machiavellian, gutter-smart, duplicitous war criminal attracted his own followers to gain control of the party. Thus began his misbegotten messianic rise to power. With an assortment of street hoodlums, he formed the *Sturmabteilung,* known as the SA, the storm troopers. These gangsters multiplied and formed the nucleus of his power, pillaging, raping, and spreading fear not only to Jews but to the general populace.

"Over the years, beginning in January 1933, he strong-armed a doddering President Hindenburg after an election that didn't give him a plurality. He was to share the chancellorship with Franz von Papen. He euchred Papen, by threats, into accepting a Vice Presidency of the Cabinet. Suffice it to say that he broke every tenet of the Versailles Treaty. He threatened Europe with bellicose speeches demanding *Lebensraum*, or more territory for existence. Europe's weakened governments, led by England's Prime Minister Chamberlain, appeased this monster. Finally, having already acquired Czechoslovakia, Austria, the Sudetenland and Danzig, on September 1, 1939, he wantonly, deliberately, and without provocation, attacked with ferocity the helpless nation of Poland, starting an aggressive World War II. He conquered most of Europe with the exception of England, Russia, Sweden, Spain, and Switzerland. Besides fighting on five fronts, he viciously and stupidly extirpated six million Jews plus millions of Christians, the weak, the elderly, women and children.

"Black Tuesday ignited it all," Bart Milburn continued. "On October 29, 1929 - eleven years after the end of World War I-the New York Stock Market crashed. It was the precursor of a worldwide depression. Millions were unemployed. People were selling apples on the streets. Men were asking passersby, 'Brother, can you spare a dime?' Suicides were at an all-time high. Soup kitchens expanded throughout America. Peddlers were operating throughout the country. Hunger was the common enemy. Prices tumbled. President Roosevelt gave us a mantra: *The only thing we have to fear is fear itself.* However, the conditions brought about a spirit of introversion. It was every man for himself. Personal survival was the order of the day. Foreign policy was a quiescent entity in a government struggling to energize the economy, while Roosevelt and Congress wrestled with the depression.

"On the other side of the Atlantic, while all the democracies were beset with the problems of the world depression, Adolf Hitler, an Austrian derelict, emigrated to Germany. With a soapbox oratorical talent, he seized on the depression as an opportunity to arouse the German people. He pandered to the dregs of humanity. Unemployment had risen to five and a half million, so this was his audience. He rose through the body politic of Germany, and when Hindenburg died in August 1934 this Austrian émigré took over complete power. He became *Der Führer*, Adolf Hitler, the most powerful dictator in the world.

"Introversion metamorphosed into complacency and apathy throughout the U.S. and Europe. Foreign policy leaders among the democracies waffled as this demonic despot quietly built up a war machine. American industries helped him. Swiss banks financed him. Britain and France appeased him as he demanded and received large pieces of European real estate. He marched into the Rhineland in 1936. He paid no attention to the draconian Versailles Treaty signed in 1918, with Germany's surrender in World War I. Then he proclaimed his war against the Jews. He took over Austria on March 12, 1938, signed a non-aggression pact with the Soviet Union and then invaded Czechoslovakia on March 14, 1939. He began a murder spree immediately after his invasion of Poland on September 1, 1939. Two days later France and England declared war on Germany, thus beginning the apocalypse of World War II.

"A study of the makeup of the hierarchy of the Third Reich, a gang of degenerates, leads one to a conclusion that defies all reason: Hitler, an Austrian failed painter, homeless street bum, and incestuous jailbird; Himmler, a chicken farmer; Goering, a postal clerk who became a flying ace in World War I; Goebbels, a crippled, dwarfish individual, who was university-educated; Hess, born in Egypt, the son of a German merchant, a college dropout and fervent anti-Semite. How did this rabble jell into a power structure that conquered half the world? They launched a campaign for a pure Aryan nation. The Western world was consumed with the threat of communism. Adolf Hitler, this bizarre little Austrian émigré, with his feral cunningness, rabble-roused Germany into an anti-Semitic frenzy. He took a page from Martin Luther and disgorged his hate virus into the Christian psyche of Germany. Luther, in the years prior to 1523, sought Jewish support for his new interpretation of the Bible and his rejection of Roman Catholic papacy claims. He was ignored by the Judaic community, and in 1526 issued a pamphlet, *Jesus Christus ein geborener Jude sei*, maintaining that there was no reason why they should not recognize Christ. The Jews avowed that the Talmud had a better interpretation of the Bible than did Luther. In 1543 he turned on them in rage, with another pamphlet, *Von den Juden und ihren Lügen,* on the Jews and their alleged lies. Savants term it the first thrust of modern anti-Semitism. He espoused a campaign of vandalism to burn synagogues, smash Jewish homes, burn their prayer books and draft them into forced labor. And that was the blueprint that this atheistic Hitler needed as a galvanizing cause for a dissolute society to loot, burn, and eventually kill Jews. Dissenters vanished. This heinous psychopath Hitler and his depraved minions amorally dispensed unspeakable tortures and death to millions, as though it was a palliative to a depression-ridden Christian Germany. These malevolent Nazis are but a minuscule part of the millions of Nazis who perpetrated crimes which have baffled criminologists, psychiatrists, psychologists, historians, and politicians. The scope of these war crimes is beyond measurement. Each and every murder needs to be judged. Each and every crime must be judged.

"The Nuremberg trials, prosecuted by Supreme Court Justice Jackson and followed by General Telford Taylor, did not get the world attention they deserved. In this trial, Nazism has been exposed to the world. What other aberration will arise in the guise of Nazism in the next millennium, or is it lurking here on this planet now?" Bart said for effect.

"To this day, in an enlightened 20th century, the horrors of their massive genocide defy all logical comprehension. The German people denied all knowledge of the Holocaust. There are hatemongers scattered around the world denying it ever took place.

"The inhumanity of man in all its aspects has been codified in our archives. The evidence presented here would take thousands of books to describe each individual victim's personal account of the terror tableaux. Himmler, sirs, became the major arbiter of death for the innocents. Hitler demonically blitzkrieged, to coin a word, his way through Europe using his young men as cannon fodder, while the SS rounded up Jews, the lame and halt in conquered countries for extirpation. Yes, sirs, without intent to offend, I must say that the so-called *civilized* nations' hands were not clean when it came to accepting migrating Jews after the infamous *Kristallnacht*, when Nazi hoodlums went berserk looting, destroying and burning everything Jewish. We Americans can't be too proud of turning away the German ship SS St. Louis, carrying over a thousand emigrating German Jews. England, France, and America do not have clean hands in this catastrophe, even though England did help the St. Louis émigrés, sharing haven for them with Holland, Belgium and Denmark after they were turned back by Cuba and the United States.

"It is clear that the draconian terms of the Versailles Treaty, a worldwide depression and runaway inflation in Germany and a doddering, senile President of the Weimar Republic, Field Marshal von Hindenburg, were the ingredients seized by these ruthless thugs to gain power. Some called Hitler a genius. If he was a genius, why did he invade Russia when he did? Why declare war on the U.S.? Why did he lead Germany to its destruction? Only the Marshall Plan is resuscitating that country from its death throes. He was a great bluffer who hoodwinked England and France into appeasement. A little bit of armed resistance could have prevented World War II. If there is a third world war in this atomic age, it will result in the end of civilization as we know it. Complacency is the devil's handiwork. Beware of *amour propre*. To quote John Philpot Curran, *The condition upon which God hath given liberty to man is eternal vigilance*. The fate of these monsters is now in your hands," Bart concluded.

"We will now hear the summation of the defense," Nimitz declared.

Hitler rose. He stared contemptuously at Bart as they passed each other.

"I will speak in my native tongue," he declared in German. Fully aware that he was about to address a world audience, Hitler turned to the press rows and extended his arm in the Nazi salute. Spectators booed. Nimitz gaveled. The deposed despot sneered. Hitler, with all of his typical mannerisms and gestures of his halcyon days, turned to the judges. "To the distinguished members of this tribunal, I thank you for your courtesy. Now, I am pleased to set the record straight and to clarify the misinformation that the prosecution has presented to this court.

"I have been pictured as a devil, a monster, a murderer, a beast, a torturer, a draft dodger, a barbarian and many other things. Let me set the record straight. I served Germany as a soldier in the First World War with distinction. I was wounded and was awarded an Iron Cross. History will tell you that Austria was part of Germany from 1215 to 1918. That despicable Versailles and the Treaty of Saint-Germain reduced Austria to a small country deprived of everything. In 1938 I brought it back to Germany. I've been called an Austrian immigrant, yet Germany elected me Chancellor, President and the *Führer*.

"I stand here proud of my accomplishments. Poland is responsible for killing our people at the border. I struck back defensively with our *Wehrmacht*. England and France stupidly declared war against Germany. We had to defend ourselves.

"Now, let's look back and study what happened to Germany after the Versailles Treaty. That was the fuse that burned slowly from 1918 to 1939. Germany suffered through a terrible depression and inflation. The country was bankrupt under the Weimar Republic. Germany became a second-rate country. Germany was a nation of supplicants who were jobless, hungry and depressed. I was sent on a mission of restoring my country to its former glory and beyond. I made it a world power and restored their pride.

I have been accused here of being responsible for what you call the Holocaust. That is a big lie. I never ordered the killing of the Jews. I was commander of our forces fighting a war against the communist Soviet Union. Himmler was crazy, killing the Jews. I wanted the Jews out of Germany and Europe. I wanted them to have their own country in Africa or the island of Madagascar."

Hitler ranted on, denying culpability for World War II and the extermination of Jews, Christian dissenters, Jehovah's Witnesses and Gypsies, and the responsibility for the war. The Western world was the villain.

Suddenly his modulated delivery turned into the familiar Hitlerian rhetoric and style he used in pre-war Germany, when rabble-rousing was his forte. "The crimes were committed by the British, the French, the Americans and, particularly, the Soviet Union. Let us look back at the last two decades. In 1918 the Allied powers reduced Germany to a sick, rudderless nation sailing on a sea of despair. The Weimar Republic had a huge debt and reparations. People were hungry and homeless, suffering through a depression and runaway inflation. Eleven years after your great victory, America had its Black Tuesday, when your stock market crumbled and triggered a world depression. It had a profound effect on Germany.

"A year later, my National Socialist Party, the Nazis, got six and a half million votes in the elections. We placed one hundred seven deputies in the

Reichstag. Germany had six years of unemployment. Yet the Jews had more jobs and professions. Doctors, lawyers, storekeepers, teachers, college professors and other occupations had Jewish percentages higher than those of the average German. I used that as a political battle cry and ran for President against Hindenburg, who barely beat me in two elections. In our next election, the Nazi Party garnered almost fourteen million votes with two hundred thirty deputies; that made my NSDAP Party the leading party in Germany. In January 1933 I was named Chancellor of Germany, which actually gave me control. I put a staff together to straighten out our economy. A little over a year later, Hindenburg died, so I became the full head of state. They called me *Der Führer*.

"My staff, sort of an oligarchy, began carrying out my campaign promises. I devoted myself to foreign affairs. Yes, I wanted an Aryan society. Half the Jews in Germany emigrated. I never ordered them killed."

Hitler began to shout and spittle sprayed from his mouth. "I didn't order them killed! That maniac Himmler did that while I was running the war!"

Then he began to ramble. "At the Evian conference of thirty-two countries, we tried to get the world to accept the Jews. They took less than one hundred fifty thousand and then set low quotas. Even your great President *Roosenvelt* turned his back on the Jews. We sent the SS St. Louis with twelve hundred Jews to Cuba. They turned them away. They went to Florida in America and *Roosenvelt* turned them away," Hitler sneered.

"I didn't want war with England and France. They declared war on Germany and it got out of hand. Our enemy was communist Russia, which is now in a Cold War with America, England and France. I am not guilty of the Holocaust. You have already tried those German traitors, Goering and Himmler. They were behind the Holocaust. I have made contributions to Israel. Now I am a philanthropist. Why I was kidnapped and put on trial here is a crime. I have been treated as a common criminal.

"Just one more thing. I tried to make peace with England after we defeated France. If that Jew-lover Churchill had agreed, my Wehrmacht would have destroyed the Soviet Union. I was also betrayed by my high command. They did not carry out my orders.

"My last statement is a warning to the world. The Nazi movement is not dead. The evil is communism. You will hang me and I will be a martyr. America, at this moment, is the most powerful country in the world. Look back at the Roman Empire and its rise and fall. How long will the American empire last? You're a nation of immigrants. There is a quiet hatred among your disparate population. The Aryans of this world will rise up against you with the help of the Asians and the Muslims. The Nazi movement by any other name will prevail. *Sieg Heil!*" he screamed, putting his arm forward in the Nazi salute. The photographers zoomed in on the raging ex-dictator. Perspiration and saliva streamed down his face. Slowly and deliberately, he took his seat. Shock was evident on the faces of the courtroom spectators and even the press.

"We will recess for lunch until 1300 hours," Nimitz declared, and he slammed the gavel down hard.

CHAPTER EIGHTEEN

Wednesday, March 25, 1953 - 1300 hours

The tribunal gaveled the court to order. Baron von Wolf rose and addressed the court. "Honorable Judges, this trial has indicated, beyond a doubt that all of the prisoners were subservient to Adolf Hitler, *Der Führer* of the Third Reich. With the court's permission, I wish to file written individual statements prepared by all the defendants, excepting Adolf Hitler and Martin Bormann."

"Objection," Bart exclaimed.

"With the court's permission, before you rule on General Milburn's objection, if I am allowed to continue, I am certain the prosecutor will withdraw his objection."

"Proceed, Mr. Wolf," Nimitz said.

"I wish to enter a change of plea for each and every one of my soldier defendants."

"Let's hear it," Nimitz responded.

"All plead *nolo contendere* and wish to place themselves on the mercy of this tribunal."

The surprise plea evoked a gasp from spectators. The prosecution huddled for a minute.

"What say you, General Milburn?" Nimitz asked.

"This is a plea of no contest, Herr Wolf? Is that your plea?" Bart asked.

"Yes, General."

"Understood. Your Honors, no objection."

"Very well, Counsel, let the record so state," Nimitz ordered. "Court is adjourned and will convene on Monday, March 30, at 0900 hours. For the record, the tribunal will meet with the other two tribunals, which have been in session simultaneously with these proceedings. On Monday we will sit *en banc*, all nine members of the triers of fact, to pronounce the sentencing of all prisoners."

Nimitz gaveled. The press raced for the doors.

As Bart was gathering his things, he waved Jacques over to the prosecution table.

"Jacques, get Sean Briscoe and join me in the conference room."

"You got it."

☆ ☆ ☆ ☆

Prosecution conference room - moments later

As the team gathered, Bart, Jacques and Briscoe huddled at the back of the room.

"Sean, I want you to arrange a covert way to move the Cobra to Israel. Ariel Rubin will be very pleased," Bart said.

"Bart, you can bet on that."

"Never mind betting on anything. Come up with a plan to get him to Israel."

"How soon can we have him?"

"As fast as you can come up with a plausible plan."

"I'll be back at you as soon as I talk to our guys at the Mossad."

"Get going, pal."

Sean raced to his special public phone booth outside the gate of the fort.

"Bart, we'll have to deliver the Cobra to a convenient airport for the pickup," Jacques said.

"Those Mossad boys are great at these schemes. Let's see what they come up with. Now let's get down to business," Bart ordered.

The team gathered at the long table, sipping coffee and nibbling on cookies.

"Well, my friends, the show is over. Now we come to the nitty-gritty. The tribunal will undoubtedly sentence quite a few to executions, others to prison sentences. Their problem with our input is where to hang them and imprison the others."

A spirited conversation began. Ideas were plentiful. Each suggestion was pitched, and some were batted down. New ideas were discussed.

"Hold it, everyone. I've got to crawl through the D.C. minefield in anticipation of the tribunal's decision. I'll be on the horn in the a.m. After that, we can discuss the ground rules," Bart said.

"Right on, General," Cartman shouted.

"All right, gang, scat and relax."

☆ ☆ ☆ ☆

Late that afternoon Jacques was walking through the corridor leading to the conference room, carrying a briefcase full of papers. Suddenly, Sean Briscoe yelled from the dark end of the passage. "Jacques, hold it one minute!"

"What's up, my Irish *landsmann?*"

"Where's Bart?"

"Why?"

"I've got it worked out to take the Cobra off your hands."

"Come with me."

Jacques poked open the door of the conference room. Bart was deep into reading the files. He looked up. Jacques beckoned him with his right forefinger. He stepped into the hall.

"What's up, Sean?"

"We have chartered a small plane. If you clear it for us to land at Sherman Field in the morning, we'll take him to the Kansas City airport and board an unmarked El Al plane to Tel Aviv. Do you approve? There's a heavy storm headed this way, Friday or Saturday."

"No good, Sean. Do it my way. A large sedan with you, the Cobra and three armed MPs will take you to the Kansas City airport."

"That's much better. I hadn't counted on an armed escort," Sean agreed.

"Now, on your El Al, will you have some guards?"

"Yes, indeed. Four of our toughest commandos. They served with the British army in the Jewish brigade during the pincer toward the Nazis with the Russians in the war. One phone call and I'll cancel the small plane."

Bart lit a cigarette and paced the hall for a few minutes.

"Sean, my friend, surprise is an important factor in a situation like this. Is the El Al plane at the airport now?"

"Yes."

"Can you reach them now?"

"The crew and the guards are at the airport hotel."

"Okay, here's the scenario. In the next hour or two, depending on how soon you're ready, we can get organized to take him out of here. He'll be gone before anyone gets wind of his disappearance. Come into my office here and make your calls on a safe phone."

Sean made his calls while Bart lined up a car and three husky Military Policemen. Ninety minutes later, Abdul "the Cobra" was on his way to Kansas City. Within hours, the shackled terrorist was en route to Israel.

☆ ☆ ☆ ☆

Thursday, March 26, 1953 - 1150 hours - Washington

General Omar Bradley returned Bart's call. "Barton, I've spoken to Ike, Attorney General Brownell, Secretary of Defense Wilson, the Joint Chiefs and the director of the Bureau of Prisons. The consensus is as follows."

"Go ahead, sir, I'll make notes."

"Does Attu island in the Aleutians have the facilities to house these rascals?"

"Eisenhower approved the plan after Admiral Prince said he can quickly erect barracks if funds are approved. Ike asked Wilson to take it out of his budget. Your buddy, Senator Bridges, will undoubtedly go along on the appropriations committee."

"Sir, this is a cold, windy and wet facility. Who will be in charge there?" Bart asked.

"Captain Roger Blake is in charge there now, but we will rotate rear admirals every six months. That area is worse than the worst weather at any of the concentration camps. The prisoners will work their butts off just to stay warm."

"Sir, I would remind you that Hitler's Revenge Plan may still be a threat. Attu should be well armed, in case an attack is attempted."

"Barton, my boy, they are on constant alert there against their Soviet neighbor. We'll beef up the defense."

"Good plan, sir. I assume you'll be talking with Nimitz soon?"

"Count on it. Good luck."

☆ ☆ ☆ ☆

March 28, 1953 - Fort Leavenworth

Strong winds delivered a heavy snowstorm as the prosecution and defense lawyers prepared pre-sentencing comments required by the tribunals. The prosecution team worked late into the night, completing their work at 0400 hours the next morning. Bart thanked his colleagues, then all hastened to their quarters, fighting the raging storm.

Bart and Jacques skipped their showers and retired to their rooms. Bart fell into a deep sleep. Three hours later, the jarring sound of the telephone pierced Jacques' restless sleep. Sleepily he answered, "Yes?"

"This is Colonel Williams. General Bradley wishes to speak with General Milburn."

The message brought Jacques to his senses. "One moment, sir. I'll transfer your call." He raced into Bart's room. "Bart, wake up. Bradley is on the line."

A somnolent Bart tried to fight off the intrusion. After several taps on his head, he absorbed the message, hurried to the bathroom and splashed his face with cold water. He picked up the phone. "This is General Milburn."

"Bart, I hope I didn't wake you up."

"Sir, if you want an honest answer, it is yes."

"Sorry about that. Do you have a pencil and paper?"

"Yes, sir."

"I spoke with Nimitz. I will repeat what I told him. President Eisenhower will sign death warrants with the names to be provided by the tribunal. As to those receiving prison sentences, that's my jurisdiction. They are to be sent to Attu Naval Base in the Aleutian Islands for hard labor. Those that the tribunal decides to send back to Germany for incarceration are herewith approved. The executions are to be conducted at the Leavenworth Federal Prison. Attorney General Brownell will notify Warden Wilson this morning. An Army photographer may film the executions. Still shots also by an Army photographer. Hand-picked members of the major media and a small pool of the secondary press will be allowed to watch. Witnesses to the executions will be composed of Army, Navy, Air Force and Marine personnel. As to civilian witnesses, prioritize survivors and clergy, if requested. Official reps of the Allied countries as well. Got it?"

"Yes, sir."

"Any problems, call me at the office at any time."

"Thank you, sir."

Bart and Jacques returned to their respective beds. Later that afternoon, Bart called Warden Wilson at the Leavenworth Federal Prison.

"General, I've been following your trial; great job. I've been briefed by the Attorney General. I am at your disposal."

"How about joining me for lunch here tomorrow at the Fort with General Fielding and Jacques Laurent, head of the Nazi desk at the CIA?"

"That's fine. I'd like to bring Liam Mahoney, our principal keeper."

"Okay. I'll see you at 12:30, my place. The provost marshal will have you escorted here. Steak and french fries."

"Perfect."

☆ ☆ ☆ ☆

Sunday, March 29, 1953 - Bart's Victorian quarters

The storm had abated, and a bright sun had turned the snow into slush. A sergeant drove the two prison officials to the Victorian house. Bart greeted the two husky ex-Marines. Warden Wilson and principal keeper Mahoney were friends of the lady of the house. Mrs. Lawrence and the two sergeants gave them a warm welcome. They kissed her.

Jacques was introduced. General Fielding greeted them. Jacques prepared martinis. Lunch was served and war experiences were exchanged. After lunch, they adjourned to the den and discussed the specifics of the executions.

"General, based on the national, or rather the international, interests, we are going to require some heavy security. I am basing that on the recent demonstration at the fort," Wilson said.

"Bart, he's right," Jacques agreed.

"We'll surround your prison with as many men as required," Fielding said.

"On the safe side, we'll need five hundred to a thousand men to surround the prison, plus local police directing traffic," Mahoney declared.

"I'll take care of the police, plus MPs added to their limited staff," Fielding said.

"General, we haven't had a hanging here since 1936. However, we can recruit some men from the Kansas State Penitentiary in Lansing, just south of here. They have the hanging expertise and will be backed up by our Military Police. We can handle it. I've seen a couple of executions there."

"Very good," Fielding responded.

"One more suggestion, sir - as soon as the sentences are handed down, let us house the condemned men in a death row," Wilson added.

"Good deal," Bart replied. "I'll fill you in later on the number of witnesses. You know all the other rules described by the Attorney General. That's your turf, Warden. We'll help in every way."

"Have we covered everything?" Wilson asked.

"A couple more gruesome items. Should there be forty or fifty hangings, can you do ten at a time?"

"With some carpenter help from the fort, we can erect a fifty-foot-long scaffold holding ten traps in a few days. Now, one of your engineers can compute the support beams needed to support the weight on the hanging platform. Say, ten men averaging two hundred pounds backed up by a guard behind each to be hanged - let's agree on two tons. Add to that five or more chaplains, three officials, that would be a possible ton. Doctors will be below to examine the men to pronounce them dead. Our hanging procedure will be based on military codes."

"Clyde, I would prefer that we use Military Police to place the hoods on the inmates and place them on the traps," Fielding said. "The Lansing men can guide us."

"No problem, General. However, we should have a run-through with them two days prior to the event. We use the standard military chart for hanging. A rehearsal is necessary. We use manila hemp ropes of one inch in diameter and approximately thirty feet in length, soaked and stretched to dry to prevent any spring, stiffness or tendency to coil."

"I am certain, Warden, that the Lansing people are experienced in that procedure, and we have some men who are knowledgeable in that process. However, you will undoubtedly have doctors examine the condemned?"

"General, we will observe all the necessary rules and precautions. We check their bodies for obesity, bone deterioration, body structure, height and weight. This is routine."

"Fine, do all by the book. Handle the noose, ligatures for hands and feet. Our MPs will do the rest. Have enough hoods and boards, in case any of them collapse. Clyde, we respect the fact that this is your turf and you're in charge. Colonel Jeremiah Brown will be in charge of Army personnel. He'll cooperate with you."

"I know the colonel. We have sipped a few together."

"Tea, I'm sure," Fielding laughed.

"Here's the last ghastly detail," Bart interjected, then lit a cigarette and took a long drag before continuing. "The Nazi virus is virulent and continues to incubate in the hearts and minds of closet haters worldwide. To avoid shrines to these pseudo-martyrs, particularly Hitler, none of these miscreants is to be buried or have their bodies turned over to families or claimants of any kind."

After a short pause, Warden Wilson asked, "Then what do we do with the remains, General Milburn?"

Bart puffed on his cigarette, emitted a cloud of smoke and replied, "As soon as the condemned are pronounced dead, I want the bodies cremated, with their ashes dumped in a garbage can. When all the hangings are completed, fill that garbage container with the ashes of all those executed."

The group was momentarily stunned. Bart's mien was austere. There was no doubt of his well-thought-out demand.

"Is there a crematorium in this area?" Fielding asked.

Warden Wilson turned to Liam Mahoney and whispered in his ear, then faced Bart and declared, "You're a man of your convictions. I agree with your rationale, sir. We have a foundry here and will accommodate your request. What do we do with the ashes?"

"First, the crematoriums are to be handled by your most trusted men. Not a leak of this procedure is to be countenanced. If you prefer, we can assign the military to handle it. An alternative is to pack the ashes in the garbage can and we'll dispose of them in our own way."

"Liam Mahoney here and I, with the help of a few of our special forces, can handle it and ensure the secret," the warden pledged.

"In that case, where do you dispose of your sewage and human waste?" Bart asked.

"Into incinerators, and when cooled down, the residue, mixed with our garbage disposal, is placed on barges and dumped in the sea somewhere. We don't know where."

"Warden, let's put that on hold for one day," Bart counseled. "I'll check with D.C. for approval or an alternate plan. For the moment, this conversation never took place, gentlemen."

All agreed. A round of brandy was served and Jacques toasted, "Here's to justice."

"Amen," they chorused.

On that note, the meeting ended.

☆ ☆ ☆ ☆

Later that afternoon

Bart called General Bradley and explained his crematorium plan.

"Barton, I agree we don't want any Nazi shrines anywhere in the world. Burying those bastards in sewage is appealing, but I'm going to change that. We have a supply plane flying to Attu after the trial. Put the garbage on that plane. We'll spill those ashes in the Bering Sea just north of the Aleutian Islands. Those rough waters will scatter them to hell. Hitler and his minions truly belong in sewage, but no one will ever know where his ashes are. The supply plane will pick up the can or cans en route to the Aleutians. Store them for a day or two. Good idea to cremate. Good luck, Barton."

"Thank you, sir."

☆ ☆ ☆ ☆

Monday, March 30, 1953 - Fort Leavenworth - 0900 hours

The tribunal members had reached agreement on trifurcation. Each tribunal would hear the defendants who were tried in their courts. They briefed Bart. Adolf Hitler was the first one to appear before the bar.

"We are going to decide your sentence, but you may speak on your behalf."

Speaking in German, Hitler arrogantly declared, "I do not recognize this tribunal as a legitimate court. I was illegally kidnapped and brought before this illegal court. You have no right to sentence me, because I was the head of a state. The Hague should have tried me. *Sieg Heil!*"

"Your remarks are noted and will appear in the record," Nimitz ruled.

"Next prisoner, General Milburn."

"We call Martin Bormann."

The stocky man nervously approached the bar.

"Have you anything to say in your behalf?" Nimitz asked.

"I will speak in my native language. At this time, I am fully aware of the heinous crimes that were perpetrated by the Nazi regime in the Third Reich. These war-crimes trials have proved, beyond a shadow of doubt, that Nazi Germany has perpetrated the worst crimes in history. The carnage was fully unveiled here in this court. I have fully cooperated with the prosecution. Only God Almighty can forgive my association with the Nazi Party. I was not an anti-Semite, nor was I a participant in the Holocaust. Not a single piece of evidence was presented here directly connecting me with the monstrosities committed by Hitler, Goering and that butcher of all butchers, Heinrich Himmler, and his killing machine. My guilt lies in my role as Hitler's assistant. As such, it was my stepping stone to power. You may not believe this, but I wanted to stop the war by making peace with our enemies. In truth, I should have killed Hitler, but with Goering, Goebbels, Himmler and the military loyal to him, it would have been suicide for me. I saved him because of my greed. I have repeated my *mea culpas,* hour by hour, day by day. I am fifty-three years old. You may opt to hang me, send me to prison or show mercy for a truly contrite person. I beg for mercy from you and, above all, from God. Thank you."

Tears rolled down Bormann's cheeks as the MPs led him back to his cell.

Sir Clive Fenwick made a very short statement. "I was the ambassador to Germany when Britain declared war against Nazi Germany. I returned to England. I candidly admit that I gave bad advice to Prime Minister Chamberlain. I was seduced by the Cliveden Set; Joseph P. Kennedy, American Ambassador to the Court of St. James's and Charles Lindbergh's dire predictions about the German Luftwaffe's ability to level London and Paris. However, I didn't know that Nordheim, who professed to be a Jew, was actually Adolf Hitler. He hired me at a munificent salary. But I must make it clear that I am not an anti-Semite. I had nothing to do with the Holocaust. It was the worst crime since the creation of this Earth. I cooperated with the prosecution. I beg for mercy. Thank you."

Next was Keith Reynolds, formerly known as Konrad Fliegel. "Your Honors, distinguished members of this war-crimes tribunal, my testimony as a prosecution witness should clearly indicate that I do not, in fair justice, belong here as a co-defendant with these Nazi vermin. I trust that, in your infinite wisdom, you will find me not guilty. I have committed no crimes. My only crime is my naiveté and guilt by association with a Mr. Nordheim, who I did not know was that fiend, Adolf Hitler. I am not, and never was, an anti-Semite. I grieve for the victims of the Holocaust. May I hand the court a letter addressed to this tribunal from Rabbi Milton Goldstein of the Institutional Synagogue of London. He addresses Your Honors, in my behalf." He handed the document to the clerk, turned and smiled at Bart, who nodded approval.

There was a parade of defendants before the three tribunals, most of whom condemned Hitler. The commandants refused to appear before the main tribunal. The soldiers appeared, one after the other, and pleaded for mercy. By nightfall, the proceedings were completed in the three courts.

The tribunals adjourned to Thursday, April 1, when they would pronounce sentencing.

☆ ☆ ☆ ☆

Thursday, April 1, 1953 - 0900 hours

A tense, crowded court waited for the tribunal to announce the sentences. All three courts would sit *en banc*. Nine chairs were in place for the tribunal members. As the door opened and the nine men entered, an MP declared, "All rise."

Another MP, acting as clerk, loudly declared, "The following prisoners will be brought to the bench: Hans Krause - Auschwitz; Wolfgang Schreiber - Buchenwald; Johann Weisst - Chelmno; Joachim Schmidt - Gross-Rosen; Franz Sauckel - Mauthausen; Hugo Schultz - Ohrdruf." He read off the names, with the exception of the Drancy commandant, René Soltere.

A platoon of Military Police, all over six feet tall, wearing their white helmets, flanked the seven concentration-camp commandants and escorted the shackled prisoners in front of the tribunal.

Marine General Holland Smith grimly eyed each one. "The evidence of your beastliness is overwhelming. All of you have been found guilty of the most heinous crimes in the history of mankind. Therefore, each and every one of you is sentenced to be hanged by the neck until pronounced dead. I will not ask God to have mercy on your souls."

Although they had expected it, six of the prisoners showed fear. Hugo Schultz, however, spouted obscenities and spit at the tribunal. He was quickly led away with the others.

A wired van from the federal penitentiary awaited the condemned men. Armed prison guards were on board. A two-mile trip delivered them along Metropolitan Avenue to the not-so-tender mercies of Warden Wilson. The seven were quickly consigned to death-row cells.

Renée Soltere was escorted to the tribunal. General Chennault addressed the French commandant. "Your egregious conduct has been reviewed, and you are sentenced to ten years on probation. However, that would apply if you ever set foot in the United States, and you would be imprisoned at Attu Island prison. You are to be tried in your native country and be immediately extradited to France. Authorities of the French government are here to take you into custody."

"Thank you, Your Honors."

Two MPs hustled him through the back doors. Chief Felix Gaumont and two French intelligence officers signed papers and removed Soltere to a waiting van. He was handed a pea jacket. Shackled, he was pushed into the van. His escorts, DGSE officers Maurice Duval and Colonel Paul Marchaud, flanked him and were driven to Sherman Army Airfield, where they boarded a chartered Air France plane.

The next defendants called before the tribunal were Franz Schwerin and Ernst Krueger. Nimitz addressed them. "You men were full-fledged Waffen SS Nazis, finally serving as guards for your *Führer*, Adolf Hitler. Your conduct cannot be condoned. You have been found guilty of war crimes. No further comment is necessary. You are each sentenced to five years of hard labor at the Attu Island prison. Based on your behavior there, you may be released at an earlier time. When released, you are to be turned over to the West German government to face the denazification court," Nimitz declared, and two MPs escorted them out.

The media and spectators tensely awaited the call for the Nazi leaders.

"The next prisoner, Sergeant, please," Nimitz ordered.

Martin Bormann, short and stocky, tried to keep pace with two six-foot MPs. His pallor and slightly palsied hands were palpable evidence of his fear.

"Herr Bormann, your plight was the subject of much study and deliberation. While there was no specificity of evidence of your direct participation in war crimes as such, you were without doubt the so-called Gray Eminence, the confidant and right-hand man to the monster of all time, Adolf Hitler. That in and of itself would be enough to find you guilty. You helped this dissolute megalomaniac, Hitler, attain his heights. You helped him escape after the defeat of Nazi Germany. You made him a rich man. You became rich yourself. In spite of the foregoing, you cooperated with the prosecution. Your greed and appetite for power deserves harsh punishment. Your Nazi membership can not be condoned. However, on the recommendation of the prosecution, you will not be executed. You are found guilty. You are fifty-three years of age. You are sentenced to serve five years at hard labor at Attu Island jail. You are also fined $3 billion, which shall be turned over to a fund for Holocaust victims. Failure to pay will delay your release indefinitely. You'll be credited with time served here."

Still shaking, Bormann uttered, "Thank you, sirs."

In groups of ten, the forty Waffen SS prisoners were brought before the tribunal. Lieutenant General Robert Eichelberg, who presided over Tribunal II, peered at the motley lineup who were once part of the Nazi elite fighting group.

"You may have been the cream of Himmler's and Hitler's special troops, but here you are a defeated group of jailbirds. Plainly stated, you are scum who pillaged and ravaged the homes of Jews, Christians, Gypsies, Jehovah's Witnesses, and killed, raped, and stole wantonly all over Europe. All of you are guilty and are sentenced to be hanged by the neck until dead."

Applause erupted from some of the spectators. Nimitz angrily gaveled for silence.

One of the ten shouted, "There is a mistake. I don't belong to this group!"

"What's your name?" Eichelberg demanded.

"I am Hans Lichter. I am not a Waffen SS member!" a short, bespectacled young man cried out.

Eichelberg ordered the other nine men away, and the MPs escorted the shaken group to the exit. He told Lichter to stay. After adjusting his reading glasses, the general scanned a loose-leaf book. He looked up at the weeping prisoner.

"I don't find your name on my list. How did you get into this group?"

The dialogue continued in German with an interpreter intervening. "I was hired two days before we were captured in Hamburg. I was a private in the war. I was a prisoner of war until late May 1945. After that, I was sent home to Stuttgart. A friend of mine got me the job in Hamburg. Up to that time I worked as a taxi driver. I don't belong here."

"Were you tried in our court?"

"No."

Bart and Jacques huddled over a large book, then Bart stood up. "May I approach the bench, sir?"

"Come ahead, General."

"General Eichelberg, a mistake has occurred here. Last night, various prisoners were moved into larger cells housing several prisoners. This young man was accidentally housed with the Waffen SS prisoners. In fact, we did not bring him to trial because we checked his story. We kept him here long enough to get information regarding the Hamburg raid. We were about to release him. In fact, sir, if you will accept the prosecution's recommendation, allow him to plead not guilty now and find him so. He can be released today. Our apologies to this tribunal."

Nimitz nodded at Eichelberg, then turned to Lichter. "Young man, you are very lucky. You are found not guilty and you are to be deported. By the way, are you a Nazi?"

"*Nein, nein, nein.* I hate them."

"Tell your friends in Germany that there is justice in the United States."

"*Danke schön.*"

Bart whispered to the MPs, "Remove Lichter's shackles. Put him in a cell, and when the lunch break comes, I'll arrange to get him clothed and turned over to Immigration for his trip back to Germany. We'll give him some money."

Four groups of ten followed. Eichelberg delivered his lecture and sentenced the forty to death. Nimitz called a recess. He gestured Bart to the bench. "After lunch, join us in our chambers about an hour from now."

Bart saluted assent. He joined the prosecution team and wordlessly wolfed a ham-and-cheese sandwich as he swigged a cold bottle of beer.

"Is something wrong, General?" Sophia Carrera asked.

"No, no, just thinking."

Silence followed. Jacques, with his innate knowledge of Bart's moods, held his hands up to the group and placed his right hand on his lips, signaling *No questions.*

"Jacques, call the penitentiary and get Warden Wilson on the phone, please."

He went to the phone in the adjoining office and placed the call. A moment later, he whistled in a low key. Bart reached for the extended phone. "Warden, sorry to disturb you."

"No problem, General. We just received the first batch of your condemned men. How can I help you?"

"The plan for the use of your foundry for cremation of the condemned has been approved. However, the garbage cans are to be stashed until a plane can pick them up here. If not garbage cans, boxes will do."

"I'll ask no questions, General."

"Good man. See you soon."

☆ ☆ ☆ ☆

Thursday, April 1, 1953 - 1300 hours

The afternoon session began with Admiral Horst von Ludwig being brought to the tribunal. The tall, handsome man stood at attention awaiting his sentence.

"Have you anything to say, Herr Ludwig?" Nimitz asked.

"In perfect English the former admiral stated, "I am not a Nazi, nor was I ever. My country was at war and I was called up to duty. I despise Hitler and his criminal minions. I admire American justice and apologize for Germany's role in this unwarranted invasion of Europe. I regret the young soldiers driven to their deaths by this maniac, and I grieve for the despicable slaughter of the Jews in the Holocaust. I am innocent of any war crimes, but I await your sentence."

"Well stated, Herr Ludwig. The tribunal has carefully studied your case. We find you not guilty. You may return to your family in Denmark."

"Thank you, sirs. You are indeed a fair and just country."

Spectators applauded. Nimitz gaveled.

Hans Langsdorff and Herman Klaus, escorted by four MPs, faced the nine-man *en banc* tribunal. Admiral William Leahy addressed the two defendants. Neither man spoke in his own behalf.

"Very well. First, I find myself distressed to see a Naval war hero like you, Herr Langsdorff. As captain of the Graf Spee, you were admired by your enemies, as well as by your Nazi countrymen. However, your involvement with Hitler's maniacal Revenge Plan resulted in your current predicament. The same applies to you, Herman Klaus. Therefore, each of you is found guilty and sentenced to five years in prison. Your sentence..."

Langsdorff shouted, "I am not guilty of anything!"

"Quiet! Let me finish. Your sentence is suspended and both of you are being deported to West Germany. Authorities are here to take you in custody to face a denazification court in your native country."

As they were about to be led back to their cells, Leahy warned them, "And do not ever attempt to return to the United States."

Nimitz declared a fifteen-minute recess. Douglas Milburn and Ed Murrow cornered Bart on his way to the men's room.

"When is Hitler coming out?" Murrow asked.

"Next," he said over his shoulder, and kept walking.

"Your brother seems preoccupied," Murrow observed to Doug.

"Do you blame him? He's been through a hell of an ordeal," Doug countered.

"I guess you're right," Murrow whispered.

The court was overrun with more members of the media. Many sat on the floor. Anticipation was high. Still cameras focused on the door as Hitler entered, flanked by four MPs.

"I challenge the authority of this kangaroo court!" he yelled in German. "I am a former head of state and…"

Admiral Nimitz gaveled. "That's enough, Adolf Hitler. You are found guilty of all charges. You have committed every war crime. You are responsible for millions of murders. You are not human. You are, as the prosecution has stated, the devil incarnate. You are to be hanged by your neck until you are pronounced dead and returned to your abode in hell."

Hitler stood there, hands on hips and his chin thrust forward. There was fire in his eyes. "My spirit will haunt you and your *bumsen* America forever!" he screamed as he was forcibly lifted off his feet by the MPs. He kept shouting epithets all the way out of the court.

A waiting car was backed up to the post vet clinic. An MP was at the wheel. Two MPs dumped Hitler's struggling body into an unmarked sedan, then sat on each side of the former tyrant. The car sped along Metropolitan Avenue to the Federal Prison, where principal keeper Liam Mahoney and two guards took the defiant man and delivered him to death row.

The sentencing continued. Sir Clive Fenwick was found not guilty. Keith Reynolds, a.k.a. Konrad Fliegel, also was found not guilty. Gunther Froelich was sentenced to five years' probation and returned to Germany for denazification. Joachim Heydrich, nephew of Reinhard Heydrich, was sentenced to death by hanging. Herman Horstman and his six employees were sentenced to five years' probation and returned to Germany for denazification. Ex-FBI man Darren Mayfield was found guilty of high treason and sentenced to death by hanging. His brother, Paul Mayfield, was turned over to the U.S. Attorney for federal prosecution. Swiss bankers Ricardo von Leute and Peter Weber were both sentenced to five years at Leavenworth Prison. Counterfeiter Karl Sturner and his five printers were turned over to the secret Service for further investigation. The next prisoner sentenced was Christopher Engel, the Gestapo soldier who had bayoneted an innocent baby at Auschwitz. He was sentenced to death by hanging.

Nimitz announced a fifteen-minute recess.

The last of the prisoners was struggling with four MPs in his cell. He lashed out at his captors. They refrained from striking his face. Jacques ran to the cell to determine the delay. He entered the fray and delivered a chop behind the prisoner's right ear. He collapsed. Quickly, the Military Police handcuffed the inert figure. They shackled his feet.

"Okay, men, he'll come to in a minute. Stand him up and carry him into the court."

The tribunal *en banc* was back on the bench. The clerk announced the groggy man as Heinrich Müller. The MPs held him in a standing position. Admiral Nimitz banged his gavel.

Bart whispered to his team, "This is the toughest bastard we've got. Nicknamed *Gestapo Müller*, a brutal son of a bitch," he added, referring to the man who had escaped from Hitler's bunker. Feared throughout Germany and Europe, Müller was the SS *GruppenFührer* and head of the Gestapo from 1939 to 1945. He was Himmler's man.

Admiral Nimitz stared at the prisoner for a few minutes. The courtroom was tense and silent. "Heinrich Müller, you are guilty of war crimes on all counts. You are undoubtedly one of the most evil of all Nazis. You are responsible for organizing mass murders of Jews in the Holocaust. You are Lucifer in the fullest sense of the word. Both Jewish and Christian theology condemn you. You are a clone of Hitler, the devil incarnate. You are herewith found guilty and are sentenced to execution." Nimitz declared.

"I'll see you all in hell!" Müller shouted in German, and spat at the bench. He was immediately lifted off his feet and carried to the exit for departure to death row.

His nephew Erich Müller was next. He was sentenced to ten years of hard labor at Attu.

"Ladies and gentlemen, this court is adjourned," Nimitz said, and he graveled.

☆ ☆ ☆ ☆

Wednesday, April 15, 1953 - 0400 hours
One thousand fully armed troops encircled the federal penitentiary on Metropolitan Avenue. It housed two thousand prisoners. All streets were shut off with wooden barriers and yellow traffic cones. MPs and local police directed traffic detours. Civilians gathered behind rope barriers. The media were carefully screened before being permitted to enter the prison. Inside, they were escorted to a large courtyard and seated in folding chairs.

Along death row, there was a flurry of activity. The condemned men had their last meals at midnight. Priests and ministers attended a number of men who sought to make peace with God. Others had rejected the prayers.

The dim lights in the courtyard indicated a fifty-foot-long and twenty-five-foot-wide scaffold with all the necessary appurtenances for a hanging. A mixture of prison guards and Military Police were testing and examining the trap door and the ropes. Television cameras were in abundance outside the prison. As the minutes completed an hour, crowds grew. Soon the dawn brought the first light of day.

Warden Wilson, Liam Mahoney, Jacques Laurent and General Warren Fielding led Adolf Hitler and the six concentration-camp commandants to the courtyard. Each man was escorted by four MPs. The courtyard was filled with witnesses composed of American officers, foreign emissaries, a dozen survivors and a large group of reporters. Two Army photographers manned 16-millimeter cameras. Ten still photographers were scattered around the scaffold. In place were six doctors on the ground alongside the scaffold. Ten Military Police stood behind the traps. A masked executioner stood at the lever.

The sun shone through. There was complete silence except for occasional footsteps. At 0600 hours, Wilson, Mahoney and Laurent led the seven condemned men up the steps, which were ten feet above the concrete pavement.

"Do you men wish to say anything?"

Epithets came from the commandants. Hitler declared, "This day you are making me a martyr. Nazi Germany will rise again!" His last words were indistinguishable.

The men were placed on the traps. General Fielding nodded at the MPs and in an instant the hoods were clamped over the heads of the condemned men and tied in place. The MPs retreated five steps. The warden nodded to the masked executioner. He pulled the lever and all ten traps were sprung open. The seven men fell to their deaths. The loud noise of the sprung traps rent the air. The bodies dangled.

A few voices yelled, "Hallelujah!"

The doctors quickly examined the bodies as they were pulled out by guards. All were pronounced dead. Televisions sets and radios the world over blared the death of Hitler and the commandants. Bold headlines were prepared in newspaper offices around the globe.

Bart Milburn, in full dress uniform, and his prosecution team watched the somber, somewhat surreal proceedings from a large window above the scaffold. He mused, *Is this the end of a bad dream or a pit stop on the highway of hate, racism, bigotry, white supremacy, communism, fascism, and tyranny?* His jaw was jutted and he was grinding his teeth.

Sophia tapped his shoulder. "You look very angry, General."

"You could say so, my dear lady. I think back to the war, our men dying and wounded. I had nightmares of the concentration camps and the Holocaust, all because of these vermin. Yet I derive no pleasure from these hangings. It's merely part of mankind's tit for tat, get even, an eye for an eye, et cetera. This is not the end of man's inhumanity to man. We're still in a Cold War with the Soviets. Will it ever stop?"

"Cynical, but true," Gideon Cartman said.

The tableau of death proceeded below with professional efficiency. Colonel Jeremiah Brown supervised the death parade as fifty-four men were executed. A special team of prison guards fed the deceased Nazi bodies into a blazing furnace.

General Fielding invited the prosecution team to his conference room. "I think we can use a drink after this ordeal."

Two sergeants served the libations.

"Dear General Milburn, in the name of justice, I toast you and your team for your dogged pursuit of these monsters," said Fielding.

"There are no qualms among millions of us who lost parents, children and grandchildren to the machinations of these lice. May they swim in the sewage of blood to their place in hell," a teary-eyed Jacques rasped.

"General Fielding, on behalf of myself and colleagues, thank you for your most gracious hospitality during our stay here at Fort Leavenworth," Bart said.

"Bart, my friend, and all here, it was a distinct honor to have you dedicated and most talented people. I drink to you."

"Hear, hear," Richard Maybrook cheered.

"Okay, gang," Bart declared, "time for you to pick up your files and pack. A plane will take you to Washington at 1430 hours. Jacques and I will clean up here and return on Friday."

At the prosecution conference room, Bart called General Bradley. "Sir, Operation Lucifer reporting. Mission accomplished."

"Congratulations, Barton, on a flawless accomplishment."

"Thank you, sir. If Friday is convenient, the supply plane to Attu can pick up that garbage can for disposal. I'll be here to see it loaded aboard."

"How many prisoners do you have going to Attu?"

"Four, sir. Bormann and three others."

"That's all?"

"Well, the cookie crumbled that way. The tribunal called the shots."

"Well, I'd better notify Attu to minimize their plans. Put them aboard the supply plane and have them blindfolded when the ashes are dumped into the Bering Sea. I'll give you an ETA on its arrival at Sherman Field. When are you coming back?"

"I'll be leaving here as soon as the garbage is put aboard the supply plane. General Fielding has a turbojet to take Jacques and me home."

"Call me on Monday. Congratulations."

★ ★ ★ ★

Friday, April 17, 1953 - 1100 hours - Sherman Army Airfield
A four-engine Lockheed Constellation was parked at a hangar. Captain Virgil Maxwell awaited the arrival of his mystery package. An Army shuttle van headed straight toward the hangar. General Milburn, Jacques Laurent and four MPs alighted, carrying a corrugated box wrapped in brown paper. Colonel Maxwell saluted Bart.

"Sir, this box can be put in the hold of my plane. Those two men over there are prepared to load it aboard. Both men have been sworn to secrecy. I am proud to deliver its contents to the Bering Sea."

"Colonel, the ashes have been transferred from a garbage can to this large box. Have those men come here."

Maxwell waved them over. They saluted Bart.

"Men, this is Jacques Laurent, chief of the CIA Nazi desk."

"This is Captain Brian Carrigan and Major Robert Goldman. They were chosen for the task of spilling these Nazi ashes into the sea," Maxwell said.

"General, I'm honored to meet you, sir. I served with General Bradley's First Army. Later, I continued with him into the liberation of the concentration camps," Major Goldman said.

"Well, this assignment should be an exclamation point to your career."

"Indeed it is, sir."

"The same goes for me," Carrigan said. "I was over there in the Army Air Corps flying bombers over Germany."

"How about you, Colonel?" Bart asked.

"I was a fighter pilot. From D-Day to the Battle of the Bulge I was in action. I was wounded by flak there. I remember seeing you at the Bulge as I was being stretchered to the medics."

"Glad to see you are okay now."

"Thank you, sir."

"Okay, men, put that box in the hold now," Bart ordered. "In a few minutes you are getting four prisoners, one of whom is Martin Bormann. They are handcuffed and shackled. Blindfold them before the ashes are dumped."

"Will do," they replied.

A van pulled up to the plane. Four MPs hustled the prisoners to the bench in the huge plane. They were strapped to the bars behind them.

Bart, Jacques and the MPs watched the plane take off for the trip to Attu Naval Base in the Aleutian Islands. Jacques and Bart shook hands with the MPs and boarded the turbojet en route to Washington.

☆ ☆ ☆ ☆

Sunday, April 19, 1953

Fifty miles from the approach to Attu, the supply plane flew five hundred feet over the turbulent Bering Sea. A trail of powdery ashes was spilled into the raging waters and scattered by high winds. One hour later, the four prisoners were incarcerated.

"So this is what I get for my cooperation?" Bormann shouted from his cramped, bitterly cold cell.

CHAPTER NINETEEN

Monday, April 20, 1953 - Washington

After a restful weekend at their Rock Creek Park home, Bart and Jacques attended a private lunch with the chairman of the Joint Chiefs of Staff, General Bradley.

"I present you with the film of the executions and the photographs of the entire scene," Bart said. "Also, here is the full record of the trial."

"Jacques, please put that material on the credenza."

"Yes, sir."

Over lunch, Bradley was filled in on the trial, then small talk followed. Finally, Bradley asked, "What are your plans, Barton and Jacques?"

"Sir, I would like to go back to my reserve status," Bart answered.

"Granted, after May 2. There is to be a special reception for you and your Operation Lucifer staff. Orders of President Eisenhower. Possibly another medal and another star," Bradley suggested, grinning.

Bart was speechless.

"And you, Jacques, what are your plans at the CIA?"

Jacques laughed, "I expect to resign before Allen Dulles fires me."

"Hold off until after the reception."

"When will that be?"

"Within the next ten days, I believe."

"How about you, General Bradley?"

"Barton, I'll be sixty in August, and that will be my retirement day. I'm looking forward to it, son."

☆ ☆ ☆ ☆

Friday, May 1, 1953 - 1100 hours - Washington - the White House
A bright spring sun bathed the nation's capital. The audience of two hundred dignitaries were seated in the Rose Garden. A pastiche of the military, senators, Congresspersons, the full Cabinet, CIA leaders, and families of the honorees were in attendance. President Eisenhower approached the podium. The crowd rose and applauded. He motioned them to be seated.

"We are here today to honor the leader and the team who brilliantly performed an historical feat in the chase, capture and successful trial of *Der Führer* and his Nazi minions. While Hitler and his Waffen SS killers have been executed, the danger of hate lurks throughout the world. This magnificent venture was headed by Major General Barton Milburn. Come forward, General."

Bart, in full dress uniform, entered from the side door of the White House. The president shook his hand as the flashbulbs clicked and the newsreel cameras focused on the two men in a filmed broadcast. The handsome, six-foot-three figure stood alongside the President during the uproarious applause and cheers in a standing ovation. As the noise subsided, Elizabeth, in the front row, was shushing Jenny and Michael.

"That's my daddy!" Michael yelled. Chuckles ensued.

The President noted Milburn's service on his staff during World War II, then said, "Step forward, General. First, I hand you a third star. You are now Lieutenant General Milburn, and I pin on you these two medals: the Presidential Medal of Freedom and a Distinguished Service Cross. Here are additional ribbons to add to your fruit-salad decorations. Congratulations, General."

The gathering roared and applauded approval, then the entire Lucifer team was called forward, and each was awarded the Presidential Medal of Freedom. The crowd roared again. The ceremony ended. Families ran forward, embracing their relatives.

That evening, General Bradley hosted a dinner reception for Bart, Jacques, and the entire team and their families. Bradley, at the conclusion of the festivities, kissed Elizabeth and handed her an envelope containing an order returning Bart to his reserve status. Elizabeth hugged the Chairman of the Joint Chiefs.

"He's a lucky man to have you, Elizabeth, and you are a lucky lady to have him. God bless you both," Bradley said.

☆ ☆ ☆ ☆

Forty-six years later - Tuesday, June 10, 1999, 7:30 p.m. - Washington
Headlines around the nation announced the end of the NATO war against Serbia. The United Nations had approved a peace pact. This was the seventy-ninth day of a merciless, devastating bombing of Belgrade and its environs. Slobodan Milosevic, President of Yugoslavia, had been indicted by The Hague tribunal as a war criminal for his actions which were translated into "ethnic

cleansing." Those two words would transpose into alleged mass murders, rape, and expelling Albanians and other Muslims from their homes in Kosovo, a state within Yugoslavia.

Barton Q. Milburn, prominent attorney, statesman, and lieutenant general (retired) of the U.S. Army was a guest on the CNN Cable Network presentation of a roundtable discussion of the breaking news. The two-hour conversation among newsmen, government officials, former cabinet members and Milburn came to its final few minutes. The anchorman turned to a head shot of Bart. "General Milburn, I'll give you the last word."

"We are reaching the termination of the most militaristic century in the history of civilization," the elderly Milburn said. "More humans were killed in the last hundred years than ever before. Let me quote the words of a survivor witness during the trial of Hitler and his Nazi minions: 'There is only one God, the Creator of the universe. One God for all of humanity. If the world would recognize that, all the enmities would stop.'"

"That's a powerful answer," the anchorman chimed in.

"One last comment, sir," Bart continued. "Just a thought for this distinguished panel and your audience. Let us not overlook the armies among these segments of society: Moslems; Sunnis fighting Shiites; Christians-Catholics and Protestants have been killing each other in Northern Ireland until recently; and, among the Semites, Arabs fighting Jews. Stamp out hate by education and we won't be shedding each other's blood in hate, anger, prejudice, persecution, terrorism, crime, or war."

"We end this program on that cogent note and await developments. Stay tuned for a statement by the President at 8 p.m. Eastern time."

☆ ☆ ☆ ☆

Friday, June 11, 1999 - Beverly Hills, California

Jacques Laurent was perusing the Los Angeles Times, checking the section dealing with the entertainment industry. His wife, Christina, intently read the front page.

"Oh, my Lord, look at this headline, Jacques!" She placed it before him on the breakfast table.

"You mean, this 'NATO halts air war'?"

"No, no, this two-column headline." She pointed to the article.

"Oh, *Mon Dieu*, I must call Bart." Jacques picked up his cellular phone and punched in the numbers.

Bart answered, "Hello?"

"Have you seen the papers yet?"

"No, Jacques, I've been concentrating on my memoirs."

"Listen to this, brother. I'll read you a large two-column headline in the L.A. Times: 'Firms Offer Fund for WWII Slave Labor.'"

"Just read me the lead paragraph, Jacques."

"More than a dozen large German corporations, including Daimler Chrysler and BMW, announced Thursday in Berlin the creation of a $1.7 billion fund for hundreds of thousands of people forced into slave labor during World War II."

"Do they name any other companies?" Bart asked.

"Yes, but first the subhead reads as follows: 'Holocaust: German companies insist on protection from lawsuits as condition. Jewish leaders decry proposal.'"

"Is that an Associated Press story?"

"No, it was written by Henry Weinstein, the Times legal-affairs writer. It's a lengthy piece, runs a long column on page one and jumps to page A35, where he names the consortium of Allianz, one of the world's largest insurance companies; BASF, the large petrochemical company; DeGussa Corp., which worked with the German government on the production of Zyklon gas for the gas chambers; Bayer, the pharmaceutical company; Deutsche Bank; Dresdner Bank; Siemens Electronics, and Thyssen-Krupp, a major arms manufacturer. What about I. G. Farben?" Jacques concluded.

"They quietly folded," Bart said.

EPILOGUE

January 1, 2001 - 12:15 a.m. - Washington

The Milburn family was gathered in the den of their Rock Creek Park home. The 80-year-old patriarch, Barton Q. Milburn, lieutenant general (retired) and his wife, Elizabeth, had invited their two sons, Michael and Quentin, daughter Jenny and their spouses to a New Year's Eve dinner. Their grandchildren were fast asleep in the guesthouse.

The group was toasting the arrival of the new millenium. They were focused on a fifty-inch television screen displaying the revelry of a million New Yorkers celebrating in world-famous Times Square. The world news was rotating on the apex of the Number One Times Square building, which had dropped the lighted big apple at the midnight hour. Two other TV monitors were carrying the New Year festivities on other channels.

Marie and George Spota's annual New Year's Eve party was in full swing at their Holmby Hills home, contiguous to Beverly Hills. Present at the party were Jacques and Christina Laurent, Douglas and Constance Milburn, Joyce Laurent Davis and her husband, Mark, and a melange of actors, writers, producers and famed musicians.

At 9 p.m. Pacific time, Spota announced a call to the Milburn home in Washington to wish Bart and Elizabeth a happy New Year. The close friends and family of the Milburns retired to the den and on a speakerphone exchanged "Happy New Years." Both coasts of gatherings chattered at each other and wound up in a chorus of "Auld Lang Syne."

At 12:23 Eastern time, Bart shouted into the speakerphone, "Quick! Turn on your TV. Talk later. 'Bye."

Twenty-three minutes into the new year, the news crawl atop the building halted for a few seconds and proclaimed three times, *Bulletin! Bulletin! Bulletin!* As the networks flashed the same bulletin, the renowned lawyer, statesman and presidential advisor declared, "Look at this."

A CNN announcer broke in, declaring, "There has been an explosion at the home of the German Chancellor. We switch you now to our Berlin bureau."

"This is Roger Jerrold. The home of the German Chancellor has been under siege for the past few hours. The time is 9:25 a.m. here in Berlin. A giant-sized wooden swastika was set afire on the lawn just before daylight. Five minutes ago, three hand grenades were hurled into the gated residence while firefighters doused the burning Nazi symbol.

"Police have surrounded the house, and evidently the situation is under control. From somewhere in the huge crowd that had gathered at the official residence, the grenades were thrown through the windows with great force. Fortunately, the Chancellor and his family escaped with minor injuries. You can see the residence ablaze while firefighters are attempting to douse the flames. Stand by...I have a report just handed to me. The police have taken two men into custody. We'll try to learn the identity of the suspects."

Bart Milburn placed his brandy glass on the bar and sighed, "That damned Nazi virus is still alive."

"Dad, when is this racial hatred ever going to end?" Michael asked.

Bart looked at Michael, Quentin and Jenny. "This world over the past millennia has experienced wars and holocausts from the beginning of time. Hitler, Stalin, Hussein, who's next? It is now up to your generation to pick up the cudgels of conscience with spoken words, print, and, if necessary, violence, to stamp out the shedding of blood caused by hatred and anger. Complacency and apathy caused World War II. We must feed the fires of outrage and destroy this virus. Eternal vigilance is the price of liberty. Remember that."

"Dad, you did your part. It's really the job of this generation. We are living in a 'me' society. We must remember, *The past is prologue,* as inscribed in our National Archives Building," Jenny asserted.

"That sums it up," Bart declared. "I'm not through either."

Another bulletin flashed on the large screen. The networks simultaneously switched to Tel Aviv. An announcer declared that a combination flight of twelve Israeli F-16s, twin fighter planes, and F-18 weather planes were engaged in a battle with six bombers twenty-five miles off the coast of Haifa over the Mediterranean Sea. The networks soon had the planes in sight.

Dan Rogers of Fox News declared, "The bombers are unidentified. Their radio gunners opened fire on the Israeli fighters. You can see the F-16s scrambling overhead."

Wilton Fallon of NBC shouted, "The Israelis are diving from four angles! Wow, three bombers are hit, afire and falling into the sea!"

Grace Teller of CBS came on the third set and excitedly declared, "The three bombers are flying away. The Israeli F-18s are zeroing in on them. There they go... three bombers exploding in midair. Wreckage is falling into the sea!"

The pictures were spectacular. An Israeli spokesman appeared on the screen.

"We haven't identified the origin of these bombers. We'll have a full statement at noon. All of our planes are returning to their base."

Bart stood up, fixed a brandy and lit a cigar.

"This looks like a Hitler Revenge Plan sortie from Iraq or Libya. A hell of a way to start the new millennium. Remembrance is a key word. The world's new generations must learn the history of World War II and never forget the Holocaust. It can happen again to every race, religion, and ethnic group. Just look at the Catholic and Protestant fight in Northern Ireland, the Sunnis and Shiites in the Middle East, the Serbs in Bosnia and Kosovo, the Albanians, and, sadly, the continuing enmity between Arabs and Jews, as well as white supremacists against blacks."

"Dad, why don't our Presidents and Congress pass a bill to imprison the practitioners of overt racism, religious and ethnic prejudice?" Michael, the lawyer, vehemently declared.

"Okay, why don't you run for Congress and try to build a consensus? You're a good public speaker. You live in New York. There is a lot of support there."

The family applauded.

Bart's attention went back to the television screen, where a spectacular display of fireworks lit up the night.

☆ ☆ ☆ ☆ ☆

LEST WE FORGET

AUTHOR'S NOTE

LEST WE FORGET

The premise of this novel is primarily a hypothetical version of the capture and trial of Adolf Hitler, Martin Bormann and their Nazi minions. The words "Lest we forget," which ends the book, is actually a creed of remembrance. In preparation for this novel, I spent almost four years researching the Holocaust and Nazism. But I had to ask the question, did anybody today care? Tests were randomly given to approximately one hundred high school and college students asking them to identify a list consisting of names such as Hitler, Goring, Goebbels, von Ribbentrop, and Bormann along with some contemporary figures of the 20th century. Shockingly, not one student attained a score of 100%; 85% of the students failed, including seven students who scored 10%. Von Ribbentrop was identified as a Dutch painter, Bormann was tagged a motion picture actor, Himmler was named a pitcher for the Boston Red Sox and sadly enough only fifteen students correctly identified Adolf Hitler.

The message here is clear: the history of the most violent century is fading into the archives. Not only in the U.S. but the world over education is being sublimated to ancient history and a myriad of other items. Where is the rationale and the outrage for our pedants, media and educational institutions? Our educational system is only concerned with political correctness and not with teaching history. This is my reason for writing an action thriller that dissects the Nazi psyche.

I hope to affect the baby boomers and all the persons born in the 20th century by refreshing their memories and kindling the fires of outrage for then and now. Hatred and racism are alive and well in this new millennium - the 21st century. Who is next for the Hitlerites, the white supremacists and the closet bigots of religious, racial and ethnic groups?

Book one of this novel contains many fictitious characters chasing Hitler and his minions. Book two has Hitler on trial. The survivors who testified against him are composites of actual persons who survived the Holocaust and lived to testify to the truth, despite the hate-monger revisionists scattered around the world. There is no fiction in the testimony about the composites, which come from historical records. Apathy and complacency on the part of our democracies are the best weapons in the hands of Nazis. Haters of every kind, in my opinion, is a synonym for Nazis.

I spoke to survivors at the Simon Wiesenthal Center's Holocaust Museum in Los Angeles. There are a hundred or more books on the subject of the Holocaust. Read them. I beg readers of this novel to pass it on to their children, grandchildren and friends of every religion, race and creed. They may face problems of fascism, hatred and racism someday in their own lives.

GLOSSARY

Abwehr. The Third Reich's secret service.

Auschwitz. Located in Oswiecim, Poland, Auschwitz was the largest and most gruesome of the 10,006 Nazi concentration camps. It is estimated that well over two million Jews and other racial enemies of the Third Reich were gassed, tortured, starved, and worked to death at Auschwitz.

Ben-Gurion, David (1886-1973). Zionist leader and first Minister President of Israel.

Bormann, Martin (1900-1945?). Hitler's right-hand man. He worked his way up the ladder to become the second most powerful Nazi at the end of World War II. No one could see Hitler unless Bormann cleared them. However, only those sent for by Hitler were admitted into his presence. There is no empirical data that Bormann was killed escaping from Berlin. In 1972 bones were unearthed which experts believe identified Hitler's gray eminence.

Canaris, Wilhelm (1887-1945). Admiral head of the Abwehr. Arrested in 1944 in connection with a plot against Hitler. He was sent to a concentration and executed before the Allies broke through.

CIA. Central Intelligence Agency, the American counterpart to M16, the British Secret Service.

Churchill, Winston (1874-1965). British Prime Minister and Allied war leader who led the English people in "their finest hour" until Nazi Germany was defeated.

Dulles, John Foster (1888-1959). Secretary of State in the Eisenhower administration and a major force in U.S foreign policy during the Cold War.

Dachau. Largest concentration camp in Germany. Over the course of its twelve-year existence, Dachau had 206,000 registered inmates of all sorts and nationalities, of whom 31,951 were officially listed as having died.

DGSE (Direction Generale Services L'Exterieur). The French intelligence agency; the counterpart to the CIA.

Eden, Anthony (1897-1977). British foreign secretary (1935-38, 40-45, 51, 55), and Prime Minister (1955-57).

Eichmann, Adolf. SS Obersturmbannführer and one of the major Holocaust murderers. As head of Jewish transportation in the Reich Main Security Office, Eichmann was responsible for rounding up well over three million Jews in all German occupied territories and drove them into the annihilation camps as part of Hitler's Final Solution to the Jewish Question. Caught in Argentina by Israeli secret agents, he was tried at Jerusalem, found guilty, and executed in 1962.

Einsatzgruppen. Special Nazi security police that followed the German army; responsible for the murder of one million Jews on their drive into Russia.

Eisenhower, Dwight D. (1890-1969). Commander of U.S. forces in the European Theater, 1942-1945. As Supreme Commander of the Allied Expeditionary Force, Eisenhower launched the most successful amphibian invasion in history at Normandy (June 6, 1944) that eventually led to the defeat of Nazi Germany. Elected to the Presidency by the largest popular vote in American history, Eisenhower served two terms (1952-60) as president.

Endlösung (Final Solution). The program authorized by Hitler to kill all Jews in Europe.

Esser, Hermann (1900-81). One of the original founders of the Nazi party and a close comrade of Adolf Hitler. His scandalous personal life, combined with his venal tendencies, made him an embarrassment even in Nazi circles. After Hitler fobbed him off with minor posts, Esser faded into obscurity during the Second World War, which may account f or the f act that he was overlooked by the Allies after World War II, though a German court sentenced him to five years of hard labor in 1949.

Fortas, Abe (1910-1982). U.S. Supreme Court justice appointed by President Lyndon B. Johnson.

Führer. German name for leader. This was the official Nazi reference to their leader, Adolf Hitler.

Gaulle, Charles de (1890-1970). French general, statesman, and President of the Fifth Republic (1958-69).

Gestapo (Geheime Staatspolizei, or State Secret Police). The dreaded Nazi political police force.

Heydrich, Reinhard (1904-42). SS Obergruppenführer and Himmler's right-hand man who chaired the infamous Wannsee Conference that led to the Holocaust.

Himmler, Heinrich (1900-45). SS Reichsführer and Hitler's ruthless bloodhound, Himmler was also the führer's executive agent, helping him in carrying out the Holocaust.

Hitler, Adolf (1889-1945). German dictator and führer, who presided over the most evil empire in history and was responsible, directly or indirectly, for the deaths of 55 million people.

Holocaust. A term derived from the Greek *holokauston* or "burnt offering" and referring to the Nazi racial program of physically annihilating the whole Jewish race. The term genocide is often used interchangeably with holocaust.

Höss, Rudolf (1900-47) SS Commandant of Auschwitz who was responsible for supervising the extermination of two million Jews in the gas chambers.

Hoover, J. Edgar (1895-1972). Head of the FBI (Federal Bureau of Investigation).

Jackson, Robert H. (d. 1954). Associate Justice of the Supreme Court and Chief U.S. Counsel at the Nuremberg War Trials.

Meissner, Otto (1878-1968). German jurist and chief of the presidential chancellery under Hindenberg and Hitler.

Mengele, Josef (1911-79). Physician and infamous "Angel of Death" at Auschwitz, where he was responsible for selecting the victims for extermination and for conducting "scientific experiments" on numerous inmates, especially identical twins. Survived the war and died in Brazil in 1979.

M16. British Secret Intelligence Service

Müller, Heinrich (1900-?). Head of the Gestapo (1939-45). Nicknamed "Gestapo Müller, " he operated the most brutal police force in Germany and later in German occupied countries. Probably survived the war.

Niemöller, Martin (1892-1984). Lutheran pastor and Nazi resister. As head of the Confessional Church, Niemöller stymied Hitler's effort to nazify the Lutheran church, but those same efforts led to his incarceration in a concentration camp.

Nimitz, Chester (1885-1966). Commander of the U.S. Pacific fleet during World War II. At the time of Japan's surrender, he commanded 6,256 ships and 4,847 combat aircraft, the largest fighting fleet in world history.

NSDAP (National Sozialistische Deutsche Arbeiterpartei, or National Socialist German Workers Party). The Nazi political party.

OSS. Office of Strategic Services, counterpart to the British M16 and predecessor of the CIA.

Papen, Franz von. Conservative Catholic politician, Weimar chancellor (1932), and the man who was instrumental in bringing Hitler into power through backdoor maneuvers. Dashing, suave and witty, he was also a sly intriguer living on thin political air. Survived the R45hm purge and held several ambassadorial posts during the Third Reich. As slippery as an eel, he survived the wrath of both Hitler and the Allies, and lived to tell the tale in his self-serving memoirs.

Peiper, Joachim (1915-1976). SS Standartenführer and tank commander of the 1st Panzer division *(Leibstandarte Adolf Hitler)* who took part in massacres against American forces at Malmedy during the battle of the Bulge. Tried for war crimes, he was sentenced to death, but the sentence was subsequently commuted to life in prison. In 1956, Peiper was released. He was murdered in 1976 in Traves, probably by a French organization called Vengeurs (Avengers).

Röhm, Ernst (1837-1934). Chief of the SA, or Sturmabteilung. He built the brownshirt storm troopers instilling fear in the German populace. Göring and Himmler warned Hitler that Röhm was a threat. Hitler personally arrested Rohm and ordered him to shoot himself with a revolver containing one bullet. Röhm refused. Theodor Eicke, on Himmler's order, fired two bullets into Röhm, killing him instantly. The SA was destroyed in what became know as "the Night of the Long Knives."

SA (Sturmabteilung, or Assault Division). Storm troopers, or brownshirts, a paramilitary organization of the Nazi party.

Schacht, Hjalmar (1877-1970). German banker and financial expert who helped Hitler in getting Germany out of the depression. After falling out with the Nazis on both economic and moral grounds, he made contact with the German resistance and ended up in a concentration camp. Survived the war and became a wealthy man in the postwar period.

Scholtz-Klink, Gertrud (1902-). The Nazi women's führer.

SD (Sicherheitsdienst, or Security Service). An SS intelligence department.

Seyss-Inquart, Artur (1892-1946). Austrian lawyer who helped lay the foundation for annexation (Anschluss) of Austria. He became reichstatthalter, or Reich governor. At Nuremberg, he was found guilty and executed for decreeing the deportation and liquidation of Jews and a variety of dissenters.

SS (Schutzstaffel, or Protective Squadron). The black uniformed elite corps of the Nazi party.

Stalin, Josef (1879-1953). Brutal leader of the Soviet Union who consolidated Communist control after the death of Lenin and imposed a rigid centralized system of totalitarianism on Russia. He was instrumental in destroying Hitler and also in ushering in the Cold War with the United States.

Taylor, Telford (1908-1998). One of the chief U.S. prosecutors at the Nazi War Tribunals at Nuremberg. He was also a law professor and prolific author of books dealing with Nazi Germany and World War II.

Truman, Harry S. (1884-1972). President of the United States, 1945-1953.

Wehrmacht. The German armed forces.

Wiesenthal, Simon (1908-). Famous "Nazi hunter." As head of the Documentation Center of the Association of Jewish Victims of the Nazi Regime and a holocaust victim himself, Wiesenthal has amassed extensive documentation relating to the holocaust. This material has proved invaluable in hunting down and capturing more than 1200 Nazis, most notably the commandant of Treblinka and Sobibor, Franz Stangl. In 1977, Yeshiva University in Los Angeles founded the Simon Wiesenthal Center, named in honor of Simon Wiesenthal and dedicated to the research and memory of Jewish persecution during the Nazi period.

BIBLIOGRAPHY

Gilbert, Martin. *The Holocaust.* 1985, Henry Holt.

Fischer, Klaus P. *Nazi Germany.* 1995, Continuum Publishing Co., 370 Lexington Avenue, New York, NY 10017.

Ortiz, Alicia Dupoune (translated by Shawn Fields). *Eva Peron.* 1996, St. Martin's Press.

Johnson, Paul. *A History of the Jews.* 1987, Harper & Row.

Höss, Rudolf. *Death Dealer Rudolph Höss - The Memoirs of the SS Kommandant at Auschwitz.* 1996, edited by Stephen Paskuly, translated by Andrew Pallinger, Da Capo Press, a subsidiary of Plenum Publishing Corp., 233 Spring Street, New York, NY 10013.

Kershaw, Ian. *Hitler: 1889-1936 Hubris..* New York: Norton, 1998.

Bower, Tom. *Nazi Gold - The Full Story of the Fifty-Year Swiss-Nazi Conspiracy to Steal Billions from Europe's Jews and Holocaust Survivors.* 1997, HarperCollins.

Cahill, Thomas. *The Gifts of the Jews - How a Tribe of Desert Nomads Changed the Way Everyone Thinks and Feels.* 1998, Nan A. Talese, an imprint of Doubleday.

Stille, Alexander. *Benevolence and Betrayal - Five Italian Jewish Families Under Fascism.* 1991, Jonathan Cape, 20 Vauxhall Bridge Road, London SWIV 2SA, England.

Taylor, Telford. *Sword and Swastika - Generals and Nazis in the Third Reich.* 1952, Barnes & Noble.

Taylor, Telford. *The Anatomy of the Nuremberg Trials.* 1992, Little, Brown.

Wiesel, Elie. *Night.* 1960, Hill & Wang.

LeBor, Adam. *Hitler's Secret Bankers - The Myth of Swiss Neutrality During the Holocaust.* 1997, Carol Publishing Group, 120 Enterprise Ave., Secaucus, NJ 07094

Pool, James. *Hitler and His Secret Partners - Contributions, Loot and Rewards, 1933-1945.* 1997, Pocket Books.

Rosenbaum, Ron. *Explaining Hitler.* 1998, Random House.

Waite, Robert G.L. *The Psychopathic God - Adolf Hitler.* 1977, Basic Books, Inc. Publishers

Hitler, Adolf. *Mein Kampf.* 1925, copyright renewed in 1971. Houghton Mifflin.

Aarons, Mark, and Loftus, John. *The Secret War Against the Jews - How Western Espionage Betrayed the Jewish People.* 1994, St. Martin's Press.

The Buchenwald Report, translated by David A Hackett. 1995, Westview Press, 5500 Central Ave., Boulder, CO 80301-2877.

Inside the Third Reich - Memoirs by Albert Speer. 1970, Macmillan.

Crankshaw, Edward. *Gestapo - Instrument of Tyranny.* 1994, Da Capo Press, a subsidiary of Plenum Publishing Corporation, 233 Spring Street, New York, NY 10013.

Dunnigan, James F., and Nofi, Albert A. *Dirty Little Secrets of World War II - Military Information No One Told You About the Greatest, Most Terrible War in History.* 1994, William Morrow.

Padfield, Peter. *Himmler - A Full-Scale Biography of One of Hitler's Most Ruthless Executioners.* 1990, MJF Books, Fine Communications, 2 Lincoln Square, 60 West 66th Street, New York, NY 10023.

Koehn, Ilse. *Mischling, Second Degree - My Childhood in Nazi Germany.* 1977, Greenwillow Books, 1350 Avenue of the Americas, New York, NY 10019.

Gilbert, G.M. *Nuremberg Diary.* 1947, copyright renewed 1974. Da Capo Press, Inc., a subsidiary of Plenum Publishing Corp., 233 Spring Street, New York, NY 10013.

Kelley, Kitty. *The Royals.* 1997, Warner Books.

Langer, Lawrence L. *Holocaust Testimonies - The Ruins of Memory.* 1991, Yale University Press.

McCullogh, David. *Truman.* 1992, Simon & Schuster.

Heiden, Konrad. *Der Fuehrer - Hitler's Rise to Power.* 1944, Houghton Mifflin.

Ziemke, Earl F. *Stalingrad to Berlin - The German Defeat in the East.* 1968 and 1996, Barnes & Noble.

Melchior, I.B., and Brandenburg, Frank. *Quest - Searching for the Truth of Germany's Nazi Past.* 1990, Presidio Press, 505 B San Marin Drive, Suite 300, Novato, CA 94949-1340.

Gilbert, Martin. *Churchill - A Life.* 1991, Henry Holt.

Shirer, William L. *The Rise and Fall of the Third Reich.* 1959, Simon & Schuster.